£2-50

Christine V.A. Russell,
Thurso 2005.

2/5

Reviews for Rankin and Rebus

QUESTION OF BLOOD

'The real strength of Rankin's work . . . is that it's a good deal more than a crime novel. The genre is simply the wrapping in which a complex story of human flaws and frailty is contained . . . Fortunately, *A Question of Blood* is just about as good as Rankin gets. As a crime novel, it stands favourable comparison with almost anything else currently being written in – or out of – the genre. Detective Inspector Rebus, I suspect, has a way to go yet' *Glasgow Herald*

'He writes with a natural rhythmn which exerts an almost hypnotic effect' *Independent*

'Exemplifies the enhanced craftmanship of the author's recent work; the sheer number of handicaps Rebus overcomes and of the puzzles he solves evinces a relishable virtuosity' *Sunday Times*

'A rich absorbing narrative in which the focus is not on who did it – that we know – but why. Artful, moving and entertaining' *Observer*

'Ian Rankin's John Rebus . . . is a flawed but very human creation, and his Edinburgh and its inhabitants beautifully drawn and utterly real' *Irish Independent*

'Exceptionally well-plotted book, which is guaranteed to hook you and keep you hooked' *Sunday Telegraph*

'Recent crime writers . . . have at their disposal all the opening for alienation afforded by the modern world – and, if one of them has to be singled out as being especially attuned to contemporary murder and social malaise, it is Ian Rankin' *The Times*

'He is an addictive writer, which accounts for his immense popularity, but he is also a serious and disturbing one . . . What he does after Rebus is an interesting question. To track back and offer us some of Rebus's earlier cases would be to reduce the novels to mere entertainment, hugely popular no doubt but a betrayal of his remarkable talent' *Spectator*

'Rankin at his raw-edged, page-turning best. Plot strands expertly twist around each other, puzzles are puzzling and the Edinburgh/South Queensferry locations are as real and atmospheric as it gets. With Rankin you can practically smell the fag-smoke and whisky fumes' *Time Out*

RESURRECTION MEN

'What is impressive in *Resurrection Men* is not just the deftness of the links between disparate crimes, but the fluency of the fugue-like counterpoint between investigations . . . On this form, nothing is beyond him.'
Sunday Times

'Rankin's Rebus novels should be required reading for anyone whose knowledge of Edinburgh has been derived from visits to the festival . . . Rankin conveys the visceral fears and hatreds lurking just below the smart Georgian surface of the "you'll have your tea" New Town.'
Sunday Telegraph

'Bears all the qualities that have established Rankin as one of Britain's leading novelists in any genre: a powerful sense of place; a redefinition of Scotland and its past; persuasive dialogue and a growing compassion among its characters.'
New Statesman

THE FALLS

'Rankin masterfully pulls his fascinating plot together, and his sense of place casts a powerful shadow over this subtle tale of the recurrence of evil.' *Guardian*

'*The Falls* pulses with vitality. Suspense vigorously propels you through its pages. Rankin's prose is crisp, laconic and witty. So is his tangy dialogue.' *Sunday Times*

'An extraordinarily rich addition to crime literature.' *Independent on Sunday*

'This is the work of a very good crime writer at his very best . . . whatever it is that makes a good crime writer. Ian Rankin has it in spades.' *Irish Times*

'*The Falls* is an inventive and absorbing book which lives up to the technical term of a rebus as an enigmatic puzzle.' *Scotsman*

'*The Falls*, the 12th full-length Inspector Rebus story, finds his creator, Ian Rankin, at his brilliant, mordant best, with the dark heart of the city featuring almost as strongly as Rebus himself.' *Sunday Telegraph*

'Few would disagree that Ian Rankin is making a contribution to crime fiction that will last. His novels are playing a significant part in redefining Scotland's image of itself in literature. He is one of a handful of British crime writers whose books are not only commercially successful but also build a strong case for why crime fiction at its best, can and should be considered as literature.' *Independent on Sunday*

SET IN DARKNESS

'Rankin is a master of his craft, handling each twist and turn of the plot with consummate skill as he takes us by the hand and leads us from the sparkling edifices of New Labour-controlled Scotland to the misty, mysterious Edinburgh alleyways, and from hip and trendy restaurants to dank pubs and bars without missing a step . . . Rankin is streets ahead in the British procedural writing field . . . our top crime writer.'

Independent on Sunday

'The book sets off at a cracking rate, with bodies piling up in the first few chapters . . . Running parallel to the excellently paced plot is the theme of Scotland's national identity, its past and future, its regeneration and re-evaluation . . . *Set in Darkness* sees Rankin in impeccable form and will undoubtedly please his legions of fans and increase his appeal even further.' *The List*

'This is, astonishingly, the eleventh Inspector Rebus novel by a writer who is still not yet 40, but whose consistent level of excellence is unmatched in the field of British crime fiction.'

Marcel Berlin, *The Times*

'Rankin exhibits his customary pitch-perfect ear for dialogue, sense of place and eye for both the seamy and grand sides of Scottish life. His books demonstrate that it is possible to take familiar elements – murder, corruption, a beautiful city, an unconventional and oddly-named detective who likes a drink and is unlucky in love – and turn them into something more original and exciting than the standard Morse code. His books are powerful, fast-moving and compulsive. Rankin is without doubt Britain's best crime novelist.' *Express*

'Rankin's particular skill is in producing a highly complex plot whose different strands cleverly come together at the end, a setting which brings to life the grim back streets of Edinburgh and a well-drawn cast of characters.' *Sunday Telegraph*

DEAD SOULS

'Rebus resurgent . . . A brilliantly meshed plot which delivers on every count on its way to a conclusion as unexpected as it is inevitable.'

Literary Review

'Rankin weaves his plot with a menacing ease . . . His prose is understated, yet his canvas of Scotland's criminal underclass has a panoramic breadth. His ear for dialogue is as sharp as a switchblade. This is, quite simply, crime writing of the highest order.'

Daily Express

'A series that shows no sign of flagging . . . Assured, sympathetic to contemporary foibles, humanistic, this is more than just a police procedural as the character of Rebus grows in moral stature . . . Rankin is the head capo of the MacMafia.' *Time Out*

'An atmospheric and cleverly plotted tale well up to Rankin's CWA Gold Dagger standard.' *Books Magazine*

'My favourite gritty page-turner was Ian Rankin's *Dead Souls*.'

Lisa Appignanesi, *Independent*

'No one captures the noirish edge of the city as well as Rankin.'

Daily Telegraph

'His fiction buzzes with energy . . . His prose is as vivid and terse as the next man's yet its flexibility and rhythm give it potential for lyrical expression which is distinctively Rankin's own.'

Scotland on Sunday

'Rankin strips Edinburgh's polite façade to its gritty skeleton.'

The Times

Capital Crimes

Dead Souls
Set in Darkness
The Falls

Also by Ian Rankin

The Inspector Rebus Series

Knots & Crosses
Watchman
Hide & Seek
Tooth & Nail
(previously published as Wolfman)
Strip Jack
The Black Book
Mortal Causes
Let it Bleed
Black & Blue
The Hanging Garden
Death is Not the End (a novella)
Dead Souls
Set in Darkness
The Falls
Resurrection Men
A Question of Blood

Other Novels

The Flood
Westwind

Short Story Collections

A Good Hanging and Other Stories
Beggars Banquet

Writing as Jack Harvey

Witch Hunt
Bleeding Hearts
Blood Hunt

Rebus: Capital Crimes

Dead Souls
Set in Darkness
The Falls

Ian Rankin

BCA

This edition published 2004
by BCA
by arrangement with Orion
an imprint of Orion Books Ltd

First Reprint 2004

CN 125739

Typeset by Deltatype Ltd, Birkenhead, Merseyside
Printed and bound in Great Britain by
Mackays of Chatham plc, Chatham, Kent

Contents

Dead Souls

To my long-suffering editor,
Caroline Oakley

The world is full of missing persons, and their numbers increase all the time. The space they occupy lies somewhere between what we know about the ways of being alive and what we hear about the ways of being dead. They wander there, unaccompanied and unknowable, like shadows of people.

Andrew O'Hagan, The Missing

Once I caught a train to Cardenden by mistake . . . When we reached Cardenden we got off and waited for the next train back to Edinburgh. I was very tired and if Cardenden had looked more promising. I think I would have simply stayed there. And if you've ever been to Cardenden you'll know how bad things must have been.

Kate Atkinson, Behind the Scenes at the Museum

Prologue

From this height, the sleeping city seems like a child's construction, a model which has refused to be constrained by imagination. The volcanic plug might be black Plasticine, the castle balanced solidly atop it a skewed rendition of crenellated building bricks. The orange street lamps are crumpled toffee-wrappers glued to lollipop sticks.

Out in the Forth, the faint bulbs from pocket torches illuminate toy boats resting on black crêpe paper. In this universe, the jagged spires of the Old Town would be angled matchsticks, Princes Street Gardens a Fuzzy-Felt board. Cardboard boxes for the tenements, doors and windows painstakingly detailed with coloured pens. Drinking straws could become guttering and downpipes, and with a fine blade – maybe a scalpel – those doors could be made to open. But peering inside . . . peering inside would destroy the effect.

Peering inside would change *everything*.

He shoves his hands in his pockets. The wind is stropping his ears. He can pretend it is a child's breath, but the reality chides him.

I am the last cold wind you'll feel.

He takes a step forward, peers over the edge and into darkness. Arthur's Seat crouches behind him, humped and silent as though offended by his presence, coiled to pounce. He tells himself it is papier-mâché. He smooths his hands over strips of newsprint, not reading the stories, then realises he is stroking the air and withdraws his hands, laughing guiltily. Somewhere behind him, he hears a voice.

In the past, he'd climbed up here in daylight. Years back, it would have been with a lover maybe, climbing hand in hand, seeing the city spread out like a promise. Then later, with his wife and child, stopping at the summit to take photos, making sure no one went too close to the edge. Father and husband, he would tuck his chin into his collar, seeing Edinburgh in shades of grey, but getting it into perspective, having risen above it with his family. Digesting the whole city with a slow sweep of his head, he would feel that all problems were containable.

But now, in darkness, he knows better.

He knows that life is a trap, that the jaws eventually spring shut on anyone foolish enough to think they could cheat their way to a victory. A police car blares in the distance, but it's not coming for him. A black coach is waiting for him at the foot of Salisbury Crags. Its headless driver is becoming impatient. The horses tremble and whinny. Their flanks will lather on the ride home.

'Salisbury Crag' has become rhyming slang in the city. It means skag, heroin. 'Morningside Speed' is cocaine. A snort of coke just now would do him the world of good, but wouldn't be enough. Arthur's Seat could be made of the stuff: in the scheme of things, it wouldn't matter a damn.

There is a figure behind him in the darkness, drawing nearer. He half-turns to confront it, then quickly looks away, suddenly fearful of meeting the face. He begins to say something.

'I know you'll find it hard to believe, but I've . . .'

He never finishes the sentence. Because now he's sailing out across the city, jacket flying up over his head, smothering a final, heartfelt cry. As his stomach surges and voids, he wonders if there really is a coachman waiting for him.

And feels his heart burst open with the knowledge that he'll never see his daughter again, in this world or any other.

Part One

Lost

We commit all sorts of injustices at every step without the slightest evil intention. Every minute we are the cause of someone's unhappiness . . .

1

John Rebus was pretending to stare at the meerkats when he saw the man, and knew he wasn't the one.

For the best part of an hour, Rebus had been trying to blink away a hangover, which was about as much exercise as he could sustain. He'd planted himself on benches and against walls, wiping his brow even though Edinburgh's early spring was a blood relative of midwinter. His shirt was damp against his back, uncomfortably tight every time he rose to his feet. The capybara had looked at him almost with pity, and there had seemed a glint of recognition and empathy behind the long-lashed eye of the hunched white rhino, standing so still it might have been a feature in a shopping mall, yet somehow dignified in its very isolation.

Rebus felt isolated, and about as dignified as a chimpanzee. He hadn't been to the zoo in years; thought probably the last time had been when he'd brought his daughter to see Palango the gorilla. Sammy had been so young, he'd carried her on his shoulders without feeling the strain.

Today, he carried nothing with him but a concealed radio and set of handcuffs. He wondered how conspicuous he looked, walking such a narrow ambit while shunning the attractions further up and down the slope, stopping now and then at the kiosk to buy a can of Irn-Bru. The penguin parade had come and gone and seen him not leaving his perch. Oddly, it was when the visitors moved on, seeking excitement, that the first of the meerkats appeared, rising on its hind legs, body narrow and wavering, scouting the territory. Two more had appeared from their burrow, circling, noses to the ground. They paid little attention to the silent figure seated on the low wall of their enclosure; passed him time and again as they explored the same orbit of hard-packed earth, jumping back only when he lifted a handkerchief to his face. He was feeling the poison fizz in his veins: not the booze, but an early-morning double espresso from one of the converted police boxes near The Meadows. He'd been on his way to work, on his way to learning that today was zoo patrol. The mirror in the cop-shop toilet had lacked any sense of diplomacy.

Greenslade: 'Sunkissed You're Not'. Segue to Jefferson Airplane: 'If You Feel Like China Breaking'.

But it could always be worse, Rebus had reminded himself, applying his thoughts instead to the day's central question: who was poisoning the zoo animals of Edinburgh? The fact of the matter was, some individual was to blame. Somebody cruel and calculating and so far missed by surveillance cameras and keepers alike. Police had a vague description, and spot-checks were being made of visitors' bags and coat pockets, but what everyone really wanted – except perhaps the media – was to have someone in custody, preferably with the tainted tidbits locked away as evidence.

Meantime, as senior staff had indicated, the irony was that the poisoner had actually been good for business. There'd been no copycat offences yet, but Rebus wondered how long that would last . . .

The next announcement concerned feeding the sea-lions. Rebus had sauntered past their pool earlier, thinking it not overly large for a family of three. The meerkat den was surrounded by children now, and the meerkats themselves had disappeared, leaving Rebus strangely pleased to have been accorded their company.

He moved away, but not too far, and proceeded to untie and tie a shoelace, which was his way of marking the quarter-hours. Zoos and the like had never held any fascination for him. As a child, his roll-call of pets had seen more than its fair share of those listed 'Missing in Action' or 'Killed in the Line of Duty'. His tortoise had absconded, despite having its owner's name painted on its shell; several budgies had failed to reach maturity; and ill-health had plagued his only goldfish (won at the fair in Kirkcaldy). Living as he did in a tenement flat, he'd never been tempted in adulthood by the thought of a cat or dog. He'd tried horse-riding exactly once, rubbing his inside legs raw in the process and vowing afterwards that the closest he'd come in future to the noble beast would be on a betting slip.

But he'd liked the meerkats for a mixture of reasons: the resonance of their name; the low comedy of their rituals; their instinct for self-preservation. Kids were dangling over the wall now, legs kicking in the air. Rebus imagined a role reversal – cages filled with children, peered at by passing animals as they capered and squealed, loving the attention. Except the animals wouldn't share a human's curiosity. They would be unmoved by any display of agility or tenderness, would fail to comprehend that some game was being played, or that someone had skinned a knee. Animals would not build zoos, would have no need of them. Rebus was wondering why humans needed them.

The place suddenly became ridiculous to him, a chunk of prime Edinburgh real estate given over to the unreal . . . And then he saw the camera.

Saw it because it replaced the face that should have been there. The man was standing on a grassy slope sixty-odd feet away, adjusting the focus on a sizeable telescopic lens. The mouth below the camera's body was a thin line of concentration, rippling slightly as forefinger and thumb fine-tuned the apparatus. He wore a black denim jacket, creased chinos, and running shoes. He'd removed a faded blue baseball cap from his head. It dangled from a free finger as he took his pictures. His hair was thinning and brown, forehead wrinkled. Recognition came as soon as he lowered the camera. Rebus looked away, turning in the direction of the photographer's subjects: children. Children leaning into the meerkat enclosure. All you could see were shoe-soles and legs, girls' skirts and the smalls of backs where T-shirts and jerseys had ridden up.

Rebus knew the man. Context made it easier. Hadn't seen him in probably four years but couldn't forget eyes like that, the hunger shining on cheeks whose suffused redness highlighted old acne scars. The hair had been longer four years ago, curling over misshapen ears. Rebus sought for a name, at the same time reaching into his pocket for his radio. The photographer caught the movement, eyes turning to match Rebus's gaze, which was already moving elsewhere. Recognition worked both ways. The lens came off and was stuffed into a shoulder-bag. A lens-cap was clipped over the aperture. And then the man was off, walking briskly downhill. Rebus yanked out his radio.

'He's heading downhill from me, west side of the Members' house. Black denim jacket, light trousers . . .' Rebus kept the description going as he followed. Turning back, the photographer saw him and broke into a trot, hindered by the heavy camera bag.

The radio burst into life, officers heading for the area. Past a restaurant and cafeteria, past couples holding hands and children attacking ice-creams. Peccaries, otters, pelicans. It was all downhill, for which Rebus was thankful, and the man's unusual gait – one leg slightly shorter than the other – was helping close the gap. The walkway narrowed just at the point where the crowd thickened. Rebus wasn't sure what was causing the bottleneck, then heard a splash, followed by cheers and applause.

'Sea-lion enclosure!' he yelled into his radio.

The man half-turned, saw the radio at Rebus's mouth, looked ahead of him and saw heads and bodies, camouflaging the approach of any other officers. There was fear in his eyes now, replacing the earlier calculation. He had ceased to be in control of events. With Rebus just about within grabbing distance, the man pushed two spectators aside and clambered over the low stone wall. On the other side of the pool was a rock outcrop atop which stood the female keeper, stooping over two black plastic pails. Rebus saw that there were hardly any spectators behind the keeper, since the rocks obstructed any view of the sea-lions. By dodging the crowd, the man could clamber back over the wall at the far side and be within striking distance of the exit. Rebus cursed under his breath, lifted a foot on to the wall, and hauled himself over.

The onlookers were whistling, a few even cheering as video cameras were hoisted to record the antics of two men cautiously making their way along the sharp slopes. Glancing towards the water, Rebus saw rapid movement, and heard warning yells from the keeper as a sea-lion slithered up on to the rocks near her. Its sleek black body rested only long enough for a fish to be dropped accurately into its mouth, before turning and slipping back into the pool. It looked neither too big nor too fierce, but its appearance had rattled Rebus's quarry. The man turned back for a moment, his camera bag sliding down his arm. He moved it so it was hanging around his neck. He looked ready to retreat, but when he saw his pursuer, he changed his mind again. The keeper had reached for a radio of her own, alerting security. But the pool's occupants were becoming impatient. The water beside Rebus seemed to flex and sway. A wave foamed against his face as something huge and ink-black rose from the depths, obliterating the sun and slapping itself down on the rocks. The crowd screamed as the male sea-lion, easily four or five times the size of its offspring, landed and looked around for food, loud snorts belching from its nose. As it opened its mouth and let out a ferocious wail, the photographer yelped and lost his balance, plunging into the pool and taking the camera bag with him.

Two shapes in the pool – mother and child – nosed towards him. The keeper was blowing the whistle strung around her neck, for all the world like the referee at a Sunday kickabout faced with a conflagration. The male sea-lion looked at Rebus a final time and plunged back into its pool, heading for where its mate was prodding the new arrival.

'For Christ's sake,' Rebus shouted, 'chuck in some fish!'

The keeper got the message and kicked a pail of food into the pool, at which all three sea-lions sped towards the scene. Rebus took his chance and waded in, closing his eyes and diving, grabbing the man and hauling him back towards the rocks. A couple of spectators came to help, followed by two plain-clothes detectives. Rebus's eyes stung. The scent of raw fish was heavy in the air.

'Let's get you out,' someone said, offering a hand. Rebus let himself be reeled in. He snatched the camera from around the drenched man's neck.

'Got you,' he said. Then, kneeling on the rocks, starting to shiver, he threw up into the pool.

2

Next morning, Rebus was surrounded by memories.

Not his own, but those of his Chief Super: framed photographs cluttering the tight space of the office. The thing with memories was, they meant nothing to the outsider. Rebus could have been looking at a museum display. Children, lots of children. The Chief Super's kids, their faces ageing over time, and then grandchildren. Rebus got the feeling his boss hadn't taken the photos. They were gifts, passed on to him, and he'd felt it necessary to bring them here.

The clues were all in their situation: the photos on the desk faced out from it, so anyone in the office could see them with the exception of the man who used the desk every day. Others were on the window-ledge behind the desk – same effect – and still more on top of a filing cabinet in the corner. Rebus sat in Chief Superintendent Watson's chair to confirm his theory. The snapshots weren't for Watson; they were for visitors. And what they told visitors was that Watson was a family man, a man of rectitude, a man who had achieved something in his life. Instead of humanising the drab office, they sat in it with all the ease of exhibits.

A new photo had been added to the collection. It was old, slightly out of focus as though smeared by a flicker of camera movement. Crimped edges, white border, and the photographer's illegible signature in one corner. A family group: father standing, one hand proprietorially on the shoulder of his seated wife, who held in her lap a toddler. The father's other hand gripped the blazered shoulder of a young boy, cropped hair and glaring eyes. Some pre-sitting tension was evident: the boy was trying to pull his shoulder from beneath his father's claw. Rebus took the photo over to the window, marvelled at the starched solemnity. He felt starched himself, in his dark woollen suit, white shirt and black tie. Black socks and shoes, the latter given a decent polish first thing this morning. Outside it was overcast, threatening rain. Fine weather for a funeral.

Chief Superintendent Watson came into the room, lazy progress belying his temperament. Behind his back they called him 'the Farmer', because he came from the north and had something of the

Aberdeen Angus about him. He was dressed in his best uniform, cap in one hand, white A4 envelope in the other. He placed both on his desk, as Rebus replaced the photograph, angling it so it faced the Farmer's chair.

'That you, sir?' he asked, tapping the scowling child.

'That's me.'

'Brave of you to let us see you in shorts.'

But the Farmer was not to be deflected. Rebus could think of three explanations for the red veins highlighted on Watson's face: exertion, spirits, or anger. No sign of breathlessness, so rule out the first. And when the Farmer drank whisky, it didn't just affect his cheeks: his whole face took on a roseate glow and seemed to contract until it became puckish.

Which left anger.

'Let's get down to it,' Watson said, glancing at his watch. Neither man had much time. The Farmer opened the envelope and shook a packet of photographs on to his desk, then opened the packet and tossed the photos towards Rebus.

'Look for yourself.'

Rebus looked. They were the photos from Darren Rough's camera. The Farmer reached into his drawer to pull out a file. Rebus kept looking. Zoo animals, caged and behind walls. And in some of the shots – not all of them, but a fair proportion – children. The camera had focused on these children, involved in conversations among themselves, or chewing sweets, or making faces at the animals. Rebus felt immediate relief, and looked to the Farmer for a confirmation that wasn't there.

'According to Mr Rough,' the Farmer was saying, studying a sheet from the file, 'the photos comprise part of a portfolio.'

'I'll bet they do.'

'Of a day in the life of Edinburgh Zoo.'

'Sure.'

The Farmer cleared his throat. 'He's enrolled in a photography night-class. I've checked and it's true. It's also true that his project is the zoo.'

'And there are kids in almost every shot.'

'In fewer than half the shots, actually.'

Rebus slid the photos across the desk. 'Come on, sir.'

'John, Darren Rough has been out of prison the best part of a year and has yet to show any sign of reoffending.'

'I heard he'd gone south.'

'And moved back again.'

'He ran for it when he saw me.'

The Farmer just stared the comment down. 'There's nothing here, John,' he said.

'A guy like Rough, he doesn't go to the zoo for the birds and the bees, believe me.'

'It wasn't even his choice of project. His tutor assigned it.'

'Yes, Rough would have preferred a play-park.' Rebus sighed. 'What does his lawyer say? Rough was always good at roping in a lawyer.'

'Mr Rough just wants to be left in peace.'

'The way he left those kids in peace?'

The Farmer sat back. 'Does the word "atonement" mean anything to you, John?'

Rebus shook his head. 'Not applicable.'

'How do you know?'

'Ever seen a leopard change its spots?'

The Farmer checked his watch. 'I know the two of you have a history.'

'I wasn't the one he made the complaint against.'

'No,' the Farmer said, 'Jim Margolies was.'

They left that in the air for a moment, lost in their own thoughts.

'So we do nothing?' Rebus queried at last. The word "atonement" was flitting about inside his skull. His friend the priest had been known to use it: reconciliation of God and man through Christ's life and death. A far cry from Darren Rough. Rebus wondered what Jim Margolies had been atoning for when he'd pitched himself off Salisbury Crags . . .

'His sheet's clean.' The Farmer reached into his desk's deep bottom drawer, pulled out a bottle and two glasses. Malt whisky. 'I don't know about you,' he said, 'but I need one of these before a funeral.'

Rebus nodded, watching the man pour. Cascading sound of mountain streams. *Usquebaugh* in the Gaelic. *Uisge*: water; *beatha*: life. Water of life. *Beatha* sounding like 'birth'. Each drink was a birth to Rebus's mind. But as his doctor kept telling him, each drop was a little death, too. He lifted the glass to his nose, nodded appreciation.

'Another good man gone,' the Farmer said.

And suddenly there were ghosts swirling around the room, just on the periphery of Rebus's vision, and chief amongst them Jack Morton. Jack, his old colleague, now three months dead. The Byrds: 'He Was a Friend of Mine'. A friend who refused to stay buried. The Farmer followed Rebus's eyes, but saw nothing. Drained his glass and put the bottle away again.

'Little and often,' he said. And then, as though the whisky had opened some bargain between them: 'There are ways and means, John.'

'Of what, sir?' Jack had melted into the windowpanes.

'Of coping.' Already the whisky was working on the Farmer's face, turning it triangular. 'Since what happened to Jim Margolies . . . well, it's made some of us think more about the stresses of the job.' He paused. 'Too many mistakes, John.'

'I'm having a bad patch, that's all.'

'A bad patch has its reasons.'

'Such as?'

The Farmer left the question unanswered, knowing perhaps that Rebus was busy answering it for himself: Jack Morton's death; Sammy in a wheelchair.

And whisky a therapist he could afford, at least in monetary terms.

'I'll manage,' he said at last, not even managing to convince himself.

'All by yourself?'

'That's the way, isn't it?'

The Farmer shrugged. 'And meantime we all live with your mistakes?'

Mistakes: like pulling men towards Darren Rough, who wasn't the man they wanted. Allowing the poisoner open access to the meerkats – an apple tossed into their enclosure. Luckily a keeper had walked past, picked it up before the animals could. He'd known about the scare, handed it in for testing.

Positive for rat poison.

Rebus's fault.

'Come on,' the Farmer said, after a final glance at his watch, 'let's get moving.'

So that once again Rebus's speech had gone unspoken, the one about how he'd lost any sense of vocation, any feeling of optimism about the role – the very existence – of policing. About how these thoughts scared him, left him either sleepless or scarred by bad dreams. About the ghosts which had come to haunt him, even in daytime.

About how he didn't want to be a cop any more.

Jim Margolies had had it all.

Ten years younger than Rebus, he was being tipped for accelerated advancement. They were waiting for him to learn the final few lessons, after which the rank of detective inspector would have been shed like a final skin. Bright, personable, a canny strategist with an eye to internal politics. Handsome, too, keeping fit playing rugby for his old school, Boroughmuir. He came from a good background and had connections to the Edinburgh establishment, his wife charming and elegant, his young daughter an acknowledged beauty. Liked by his fellow officers, and with an enviable ratio of arrests to convictions. The family lived quietly in The Grange, attended a local church, seemed the perfect little unit in every way.

The Farmer kept the commentary going, voice barely audible. He'd started on the drive to the church, kept it up during the service, and was closing with a graveside peroration.

'He had it all, John. And then he goes and does something like that. What makes a man . . . I mean, what goes through his head? This was someone even older officers looked up to – I mean the cynical old buggers within spitting distance of their pension. They've seen everything in their time, but they'd never seen anyone quite like Jim Margolies.'

Rebus and the Farmer – their station's representatives – were towards the back of the crowd. And it was a good crowd, too. Lots of brass, alongside rugby players, churchgoers, and neighbours. Plus extended family. And standing by the open grave, the widow dressed in black, managing to look composed. She'd lifted her daughter off the ground. The daughter in a white lace dress, her hair thick and long and ringlet-blonde, face shining as she waved bye-bye to the wooden casket. With the blonde hair and white dress, she looked like an angel. Perhaps that had been the intention. Certainly, she stood out from the crowd.

Margolies' parents were there, too. The father looking ex-forces, stiff-backed as a grandfather clock but with both trembling hands gripping the silver knob of a walking-stick. The mother teary-eyed, fragile, a veil falling to her wet mouth. She'd lost both her children. According to the Farmer, Jim's sister had killed herself too, years back. History of mental instability, and she'd slashed her wrists. Rebus looked again at the parents, who had now outlived both their offspring. His mind flashed to his own daughter, wondering how scarred *she* was, scarred in places you couldn't see.

Other family members nestled close to the parents, seeking comfort or ready to offer support – Rebus couldn't tell which.

'Nice family,' the Farmer was whispering. Rebus almost perceived a whiff of envy. 'Hannah's won competitions.'

Hannah being the daughter. She was eight, Rebus learned. Blue-eyed like her father and perfect-skinned. The widow's name was Katherine.

'Dear Lord, the sheer waste.'

Rebus thought of the Farmer's photographs, of the way individuals met and interlaced, forming a pattern which drew in others, colours merging or taking on discernible contrasts. You made friends, married into a new family, you had children who played with the children of other parents. You went to work, met colleagues who became friends. Bit by bit your identity became subsumed, no longer an individual and yet stronger somehow as a result.

Except it didn't always work that way. Conflicts could arise: work perhaps, or the slow realisation that you'd made a wrong decision some time back. Rebus had seen it in his own life, had chosen profession over marriage, pushing his wife away. She'd taken their daughter with her. He felt now that he'd made the right choice for the wrong reasons, that he should have owned up to his failings from the start. His work had merely given him a reasonable excuse for bailing out.

He wondered about Jim Margolies, who had thrown himself to his death in the dark. He wondered what had driven him to that final stark decision. No one seemed to have a clue. Rebus had come across plenty of suicides over the years, from bungled to assisted and all points in between. But there had always been some kind of explanation, some breaking point reached, some deep-seated sense of loss or failure or foreboding. Leaf Hound: 'Drowned My Life in Fear'.

But when it came to Jim Margolies . . . nothing clicked. There was no sense to it. His widow, parents, workmates . . . no one had been able to offer the first hint of an explanation. He'd been declared A1 fit. Things had been fine on the work front and at home. He loved his wife, his daughter. Money was not a problem.

But something had been a problem.

Dear Lord, the sheer waste.

And the cruelty of it: to leave everyone not only grieving but questioning, wondering if they were somehow to blame.

To erase your own life when life was so precious.

Looking towards the trees, Rebus saw Jack Morton standing there, seeming as young as when the two had first met.

Earth was being tossed down on to the coffin lid, a final futile wake-up call. The Farmer started walking away, hands clasped behind his back.

'As long as I live,' he said, 'I'll never understand it.'

'You never know your luck,' said Rebus.

3

He stood atop Salisbury Crags. There was a fierce wind blowing, and he turned up the collar of his coat. He'd been home to change out of his funeral clothes and should have been heading back for the station – he could see St Leonard's from here – but something had made him take this detour.

Behind and above him, a few hardy souls had achieved the summit of Arthur's Seat. Their reward: the panoramic view, plus ears that would sting for hours. With his fear of heights, Rebus didn't get too close to the edge. The landscape was extraordinary. It was as though God had slapped his hand down on to Holyrood Park, flattening part of it but leaving this sheer face of rock, a reminder of the city's origins.

Jim Margolies had jumped from here. Or a sudden gust had taken him: that was the less plausible, but more easily digested alternative. His widow had stated her belief that he'd been 'walking, just walking', and had lost his footing in the dark. But this raised unanswerable questions. What would take him from his bed in the middle of the night? If he had worries, why did he need to think them out at the top of Salisbury Crags, several miles from his home? He lived in The Grange, in what had been his wife's parents' house. It was raining that night, yet he didn't take the car. Would a desperate man notice he was getting soaked . . . ?

Looking down, Rebus saw the site of the old brewery, where they were going to build the new Scottish parliament. The first in three hundred years, and sited next to a theme park. Nearby stood the Greenfield housing scheme, a compact maze of high-rise blocks and sheltered accommodation. He wondered why the Crags should be so much more impressive than the man-made ingenuity of high-rises, then reached into his pocket for a folded piece of paper. He checked an address, looked back down on to Greenfield, and knew he had one more detour to make.

Greenfield's flat-roofed tower blocks had been built in the mid-1960s and were showing their age. Dark stains bloomed on the discoloured harling. Overflow pipes dripped water on to cracked paving slabs.

Rotting wood was flaking from the window surrounds. The wall of one ground-floor flat, its windows boarded up, had been painted to identify the one-time tenant as 'Junky Scum'.

No council planner had ever lived here. No director of housing or community architect. All the council had done was move in problem tenants and tell everyone central heating was on its way. The estate had been built on the flat bottom of a bowl of land, so that Salisbury Crags loomed monstrously over the whole. Rebus rechecked the address on the paper. He'd had dealings in Greenfield before. It was far from the worst of the city's estates, but still had its troubles. It was early afternoon now, and the streets were quiet. Someone had left a bicycle, missing its front wheel, in the middle of the road. Further along stood a pair of shopping trolleys, nose to nose as though deep in local gossip. In the midst of the six eleven-storey blocks stood four neat rows of terraced bungalows, complete with pocket-handkerchief gardens and low wooden fences. Net curtains covered most of the windows, and above each door a burglar alarm had been secured to the wall.

Part of the tarmac arena between the tower blocks had been given over to a play area. One boy was pulling another along on a sledge, imagining snow as the runners scraped across the ground. Rebus called out the words 'Cragside Court' and the boy on the sledge waved in the direction of one of the blocks. When Rebus got up close to it, he saw that a sign on the wall identifying the building had been defaced so that 'Cragside' read 'Crap-site'. A window on the second floor swung open.

'You needn't bother,' a woman's voice boomed. 'He's not here.'

Rebus stood back and angled his head upwards.

'Who is it I'm supposed to be looking for?'

'Trying to be smart?'

'No, I just didn't know there was a clairvoyant on the premises. Is it your husband or your boyfriend I'm after?'

The woman stared down at him, made up her mind that she'd spoken too soon. 'Never mind,' she said, pulling her head back in and closing the window.

There was an intercom system, but only the numbers of flats, no names. He pulled at the door; it was unlocked anyway. He waited a couple of minutes for the lift to come, then let it shudder its way slowly up to the fifth floor. A walkway, open to the elements, led him past the front doors of half a dozen flats until he was standing outside 5/14 Cragside Court. There was a window, but curtained with what looked like a frayed blue bedsheet. The door showed signs of abuse: failed break-ins maybe, or just people kicking at it because there was no bell or knocker. No nameplate, but that didn't matter. Rebus knew who lived here.

Darren Rough.

The address was new to Rebus. When he'd helped build the case against Rough four years before, Rough had been living in a flat on Buccleuch Street. Now he was back in Edinburgh, and Rebus was keen for him to know just how welcome he was. Besides, he had a couple of questions for Darren Rough, questions about Jim Margolies . . .

The only problem was, he got the feeling the flat was empty. He tried one half-hearted thump at both door and window. When there was no response, he leaned down to peer through the letterbox, but found it had been blocked from inside. Either Rough didn't want anyone looking in, or else he'd been getting unwelcome deliveries. Straightening up, Rebus turned and rested his arms on the balcony railing. He found himself staring straight down on to the kids' playground. Kids: an estate like Greenfield would be full of kids. He turned back to study Rough's abode. No graffiti on walls or door, nothing to identify the tenant as 'Pervo Scum'. Down at ground level, the sledge had taken a corner too fast, throwing off its rider. A window below Rebus opened noisily.

'I saw you, Billy Horman! You did that on purpose!' The same woman, her words aimed at the boy who'd been pulling the sledge.

'Never did!' he yelled back.

'You fucking did! I'll murder you.' Then, tone changing: 'Are you all right, Jamie? I've told you before about playing with that wee bastard. Now get in here!'

The injured boy rubbed a hand beneath his nose – as close as he was going to get to defiance – then made his way towards the tower block, glancing back at his friend. Their shared look lasted only a second or two, but it managed to convey that they were still friends, that the adult world could never break that bond.

Rebus watched the sledge-puller, Billy Horman, shuffle away, then walked down three floors. The woman's flat was easy to find. He could hear her shouting from thirty yards away. He wondered if she constituted a problem tenant; got the feeling few would dare to complain to her face . . .

The door was solid, recently painted dark blue, and boasting a spy-hole. Net curtains at the window. They twitched as the woman checked who her caller was. When she opened the door, her son darted back out and along the walkway.

'Just going to the shop, Mum!'

'Come back here, you!'

But he was pretending not to have heard; disappeared around a corner.

'Give me the strength to wring his neck,' she said.

'I'm sure you love him really.'

She stared hard at him. 'Do we have any business?'

'You never answered my question: husband or boyfriend?'

She folded her arms. 'Eldest son, if you must know.'

'And you thought I was here to see him?'

'You're the police, aren't you?' She snorted when he said nothing.

'Should I know him then?'

'Calumn Brady,' she said.

'You're Cal's mum?' Rebus nodded slowly. He knew Cal Brady by reputation: regal chancer. He'd heard of Cal's mother, too.

She stood about five feet eight in her sheepskin slippers. Heavily built, with thick arms and wrists, her face had decided long ago that make-up wasn't going to cure anything. Her hair, thick and platinum-coloured, brown at the roots, fell from a centre parting. She was dressed in regulation satin-look shell suit, blue with a silver stripe up the arms and legs.

'You're not here for Cal then?' she said.

Rebus shook his head. 'Not unless you think he's done something.'

'So what *are* you doing here?'

'Ever have any dealings with one of your neighbours, youngish lad called Darren Rough?'

'Which flat's he in?' Rebus didn't answer. 'We get a lot of coming and going. Social Work stuff them in here for a couple of weeks. Christ knows what happens to them, they go AWOL or get shifted.' She sniffed. 'What's he look like?'

'Doesn't matter,' Rebus said. Jamie was back down in the playground, no sign of his friend. He ran in circles, pulling the sledge. Rebus got the idea he could run like that all day.

'Jamie's not in school today?' he asked, turning back towards the door.

'None of your bloody business,' Mrs Brady said, closing it in his face.

4

Back at St Leonard's police station, Rebus looked up Calumn Brady on the computer. At age seventeen, Cal already had impressive form: assault, shoplifting, drunk and disorderly. There was no sign as yet that Jamie was following in his footsteps, but the mother, Vanessa Brady, known as 'Van', had been in trouble. Disputes with neighbours had become violent, and she'd been caught giving Cal a false alibi for one of his assault charges. No mention anywhere of a husband. Whistling 'We Are Family', Rebus went to ask the desk sergeant if he knew who the community officer was for Greenfield.

'Tom Jackson,' he was told. 'And I know where he is, because I saw him not two minutes ago.'

Tom Jackson was in the car park at the back of the station, finishing a cigarette. Rebus joined him, lit one for himself and made the offer. Jackson shook his head.

'Got to pace myself, sir,' he said.

Jackson was in his mid-forties, barrel-chested and silver-haired with matching moustache. His eyes were dark, so that he always looked sceptical. He saw this as a decided bonus, since all he had to do was keep quiet and suspects would offer up more than they wanted to, just to appease that look.

'I hear you're still working Greenfield, Tom.'

'For my sins.' Jackson flicked ash from his cigarette, then brushed a few flecks from his uniform. 'I was due a transfer in January.'

'What happened?'

'The locals needed a Santa for their Christmas do. They have one every year at the church. Underprivileged kids. They asked muggins here.'

'And?'

'And I did it. Some of those kids . . . poor wee bastards. Almost had me in tears.' The memory stopped him for a moment. 'Some of the locals came up afterwards, started whispering.' He smiled. 'It was like the confessional. See, the only way they could think to thank me was to furnish a few tip-offs.'

Rebus smiled. 'Shopping their neighbours.'

'As a result of which, my clear-up rate got a sudden lift. Bugger is, they've decided to keep me there, seeing how I'm suddenly so clever.'

'A victim of your own success, Tom.' Rebus inhaled, holding the smoke as he examined the tip of his cigarette. Exhaling, he shook his head. 'Christ, I love smoking.'

'Not me. Interviewing some kid, warning him off drugs, and all the time I'm gasping for a draw.' He shook his head. 'Wish I could give it up.'

'Have you tried patches?'

'No good, they kept slipping off my eye.'

They shared a laugh at that.

'I'm assuming you'll get round to it eventually,' Jackson said.

'What, trying a patch?'

'No, telling me what it is you're after.'

'Am I that transparent?'

'Maybe it's just my finely honed intuition.'

Rebus flicked ash into the breeze. 'I was out at Greenfield earlier. You know a guy called Darren Rough?'

'Can't say I do.'

'I had a run-in with him at the zoo.'

Jackson nodded, stubbed out his cigarette. 'I heard about it. Paedophile, yes?'

'And living in Cragside Court.'

Jackson stared at Rebus. 'That I didn't know.'

'Neighbours don't seem to know either.'

'They'd murder him if they did.'

'Maybe someone could have a word . . .'

Jackson frowned. 'Christ, I don't know about that. They'd string him up.'

'Bit of an exaggeration, Tom. Run him out of town maybe.'

Jackson straightened his back. 'And that's what you want?'

'You really want a paedophile on your beat?'

Jackson thought about it. He brought out his pack of cigarettes and was reaching into it when he checked his watch: ciggie break over.

'Let me think on it.'

'Fair enough, Tom.' Rebus flicked his own cigarette on to the tarmac. 'I bumped into one of Rough's neighbours, Van Brady.'

Jackson winced. 'Don't get on the wrong side of that one.'

'You mean she has a *right* side?'

'Best seen when retreating.'

Back at his desk, Rebus put a call in to the council offices and was eventually put through to Darren Rough's social worker, a man called Andy Davies.

'Do you think it was a wise move?' Rebus asked.

'Care to give me some clue what you're talking about?'

'Convicted paedophile, council flat in Greenfield, nice view of the children's playground.'

'What's he done?' Sounding suddenly tired.

'Nothing I can pin him for.' Rebus paused. 'Not yet. I'm phoning while there's still time.'

'Time for what?'

'To move him.'

'Move him where exactly?'

'How about Bass Rock?'

'Or a cage at the zoo maybe?'

Rebus sat back in his chair. 'He's told you.'

'Of course he's told me. I'm his social worker.'

'He was taking photos of kids.'

'It's all been explained to Chief Superintendent Watson.'

Rebus looked around the office. 'Not to my satisfaction, Mr Davies.'

'Then I suggest you take it up with your superior, Inspector.' No hiding the irritation in the voice.

'So you're going to do nothing?'

'It was your lot wanted him here in the first place!'

Silence on the line, then Rebus: 'What did you just say?'

'Look, I've nothing to add. Take it up with your Chief Superintendent. OK?'

The connection was broken. Rebus tried Watson's office, but his secretary said he was out. He chewed on his pen, wishing plastic had a nicotine content.

It was your lot wanted him here.

DC Siobhan Clarke was at her desk, busy on the phone. He noticed that on the wall behind her was pinned up a postcard of a sea-lion. Walking up to it, he saw someone had added a speech balloon, issuing from the creature's mouth: 'I'll have a Rebus supper, thanks.'

'Ho ho,' he said, pulling the card from the wall. Clarke had finished her call.

'Don't look at me,' she said.

He scanned the room. DC Grant Hood reading a tabloid, DS George Silvers frowning at his computer screen. Then DI Bill Pryde walked into the office, and Rebus knew he had his man. Curly fair hair, ginger moustache: a face just made for mischief. Rebus waved the card at him and watched Pryde's face take on a look of false wounded innocence. As Rebus walked towards him, a phone began sounding.

'That's yours,' Pryde said, retreating. On his way to the phone, Rebus tossed the card into a bin.

'DI Rebus,' he said.

'Oh, hello. You probably won't remember me.' A short laugh on the line. 'That used to be a bit of a joke at school.'

Rebus, immune to every kind of crank, rested against the edge of the desk. 'Why's that?' he asked, wondering what kind of punch-line he was walking into.

'Because it's my name: Mee.' The caller spelled it for him. 'Brian Mee.'

Inside Rebus's head, a fuzzy photograph began to develop – mouthful of prominent teeth; freckled nose and cheeks; kitchen-stool haircut.

'Barney Mee?' he said.

More laughter on the line. 'I never knew why everyone called me that.'

Rebus could have told him: after Barney Rubble in *The Flintstones*. He could have added: because you were a dense wee bastard. Instead, he asked Mee what he could do for him.

'Well, Janice and me, we thought . . . well, it was my mum's idea actually. She knew your dad. Both my parents knew him, only my dad passed away, like. They all drank at the Goth.'

'Are you still in Bowhill?'

'Never quite escaped. I work in Glenrothes though.'

The photo had become clearer: decent footballer, bit of a terrier, the hair reddish-brown. Dragging his satchel along the ground until the stitching burst. Always with some huge hard sweet in his mouth, crunching down on it, nose running.

'So what can I do for you, Brian?'

'It was my mum's idea. She remembered you were in the police in Edinburgh, thought maybe you could help.'

'With what?'

'It's our son. Mine and Janice's. He's called Damon.'

'What's he done?'

'He's vanished.'

'Run away?'

'More like a puff of smoke. He was in this club with his pals, see—'

'Have you tried calling the police?' Rebus caught himself. 'I mean Fife Constabulary.'

'Thing is, the club's in Edinburgh. Police there say they looked into it, asked a few questions. See, Damon's nineteen. They say that means he's got a right to bugger off if he wants.'

'They've got a point, Brian. People run away all the time. Girl trouble maybe.'

'He was engaged.'

'Maybe he got scared.'

'Helen's a lovely girl. Never a raised voice between them.'

'Did he leave a note?'

'I went through this with the police. No note, and he didn't take any clothes or anything.'

'You think something's happened to him?'

'We just want to know he's all right . . .' The voice fell away. 'My mum always speaks well of your dad. He's remembered in this town.'

And buried there, too, Rebus thought. He picked up his pen. 'Give me a few details, Brian, and I'll see what I can do.'

A little later, Rebus visited Grant Hood's desk and retrieved the discarded newspaper from the bin. Turning the pages, he found the editorial section. At the bottom, in bold script, were the words 'Do you have a story for us? Call the newsroom day or night.' They'd printed the telephone number. Rebus jotted it into his notebook.

5

The silent dance resumed. Couples writhed and shuffled, threw back their heads or ran hands through their hair, eyes seeking out future partners or past loves to make jealous. The video monitor gave a greasy look to everything.

No sound, just pictures, the tape cutting from dancefloor to main bar to second bar to toilet hallway. Then the entrance foyer, exterior front and back. Exterior back was a puddled alley boasting rubbish bins and a Merc belonging to the club's owner. The club was called Gaitano's, nobody knew why. Some of the clientele had come up with the nickname 'Guiser's', and that was the name by which Rebus knew it.

It was on Rose Street, started to get busy around ten thirty each evening. There'd been a stabbing in the back alley the previous summer, the owner complaining of blood on his Merc.

Rebus was seated in a small uncomfortable chair in a small dimly lit room. In the other chair, hand on the video's remote, sat DC Phyllida Hawes.

'Here we go again,' she said. Rebus leaned forward a little. The view jumped from back alley to dancefloor. 'Any second.' Another cut: main bar, punters queuing three deep. She froze the picture. It wasn't so much black and white as sepia, the colour of dead photographs. Interior light, she'd explained earlier. She moved the action along one frame at a time as Rebus moved in on the screen, bending so one knee touched the floor. His finger touched a face.

'That's him,' she agreed.

On the desk was a slim file. Rebus had taken from it a photograph, which he now held to the screen.

'All right,' he said. 'Forward at half-speed.'

The security camera stayed with the main bar for another ten seconds, then switched to second bar and all points on the compass. When it returned to the main bar, the crush of drinkers seemed not to have moved. She froze the tape again.

'He's not there,' Rebus said.

'No chance he got served. The two ahead of him are still waiting.'

Rebus nodded. 'He should be there.' He touched the screen again.

'Next to the blonde,' Hawes said.

Yes, the blonde: spun-silver hair, dark eyes and lips. While those around her were intent on catching the eyes of the bar staff, she was looking off to one side. There were no sleeves to her dress.

Twenty seconds of footage from the foyer showed a steady stream entering the club, but no one leaving.

'I went through the whole tape,' Hawes said. 'Believe me, he's not on it.'

'So what happened to him?'

'Easy, he walked out, only the cameras didn't pick him up.'

'And left his pals gasping?'

Rebus studied the file again. Damon Mee had been out with two friends, a night in the big city. It had been Damon's shout – two lagers and a Coke, this last for the designated driver. They'd waited for him, then gone looking. Initial reaction: he'd scored and slunk off without telling them. Maybe she'd been a dinosaur, not something to brag about. But then he hadn't turned up at home, and his parents had started asking questions, questions no one could answer.

Simple truth: Damon Mee had, as the timer on the camera footage showed, vanished from the world between 11.44 and 11.45 p.m. the previous Friday night.

Hawes switched off the machine. She was tall and thin and knew her job; hadn't liked Rebus appearing at Gayfield cop shop like this; hadn't liked the implication.

'There's no hint of foul play,' she said defensively. 'Quarter of a million MisPers every year, most turn up again in their own sweet time.'

'Look,' Rebus assured her, 'I'm doing this for an old friend, that's all. He just wants to know we've done all we can.'

'What's to do?'

Good question, and one Rebus was unable to answer right that minute. Instead, he brushed dust from the knees of his trousers and asked if he could look at the video one last time.

'And something else,' he said. 'Any chance we can get a print-out?'

'A print-out?'

'A photo of the crush at the bar.'

'I'm not sure. It's not going to be much use though, is it? And we've decent photos of Damon as it is.'

'It's not him I'm interested in,' Rebus said as the tape began to play. 'It's the blonde who watched him leave.'

That evening, he drove north out of Edinburgh, paid his toll at the Forth Road Bridge, and crossed into Fife. The place liked to call itself 'the Kingdom' and there were those who would agree that it was another country, a place with its own linguistic and cultural currency. For such a small place, it seemed almost endlessly complex, had seemed that way to Rebus even when he'd been growing up there. To outsiders the place meant coastal scenery and St Andrews, or just a stretch of motorway between Edinburgh and Dundee, but the west central Fife of Rebus's childhood had been very different, ruled by coal mines and linoleum, dockyard and chemical plant, an industrial landscape shaped by basic needs and producing people who were wary and inward-looking, with the blackest humour you'd ever find.

They'd built new roads since Rebus's last visit, and knocked down a few more landmarks, but the place didn't feel so very different from thirty-odd years before. It wasn't such a great span of time after all, except in human terms, and maybe not even then. Entering Cardenden – Bowhill had disappeared from road-signs in the 1960s, even if locals still knew it as a village distinct from its neighbour – Rebus slowed to see if the memories would turn out sweet or sour. Then he caught sight of a Chinese takeaway and thought: both, of course.

Brian and Janice Mee's house was easy enough to find: they were standing by the gate waiting for him. Rebus had been born in a pre-fab but brought up in a terrace much like this one. Brian Mee practically opened the car door for him, and was trying to shake his hand while Rebus was still undoing his seat-belt.

'Let the man catch his breath!' his wife snapped. She was still standing by the gate, arms folded. 'How have you been, Johnny?'

And Rebus realised that Brian had married Janice Playfair, the only girl in his long and trouble-strewn life who'd ever managed to knock John Rebus unconscious.

The narrow low-ceilinged room was full to bursting – not just Rebus, Brian and Janice, but Brian's mother and Mr and Mrs Playfair, plus a billowing three-piece suite and assorted tables and units. Introductions had to be made and Rebus guided to 'the seat by the fire'. The room was overheated. A pot of tea was produced, and on the table by Rebus's armchair sat enough slices of cake to feed a football crowd.

'He's a brainy one,' Janice's mother said, handing Rebus a framed photograph of Damon Mee. 'Plenty of certificates from school. Works hard. Saving to get married.'

The photo showed a smiling imp, not long out of school.

'We gave the most recent pictures to the police,' Janice explained. Rebus nodded: he'd seen them in the file. All the same, when a packet of holiday snaps was handed to him, he went through them slowly: it saved having to look at the expectant faces. He felt like a doctor, expected to produce both immediate diagnosis and remedy. The photos showed a face more careworn than in the framed print. The impish smile remained, but noticeably older: some effort had gone into it. There was something behind the eyes, disenchantment maybe. Damon's parents were in a few of the photos.

'We all went together,' Brian explained. 'The whole family.'

Beaches, a big white hotel, poolside games. 'Where is it?'

'Lanzarote,' Janice said, handing him his tea. 'Do you still take sugar?'

'Haven't done for years,' Rebus said. In a couple of the pictures she was wearing her bikini: good body for her age, or any age come to that. He tried not to linger.

'Can I take a couple of the close-ups?' he asked. Janice looked at him. 'Of Damon.' She nodded and he put the other photos back in the packet.

'We're really grateful,' someone said: Janice's mum? Brian's? Rebus couldn't tell.

'You said his girlfriend's called Helen?'

Brian nodded. He'd lost some hair and put on weight, his face jowly. There was a row of cheap trophies above the mantelpiece: darts and pool, pub sports. He reckoned Brian kept in training most nights. Janice . . . Janice looked the same as ever. No, that wasn't strictly true. She had wisps of grey in her hair. But all the same, talking to her was like stepping back into a previous age.

'Does Helen live locally?' he asked.

'Practically round the corner.'

'I'd like to talk to her.'

'I'll give her a bell.' Brian got to his feet, left the room.

'Where does Damon work?' Rebus asked, for want of a better question.

'Same place as his dad,' Janice said, lighting a cigarette. Rebus raised an eyebrow: at school, she'd been anti-tobacco. She saw his look and smiled.

'He got a job in packaging,' her dad said. He seemed frail, chin quivering. Rebus wondered if he'd had a stroke. One side of his face looked slack. 'He's learning the ropes. It'll be management soon.'

Working-class nepotism, jobs handed down from father to son. Rebus was surprised it still existed.

'Lucky to find any work at all around here,' Mrs Playfair added.

'Are things bad?'

She made a tutting sound, dismissing the question.

'Remember the old pit, John?' Janice asked.

Of course he remembered it, and the bing and the wilderness around it. Long walks on summer evenings, stopping for kisses that seemed to last hours. Wisps of coal-smoke rising from the bing, the dross within still smouldering.

'It's all been levelled now, turned into parkland. They're talking about building a mining museum.'

Mrs Playfair tutted again. 'All it'll do is remind us what we once had.'

'Job creation,' her daughter said.

'They used to call Cowdenbeath the Chicago of Fife,' Brian Mee's mother added.

'The Blue Brazil,' Mr Playfair said, giving a croaking laugh. He meant Cowdenbeath football club, the nickname a self-imposed piece of irony. They called themselves the Blue Brazil because they were rubbish.

'Helen'll be here in a minute,' Brian said, coming back in.

'Are you not eating any cake, Inspector?' added Mrs Playfair.

On the drive back to Edinburgh, Rebus thought back to his chat with Helen Cousins. She hadn't been able to add much to Rebus's picture of Damon, and hadn't been there the night he'd vanished. She'd been out with friends. It was a Friday ritual: Damon went out with 'the lads', she went out with 'the girls'. He'd spoken with one of Damon's companions; the other had been out. He'd learned nothing helpful.

As he crossed the Forth Road Bridge, he thought about the symbol Fife had decided upon for its 'Welcome to Fife' signs: the Forth Rail Bridge. Not an identity so much as an admission of failure, recognition that Fife was for many people a conduit or mere adjunct to Edinburgh.

Helen Cousins had worn black eyeliner and crimson lipstick and would never be pretty. Acne had carved cruel lines into her sallow face. Her hair had been dyed black and fell to a gelled fringe. When asked what she thought had happened to Damon, she'd just shrugged and folded her arms, crossing one leg over the other in a refusal to take any blame he might be trying to foist on her.

Joey, who'd been at Guiser's that night, had been similarly reticent.

'Just a night out,' he'd said. 'Nothing unusual about it.'

'And nothing different about Damon?'

'Like what?'

'I don't know. Was he maybe preoccupied? Did he look nervous?'

A shrug: the apparent extent of Joey's concern for his friend . . .

Rebus knew he was headed home, meaning Patience's flat. But as he stop-started between the lights on Queensferry Road, he thought maybe he'd go to the Oxford Bar. Not for a drink, maybe just for a cola or a coffee, and some company. He'd drink a soft drink and listen to the gossip.

So he drove past Oxford Terrace, stopped at the foot of Castle Street. Walked up the slope towards the Ox. Edinburgh Castle was just over the rise. The best view you could get of it was from a burger place on Princes Street. He pushed open the door to the pub, feeling heat and smelling smoke. He didn't need cigarettes in the Ox: breathing was like killing a ten-pack. Coke or a coffee, he was having trouble making up his mind. Harry was on duty tonight. He lifted an empty pint glass and waved it in Rebus's direction.

'Aye, OK then,' Rebus said, like it was the easiest decision he'd ever made.

He got in at quarter to midnight. Patience was watching TV. She didn't say much about his drinking these days: silence every bit as effective as lectures had ever been. But she wrinkled her nose at the cigarette smoke clinging to his clothes, so he dumped them in the washing basket and took a shower. She was in bed by the time he got out. There was a fresh glass of water his side of the bed.

'Thanks,' he said, draining it with two paracetamol.

'How was your day?' she asked: automatic question, automatic response.

'Not so bad. Yours?'

A sleepy grunt in reply. She had her eyes closed. There were things Rebus wanted to say, questions he'd like to ask. What are we doing here? Do you want me out? He thought maybe Patience had the same questions or similar. Somehow they never got asked; fear of the answers, perhaps, and what those answers would mean. Who in the world relished failure?

'I went to a funeral,' he told her. 'A guy I knew.'

'I'm sorry.'

'I didn't really know him that well.'

'What did he die of?' Head still on the pillow, eyes closed.

'A fall.'

'Accident?'

She was drifting away from him. He spoke anyway. 'His widow, she'd dressed their daughter to look like an angel. One way of dealing with it, I suppose.' He paused, listening to Patience's breathing grow regular. 'I went to Fife tonight, back to the old town. Friends I haven't seen in years.' He looked at her. 'An old flame, someone I could have ended up married to.' Touched her hair. 'No Edinburgh, no Dr Patience Aitken.' His eyes turned towards the window. No Sammy . . . maybe no job in the police either.

No ghosts.

When she was asleep, he went back through to the living room and plugged headphones into the hi-fi. He'd added a record deck to her CD system. In a bag under the bookshelf he found his last purchases from Backbeat Records: Light of Darkness and Writing on the Wall, two Scottish bands he vaguely remembered from times past. As he sat to listen, he wondered why it was he was only ever happy on rewind. He thought back to times when he'd been happy, realising that at the time he hadn't felt happy: it was only in retrospect that it dawned on him. Why was that? He sat back with eyes closed. Incredible String Band: 'The Half-Remarkable Question'. Segue to Brian Eno: 'Everything Merges with the Night'. He saw Janice Playfair the way she'd been the night she'd laid him out, the night that had changed everything. And he saw Alec Chisholm, who'd walked away from school one day and never been seen again. He didn't have Alec's face, just a vague outline and a way of standing, of composing himself. Alec the brainy one, the one who was going to go far.

Only nobody'd expected him to go the way he did.

Without opening his eyes, Rebus knew Jack Morton was seated in the chair across from him. Could Jack hear the music? He never spoke, so it was hard to know if sounds meant anything to him. He was waiting for the track called 'Bogeyman'; listening and waiting . . .

It was nearly dawn when, on her way back from the toilet, Patience removed the headphones from his sleeping form and threw a blanket over him.

6

There were three men in the room, all in uniform, all wanting to hit Cary Oakes. He could see it in their eyes, in the way they stood half-tensed, cheekbones working at wads of gum. He made a sudden movement, but only stretching his legs out, shifting his weight on the chair, arching his head back so it caught the full glare of the sun, streaming through the high window. Bathed in heat and light, he felt the smile stretch across his face. His mother had always told him, 'Your face *shines* when you smile, Cary.' Crazy old woman, even back then. She'd had one of those double sinks in the kitchen, with a mangle you could fix between them. Wash the clothes in one sink, then through the mangle into the other. He'd stuck the tips of his fingers against the rollers once, started cranking the handle until it hurt.

Three prison guards: that's what they reckoned Cary Oakes was worth. Three guards, and chains for his legs and arms.

'Hey, guys,' he said, pointing his chin at them. 'Take your best shot.'

'Can it, Oakes.'

Cary Oakes grinned again. He'd forced a reaction: of such small victories were his days made. The guard who'd spoken, the one with the tag identifying him as SAUNDERS, did tend towards the excitable. Oakes narrowed his eyes and imagined the moustached face pressed against a mangle, imagined the strength needed to force that face all the way through. Oakes rubbed his stomach; not so much as an ounce of flab there, despite the food they tried to serve him. He stuck to vegetables and fruit, water and juices. Had to keep the brain in gear. A lot of the other prisoners, they'd slipped into neutral, engines revving but heading nowhere. A stretch of confinement could do that to you, make you start believing things that weren't true. Oakes kept up with events, had magazine and newspaper subscriptions, watched current affairs on TV and avoided everything else, except maybe a little sport. But even sport was a kind of novocaine. Instead of watching the screen, he watched the other faces, saw them heavy-lidded, no need to concentrate, like babies being spoon-fed contentment, bellies and brains filled to capacity with warmed-over gunk.

He started whistling a Beatles song: 'Good Day, Sunshine', wondering if any of the guards would know it. Potential for another reaction. But then the door opened and his attorney came in. His fifth lawyer in sixteen years, not a bad average, batting .300. This lawyer was young – mid-twenties – and wore blue blazers with cream slacks, a combination which made him look like a kid trying on his dad's clothes. The blazers had brass-effect buttons and intricate designs on the breast pocket.

'Ahoy, shipmate!' Oakes cried, not shifting in his chair.

His lawyer sat down opposite him at the table. Oakes put his hands behind his head, rattling the chains.

'Any chance of removing those from my client?' the lawyer asked.

'For your own protection, sir.' The stock response.

Oakes used both hands to scratch his shaved head. 'Know those divers and spacemen? Use weighted boots, necessary tool of the trade. I reckon when I lose these chains, I'm going to float up to the ceiling. I can make my living in freak shows: the human fly, see him scale the walls. Man, imagine the possibilities. I can float up to second-floor windows and watch all the ladies getting ready for bed.' He turned his head to the guards. 'Any of you guys married?'

The lawyer was ignoring this. He had his job to do, opening the briefcase and lifting out the paperwork. Wherever lawyers went, paper went with them. Lots of paper. Oakes tried not to look interested.

'Mr Oakes,' the lawyer said, 'it's just a matter of detail now.'

'I've always enjoyed detail.'

'Some papers that have to be signed by various officials.'

'See, guys,' Oakes called to the guards, 'I told you no prison could hold Cary Oakes! OK, so it's taken me fifteen years, but, hey, nobody's perfect.' He laughed, turning to his lawyer. 'So how long should all these . . . details take?'

'Days rather than weeks.'

Inside, Oakes's heart was pumping. His ears were hissing with the intensity of it, the swell of apprehension and anticipation. *Days . . .*

'But I haven't finished painting my cell. I want it left pretty for the next tenant.'

Finally the attorney smiled, and Oakes knew him in that instant: working his way up in Daddy's practice; reviled by his elders, mistrusted by his peers. Was he spying on them, reporting back to the old man? How could he prove himself? If he joined them for drinks on a Friday night, loosening his tie and mussing up his hair, they felt uncomfortable. If he kept his distance, he was a cold fish. And what about the father? The old man couldn't have anyone accusing him of nepotism, the boy had to learn the hard way. Give him the shitty-stick cases, the no-hopers, the ones that left you needing a shower and change of clothes. Make him prove himself. Long hours of thankless toil, a shining example to everyone else in the firm.

All this discerned from a single smile, the smile of a half-shy, self-conscious drone who dreamt of being King Bee, who perhaps even harboured little fantasies of patricide and succession.

'You'll be deported, of course,' the prince was saying now.

'What?'

'You were in this country illegally, Mr Oakes.'

'I've been here nearly half my life.'

'Nevertheless . . .'

Nevertheless . . . His mother's word. Every time he had an excuse prepared, some story to explain the situation, she'd listen in silence, then take a deep breath, and it was like he could see the word forming in the air that issued from her mouth. During his trial, he'd rehearsed little conversations with her.

'Mother, I've been a good son, haven't I?'

'Nevertheless . . .'

'Nevertheless, I killed two people.'

'Really, Cary? You're sure it was only two . . . ?'

He sat up in his chair. 'So let them deport me, I'll come straight back.'

'It won't be so easy. I can't see you securing a tourist visa this time, Mr Oakes.'

'I don't need one. You're behind the times.'

'Your name will be on record . . .'

'I'll walk across from Canada or Mexico.'

The lawyer shifted in his seat. He didn't like to hear this.

'I have to come back and see my pals,' nodding towards the guards. 'They'll miss me when I'm gone. And so will their wives.'

'Fuck you, slime.' Saunders again.

Oakes beamed at his lawyer. 'Isn't that nice? We have nicknames for each other.'

'I don't think any of this is very helpful, Mr Oakes.'

'Hey, I'm the model prisoner. That's the way it works, right? I learned a fast lesson: use the same system they used to put you where you are. Read up on the law, go back over everything, know the questions to ask, the objections that should have been made at the original trial. The lawyer they had representing me, I'll tell you, he couldn't have presented a school prize, never mind my case.' He smiled again. 'You're better than him. You're going to be all right. Remember that next time your pop is chewing you out. Just say to yourself: I'm better than that, I'm going to be all right.' He winked. 'No charge for my time, son.'

Son: as if he was fifty rather than thirty-eight. As if the knowledge of the ages was his for the dispensing.

'So I get a free flight back to London?'

'I'm not sure.' The lawyer looked through his notes. 'You're from Lothian originally?' Pronouncing it *loathing*.

'As in Edinburgh, Scotland.'

'Well, you might end up back there.'

Cary Oakes rubbed at his chin. Edinburgh might do for a while. He had unfinished business in Edinburgh. Was going to leave it till the heat had died down, but nevertheless . . . He leaned forward over the table.

'How many murders did they pin on me?'

The lawyer blinked, sat there with palms flat on the table. 'Two,' he said at last.

'How many did they start with?'

'I believe it was five.'

'Six actually.' Oakes nodded slowly. 'But who's counting, eh?' A chuckle. 'They ever catch anyone for the others?'

The lawyer shook his head. There were beads of perspiration at his temples. He'd be making a detour home for a shower and fresh clothes.

Cary Oakes sat back again and angled his face into the sun, turning his head so every part felt the warmth. 'Two's not much of a tally, is it, in the scheme of things? You kill your old man, you'll only be one behind.'

He was still chuckling to himself as his lawyer was led out of the room.

7

Younger runaways tended to take the same few routes: by bus, train or hitching, and to London, Glasgow or Edinburgh. There were organisations who would keep an eye open for runaways, and even if they wouldn't always reveal their whereabouts to the anxious families, at least they could confirm that someone was alive and unharmed.

But a nineteen-year-old, someone with money to hand . . . could be anywhere. No destination was too distant – his passport hadn't turned up. He took it with him to clubs as proof of age. Damon had a current account at the local bank, complete with cashcard, and an interest-bearing account with a building society in Kirkcaldy. The bank might be worth trying. Rebus picked up the telephone.

The manager at first insisted that he'd need something in writing, but relented when Rebus promised to fax him later. Rebus held while the manager went off to check, and had doodled half a village, complete with stream, parkland and pit-head, by the time the man came back.

'The most recent withdrawal was a cash machine in Edinburgh's West End. One hundred pounds on the fifteenth.'

The night Damon had gone to Gaitano's. A hundred seemed a lot to Rebus, even for a good night out.

'Nothing since then?'

'No.'

'How up to date is that?'

'Up to the close of play yesterday.'

'Could I ask you a favour, sir? I'd like tabs kept on that account. Any new withdrawals, I'd like to know about them pronto.'

'I'd need that in writing, Inspector. And I'd probably also need the approval of my head office.'

'I'd appreciate it, Mr Brayne.'

'It's Bain,' the bank manager said coldly, putting down the phone.

Rebus called the building society and endured the same rigmarole before learning that Damon hadn't touched his account in more than a fortnight. He made one last call to Gayfield police station and asked for DC Hawes. She didn't sound too thrilled when he identified himself.

'What's the word on Gaitano's?' he asked.

'Everyone calls it Guiser's. Pretty choice establishment. Two stabbings last year, one in the club itself, one in the alley out back. Been quieter this year, which is probably down to a stricter door policy.'

'You mean bigger bouncers.'

'Front-of-house managers, if you please. Locals still complain about the noise at chucking-out time.'

'Who owns it?'

'Charles Mackenzie, nicknamed "Charmer".'

A couple of uniforms had talked to Mackenzie about Damon Mee, and he'd offered up the security tape which had languished in Gayfield ever since.

'Know how many MisPers there are every year?' Hawes said with a sigh.

'You told me.'

'Then you should know that if there's no suspicion of foul play, they're not exactly a white-hot priority. God knows there are times I've felt like doing a runner myself.'

Rebus thought of his night-time car-rides, long, directionless hours, just filling in the blank spaces of his life. 'Haven't we all?' he said.

'Look, I know you're doing this as a favour . . .'

'Yes?'

'But we've done all we can, haven't we?'

'Pretty much.'

'So what's the point?'

'I'm not sure.' Rebus could have told her that it had to do with the past, with some debt he felt he owed to Janice Playfair and Barney Mee – and to the memory of a friend he'd once had called Mitch. Somehow, he didn't think explaining it to an outsider would help. 'One last thing,' he asked instead. 'Did you get me a still of that woman?'

Gaitano's was little more than a solid black door with a neon sign above it, flanked either side by pubs and with a hi-fi shop across the road. There were valve amplifiers and an outsized record deck in the shop window. The deck had an outsized price-tag to match. One of the pubs was called The Headless Coachman. It had changed its name a couple of years back and was touting for tourists.

Rebus pushed the door-buzzer to Gaitano's and a woman opened it for him. She was the cleaner, and Rebus didn't envy her the job. Glasses had been cleared from the tables, but the place still looked like a wreck. There was an industrial vacuum cleaner on the carpet which encircled the dance floor. The floor was littered with cigarette stubs, cellophane, the occasional empty bottle. She'd finished cleaning the foyer, but was only halfway through the main dance area. There were mirrors on all the walls, and in the right light the place would look many times its actual size. In bare white light and with no music, no punters, it looked and felt desolate. There was a fug of stale sweat and beer in the air. Rebus saw a security camera in one corner and gave it a wave.

'Inspector Rebus.'

The man walking towards him across the dancefloor was about five feet four inches and as thin as a swizzle-stick. Rebus placed him in his mid-fifties. He wore a powder-blue suit and open-necked white shirt to show off his suntan and gold jewellery. His hair was silver and thinning, but as well-cut as the suit. They shook hands.

'Do you want a drink?'

He was leading Rebus towards the bar. Rebus looked at the row of optics.

'No thank you, sir.'

Charmer Mackenzie went behind the bar and poured himself a cola.

'Sure?' he said.

'Same as you're having,' Rebus said. He examined one of the bar stools for cigarette ash, then pulled himself up on to it. They faced one another across the bar.

'Not your normal tipple?' Mackenzie guessed. 'In my trade, you get a nose for these things.' And he tapped his nose for effect. 'The kid hasn't turned up then?'

'No, sir.'

'Sometimes they get a notion . . .' He shrugged, dismissing the foibles of a generation.

'I've got a photograph.' Rebus reached into his pocket, handed it over. 'The missing person is second row.'

Mackenzie nodded, not really interested.

'See just behind him?'

'Is that his doll?'

'Do you know her?'

Mackenzie snorted. 'Wish I did.'

'You haven't seen her before?'

'Picture's not the best, but I don't think so.'

'What time do the staff clock on?'

'Not till tonight.'

Rebus took the photo back, put it in his pocket.

'Any chance of getting my video back?' Mackenzie asked.

'Why?'

'Those things cost money. Overheads, that's what can cripple a business like this, Inspector.'

Rebus wondered how he'd merited the nickname 'Charmer'. He had all the charm of sandpaper. 'We wouldn't want that now, would we, Mr Mackenzie?' he said, getting to his feet.

Back at the office, he played the tape again, watching the blonde. The way her head was angled, strong jawline, mouth open slightly. Could she be saying something to Damon? A minute later, he was gone. Had she said she'd meet him somewhere? After he'd gone, she'd stayed at the bar, ordering a drink for herself. At dead on midnight, fifteen minutes after Damon had vanished, she'd left the nightclub. The final shot was from a camera mounted on the club's exterior wall. It showed her turning left along Rose Street, watched by a few drunks who were trying to get into Gaitano's.

Someone put their head round the door and told him he had a call. It was Mairie Henderson.

'Thanks for getting back to me,' he said.

'I take it you've a favour to ask?'

'Quite the reverse.'

'In that case, lunch is on me. I'm in the Engine Shed.'

'How convenient.' Rebus smiled: the Engine Shed was just behind St Leonard's. 'I'll be there in five minutes.'

'Make it two, or all the meatballs will have gone.'

Which was a joke of sorts, in that there was no meat in the meatballs. They were savoury balls of mushroom and chickpea with a tomato sauce. Though a one-minute walk from his office, Rebus had never eaten in the Engine Shed. Everything about it was too healthy, too nutritious. The drink of the day was organic apple juice, and smoking was strictly forbidden. He knew it was run by some sort of charity, and staffed by people who needed a job more than most. Typical of Mairie to choose it for a meeting. She was seated by a window, and Rebus joined her with his tray.

'You look well,' he said.

'It's all this salad.' She nodded towards her plate.

'Lifestyle still suit you?'

He meant her decision to quit the local daily paper and go freelance. They'd helped one another out on occasion, but Rebus was aware he owed her more brownie points than she owed him. Her face was all clean, sharp lines, her eyes quick and dark. She'd restyled her hair to early Cilla Black. On the table beside her sat her notebook and cellphone.

'I get the occasional story picked up by the London papers. Then my old paper has to run its own version the next day.'

'That must annoy them.'

She beamed. 'Have to let them know what they're missing.'

'Well,' Rebus said, 'they've been missing a story that's right under their noses.' He pushed another forkful of food into his mouth, having to admit to himself that it wasn't at all bad. Looking around the other tables, he realised all the other diners were women. Some of them were tending to kids in high chairs, some were involved in quiet gossip. The restaurant wasn't big, and Rebus kept his voice down when he spoke.

'What story's that?' Mairie said.

Rebus's voice went lower. 'Paedophile living in Greenfield.'

'Convicted?'

Rebus nodded. 'Served his time, now they've plonked him in a flat with a lovely view of a kids' play-park.'

'What's he been up to?'

'Nothing yet, nothing I can pin him for. Thing is, his neighbours don't know what's living next door to them.'

She was staring at him.

'What is it?' he said.

'Nothing.' She munched on more salad, chewing slowly. 'So where's the story?'

'Come on, Mairie . . .'

'I know what you want me to do.' She pointed her fork at him. 'I know why you want it.'

'And?'

'And what has he done?'

'Christ, Mairie, do you know what the reoffending rate is? It's not something you cure by slapping them in prison for a few years.'

'We've got to take a chance.'

'*We?* It's not us he'll be after.'

'All of us, we've all got to give them a chance.'

'Look, Mairie, it's a good story.'

'No, it's your way of getting to him. Does this all come back to Shiellion?'

'It's got bugger all to do with Shiellion.'

'I hear they've got you down to give evidence.' She stared at him again, but all he did was shrug. 'Only,' she went on, 'the knives are out as it is. If I do a story on a paedophile living in Greenfield of all places . . . it'd be incitement to murder.'

'Come on, Mairie . . .'

'Know what I think, John?' She put down her knife and fork. 'I think something's gone bad inside you.'

'Mairie, all I want . . .'

But she was on her feet, unhooking her coat from the back of the chair, collecting her phone, notebook, bag.

'I don't have much of an appetite any more,' she said.

'Time was, you'd have gnawed a story like this to the bone.'

She looked thoughtful for a moment. 'Maybe you're right,' she said. 'I hope to God you're not, but maybe you are.'

She walked the length of the restaurant's wooden floorboards on noisy heels. Rebus looked down at his lunch, at the untouched glass of juice. There was a pub not three minutes away. He pushed the plate away. He told himself Mairie was wrong: it had nothing to do with Shiellion. It was down to Jim Margolies, to the fact that Darren Rough had once made a complaint against him. Now Jim was dead, and Rebus wanted something back. Could he lay Jim's ghost to rest by tormenting Jim's tormentor? He reached into his pocket, found the sliver of paper there, the telephone number still perfectly legible.

I think something's gone bad inside you.

Who was he to disagree?

8

Four years before, Jim Margolies had been passing through St Leonard's, seconded to help with a staff shortfall. Three of the CID were down with flu, and another was in hospital for a minor op. Margolies, whose usual beat was Leith, came highly recommended, which made his new colleagues wary. Sometimes a recommendation was made so a station could offload dead weight elsewhere. But Margolies had proved himself quickly, handling a paedophile inquiry with dedication and tact. Two boys had been interfered with on The Meadows during, of all things, a children's festival. Darren Rough was already in police files. At twelve, he'd interfered with a neighbour's son, aged six at the time. He'd had counselling, and spent time in a children's home. At fifteen, he'd been caught peeping in at windows at the student residences in Pollock Halls. More counselling. Another mark in his police file.

The schoolboys' description of their attacker had taken police to the house Rough shared with his father. At nine in the morning, the father was drunk at the kitchen table. The mother had died the previous summer, which looked to be the last time the house had been cleaned. Soiled clothes and mouldy dishes were everywhere. It looked like nothing ever got thrown out: burst and rotting binbags stood inside the kitchen door; mail was piled high in a corner of the front hall, where damp had turned it into a single sodden mass. In Darren Rough's bedroom, Jim Margolies found clothing catalogues, crude penned additions made to the child models. There were collections of teen magazines under the bed, stories about – and pictures of – teenage girls and boys. And best of all from the police point of view, tucked under a corner of rotting carpet was Darren's 'Fantasy League', detailing his sexual proclivities and wish lists, with his Meadows exploit dated and signed.

For all of which the Procurator Fiscal was duly grateful. Darren Rough, by now twenty years old, was found guilty and sent to jail. A crate of beer was opened at St Leonard's, and Jim Margolies sat at the top of the table.

Rebus was there, too. He'd been part of the shift team interviewing

Rough. He'd spent enough time with the prisoner to know that they were doing the right thing locking him up.

'Not that it ever helps with those bastards,' DI Alistair Flower had said. 'Reoffend as soon as they're out.'

'You're suggesting treatment replaces incarceration?' Margolies had asked.

'I'm suggesting we throw away the fucking key!' To which there had been cheers of agreement. Siobhan Clarke had been too canny to add her own view, but Rebus knew what she'd been thinking. Nothing was said of the complaint Rough had made. Bruising to his face and body: he'd told his solicitor Jim Margolies had given him a beating. No witnesses. Self-inflicted was the consensus. Rebus knew he'd felt like giving Rough a couple of slaps himself, but Margolies had no history of aggression against suspects.

There'd been an internal inquiry. Margolies had denied the accusation. A medical examination had been unable to determine whether Rough's bruises were self-inflicted. And that's where it had ended, with the faintest of blots on Margolies' record, the faintest doubt hanging over the rest of his career.

Rebus closed the case file and walked back to the vault with it.

Mairie: *I think something's gone bad inside you.*

Rough's social worker: *Your lot wanted him here.*

Rebus went to the Farmer's office, knocked on the door, entered when told.

'What can I do for you, John?'

'I had a word with Darren Rough's social worker, sir.'

The Farmer looked up from his paperwork. 'Any particular reason?'

'Just wanted to know why Rough had been given a flat with a view of a kiddies' playground.'

'I bet they loved you for that.' Not sounding disapproving. Social workers rated only a rung or two above paedophiles on the Farmer's moral stepladder.

'They told me that we wanted him here in the first place.'

The Farmer's face furrowed. 'Meaning what?'

'They suggested I ask you.'

'I haven't the faintest idea.' The Farmer sat back in his chair. '*We* wanted him here?'

'That's what they said.'

'Meaning Edinburgh?'

Rebus nodded. 'I've just been through the file on Rough. He was in a children's home for a while.'

'Not Shiellion?' The Farmer was looking interested.

Rebus shook his head. 'Callstone House, other side of the city. Just for a short spell. Both parents were alcoholic, neglecting him. There was nowhere else for him to go.'

'What happened?'

'Mother dried out, Rough went back home. Then, later on, she was diagnosed with liver disease, only nobody bothered moving Rough.'

'Why?'

'Because by that time, he was looking after his father.'

The Farmer looked towards his collection of family snaps. 'The way some people live . . .'

'Yes, sir,' Rebus agreed.

'So where's this leading?'

'Only this: Rough comes back to Edinburgh, apparently because we want him here. Next thing, the officer who put him away ends up walking off Salisbury Crags.'

'You're not suggesting a connection?'

Rebus shrugged. 'Jim goes out to dinner at some friends' with his wife and kid. Drives home. Goes to bed. Next morning he's dead. I'm looking for reasons why Jim Margolies would take his own life. Thing is, I'm not finding any. And I'm also wondering who'd want Darren Rough back here and why.'

The Farmer was thoughtful. 'You want me to talk to Social Work?'

'They wouldn't talk to me.'

The Farmer reached for paper and a pen. 'Give me a name.'

'Andy Davies is Rough's social worker.'

The Farmer underlined the words. 'Leave it with me, John.'

'Yes, sir. Meantime, I'd like to take a look at Jim's suicide.'

'Mind if I ask why?'

'To see if it *does* tie in with Rough.' And maybe, he could have added, to satisfy his own curiosity.

The Farmer nodded. 'On the subject of Shiellion . . . when do you give evidence?'

'Tomorrow, sir.'

'Got your spiel rehearsed?'

Rebus nodded.

'Remember the secret of a good court appearance, John.'

'Presentation, sir?'

The Farmer shook his head. 'Make sure you take plenty of reading matter with you.'

That evening, on his way home, he dropped in to see his daughter. Sammy had moved out of her first-floor colony flat into a newish ground-floor flat in a brick-built block off Newhaven Road.

'Downhill all the way to the coast,' she'd told her father. 'And you should see this thing with the brakes off.'

Referring to her wheelchair. Rebus had wanted to put his hand in his pocket for a motorised one, but she'd waved away the offer.

'I'm building up my muscles,' she'd said. 'And besides, I won't be in this thing for long.'

Perhaps not, but the road back to full mobility was proving hard going. She was receiving physio only twice a week, spending the rest of her time concentrating on home exercises. It was as if the accident had affected both her spine and her legs.

'My brain tells them what to do, but they don't always listen.'

There was a little wooden ramp at the main door to her block. A friend of a friend had constructed it for her. One of the bedrooms in the flat had been turned into a makeshift gym, a large mirror placed against one wall, and parallel bars taking up most of the available space. The doorways were narrow, but Sammy had proved adept at manoeuvring her wheelchair in and out without grazing knuckles or elbows.

When Rebus arrived, Ned Farlowe opened the door. He had a job subbing for one of the local freesheets. The hours were short, which gave him time to help Sammy with her workouts. The two men still didn't trust one another – did fathers ever really come to trust the men who were sleeping with their daughters? – but Ned seemed to be doing his damnedest for Sammy.

'Hi there,' he said. 'She's working out. Fancy a cuppa?'

'No thanks.'

'I'm just making some dinner.' Ned was already retreating to the long, narrow kitchen. Rebus knew he'd only be in the way.

'I'll just go and . . .'

'Fine.'

The smells from the kitchen were like those in the Engine Shed: aromatic and vegetarian. Rebus walked down the hall, noting graze-marks on the walls where the wheelchair had connected. Music was coming from the spare bedroom, a disco beat. Sammy was lying on the floor in her black leotard and tights, trying to get her legs to do things. Her face was flushed with effort, hair matted to her forehead. When she saw her father, she rested her head against the floor.

'Turn that thing off, will you?' she said.

'I could just watch.'

But she shook her head. She didn't like him watching her at work. This was *her* fight, a private battle with her own body. Rebus switched off the tape machine.

'Recognise it?' she asked.

'Chic, "Le Freak". I went to enough bad discos in the seventies.'

'I can't imagine you in flares.'

'Distress flares.'

She had pushed herself up to sitting. He made just the one step forward to help her, knowing if he got any closer she'd shoo him away.

'How's your claim for disability going?'

She rolled her eyes, reached a hand out for a towel, starting wiping her face. 'I thought I knew all about bureaucracy. Thing is, I'm going to get better.'

'Sure.'

'So there are all kinds of complications. Plus my job at SWEEP's still open.'

'But the office is three floors up.' He sat on the floor beside her.

'I can work from home.'

'Really?'

'Only I don't want to. I don't want to become dependent on just these four walls.'

Rebus nodded. 'If there's anything you need . . .'

'Got any disco tapes?'

He smiled. 'I was more Rory Gallagher and John Martyn.'

'Well, nobody's perfect,' she said, wrapping the towel around her neck. 'Speaking of which, how's Patience?'

'She's fine.'

'I talk to her on the phone.'

'Oh?'

'She says I speak to her more than you do.'

'I don't think that's true.'

'Don't you?'

Rebus looked at his daughter. Had she always had this edge to her? Was it something to do with the accident?

'We get along fine,' he said.

'On whose terms?'

He stood up. 'I think your dinner's nearly ready. Want me to help you into the chair?'

'Ned likes to do it.'

He nodded slowly.

'You didn't answer my question.'

'I'm a policeman. Usually *we* ask the questions.'

She draped the towel over her head. 'Is it because of me?'

'What?'

'Ever since . . .' She looked down at her legs. 'It's like you blame yourself.'

'It was an accident.' He wasn't looking at her.

'It pushed the two of you back together. Do you see what I'm saying?'

'You're saying I'm busy blaming myself for your accident, while you're busy blaming yourself for Patience and me.' He glanced towards her. 'Does that just about sum it up?'

She smiled. 'Stay and have something to eat.'

'Don't you think I should head home to Patience?'

She lifted the towel from her eyes. 'Is that where you're going?'

'Where else?' He gave her a wave as he left the room.

9

Being down Newhaven Road, he stopped off at a couple of waterfront bars, a pint in one, nip of whisky in the other. Plenty of water in the whisky. It was dark, but he could see streetlights across the Forth in Fife. He thought of Janice and Brian Mee, who had never left their home town. He wondered how he'd have turned out if he'd stayed. He thought again of Alec Chisholm, the boy who had never been found. They'd scoured the countryside, sent men down into disused coal-shafts, dredged the river. A long hot summer, the Beatles and the Stones on the café jukebox, ice-cold bottles of Coke from the machine. Glass coffee cups topped with frothed milk. And questions about Alec, questions which showed that none of them had ever really known him, not deep down, not the way they thought they knew each other. And Alec's parents and grandparents, walking the streets late at night, stopping to ask strangers the same thing: have you seen our boy? Until the strangers became acquaintances, and they ran out of people to stop.

Now Damon Mee had stepped away from the world, or had been yanked out of it by some irresistible force. Rebus got back in his car and drove along the coast, came up on to the Forth Bridge, and headed into Fife. He tried telling himself he wasn't escaping – from Sammy's words and Patience and Edinburgh, from all the ghosts. From thoughts of paedophiles and suicide leaps.

When he got to Cardenden, he slowed the car, finally coming to a stop on the main drag. There seemed to be flyers in every shop window: Damon's picture and the word MISSING. There were more taped to lamp-posts and the bus shelter. Rebus started the car again and headed for Janice's house. But there was no one at home. A neighbour supplied the information Rebus needed, information which sent him straight back to Edinburgh and Rose Street, where he found Janice and Brian sticking more flyers on to lamp-posts and walls, pushing them through letterboxes. Photocopied sheets of A4. Holiday photo of Damon, and handwritten plea: DAMON MEE IS MISSING: HAVE YOU SEEN HIM? Physical description, including the clothes he'd been wearing, and the Mees' telephone number.

'We've covered the pubs,' Brian Mee said. He looked tired, eyes dark, face unshaven. The roll of sellotape he held was nearly finished. Janice leaned against a wall. Looking at the pair of them was far from like stepping into the past – present worries had scarred them.

'The one place they don't want to know,' Janice said, 'is that club.'

'Gaitano's?'

She nodded. 'Bouncers wouldn't let us in. Wouldn't even take flyers from us. I stuck one on the door but they took it down.' She was almost in tears. Rebus looked back along the street towards the flashing neon sign above Gaitano's.

'Come on,' he said. 'Let's try the magic word this time.'

And when he got to the door, he flashed his ID and said, 'Police.' The three were ushered inside while someone got on the phone to Charmer Mackenzie. Rebus looked to Janice and winked.

'Open Sesame,' he said. She was looking at him as if he'd done something wonderful.

'Mr Mackenzie's not here,' one of the bouncers said.

'So who's in charge?'

'Archie Frost. He's assistant manager.'

'Lead me to him.'

The bouncer looked unhappy. 'He's having a drink at the bar.'

'No problem,' Rebus said. 'We know our way.'

Bass music was pulsing, the club's interior dark and hot. Couples were hitting the dancefloor, others smoking furiously, knees pumping as they scanned the dimness for action. Rebus leaned towards Janice, so his mouth was an inch from her ear.

'Go round the tables, ask your questions.'

She nodded, passed the message along to Brian, who was looking uncomfortable with the noise.

Rebus walked towards the bar, walked through beams of indigo light. There were people waiting for drinks, but only two men actually drinking at the bar. Well, one of them was drinking. The other – who looked thirsty – was listening to what was being said to him.

'Sorry to butt in,' Rebus said.

The speaker turned to him. 'You will be in a minute.'

Maybe twenty or twenty-one, black hair pulled back into a ponytail. Stocky, wearing a suit with no lapels and a dazzling white T-shirt. Rebus pushed his warrant card into the face, identified himself.

'Been taking charm-school lessons from your boss?' he asked. Archie Frost said nothing, just finished his drink. 'I want a word, Mr Frost.'

'They don't look like polis,' Frost said, nodding towards where Janice and Brian Mee were working the room.

'That's because they're not. Their son went missing. Disappeared from here, in fact.'

'I know.'

'Well then, you'll know why I'm here.' Rebus brought out the photograph of the mystery blonde. 'Seen her before?'

Frost shook his head automatically.

'Take a closer look.'

Frost took the photo grudgingly, and angled it towards the light. Then he shook his head and tried handing it back.

'What about your pal?'

'What about him?'

The 'pal' in question, the young man without a drink, had half-turned from them, so he was watching the dancefloor.

'He's not in here much,' Frost said.

'All the same,' Rebus persisted. So Frost stuck the photo in front of his friend's nose. An immediate shake of the head.

'I'm going to take this around your punters,' Rebus said, lifting the photo from Frost's hand, 'see if their memories are any better.' He wasn't looking at Frost; he was looking at his companion. 'Do I know you from somewhere, son? Your face looks familiar.'

The young man snorted, kept his eyes on the dancing.

'I'll let you get back to your business then,' Rebus said. He did a circuit of the room, following behind Janice and Brian. They'd left flyers on most of the tables. A couple had already been crumpled up. Rebus fixed the culprits with a stare. He wasn't faring any better with his own picture, but saw that ahead of him Janice and Brian had seated themselves at a table and were deep in conversation with two girls there. Eventually, he caught up with them. Janice looked up at him.

'They say they saw Damon,' she yelled, fighting the music.

'He was getting into a taxi,' one of the girls repeated for the newcomer's benefit.

'Where?' Rebus asked.

'Outside The Dome.'

'Other side of the road,' her friend corrected. They were wearing too much make-up, trying for a look they'd probably call 'sophisticated', trying to look older than their years. Soon enough, they'd be reversing the process. They wore incredibly short skirts. Rebus could see Brian trying not to stare.

'What time was this?'

'About quarter past twelve. We were late for a party.'

'You're sure about the date?' Rebus asked. Janice looked at him accusingly, not wanting this fragile bubble to burst.

One girl got a diary out of her handbag, tapped a page. 'That's the party.'

Rebus looked: it was the same date Damon had disappeared. 'How come you noticed him?'

'We'd seen him in here earlier.'

'Just standing at the bar,' her friend added. 'Not dancing or anything.'

A couple of young men, still in their day-job suits, had peeled off from an office party and were approaching, ready to ask for a dance.

The girls tried to look disinterested, but a glower from Rebus sent the suitors back in the direction they'd come.

'We were after a taxi ourselves,' one girl explained. 'Saw them waiting across the road. Only they got lucky, we ended up walking.'

' "They"?'

'Him and his girl.'

Rebus looked to Janice, then handed over the photo.

'Yeah, that looks like her.'

'Blonde out of a bottle,' the other agreed.

Janice took the photo from them, looked at it herself.

'Who is she, John?'

Rebus shook his head, telling her he didn't know. Glancing towards the bar, he saw two things. One was that Archie Frost was watching him intently over the rim of a fresh glass. The other was that his non-drinking friend had gone.

'Maybe they've run off together,' one of the girls was saying, trying hard to be helpful. 'That would be romantic, wouldn't it?'

Janice and Brian hadn't eaten, so Rebus took them to an Indian on Hanover Street, where he explained the little he knew about the woman in the photograph. Janice kept the photo in one hand as she ate.

'It's a start, isn't it?' Brian said, pulling apart a nan bread.

Rebus nodded agreement.

'I mean,' Brian went on, 'we know now he left with someone. He's probably still with her.'

'Only he didn't go off with her,' Janice said. 'John's already told us, Damon left on his own.'

In fact, Rebus hadn't even gone that far. They only had the girls' word for it that Damon had left the club at all . . .

'Well,' Brian stumbled on, 'thing is, he wouldn't want his mates seeing them together, not when he was supposed to be engaged.'

'I can't believe it of Damon.' Janice's eyes were on Rebus. 'He loves Helen.'

Rebus nodded. 'But it happens, doesn't it?'

She gave a rueful smile. Brian saw a look passing between them, but chose to ignore it.

'Anyone want any more rice?' he asked instead, lifting the salver from its hotplate.

'We should be getting home,' his wife said. 'Damon might have tried phoning.' She was getting to her feet. Rebus gestured towards the photo, and she handed it back. It was smudged, creased at the corners. Brian was looking down at the food still on his plate.

'Brian . . .' Janice said. He sniffed and got up from his chair. 'Get the bill, will you?'

'This is on me,' Rebus said. 'They'll stick it on my tab.'

'Thanks again, John.' She held out her hand and he took it. It was long and slender. Rebus remembered holding it when they danced, remembered the way it would be warm and dry, unlike other girls' hands. Warm and dry, and his heart pounding in his chest. She'd been so slender at the waist, he'd felt he could encircle her with just his hands.

'Yes, thanks, Johnny.' Brian Mee laughed. 'You don't mind me calling you Johnny?'

'Why should I mind?' Rebus said, still looking into Janice's eyes. 'It's my name, isn't it?'

10

First thing, Rebus looked through the newspapers, but he didn't find anything to interest him.

He headed down to Leith police station, where Jim Margolies had been stationed. He'd told the Farmer he was looking for a connection between Rough's reappearance and Jim's death, but he wasn't particularly confident of finding one. Still, he really *did* want to know why Jim had done it, had done something Rebus had thought about doing more than once – taking the high walk. He was met in Leith by a wary Detective Inspector Bobby Hogan.

'I know I owe you a favour or two, John,' Hogan began. 'But do you mind telling me what it's all about? Margolies was a good man, we're missing him badly.'

They were walking through the station, making for CID. Hogan was a couple of years younger than Rebus, but had been on the force for longer. He could take retirement any time he wanted, but Rebus doubted the man would ever want it.

'I knew him, too,' Rebus was saying. 'I'm probably just asking myself the same question all of you have been asking.'

'You mean why?'

Rebus nodded. 'He was headed for the top, Bobby. Everyone knew it.'

'Maybe he got vertigo.' Hogan shook his head. 'The notes aren't going to tell you anything, John.'

They had stopped outside an interview room.

'I just need to see them, Bobby.'

Hogan stared at him, then nodded slowly. 'This makes us even, pal.'

Rebus touched him on the shoulder, walked into the room. The manila file was sitting on the otherwise empty desk. There were two chairs in the room.

'Thought you'd like some privacy,' Hogan said. 'Look, if anyone wonders . . .'

'My lips are sealed, Bobby.' Rebus was already sitting down. He examined the folder. 'This won't take long.'

Hogan fetched a cup of coffee, then left him to it. It took Rebus precisely twenty minutes to sift through everything: initial report and back-up, plus Jim Margolies' history. Twenty minutes wasn't long for a CV. Of course, there was little about his home life. Speculation was for after-work drinks, for cigarette breaks and coffee-machine meetings. The bare facts, set down between double margins, gave no clues at all. His father was a doctor, now retired. Comfortable upbringing. The sister who'd committed suicide in her teens . . . Rebus wondered if his sister's death had been at the back of Jim Margolies' mind all these years. There was no mention of Darren Rough, no mention of Margolies' short time at St Leonard's. His last night on earth, Jim had been out to dinner at some friends' house. Nothing out of the ordinary. But afterwards, in the middle of the night, he'd slipped from his bed, got dressed again, and gone walking in the rain. All the way to Holyrood Park . . .

'Anything?' Bobby Hogan asked.

'Not a sausage,' Rebus admitted, closing the file.

Walking in the rain . . . A long walk, from The Grange to Salisbury Crags. No one had come forward to say they'd seen him. Inquiries had been made, cabbies questioned. Perfunctory for the most part: you didn't want to linger over a suicide. Sometimes you could find out things that were better left undisturbed.

Rebus drove back into town, parked in the car park behind St Leonard's and went into the station. He knocked on Farmer Watson's door, obeyed the command to enter. Watson looked like the day had started badly.

'Where have you been?'

'I had a bit of business down at D Division, looking at Jim Margolies' file.' Rebus watched the Farmer pace behind his desk. He cradled a mug of coffee in both hands. 'Did you speak to Andy Davies, sir?'

'Who?'

'Andy Davies. Darren Rough's social worker.'

The Farmer nodded.

'And, sir?'

'And he told me I'd have to speak to his boss.'

'What did his boss say?'

The Farmer swung round. 'Christ, John, give me time, will you? I've got more to deal with than your little . . .' He exhaled, his shoulders slumping. Then he mumbled an apology.

'No problem, sir. I'll just . . .' Rebus headed for the door.

'Sit down,' the Farmer ordered. 'Now you're here, let's see if you can come up with any clever ideas.'

Rebus sat down. 'To do with what, sir?'

The Farmer sat too, then noticed that his mug was empty. He got up again to fill it from the pot, pouring for Rebus too. Rebus examined the dark liquid suspiciously. Over the years, the Farmer's coffee had definitely improved, but there were still days . . .

'To do with Cary Dennis Oakes.'

Rebus frowned. 'Should I know him?'

'If you don't, you soon will.' The Farmer tossed a newspaper in Rebus's direction. It fell to the floor. Rebus picked it up, saw that it was folded to a particular story, a story Rebus had missed because it wasn't the one he'd been looking for.

KILLER IS SENT 'HOME'.

'Cary Oakes,' Rebus read, 'convicted of two murders in Washington State, USA, will today board a flight back to the United Kingdom after serving a fifteen-year sentence in a maximum-security prison in Walla Walla, Washington. It is believed that Oakes will make his way back to Edinburgh, where he lived for several years before going to the United States.'

There was a lot more. Oakes had flown to the States toting a rucksack and a tourist visa, and then had simply stayed put, taking a series of short-term jobs before embarking on a mugging and robbery spree which had climaxed with two killings, the victims clubbed and strangled to death.

Rebus put down the paper. 'Did you know?'

The Farmer slammed his fists down on the table. 'Of course I didn't know!'

'Shouldn't we have been told?'

'Think about it, John. You're a cop in Wallumballa or whatever it's called. You're sending this murderer back to *Scotland*. Who do you tell?'

Rebus nodded. 'Scotland Yard.'

'Not realising for one minute that Scotland Yard might actually be in another country altogether.'

'And the brainboxes in London decided not to pass the message on?'

'Their version is, they got their wires crossed, thought Oakes was only travelling as far as *their* patch. In fact, his ticket only goes as far as London.'

'So he's their problem.' But the Farmer was shaking his head. 'Don't tell me,' Rebus said, 'they've had a whip-round and added the fare to Edinburgh?'

'Bingo.'

'So when does he get here?'

'Later on today.'

'And what do we do?'

The Farmer stared at Rebus. He liked that *we*. A problem shared – even if with a thorn like Rebus – was a problem that could be dealt with. 'What would you suggest?'

'High-visibility surveillance, let him know we're watching. With any luck he'll get fed up and slope off somewhere else.'

The Farmer rubbed at his eyes. 'Take a look,' he said, sliding a folder across the desk. Rebus looked: sheets of fax paper, about twenty of them. 'The Met took pity on us at the last, sent what they'd been sent by the Americans.'

Rebus started reading. 'How come he's been released? I thought in America "life" meant till death.'

'Some technicality to do with the original trial. So arcane, even the American authorities aren't sure.'

'But they're letting him go?'

'A retrial would cost a fortune, plus there's the problem of tracing the original witnesses. They offered him a deal. If he gave it up, signed away the right to any retrial or compensation, they'd fly him home.'

'In the news story, "home" had inverted commas.'

'He hasn't spent much time in Edinburgh.'

'So why here?'

'His choice, apparently.'

'But why?'

'Maybe the fax will tell you.'

The message of the fax was clear and simple. It said Cary Oakes would kill again.

The psychologist had warned the authorities of this. The psychologist said, Cary Oakes has little concept of right and wrong. There were lots of psychological terms applied to this. The word 'psychopath' wasn't used much any more by the experts, but reading between the lines and the jargon, Rebus knew that was what they were dealing with. Anti-social tendencies . . . deep-seated sense of betrayal . . .

Oakes was thirty-eight years old. There was a grainy photo of him included with the file. His head had been shaved. The forehead was large and jutting, the face thin and angular. He had small eyes, like little black beads, and a narrow mouth. He was described as above-average intelligence (self-taught in prison), interested in health and fitness. He'd made no friends during his incarceration, kept no pictures on his walls, and his only correspondence was with his team of lawyers (five different sets in total).

The Farmer was on the telephone, finding out Oakes's flight schedule, liaising with the Assistant Chief Constable at Fettes. When he'd finished, Rebus asked what the ACC thought.

'He thinks we should ca' canny.'

Rebus smiled: it was a typical response.

'He's right in a way,' the Farmer continued. 'The media will be all over this. We can't be seen to be harassing the man.'

'Maybe we'll get lucky and the reporters will scare him off.'

'Maybe.'

'It says here he was originally questioned about another four murders.'

The Farmer nodded, but seemed distracted. 'I don't need this,' he said at last, staring at his desk. The desk was a measure of the man: always carefully ordered, reflecting the room as a whole. No piles of paperwork, no mess or clutter, not so much as a single stray paperclip on the carpet.

'I've been at this job too long, John.' The Farmer sat back in his chair. 'You know the worst kind of officers?'

'You mean ones like me, sir?'

The Farmer smiled. 'Quite the opposite. I mean the ones who're biding their time till pension day. The clock-watchers. Recently, I've been turning into one. Another six months, that's what I was giving myself. Six more months till retirement.' He smiled again. 'And I wanted them quiet. I've been praying for them to be quiet.'

'We don't know this guy's going to be a problem. We've been here before, sir.'

The Farmer nodded: so they had. Men who'd done time in Australia and Canada, and hardmen from Glasgow's Bar-L, all of them settling in Edinburgh, or just passing through. All of them with pasts carved into their faces. Even when they weren't a problem, they were still a problem. They might settle down, live quietly, but there were people who knew who they were, who knew the reputation they carried with them, something they'd never shake off. And eventually, after too many beers down the pub, one of these people would decide it was time to test himself, because what the hardman brought with him was a parameter, something you could measure yourself against. It was pure Hollywood: the retired gunslinger challenged by the punk kid. But to the police, all it was was trouble.

'Thing is, John, can we afford to play a waiting game? The ACC says we can have funding for partial surveillance.'

'How partial?'

'Two teams of two, maybe a fortnight.'

'That's big of him.'

'The man likes a nice tight budget.'

'Even when this guy might kill again?'

'Even murder has a budget these days, John.'

'I still don't get it.' Rebus picked up the fax. 'According to the notes, Oakes wasn't born here, doesn't have family here. He lived here for, what, four or five years. Went to the States at twenty, he's been almost half his life there. What's for him back here?'

The Farmer shrugged. 'A fresh start?'

A fresh start: Rebus was thinking of Darren Rough.

'There has to be more to it than that, sir,' Rebus said, picking up the file again. 'There has to be.'

The Farmer looked at his watch. 'Aren't you due in court?'

Rebus nodded agreement. 'Waste of time, sir. They won't call me.'

'All the same, Inspector . . .'

Rebus got up. 'Mind if I take this stuff?' Waving the sheets of fax paper. 'You told me I should take something to read.'

11

Rebus sat with other witnesses, other cases, all of them waiting to be called to give evidence. There were uniforms, attentive to their notebooks, and CID officers, arms folded, trying to be casual about the whole thing. Rebus knew a few faces, held quiet conversations. The members of the public sat there with hands clasped between knees, or with heads angled to the ceiling, bored out of their minds. Newspapers – already read, crosswords finished – lay strewn around the room. A couple of dog-eared paperbacks had attracted interest, but not for long. There was something about the atmosphere that sucked all the enthusiasm out of you. The lighting gave you a headache, and all the time you were wondering why you were here.

Answer: to serve justice.

And one of the court officers would wander in and, looking at a clipboard, call your name, and you'd creak your way to the court, where your numbed memory would be poked and prodded by strangers playing to a judge, jury, and public gallery.

This was justice.

There was one witness, seated directly across from Rebus, who kept bursting into tears. He was a young man, maybe mid-twenties, corpulent and with thin strands of black hair plastered to his head. He kept emptying his nose loudly into a stained handkerchief. One time, when he looked up, Rebus gave him a reassuring smile, but that only started him off again. Eventually, Rebus had to get out. He told one of the uniforms that he was going for a ciggie.

'I'll join you,' the uniform said.

Outside, they smoked furiously and in silence, watching the ebb and flow of people from the building. The High Court was tucked in behind St Giles' Cathedral, and occasionally tourists would wander towards it, wondering what it was. There were few signs about, just Roman numerals above the various heavy wooden doors. A guard on the car park would sometimes point them back towards the High Street. Though members of the public could enter the court building, tourists were actively discouraged. The Great Hall was enough of a cattle market as it was. But Rebus liked it: he liked the carved wooden ceiling, the statue of Sir Walter Scott, the huge stained-glass window. He liked peering through the glass door into the library where the lawyers sought precedents in large dusty tomes.

But he preferred the fresh air, setts below him and grey stone above, and the inhalation of nicotine, and the illusion that he could walk away from all this if he chose. For the thing was, behind the splendour of the architecture, and the weight of tradition, and the high concepts of justice and the law, this was a place of immense and continual human pain, where brutal stories were wrenched up, where tortured images were replayed as daily fare. People who thought they'd put the whole thing behind them were asked to delve into the most secret and tragic moments of their past. Victims rendered their stories, the professionals laid down cold facts over the emotions of others, the accused wove their own versions in an attempt to woo the jury.

And while it was easy to see it as a game, as some kind of cruel spectator sport, still it could not be dismissed. Because for all the hard work Rebus and others put into a case, this was where it sank or swam. And this was where all policemen learned an early lesson that truth and justice were far from being allies, and that victims were something more than sealed bags of evidence, recordings and statements.

It had probably all been simple enough once upon a time; the concept still was fairly simple. There is an accused, and a victim. Lawyers speak for both sides, presenting the evidence. A judgment is made. But the whole thing was a matter of words and interpretation, and Rebus knew how facts could be twisted, misrepresented, how some evidence sounded more eloquent than others, how juries could decide from the off which way they'd vote, based on the manner or styling of the accused. And so it turned into theatre, and the cleverer the lawyers became, the more arcane became their games with language. Rebus had long since given up fighting them on their own terms. He gave his evidence, kept his answers short, and tried not to fall for any of the tried and tested tricks. Some of the lawyers could see it in his eyes, could see that he'd been here too often before. They detained him only briefly, before moving on to more amenable subjects.

That was why he didn't think they'd call him today. But all the same, he had to sit it out, had to waste his time and energy in the great name of justice.

One of the guards came out. Rebus knew him, and offered a cigarette. The man took it with a nod, accepting Rebus's box of matches.

'Fucking awful in there today,' the guard said, shaking his head. All three men were staring across the car park.

'We're not allowed to know,' Rebus reminded him with a sly smile. 'Which court are you in?'

'Shiellion,' Rebus said.

'That's the one I'm talking about,' the guard said. 'Some of the testimony . . .' And he shook his head, a man who'd heard more horror stories than most in his working life.

Suddenly, Rebus knew why the man across from him had been crying. And if he couldn't put a name to the man, at least now he knew who he was: he was one of the Shiellion survivors.

Shiellion House lay just off the Glasgow Road at Ingliston Mains. Built in the 1820s for one of the city's Lord Provosts, after his death and various family wranglings it had passed into the care of the Church of Scotland. As a private residence it was found to be too big and draughty, its isolation – distant farms its only neighbours – driving away most of its residents. By the 1930s it had become a children's home, dealing with orphans and the impoverished, teaching them Christianity with hard lessons and early rises. Shiellion had finally closed the previous year. There was talk of it becoming a hotel or a country club. But in its later years, Shiellion had garnered something of a reputation. There had been accusations from former residents, similar stories told by different intakes about the same two men.

Stories of abuse.

Physical and mental abuse to be sure, but eventually sexual abuse too. A couple of cases had come to the attention of the police, but the accusations were one-sided – the word of aggressive children against their quietly spoken carers. The investigations had been half-hearted. The Church had carried out its own internal inquiries, which had shown the children's stories to be tissues of vindictive lies.

But these inquiries, it now transpired, had been fixed from the start, comprising little more than cover-ups. Something *had* been happening in Shiellion. Something bad.

The survivors formed a pressure group, and got some media interest. A fresh police investigation was implemented, and it had led to this – the Shiellion trial; two men up on charges ranging from assault to sodomy. Twenty-eight counts against either man. And meantime, the victims were readying to sue the Church.

Rebus didn't wonder that the guard was pale-faced. He'd heard whispers about the stories being retold in court number one. He'd read some of the original transcripts, details of interviews held at police stations up and down the country, as children who'd been held in Shiellion were traced – adults now – and questioned. Some of them had refused to have anything to do with it. 'That's all behind me,' was an oft-used excuse. Only it was more than an excuse: it was the simple truth. They'd worked hard to lock out the nightmares from their childhood: why would they want to relive them? They had whatever peace would ever be available to them in life: why change that?

Who would face terror across a courtroom, if they could choose to avoid it?

Who indeed.

The survivors' group comprised eight individuals who had chosen the more difficult path. They were going to see to it that after all these years justice was finally done. They were going to lock away the two monsters who'd ripped apart their innocence, monsters who were still there in the world whenever they woke from their nightmares.

Harold Ince was fifty-seven, short and skinny and bespectacled. He had curly hair, turning grey. He had a wife and three grown children. He was a grandfather. He hadn't worked in seven years. He had a dazed look to him in all the photographs Rebus had seen.

Ramsay Marshall was forty-four, tall and broad, hair cut short and spiky. Divorced, no children, had until recently been living and working (as a chef) in Aberdeen. Photographs showed a scowling face, jutting chin.

The two men had met at Shiellion in the early 1980s, formed a friendship or at the very least an alliance. Found they shared a common interest, one that could, it seemed, be carried out with impunity in Shiellion House.

Abusers. Rebus was sickened by them. They couldn't be cured or changed. They just went on and on. Released into the community, they'd soon revert to type. They were control junkies, weak-minded, and just awful. They were like addicts who couldn't be weaned off their fix. There were no prescription drugs, and no amount of psychotherapy seemed to work. They saw weakness and had to exploit it; saw innocence and had to explore it. Rebus had had a bellyful of them.

Like with Darren Rough. Rebus knew he'd snapped in the zoo because of Shiellion, because of the way it wasn't going away. The trial had lasted two weeks so far, heading into week three, and still there were stories to be told, still there were people crying in the waiting room.

'Chemical castration,' the guard said, stubbing out his cigarette. 'It's the only way.'

Then there was a cry from the courthouse door: one of the ushers.

'Inspector Rebus?' she called. Rebus nodded, flicked his cigarette on to the setts.

'You're up,' she called. He was already moving towards her.

Rebus didn't know why he was here. Except that he'd interviewed Harold Ince. Which was to say, he'd been part of the team interviewing Ince. But only for one day – other work had pulled him away from Shiellion. Only for one day, early on in the inquiry. He'd shared the sessions with Bill Pryde, but it wasn't Bill Pryde the defence wanted to examine. It was John Rebus.

The public gallery was half-empty. The jury of fifteen sat with glazed expressions, the effect of sharing someone else's nightmare, day in, day out. The judge was Lord Justice Petrie. Ince and Marshall sat in the dock. Ince leaned forward, the better to hear the evidence, his hands twisting the polished brass rail in front of him. Marshall leaned back, looking bored by proceedings. He examined his shirt-front, then would turn his neck from side to side, cracking it. Clear his throat and click his tongue and go back to studying himself.

The defence lawyer was Richard Cordover, Richie to his friends. Rebus had had dealings with him before; he'd yet to be invited to call the lawyer 'Richie'. Cordover was in his forties, hair already grey. Medium height and with a muscular neck, face tanned. Health club regular, Rebus guessed. Prosecution was a fiscal-depute nearly half Rebus's age. He looked confident but careful, browsing through his case notes, jotting points down with a fat black fountain pen.

Petrie cleared his throat, reminding Cordover that time was passing. Cordover bowed to the judge and approached Rebus.

'Detective Inspector Rebus . . .' Pausing immediately for effect. 'I believe you interviewed one of the suspects.'

'That's right, sir. I was present at the interview of Harold Ince on October the twentieth last year. Others present included—'

'This was where exactly?'

'Interview Room B, St Leonard's police station.'

Cordover turned away from Rebus, walked slowly towards the jury. 'You were part of the investigating team?'

'Yes, sir.'

'For how long?'

'Just over a week, sir.'

Cordover turned to Rebus. 'How long did the investigation last in total, Inspector?'

'A matter of some months, I believe.'

'Some months, yes . . .' Cordover went as if to check his notes. Rebus noticed a woman seated on a chair near the door. She was a CID detective called Jane Barbour. Though she sat with arms folded and legs crossed, she looked as tense as Rebus felt. Normally, she worked out of Fettes, but halfway through Shiellion she'd been put in charge: after Rebus's time; he hadn't had any dealings with her.

'Eight and a half months,' Cordover was saying. 'A decent period of gestation.' He smiled coldly at Rebus, who said nothing. He was wondering where this was leading; knew now that the defence had some bloody good reason for bringing him here. Only he didn't yet know what.

'Were you pulled from the inquiry, Inspector Rebus?' Asked casually, as if to satisfy curiosity only.

'Pulled? No, sir. Something else came up—'

'And someone was needed to deal with it?'

'That's right.'

'Why you, do you think?'

'I've no idea, sir.'

'No?' Cordover sounded surprised. He turned towards the jury. 'You've no idea why you were pulled from that inquiry after just one—'

The prosecution counsel was on his feet, arms spread. 'The detective inspector has already stated that the word "pulled" is an inaccuracy, Your Honour.'

'Well then,' Cordover went on quickly, 'let's say you were *transferred*. Would that be more accurate, Inspector?'

Rebus just shrugged, unwilling to agree to anything. Cordover was persistent.

'Yes or no will do.'

'Yes, sir.'

'Yes, you were transferred from a major inquiry after one week?'

'Yes, sir.'

'And you've no idea why?'

'Because I was needed elsewhere, sir.' Rebus was trying not to look towards the fiscal-depute: any glance in that direction would have Cordover scenting blood, scenting someone who needed rescuing. Jane Barbour was shifting in her seat, still with arms folded.

'You were needed elsewhere,' Cordover repeated in a flat tone of voice. He returned to his notes. 'How's your disciplinary record, Inspector?'

The fiscal-depute was on his feet. 'Inspector Rebus is not on trial here, Your Honour. He has come to give evidence, and so far I can't see any point to the—'

'I withdraw the remark, Your Honour,' Cordover said airily. He smiled at Rebus, approached again. 'You conducted how many interviews with Mr Ince?'

'Two sessions over a single day.'

'Did they go well?' Rebus looked blank. 'Did my client co-operate?'

'His answers were deliberately obtuse, sir.'

'"Deliberately"? Are you some kind of expert, Inspector?'

Rebus fixed his eyes on the advocate. 'I can tell when someone's being evasive.'

'Really?' Cordover was making for the jury again. Rebus wondered how many miles of floor he covered in a day. 'My client is of the opinion that you were "a threatening presence" – his words, not mine.'

'The interviews were recorded, sir.'

'Indeed they were. And videotaped, too. I've watched them several times, and I think you'd have to agree that your method of questioning is *aggressive*.'

'No, sir.'

'No?' Cordover raised his eyebrows. 'My client was obviously terrified of you.'

'The interviews followed every procedure, sir.'

'Oh, yes, yes,' Cordover said dismissively, 'but let's be honest here, Inspector.' He was in front of Rebus now, close enough to hit. 'There are ways and ways, aren't there? Body language, gestures, ways of phrasing a question or statement. You may or may not be expert at divinating obtuse answers, but you're certainly a ruthless questioner.'

The judge peered over the top of his glasses. 'Is this leading somewhere, other than to an attempt at character assassination?'

'If you'll bear with me a moment longer, Your Honour.' Cordover bowed again, consummate showman. Not for the first time, Rebus was struck by the utter ridiculousness of the whole enterprise: a game played by well-paid lawyers using real lives as the pieces.

'A few days ago, Inspector,' Cordover went on, 'were you part of a surveillance team at Edinburgh Zoo?'

Oh, hell. Rebus knew now *exactly* where Cordover was leading, and like a bad chess-player put against a master, he could do little to forestall the conclusion.

'Yes, sir.'

'You ended up in pursuit of a member of the public?'

The fiscal-depute was on his feet again, but the judge waved him aside.

'I did, yes.'

'You were part of an undercover team trying to catch our notorious poisoner?'

'Yes, sir.'

'And the man you chased . . . I believe it was into the sea-lion enclosure?' Cordover looked up for confirmation. Rebus nodded dutifully. 'Was this man the poisoner?'

'No, sir.'

'Did you suspect him of being the poisoner?'

'He was a convicted paedophile . . .' There was anger in Rebus's voice, and he knew his face had reddened. He broke off, but too late. He'd given the defence lawyer everything he wanted.

'A man who had served his sentence and been released into the community. A man who has not reoffended. A man who was enjoying the pleasures of a trip to the zoo until *you* recognised him and chased after him.'

'He ran first.'

'He ran? From *you*, Inspector? Now why would he do a thing like that?'

All right, you sarky bastard, get it over with.

'The point I'm making,' Cordover said to the jury, approaching them with something close to reverence, 'is that there is prejudice against anyone even *suspected* of crimes against children. The Inspector happened to catch sight of a man who had served a single custodial sentence, and immediately suspected the worst, and *acted* on that suspicion – quite wrongly, as it turned out. No charges were made, the poisoner struck again, and I believe the innocent party is considering suing the police for wrongful arrest.' He nodded. 'Your tax money, I'm afraid.' He took a deep breath. 'Now, it may be that we can all understand the Inspector's feelings. The blood rises where children are involved. But I'd ask you: is it morally right? And does it contaminate the entire case against my clients, seeping down through the tools of the investigation, coming to rest with the very officers who conducted the inquiry?' He pointed towards Rebus, who felt now that he was in the dock rather than the witness box. Seeing his discomfort, Ramsay Marshall's eyes were twinkling with pleasure. 'Later, I shall produce further evidence that the initial police investigation was flawed from the outset, and that Detective Inspector Rebus here was not the only culprit.' He turned to Rebus. 'No more questions.'

And Rebus was dismissed.

'That was a tough one.'

Rebus looked up at the figure walking slowly towards him. He was lighting a cigarette, inhaling deeply. He offered one over, but she shook her head.

'Have you come across Cordover before?' Rebus asked.

'We've had our run-ins,' Jane Barbour said.

'Sorry I couldn't . . .'

'Not much you could have done about it.' She exhaled noisily, clutching a briefcase to her chest. They were outside the court building. Rebus felt gritty and exhausted. He noticed she was looking pretty tired herself.

'Fancy a drink?'

She shook her head. 'Things to do.'

He nodded. 'Think we'll win?'

'Not if Cordover has anything to do with it.' She scraped the heel of one shoe across the ground. 'I seem to be losing more than I'm winning lately.'

'You still at Fettes?'

She nodded. 'Sex Offences.'

'Still a DI?'

She nodded again. Rebus remembered a rumour about a promotion. So Gill Templer remained the only female chief inspector in Lothian. Rebus studied her from behind his cigarette. She was tall, what his mother would have called 'big-boned'. Shoulder-length brown hair fashioned into waves. Mustard-coloured two-piece with a light silk blouse. She sported a mole on one cheek and another on her chin. Mid-thirties . . . ? Rebus was hopeless with ages.

'Well . . .' she said, ready to leave but looking for an excuse not to.

'Goodbye then.' A voice sounded behind them. They turned and watched Richard Cordover walking to his car. It was a red TVR with personalised plate. By the time he was unlocking the car, he seemed to have forgotten about them.

'One cold bastard,' Barbour muttered.

'Must have saved him a few bob.'

She looked at Rebus. 'How's that?'

'He could skip the TVR's air-conditioning option. Sure about that drink? There's something I wanted to ask you . . .'

They bypassed Deacon Brodie's – too many 'clients' drank there – and headed for the Jolly Judge. Rebus had once had a drink there with an advocate who drank advocaat. Now Rangers had signed a Dutch manager called Advocaat and the jokes were being dusted off . . . He bought a Virgin Mary for Barbour and a half of Eighty for himself. They sat at a table below the stairs, well out of the way.

'Cheers,' she said.

Rebus raised his glass to her, then to his lips.

'So what can I do for you?'

He put down the glass. 'Just some background. You used to work MisPers, didn't you?'

'For my sins, yes.'

'What did you do exactly?'

'Collect, collate, stick them all into filing cabinets and computer memories. A bit of liaison, punting our MisPers to other forces and receiving theirs in return. Lots of meetings with the various charities . . .' She puffed out her cheeks. 'Lots of meetings with families, too, trying to help them understand what had happened.'

'Job satisfaction?'

'Up there with sewing mailbags. Why the interest?'

'I've got a missing person.'

'How old?'

'He's nineteen. Still lives at home; his parents are worried.'

She was shaking her head. 'Needle in a haystack.'

'I know.'

'Did he leave a note?'

'No, and they say he'd no reason to leave.'

'Sometimes there aren't reasons, not any that would make sense to the family.' She straightened in her chair. 'Here's the checklist.' She counted fingers as she spoke. 'Bank accounts, building society, anything like that. You're looking for withdrawals.'

'Done.'

'Check with hostels. Local, plus the usual cities – anything between Aberdeen and London. Some of them have charities who deal with the homeless and runaways: Centrepoint in London, for example. Get a description out. Then there's the National Missing Persons Bureau in London. Fax any details to them. You might ask the Sally Army to keep their eyes open too. Soup kitchens, night shelters, you never know who'll turn up.'

Rebus was jotting in his notebook. He looked up, watched her shrug.

'That's about it.'

'Is it a big problem?'

She smiled. 'Thing is, it's not a problem *at all*, not unless you're the one who's lost somebody. A lot of them turn up, some don't. Last estimate I saw said there could be as many as a quarter of a million MisPers out there. People who've just dropped out, changed their identity, or been dumped by the so-called "caring" services.'

'Care in the community?'

She gave her bitter smile again, drank some of her drink, checked her watch.

'I can see Shiellion must have come as a welcome break.'

She snorted. 'Oh yes, like a camping trip. Abuse cases are always a breeze.' She turned thoughtful. 'I had a double rapist a few weeks back, he ended up walking. Crown cocked it up, prosecuted it as a summary case.'

'Maximum sentence three months?'

She nodded. 'He wasn't up for rape this time, just indecent exposure. The Sheriff was furious. By the time remand was taken into account, the bastard had under two weeks to serve, so the Sheriff put him back on the streets.' She looked at Rebus. 'Psych report said he'd do it again. Probation and community service, with a bit of counselling thrown in. And he'll do it again.'

He'll do it again. Rebus was thinking of Darren Rough, but of Cary Oakes too. He checked his own watch. Soon Oakes would be touching down at Turnhouse. Soon he'd be a problem . . .

'Sorry I can't be more help about your MisPer,' she said, beginning to stand. 'Is it someone you know?'

'Son of some friends.' She was nodding. 'How did you know?'

'No offence, John, but you probably wouldn't be bothering otherwise.' She lifted up her briefcase. 'He's one out of quarter of a million. Who's got the time?'

12

There were reporters waiting inside the terminal building. Most carried mobile phones with which they kept in touch with the office. Photographers chatted to each other about lenses and film speeds and the impact digital cameras would eventually have. There were three TV crews: Scottish, BBC and Edinburgh Live. Everyone seemed to know everyone else; they were all pretty relaxed, maybe even looking a bit tired by the wait.

The flight was subject to a twenty-minute delay.

Rebus knew the reason why. The reason was that the Met officers at Heathrow had taken their time transferring Cary Oakes. Oakes had spent over an hour in Heathrow. He'd visited the toilet, had a drink in one of the bars, bought a newspaper and a couple of magazines, and taken a telephone call.

The telephone call had intrigued Rebus.

'He was paged,' the Farmer had informed him. 'Someone got a call through to him.'

'Who would that be?'

The Farmer had shaken his head.

Now Oakes was bound for Edinburgh. Detectives had accompanied him on to the flight, then had left again, keeping their eyes on the plane right up until it left London air space. Then they'd called their colleagues at Lothian and Borders HQ.

'He's all yours,' was the message.

The ACC (Crime) was putting the Farmer in charge. The Farmer didn't usually stray from his office: he was happy to delegate; trusted his team. But tonight . . . tonight was a bit special. So he was seated alongside Rebus in the squad car. DC Siobhan Clarke sat in the back. It was a marked car: they wanted Oakes to know about it. Rebus had been out to recce the scene, reporting back with news of the journos.

'Anyone we know?' Clarke asked.

'Usual faces,' Rebus said, accepting another piece of chewing gum from her. This was the bargain they'd made: he wouldn't smoke so long as she bought the gum. His reconnaissance had been an excuse for a ciggie.

The dashboard clock said the plane would be touching down any minute. They heard it before they saw it: a dull whine, lights flashing in the dark sky. They had one window down, stopping the car from steaming up.

'Could be the one,' the Farmer stated.

'Could be.'

Siobhan Clarke had all the paperwork beside her; she'd been doing her reading on Cary Dennis Oakes. She wasn't sure that they were serving any purpose here other than curiosity. Still, she *was* curious.

'Shouldn't take long,' she said.

'Don't bet on it,' Rebus said, opening his door again. He was digging in his pocket for a cigarette as he made towards the terminal doors.

He circumvented the huddle of pressmen and made for a No Entry sign. Showing his ID, he made his way towards the arrivals hall. He'd already had a word, and Customs and Immigration were waiting for him. He knew what happened with international transfers: there were no checks at Heathrow. Often, there were no checks at Edinburgh either: it depended on staff rotas; the cutbacks had bitten hard. But there'd be the full panoply of checks tonight. Rebus watched as the passengers from the Heathrow flight filtered into the terminal and began the wait for baggage. Businessmen mostly, carrying briefcases and newspapers. Half the flight carried hand-luggage only. They made their way briskly through Customs, cars waiting in the car park, families waiting at home.

Then there was the man wearing casual clothes: denims and trainers, red and black check shirt, white baseball cap. He carried a sports holdall. It didn't look particularly full. Rebus nodded to the Customs officer, who stepped out and stopped the man, bringing him over to the counter.

'Passport, please,' the Immigration officer said.

The man dug into his shirt-breast pocket and produced a new-looking passport. It had been applied for over a month back, when the Americans had known they'd be freeing him. The Immigration officer flipped through it, finding little but empty pages.

'Where are you travelling from, sir?'

Cary Oakes's eyes were on the man in the background, the man who'd arranged all this.

'United States,' he said. His voice was an odd mix of transatlantic inflexions.

'And what were you doing there, sir?'

Oakes smirked. He had the face of a weathered schoolboy, the classroom joker. 'Passing time,' he said.

The Customs officer had decanted the contents of his bag on to the counter. Washbag, change of clothes, a couple of razzle mags. A manila folder was full of drawings and photos clipped from magazines. They looked like they'd been pinned to a wall for a long time. There was a good luck card, too, telling him to 'fly high and straight' and signed by 'your buddies on the wing'. Another folder contained trial notes and newspaper court reports. There were two paperback books, one a Bible, the other a dictionary. Both looked well-used.

'Travel light, that's my motto,' Oakes informed them.

The Customs officer looked to Rebus, who nodded, keeping his stare fixed on Oakes. Everything was put back into the bag.

'This is actually pretty low-key,' Oakes said. 'And don't think I don't appreciate it. Quiet life's going to suit me for a while.' He was nodding to himself.

'Don't plan on sticking around,' Rebus said quietly.

'I don't think we've been introduced, Officer.' Oakes thrust out a hand. Rebus saw that the back of it was dotted with ink tattoos: initials, crosses, a heart. After a moment, Oakes withdrew the hand, laughing to himself. 'Not so easy to make new friends, I guess,' he mused. 'I've lost the old social skills.'

The Customs officer was zipping the holdall. Oakes grabbed its handles.

'Now, gentlemen, if you've had your fun . . .?'

'Where are you headed?' the Immigration man asked.

'A nice hotel in the city. Hotels for me from now on. They wanted to put me in some palace out in the country, but I said no, I want lights and action. I want some *buzz*.' He laughed again.

'Who's they?' Rebus couldn't help asking.

Oakes just grinned and winked. 'You'll find out, partner. Won't even have to do much detecting.' He hefted the bag and slung it over his shoulder, whistling as he walked away, joining the throng headed for the exit.

Rebus followed. The reporters outside were getting their photos and footage, even if Oakes had slid the baseball cap down over his face. Questions were hurled at him. And then an overweight man was pushing his way through, cigarette dangling from his mouth. Rebus recognised him: Jim Stevens. He worked for one of the Glasgow tabloids. He grabbed Oakes by the arm and said something into his ear. They shook hands, and then Stevens was in charge, manoeuvring Oakes through the huddle, proprietorial hand on his shoulder.

'Oh, Jim, for Christ's sake,' one of the other reporters cried.

'No comment,' Stevens said, the cigarette flapping at one corner of his mouth. 'But you can read our exclusive serialisation, starting tomorrow.'

And with a final wave, he was through the doors and off. Rebus made for another exit, got into the car beside the Farmer.

'Looks like he's made a friend,' Siobhan Clarke commented, watching Stevens put Oakes's bag into the boot of a Vauxhall Astra.

'Jim Stevens,' Rebus told her. 'He works out of Glasgow.'

'And Oakes is now his property?' she guessed.

'So it would seem. I think they're heading into town.'

The Farmer slapped the dashboard. 'Should have guessed one of the papers would nab him.'

'They won't hang on to him forever. Soon as the story's done . . .'

'But till then, they've got their lawyers.' The Farmer turned to Rebus. 'So we can't do *anything* that could be construed as harassment.'

'As you wish, sir,' Rebus said, starting the engine. He turned to the Farmer. 'So do we head home now?'

The Farmer nodded. 'Just as soon as we've tailed them. Let Stevens know the score.'

'There's a cop car after us,' Cary Oakes warned.

Jim Stevens reached for the cigarette lighter. 'I know.'

'Welcoming committee at the airport, too.'

'He's called Rebus.'

'Who is?'

'Detective Inspector John Rebus. I've had a few run-ins with him. What did he say to you?'

Oakes shrugged. 'Just stood there trying to look mean. Guys I met in prison, they'd have given him a nervous breakdown.'

Stevens smiled. 'Save it till the recorder's running.'

Oakes had the passenger-side window open all the way, angling his head into the fierce cold air.

'Does smoking bother you?' Stevens said.

'No.' Oakes moved his head to and fro, as if under a hair dryer. 'Clever of you to have me paged at Heathrow.'

'I wanted to be the first to make you an offer.'

'Ten grand, right?'

'I think we can manage ten.'

'Exclusive rights?'

'Got to be, for that price.'

Oakes brought his head back into the car. 'I'm not sure how good I'll be.'

'You'll be fine. You're a Scot, aren't you? We're born storytellers.'

'I guess Edinburgh's changed.'

'You've been away a while.'

'Oh, yes.'

'Do you still know anyone here?'

'I can think of a couple of names.' Oakes smiled. 'Jim Stevens, John Rebus. That's two, and I've only been in the country half an hour.' Jim Stevens started to laugh. Oakes rolled the window back up, leaned down to switch off the music. Turned in his seat so Stevens had his full attention. 'So tell me about Rebus. I'd like to get to know him.'

'Why?'

Oakes's eyes never left the reporter's. 'Someone takes an interest in me,' he said, 'I take an interest back.'

'Does that put me in the frame too?'

'You never know your luck, Jim. You just never know your luck.'

Stevens had wanted Oakes out of Edinburgh. He'd wanted him in seclusion for as long as it took to do the interviews. But Oakes had told him on the phone: it has to be Edinburgh. It just has to be. So Edinburgh it was; a discreet hotel in a New Town terrace. Stevens had to smile at 'New Town': everywhere else in Scotland, it meant the likes of Glenrothes and Livingston, places built from nothing in the fifties and sixties. But in Edinburgh, the New Town dated back to the eighteenth century. That was about as new as the city liked things. The hotel would have been a private residence at one time, spread over four floors. Understated elegance; a quiet street. Oakes took one look at it and decided it wouldn't do. He didn't say why, just stood on the steps outside, taking in the air, while Stevens made a couple of frantic calls on his mobile.

'It would help if I knew what you wanted.'

Oakes just shrugged. 'I'll know when I see it.' He waved a little wave towards where the police car had parked, its lights still on.

'Right,' Stevens said at last. 'Back in the motor.'

They headed down Leith Walk, towards the port of Leith itself.

'This still a rough part of town?' Oakes said.

'It's changing. New developments, Scottish Office. New restaurants and a couple of hotels.'

'But it's still Leith, right?'

Stevens nodded. 'Still Leith,' he conceded. But when they hit the waterfront and Oakes saw their hotel, he started nodding straight away.

'Atmosphere,' he said, looking out across the docks. There was a container ship tied up there, arc lights on as men worked around it. A couple of pubs, both with restaurants attached. Across the basin was a permanent mooring, a boat which had become a floating nightclub. New flats being built across there too.

'Scottish Office is just down there,' Stevens said, pointing.

'How long do you think they'll keep this up?' Oakes asked, watching the police car come to a stop.

'Not long. If they try it on, I'll phone our lawyers. I need to call them anyway, get your contract sorted.'

'Contract.' Oakes tried out the word. 'Long time since I've had a job.'

'Just talking into a microphone, posing for a few pictures.'

Oakes turned to him. 'For ten thou, I'll do re-enactments for you.'

Some of the colour slid from Stevens' face. Oakes was watching him intently, measuring the reaction.

'That probably won't be necessary,' Stevens said.

Oakes laughed, liking that 'probably'.

Inside the hotel, he approved of his room. Stevens couldn't get one next door, had to settle for down the hall. Stuck the rooms on plastic and said they'd need them for a few days. He found Oakes lying on the bed in his room, shoes still on, holdall on the bed beside him. He'd taken one item from it: a battered Bible. It lay on the bedside table. Nice touch: Stevens would use it in his intro.

'You a religious man, Jim?' Oakes asked.

'Not especially.'

'Shame on you. Bible'll teach you a lot of things. I got my first taste in prison. Time was, I'd no time for the Good Book.'

'Did you go to church?'

Oakes nodded, seeming distracted. 'We had Sunday service in the jail. I was a regular.' He looked to Stevens. 'I'm not a prisoner, right? I mean, I can come and go?'

'Last thing I want is for you to feel like a prisoner.'

'Makes two of us.'

'But there are a few rules, so long as *I'm* paying your way. If you go out, I want to know. In fact, I'd like to tag along.'

'Afraid the competition will hook me?'

'Something like that.'

Oakes turned his head, grinned. 'Supposing I want a woman? You going to be sitting in the corner while I hump her?'

'Listening at the door will be fine,' Stevens said.

Oakes laughed, wriggled on the mattress. 'Softest bed I ever had. Smells nice too.' He lay a moment longer, then swung swiftly to his feet. Stevens was surprised at the turn of speed.

'Come on then,' Oakes told him.

'Where?'

'Out, man. But don't fret, I'm not going more than fifty yards.'

Stevens followed him outside, but stayed by the hotel, could see where Oakes was headed.

The police car; lights still on; three figures inside. Oakes peered through the windscreen, headed for the driver's side, tapped on the glass. The one he now knew as Rebus wound down the window.

'Hey,' Oakes said by way of greeting, nodding his head to the other two – young woman, and a senior-looking man with a huge scowl on his face. He gestured towards the hotel. 'Nice place, huh? Any of you ever stay someplace like that?' They said nothing. He leaned one arm on the roof of the car, the other on the door panel.

'I was . . .' All at once he looked a little shy. 'Yeah,' knowing now how to put it, 'I was real sorry to hear about your daughter. Man, that's got to be a bitch.' Looking at Rebus with liquid, soulless eyes. 'One of the killings they pinned me for, girl would have been about the same age. I mean, same age as your daughter. Sammy, that's her name, right?'

Rebus pushed open his door so hard, it propelled Oakes back almost to the water's edge. The other man – Rebus's boss – was calling out a warning; the young woman was coming out of the car behind Rebus. Rebus himself was up in Cary Oakes's face. Jim Stevens was sprinting from the hotel.

Oakes had his hands raised high over his head. 'You touch me, it's assault.'

'You're a liar.'

'Say again?'

'They didn't charge you with anybody my daughter's age.'

Oakes laughed, rubbed his chin. 'Well, you've got something there. Guess that gives you the first round, huh?'

The woman officer was gripping one of Rebus's arms. Jim Stevens was panting after the short jog. The chief stayed sitting in the car, watching.

Oakes bent a little to peer in. 'Too important for all this, huh? Or no stomach for it? Your call, man.'

Stevens grabbed him by the shoulder. 'Come on.'

Oakes shrugged free. 'Nobody touches me, that's rule one.' But he allowed himself to be steered back across the road towards the hotel. Stevens turned round, found Rebus staring at him hard, knowing who'd told Oakes about him, about his family.

Oakes started laughing, laughed all the way to the hotel's glass doors. He stood on the inside, looking out.

'That Rebus,' he said quietly. 'He's not exactly what you'd call a slow burner, now is he?'

Back at Patience's flat in Oxford Terrace, Rebus poured himself a whisky and added water from a bottle in the fridge. She came through from the bedroom, eyes slanted in the sudden light, a pale yellow nightdress falling to her ankles.

'Sorry if I woke you,' Rebus said.

'I wanted a drink anyway.' She took grapefruit juice from the fridge door, poured herself a large glass. 'Good day?'

Rebus didn't know whether to laugh or cry. They took the drinks into the living room, sat together on the sofa. Rebus picked up a copy of *The Big Issue*: Patience always bought it, but he was the one who read it. Inside, there were fresh appeals for MisPer information. He knew if he turned on the TV and went to Teletext, there was a listing for missing persons. He'd watched it from time to time, scanning a few pages. It was run by the National MisPer Helpline. Janice had said she'd contact them . . .

'What about you?' he asked.

Patience tucked her feet beneath her. 'Same old story. Sometimes, I almost think a robot could do the work. Same symptoms, same prescriptions. Tonsils, measles, dizzy spells . . .'

'Maybe we could go away.' She looked at him. 'Just for a weekend.'

'We tried it, remember? You got bored.'

'Ach, that was the country.'

'So which romantic interlude did you have in mind? Dundee? Falkirk? Kirkcaldy?'

He got up for a refill, asked her if she wanted one. She shook her head, her eyes on his empty glass.

'Second one today,' he said, making for the kitchen.

'What's brought this on anyway?' She was following him.

'What?'

'The sudden notion of a holiday.'

He glanced towards her. 'I went to see Sammy yesterday. She said she speaks to you more than I do.'

'A bit of an exaggeration . . .'

'That's what I said. But she has a point all the same.'

'Oh?'

He poured less water into the glass this time. And maybe a drop more whisky too. 'I mean, I know I can be . . . distracted. I know I'm a pretty lousy proposition.' He closed the fridge, turned to her and shrugged. 'That's about it, really.'

Kept his eyes on the glass as he spoke, wondering why it was that as he said the words, a holiday snap of Janice Mee flashed across his mind.

'I keep thinking you'll come back,' Patience said. He looked at her. She tapped her own head. 'From wherever it is you've gone.'

'I'm right here.'

She shook her head. 'No you're not. You're not really here at all.' She turned away, walked back through to the living room.

A little later, she went to bed. Rebus said he'd stay up a bit longer. Flipped TV channels, finding nothing. Went to Teletext, page 346. Stuck the headphones on so he could listen to Genesis: 'For Absent Friends'. Jack Morton sitting on the arm of the sofa as screen after screen of missing persons appeared. No sign of Damon yet. Rebus lit a cigarette, blew smoke at the television, watching it dissolve. Then remembered this was Patience's flat, and she didn't like smoking. Back into the kitchen to extinguish his guilty pleasure. After Genesis, he switched to Family: 'Song for Sinking Loves'.

Something's gone bad inside you.

It was your lot wanted him here.

Saw two men in the dock, their lawyer working on the jury. Saw Cary Oakes leaning into the car.

He'll do it again.

Saw Jim Margolies take that final flight into darkness. Maybe there was no way to understand any of it. He turned to Jack. Often he'd phoned Jack – didn't matter what time of night it was, Jack never complained. They'd talk around subjects, share worries and depressions.

'How could you do that to me, Jack?' Rebus said quietly, drinking his drink as the room filled with ghosts.

It was late, but Jim Stevens knew his editor wouldn't mind. He tried the mobile number first. Bingo: his boss was at a dinner party in

Kelvingrove. Politicos, the usual movers and shakers. Stevens's boss liked all that crowd. Maybe he was the wrong man for a tabloid.

Or maybe, all these years down the road, it was Jim Stevens who was out of touch. He seemed surrounded by journalists younger, brighter, and keener than him. These days, you could be washed up at fifty. He wondered how long it would be till the cheque for services rendered was being countersigned at his editor's desk, how long before the young bloods in the office were having a whip-round to see off 'good old Jim'. He knew the drill, even knew the speeches they'd make – stuff any self-respecting sub would block and delete. He knew because he'd been there himself, back in the days when *he'd* been a young blood and the old-timers had been complaining about falling standards and the changing world of journalism.

Soon as Jim had heard about Cary Oakes, he'd taken his boss aside for a private word, then had checked flight schedules, brown-nosing Heathrow Information so they'd page the prodigal son.

'It's yours, Jim,' his editor had said, but with a warning finger. 'Could be the cream on the cake. Just make sure it doesn't turn sour.'

Now the boss was giving him a couple of snippets of gossip from the dinner party. He'd obviously had a few drinks. They wouldn't stop him heading into the newsroom afterwards. Twelve-hour days: a while since Jim Stevens had worked any of those.

'So what can I do you for, Jim?'

At last. Stevens took a deep breath. 'I've got us settled in at the hotel.'

'How does he seem?'

'All right.'

'Not a slavering monster or anything?'

'No, pretty quiet really.' Stevens deciding his boss needn't know about the blow-up with Rebus.

'And ready to give us the exclusive?'

'Yes.' Stevens lit a cigarette for himself.

'You might try to sound a bit more enthusiastic.'

'Just been a long day, boss, that's all.'

'Sure you've got the stamina, Jim? I could lend you one of the newsroom crew . . . ?'

'Thanks but no thanks.' Stevens heard his boss laughing. Ha bloody ha. 'That's not the kind of back-up that worries me.'

'You mean corroboration?'

'Lack of it, more like.'

'Mmm.' Thoughtful now. 'Got a game plan?'

'You worked for a year or two in the States, didn't you?'

'While back.'

'Still got friends there?'

'Might have one or two.'

'I need to hook up with someone on a Seattle paper, see if I can talk to one of the cops who worked the Oakes case.'

'One guy I knew now works news for CBS.'

'That'd be a start.'

'Soon as I get to the office, OK, Jim?'

'Thanks.'

'And Jim? Don't worry too much about confirmation. First thing you need to get from our friend Oakes is a bloody good story. Whatever it takes.'

Stevens put the phone down, lay back on his bed. Part of him wanted to chuck the job right now. But the other part was still hungry. It *wanted* those kids in the office to stare at him, wondering if they'd ever be as good, as sharp. It wanted Oakes's story. Afterwards, he could walk away if he liked: crowning glory and all that. He thought again of Rebus. Wondered what Oakes had to gain from sparring with him. From what Stevens knew, no one had ever got into the ring with Rebus and come away without at least a few cuts and bruises. And sometimes . . . sometimes there'd be traction and a hospital waiting.

But Oakes had looked keen. Oakes had looked ready, *making* Rebus come at him like that.

Jim Stevens was supposed to be Oakes's baby-sitter. But it seemed to him that Oakes had either an agenda or a death wish. Difficult to baby-sit either one.

'This is your last job, Jim,' Stevens promised himself. Decided a raid on the mini-bar would seal the contract.

13

The surveillance budget was so tight, they were reduced to singles. Four in the morning, Rebus couldn't sleep, so he drove down to the waterfront, stopping off at an all-night garage. Siobhan Clarke was in an unmarked Rover 200. She'd dressed for a mountain trek: trousers tucked into thick socks and climbing boots; thermal jacket and bobble hat. On the passenger seat: notebook and pen; three empty packets of lo-fat crisps; two flasks. Rebus climbed into the back and offered a microwaved pasty and beaker of coffee.

'Cheers,' she said.

Rebus looked out at the hotel. 'Any movement?'

She shook her head, chewed and swallowed. 'I'm a bit worried though. There are service exits to the back of the building. No way I can cover those.'

'He's probably jet-lagged anyway.'

'Meaning awake all night, asleep all day?'

'I hadn't thought of that.' Rebus leaned forward. 'He hasn't been out *at all*?'

She shook her head. 'All those years in jail, maybe he's turned agoraphobic.'

'Maybe.' Rebus knew she might have a point. He'd known ex-cons who just couldn't cope with the outside world – all that space and light. They ended up reoffending, only way they could get put away again.

'He ate dinner in the restaurant.' She nodded towards the plate-glass windows of the hotel's dining room.

'Did he spot you?'

'Not sure. His room's on the second floor. That window at the far end.'

Rebus looked. Twelve small square panes of glass. The window was open an inch at the bottom. 'How do you know?'

'I asked the manager.'

Rebus nodded: orders from the Farmer – no need to be subtle. 'How did the manager take it?'

'He seemed uncomfortable.' She took a final bite of pasty.

'Don't want to make Oakes's stay too pleasant, do we?'

'No, sir,' Clarke said.

Rebus opened his door. 'Just going for a recce.' He paused. 'What do you do when you need to . . .?'

She lifted one of the flasks, reached to the floor for a kitchen funnel.

'And what if . . .?'

'Self-control, sir.'

He nodded. 'Don't get your flasks mixed up, will you?'

Outside, the air was fresh. Sounds of night traffic at the port, the occasional taxi cruising past the end of the road. Taxis: he had to ask them about Damon and the woman. He walked around the side of the hotel, wandered into the car park. The service exits were locked. Beside them were four rubbish skips, separated by a high wooden fence from the guests' cars. Jim Stevens's Astra was easy to spot. Rebus tore a page from his notebook, scribbled a couple of words, folded the sheet and fixed it beneath a wiper blade. Back at the service doors, Rebus checked they couldn't be opened from outside. He left satisfied that even if Oakes used them to get out of the hotel, he'd have to use the front entrance to get back in.

Always supposing he'd come back. Maybe he'd just scarper: wasn't that what they wanted? No, not exactly: they wanted to be *certain* he'd left Edinburgh. Oakes missing from his hotel wasn't quite the same thing. Rebus went back to Clarke's car, got out his mobile and made a call. Hotel reception answered.

'Good evening,' Rebus said. 'Could you put me through to Mr Oakes's room, please?'

'One moment.'

Rebus winked at Clarke. He held the mobile between them so she could listen. A buzzing noise repeated three or four times. Then the pick-up.

'Yeah? What is it?' Sounding authentically groggy.

'Tommy, is that you?' Mock-Glaswegian. 'We're having a bit of a bevvy in my room. Thought you were coming up.'

Silence for a moment. Then: 'What room is it again?'

Rebus pondered an answer, cut the connection instead. 'At least we know he's there.'

'And awake now.'

Rebus checked his watch. 'Your shift ends at six.'

'If Bill Pryde doesn't sleep in.'

'I'll give him an alarm call for you.' Rebus made to leave the car again.

'Look, sir.' Clarke was nodding towards the hotel.

Rebus looked: second-floor window, right at the far end. No light on, but curtains open and a face at the window, peering out. Looking straight at them. Rebus gave Cary Oakes a wave as he made for his own car.

No need to be subtle.

At eight sharp he was in the office, typing up details of Damon Mee, preparing a blitz on charities, hostels and organisations for the homeless. At nine there was a message from the front desk. Someone to see him.

Janice.

'You must be psychic,' Rebus told her. 'I was just working on Damon. Any news?'

He was guiding her down Rankeillor Street. They'd find a café on Clerk Street. He didn't want to talk to her in the cop-shop. A bundle of motives: didn't want anyone to suspect he was working on a case that wasn't official L&B business; didn't want her seeing some of the stuff in St Leonard's – photos of MisPers and suspects, cases dealt with without emotion or (often) enthusiasm; and maybe, just maybe, he didn't want to share her. Didn't want the part of her that belonged to his past intruding on his here and now, his workplace.

'No news,' she said. 'I thought I'd spend the day in Edinburgh, see if I couldn't . . . I don't know. I have to do *something*.'

Rebus nodded. There were dark half-moons beneath her eyes. 'Are you getting much sleep?' he asked.

'The doctor gave me some pills.'

Rebus remembered the way her replies to questions could sometimes only *seem* to be answers.

'Do you take them?' She smiled, glanced at him. 'Thought not,' he said. It wasn't that Janice would lie to you, but you had to know how to phrase a question to make sure of getting a truthful response.

'We used to have these conversations all the time, didn't we?'

She was right, they did. Rebus wondering if she fancied any of his friends, trying to find ways of asking without seeming jealous. She telling him versions of her life before they'd started dating. Dialogues of the left-unsaid.

He guided her into the café. They took a corner table. The owner, recently arrived, had only unlocked the door because he recognised Rebus.

'I can't cook anything,' he warned them.

'Coffee's fine for me,' Rebus said. He looked to Janice, who nodded. Their eyes stayed on one another as the café owner walked away.

'Have you ever forgiven me?' she asked.

'For what?'

'I think you know.'

He nodded. 'But I want to hear you say it.'

She smiled. 'For knocking you out.'

He looked around. 'Keep your voice down, someone might hear.'

She laughed, the way he'd meant her to. 'You were always the joker, Johnny.'

'Was I?' He tried to remember.

'Did you keep in touch with Mitch?'

He puffed out his cheeks. 'Now there's a name from the past.'

'The two of you were like this.' She twisted two fingers together.

'I'm not sure that's legal these days.'

She smiled, looked down at the tabletop. 'Always the joker.' There were spots of red high on her cheeks. Yes, he'd been able to make her blush back then too.

'What about you?' he asked.

'What about me?'

'You and Barney.'

'Nobody calls him Barney these days.' She sat back in her chair. 'We were just friendly, stayed that way for a few years. One night he asked me out. Started seeing one another.' She shrugged. 'That's how it works sometimes. No Cupid's arrow, no fireworks. Just . . . nice.' She looked up at him, smiled again. 'As for the rest of the crew . . . Billy and Sarah are still around. They got married but split up, three kids. Tom's still around, got some industrial injury, hasn't been back to work in years. Cranny – you remember her?' Rebus nodded. 'Some moved away . . . a few died.'

'Died?'

'Car smashes, accidents. Wee Paula got cancer. Midge had a heart attack.' She paused as their coffees arrived, topped with a froth of milk.

'I've got some biscuits . . . ?' the café owner suggested. They shook their heads.

Janice blew on the coffee, sipped. 'Then there was Alec . . .'

'Never turned up?' Alec Chisholm, who'd gone to play football. Alec, who'd never reached the park.

'His mum's still alive, you know. She's in her eighties. Still wonders what happened to him.'

Rebus said nothing. He could see what she was thinking: *maybe that's my future too*. He leaned across the table, squeezed her hand. It was warm, pliant.

'You can help me,' he said.

She looked in her bag for a handkerchief. 'How?'

Rebus took out the list he'd printed that morning. 'Hostels and charities,' he told her. She blew her nose and examined the list. 'They all need contacting. I was going to do it myself, but we'd save time if you made a start.'

'OK.'

'Then there are the taxis. That means putting the word out, visiting each rank and letting them know what we need. Damon and the blonde, across the road from The Dome.'

Janice was nodding. 'I can do that,' she said.

'I'll give you a list of where to find them.'

The café owner was standing by the counter, smoking a breakfast cigarette and opening the morning's paper. Rebus caught a headline, knew he had to buy the paper for himself. Janice was checking in her purse.

'I'll get these,' Rebus told her.

'I'll need coins for the phone,' she said.

Rebus thought for a moment. 'Why not use my flat as a base? It's not that much more comfortable than most phone boxes, but at least you can sit down, have a cup of coffee . . .' He held out a bunch of keys to her. She looked at him.

'Are you sure?'

'Sure I'm sure.' He wrote his address on a page of his notebook, added his work and mobile phone numbers, tore the page out and handed it to her. She studied it.

'No secrets there you don't want anyone to see?'

He smiled. 'I don't use the place much, to be honest. There's a couple of local shops if you need—'

'So where do you usually stay?'

He cleared his throat. 'With a friend.'

Her turn to smile. 'That's nice.'

Why had he said 'friend' rather than 'lover'? Rebus wondered if they sounded as awkward as he felt: kids again, language the clumsiest form of communication.

'I'll give you a lift,' he said.

'Remember the list of taxi ranks,' she told him. 'And an A to Z if you've got one.'

Rebus went to pay. The owner rang it up on the till. His paper was open at a court headline: previous day's testimony from the Shiellion case. KIDS' BOSS BRANDED MONSTER. There was a photograph of Harold Ince being led to a police van by the court guard Rebus had shared a smoke with. Ince looked tired, ordinary.

That was the trouble with monsters. They could be every bit as ordinary as anyone else.

Jim Stevens couldn't hide the relief on his face when he walked into the dining room. He made for one of the window tables. A couple of guests nodded and smiled at him as he passed them. He got the idea they'd been in the bar last night.

'Morning, Jim,' Cary Oakes said, wiping egg yolk from the corners of his mouth. He gazed out of the window. 'Grey old day, just the way I remember.' He picked up the last triangle of fried bread and started working on it. 'Cops are still out there.'

Jim Stevens looked out of the window. An unmarked car, but unmistakable. A man in the driver's seat, chewing on a roll.

'How long do you think they'll keep it up?' Oakes asked.

Stevens looked at him. 'I tried phoning your room.'

'When?'

'Fifteen, twenty minutes ago.'

'I was down here, partner, soaking up the *ambience*.'

Stevens looked around for a waiter.

'You help yourself to fruit juices and cereals,' Oakes explained, nodding towards a self-serve area. 'Then they take your order for the hot breakfast.'

Stevens looked at Oakes's greasy plate. 'After last night, I think I'll stick to orange juice and coffee.'

Oakes laughed. 'That's why I don't drink.' Last night he'd been on pints of orange and lemonade: Stevens remembered now. 'Besides,' Oakes said, leaning over the table towards the reporter, 'when I drink I do crazy things.'

'Save it for the tape machine, Cary.'

When the waiter came, Oakes asked if he could have another cooked breakfast. 'Just the bits I missed out on last time.' He studied the menu. 'Uh, how about fried liver, some onions and maybe some fried haggis and black pudding.' He patted his stomach, smiling at Stevens. 'Just today, you understand. The fitness regime recommences tomorrow.'

When the food arrived, Stevens, who'd been knocking back orange juice and trying to steel himself for toast, took one look at the plate and made his excuses. He drifted outside, lit a cigarette. There was a cold breeze blowing in from the docks. Just through the dock gates, he could see the Scot FM building. Turning his head, he saw the cop in the car watching him. He didn't recognise the face. Through the dining room window, Oakes was tucking in with exaggerated relish, teasing the detective. Smiling, Stevens walked around to the car park, examined the executive motors: Beamers, Rover 600s, an Audi. Noticed something on the windscreen of his own car. At first he took it for a piece of rubbish, gusted there. Then thought maybe it was a flyer for a carpet sale or antique show. But when he unfolded it, he knew who it was from. Two words:

DROP HIM.

Stevens tucked the note in his pocket, headed back to the hotel. Oakes had finished breakfast and was sitting on one of the sofas in reception, flicking through a newspaper: one of the broadsheets.

'I'm hurt,' he said. 'After that scrum at the airport . . .'

'Try the tabloids,' Stevens said, sitting down opposite him. 'Plenty of coverage there. I think my favourite is "Killer Cary Comes Home".'

'Well, isn't that nice?' Oakes tossed the paper aside. 'So when do we get down to work?'

'Let's say fifteen minutes in your room?'

'Fine by me. Before that, though, I've another favour to ask.'

'What?'

'Someone I want to find. His name's Archibald.'

'Plenty of those around.'

'That's his surname. First name, Alan.'

'Alan Archibald? Should I know him?'

Oakes shook his head.

'Care to tell me who he is?'

'He was a policeman – maybe still is. Got to be getting on a bit, though.'

'And?'

Oakes shrugged. 'For now, that's all you need. If you're a good boy, I'll maybe tell you the story.'

'For what we're paying you, we want *all* the stories.'

'Just find him, Jim. You'll make me happy.'

Stevens studied his charge, wondering just who was pulling the strings. He knew it should be him. But all the same . . .

'I can make a couple of calls,' he conceded.

'That's my boy.' Oakes got to his feet. 'Fifteen minutes in my room. Bring all the papers with you. I like being the day's news.'

And with that he set off towards the stairs.

14

It was Jamie's job to fetch milk, papers and breakfast rolls from the shop. He'd turned it into an art, skimming cash by lying about the prices. His mum complained, knew they could be found cheaper elsewhere, but 'elsewhere' wasn't walking distance for Jamie. She didn't like him straying too far. That was fine: whenever he wanted to wander the city, he had Billy Boy to say he'd been round at his house.

Jamie thought he was pretty smart.

He stopped outside the shop for a cigarette. He didn't buy them there – it was against the law and the Paki owner wouldn't let him. Instead, he had a deal with an older kid at school, who supplied packets of twenty in exchange for scud mags. Jamie got the mags from under Cal's bed. There were so many of them, Cal never seemed to notice. Even in freezing weather, Jamie liked his smoke outside the shop. Early-rise kids on their way to school would stare at him. Friends would sometimes join him. He got noticed.

A neighbour once told his mum, and she'd tried whacking him, but he was super-fast and dodged beneath her arm, spinning out of the door, laughing at her curses. One time she'd really gone for him had been when the school had sent the letter home. He'd been skiving, whole weeks at a time. His mum had belted him purple and sent him crying to his room, face red with shame at his own tears.

He'd probably go to school some time today. Cal was good at forging letters. He'd been doing it so long, the school thought *his* signature was their mum's, and when she'd signed some note about going on a school trip, the headmaster had quizzed Jamie about its origins. He'd even picked up the phone to talk to Jamie's mum, which had made Jamie smile: they didn't have a telephone in the flat. About two dozen ashtrays, most of them from holidays or nicked from pubs, but no telephone. Cal had a mobile, and that's what they used in emergencies – when Cal was in a mood to let them.

That was the problem with Cal. He could be great . . . and then he could lose the rag. Boom: like a bottle exploding against a wall. Or he'd get all quiet and lock himself in his room and refuse to write notes to the school. Jamie would go out and get him something, maybe nick it from a shop: peace offerings for some wrong he hadn't done. On good days, Cal would rub knuckles hard against Jamie's head, tell him he was the peacemaker: Jamie liked the sound of that. Cal would say he was the United Nations, sustaining an uneasy truce. He got stuff like that from the papers: 'United Nations'; 'uneasy truce'. Jamie asked him once: 'If nations are supposed to be united, how come we want to split away?'

'How do you mean, pal?'

'Split from England.'

Cal had folded the newspaper on his lap, flicked ash into an ashtray on the arm of his chair. 'Because we don't like the English.'

'How no?'

'Because they're *English.*' An edge to Cal's voice, telling Jamie to back off.

'We've got cousins in England, haven't we? We don't hate them, do we, Cal?'

'Look . . .'

'And fighting the Germans, we fought with the English, didn't we?'

'Look, Jamie, we want to run our own country, OK? That's all it is. Scotland's a country, isn't it?' He'd waited for Jamie's nod. 'Then who should be in charge of it? London or Edinburgh?'

'Edinburgh, Cal.'

'Right then.' Picking up the paper: discussion adjourned.

Jamie had a lot more questions, but never seemed to get answers. His mum was useless: 'Don't talk to me about politics,' she'd say. Or 'Don't talk to me about religion.' Or anything, really. As if she'd done all the hard thinking in her life, found satisfactory answers, and wasn't about to start over again for *his* benefit.

'That's why you've got teachers,' she'd say.

Which was fair enough, but at school Jamie had a rep to maintain. He was *Cal Brady's brother*. He couldn't go asking the teachers questions. They'd begin to wonder about him. Cal had told him a long time ago: 'With school, Jamie, it's definitely "us" and "them", know what I mean? A battlefield, pal, take no prisoners, understood?'

And Jamie had nodded, understanding nothing.

As he stood at the shop, tapping the toe of one shoe against a rubbish bin, along came Billy Horman. Jamie straightened a bit.

'All right, Billy Boy?'

'No' bad. Got a fag?'

Jamie handed over one of his precious cigarettes.

'See the football last night?'

Jamie shook his head, sniffed. 'Not bothered,' he said.

'Hearts, ya beauties.' The way Billy looked at him as he said this, seeking approval or something, Jamie knew Billy had heard it from someone else, maybe his mum's boyfriend, and wasn't sure about it.

'They're doing OK,' Jamie conceded as Billy mimed a blazing shot at goal.

'You going home?' Billy asked.

Jamie tapped the paper and rolls, held under one of his arms.

'Wait a minute, I'll come with you.' Billy marched into the shop, came out again with milk and a carton of marge. 'Mum went spare this morning. Her new man got in from the pub and had about ten slices of toast.' He tossed the marge and caught it. 'Finished the tub.'

Jamie didn't say anything. He was thinking about fathers, how it was funny neither Billy nor he had one. Jamie wondered where his was, which story about him to believe.

'Who was that you were with yesterday?' he asked as they began walking.

'Eh?'

'Bottom of St Mary's Street. An uncle or somebody?'

'Aye, that's it. My Uncle Bill.'

But Billy Boy was lying. His ears always went red when he lied . . .

Back at the flat, Jamie took the paper into Cal's bedroom.

'About fucking time, wee man.' Cal lying in bed, portable telly on. The room smelled stale. Jamie sometimes tried to hold his breath. Cal had a mug of tea on the floor beside his ashtray.

'Switch the channel, will you?'

The TV was on a chest of drawers at the bottom of the bed. It didn't have a remote. Cal had just brought it home one night, said he won it in a bet at the pub. There was a little square beside the panel of buttons. It said 'Remote Sensor'. So Jamie knew there should be a remote with it. He had to jump over a pile of Cal's clothes on the floor to get to the TV. Pressed the button for Channel 4. You got some dolls on the breakfast show – Cal had taught him the word: dolls.

Jamie leapt back over the clothes and fled the room, letting out a huge exhalation in the hallway. Twenty-five seconds: not even near his record for breath-holding. His mum was buttering rolls at the kitchen table. She handed him one. He got himself a mug of milk and sat down. He'd told his mum that because of cutbacks, his school didn't start till half past nine. Either she'd believed him, or hadn't been up to arguing. She looked tired, his mum, looked like she needed a treat. But he knew looks could deceive: she could go from tired to mental in two seconds flat. He'd seen her do it with one of the old hoors from upstairs who'd come to complain about the noise. Pure mental. Same thing with the old guy who'd complained of the ball landing in his garden.

'Next time I'll put a garden fork through it, so help me.'

'Do that,' Jamie's mum had said, 'and I'll take your fucking fork and stick it through your balls.' Right up close to him, growing huge as he seemed to shrink.

Jamie had a lot of respect for his mum. Last time she'd clipped him, it had been because he'd tried calling her Van. Cal called her Van, but that was all right because he was grown up, same as she was. Jamie couldn't wait to grow up.

With a mug of tea in her hand, his mum went through her morning ritual: trying to remember where she'd put her cigarettes.

'Maybe Cal's got them,' Jamie suggested.

'Finish what's in your mouth before you speak.' She yelled towards Cal's room, got a yelled denial back. In the living room, she pulled cushions off the sofa and chair, kicked the pile of car and music magazines sitting on the floor. Found half a packet on top of the hi-fi. The top of the flip-pack was missing. Cal used them for his 'special roll-ups'. His mum pulled out a cigarette, but most of it was missing too. She sighed heavily, stuck it in her mouth anyway and lit it with the lighter she found inside the packet.

She didn't have any pockets, so put the cigarettes on the arm of her chair. She was wearing silver-grey shell-suit bottoms with a purple zip-up jogging top. The top was old, the lettering on its back – SPORTING NATION – cracked and peeling. Jamie wondered if Sporting Nation meant Scotland.

Roll and milk finished, he slid off his chair. He had plans for today: Princes Street maybe, or a bus out to The Gyle. On his own, or with anyone he could round up. Problem with The Gyle was, it was in the middle of nowhere. There was a games arcade on Lothian Road, he liked it there, but there were other regulars who were better than him at the games, and even if he didn't want to play against them, they'd stand and watch him on his machine, then tell him what mistakes he was making and say they could do better with their wrists in plaster.

Just as well, he knew he should tell them, *because the way you're going, your whole body's going to end up in plaster*. But he never did: most of them were bigger than him. And they didn't know Cal, so he was no use as a threat. Which was why Jamie didn't go in there so much any more . . .

Cal's bedroom door flew open and he stalked into the kitchen. He had his jeans on, but had forgotten to zip them up or buckle his belt. No shoes or socks, no T-shirt. He had nicks and bruises on his chest and arms. You could see the muscles moving beneath his skin. He flung the paper on to the table and slapped a hand down on it.

'Look at this,' he hissed, face pink with anger. 'Just take a look at this.'

Jamie looked: double-page story. SEX OFFENDER WITH PLAY-GROUND VIEW. There were photos. One showed a block of flats, an arrow pointing to one of the storeys. The other showed a patch of tarmac and a couple of kids playing.

'That's here,' he said, amazed. He'd never seen Greenfield in the papers before, never seen photos of the place. His mum came over.

'What is it?' she asked.

'Fucking pervert living right under our noses,' Cal spat. 'Nobody told us.' He stabbed the paper. 'Says so right here. Nobody bothered to tell us.'

Van studied the story. 'There's no picture of him.'

'No, but they as good as point at the bastard's door.'

She remembered something. 'Cops came round the other day. I thought they were looking for you.'

'What did they want?'

'Just the one of them. Asked if I knew somebody called . . .' She squeezed shut her eyes. 'Darren something-or-other.'

'Darren Rough,' Jamie said. Cal stared at him.

'You know him?'

Jamie didn't know what answer would please Cal. He shrugged. 'Seen him around the place.'

'How do you know his name?' Eyes burning into him.

'He . . . I don't know.'

'He what?' Cal was facing him now, fists bunched. 'Which flat's he in?' Jamie started to tell him, but Cal snatched the neck of his shirt. 'Better still, show me.'

But as they walked along the landing to Darren Rough's flat, they saw that others had the same idea. A group of seven or eight residents stood outside Rough's door. Most of them had the morning paper with them, rolled up and brandished like a weapon. Cal was disappointed they weren't the first.

'Is he no' in?'

'No' answering anyway.'

Cal kicked at the door, saw from the looks around him that they were impressed. Stood back and shouldered the door, kicked it again. Two locks: Yale and mortice. No way to see inside: letterbox was blocked up; a sheet pinned across the window. Everyone was talking about it.

'Wake up, ya bastardin' pervert!' Cal Brady shouted at the window. 'Come and meet your fan club!' There were smiles around him.

'Maybe he works shifts,' someone offered. Cal couldn't think of a smart remark to make back. He thumped on the window instead, then went back to kicking the door. A few more residents arrived, but more began to drift away. Soon there were just a couple of kids, plus Cal and Jamie.

'Jamie,' Cal said, 'go get me a spray can. Try under my bed.'

Jamie already knew there were a couple of cans under there. 'Blue or black?' he asked, before he realised what he'd done.

But Cal didn't notice. He was busy staring at the door. 'Doesn't matter,' he said. Jamie went off to fetch the can. His mum was outside, arms folded, talking with a couple of women from the landing. Jamie trotted past them.

'Well?' his mum said.

'Nobody's in.'

She turned back to her friends. 'Could be anywhere. Scum like that, there's no telling.'

'What we need's a petition,' one of the women said.

'Aye, get the council to rehouse him.'

'Think they'll listen to us?' Van said. 'Direct action, that's what we want. Our problem, we deal with it, never mind what anyone else says.'

'People's Republic of Greenfield,' another woman offered.

'I'm serious, Michele,' Van said, 'deadly serious.' Behind her, Jamie disappeared into the flat.

15

'Mum and me, we seemed to move around a lot in the early days.'

Cary Oakes was in a chair by his bedroom window, feet up on the table in front of him. Jim Stevens sat on a corner of the bed, holding the tape recorder at arm's length.

'Places? Dates?'

Oakes looked at him. 'I don't remember the names of towns, people we stayed with. When you're a kid, that sort of thing doesn't matter, does it? I had my own life, my own little fantasy world. I'd be a soldier or a fighter pilot. Scotland would be full of aliens, and I'd be out to get them, a vigilante sort of scenario.' He gazed out of the window. 'Because we moved so much, I never really made any friends. Not close friends.' He saw that Stevens was about to interrupt. 'Again, I can't give any names. I remember coming to Edinburgh, though.' He paused, stretched to rub his thumb across the toe of one shoe, removing a trace of dirt. 'Yes, Edinburgh sticks in my mind. We stayed with family. My aunt and her husband. Don't remember which part of town they lived in. There was a park nearby. I went there a lot. Maybe we could get a picture of me there.'

Stevens nodded. 'If you can remember where it is.'

Oakes smiled. 'Any park would do, wouldn't it? We'd just pretend. That's what I did in that park. It was my universe. *Mine*. I could do whatever the hell I liked there. I was God.'

'So what did you do?' Stevens was thinking: this is easy, fluid. Oakes was either a born storyteller or else . . . or else he'd been rehearsing. But something had jarred, something about family: *my aunt and her husband*. A strange way of putting it.

'What did I do? I played games, same as every other kid. I had an imagination, I'll tell you that. When you're a kid, nobody minds if you run around shooting up the world, know what I'm saying? In your head, you can kill whole populations. I'll bet there isn't one damned person on this planet hasn't thought about murdering someone at *some* time. I'll bet you have.'

'I'll show you my collection of voodoo dolls.'

Oakes smiled. 'My mum, she did her best for me.' He paused. 'I'm sure of that.'

'What happened to her?'

'She died, man.' His eyes bored into the reporter's. 'But then everybody dies.'

'You played these games by yourself?'

Oakes shook his head. 'The other kids got to know me. I joined a gang, rose through the ranks.'

'See much action?'

Oakes shrugged. 'There were a few fights. Mostly we just played football and glowered at strangers. Offed a few of the neighbourhood cats too.'

'How?'

'Sprayed them with lighter fluid, torched them.' Oakes's eyes fixed on Stevens. 'Typical start to your basic serial killer. I read about it in jail. Loner who torches animals.'

'But you weren't alone, you were with your gang.'

Oakes smiled again. 'But I was the one with the lighter, Jim. And that made all the difference.'

When they took a break, Stevens returned to his own room. Two sachets of coffee into a cup of boiling water. He'd been wakened at four that morning by the telephone. His boss had worked a miracle, and Stevens found himself speaking to a Seattle journalist who'd followed the Oakes case all the way along. The journalist, Matt Lewin, confirmed that Oakes had attended regular Sunday services in the Walla Walla penitentiary.

'A lot of them do, doesn't mean they've seen the light.'

Now Stevens lay back on the bed and sipped his coffee. He wanted to track down Oakes's teenage gang. It would be good background, another insight into Cary Oakes. If they ran the story, maybe someone from the gang would read it and come forward. Then Stevens could interview them for the book. He'd asked Matt Lewin if any American publishers would be interested.

'Not when he's not one of ours. We like home-grown product. Besides, Jim, serial killers went out of fashion a while back.'

Stevens was hoping for a fashion revival. The book deal would be his gold watch, a little retirement gift to himself. He knew he should do some research, try to check the stories Oakes had been telling. But he felt so tired, and his boss had told him: get the story first, confirm it later. He finished his coffee and reached for a cigarette. Swung his legs off the bed.

Showtime.

Janice Mee took a break, ate at the restaurant at the top of John Lewis's. From one window, the view was of Calton Hill. They'd climbed it with Damon one day, back when he was seven or eight. She had photos of the trip in one of her albums: Calton Hill, the Castle, Museum of Childhood . . . There were dozens of albums. She kept them in the bottom of the wardrobe. She'd taken them out recently, brought the whole lot downstairs so she could go through them, reviving memories of holiday camps and days at the seaside, birthday parties and sports days. From one of the restaurant's other windows, she had a good view of the Fife coastline. She couldn't see as far inland as her home town. There were times in the course of her life when she'd contemplated a move: south to Edinburgh, north to Dundee. But there was something comfortable about the place where you were born, where your family and friends were. Her parents and grandparents had been born in Fife, the history of the place inextricably linked to her own. Her mother had been a little girl at the time of the General Strike, but remembered them putting up barricades around Lochgelly. Her father had clung to a lamp-post to watch Johnny Thomson's funeral. The way a family stretched back in time could be measured. But that sense of history misled you into thinking the future would be the same. As Janice was finding out, the thread of continuity could be snapped at any point along the way.

She ate the roll, filled with prawn mayonnaise, without any pleasure or sense of taste. She knew she'd drunk her coffee only because the cup was empty. One pale prawn sat on the rim of the plate, where it had fallen from the roll. She left it where it was and got up from the table.

Outside the St James' Centre she crossed Princes Street and headed for Waverley Station. A line of taxi cabs snaked from the underground concourse back up on to Waverley Bridge. The drivers sat behind their wheels, some reading or eating or listening to their radios. Others staring into space or sharing news with fellow drivers. She started at the back of the queue and worked her way forwards. John Rebus had given her some names. One of them was Henry Wilson. The drivers all seemed to know him, called him 'The Lumberjack'. They put out a call to him. Meantime, she showed them her pictures of Damon and explained that he'd been picked up on George Street.

'Anyone with him, love?' one driver asked.

'A woman . . . short blonde hair.'

The driver shook his head. 'I've a good memory for blondes,' he said, handing back the flyer.

The problem was, a couple of trains had just arrived – London and Glasgow. The taxis were moving faster than she could, heading down to where their passengers waited. She looked back up the slope. More taxis were joining the back of the queue. She couldn't tell who she'd talked to and who was new. Engines were starting, fumes getting into her lungs. Cars sounding their horns as they moved past her, heading down into the station, wondering what she was doing on the roadway when there was a pavement the other side. Day-trippers looked at her, too. They knew she'd never get a taxi here, knew the system: you queued at the rank.

Her mouth felt sour and gritty. The coffee had been strong: she could feel her heart pounding. And then another car sounded its horn.

'All right, all right,' she said, passing down the line to the next taxi, which was already moving off. The car-horn sounded again: right behind her. She turned on it, glowering, saw it was another black cab, window open. Nobody in the back, just the driver, leaning towards her. Short black hair, long black beard, green tartan shirt.

'Lumberjack?' she said.

He nodded. 'That's what they call me.'

She smiled. 'John Rebus gave me your name.' Cars were held up behind him. One flashed its lights.

'You better get in,' he said. 'Before they have my licence off me for obstruction.'

Janice Mee got in.

The taxi went down into the station, and took the exit ramp back up, then turned right and crossed the traffic, settling at the back of the queue of cabs. Henry Wilson pulled on the handbrake and turned in his seat.

'So what does the Inspector want this time?'

And Janice Mee told him.

It had to be serious: instead of summoning him, the Farmer had come looking for Rebus, who was out in the car park having a cigarette and thinking about Janice Playfair aged fifteen . . .

'Is it the surveillance?' Rebus asked, thinking maybe something had happened.

'No, it bloody well isn't.' The Farmer stuck his hands in his pockets: he meant business.

'What have I done this time?'

'The press have got hold of Darren Rough. One paper printed the story this morning, the rest are busy catching up. My secretary's fielded so many calls, she doesn't know if she's in St Leonard's or St Pancras.'

'How did they get the story?' Rebus asked, ditching his cigarette.

The Farmer narrowed his eyes. 'That's what Rough's social worker wants to know. He's ready to make a formal complaint.'

Rebus rubbed at his nose. 'He thinks I did it?'

'John, I know bloody well you did it.'

'With respect, sir—'

'John, just shut up, will you? The reporter you spoke to, first thing he did when you'd put the phone down was hit 1471. He got the number you were calling from.'

'And?'

'And it was The Maltings.' Public house: almost directly across the street from St Leonard's. 'But better than that, our intrepid reporter asked the punter who answered about the person who'd last used the phone. Want me to read you the description?'

'Male, white, middle-aged?' Rebus guessed. 'Could be a thousand blokes.'

'Could be. Which hasn't stopped Rough's social worker thinking it's you.'

Rebus looked out towards Salisbury Crags. 'I'm glad somebody shopped him.' He paused. 'If that was what it was going to take.'

'Take to do what? To run him out of town? To get a mob baying for his blood? John, I'd hate to see what you'd do to Ince and Marshall.'

Ince and Marshall: the Shiellion accused.

'You wouldn't have to watch,' Rebus said. He squared up to his boss. 'What do you want me to do?'

'Steer clear of Rough, that's number one. Stay on the Oakes surveillance, at least that way you'll keep out of trouble for six hours at a stretch. And give Jane Barbour a bell.' He handed Rebus a slip of paper with a phone number on it.

'Barbour? What does she want?'

'No idea. Probably something to do with Shiellion House.'

Rebus stared at the phone number. 'Probably,' he said.

The Farmer left him to it, and instead of going back into the station, Rebus walked down the lane towards the main road, checked for traffic and walked briskly across. Stepped into The Maltings. It was quiet most daytimes. When he'd made the call, there'd only been one other drinker in the place. A minute after opening time, the same man was alone at the bar with a half-pint and a whisky in front of him.

'Alexander,' Rebus said, 'a word with you, please.' He pulled the drinker by his arm towards the gents' toilets: didn't want the barmaid listening in.

'Christ, man, what is it?' The drinker's name was Alexander Jessup. He didn't like Alex or Alec or Sandy or Eck: it had to be Alexander. He'd run his own business at one time: a printer's. Did headed paper, account books, raffle tickets and the like. Sold it on and was quietly drinking the proceeds away. As a man about town, he heard things, but never gave Rebus much that proved useful. He did like to talk though; he'd talk to anyone who'd listen.

'Any reporters been after you?' Rebus asked.

Jessup looked at him with rheumy eyes, like those of an old dog. He shook his head. His face was a mess of puffiness and burst capillaries.

'You spoke to one on the phone,' Rebus reminded him.

'Was he a reporter?' Jessup looked stung. 'He never said.'

'You gave him my description.'

'I might've done.' He thought about it, nodded, then held up a finger. 'But no names, you know me, John. I never gave him your name.'

Rebus kept his voice low. 'If anyone comes looking, keep the description as vague as you can, understood? You never saw the guy on the phone before, he's not a regular.' He waited for the message to sink in. Jessup gave him an enormous wink.

'Message received.'

'And understood?'

'And understood,' Jessup confirmed. 'I didn't get you into trouble, did I?' Dying to know. 'You know I'd never do something like that.'

Rebus patted his shoulder. 'I know, Alexander. Just remember who brings you your breakfast when they've put you in the cells for the night.'

'Right enough, John.' Jessup gave an 'OK' sign with his hand. 'Sorry if I got you into any bother.'

Rebus pulled open the door. 'Here, let me buy you one, eh?'

'Only if you'll take one back.'

'It's tempting,' Rebus said, as they headed for the bar. 'I'd be lying if I said that it wasn't.'

'Have you been drinking?' Janice Mee asked.

Rebus didn't reply straight away; he was too busy looking around his living room. Janice laughed.

'Sorry,' she said. 'Couldn't help myself.'

The place had been tidied: newspapers and magazines now took up space on the bottom bookshelf. Books which had been scattered across the floor were on the second and third shelves up. Mugs and plates had vanished into the kitchen, takeaway wrappers and beer cans deposited in the bin. Even the ashtray had been cleaned. Rebus picked it up.

'I think that's the first time I've been able to make out what it says.'

It was lifted from a pub, advertising some new beer which hadn't made the grade.

Janice smiled. 'It's something I do when I'm nervous.'

'You should be nervous round here more often.'

She gave him a punch.

'Careful,' he said, 'last time you tried that, I was out cold for ten minutes.'

'I bought teabags and milk while I was out,' she told him, making for the kitchen. 'Do you want a cup?'

'Please.' He followed the trail of her perfume. He hadn't brought Patience here in over a year; had never entertained many women here. 'So how did it go?'

'I liked The Lumberjack.'

'But was he any help?'

She made herself busy with the kettle. 'Oh, you know . . .'

'Did you get round all the cab ranks?'

'Your friend said I didn't need to. He'd do it for me.'

'Which left you feeling useless again?'

She tried to smile. 'I thought . . . I thought coming here I could . . .' She bowed her head, voice dropping to a whisper. 'I'd have been better off staying at home.'

'Janice.' He turned her so she was facing him. 'You're doing your best.' Her height, her softness and slenderness. They stood as close together now as they had done when they'd danced at the school leaving party, their last night as a couple. Formal dances: waltzes and military two-steps and the Gay Gordons. She wanting each dance to last; he wanting to take her round the back of the school, to their secret place – the same secret place everyone else used.

'You're doing your best,' he repeated.

'But it's not helping. Know what I found myself thinking today? I thought: I'll kill him for putting me through this.' Bitter twist of a smile. 'Then I thought: what if he's already dead?'

'He's not dead,' Rebus said. 'Trust me on this. He's not.'

They took the tea through to the living room, sat at the dining table.

'What time are you headed back?' he asked.

'I thought six. There's a train around then.'

'I'll drive you.'

She shook her head. 'Even a country girl like me knows what the traffic's like that time of day. I'd be quicker on the train.'

Which was true. 'I'll run you to the station then.' What else had he to do before his shift started, other than try to doze for a while?

She placed her hands around the mug. 'Why a policeman, Johnny?'

'Why?' He tried to form an answer she'd accept. 'I'd been in the army, didn't like it, didn't know what I wanted to do.'

'It's not exactly the kind of job you drift into.'

'For some of us it is. See, I really got into it.'

'And you're good at what you do?'

He shrugged. 'I get results.'

'Is that not the same thing?'

'Not exactly. Keeping your head down and your nose clean, being good at the office politics . . . I fall down there.' He shifted in his chair. 'You always said you were going to be a teacher.'

'I was a teacher . . . for a while.'

Rebus refrained from saying that his ex-wife had been a teacher too.

'Then you married Brian?' he asked instead.

'The two aren't connected.' She looked down into her tea, seemed relieved when the phone rang. Rebus picked it up.

'Evening, Mr Rebus.'

'Henry,' Rebus said for Janice's benefit, 'got anything for us?'

'Might have. Two fares, picked up on George Street. Driver remembered the blonde. Distinctive face, he said. Kind of hard. Cold eyes. He thought maybe she was a pro.'

'Where did he take them?' Rebus looking at Janice, who had stood up, still clutching the mug.

'Down to Leith, dropped them by The Shore.'

Leith: where the city's working girls plied their trade. The Shore: where Cary Oakes's hotel was.

'Did he see where they went?'

'The lad wasn't a big tipper. My mate got straight back on the road. Someone had tried flagging him down on Bernard Street. Not many places they could have been going. That time of night, the pubs would be on last orders if they weren't already shut. There are flats down there, though.'

Rebus agreed. Flats . . . and the hotel.

'Unless they were going to that boat,' Wilson said.

'What boat?'

'The one that's tied up down there.' Yes: Rebus had seen it, looked like a semi-permanent mooring. 'They use it for parties,' Wilson was saying. 'Not that I've ever been to one . . .'

He dropped Janice off at Waverley's concourse. They'd arranged to meet the next afternoon, go look at the boat.

'May be something or nothing,' Rebus had felt obliged to warn her.

'I'll settle for that,' she'd said.

As she made to leave the car, she hesitated, then leaned towards him and planted a kiss on his cheek.

'What, no tongues?' he said, smiling. She made to thump his arm, thought better of it. 'Say hello to Brian from me.'

'I will. If he's not out with his pals.' Something in her tone made Rebus want to pursue the subject, but she was out of the car, closing the door. She waved, blew him a kiss, turned and walked towards her platform with the look of a woman who knows she's being watched. Rebus realised he had one hand on his door handle.

'Forget it,' he told himself. Instead, he picked up his mobile, told Patience's machine that he was on night shift and was headed back to his own flat for a bit of kip.

But first, a pit-stop at the Oxford Bar: whisky with plenty of water. Just the one: responsible car-driver. He caught up on the gossip, adding little to the conversation. George Klasser chastised him for a lapse of faith.

'You're becoming an irregular regular, John.'

'I always was, Doc.'

Further along the bar, a rugby argument was developing, drawing other drinkers in. Everyone had an opinion, everyone but Rebus himself. He stared at a print on the wall: portrait of Robert Burns. There was another on the far wall: Burns meeting a young Walter Scott. It looked like a fairly awkward affair, the artist working with benefit of hindsight. It was as if Burns knew the child before him was destined to outsell him, knew the runt would get a knighthood, build Abbotsford and cosy up to the King.

It was a great thing, hindsight.

He looked into his glass and saw the leavers' dance. Saw a gangly kid called Johnny leading his girlfriend out of the hall, out the school doors and down the steps. Making like it was a game, but tugging her hard by both hands. Both of them pretending it was all right, because that was part of the whole ritual. And back in the hall, Johnny's pal Mitch – best friends; always sticking up for one another – not realising he was being stalked by three boys who'd become his enemies. Boys who knew this might be their last chance for revenge. Revenge for what? They probably didn't know themselves. Maybe for some ugly feeling that life had already short-changed them; that people like Mitch were going to succeed where they'd taste only failure.

Three against one.

While Johnny Rebus played out another fate entirely.

Rebus finished his drink, drove home. Sank into his chair, a double malt in his fist. Listened to Tommy Smith, *The Sound of Love*. Pondered whether or not you really could *hear* love.

Fell asleep in the orange sodium glow of the streetlights.

As close to being at peace as he got.

It had taken them a while to find a church with an unlocked door.

'No one has any trust these days,' Cary Oakes had said, 'not even God.'

They'd walked through Leith and up the Walk to Pilrig. It was a Catholic church, nobody around but them. Cool and dark inside. There were plenty of windows, but the church was surrounded on three sides by tenement buildings. Time was, as Stevens recalled, you weren't allowed to build anything higher than a church. Oakes was sitting in a pew near the front, head bowed. He didn't look exactly peaceful or contemplative: his neck and shoulders were tensed, his breathing fast and shallow. Stevens wasn't comfortable. The door might not have been locked, but he felt like a trespasser. A Catholic church, too: he didn't think he'd been in one of those his whole life. Didn't look much different from the Presbyterian model: no smell of incense. Confession boxes, but he'd seen those before in films. One of them, the curtain was open. He glanced in, trying not to think that it looked like a Photo-Me booth. He tried to take soundless steps; didn't want a priest appearing, having to explain what they were doing there.

Oakes's request: 'I'd like to go to church.'

Stevens: 'Can't it wait till Sunday?'

But Oakes's eyes had told him it was no joking matter. So they'd headed off on foot, the surveillance car following at a crawl, drawing attention to itself and to them.

'They want to play it that way,' Oakes had said, 'that's fine by me.'

Ten, fifteen minutes passed. Stevens wondered if maybe Oakes had nodded off. He walked down the aisle, stopped beside him. Oakes looked up.

'A couple more minutes, Jim.' Oakes motioned with his head. 'Take a break, if you like.'

Stevens didn't need telling twice. Stepped outside for a cigarette. Cop car parked at the end of the street, driver watching him. He'd just got one lit when the thought struck him: you're a reporter on a story. You should be in there, trying to find an angle, running phrases through your head. Oakes in church: it could open one of the book chapters. So he nipped the cigarette, slipped it back into the packet. Pushed open the door and went inside.

There was no sign of Oakes in any of the pews. Sound of running water. Stevens peered into the gloom, eyes adjusting slowly. A shape over by the confessional. Oakes standing there, looking over his shoulder towards Stevens, body arched as he urinated through the curtain. Oakes grinned, winked. Finished his business and zipped himself up. He was walking back up the aisle, back to where Stevens stood, face failing to disguise his shock. Oakes pointed up towards the ceiling.

'Got to remind Him just who's boss, Jim.' He moved past Stevens and out into daylight. Stevens stood there a moment longer. Pissing into the confessional: a message to God, or to the reporter himself? Stevens turned and left the church, wondering how the hell his world had come to this.

16

A young DS called Roy Frazer was the fourth member of the surveillance team. He'd arrived at St Leonard's the previous month, a rare recruit from F Division, based in Livingston. Edinburgh city cops knew the Livingston operation as 'F Troop'. They'd had a few digs at Frazer, but he'd been able – or at least willing – to take them. The Farmer had chosen Frazer for the team. The Farmer thought Frazer was a bit special.

Rebus sat beside him in the Rover, listening to his report.

'Only real highlight,' Frazer was saying, 'that restaurant next to the pub back there, they took pity on me, brought me out a meal.'

'You're kidding.' Rebus looked back towards the pub in question. Just past closing time, and drinkers were taking their grudging leave.

'Carrot soup, then some chicken thing in puff pastry. Wasn't bad at all.'

Rebus looked down at the carrier bag he'd brought with him: flask of strong coffee; two filled rolls (corned beef and beetroot); chocolate and crisps; some tapes and his Walkman; an evening paper and a couple of books.

'Brought it out on a tray, came back half an hour later with some coffee and mints.'

'You want to be careful, son,' Rebus cautioned. 'No such thing as a free dinner. Once you start taking bribes . . .' He shook his head ruefully. 'I mean, it might have been the done thing in Livingston, but you're not in the sticks now.'

Frazer saw at last that he was joking, produced a grin which was two parts relief to one part humour. He was strong-looking, played rugby for the police team. Cropped black hair, square-jawed. When he'd arrived at St Leonard's, he'd sported a thick moustache, but had shaved it off for some reason. The skin beneath still looked pink and delicate. Rebus knew he came from farming stock – somewhere between West Calder and the A70. His father still farmed there. Something he had in common with The Farmer, whose family had worked the land around Stonehaven. Another thing the two men shared: regular church-going. Rebus, too, went to churches, but seldom on a Sunday. He liked them empty except for his thoughts.

'Have you got the log?' Rebus asked. Frazer produced the A4-sized notebook. Bill Pryde had taken over from Siobhan Clarke at 6 a.m., recorded that Oakes and Stevens had stayed in the hotel until eleven. Up till then, they hadn't come downstairs – he'd checked with the front desk. Morning coffee for two had been ordered for Oakes's room. Pryde's interpretation: they were working. A cab had arrived at eleven, and both men had come out of the hotel. Stevens had handed a large envelope to the cabbie, who'd driven off again. Pryde's guess: tape of first interview, heading for the newspaper office.

With the taxi gone, Stevens and Oakes had walked into Leith Docks, Pryde following on foot. They looked like they were killing time, taking a breather. Then it was back to the hotel. Siobhan Clarke took over at noon: Rebus had persuaded her to change shifts with him. Not that it had been difficult: 'I like my own bed at night,' she'd admitted.

The afternoon had gone much as the morning: the two men ensconced in the hotel; taxi taking delivery of an envelope; the two men taking a break. Except this time they'd headed into town, stopping at a church in Pilrig. Rebus looked at Frazer.

'A church?'

Frazer just shrugged. After the church, they'd headed to the top of the Walk and John Lewis's, where they shopped for clothes for Oakes. New shoes, too. Stevens put everything on his plastic. Then they'd hit a couple of pubs: the Café Royal, Guildford Arms. Clarke had stayed outside: 'Didn't know whether to go in or not. It's not as if they didn't know I was there.'

Back to the hotel, Oakes giving her a wave as she pulled up outside.

Relieved by Frazer at 6 p.m. The two men, Stevens and Oakes, had walked to one of the new restaurants built facing the Scottish Office. One wall was all glass, affording them a view of Frazer as he kicked his heels outside. Apart from his own surprise dinner – not mentioned in the notebook – that was about it.

'Would I be right in thinking this is a complete waste of time?' Frazer stated when Rebus had finished reading.

'Depends on your parameters,' Rebus said. He'd lifted the line from a training course at Tulliallan.

'Well, they're obviously here for the duration, aren't they?'

'We just want Oakes to know.'

'Yes, but surely the time to let him know is when he's left to his own devices. Once he's found himself a place to live, and all the media stuff's finished.'

Frazer had a point. Rebus conceded as much with a slow nod of his head. 'Don't tell me,' he said, 'tell the Chief Super.'

'That's just what I did.' Rebus looked at him, waiting for more. 'He turned up about nine o'clock, wanting to know how things were going.'

'And you told him?'

Frazer nodded; Rebus laughed.

'What did he say?'

'He said to give it a few more days.'

'You know they think Oakes might kill again?'

'Only person within range at the moment is that reporter. Anything happened to him, I'd be heartbroken.'

Rebus burst out laughing again. 'Know something, Roy? You're going to be all right.'

'The power of prayer, sir.'

Rebus had been in the car by himself for an hour, cold seeping inside his three pairs of socks, when he saw someone push open the door of the hotel and step outside. The hotel bar was still open, wouldn't close till the last guest had had enough. Stevens wore his tie loose around his neck, top two shirt buttons open. He was blowing cigarette smoke up into the sky, shuffling his feet to keep his balance. Been there, done that, Rebus thought. Eventually, Stevens focused on the police car, seemed to find it amusing. Chuckled to himself, bending forward at the waist, shaking his head slowly. Came walking towards the car. Rebus got out, waited for him.

'So we meet at last, Moriarty,' Stevens said. Rebus folded his arms, leaned against the car.

'How's the baby-sitting?'

Stevens puffed out his cheeks. 'To tell you the truth, I'm having trouble getting a handle on him.'

'How do you mean?'

'All that time behind bars – no pun intended – you'd think he might want to celebrate.'

'I'm guessing he doesn't drink.'

'Your guess is correct. Says drink contaminates his mind, makes him feel dangerous.' A humourless laugh.

'How much longer?' Rebus could smell the whisky on Stevens' breath. Give him a minute or two, he'd place the brand.

'Couple more days. It's good stuff, wait till you read it.'

'Know what the Yanks told us? They said he'll kill again.'

'Really?'

'Has he said anything?'

Stevens nodded. 'Gave me a list of his next victims. Nice tie-in with the story.' Stevens grinned lopsidedly, saw the look on Rebus's face. 'Sorry, sorry. Not in very good taste. I've got a publisher interested, did I tell you? Coming back to me tomorrow or the day after with an offer.'

'How can you do it?' Rebus asked quietly.

Stevens got his balance back. 'Do what?'

'Do what you do.'

'Sounds like a Motown line.' He sniffed, coughed. 'It's an interesting story, Rebus. That's what he means to me: a story. What does he mean to you?' He awaited a response, didn't get one, wagged a finger. 'That note you left me: "Drop him". Think I'd suddenly see the light, hand him over to somebody else, some other paper? No chance, pal. This isn't the Damascus Road.'

'I'd noticed.'

'And my boy's not the only ex-offender in the news, is he? I see someone outed a paedophile. Word is, it was a cop.' He tutted, wagged his finger again. 'Any comment to make, Inspector?'

'Go fuck yourself, Stevens.'

'Ah, now there's another thing. Guy's been in the nick fourteen years, and here we are in Leith, Edinburgh's knocking-shop, and he's not interested. Can you credit that?'

'Maybe he's got other things on his mind.'

'Wouldn't bother me if he preferred chickens, just so long as he gets me a book deal.' He rubbed his hands together. 'Look at us, eh? You out here, me in that big hotel. Makes you think.'

'Go to bed, Stevens. You need all the beauty sleep you can get.'

Stevens turned away, remembered something and turned back. 'OK for a wee photo-shoot tomorrow night? Photographer's coming anyway, and I thought it'd make a nice sidebar: cop who'll never sleep while killer's at large.'

Rebus said nothing, waited till the reporter had turned away again. 'What did he want in the church?' The question stopped Stevens cold. Rebus repeated it. Stevens half-turned towards him, shook his head slowly, then walked back across the road. There was something tired in the walk now, something Rebus couldn't interpret. He reached into the car for his cigarettes, lit one. Closed the driver's door and walked fifty yards to the end of the road, then across the bridge to the other side of the basin, where a boat was moored. There was a sign telling patrons to respect the neighbours and keep the noise down late at night. But the boat wasn't being used tonight, no private party or celebration. Nearby, they were building more 'New York loft-style apartments' for young professionals, part of Leith's revival. Rebus crossed back to the pub, but it was closed now. The bar staff would probably be inside, enjoying a drink as they replayed the evening's highlights. Rebus walked back to the car.

An hour later, a taxi pulled up outside the hotel. His first thought: another tape for the newspaper. But someone was in the taxi. They paid the driver, got out. Rebus checked his watch. Two fifteen. One of the guests who'd been out on the town. He took a nip from his quarter-bottle, slipped the headphones back on to his ears. String Driven Thing: 'Another Night in This Old City'.

That's all it ever was . . .

Forty minutes later, the man from the taxi exited the hotel. He waved back to the night porter. Window down, Rebus heard him say, 'Good night.' He stood outside, glanced at his watch, looked up and down the street. Looking for a taxi, Rebus thought. Who would be visiting a hotel this time of night? *Who* would he be visiting?

The man's gaze fell on the police car. Rebus wound the window down further, flicked ash on to the roadway. The man was making his way towards the car. Rebus opened his door, got out.

'Inspector Rebus?' The man held out his hand. Rebus gave him a once-over. Late fifties, well-dressed. Didn't look the type to pull a stunt, but you could never be sure. The man read his thoughts, smiled.

'I don't blame you. Middle of the night, stranger wants to make friends, already knows your name . . .'

Rebus narrowed his eyes. 'We've met before, haven't we?'

'A while back. You've got a good memory. My name's Archibald. Alan Archibald.'

Rebus nodded, finally shook Archibald's hand. 'You had a posting at Great London Road.'

'For a couple of months, yes. Before I retired, I was based at Fettes, pushing paper around a desk.'

Alan Archibald: tall, cropped salt-and-pepper hair. A face full of strong features, a body resisting the ageing process.

'I heard you'd retired.'

Archibald shrugged. 'Twenty years in, I thought it was time.' His look said: what about you? Rebus's mouth twitched.

'It's warmer in the car. I can't offer you a lift, but I could probably . . .'

'I know,' Alan Archibald was saying. 'Cary Oakes told me.'

'He what?'

Archibald nodded towards the car. 'I'll take you up on your offer, though. I'm not used to night shifts these days.'

So they got into the car, Archibald tucking his black woollen overcoat around him. Rebus ran the engine, stuck the heating on, offered Archibald a cigarette.

'I don't, thanks all the same. But don't let me stop you.'

'You'd need heavy artillery to stop me,' Rebus said, lighting another for himself. 'So what's the story with Oakes?'

Archibald touched his fingers to the dashboard. 'He called me, told me where he was.' He looked at Rebus. 'He knows all about you.'

Rebus shrugged. 'That's the point.'

'Yes, he knows that too. But he knew *you* were on the late shift.'

'Not difficult. He can see me from his bedroom window.' Rebus pointed towards it. 'Or maybe his minder told him.'

'The journalist? I didn't meet him.'

'Probably in bed.'

'Yes, I had to ring up to Oakes's bedroom. He wasn't sleeping, though, told me it's jet-lag.'

'How did he get your number?'

'It's unlisted.' Archibald paused. 'I'm guessing the journalist pulled a few strings.'

Rebus inhaled smoke, let it pour down his nostrils. 'So what's the story?'

'My guess is, Oakes wants to play some game.'

Rebus looked at his passenger. 'What sort of game?'

'The sort that gets me out of bed at one in the morning. That's when he phoned, said we had to meet now or never at all.'

'What about?'

'The murder.'

Rebus frowned. 'Murder singular?'

'Not one of the ones he committed in the States. This happened right here in Edinburgh. More specifically, out at Hillend.'

Hillend: at the northern tip of the Pentland Hills – hence the name. Known locally for its artificial ski-slope. From the bypass, you could see the lights at night. Suddenly, Rebus remembered the case. An outcrop of rocks, a woman's body. Young woman: student at a teacher-training college. Rebus had helped with the initial search. The search had taken him from Hillend to Swanston Cottages, an extraordinary cluster of homes, seemingly untouched by modernity. All at once he'd wanted to buy a place there, but it had been too isolated for his wife – and outwith their means anyway.

'This was fifteen years ago?' Rebus said.

Archibald shook his head. He'd slipped his hands into his pockets, was staring at the windscreen. 'Seventeen years,' he told Rebus. 'Seventeen years this month. Her name was Deirdre Campbell.'

'Were you on the case?'

Archibald shook his head again. 'Wasn't possible at the time.' He took a deep breath. 'Never found the killer.'

'She was strangled?'

'Beaten about the head, then strangled.'

Rebus remembered Oakes's *modus operandi*. Again, it was as if Archibald could read his mind.

'Similar,' he said.

'Was Oakes here at the time?'

'It was just before he left for the States.'

Rebus gave a low whistle. 'He's owned up?'

Archibald shifted in his seat. 'Not exactly. When he was arrested in the States, I followed his trial, noticed similarities. I went out there to interview him.'

'And?'

'And he played his little games. Hints, smiles and half-truths and stories. He led me a merry little dance.'

'I thought you weren't on the case?'

'I wasn't. Not officially.'

'I don't get it.'

Archibald examined his fingertips. 'All these years he's been inside, we've played his games. Because I know I can wear him down. He doesn't know how persistent I can be.'

'And now he phones you in the middle of the night?'

'And feeds me more stories.' A half-smile. 'But he doesn't seem to realise, the gameboard has changed. He's in Scotland now. *My* rules.' A pause. 'I've asked him to come out to Hillend with me.'

Rebus stared at Archibald. 'The man's a killer. Psych reports say he'll do it again.'

'He kills the weak. I'm not weak.'

Rebus wondered about that. 'Maybe he's switched games,' he said.

Archibald shook his head. He looked like a man obsessed. Jesus, Rebus could write the book on that one: cases which grabbed you and wouldn't let go; unsolveds which stayed with you all the long sleepless nights. You sifted through them time and again, examining the grains of sand, seeking anomalies . . .

'I still don't get it,' Rebus said. 'You weren't on the original case . . . how come you're . . .'

Then he remembered. It should have come to him sooner. The story had gone around at the time, had been passed between the searchers on the hillside.

'Oh shit,' Rebus said. 'She was your niece . . .'

17

It had been easy, finding an unoccupied room in the hotel. Simplicity itself to pick the door lock. So it was that Cary Oakes sat in darkness at the window, a window unwatched by Detective Inspector John Rebus. He had to smile: the watcher had become the watched, without realising it.

There was an *A–Z* on his lap. He'd told Stevens he needed it so he could reacquaint himself with his city. Earlier, Stevens had let slip that Rebus used to live in Arden Street, and maybe still did. Arden Street in Marchmont. Page 15, square 6G. Alan Archibald lived in Corstorphine, or had done when he'd written to Oakes in prison. All those letters, he'd never once let the prisoner know his phone number. It had taken Oakes less than a day to discover it. Strength in knowledge; always surprise your opponent – that's how games were played.

Oakes watched the two men talking in the car. He felt a certain pride, almost like running a dating agency. He'd brought the two of them together; he felt sure they'd get along. They sat there for an hour, even sharing a hot drink from a flask. Then a patrol car turned up – Rebus must have radioed for it. Wasn't that thoughtful: a free ride home for the retired detective. Archibald had aged well, maybe out of spite. Oakes knew *he* didn't look as fresh as the day he'd been incarcerated. Flesh sagged from his face, and there was a dead look to his eyes, despite the regular vitamins and exercise regime.

He slipped a hand into his pocket, felt a fold of banknotes there. He'd been drinking at the bar, spinning a line to some business types, Stevens his quiet partner. Stevens had given up eventually, left them to it. Oakes had learned many trades during his time inside. Lock-picking was one; pocket-picking another. He'd left the credit cards alone: that was the sort of thing that could be traced, get him in trouble. He let cash alone be his guide. He knew Stevens wanted him to be dependent on the paper, knew that was why Stevens was holding back payment. Well, for now he needed Stevens, but that would change. And meantime, he had work to do.

And the money would be his means.

He left the room and made his way down the stairs to the first-floor landing. At the end was a window which opened on to a line of lock-up garages. Eight-foot drop to the roof of the nearest garage. He crouched on the windowledge, waited for the taxi to come. Heard its engine as it rolled towards the hotel. He'd given the name and room number of one of his drinking companions. He listened for the moment when the taxi would pass Rebus's car, the moment when the detective would be least likely to hear anything, then dropped through the darkness on to the roof, sliding down and on to solid tarmac. Not even pausing for breath or to dust himself off, immediately jogging towards the wall which would take him into the lane, the lane which would take him away from the hotel.

With any luck, he'd pick up a taxi. There'd be one coming along in a minute, its driver disgruntled and seeking a fare . . .

Four in the morning, Darren Rough reckoned it would be safe. Everyone would be asleep. He counted himself lucky: out late the night before this, picking up an early edition of his paper on the way home, seeing his story twisted there. He'd been in the flat, Radio Two playing quietly so as not to disturb the neighbours: they had kids, kids needed sleep, everyone knew that. Radio barely audible, tea and toast, sitting by the gas fire.

Then coming upon those pages. Reading just the first couple of paragraphs, enough to make him screw the paper up, pace the floor, start hyperventilating. He breathed into a paper bag until the attack passed. Felt weak, crawling into the bathroom on hands and knees. Splashed water from the toilet on to his face and neck. Hauled himself up on to the pan, sat there for a while, head bowed under its massive weight. When he got back the use of his legs, he uncrumpled the paper, spread it out on the floor. Read the story through.

So it starts again, he thought to himself.

Knew he had to get out before morning. Spent the rest of the night walking the streets, bones cold and aching with tiredness. A café first thing for breakfast. His social worker didn't get into the office till nine, said he'd talk to a solicitor, see what grounds they had for a complaint. Said everything would be fine.

'We just have to ride it out.'

Easy words from a warm office; warm family probably waiting at home too. The car his social worker drove was an estate; kids' football boots in the back. Family man, doing his nine-to-five.

The rest of that day, Darren kept his distance from Greenfield. Walked as far as the Botanics, pretended to be interested in the plants. Kept warm in the hothouses: did about a dozen circuits. Back into town, Princes Street Gardens: he managed an hour's kip on a bench, until a policeman told him to move on. His plight was remarked on by a group of travellers. They offered him cigarettes and strong lager. He stayed with them for an hour, but didn't like them: too scruffy; not his kind of people at all.

Art galleries; churches: there was a lot that was free in Edinburgh. By evening, he reckoned he could write his own guidebook. Ate in a fast-food restaurant, taking as long as he could over the meal. Then a pub on Broughton Street. Waiting for a day to pass . . . it made you realise why people needed goals, needed work. He liked a structure to his day. Liked not to feel hunted.

After closing time, he'd met some more travellers, listened to more of their stories. Then had made his way carefully back towards Greenfield, turning away three times before finally confronting his own fear and overcoming it. Goal achieved.

He crept up the stairwell, expecting at every turn to find a waiting face, a knife-blade. Nothing. Just shadows. Along the landing, past closed doors, sleeping windows. His key sounded like a wood-saw as he slipped it into the lock. Then he noticed his hands were sticky. Stood back, noticed for the first time that his door was smeared with mud . . . No, not mud: excrement. He could smell it on the back of his hand, his knuckles, fingers. And beneath the shit, something in black paint, some writing. He crouched, wiped his hands on the concrete flooring, looked up at the message.

MONSTER YOU DIE.

The word DIE was underlined twice, just so he wouldn't miss it.

This was the park.

It hadn't changed. They'd installed some swings and a roundabout, but the roundabout was gone, leaving only a metal stump. The swings were thick rubber tyres. Tarmac underfoot, playing field off to the left. Trees had been planted, but looked stunted. His aunt's house . . . you could see a thin vertical slice of the park from the upstairs bathroom window, peering between two blocks of terraced housing. The house was still there, in darkness, curtains closed. He'd shared a bedroom with his mother at the back of the house, with a view down on to a small neglected garden, the hut which had become his refuge.

There hadn't been much refuge in the park. The local gang hung out there, and Cary was never allowed to join. He was an 'incomer', an 'outsider', the two terms sounding like opposites. He stayed on the periphery, clinging to the park railings, until one of them, fed up of cursing him, would come over to administer a kicking.

And he'd take it. Because it was better than nothing.

The one time he'd stalked a cat, squirting lighter fluid on it, watching the tail catch fire . . . there'd been no one there to see him. Police had questioned the gang, but no one had bothered with Cary Oakes. No one had bothered to ask 'the runt'.

He stood by the fence now. Half of it was missing. Middle of the night, no one was about. No cars passed. No one to see him as his hands worked at the rusted railings, turning them in their sockets.

Then a sound: drunken laughter. Three of them, young, wandering, not bothered who heard them, whose sleep they might be disturbing. The teenage Cary had lain awake late into the night, hearing above his mother's breathing the sounds of revellers as they headed home, some singing songs about King Billy and the Sash.

Three of them, not worried about waking anyone because *they* ruled this place. They ran in the local gang. *They* were all that mattered.

They were on the other side of the road, but saw Oakes, saw him looking at them.

'What you staring at?'

No answer. They started a conversation among themselves, didn't seem to be stopping.

'One of them paedophiles.'

'Always hang out in parks.'

'Or maybe a poof like.'

'This time of night, just standing there . . .'

Now they'd stopped. Turning back, crossing the road. Three of them. Excellent odds.

'Hiy, pal, what you up to, eh?'

'Thinking about things,' Oakes said quietly, one hand still working at the railing. The three youths looked at each other. They'd spent the night in town, pubbing and clubbing. Booze and some drugs maybe. A mix to up the aggression and confidence. While they were still considering what to do with this stranger, and which one of them should take the lead, Oakes hauled the steel rail up out of the fence and swung it. Caught the first one across the nose, which burst open like a flower in one of those speeded-up film jobs. Hands went to face as the young man screeched and dropped to his knees. As the rail finished one arc, Oakes swung it back again, pendulum-style, caught number two on the ear. Number three swung a kick, but the rail whacked against his shin, then swung upwards to smash into his mouth, breaking teeth. Oakes dropped the weapon. Broken Nose he felled with a kick to the throat. Eardrum he smashed with his fist. Shin and Teeth was limping away, but Oakes walked after him, tripped him, then sent a flurry of kicks to his head.

He stood up straight afterwards, got his breathing under control. Looked around at the houses he remembered so well. No one had moved from bed. No one had seen him in his moment of victory. He wiped the toes of his shoes against the prone figure's shirt, examined them to make sure they hadn't been scuffed in the fight. Walked over to Eardrum and pulled him up by the hair. Another squeal. Oakes put his lips close to the ear that wasn't bleeding.

'This is *my* place now, understood? Anyone fucks with me gets tenfold back.'

'We didn't—'

Oakes pressed his thumb hard against the bleeding ear.

'None of you would ever listen.' He was looking towards the gap in the terrace, where his aunt's house stood. He threw the youth's head hard against the ground. Patted it once, then turned to walk away.

At twenty past six, Rebus crept into Patience's flat on Oxford Terrace, armed with bread still warm from the oven, fresh milk and newspaper. He made himself a mug of tea and sat in the kitchen, reading the sports pages. At six forty-five he put the radio on, just as the central heating was kicking in. Made a fresh pot of tea, poured out a glass of orange juice for Patience. Sliced the bread and got a tray ready. Took it into the bedroom. Patience peered at him with one eye.

'What's this?'

'Breakfast in bed.'

She sat up, arranged the pillows behind her. He laid the tray on her lap.

'Have I forgotten some anniversary?'

He pushed a strand of hair back from her eyes. 'I just didn't want you oversleeping.'

'Why not?'

'Because as soon as you get up, I'm into that bed and asleep.'

He dodged the butter-knife as she swiped it at him. They were both laughing as he started to unbutton his shirt.

Jim Stevens went down to breakfast, expecting to find Cary Oakes halfway through another fry-up. But there was no sign of him. He asked at reception, but nobody had seen him. He called up to Oakes's room: no answer. He went up and banged on the door: ditto.

He was back in reception, ready to demand a duplicate key, when Cary Oakes came walking in through the hotel door.

'Where the hell have you been?' Stevens asked, feeling almost dizzy with relief.

'No caffeine for you this morning, Jim,' Oakes said. 'Look at you, you've got the shakes already.'

'I asked where you'd been.'

'Got up early. Guess I'm still on US time. Walked down by the docks.'

'Nobody here saw you leave.'

Oakes looked over towards the reception desk, then back to Stevens. 'Is there a problem? I'm here now, aren't I?' He opened his arms wide. 'Isn't that what counts?' He placed a hand on Stevens' shoulder. 'Come on, let's eat.' Started leading them towards the dining room. 'Have I got some great stuff for you this morning. Your editor's going to offer to blow you when he reads it . . .'

'Just another day at the office then,' Stevens said, wiping sweat from his brow.

18

The businessman who owned the Clipper Night-Ship asked Rebus if he wanted to make him an offer.

'I'm serious. I'd be happy to make a loss, only no one wants to buy her.'

He explained that the Clipper had brought him little but headaches. Licensing hassles, complaints from local residents, a council investigation, police visits . . .

'All that so punters can have a piss-up on a boat. I could run a pub with less grief and bigger takings.'

'So why don't you?'

'I used to: the Apple Tree in Morningside. But at that time it seemed like every pub had to have a gimmick. God knows what it's all about with Irish pubs: whoever came up with the notion they're any better than Scottish ones? Then there's the other theme pubs – Sherlock Holmes or Jekyll and Hyde, or pubs for Australians and South Africans.' He shook his head. 'I took one look at the Clipper and thought I was on a winner. Maybe I am, only sometimes it seems like a lot of hard work and sweet FA to show for it.'

They were seated in the offices of PJP: Preston-James Promotions. Rebus and Janice Mee were one side of the desk, Billy Preston the other side. Rebus didn't think Preston would appreciate being informed that his namesake used to play keyboards for the Beatles and the Stones.

Billy Preston was in his mid-thirties, immaculately turned out in a grey collarless suit with a metallic shine to it. You got the feeling nothing would stick to him, a regular Teflon Man. His head was shaved, but his long square chin sported a Frank Zappa beard. The offices of PJP took up two rooms on the first floor of a building halfway down Canongate. Below was a shop specialising in antiquarian maps.

'We'd move,' Preston had told them, 'find somewhere bigger, somewhere with parking, only my partner says to hold fire.'

'Why?' Rebus had asked.

'The Parliament.' Preston had pointed out of the window. 'Two hundred yards that way. Property around here is rocketing. We'd be mugs to sell.' He kept playing with his computer mouse, running it over its mat, clicking and double-clicking. It annoyed Rebus, who couldn't see the screen. 'Now if they'd chosen Leith instead of Holyrood . . .' Preston rolled his eyes.

'The Clipper wouldn't be causing you this grief?' Rebus guessed.

'Bingo. We'd have bided our time, waited for the MPs and their staff, all on healthy salaries and looking to spend.'

'The Clipper's like a private club?' Janice asked.

'Not exactly. She's for hire. If you guarantee me a minimum of forty punters on a week day, sixty at weekends, she's yours gratis, so long as they're drinking at the ship's bar. You pay for the disco, that's it.'

'You say a minimum of forty. What's the maximum?'

'Public Safety regulations stipulate seventy-five.'

'But forty guarantees you a profit?'

'Just barely,' Preston said. 'I've got staff, overheads, power . . .'

'So some nights you don't open?'

'It comes in waves, if you'll pardon the pun. We've had good times. Now we're in . . .'

'The doldrums?' Rebus offered.

Preston snorted, reached into a drawer for a ledger book. 'So what date is it you're interested in?'

Janice told him. She had both hands cupped around a mug of coffee. It had been tepid and stewed on delivery. Rebus wondered at the qualifications of the tall blonde secretary in the outer office. Paperwork all over the floor, unopened mail . . . If Preston wasn't helpful, Rebus could foresee a phone call to the VAT inspectors.

But in fact he flicked quickly through the ledger. 'Found this here when we moved in,' he explained. 'Thought I'd try to find a use for it.' He looked up. 'You know, a continuity kind of thing.'

His finger found the date, ran along the line.

'Booking that night, private party. Fancy dress.' He looked up at Janice. 'Sure your son was headed for the Clipper?'

She shrugged. 'It's possible.'

'Whose party was it?' Rebus asked. He was already out of his chair. Preston, eyes on the ledger, didn't seem to notice Rebus coming around the side of the desk. Rebus's first impulse: look at the screen. A game of patience, sitting waiting for the player to start.

'Amanda Petrie,' Preston said. 'I was there that night. I remember it. There was a theme . . . pirates or something.' He rubbed his chin. 'No, it was *Treasure Island*. Some arsehole turned up dressed as a parrot. By the end of the night, he was as sick as one.' He looked at Janice. 'Can I see those photos again?'

She handed them over: Damon and the blonde from the security cameras; then Damon in a holiday snap.

'They weren't in fancy dress?' Preston asked.

Janice shook her head.

Preston's hands were busy with the ledger and the photos. Rebus, leaning over to examine the ledger, found that his elbow had nudged the mouse up the screen, to where it could close the game. Slight pressure on the mouse, and the screen changed. From a game of patience to the image of a woman on all fours. The photo had been taken from behind, the model turning her head to pout at the photographer. She was wearing white stockings and suspenders, nothing else. The pout was exaggerated. On the floor nearby, an empty champagne bottle. Rebus looked up to the windowsill, where an empty champagne bottle sat.

'But is she any good at shorthand?' Rebus said. Preston saw what he was looking at, switched the screen off. Rebus took the opportunity to lift the heavy ledger from the desk, walk back around to his chair with it.

'So you were there that night?' he asked.

Preston looked flustered. 'Keeping an eye on things.'

'And you didn't see either Damon or the blonde?'

'I don't remember seeing them.'

Rebus glanced up. 'Not quite the same thing, is it?'

'Look, Inspector, I'm trying to help . . .'

'Amanda Petrie,' Rebus said. Then he saw her address, recognised it. He looked up at Preston again.

'The judge's daughter?'

Preston was nodding. 'Ama Petrie.'

'Ama Petrie,' Rebus echoed. He turned to Janice, saw the question in her eyes. 'Edinburgh's original wild child.' Back to Preston: 'I see you didn't charge her for the boat.'

'Ama always brings a good crowd.'

'She uses the Clipper a lot?'

'Maybe once a month, usually fancy dress of some kind.'

'Does everyone play along?'

Preston saw what he was getting at. 'Not all the time.'

'So this night, there'd have been guests in normal clothes?'

'Some, yes.'

'And they wouldn't have been quite as eye-catching as pirates and parrots?'

'Agreed.'

'So it's possible . . . ?'

'It's possible,' Preston said with a sigh. 'Look, what do you want me to say? Want me to lie and say I saw them there?'

'No, sir.'

'Best person to talk to is Ama herself.'

'Yes,' Rebus said thoughtfully. Thinking of Amanda Petrie, her reputation. Thinking too of her father, Lord Justice Petrie.

'She runs with a pretty fast bunch,' Preston said.

Rebus nodded. 'Pretty rich too.'

'Oh yes.'

'The kind of customers you could do with more of.'

Preston glared at him. 'I wouldn't lie for her. Besides, I'm not sure the old ticker could cope with more than one Ama. Takes an age to clean up after her – more expense for me. And I always seem to get the bulk of complaints after Ama's parties. God knows, they're loud enough when they arrive . . .'

'Anything out of the ordinary that night?'

Preston stared at Rebus. 'Inspector, this was *Ama Petrie*. With her, there *is* no "ordinary".'

Rebus was copying her phone number from the ledger into his notebook. His eyes ran down other bookings, saw nothing to interest him.

'Well, thanks for your time, Mr Preston.' A final glance towards the computer. 'We'll let you get back to your game.'

Outside, Janice turned to him. 'I get the feeling I missed something back there.'

Rebus shrugged, shook his head. The car was parked on a sideroad. Drizzle was being blown into their faces as they walked.

'Ama Petrie,' Rebus said, keeping his head bowed. 'She doesn't fit my picture of Damon.'

'The mystery blonde,' Janice stated.

'Friend of hers, you reckon?'

'Let's ask Ms Petrie.'

Rebus tried the number from his cellphone: got an answering machine, and didn't leave a message. Janice looked at him.

'Sometimes it helps not to give too much advance warning,' he explained.

'Gives people time to concoct a story?'

He nodded. 'Something like that.'

She was still looking at him. 'You're good at this, aren't you?'

'I used to be.' He thought of Alan Archibald: all those years on the force, all that persistence, pursuing Deirdre Campbell's killer . . . It might be a kind of madness, but you had to admire it. It was what Rebus liked about cops. Only thing was, most of them weren't like that at all . . .

'Back to Arden Street,' he told Janice. There were calls she still had to make; his flat was still her base.

'What about you?' she asked.

'Things to do, people to see.'

She took his hand, squeezed it. 'Thanks, John.' Then reached up to touch his face. 'You look tired.' Rebus removed her fingers from his cheek, held them to his mouth, kissed them. Reached down with his free hand to turn the ignition.

The first instalment of Cary Oakes's 'Lifer Story' was perfunctory: a couple of paragraphs about his return to Scotland, a couple more about his incarceration, and then early biography. Rebus noted that place-names were kept to a minimum. Oakes's explanation: 'I don't want anywhere getting a bad rep just because Cary Oakes once spent a wet winter there.'

Thoughtful of him.

Several times, revelations were hinted at – teasers to keep the audience coming back for more – but on the whole it looked like whatever the paper had paid Oakes, they'd got themselves a pig in a poke. Rebus doubted Stevens' editor would be chuffed. There were photos: Oakes at the airport; Oakes on his release from the penitentiary; Oakes as a baby. A small photo too of 'reporter James Stevens', alongside his byline. Rebus noted that the photographs took up more space than the actual story. Looked like the reporter would be struggling to get a book's worth.

He folded the paper and looked out of his car window. He was parked at the gateway to a Do-It-Yourself superstore, one of those thinly disguised warehouses which, cheaply and quickly built, seemed to surround the city. There were only four cars in the capacious car park. He didn't know this part of the city well: Brunstane. Just to the west was The Jewel, with its mandatory shopping centre; to the east stood Jewel and Esk College. The message Jane Barbour had left for him at the office had been perfunctory: time and place, telling him to meet her. Rebus lit another cigarette, wondering if she was ever coming. Then a car pulled up alongside him, sounded its horn, and proceeded into the car park. Rebus started his engine and followed.

DI Jane Barbour drove a cream-coloured Ford Mondeo. She was getting out as Rebus parked alongside her. She reached back into the car for an A4 envelope.

'Nice car,' Rebus said.

'Thanks for coming.'

Rebus closed the car door for her. 'What's up? Run out of rawlplugs?'

'Have you been here before?'

'Can't say that I have.'

The wind blew her hair across her face. 'Come on,' she said, all businesslike, verging on the hostile.

He let himself be led round the side of the building. This was where staff parked their cars and bikes. There were two fire-exit doors, painted a green as drab as the grey of the corrugated walls. The back of the warehouse was a waste and delivery area. Skips spilled out flattened cardboard boxes. A dozen terracotta pots waited to be taken inside and displayed for sale. A low brick wall surrounded the area.

'Is this where you mug me?' Rebus asked, sticking his hands in his pockets.

'Why have you got it in for Darren Rough?'

'What's it to you?'

'Just tell me.'

He tried for eye contact, but she wasn't playing. 'Because of what he is, what he was doing at the zoo. Because he slandered a fellow officer. Because of . . .'

'Shiellion?' she guessed, her eyes meeting his at last. 'You couldn't touch Ince and Marshall, but suddenly there was *someone* you could replace them with.'

'It wasn't like that.'

Barbour reached into the envelope, lifted out a black and white photograph. It looked old, showed a three-storey Georgian house. A family posed in front of it, proud of their new motor car. The car was a 1920s model.

'They knocked it down six years ago,' Barbour explained. 'It was either that or wait for it to disintegrate of its own accord.'

'Nice-looking house.'

'The patriarch there,' Barbour said, tapping the man with one foot on the car's running-board, 'he went bankrupt. Mr Callstone, he was called. Worked in jute or something. The family home had to be sold. Church of Scotland snapped it up. But part of the deal was, they had to retain the family's name. So it stayed Callstone House.'

She waited for him to get the name. 'Children's home,' he said at last, watching her nod.

'Ramsay Marshall worked there, prior to his transfer to Shiellion. He already knew Harold Ince before the move.' She handed him more photos.

Rebus looked through them. Callstone House as a children's home, run by the Church of Scotland. Kids grouped outside the same front door, kids photographed inside, seated at long tables, looking hungry. Dormitory beds. Some photos of stern-looking staff. Rebus's mind was working now. 'Darren Rough spent some time at Callstone . . .'

'Yes, he did.'

'During Ramsay Marshall's reign?'

She nodded again.

'You . . .' he said, suddenly getting it. 'It was you that wanted Darren Rough back here.'

'That's right.'

'For the trial?'

She nodded. 'Arranged a flat for him, wanted him amenable. Worked on him for weeks.'

'He was abused?' Rebus frowned. 'He's not on the list.'

'The Procurator Fiscal didn't think he'd make a good witness.'

Rebus nodded. 'Criminal record. Couldn't risk cross-examination.'

'That's right.'

Rebus handed back the photographs. He knew where this was leading now. 'So what happened to him?'

She busied herself putting the photos back in their envelope. 'One night, Marshall went into the dorm. Darren wasn't asleep. Marshall said they were going on a drive. He took Darren to Shiellion.'

'Proving that Marshall and Ince were already in cahoots?'

'That's how it looks. The two of them and a third man took turns.'

'Christ.' Rebus stared at the warehouse, imagining it as a children's home, a supposed refuge. He wondered what Mr Callstone's ghost would be making of it. 'Who was the third man?'

Barbour shrugged. 'They had Darren in a blindfold.'

'How come?'

'The thing is, John, I made certain promises to him.'

'To a convicted paedophile,' Rebus felt bound to add.

'Ever heard of environment working on character?'

'The abused becoming the abuser? You think that's a reasonable excuse?'

'I think it's a reason.' She was calmer now. 'Professor Calder in Glasgow, he has this test. It shows how likely it is someone will reoffend. Darren came out low-risk. All his time inside, he went to the meetings, kept the therapy going.'

Rebus wrinkled his nose. 'How come he's not registered?' He'd checked: forty-nine sex offenders registered with police in Edinburgh; Rough wasn't among them.

'That was part of the deal. He's terrified they'll get him.'

'"They"?'

'Ince and Marshall. I know they're locked up, but he still has nightmares about them.' She waited for him to say something, but Rebus was thoughtful. 'What's happening down at Greenfield,' she pressed on, 'it's not right. Is that your answer: hound them, chase them out? They'll end up *somewhere*, John. We need to deal with them, not hand them to the mob.'

Rebus looked down at his shoes. As ever, they needed a clean. 'Did Rough tell you?'

She shook her head. 'When I saw the paper, I tried to find him. Then I spoke to his social worker. Andy Davies is pretty sure it was you.'

'You believe him?'

She shrugged. They were walking back towards their cars. 'So what do you want?' Rebus asked. 'An apology?'

'I just want you to understand.'

'Well, thanks for the therapy. I think I'm ready to be released back into the community.'

'I'm glad you can make a joke of it,' she said coldly.

He turned to her. 'Rough comes back to Edinburgh, and Jim Margolies, the cop he accused of beating him up, decides to take a walk from Salisbury Crags. I think there might be a connection. *That's* why I'm interested in . . .' He saw her face change at Jim Margolies' name. 'What?' he asked. She shook her head. Rebus narrowed his eyes. 'You spoke to Jim, didn't you? Had the same conversation we've just had?'

She hesitated, then nodded. 'I was bringing Darren back to Edinburgh. He was reluctant, wanted to know if DI Margolies was still around.'

'So you met with Jim, explained it all?'

'I wanted to know there'd be no . . . conflict, I suppose.'

'So Margolies knew Rough was coming back?' Rebus was thoughtful. A mobile phone sounded: hers. She lifted it from her pocket, listened for a moment.

'I'll head straight there,' she said, terminating the call. Then to Rebus: 'You'd better come too.'

He looked at her. 'What is it?'

She opened her car door. 'Ugly scenes in Greenfield. Looks like Darren's finally gone home.'

19

There was a mob on the landing outside Darren Rough's flat, and the only thing standing between them and it was PC Tom Jackson. Van Brady was at the front of the queue, brandishing a crowbar. Other women crowded behind her. A local TV crew jockeyed for position. A news photographer was snapping a cluster of kids holding up a banner. The banner was homemade: half a bedsheet and black spray-paint. The message read: SAVE US FROM THE BEAST.

'Lovely,' Jane Barbour said.

People in the other blocks were watching from their windows, or had opened them to shout encouragement. Rebus saw that paint had been daubed on the door of the flat. Eggs and grease had been smeared on the window. The crowd was baying for blood, and more people seemed to be joining in all the time.

Rebus thought: *What in God's name have I done?*

Tom Jackson glanced in Rebus's direction. His face was red, lines of sweat trickling from both temples. Jane Barbour was pushing her way to the front.

'What's going on here?' she shouted.

'Just bring the bastard out here,' Van Brady yelled back. 'We'll bloody well lynch him!'

There were cries of agreement – 'String him up!'; 'Hanging's too good!' Barbour held up both hands, appealing for quiet. She saw that most of the protestors were wearing white sticky labels on their jackets and jumpers. Plain labels on which had been written three letters – GAP.

'What's that?' she asked.

'Greenfield Against Perverts,' Van Brady told her.

Rebus saw a kid handing the labels out. Recognised him as Jamie Brady, Van's youngest.

'Since when was it your job to stick up for sick bastards like him?' one woman asked.

'Everybody's got certain rights,' Barbour replied.

'Even sickos?'

'Darren Rough served his sentence,' Barbour went on. 'He's now on a rehab programme.' She saw the film crew getting close, whispered something to Tom Jackson. He pushed his way to the camera, held a hand in front of it.

'We want answers,' Van Brady was shouting. 'Why was he put here? Who knew about it? Why weren't we told?'

'And we want him out!' a male voice called. A newcomer, the sea of bodies parting to let him through. A young man, chiselled face, bare-armed. He stood shoulder to shoulder with Van Brady, ignoring Barbour and directing his comments towards the film crew.

'This is our community here, not the police's.' Applause and cheers. 'If they can't deal with scum,' jerking his thumb back towards Rough's front door, 'no problem – we'll deal with it ourselves. We've always been tidy that way in Greenfield.'

More cheers; nods of agreement.

One protestor: 'You said it, Cal.'

Cal Brady, standing next to his mum, who looked on with pride at her son's oratory. Cal Brady: Rebus's first sighting in the flesh.

Well, not exactly: first sighting with the knowledge of who he was. But Rebus had seen Cal Brady before. At Gaitano's nightclub, standing at the bar with the undermanager, Archie Frost. Frost with his pigtail and bad manners; his friend saying nothing, then making himself scarce . . .

'Could we talk about it?' Jane Barbour asked.

'What's there to talk about?' Van Brady asked, folding her arms.

'This whole situation.'

Cal Brady ignored her, spoke to his mother. 'Is he in there?'

'One of his neighbours heard sounds.'

Cal Brady thumped on the window, then had to wipe grease off on his jeans.

'Look,' Jane Barbour was saying, 'if we could all—'

'Right you are,' Cal Brady said. Then, swiping the crowbar from his mother, he swung it at the window, shattering the glass. Grabbed at the soiled sheet, pulling it down from where drawing-pins held it in place. He was halfway over the windowsill and into the room, crowbar still in his hand. Rebus grabbed him by the feet, pulled him back. Glass shards ripped the front from Brady's T-shirt.

'Hey, you!' Van Brady yelled, swinging a punch at Rebus. Cal Brady wriggled free, pulled himself up and got into Rebus's face.

'You want it, do you?' Brandishing the crowbar. Not recognising the policeman.

'I want you to calm down,' Rebus said quietly. He turned to Van. 'And you, behave yourself.'

The crowd had formed around the window, keen for a view of the flat's interior. It looked much like any other: emulsioned walls, sofa, chair, bookcase. No TV, no hi-fi. Books piled on the sofa: photography texts; fiction titles. Newspapers on the floor, empty pot noodle containers, a pizza box. Cans and lemonade bottles on the bookcase. They all looked disappointed with this haul.

'He's polis,' Van warned her son.

'Listen to your mother, Cal,' Rebus said.

Cal Brady was lowering the crowbar as half a dozen uniforms came out of the stairwell.

First thing they did was disperse the crowd. Van Brady shouted that there'd be a GAP meeting in her flat. The TV crew looked ready to follow. The photographer lingered to take shots of Darren Rough's living room, until uniforms moved him on too. Barbour was on her mobile, calling for someone to come and board up the window.

'And pronto, before someone tips a can of petrol into the place.'

Tom Jackson, mopping his brow, came over to where Rebus was standing.

'Christ almighty,' he said. 'I think I preferred it the way it was before.'

When Rebus looked up, Jackson's eyes were on him.

'You're blaming me for this?' Rebus asked.

'Did I say that?' Jackson was still busy with his handkerchief. 'I don't remember saying that.' He turned and walked away.

Rebus looked in through the window. There was a musty smell from the room; hardly surprising, when it got neither fresh air nor sunlight. In for a penny, he thought to himself, lifting a foot on to the sill and pulling himself up.

Broken glass crunched underfoot. No sign of Darren Rough.

This is what you wanted, John. The voice in his head: not his own, but Jack Morton's. *This is what you wanted, and now you've got it . . .*

No, he thought, I didn't want *this*.

But Jack was right to a degree: here it was anyway.

A narrow archway from the living room led into the kitchenette. Rebus felt the electric kettle: a trace of warmth. Looked in the fridge: bread, marge, jam. No milk. In the swing-top bin: empty milk carton, baked bean tins.

Jane Barbour looked in at him. 'Anything?'

'Nothing much.'

'How about opening the door?'

'Sure.' He opened the door to the hall, which was in darkness. Fumbled and found a light switch. Bare forty-watt bulb. He tried opening the door, but the mortice had been locked, no sign of a key anywhere. The letterbox was protected by a block of wood. Not that Rough would get much mail. He went back to the window, let Barbour know she'd have to climb in if she wanted the tour.

'No thanks,' she said. 'Once was enough.' Rebus looked at her. 'When I first brought him here.'

Rebus nodded, went back into the hall. Just the two bedrooms, plus bathroom and separate toilet. The first bedroom contained a sleeping bag on the floor. Bedtime reading: the Bible, Good News version. Empty crisp packets. Rebus picked them up. There was a used condom inside one. Curtain across the window: Rebus pulled it open, looked down on to a roadway. Second bedroom was empty, not even a lightbulb. Same view as bedroom one. The bathroom needed a clean. There was mould on the walls. The only towel was a pitifully small and frayed affair, hospital knock-off or similar. Rebus tried the toilet door. It was locked. He pushed harder, definitely locked. He tapped on the wood.

'Rough? You in there?' No way of locking the door from the outside. 'Police,' Rebus called. 'Look, we're about to move out, and your front window's smashed. Minute we're gone, the barbarians will be back.' Silence. 'Fine and dandy,' Rebus said, turning away. 'By the way, DI Barbour's outside. Cheers, Darren.'

Rebus was half out of the window when he heard the noise behind him. Turned and saw Darren Rough standing in the doorway, face gaunt, eyes flickering in terrified expectation. Looking both haunted and hunted. He held shivering hands up to his chest, like they'd protect him from a crowbar's blows.

Rebus, immune to most things, felt a sudden stab of pity. Jane Barbour was out on the walkway, talking to Tom Jackson. She saw Rebus's look, broke off the conversation.

'DI Barbour,' he called. 'One of yours, I believe.'

Jim Stevens tried to put from his mind the sight of Cary Oakes urinating in the church. Now that he had Oakes, he needed the story, needed it to be *big*. His boss had complained about the first instalment, called it a 'cock-tease', hoped there was better to come. Stevens had given him his word.

Oakes had a Bible beside his bed. Yet in the church . . . Stevens didn't want to think about what it might mean. There was something about Oakes . . . you looked into his eyes sometimes and saw it, and if he caught you watching, he was able to blink it away. But for seconds at a time, his mind would be somewhere else, somewhere the reporter didn't want to be.

Just do your job, he kept telling himself. A few more days, plenty of time to score maximum brownie points with his boss, show the other rags that he could still cut it, and put together a proposal for whichever publisher made the highest bid. He was already in negotiation with two London houses, but four more had turned the idea down.

'Killers' life stories,' one editor had said dismissively, 'been there, done that.'

To get a bidding war going, he needed more offers. Two interested parties barely qualified as a tiff.

And now this.

Oakes had said he was going to his room for half an hour after lunch. The morning session had been good; not brilliant, but all right. Enough nuggets for the next instalment. But Oakes had complained of a headache, said he wanted to soak in a bath. After half an hour, Stevens had tried his room: no one answering. Reception hadn't seen him. Stevens had thought about going out and asking the surveillance, but that would have been rash. He persuaded the manager that he was worried about his colleague's health. A skeleton key got them into the room. No one there, no one at all. Stevens had apologised to the manager, gone back to his own room. Where he now sat, nipping at his fingernails and wondering where his story had gone.

It had to be bravado.

Caught snivelling and shivering like that by the police . . . The only way for Darren Rough to scrape together any self-esteem was to turn down Barbour's offer of a move. She could offer a police cell until something better came up; could no longer guarantee his safety in Greenfield.

Rough had smiled as she said 'no longer', both of them knowing she was playing with words.

'I'm staying,' he'd said. 'Got to stop running some time, might as well be here and now.' And he'd chuckled. 'Like some old Western, isn't it? Whatsisface, John Wayne.' He made his fingers into a six-shooter, blasted the air. Then he looked around and sniffed, his face losing its animation.

'I don't think it's a good idea,' Barbour said.

'I agree,' Andy Davies said. It was the first time Rebus had met Darren Rough's social worker. He was tall and thin and bearded, red hair going bald at the dome. Laughter lines around his eyes; small pink mouth.

'There *is* something you could do for me,' Rough said.

Davies leaning forward on the sofa, hands pressed between his knees. 'What's that, Darren?'

'A dustpan and brush, so I can clear up all this shit.' Kicking at a fragment of glass.

A council workman had arrived to put boards across the window. There was a dull loathing in his eyes. Someone down below had pressed a GAP label on to his toolbox. He used a cordless screwdriver, saw and hammer to fix the sheets of board to the windowframe, blotting out the last of the daylight.

When Rough went into the kitchenette, Rebus made to follow. The social worker stood up.

'It's OK,' Rebus told him, 'I just want a word.' The two men fixed one another with a stare. Rebus motioned for Davies to sit back down, but instead Davies walked to the window. Rebus made his way to the kitchenette's archway. Rough was opening and closing cupboards, not really sure what he was doing or why. He knew Rebus was there, but wouldn't look at him.

'Got what you wanted,' he muttered.

'What I want are some answers.'

'Funny way to go about it.'

Rebus slid his hands into his pockets. 'How long have you been back?'

'Three, four weeks.'

'I don't suppose you've seen DI Margolies?'

'He's dead. I saw it in the paper.'

'Yes, but before then.'

Rough slammed shut one of the doors, turned on Rebus, voice shaking. 'Christ, what now? He topped himself, didn't he?'

'Maybe.'

Rough rubbed a hand over his forehead. 'You think I . . .?'

Andy Davies had come over. 'What the hell is it now?'

'He's trying to set me up,' Rough blurted out.

'Look, Inspector, I don't know what you think—'

'That's right,' Rebus snapped back, 'you don't. So why don't you just keep out of it?'

'I can't handle this,' Rough bawled, on the verge of tears.

Jane Barbour came in from the hall. Rebus read her look: four parts accusation to one part disappointment. He remembered what she'd told him about Rough. The man was sniffing now, rubbing the back of his hand beneath his nose. His knees looked like they were about to give way. The workman was nearly finished, leaving the room in twilight. Each screw that went home was like fixing the lid on a coffin.

'Did DI Margolies come to see you?' Rebus persisted.

Rough fixed him with a defiant look. 'No.'

Rebus stared him out. 'I think you're lying.'

'So slap me around a bit.'

Rebus took a step towards him. The social worker was pleading with Barbour.

'DI Rebus,' Barbour warned.

Rebus got right up into Rough's face. Rough had backed all the way into the kitchenette, nowhere else to go.

'Did he come to see you?'

Rough looked away, bit his lip.

'Did he?'

'Yes!' Darren Rough screamed. He bowed his head, pulled a hand through his hair. Incessant hammering of nails into wood. He pushed both palms against his ears. Rebus pulled them away, using as little force as possible. Kept his voice quiet when he spoke.

'What did he want?'

'Shiellion,' Rough groaned. 'It's always been Shiellion.'

Rebus frowned. 'DI Rebus . . .' Barbour's voice growing taut, breaking point almost reached.

'What about Shiellion?'

Rough looked to Jane Barbour, his words directed at her. 'You told him what happened to me.'

'And?' Rebus probed.

'He wanted to know why they'd blindfolded me . . . kept asking who else was there.'

'Who else *was* there, Darren?'

Through gritted teeth: 'I don't know.'

'That what you told him?'

A slow nod. 'Could have been anyone.'

'Someone they didn't want you to see. Maybe you knew them.'

Rough nodded. His voice was calmer. 'I've often wondered. Maybe I'd have recognised . . . I don't know, a uniform or something. Priest's dog collar.' He looked up. 'Maybe even one of your lot.'

But Rebus had stopped listening. 'Priest?' he said. 'Callstone and Shiellion were run by the Church of Scotland. They don't have priests.'

But Rough nodded. 'We had one.'

Barbour, looking intrigued now, frowned. 'You had a priest?'

'Visited for a while, then stopped coming. I liked him. Father Leary, his name was.' A weak smile. 'Told us to call him Conor.'

When Rebus headed downstairs, Jane Barbour followed.

'What do you make of it?' she asked.

Rebus shrugged. 'Why was Jim Margolies interested in Shiellion?'

Her turn to shrug.

'You told Jim that Rough was abused there?'

She nodded. 'You think it has something to do with his suicide?'

'If it *was* suicide.'

She blew air from her cheeks. 'I'd better talk to the vigilantes,' she told him. 'Keep the lid on the pressure cooker.'

'Tom Jackson's already had a word.'

They turned, hearing footsteps behind them on the stairwell: Andy Davies.

'We should move him,' Davies said. 'It's not safe for him to stay here.'

'He doesn't want to leave.'

'We could insist.'

'If that mob up there couldn't make him leave, what chance have *we* got?'

'You could arrest him.'

Rebus burst out laughing. 'A couple of days back—'

Davies turned on him. 'I'm talking about *protecting* him, not harassment.'

'We'll keep someone in the vicinity,' Barbour said.

'Tom Jackson's got to go home some time,' Rebus commented.

'I'll do guard duty myself if need be.' She turned to Davies. 'At the moment, I'm not sure what more we can be expected to do.'

'And if he'd proved useful to you in court . . .?'

'I'll ignore that remark, Mr Davies.' Said with ice in her voice, and eyes like weaponry.

'They'll kill him,' the social worker said. 'And I don't suppose you'll be shedding too many tears.'

Barbour looked to Rebus, wondering if he would respond. All Rebus did was shake his head and light up a cigarette.

Rebus had known Father Conor Leary for years. For a time, he'd visited the priest regularly, sharing conversation and cans of Guinness. But when Rebus called Leary's number, another priest answered.

'Conor's in hospital,' the young priest explained.

'Since when?'

'A few days ago. We think it was a heart attack. Fairly mild, I think he'll be fine.'

So Rebus drove to the hospital. Last time he'd visited Leary, there'd been a fridge full of medicine. The priest had explained that they were for minor ailments.

'How long have you known?' Rebus asked, drawing a chair over to his friend's bedside. Conor Leary looked old and pale, his skin slack.

'No grapes, I notice,' Leary said, his voice lacking its usual gruff power. He was sitting up in the bed, surrounded by flowers and get-well cards. On the wall above his head Christ on the cross gazed down.

'I only heard half an hour ago.'

'Nice of you to drop by. Can't offer you a drink, I'm afraid.'

Rebus smiled. 'They say you'll be out in no time.'

'Ah, but did they say whether I'd be leaving in a box?'

Rebus managed a smile. Inside, he saw a carpenter, hammering home nails.

'I've a favour to ask,' he said. 'If you're up to it.'

'You want to turn Catholic?' Leary joked.

'Think the confessional could cope?'

'True enough. We'd need a relay team of priests for a sinner like yourself.' He rested his eyes. 'So what is it then?'

'Sure you're up to it? I could come back . . .'

'Cut it out, John. You know you're going to ask me anyway.'

Rebus leaned forward in his chair. His old friend had flecks of white at the corners of his mouth. 'A name you might remember,' he said. 'Darren Rough.'

Leary thought for a moment. 'No,' he said. 'You'll need to give me a clue.'

'Callstone House.'

'Now that was a while back.'

'You spent time there?'

Leary nodded. 'One of those multi-faith things. God knows whose idea it was, but it wasn't mine. A minister would visit Catholic homes, and I got to spend time in Callstone.' He paused. 'Was Darren one of the kids?'

'He was.'

'The name doesn't mean anything. I spoke with a lot of them.'

'He remembers you. Says you told him to call you Conor.'

'I'm sure he's right. Is he in trouble, this Darren?'

'You haven't heard?'

'This place tends to swaddle you. No newspapers, no news.'

'He's a paedophile, released into the community. Only the community doesn't want him.'

Conor Leary nodded, eyes still closed. 'Did he abuse another child?'

'When he was twelve. The victim was six.'

'I remember him now. Whey-faced, wouldn't say boo to a goose. The man who ran Callstone . . .'

'Ramsay Marshall.'

'He's on trial, isn't he?'

'Yes.'

'Did he . . . ? With Darren?'

'Afraid so.'

'Ah, dear Lord. Probably going on under my very nose.' He opened his eyes. 'Maybe the boys . . . maybe they tried to tell me, and I couldn't hear what they were saying.' When the priest's eyes closed again, a tear escaped from one and trickled down his cheek.

Rebus felt bad, which hadn't been his intention in coming here. He squeezed his friend's hand. 'We'll talk again, Conor. But you need to rest now.'

'John, when do the likes of you and me ever rest?'

Rebus got up, looked down at the figure on the bed. *Priest's dog collar* . . . Maybe, but never Conor Leary. *Even one of your lot* . . . Someone in uniform. Rebus didn't want to think about it, but Jim Margolies had put some thought into it. And soon afterwards, he'd died.

'John,' the priest was saying, 'remember me in your prayers, eh?'

'Always, Conor.'

Hadn't the heart to admit he'd stopped praying long ago.

20

Back at his flat, he made two mugs of coffee and took them through to the living room. Janice was on the phone to yet another charity, giving them details of Damon. Rebus sat at the dining table. It was a big room, twenty-two feet by fourteen. Bay window (still with the original shutters). High ceiling – maybe eleven feet – with cornicing. Rhona, his ex-wife, had loved the room, even with the original wallpaper from when they'd bought it (purple wavy lines which made Rebus feel seasick whenever he walked past). The wallpaper had gone, as had the brown carpet with matching paintwork.

He thought of Darren Rough's flat. He'd seen worse in his time, of course, but not much worse. Janice put down the receiver and scratched at her hair with a pen, before scribbling a note on a pad of paper. Having scored a line through the charity's phone number, she threw the pen on to the table.

'Coffee,' Rebus told her. She took the mug with a smile of thanks.

'You look glum.'

'My natural disposition,' he said. 'Mind if I use the phone?'

She shook her head, so he moved over to the chair, sat down and picked it up. A cordless model; he'd only had it a few months. He called Ama Petrie's number again. A flustered male voice told him to try one of the function rooms at the Marquess Hotel, told him what he'd find there.

'You got a message from Damon's bank manager,' Janice told him, when the call was finished.

'Oh yes?'

'Head office approval. If there are any debits from Damon's account, he'll let you know.'

'Nothing so far?'

'No.'

'Night he vanished, he took out a hundred.'

'How far does that go these days?'

'If he's sleeping rough, quite a way.'

'We're talking as if he's a runaway.'

'Until proved otherwise, that's what he is.'

'But why would he . . . ?' She broke off, smiled. 'Same old questions. You must be sick of hearing them.'

'The only one who can explain is Damon himself. Doing your head in isn't going to help in the interim.'

She looked at him. 'Right as ever, Johnny.'

He shrugged. 'Pleased to be of service.'

When Janice had finished her coffee, using the last mouthfuls to wash down two paracetamol tablets, he told her they were going out.

'Where?' she asked, looking around for her jacket.

'A beauty contest,' Rebus told her. Then he winked. 'Brought your swimsuit with you?'

'No.'

'Doesn't matter, you wouldn't be eligible anyway: too old.'

'Thanks very much.'

'You'll see,' he said, leading her to the door.

Cary Oakes had a newspaper cutting. It was old and fragile. These days, he didn't look at it much for fear that it would crumble between his fingers. But today was a special occasion, sort of, so in the café he withdrew it from his pocket and read it through. Faded words on grey paper. A report of his trial and verdict, clipped from one British tabloid. And words of hate: 'He should have had the electric chair.' A simple statement of belief.

But they hadn't given him 'Old Sparky', and here he was, back in the same town as the person who'd wanted them to fry him. The anger rising in him again, his hands trembled a little as he folded the cutting along its well-creased lines, slipping it back into his pocket. One day very soon, he'd make someone eat those words. He'd sit there watching them chew, seeing fear and knowledge in their eyes.

And then he'd spark out *their* life.

Leaving the café, he headed uphill, wandering past bungalows, along quiet pavements. Until he reached his destination. Stared at the building.

He was in there. Oakes could almost taste and smell him. Maybe he was alone in his room, resting or asleep. Or reading the newspaper, catching up on the exploits of Cary Oakes.

'Soon,' Oakes said quietly to himself, turning away, not wanting to seem conspicuous. 'Soon,' he repeated, beginning to walk back down the hill towards the town.

The hotel was a 1930s design, next to a roundabout on the western edge of Edinburgh.

'Looks like the Rex, doesn't it?' Janice said.

She had a point. The Rex had been one of Cardenden's three cinemas, perched on a prominent site on the town's main street. As a kid, it had looked to Rebus like one of those state buildings you saw in films about the Iron Curtain: forbidding, all straight lines and right angles. This hotel was an elongated version of the Rex, as though someone had gripped its sides and pulled. The spaces in the car park were taken, so Rebus did what others before him had done: bumped the Saab up on to the grass verge so that its nose touched the flower beds.

There was a large noticeboard in the middle of the hotel lobby. It told them that Our Little Angels could be found in the Devonshire Suite. Through a double set of doors and along a corridor, hearing a smattering of applause. At the door to the Devonshire Suite was a large woman in a fuchsia two-piece. She sat behind a small table with half a dozen name-tags left lying on it. She asked them their names.

'We're not expected,' Rebus told her, taking out his warrant card. Her eyes widened, and stayed that way as Rebus led Janice into the room.

There was a temporary stage at one end, rows of chairs arranged in front of it, pink and blue drapes hanging behind it. Burgeoning vases of flowers sat along the front of the stage and at the ends of each row of chairs. The room was about half-full. Around the walls sat bags and coats. Mothers and daughters were busy at work, primping and preening. Hair was brushed and teased, make-up perfected, a dress straightened or a ribbon retied. The daughters looked around the room, studying the competition nervously – or occasionally with a hint of contempt. None of them could have been older than eight or nine.

'It's like a dog show,' Janice whispered to Rebus.

A man at a microphone was reading from a prompt-card, introducing the next contestant.

'Molly comes from Burntisland and attends the local primary school. Her hobbies are pony-trekking and dress-designing. She designed her own dress for today's competition.' He looked up at his audience. 'How about that, eh, folks? The next Dior. Please welcome Molly.'

The mother patted her daughter on the shoulder, and with hesitant tread Molly made her way up the three wooden steps to the stage. The compère crouched down, microphone in hand. Fake tan and hair-weave – or maybe Rebus was just jealous. The judges were in the front row, trying to hide their voting papers from prying eyes.

'And how old are you, Molly?'

'Seven and three-quarters.'

'Seven and three-quarters? You're sure it's not seven-eighths?' The compère was smiling, but Molly's face had turned panicky, unsure how to respond. 'Not to worry, my darling,' the compère went on. 'So tell us about that lovely dress you're wearing.'

Rebus looked around him. Make-up applied to faces not yet ready for it, so that the girls looked like clowns. Hair spun into grown-up shapes. Mothers fussing, looking fraught and expectant. The mothers wore make-up too, and bright clothes. Some of them had dyed hair. A few had probably been under the knife. Nobody was paying any attention to Rebus and Janice: there were plenty of couples in evidence. But this was a mother-and-daughter show, no doubt about that.

No sign of Ama Petrie, and he'd no idea what she'd be doing here anyway. The voice on the phone hadn't had time to explain. Then he saw two figures he recognised. Hannah Margolies, long blonde hair curling past her shoulders. At her father's funeral she'd worn white lace. Today she was in a pale-blue dress with white tights and glossy red shoes. There were blue bows in her hair, her mouth a glistening crimson button. Her mother, Katherine Margolies, was kneeling in front of her, giving a final pep-talk. Hannah kept her eyes on her mother's, nodding slightly from time to time. Katherine took her hands and squeezed them, then stood up.

Jim Margolies' widow had looked composed at the funeral; she looked more nervous now. She was still wearing black – skirt and jacket over a white silk blouse. She glanced towards the stage where Molly, aided by tape-recorded backing, was singing 'Sailor', a song Rebus associated with Petula Clark. Janice, who had found a seat at the end of a row, turned to look up at Rebus with disbelieving eyes. When he looked back at Hannah, he saw Katherine Margolies studying him, as if trying to work out where she'd met him before. Molly was finishing her act, taking the applause with a curtsey. She fairly skipped off the stage, grinning to show wide-spaced teeth.

'Our next contestant,' the compère was saying, 'is Hannah, who lives right here in Edinburgh . . .'

When Hannah had taken the stage, Rebus wandered across to her mother.

'Hello, Mrs Margolies.'

She put a finger to her lips, her concentration focused on the stage. She pressed her hands together in something like prayer as she watched Hannah's performance, her mouth twisting when the compère asked what seemed to her a tricky question. Finally, the mother reached down into one of her bags and walked to the stage with a recorder, handing it to her daughter with a smile. Unaccompanied, Hannah played a tune which Rebus suspected was classical. He'd heard it on an advert somewhere, couldn't think what the advert was for. Looking towards Janice, Rebus saw that seated next to her were an elderly couple, beaming at the stage. They held hands. In the man's free hand was a walking stick. Rebus recognised them: Jim Margolies' parents.

Finally: applause, and Hannah came back to her mother, who kissed her hair.

'You were perfect,' Katherine Margolies said. 'Just perfect.'

'I played a wrong note.'

'I didn't hear it.'

Hannah turned to Rebus. 'Did you hear it?'

Rebus shook his head. 'Sounded fine to me.'

Hannah's face relaxed a little. She whispered something to her mother.

'Off you go then.'

As Hannah made her way to her grandparents, Katherine Margolies got slowly to her feet, watching her leave.

'We haven't actually met, Mrs Margolies,' Rebus said, 'but I was at Jim's funeral. I used to work with him. My name's John Rebus.'

She nodded distractedly. 'You must think I'm . . .' She sought the words. 'I mean, so soon after Jim's accident. But I thought it might take Hannah's mind off things.'

'Of course.'

'She's been so upset.'

'I'm sure.' He noticed that she was now studying the judges, the members of the audience, as if looking for some clue as to Hannah's success. 'You think Jim fell?' he asked.

She looked at him. 'What?'

'People seem to think it was suicide.'

'Let them think what they like,' she snapped. Then she turned to him. 'You want me to tell Hannah her father took his own life?'

'Of course not . . .'

'He was out walking, got too close to the edge. It was dark . . . a gust of wind maybe.'

'Is that what you believe?' She didn't reply. 'Did Jim often go out walking at night?'

'What business is it of yours?'

He looked down at the carpet. 'Frankly, none.'

'Well then.'

'It's just that I've been trying to make sense of it.'

She looked at him again. 'Why?'

'For my own satisfaction.' He held her stare. She was beautiful. Black hair pulled back to show the geometry of her face. Thin arched eyebrows, good cheekbones. Hannah's eyes were blue, same as her father's, but Katherine Margolies' were hazel. 'And because,' Rebus went on, 'I thought it might have something to do with Darren Rough.'

'Who's he?'

'Didn't Jim mention him?'

She shook her head, sighed with impatience, and turned her gaze towards the judges again. One of them was having a conversation with the compère, who had switched his microphone off.

Rebus thought she was about to say something. When she didn't, he tried another question.

'He didn't take his car, did he?'

'What?'

'It was raining that night.'

'When you go for a walk, do you take *your* car?'

'I wouldn't head up Salisbury Crags in a downpour, day or night.'

'Well, Jim did, didn't he?'

'Yes, he did . . . and I still don't understand why.'

'Well, Mr Rebus, I've enough to worry about, so if you'll excuse me . . .' She looked over his shoulder and her face brightened. 'Amanda, darling!'

A young woman had breezed through the door, completely ignoring the woman at the desk. She now came forward with arms open, shopping bags swinging from both hands, and embraced Katherine Margolies.

'Sorry I'm late, Katy. Traffic was murder. Tell me I haven't missed her.'

'Afraid so.'

'Oh, fuck it!' Loud enough for heads to turn. From a distance of four feet, Rebus could smell the cigarettes and booze. The shopping bags: Jenners, Cruise, Body Shop. 'How was she? I'll bet she was brilliant . . .' Looking around. 'Where is she anyway?'

Hannah was coming towards them, leading her grandmother by the hand, her grandfather following. Her face lit up at the sight of her new visitor. Amanda crouched down and opened her arms again, and Hannah ran into them.

'Careful with her make-up, Ama,' Katherine Margolies warned.

'You look like an angel,' Amanda told Hannah. 'Not that angels ever wore lipstick.'

Katherine Margolies was looking at Rebus. 'I'm sorry, I thought we'd finished chatting.' A polite dismissal.

'We had,' Rebus said. 'But it's Miss Petrie I've come here to see.'

Amanda Petrie stood up. She was wearing a clinging black mini-dress and black leather jacket with zips to spare. Black high heels and bare legs. She looked Rebus up and down.

'Who do I owe money to?' she asked. Her attention shifted to Dr and Mrs Margolies. 'Hello, you two.' She kissed and embraced both of them. 'How are you bearing up?'

'Well, you know, dear,' Mrs Margolies said.

'Hannah was *splendid*,' Dr Margolies said. 'We haven't been introduced.' He held a hand towards Rebus.

'DI Rebus,' Rebus said, watching the old man's face fall. And now Ama Petrie was studying him. He smiled. 'I've been taken for worse things than a loan-shark's muscle,' he told her. 'Maybe we could have a drink at the bar . . . ?'

But Amanda Petrie wasn't that stupid. Rebus's thinking: a couple more drinks would loosen her up even more. Amanda, however, had insisted on a pot of tea and several glasses of orange juice. Rebus, Janice and Ama Petrie: just the three of them, seated in the hotel lounge. Ama tucking a strand of blonde hair behind one ear. Rebus looking at her, knowing what Janice was thinking: could she be the mystery blonde? He didn't think so; her build was different, not so tall, narrower at the shoulders. He couldn't see any resemblance to her father . . .

She played with one of the shoulders of her dress. Her eyes kept scanning the lounge, looking for anyone more interesting, more glamorous, anyone she should know.

'I want to be back for the judging,' she reminded them. 'Hannah's bound to win.'

'Why do you say that?'

'She's got breeding. It's not something you can paint on to a face or run up with a sewing-machine.'

'Ever done any sewing yourself?' Rebus asked.

She pulled her attention back to him. 'Needlework and home economics. My school wanted to make little women of us.' She lit a cigarette, tucked her legs under her. Since she hadn't offered, Rebus made a show of taking out his own pack, lighting one for himself and offering another to Janice.

'Sorry,' Ama Petrie said, offering them her pack. Rebus waved his already lit cigarette at her. 'How did you find me?' she asked.

'Phoned your number.'

'You probably spoke to Nick.' She blew out smoke. 'He's my brother. Always ready to shop his sis to the filth.'

Rebus let that one go. 'How do you know Hannah?' he asked.

'We're cousins or something. Twice removed, you know how it is with families.'

Rebus knew Jim Margolies had married someone with 'society connections'. He hadn't known Katherine was related to Lord Justice Petrie.

'Not that I'd have anything to do with most of my family,' Ama Petrie went on, 'but Hannah's just adorable, don't you think?' She asked the question of Janice, who nodded.

'I'm not sure about these shows, though,' Janice said.

Ama seemed to agree. 'Yes, but Katy loves them, and I think Hannah does too.'

'All those mothers . . .' Janice mused. 'Pushing their daughters.'

'Yes, well . . .' Ama tapped her cigarette against the ashtray. 'What is it you want, anyway?'

Rebus explained the situation. As he talked, Ama's attention moved to Janice. At one point, she leaned forward and took her hand, squeezing it.

'You poor dear.'

An agony aunt's look on her face; someone who'd been touched by loss only at one remove.

'I did have a party that night,' she agreed. 'Not that I remember it too well. Bit too much to drink, too many people . . . as per. Word gets around, I do get the occasional gatecrasher. I don't mind, so long as they're interesting, but the boat's owner goes on about overcrowding.

He's always asking me if I know this or that person, did I invite them?' She drained her second glass of orange. 'Christ knows why I bother.'

'Why do you bother?'

A smirk. 'Because it's fun, I suppose. And because while I'm doing it, I'm *somebody*.' She thought about this, shrugged the thought aside as if it were the wrong jacket. 'You're sure he was coming to *my* party?'

'It's the last time he was seen,' Janice confirmed.

Rebus got out the photographs: Damon; Damon and the mystery blonde. As Ama studied them, he asked casually if she'd ever been to Gaitano's.

'Do people call it Guiser's?' He nodded confirmation. 'Yes, once or twice. Lots of sweaty job-creation-schemers and dole-fiddlers. Off their faces on happy-hour cocktails, dropping E in the lavs.' She smiled. 'Not my scene, I'm afraid.' She handed back the photos. 'Sorry, don't mean a thing to me.'

'Not even the woman?'

She wrinkled her nose. 'Looks a bit tarty.'

'It couldn't be someone you know?'

'Inspector.' A throaty laugh. 'That's hardly narrowing things down. I know *everybody*.'

'But you don't know my son,' Janice said grimly.

'No,' Ama said, face making a show of contrition. 'I'm very much afraid I don't.' She sprang to her feet. 'I'd better get back. They'll have started the judging.'

Rebus and Janice followed her, stood in the doorway as the prizes were handed out. Hannah was runner-up. As the winner was announced, and went forward to receive a sparkling tiara, everyone clapped and cheered. Everyone except Ama Petrie, who bounced on her toes, booing at the top of her voice as she gave an enthusiastic thumbs-down to the little girl with voluminous black hair, shimmering with glitter.

Katherine Margolies tried to stop Ama making a scene, but to Rebus's eyes she didn't try very hard . . .

'Where the hell have you been?'

Stevens found Cary Oakes in the bar, where he was drinking orange juice and talking to the staff.

'Walking, thinking.' Oakes looked at him. 'Want to make sure I don't forget anything.'

Stevens picked up Oakes's glass. 'Then don't forget this: that's *my* juice you're drinking, *my* money paying for it. We've lost a whole session.'

'I'll make it up to you.' Oakes blew Stevens a kiss, grinned and winked at the barman. Turned back to Stevens. 'Look at you, man, all trembling and sweating. A cardiac arrest's having your name paged as we speak. You got to slow down, Jim. Go with the flow.'

'My editor wants better copy.'

'You could give him Kennedy's assassin, he'd say he wanted better copy. You and I know, Jim, the best stuff has to wait for the book, right? The book's what's going to make us rich.'

'If I find a publisher.'

'It'll happen, trust me. Now sit down here beside me and let me buy you one. Hell, I don't mind putting my hand in my pocket for a friend.' He wrapped an arm around Stevens' shoulders. 'You're with Cary now, Jim. You're part of my exclusive circle. Nothing bad's going to happen.' Oakes made eye contact, held it. 'You can depend on that,' he said. 'Cross my heart.'

'Just drop me off at Haymarket,' Janice said. They were back in the car, heading into town.

'You sure? I could drive you—'

She was shaking her head.

'Look, Janice, a trail like this . . . we're bound to run into dead ends. Maybe a lot of them. It's something you'll have to accept.'

She shook her head. 'I was thinking of all those kids . . . wondering what they'll be like when they grow up. If I'd had a daughter . . .' She shook her head again.

'It was pretty ghastly,' Rebus agreed.

She looked at him. 'Did you think so? I thought so too, at first. But then I kept looking . . . and they all looked so beautiful.' She took out a handkerchief, dabbed at her eyes.

'I think I'd better drive you home,' he said.

'No, I don't want that.' She paused, put a hand on his arm. 'I just mean . . . I don't want to put you . . . Oh Christ, I don't know what I want any more.'

'You want Damon back.'

'Yes, I want that.'

'What else?'

She seemed to consider the question. But in the end she made no answer, just turned to him again and smiled, eyes shiny from crying.

'In a funny way, it's like you've never been away,' she told him.

He nodded. 'Just the thirty-odd years. What's that between friends?'

They shared the laughter; he touched the back of her hand with his fingers. Parked outside Haymarket station, they sat in silence for a while. Then she opened the door, got out. Smiled one last time and walked away.

Rebus sat for another minute or two, imagining himself running down to the platform, seeking her amongst the crowds . . . Like in a film. Real life was never like that. In films, there was nothing you couldn't do; in the real world . . . in the real world it always got messy.

He went back to Oxford Terrace. Patience wasn't home. They'd passed beyond the stage of leaving notes. He soaked in a bath for half an hour, drifting off to sleep, startling himself awake as his chin dipped beneath the water. He saw the headline: dog-tired cop in bathtime tragedy. One for Jim Stevens to relish.

He lay on the sofa, put some music on. Pete Hammill: 'Two or Three Spectres'. He knew they were there, his ghosts, settling around him, getting comfortable. More comfortable than he could ever be. Patience, Sammy, Janice . . . A point was coming, between Patience and him. A crisis point maybe, but then they'd been there before. But was there some point coming between Janice and him too? Something very different . . . ? He picked up a book, covered his eyes with it.

Slept.

21

Ama Petrie wasn't the only one who'd thought the mystery blonde looked 'tarty' or a bit like a pro. On his way down to The Shore that evening, Rebus decided on a slight detour.

A few of the working girls still plied their trade dockside. Most of the city's prostitutes worked in licensed premises masquerading as saunas, but a few still took risks by walking the streets. Sometimes it was because they were desperate or unemployable – which meant they had an obvious drug habit – while others just liked to do their own thing, despite the dangers. Over in Glasgow, there were fewer saunas and more girls on the street. Result: seven murders in as many years.

Rebus's thinking: street girls worked Leith; the blonde looked 'tarty'; the taxi had brought her and Damon to Leith. It was another possibility. Say they hadn't been making for the Clipper. Say they'd been heading for her room.

Her room, or maybe a hotel . . .

There were only three women out this evening on Coburg Street, but he knew one of them. Stopped the car and called her over. She got into the passenger seat, bringing waves of perfume with her.

'Long time no see,' she said. Her name was Fern. Punters assumed it was made up, but Rebus knew from her records that she'd been born Fern Bogot. He knew too that she worked the streets because she liked to be her own boss. In saunas, the proprietor was always taking a cut. She had her regulars; didn't often go with strangers. Mature gentlemen preferred. She found them less aggressive.

Her mane of red hair was a wig, though it looked natural enough. Rebus put the car into gear and signalled to move off. She took her punters to some waste ground in Granton. If Rebus stuck around, he wasn't a punter, and that made everyone uneasy. Looking in his rearview, he saw one of the remaining women peering at the car, then turning to scrawl something on a wall.

'What's she doing?' he asked.

Fern turned back. 'Good old Lesley,' she said. 'She's taking your registration. That way, if my body turns up, there's something for the cops to go on. We call it our insurance policy. Can't be too careful these days.'

Rebus nodded agreement, drove them around the streets, asking his questions. She studied the photographs in detail, but was forced to shake her head.

'Nobody like that works down here.'

'What about the lad?'

'Sorry.' She handed the photos back. Rebus exchanged them for one of Janice's flyers.

'Just in case,' he said.

When he dropped her back at her patch, he got out of the car and went to look at the wall. Sure enough, there were rows of car registration numbers scrawled there, most of them in various shadings of lipstick, some worn away by the elements. His own was at the bottom of the last column. He looked up the column, started to frown. At the top was a number he thought he recognised. Where did he know it from . . . ?

Suddenly it dawned on him: he'd seen it in a file at Leith police station. Leith: where Jim Margolies had been stationed. It was mentioned in the file on Jim's suicide.

It was the registration number of his car.

'What is it?' Fern asked.

Rebus tapped the wall. 'This one. Belongs to a guy called Jim. A cop.'

She frowned in concentration, then shrugged. 'Not one of mine,' she said. 'But it's orange lipstick.'

'So?'

'Lesley has a code, her way of telling who's gone in which car.'

'And who does orange lipstick mean?'

She was shaking her head. 'Not a who so much as a what. Orange means whoever it was, he liked them young . . .'

Roy Frazer wasn't the only one waiting for Rebus down at The Shore. Sitting in the car alongside him was the Farmer.

'Checking up on us, sir?' said Rebus, getting into the back seat. As he got in, Frazer got out, closing the door after him.

'Where the hell have you been?' the Farmer said. 'I've spent half the day trying to find you.' He handed Rebus the day's surveillance notes. 'First entry,' he snapped.

Rebus looked. Bill Pryde recorded himself taking over from Rebus at 0600. His next entry: 'Cary Oakes entered hotel at 0745.'

'Which means,' the Farmer said, 'he left the hotel at some point, and one of you missed him.'

'I saw his bedroom light go off,' Rebus said.

'That's right, you did. It's in the log.'

'Which means he sneaked out on my shift?' Rebus's fingernails dug into his palms.

'Or during the first hour of Bill Pryde's.'

'Either's possible. We're only covering the front of the building. Plenty of access points at the rear.'

The Farmer turned to face him. 'Access isn't our problem, John. Our problem is that he seems to be able to leave whenever he likes.'

'Yes, sir. But a single-officer surveillance . . .'

'Is no bloody use at all if we're not keeping tabs on him.'

'I thought the point was to needle him, let him know we can make things difficult.'

'And does it look to you like we're succeeding, Inspector?'

'No, sir,' Rebus conceded. 'Thing is, if he's got a way of getting out undetected, why not go back the same way?'

'Because the doors at the back can only be opened from within.'

'That's one possibility, sir.'

'And the other?'

'He's playing with us, having a little joke at our expense. He *wants* us to know what he's been doing.'

'And what has he been doing, all the time he's been out roaming?'

Rebus shook his head. 'I don't know, sir. Why don't we ask him?'

When Frazer and the Farmer had left, Rebus decided to follow his own advice. He found Cary Oakes in the bar: no sign of Jim Stevens. Oakes was sitting on a stool, chatting with the two barmen. There were a few other drinkers scattered round the tables, business types, discussing deals even in their cups.

Oakes waved for Rebus to join him, asked him what he was drinking.

'Whisky,' Rebus said. 'A malt.'

'Take your pick, Mr Stevens is paying.' Oakes allowed himself a little chuckle, chin tucked into his neck. He looked like he'd had a few, but Rebus saw he was drinking cola. 'What about something to chase it down?'

Rebus shook his head. 'And I pay for my own,' he said.

There was plenty of choice behind the bar. Rebus decided on something fiery: Laphroaig, with a splash of water to damp the flames. Cary Oakes tried signing for the drink, but Rebus was insistent.

'Your good health then,' Oakes said, lifting his own glass.

'You like playing games, don't you?' Rebus asked.

'Not much else to do in jail. I taught myself chess.'

'I don't mean board games.'

'What then?' Oakes' eyes were heavy-lidded.

'Well, you're playing a game right now.'

'Am I?'

'Bar-room raconteur. A couple too many, telling stories to anyone who'll listen.' He nodded towards the barmen, who'd moved to the far end to wash glasses. 'Just another piece of play-acting.'

'You could go on TV with this stuff. No, I mean it. You're *so* shrewd. Guess you have to be in your profession.'

'Is Jim Stevens falling for it?'

'For what?'

'The stories you're telling him. How much of the truth are you giving him?'

Oakes narrowed his eyes. 'How much truth do you think he can take? If I went into details, think his newspaper would publish them?' He shook his head slowly. 'People can only take so much truth, John.' He leaned towards Rebus. 'Want me to tell *you* about it, John? Want me to tell you how many I really did kill?'

'Tell me about Deirdre Campbell.'

Oakes sat back, took a sip of his drink. 'Alan Archibald thinks I killed her.'

'And did you?' Rebus tried to keep the question casual. Lifted his glass to his lips.

'Does it matter?' Oakes smiled. 'It matters to Alan, doesn't it? Why else would he have come running when I called?'

'He wants the truth – all of it.'

'Maybe you're right. And what do you want, John? What brought *you* running in here? Shall I tell you?' He made himself comfortable on the stool. 'The morning shift saw me coming back. I wasn't sure he was awake: arms folded, head over on one shoulder. I thought he'd nodded off.' He tutted. 'I'm not sure his heart's in it. The job, I mean, police work. He looks the type who's coasting to retirement.'

Which just about summed up Bill Pryde; not that Rebus was about to admit it.

'I think you have problems with your job, too, but not in the same way.'

'Taught yourself psychology along with the chess?'

'When there were no new books to read, I started reading people.'

'You killed Deirdre Campbell, didn't you?'

Oakes put a finger to his lips. Then: 'Did *you* kill Gordon Reeve?'

Gordon Reeve: another ghost; a case from years back . . . Jim Stevens had been shooting his mouth off.

'Tell me,' Rebus said, 'do you trade with Stevens? You tell him a story, he has to tell you one?'

'I'm just interested in you.'

'Then you'll know I killed Gordon Reeve.'

'Did you mean to?'

'No.'

'Are you sure about that? You stabbed a drug-dealer . . . he died.'

'Self-defence.'

'Yes, but did you want him dead?'

'Let's talk about you, Oakes. What made you pick Deirdre Campbell?'

Oakes gave another wry smile. Rebus wanted to rip his lips from his face. 'See, John? See how easy it is to play the game? Stories, that's all they are. Way back in the past, things we'd like to think we can forget.'

He slipped off the stool. 'I'm going to my room now. A nice hot bath, I think, then maybe one of the in-room movies. I might call down for a sandwich later. Would you like something sent out to the car?'

'I don't know, what's the menu like?'

'No menu, you just order what you like.'

'Then I'll have your head on a plate, no garnish required.'

Cary Oakes was laughing as he left the bar.

There was someone in the car.

Rebus started forward, saw they were in the passenger seat. As he got close, he saw it was Alan Archibald. Rebus opened the driver's-side door and got in.

'Car wasn't locked,' Archibald said.

'No.'

'Didn't think you'd mind.'

Rebus shrugged, lit a cigarette.

'Have you been talking to him?' Archibald needed no confirmation. 'What did he say?'

'He's playing a game with you, Alan. That's all it is to him.'

'He told you that?'

'He didn't need to. It's what he does. Stevens, you, me . . . we're how he gets his kicks.'

'You're wrong there, John. I've seen how he gets his kicks.' He leaned down to the floor, brought out a green folder. 'Thought you might like something to read.'

Alan Archibald's file on Cary Dennis Oakes.

Cary Oakes had travelled to the USA on a tourist visa. His biography prior to this time was sketchy: a father who'd died when he was young; a mother who'd had psychological problems. Cary had been born in Nairn, where his father had worked as a green-keeper at one of the local golf courses, and his mother as a maid at a hotel in the town. Rebus knew Nairn as a windswept coastal resort, the kind of destination that had lost out as cheap foreign holidays had prospered.

When Oakes's father had died following a stroke, the mother had experienced a breakdown. Her employers had let her go, and she'd headed south with her son, finally stopping in Edinburgh, where she had a half-sister. They'd never been particularly close, but there was no one else, no other family, so mother and son had been squeezed into a room in the house in Gilmerton. Soon afterwards, Cary had started running away. His school had notified his mother that his attendance was irregular at best. There were nights and weekends when he just didn't bother going home at all. His mother was beyond caring, and her half-sister preferred him out of the house anyway, since her husband had taken a furious dislike to the boy.

Where did the money come from for his trip to the States? Alan Archibald had done some digging, uncovering a series of muggings and break-ins in Edinburgh, unsolved, but tailing off at about the time Cary Oakes made his trip. The mystery of his niece's murder made for a file in itself. Archibald had interviewed Oakes's mother and half-sister (both now deceased) and the husband (still alive; living alone in sheltered accommodation in East Craigs). They hadn't remembered anything specific about the night of the murder, couldn't even be sure that Cary had been near the house that day or the next.

Deirdre Campbell had been out dancing in town, ending up at a club on the corner of Rose Street – not a hundred yards from where Gaitano's was now sited. She'd been picked by one particular man, had danced the last four or five dances with him. She'd introduced him to her friends. She had exams coming up, shouldn't have been there in the first place. The club was for over-twenty-ones only, and Deirdre had been underage. The owner had got into trouble afterwards. His defence: 'If she hadn't come in here, they'd have let her in someplace else.' Which was true: make-up, choice of clothes and hairstyle could add half a dozen years to a teenage girl. After the club, the group had headed out to Lothian Road, trying hard not to let the night die. A pizza restaurant, and then taxis. Deirdre had said she'd walk. She lived in Dalry, it would only take her twenty minutes.

Police questioned the young man who'd been with her, the one she'd danced with. He'd asked if he could see her home, but she'd shaken her head. He lived way out at Comiston, so had accepted a ride in one of the taxis. Deirdre had started walking home.

Only to end up murdered on a hillside. Clothing interfered with, but no sign of rape or assault. A blow to the head, then strangulation.

Three days later, Cary Oakes had been heading out of Scotland, taking with him a rucksack and sports holdall. None of his family knew what he was up to. First they'd heard was when he'd been arrested, over two months later.

They hadn't bothered contacting police, registering him as missing. 'He was old enough to make his mind up what he wanted to do,' his uncle had told Alan Archibald. 'We knew he'd taken some clothes and stuff, figured he'd just took off.'

Archibald had used police reports and trial evidence to piece together Cary Oakes's American travels. From New York he'd taken a bus cross-country. At his trial, Oakes stated that he did this 'because it's what all the pioneers did: headed west'. He spent a week in Chicago, just criss-crossing the city on foot and by means of public transport. Then, hitching rides west, he stopped at Minneapolis, where he decided he needed more money and tried his hand at mugging. A couple of minor successes, and one major setback: picked on a woman with Mace in her coat pocket and a lethal left hook. He left Minneapolis with a swollen left eye and the right bloodshot and stinging. He ate at truck stops along I-94, passing through Fargo and Billings, making it as far as Spokane before his need for dollars became desperate. He broke into a couple of houses, tried pawning his meagre findings. The brokers knew swag when they saw it, offered him a few dollars, then, when he bad-mouthed them, called his description in to the police.

He'd taken to sleeping rough, finding like-minded individuals. Joined a little shoplifting gang. With his 'funny accent', he'd keep the staff busy and interested while the others went about their work undetected. Already, he was boasting that he was on the run, that he'd 'offed' someone back in Scotland. No details, the assertion taken for bravado. Everyone on the street hid behind a shield of lies and fantasies. They'd all tasted the good life; all fallen from a state of grace.

In Spokane, he'd murdered Dorothy Anne Wreiss, a forty-two-year-old divorcee who taught kindergarten three days a week. She lived in a sprawling suburban tract. It was thought Oakes had spotted her at the mall, followed her home or trawled the neighbourhood until he'd spotted her station wagon parked in the drive.

She was found in her kitchen, groceries still in their bags on the breakfast bar. Her two cats had curled up on her back and were sleeping. She'd been beaten with a rock, then strangled with a dishtowel. Her purse had been emptied, as had the jewellery box in her bedroom. Next day, Oakes had tried pawning her watch. At the trial, he'd say it had been gifted to him by one of his drifter friends, the one called Otis. But no one who'd known him had known anyone called Otis.

He ran towards Seattle, stayed there over a week. There was one unsolved they'd tried pinning on him: man found unconscious in the car park of the King Dome. He'd been beaten around the head, his car stolen. Died in hospital of his injuries. The car turned up in Ballard, as did Cary Oakes. By now, the police forces of several states were interested in the 'Scottish drifter'. A couple of serious assaults in Chicago; a known homosexual found dead in his car in the La Grange district of the city. A woman attacked and left for dead in a mall on the outskirts of Bloomington, Minneapolis. The death of a seventy-eight-year-old following a break-in at her home in Tacoma, Washington. Sometimes, police had physical descriptions of someone at or near the scene; sometimes all they had was an MO. No useful fingerprints, no positive IDs of Cary Oakes.

The final killing: another homosexual, Willis Chadaran, age sixty. The attack had taken place in the master bedroom of his home in Bellevue. A heavy statuette, which Chadaran had won for his editing work on a documentary film back in 1982, was the weapon. He'd been beaten senseless with it, then finished off with the belt from his red silk *yakuta*. Cary Oakes's fingerprints were found on the headboard. When arrested and presented with the fingerprint match-up, he admitted he'd been to Chadaran's home, but denied killing him. Detectives had asked how his prints had ended up on the headboard.

Oakes said he'd sneaked into the room looking for stuff to steal, maybe he'd touched it then.

He was finally arrested at Pike Place Market. Traders had complained that he'd looked ready to swipe something. Police had asked for his ID. He'd offered his passport, with its invalid tourist visa, then made a run for it. They'd caught him, taken him in, and someone had connected him to various descriptions which had been coming in from all across the country.

At the trial, the prosecution's summing-up had been succinct.

'This is a man for whom brutal murder has become a way of life, a commonplace. If he needs something, wants something, covets something . . . he kills for it. He sees us all as potential victims. We're not fellow humans to him; he's ceased to think of us in those terms, the terms by which we co-ordinate and validate our society, terms without which we cannot call ourselves *civilised*. His soul has shrivelled to the size of a walnut, maybe not even that big. Cary Oakes, ladies and gentlemen of the jury, has stepped outside our society, our laws, our civilisation, and he must pay the price.'

The price being two life sentences.

Rebus put down the file. 'Lots of circumstantial evidence,' he mused.

'It all adds up though. More than enough to make a case.'

Rebus nodded agreement. 'But I can see where he found his loopholes.' He tapped the folder, thought of the summing-up. 'Wonder how big a soul usually is . . .' He turned to Archibald. 'He plays games.'

'I know that. The version Jim Stevens' paper is printing . . . Oakes is spinning them a line.'

'He told me one of his victims was the same age as my daughter. Nobody in here fits with that.'

Alan Archibald shrugged. 'Your daughter's mid-twenties, Deirdre was eighteen.' He paused. 'Maybe there are others we don't know about.'

Yes, thought Rebus, and maybe it had been just another lie. 'So what are you going to do?' he asked.

'Keep at him.'

'Play along with him?'

'I don't see it that way.'

'I know you don't; that's what worries me.'

'She wasn't *your* niece.'

Rebus looked into Alan Archibald's eyes; saw courage and grit, the vital energies which had stayed with him all his working years, not about to be jettisoned now.

'How can I help?'

'What makes you think I want any help?'

'Because you came back tonight. Not to talk to him, but to see me.'

Alan Archibald smiled. 'I know a bit about you, John. I know we're not so very different.'

'So how can I help?'

'Help me make him come to Hillend.'

'What good do you think it would do?'

'He ran from the crime, John. Ran as far as he could from the memory of it. Take him back there, back to his *first* killing . . . I think it would bring it all back: the terror, the uncertainty. I think he'd start to unravel.'

'Is that what we want?' Rebus thinking: *He'll kill again . . .*

'It's what I want. I just need to know if I'll have your help.'

Rebus rubbed his hands over the steering-wheel. 'I'll need to think.'

'Well, don't be too long about it. I get the feeling maybe you need this as much as I do.'

Rebus looked at him.

'We can't always live by faith alone,' Archibald went on. 'Now and then, there has to be something more.'

22

After a further hour of conversation, Archibald left, saying he'd find himself a taxi. He'd talked about his niece, his memories of her, the way her murder had affected the family.

'We disintegrated,' he'd said. 'So slowly, I don't think anybody noticed. I think we felt guilty whenever we met, like we were to blame. Because when we got together, there was only one possible subject, one thing on our minds, and we didn't want that.'

He'd talked too about his work on the case: weeks spent in police archives; months spent piecing together Cary Oakes's history; trips to the US.

'It must all have cost a lot,' Rebus had said.

'Worth every penny, John.'

Rebus hadn't added that money wasn't his point. He knew all about obsession, knew how it could rob you of everything. He'd been given a jigsaw one year as a Christmas present, back when Sammy was just a kid. He'd cleared a table and started work on it, found he worked late into the night, even though he knew the picture he was making – knew because it was right there on the box. Only he tried not to look at it, wanting to complete the puzzle without any help.

And one piece was missing. He'd asked Rhona, questioned Sammy: had she taken it? Rhona told him maybe it wasn't in the box to start with, but he couldn't accept that. He'd stripped the sofa and chairs, pulled up the carpet, gone over the room inch by inch, then the rest of the flat – just in case Sammy *had* put it somewhere. Never found it. Even years later, he would find himself wondering if maybe it had slipped between the floorboards, or under the skirting-board . . .

Police work could affect you like that, if you let it. Unsolved cases; questions that niggled; people you *knew* were the culprits but couldn't incriminate . . . He'd had more than his fair share of those. But eventually he let them go, even if it meant drinking them into oblivion. Alan Archibald didn't look capable of putting Cary Oakes behind him. Rebus got the feeling that even if Oakes were proved innocent, Archibald would go on believing in his guilt. It was in the nature of obsession.

Alone with his thoughts, Rebus reached into his pocket for the quarter-bottle, drained it dry.

Proved innocent . . . He thought of Darren Rough, shaking with fear, holed up in his locked toilet. All because Social Work had put him in a flat above a kids' playground. And because John Rebus had placed on Rough's shoulders the sins of others – the sins of men who had themselves abused Rough.

Rebus rubbed at his eyes. It wasn't unusual for him to feel a weight of guilt. He carried Jack Morton's death with him. But something had changed. In the old days, he wouldn't have given much thought to Darren Rough. He'd have told himself Rough deserved what he got, for being what he so evidently was. But go back further . . . back to the cop he had once been, so long ago now, and he wouldn't have taken Rough's story to the tabloids. Maybe Mairie Henderson was right: *something's gone bad inside you*.

He admired Alan Archibald's persistence, but wondered what would happen if he were proved *wrong*. Would he still pursue Cary Oakes? Would he take things further than mere pursuit . . . ? Rebus stared out at the night sky.

It's all pretty tricky down here, isn't it, Big Man?

He wondered what point the surveillance was serving. Oakes seemed to be turning it to his own advantage, coming and going as he pleased, letting them know he could do it. So that all their efforts seemed so much waste. He closed his eyes, listened to the occasional message on the police radio, his thoughts turning to Damon Mee. The boat looked like another dead end. Damon had walked out of the world, given his life the slip. Thoughts of Damon took him to Janice, and from there to his schooldays, when everything had just started to get complicated in his life.

Alec Chisholm had disappeared one day; never found.

Rebus had gone to the school leaving dance, with something he wanted to tell Mitch.

Then Janice had knocked him cold, a gang had descended on Mitch, and suddenly Rebus's whole life was decided . . .

A noise brought him out of his reverie. He thought it had come from the back of the hotel. He decided to investigate. The car park and service entrance in darkness, but he swept his torch around. Looked up at the hotel windows. You could tell the corridors: lights still burned in those windows. One of the windows was open, curtains flapping. Rebus moved his torch in a downward arc, its beam landing on the roof of a lock-up garage, one of a row of three. They were separated from the hotel property by a wall. Rebus pulled himself up and over it. A narrow alley, puddles and rubbish underfoot. No sign of life, but footprints in the mud. He followed the path. It led him around the back of a factory unit and tenement, then up on to the busy thoroughfare of Bernard Street, where late-night cars and taxis idled at traffic lights. Where drunks stumbled their way home. One man was doing an elaborate dance and providing his own musical accompaniment. The woman with him thought he was hilarious. Can: 'Tango Whiskyman'.

There was no sign of Cary Oakes, no sign at all, but Rebus got the feeling he was out there. He retraced his steps, stopped at a rubbish skip parked next to one of the service doors, took the empty bottle from his pocket and tossed it in.

Felt his head jerk forward as a blow hit him from behind. Searing pain, his eyes screwing shut. He raised a hand, half-turned. A second blow laid him out cold.

It was pitch black, and when he moved there was a dull steel echo.

And a smell.

He was lying on something soft. Voices above him, then blinding light.

'Dear oh dear.'

Second voice, amused: 'Sleeping it off, sir?'

Rebus shielded his eyes, peered up at sheer walls. Two heads bobbing over the rim. He pulled his knees up, slithered as he tried to stand. His hands were tingling. His head pulsed with pain.

He was . . . he knew where he was. In a rubbish skip, the one behind the hotel. Wet cardboard boxes beneath him, and Christ knew what else. Hands were helping him to his feet.

'Come on then, sir. Let's . . .' The voice died as the torch found his face again. Two uniforms, probably from Leith cop shop. And one of them had recognised him.

'DI Rebus?'

Rebus: dishevelled, whisky on his breath, being helped from a skip. Supposedly on surveillance. He knew how it must look.

'Christ, sir, what happened to you?'

'Get that torch out of my face, son.' Their faces were shadows to him, no way to tell if he knew them. He asked the time, worked out that he'd been unconscious only ten or fifteen minutes.

'Call from a public box on Bernard Street,' one of the uniforms was explaining. 'Said there was a fight going on at the back of the hotel.'

Rebus examined the back of his head: no blood on his palm. Hands still tingling. He rubbed at the fingers. They hurt when he worked them. Lifted them into the torchlight. One of the uniforms whistled.

The knuckles were grazed, bruised. A couple of the joints seemed to be swelling.

'Gave him a sore one, whoever he was,' the uniform said.

Rebus studied the scrapes. Like he'd been punching concrete. 'I didn't hit anyone,' he said. The uniforms shared a glance.

'If you say so, sir.'

'I suppose it's asking too much to tell you to keep this to yourselves.'

'We won't breathe a word, sir.'

An outright lie; it didn't do to beg favours from uniforms.

'Anything else we can do, sir?'

Rebus started to shake his head, felt a wave of nausea as the pain slammed in. Steadied himself with a hand on the skip.

'My car's round the corner,' he said, voice brittle.

'You'll want a shower when you get home.'

'Thank you, Sherlock.'

'Only trying to help,' the uniform muttered.

Rebus walked slowly around the building. The receptionist looked ready to call security until Rebus produced ID and asked her to buzz Oakes's room. There was no reply.

'Will there be anything else, sir?'

Rebus was looking in his wallet. His cards were there, but the cash had gone.

'Any idea where Mr Oakes is?' he asked.

She shook her head. 'I didn't see him leave.'

Rebus thanked her and walked over to a sofa, fell down on to it. A little later, he asked for aspirin. When she brought them, she had to shake his shoulder to wake him up.

He headed for Patience's: sod the surveillance. Oakes wasn't in his room. He was out on the streets. Rebus needed clean clothes, a shower, and more painkillers. As he stumbled through the door, Patience came into the hall, blinking her eyes sleepily. He held up both hands to pacify her.

'It's not what you think,' he said.

She came forward, held his hands, looking at the swelling.

'Explain,' she said. So Rebus did just that.

He lay in the bath, a cold compress on the back of his skull. Patience had rigged it up from a sandwich bag, some ice cubes, and a bandage. She was treating his hands with antiseptic cream, having cleaned them and established nothing was broken.

'This man Oakes,' she said, 'I'm still not sure why he'd do it.'

Rebus adjusted the ice-pack. 'To humiliate me. He made sure I'd be found by uniforms, out cold in a rubbish skip.'

'Yes?' She dabbed on more ointment.

'Knuckles bruised like I'd been fighting. And whoever I'd fought had whipped me. Found like that at the back of the hotel, there's only one real candidate. By morning, it'll be round every station in the city.'

'Why would he do that?'

'To show me he can. Why else?' He tried not to flinch as she rubbed cream into a cut.

'I don't know,' she said. 'Maybe to distract you.'

He looked at her. 'From what?'

She shrugged. 'You're the detective here.' She examined her handiwork. 'I need to wrap your hands.'

'So long as I can still drive.'

'John . . .' Knowing he'd pay no attention.

'Patience, if I go round with hands looking like a mummy's, he's won this round.'

'Not if you refuse to play.'

He saw the depth of concern in her eyes, brushed her cheek with the back of his hand. Saw Janice doing the self-same thing to him, and withdrew his hand guiltily.

'Hurts, does it?' Patience asked, misreading the gesture. He nodded, not trusting himself to speak.

Later, he sat on the sofa with a mug of weak tea. He'd washed down two more painkillers, prescription-strength. His soiled clothes had been bundled into a black bin-liner, ready for a trip to the cleaner's. Such a shame, he thought, that his soiled thoughts couldn't be steam-pressed so easily.

When his mobile phone sounded, he stared at it hard. It lay on the coffee table in front of him, alongside his keys and small change. Patience was standing in the doorway as he finally picked the phone up. There was a little smile on her lips, but no humour in her eyes. She'd known all along he would answer it.

Cal Brady came home from Guiser's feeling pretty good. The buzz lasted all of ten seconds. As he flopped on to his bed, he remembered about the pervert. His mum was in her bedroom with some bloke; walls were so thin they'd have been as well having it off in front of him. All the flats were like that, so that things you wanted done in secrecy you had to do quietly. He put his ear to one wall, then another: his mum and her bloke; a couple of television stations – Jamie was still awake, watching the box in the living room, and the portable was on in Van's room, a weak attempt to mask other sounds. He put his ear to the floor. He could still hear all of it, plus the people below's movements, coughs and conversations. He'd gone to the doctor a while back, asked if maybe he had ears that were more sensitive than the norm.

'I keep hearing things I don't want to.'

When he'd explained that he lived in one of the high-rises in Greenfield, the doctor had suggested a personal stereo.

But it was the same on the street: he overheard snippets of conversation, stuff the talkers didn't think he could hear. Sometimes he thought it was getting worse, thought he could hear people's hearts beating, the quick flow of blood around their bodies. He thought he could hear their *thoughts*. Like at Guiser's, when girls looked at him and he smiled back. They were thinking: he might not look much, but he's with Archie Frost, so he must be important in some way. They'd think: if I dance with him, let him buy me a drink, I'll be closer to the *power*.

Which was why he seldom did anything, just stayed by the bar, affecting a cool poise and saying nothing. But listening, always listening.

Always hearing things . . . Things about Charmer, things about the clients – Ama Petrie, her brother and the rest. His own version of the *power*.

It had been quiet in the club tonight. If it hadn't been for a busload from Tranent, the place would have been dead. They hadn't looked too impressed: nobody to dance with but themselves. Archie doubted they'd be back. Archie was already looking for other work: plenty more clubs in the city. Cal hadn't started looking though. Cal believed in loyalty.

'I know Charmer's trying to collect on some debts,' Archie had said, 'but the problem is, he's got debts of his own. Only a matter of time before people come calling . . .'

Cal had straightened his back, as if to say: fine by me.

He wanted to think things through, get them straight in his head, which was why he'd come into his bedroom rather than sitting up with Jamie. But even before he'd reached that sanctuary, his thoughts had turned to Darren Rough. The hall was half-full of placards. They sat against the wall, still smelling of fresh paint. Cardboard boxes had been cut up flat, messages written on their blank sides. DESTROY ALL MONSTERS; KEEP AWAY FROM OUR KIDS; LET'S PLAY HANG THE PERV.

Destroy all monsters, Cal was thinking, lying on his bed, smoking a cigarette. He got up abruptly, thumped on the far wall.

'Will you fucking well shut up, the pair of you!'

Silence, then muffled laughter. For a moment, Cal was ready to burst in on them, but he knew what his mum would do to him. And besides, last thing he wanted was to see her like that.

Destroy all monsters.

The doorbell. Who the fuck at this time of night . . . ? Cal went to see. Recognised the woman. She looked agitated, rubbing her hands like she was doing the washing-up.

'You haven't seen our Billy, have you?' She was Joanna Horman, Billy's mum. Billy was one of Jamie's pals. Cal called for him and Jamie came out of the living room.

'Have you seen Billy Boy?' Cal asked. Jamie shook his head. He had a packet of crisps in his hand. Cal turned back to Joanna Horman. Some of his friends reckoned she looked all right. Right now, though, she looked a mess.

'What's up?' he asked.

'He went out to play about seven, I haven't seen him since. I thought maybe he'd gone to his gran's, but when I checked she hadn't clapped eyes on him.'

'I'm just in. Hold on a minute.' He went and banged on Van's door: as good an excuse as any to break things up in there. 'Hiy, Maw, has Billy Horman been round here the night?'

Noises from within. Joanna Horman was leaning against the door, looking ready to fall down. Not a bad body, Cal decided. Bit squishy, but he didn't like them all skin and bones. His mother's bedroom door opened. Van was wearing her dress, arranging it over her. Nothing on underneath, he'd bet. She closed the door quickly behind her; no way to tell who else was in the room.

'Something the matter, Joanna?' Pushing past Cal, ignoring him altogether.

'It's wee Billy, Van. He's disappeared.'

'Aw, Christ. Come into the living room.'

'I just don't know what to do.'

'Where have you looked?'

Cal followed the two women into the living room.

'Everywhere. I think maybe it's time I called the police.'

Van snorted. 'Oh aye, they'd be round here like a shot. Only thing those buggers are interested in is protecting perverts . . .' Her voice died away; for the first time, she looked at her son. They knew one another so well, no words were needed.

'Joanna, pet,' Van said quietly, 'you stay there. I'm going to round up the troops. If your Billy's anywhere on the estate, we'll find him, don't you worry.'

Within half an hour, Van Brady had the search parties organised. People were going from door to door, asking questions, getting new volunteers. Jamie had been sent to bed, but wasn't asleep, and Joanna Horman was in the living room with a tumbler of rum and Coke. Cal had offered to keep an eye on her. She was on the sofa, and he was in the chair. He couldn't think of anything to say. Wasn't normally this tongue-tied. He found himself aroused by her grief, the way it softened her. But he felt ashamed to be so affected by her, and his brain was spinning the way it did when he'd drunk too much or taken some speed.

He got up, opened the door to Jamie's room.

'Get up, you, and keep an eye on Billy's mum. I've got to go out.'

Then he opened the main door and stalked down the hallway. Down the stairwell and out into the night. There were some lock-ups across the way. He had the key to one of them. He was keeping some stuff there. Jerry Langham's lock-up it was, but Jerry was serving three-to-five in Saughton, another six months before he'd have even a whiff of roly-paroley. He kept his car in the lock-up. It was a 1970s Merc with rusty sills and a custard-yellow paint job, but Jerry loved it.

'I don't keep my missus under lock and key, but no way am I letting any bastard near my Merc.'

This was by way of a warning: use the lock-up, keep an eye on the motor, but never think of touching it. Not that Cal had heeded the advice. He unlocked the car sometimes and sat in it, pretending to be driving. And he'd opened the boot once, too, so he knew what was inside.

He unlocked it now, lifted out the jerrycan and gave it a shake. He was sure there'd been more than that; it was barely half-full now. Evaporation or something. He supposed petrol could do that. On a stack of shelves he found some oily rags. Stuffed them into his pockets and he was ready.

Back to the block of flats, taking the steps two at a time. He had a purpose now, jerrycan making quiet sloshing sounds. Close your eyes, you could almost be at the seaside. Crept along to Darren Rough's flat. Fresh lengths of board across his window. The kids had already been busy with their aerosols. GAP had made the flat their first stop tonight: no answer, nobody home. Cal opened the mouth of the can, held it high so the petrol trickled out of it, running it the length of the boarded window, then across the door. Took a ball of rag from his pocket and doused it in petrol. Stuffed it into the narrow gap between board and wall. Then another and another. Chucked the empty can over the balcony, then cursed to himself: there'd be prints on it. And besides, Jerry might want it. He'd go retrieve it in a minute.

Took out his cigarette lighter, the one Jamie had given him for Christmas. Jamie . . . he was doing this for Jamie and his pals, for all the kids. Jamie was bright. Didn't like school, but then who did? Didn't make him thick. He could go places, do things with his life: a couple of times when drunk, Cal had tried to tell him as much. He got the feeling it hadn't come out right, had come out like he was envious. Maybe he was, just a little. A kid like Jamie, the world was his oyster. Cal looked at the lighter. Another thing about his wee brother: he had shoplifting down to an art.

23

When Rebus got to Greenfield, half the estate was out watching the fire, or what was left of it.

Rebus knew one of the firemen, guy called Eddie Dickson. Dickson nodded a greeting. He was in full uniform, standing guard by his engine.

'If I move, they'll be in about it.' Meaning the local kids; meaning they'd strip it of anything they could find. 'We got bottled coming in.'

'Who by?'

Dickson shrugged. 'Came flying out of the dark. I get the feeling we weren't wanted.'

Uniforms from St Leonard's were trying to get the spectators to go back to bed.

'Any casualties?'

Dickson shrugged again. 'You mean from the bottles?'

Rebus stared at him. 'I mean in there.' Pointing towards Darren Rough's flat.

'Place was empty when we got here.'

'Door open?'

Dickson shook his head. 'Had to kick in what was left of it. Grudge thing, is it?'

'Don't you read the papers?'

'When do I get the time, John?'

'Paedophile.'

Dickson nodded. 'Remember it now. Frying's too good for them, eh?'

Rebus left him to his guard duty, headed for Cragside Court. The uniform in the lobby told him not to bother with the lifts.

'One's buggered, the other's a toilet.'

Rebus would have taken the stairs anyway. Nothing left of the boards across Rough's window but a few charred scraps clinging to their screws. The door had been torched, too. DC Grant Hood was standing in the hallway of the flat. Rebus toed open the toilet door: nobody home.

'Your pal,' Hood said. He was young, bright. Followed Glasgow Rangers with a passion, but nobody was perfect.

'Wasn't me,' Rebus commented. 'But thanks for the call.'

Hood shrugged. 'Thought you might be interested.' He nodded towards Rebus's bandaged hands. 'Had an accident yourself?'

Rebus ignored the question. 'No chance *this* was an accident, I suppose?'

'Bits of rag hanging from the windowframe. Petrol spilt on the walkway . . .'

'No sign of the occupier?'

Hood shook his head. 'Any ideas?'

'Look around, Grant. It's the Wild West out here. Any one of them's capable.' Rebus had walked back through what remained of the door, was leaning over the balcony. 'But if it was me, I'd be asking Van Brady and her eldest son.'

Hood jotted the names down. 'I don't suppose Mr Rough will be coming back.'

'No,' Rebus said. Which had been the point all along. But now that they'd come to that point, Rebus wondered why he felt so lousy inside . . . Jane Barbour's words came back to him: low chance of reoffending . . . abused as a child himself . . . need to give him a chance.

Then he saw Cal Brady, down amongst the thinning crowd. He was fully clothed, looked like he hadn't yet been to bed. Rebus went back downstairs. Cal was handing out GAP stickers to anyone who didn't have one. Women with coats thrown over their nighties were getting them. Cal placed each one on its recipient with exaggerated gentleness, causing some of the women – not exactly coy maidens – to blush.

'All right, Cal?' Rebus said. Cal looked round at him, peeled off a sticker and slapped it on Rebus's jacket.

'I hope you're with us, Inspector.'

Rebus started removing the sticker. Cal put out a hand to stop him, and Rebus caught it, lifted it to his nose. Cal pulled away quickly, but not quickly enough.

'Soap and water's usually a good idea,' Rebus told him.

'I haven't done anything.'

'You stink of petrol.'

'Not guilty, Your Honour.'

'I'm not one to prejudge, Cal—'

'Not what I hear.'

'But in your case I'll definitely make an exception.' Thinking: who had Cal been talking to? Who'd been telling him about Rebus? 'DC Hood's going to want to ask you some questions. Be nice to him.'

'Fuck the lot of you.'

'Think your dick's long enough?' Said with a smile.

Cal stared him out; then broke off and laughed. 'You're a clown. Go home to your circus.'

'What do you think *you* are, Cal? The ringmaster?' Rebus shook his head. 'No, son, you'll do tricks for whoever's cracking the whip.' Rebus turned away. 'Whether it's your mum or Charmer Mackenzie.'

'What do you mean?'

'You work for him, don't you?'

'What's it to do with you?'

Rebus just shrugged and went back to his car. He'd parked it right next to the fire engine: didn't want to find it up on bricks.

'Hey, John,' Eddie Dickson said, 'won't it be perfect?'

'What?'

'When they build the Parliament.' He swept an arm before him. 'Right next door to all this.'

Rebus looked up, saw the dark form of Salisbury Crags. Once more he felt like he was in a canyon of some kind, sheer walls affording no escape. Your fingers would be raw and bleeding from trying.

Either that or stained with four-star.

Hood came running up as Rebus was flexing his hands. 'I think we've got a problem.'

'Be a miracle if we didn't.'

'There's a kid missing. They weren't even going to tell us.'

Rebus was thoughtful. 'It's UDI,' he said. Hood looked puzzled. 'A Unilateral Declaration of Independence, son. So who spilt the beans?'

'I went to Van Brady's flat. Door was open, young woman in the lounge.' He checked his notebook. 'Name's Joanna Horman. Kid's name is Billy.'

Rebus remembered his first visit to Greenfield, Van Brady leaning out of her window: *I saw you, Billy Horman!* He couldn't remember much about the kid, only that he'd been playing with Jamie Brady.

'Now we know why they torched the flat,' Hood went on.

'A brilliant deduction, Grant. Maybe we better go talk to the lady in question.'

'The kid's mum?'

Rebus shook his head. 'Van Brady.'

Having opened negotiations with Van Brady, her kitchen providing an unpromising table for such a high-powered summit, Rebus called for reinforcements. They'd organise more search parties, police and residents working together.

'This is your patch,' Rebus had conceded, washing down more pills with a mug of cheap chicory coffee. 'You know the place better than any of us: any hidey-holes, gang huts, anywhere he might stop the night. If his mum gives us a list of his school pals, we can contact their parents, see if he's maybe staying with one of them. There are things we can do best, and things you can do.' He'd kept his voice level, and maintained eye-contact throughout. There were eight bodies in the kitchen, and more in the hallway and living room.

'What about the pervert?' Van Brady had asked.

'We'll find him, don't worry. But right now, I think we should concentrate on Billy, don't you?'

'What if he's the one who's *got* Billy?'

'Let's wait and see, eh? First thing is to get the search going again. We're not going to find anyone sitting here.'

Meeting over, Rebus had sought out Grant Hood.

'This is yours, Grant,' he said. 'I shouldn't even be here.'

Hood nodded. 'Sorry I got you involved.'

'Don't be. But keep yourself straight: wake up DI Barbour and let her know the score.'

'What happens if they find him first?' Meaning Darren Rough rather than the kid.

'Then he's dead,' Rebus said. 'It's as simple as that.'

He drove out of Greenfield, wondering at what point Darren Rough had vacated his flat. Wondering where the young man would go. Holyrood Park: once, centuries back, it had been sanctuary for convicts. As long as you didn't cross the boundary, you were on Crown Estate and couldn't be touched by the law. Debtors would flee there, live there for years, existing on charity, fish from the lochs and wild rabbits. When their debts were finally paid or written off, they'd cross the boundary, step back into society. The park had provided them with an illusion of freedom; in reality, they'd merely been in an open prison.

Holyrood Park: a road wound its way around the base of Salisbury Crags and Arthur's Seat. There were car parks near the lochs, popular with families and dog-owners during the day. At night, couples drove there for sex. The Royal Parks Police made irregular patrols. There had been talk of their disbanding, of the park falling within Lothian and Borders jurisdiction. It hadn't happened yet.

Rebus made three circuits of the park. Driving slowly, not really interested in the few parked cars he passed. Then, by St Margaret's Loch, just as he was readying to exit at Royal Park Terrace, he thought he caught shadow play at the edge of his vision. Decided to stop the car. Maybe just the headache and the pills, tricking his vision. He kept the engine running, wound down the window and lit a cigarette. Foxes, maybe even badgers . . . he could have been mistaken. There were all kinds of shadows in the city.

But then a face appeared at the open window.

'Any chance of a ciggie?'

'No problem.' Rebus averted his face as he searched his pockets.

'Eh . . . look, I'm not sure . . .' A clearing of the throat. 'I mean, you're not looking for company, are you?'

'As a matter of fact, I am.' Now Rebus looked up. 'Get in, Darren.'

Shock hit Darren Rough's face as he recognised Rebus. His face was blackened. He coughed again, doubling over.

'Smoke inhalation,' Rebus observed. 'You left it pretty late getting out.'

Rough wiped his mouth. The sleeves of his green raincoat were singed where he'd held them in front of his face.

'I thought they'd be waiting for me outside. I kept listening for a fire engine.'

'Somebody called one eventually.'

He snorted. 'Probably afraid it would spread to their flat.'

'Nobody was waiting outside?'

Rough shook his head. No, Rebus thought, because they'd all been out searching for Billy Horman. Cal Brady had torched the flat alone, and hadn't stuck around to be spotted.

It had started to rain; sudden gobbets which bounced off Rough's shoulders. He lifted his face to the sky, opened his scorched mouth to the drops.

'You better get in,' Rebus told him.

He angled his head, stared at Rebus. 'What am I charged with?'

'A kid's gone missing.'

Rough lowered his eyes. Said something like 'I see', but so quietly Rebus didn't catch it. 'They think I . . . ?' He stopped. 'Of course they think I did it. In their shoes, I'd think the same.'

'But it wasn't you?'

Rough shook his head. 'I don't do that any more. That's not me.' He was getting soaked.

'Get in,' Rebus repeated. Rough got into the passenger seat. 'But you still think about it,' Rebus said, watching for a response.

Rough stared at the windscreen, his eyes glinting. 'I'd be a liar if I said I didn't.'

'So what's changed?'

Rough turned to him. 'Are you charging me?'

'No charge,' Rebus said, putting the car into gear. 'Tonight, you ride for free.'

24

Rebus took Darren Rough to St Leonard's.

'Don't worry,' he said. 'Call it protective custody. I just want to make your answers on the missing kid official.'

They sat in an interview room with the recording machine running and a uniform on the door, drinking watery tea and with the rest of the station practically empty. All the spare bodies were down at Greenfield, looking for Billy Horman.

'So you don't know anything about a missing child?' Rebus asked. Because there was no one around to tell him not to, he'd lit himself a cigarette. Rough didn't want one, but then changed his mind.

'Cancer's probably the least of my problems right now,' he surmised. Then he told Rebus that all he knew was what he'd heard from the detective himself.

'But the locals warned you off, and you stayed put. There must have been a reason.'

'Nowhere else to go. I'm a marked man.' Glancing up. 'Thanks to you.' Rebus stood up. Rough flinched, but all Rebus did was lean against the wall, so he was facing the video camera. Not that it mattered: the camera wasn't on.

'You're a marked man because of what you are, Mr Rough.'

'I'm a paedophile, Inspector. I suppose I'll always be one. But I have ceased to be a *practising* paedophile.' A shrug. 'Society's going to have to get used to it.'

'I don't think your neighbours would agree.'

Rough allowed himself a condemned man's smile. 'I think you're right.'

'What about friends?'

'Friends?'

'Others who share your interests.' Rebus flicked ash on to the carpet; the cleaners would be in before morning. 'Had any of them round to the flat?'

Rough was shaking his head.

'Sure about that, Mr Rough?'

'Nobody knew I was there till the papers splashed me across a double-page spread.'

'But afterwards . . . nobody from the old days got in touch?'

Rough didn't answer. He was staring into space, still thinking of newspapers. 'Ince and Marshall . . . I see the stories about them. Where they are . . . in the cells . . . do they get to see the news?'

'Sometimes,' Rebus admitted.

'So they'll know about me?'

Rebus nodded. 'Don't worry about them. They're on remand in Saughton Prison.' He paused. 'You were going to testify against them.'

'I wanted to.' He stared into space again, his face tightening with memories. Rebus knew the story: the abused became abusers themselves. He'd always found it easy to discard. Not every victim turned abuser.

'That time they took you to Shiellion . . .' Rebus began.

'Marshall took me. Ince told him to.' His voice was trembling. 'Didn't pick on me specially or anything – could have been any one of us. Only I think I was the quietest, the least likely to do anything about it. Marshall was right under Ince's thumb at that time, loved the way Ince ordered him about. I saw a photo of Ince, he hasn't changed. Marshall's got a lot tougher-looking, like he's grown an extra skin.'

'And the third man?'

'I told you, could have been anybody.'

'But he was already there, waiting at Shiellion when you arrived.'

'Yes.'

'So probably a friend of Ince, rather than Marshall.'

'They took it in turns.' Rough's hands were holding the edge of the desk. 'Afterwards, I tried telling people, but nobody would listen. It was: "You mustn't say that"; "Don't tell such stories." Like it was all *my* fault. I'd touched up a neighbour's kid, so I deserved everything I got . . . Even worse, some of them thought I was lying, and I never lied . . . never.' He closed his eyes, rested his forehead on his hands. He muttered something that might have been 'Bastards.' And then he started to cry.

Rebus knew he had choices. Phone Social Work and have them take Rough somewhere. Put him in a cell. Or drop him off somewhere . . . anywhere. But when he tried the Social Work emergency number, no one answered. They'd be out on a call. The recorded message told him to keep trying the number every ten minutes or so. It told him not to panic.

There were empty cells in the station, but Rebus knew word would get out, and when it came time to release Darren Rough, there'd be a crowd waiting. So he lit another cigarette and went back to the interview room.

'Right,' he said, opening the door, 'you're coming with me.'

'Nice room,' Darren Rough said. He looked around, examining the high cornicing. 'Big,' he added, nodding to himself. He was trying to be pleasant, make conversation. He was wondering what Rebus was going to do with him, here in Rebus's own flat.

Rebus handed over a mug of tea and told him to sit down. He offered Rough another cigarette, the offer refused this time. Rough was sitting on the sofa. Rebus wanted to tell him to move on to one of the dining chairs. It was as if Rough could contaminate everything he touched.

'Your social worker better find you something in the morning,' Rebus said. 'Something far from Edinburgh.'

Rough looked at him. His eyes were dark-ringed, his hair needing a wash. The green raincoat was draped over the back of the sofa. He wore a check suit-jacket with jeans and baseball boots, white nylon shirt. He looked like he'd won a ninety-second dash through an Oxfam shop.

'Keep moving, eh?'

'A moving target's harder to hit,' Rebus told him.

Rough smiled tiredly. 'I see you've been hitting a target yourself.'

Rebus flexed his fingers again, trying to stop them seizing up.

Rough sipped his tea. 'He did beat me up, you know.'

'Who?'

'Your friend.'

'Jim Margolies?'

Rough nodded. 'All of a sudden he got this look in his eyes. Next thing the fists were flying.' He shook his head. 'When he killed himself, I read the obituaries. They all said he was a "fine officer", a "loving father". Attended church regularly.' A half-smile. 'When he laid into me, he must have been demonstrating muscular Christianity.'

'Careful what you say,'

'Yes, he was your friend, you worked with him. But I wonder if you *knew* him.'

He didn't say as much, but Rebus was beginning to wonder the same thing. Orange lipstick, meaning he liked them young. He'd asked Fern how young. Nothing illegal, she'd told him.

'Why do you think he died?' Rebus asked.

'How should I know?'

'When the two of you talked . . . how did he seem?'

Rough was thoughtful. 'Not angry with me or anything. Just wanting to know about Shiellion. How often I'd been . . . you know. And who by.' He glanced towards Rebus. 'Some people get a kick that way, listening to stories.'

'You think that's why he was asking?'

'Why are *you* asking all these questions, Inspector? Outing me to the papers, then coming to the rescue. I think maybe that's how *you* get your kicks, fucking with people's heads.'

Rebus thought of Cary Oakes and his games. 'I think you had something to do with Jim Margolies' death,' he said. 'Whether you know it or not.'

They sat in silence after that, until Rough asked if there was anything he could eat. Rebus went through to the kitchen, stared at one of the cupboard doors, wanting to punch it. But his knuckles wouldn't thank him for that. He looked at them. He knew what Oakes had done, rubbed them hard over the floor of the car park, maybe bunched them into fists and driven them into the steel skip. Twisted little bastard that he was. And Patience wondered if it was all a blind, some way of diverting Rebus from some other scheme. His head seemed full of diversions. How could he trust what Rough was telling him? He didn't see Rough as a schemer; too weak. But Jim Margolies . . . had *he* been playing some game?

And had it killed him?

Rebus opened the cupboard door, called out that he could do beans on toast. Rough said that would be fine. There was no marge for the toast, but Rebus reckoned the tomato sauce would soften it up. He emptied the beans into a pot, stuck the bread under the grill, and went to sort out the sleeping accommodation.

Not his own room; definitely not his own room. He opened the door to what had been the guest room, and – long before that – Sammy's room. Her single bed was still there; posters on the walls; teenage girls' annuals on a bookshelf. One of the last people to use the room had been Jack Morton. No way was Darren Rough sleeping there.

Rebus opened the wardrobe, found an old blanket and pillow, took them through to the living room.

'You can have the sofa,' he said.

'Fine. Whatever.' Rough was standing at the window. Rebus crossed over to him. A couple of kids lived across the street, but their shutters were closed, no peep-show available.

'It's so quiet here,' Rough said. 'In Greenfield, there always seems to be a row going on. Either that or a party, and most of the parties turn into a row.'

'But you're a good neighbour, eh?' Rebus said. 'Quiet, keep yourself to yourself?'

'I try to.'

'What about when the kids are noisy: don't you want to do something about them?'

Rough closed his eyes, pressed his forehead to the glass. 'I won't make any excuses,' he whispered.

'And no apologies either?'

Another smile, eyes still shut. 'I can apologise until the cows come home. It doesn't change anything. It doesn't change how I feel.' He opened his eyes, turned to Rebus. 'But you don't want to hear about that, do you?'

Rebus stared at him. 'The toast's burning,' he said, turning away.

At five o'clock, with Rough hidden under the blanket on the sofa, Rebus telephoned Bill Pryde.

'Sorry to wake you, Bill.'

'The alarm was about to go off anyway. What's up?'

'The surveillance car.'

'What about it?'

'It's not at The Shore.' He explained where it was.

'Christ, John, what about Oakes?'

'He comes and goes as he likes, Bill. The only thing we were doing there was keeping him amused.'

'You better tell that to the Farmer.'

'I will.'

'Meantime, you want me to pick up the car from your flat?'

'I've filled in the log, explained everything.'

'What about the keys?'

'Under the front seat, same place the log is. I've left it unlocked.'

'And now you're about to get your head down?'

'Something like that.' He stared at Darren Rough, watching the rise and fall of the blanket. He looked about as dangerous as pastry dough. Rebus cut the connection, tried the station. There was still no sign of Billy Horman. They'd looked everywhere. The search was being called off until daylight. Rebus called the hotel, asked for Cary Oakes's room: still no answer. He put down the phone, went into his bedroom. Lay on his bed – a mattress on the floor. He'd thought about going back to Patience's, but didn't like the thought of Rough being here by himself. He might explore, find Sammy's room. Pull open drawers, touch things. As soon as feasible, Rebus wanted him out.

You brought him here, a voice in his head seemed to say. *You brought him to this.* Sticks and crowbars and angry voices. The residents of Greenfield roused to a mob. Cal Brady with his petrol and denials. He worked for Charmer Mackenzie, worked the door at Guiser's. Damon Mee had left there, got into a taxi with a blonde. Last seen in the vicinity of the Clipper, the night of one of Ama Petrie's parties. Her father was presiding over Shiellion, where Darren Rough should have given evidence, where Rebus had been steamrollered by Richard Cordover. Lord Justice Petrie . . . who was related to Katherine Margolies.

Ama, Hannah, Katherine . . . Sammy, Patience, Janice . . . The never-ending dance of relationships and criss-crossings which took up so much space in his head. The party that never stopped, the invitations guilt-edged.

Life and death in Edinburgh. And space still left over for a few ghosts, their numbers increasing.

If I'd stuck around Fife, he thought, *not joined the army . . . what would I be thinking now? Who would I be?*

The voice in his head again – was it Jack Morton's? *It was never going to happen. This is where you were always headed.* He looked around the room for whisky, but he was all cleaned out. Closed his eyes instead. Still that dull pain at the back of his skull. *Please, Lord, let my sleep be dreamless.*

His first prayer in a while.

Cary Oakes had been in Arden Street for Rebus's return, had seen him get out of his car with another man, lead the man into his tenement. He wondered who this stranger was, wondered where Rebus had met him. He'd been standing across the road, hidden in the shadow of a tenement doorway. He had a plastic bag with him, a paperback book inside to give it weight. If anyone saw him, he had his story ready: working shifts, waiting for his lift to turn up. They were late, he'd say.

Only no one saw him. No one entered or left the building. But he saw the lights come on in Rebus's living room. Saw the stranger approach the window, put his head to it. Saw Rebus over the man's shoulder, staring down. Oakes stood his ground, felt he hadn't been spotted. The beauty was, even if Rebus *did* see him, well, that was all right too. Then Rebus had come out of the tenement, gone to his car to fetch something: a book of some kind. Way he was moving, acting, Oakes hadn't done too much damage. Rebus took the book upstairs with him, then came back down half an hour later, put it back in the car. When he'd gone back up again, Oakes crossed to where the car was parked, tried the driver's door. It wasn't locked. He got in, felt on the floor for where Rebus had put the book. Found it. And the car keys. Smiled to himself. He turned the ignition, powered up the police radio: easy listening while he perused the surveillance notes. Rebus hadn't put in anything about Alan Archibald. That was interesting.

Fifty minutes later, when the tenement door rattled open, he slid down in his seat, rose up again to watch the stranger walk away from the building. He looked dirty and dishevelled. Some secret little vice of Rebus's? Oakes didn't think so. But it intrigued him all the same. He waited till the man had rounded the corner, then started the engine and began to follow . . .

At six o'clock, Rebus was wakened by the front buzzer. He went to the door, pushed the intercom.

'Who is it?'

'It's me.' Bill Pryde, not sounding happy.

'What's the matter?'

'This car I'm supposed to pick up. Just where exactly have you hidden it?'

'Hang on.'

Rebus walked into the living room, glanced at the sofa. Saw the blanket had been folded neatly; no sign of Darren Rough. Peered out of the window. A space where the car had been. He cursed under his breath. Put his shoes on and headed downstairs.

'I think someone took it,' he told Bill Pryde.

'This isn't my fuck-up, John.' Pryde: ticking off the days till retirement.

'I know,' Rebus said, unwilling to add that he might know who'd taken it: Darren Rough.

Pryde pointed at his hands. 'Word's out you lost the punch-up. How does Oakes look?'

'That's not what happened,' Rebus said.

'You were found KO'd in a skip, way I heard it.'

Rebus stared at him. 'You want to walk to work, Bill?'

Pryde shook his head. 'I want to be ringside for the main bout: you telling the Farmer how you came to lose the car.'

Rebus stared up and down the road again. 'Better slip a horseshoe into my glove for that one,' he said, turning back into the tenement.

25

Rebus drove them to St Leonard's in his Saab and reported the theft, cheering up the day shift who'd just come on. At quarter to nine, he was in the Farmer's office, explaining the whole thing yet again, including the scrapes on his hands. The Farmer busied himself at his coffee machine all the time Rebus was making his report. It was an espresso-maker with a spout for steamed milk. He hadn't offered Rebus a cup. When Rebus stopped talking, the Farmer poured the foamy milk into his mug, switched off the machine, and sat behind his desk. Holding the mug in both hands, he looked at Rebus.

'I always thought surveillance was a fairly simple procedure. Once more, you've managed to prove me wrong.'

'It wasn't going anywhere, sir.'

'Unlike the missing car.'

Rebus looked down at the floor.

'So let me see where we stand,' the Farmer continued, taking another sip. 'I tell you to lay off Darren Rough. You go out looking for him. I tell you to keep an eye on a man whom experts say may murder someone. You end up unconscious in a rubbish skip.' The Farmer's voice was rising. 'You find Darren Rough and take him to your flat. He then leaves, taking one of our cars with him, along with the surveillance log. Does that just about cover it?' His face was growing red with anger.

'Clear and concise, sir.'

'*Don't you dare be amused!*' The Farmer slapped a hand down on the desk.

'I'm anything but, sir.' Rebus gritted his teeth. 'But I thought I was doing the right thing at the time.'

'No, Inspector. As usual, what you were doing was following your own agenda, and to hell with the rest of us. Isn't that nearer the mark?'

'With respect, sir—'

'Don't give me that. You've no respect for me, no respect for the job we're supposed to be doing here!'

'Maybe you're right, sir,' Rebus said quietly, his head beginning to throb again.

The Farmer looked at him, leaned back in his chair and took another mouthful of coffee. 'So what are we going to do about that?'

'I don't know, sir. I mean, you're right: I've been having doubts about the job for months. Ever since Jack Morton . . .'

'Maybe even before then?' Sounding calmer now.

'Maybe, sir. More than once, I've thought about chucking it.' He looked at his boss. 'Make your life a bit easier.'

'But you haven't chucked it.'

'No, sir.'

'Must be a reason.'

'Maybe a bit of me still believes, sir. And funnily enough, that part's been growing.'

'Oh?'

Alan Archibald; Darren Rough: he hadn't mentioned Archibald to the Farmer, hadn't seen the point.

'I was wrong about Rough, I admit that. Well . . . I'm not sure I was wrong, to tell you the truth. But I know now why he's in Edinburgh. I know a bit more about his background.'

'What are you saying?' The Farmer narrowed his eyes. 'You *understand* him, is that it?' A smile with an edge of cruelty to it. 'Compassion? *You*, John? I didn't know dinosaurs could evolve.'

'Either that or the species dies,' Rebus said, pressing his hands to his knees. How could he explain it, explain what he was learning: that the past shapes the present, that free will is a fantasy, that a force we could call Fate or God controls the paths we take? Janice throwing a punch . . . young Darren Rough in a car on the way to Shiellion . . . Alan Archibald and his niece. All seemed connected in some strange and intricate way.

'You'll want a full report,' Rebus said, straightening in his chair.

The Farmer nodded. 'I was about to pull the surveillance anyway.' He put down his mug. 'Do you think Cary Oakes is dangerous?'

'Definitely. But I think he's changed.'

'Changed how?'

'His spree in the States, it wasn't planned. There was a lack of deliberation, and it always seemed to be part of some other strategy.'

'Explain.'

'He killed because he needed things: money, a car, whatever. But towards the end, I think he was really getting a taste for it. Then he got caught. He's been all these years in jail, remembering that buzz.'

'So now he might kill for no other reason than the buzz?'

'I'm not sure. I think he has some sort of plan, something that involves Edinburgh.' And Alan Archibald, he might have added. 'I think he's getting all sorts of tingly feelings just planning it.'

'Maybe he'll put it off indefinitely.'

Rebus smiled. 'I don't think so. This is foreplay to him.'

The Farmer seemed embarrassed by the image, relieved when his phone sounded. He picked up the receiver, listened.

'Good,' he said at last. 'I'll let him know.'

He put down the receiver, looked up at Rebus. 'The car's turned up.'

'Great.'

'Handily parked, too.'

Rebus asked what the Farmer meant. The answer gave him the shock of his life.

A couple of uniforms were already on the scene when Rebus, the Farmer and Bill Pryde arrived at The Shore. The Rover was sitting in its usual spot, opposite the hotel.

'I don't believe it,' Rebus said for the fifth or sixth time.

'This isn't some joke of yours?' Bill Pryde asked.

The Farmer looked inside. 'Where's the log?'

'It was under the seat, sir.'

The Farmer reached in, pulled out the log and a set of car keys.

'Did you say anything to Rough about the surveillance?' he asked. Rebus shook his head. 'So can we assume Rough did *not* take the car?' Rebus shrugged.

'Looks like it was someone who knew what we were up to,' Bill Pryde admitted.

'Or simply read about it in the log,' Rebus said. 'Anyone finding the keys would have found the log.'

'True,' Pryde conceded.

'Which might put Rough back in the frame,' the Farmer said. 'Thing is, it also means whoever stole the car read the surveillance notes.'

'Red faces all round, sir,' Pryde said.

'More than that if Fettes get to hear about it.'

'Who's going to tell them?'

The Farmer had flipped through the notes, coming to Rebus's final section – or what should have been the final section. He opened the book wide, held it out so Rebus and Pryde could see it.

'What's this?'

Rebus looked. Written in big capitals, red felt pen. Someone had added a postscript to Rebus's thoughts on the case:

NAUGHTY, NAUGHTY. WHERE'S MR ARCHIBALD????

The Farmer was staring at him.

'Who's Mr Archibald?'

Pryde was shrugging. 'Search me.'

But the Farmer had eyes only for John Rebus.

'Who's Mr Archibald?' he repeated, red rising to his cheeks. Rebus said nothing, crossed the street and looked in through the large windows of the restaurant. They were serving late breakfasts, tables half-hidden behind potted plants and hanging baskets. But there, at a window table and enjoying the show, sat Cary Oakes. He waved a fork at Rebus, sat beaming a grin as he lifted a glass of orange juice and toasted him. Rebus made for the hotel door, pushed it open, strode inside. Cooking smells were wafting from the restaurant. A waiter asked if he wanted a table for one. Rebus ignored him, walked straight up to the table where Cary Oakes was seated.

'Care to join me, Inspector?'

'Not even if you were coming apart at the seams.' Rebus pushed his knuckles into Oakes's face. 'Remember these?'

'Looks nasty,' Oakes said. 'I'd get a doctor to look at them. Lucky you already know one.'

'You know where I live,' Rebus hissed. 'Jim Stevens told you.'

'Did he?' Oakes started cutting up a sausage. Rebus noticed that he sliced it lengthwise first, as though dissecting it.

'You took the car.'

'Bit early for riddles.' Oakes lifted a morsel of meat to his lips. Rebus flung out a hand, sent fork and sausage flying. Then he hoisted Cary Oakes to his feet.

'What the fuck are you up to?'

'Shouldn't that be my line?' Oakes said, grinning. There was a sudden explosion of light. Rebus half-turned his head. Jim Stevens was behind him. Next to him stood a photographer.

'Now,' Stevens was saying, 'if we could have the two of you shaking hands in the next one.' He winked at Rebus. 'Told you I wanted some pictures.'

Rebus dropped Oakes, flew towards the journalist.

'Inspector!'

The Farmer's voice. He was in the restaurant doorway, face like fury. 'A word with you outside, if you don't mind.' A voice not to be disobeyed. Rebus stared hard at Jim Stevens, letting him know this wasn't the end of anything. Then he walked out of the dining room and into reception. The Farmer was after him.

'I'm still waiting for an answer. Who is Mr Archibald?'

'A man with a mission,' Rebus told him. In his mind, he could still see the grin on Oakes's face. 'Problem is, he's not the only one.'

Rebus spent till lunchtime 'in conference' with the Farmer. Just before midday, Archibald himself joined them, the Farmer having dispatched a squad car to Corstorphine to pick him up. The two men knew one another of old.

'Thought you'd have had the gold watch by now,' Archibald said, shaking the Farmer's hand. But the Farmer was not to be mollified.

'Sit down, Alan. For a retired copper, you haven't half been busy.'

Archibald glanced at Rebus, who was staring at the window-blind. 'I'm going to nail him, that's all.'

'Oh, that's all, is it?' The Farmer looked mock-astonished. 'John tells me you've seen the files on Cary Oakes. In fact, you've got more gen on him than we have. So you should know who you're dealing with.'

'I know *what* I'm dealing with.'

The Farmer's gaze went from Archibald to Rebus and back again. 'It's bad enough I'm lumbered with this one,' he said, nodding towards Rebus. 'Last thing I need is yet another headcase out there trying to take the law into his own hands. You think Oakes killed your niece, show me the evidence.'

'Come on, man . . .'

'Show me the evidence!'

'I would if I could.'

'Would you, Alan?' The Farmer paused. 'Or would you want to keep it personal, right to the bitter end?' He turned to Rebus. 'What about you, John? Were you going to lend a hand burying the body?'

'If I'd wanted him dead,' Archibald said, 'he'd be in the ground by now.'

'But what if he confesses, Alan? Just you and him, no third party.' The Farmer shook his head. 'Wouldn't be enough to go to court with, so what would you do?'

'It'd be enough,' Archibald said quietly.

'For what?'

'For me. For Deirdre's memory.'

The Farmer waited, turned to Rebus. 'Do you buy that? You think Alan here would listen to Oakes's confession and then just walk away?'

'I don't know him well enough to comment.' Rebus still seemed mesmerised by the window-blind.

'Two peas in a pod,' the Farmer said. Rebus glanced at Archibald, who was looking at him. There was a knock at the door. The Farmer barked an order to enter. It was Siobhan Clarke.

'Come to intercede?' the Farmer asked.

'No, sir.' She seemed unwilling to come in; stood with only her head showing round the door.

'Well?'

'Suspicious death, sir. Up on Salisbury Crags.'

'How suspicious?'

'First reports say very.'

The Farmer pinched the bridge of his nose. 'This is one of those weeks that seem to last a fortnight.'

'Thing is, sir, from the description, I'd say we have an ID.'

He looked at her, hearing something in her tone. 'Someone we know?'

Clarke was looking towards Rebus. 'I'd say so, sir.'

'This isn't a parlour game, DC Clarke.'

She cleared her throat. 'I think it might be Darren Rough.'

26

'Start any time you're ready.'

Jim Stevens' room was beginning to look messy and lived-in, just the way he liked. But they weren't in Stevens' room, they were in Oakes's, and it looked like its occupant hadn't spent any time there at all. There were two chairs at a small circular table by the window. The complimentary book of matches still sat folded open in its ashtray. Two magazines of interest to visitors to Edinburgh sat beside it, and lying on top of them was the guests' comment card, yet to be filled in, or even perused.

Most people, Stevens guessed, even people who'd spent a third of their life enjoying the facilities of a foreign country's prison service, would do what he'd done in his own room: explore it, try out and touch everything, flick through every piece of literature.

But not Cary Oakes, who now cleared his throat.

'Aren't you curious about what Rebus wanted?'

Stevens looked at him. 'I just want this finished.'

'Lost the old vigour and vim, eh, Jim?'

'You have that effect on people.'

'Tracked down any of my old teenage gang?' Oakes laughed at the look on Stevens' face. 'Thought not. Probably scattered to the four winds by now.'

'Last time we broke off,' Stevens said coldly, checking the spools were turning, 'you were crossing America.'

Oakes nodded. 'I got to a place called, believe it or not, Opportunity, a ratty little truck-stop on the Washington–Idaho border. That's where I met the trucker, Fat Boy. I never learned his real name; I think even the ID he carried was fake.'

'What name was on the ID?'

Oakes ignored the question. 'Fat Boy had these notions about a government conspiracy, told me he kept his home booby-trapped whenever he was working long-distance. He said truckers got a real good view of the world – by which he meant the USA; that's as far as his world stretched – a real good view from behind the wheel of a truck. He knew a trucker would make a damned good President.

'So that was Fat Boy. My introduction to him. Opportunity, Washington. Lots of names like that in the States. Lots of Fat Boys, too. We got talking about murder. The radio was on, and every other station had news flashes about unlawful killing. He said the word "unlawful" was a misnomer. There was "wrong" killing and "right" killing, and which was which was down to the individual, not the lawmakers.'

'And what kind did you do?'

Oakes didn't like his flow being interrupted. 'I'm talking about Fat Boy, not me.'

'How long did you travel with him?' Stevens was trying to keep the chronology right.

'Three, four days. We headed south to make a delivery, then back up on to I-90.'

'What was he carrying?'

'Electrical goods. He worked for General Electric. Meant he travelled all over. He said that was good, considering his hobby. His hobby was killing people.' Oakes looked to Stevens. 'It was supposed to unnerve me, him saying something like that while we're travelling fifty-five on an interstate. Maybe if it had, that would have been it: he'd have tried skinning me. But I just looked at him, told him that was interesting.' A laugh. 'Mild understatement, right? Someone tells you they're a serial killer and you say "Mm, that's interesting."'

'But you believed him?'

'After a while, yes. And I thought: all this stuff he's telling me, no way is he letting me go. Every time we stopped, I thought he was about to whack me.'

'You were ready for him?' Stevens was staring at Oakes, trying to gauge how much of the story was true. Did it relate in some way to the relationship between Oakes and the reporter himself?

'You know the strange part? I just let myself relax into it. Like, if he was going to kill me, OK, that's what was going to happen. It was as if I didn't care; I could have died right then, and it would have been poetic justice or something.'

'Did he kill anyone while you were on the road?'

'No.'

'But he convinced you he wasn't lying?'

'You think he was lying, Jim?'

'When they arrested you, did you tell the police about him?'

'Why the hell would I do that?'

'Might have scored you some points.'

'Truth is, I never thought about it.'

'But he made you think about killing?'

'He knew what he was talking about. I mean, you can always tell when someone's making it up, can't you?' Oakes beamed a smile. '"Can the world really be like this?" I remember asking myself that as I listened to him. And the answer came back: yes, of course. Why should it be any different?'

'You're saying Fat Boy made you feel all right about killing?'

'Am I?'

'Then what are you saying?'

'Just telling you my story, Jim. It's up to you how you read it.'

'What about in jail, Cary? All that time to yourself, thoughts that you're thinking . . . ?'

'Jim, you get no time to yourself. There's always noise, disruption, routine. You sit there trying to think, they send you for psychiatric evaluation.' Oakes took a final sip of orange juice. 'But I see what you're getting at.' He examined his empty glass. 'How's the background check going, by the way? Spoken to anyone at Walla Walla?' Turned the empty glass in his hand. 'Take away the juice and the ice, you're left with a lethal weapon.' He pretended to smash the glass against the edge of the table, and then laughed a laugh which sent a shiver right along Jim Stevens' arms.

Climbing back up Salisbury Crags, Rebus kept his hands in his pockets and his thoughts to himself. He knew what the Farmer was thinking. This morning, Darren Rough had been in Rebus's flat. As far as they knew, Rebus was the last person to have seen him alive.

And Rebus had been his tormentor, his nemesis. The Farmer wouldn't make anything of it, but others might: Jane Barbour; Rough's social worker.

Radical Road was a stony footpath which led around the Crags. You could start near the student residences at Pollock Halls and end up at Holyrood. Along the way, you had the city skyline for company, stretching from the south and west to the city centre and beyond. All spires and crenellations. Manfred Mann: 'Cubist Town'. With Greenfield almost directly below.

'You picked him up here, didn't you?' the Farmer asked as they walked.

Rebus shook his head. 'St Margaret's Loch.' Which lay around a long curve in the rock and down an impossibly steep bank. 'Tell you what, though,' he added. 'Jim Margolies jumped from up there.' And he pointed with his finger, way up to where the rock-face ended in something akin to a clifftop. People took their dogs for walks across the plateau, not straying too close to the edge. Edinburgh was prone to sudden, malevolent gusts, any one of which could have you over the side.

The Farmer was breathing hard. 'You still see a connection between Rough and Jim Margolies?'

'Now more than ever, sir.'

The body lay a little further along the path, cordoned off by warning tape. A few walkers, wrapped up against the weather, had gathered at the cordon, stretching their necks for a view. A white plastic contraption like a windbreak had been placed around the body, so that only those who needed to see it would. A woman with a black springer spaniel was being interviewed: she'd been the one to find the body. Out walking the dog, a daily ritual which both had looked forward to. From now on, she'd find another route, a long way from Salisbury Crags.

'Hard to believe they're putting our Parliament there,' the Farmer commented, looking down towards Holyrood Road. 'A real old backwater. Traffic's going to be a nightmare.'

'And it's on our patch.'

'Not my problem, thank God.' The Farmer sniffed. 'I'll have that gold watch on one hand and a golfing glove on the other.'

They passed through the cordon. The scene-of-crime team was at work, securing the *locus* and ensuring what they liked to call its 'purity'. This meant Rebus and the Farmer had to don coveralls and overshoes, so they'd leave no trace elements at the scene.

'The wind up here will probably have scattered them to the four corners anyway,' Rebus said. But it was a half-hearted grouch: he knew the worth of scene-of-crime work, knew that science and forensics were his friends. A police doctor had declared the victim deceased. Dr Curt was the usual pathologist, but he was in Miami to give a paper at some convention. His superior, Professor Gates, had stepped in, and was examining the body *in situ*. He was a large man with thick brown hair slicked back from his forehead. He carried a hand-held tape recorder, talking into it as he moved around. He was forced to jostle for space: a photographer and video cameraman both wanted shots of the corpse.

DS George Silvers came over. He nodded a greeting to his Chief Superintendent, but took it further, so that it turned into something more akin to a ceremonial bow. That was typical of Silvers, whose station nickname was 'Hi-Ho'. He was in his late thirties, always smartly dressed and coiffed, always on the eye for promotion without the necessary concomitant of hard work. His black hair and deep-set eyes gave him the look of football pundit Alan Hansen.

'We think we've got the murder weapon, sir. A rock with some blood and hair on it.' He pointed up the path. 'Forty yards or so that way.'

'Who found it?'

'A dog, sir.' One eye twitching. 'Licked most of the blood off before we could get to it.'

Professor Gates looked up from his work. 'So if the lab gets a match,' he said, 'and tells you the victim had a lovely shiny coat, you'll know what the problem is.'

He laughed, and Rebus laughed with him. It was like that at the *locus*, everyone pretending nothing was out of the ordinary, erecting barriers to separate them from the glaring fact that *everything* was out of the ordinary.

'I'm told you might manage an informal ID,' Gates said. Rebus nodded, took a deep breath and stepped forward. The body was lying where it had fallen, the back of the skull smashed open and caked with blood. The face rested against the jagged path, one leg bent at the knee, the other straight. One arm was trapped beneath the body, the other stretching so the fingers could claw at the cold earth. Rebus could tell from the clothes, but crouched down to study what could be seen of the face. Gates lifted it a little to help. Light had died behind the eyes; the three-day growth of beard would need to be shaved by the undertaker. Rebus nodded.

'Darren Rough,' he said, his voice growing thick.

Having taken a break from recording, Jim Stevens sat naked on the edge of his bed, discarded clothes strewn around him, two empty miniatures of whisky on his bedside cabinet. The empty glass was clutched in one hand, and he stared at it and through it, focusing on things the world couldn't see . . .

Part Two

Found

I invite you to examine more closely your duty and the obligations of your earthly service because that is something which all of us are only dimly aware of, and we scarcely . . .

27

One of Rough's shoes had come off at some point, about halfway between the spot where his body had fallen and where the rock had been found. One early theory: someone had thumped him hard. He'd stumbled, staggered on, trying to get away from his attacker. His shoe had come off and been discarded. Finally, he'd fallen to the ground, where he'd died from the earlier blows. A barking dog approaching had alerted the attacker to the need to flee.

Another theory: after being hit, Rough had died instantly. His attacker had then dragged him along the path, the shoe coming free. Maybe intending to set things up so it looked like Rough had jumped or fallen from the Crags. But the dog-walker had come along, scaring off the killer.

'What was he doing up there anyway?' someone back at the station asked.

'I think he liked it there,' Rebus said. He was now officially the St Leonard's expert on Darren Rough. 'It was like a sanctuary, somewhere he felt safe. And he could look down on Greenfield from there, see what was happening.'

'So someone followed him? Sneaked up on him?'

'Or persuaded him to go there.'

'Why?'

'To make it look like suicide. Maybe they read about Jim Margolies in the paper.'

'It's a thought . . .'

There were plenty of thoughts, plenty of theories. One thought was: good riddance to the bastard. A week ago, it would have been Rebus's view, too.

The murder room was being prepared, computers moved from other parts of the building into the room set aside for such work. The Farmer had put Chief Inspector Gill Templer in charge. Rebus had been her lover for a time, so long ago now it might have been in some past life. Her hair was a dark-streaked feather-cut. Her eyes were emerald green. She moved confidently across the room, checking preparations.

'Good luck,' Rebus told her.

'I want you on the team,' she said.

Rebus thought he could understand. She was circling the wagons, and it was better to have him in the ring shooting out, than outside shooting in.

'And I want a report on my desk: everything you can tell me about you and the deceased.'

Rebus nodded, got to work on one of the computers. *Everything you can tell me*: Rebus liked her wording, it gave him an escape clause – not everything he *knew* necessarily, but all he felt able to divulge. He looked across to where Siobhan Clarke was compiling a wall-mounted duty roster. She saw him and made a T sign with her hands. He nodded, and five minutes later she was back with two scalding beakers.

'Here you go.'

'Thanks,' he said. She was looking over his shoulder at the screen.

'Nothing but the truth?' she asked.

'What do you think?'

She blew on her cup. 'Any idea who'd want him dead?'

'I can't think of many who didn't. We've got half the population of Greenfield to start with.' Especially Cal Brady, with his previous convictions; and not forgetting his mother . . .

'Chasing him out and killing him aren't quite in the same league.'

'No, but something like that can escalate. Maybe Billy Horman was all it took.'

She rested against the corner of the desk. 'Hit with a rock . . . doesn't sound premeditated, does it?'

Hit with a rock . . . Deirdre, Alan Archibald's niece, had been killed in a similar way: smashed over the head with a rock and then strangled. Clarke could read his mind.

'Cary Oakes?'

'Have we got a time of death yet?' Rebus asked, reaching for a telephone.

'Not that I know of. Body was found at eleven thirty.'

'And we're guessing the killer heard someone coming and ran for it.' Rebus had pressed the digits and was waiting. Connected. 'Hello, could you put me through to James Stevens, please?'

Clarke looked at him. He put his hand over the mouthpiece. 'I want to know what happened after breakfast.' He listened again, took his hand away. 'Could you try Cary Oakes's room for me?' Shook his head to let Clarke know Stevens wasn't in his own room. This time the call was answered.

'Oakes, is that you? It's Rebus here, put Stevens on.' He waited a moment. 'One question: what happened after breakfast?' Listened again. 'Was he out of your sight? You've been there all morning?' Listened. 'No, it's all right. You'll find out soon enough.'

Replaced the receiver.

'They've been working all morning.'

'No chance it was Oakes then.' She looked at the computer screen. 'What would be his motive anyway?'

'Christ knows. But he was at my flat. He took the patrol car. Maybe he saw Rough leave, worked out he was connected to me.'

'Can you prove that?'

'No.'

'Then all he has to do is deny it.'

Rebus exhaled noisily. 'It's all games with him.'

Gill Templer was staring at them from across the room.

'I'd better get back to work,' Clarke said, taking her tea with her. Rebus finished his report, printed it out, handed it personally to Gill Templer.

'When's the post-mortem?'

She checked her watch. 'I was just about to head over there.'

'Need a driver?'

She studied him. 'Has your driving improved?'

'I'll let you be the judge, ma'am.'

The city mortuary wasn't in business. Health and Safety; changes needed to be made. Meantime, they were using the Western General Hospital. Because they couldn't find any relatives or friends, Andy Davies had been called to verify Rebus's identification. The social worker was waiting when Rebus and Gill Templer arrived. He made the ID, said nothing to Rebus but shot him a cold look before leaving.

'Bad blood?' Templer asked.

'Better than none at all, Gill.'

Professor Gates was already at work by the time they'd got their gowns and masks on. For the official ID, Rough's corpse had worn a shroud. Now, lying on the stainless-steel bench, it wore nothing at all. Prominent ribs, Rebus noted. He was thinking of the meal he'd made for Rough. Grudgingly made. Beans on toast. Probably the man's last meal ever. And eventually, Gates would reveal it to the world again. Rebus half-turned his face.

'Seasick, Inspector?' Gates asked.

'I'll be fine so long as we keep out of the bilges.'

Gates chuckled. 'But below decks is the most interesting part.' He was measuring, muttering his findings to his assistant, a young man with a face the colour of a cancer bed.

'And how are you, Gill?' he asked at last.

'Overworked.'

Gates glanced up. 'Fine lassie like you should be at home, bringing up strong healthy bairns.'

'Thanks for the vote of confidence.'

Gates chuckled again. 'Don't tell me you lack suitors?'

She chose to ignore the remark.

'What about you, John?' Gates persisted. 'Love life satisfactory?

Maybe I should play Cupid, put the two of you together. What do you say to that now, eh?'

Rebus and Templer shared a look.

'Professions like ours,' Gates drawled on, 'aren't the same as being a lawyer or a novelist, are they? Not much of an ice-breaker at parties.' He nodded towards his assistant. 'Bear that in mind, Jerry. No nookie unless you lie about what you do.' Gates's final chuckle turned into a choking bark, a bronchial cough which almost doubled him over. He wiped his eyes afterwards.

'Time to stop smoking,' Templer warned him.

'I can't do that. It would spoil the bet.'

'What bet?'

'Dr Curt and myself: who'll live the longer on twenty a day.'

'That's . . .' Templer had been about to say 'sick', but then she saw that the body had been opened up almost without her noticing, and she realised why Gates kept the conversation going: it was to take everyone's mind off the task at hand. And for a few moments, it had worked.

'I'll tell you one thing straight off,' the pathologist said. 'His clothes were damp, and to me that means rain. I've checked: we had a short shower early this morning and nothing since.'

'Could he have got wet lying on the path?'

'He was lying on his front. The back of his clothing was damp. So he was out in that shower, whether alive or dead I can't say. But his hair was wet, too. Now, if you're caught in a sudden downpour, wouldn't you usually pull your jacket up over your head?'

'Depends on your state of mind,' Rebus said.

Gates shrugged. 'I'm only surmising. But one thing I'm sure of.' He ran a finger along the body, tracing patches of pale bluish markings. '*Livor mortis*. It was present at the scene. I arrived forty-five minutes after the body was discovered.'

'But lividity starts . . . ?'

'Well, it starts from the moment the heart stops pumping, but it becomes visible somewhere between half an hour and an hour after death. This was well-established by the time I arrived.'

'What about rigor mortis?'

'Eyelids had stiffened, as had the jaw. I'll take a potassium sample from the eye, to get a better idea of timing, but right now I'd guess the body had been lying there for three hours, maybe more.'

Rebus took a step forward. If Gates was right – and he invariably was – the dog-walker had not disturbed the killer. The killer had been long gone by the time the spaniel and its owner had arrived, and Darren Rough had died around seven or eight in the morning. At five he'd been asleep on Rebus's couch; by six he'd gone . . .

'Did he die where we found him?' Rebus asked, wanting to be sure.

'Judging by the patterns of lividity, I'd say it's a racing certainty.'

The pathologist paused. 'Of course, I've lost a few pounds on horses in my time.'

'We need a more specific time of death.'

'I know you do, Inspector. You *always* do. I'll do what tests the budget will stretch to.'

'And ASAP.'

Gates nodded. He was about ready to begin removing the inner organs. Jerry was fussing with the necessary tools.

Rebus was thinking: three, maybe four hours.

Thinking: Cary Oakes was back in the running.

28

They took him in for questioning, Rebus keeping out of the way, listening to the tapes afterwards. Stevens' paper had provided their client with a solicitor from one of the city's top firms, despite Templer's insistence that all they had were a few questions, easily cleared up. But Oakes was saying nothing. Templer was good, and she had Pryde with her: their routine was well-honed, but Rebus got the feeling Oakes had seen all the moves before. He'd been examined and cross-examined and called to the stand again, he'd been through all that in an American courtroom. He just sat there and said he knew nothing about the patrol car, nothing about where Rebus lived, and nothing about any dead paedophile. His final comment:

'What's all the fuss about a kiddie-fucker?'

Pryde, listening to the tape, folded his arms at that and puckered his lips, most of him agreeing with the sentiment. When Pryde asked if Rebus was heading outside for a smoke, Rebus, inwardly gasping for one, shook his head. Later, he went out into the car park alone, pacing as he sucked hungrily on first one Silk Cut and then a second. Ten a day, he was keeping to ten a day. And if he went as high as twelve today, that meant only eight tomorrow. Eight was fine, he could handle that. It gave him a margin for today, a margin he reckoned he'd need.

Only thing was, he was already in arrears for the week; for the whole month, truth be told.

Tom Jackson came out, lit one of his own. They didn't speak for the first couple of minutes. Jackson scuffed his shoes on the tarmac and broke the silence.

'I hear you took him in.'

Rebus blew smoke from his nose. 'That's right.'

'Rescue act, let him stay the night.'

'So?'

'So not everyone would have been so charitable.'

'I'm not sure it was charity.'

'What then?'

What then? It was a good question.

'Thing is,' Jackson went on, 'a few days back, you were all for stringing him up.'

'Don't exaggerate.'

'You set that pack of wild dogs on him.'

'You mean the papers or his neighbours?'

'Both.'

'Careful, Tom. You're their community officer. That's your flock you're talking about.'

'I'm talking about *you*: what happened?'

'He only slept on my couch, Tom. It's not like I gave him a gam or anything.' Rebus flicked his third cigarette on to the ground, stubbed it out. Only half-smoked, so he'd count two and a half; round it down to two.

'We still haven't turned up the kid.'

'How's his mother doing?'

Jackson knew the question's subtext, answered accordingly. 'Nobody seems to think she's a suspect.'

'What's her history?'

'Billy's her only kid. Had him at nineteen.'

'Is the father around?'

'Did the usual vanishing act before the baby was born. Ran off to Ulster to join the paramilitaries.'

'He'll be running for office now then.'

Jackson snorted. 'She's had half a dozen blokes since; been living with the latest for the past few weeks.'

'The three of them in the flat together?'

Jackson nodded. 'He's being interviewed. We're digging into his history.'

'A fiver says he's got form.'

'What? Living in Greenfield?' Jackson smiled. 'Keep your money in your pocket.' He paused. 'You really don't think this connects to our deceased friend?'

'It might do, Tom. But just maybe not in the way we think.'

'What do you mean?'

'Be seeing you,' Rebus said, moving away.

Thinking of an old Gravy Train song: 'Won't Talk About It'.

He told Patience he wouldn't be seeing her. There must have been something in his tone of voice.

'Out on the ran-dan?' she said.

'You know me too well.' He put the receiver down before she could say anything else. He started at The Maltings, headed up Causewayside to Swany's, then took a taxi to the Ox. His car was back at St Leonard's: no problem, he could walk into work next morning. Salty Dougary, one of the Young Street regulars, had just been in hospital: a coronary; they'd operated, angioplasty or something like that. He was telling the bar all about it. For some reason Rebus couldn't fathom, the operation had apparently started at Dougary's groin.

'Way to a man's heart,' Rebus commented, sinking another whisky. He was diluting them with water, but not overly so. He felt fine, as in not drunk; mellow, kind of. But he knew if he walked out of the bar, he'd start to feel the alcohol. A good excuse to stay put, like that character in *Apocalypse Now*: 'Never get out of the boat.' It was only when you left the boat that you got into trouble. The same thing, in Rebus's experience, was true of pubs, which was why he was still in the Ox at half past midnight. The back room had been taken over by musicians, a dozen or more of them; guitars mostly, twelve-bar blues. One guy with a beard was playing the harmonica like he was in front of a Madison Garden crowd. Janis Joplin: 'Buried Alive in the Blues'.

Rebus was talking with George Klasser, a doctor at the Infirmary. Klasser usually left early – sevenish or a little after. When he stayed late, it was a sign things were fraught at home. He'd started the evening advising Salty Dougary to regulate his alcohol intake.

'The pot calling the kettle black,' had been Dougary's riposte. Dougary looking like he'd just been on holiday rather than in surgery: face tanned, ciggies cut down from forty a day to ten. Klasser with dark shadows under his eyes, a slight trembling to the hand when he picked up his glass. Rebus had had an uncle who'd smoked a pack of cigarettes every day of his life and lived to be eighty. His own father had died younger, having given up cigarettes two decades previously. You never could tell.

There were only four of them in the front bar, five including Harry. Dougary, who'd drunk in every pub in the city, reckoned Harry was Edinburgh's rudest barman, which was quite a feat, considering the competition.

'I wish youse lot would bugger off home,' Harry said, not for the first time that evening.

'Night's young yet, Harry,' Dougary said.

'How come they let you out of intensive care?'

Dougary winked. 'Intensive care's what I come in here for.' He toasted them with his glass and raised it to his lips. Twenty minutes before, Rebus had told Klasser about Darren Rough. Now Klasser turned to him, eyes heavy-lidded.

'There was a famous murder case. Turn of the century, I think it was. German couple came here on their honeymoon, only it turned out he wanted her money rather than love. He planned to kill her, make it look like suicide. So they went for a walk up on Arthur's Seat, and he pushed her off the Crags.'

'But he didn't get away with it?'

'Obviously not, or there'd be no story to tell.'

'So how was he caught?'

Klasser stared into his glass. 'I can't recall.'

Dougary laughed. 'Don't let him start telling any jokes, he always forgets the punchline.'

'I'll punch *you* in a minute, Salty.'

'Get in the queue,' Harry commented.

Some nights it was like that in the Oxford Bar. When the guitar-players packed up, Rebus put his coat on. There was a stiff breeze outside, and it had been raining again, the streets black and shiny as a beetle's back. He'd meant to phone Janice, but what would he have said? There was no news of Damon. He walked along Princes Street, deciding he liked the city best like this: all the visitors tucked up in bed. Outside the Balmoral Hotel, a line of Jags and Rovers sat, their chauffeurs waiting for some function to finish. A young couple walked past, sharing a bottle of cheap cider. The male wore a jacket with a badge on it. The badge said Stockholm Film Festival. Rebus had never heard of it. Maybe it was the name of a band: you couldn't be sure these days.

He walked up the Bridges, stopped at some railings so he could look down on to the Cowgate. There were clubs still open down there, teenagers spilling on to the road. The police had names for the Cowgate when it got like this: Little Saigon; the blood bank; hell on earth. Even the patrol cars went in twos. Whoops and yells: a couple of girls in short dresses. One lad was down on his knees in the road, begging to be noticed.

Pretty Things: 'Cries from the Midnight Circus'.

In Edinburgh, sometimes it could be midnight in the middle of the day . . .

He didn't know where he was going, what he was doing. If he was going home, he was doing so only by degrees. When a taxi came, he flagged it down. On sudden impulse, he named his destination.

'The Shore.'

29

The idea was . . .

The idea was to stand in the freezing cold outside the hotel, call up to Oakes's room on the mobile. Get him downstairs . . . no crack to the back of the head this time. Face to face. But it was the drink, that was all. Rebus knew he wouldn't do it; knew Oakes wouldn't fall for it anyway. Looking across from The Shore, he saw there were lights from the Clipper, and a minder on the door. So Rebus crossed the bridge, introduced himself. The minder was wiping sweat from his face. From within, Rebus could hear raised voices, laughter.

'Party?' he asked.

'Don't tell me there've been complaints,' the minder growled. His accent was Liverpudlian. From his size, Rebus would bet his family had worked dockside. 'That's all I need right now.'

'What's up?'

'Buggers don't want to leave, do they?'

'Have you tried asking nicely?'

The man snorted.

'Nobody here to help you?'

'When we turned the music off, looked like they weren't going to stick around. DJ packed up and sodded off home. So did Mr Frost – my boss. Told me all I had to do was switch off the lights and lock up after me.'

'You're new to this game.'

The bouncer smiled. 'Does it show?'

'I take it you've got a mobile about your person. Why not call Mr Frost?'

'Don't have his home number.'

Rebus rubbed his chin. 'Is that as in Archie Frost?'

'That's him.'

Rebus was thoughtful for a moment. 'Want me to talk to them?' He nodded towards the boat. 'See if I can get them to pack up?'

The minder stared at him. He was well-educated in the relationship that should exist between his profession and Rebus's: a favour done now might mean a favour asked later. He turned towards a noise. One of the revellers had come up on deck and was preparing to urinate off the side. He sighed.

'Why not?' he said.

And Rebus was in.

One guy had pegged out on the deck, champagne bottle held to his chest. His bow tie was hanging from his neck; his watch was a gold Rolex. The guest using the Albert Basin as his own private loo rocked to and fro on his heels. He was humming the chorus of some pop song. Seeing Rebus, he beamed a smile. Rebus ignored him, headed down the steps into the main body of the boat. It was set up for a party: chairs and tables around a long narrow dancefloor. Bar at one end, makeshift stage at the other. There was a lighting rig, a mirror-ball over the dancefloor. Shutters had been brought down across the bar and fixed with a padlock, which another drunk was trying to pick with a plastic toothpick. A couple of the tables had been knocked over, along with a dozen or so chairs. There were forgotten items of clothing strewn across the floor, along with crisps, peanuts, empty bottles, and bits of sandwich and squashed quiche. The main action was centred on two tables which had been pushed together. Fourteen or fifteen people sat here. Women sat on men's laps, kissing deeply. A few couples were indulging in muted conversations. One or two individuals were fast asleep. A hard core of five – three men, two women – were telling slurred stories, detailing the party highlights, mostly involving drink, vomit and snogging.

'Hello again,' Rebus said to Ama Petrie. 'This your do, is it?'

She had her head on the shoulder of the young man next to her. Her mascara was smeared, making her look tired. Her short dress was a meshing of black gauzy layers. Her bare feet were in the lap of the man on the other side of her. He was playing with her toes.

'Oh, Christ,' this man said, eyes drooping, 'they've sent in the heavy brigade. Look, my good man, we've paid for this evening – cash, and upfront. So kindly bugger off and—'

'Oscar, you arse, he's a policeman,' Ama Petrie said. Then, to Rebus: 'Nice to see you again.' It was an automatic greeting, something she couldn't help but say, even though her eyes told a different story. Her eyes told Rebus she wasn't in the least pleased to see him.

'Well,' Oscar said, smiling to the assembly, 'in that case, it's a fair cop, guv, but society's to blame. I never had a chance.' He slipped into the role effortlessly, drawing smiles and laughter from his audience. Rebus looked at the faces around him: the faces of Edinburgh's rich young things. They'd have their own flats in the New Town, gifts from indulgent parents. They had their parties and their nights out. Maybe by day they shopped or lunched or attended a couple of lectures at the university. Maybe they drove their sports cars out to the country. Their lives were predestined: a job in the family business, or something 'arranged' – a position they could cope with, something requiring inbred charm and minimal effort. Everything would fall into their laps, because that's the way the world was.

'Shame he's not in uniform, eh, Nicky?'

'What have we done, Officer?' another of the men asked.

'Well, you've overstayed your welcome,' Rebus said. 'But that doesn't really concern me. Might I ask whose party this is?' He was looking at Ama.

'Mine, actually,' the man with the toothpick said, turning away from the bar. He pushed his thick fair hair back from his forehead. A thin face, soft-featured. 'I'm Nicol Petrie, Ama's brother.' Rebus guessed this was 'Nicky': *Shame he's not in uniform, eh, Nicky?*

He was in his early twenties, fashionably unshaven so his face shone a spiky gold. 'Look,' he said, 'I'll move this lot off the boat, promise.' And to his friends: 'We'll go back to my place. Plenty of drink there.'

'I want to go to a casino,' one woman complained. 'You *said* we'd go.'

'Darling, he only said that so you'd give him a blow job.'

Hoots of laughter, pointed fingers. Ama had her eyes closed but was chuckling, her feet grinding against her companion's groin.

Everyone seemed to have forgotten Rebus. The conversations were starting up again. He reached into his pocket, handed two photographs to Nicol Petrie.

'His name's Damon Mee. He left a nightclub with the blonde woman. We think they were on their way to a party on this boat, hosted by your sister.'

'Yes,' Nicol Petrie said, 'Ama told me.' He studied the photos, shook his head. 'Sorry.' Handed them back.

'You were at the party in question?' Petrie nodded. 'All of you?'

They looked to Ama, who told them which party it had been. A couple hadn't been present – previous commitments. Rebus handed the photos out anyway. Nobody paid much attention to them; they kept talking to each other as they passed them round.

'I could just go some smoked salmon.'

'Alison's bash next Friday: are you going?'

'Hair extensions, they change your whole face instantly . . .'

'Thought about putting a consortium together, buy a racehorse . . .'

Ama Petrie didn't even glance at the pictures, just passed them along.

'Sorry,' the last of the group said, handing them back to Rebus before continuing a conversation. Nicol Petrie looked apologetic.

'I promise we'll leave soon, assemble some taxis.'

'Right, sir.'

'And I'm sorry we couldn't be more help.'

'Not to worry.'

'I ran away from home once . . .'

'Nick, you were only *twelve*,' Ama Petrie drawled.

'All the same, I know how much it hurt our mother and father.'

Ama disagreed. 'They hardly noticed you were gone.' She looked up at him. 'It was me who called the police.'

'What happened?' Rebus asked.

'I'd been staying at a friend's house,' Nicol Petrie explained. 'When his parents heard I was supposed to be missing, they drove me home.' He shrugged. A couple of his friends laughed.

'Right,' he said, raising his voice slightly. 'Back to my place. The night is still young, and so are we!'

There were cheers at this. Rebus got the feeling Nicol had roused the troops like this before.

'Where's Alfie?' Ama asked.

'Taking a leak,' she was told.

Rebus made for the stairs. 'Thanks anyway,' he said to her brother. Nicol Petrie shot out a hand, which Rebus shook.

Shame he's not in uniform . . . What the hell had that meant? Some private joke? Rebus climbed back up into fresh air. The man who'd been relieving himself – Alfie – was sitting on the floor of the boat, legs splayed. He'd forgotten to button his flies.

'Leaving so soon?' he asked.

'Everyone's going back to Nicky's,' Rebus said, like he was one of the gang.

'Good old Nicky,' Alfie said.

'You're Alfie, aren't you?'

The young man looked up, trying to place Rebus. 'Sorry,' he said, 'can't seem to . . .'

'John,' Rebus said.

'Of course, John.' Nodding briskly. 'Never forget a face. You're in the finance sector?'

'Securities.'

'Never forget a face.' Alfie started to get up. Rebus helped him. He still had his photos in one hand.

'Here,' he said. 'Take a look.' Didn't say any more than that, just handed them over.

'Photographer must have been pissed,' Alfie said.

'Not very good, are they?'

'Bloody awful. I've got a friend who's a photographer. Let me give you his number.' Reaching into his jacket.

'You'll know his face, though,' Rebus said, tapping the holiday snap of Damon.

Alfie squinted at the photo, brought it close to his nose, moved it to pick up the available light.

'I pride myself,' he said, 'on never forgetting a face. But in this chap's case, I'll make an exception.' Smiled crookedly at his own little joke. 'Now the lady, on the other hand . . .'

'Alfie!' Ama Petrie was standing at the top of the stairs, arms folded against the chill. 'Come on, we're getting ready to go.'

'Super idea, Ama.' Alfie blinked so slowly, Rebus thought he'd nodded off.

'About the blonde . . .' Rebus persisted.

Ama had come up to them, was tugging on Alfie's sleeve. Alfie patted Rebus's arm. 'See you at Nicky's, old boy.'

'Come on, Alfie.' Ama pecked his cheek, led him to the stairs. A quick backward glance towards Rebus. Looking . . . angry? Relieved? A mix of the two? When they disappeared from view, Rebus walked off the boat.

'They're on their way,' he told the minder.

'Cheers.'

'That's one you owe me,' Rebus said, waiting till the minder had nodded. 'To square things, I want you to tell me what Archie Frost has to do with Billy Preston.'

'He just works for him, same as I do.'

'But he runs Gaitano's for Charmer Mackenzie.'

The minder was nodding. 'That's right.'

'No conflict of interests?'

'Should there be?'

Rebus narrowed his eyes. 'Mackenzie owns this boat?'

The minder licked his lips. 'Part-owns. Mr Preston has the other half.'

Charmer Mackenzie had a half-share in the Clipper. And he owned Gaitano's. Damon had been at Gaitano's, and was last seen near the Clipper. Rebus was beginning to wonder . . .

'That's us quits,' the minder said, as the party-goers did a conga towards the gangway.

He went back to his flat but couldn't sleep. The blanket Darren Rough had slept under was still folded on the sofa. He couldn't bring himself to move it. Instead, he sat in his chair, waiting for the ghosts to come. Maybe Darren would be with them, or maybe he'd have other souls to haunt.

But no ghosts came. Rebus dozed, came awake with a start. Decided he'd be better off out of doors. He cut through The Meadows, past the Infirmary. It was due to move out of town, south to Little France. There was talk the old Infirmary site would be turned into upmarket flats, or maybe a hotel. Prime city-centre site, but who'd want a flat where a hospital ward had been?

He paused at the statue of Greyfriars Bobby. When you thought of it, Bobby was just a dog with nowhere better to go, nothing better to be doing. Rebus reached out and patted the statue's head.

'Stay,' he said, heading down George IV Bridge. A couple of taxis slowed beside him, touting for custom, but he waved them on, took the Playfair Steps down to the National Gallery and Royal Academy. He passed a couple of people sleeping rough, watched the Castle beginning to assume shape again against the sky as night segued into morning. He thought of his grandfathers, whose names were buried somewhere in the Castle's Books of Remembrance. He couldn't even recall what regiments they'd served in. Both had died in the 1914–18 campaign, long before Rebus's parents had even met.

Princes Street had the usual haphazard look to it. The pavements seemed plenty wide when there was no one else about. He nipped up the side of Burger King and into the Penny Black, which opened for business at five. There were a couple of drinkers already in. Rebus ordered a whisky, added plenty of water.

'Man, you're drowning it,' one drinker commented.

Rebus just smiled; didn't tell the man that water was his lifeline. An early edition of the *Scotsman* sat on the bar. Rebus flicked through it. A report of the previous day's doings in the Shiellion trial, plus the 'suspicious death' of Darren Rough and the disappearance of Billy Horman. There was an anonymous quote from a member of GAP, to the effect that they blamed Rough for the boy's disappearance.

'And we're just glad and relieved that one piece of vermin has departed this earth. May all the others do the same.'

Van Brady in preaching mode. There was talk of a residents' committee, of new arrivals in Greenfield being vetted by their neighbours. There was going to be discussion of neighbourhood patrols, spot checks, and even some kind of barrier to stop 'undesirables' from entering Greenfield and 'defacing' it.

Rebus knew Scotland was gearing up for self-rule, but this was taking it to extremes.

'We've got a computer in the community centre,' the spokesperson said, 'and now we want to get hooked up to the Internet so we can ask the Guardian Angels for advice. We're hoping a lottery grant will get us the software. This community deserves no less.'

If there was going to be a private police force in Greenfield, Rebus wondered who'd be best placed to operate it. The name Cal Brady came readily to mind . . .

He finished his drink and decided to have breakfast down in Leith, where there was a café open at six with huge portions and little fuss. He walked the length of Leith Walk, found the café and settled down. With the paper already read, he'd nothing to do but chew on a half-slice of fried bread and stare out of the window. When a taxi stopped at the lights outside the café, Rebus caught a glimpse of the passenger. He tried for a better look, but the taxi was already on the move, taking Cary Oakes back to his hotel. He got the licence number, jotted it on the back of his hand. A mouthful of scalding tea helped him wash down the bread, then he asked to use the owner's phone. Called a cab company and asked about the reg.

'You kidding? Know how many cabs we've got?'

'Do your best, eh?' He gave them his mobile number, then tried the other companies in the city. They all seemed to think he was asking a lot, but by the time he got to St Leonard's, he had a result. The cabbie was actually back at base, his shift over. Rebus spoke to him.

'You took a fare down to Leith, I'm guessing The Shore. About an hour ago.'

'Yeah, last pick-up I had.'

'Where exactly did you pick him up?'

'Out Corstorphine way, just before the Maybury roundabout. What's he done?'

Corstorphine: where Alan Archibald lived. Rebus thanked the driver and terminated the call. He went to the toilets for a wash and shave, swallowed two paracetamol with some coffee. The murder room was empty, no one yet at work. He examined the photos on the wall. Archibald's niece had been murdered on a hillside; Darren Rough had been murdered on a hillside. Was it a connection? He thought of Cary Oakes, roaming freely through the city. Picked up one of the phones and called Patience.

'Morning,' she said sleepily.

'This is your alarm call.'

He could hear her stretch her back, sitting up in bed. 'What time is it?'

He told her. 'I couldn't get back for breakfast, thought I'd phone instead.'

'Where are you?'

'St Leonard's.'

'Did you sleep at Arden Street?'

'I managed a nap.'

'I don't know how you do it.' She was probably pushing hair out of her eyes. 'I need eight hours minimum.'

'They say it's the sign of a clear conscience.'

'What does that say about you?' She knew he wasn't going to answer that, asked instead if she'd see him for dinner.

'Sure,' he told her. 'Unless you don't, of course.'

'Of course,' she said. Then: 'How's the head?'

'Fine.'

'You liar. Try one day off the booze, John, just for me. One day, and tell me you don't feel better in the morning.'

'I know I'll feel better in the morning. Problem is, as soon as I have a drink, I forget.'

'Bye, John.'

'Bye, Patience.'

Patience: more than living up to her name . . .

30

Rebus and Gill Templer, in Interview Room B with Cal Brady.

Interview Room B: same room Rebus had taken Darren Rough. Same room he'd first met Harold Ince during the Shiellion inquiry. They were talking to Cal Brady again because Templer had a few things to clear up.

'You started that fire,' she said.

'Did I?' Brady looked around, wide-eyed. 'Maybe we better get a solicitor in here then.'

'Don't try to be funny, Mr Brady.'

'Only jokers I see around here are you lot.'

'Billy Horman is reported missing, next thing you're out torching Darren Rough's flat. If I was of a mind, I might think *you* had something to gain from that.' She paused, shifting the paperwork in front of her. 'Or something to hide.'

'Such as?' Brady sat back in his chair, arms folded.

'That's what I'm wondering.'

Brady snorted, looked to where Rebus was standing. 'Lost your voice or what?'

Rebus didn't rise to it. Gill Templer was quite capable of dealing with the likes of Cal Brady.

'Everyone else went out looking for Billy,' she continued, 'but you held back. Why's that, Mr Brady?'

Brady shifted in his seat. 'Kept an eye on Billy Boy's mum.'

Templer made a show of checking her notes. 'Joanna Horman?' She waited for Brady to nod agreement. 'That's women's work, isn't it, Calumn? Holding the mother's hand, offering sympathy and a rum and Coke. Thought you were more of an Action Man.'

'Someone had to do it.'

'But why *you*, that's what I'm getting at? Maybe you fancied her. Maybe the two of you know one another . . . ?' She paused. 'Or could it be that you already knew there was no point looking for Billy Horman . . . ?'

Brady thumped the desk. 'Don't you start on this!' Quick to ignite.

'Everybody knows what happened to Billy Boy. He got snatched by Rough or one of his cronies.'

'Then where is he?'

'How the hell should I know?'

'And who killed Darren Rough?'

'If it had been me, he'd've been missing some bits.'

'What if I tell you he was?' Templer playing a little game.

Brady looked surprised. 'Was he? Nobody said . . .'

Templer looked at her notes. Then: 'DI Rebus, I believe you have a few more questions for Mr Brady.'

Rebus having cleared things with her first, explaining his interest. He moved towards the desk, rested his knuckles on it.

'How do you come to know Archie Frost?'

'Archie?' Brady looked at Templer. 'What's this got to do with anything?'

'Another inquiry, Mr Brady. Unconnected to the other two, except, perhaps, by you.'

'I don't get it.'

'You want that solicitor now?'

He thought about it, shrugged his shoulders. 'I do some work for him.'

'For Mr Frost?'

'That's right. I work on the door some nights.'

'You're a bouncer?'

'I keep an eye out for trouble.'

Rebus produced the photographs again. They had curled and creased at the edges, and were smeared with fingerprints.

'Do you remember me asking about these people?'

Brady looked at the photos, nodded. 'I wasn't on the door that night.'

'And which night is that?' Brady looked up from the photos. Rebus was smiling. 'I don't recall giving Mr Frost any particular night.'

'If I'd been working that night I'd have spotted him. I had a run-in with him once before. No way he would have got past the door with me there.'

Rebus narrowed his eyes. 'What sort of run-in?'

Brady shrugged. 'Nothing much. He was just a bit pissed, making too much noise. I told him to calm down and he didn't, so a couple of us escorted him off the premises.'

Brady liked this last phrase; smiled at it. A nice official ring to it: 'escorted', 'premises'.

'You ever do any door work at the Clipper?'

Brady shook his head.

'But you work for its owner.'

'Mr Mackenzie has a share of the boat, that's all.'

'But he provides the bouncers too.'

'I tried it once, didn't like it.'

'Why not?'

'All these stuck-up tarts and Hooray Henries, thinking they could walk all over you because they had a bit of cash.'

'I know what you mean.' Brady looked at him. 'No, really. I've seen them for myself.' Rebus was still thinking about Brady's run-in with Damon Mee. He'd thought it was Damon's first visit to Gaitano's; no one had told him any different. 'Thing is, Cal, Damon's a missing person, and I'm a bit like Gulliver in one of Lilliput's toilets.'

'Eh?'

'I've not got much to go on.' Gill Templer groaned at the joke, while Rebus counted off on his fingers. 'I've got Damon going missing, last seen with a blonde being dropped by taxi outside the Clipper. The boat's part-owned by Charmer Mackenzie, who also owns Guiser's, which is where Damon and the blonde seemed to meet. See, there's a connection there. Right now, it's the only thing I've got, which is why I'm going to keep working away at it until I've got some answers.' He paused. 'Only you don't have any of the answers, do you?'

Brady stared at him. Rebus turned to Templer.

'No further questions, m'lud.'

'All right, Mr Brady,' she said. 'You can go now.'

Brady walked to the door, opened it, turned his head back towards Rebus.

'Gulliver,' he said. 'Is he the one in the cartoon with the little people?'

'That's him,' Rebus acknowledged.

Brady nodded thoughtfully. 'I still don't get it,' he said, closing the door after him.

At lunchtime, Rebus sat in his car and slept for half an hour, before heading back to the office with a beaker of tomato soup and a cheese and Branston sandwich.

'We've got something,' Roy Frazer informed him. 'Sighting of a white saloon car, exiting Holyrood Park at the Dalkeith Road end. Someone from maintenance at the Commonwealth Pool noticed it. Early morning, no traffic about. This car was doing a fair lick, went through a red light. He's a cyclist, pays attention to that sort of thing.'

'And a model citizen too, I'll bet. Never sneaks through a red on his bike when nobody's watching.' Rebus thought for a moment. 'Any surveillance cameras that might have caught it?'

'I'll check.'

'Clear it with DCI Templer first. She's in charge.'

'Yes, sir.' Frazer bounded off in search of her. He reminded Rebus of a pet spaniel, always ready for attention and praise. White saloon car . . . Something was niggling Rebus. He put in a call to Bobby Hogan at Leith police station.

'If I say the words "white saloon car" to you, what would you say to me?'

'I'd say my brother's got one, a Ford Orion.'

'I'm thinking of Jim Margolies.'

'Something in the notes?'

'Yes. I'm sure there was a white saloon.'

'Can I call you back?'

'Soon as poss.' He put down the receiver, scribbled circles within circles on his pad, then sent lines radiating out from the centre. He couldn't decide if it looked more like a spider's web or a dartboard, came to the answer: neither. The telescopic sight from a warplane maybe? Or a section through a tree-trunk? All possibilities, but really all it was in the end was a meaningless squiggle. And when he ran over it a few times with the pen, it became clotted past interpretation.

His phone rang and he picked up.

'Is it important?' Bobby Hogan asked.

'I don't know. Might connect to something else.'

'Want to tell me what?'

'You go first.'

He seemed to be considering the offer, then began to recite from the case-notes. 'Light-coloured saloon car, possibly white or cream. Seen parked on Queen's Drive.'

'Where on Queen's Drive?' Queen's Drive being the roadway that wound around Holyrood Park.

'You know The Hawse?'

'Not by name.'

'It's at the foot of the Crags, near where the path starts. This car was parked there, lights on, apparently nobody in it. Someone came forward when they heard about the suicide. But the timing was wrong. They spotted it at around ten thirty that night. It was gone by the time a patrol went past at midnight. Margolies didn't head up there until later.'

'According to his widow.'

'Well, she should know, shouldn't she? So are you going to tell me what this is all about?'

'Another sighting of a white saloon, the morning Darren Rough was killed. Seen haring out of Holyrood Park.'

'What's that got to do with Jim's suicide?'

'Probably nothing,' Rebus said, thinking of the doodle again. 'Maybe I'm just seeing things.' He saw the Farmer standing in the doorway, beckoning. 'Thanks anyway,' he said.

'Any other fantasies you get, they've got special phone numbers these days.'

Rebus put down the receiver, started towards the door.

'My office,' the Farmer said, moving away before Rebus could reach him. There was a mug of coffee already sitting on the Farmer's desk. He poured Rebus one, handed it over.

'What have I done this time?' Rebus asked.

The Farmer motioned for him to sit. 'It's Darren Rough's social worker. He's made an official complaint.'

'About me?'

'He reckons you "outed" his client, and brought this whole thing on. He's asking questions about how closely you tie in to Rough's death.'

Rebus rubbed his eyes, managed a tired smile. 'He's welcome to his opinions.'

'No danger he can back them up with hard proof?'

'Not a chance in hell, sir.'

'It's still not going to look good. You were the last person Rough had any contact with.'

'Only if you discount the killer. Have forensics turned up anything?'

'Only that the killer probably got some of Rough's blood on him.'

'What if I put forward a proposal?'

The Farmer picked up a pen, studied it. 'What sort of proposal?'

'That we bring in Cary Oakes again. I'm positive he nicked my car, which puts him in Arden Street around the time Darren Rough was leaving. What was he doing there in the first place? Staking the place out? In which case, he'd been there a while, maybe saw us going in, took Rough for a friend of mine . . .'

The Farmer was shaking his head. 'We can't bring in Oakes, not without something solid.'

'How about a mallet?'

It was the Farmer's turn to smile. 'Stevens' paper has lawyers, John. And you've said yourself, Oakes is a pro. He'll sit there keeping schtum till they spring him. At which point, the daily rags have got themselves another story about police harassment.'

'I thought we were *trying* to harass him?'

The Farmer dropped the pen on the floor, stooped to pick it up. 'We've been through all this.'

'I know.'

'So now we're going in circles. Bottom line, a complaint from Social Work has to be followed up.'

'And meantime, I can't work the investigation.'

'It would look bloody odd under the circumstances. What other work have you got?'

'Officially, not a lot.'

'I heard you had a MisPer.'

'I was working it in my own time.'

'So spend a bit more time on it. But – and this is off the record, mind – keep close to Gill and the team. You seem to know more about Rough and Greenfield than most.'

'In other words, you need me, but can't afford to be seen with me?'

'You always had a way with words, John. Off you go now. POETS day, you know, weekend coming up. Go and enjoy yourself.'

31

Janice Mee turned up at Arden Street for want of anything more constructive to do. She had all this time to herself, and over in Fife she felt she was accomplishing nothing. If she sat at home, the patterns on the wallpaper started swirling, and the clock's tick seemed amplified beyond all enduring. But if she went out, there were questions to be answered by neighbours and passers-by – 'Is he no' back yet?'; 'Where do you think he'd have went?' – and comments to be fielded – usually to do with having patience or keeping fingers crossed. Besides, she had a feeling whenever she stepped off the train at Waverley that Damon was nearby. It was true people had a sixth sense: you could feel when someone was creeping up behind you. And every time she stepped on to the platform, stopping there while the workers and shoppers made to pass her, hurried lives they had to be getting on with . . . when she stopped there, it was as if her world stopped turning, and everything became still and peaceful. In those moments, with the city hushed and the blood singing in her heart, she could almost hear him, smell him – everything but reach out and touch his arm. She saw herself pulling him to her, scolding him as she poured kisses on his face, and him all grown-up and trying to resist, but pleased, too, to be wanted like this and loved like this, loved the way no one in the universe would ever love him.

Since he'd gone missing, she'd been sleeping in his room. At first, she'd reasoned to Brian that Damon might sneak back in the night for his things. This way, she'd be there to confront him, to snare him. But then Brian had said he'd move into the room too, and she'd pointed out there was just the single bed, and he'd countered that he'd sleep on the floor. On and on the discussion had gone, until she'd lost it and blurted out that she'd rather be on her own.

The first time she'd spoken the words.

'Frankly, Brian, I'd much rather be on my own . . .'

His face had lost all rigidity, had folded in on itself, and she'd felt sick in her stomach. But she'd been right to say the words, wrong to keep them inside the past months and years.

'It's Johnny, isn't it?' Brian, face averted, had plucked up the courage to ask.

And in a way it was, though not quite the way Brian meant. It was that Johnny had shown her another road she might have taken, and in doing so had opened up the possibility of all the other roads left untravelled, all the places she'd never been. Places like Emotion and High and Elation. Places like Myself and Free and Aware. She knew she'd never say these things to anyone; they sounded too much like stuff from the magazines. But that didn't stop her feeling they were true. Born and bred in the town, lived most of her days there: did she really want to die there? Did she want it that thirty-odd years of her life could be summarised in five minutes to a friend she hadn't seen since secondary school?

She wanted more.

She wanted out.

Of course, she knew what people would say: you're just emotional, dear. It's bound to be upsetting, something like this. And it was. Oh, Jesus sweet Christ almighty, it was. Yet she felt more powerless and aimless than ever. She'd told her story to all the charities, she'd done her bit talking to the taxi drivers, but what was left? She knew there must be something she hadn't tried, but couldn't think what. All she knew was, this was where she had to be.

Now that she had a feel for the city, she enjoyed the walk to Marchmont. The steep climb up Cockburn Street, full of 'alternative' shops – some of them had even taken her flyers. Then up the High Street to George IV Bridge, and down past libraries and bookshops to Greyfriars Bobby. Past the university and the milling students, carrying books with them or pushing their bicycles. Then The Meadows, flat and green and with Marchmont rising in the distance. She liked the shops near Johnny's flat; liked the tenement itself and all the streets around it. The roofs seemed to her like castle turrets. Johnny said the area was full of students. She'd always imagined students living in poorer places.

She opened the main door and climbed to Johnny's landing. There was mail behind his door. She picked it up, took it through to the living room. It looked like bills and junk; no real letters. No photos in his living room; gaps in the wall-units which she would have filled with ornaments. Books tidied away into piles: before she moved them, they'd been lying everywhere. There was a time Brian wouldn't have stood for it if she'd moved his stuff around; these days, he probably wouldn't even notice. Johnny had noticed when she'd tidied up, but she wasn't sure he'd been pleased, even though he'd said 'Thanks.'

She took mugs, plate and ashtray through to the kitchen. Took a blanket from the sofa and put it on the bed in the spare room. When everything was to her satisfaction, she wondered what to do next. Clean the windows? With what? Make herself a cup of something? Listen to some music . . . when had she last sat down and listened to music? When had she last had time? She looked through Johnny's collection. Pulled out an album – one of the first by the Rolling Stones. It looked the same copy he'd had when they'd been going out together. On the back she found an ink doodle: JLJ – Janice Loves Johnny. She'd put it there one night, wondering if he'd notice. He always liked to study his LP sleeves. And when he had noticed, he hadn't been too thrilled, had tried taking a rubber to it. You could still see the smudge . . .

Summers in the café, long evenings with the Coke machine and the jukebox. Then a bag of chips, salt and vinegar. Maybe a film some nights, or just a stroll in the park. The youth club was run by the local church. Johnny hadn't liked that; hadn't been churchy. Yet here was a copy of the Bible, sitting alone on the mantelpiece. And other books that looked religious: *The Confessions of St Augustine; The Cloud of Unknowing*. She liked the sound of that last one. Lots of books, yet he didn't seem much of a reader, and the books looked brand new, most of them.

His bedroom . . . she'd sneaked a peek in there. Not the most inviting of rooms: mattress on the floor, clothes in piles in a corner, waiting to be decanted into the chest of drawers. Odd socks: what was it with men and odd socks? The whole flat had an unloved feel to it, despite some redecoration in the living room. His chair, positioned next to the bay window, phone on the floor next to it – the whole flat seemed to revolve around that one space. Kitchen cupboards: bottles of whisky and brandy and vodka and gin. More vodka in the freezer; beer in the fridge, along with cheese, marge, and an unpromising quarter of corned beef. Jars of beetroot and raspberry jam on the worktop, breadbin with two stale rolls and the heel of a loaf.

They said you could tell a lot about a man from his home. She got the feeling Johnny was lonely, but how could that be when he had the doctor, Patience whatsername?

The doorbell. She wondered who it could be. Went and opened the door, not even bothering with the spy-hole. A man standing there, smiling.

'Hiya,' he said. 'Is John in?'

'No, I'm afraid not.'

The smile disappeared; the man checked his watch. 'I hope he's not going to stand me up again.'

'Well, in his job . . .'

'Oh, that's true enough. You'll know all about it, I suppose.'

She felt herself blushing under his gaze. 'I'm not his girlfriend or anything.'

'No? And here I was thinking he'd struck lucky, the old devil.'

'No, I'm just a friend.'

'Just good friends, eh?' He tapped his nose. 'You can trust me, I won't tell Patience.'

Her blush spread. 'We were at school, Johnny and me. Met up again recently.' She was babbling, and knew it, but somehow couldn't stop herself.

'That's nice: old friends getting together. Plenty to catch up on, eh?'

'Plenty.'

'I know the feeling. I was out of touch with John for years too.'

'Really?'

'Working in the States.'

'How interesting. Were you there long . . .?' She caught herself. 'Sorry, I can't keep you standing out there, can I?'

'I was beginning to wonder.'

She opened the door wider, took a step back. 'You better come in. My name's Janice, by the way.'

'You'll laugh when I tell you my name. All I can say is, nobody consulted *me*.'

'Why, what's your name?' Laughing now as he stepped past her into the hall.

'Cary,' he told her. 'After the actor. Only I've never managed to be quite so suave.'

He was winking at her as she closed the door.

The flat was empty when Rebus got home, but he sensed someone had been there: things moved, things tidied. Janice again. He looked for a note, but she hadn't left one. He took a beer from the fridge, then turned on the hi-fi. The Stones: 'Goat's Head Soup'. On the album cover, David Bailey had photographed them with their made-up faces covered by some diaphanous material, making Jagger look more feminine than ever. Rebus turned the volume down and called Alan Archibald's number. Nobody home but the answering machine. Archibald's voice sounded clipped and distant.

'It's John Rebus here. A simple message: ca' canny. A taxi driver picked Oakes up near your home. I can't think of any other reason he'd have been in the neighbourhood. He's also been in my street. I don't know what his thinking is, maybe he just wants to rattle us. Anyway, consider yourself forewarned.'

He put down the phone. Forewarned is forearmed, he thought, wondering how Alan Archibald would arm himself.

He turned up the volume, sat by the window and stared out at the opposite tenement. The kids were home from school, playing at their living room table. Some card game, it looked like. Happy Families maybe. Rebus had never been much good at that. When he turned from the window, he saw a shape in the doorway.

'Christ,' he said, putting a hand to his chest, 'don't do that to me.'

'Sorry,' Janice said, smiling. She raised a carton of milk for him to see. 'You were running out.'

'Thanks.' He followed her through to the kitchen, watched her put the milk in the fridge.

'Did you forget your appointment?' she asked.

'Appointment?' Rebus was thinking: doctor? Dentist?

'You stood your friend up. He was round here an hour ago. I went with him for a coffee.' She tutted at Rebus's fecklessness.

'You've lost me,' he said.

'Cary,' she told him. 'The two of you were going out for a drink.'

Rebus felt his spine turn cold. 'He came here?'

'Looking for you, yes.'

'And you went out with him?'

She'd been wiping the worktop, but turned towards him, saw the look on his face.

'What is it?' she asked.

He looked towards the cupboards, made a show of opening one to check for something. He couldn't tell her. She'd have a fit. He closed the cupboard door.

'Have a nice chat, the two of you?'

'He told me about his job in the States.'

'Which one? I think he had a couple.'

'Did he?' She frowned. 'Well, the only one he told me about was being a prison guard.'

'Oh, right.' Rebus nodded. 'I suppose you told him about us?'

She gave him a sly glance. There were spots of red on her cheeks. 'What's to tell?'

'I mean, told him about yourself, how we know one another . . . ?'

'Oh, yes, all that.'

'And Fife?'

'He seemed really interested in Cardenden. I told him off, thought he was taking the mickey.'

'No, Cary's always interested in people.'

'That's exactly what he said.' She paused. 'Sure you're all right?'

'Fine. It's just . . . work-related problems.' Namely, Cary Oakes, who had now pulled Janice into his game. And Rebus, himself in the middle of the board, had yet to be told the rules.

'Want some coffee or something?'

Rebus shook his head. 'We're going somewhere.' *We?* If Cary Oakes had gone to Fife, it was safer for Janice to stay in Edinburgh. But stay where? Rebus's flat was proving no sanctuary. She was safer with Rebus, and Rebus had somewhere he needed to be.

'Where?'

'Back to Fife. I've a few more questions for Damon's friends.' And terrain to scout, seeking signs of contamination by Oakes.

She stared at him. 'Have you . . . are you on to something?'

'Hard to tell.'

'Try me.'

He was shaking his head. 'I don't want to raise your hopes. It might turn out to be nothing.' He started to move out of the kitchen. 'Give me a minute to do some packing.'

'Packing?'

'Weekend's coming, Janice. Thought I might stay over till tomorrow. Is there still a hotel in town?'

She hesitated for a moment. 'You can stay with us.'

'A hotel will be fine.'

But she shook her head. 'You'll understand, I couldn't let you have Damon's room, but there's always the couch.'

Rebus pretended to be torn. 'OK then,' he said at last. Thinking: I want to be there overnight; I want to be close to her. Not for any obvious reasons – reasons he might have put to himself a day or two ago – but because he wanted to know if Cary Oakes would travel to Cardenden, stake out her home. Whatever Oakes was planning, it was moving apace. If he was going to move on Janice, Rebus reckoned it would be at the weekend.

If anything happened, Rebus needed to be there.

'I'll just throw some stuff in a bag,' he said, heading for his bedroom.

32

Rebus took Janice to Sammy's first of all. He just wanted to check on her. She was doing pull-ups with the help of her parallel bars, hoisting herself to standing, locking her knees, then easing herself back into the wheelchair. The front door was unlocked: she kept it that way when Ned wasn't home. Rebus had been worried, until she'd explained her reasoning.

'I had to weigh up the chances, Dad: me needing help, versus someone breaking in. If I'm lying paralysed on my back, I want any Good Samaritans to be able to get in.'

She wore a grey sleeveless T-shirt, its back turned a darker grey by sweat. There was a towel around her shoulders, and her hair was matted to her forehead.

'God knows if this is helping my legs,' she said, 'but I'm getting a shot-putter's biceps.'

'And not an anabolic steroid in sight,' he said, leaning down to kiss her. 'This is Janice, old school-pal of mine.'

'Hello, Janice,' Sammy said. When she looked back at her father, he felt embarrassed, and wasn't sure why.

'Her son's disappeared,' he explained. 'I'm trying to help.'

Sammy wiped her face with the towel.

'I'm sorry,' she said. Janice smiled and shrugged.

'Janice still lives in Cardenden,' Rebus went on. 'We're headed back there, in case you were thinking of phoning me tonight.'

'Right,' Sammy said, her face still busy in the towel. Now that he was here, he knew he'd made some kind of mistake, knew Sammy was jumping to all the wrong conclusions, and couldn't think of a way out without embarrassing Janice.

'So I'll see you some time,' he said.

'I'm not going anywhere.' She had finished with the towel; was studying the bars, the extent of her current universe.

'We'll have to go through there some day. I can show you my old hunting-ground.'

She nodded. 'We can take Patience, too. I'm sure she wouldn't want to be left out.'

'Have a nice weekend, Sammy,' he said, making for the door.

She neglected to tell him to do the same.

'I'll just phone Patience,' he said, easing his mobile out of his pocket. They were back in the car, heading for the A90. Patience sometimes went out with friends on a Friday night; it was a regular thing – drinks and a meal, maybe a play or concert. Three other women doctors: two of them divorced, one still apparently happily married. She answered on the fourth ring.

'It's me,' he said.

'What have I told you about using that thing when you're driving?'

'I'm stalled at lights,' he lied, giving Janice a conspirator's wink. She looked uncomfortable.

'Got plans?'

'I have to go to Fife, couple of interviews I want to get out of the way. I'll probably stay the night. Are you going out?'

'In about twenty minutes.'

'Say hello to the gang from me.'

'John ... when are we going to see one another?'

'Soon.'

'This weekend?'

'Almost certainly.'

'I'm going over to Sammy's tomorrow.'

'Right,' he said. Sammy would tell Patience about Janice. Patience would know Janice had been in the car when he'd called her. 'I'm staying the night with some friends: Janice and Brian.'

'The ones you were at school with?'

'That's right. I didn't realise I'd mentioned them.'

'You hadn't. Thing is, as far as I'm aware you haven't *made* any friends since school.'

'Bye, Patience,' he said, easing into the outside lane and putting his foot down.

Dr Patience Aitken had a taxi ordered. When it arrived, the driver pushed open her gate, headed down the steep and winding set of stone steps which led to her garden flat. He rang the doorbell and waited, scuffing his feet on the flagstones. He liked the New Town's garden flats, the way they were below street level at the front, but had gardens at the back. And they had these little courtyards at the front, with cellars built into the facing wall. Not that you'd use the cellars for much; too damp. Certainly not for keeping wine in. He'd taken the wife to the Loire the previous summer, learned all about the wines. He had three mixed cases now, stored in the cupboard beneath his stairs. Far from ideal conditions: a modern two-storey semi out at Fairmilehead. Too dry, too warm. What he needed was a flat like this one – he'd bet there'd be cupboards inside just right for laying down wine, cool and dryish with thick stone walls.

He noticed that the doctor had tried for a sort of garden feel in the courtyard: hanging baskets, terracotta pots. Nothing down here would get too much light, that was the thing. First thing he'd done with his front garden when he'd moved in: put flagstones over most of it, leaving just a square of earth in the middle, couple of roses planted in there. Minimum maintenance.

The door opened and the doctor stepped out, pulling a shawl around her shoulders. Perfume wafted out with her: nothing too overbearing.

'Sorry I've kept you,' she said, pulling the door closed and making for the steps.

'I'd double-lock it if I were you,' he suggested.

'What?'

'Yales,' he explained, shaking his head. 'A kid could be inside in ten seconds flat.'

She thought about it, shrugged her shoulders. 'What's life without a bit of a risk?'

'As long as you're insured,' he said, studying her ankles as he climbed the steps after her.

Jim Stevens lay on his bed, one hand covering his eyes, the other holding the telephone receiver to his ear. He was listening to Matt Lewin, who had just told him how good the weather was in Seattle. Stevens had faxed him portions of Cary Oakes's 'confession', and Lewin was giving his views.

'Well, Jim, bits of it seem to tally all right. The truck driver story is new, and frankly, I don't think it's worth chasing.'

'You think he made it up?'

'Not my problem, thank God. I tell you, Jim, no disrespect, but I wouldn't trust anything that bastard told me, and I sure as hell wouldn't give him the satisfaction of seeing it in print.'

Which seemed to be Stevens' boss's view, too. The projected eight-parter had been cut to just five.

'I'm sure as hell glad he's your problem now and not ours,' Lewin went on.

'Thanks.'

'He giving you any trouble?'

Stevens didn't see the point in telling Lewin that Oakes was proving more awkward by the day. He'd slipped away from the hotel again that afternoon, stayed out the best part of three hours and wouldn't say where he'd been.

'It's nearly over anyway,' Stevens said, rubbing his hand over his brow.

'Good riddance, that's my advice.'

'Yes.' But Stevens couldn't help but worry. He worried about what Oakes would do with himself afterwards, once he was out on the street. No way was Stevens' paper going to come up with ten K, not for the scraps Oakes had given them. Stevens still had to break that news to Oakes.

He worried for himself too. He was part of Oakes's sphere now, and was just hoping Oakes would let him go.

He got the feeling, God help him, that it might not be all that easy . . .

Cary Oakes watched the taxi leave. Dr P, he presumed. Getting on a bit, but then the state Rebus was in, he doubted he'd be complaining. Basement apartment too: perfect for what he had in mind. He came out from behind the parked car and looked up and down the street. The place was dead. Half of Edinburgh seemed dead to him: you could wander around for ages and not go noticed, never mind raise suspicion.

Jim Stevens had been in a foul mood, watching the Cary Oakes story relegated as the editor decided to run a special on vigilanteism. Stevens blamed the paedophile murder.

'Bloody Rebus again,' he'd muttered, and Oakes had asked him to explain.

Stevens' theory: Rebus had outed Darren Rough, raised the mob against him. And now one of them had taken it too far. Everything Oakes learned about the detective made Rebus seem more interesting, more complicated.

'What sort of code does he live by, do you think?' he'd asked.

Stevens had snorted. 'Could be Morse or Highway for all I know.'

'Some people make up their own rules,' Oakes had mused.

'You mean like the serial killer?'

'Hmm?'

'The one who picked you up in his truck.'

'Oh, him . . . Well, yes, of course.'

And Stevens had looked at him. And Cary Oakes had stared back.

He crossed the road now. No houses across the street from where he'd be working, just a wrought-iron fence, a bank of grass behind it. No neighbours to spot him as he went about his business.

He expected no interruptions at all.

The batteries were fading anyway, Rebus rationalised, and he didn't have the recharger with him. So he switched off his mobile.

'The weekend starts here,' he said, as they crossed the Forth Road Bridge into Fife.

Later: 'Roads have changed,' as they came off the dual carriageway outside Kirkcaldy. But the old Kirkcaldy–Cardenden road seemed much the same, same twists and turns, potholes and bumps.

'Remember we walked to Kirkcaldy once to go to the pictures?' Janice said.

Rebus smiled. 'I'd forgotten that. Why didn't we just take the bus?'

'I think we didn't have enough money.'

He frowned. 'Was it just us?'

'Mitch and his girlfriend too. Can't remember who he was dating at the time.'

'He went through them, all right.'

'Maybe *they* got fed up of *him*.'

'Maybe.' They sat in silence for a minute. 'What was the film?'

'Which film?'

'The one we walked six miles to see.'

'I don't recall watching much of it.'

They glanced at one another, burst out laughing.

Brian Mee heard the car, came out to meet them.

'This is a surprise,' he said, shaking Rebus's hand.

'I need to talk to Damon's pals,' Rebus explained.

Janice touched her husband's arm. 'He said he wanted to go to the hotel.'

'Rubbish, you can stay with us. Damon's room's . . .'

'I thought maybe the sofa,' Janice interjected.

Brian recovered well. 'Oh aye, it's not that old. Comfy too. I should know: I nod off on it most nights myself.'

'That's settled then,' Janice said. She had a man on either arm as she walked up the front path.

They ordered Chinese from the takeaway, opened a couple of bottles of wine. Old stories, rekindled memories. Half-remembered names; the exploits of those who'd grown old in the town; changes to the fabric of the place. Rebus had phoned Damon's friends, the ones who'd been with him at Gaitano's, but neither of them was in. He'd left messages, saying he had to see them in the morning.

'We could go out for a drink,' he told his hosts. His eyes were on Janice as he spoke. 'Be the first time we had a drink together in the Goth without being underage.'

'The Goth's shut, John,' Brian said.

'Since when?'

'They're turning it into a centre for the unemployed.'

'Isn't that what it always was?'

They smiled at that. The Goth closed: his dad's watering-hole; the first place John Rebus had ever bought a round.

'Railway Tavern's still going,' Brian added. 'We'll be there tomorrow night for the karaoke.'

'You'll stay for that, won't you?' Janice asked.

'I'm kind of allergic to karaokes, actually.' Rebus was once again in the 'seat by the fire', the one he'd been made to sit in on his first visit. The TV was playing, sound turned down. It was like a magnet, their eyes sliding towards it throughout the conversation. Janice cleared away the dishes – they'd eaten with the plates on their laps. He helped her take the things through to the kitchen, saw it was too small for three people to eat in. There was a dining table in front of the living room window, but set with ornaments, its leaves folded. Used for special occasions only. With the leaves opened, it would all but fill the room. They ate all their meals on their laps, in front of the TV. He imagined the three of them – mother, father, son – staring at the screen, using it to excuse the lengthening gaps in conversation.

After coffee, Janice said she was going up to bed. Brian said he'd be up in a while. She brought down blankets and a pillow for Rebus, told him where the bathroom was. Told him where the light-switch was in the hall. Told him there was plenty of hot water if he wanted a bath.

'See you in the morning.'

Brian reached for the remote, switched off the TV, then caught himself.

'There wasn't something you wanted to . . . ?'

Rebus shook his head. 'I'm not a big fan.'

'And what would you say to a wee whisky?'

'More my cup of tea altogether,' Rebus acknowledged with a smile.

They sipped the whisky in silence. It wasn't a malt: maybe Teacher's or Grant's. Brian had added a dollop of water to his, but Rebus hadn't bothered.

'Where do you think he is?' Brian asked at last, swirling the drink around the rim of his glass. 'Just between us, like.'

As if Janice couldn't take it; as if he were stronger than her.

'I don't know, Brian. I wish I did.'

'They normally go to London, though.'

'Yes.'

'And most of them do OK for themselves?'

Rebus nodded, not wanting any of this, wishing of a sudden that he was back in his flat with his own whisky, his music and books. But Brian had a need to talk.

'I blame us, you know.'

'I'd guess most parents do.'

'I think he picked up on the atmosphere, and it drove him away.' He sat on the edge of the sofa, hands squeezing his glass. He was looking at the floor as he spoke. 'I got the feeling Janice was just waiting for Damon to go. You know, get a place of his own. That's what she was waiting for.'

'And then what?'

Brian glanced up at him. 'Then she'd have no reason to stay. Every time she goes to Edinburgh, I think that's it: she won't be back.'

'But she always comes back.'

He nodded. 'But it's different now. She comes back in case Damon's here. Nothing to do with me.' He coughed, cleared his throat, drained the whisky. 'Want a refill?' Rebus shook his head. 'No, suppose not. Time for kip, eh?' Brian got to his feet, managed a smile. 'Schooldays, eh, Johnny?'

'Schooldays, Brian,' Rebus agreed. He watched something brighten behind Brian Mee's eyes, then die again.

Rebus brushed his teeth in the kitchen – didn't want to intrude upstairs, not with Brian readying for bed. He laid the blankets out on the sofa. Sat there with the lights out, then got up and went to the window. Peered through the curtains. Outside, the street-lamps cast a faint orange glow. The street itself was empty. He crept into the hall, opened the front door quietly, leaving it on the latch. Five minutes outside told him Cary Oakes wasn't in the vicinity. He headed back indoors, needed the toilet. The kitchen sink seemed inappropriate, so he listened at the foot of the stairs then headed up. He knew the bathroom door, went in and did his business. One bedroom door was closed, the other slightly open. The open door had a football scarf pinned to it, and half a dozen used concert tickets from a few years before. Rebus pushed his head around the door: saw the outlines of posters, a wardrobe and chest of drawers. Saw the window with the curtains drawn. Saw the single bed, and Janice sleeping in it, her breathing regular.

Crept downstairs again feeling like a housebreaker.

33

Next morning after breakfast, he had a meeting with Damon's friends.

They came round to the house, while Janice and Brian were out shopping. Joey Haldane was tall and skinny with closely cropped bleached hair and dark bushy eyebrows. He wore all denim – jeans, shirt, jacket – with black Dr Marten shoes. Rebus noticed that his mouth hung open most of the time, as though he had trouble breathing through his nose.

Pete Mathieson was as tall as Joey but a lot broader, the kind of son a farmer would be proud of (and probably exploit). He wore red jogging pants and a blue sweatshirt, Nike trainers with the soles almost rubbed away. They sat on the sofa. Rebus's sheets and pillow had disappeared upstairs before breakfast, while he'd been soaking in the bath.

'Thanks for coming,' Rebus began. Instead of one of the overstuffed armchairs, he was seated on a straight-backed dining chair, planted in the middle of the room. Below him, the boys sank into the sofa. He'd turned his chair so he could straddle it, leaning his arms on its back.

'I know we've talked before, Joey, but I've got a couple of back-up questions. So-called because when I think someone's not playing straight with me, it tends to get my back up.'

Joey wet his lips with his tongue, Pete twitched a shoulder, angled his head and tried to look bored.

'See,' Rebus went on, 'I was told the three of you had gone just that once to Edinburgh for your night out. But now I think I know differently. I think you'd been there before. I think maybe it was a regular thing, which makes me wonder why you'd lie. What is it you're trying to hide? Remember, this is a missing person investigation. No way you're not going to be found out.'

'We haven't done nothing.' This from Joey, his voice a hoarse local accent, the sound of carpentry work.

'Know what a double negative is, Joey?'

'Should I?' Holding Rebus's stare for the briefest of moments.

'If you say you haven't done nothing, it means you've done *something*.'

'I've told you, we haven't done nothing.'

'You haven't lied about that night? You hadn't been to Edinburgh for a night out before . . . ?'

'We'd been before,' Pete Mathieson said.

'Hello there, Pete,' Rebus said. 'Thought you'd lost the power of speech for a minute there.'

'Pete,' Joey spat, 'for fuck's—'

Mathieson gave his friend a look, but when he spoke it was for Rebus's benefit.

'We'd been before.'

'To Guiser's?'

'And other places – pubs, clubs.'

'How often?'

'Four, five nights.'

'Without telling your girlfriends?'

'They thought we were down Kirkcaldy, same as always.'

'Why not tell them?'

'That would have spoiled it,' Joey said, folding his arms. Rebus thought he knew what he meant. It was only an adventure if it was furtive. Men liked to have their little secrets and tell their little lies. They liked a sense of the illicit. All the same, he got the feeling it went further. It was the way Joey was leaning back in the sofa, crossing one ankle over the other. He was thinking of something, something about the nights out, and the thought was making him feel good . . .

'Was it just you that was cheating, Joey, or was it all of you?'

Joey's face grew darker. He turned to his friend.

'I never said nothing!' Pete blurted out.

'He didn't need to, Joey,' Rebus said. 'It's written on your face.'

Joey wriggled in his seat, less comfortable by the second. Eventually he sat forward, arms on knees. 'If Alice finds out she'll kill me.'

So much for the thrill of the illicit.

'Your secret's safe with me, Joey. I just need to know what happened that night.'

Joey glanced towards Pete, as though giving him permission to do the talking.

'Joey met a girl,' Pete began. 'Three weeks before. So every time we went across, he hooked up with her.'

'You weren't in Guiser's?'

Joey shook his head. 'Went back to her flat for an hour.'

'The plan was,' Pete explained, 'we'd all meet up later at Guiser's.'

'You weren't there either?'

Pete shook his head. 'We were in a pub beforehand, I got chatting to this lassie. I think Damon was a bit bored.'

'More likely jealous,' Joey added.

'So he headed off to Guiser's on his own?' Rebus asked.

'By the time I got there,' Pete said, 'there was no sign of him.'

'So he wasn't at the bar for a round of drinks? You made that up so nobody would know you were busy elsewhere?' He was looking at Joey.

'That's about it,' Pete answered. 'Didn't think it made any difference.'

Rebus was thoughtful. 'What about Damon? Did he ever hook up with anyone?'

'Never seemed to get lucky.'

'It wasn't because he was thinking of Helen?'

Joey shook his head. 'He was just useless with birds.'

And he'd gone off to Guiser's on his own . . . thinking what? Thinking about how of the three, he was the only one who couldn't pick up a girl for the night. Thinking he was 'useless'. Yet somehow he'd ended up sharing a taxi with the mystery blonde . . .

'Does it matter?' Pete asked.

'It might. I'll have to think about it.' It mattered because Damon had been there alone. It mattered because now Rebus had no idea what had happened to him between leaving Pete in the pub and standing at the bar in Guiser's waiting to be served, with a blonde at his shoulder. They might have met en route. Something might have happened. And Rebus couldn't know. Just when the picture should have been becoming clearer, it had been torn apart.

When Janice and Brian started bringing bags in from the car, Rebus dismissed Pete and Joey. Something else they'd said: Damon wouldn't have minded finding a girl for the night. What did that say about his relationship with Helen?

'All right, John?' Janice said, smiling.

'Fine,' he replied.

After lunch, Brian invited him to the pub. It was a regular thing – Saturday afternoon, football commentary on the radio or TV. A few drinks with the lads. But Rebus declined. He had the excuse that Janice had offered to take a walk around the town with him. Rebus didn't want to be out drinking with Brian, a time when bonds could be made or tightened, secrets could dribble out 'in confidence'. Now that he'd seen Janice sleeping in a separate room, Rebus felt he knew things he shouldn't.

Of course, she might be sleeping there because of Damon, because she missed him. But Rebus didn't think that was it.

So Brian went off to the pub, and Janice and Rebus went walking. Rain was falling, but lightly. She wore a red duffel coat with a hood. She offered Rebus an umbrella, but he declined, explaining that ever since he'd seen someone almost get their eye taken out with one on Princes Street, he'd regarded them as offensive weapons.

'Where we're walking won't be quite so crowded,' she told him.

And it was true. The streets were empty. Locals went to Kirkcaldy or Edinburgh for their shopping. When Rebus had been young his family hadn't owned a car. The shops on the main street had catered for all their needs. The needs these days seemed to be videos and takeaway food. The Goth was indeed closed, its windows boarded up, reminding Rebus of Darren Rough's flat. The flats on Craigside Road had been demolished, new houses replacing them. Some of them were owned by the local housing association, the others were private.

'Nobody owned their own house when we were growing up,' Janice stated. Then she laughed. 'I must sound about seventy-eight.'

'The good old days,' Rebus agreed. 'Places do change, though.'

'Yes.'

'And people are allowed to change too.'

She looked at him, but didn't ask what he meant. Maybe she already knew.

They climbed up to The Craigs, a high ridge of wilderness above Auchterderran, and walked along it until they could see the old school.

'Not that it's used as a school any more,' Janice explained. 'Kids these days go to Lochgelly. Remember the school badge?'

'I remember it.' Auchterderran Secondary School: ASS. Kids from other schools used to bray at them, poking fun.

'Why do you keep looking round?' she asked. 'Think someone's following us?'

'No.'

'Brian's not like that, if that's what you're thinking.'

'No, no, nothing—'

'Sometimes I wish he was.' She strode ahead of him. He took his time catching up.

They walked back into town past the Auld Hoose pub. Cardenden as it now was had at one time been four distinct parishes known as the ABCD – Auchterderran, Bowhill, Cardenden and Dundonald. When they'd been going out together, Rebus had lived in Bowhill, Janice in Dundonald. He would take this route walking her home, going the longest way round they could think of. Crossing the River Ore at the old humpbacked bridge – now long replaced by a tarmac road. Sometimes, in summer, say, cutting through the park, crossing the river further up at one of the wide-diameter pipes. Those pipes had provided a test for the local kids. Rebus had known boys freeze halfway across, until their parents had to be fetched. He'd known one boy pee in his trousers with fear, but keep on moving his feet inch by inch along the pipe, while the river surged below him. Others took the crossing at a canter, hands in their pockets, needing no help with balancing.

Rebus had been one of the cautious ones.

The same pipe ran the length of the park before disappearing into the undergrowth beyond. You could follow it all the way to the bing – the hill-sized mound of dross and coal-shavings which the local colliery had deposited. Fires started on the bing could smoulder for months, wisps of smoke rising from the surface as from a volcano. In time, trees and grass had grown on the slopes, so that more than ever the bing came to resemble a natural hill. But if you climbed to the top, there was a plateau, an alien landscape, wired off for safety's sake. It was like a small loch, its surface oily, thick-looking, and black. Nobody knew what it was, but they respected it – kept their distance and threw stones, watching them sink slowly from view as they were sucked beneath the surface.

Boys and girls went into the wild areas behind the park and found secret places, flattened areas of fields which they could call their own. And that had been Janice and Johnny, too, once upon a time . . .

The Kinks: 'Young and Innocent Days'.

Now, the place had changed. The bing had gone, the whole area landscaped. The colliery had been demolished. Cardenden had grown up around coal, hurried streets constructed in the twenties and thirties to house the incoming miners. These streets hadn't even been given names, just numbers. Rebus's family had moved into 13th Street. Relocation had taken the family to a pre-fab in Cardenden, and from there to a terraced house in a cul-de-sac in Bowhill. But by the time Rebus had been at secondary school, the coal was proving difficult to mine: fractured strata, so that a face might yield low tonnage. The colliery had become uneconomic. The daily siren signalling the change of shifts had been silenced. Schoolfriends of Rebus, boys whose fathers and grandfathers had been miners, were left wondering what to do.

And Rebus too had been asking himself questions. But with Mitch's help he'd come to a decision. They'd both join the army. It had seemed so simple back then . . .

'Is Mickey still around?' Janice asked.

'Lives in Kirkcaldy.'

'He was a pest, your wee brother. Remember him charging into the bedroom? Or opening the bowley-hole all of a sudden so he could catch us?'

Rebus laughed. *Bowley-hole*: a word he hadn't heard in years. The serving-hatch between kitchen and living room. He could see Mickey now. He'd be up on the worktop in the kitchen, trying to spy on Rebus and Janice while they were alone in the living room.

Rebus looked around again. He didn't think Cary Oakes was in town. A place this size, where everyone knew everyone, it was hard to hide. He'd already had a couple of people come up and say hello, like they'd seen him just the other day, rather than a dozen or more years ago. And Janice had been stopped by half a dozen people – neighbours or the plain curious – and asked about Damon. It was hard to escape him: every wall, lamppost and window seemed to have his picture stuck to it.

'I was here a few years back,' he told Janice. 'Hutchy's betting shop.'

'You were after Tommy Greenwood?'

He nodded. 'And I bumped into Cranny.' Their old nickname for Heather Cranston.

'She's still around. So's her son.'

Rebus sought the name. 'Shug?'

'That's it,' Janice said. 'If you're lucky, you might see Heather tonight.'

'Oh?'

'She often comes to the karaoke.'

Rebus asked Janice if they could turn back. 'I want to see the cemetery,' he explained. And backtracking, he might have added, as he'd learned in the army, was a good way to find if you were being followed. So they headed back through Bowhill, and up the cemetery brae. He was thinking of all the stories buried in the graveyard: mining tragedies; a girl found drowned in the Ore; a holiday car crash which had wiped out a family. Then there was Johnny Thomson, Celtic goalkeeper, fatally injured during an Old Firm derby, only in his twenties when he died.

Rebus's mother had been cremated, but his father had insisted on a 'proper burial'. His headstone was over by the end wall. Loving husband to . . . and father of . . . And at the bottom, the words *Not Dead, But at Rest in the Arms of the Lord*. But as they approached, Rebus saw that something was wrong.

'Oh, John,' Janice gasped.

White paint had been poured down the headstone, covering most of the lettering.

'Bloody kids,' Janice said.

Rebus saw tracks of paint on the grass, but no sign of the empty tin.

'This wasn't kids,' he said. Too much of a coincidence.

'Who then?'

He touched his finger to the headstone: the paint was still viscous. Oakes *had* been in town. Janice was squeezing his arm.

'I'm so sorry.'

'It's only a bit of stone,' he said quietly. 'It can be fixed.'

They drank tea in the living room. Rebus had tried Oakes's hotel – Stevens' room, the bar, no one was there.

'We've had phone calls,' Janice told him.

'Cranks?' he guessed.

She nodded. 'Telling us Damon's dead, or we killed him. Thing is, the callers . . . their voices sound local.'

'Probably are local then.'

She offered him a cigarette. 'It's pretty sick, isn't it?'

Rebus, looking around, nodded his agreement.

They were still sitting in the living room when Brian came back from the pub.

'I'll just take a shower,' he said.

Janice explained that he always did this. 'Clothes in the washing basket, and a good wash. I think it's the cigarette smoke.'

'He doesn't like it?'

'Hates it,' she said. 'Maybe that's why I started.' The front door was opened again. It was Janice's mum. 'I'll fetch a cup,' Janice said, getting to her feet.

Mrs Playfair nodded a greeting towards Rebus and sat down opposite him.

'You haven't found him yet?'

'Not for want of trying, Mrs Playfair.'

'Ach, I'm sure you're doing your best, son. He's our only grandchild, you know.'

Rebus nodded.

'A good laddie, wouldn't harm a fly. I can't believe he'd get into trouble.'

'What makes you think he's in trouble?'

'He wouldn't do this to us otherwise.' She was studying him. 'So what happened to you, son?'

'How do you mean?' Wondering if she'd read his thoughts.

'I don't know . . . the way your life's gone. Are you happy enough?'

'I never really think about it.'

'Why not?'

He shrugged his shoulders. 'I like looking into people's lives. That's what detective work is.'

'The army didn't work out?'

'No,' he said simply.

'Sometimes things don't work out,' she said, as Janice came back into the room. She watched her daughter pour the tea. 'A lot of marriages break up round here.'

'Do you think Damon and Helen would have made a go of it?'

She took a long time thinking about it, accepted the cup from Janice. 'They're young, who knows?'

'What odds would you give them?'

'You're talking to Damon's gran, John,' Janice said. 'No girl in the world's good enough for Damon, eh, Mum?' She smiled to let him know she was half-joking. Then, to her mother again: 'Johnny's had a shock.' Describing the vandalised grave. Brian came in rubbing his hair. He'd changed his clothes. Janice repeated the story for him.

'Wee bastards,' Brian said. 'It's happened before. They push the stones over, break them.'

'I'll fetch you a mug,' Janice said, making to get up again.

'I'm fine,' Brian said, waving her back. He looked towards Rebus. 'Probably don't feel like eating out then? Only we were going to treat you.'

After a moment's thought, Rebus said, 'I'd like to get out. But I should be paying.'

'You can pay next time,' Brian said.

'Judging on past history,' Rebus said, 'that'll be roughly thirty years from now.'

Rebus drank nothing but mineral water with his curry. Brian was on the beers, and Janice managed two large glasses of white wine. Mr and Mrs Playfair had been invited, but had declined.

'We'll let you young things get on with it,' Mrs Playfair had said.

From time to time, when Janice wasn't looking, Brian would glance in her direction. Rebus thought he was worried: worried his wife was going to leave him, and wondering what he was doing wrong. His life was falling apart, and he was on the lookout for clues as to why.

Rebus considered himself something of an expert on break-ups. He knew sometimes a perspective could shift, one partner could start wanting things that seemed outwith their reach as long as they stayed married. It hadn't been that way with his own marriage. There, it had been down to the fact that he never should have married in the first place. When work had begun to consume him, there hadn't been much left to sustain Rhona.

'Penny for them,' Janice said at one point, tearing apart a nan bread.

'I'm wondering about getting the headstone clean.'

Brian said he knew a man who could do it: worked for the council, took graffiti off walls.

'I'll send you the money,' Rebus told him. Brian nodded.

After the meal, he drove them back to Cardenden. The karaoke night was held in a back room at the Railway Tavern. The equipment sat on a stage, but the singers stayed on the dancefloor, eyes on the TV monitor with its syrupy videos and the words appearing along the bottom of the screen. Sheets came round, printed with all the songs. You wrote your choice on a slip of paper and handed it to the compère. A skinhead got up and did 'My Way'. A middle-aged woman had a go at 'You to Me are Everything'. Janice said she always took 'Baker Street'. Brian switched between 'Satisfaction' and 'Space Oddity', depending on his mood.

'So most people sing the same song every week?' Rebus asked.

'That guy getting up just now,' she said, nodding towards the corner of the room, where people were shifting their seats to allow someone out, 'he always chooses REM.'

'So he's probably pretty good at it by now?'

'Not bad,' she agreed. The song was 'Losing My Religion'.

Drinkers were wandering through from the front bar, standing in the doorway to watch. There was a small bar specially for the karaoke: a hatch, manned by a teenager who kept testing the acne on his cheeks. People seemed to have their regular tables. Rebus, Janice and Brian were seated near one of the loudspeakers. Brian's mum was there, alongside Mr and Mrs Playfair. An elderly man came over to talk to them. Brian leaned towards Rebus.

'That's Alec Chisholm's dad,' he said.

'I wouldn't have known him,' Rebus admitted.

'They don't like talking to him. He's always on about how long Alec's been gone.'

It was true that the Playfairs and Mrs Mee sat stony-faced as they listened to Chisholm. Rebus got up to get a round in. He felt numb, remembering the scene which had greeted him in the cemetery, Oakes letting him know he was one step ahead, making it *personal*. Rebus saw it as another part of the test, knew Oakes was trying to break him. Rebus was more determined than ever not to let that happen.

Janice's mum was drinking Bacardi Breezes, watermelon flavour. Rebus doubted she'd ever seen a watermelon in her life. He saw Helen Cousins standing in the doorway with a couple of friends, went up to say hello.

'Any news?' she asked.

He shook his head, and she just shrugged, like she'd already given up on Damon. So much for the big romance. She was holding a bottle of Hooch, lemon flavour. All these sugary drinks, perfect for Scotland: a sweet tooth and a kick. Through in the saloon, he'd noticed they kept the bottles of mixers – lemonade and Irn Bru – on the bar, to be used freely by the punters. Not many pubs did that any more. Another thing: cheap beer. A lesson in economics: where you had a depressed area, you had to make your beer affordable. He'd spotted Heather Cranston through in the bar, seated on a stool, eyes drooping as some man talked into her ear and rested his hand on the back of her neck.

Helen handed her bottle to one of her friends, said she was off to the loo. Rebus hung around. The two girls were staring at him, wondering who he was.

'She must be taking it hard,' he said.

'What?' the one chewing gum asked, face creasing into puzzlement.

'Damon disappearing.'

The girl shrugged.

'More embarrassed than anything,' her friend commented. 'Doesn't do much for your morale, does it, your boyfriend doing a runner?'

'I suppose not,' Rebus said. 'I'm John, by the way.'

'Corinne,' the gum-chewer said. She had long black hair crimped with curling-tongs. Her pal was called Jacky and was tiny with dyed platinum hair.

'So what do you think of Damon?' he asked. He meant about Damon disappearing, but they didn't take it that way.

'Ach, he's all right,' Jacky said.

'Just all right?'

'Well, you know,' Corinne said. 'Damon's heart's in the right place, but he's a bit thick. A bit slow, like.'

Rebus nodded, as if this were his impression too. But the way Damon's family had spoken of him, he'd been more of a genius in waiting. Rebus realised suddenly just how superficial his own portrait of Damon was. So far, he'd heard only one side of the story.

'Helen likes him, though?' he asked.

'I suppose so.'

'They're engaged.'

'It happens, doesn't it?' Jacky said. 'I've got girlfriends who got engaged just so they could throw a party.' She looked at her pal for support, then leaned towards Rebus to utter a confidentiality. 'They used to have some mega arguments.'

'What about?'

'Jealousy, I suppose.' She waited till Corinne had nodded confirmation. 'She'd see him notice someone, or he'd say she'd been letting some guy chat her up. Just the usual.' She looked at him. 'You think he's gone off with someone?' Rebus saw behind her eyeliner to a sharp intelligence.

'It's possible,' he said.

But Corinne was shaking her head. 'He wouldn't have had the guts.'

Looking along the corridor, Rebus saw that Helen hadn't made it to the toilets. She was chatting to some guy, her back to the wall, hands behind her. Rebus asked Corinne and Jacky what they were drinking. Two Bacardi-Cokes. He added them to the shopping list.

When he got back to his table, Janice was taking the floor. She sang 'Baker Street' with real emotion, eyes closed, knowing the words by heart. Brian watched her, his face giving away little. He probably didn't realise he spent the whole song tearing a beer-mat into tinier and tinier pieces, piling them on the table before sweeping them on to the floor as the number finished.

Rebus stepped outside, took deep gulps of the crisp night air. He was sticking to whisky, heavily watered. There were shouts in the distance, football chants. UVF spray-painted on the side wall of the pub. A man was urinating there. Afterwards, he reeled towards Rebus, asked if he could borrow a cigarette. Rebus gave him one, lit it.

'Cheers, Jimmy,' the drunk said. Then he studied Rebus's face. 'I knew your father,' he said, walking away before Rebus could quiz him further.

Rebus stood there. This wasn't where he belonged, he knew that now. The past was a place you could visit, but it didn't do to linger there. He'd drunk too much to drive, but first thing . . . first thing he would head back. Cary Oakes wasn't here. He'd visited only long enough to leave a message. Rebus felt sorry for Janice and Brian, the way things had gone for them. But right now they were the least important of his many problems. He'd allowed his perspective to skew, and Oakes had made far too much capital from that.

Back indoors, no one tried to press the microphone on him. By now they all knew who he was, knew about the act of desecration. Stories passed quickly through a town the size of Cardenden. What else was history made up of?

34

It was still dark when he awoke. He dressed, folded the blankets, left a note on the dining table. Then headed out to his car, drove through the quiet streets and quieter countryside, hitting dual carriageway and giving the Saab's engine a proper work-out as he sped south towards Edinburgh.

He found a space round the corner from Oxford Terrace and walked back to Patience's flat. It was still too dark to see the door; he ran his fingers over it, found the lock and keyed it open. The hall was in darkness too. He walked on tiptoe, headed for the kitchen, poured water into the kettle. When he turned round, Patience was standing in the doorway.

'Where the hell have you been?' she said, tiredness failing to dampen her irritation.

'Fife.'

'You didn't call.'

'I told you I was going.'

'I tried your mobile.'

He switched the kettle on. 'I had it turned off.' He saw pain suddenly crease her face. Took her by the arms. 'What is it, Patience?'

She shook her head. There were tears in her eyes. She sniffed them back, took him by the hand into the hallway, where she switched on the light. He saw marks on the floor, a trail of them leading to the front door.

'What happened?' he asked.

'Paint,' she said. 'It was dark, I didn't see I was treading it in. I've tried cleaning it off.'

A white snail's trail of footprints . . . Rebus thought of the white tracks leading to his father's grave. He stared at her, then went to the front door and opened it. Behind him, she reached for the light-switch, illuminating the patio. Rebus saw the paint. Words daubed in foot-long letters on the paving-stones. He angled his head to read them.

YOUR COP LOVER KILLED DARREN.

The whole message underlined.

'Christ,' he gasped.

'Is that all you can say?' Her voice trembled. 'I've been trying to get you all weekend!'

'I was . . . When did it happen?' He was walking around the message.

'Friday night. I came home late, went to bed. About three, I woke up with a headache. Went to get some water, put the hall light on . . .' She was pulling back her hair with her hands, her face stretching, tightening. 'I saw the paint, came out here, and . . .'

'I'm sorry, Patience.'

'What does it mean?'

'I'm not sure.' Oakes again. All the time Rebus had been in Fife, Oakes had been right here, making his next move. He didn't just know about Janice, he knew about Patience too. And had told Rebus as much, telling him it was lucky he knew a doctor.

He'd telegraphed the move, and Rebus hadn't read it.

'You're lying,' Patience said. 'You know damned well. It's *him*, isn't it?'

Rebus tried putting his arms round her, but she shrugged him off.

'I called St Leonard's,' she said. 'They sent someone round. Two kids in uniform. In the morning, Siobhan turned up.' She smiled. 'She took me out for breakfast. I think she knew I hadn't been to sleep. It made me realise how vulnerable this place is. Garden at the back: anyone could scale the wall, get in through the conservatory. Or break down the front door: who's going to notice?' She looked at him. 'Who am I going to call?'

He made again to put his arms around her. This time she allowed it, but he could feel resistance.

'I'm sorry,' he repeated. 'If I'd known . . . if there'd been any way . . .' Friday night he'd switched off his mobile. Now he asked himself why. To conserve the battery? It was what he'd told himself back then, but maybe he'd been trying to block Fife off from everything else in his life; so busy thinking about Janice, he'd ignored Oakes's more obvious move. He kissed Patience's hair. Skewed perspectives, not thinking straight. Oakes was winning every fucking round. The bond Rebus felt with Janice was undeniable, but was all about failed chances. In the here and now, Patience was his lover. Patience was the one he was holding and kissing.

'It'll be all right,' he told her. 'Everything's going to be OK.'

She pulled away from him, wiped her eyes with the sleeve of her gown. 'Something funny's happened to your voice. You've gone all Fife.'

He smiled. 'I'll make us some tea. You go back to bed. If you need me, you know where I'll be.'

'And where's that?'

'Ben the scullery, hen.'

'It's got to be Oakes,' he said.

He'd called Siobhan to thank her. Patience had told him to ask her to lunch. So now, with the sun overhead, they were seated at the table in the conservatory. The Sunday papers lay unread in a pile in the corner. They ate Scotch broth, cooked ham and salad. A couple of bottles of wine had taken a pasting.

'Know what she did last night?' Patience had said – meaning Siobhan; talking to Rebus. 'Phoned to check I was all right. Said if I wasn't, I could sleep round at her place.' A lazy half-drunken smile, and she got up to make the coffee. It was then that Rebus voiced his suspicions to Siobhan.

'Evidence?' she replied, before finishing her wine: just the two glasses – she was driving.

'Gut feeling. He's been watching my flat. He knows I was the last person to see Rough alive. He took Janice out, and now it's Patience's turn.'

'What has he got against you?'

'I don't know. Maybe it could have been any one of us; just so happens I got the short straw.'

'From what you say, he's more calculating than that.'

'Yes.' Rebus pushed a cherry tomato around the bed of lettuce on his plate. 'Patience said something a while back. She said it all could be some kind of tactic to keep us from seeing what he's really up to.'

'And what might that be?'

Rebus sighed. 'I wish to God I knew.' He studied the salad again. 'Remember when you could only get one kind of lettuce? One kind of tomato?'

'I'm too young.'

Rebus nodded thoughtfully. 'Do you think she'll be OK?' Meaning Patience.

'She'll be fine.'

'I should have been here.'

'She said you were in Fife. What were you doing there?'

'Living in the past,' he said, finally stabbing the tomato with his fork.

He spent the rest of the day with Patience. They took a walk in the Botanic Gardens, then dropped in on Sammy. Patience hadn't gone to see her on Saturday – had phoned to say something had come up, not elaborating. She had a lie prepared for their visit, briefed Rebus so he'd back her up. Another walk: this time with Sammy in the wheelchair. Rebus still felt awkward, going out with her in public. She teased him about it.

'Ashamed to be seen with a cripple?'

'Don't talk like that.'

'What is it then?'

But he had no answer for her. What was it? He didn't know himself. Maybe it was other people, the way they stared. He wanted to say: she's going to get better, she won't be in this thing forever. He wanted to explain how it had happened and how well she'd taken it. He wanted to tell them she was *normal*.

With Sammy in a wheelchair . . . it was like she was a toddler again, and he felt himself watching for bumps and dips in the pavement, for awkward kerbs and safe crossing-places. He was insistent they wait for the green man, even when there was no traffic in sight.

'Dad,' she would say, 'what are the odds of me getting hit again?'

'Don't forget, the bookies had us odds-on for Culloden.'

And she would laugh.

Her boyfriend Ned was with them, but Sammy insisted on pushing herself, leaning back to do wheelies and show her mastery of the vehicle. Ned laughed with her, walked alongside with hands in pockets. Patience slipped her hand into Rebus's.

A Sunday outing: that's what it was.

And afterwards, back at the flat there were cream cakes and mugs of Darjeeling, football highlights on the TV with the sound turned down. Sammy talking to Patience about her latest exercise regime. Ned talking to Rebus. Rebus not listening, his eyes half-turned to the window, wondering if Cary Oakes was out there . . .

That evening, he told Patience he had to go home. 'Couple of things I need. I'll be back later.' He kissed her. 'You all right here, or do you want to come with me?'

'I'll stay,' she said.

So Rebus got into his car and drove. Not to Arden Street but down to Leith. He walked into the hotel and asked to speak to Cary Oakes. Reception tried his room: no answer.

'Maybe he's in the bar,' the woman said.

But Cary Oakes was not in the bar – Jim Stevens was.

'Let me get you a drink,' he said. Rebus shook his head, noticed Stevens was on large G and Ts.

'Where's your boy?'

Stevens just shrugged.

'I thought you'd want to keep tabs on him,' Rebus said, trying to control his anger.

'I do, believe me. But he's a slippery little bugger.'

'How much more can you milk out of him?'

Stevens smiled, shaking his head. 'Something strange and wonderful has happened. You know me, Rebus, I'm what they call a seasoned hack, meaning I'm tough and I'm relentless and I don't take shit.'

'And?'

'And I think he's been giving me shit.' Stevens shrugged. 'It's not bad stuff, don't get me wrong. But where's the corroboration?'

'Since when has that stopped you?'

Stevens bowed his head, acknowledging the point. 'For my own satisfaction,' he added, 'I'd like to know. And along the way, dear old Cary seems to have managed to weasel almost as many stories out of me as I've had from him.'

'Oh, you've always been known for your reticence.'

'I don't mind telling stories . . . bit of repartee at the bar. But Oakes . . . I don't know. It's not the stories themselves that interest him so much as what they say about the people involved.' He picked up his drink. There were three empty glasses beside it. He'd decanted all the lemon slices into the most recent arrival. 'That probably makes no sense. I don't care: I'm off duty.'

'So are you finished with him?'

Stevens smacked his lips. 'I'd say we're getting there. The question is: is *he* finished with *me*?'

Rebus took out a cigarette and lit it, offered one to the reporter. 'He's been tailing me, people I know.'

'What for?'

'Maybe he wants another story for you.' Rebus moved closer. 'Listen, off the record, just two old bastards talking . . .'

Stevens blinked away some of the alcohol. 'Yes?'

'Has he said *anything* about Deirdre Campbell?' Stevens couldn't place the name. 'Alan Archibald's niece.'

'Oh, right.' An exaggerated nod, face dipping towards the gin glass, then a frown of concentration. 'He did say something about clear-up rates. Said that's what happened when they pinned you for something: they tried to tidy away a few unsolveds by sweeping them into your case-file.'

Rebus had eased himself on to a stool. 'He didn't mention specifics?'

'You think there's something I've missed?'

Rebus was thoughtful. 'You've said it yourself: you think he's using you.'

'By putting clues in his story that I'm not going to get? Give me a bit of credit.'

'He likes *games*,' Rebus hissed. 'That's all we are to him.'

'Not me, pal. I'm his sugar daddy.'

'Sugar daddies get cheated on.'

'John . . .' Stevens sat up straight, took a reviving lungful of air. 'This story's put me back on the map. *I* got to him first. Me, washed-up old Jim Stevens, gold-watch contestant. Even if he buggered off tonight, I'd have the best part of a book's-worth.' He nodded to himself, eyes on the glass he was picking up. Rebus found himself not believing the reporter. 'See, when I make a toast these days,' Stevens went on, raising his glass, 'it's only ever to Number One. As far as I'm concerned, pal, the rest of you can go straight to hell, no Just Visiting and no Free Parking.' He drank, drained the glass dry.

He was ordering another as Rebus made for the door.

35

When Rebus left Patience's next morning, she was out on the patio, discussing with two workmen how best to clean the paint off the flagstones. As he walked into St Leonard's and made for the CID suite, he could feel that something had happened. There was activity around him and the air felt charged. Siobhan Clarke was first with the news.

'Joanna Horman's lover.' She handed Rebus a report. 'He's dirty.'

Rebus glanced down the sheet. The lover's name was Ray Heggie. He'd done time for housebreaking and assorted acts of drunken violence. He was ten years older than Joanna. He'd been living with her for six weeks.

'Roy Frazer's got him in the interview room.'

'How come?' Rebus handed back the report.

'A previous girlfriend of Heggie's. She read about the kid going missing, phoned to tell us he'd abused her little girl. That was why they broke up.'

'She didn't think to tell us before?'

Clarke shrugged. 'She's told us now.'

Rebus twitched his nose. 'How old's the girl?'

'Eleven. Someone from Sex Offences is talking to her at home.' She looked at him. 'You're not buying it, are you?'

'*Caveat emptor*, Siobhan. I'll decide after the test drive.' He winked, moved away. An old girlfriend with a grudge, probably all it was. Saw a chance to make mischief . . . All the same, if Heggie was an abuser, maybe he'd known Darren Rough. Rebus knocked on the interview room door.

'Detective Inspector Rebus enters the room,' Frazer said, for the benefit of the recording tape. He was following procedure: audio- *and* video-taping. 'Hi-Ho' Silvers sat beside him at one side of the table, arms folded, looking unimpressed by everything he'd heard. That was Silvers's role: say nothing, but make the suspect uncomfortable. Across the table sat a man in his forties, black curly hair with a pronounced bald spot. He hadn't shaved for a couple of days. His eyes were dark-ringed. He wore a black T-shirt, and ran his hands over thickly haired arms.

'Join the party,' was his comment to Rebus. The room was so small, Rebus stood by the wall, folding his own arms and preparing to listen.

'The locals organised a search party,' Frazer went on, 'you weren't part of it. How come?'

'I wasn't there.'

'Where were you?'

'Glasgow. I went out drinking with a mate, stayed the night at his place. Ask him, he'll tell you.'

'I'm sure he will. Mates are good that way, aren't they?'

'It's the truth.'

Frazer scribbled a note to himself. 'You went out drinking, that means there'll be witnesses.' He looked up from his notebook. 'So name me some.'

'Give me a break. Look, the pubs were all dead, so we got a carry-out and went back to his flat. Sat watching some videos.'

'Anything good?'

'Top-shelf stuff.' Heggie winked. Frazer just glared back.

'Porn?'

'That's what I said.'

'Straight?'

'I'm not a poof.' Heggie stopped rubbing his arms.

'I meant, was there any lezzie action?'

'Might have been.'

'Bondage? Animals? Kids?'

Heggie saw where this was leading. 'I'm not into any of that, I've told you.'

'Your ex says different.'

'That slut'd say anything. Wait till I see her . . .'

'Anything happens to her, Mr Heggie, if she so much as catches a cold, I'll have you back in here. Understood?'

'I didn't mean anything. It's just a saying, isn't it? But she's been slagging me off, telling people I've got AIDS, you name it. Vindictive, she is. Any chance of a cuppa?'

Frazer made a show of checking his watch. 'We'll take a break in five minutes.' Rebus had to stifle a smile, knowing they'd only break when Frazer was good and ready. 'You've got a record of violence, Mr Heggie. My thinking is: you lost patience with the kid, didn't mean to hurt him. But a valve blew, and next thing you knew he was dead.'

'No.'

'So you had to hide him somewhere.'

'No. I keep telling you—'

'Where is he then? How come he goes missing and you turn out to have a record of hurting kids?'

'All you've got is Belinda's word for it!' Belinda: the ex. 'I'm telling you, get a doctor to look at Fliss.' Fliss: the ex's daughter. 'And even if it turns out someone's been poking her, no way it was me. No fucking way. Ask her.' He scratched at his hair with one hand.

'We're doing that, Mr Heggie.'

'And if she says I did anything, her mum's put her up to it.' He was growing more agitated. 'I don't believe this, really I don't.' He shook his head. 'You lot told Joanna. Now what's she going to think?'

'Why do you always shack up with single mothers?'

Heggie raised his eyes to the ceiling. 'Tell me this is a bad dream.'

Frazer, who'd been resting his arms on the table, now sat back, glanced towards Rebus. It was the signal Rebus had been waiting for. It meant Frazer was finished for the moment.

'Did you know Darren Rough, Mr Heggie?' Rebus asked.

'He's the one that got topped?' He waited for Rebus to nod confirmation. 'Never knew him.'

'Never spoke to him?'

'We weren't in the same block.'

'You knew where he lived then?'

'It's been all over the papers. Perverted little bastard, whoever did it deserves a medal.'

'Why do you say he was "little"? He was, by the way. Not tall, at any rate. But it wasn't in the papers.'

'It's just . . . it's something you say, isn't it?'

'It's certainly something *you* say. Makes me think you'd seen him.'

'Maybe I had. It's not that big a scheme.'

'No, it's not,' Rebus said quietly. 'Everyone knows everyone else.'

'Until the council move in bastards they can't put anywhere else.'

Rebus nodded. 'So you might have seen Darren Rough around?'

'What difference does it make?'

'It's just that he liked young kids too. Paedophiles seem to be good at recognising one another.'

'I'm not a paedophile!' Losing it. His voice was trembling as he got to his feet. 'I'd kill every last one of them.'

'Did you start with Darren?'

'What?'

'Get rid of him, you'd be a hero.'

A burst of nervous laughter. 'So now I didn't just do in Billy, I topped the pervert as well?'

'Is that what you're telling us?' Rebus asked.

'I haven't killed anyone!'

'How did you get on with Billy, by the way? Must've been awkward, having him around, you wanting Joanna all to yourself.'

'He's a nice kid.'

'Sit down, Mr Heggie,' Frazer commanded.

Eventually Heggie sat down, but then leapt up again, his finger pointing at Rebus. 'He's trying to set me up!'

Rebus shook his head, gave a wry smile. He pushed off from the wall.

'I'm just after the truth,' he said, making to leave the room.

'Inspector Rebus leaving the interview room,' he could hear Frazer saying behind him.

Later, Frazer stopped off at Rebus's desk. 'You don't really make him for Darren Rough, do you?'

Rebus shrugged. 'Do you make him for the kid?'

'Maybe if Sex Offences come up with something. From what I hear, her mum's sticking to her like glue, answering for her, putting words in her mouth.'

'Doesn't mean she's lying.'

'No.' Frazer was thoughtful. 'Heggie doesn't give a shit about Billy Horman. All he's worried about is that Joanna will boot him out.' He shook his head slowly. 'People like him, you never get through to them, do you?'

'No.'

'And you can't get them to change.' He looked at Rebus. 'That's what you think too, isn't it?'

'Welcome to my world, Roy,' Rebus said, reaching for the telephone.

He had to keep working; had to stop letting thoughts of Cary Oakes consume him. So Rebus phoned Phyllida Hawes at Gayfield station.

'Has your MisPer turned up?' she asked.

'Not a bloody sign of him.'

'Well, that can be good news too, can't it? Means he's probably still alive.'

'Or the body's been well-hidden.'

'I do like an optimist.'

Another time, Rebus might have kept the banter going. 'You know Gaitano's?' he said instead, getting to the point.

'Yes.' Sounding curious, wondering what he was after.

'As owned by Charmer Mackenzie?'

'The same.'

'What have you got on him?'

Silence for a moment. 'Is he connected to your MisPer?'

'I'm not sure.' Rebus told her about the boat.

'Yes, I knew about that,' she said. 'But it's strictly a money thing. I mean, Mackenzie has a share, but he doesn't interfere with the business. You've met Billy Preston?' Rebus admitted he had. 'Charmer leaves him to get on with it.'

'Not quite. The under manager at Gaitano's, young guy called Archie Frost, he keeps an eye on the Clipper. Plus provides muscle for the door.'

'Is that so?' Rebus could hear her scribbling a note to herself.

'Does he have any other interests?' he asked.

'You might want to take this conversation to NCIS.'

NCIS: the National Criminal Intelligence Service. Rebus leaned forward in his chair. 'They have something on Mackenzie?'

'They have a file, yes.'

'So he's got dirt under his fingernails: what is it exactly?'

'Farmyard mud for all I know. Go talk to NCIS.'

'I will.' Rebus put the phone down, logged on at one of the computer terminals and entered Mackenzie's details. At the bottom of the screen there was a reference number and an officer's name. Rebus called NCIS and asked to speak to the name: Detective Sergeant Paul Carnett.

'That's a misprint,' the switchboard told him. 'It's not Paul, it's Pauline.' She put him through anyway, where a male voice told Rebus DS Carnett would be in a meeting for another hour, maybe an hour and a half. Rebus checked his watch.

'Has she anything after that?'

'Not that I can see.'

'Then I'd like to make a reservation: table for two, the name's DI Rebus.'

36

The Scottish office of NCIS was based at Osprey House in Paisley, not far off the M8. Last time Rebus had been this way had been to drop his ex-wife off at Glasgow Airport. She'd come up from London to see Sammy, and all the Edinburgh flights had been full. He couldn't remember what they'd talked about on the drive.

Osprey House was supposed to be the future of high-profile policing in Scotland, housing as it did the Scottish Crime Squad and Customs and Excise as well as NCIS and the Scottish Criminal Intelligence Office. Its remit was intelligence-gathering. Having started with just the two officers, NCIS now had a staff of ten. There had been bad feeling when the office had opened, due to the fact that the Scottish NCIS team reported not to a Scottish chief constable but to the London-based director of the whole UK operation, who in turn reported to the Scottish Secretary. NCIS dealt with counterfeiting, money-laundering, organised drug and vehicle crime, and, if Rebus remembered correctly, paedophile gangs. Rebus had heard the officers at NCIS called 'anoraks' and 'computer nerds', but not by anyone who'd actually met them.

'It's fairly irregular,' Pauline Carnett said, as Rebus explained why he was there.

They were seated in an open-plan office, around them the incessant humming of computer fans and quiet telephone conversations. The occasional flurry of keyboard strokes. Young men in shirtsleeves and ties; two women, both dressed for business. Pauline's desk was at the opposite end of the room from the other woman officer. Rebus wondered if there was any significance in this.

Pauline Carnett was in her mid-thirties with short blonde hair brushed out from a centre parting. Tall and broad-shouldered, she had offered a handshake firmer than most Masons Rebus knew. She had a gap between her two front teeth and seemed overly conscious of the fact, which made Rebus want to make her smile.

Like all the others, her desk was L-shaped, with one surface given over to a computer, the other to paperwork. The office shared a printer. It was churning out work, a young man standing beside it, looking bored.

'So this is the heart of the machine,' had been Rebus's comment on entering the room.

Carnett put her cup down on a mouse pad stained with dozens of coffee rings. Rebus set his own cup on the worktop.

'Irregular,' she said again, as if he might be persuaded to leave. Instead, he just shrugged. 'Information is usually requested by telephone or fax.'

'I've always preferred the personal touch,' Rebus said. He handed her a scrap of paper on which he'd jotted the reference number concerning Charmer Mackenzie. She slid her chair closer to the desk and hammered on the keys, as if meaning to do violence to the keyboard. Then she slid the mouse around the pad, expertly avoiding the coffee cup, and double-clicked.

Charmer Mackenzie's file came up. Rebus saw straight away that there was a lot of stuff there. He moved his own chair closer to hers.

'Initially,' she said, 'it looks like we got on to him because Crime Squad had him hosting private parties for someone called Thomas Telford.'

'I know Telford,' Rebus said. 'I helped put him away.'

'Good for you. Telford used Mackenzie's club for meetings, and also rented a boat part-owned by Mackenzie. The boat was used for parties. Crime Squad kept tabs on it because you never knew who might turn up. Didn't get much joy, though: operation suspended.' She hit the return key, bringing up another page. 'Ah, here we go,' she said, leaning in towards the screen. 'Money-lending.'

'Mackenzie?'

She nodded. Rebus read over her shoulder. NCIS suspected Mackenzie of running a little business on the side, fronting money for criminal schemes – guaranteed payback, one way or another – but also loaning cash sums to people who either couldn't get the money elsewhere or had reasons not to go walking into a bank or building society.

'How accurate is this?' Rebus asked.

'It wouldn't be here if it wasn't one hundred per cent.'

'All the same . . .'

'All the same, there's obviously not enough to go on, or we'd have had him in court.' She pointed to an icon at the foot of the screen. 'Case-notes went to the Procurator Fiscal, who decided there wasn't enough for a prosecution.'

'So is the case ongoing?'

She shook her head. 'We have patience, we can wait. We'll see what else filters down to us, decide when the time's right to try again.' She glanced at him. 'Robert the Bruce and all that.'

Rebus was still studying the screen. 'Have you got names?'

'You mean people who've borrowed from him?'

'Yes.'

'Hang on.' She hit more keys, studied the information as it came up on the screen. 'Hard copies,' she mumbled at last. Then she got up from her seat and told him to follow her. They went to a storeroom filled with filing cabinets.

'So much for the paperless office,' Rebus said.

'I'm with you on that.' She found the cabinet she was looking for, pulled out the top drawer and started riffling through the file-holders, found the one she was looking for and pulled it out.

Inside the green file were about three dozen sheets of paper. Two of the sheets listed 'suspected' users of Charmer Mackenzie's loan scheme.

'No statements,' Rebus said, sifting the sheets.

'Case probably didn't get that far.'

'I thought it was your case.'

She shrugged. 'We get sent a lot of stuff from Crime Squad, Customs, wherever. It goes into the computer and into a drawer – that's my job.'

'You're a filing clerk?' Rebus suggested. Her eyes narrowed aggressively. 'Sorry,' he said. 'Trying to make a joke.' He went back to the file. 'So how did you come by these names?'

'Probably one or two people talked.'

'But didn't make reliable witnesses?'

She nodded. 'People who need to go to a loan shark, we're not talking public-minded citizens here.'

Rebus recognised a couple of names: known housebreakers. Maybe looking to finance some bigger scheme.

'Others on the list,' Carnett was saying, 'could be they got thumped by Mackenzie or his men, and Crime Squad got wind of it.'

'And nobody would talk?' Rebus guessed. She nodded again. He'd come across this before; they both had. It was fine to have seven bells knocked out of you, but a black mark to talk to the filth about it. You'd get 'GRASS' sprayed on your front door. People would cross the road to avoid you. Rebus started jotting down names and addresses, sure none of it was going to be any use. But he'd come all this way, after all.

'I can make copies,' Carnett suggested.

Rebus nodded. 'I'm a bit of a dinosaur, need to have the gist in my wee book.' He tapped one entry. No name, just a series of numbers. 'Is this what we're supposed to call Prince now?'

She smiled, covered it quickly with her hand. 'Looks like another reference,' she said. 'I'll check it back at my desk.'

So they went back there, and while Rebus finished his cold coffee, he watched her work.

'Interesting,' she said at last, leaning back in her chair. 'It's our way of keeping certain names quiet. Computers aren't always safe from prowlers.'

'Hackers.'

She looked at him. 'Not quite a dinosaur,' she commented. 'Wait here a minute.'

She was actually gone three minutes, long enough for her screen-saver to activate. When she returned, she had a single sheet of paper with her, which she handed to Rebus.

'We use numbers as codes when a name is judged too hot: that means someone we don't want everyone knowing about. Any idea who he is?'

Rebus was looking at the name on the sheet. There was nothing else printed there.

'Yes,' he said at last. 'He's a judge's son.'

'That would explain it then,' Pauline Carnett said, lifting her cup.

The name on the sheet was Nicol Petrie.

When they delved a little deeper, they found a Crime Squad report detailing a mugging attack. Nicol Petrie had been found unconscious in one of the shadowy back lanes off Rose Street – about a hundred yards from Gaitano's nightclub. Petrie had been taken by ambulance to hospital, a uniformed officer waiting to talk to him. But when he'd regained consciousness, he had had nothing to say.

'I can't remember,' had been his refrain. He couldn't even say if anything had been stolen from him. But a couple of eye-witnesses gave descriptions of two men leaving the lane. They were laughing, lighting cigarettes. One of them even complained that he'd scraped his knuckles. Police got as far as holding an ID parade for the witnesses, but by then they'd long since sobered up and wanted nothing to do with it, refused to identify anyone.

Two bouncers from Gaitano's had been in the parade: one of them was named as Calumn Brady.

Rebus went through the witness statements. The descriptions of the attackers were vague. He could just about see one of them – the shorter of the two – as Cal Brady. But it didn't matter. Nicol Petrie wasn't about to say anything, and the witnesses had either been warned off, paid off, or had just come to their senses.

Crime Squad put it down to a 'warning' from Mackenzie, and let it go at that. Speculation: that's all it was. But Rebus was willing to go along with it. All the same . . . something refused to click into place.

'Nicol's dad's a judge, plenty of money. Why didn't he just borrow from him?'

Pauline Carnett didn't have an answer for that.

Later, he asked if he could speak to someone from the paedophile unit. He was introduced to a woman officer called DS Whyte. He asked her about Darren Rough. She brought the details up on her screen.

'What about him?' she said.

'Known associates.'

She hammered keys, shook her head. 'He was a loner. NKA.'

NKA: No Known Associates. Rebus scratched his chin. 'How about Ray Heggie.'

She hit more keys. 'No record,' she said at last. 'Is he someone I should know about?'

Rebus shrugged.

'In that case . . .' she said, adding the name to her screen. Rebus's name went there too. 'Just so I know where I first heard of him.'

Rebus nodded. 'Have you been following Shiellion?'

'I hear the jury's out. Looking good for guilty.'

'Not if Richie Cordover has anything to do with it.'

'He's good, but I've come across Lord Justice Petrie before, and if there's one thing he can't stand, it's a paedophile. The way Petrie summed up, Ince and Marshall are fucked.'

'Not before time,' Rebus added, getting up to go.

37

Back in Edinburgh, he was wanted at Fettes – by the ACC, no less.

The Assistant Chief Constable (Crime) was known to be scrupulous, fair, and to have no record of suffering fools gladly. He had a nice fat file on Rebus which told him the officer was 'difficult but useful'. Rebus had made a career out of making enemies. The ACC, whose name was Colin Carswell, liked to think of himself as not among them.

There was an identifying plaque on the door, and the room number below it: 278. The room itself was large, with institutional carpet and curtains, and a bowl of flowers on the windowsill. There was little other decoration. Carswell, tall and thin with a good head of salt-and-pepper hair and moustache to match, rose from his chair just long enough to shake Rebus's hand. Typically, he didn't sit behind his desk for interviews, but conducted them in two chairs by the window. The chairs were swivel designs and sat on castors, so that unwary officers could find themselves spinning a hundred and eighty degrees or sliding backwards towards Carswell's desk. After an interview like that, most agreed they'd have settled for the old-fashioned kind.

Which, the ACC might have told them, was the whole point of the exercise.

The dark eyes spoke of lost sleep. Despite his advancing years, the ACC had recently become a father for the fourth time. As his other kids were all grown-up, the conclusion reached by every station in the city was that the new addition was an accident, which would make it practically the only thing in the ACC's life that he'd not been able to orchestrate or control.

'How are you, John?' he asked.

'Not bad, sir. How's the wee one?'

'Fit as a fiddle. Look, John . . .' Carswell never wasted time on preliminaries. 'I've been asked to look into this murder case.'

'Darren Rough?'

'That's the one.'

'Social Work, was it, sir?' Rebus settled his hands on the arm rests.

'Fellow called Andrew Davies. Made a sort of complaint.'

'Sort of?'

'Couched fairly ambiguously.'

'He's probably got a point, sir.'

The ACC held his breath for a second. 'Am I hearing you right?'

'I chased Rough through the zoo without probable cause, giving our poisoner the chance to strike again. Then when I found out Rough was living upstairs from a playground, I put word out on the street.'

Carswell put his hands together, as if in prayer. Knowing Rebus's reputation, a confession was the last thing he'd been expecting. 'You outed him?'

'Yes, sir. I wanted him off my patch. At the time . . .' Rebus paused. 'I didn't work through the consequences. Later on, I helped him get away from Greenfield – at least, that was the plan. Only he left my flat and got himself murdered. Right at the end, though . . . I think I did try to make amends.'

'I see. You want me to take this to Social Work?'

'That's up to you, sir.'

'Then what *do* you want?'

Rebus looked at him. It was bright outside: another ploy of the ACC's – he tended to use the chair trick when it was sunny. All Rebus could see of his superior was a haze of light.

'For a while, I thought I wanted out, sir. Maybe that was in my mind when I went after Rough: if I went after him hard, I might end up kicked off the force, but still feel all right about it.'

'But that didn't happen.'

'It hasn't happened yet, sir, no.'

Carswell was thoughtful. 'How do you feel now?'

Rebus squinted into the light. 'I'm not sure. Tired, mostly.' He managed a smile.

'A long time back, John – I know you all like to think I've spent my whole life behind a desk – but a long time back there was this man got himself into a fight down in Leith. Clean-cut type, suit and everything. Wife and kids at home. And he'd walked into a pub by the dockside, looked for the biggest, meanest-looking bugger he could find, and started having a go at him. I was young back then, they sent me to interview him in hospital. Turned out he'd been trying to commit suicide, hadn't had the guts. So he'd gone looking for someone to do the job for him. Sounds a bit like what you were up to with Darren Rough: assisted career suicide.'

Rebus smiled again, but he was thinking: *Suicide again . . . like with Jim Margolies. Assisted career suicide . . .*

'I don't think I'm going to give this to our friends in Social Work,' the ACC said finally. 'I think I'm going to sit on it for a while. Maybe there's room for some sort of apology . . . that'll be up to you.'

'Thank you, sir.'

'And John,' rising to his feet, taking Rebus's hand again, 'I appreciate you not trying to spin me some yarn.'

'Yes, sir.' Rebus was on his feet, too. 'And maybe, with respect, sir, there's a way you could show your appreciation . . .'

Nicol Petrie lived in a West End flat, sprawling over the top two floors of a Georgian pile. There was a shared entrance hall with occasional tables and rugs. The tables had vases and things on them. It was a far cry from the tenement stairwells Rebus was used to.

And there was a lift, its mirrored interior highly polished, the wooden surrounds gleaming. Beside the buttons for each floor were printed labels listing the occupants. There were two Petries: N and A. Rebus guessed that A stood for Amanda.

The lift brought Rebus out on to a landing, glass cupola above. Pot plants surrounded him. And more carpeting. Nicol Petrie opened the door and gave a little nod, leading Rebus inside.

Rebus had been expecting antiquity, but was disappointed. The flat's walls were painted an almost luminous white and were devoid of paintings or posters. The floors had been stripped and varnished. It was like stepping into an Ikea catalogue. An internal stairway led up to the top floor, but Nicol led Rebus past it and into the living room, fully thirty-five feet long and twelve high, and with double sash windows giving uninterrupted views across Dean Valley and the Water of Leith. The Fife coastline was visible in the distance. Walking into the room, taking it all in, Rebus missed the doll on the floor and ended up giving it a kick, sending it flying towards its owner.

'Jessica!' the little girl squealed, moving on hands and knees to pick up her property and nurse it to her bosom. Then she slid back across the floor to where a toys' tea-party was in progress. Rebus apologised, but Hannah Margolies wasn't listening.

'Hello again,' Hannah's mother said. She was seated on a white sofa. 'Sorry about that. Hannah's toys get everywhere.' She sounded tired. Rebus noted that she still wore black, albeit a short black dress with black tights. Mourning as fashion statement.

'Sorry,' he said to Nicol Petrie, 'I didn't know you had company.'

'You know one another?' Petrie bowed his head at the stupidity of the question. 'Through Jim, of course. Sorry.'

It seemed to Rebus that all anyone had done so far was make apologies. Katherine Margolies got to her feet in a sudden elegant movement.

'Come on, Han-Han. Time to go.'

Hannah didn't argue or complain, just rose to her feet and joined her mother.

'Nicky,' Katherine said, kissing both his cheeks, 'thanks as ever for listening.'

Nicol Petrie embraced her, then crouched down for a kiss from Hannah. Katherine Margolies lifted Hannah's coat from the back of the sofa.

'Goodbye, Inspector.'

'Bye, Mrs Margolies. Bye, Hannah.'

Hannah gave him a look. 'You think I should have won, don't you?'

Katherine stroked her daughter's hair. 'Everyone knows you were robbed, sweetheart.'

Hannah was still staring at Rebus. 'Someone stole my father,' she said.

Nicol Petrie made a fuss of her as he showed mother and daughter to the door. When he returned to the room, Rebus was standing at one of the windows, looking down into the street immediately below. Petrie began tidying the toys into a cardboard box.

'Sorry again if I disturbed you, sir,' Rebus said, not managing much enthusiasm for the lie.

'That's all right. Katy often pops in unannounced. Especially since . . . well, you know.'

'Do you make a good listener, Mr Petrie?'

'No more than most, I don't suppose. Usually it's because I can't think of anything helpful to say, so all I do is fill the gaps with questions.'

'You'd make a good detective then.'

Petrie laughed. 'I rather doubt that, Inspector.' He opened one of the doors leading off the living room. It led to a walk-in cupboard. There were shelves inside, and he placed the box of toys on one of them. Everything tidied away. Rebus would bet the box always went back on the same shelf, always the same spot. He'd known people like that, people who managed their lives by compartments. Siobhan Clarke was just the same: if you wanted to annoy her, you only had to move something of hers from one desk-drawer to its neighbour.

Below him, Katherine Margolies and her daughter emerged from the building. Their car had remote locking. It was a Mercedes saloon, new-looking. The number plate was the same one he'd seen lipsticked on the wall in Leith.

It was a white Mercedes.

White . . .

'Has it hit her hard?' he asked, still watching from the window.

'Devastated, I should think.'

'And the little one?'

'I'm not sure Han-Han's taken it in yet. Like she said, she thinks he's been stolen from her.'

'She's right in a way.'

'I suppose so.' Petrie came to the window, watched with Rebus as the car drove off. 'Nobody could fail to be shocked by something like that.'

'Why do you think he did it?'

Petrie looked at him. 'I haven't the faintest idea.'

'His widow hasn't said anything?'

'That's between her and me.'

'Sorry,' Rebus said. 'It's just curiosity. I mean, someone like Jim Margolies . . . it makes you ask questions of yourself, doesn't it?'

'I think I know what you mean.' Petrie turned back into the room. 'If you've got it all and you're still unhappy, what's the point of everything?' He slumped into a chair. 'Maybe it's a Scottish thing.'

Rebus took a seat on the sofa. 'What is?'

'We're just not supposed to have it all, are we? We're supposed to fail gloriously. Anything we succeed at, we keep low-profile. It's our failures we're allowed to trumpet.'

Rebus smiled. 'Might be something in that.'

'It runs right through our history.'

'And ends at the national football team.'

It was Petrie's turn to smile. 'I've been very rude: can I offer you something to drink?'

'What are you having?'

'I thought maybe a glass of wine. I'd opened a bottle for Katy, thinking she'd come by taxi. Parking around here is hellish.' He left the room, Rebus following. The kitchen was long and narrow and spotless. The hob looked like it had never been used. Petrie went to the fridge, lifted out a bottle of Sancerre.

'Lovely flat,' Rebus said, as Petrie reached into a cupboard for two glasses.

'Thank you. I like it.'

'What do you work at, Mr Petrie?'

Petrie glanced at him. 'I'm a student, second year into my PhD.'

'Was your first degree at Edinburgh?'

'No, St Andrews.' Pouring now.

'Not many students with flats as grand as this – or am I behind the times?'

'It's not mine.'

'Your father's?' Rebus guessed.

'That's right.' Pouring the second glass; looking a little less serene now.

'He must like you.'

'He loves his children, Inspector. I'd assume most parents do.'

Rebus thought of himself and Sammy. 'Not always a two-way thing, though, is it?'

'I don't know what you mean.'

Rebus shrugged, accepted the glass. 'Cheers.' He took a sip. Petrie was at the end of the narrow kitchen: no way out of there except past Rebus. And Rebus wasn't moving. 'Funny thing is, if I'd a father who loved me, who'd spent a fortune on a flat for me, any time I got into trouble I'd probably turn to him to bail me out.'

'Look, what's—'

'Say, if I needed money. I wouldn't go to a loan shark.' Rebus paused, took another sip. 'How about you, Mr Petrie?'

'Christ, is that what this is about? Those two thugs giving me a kicking?'

'Maybe it wasn't about money. Maybe they just didn't like your looks.' Nicol Petrie: face unblemished, thin dark eyebrows, high cheekbones. A face so perfect you might just want to damage it.

'I don't know what they wanted.'

Rebus smiled. 'Yes you do. That handy amnesia of yours, you let it slip. You shouldn't have known there were two of them.'

'The police said as much at the time.'

'Two men employed by Charmer Mackenzie. We call them "frighteners", and believe me, I'd have been frightened too. He's a hard bastard, Cal Brady, isn't he?'

'Who?'

'Cal Brady. You must have come across him.'

Petrie shook his head. 'I don't think so.'

'How much was it you owed? I'm assuming you've paid it off by now. And why didn't you tap your dad for a loan in the first place? See, I'm curious, Mr Petrie, and when I start asking questions, I tend not to give up till I've found answers.'

Petrie put his glass down on the worktop. He wasn't looking at Rebus when he spoke. 'This is strictly between us? No way I'm taking this any further.'

'Fair enough,' Rebus said.

Petrie folded his arms around himself, looking skinnier than ever. 'I did borrow money from Mackenzie. We knew, those of us who frequented the Clipper, knew he'd lend money. And I found myself needing some. My father can be generous when it suits him, Inspector, but I'd managed to fritter away a good deal of his money. I didn't want him knowing. So I went to Mackenzie instead.'

'Surely you could have arranged an overdraft?'

'I dare say I could.' Petrie looked away. 'But there was something . . . the idea of dealing with Mackenzie was so much more appealing.'

'How so?'

'The danger, the whiff of the illicit.' He turned back towards Rebus. 'You know Edinburgh society loves that sort of thing. Deacon Brodie didn't need to break into people's houses, but that didn't stop him. Strait-laced old town, how else are we going to get our thrills?'

Rebus stared at him. 'Know something, Nicky? I almost believe you. Almost, but not quite.' He raised a hand towards Petrie, who flinched. But all Rebus did was place a fingertip against the young man's temple. It came away with a bead of perspiration clinging to it. The droplet fell, splashed onto the worktop.

'Better wipe that up,' Rebus said, turning away. 'You wouldn't want anything marking that stainless surface of yours, would you?'

38

There was still no sign of Billy Horman.

His mother Joanna had cried at the press conference, ensuring TV coverage. Ray Heggie, Joanna's lover, had sat beside her, saying nothing. When the crying started, he'd tried to comfort her, but she'd pushed him away. Rebus knew he'd drift away eventually, as long as he was innocent.

GAP was as active as ever. They were holding a vigil outside the High Court while the jury retired to reach a verdict in the Shiellion case. They'd lit candles and tied placards to the railings. The placards detailed child-killers and paedophiles and their victims. The police were instructed not to move the protesters on. Meantime, there were fresh news reports of paedophiles being released from prison. GAP sent members to the relevant towns. It had become a movement now, Van Brady its unlikely figurehead. She hosted her own news conferences, blown-up photos of Billy Horman and Darren Rough on the wall behind her.

'The world,' she'd said at one meeting, 'should be a green field without limits, where our children can play free from harm, and where parents can leave their children without fear. That is the purpose and intention of the Green Field Project.'

Rebus wondered who was writing her speeches for her. GFP was a departure for GAP, a funding application to set up patrolled play areas with security cameras and the like. To Rebus, it sounded less like the world as green field, more like the world as prison camp. They were applying to the Lottery and the EC for cash. Other housing schemes had made successful bids in the past, and were lending a hand to Greenfield. They wanted something like two million quid. Rebus shuddered to think of Van and Cal Brady in charge of such a fund.

But then it wasn't his problem, was it?

His immediate problem, as he knew when he picked up the ringing phone, was Cary Oakes.

The voice on the line belonged to Alan Archibald. 'He's agreed.'

'Agreed to what?'

'To go out to Hillend with me. To walk across the hills.'

'He's admitted it?'

'As good as.' Archibald's voice shook with excitement.

'But has he said anything *specific*?'

'Once we get out there, John, I know he'll tell me, one way or the other.'

'You're going to torture him, are you?'

'I don't mean it like that. I mean once he's there, the scene of the crime, I think he'll crack.'

'I wouldn't be so sure. What if it's a trap?'

'John, we've been through this.'

'I know.' Rebus paused. 'And you're still going.'

The voice quiet now, calm. 'I've got to, whatever happens.'

'Yes,' Rebus said. Of course Archibald would go. It was his destiny. 'Well, count me in.'

'I'll ask him—'

'No, Alan, you'll *tell* him. It's both of us or no go.'

'What if he—'

'He won't. Trust me on this. I think he'll want me out there too.'

The tape was still running, but Cary Oakes hadn't spoken for a couple of minutes. Jim Stevens was used to it, used to long pauses as Oakes gathered his thoughts. He let another sixty seconds spool on before asking: 'Anything else, Cary?'

Oakes looked surprised. 'Should there be?'

'That's it then?' Still Stevens left the tape running. Oakes only nodded, and reached his hands behind his head, job done. Stevens checked his watch, spoke the time into the machine, then squeezed the Stop button. He slipped the recorder into the breast pocket of his pale mauve shirt. It was pale because it had been through about three hundred washes in the five years since Stevens had bought it. He knew the other reporters thought he'd filled out in the past half-decade. The shirt could have proved them wrong, but would also have proved how seldom he bought new clothes.

'Satisfied?' Oakes said, getting to his feet, stretching as if after a long day at the coal-face.

'Not really. Journalists never are.'

'Why's that?'

'Because no matter how much we're told, we *know* we're not getting everything.'

Oakes held his hands out. 'I've given you blood, Jim. I feel like you've taken a transfusion from me.' That unnerving grin again; so lacking in humour. Stevens wrote date and time on a sticker, peeled it off and placed it down one edge of the cassette case. He made this tape number eleven. Eleven hours of Cary Oakes. It wasn't enough for a book, but it might get him the contract, and the rest of the book could be padded: trial reports, interviews, photographs.

Only thing was, he didn't think he was going to find a publisher. He wasn't even going to try.

'What are you thinking, big man?' Oakes asked. He'd taken to calling Stevens 'big man'. Stevens wasn't naive enough to take it as a compliment; at best it was weighted with irony.

'I'm . . . not really thinking at all.' Stevens shrugged. 'Just that it's over, that's all.'

'So now it's pay-off time for old Cary.'

'You'll get your cheque.'

'What good's a cheque? I said cash.'

Stevens shook his head. 'A cheque, has to be or our accounts department would have a breakdown. You can use it to open a bank account.'

'And sit around how long waiting for it to clear?' Oakes had been pacing the room. Now he came to Stevens' chair and leaned down over him, staring him out. Stevens blinked first, which seemed victory enough for Oakes. He propelled himself back upright and angled his head to the ceiling, letting out a whoop of laughter. Then he leaned down again long enough to pat one of Stevens' resilient cheeks.

'It's OK, Jim, really it is. I never really needed the money anyway. What I needed was for you to think you had me by the balls.'

'I never ever thought that, Oakes.'

'No more first names, huh? Did I upset you or something?'

Stevens shook the tape box. 'How much of this is crap?'

Oakes grinned again. 'How much do you think, partner?'

'I don't know. That's why I'm asking.' He saw Oakes glance towards the clock by the bed. 'Going somewhere?'

'My work here's finished. Nothing to keep me.'

'Where are you going?' Stevens didn't know why, but while Oakes had been laughing, he'd switched the recorder back on. Situated as it was in his shirt pocket, he didn't know how much it would pick up. He could hear its small motor working, feel it grinding against his chest.

'Why should you care?'

'I'm a reporter. You're still a story.'

'You haven't seen the best of it, Jimmy baby.'

Stevens ran a dry tongue over his lips.

'Do I scare you, Jim?'

'Sometimes,' Stevens admitted.

'You're bigger than me, heavier anyway. You could take me, couldn't you?'

'It's not always down to size.'

'True, true. Sometimes it's down to just how rip-roaring crazy and ferocious your opponent is. Is there a touch of madness in me, Jimbo?'

Stevens nodded slowly. 'And ferocity too,' he added.

'You better believe it.' Oakes was examining himself in the wall-mirror, running a hand over his cropped head. 'And it's a hungry madness, Jim. It wants me to eat people up.' A sly sideways look. 'Not you, though, don't worry on that score.'

'What score should I worry on?'

'You'll find out soon enough.' He studied himself in the mirror again. 'I have a date with my past, Jim. A date with destiny, as you and your fellow hacks might put it. With someone who never listened to me.' He was nodding to himself. 'Just one last thing, Jim.' Turning towards the journalist. 'I knew when I came out I'd be telling my story. I've had a long time to get it straight.'

' "Straight" rather than true?'

'You're smarter than you look, Jimbo.' Oakes laughed.

Stevens' heart beat a little faster. It was what he'd suspected for some days, but that didn't make it any easier to hear.

'Some of it must have been accurate,' he managed to utter.

'Scots are a nation of storytellers, Jim, isn't that right?' He patted Stevens' cheek again, then headed for the door. 'It was all shit, Jim. Remember that till the day you die.'

After the door had closed on Oakes, Stevens put his head in his hands and sat there for a few moments, relieved it was all over, whatever the outcome. When his phone rang, he remembered the recorder in his pocket. Removed it and switched it off, rewound and hit Play.

Oakes's voice had grown small and tinny, but no less devilish. *It was all shit, Jim.* He turned off the tape and went to answer the phone. Cleared his throat first, sat down on the edge of the bed.

'Hello?' he said into the receiver.

'Jim, is that you? Peter Barclay here.'

Barclay worked for a rival tabloid. 'What do you want, Peter?'

'Caught you at a bad time?' Barclay chuckled. He always spoke with a cigarette in his mouth. It made him sound like a bad ventriloquist.

'You might say that.'

'I do say that. Your boy's been telling tales out of school.'

'What?' Stevens stopped rubbing the back of his neck.

'He's sent a letter to all your lovely competitors, saying his "autobiography" is complete bollocks. Any comment to make, Jim? On the record, naturally.'

Stevens slammed the receiver back into its cradle, then swiped the apparatus off the bedside table and on to the floor.

'Number disconnected,' he said, giving it a kick for good measure.

39

There was mist on the Pentland Hills, leaching colour from the landscape and threatening to cut Hillend and Swanston off from the city just north of them.

'I don't like it,' Rebus said as they parked.

'Afraid we'll get lost?' Cary Oakes smiled. 'Wouldn't that be a blow to humanity?'

He was sitting in the passenger seat, Alan Archibald in the back. Rebus hadn't wanted Oakes in the back; had wanted him where he could see him. Before setting off, he'd insisted on patting Oakes down. Oakes had asked if Rebus would reciprocate.

'I'm not the killer here,' Rebus had said.

'I'll take that as a no.' Oakes had turned to Archibald. 'I thought it would just be the two of us. More intimate that way.' Nodding towards Rebus. 'No need for outsiders, Mr Archibald.'

'You're going nowhere without me,' Rebus had said.

And here they were. Archibald seemed nervous. Getting out of the car, he dropped his Ordnance Survey map. Oakes picked it up for him.

'Maybe we should leave a little trail of breadcrumbs,' he suggested.

'Let's just get on with it,' Archibald answered, nerves lending his voice an edge of irritation.

Rebus was looking around. No other cars in the vicinity; no hill-walkers; no sounds of dogs being exercised.

'Creepy, isn't it?' Oakes said. He was donning a cheap green kagoul.

Rebus's jacket had an integral hood. He rolled it out but didn't put it over his head. He knew it would work like a pair of blinkers, and didn't want to be deprived of his peripheral vision. Archibald had a flat tweed cap with him, and was wearing hiking boots. Cap and boots looked brand new: they'd been waiting on this day for a while.

'Drinkie anyone?' Oakes said, taking out a hip flask. Rebus stared at him. 'You going to be scowling like that all day?' Oakes laughed. 'Got something you want to get off your mind, maybe?'

'Plenty.' Rebus's fists were clenched.

'Not here, John,' Archibald pleaded. 'Not now.'

Eyes on Rebus, Oakes held out the flask to Archibald, who shook his head. Oakes tipped the flask to his own mouth, showing them the liquid trickling in. He swallowed noisily.

'See,' he said, 'it's not poisoned.' He made the offer again, and this time Archibald took a sip. 'I had them fill it at the hotel bar.' He took the flask back from Archibald. 'And yourself, Inspector?'

Rebus took the flask, sniffed its contents. Christ, it did smell good, but he handed it back untouched.

'Balvenie,' he said. 'If I'm not mistaken.'

Oakes laughed again; Archibald forced a smile.

'I thought you didn't drink,' Rebus said.

'I don't, but this is in the nature of a special occasion, wouldn't you say?'

Then Archibald started unfolding the map, and it became business, Oakes studying the area intently, aware of Rebus immediately behind him, and finally saying: 'I'm not sure this is going to be much use.' He looked around. 'I think I'm going to have to follow my nose.' He glanced at Archibald. 'Sorry about that.'

'Just take me to where she was killed,' the older man said.

'Maybe you should lead the way,' Oakes said. 'After all, I've never been here before.' And he gave a wink.

They started walking.

Eventually Rebus said: 'Another game, Oakes?'

Oakes stopped walking, caught his breath. 'You know how the song goes, Inspector: we can't go on together, if you're going to have a suspicious mind. Far as I'm concerned, we're just out for a breath of country air. Besides, I'm curious to see where the body was found.'

'You know damned well where the body was found!' Alan Archibald snapped.

Oakes turned his lips into a pout. Rebus wanted to see blood there, wanted teeth dislodged and a gushing nose. Instead, his fingernails bit more deeply into his palms.

'Did you kill her?' he asked.

'Kill her when?'

Rebus felt his voice rising. 'Did you kill her?'

Oakes wagged a finger. 'I might not have been back that long, but don't think I don't know how it's played. There are two of you. Anything I admit, you've got corroboration.'

'This is between ourselves,' Alan Archibald said. 'It's gone beyond anything I'd take to the police.'

Oakes smiled. 'How long have you been chasing ghosts? If I say I killed her, will you rest easy in your bed?' Archibald didn't answer. 'How about you, Inspector: any ghosts keeping *you* awake at night?'

As if he knew. Rebus tried not to show anything, but Oakes was nodding, smiling to himself. 'A career littered with bodies, man,' Oakes went on, 'and *I'm* the one they lock up.' He paused. 'Tell me something,' folding his arms, eyes on Archibald now, 'how did the killer get her up here? Long way to bring a victim.'

'She was terrified.'

'What if she wasn't? What if she was willing? She'd been out drinking, right? Feeling a bit horny . . .'

'Shut up, Oakes.'

'I thought you *wanted* me to talk?' He opened his arms wide. 'I might just be speculating here, but say he picked her up, drove her up here. Say it's exactly what she wanted. I mean, this is a complete stranger she's in the car with, but tonight she's in the mood for *danger*. She feels reckless. Who knows, maybe she even *wants* it to happen.'

Archibald turned on him, waving his fist. 'Don't talk about her like that.'

'I'm just—'

'You abducted her. Knocked her cold and dragged her up here.'

'Any signs of a struggle, Al? Huh? Did the post-mortem show she'd been dragged anywhere?'

Archibald looked at him. 'You know it didn't.'

More laughter. 'No, Al, I don't know jack-shit. I'm just guessing, that's all. Same as you are.'

Oakes started walking again. The wind was rising, a fine rain blowing into their faces, threatening to drench them. Rebus looked back. Already the car was lost to view.

'It's OK,' Archibald assured him. 'I'm marking our route as we go.' He had the map folded, tapped a pen against one of the contour lines.

Rebus took the map from him, wanting to be sure. He'd done map-reading in the army. It looked like Archibald knew what he was doing. Rebus nodded and handed the map back. But the look in Archibald's eyes, that mix of fear and expectation . . . Rebus patted his shoulder.

'Come on, slowcoaches,' Oakes said, waiting till they caught up.

'You took it too far,' Rebus told him.

'Huh?'

'Your little joke with the skip, I didn't mind that so much. But the cemetery, the patio . . . no way you're getting away with those.'

'You're forgetting your old flame.' Oakes turned towards him. There wasn't more than a foot or two between them. 'I talked to her, remember? How come she's not on your little hit-list? She told me the two of you might be hooking up again.' He tutted. 'Don't tell me you're going to let her down? Does she know?'

Rebus caught Oakes a glancing blow. Fist barely connected with cheek, Oakes arching back on the balls of his feet. Fast, he was hellish fast. Didn't change his stance, so confident, so sure of his opponent. Archibald's arms wrapped themselves around Rebus, but Rebus shrugged them off.

'I'm fine,' he said, voice lacking emotion.

'Want some more?' Oakes threw open his arms. 'I'm right here, man.' There was a graze on his cheek, but he paid it no notice.

Rebus *knew* he couldn't afford to lose it; had to stay calm. But Oakes had crawled all the way under his skin. Laughing at him now, putting a theatrical hand to his face.

'Ouch! That *stings*.' Laughing all the time. Then walking away, and now it was Archibald's turn to pat Rebus's shoulder.

'I'm OK,' Rebus told him, making after Oakes.

A little later, Oakes stopped. Visibility was down to a hundred yards, maybe less. 'Where's Swanston Village from here?' he asked. He seemed to have forgotten all about Rebus. Archibald checked the map, pointed with his finger. He was pointing into swirling smoke, pointing into nothingness.

'It's like bloody *Brigadoon*,' Rebus said, lighting a cigarette. Oakes took a bar of chocolate from his pocket, offered it around.

'You know,' he said, 'I'm amazed you're trusting me. Not you, Mr Archibald, you've got no choice. But the Inspector here.' Oakes fixed Rebus with his dark, peering eyes. 'You're a hard man to figure.'

'And you're full of shite.'

'Please, John . . .' Archibald had a hand on Rebus's shoulder. Despite his clothing, he looked cold and tired and suddenly so very old. Rebus realised what this meant to him: an answer, one way or another. Either Oakes had killed his niece – in which case there could be proper grieving – or someone else had, in which case he'd wasted these years with his pet theory, and her killer was still out there somewhere . . .

'OK, Alan,' Rebus said. The three of them out here: an old man, a nutter with shorn head and piercing eyes, and John bloody Rebus. Oakes enjoying every moment, Archibald looking as brittle as the chocolate bar.

And Rebus? Trying hard not to add another body to the hill's death toll.

Oakes offered Archibald his flask, and Archibald took a grateful drink. Rebus declined, and Oakes screwed the top back on.

'Not having one yourself?' Rebus asked.

Oakes ignored him, offered him chocolate instead. Rebus again refused.

'So where exactly are we going?' Oakes asked.

'It's not far now,' Archibald told him.

Oakes saw Rebus studying him. 'Got any questions for me yourself, John? Any unsolveds you want to pin on me?'

'Anything in particular you want me to ask?'

'Nicely put, sir. I see someone killed Darren Rough.'

'You were outside my flat that night.'

'Was I?'

'You took the car.' Rebus paused. 'You saw Rough leave.'

'Man, I was busy that night, wasn't I?' Rebus stared him out. Oakes came close, leaned in towards him as if to speak confidentially. Rebus moved away. 'I'm not going to bite,' Oakes said.

'Say what you were going to say.'

Oakes put on a wounded look. 'I don't know if I want to now.' Then he grinned. 'But I will anyway. I saw him leave your place, even followed him for a while. I wondered who he was, only found out later when I saw his picture in the paper.'

'What happened?'

'You tell me. I lost him.' Oakes shrugged. 'He cut across The Meadows. No way to follow in a car.' He gave another wink.

'This is all just another part of your little—'

'Don't say it!' Alan Archibald screeched. 'Don't say it's a game! It's not a game, not to me!' He was shaking.

Rebus pointed to Oakes, but spoke to Archibald. 'This is what he wants. You thought by bringing him up here you'd have the upper hand. Don't you think he knew that, played on it? Look at him, Alan, he's laughing at you. He's laughing at all of us!'

'I'm not laughing.' And it was true: Oakes was stony-faced, his eyes on Archibald. He walked up to him, touched his arm. 'Sorry,' he said. 'Come on, you're right – we've got work to do.'

He started walking again. Archibald made to apologise to Rebus, but Rebus waved it aside. Oakes was moving off at a brisk pace, as if determined to finish things. That look on his face . . . Rebus couldn't read it. There had been something there, a gloss of sympathy. But beneath it he thought he detected something more feral, itself mixed with something like the curiosity of the scientist when faced with some unexpected result.

Visibility was decreasing as they climbed.

'You've been playing a little game with *me*, haven't you, Al?'

'What do you mean?'

'Come on, Al, the route you've brought us, we've already been past the spot where she was killed. I bet you've got it all planned so we'll end up circling it. You want me rattled, don't you, Al? It's not going to happen.'

'How do you know where she was killed?' Rebus asked.

'I got all the newspapers. Plus Al kept sending me stuff, didn't you, Al?'

'You said you never read any of it,' Archibald said, trying to catch his breath.

'So I lied. Thing is, I'm getting a picture in my head . . . They had sex further up the slope. Then she panicked, ran back down. That's when he hit her. But where they had sex . . . he left something behind.'

'What?'

'Hidden.'

'What?'

'Alan, he's—'

Archibald turned on Rebus. 'Shut up!' he hissed.

'I'm seeing three hillocks,' Oakes called back. 'If there's a line of hillocks anywhere nearby, I'd be interested to see them.'

'Hillocks . . . ?' Archibald broke into a trot, trying to reach Oakes. He had the map in front of his face, seeking the corresponding contours. 'Maybe just to the west.'

Rebus hadn't seen him mark anything on the map with his pen, not for a while.

'How's our position, Alan?'

But Archibald wasn't listening, not to Rebus.

'Maybe three-quarters of the way up the slope,' Oakes was saying. 'A line of three . . . maybe four . . . but three distinct outcrops, similar heights.'

'Hang on a second,' Archibald said. His finger scratched over the map. He folded it smaller, brought it closer to his face, blinked so as to focus better. 'Yes, just to the west. That way, about a hundred yards.'

He started to climb. Oakes was already on his way, Rebus bringing up the rear. He looked behind him: couldn't see a damned thing. It was a landscape out of time. Kilted warriors might have emerged from that mist and he wouldn't have been surprised. He rounded some bracken and kept moving, his joints aching, a slight burning in his chest. Archibald was moving faster, moving with the zeal of the possessed.

Rebus wanted to tell him: *you've* got a map, what's to say Oakes didn't buy one too? What's to say he didn't study it, looking for certain features? He might even have been here already on a recce – he'd given his minders the slip plenty of times.

'Hang on!' he called, quickening his pace.

'John!' Archibald called back, his form ghostlike up ahead. 'You try that way, we'll take the other two!' Meaning Rebus was to explore the easternmost outcrop.

'Will I need to dig?' he called out. Receiving laughter in reply: Oakes's laughter. The more unsettling for the fact he could barely be seen.

'Will we?' he heard Archibald asking Oakes.

'Oh, I don't think so,' Oakes answered. 'We'll just leave the bodies where they fall.'

Rebus was still wondering if he'd misheard when he heard the dull sound of an impact, and a distant groan.

'Oakes!' he roared, upping his pace. He could make out the shadowy silhouette: Oakes standing over the fallen Archibald, a rock in his hand, raised to strike again.

'Oakes!' he repeated.

'I hear you!' Oakes yelled back, bringing the rock down on to Archibald's head.

By now Rebus was almost upon him. Oakes tossed the rock on to the ground and was licking his lips as Rebus reached him. 'You'll never know the satisfaction,' he said. 'A flea's been biting me for years, and now I've squashed it.' He slipped a hand into his waistband and brought out a folding knife.

'Amazing what the human body can hide,' Oakes said, grinning now. 'A rock was good enough for the old man, but I thought maybe you deserved something with a bit more bite.' He lunged. Rebus jumped back, lost his footing and was skidding back down the slope. Above him, he saw Oakes in pursuit, bounding like a mountain goat.

'I'm going to enjoy this!' Oakes called. 'You'll never know how much!'

Rebus kept himself rolling until bracken stopped him. He clambered to his feet, picking up a stone and hurling it. His aim was wild. Oakes dodged it easily, only ten yards away now and slowing his descent.

'Ever skinned a rabbit?' Oakes said, breathing heavily, sweat glistening on his skull.

'You're just where I want you,' Rebus hissed.

Oakes gave a look of mock surprise. 'And where's that?'

'Committing an offence. Now I get to arrest you, and it's clean.'

'You get to *arrest* me?' Spluttering laughter. He was so close, his saliva hit Rebus's face. 'Man, you've got balls.' Moving the knife. 'Enjoy them while you can.'

'All these games,' Rebus was saying. 'There's something else, isn't there? Something you don't want us to know. Keeping us all busy so we don't go looking.'

'No shit?'

'What is it?'

But Oakes was shaking his head, working the knife. Rebus turned and ran. Oakes was after him, whooping, bounding through bracken. Rebus looking around, seeing nothing but hillside and a killer with a knife. He stumbled, came to a stop and turned to face Oakes.

'Gotcha,' Oakes called out.

Rebus, almost out of breath, just nodded.

'Know what you are, man?' Oakes asked. 'You're my spot of R&R, that's all.'

Rebus, walking backwards, started tugging his shirt out of his waistband. Oakes looked puzzled, until Rebus pulled the shirt up, revealing a tiny mike taped to his chest. Oakes looked at him, Rebus holding the stare. Then looked around, seeking shapes.

Voices approaching at speed.

'Thanks for all that shouting,' Rebus said. 'Better than a trail of breadcrumbs any day.'

With a roar, Oakes took a final lunge at him. Rebus sidestepped it, and Oakes was past him and running. Downhill to start with, then changing his mind and making an arc, climbing now, further into the hills. The first uniforms appeared out of the mist. Rebus pointed after Oakes.

'Get him!' he called. Then he started climbing too, making his way back to where Alan Archibald lay, still conscious but with blood pouring from his wounds. Rebus crouched beside him as more uniforms ran past.

'Radio down for help!' Rebus called out to them. One of the uniforms turned back to him.

'Don't need to, sir. You've already done it.'

Rebus looked at the mike on his chest and realised this was true.

'Where did the cavalry come from?' Archibald asked, his voice faint.

'I got them from the ACC,' Rebus told him. 'He promised me a chopper too, but it would have needed X-ray eyes.'

Archibald managed a smile. 'Do you think . . . ?'

'I'm sorry, Alan,' Rebus said. 'It was all crap, that's what I think. He just wanted a couple more scalps.'

Archibald touched shaking fingers to his head. 'He nearly got one,' he said, closing his eyes to rest.

Alan Archibald went to hospital, and Rebus went in search of Jim Stevens. He'd already checked out of the hotel, and wasn't at the newspaper office. Eventually, Rebus tracked him down to The Hebrides, a furtive little bar behind Waverley station. Stevens was sitting alone in a corner with only a full ashtray and glass of whisky for company.

Rebus got himself a whisky and water, gulped it down, ordered another and went to join him.

'Come to gloat?' Stevens asked.

'About what?'

'That wee shite set me up.' He told Rebus what had happened.

'Then I'm an angel straight from heaven,' Rebus said.

Stevens blinked. 'How do you make that out?'

'I bring glad tidings. Or more accurately, a news story, and I'd say you're ahead of the pack.'

Rebus had never seen a man sober up so quickly. Stevens pulled a notebook from his pocket and folded it open. His pen ready, he looked up at Rebus.

'It'll have to be a trade,' Rebus told him.

'I need this,' Stevens said.

Rebus nodded, told him the story. 'And I'd have been next if he got his way.'

'Jesus Christ.' Stevens exhaled, took a gulp of whisky. 'There are probably dozens of questions I should be asking you, but right now I can't think of any.' He took out a mobile phone. 'Mind if I call this in?'

Rebus shook his head. 'Then we talk,' he said.

While Stevens read from his notes, turning them into sentences and paragraphs, Rebus listened, nodding confirmation when it was demanded of him. Stevens listened while the story was read back to him. He made a few changes, then finished the call.

'I owe you,' he said, putting the phone on the table. 'What'll it be?'

'Another whisky,' Rebus said, 'and the answers to some questions.'

Half an hour later he had a pair of headphones on and was listening to the tape of Oakes's last interview.

' "A date with my past",' he recited, slipping the headphones off his ears. ' "A date with destiny".'

'That's Archibald, isn't it? Archibald's been hassling him for years.'

Rebus thought back to Alan Archibald . . . the way he'd looked as they'd lifted him into the ambulance. He'd looked spent and stunned, as if his dearest possession had been torn from him. Easy to steal away a dream, a hope . . . Cary Oakes had done that.

And had gotten away.

'They didn't catch him then?' Stevens asked, not for the first time.

'He ran into the hills, could be anywhere.'

'It's a hell of an area to search,' Stevens conceded. 'What made you take reinforcements?'

Rebus shrugged.

'You know, John, once upon a time you wouldn't have thought you needed them.'

'I know, Jim. Things change.'

Stevens nodded. 'I suppose they do.'

Rebus rewound the tape, listened to the last half again. *'A date with destiny, as you and your fellow hacks might put it. With someone who never listened to me . . .'* This time, he was frowning when he finished.

'You know,' he said, 'I'm not sure he means Archibald and me. He called us his spot of R&R.'

Stevens had drained his glass. 'What else could it be?'

Rebus shook his head slowly. 'There was some reason for him coming back here.'

'Yes, me and my chequebook.'

'Something more than that. More than the chance to play games with Alan Archibald . . .'

'What?'

'I don't know.' He looked at Stevens. 'You could find out.'

'Me?'

'You know the city inside out. It has to be something from his past, something from before he went to America.'

'I'm not an archaeologist.'

'No? Think of all the years you've spent digging dirt. And Alan Archibald has a lot of stuff on Oakes, better than anything the bastard gave you.'

Stevens snorted, then smiled. 'Maybe . . .' he said to himself. 'It would be a way of getting back at him.'

Rebus was nodding. 'He's given you a tissue of lies, you bounce back with a whole boxful of truth.'

'The truth about Cary Oakes,' Stevens said, measuring it up for a headline. 'I'll do it,' he said at last.

'And anything you find, you share with me.' Rebus reached for Stevens' notepad. 'I'll give you my mobile number.'

'Jim Stevens and John Rebus, working together.' Stevens grinned. 'I won't tell if you don't.'

40

There were messages for Rebus. Janice had called three times; Damon's bank manager once. Rebus spoke to the bank manager first.

'We have a transaction,' the man said.

'What, when and where?' Rebus reached for paper and pen.

'Edinburgh. A cash machine on George Street. Withdrawal of one hundred pounds.'

'Today?'

'Yesterday afternoon at one forty precisely. It's good news, isn't it?'

'I hope so.'

'I mean, it proves he's still alive.'

'It proves someone's used his card. Not quite the same thing.'

'I see.' The manager sounded a little dispirited. 'I suppose you have to be cautious.'

Rebus had a thought. 'This cash machine, it wouldn't be under surveillance, would it?'

'I can check for you.'

'If you wouldn't mind.' Rebus wound up the call and phoned Janice.

'What's up?' he asked.

'Nothing.' She paused. 'It's just you ran off so early that morning. I wondered if it was something we'd . . .'

'Nothing to do with you, Janice.'

'No?'

'I just needed to get back here.'

'Oh.' Another pause. 'Well, I was just worried.'

'About me?'

'That you were disappearing from my life again.'

'Would I do that?'

'I don't know, John: would you?'

'Janice, I know things are a bit rocky between you and Brian . . .'

'Yes?'

He smiled, eyes closed. 'That's it really. I'm not exactly an expert on marriage guidance.'

'I'm not in the market for one.'

'Look,' he said, rubbing his eyes, 'there's a bit of news about Damon.'

A longer pause. 'Were you planning on telling me?'

'I just did tell you.'

'Only so you could change the subject.'

Rebus felt like he was in the boxing-ring, cornered on the ropes. 'It's just that his bank account's been used.'

'He's taken out?'

'Someone's used his card.'

Her voice was rising, filling with hope. 'But nobody else knows his number. It has to be him.'

'There are ways of using cards . . .'

'John, don't you *dare* take this away from me!'

'I just don't want you getting hurt.' He saw Alan Archibald again, saw that look of final inescapable defeat.

'When was this?' Janice said; she was barely listening to him now.

'Yesterday afternoon. I got word about ten minutes ago. It was a bank on George Street.'

'He's still in Edinburgh.' A statement of belief.

'Janice . . .'

'I can feel it, John. He's there, I know he's there. What time's the next train?'

'I doubt he's still hanging around George Street. The withdrawal was a hundred pounds. Might have been travelling money.'

'I'm coming anyway.'

'I can't stop you.'

'That's right, you can't.' She put down the telephone. Seconds later, it rang again. Damon's bank manager.

'Yes,' he said, 'there's a camera.'

'Trained on the machine?'

'Yes. I've already asked: the tape's waiting for you. Talk to a Miss Georgeson.'

As Rebus finished the call, George Silvers brought him a cup of coffee. 'Thought you'd have gone home,' he said: Hi-Ho's way of showing he cared.

'Thanks, George. No sign of him yet?'

Silvers shook his head. Rebus stared at the paperwork on his desk. There were cases to write up, he could barely recall them. Names swimming in front of him. All of them demanding an ending.

'We'll catch him,' Silvers said. 'Don't you worry about that.'

'You've always been a comfort to me, George,' Rebus said. He handed back the cup. 'And one of these days you'll remember that I don't take sugar.'

He went to talk to Miss Georgeson. She was plump and fiftyish and reminded Rebus of a school dinner-lady he'd once dated. She had the videotape ready for him.

'Would you like to view it here?' she asked.

Rebus shook his head. 'I'll take it back to the station, if you've no objection.'

'Well, really I should make you a copy . . .'

'I don't intend losing it, Miss Georgeson. And I *will* bring it back.'

He left the bank with the tape held tightly in one hand. Checked his watch, then headed down to Waverley. He sat on one of the benches on the concourse, drinking a milky coffee – or *caffe latte* as the vendor had called it – and keeping an eye open. He had the tape in his raincoat pocket; no way he was leaving it in the car. He flicked through the evening paper. Nothing about Cary Oakes – it would be an exclusive in Stevens' paper first thing in the morning, and Stevens would have answered his detractors with one mighty two-fingered salute.

A date with destiny . . .

What the hell did that mean? Was Oakes laying yet another false trail? Rebus would put nothing past him. He'd sold Stevens, Archibald, and himself dummies like he was vintage George Best and they were Sunday league.

Finally he saw her. Late-afternoon trains into Edinburgh weren't busy; the traffic was all the other way. She was walking against the crowds as she came off the platform. He got into step beside her before she'd noticed him.

'Needing a taxi?' he said.

She looked surprised, then bemused. 'John,' she said. 'What brings you here?'

For answer, he took the video out and held it in front of her.

'A peace offering,' he said, leading her back to his car.

They sat in the CID suite. It too was quiet. Most people had gone home for the day. Those who were left were trying to finish reports or catch up with themselves. No one was in the mood to dawdle. The video monitor sat in one corner. Rebus pulled two chairs over. He'd fetched them coffee. Janice was looking excited and fearful at the same time. Again, he was reminded of Alan Archibald on the hillside.

'Look, Janice,' he warned her, 'if it's not him . . .'

She shrugged. 'If it's not him, it's not him. I won't blame you.' She flashed him a momentary smile. He started the tape. Miss Georgeson had explained that the camera was motion-sensitive, and would only begin recording when someone approached the machine. Back at the bank, Rebus had taken a look at the cash machine. The camera was above it, shooting from behind one of the bank's glass windows. When the first face came on the tape, Rebus and Janice were looking at it from above. The time-counter said 08.10. Rebus used the remote to fast forward.

'We're looking for one forty,' he explained. Janice was sitting on the edge of her chair, the coffee cup held in both hands.

This, Rebus thought, was the way it had started: with security footage, grainy pictures. Towards the middle of the day, more people were using the machine. There was a lot of tape to get through. Lunchtime queues built up, but by one thirty it was a little quieter.

The time-counter said 13.40.

'Oh, dear Lord, there he is,' Janice said. She'd placed her cup on the floor, clapped her hands to her face.

Rebus looked. The face was angled down, looking at the machine's keypad. Then it turned away, as if staring down the street. Fingers were tapped impatiently against the screen of the cash machine. The card was retrieved, a hand went to the slot to extract the notes. Didn't linger; didn't wait for a receipt. The next customer was already moving forward.

'Are you sure?' he asked.

A tear was falling from Janice's cheek. 'Positive,' she said, nodding.

Rebus found it hard to tell. All he had were photos of Damon and the footage from Gaitano's; he'd never met him. The hair looked similar . . . maybe the nose too, the shape of the chin. But it wasn't as though they were unusual. The person on view now, they looked much like the customer who'd just left. But Janice was blowing her nose. She was satisfied.

'It's him, I'd swear to it.' She saw uncertainty on his face. 'I wouldn't say it was if it wasn't.'

'Of course not.'

'It's not just the face or hair or clothes . . . it's the way he stood, the way he held himself. And those little twitches of impatience.' She used a corner of the hankie to wipe her eyes. 'It was him, John. It was him.'

'OK,' Rebus said. He rewound the tape, played the minutes leading up to 13.40. He was studying the background to see if he could spot Damon making for the machine. He wanted to know if he'd been alone. But he entered the picture suddenly, and from the side. That look again, towards where he'd just come from. Was there a slight nod of the head . . . some signal to another person just out of shot . . . ? Rebus rewound and watched again.

'What are you looking for?' Janice asked.

'Anyone who might have been with him.'

But there was nothing. So he let the tape play on, and was rewarded a minute or two later by legs moving across the top of the picture, just behind the person at the machine. Two pairs, one male, one female. Rebus pressed freeze-frame, but couldn't get the picture to stay absolutely still and focused. So instead, he rewound and played it again, following the feet with his finger.

'Recognise the trousers, the shoes?'

But Janice shook her head. 'They're just a blur.'

And so they were.

'Could be anybody,' she added.

And so it could.

She got to her feet. 'I'm going to George Street.' He made to say something but she cut him off. 'I know he won't be there, but there are shops, pubs – I can show them his picture at least.'

Rebus nodded. She gripped his forearm.

'He's still here, John. That's *something*.'

As she left, she held the door open to someone just coming in: Siobhan Clarke.

'Any sign of him?' Rebus asked.

Siobhan slumped into a chair. 'Billy Horman?'

Rebus shook his head. 'Cary Oakes.'

She stretched her neck. He heard the snap. 'Another day down,' he told her.

She nodded. 'I'm not working Oakes. I'm on Billy Boy.'

'No progress?'

She shook her head. 'We need another dozen officers. Maybe a couple of dozen.'

'I can see the budget stretching to that.'

'Maybe if we got rid of a few of the bean-counters.'

'Careful, Siobhan. That's anarchist talk.'

She smiled. 'How are you? I hear Oakes was ready to kill the pair of you.'

'The tremors have stopped,' he told her. 'Buy you a drink?'

'Not tonight. I've a date with a hot bath and a takeaway. What about you?'

'Straight home, same as yourself.'

'Well . . .' She stood up as though the effort was costing her. 'See you tomorrow.'

'Night, Siobhan.'

She waved fingers over her shoulder as she left.

Rebus was almost as good as his word – just the one stop-off to make beforehand. He climbed the stairwell of Cragside Court. Darkness was falling, but there were still children out playing, albeit supervised by a member of GAP. They'd had T-shirts printed up with a logo on the front, getting more organised by the day. The woman in the T-shirt had studied Rebus, knowing she'd seen him somewhere before, but not recognising him as a resident.

He stood looking out over Greenfield. On one side, Holyrood Park; on the other, the Old Town, and the site of the new Parliament. He wondered if the estate would be allowed to survive. He knew that if the council wanted it run down, they would work by stealth. Repairs would not be carried out, or would be botched. Flats would be found to be uninhabitable, tenants rehoused, windows and doors blocked and padlocked. Things would slowly deteriorate, causing residents to rethink their options. More of them would move out. The state of the high-rises would become a 'cause for concern'. There'd be a media outcry about conditions. The council would move in with offers of help – meaning relocation: cheaper than shoring up the estate. And eventually it would be deserted, a demolition site from which new buildings could rise. Expensive *pieds-à-terre* for parliamentarians, perhaps. Or offices and select shops. It was a prime site, no doubt about it.

As for Salisbury Crags . . . he didn't doubt there'd be people who would build on it too, given the chance. But that chance would be a long time coming. All the centuries of change, and the park was much as it ever had been. It made no judgements on the work around it, but merely sat there, above it all. And the people who tramped over it were minor irritations, dead by the age of seventy if not before. They made no impression on it, not when measured in millennia.

Rebus was outside Darren Rough's flat now. Darren had come home to give evidence against two evil men. As recompense, he'd been harried, cursed and eventually killed. Rebus didn't feel proud that he'd been the first player. He hoped Darren might one day forgive him. He almost said as much to the ghostly shape at the end of the walkway, but when it came towards him, he saw it was flesh and blood, very much alive.

It was Cal Brady, his face an angry scowl.

'What do you want?'

'Just taking a look.'

'I thought you were another pervert.'

Rebus nodded towards the mobile phone in Brady's hand. 'Did the playground guard tell you?' He nodded to himself. 'Nice little operation you've got here, Cal. Anything in it for you?'

'It's my public duty,' Brady said, puffing out his chest.

Rebus took a step closer, hands in coat pockets. 'Cal, the day people like you are deciding what's right and what's wrong, we're all in Queer Street.'

'You calling me a poof?' Cal Brady yelled, but Rebus was already past him and heading for the stairs.

41

'Tell me about Janice,' Patience said.

They were seated in the living room, a bottle of red wine open on the carpet between them. Patience was lying along the sofa. There was a paperback novel folded open on her chest. She had placed it there some time ago; had been staring into space, listening to the music on the hi-fi. Nick Drake, 'Pink Moon'. Rebus was in the armchair, legs hanging over its side. He had kicked off his shoes and socks, was catching up with the football news in that day's paper.

'What?'

'Janice, I'd like to know about her.'

'We were at school together.' Rebus stopped reading. 'She's married with just the one son. She used to work as a teacher. I was at school with her husband, too. His name's Brian.'

'You went out with her?'

'At school, yes.'

'Sleep together?'

Rebus looked at her. 'Didn't quite get that far.'

She nodded to herself. 'Are you curious about what it would have been like?'

He shrugged.

'I think I would be,' she went on. Her glass was empty, and she leaned over to refill it. The book slid on to the floor, but she paid it no heed. Rebus was still on his first helping of the Rioja. The bottle was nearly empty.

'Anyone would think you were the one with the drink problem,' he said, making sure he was smiling as he spoke.

She was getting comfortable again. A splash of wine fell on to the back of her hand, and she put her mouth to it.

'No, I just like a little bit too much now and again. So, have you thought about sleeping with her?'

'Christ, Patience . . .'

'I'm interested, that's all. Sammy says Janice had a look about her.'

'What sort of look?'

Patience frowned, as if trying to recall the exact words. 'Hungry. Hungry and a little desperate, I think. How's the marriage?'

'Rocky,' Rebus admitted.

'And you going to Fife . . . did that help?'

'I didn't sleep with her.'

Patience wagged a finger. 'Don't go defending yourself before an accusation's made. You're a detective, you know how it looks.'

He glared at her. 'Am I a suspect?'

'No, John, you're a man. That's all.' She took another sip of wine.

'I wouldn't hurt you, Patience.'

She smiled, stretched out a hand as if to squeeze his, but he was too far away. 'I know that, sweetheart. But the thing is, you wouldn't even be thinking of me at the time, so the idea of hurting me or not hurting me wouldn't enter into it.'

'You're so sure.'

'John, I get it every single day. Wives coming into the surgery, wanting anti-depressants. Wanting *anything* that'll help them get through the bloody awful marriages they've found themselves in. They tell me things. It all spills out. Some of them turn to drink or drugs, some slash their wrists. It's bizarre how seldom they just walk out. And the ones who do walk out are usually the ones married to the violent cases.' She looked at him. 'Do you know what *they* do?'

'End up going back?' he guessed.

She focused on him. 'How do you know?'

'I get them too, Patience. The domestics, the neighbours who complain of screams and punches. The same wives *you* get, only further down the road. They won't press charges. They get put into a hostel. And later, they walk back to the only life they really know.'

She blinked away a tear. 'Why does it have to be like that, John?'

'I wish I knew.'

'What's in it for us?'

He smiled. 'A paycheque.'

She had stopped looking at him. Picked her book off the floor, put down her wine glass. 'The man who painted that message . . . What was he trying to do?'

'I'm not sure. Maybe he wanted me to know he'd been here.'

She had found her page, stared at the words without moving her eyes. 'Where is he now?'

'Lost on the hills and freezing to death.'

'You really think so?'

'No,' he admitted. 'Someone like Oakes . . . that would be too easy.'

'Will he come after you?'

'I'm not at the top of his list.' No, because Alan Archibald was still alive. X-rays had shown a skull fracture; Archibald would be in hospital a little longer. There was a police guard on his bed.

'Will he come here?' Patience asked.

The CD had finished; there was silence in the room. 'I don't know.'

'If he tries painting my flagstones again, I'll give him a bloody good kicking.'

Rebus looked at her, then began laughing.

'What's so funny?' she said.

Rebus was shaking his head. 'Nothing really. I'm just glad you're on my side, that's all.'

She raised the wine glass to her lips again. 'What makes you so sure of that, Inspector?'

Rebus raised his own glass to her, pleased that until Patience had mentioned her, he hadn't thought once that evening of Janice Mee. He hit 'Replay' on the CD remote. 'This guy sounds like he needs help,' Patience said.

'He did,' Rebus told her. 'He OD'd.' She looked at him and he shrugged. 'Just another casualty,' he said.

Later, he headed outside for a cigarette. The message was still there on the patio: YOUR COP LOVER KILLED DARREN. The workmen would start cleaning it off tomorrow. Oakes said he'd followed Darren but lost him. Well, someone had found him. Rebus wasn't going to take the blame for that. Cigarette lit, he climbed the steps. There was a marked patrol car parked directly outside, a message to Cary Oakes should he think about paying a visit. Rebus had a word with the two officers inside, finished his cigarette and headed back indoors.

42

'Fancy a run?' Siobhan Clarke offered.

'I trust you mean "run" as in "drive"?'

'Don't worry, I don't have you down as the jogging type.'

'Perceptive as ever. Where are you going?'

It was morning in St Leonard's. The weather up on the Pentlands had cleared, and Rebus had made sure the helicopter would be out scanning the area for signs of Cary Oakes. Villages and farms in the foothills had been warned to be on the look out.

'Don't try to corner him,' the message had gone. 'Just let us know if you see him.'

So far, no one had called in.

Rebus felt like dead weight. He'd made breakfast for Patience – orange juice and two sachets of Resolve – and had been complimented on both his diagnosis and his bedside manner. She'd said she'd make the surgery OK.

'I just hope no one expects me to do my Agony Aunt bit today.'

And now Rebus was in the CID suite with his coffee and a Mars Bar.

'Breakfast of coronaries,' he said, noting Siobhan's distaste.

'We've had a sighting of Billy Boy. It'll probably turn out to be a waste of time . . .'

'And you'd rather waste it with me?' Rebus smiled. 'Isn't that thoughtful?'

'Never mind,' she said, turning away.

'Whoa, hold on. What side of the bed did you fall out of?'

'I didn't quite reach bed last night,' she snapped. Then she melted a little. 'It's a long story.'

'Just right for a car-ride then,' he said. 'Come on, you've got me hooked.'

The story was, her upstairs neighbours' washing-machine had sprung a leak. They'd been out, and hadn't noticed. And she'd only found out when she'd gone into her bedroom.

'Their washing-machine's above your bedroom?' Rebus asked.

'That's another bone of contention. Anyway, I noticed this stain on the ceiling, and when I touched the bed it was soaked through. So I ended up on the couch in a smelly old sleeping-bag.'

'Poor you.' Rebus was thinking of all the times he'd slept in his chair – but that had been voluntary. He looked in the wing mirror as they crawled westwards out of town. 'Tell me something: why are we going to Grangemouth? Couldn't the locals handle it?'

'I'm reluctant to delegate.'

Rebus smiled: she'd stolen one of his lines. 'What you mean is, you don't trust anyone to do the job thoroughly.'

'Something like that,' she said, glancing at him. 'I had a good teacher.'

'Siobhan, it's been quite some time since I could teach you anything.'

'Thanks.'

'But that's because you've stopped listening.'

'We are not amused.' She craned her neck. 'What is with this traffic?'

The vehicles ahead were barely moving.

'It's part of the new council initiative. Make things bloody awful for drivers, and they'll stop coming into town and making everything look untidy.'

'They want a conservation village.'

Rebus nodded. 'And just the half a million villagers.'

Eventually they got moving. Grangemouth lay out to the west along the Forth estuary. Rebus hadn't been to the town in years. As they approached, Rebus's first impression was that they'd wandered on to the set of *Blade Runner*. A vast petrochemical complex dominated the skyline, throwing up jagged chimneys and weird configurations of pipes. The complex looked like some encroaching alien life-form, about to throw its many mechanical arms around the town and squeeze the life out of it.

In fact, the contrary was true: the complex and all that went with it had brought employment to Grangemouth. The streets they eventually drove through were dark and narrow, with architecture from much earlier in the century.

'Two worlds collide,' Rebus muttered, taking it all in.

'I feel they've spoiled their chances in the conservation village stakes.'

'I'm sure the townsfolk are grieving.' He was peering at the street names. 'Here we go.' They parked outside a row of cottage-type houses, all of which had added bedrooms and windows to their roof-space.

'Number eleven,' Siobhan said. 'Woman's name is Wilkie.'

Mrs Wilkie had been waiting for them. She seemed the type of neighbour every street has: interested to the point of nosiness. Her kind could be a distinct asset, but Rebus would bet some of her neighbours didn't see it that way.

Her living room was a tiny box, overheated and with pride of place given to a large and ornate doll's-house. When Siobhan, out of politeness, showed interest in it, Mrs Wilkie delivered a ten-minute speech concerning its history. Rebus could swear she didn't once draw breath, giving neither of her prisoners the chance to jump in and take the conversation elsewhere.

'Well, isn't that lovely?' Siobhan said, glancing towards Rebus. The look on his face had her sucking in her cheeks to stop from laughing. 'Now, about this boy you saw, Mrs Wilkie . . . ?'

They all sat down, and Mrs Wilkie told her story. She'd seen the laddie's picture in the paper, and as she was coming back from the shops around two, caught him playing football in the street.

'Kicking the ball against the wall of Montefiore's Garage. There's this low stone wall around the . . .' She made motions with her hands. 'What do you call it?'

'Forecourt?' Siobhan suggested.

'That's the word.' She smiled at Siobhan. 'I'll bet you're a dab hand at crosswords, brain like that.'

'Did you say anything to the boy, Mrs Wilkie?'

'It's Miss Wilkie actually. I never married.'

'Really?' Rebus managed to put on a surprised look. Siobhan coughed into her hand, then handed some snaps of Billy Horman over to Miss Wilkie.

'Well, these certainly look like him,' the old woman said, sorting through the photos. She lifted one out. 'Except for this, that is.'

Siobhan took the proffered photo, stuck it back in her folder. Rebus knew she'd sneaked in a picture of a different kid to assess how alert her witness actually was. Miss Wilkie had passed.

'To answer your question,' Miss Wilkie said, 'no, I didn't say anything. I came back here and took another look at the paper. Then I phoned the number it said to call. Spoke to a very nice young man at the police station.'

'This was yesterday?'

'That's right, and I haven't seen the laddie today.'

'And you just saw him the once?'

Miss Wilkie nodded. 'Playing all by himself. He looked so lonely.' She had handed back the photos, and got up to look out of her window. 'You notice strangers on a street like this.'

'I'm sure not much gets past you,' Rebus said.

'All these cars nowadays . . . I'm surprised you found a space.'

Rebus and Siobhan looked at one another, thanked Miss Wilkie for her time, and left.

Outside, they looked to left and right. There was a garage on the corner at the far end of the street. They walked towards it.

'What did she mean about the cars?' Siobhan asked.

'My guess is, there's always someone parked outside her window. Makes it harder for her to see everything that's going on.'

'I'm impressed.'

'Not that I speak from experience, you understand.'

But back in the cottage, Rebus had felt a sudden depression. He, too, was a watcher. All the nights he sat in his flat, lights off, watching from the window . . . As he got older, would he turn into a Miss Wilkie: the street's nosy neighbour?

Montefiore's Garage consisted of a single line of petrol pumps, a shop, and a double work-bay. A man in blue overalls was in one of the work-bays, his head just visible as he stood in the pit, a blue Volkswagen Polo above him. There was another, older man behind the counter in the shop. Rebus and Siobhan stopped on the pavement.

'Might as well ask if they saw him,' Siobhan said.

'Suppose so,' Rebus replied, with little enthusiasm.

'I told you it was a wild shot.'

'Could be a neighbourhood kid. New family moved in, hasn't had time to make friends.'

'It was two o'clock she saw him. He should have been at school.'

'True,' Rebus said. 'She seemed so certain, didn't she?'

'Some people do. They want to be helpful, even if it means making up a story.'

Rebus tutted. 'You didn't learn cynicism like that from me.' He looked around at the bumper-to-bumper parking. 'I wonder . . .'

'What?'

'He was kicking the ball off the forecourt wall.'

'Yes.'

'Not much of a game if all these cars were here. Pavement's not wide enough.'

Siobhan looked at the wall, the pavement. 'Maybe the cars weren't here.'

'According to Miss Wilkie, that would be unusual.'

'I can't see what you're getting at.'

Rebus pointed to the forecourt. 'What if he was in there? Plenty of space so long as no cars are using the pumps.'

'They'd chase him off.' She looked at him. 'Wouldn't they?'

'Let's go ask them.'

They went to the shop first, identified themselves to the man behind the counter.

'I'm not the owner,' he said. 'I'm his brother.'

'Were you here yesterday?'

'Been here the past ten days. Eddie and Flo are on their hols.'

'Somewhere nice?' Siobhan asked, making out they were just having a normal conversation.

'Jamaica.'

'Do you remember a young boy?' Rebus asked. Siobhan held up one of the photographs. 'Playing kickabout in the forecourt?'

The owner's brother nodded. 'Gordon's nephew.'

Rebus tried to keep his voice level. 'Gordon who?'

The man laughed. 'Gordon Howe, actually.' He spelt the name for them, and they laughed along with him.

'Bet he gets jokes about that,' Siobhan said, wiping an imaginary tear from her eye. 'Any idea where we could find Mr Howe?'

'Jock will know.'

Siobhan nodded. 'And who's Jock?'

'Sorry,' the man said. 'Jock's the other mechanic.'

'Under the Polo?' Rebus asked. The man nodded.

'So Mr Howe works for the garage?'

'Yes, he's a mechanic. He's got the day off today. Well, we're not busy, and with him looking after young Billy . . .' He waved the picture of Billy Horman.

'Billy?' Siobhan said.

Sixty seconds later they were out on the forecourt again and Siobhan was using Rebus's mobile. She got through to St Leonard's and asked if Billy Horman had an uncle called Gordon Howe. Listening to the answer, she shook her head to let Rebus know what she was hearing. They walked towards the work-bay.

'Could we have a word?' Rebus called. They had their IDs ready as the mechanic called Jock crawled out from under the Polo and started wiping his hands on an impossibly oil-blackened rag.

'What have I done?' He had ginger hair, curling to the nape of his neck, and a long earring dangling from one ear. The backs of his hands were tattooed, and Rebus noticed he was missing the pinkie on his left hand.

'Where can we find Gordon Howe?' Siobhan asked.

'Lives on Adamson Street. What's the matter?'

'Will he be there just now, do you think?'

'How should I know?'

'He's got the day off,' Rebus said, taking a step closer. 'Maybe he told you how he planned to spend it?'

'Taking Billy out.' The mechanic's eyes flicked from one detective to the other.

'Billy being . . .?'

'His sister's kid. She's been poorly, one-parent family and that. Billy either went into care for the duration or Gordy looked after him. Is it Billy? Has he been up to something?'

'Do you think he's the type?'

'Not at all.' The mechanic smiled. 'Very quiet kid, actually. Didn't want to talk about his mum . . .'

'Didn't want to talk about his mum,' Siobhan repeated, as they walked up the path to the house in Adamson Street. It was a sixties-built semi in an estate on the edge of town. Council-owned for the most part. You could tell the homes that had been purchased by their tenants: replacement windows and better doors. But they all had the same grey harled walls.

'Uncle Gordon's orders, no doubt.'

They rang the bell and waited. Rebus thought he detected movement at an upstairs window. Took a step back to look, but couldn't see anything.

'Try again,' he said, opening the letterbox while Siobhan pushed the doorbell. There was a door at the end of the corridor, half-open. He saw shadows beyond it, snapped the letterbox shut.

'Round the back,' he said, heading for the side of the house. As they entered the back garden, a man was disappearing over a high bark fence.

'Mr Howe!' Rebus shouted.

By way of response, the man called out, 'Run for it!' to the boy who was with him. Rebus let Siobhan climb the fence. He headed back round to the front, ran down the road, wondering where the two would appear.

Suddenly they were ahead of him. Howe was limping, clawing at one leg. The boy was off like a shot, Howe spurring him on. But when the boy looked back, saw the distance widening between himself and Howe, his pace slowed.

'No! Keep running, Billy! Keep running!'

But the boy wasn't listening to Howe. He came to a dead stop, waited for the man to catch up. Siobhan came into view, a rip in the knee of her trousers. Howe saw he was going nowhere and put up his hands.

'All right,' he said, 'all right.'

He looked despairingly at Billy, who was walking back towards him. 'Billy, will you never listen?'

As Gordon Howe dropped to his knees, Billy slid his arms around his neck, man and boy embracing.

'I'll tell them,' Billy was wailing. 'I'll tell them it's all right.'

Rebus looked down at them, saw the tattoos on Gordon Howe's bare arms: No Surrender; UDA; the Red Hand of Ulster. He recalled Tom Jackson's story: *ran off to Ulster to join the paramilitaries* . . .

'You'll be Billy's dad then,' Rebus guessed. 'Welcome back to Scotland.'

43

On the way back into Edinburgh, Rebus sat in the back with Howe, while Billy sat in the front with Siobhan.

'You read about Greenfield in the paper?' Rebus guessed. Gordon Howe nodded. 'What's your real name?'

'Eddie Mearn.'

'How long have you been back from Northern Ireland?' Siobhan asked.

'Three months.' He reached out a hand to ruffle his son's hair. 'I wanted Billy back.'

'Did his mother know?'

'That cow? It was our secret, wasn't it, Billy?'

'Aye, Dad,' Billy said.

Mearn turned to Rebus. 'I used to visit him on the quiet. If his mum had found out, she'd've put a stop to it. But we kept it hush-hush.'

'Then you read about Darren Rough?' Rebus added.

Mearn nodded. 'Looked too good to be true. I knew if I snatched Billy, they'd just assume that wanker had him – at least for a while. Give us a chance to get settled. We were getting on fine, weren't we, Billy?'

'Grand,' his son agreed.

'Your mum's been at her wits' end, Billy,' Siobhan said.

'I hate Ray,' Billy said, tucking his chin into his neck. Ray Heggie: Joanna Horman's lover. 'He hits her.'

'Why do you think I wanted Billy out of there?' Mearn said. 'It's not right for a kid to have to deal with. It's not right.' He bent forward to kiss the top of his son's head. 'We were all fixed up, though, weren't we, Billy Boy? We'd've managed.'

Billy turned in his seat, tried to hug his father, the seatbelt restricting him. Looking in the rearview, Siobhan fixed her eyes on Rebus's. Both knew what would happen: Billy would go back to Greenfield; Mearn would probably be charged. Neither officer felt especially great about it.

As they headed into central Edinburgh, Rebus asked Siobhan to make a detour along George Street. There was no sign of Janice . . .

'You know something?' Rebus asked Mearn.

They were in an interview room at St Leonard's. Mearn had a cup of tea in front of him. A doctor had looked at his leg: just a sprain.

'What?'

'You said you knew they'd all blame Billy's disappearance on Darren Rough, and that would give you some time to get settled.'

'That's right.'

'But I can think of a better way, a plan that would mean they'd *give up* looking for Billy.'

Mearn looked interested. 'What's that then?'

'If Rough was dead,' Rebus said quietly. 'I mean, we'd look for Billy for a while, even if all we expected to find was a body hidden somewhere. But we'd call a halt eventually.'

'I thought of that.'

Rebus sat down. 'You did?'

Mearn was nodding. 'You know, after I read about him being topped. I thought it was the answer to our prayers.'

Rebus was nodding. 'And that's why you did it?'

Mearn frowned. 'Did what?'

'Killed Darren Rough.'

The two men stared at one another. Then a look of horror spread across Mearn's face. 'N-n-no,' he stammered. 'No way, no way . . .' His hands gripped the edge of the table. 'Not me, I didn't do it.'

'No?' Rebus looked surprised. 'But you've got the perfect motive.'

'Christ, I was starting a *new* life. How could I contemplate *that* if I'd topped someone?'

'Lots of people do it, Eddie. I see them in here several times a year. I'd've thought it would be easy for someone with paramilitary training.'

Mearn laughed. 'Where did you get that idea?'

'It's what they're saying on the estate. When Joanna got pregnant with Billy, you ran off to join the terrorists.'

Mearn calmed down, looked around. 'I think I want a solicitor,' he said quietly.

'One's on its way,' Rebus explained.

'What about Billy?'

'They've phoned his mum. She's on her way too. Probably smartening herself up for the press conference.'

Mearn squeezed his eyes shut. 'Shit,' he whispered. Then: 'Sorry, Billy.' He was blinking back tears as he looked towards Rebus. 'What gave us away?'

A nosy old lady and a line of parked cars, Rebus could have told him. But he hadn't the heart.

There were cameras and microphones outside St Leonard's; so many that the journalists were spilling on to the road. Cars and vans were sounding their horns, making it hard to hear Joanna Horman speaking of her emotional reunion with her son. No sign of Ray Heggie: Rebus wondered if she'd given him the push. And not much sign of emotion from young Billy Boy. His mother kept hugging him to her, almost smothering him as the cameramen bayed for another shot. She pockmarked his face with lipstick kisses. As she made to answer another question, Rebus noticed Billy trying to wipe his face clean.

There were civilians mixed in with the reporters: passers-by and the curious. A woman in a GAP T-shirt was trying to hand out leaflets: Van Brady. Across the road, a kid sat balanced on his bike, one hand touching a lamp-post for support. Rebus recognised him: Van's youngest. No leaflets; no T-shirt – Rebus wondered about that. Was the boy less easily swayed than those around him?

'And I'd like to thank the police for all their hard work,' Joanna Horman was saying. You're welcome, Rebus thought to himself, pushing through the scrum and crossing the road. 'But most of all, I'd like to thank everyone at GAP for their support.'

A loud roar of agreement went up from Van Brady . . .

'It's Jamie, isn't it?'

The boy on the bike nodded. 'And you're the cop who came looking for Darren.'

Darren: first name only. Rebus took out a cigarette, offered one to Jamie, who shook his head. Rebus lit up, exhaled.

'I suppose you saw Darren around a bit?'

'He's dead.'

'But before then. Before the story got out.'

Jamie nodded, eyes guarded.

'Did he ever try anything?'

Now Jamie shook his head. 'He just said hello, that's all.'

'Did he hang around the playground?'

'Not that I saw.' He was staring at the scene across the road.

'Looks like Billy's the centre of attention, eh?' Rebus got the feeling Jamie was jealous, but trying not to let it show.

'Yeah.'

'I bet you're glad he's back.'

Jamie looked at him. 'Cal's moved in with his mum.'

Rebus took another draw on his cigarette. 'She's booted Ray out then?' Jamie nodded again.

'And moved your brother in?' Rebus looked impressed. 'That's fast work.'

Jamie just grunted. Rebus saw an opening.

'You don't sound too chuffed: are you going to miss him?'

Jamie shrugged. 'Not bothered.' But he was. His brother had moved out; his mother was busy with GAP; and now Billy Boy Horman was getting all the attention.

'You ever see Darren with anyone? I don't mean kids, I mean visitors.'

'Not really.'

Rebus angled his face so Jamie had little choice but to look at him. 'You don't sound too sure.'

'Someone came looking for him.'

'When?'

'When all the stuff about GAP started.'

'Friend of Darren's?'

Another shrug. 'He didn't say.'

'Well, what did he say, Jamie?'

'Said he was looking for the guy from the newspaper. He had the paper with him.' The paper: the story outing Darren Rough.

'Were those his exact words: "the guy from the newspaper"?'

Jamie smiled. 'I think he said "chap".'

'Chap?'

Jamie put on a posh voice. ' "The chap who was in the newspaper." '

'Not a local then?'

Now Jamie let out a stuttering laugh.

'What did he look like?'

'Old, quite tall. He had a moustache. His hair was grey, but the moustache was black.'

'You'd make a good detective, Jamie.'

Jamie wrinkled his nose in distaste. His mother had spotted the conversation, was making to cross the road towards them.

'Jamie!' she called, trying to weave between traffic.

'What did you tell him, Jamie?'

'I pointed to Darren's flat. Told him I knew Darren wasn't in.'

'What did the man do?'

'Gave me a fiver.' He looked around, almost furtively. 'I followed him back to his car.'

Rebus smiled. 'You really would make a detective.'

Another shrug. 'It was a big white car. I think it was a Merc.'

Rebus backed off as Van Brady reached them.

'What's he been saying, Jamie?' she asked, staring daggers at Rebus. But Jamie looked at her defiantly.

'Nothing,' he said.

She looked at Rebus, who just shrugged. When she turned back to her son, Rebus winked at him. Jamie gave the flicker of a smile. For a few moments, *he'd* been the centre of someone's attention.

'I was just asking about Cal,' Rebus told Van Brady. 'I've heard he's moving in with Joanna.'

She turned on him. 'What's it to you?'

He nodded towards the leaflet in her hand. 'Got one of those for me?'

'If you did your job right,' she sneered, 'we wouldn't need GAP.'

'What makes you think we need it anyway?' Rebus asked her, turning to walk away.

Rebus got on the computer, and decided to cover his bets by talking to the area's Merc dealerships. He already knew one person who drove a white Merc: the widow Margolies. Rebus tapped his pen against his desk, started calling. He got lucky with the first number he tried.

'Oh, yes, Dr Margolies is a regular customer. He's been buying nothing but Mercedes for donkey's years.'

'Sorry, I'm talking about a Mrs Margolies.'

'Yes, his daughter-in-law. Dr Margolies bought that car, too.'

Dr Joseph Margolies . . . 'He bought one for his son and daughter-in-law?'

'That's right. Last year, was it?'

'And for himself?'

'He likes to part-ex: keeps the model a year or two, then trades for something brand new. That way you don't get the same scale of depreciation.'

'So what's he driving just now?'

The sales manager turned cautious. 'Why don't you ask him yourself?'

'Maybe I'll do that,' Rebus said. 'And I'll be sure to tell him you could have saved me the trouble.'

Rebus listened to the receiver making a sighing sound. Then: 'Hang on a sec.' He heard fingers on a keyboard. A pause, then: 'An E200, purchased six months ago. Happy?'

'As a kid on Christmas morning.' Rebus scribbled the details down. 'And the colour?'

Another sigh. 'White, Inspector. Dr Margolies always buys white.'

As Rebus put down the phone, Siobhan Clarke came over. She rested against the corner of his desk.

'Looks like someone got lazy,' she said.

'How do you mean?'

'Eddie Mearn. As far as the inquiry was concerned, he was still in Northern Ireland. Someone made a phone call to Lisburn, and took it as gospel when he was told Mearn was still around.'

'Who made the call?'

'Roy Frazer, I'm sorry to say.'

'It's the only way he'll learn.'

'Sure, like you've learned from past mistakes.'

He smiled. 'That's why I never make the same one twice.'

She folded her arms. 'You think Mearn had this planned all along?'

Rebus nodded slowly. 'I'd say it's likely. Moved back from Lisburn, maybe it's true he didn't tell anyone there he was leaving. Sets up a new identity for himself in Grangemouth – striking distance of Edinburgh. Why lie about who he was? Only reason I can think of is, he was going to snatch Billy. New life for both of them.'

'Would that have been so bad?' Siobhan asked.

'No worse than where Billy is now,' Rebus admitted. He looked at her. 'Careful there, Siobhan. You're in danger of thinking the law's an ass. That's only one step away from making up your own rules.'

'The way you've done.' It was statement rather than question.

'The way I've done,' Rebus was forced to agree. 'And look where it's got me.'

'Where's that?'

He tapped his sheet of notes. 'Seeing white cars everywhere.'

44

A white car had been spotted the night Jim Margolies had flown from Salisbury Crags. Fair enough, Jim himself owned a white car, but according to his wife the car had stayed in the garage. He'd walked all the way to the Crags. How likely was that? Rebus didn't know.

Another white car had been spotted in Holyrood Park around the time Darren Rough was bludgeoned to death.

And prior to this, someone in a white car had been looking for Darren.

Rebus told the story to Siobhan, and she pulled over a chair so they could work through some theories.

'You're thinking they're all the same car?' she asked.

'All I know is, they're in the park when two apparently unconnected deaths occur.'

She scratched her head. 'I'm not seeing anything. Any other owners of white Mercs?'

'You mean, have any serial killers bought or hired one lately?' She smiled at this. 'I'm checking,' Rebus went on. 'So far, the only name I have is Margolies.' He was thinking: Jane Barbour drove a cream-coloured car, a Ford Mondeo . . .

'But there are more white Mercs than that out there?'

Rebus nodded. 'But Jamie's description of the man sounds awfully like Jim's father.'

'You saw him at the funeral?'

Rebus nodded. And at a children's beauty show, he might have added. 'He's a retired doctor.'

'Racked with grief at his son's suicide, he decides to become a vigilante?'

'Ridding the world of corruption to protest at the iniquity of life.'

Her smile broadened. 'You don't see it, do you?'

'No, I don't.' He tossed his pen on to the desk. 'To tell you the truth, I'm not seeing anything at all. Which must make it time for a break.'

'Coffee?' she suggested.

'I was thinking of something stronger.' He saw the look on her face. 'But coffee will do in the meantime.'

He went out to the car park for a cigarette, but ended up jumping into the Saab and heading down The Pleasance, across the High Street and past Waverley station. He drove west along George Street, then made an illegal turn to head back east along it. Janice was sitting on the kerb, head in her hands. People were looking at her, but no one stopped to ask if they could help. Rebus pulled up alongside and got her into the car.

'I know he's here,' she kept repeating. 'I know it.'

'Janice, this isn't doing either of you any good.'

Her eyes were bloodshot, looking sore from all the crying. 'What would you know about it? Have you ever lost a child?'

'I nearly lost Sammy.'

'But you didn't!' She turned away from him. 'You've never been any good, John. Christ, you couldn't even help Mitch, and he was supposed to be your best friend. They nearly blinded him!'

She had plenty left to say, plenty of poison. He let her talk, resting his hands lightly on the steering-wheel. At one point, she tried to get out, but he pulled her back into the car.

'Come on,' he said. 'Give me more. I'm listening to you.'

'No!' she spat. 'Know why? Because so help me, I think you're enjoying it!' This time when she opened the door, he didn't try to stop her. She took a left at the corner, heading down into the New Town. Rebus turned the car again, took a right into Castle Street and a left into Young Street. Stopped outside the Oxford Bar and walked in. Doc Klasser was standing in his usual spot. The afternoon drinkers were in: most of them would clear out by five or six, when the place filled with office workers. Harry the barman saw Rebus and lifted a pint glass. Rebus shook his head.

'A nip, Harry,' he said. 'Better make it a large one.'

He sat in the back room. Nobody there but the writer, the one with the big bag of books. He seemed to use the place as an office. A couple of times Rebus had asked him what books he should be reading. He'd bought the suggestions, but hadn't read them. Today, neither man seemed in need of company. Rebus sat with his drink and his thoughts. He was thinking back over thirty years, back to the last school party. His own version of the story . . .

Mitch and Johnny had a plan. They'd join the army, see some action. Mitch had sent away for the literature, then had dropped into the Army Careers Office in Kirkcaldy. The following week, he'd taken Johnny with him. The recruiting sergeant told them jokes and stories from his time 'in the field'. He told them they'd breeze through basic training. He had a moustache and a paunch and told them there'd be 'shagging and boozing galore': 'two good-looking lads like you, it'll be dripping out of your ears'.

Johnny Rebus hadn't been sure what that meant exactly, but Mitch had rubbed his hands together and chuckled with the Sarge.

So that was that. All Johnny had to do was tell his dad and Janice.

His dad, it turned out, wasn't keen. He'd done some time in the Far East in World War II. He had some photographs and a black silk scarf with the Taj Mahal sewn into it. He had a scar on his knee that wasn't really a bullet wound, even though he said it was.

'You don't want that,' Johnny's dad said. 'You want a proper job.' They kicked it back and forth between them. His dad's final shot at goal: 'What will Janice say?'

Janice didn't say anything; Rebus kept putting off telling her. And then one day she learned from her mum, who'd been talking to Johnny's dad, learned Johnny was thinking of leaving.

'It's not like I'm going for good,' he argued. 'I'll have plenty of home visits.'

She folded her arms, the way her mother did when she had right on her side. 'And am I supposed to just wait for you?'

'Please yourself,' Johnny said, kicking a stone.

'That's the plan,' she said, walking off.

Later, they made it up. He went to her house, went up to her bedroom with her: it was the only place they could talk. Her mum brought up juice and biscuits; gave them ten minutes then came up again to check they didn't need anything. Johnny said he was sorry.

'Does that mean you've changed your mind?' Janice asked.

He shrugged. He wasn't sure. Who did he want to let down: Janice or Mitch?

By the night of the dance, he'd made his mind up. Mitch could go alone. Johnny would stay behind, get a job of some kind and marry Janice. It wouldn't be a bad life. Plenty before him had done the same thing. He would tell Janice, tell her at the dance. And Mitch too, of course.

But first they had a drink. Mitch had got some bottles and an opener. They sneaked into the churchyard next to the school, drank a couple each, lay there in the grass, the headstones rising all around them. And it felt good, felt comfortable. Johnny swallowed back his confession. It could wait; he couldn't spoil this moment. It was like their whole lives had been sorted out, and everything was going to be fine. Mitch talked about the countries they'd visit, the things they'd see and do.

'And they'll all be gutted, just you wait.' Meaning everyone who stayed in Bowhill, all their friends who were going off to college or down the pit or into the dockyard. 'We'll see the whole fucking world, Johnny. And all they'll ever see is this place.' And Mitch stretched his arms out until his fingertips brushed the rough surfaces of two headstones. 'All they'll ever have to look forward to is this . . .'

They were untouchable as they marched into the playground. A teacher and the deputy head were on the door, collecting tickets.

'I smell beer,' the deputy head said, catching them off guard. Then he winked. 'You might have saved one for me.'

Johnny and Mitch were laughing, all grown-up now, as they walked into the assembly hall. There was music playing, people up dancing. Soft drinks and sandwiches on trellis tables in the dining hall. Chairs around the perimeter of the assembly hall; huddles of conversation, eyes darting everywhere. It felt – just for a moment – as if everyone was looking at the new arrivals . . . looking at them, *envying* them. Mitch slapped Johnny's arm, headed towards his girlfriend Myra. Johnny knew he'd tell him at the end of the dance.

He looked for Janice, couldn't see her. He had to tell her . . . had to find the words. Then someone told him there was whisky in the toilets, and he decided to stop there first. Two cubicles, side by side. Three boys in each, passing the bottle back and forth over the partition. Keeping silent so they wouldn't be caught. The stuff tasted like fire. Its fumes came rolling down Johnny's nostrils. He felt drunk; elated; unstoppable.

Back in the hall, it was ladies' choice. A girl called Mary McCutcheon asked him up. They danced well together. But the reel made Johnny light-headed. He had to sit down. He hadn't noticed some recent arrivals – three boys from his year; boys who had over time become Mitch's implacable enemies. The leader of the three, Alan Protheroe, had gone one-on-one with Mitch. Mitch had pulverised him, eventually. Johnny didn't see them eyeing up Mitch. Didn't think that the last dance of schooldays might be a time for settling scores, for ending things as well as beginning them.

Because now Janice was in the hall. Seated next to him. And they were kissing, even when Miss Dysart stood in front of them clearing her throat in warning. When Janice drew away eventually, Johnny stood up, pulling her to her feet.

'I've something to tell you,' he said. 'But not here. Come on.'

And had led her outside, round the back of the old building to where the bike-sheds – now largely unused – still stood. Smokers' Corner, they called it. But it was a place for lovers too, for quick snogs at lunchtime. Johnny sat Janice down on a bench.

'Aren't you going to tell me how lovely I look?'

He drank her in. She did look lovely. Light from the school windows made her skin seem to glow. Her eyes were dark invitations, her dress rustled with layers waiting to be unpeeled. He kissed her again. She tried to break away, asked him what it was he wanted to tell her. But now he knew that could wait. He was light-headed and full of dreams and desire. He touched her neck where it was bare at the shoulders. He ran his hand down her back, slipping it beneath the material. Her mum had made the dress; he knew it had taken hours. When he pressed harder, he felt the stitching in the zip give way. Janice gave a gasp and pushed him away.

'Johnny . . .' Craning her neck to try to assess the damage. 'You silly bugger, see what you've done.'

His hands on her legs, sliding the dress up past the knee. 'Janice.' She was standing now. He stood, too, pressing in on her for another kiss. She turned her face away. He seemed all limbs, sliding up her legs, slithering around her neck and down her back . . . She knew he tasted of beer and whisky. Knew she didn't like it. When she felt his hand trying to prise her legs apart, she pushed him away again, and he stumbled. Regaining balance, he wasn't so much smiling as leering as he moved in on her again.

And she swung back her hand, made a fist of it, and hit him a solid blow, almost dislocating her wrist in the process. She rubbed her knuckles, mouthing silent words of pain. He was flat out on the ground; knocked cold. She sat down again on the bench and waited for him to get up. Then heard what sounded like a commotion, and felt she'd much rather investigate than stay out here . . .

It was a fight. Slaughter might have been nearer the mark. The gang of three had somehow got Mitch on his own. They were at the edge of the playing-field, The Craigs silhouetted behind them. The sky was dark blue, bruise-coloured. Maybe Mitch had felt that tonight of all nights, he could take all three. Maybe they'd offered him a rematch, promising one-on-one. But it was three against one, and Mitch was on his hands and knees as the kicks rained in on his face and ribs. Janice was running forward, but a small, wiry figure beat her to it, legs and arms working like a windmill, head smashing into an unprotected nose, teeth bared with determination. She was amazed to identify the figure as Barney Mee, everyone's joker. What he lacked in elegance and precision, he more than made up for in sheer bloody-mindedness. He was like a machine. It only lasted a minute, maybe less, and at the end he was exhausted, but three figures were slouching off into the encroaching darkness as Barney slumped to the ground and lay on his back, staring up at the moon and the stars.

Mitch had pulled himself into a sitting position, one hand on his chest, the other covering an eye. Both hands were smeared with his own blood. His lip was split, and his nose was dripping red. When he spat, half a tooth was attached to the string of thick saliva. Janice stood above Barney Mee. He didn't seem so small, lying stretched out like that. He seemed . . . compact, but heroic. He opened his eyes and saw her, gave her one of his toothy grins.

'Lie down here,' he told her. 'There's something you should see.'

'What?'

'You won't see it standing up. You've got to lie down.'

She didn't believe him, but she lay down anyway. What did it matter if her dress got mucky: it was already split at the back. Her face was inches from his.

'What am I supposed to be looking at?' she asked.

'Up there,' he said, pointing.

And she looked. The sky wasn't black, that was the first strange thing. It was dark, certainly, but streaked with seams of white stars and clouds. And the moon seemed huge and orange rather than yellow.

'Isn't it amazing?' Barney Mee said. 'Every time I look at it, I can't help saying that.'

She turned to him. '*You're* amazing,' she said.

He smiled at the compliment. 'What are you going to do?'

'You mean when I leave?' She shrugged. 'Don't know. Look for a job, I suppose.'

'You should go to college.'

She looked at him more closely. 'Why?'

'You'd make a good teacher.'

She laughed out loud, but only for a second. 'What makes you say that?'

'I watch you in class. You'd be good, I know you would. Kids would listen to you.' He was looking at her now. 'I know I would,' he said.

Mitch cleared some blood from the back of his throat. 'Where's Johnny?' he asked.

Janice shrugged. Mitch eased his hand away from his eye. 'I'm fucking blind,' he said. 'And it hurts.' He bent over and began to cry. 'It hurts inside my head.'

Janice and Barney got up, helped him to his feet. They got one of the teachers to drive him to hospital. By the time Johnny Rebus came round, the show was over. He didn't even notice Janice dancing with Barney Mee. He just wanted a lift to the hospital.

'There's something I need to tell him.'

Eventually Mitch's parents came, and gave Johnny a lift to Kirkcaldy.

'What in God's name happened?' Mitch's mum asked.

'I don't know. I wasn't there.'

She turned to look at him. 'Weren't there?' He shook his head, ashamed. 'Then how did you get that bruise . . . ?'

His cheekbone, all the way down to his chin: a long purple trail. And he couldn't tell anyone how he'd come by it.

They had a long wait at the hospital. X-rays were mentioned. Cracked ribs.

'When I find whoever did this . . .' Mitch's dad said, balling his fists.

And then later, the bad news: a retina had been dislodged, maybe even worse. Mitch would lose the sight in one eye.

And by the time Johnny was allowed in to see him – with warnings not to stay too long, not to wear him out – Mitch had heard the news and was in tears.

'Christ, Johnny. Blind in one eye, how about that?'

There was a gauze patch over the eye in question.

'Long John fucking Silver and no mistake.' One of the patients on the ward coughed at the swear-word. 'And you can fuck off too!' Mitch yelled at him.

'Jesus, Mitch,' Johnny whispered. Mitch grabbed his wrist, squeezed it hard.

'It's you now. For both of us.'

Johnny licked his lips. 'How do you mean?'

'They won't take me, not blind in one eye. I'm sorry, pal. You know I am.'

Johnny was shaking, trying to think his way out. 'Right,' he said, nodding. It was all he could say, and he kept repeating it.

'You'll come back and see us, though, eh?' Mitch was saying. 'Tell me all about it. That's what I'd like . . . as if I was there with you.'

'Right, right.'

'You're going to have to live it for me, Johnny.'

'Sure, right.'

A smile from Mitch. 'Thanks, pal.'

'Least I can do,' said Johnny.

So he'd joined up. Janice hadn't seemed to mind. Mitch had waved him off at the station. And that was that. He sent Mitch and Janice letters; received none in return. By the time of his first leave, Mitch was nowhere to be found, and Janice was on holiday with her parents. Later, he found out Mitch had run off somewhere, no one seemed to know why or where. Johnny had half an idea: those letters, the visits home – reminders of the life Mitch could now never have . . .

Then his brother Mickey wrote to him, told him Janice had said to tell him she was going out with Barney Mee. And Johnny hadn't gone home after that for a while, had found other places to be when he was on leave, writing lies home so his father and brother wouldn't suspect, coming to think of the army as his home now . . . the only place he could be understood.

Drifting further in his mind from Cardenden and the friends he'd once had, and the dreams he'd once thought were within his reach . . .

45

It was dark and Cary Oakes was hungry and the game still wasn't over.

In prison, he'd been given lots of good advice about evading capture, all of it from men who'd been caught. He knew he needed to change his appearance: easily achieved with a visit to a charity shop. A new outfit of jacket, shirt and trousers for less than £20, topped off with a flat tweed cap. After all, he couldn't suddenly make his hair grow. When he saw his likeness in the newspaper, he made further adjustments, shaving himself scrupulously in a public convenience. He found a few stray carrier bags and filled them with rubbish. Examining himself in a shop window, he saw an unemployed man, a little bitter but still with enough money to buy the shopping.

He found the places where the down-and-outs spent their days: drop-in centres in the Grassmarket; the bench beside the toilets at the Tron Kirk; the foot of The Mound. These were safe places for him. People shared a can and a cigarette and didn't ask questions he couldn't make up answers to.

He was shivery and achy, made soft from his stay in the hotel. The windswept night on the hills had skimmed off some of his strength. It hadn't played the way he'd wanted it to. Archibald was still alive. Two spirits needed cleansing from his life: both were still to be dealt with.

And Rebus . . . Rebus had turned out to be something more than the 'wild operator' described by Jim Stevens. The way the reporter had talked, Oakes had expected Rebus to turn up naked to do battle. But Rebus had brought a whole goddamned army with him. Oakes had escaped by dint of good fortune and the weather. Or because the gods wanted his mission to succeed.

He knew things now would be difficult. In the centre of the city, he could remain anonymous, but further out there'd be more danger of discovery. The suburbs of Edinburgh remained places where strangers did not go undetected for long. It was as if people sat with their chairs at their windows in a constant state of alert. Yet one such suburb was his ultimate destination, as it had been all along.

He could have taken a bus, but in the end he walked. It took him well over an hour. He passed Alan Archibald's bungalow: 1930s styling with a bow window and white harled walls. There was no sign of life within. Archibald was in a hospital bed, and – according to one newspaper – under police guard. For the moment, Oakes had scratched him from his plans. Maybe the old bastard would die in hospital anyway. No, he was heading uphill and along another winding road into East Craigs. He'd been here just twice before, knowing people would get suspicious if he suddenly started frequenting the area. Two trips, one at night, one in the daytime. Both times he'd taken taxis from the foot of Leith Walk, making sure he was dropped off a few streets from his destination, not wanting the cabbies to know. In the dead of night, he'd walked right up to the walls of the building and touched trembling fingers to the stonework, trying to feel for a single life-force within.

He knew he was in there.

Couldn't stop shaking.

Knew he was in there, because he'd called to ask, identifying himself as the son of a friend. Asked if he could keep his call a secret: he wanted his visit to be a surprise.

He wondered if it *would* be a surprise . . .

Now, he was level with the car park. He sauntered past, just another tired worker on his way home. From the corner of his eye, he checked for police cars. Not that he thought they'd have guessed, but he wasn't going to underestimate Rebus again.

And saw instead a car he thought he recognised. Stopped and put his bags down, making to change hands, making out they were heavier than they were. And studied the car. A Vauxhall Astra. Numberplate the same. Oakes bared his teeth and let out a hiss of air. This was too much, the bastards were determined to wreck his plans.

Only one thing for it. He fingered the knife in his pocket, knowing he'd have to do some killing.

He had ditched the carrier bags and was lying beneath the car when he heard footsteps. Turned his head to watch them coming closer. He reckoned he'd been lying on the ground for a good hour and a half. His back was chilled, and the shivers were starting again. When he heard the clunk of the locks disengaging, he slid out from his hiding-place and tugged open the passenger door. Seeing him, the driver made to get out again, but Cary Oakes had the knife in his right hand while his left grabbed at Jim Stevens's sleeve.

'Thought you'd be pleased to see me again, Jimbo,' Oakes said. 'Now close the door and get this thing moving.' He took off his jacket, tossed it on to the back seat.

'Where are we going?'

'Just drive, man.' His shirt followed.

'What are you doing?' Stevens asked. But Oakes ignored him, loosed his trousers and threw them into the back too.

'This is all a bit sudden for me, Cary.'

'A man who likes a joke, huh?' As they left the car park, Oakes realised he was sitting on something. Pulled out the reporter's notebook and pen.

'Been working, Jim?' He opened the notebook, and was disappointed to see Stevens had used shorthand.

'Why'd you go see him?' Oakes asked, beginning to tear each page of the notebook into four.

'See who? I was visiting an old neighbour of mine, and—'

The knife arced into Stevens's side. He took his hands off the wheel, and the car veered towards the kerb. Oakes straightened it up.

'Keep your foot down, Jim! If this car stops, you're a dead man!'

Stevens examined his palm. It was wet with blood. 'Hospital,' he croaked, face twisted with pain.

'You'll get a hospital *after* I've had my answers! What made you go to see him?'

Stevens hunched over the wheel, taking control again. Oakes thought he was going to pass out, but it was just the pain.

'I was checking details.'

'That all?' Ripping at the notebook.

'What else would I be doing?'

'Well, that's why I'm asking, Jim-Bob. And if you don't want knifing again, you'll convince me.' Oakes reached for the heater switch, slid it to full.

'It's for the book.'

'The book?' Oakes narrowed his eyes.

'I don't have enough material with just the interviews.'

'You should have asked me first.' Oakes was silent for a minute.

'Where are we going?' Stevens had one hand on the steering-wheel, one pressed to his side.

'Turn right at the roundabout, head out of town.'

'The Glasgow road? I need a hospital.'

Oakes wasn't listening. 'What did he say?'

'What?'

'What did he say about me?'

'Probably what you'd expect.'

'He's *compos mentis* then?'

'Pretty much.'

Oakes wound down the window, scattering the scraps of paper. When he turned round again, Stevens was scrabbling on the floor with his hand.

'What are you doing?' Oakes brandished the knife.

'Paper hankies. I thought I'd a box somewhere.'

Oakes examined his handiwork. 'Just between you and me, Jim, I don't think paper tissues are going to do the job.'

'I feel faint. I've got to stop.'

'Keep going!'

Stevens' eyelids looked heavy. 'See if they're in the back.'

'What?'

'The box of hankies.'

So Oakes turned in his seat, pushed his clothes around. 'Nothing here.'

Stevens was rooting in his pockets. 'Must be something . . .' Eventually he found a large cotton handkerchief, eased it inside his shirt.

'Take the airport exit,' Oakes commanded.

'You leaving us, Cary?'

'Me?' Oakes grinned. 'When I'm just beginning to enjoy myself?' He sneezed, spraying the windscreen with spittle.

'Bless you,' Stevens said. There was silence in the car for a moment, then both men laughed.

'That's funny,' Oakes said, wiping an eye. 'You blessing me.'

'Cary, I'm losing a lot of blood.'

'It's all right, Jimbo. I've seen people bleed to death before. You've got hours left in you.' He sat back in his seat. 'So you were out there all by yourself, checking background . . . ? Who knew you were going?'

'Nobody.'

'Not your editor?'

'No.'

'And John Rebus?'

Stevens snorted. 'Why would I tell him?'

'Because I made you mad.' Oakes pushed out his bottom lip. 'Sorry about that, by the way.'

'Was it really all lies?'

'That's between me and my conscience, man.'

The car hit a bump and Stevens grimaced.

'Know what they say about pain, Jim? They say it makes you see colour for the very first time. Makes everything really *vivid*.'

'The blood certainly looks vivid.'

'There's nothing like it,' Oakes said quietly, 'not in the whole world.'

They were coming to another roundabout. Off to their left sat Ingliston Showground, unused for the most part of the year. Unused tonight.

'Airport?' Stevens asked.

'No, take a left.'

So Stevens did, and found himself approaching a building site. Another new hotel was being thrown up, to complement the one at the airport exit. Around it lay farmland, the dwellings few and far between. There were no visible lights at all, not even from planes landing and taking off.

'No hospitals near here,' Stevens said, dread overcoming him.

'Pull over.'

Stevens did as he was told.

'They'll have a doctor at the airport,' Oakes told him. 'I'll need your car, but you can walk it.'

'Better still, you could drop me off.' Jim Stevens licked his dry lips.

'Or better yet . . .' Cary Oakes said. And his hand flew, and the knife went into Stevens' side again.

And again and again, as the journalist's words became twisted sounds, finding a new vocabulary of terror, resignation and pain.

Oakes dragged the corpse out and dumped it behind a mound of earth. Searched in the pockets and found Stevens' cassette recorder. There wasn't much light, but he was able to prise it open, remove the tape. Left the recorder behind; took the tape. Little money in Stevens' wallet: credit cards, but he wanted neither to use them nor be caught with them in his possession. He bent down again, wiped the recorder on Stevens' jacket, getting rid of prints.

The wind was cutting through him. If he tried concealing the body, he might die of hypothermia. He raced back to the car, got into the driver's seat and headed off. The heater wouldn't go any higher. The blood was sticking his underpants to the seat. He could feel it against his skin. Couldn't put his clothes on yet: had to keep them clean. Couldn't go wandering around Edinburgh with bloodstained clothes.

Another trick from prison. Maybe his fellow inmates hadn't been so stupid after all.

On the way back into town, he stopped in a deserted supermarket car park, threw the tape into a bin.

Then he was on his way. Knew he had at least one night before the body was found. One night when he'd have some shelter, courtesy of Jim Stevens' car.

46

Anything out west was a Torphichen call, but news travelled fast. Roy Frazer drove Rebus out to the scene. The whole drive, Rebus only said one thing to the young man.

'You screwed up about Eddie Mearn. It happens. Best to have it happen young when you can still learn from it. Otherwise you get intimations of infallibility, which translates to your colleagues as "smart-arse".'

'Yes, sir,' Frazer said, frowning as though trying to memorise the advice. Then he reached into his pocket. 'Message from DS Clarke.' He handed over the note. Rebus unfolded the piece of paper. At first he didn't take it in. His brain was overloaded as it was. But eventually the words hit him with the force of electricity.

I did a bit of digging. Joseph Margolies wasn't just a doctor. He worked for the council for a time, had special responsibility for children's homes. Don't know if it means anything, but I get the feeling you had him down as a GP. Cheers, S.

He read the note half a dozen times. He wasn't sure if it *did* mean anything. But he could see definite connections beginning to appear. And connections could always be exploited . . .

The DI from Torphichen was Shug Davidson. He offered a brief smile as Rebus got out of the car.

'They say the culprit always returns to the scene of the crime.'

'That's not funny, Shug.'

'Way I hear it, you and the deceased weren't exactly bosom buddies.'

'Maybe towards the end,' Rebus said. 'Have they moved him yet?'

Davidson shook his head. Work on the construction site had stopped. There were faces at the portakabin windows. Other workers milled around outside, wearing hard hats, drinking tea from their flasks. Their gaffer was complaining that work was a fortnight behind as it was.

'Then a few more hours isn't going to make much of a dent, is it?' Davidson said.

Rebus had ducked beneath the *locus* tape. The victim had been pronounced dead. They were photographing the body. Forensics had already completed taping it. Uniforms were spreading out from the *locus*, seeking clues. Davidson had the whole situation under control.

'Any ideas?' Davidson asked Rebus.

'One fairly big one.'

'Oakes?' Rebus looked at Davidson, who smiled. 'I read the papers too, John. Friend of a friend told me Oakes had dumped on Stevens. Next thing, Oakes is on the run after the attack on Alan Archibald.' He broke off. 'How is he, by the way?'

'Doing better than this poor bugger,' Rebus said, moving closer to the body. Professor Gates was crouched – or as Gates himself liked to say, on his 'cuddy-hunkers' – at Stevens' head. He nodded a greeting towards Rebus, but carried on with his initial appraisal of the scene. One of the forensics team held out a clear plastic bag, into which Jim Stevens' possessions were being dropped.

'No car keys?' Rebus asked. The forensics woman shook her head.

'No car either,' Davidson added.

'Stevens drives a Vauxhall Astra.'

'I know, John. It's being hunted.'

'Must have been brought here in a car. Oakes doesn't have one.'

'Probably lost a lot of blood en route,' Gates said. 'His shirt and trousers are soaked, but there's not that much lying beneath him.'

'You think he was stabbed somewhere else?'

'That would be my guess.' Gates turned to the forensics officer. 'Let Inspector Rebus see the machine.'

She lifted a small metal box from the bag. Rebus looked at it closely, but knew better than to touch.

'It's his recorder.'

'Yes,' Gates said. 'And in his right-hand pocket, well away from the wounds and the blood.'

'But there's blood on it,' Rebus said.

Gates nodded. 'And no tape inside.'

'The killer took the tape?'

'Or it was important enough for the deceased to take time to remove it, even though by that time he'd already been stabbed and was probably entering a state of shock.'

Rebus turned to Davidson. 'Any sign of it?'

'That's what they're looking for.' Davidson motioned towards the uniforms. 'John, have you any idea what Stevens was up to?'

'Last time I spoke to him, he was going to look into Oakes's past.'

'Wonder what he found.'

Rebus shrugged. 'Bringing in Oakes *has* to be the priority.'

'After his attack on you, it already was.'

Rebus stared down at the lifeless body of Jim Stevens. Stevens, who had been Rebus's shadow for so long, and who had come back into his life only recently.

'I'd only just started liking him,' Rebus said. 'That's the funny thing.'

He looked at Davidson. 'I get the feeling the game's not over, Shug. Not by a long chalk.'

One of Davidson's officers sprinted towards them. 'Car's been found,' he called.

'Where?' Rebus was first to ask.

The officer blinked, shook his head. 'You're not going to like it . . .'

Jim Stevens' Astra sat on a single yellow line on a street called St Leonard's Bank, just round the corner from St Leonard's cop shop. St Leonard's Bank boasted a single row of higgledy-piggledy houses, all of them facing a wrought-iron fence behind which sat Holyrood Park and Salisbury Crags. The car was parked outside a double-fronted three-storey house painted a vivid pink. The key was in the ignition. This was what had first alerted one of the neighbours. They'd gone next door to ask if anyone there had left their keys in their car. Heading out to investigate, they'd found the doors to be unlocked. On opening the driver's side, they'd noticed how wet and stained the seat seemed to be. Pressing fingers down into the fabric, lifting them away to find them stained viscous red . . .

'Is he taking the piss or what?' Roy Frazer said. A crowd from St Leonard's had gathered, though more, it seemed, out of curiosity than from a desire to help. Rebus started shooing most of them away. He'd brought three of the forensics team with him; the rest would follow when they'd finished at the construction site. Chief Superintendent Watson came to gawp, and to make sure everything was 'under control'.

'It's Shug Davidson's call really, sir,' Rebus informed him. 'He's on his way.'

The Farmer nodded. 'Fair enough, John. But let's get the car moved ASAP, even if only into our car park. It's already been on Lowland Radio. Leave it much longer, we can start selling tickets.'

It was true that the crowd around the car was swelling. Rebus recognised a few faces from Greenfield. The estate was only a short walk away.

Roy Frazer was repeating his question.

'He's taunting us,' Rebus answered. He went to see how the forensics team was doing.

'Found this on the floor under the driver's seat,' one of them said. Inside a plastic bag he had a cassette tape, unlabelled. There was a single bloody thumb print clearly visible on its casing.

'I need this,' Rebus said.

'We need to print it.'

Rebus shook his head. 'The print belongs to the victim.' He was managing to smile. *You clever bugger, Jim*, he was thinking. *He didn't get your tape . . .*

At least, that was what he hoped.

'Something else,' another of the team said, pointing to show Rebus a spread of tiny spots on the windscreen. 'These are on the inside. The way the pattern is . . . it's like someone coughed or sneezed. If it was the killer . . .'

'Is there enough for DNA?'

'It's a hell of a long shot, but you never know. Don't know if this is relevant.' Now he pointed to a notebook on the floor of the passenger side. It had a tin spiral holding the loose-leaf pages in place. Shreds of paper clung to the spiral, showing where pages had been torn out.

Rebus patted the man's shoulder. He didn't like to say *It doesn't matter. I know who killed him . . . I may even know why* . . . When he turned away, he was carrying the cassette tape in its little poly-bag, for all the world like a solemn kid who'd won a goldfish at the fair.

Because it was quieter there, Rebus used one of the interview rooms. He'd slotted the tape into one of the recorders, being careful to hold it by its edges. No point destroying trace evidence. He had a pair of Sennheiser headphones on, and spread out in front of him the contents of Cary Oakes's file, as well as cuttings of his recent newspaper interviews. He'd telephoned Stevens' old employer, and they were faxing over the unused portions of transcript. Every now and then, a uniform would stick his or her head round the door and hand him the latest fax sheets, so that the table became covered.

Siobhan Clarke went so far as to bring him a mug of coffee and a BLT, but otherwise left him to it, which was just what he wanted. His mind was on nothing but the interview he was listening to.

'Little bugger came to us with his mum . . . my wife's sister, she was. Right little runt he was.' The man's voice sounded old, wheezy.

'You didn't get on with him?' Jim Stevens' voice, making the hairs rise on Rebus's arms. He looked around but Stevens' ghost was nowhere to be seen; not yet . . . Occasional background noises: coughs, voices, a television playing. An audience . . . no, spectators. Spectators at what sounded like a football match. Rebus went through to CID and dug in bins, looked through the papers sitting folded and forgotten on window ledges, until he found one for the previous day. Seven thirty: UEFA Cup action. That seemed to fit the bill. He tore out the TV page, took it back with him to the interview room, turned the tape on again.

'I hated him, to be frank with you. Bloody disruption, that's all it was. I mean, we had ourselves sorted out, everything going smoothly, everything just so . . . and then the two of them come waltzing in. Couldn't very well kick them out, being family and all, but I made sure they knew I wasn't happy. Oi, I'm watching that!'

Someone had changed channels. Studio laughter. Rebus checked the paper: a sitcom on the BBC.

Back to the sound of crowd and commentator.

'We had some high old ding-dongs, him and me.'

'What about?'

'Everything: him staying out, him thieving. Money kept disappearing. I laid a few traps, but I never caught him, he was too canny for that.'

'Did your fights ever become physical?'

'I should say so. Tough little runt, I'll give him that. You see me the way I am now, but back then I was fighting fit.' He coughed loudly; sounded like his lungs were being turned inside out. 'Give me that water, will you?' The old man took a drink, then broke wind. 'Anyway,' he went on, not bothering to apologise, 'I made sure he knew who was boss. It was my house, remember.' As if Stevens were accusing him.

'You were the boss,' Stevens reassured him.

'I was and all. Take my word for it.'

'And if you thumped him, it was just so he'd understand.'

'That's what I'm telling you. And he was no angel, believe you me. Mind you, try telling the women that.'

'His mother and her sister?'

'My wife, aye. She never saw any harm in anyone, did Aggie. But I'd have to say, even back then I knew there was badness in him. Deep-rooted badness.'

'You tried knocking it out of him.'

'I'd have needed a sledgehammer, son. Did use a hammer on him once, as it happens. Bastard was tough by then, ready to give as good as he got.' Rebus thinking: *The poison passed from one generation to the next. As with abuse, so with violence.*

'Did he run with a gang?'

'Gang? Nobody would have him, son. What did you say your name was?'

'Jim.'

'And you're with the papers? I spoke to some of your lot when he was put away.'

'What did you tell them?'

'That he should've had the electric chair. We could do a lot worse ourselves than bring back hanging.'

'You think it's a deterrent?'

'Once they're dead, son, they don't do it again, do they? What more proof do you want?'

There were sounds of someone bringing Stevens a cup of coffee or tea.

'Aye, they're good to me in here.'

Nursing home . . . Cary Oakes's uncle . . . What was his name? Rebus found it in the notes: Andrew Castle. Alongside it, the name of his nursing home. Rebus got on the phone, found a number for the home and rang them.

'You've got a resident called Andrew Castle.'

'Yes?'

'He had a visitor last night.'

'He did, yes.'

'Did you see him leave?'

'I'm sorry, who is this?'

'My name's Detective Inspector Rebus. Only Mr Castle's visitor has turned up dead, and we're trying to trace his last movements.'

There was a tapping at the door. Shug Davidson came in. Rebus nodded for him to sit.

'Gracious,' the woman at the nursing home was saying. 'You mean the reporter?'

'That's who I mean. What time did he leave?'

'It must have been . . .' She broke off. 'How did he die?'

'He was stabbed, madam. Now, what time did he leave?'

Davidson, seated across the table from Rebus, turned some of the fax sheets round so he could read them.

'Just before bedtime . . . say, nine o'clock.'

'Did he have a car with him?'

'I think so, yes. He parked it outside.'

'Was anyone seen hanging around?'

She sounded puzzled. 'No, I don't think so.'

'Any suspicious sightings the past day or two?'

'Gracious me, Inspector, what's this about?'

Rebus thanked her for her time, said someone would be coming to get her statement. Then he put down the phone, checked the home's address against an *A–Z*.

'Shug,' he said, 'I've got Stevens at a nursing home near the Maybury roundabout, probably from around seven thirty last night till nine.'

'Maybury's on the road out to the airport.'

Rebus nodded. 'I think Oakes was already there.'

'Where?'

'The nursing home.'

'Who was Stevens seeing there?'

'Oakes's uncle. The questions Jim used on the tape . . . I think he'd already talked to the uncle, already made up his mind about him.'

'How do you mean?'

'The questions were angled a certain way, letting the uncle show himself as a sadist.'

'You're going to tell me this uncle turned Cary Oakes into a psychopath?'

Rebus shrugged. 'That's you talking, not me. What I *do* think is, Oakes has a grudge.' He thought for a moment. *I have a date with my past. A date with destiny . . . with someone who wouldn't listen . . .* Oakes's words to Stevens at the end of their last interview . . . 'Alan Archibald lives out that way.' He opened the *A–Z* again, pointed to Archibald's street, then the cul-de-sac which housed the nursing home. They were barely half a dozen streets apart. 'I thought Oakes went there to scope out Alan Archibald.'

'Now you think different?'

'He came back to Edinburgh to settle old scores. There's none older than his uncle.' He looked up at Davidson. 'I think he'll try to kill him.'

Davidson rubbed a palm over his jaw. 'And Jim Stevens?'

'Was in the wrong place at the wrong time. If Oakes thought Jim was on to his plan, he'd have to deal with him. Oakes took the tape from Jim's recorder, only Jim had switched tapes. Then Oakes tore out the pages from Jim's notebook. He didn't want us knowing.'

'But we were bound to find out where Stevens had been.'

'Eventually, yes.' Rebus tapped the tape machine. 'But without this, it would have taken a while.'

Davidson was starting to rise. 'Long enough to let him carry out his plan?'

'Which means it's got to be soon.' Rebus was on his feet too.

As Davidson reached for the phone, Rebus sprinted from the room.

47

They had undercover officers on the scene. It was difficult to blend in: most of the staff were middle-aged women. Young, wary-looking men with CID haircuts looked out of place. The officers came from the Scottish Crime Squad. Andrew Castle was confined to his room. There were two men in there with him: one participating in a game of cards – twopenny bets – while the other sat in the corner, affording the best view of door and window. The window was curtained. There was another man in a parked car outside.

'Would he try a sniper shot?' had been one of the questions at the briefing. Rebus had doubted it: he'd no known access to guns, and besides, it was personal with him. His uncle would have to know the why and the who before any killing could be done.

One of the other officers was pushing a mop up and down the corridor outside. Rebus and Davidson were satisfied.

Another question from the briefing: 'What if all we do is scare him off?'

Rebus's response: 'Then we've saved an old man's life . . . for now.'

He'd listened once more to the whole tape, and didn't doubt that Oakes's uncle had been – and probably still was – rotten to the marrow, despite his senility and frailty. Now he had questions.

If Cary had ended up in a home where he'd been loved, would everything have been changed? Were people programmed from birth to become killers, or did other people – and sets of circumstances – conspire to make killers of them, turning the potential that was in most people into something more tangible?

They weren't new questions, certainly not to him. He thought of Darren Rough, the abused becoming abuser. Not all abuse victims took that road, but plenty did . . . And what about Damon Mee? What *had* made him leave home? His parents' failing marriage? Fear of getting married himself? Or had he been coerced away, forcibly stopped from returning?

And why had Jim Margolies died?

And would Cary Oakes walk into the trap?

My, my, my, said the spider to the fly . . .

Oakes had been the spider for far too long.

Rebus dropped into hospital to check on Alan Archibald. There was nothing for him to do at the nursing home. In fact, as one of the Crime Squad officers had succinctly put it, he was 'a positive hindrance'. Meaning that because Oakes knew Rebus, his presence on the scene could spoil everything.

'Soon as anything happens, we'll call.'

Rebus had made the officer write his mobile number on the back of his hand. Then had handed him a business card anyway: 'Just in case you wash it off by mistake.'

Archibald was at the far end of an open ward, with a screen around his bed. Bobby Hogan from Leith CID was sitting bedside, flicking through a copy of *Mass Hibsteria*.

'Your team's going down, Bobby,' Rebus told him.

Hogan looked up. 'It's not mine.' He waved the football fanzine at Rebus. 'Someone left it on the ward.'

The two men shook hands, and Rebus went to fetch another chair. Alan Archibald was snoring gently, head propped up on three pillows.

'How is he?' Rebus asked. Archibald's head was bandaged and there was a gauze compress taped to one ear.

'Thumping headache.'

'Well, his head *did* take a thumping.'

'They did some tests, say he'll be fine.' Hogan smiled. 'They tried testing his memory, but as Alan said, at his age he's lucky to remember which day it is, dunt on the heid or no'.'

Rebus smiled too. 'You know him then?'

'Worked together years ago. That's why I asked for this detail.'

'Were you with him when his niece was murdered?'

Hogan stared at the sleeping figure. 'It took all the juice out of him, like his batteries were flat after that.'

'He wanted it to be Cary Oakes.'

Hogan nodded. 'I think anyone would have done as far as Alan was concerned, but Oakes was the obvious choice.'

'Still could be.'

Hogan looked at him. 'Not according to Alan.'

'I wouldn't trust anything Oakes said. Everything in his world has to be twisted round.'

'But he thought he was going to kill Alan . . . why bother lying to him?'

'To amuse himself.' Rebus crossed one leg over the other. 'That seems to be what he's been doing ever since he hit town, spinning stories . . .' And now Rebus was surplus to requirements; other officers would bring in Cary Oakes.

'Did you ever get anywhere with Jim's suicide?'

Rebus looked at Hogan. 'I was beginning to. I got sidetracked.'

'So what can you tell me?'

Alan Archibald grunted, and his lips started moving as though savouring something. Slowly his eyes opened. He looked to his left and saw his two visitors.

'Any sign of him?' he asked, voice dry and brittle. Hogan poured him some water.

'Do you want any more tablets, Alan?'

Archibald made to shake his head, then screwed shut his eyes with the sudden pain. 'No,' he said instead. As Hogan trickled the water into his mouth, it dribbled either side of the plastic cup and down his chin. Hogan dabbed it with a napkin.

'He'd make a great nurse.' Archibald winked at Rebus. His eyes looked unfocused; Rebus wondered what kind of painkillers they had him on. 'They haven't caught him?'

'Not yet,' Rebus admitted.

'But he's been busy, hasn't he?'

Rebus didn't know if it was pure instinct or whether something in his voice had alerted Archibald. He nodded, told Archibald about Jim Stevens, about the nursing home and Oakes's uncle.

'I remember the uncle,' Archibald said. 'I interviewed him a while back. I think he hated Oakes almost more than I did.'

'You didn't happen to mention him to Oakes, did you?'

Archibald was thoughtful for a moment. 'Not for a while. He might have been in one of the letters I sent.' His eyes widened. 'How did Oakes know where he was? You think I . . . ?' Pain coursed across his face. 'I should have twigged. But I wasn't thinking like a copper, that's the bottom line. I had my own motives. I wasn't really interested in the uncle, only in what he could tell me about Oakes. There was that one question always at the back of my mind . . . that one question I needed the answer to.'

'Yes,' Rebus agreed.

'Everything I'd learned went out the window.' Tears were welling in Archibald's eyes.

'Don't blame yourself,' Hogan said, touching his shoulder.

Archibald was looking past him, towards the seated figure of John Rebus. 'Whether he killed her or not . . . I'll never know for sure, will I?'

Tears dropped on to Archibald's cheeks and down his chin. Bobby Hogan dabbed at them with the already damp napkin.

'All these years not knowing . . . damned fool to think I could . . .' He closed his eyes, crying softly. In the other beds, no one stirred. Crying in the night maybe wasn't so unusual here. Bobby Hogan had taken hold of both the old man's hands. It looked like Archibald was squeezing with all his might.

Alan Archibald was in hospital because he'd become obsessed with an idea. Rebus, knowing what he knew now, was wondering if Jim Margolies had become obsessed too. With nothing else to do, he headed back to St Leonard's. It took a couple of hours, several phone calls, and a lot of grudging help before Rebus got what he wanted.

He sat at his desk scoring through points on his notepad. The people he'd spoken to from the Health Board and Social Work had all asked if it couldn't wait till morning. Rebus had insisted it could not.

'It's a murder inquiry,' had been his only line of attack. When pressed for details, he'd said he couldn't add anything 'at the present moment in time', trying to sound like the sort of detective they'd expect him to be: a bureaucrat, a man following a preordained path of investigation where no overnight rest-stops could be taken.

In the end, he'd had to drive to the various offices himself to pick up the information he'd asked for. On each occasion, he'd been met by the official he'd spoken to on the phone. They'd all stared at him with ill-will and irritation. But they'd all handed over the documents. Which gave Rebus little to do but head back to St Leonard's and plough through the field of information on Dr Joseph Margolies.

Dr Margolies had been born in Selkirk, and educated in the Borders and at Fettes. His medical degree was completed at the University of Edinburgh, with stints working in Africa for a Christian charity. He'd become a general practitioner, then had taken to lecturing, specialising in paediatrics. And eventually, as Siobhan's note had said, he'd been employed to 'look after' the council-run children's homes in Lothian, a job which also took him into private homes licensed by the council – such as those owned and operated by churches and charities.

What his job meant in effect was that he checked the children for signs of abuse, and would be brought in to make a physical examination should any accusations of abuse be made. Also, some of the kids were classed as 'difficult cases', and a medical prognosis would be part of their ongoing record. Dr Margolies might recommend psychiatric consultation, or a move to some other type of institution. He could prescribe treatments and medication. His powers, in effect, were almost without limit. His word was law.

About halfway through his reading, Rebus began to get a queasy feeling in his gut. He hadn't eaten for hours, but didn't think that had anything to do with it. Nevertheless, he forced himself to get some fresh air, visited Brattisani's for a fish supper with buttered bread and tea. Afterwards, he knew he'd been away from the station for the best part of an hour, but couldn't recall any of that time: no faces, no voices. Brain busy with other things.

He remembered a recent case, a priest who'd abused children for years. The children had been in the care of nuns, and when any of them complained they were thrashed by the nuns, told they were liars, and made to attend confession – where, listening to them, would be the same priest they'd just accused of abuse.

He knew that oftentimes paedophiles were well able to hide their true natures for months and years as they trained for positions in children's homes and the like. They would pass all the checks and psychological tests, only later for the mask to slip. Their need was so great, they would go to extraordinary lengths to fulfil it. And sometimes it might have remained latent had they not encountered at some point a fellow traveller, each spurring the other on . . .

Like Harold Ince and Ramsay Marshall. Rebus could believe that either one, left in isolation, would never have found the strength to begin their eventual programme of systematic abuse. But together, working as a team, the effect had been to intensify their lusts and desires, making the eventual abuse so much more appalling.

Rebus looked back through all the paperwork on Dr Joseph Margolies, until he was sure of what he saw.

That Margolies had been attached to the city's children's homes at the time of the Shiellion scandal.

That he had retired soon afterwards – and prematurely – on 'health grounds'.

That he was considered courageous by those he worked with for the way he'd kept going following his daughter's suicide.

Rebus didn't find much about the daughter. She'd killed herself at fifteen, hadn't left a note. She'd been a quiet child, withdrawn. Adolescence had done her few favours. She'd been worried about upcoming exams. Her brother Jim had been devastated by her death . . .

She hadn't leapt from some high spot. She'd slashed her wrists in the bathroom of her home. Her father had kicked open the door and found her there. It was believed she'd done the deed in the dead of night. Her father was always the first to rise in the morning.

Rebus put a call through to Jane Barbour. By dint of white lies and stubbornness, he secured her mobile number. When she picked up, he could hear loud music and cheering in the background.

'Good party, is it?'

'Who's this?'

'DI Rebus.'

Another wave of cheering behind her. 'Hang on, I'll just take this outside.' The sounds died away. Barbour exhaled noisily. She sounded drunk. 'We're at the Police Club.'

'What's the celebration?'

'Take a guess.'

'Guilty verdicts?'

'On both the bastards. Not a single juror went against us.'

Rebus sat back in his chair. 'Congratulations.'

'Thanks.'

'Cordover must be seething.'

'Bugger Cordover. Petrie pronounces tomorrow. He'll stick them away for ever and a day.'

'Well, congratulations again. It's a hell of a result.'

'Why don't you come down? We've enough booze here—'

'Thanks all the same. But it's a coincidence, I'm phoning about Ince and Marshall.'

'Oh?'

'Indirectly anyway. Dr Joseph Margolies.'

'Yes?'

'You know who he is?'

'Yes.'

'Was he called to give evidence?'

'No, he wasn't. Christ, it's so mild out here tonight.'

Rebus wondered if she was on anything other than a natural high. 'Why wasn't he called?'

'Because of the facts of the case. It's true a few of the Shiellion kids made accusations at the time, but they weren't believed.'

'There'd be a medical check, though.'

'Of course, carried out by Dr Margolies. I interviewed him several times. But the boys were known to be gay, insofar as they worked as occasional rent boys around Calton Hill. If they ran from Shiellion, that's where everyone knew to find them. So you see, evidence of anal sex was not in itself evidence of abuse – I'm quoting the Procurator Fiscal's line. To my mind, these kids were underage and in care, and anyone who had sex with them was guilty of abuse.' She paused. 'End of rant.'

'Sooner you're free of this case the better.'

'So why are you dragging it all up again?'

'I'm trying to get a fix on Dr Margolies.'

'Why?'

'When you talked to him, was he helpful?'

'As much as he could be. He said himself the kids had been caught lying before, so who was going to believe them next time? And a lot of the abuse claims referred to oral sex and masturbation . . . not many medical tests for those, Inspector.'

'No,' Rebus said thoughtfully. 'So he didn't give evidence?'

'Not in court. Fiscal said it would be a waste of time. Might even have harmed our case by casting doubt in the jury's mind.'

'In which case Cordover might have wanted the doctor as a witness.'

'Yes, but he didn't, and I wasn't about to give him a hand.' She paused. 'You think Margolies was involved in a cover-up?'

'What makes you ask?'

'I wondered about it myself. I mean, chances are there were people working at Shiellion who had a good idea what was happening. But nobody stuck their head above the parapet.'

'Afraid to cause trouble?'

'Or warned off by the Church. It's not been unknown in the past. Of course, there's an even worse scenario.'

Rebus dreaded to think what it might be. But he asked anyway.

'Just this,' she said. 'People knew it was happening, but they just didn't care. Now if you'll excuse me, I'm heading back indoors to get blisteringly drunk.'

Rebus thanked her and rang off. Sat with his head in his hands, staring at his desk.

People knew . . . they just didn't care . . .

48

Just as during their actual trial, Ince and Marshall were being held in Saughton Prison. The difference was, now they'd been found guilty they were no longer on remand. As remand prisoners, they'd been able to wear their own clothes, phone out for food, and go about their business. Now they'd be getting used to prison garb and all the other comforts of the prison regime proper.

They were being held in separate cells, with an empty cell between so there was less chance of them communicating. Rebus didn't know why anyone bothered: they'd probably end up in the same sex offender programme.

He had a difficult choice to make: Ince or Marshall? Of course, if one failed him, there was nothing to stop him trying the other. But that would mean going through the same process again, asking the same questions, playing the same games. The right choice might save him all that grief.

He chose Ince. His reasoning: Ince was the elder, with the higher IQ. And though early on in the relationship, there was no doubt that he'd been the leader, the pupil had soon become the master. In the courtroom, Marshall had been the one who'd scowled and grunted and played to the gallery; the one who'd looked as though the trial had nothing to do with him.

The one with no visible show of shame, even as his victims told their stories.

The one who'd fallen down the stairs a couple of times on his way back to the cells.

Yes, Marshall had learned a lot from Harold Ince, but he'd added ingredients of his own. He was the more savage, the more amoral, the less penitent. He was the one who thought it was the world's problem, not his. At the trial, he'd tried quoting Aleister Crowley, to the effect that only *he* had the right to judge his actions right or wrong.

The court hadn't thought much of that.

Rebus sat in the visitors' room and smoked a cigarette. He'd called Patience, got the machine: a message telling callers to try her mobile.

He did so, found she was at a friend's. Another woman doctor, off on prenatal leave.

'I might stay the night,' Patience told him. 'Ursula's offered.'

'How is she?'

'Sick.'

'Oh dear.'

'You misunderstand: she's sick she can't drink. Never mind, I'm drinking for two.'

Rebus smiled. 'I'll go to Arden Street,' he said. 'If you're going home, let me know.'

'You think I should stay away?'

'It might be an idea.' He meant until Cary Oakes was caught. When he rang off, he got through to St Leonard's, who confirmed that the patrol car was now stationed outside Patience's friend's.

'Safe as houses, John.'

So he sat in the visitors' room and smoked a cigarette, defying the sign on the wall, flicking ash on to the carpet. The uniform brought Harold Ince in. Rebus thanked him, told him to wait just outside. Not that Rebus expected anything from Ince: no violence, no escape attempt. He looked resigned to his fate. Since Rebus had seen him at the trial, his face had grown longer and thinner, the pallid skin hanging from it. His stomach bulged, but his chest seemed to have caved in, as though the heart had been removed. Rebus knew that at least one of Ince's victims had committed suicide. There was a smell from the man: sulphur mixed with Germolene.

Rebus offered him a cigarette. Ince, slumping into a chair, shook his head.

'You gave evidence, didn't you?' The voice was thin and reedy.

Rebus nodded, flicked ash. 'Your lawyer tried carving me up.'

The brief flicker of a smile. 'I remember now. Didn't work, did it?'

'And now you've been found guilty.'

'Come to rub it in?' Ince's eyes found Rebus's for the briefest moment.

'No, Mr Ince, I've come to ask for your help.'

Ince snorted, folded his arms. 'Yeah, I'm well in the mood to help the police.'

'I wonder if he's already made up his mind?' Rebus asked, as if wondering aloud.

Ince's forehead creased. 'Who?'

'Lord Justice Petrie. He's a tough old buzzard.'

'So I've heard.'

But soft on his kids, Rebus thought to himself. *Or is he . . .?*

'My money's on Peterhead for the pair of you,' he said. 'You'll be there a long time. That's where they take the sex offenders.' Rebus sat forward. 'It's also where a lot of the real hard cases are kept, the ones who rate kiddie-fuckers slightly lower than the amoeba on the evolutionary ladder.'

'Ahh . . .' Ince sat back, nodded. 'So that's it: you've come to scare me. Let me save you the effort: the guards at the trial told me what I could expect, whichever jail I'm sent to. A couple of them said they'd be coming to see me themselves.' Another glance at Rebus. 'Isn't that thoughtful?'

Behind the show of bravado, Rebus could tell Ince was terrified. Terrified of the unknown. Every bit as scared as the kids must have been, every time they heard him approaching . . .

'I don't want to scare you, Mr Ince. I want you to help me. But I'm not stupid, I know I have to offer something in return.'

'And what would that be, Inspector?'

Rebus stood up, walked over to where the video camera covered the room.

'You'll notice I'm not taping this,' he said. 'Good reason for that. This stays off the record, Mr Ince. Anything you tell me, it's for my own satisfaction only. Nothing to do with building a case. If I ever tried using it, it would be my word against yours: inadmissible.'

'I know the law, Inspector.'

Rebus turned towards him. 'Me too. What I'm saying is, this is strictly between us. I could get into trouble just for making you an offer.'

'What offer?' Sounding interested now.

'Peterhead, I know a few of the villains up there. I'm owed favours.'

There was silence while Ince digested this. 'You'd put in a word on my behalf?'

'That's right.'

'But they might choose not to heed it.'

Rebus shrugged, sat down again, arms resting along the edge of the desk. 'It's the best I can do.'

'And I only have your word that you'd do it anyway.'

Rebus nodded slowly. 'That's right, you do.'

Ince was studying the backs of his own hands, his fingers gripping the desk.

'Well, I must say, that's a very generous offer.' A touch of humour in the voice.

'It could save your life, Harold.'

'Or it could be totally meaningless.' He paused. 'What is it you want to ask me?'

'I need to know who the third man was.'

'Wasn't it Orson Welles?'

Rebus made himself smile. 'I mean the night Ramsay Marshall brought Darren Rough to Shiellion.'

'Long time ago. I was on the drink back then.'

'You made Darren wear a mask.'

'Did we?'

'Because of the other man. Maybe it was his idea. Didn't want Darren recognising him.' Rebus lit another cigarette. 'You'd been drinking. Maybe with this man. Chatting about this and that. Eventually telling him your secret.' Rebus studied Ince. 'Because you thought you could see something . . .'

Ince licked his lips. 'What?' Said so quietly it was barely above a whisper. Rebus lowered his own voice.

'You thought he was like you. You could see a potential. The more you talked, the clearer you saw it. You told him Marshall was bringing some kid along. Maybe you suggested he stay.'

'You're making this up, aren't you?'

Rebus nodded. 'Insofar as I can't prove any of it, yes, I'm making it up.'

'This potential you speak of . . . I'd contend it's in every one of us.' Now Ince looked at Rebus, and his eyes seemed harder. He held Rebus's gaze, returned it. 'Do you have any children, Inspector?'

'I've a daughter,' Rebus admitted, knowing the danger of letting Ince into his personal life, letting him inside his head. But Ince was no Cary Oakes. 'She's grown up now.'

'I bet at some point in your relationship you've thought about what it would be like to bed her, to have sex with her. Haven't you?'

Rebus could feel the pressure behind his eyes: anger and revulsion. Strong enough to make him blink away the smoke.

'I don't think so.'

Ince grinned. 'That's what you tell yourself. But I think you're lying, even if you don't know it. It's human *instinct*, nothing to be ashamed of. She might have been fifteen, or twelve, or ten.'

Rebus got to his feet. Had to keep moving, otherwise he'd pound Ince's head into the desk. He wanted to light another cigarette, but was only halfway through the current one.

'This isn't about me,' he said. Even to his ears, it sounded weak.

'No? Perhaps . . .'

'It's about Darren Rough.'

'Ah . . .' Ince leaned back on his chair. 'Poor Darren. They had him down on the list of witnesses, but didn't use him. I'd have liked to see him again.'

'Not possible. Someone murdered him.'

'What? Before the trial?'

Rebus shook his head. 'During it. I've been trying to find a motive, only now I think I was looking in all the wrong places.' He rested a hand on the desk, leaned down over Ince. 'I had a look at the charge sheets, the evidence. Just you and Marshall; none of the other victims mention a third abuser. Was it just that one night? Someone who tried it just the once . . . ?' Rebus sat back down in his seat. He'd finished the cigarette at last; lit himself another from its stub, chain-smoking now. 'I found Darren at the zoo. Found out where he lived. It leaked to the newspapers. This third man . . . he knew you weren't going to mention him in court. I don't know why, but I can guess. But the one thing he was scared of was Darren. Which was fine – as far as he knew, Darren

Rough was well out of things. Then suddenly he reads that Darren's here, and he can guess why: Darren's helping with Shiellion. There's half a chance he saw something or heard something, maybe without knowing it. There's half a chance our third man's picture might end up in the paper after the trial, and Darren will recognise it.

'Suddenly there's danger. So he has to strike.' Rebus blew a thin column of smoke at Ince. 'We both know who I'm talking about. But for my own satisfaction, I'd be happier to hear a name.'

'That's why Darren died?'

Rebus nodded. 'I think so.'

'But you've no proof?'

Rebus shook his head. 'And I'm unlikely to find it. With you or without you.'

'I'd like a mug of coffee,' Harold Ince said. 'Milk, two sugars. If you order it, it might come *sans* saliva.'

Rebus looked at him. 'Anything to eat?'

'I'm partial to a chicken korma curry. Nan bread, no rice. Sag aloo as a side dish.'

'I can phone out for it.'

'Again, I'd prefer it unadulterated.' There was confidence in Ince's voice now. He'd made a decision.

'And meantime we'll talk?' Rebus asked.

'For your own peace of mind, Inspector . . . yes, we'll talk.'

49

Rebus sat in the darkness of his living room, sipping from a glass of whisky and water. The street outside was night-time quiet, interrupted by the occasional dull crunching sound of car tyres passing over the setts. He didn't know how long he'd been sitting there, maybe a couple of hours. He'd put a CD on, but hadn't bothered getting up to change it. It had been on the repeat function for three or four plays. 'Stray Cat Blues' had never felt so sordid. It affected him more than the literate and well-mannered 'Sympathy for the Devil', which had an air of desperation to it. There was no desperation in 'Stray Cat Blues', just the certainty of underage sex . . .

When the phone rang, he was slow to answer. It was Siobhan, relaying a message. Patience's flat had been broken into.

'Did they get anyone?'

'No. A couple of uniforms are still there. They're waiting for someone who can deal with the alarm . . .'

Rebus called St Leonard's, and a patrol car arrived to take him to Oxford Terrace. The driver could smell whisky on Rebus's breath.

'Been out partying, sir?'

'Your basic party animal, that's me.' Rebus's tone ensured no more questions came from the front of the car.

The alarm was still ringing. Rebus went down the steps and pushed open the front door. The two uniforms were in the kitchen, far away from the noise. They'd made themselves tea, and were searching the cupboards for biscuits.

'Milk, no sugar,' Rebus told them. Then he went back into the hall and used his key to disable the alarm. One of the uniforms handed him a mug.

'Thank God for that. It was driving us mental.'

Rebus was at the front door, examining it.

'Clean job,' the uniform said. 'Looks like they had a key.'

'More likely he picked it.' Rebus went back into the hall. 'But he couldn't pick the alarm box . . .' He walked from room to room.

'Anything missing, sir?'

'Yes, son: some hot water from the kettle, two tea-bags and a spot of milk.'

'Maybe the alarm scared him off.'

'If he picked one lock, why not another?' Rebus thought he knew the answer: because the very fact the alarm was set had told the intruder something.

Told him no one was home.

And he wanted *someone* to be home – Rebus or Patience – that was the whole point of the exercise. Cary Oakes hadn't broken in with the intention of stealing anything. He'd had other plans altogether . . .

When they left, Rebus reset the alarm and made sure the mortice lock was engaged as well as the Yale.

In the trade, it was known as shutting the stable door.

He got the patrol car to take him home by way of Sammy's. Not that he went into her flat – he just wanted to see everything was OK. She wouldn't be on her own; Ned would be sleeping beside her. Not that Ned would give Oakes many problems . . .

'Do me a favour, will you?' Rebus asked the driver. 'Arrange for a car to come past here once an hour until morning.'

'Will do, sir. You think he'll try it again?'

Rebus didn't even know if Oakes knew Sammy's address. He didn't know if Stevens had known it. He used the car's two-way to talk to the nursing home.

'Quiet as the grave here,' he was told.

Then he tried the hospital, got one of the night staff, who assured him there was someone with Mr Archibald and, yes, they were wide awake. From her description, Rebus guessed it was still Bobby Hogan.

Everyone was safe. Everyone was covered.

The patrol car dropped him off, and he climbed the stairs to his flat. Unlocking the door, he thought he heard a sound on the stairwell below him. He peered over the banister, but couldn't see anything. Mrs Cochrane's tabby probably, rattling the cat-flap as it went in or out.

He closed the door after him, didn't bother with the light in the hallway. He knew it well enough in the dark. Switched the light on in the kitchen and boiled the kettle. His head was thick from the whisky. He made tea, took it through to the living room. Too late for music, really. He walked over to the window and stood there, blowing on the tea.

Saw a shape move. On the pavement across the road. The outline of a man. He cupped his hands to the window, put his face between them, trying to block out the light from the streetlamp.

It was Cary Oakes. He was swaying slightly, like he could hear music. And he had a huge smile on his face. Rebus turned from the window, looked for his phone. Couldn't see it anywhere. He kicked books across the floor. Where the hell was it?

His mobile then: where was that? He'd forgotten to take it with him;

probably in a coat pocket. He went to the hall cupboard: no sign of it. Kitchen? No. Bedroom? Not there either.

Cursing, he ran back to the window to check if Oakes had gone. No, he was still there, only now he had his hands raised, as though in surrender. Then Rebus saw he was holding two small dark objects. He knew what they were.

His cordless phone and his mobile.

'Bastard!' Rebus roared. Oakes had been in the flat; picked the stairwell Yale and the front door.

'Bastard,' Rebus hissed. He ran to the door, yanked it open. He was halfway down the stairs when he heard the main door creaking open. Had it been locked? If so, Oakes had dealt with it quickly.

Suddenly Oakes was there at the foot of the stairwell, backlit by a single bulb on the wall. All the walls were painted a weak-custard yellow, making his face seem jaundiced. His teeth were bared, mouth open to expose his tongue. He dropped the phones on the stone floor, reached into his waistband.

'Remember this?'

He was holding the knife. Purposefully, eyes on Rebus, he started climbing the steps, his feet making the sound of sandpaper on wood.

Rebus turned and ran.

'Where you going, Rebus?' He was laughing, not worried about keeping his voice down. The neighbours were students and old-age pensioners: he probably fancied his luck against the whole lot of them.

Mrs Cochrane had a telephone. Rebus thumped on her door as he passed, knowing it to be a futile gesture. She was stone deaf. The students on his landing: would they have a phone? Would they even be home? He ran in through his own door, shut it after him. The Yale clicked, but he knew it would take more than that to keep Oakes out. He slid the chain across, knew a good kick would probably smash it and the Yale both. Where was the key for the mortice? It was usually in its lock. He looked on the floor, then realised Oakes must have taken it. He'd studied the locks, known the mortice would keep him out . . . Rebus put his eye to the spy-hole. Oakes's face appeared from nowhere. Rebus could hear what he was saying.

'Little pigs, little pigs, let me in.'

Lines from *The Shining*.

Rebus went into the kitchen, opened the cutlery drawer. He found a twelve-inch-long Sabatier with a riveted black handle. He didn't think it had ever been used. He ran his thumb over its blade and cut himself.

It would do.

Rebus had come up against knife attackers before. But he'd been able to reason with most of them. The others, he'd been able to deal with . . . But that was then and this was altogether different. Back out in the hall, he decided to take the fight to Oakes. With the carving-knife in his fist, he slid the chain off, threw open the door. He was expecting an immediate attack, but none came. He craned his neck, couldn't see Oakes on the landing.

'Piggy going walkies.'

Oakes's voice: halfway down to the first landing. Rebus was out of the door, not hurrying, trying to keep calm. Eyes boring into Oakes's, peripheral vision fixed on Oakes's knife.

'Ooh, that *is* a big one,' Oakes mocked. He was moving backwards down the stairs, seeming sure of himself. 'Let's take it outside, Rebus. Let's give it some air.'

He turned and jogged out of the tenement. Rebus thought for a moment. His telephones were lying there. He should pick up his mobile and call in, get officers here pronto. Then he thought of Alan Archibald and Patience and Janice . . . and of his parents' grave. Of Jim Stevens. Time to end it. He had to keep Oakes in his sight, couldn't let him slip away again.

He reached down, pocketed the mobile, and headed for the door.

Oakes was standing on the pavement, nodding.

'That's right. Just the two of us.'

He started walking. Rebus followed. The pace was brisk, without either man ever breaking into a jog. Oakes kept his head angled back towards his pursuer. He looked pleased that things were turning out this way. Rebus couldn't see the logic, but he was wary. So far, Oakes had done nothing without good reason. Bouncing around Rebus's head, the words *Finish it! This is the last round* . . .

'Good for the arteries, an early-morning constitutional. Helps make up for the Scottish diet. I looked in your fridge, man. I had more food in my fucking cell back in Walla Walla. Whisky by the chair in the lounge, though: I have to give you credit for that.' He laughed. 'What are you, Sam Spade or something?'

Rebus said nothing. Oakes was a lot younger than him, and fitter too. Last thing Rebus wanted was to tire himself out yapping.

They were crossing Marchmont Road, heading along Sciennes and past the Sick Kids Hospital. Rebus cursed himself for living in such a quiet area. The pubs had all emptied; the chip shops were closed. There were no clubs, not so much as a massage parlour. Then, on the other side of the road: two young men walking home, knees just locking and no more – the end of a good night's drinking. One of them was demolishing a kebab. They looked at the strange pursuit. Oakes's knife was in his pocket, but Rebus brandished his.

'Call the police!' he called out.

Oakes just laughed, as if his buddy was drunk and joking, waving his rubber dagger around.

One man grinned; the other, the one with kebab sauce on his chin, stared, still chewing.

'I'm not joking!' Rebus shouted, not caring who he woke up. 'Call the cops!'

He couldn't stop to show them ID, couldn't risk letting Oakes out of his sight: there were too many potential victims out there. And he couldn't take his eyes off Oakes for a second.

So they kept moving, leaving the two young men far behind.

'By the time they get home,' Oakes said, 'they'll have forgotten the whole thing. It'll be drinks from the fridge and Jerry Springer on TV. That's how it is these days, Rebus. Nobody gives a shit.'

'Nobody but me.'

'Nobody but you. Ever wondered why that is?'

Rebus shook his head. He didn't mind Oakes talking: while Oakes was talking, he was using up energy.

'You never think about it? It's because you're a fucking dinosaur, man. Everyone knows it – you, your bosses, the people you work with. Probably even your doctor friend. What's with her: she likes to screw prehistoric things?' Oakes laughed again. 'In case you're wondering, I kept fit in the pen. I can bench-press your ass. I can keep this pace up all day and night. How about you? You look about as fit as something extinct.'

'Sometimes all you need is attitude.'

They were cutting through narrow passageways now, coming out on Causewayside.

'Where are we going?'

'Nearly there, Rebus. Wouldn't want to tire you out . . . what's the Scots word again: puggle?' He laughed. There were cars on Causewayside. Rebus made sure they saw him holding the knife. Maybe they'd stop at a phone box or flag down a patrol car. But he knew the odds weren't good – not many patrol cars round here. Probably no foot patrols either. They'd drive home, and then *maybe* they'd phone to report it.

And *maybe* someone from St Leonard's would come to investigate.

It would be too late. Whatever was being played out, he got the feeling it was coming to its conclusion right now. For some reason, it had to do with . . . no . . . he knew where they were. The far end of Salisbury Place: they were at the junction with Minto Street.

'It was here, wasn't it?' Oakes asked, stopping because Rebus had stopped too. 'She was crossing the road or something?'

Sammy . . . crossing the road when the driver hit her. Twenty yards down Minto Street.

Rebus stared at Oakes. 'Why?'

Oakes just shrugged. Rebus was trying to focus again on *this* moment. This was what counted; he could think about Sammy later. He had to stop letting Oakes *play* with him.

'He sent her flying, huh?' Oakes was saying. He had his hands in his pockets, as if they were just stopping to chat. Rebus couldn't remember which pocket the knife was in. His own weapon hung from his right hand, useless for the moment. Crossing the road and she . . . she never had a chance.

He realised he hadn't been here since the day after the collision. He'd been avoiding the place.

And somehow Oakes had known the effect this place would have on him. Rebus blinked a few times, tried clearing his head.

'You've been to check on her, haven't you?' Oakes asked.

'What?' Rebus narrowed his eyes.

'You went to your girlfriend's flat, knew I'd been there. Next thing you did was go to your daughter's. But you didn't go in, did you?'

It was like staring into a devil's eyes. 'How do you know?'

'You wouldn't be here otherwise.'

'Why not?'

'Because I've *been* there, Rebus. Earlier tonight.'

'You're lying.' Rebus's voice was dry, his throat acrid. *Trying to get you off your guard, same trick worked with Archibald . . .*

Oakes just shrugged. They were at the corner. Diagonally across from them, two cars had drawn up side by side at a red light. Taxi on the inside lane; boy racer revving beside him. The taxi driver was watching what looked like a fight about to break out: nothing he hadn't seen before.

'You're lying,' Rebus repeated. He slipped his free hand into his pocket, brought out the mobile. Used his thumb to press the digits, holding the phone to his face so he could watch it and Oakes at the same time.

'She didn't need her legs anyway,' Oakes was saying. The phone was ringing. 'There's no answer, is there?'

Sweat was trickling into Rebus's eyes. But if he shook his head to clear the drops, Oakes would think he was answering his question.

The phone stopped ringing.

'Hello?' Ned Farlowe's voice.

'Ned! Is Sammy there? Is she all right?'

'What? Is that you, John?'

'*Is she all right?*' Knowing the answer; needing to hear it anyway.

'Of course she's—'

Oakes flew at him, the knife emerging from his right-hand pocket. Missing Rebus's chest by centimetres. Rebus stepped back, dropped the phone. He had the longer reach. The taxi driver had his window down.

'Cut that out, the pair of you!'

'I'll cut it out all right,' Oakes hissed. 'I'll dice it and slice it.' He made another sweep with the knife. Rebus tried to kick it away, almost lost his footing. Oakes laughed at him. 'You're no Nureyev, pal.' A quick thrust took the knife into Rebus's arm. Rebus felt his nerves go dull: prelude to agony. *Finish it.*

Rebus took a step forward, feinted with the knife, so that Oakes had to move position. On the edge of the pavement now. Rebus saw the traffic lights behind Oakes were changing. Oakes leaned forward, slashed at his chest. Thin whistling sound as Rebus's shirt split. Blood warm on his arm, more blood trickling from the fresh wound. Red to red/amber.

To green.

Rebus charged in with his foot up and hit Oakes solid in the chest with his sole. Oakes got in a swipe before he was propelled back into the road, where the boy racer, oblivious to the fight, radio on full-blast and his girl with her arm around him, was showing off his car's acceleration from a flat start. The car clipped Oakes, sent him flying, breaking his hip and, Rebus hoped, a few more bones to boot. The car screeched to a halt, the young man's head appeared through the window. He saw knives. He pulled his foot off the clutch and roared off.

Rebus didn't bother to catch the licence plate. He stood on Oakes's knife-hand, forcing the fingers open, then lifted the knife and pocketed it. The taxi driver was still at the lights.

'Phone for police assistance!' Rebus called to him. He held his injured arm to his chest.

Oakes was rolling on the ground, hand to his thigh and side, teeth bared not in a grin now but in a grimace of pain.

Rebus stood up, took a step back, and kicked him in the groin. As Oakes groaned and retched, Rebus gave him another kick, then crouched down again.

'I'd like to say that was for Jim Stevens,' he said. 'But if I'm being entirely honest with you, really it was for me.'

Rebus spent an hour in the casualty department – four stitches to his arm, eight to his chest. The arm wound was deepest, but both were clean. Oakes was somewhere nearby, being treated for breaks and fractures. Six of Crime Squad's finest on guard detail.

A patrol car took Rebus back to his flat, where he retrieved his cordless phone – didn't want any of the students pocketing it – and had a mouthful of whisky. Then another after that.

The rest of the night he spent at St Leonard's, typing his report one-handed, giving an additional verbal briefing to Chief Superintendent Watson, who'd been summoned from bed and whose hair sported a cow's-lick which flapped when he moved his head.

There was little certainty that Oakes could be charged with Jim Stevens' murder. It would depend on forensic evidence: fingerprints, fibres, saliva. Stevens' cassette had been bagged and handed over to the white-coat brigade.

'But he'll go down for the attack on me and Alan Archibald?' Rebus asked his superior.

Farmer Watson nodded. 'For the Pentland attack, yes.'

'What about the attempted murder of three hours ago?'

The Farmer shuffled paperwork. 'You've said yourself, most of the witnesses will have seen *you* with the knife, not him.'

'But the taxi driver . . .'

The Farmer nodded. 'He'll be crucial. Let's hope he gets his story straight.'

Rebus saw what his boss was getting at. 'Sir, you do believe I acted in self-defence?'

'Of course, John. Goes without saying.' But the Farmer wouldn't meet his eyes.

Rebus tried to think of something to say; decided it wasn't worth his breath.

'Crime Squad are pissed off,' the Farmer added with a smile. 'They hate an anti-climax.'

'I might not look it, but inside I'm crying for them.' Rebus turned to leave the room.

'No going back to the hospital, John,' the Farmer warned. 'Don't want him falling out of bed and saying he was pushed.'

Rebus snorted, went downstairs and into the car park. It would be growing light soon. He dry-swallowed some more painkillers, lit a cigarette and stared in the direction of Holyrood Park. They were there – Arthur's Seat, Salisbury Crags – it was just, you couldn't always see them. It didn't mean they weren't there.

Easy to lose your footing in the dark . . . Easy for someone to come up behind you . . .

Rebus left the car park and headed into St Leonard's Bank. Stevens' car had been taken away for examination at Howdenhall. At the end of the road, there was a gap in the fence, allowing passage into the park itself. Rebus headed down the slope towards Queen's Drive. Once across it, he started to climb. Away from the street-lighting now, his steps were more tentative. He sensed more than saw the starting-point of Radical Road, above which loomed the irregular rockface of the Crags themselves. Rebus ignored the path, kept climbing until he was on top of the Crags, the city spread out below him in a grid of orange sodium and yellow-white halogen. The beast was definitely beginning to awake: cars heading into the city. Turning round, he saw that the sky was a lighter shade of black than the mass of rock below it. Some people said Arthur's Seat looked like a crouched lion, ready to pounce. It never did pounce, though. There was a lion on the Scottish flag too – not crouched but rampant . . .

Had Jim Margolies come up here with the express intention of leaping off? Rebus thought he knew the answer now. And he knew because of the Margolies' dinner engagement that evening, across the park from where they lived.

That, and the fact of a white saloon car . . .

50

Dr Joseph Margolies lived with his wife in a detached house in Gullane, with an uninterrupted view of Muirfield golf course. Rebus didn't play golf. He'd tried a few times as a kid, dragging a half-set of clubs around his local course, losing half a dozen balls in Jamphlars Pond. He knew some of his colleagues had taken up the game thinking it would help their careers, making sure to concede defeat to their superiors.

That didn't sound like a game to Rebus.

Siobhan Clarke parked the car, and switched off the radio news. It was ten in the morning. Rebus had managed a couple of hours' shut-eye in his Arden Street flat, and had phoned Patience to let her know Cary Oakes was behind bars.

'Stay in the car,' he told Clarke, manoeuvring himself out of the door. Not easy with one arm strapped up and his chest giving him grief every time he stretched.

Mrs Margolies answered the door. Close up, she resembled her son. Same flat chin, same narrow eyes. She even had the same smile.

Rebus introduced himself and asked if he could have a word with her husband.

'He's in the greenhouse. Is there a problem, Inspector?'

He smiled at her. 'No problem, madam. Just a couple of questions, that's all.'

'I'll show you the way,' she said, standing back to let him in. She'd glanced at his arm, but wasn't going to comment on it. Some people were like that: didn't like to ask questions . . . As he followed her down the corridor, he glanced through open doorways, seeing domestic order everywhere: knitting on a chair; magazines in a paper-rack; dusted ornaments; gleaming windows. The house dated from the 1930s. From the outside, it seemed to be all eaves and gables. Rebus asked her how long they'd lived there.

'Over forty years,' Mrs Margolies replied, proud of the fact.

So this was the house Jim Margolies had grown up in. And his sister too. From the notes, Rebus knew she'd committed suicide in the family bathroom. Often, in a situation like that, the families elected to sell up and move somewhere new. But he knew other families would elect to stay, because something of their loved one still remained in the home, and would be lost forever if they abandoned it.

The kitchen was tidy too, not so much as a cup and saucer drying on the draining-board. A message-list had been fixed to the fridge with a magnet in the shape of a teapot. But the list remained blank. Mrs Margolies asked him if he'd like some tea. He shook his head.

'I'm fine, thanks anyway.' Still smiling, but studying her. Thinking: *The wife often knows* . . . Thinking: *Some people just don't ask questions* . . .

Outside the kitchen door was a short hall with two walk-in cupboards – both open to display garden tools – and the back door, which also stood open. They stepped outside and into a walled garden, obviously much worked-on. There was a rockery, and next to it some flowerbeds. These were separated by a trimmed lawn from a long, narrow vegetable bed. Towards the bottom of the garden were trees and bushes, and tucked away in one corner a small greenhouse with a figure moving around inside.

Rebus turned to his guide. 'Thank you, I'll be fine.'

And he walked across the lawn. It was like walking across luxury Wilton. He looked back once, saw Mrs Margolies watching him from the doorway. In a neighbouring garden, someone was having a bonfire. Smoke crackled over the wall, white and pungent. Rebus walked through it as he neared the greenhouse. A black labrador pricked up its ears at his approach, then pushed itself up to sitting and gave a half-hearted bark. Its nose and whiskers were grey, and it had about it a pampered look: overfed and, in its declining years, underexercised. The door of the greenhouse slid open and an elderly man peered through half-moon glasses at his visitor. Tall, grey hair, black moustache – just the way Jamie Brady had described him: the man who'd gone to Greenfield looking for Darren Rough.

'Yes? Can I help you?'

'Dr Margolies, I'm Detective Inspector John Rebus.'

Margolies held up his hands. 'You'll forgive me for not shaking.' The hands were blackened with soil.

'Me too,' Rebus said, gesturing to his arm.

'Looks nasty. What happened?' Not sharing his wife's reticence. But then maybe she'd had half a lifetime of biting back questions. Rebus leaned down to rub the labrador's head. Its heavy tail thumped the ground in appreciation.

'Got into a fight,' Rebus explained.

'Line of duty, eh? We've met before, I think.'

'Hannah's competition.'

'Ah, yes.' Nodding slowly. 'You wanted to speak to Ama.'

'I did then, yes.'

'Is this something to do with her?' Margolies was retreating back into the greenhouse. Rebus followed, and saw that the old man was potting seedlings. It was warm in the greenhouse, despite the day being overcast. Margolies asked Rebus to close the door.

'Keep the heat in,' he explained.

Rebus slid the door shut. Most of the available space was taken up with work surfaces, trays of seedlings laid along them in rows. A bag of potting compost lay open on the ground. Dr Margolies was scooping a black plastic flowerpot into it.

'How does it feel to get away with murder?' Rebus asked.

'I'm sorry?' Margolies took a seedling, pushed it into its new pot.

'You murdered Darren Rough.'

'Who?'

Rebus took the pot from Margolies' fingers. 'It's going to be a devil trying to prove it. In fact, I don't think it will happen. I really do think you've got away with it.'

Margolies met his eyes, reached to take his pot back.

'I'm sorry,' he said. 'I haven't the faintest idea what you're talking about.'

'You were seen in Greenfield. You were asking about Darren Rough. Then off you drove in your white Mercedes. A white saloon car was seen in Holyrood Park around the time Darren was killed. I think he went there for sanctuary, but you found it an ideal site for a murder.'

'These riddles, Inspector . . . Do you know who I am?'

'I know exactly who you are. I know both your children committed suicide. I know you were part of the Shiellion set-up.'

'I beg your pardon?' A slight trembling in the voice now. A seedling slipped from parchment fingers.

'Don't worry, Harold Ince is going to keep his side of the bargain. He talked to me, but it wouldn't be admissible, and he won't tell anyone else. He told me you were at Shiellion that night. Ince had talked with you often, had come to know you. He'd told you what he did to the kids in his care. He *knew* you wouldn't say anything, because the two of you were alike. He knew how useful it would be to him if a doctor, the man responsible for examining the children, were part of the whole enterprise.' Rebus leaned close to Margolies' ear. 'He told me *all* of it, Dr Margolies.'

The after-hours drinking, loosening up the doctor. Then the arrival of Ramsay Marshall with a fresh new kid, Darren Rough. Making the kid wear a blindfold so he wouldn't recognise Margolies – this at the doctor's insistence. Sweating and trembling . . . knowing this night changed everything . . .

And afterwards: self-loathing perhaps; or maybe just fear of exposure. He hadn't been able to cope, had feigned ill-health, opting for early retirement.

'But you could never loose Ince's grip on you. He'd been blackmailing you, him and Marshall both.' Rebus's voice was little more than a whisper, his lips almost touching the old man's ear. 'Know what? I'm so fucking *glad* he's been sucking you dry all these years.' Rebus stood back.

'You don't know anything.' Margolies' face was blood-red. Beneath the checked shirt, he was breathing hard.

'I can't *prove* anything, but that's not quite the same thing. I *know*, and that's what matters. I think your daughter found out. The shame of it killed her. You were always the first one awake in the morning; she knew *you'd* be the one to find her. And then somehow Jim found out, and he couldn't live with it either. How come *you* can live with it, Dr Margolies? How come you can live with the deaths of both your children, and the murder of Darren Rough?'

Margolies lifted a gardening fork, held it to Rebus's throat. His face was squeezed into a mask of anger and frustration. Beads of perspiration dripped from his forehead. And outside, the billowing smoke seemed to be cutting them off from everything.

Margolies didn't say anything, just made sounds from behind gritted teeth. Rebus stood there, hand in pocket.

'What?' he said. 'You're going to kill me too?' He shook his head. 'Think about it. Your wife's seen me. There's another officer waiting for me out front. How will you talk your way out of it? No, Dr Margolies, you're not going to kill me. Like I say, I can't prove anything I've just said. It's between you and me.' Rebus lifted the hand from his pocket, pushed the fork aside. The black lab was watching through the door, seemed to sense all was not well. It frowned at Rebus, looking disappointed in him.

'What do you want?' Margolies spluttered, gripping the work-bench with both hands.

'I want you to live the rest of your life knowing that I know.' Rebus shrugged. 'That's all.'

'You want me to kill myself?'

Rebus laughed. 'I don't think you've got it in you. You're an old man, you're going to die soon enough. Once you're dead, maybe Ince and Marshall will rethink their loyalty to you. You won't be left with any reputation at all.'

Margolies turned towards him, and now there was clear, focused hatred in his eyes.

'Of course,' Rebus said, 'if any evidence does turn up, you can be assured I'll be back here at the double. You might be celebrating the millennium, you might be getting your card from the Queen, and then you'll see me walking through the door.' He smiled. 'I'll never be very far away, Dr Margolies.'

He slid open the greenhouse door, manoeuvred his way past the dog. Walked away.

It didn't feel like any sort of victory. Unless something turned up, there'd be no justice for Darren Rough, no public trial. But Rebus knew he'd done what he could. Mrs Margolies was in the kitchen, making no pretence of doing anything other than waiting for him to return.

'Everything all right?' she asked.

'Fine, Mrs Margolies.' He headed down the hall, making for the front door. She was right behind him.

'Well, I just was wondering . . .'

Rebus opened the door, turned to her. 'Why not ask your husband, Mrs Margolies?'

The wife often knows, never brings herself to ask.

'Just one thing, Mrs Margolies . . . ?'

'Yes?'

Your husband's a cold-blooded murderer. His mouth opened and closed, but no words came. He shook his head, started down the garden path.

Clarke drove him to Katherine Margolies' house, in the Grange area of Edinburgh. It was a three-storey Georgian semi in a street half of whose homes had been turned into bed-and-breakfast establishments. The white Merc was parked in front of the gate. Rebus turned to Clarke.

'I know,' she said: 'stay in the car.'

Katherine Margolies looked less than thrilled to see him.

'What do you want?' She seemed ready to keep him on the doorstep.

'It's about your husband's suicide.'

'What about it?' Her face was narrow and hard, hands long and thin like butcher's knives.

'I think I know why he did it.'

'And what makes you think *I'd* want to know?'

'You already do know, Mrs Margolies.' Rebus took a deep breath. Well, if she didn't mind them talking like this on her doorstep . . . 'When did he find out his father was a paedophile?'

Her eyes widened. A woman emerged from the neighbouring house, preparing to walk her Jack Russell terrier. 'You better come in,' Katherine Margolies said sharply, eyes darting up and down the street. After he walked in, she closed the door and stood with her back to it, arms folded.

'Well?' she said.

Rebus looked around. The hall had a grey marble floor veined with black lines. A stone staircase swept upwards. There were paintings on the walls: Rebus got the feeling they weren't prints. She didn't seem to have noticed his arm, had no interest in him that way.

'Hannah not home?' he asked.

'She's at school. Look, I don't know what it is—'

'Then I'll tell you. It's been gnawing at me, Jim's death. And I'll tell you why. I've been there myself, standing at the top of a very high place, wondering if I'd have the guts to jump off.'

Her face softened a little.

'Usually it was the booze doing it,' he went on. 'These days, I think I've got that under control. But I learned two things. One, you have to be incredibly brave to pull it off. Two, there's got to be some crunch reason for you not to go on living. See, when it comes to it, going on living is the easier of the two options. I couldn't see any reason why Jim would take his life, no reason at all. But there had to be one. That's what got to me. There *had* to be one.'

'And now you think you've found it?' Her eyes were liquid in the cool dimness of the hall.

'Yes.'

'And you felt it worth sharing with me?'

He shook his head. 'All I need from you is confirmation that I'm right.'

'And then you'll have contentment?' She waited till he'd nodded. 'And what right do you have to that, Inspector Rebus? What gives you the right to sleep easy?'

'I never find sleep very easy, Mrs Margolies.' It seemed to him then – and maybe it was a trick of the light – that he was seeing her at the end of a long dark tunnel, so that while she stood out clearly, everything between and around them was a blur of indistinct shading. And things were moving and gathering on the periphery: the ghosts. They were all here, providing a ready-made audience. Jack Morton, Jim Stevens, Darren Rough . . . even Jim Margolies. They felt so alive to him he could scarcely believe Katherine Margolies couldn't make them out.

'The night Jim died,' Rebus went on, 'you'd been out to dinner with friends in Royal Park Terrace. I wondered about that . . . Royal Park Terrace to The Grange.'

'What about it?' Looking bored now more than anything. Rebus thought it was bravado.

'Easiest route is to cut through Holyrood Park. Is that the way you drove home?'

'I suppose so.'

'In your white Mercedes?'

'Yes.'

'And Jim stopped the car, got out . . .'

'No.'

'Someone saw the car.'

'No.'

'Because something had been making his life hell, something he'd maybe just discovered about his father . . .'

'No.'

Rebus took a step towards her. 'It was bucketing down that night. He wouldn't have gone out walking. That's your version, Mrs Margolies: in the middle of the night he got up, got dressed, and went out walking. He walked all the way to Salisbury Crags in the rain, just so he could throw himself off.' Rebus was shaking his head. 'My version makes more sense.'

'Maybe to you.'

'I'm not about to go shouting from the chimney-pots, Mrs Margolies. I just need to know that that's how it happened. He'd been talking to one of the Shiellion victims. He found out his father was involved in the Shiellion abuse and he was afraid it would come out, afraid the shame would rebound on to him.'

She exploded. 'Christ, you couldn't be more wrong! It had nothing to do with that. What's any of this got to do with Shiellion?'

Rebus collected himself. 'You tell me.'

'Don't you see?' She was crying now. 'It was Hannah . . .'

Rebus frowned. 'Hannah?'

'Hannah was his sister's name. Our Hannah was named after her. Jim did it to get back at his father.'

'Because Dr Margolies had . . .' Rebus couldn't bring himself to say the word. 'With Hannah?'

She rubbed the back of her hand across her face, smudging mascara. 'He interfered with his own daughter. God knows whether it was just once. It might have been going on for years. When she killed herself . . .'

'She did so knowing who'd be first to find her?'

She nodded. 'Jim knew what had happened . . . knew why she'd done it. But of course nobody ever talks about it.' She looked at him. 'You just don't, do you? Not in polite society. Instead he tried shutting it out, accepting that there was no remedy.'

'I'm not sure I understand.' But he understood something, knew now why Jim had beaten up Darren Rough. Displaced anger: he hadn't been hitting Rough; he'd been hitting his father.

She slid down the door until she was crouching, arms hugging her knees. Rebus lowered himself on to the bottom step of the staircase, tried to make sense of it: Joseph Margolies had abused his own daughter . . . what would have made him turn to a boy like Darren Rough? Ince's insistence, perhaps; or simple lust and curiosity, the thought of more forbidden fruit . . .

Katherine Margolies' voice was calm again. 'I think Jim joined the police as another way of telling his father something, telling him he'd never forget, never forgive.'

'But if he knew all along about his father, why did he kill himself?'

'I've told you! Because of Hannah.'

'His sister?'

She gave a wild, humourless laugh. 'Of course not.' Paused for breath. 'Our daughter, Inspector. I mean Hannah, our daughter. Jim had . . . he'd been worried for some time.' She took a deep breath. 'I'd noticed he wasn't sleeping. I'd wake in the night and he'd be lying there in the darkness, eyes open, staring at the ceiling. One night he told me. He felt I ought to know.'

'What was he worried about?'

'That he was turning into his father. That there was some genetic component, something he had no control over.'

'You mean Hannah?'

She nodded. 'He said he tried not to have the thoughts, but they came anyway. He looked at her and no longer saw his daughter.' Her eyes were on the pattern in the floor. 'He saw something else, something to be desired . . .'

Finally Rebus saw it. Saw all Jim Margolies' fears, saw the past which had haunted him and the expectation of recurrence. Saw why the man had turned to young-looking prostitutes. Saw the dread of history. *Not in polite society*. If families like the Margolies and the Petries represented polite society, Rebus wanted nothing to do with it.

'He'd been quiet all evening,' Katherine Margolies went on. 'Once or twice I caught him looking at Hannah, and I could see how scared he was.' She rubbed the palm of either hand over her eyes, looked up to the ceiling, demanding something more from it than the comfort of cornice and chandelier. The noise that escaped from her throat was like something from a caged animal.

'On the way home, he stopped the car and ran. I went after him, and he was just standing there. At first, I didn't realise he was at the very edge of the Crags. He must have heard me. Next thing, he'd vanished. It was like a stunt, something a stage magician would do. Then I realised what it was. He'd jumped. I felt . . . well, I don't know what I felt. Numb, betrayed, shocked.' She shook her head, unsure even now what her feelings were towards the man who had killed himself rather than give in to his most feral craving. 'I walked back to the car. Hannah was asking where her daddy was. I said he'd gone for a walk. I drove us home. I didn't go down to help him. I didn't do anything. Christ knows why.' Now she ran her hands through her hair.

Rebus got up, pushed open a door. It led into a formal dining room. Decanters on a polished sideboard. He sniffed one, poured a large glass of whisky. Took it through to the hall and handed it to Katherine Margolies. Went back to fetch another for himself. He saw the sequence now: Jane Barbour telling Jim that Rough was coming back to town; Jim dusting off the case, becoming intrigued by the third man. Knowing his father had been working in children's homes. Wanting to know, quizzing Darren Rough, his world collapsing in on him . . .

'You know,' his widow was saying, 'Jim wasn't scared of dying. He said there was a coachman.'

'Coachman?'

'He took you to wherever it was you went when you died.' She looked up at him. 'Do you know that story?'

Rebus nodded. 'An old Edinburgh ghost story, that's all it is.'

'You don't believe in ghosts then?'

'I wouldn't say that necessarily.' He raised his glass. 'Here's to Jim,' he said. When he looked around, there wasn't a ghost to be seen.

51

A week later, Rebus received a phone call from Brian Mee.

'What's up, Brian?' Rebus already guessing from the tone of voice.

'Ah, shite, John, she's left me.'

'I'm sorry to hear that, Brian.'

'Are you?' There was a hint of disbelief in the laugh that followed.

'I really am, I'm sorry.'

'She told you, though?'

'In a roundabout sort of way.' Rebus paused. 'So do you know where she is?'

'Cut the crap, John. She's at your flat.'

'What?'

'You heard me. She's biding with you.'

'First I've heard of it.'

'She doesn't know anybody else over there.'

'There are bed and breakfasts, rooms to rent . . .'

'You're not putting her up?'

'You've got my word for it.'

There was a long silence on the line. 'Christ, man, I'm sorry. I'm off my head with worry here.'

'Only to be expected, Brian.'

'Think it's worth my while coming to look for her?'

Rebus exhaled. 'What do you think?'

'I think she used to love me.'

'But not any more?'

'She wouldn't have left otherwise.'

'True enough.'

'Even if she finds Damon, I don't think she's coming back.'

'Give her some time, Brian.'

'Aye, sure.' Brian Mee sniffed. 'Know something? I used to like it that folk called me Barney. I know how I got the name, you know.'

'I thought you said you didn't?'

'Oh aye, but I know all the same. Barney Rubble. Because folk thought I was like him. Somebody said it to me once, not just "Barney" but "Barney Rubble".'

Rebus smiled. 'But you liked the name anyway?'

'I didn't say that. I said I liked that I had a nickname. It was a sort of identity, wasn't it? And that's better than nothing.'

Rebus's smile stretched. He was seeing Barney Mee, the tough little battler, wading in to save Mitch. The years separating the present from that long-ago event seemed to fall away. It was as if the two could live side by side, the past a ghostly presence forever of the here and now. Nothing lost; nothing forgotten; redemption always a possibility.

But if that was true, how could he explain that Dr Margolies would never see a court of law, his crimes known only to the few? And how to explain that the Procurator Fiscal seemed able to prosecute Cary Oakes only for the attempted murder of Alan Archibald? All the forensic evidence connecting him to Jim Stevens could be explained away: fingerprints and fibres in Stevens' car – Oakes had ridden in it before. Hell, three police officers had watched him being driven away from the airport in it. The Stevens file would be kept open, but no one would be investigating. Everyone knew who'd done it. But short of a confession, there was nothing they could do.

'Let's stick to our strongest suit,' the fiscal depute had said. This meant discarding the attack on Rebus, too, even though the taxi driver had been willing to testify.

'Too many possible arguments for the defence,' the fiscal depute had said. Rebus tried not to take it personally. He knew prosecution was a game all to itself, where the best player might lose, the cheat prosper. He knew it was the job of the police to investigate and present the facts. It was the job of lawyers like Richie Cordover to then twist everything around until they could persuade juries and witnesses that Celtic fans sang 'The Sash' and Cowdenbeath was an ideal holiday location.

'Hey, John?' Brian Mee was saying.

'Yes, Barney?'

Brian laughed at that. 'What about coming through some weekend, just you and me, eh? Double-act at the karaoke, and see if we can dust off some chat-up lines.'

'Sounds tempting, Barney. I'll give you a bell some time.' Both men knowing he wouldn't.

'Right then, that's you on a promise.'

'Cheers, Barney.'

'Bye, John. It was good to catch up with you . . .'

Another paedophile had been released from prison, this time in Glasgow. GAP had organised a bus and headed off for Renfrew, where he was rumoured to be holed up. Some of the younger males in the company had gone for a night on the town, which had ended with a full-scale battle raging through the streets.

It was hoped, at least in some quarters, that the resulting negative publicity would sound the organisation's death knell. But Van Brady was still giving interviews and getting her picture in the papers, still applying to the Lottery for funding. Journalists liked that she talked almost exclusively in sound-bites, even if half of them had to be toned down for publication.

There was a memorial service for Jim Stevens. Rebus went along. He suspected that in his day Stevens had probably fallen out with at least three-quarters of the mourners. But there were eulogies and sombre faces, and Rebus couldn't help feeling that Jim wouldn't have wanted it that way. Afterwards, he held a little wake of his own in the Oxford Bar's back room with three or four of the loudest, rudest, and funniest hacks around. They drank till well after midnight, their laughter almost drowning out the music from the ceilidh band in the corner.

Rebus stumbled down the road to Oxford Terrace, dumped his clothes in the washing basket and had a shower.

'You still reek,' Patience told him as he climbed into bed.

'I'm keeping up traditions,' Rebus said. 'Edinburgh's not called "Auld Reekie" for nothing.'

He thought it curious that Cal Brady should want to speak to him. Cal was out on bail, awaiting trial for various offences against the person on the night of the Renfrew stramash. The morning phone call was so unexpected, Rebus walked out of the station without telling anyone where he was going. They met up on Radical Road. Cal had wanted somewhere not too far from home, but not a cop-shop, somewhere they could talk without anyone hearing.

The wind was flying, stinging Rebus's ears. There were occasional blasts of sunshine as the fast-moving clouds broke, only to blot out the sun again moments later. Cal Brady had deep bruises beneath both eyes, and a burst lip. His left hand sported a bandage and he seemed to limp ever so slightly as he walked.

'Bad one, was it?' Rebus asked.

'Those weegies . . .' Cal shook his head.

'I thought it was Renfrew?'

'Renfrew, Glasgow . . . all the same, man. Mad bastards, each and every one. Their idea of a square go is to rip your face off with their teeth.' He shivered, pulled his denim jacket tighter around him.

'You could button it up,' Rebus told him.

'Eh?'

'The jacket . . . if you're cold.'

'Aye, but it looks stupid when you do that. Levi jackets are only cool when they're open.' Rebus had no answer to that. 'I hear you got a bit of a scrape yourself.'

Rebus looked at his arm. No sling now, just a taped compress. Another week or so, the stitches would dissolve. 'What did you want to see me for, Cal?'

'These fucking charges.'

'What about them?'

'I'll probably end up going down, record I've got.'

'So?'

'So, I could do without it.' He twitched a shoulder. 'Gonny help me out?'

'You mean put in a good word?'

'Aye.'

Rebus stuck his hands in his pockets, as if relaxing. In truth, he'd been on his guard ever since arriving at the meeting-point five minutes before Brady: on the lookout for traps or a possible ambush. Lessons learned from Cary Oakes. 'Why should I do that?' he asked.

'Look, I'm no fucking snitch, right?'

Rebus nodded agreement, as seemed to be expected.

'But I hear things.' He paused. 'Try not to, but sometimes I can't help it.'

'Such as?'

'So you'll put a word in?'

Rebus stopped walking. He seemed to be admiring the vista. 'I could tell them you're one of mine. I could make you sound important.'

'But I wouldn't *be* your grass, right? That's the crux.'

Rebus nodded. 'But you've got something to trade?'

Cal looked around, as if even here he might be overheard. When he lowered his voice, Rebus had to move close to him to hear what he was saying over the noise of the wind.

'You know I work for Mr Mackenzie?'

'You're his enforcer.'

Brady prickled at that. 'Sometimes he's owed money. Happens to a lot of businesses.'

'Sure.'

'I make sure his debtors know the risks they're taking.'

Rebus smiled. 'A nice way of putting it.'

Brady looked around again. 'Petrie,' he said, like this would explain everything.

'I know,' Rebus said. 'Nicky Petrie owed Charmer money, got beaten up in lieu of a final reminder.'

But Brady was shaking his head. 'It was his sister owed the money.'

'Ama?' Brady nodded. 'So why thump Nicky?'

Brady snorted. 'She's a cold, hard bitch. Maybe you haven't noticed. But she likes her little brother. She *loves* little Nicky . . .'

'So you were sending the message to her?' Rebus thought about it, remembered something Ama had said to him at the beauty contest: *Who do I owe money to?* 'Why didn't she get the money from her father?'

'Story is, she wouldn't ask him for the time of day, and he wouldn't give it to her if he'd a watch on either arm.'

'I still don't know what this has to do with me.'

'That flat of theirs.'

'What about it?'

'*She* lives there. The blonde you were looking for.'

Rebus stared at Brady. 'She's in that flat?' Brady was nodding. 'What's her name?'

'I think it's Nicola.'

'How do you know all this?'

Brady shrugged. 'They can't help talking, that little gang.'

Rebus thought of the scene on the boat . . . the way the drunk had been about to say something until warned off by Ama Petrie . . .

'They know about this Nicola?'

'They *all* know.'

Which meant they'd all lied to Rebus . . . including the brother and sister, Nicky and Ama.

'Is she Nicky's girlfriend?'

Brady shrugged again.

'Or Ama's maybe?'

'I don't get involved,' Brady said, waving his hand as though to cut the discussion dead.

'How about you, Cal? Still living with Joanna?'

'Nothing to do with you.'

'How's Billy Boy? Don't you think he'd be better off with his dad?'

'That's not what Joanna wants.'

'Has anyone asked Billy what *he* wants?'

Brady's voice rose. 'He's just a kid. How's he supposed to know what's best for him?'

'I bet when you were his age you knew what you wanted.'

'Maybe,' Brady conceded after a moment's thought. 'But I'll give you odds-on I didn't get it.' He laughed. 'Maybe I'm *still* not getting it. Know what I think about that?'

'What?'

'Just watch.'

And Rebus did watch, as Cal Brady unzipped his fly, took out his penis, and began to urinate off the edge of Radical Road. Standing well back from the performance, it seemed to Rebus that he was pissing on Holyrood and Greenfield and St Leonard's, pissing in a giant arc over the whole city.

And if Rebus had been able, at that exact moment he might have joined him.

52

Returning to St Leonard's with Siobhan Clarke after a call-out, Rebus made a detour to the New Town. Clarke knew better than to ask why: he'd tell her in his own good time and not before.

It was late afternoon, and he sat kerbside, indicators flashing, wondering about Nicky Petrie. To pay a visit, or not to pay a visit? Would the girlfriend be there? Would Petrie string together another series of lies and half-truths? Clarke was about to open her mouth to say something when she saw his hands tighten on the steering-wheel.

A woman was coming down the steps from Petrie's building. Rebus saw for the first time that a taxi was waiting. She stepped into it. He'd caught only a glimpse of her: tall, willowy. A blonde pageboy cut. Black dress and tights beneath a billowing black wool coat. Rebus switched off the indicators, made to follow the cab, started explaining the situation to Clarke.

'Where do you think she's going?'

'Only one way to find out.'

The taxi headed towards Princes Street, crossed it and crawled up The Mound. Through traffic lights at the top and took a right down Victoria Street. Grassmarket was the destination. Nicola paid the driver, got out. She looked around, somewhat uncertainly. Her face was like a mask.

'Bit heavy on the make-up,' Clarke commented. Rebus was trying to find a parking space. Finding none, he left the car on a single yellow line. If he got a ticket, it could join the others in the glove compartment.

'Where did she go?' he asked, getting out of the car.

'Down Cowgate, I think,' Clarke said.

'Hell does she want down there?'

While Grassmarket itself had been gentrified, the area immediately to the east was still Hostel City: a place the city's dispossessed could, for the moment, call its own. Things would doubtless be different once the politicians moved in down the road.

They stood on street corners, or sat on the steps of disused churches – baggy-trousered and grim-bearded, with too few teeth, and stooped backs. As Rebus and Clarke rounded the corner, they saw that the woman was walking with exaggerated slowness through a phalanx of admirers, only a smattering of whom bothered asking her for spare change and cigarettes.

'Likes to show off,' Clarke said.

'And not too fussy with it.'

'Just one thing bothering me, sir . . .'

But Nicola had turned to acknowledge a wolf-whistle, and as she did so she saw them. She turned again quickly and upped her pace, keeping a tight hold of her zebra-skin shoulder-bag.

'Not the world's greatest surveillance,' Clarke said.

'She knows us,' Rebus hissed. They broke into a trot, ran along the pavement below George IV Bridge. She wore flat-heeled shoes, ran well despite the tangle of her long coat. She found a gap in the traffic and darted across the road. Cowgate was horrible: a narrow canyon, with high-sided buildings. When traffic built up, the carbon monoxide had no place to go. The stitches in Rebus's chest slowed him down.

'Guthrie Street,' Clarke said. That was where Nicola was headed. It would bring her up on to Chambers Street, where she could more easily lose her pursuers. But as she turned into the steep wynd, she bumped into someone. The collision sent her spinning. Something fell to the ground, but she kept running. Rebus paused to scoop it up. A short blonde wig.

'What the hell?'

'That's what I was trying to tell you, sir,' Clarke said. Ahead of them, Nicola was tiring, holding the wall for support as she hauled herself up the incline. Limping, too, an ankle twisted in the collision. Eventually, just as she reached Chambers Street, her hair short and merely fair now rather than blonde, she gave up, stood with her back to the wall, panting noisily. Perspiration was streaking the make-up. Behind the mask, Rebus saw someone he knew only too well.

Not Nicola, Nicky. Nicky Petrie.

Petrie's words: *Straitlaced old town, how else are we going to get our thrills . . . ?*

Rebus's heart was on fire as he stopped in front of him. He could hardly get the words out.

'It's story time, Mr Petrie.' He slapped the wig down on Nicky Petrie's head. Petrie, with a show of disgust, removed the wig, held it to his face. It was hard to make out now what was sweat and what was tears.

'Oh God, oh God, oh God,' he kept saying.

'Where's Damon Mee?'

'Oh God, oh God, oh God.'

'I don't think He's in a position to help you, Nicky.'

Rebus looked at the clothes. They could belong to Ama Petrie: brother and sister were of similar build, Nicky slightly taller and broader. The black dress looked tight on him.

'This is what you like to do, Nicky? Dress up as a woman?'

'No harm in it,' Clarke added quickly. 'We're all different.'

Nicky looked at her, blinking to refocus his eyes.

'You could do with a makeover, sweetheart,' he said.

She smiled. 'You're probably right.'

'Who does your make-up, Nicky?' Rebus asked. 'Ama?'

He straightened up. 'All my own work.'

'And then you head for this side of town? Walk up and down and soak up the admiration?'

'I don't expect you to—'

'Nobody's asking what you expect, Mr Petrie.' He turned to Clarke. 'Go fetch the car.' Handed her the keys. 'We'll need to take Mr Petrie here to the station.'

Petrie's eyes widened with fear. 'Why?'

'To answer a few questions about Damon Mee. And to explain why you've been lying to us all along.'

Petrie made to say something, then bit his lip.

'Suit yourself,' Rebus told him. Then, to Clarke: 'Go get the car.'

Rebus questioned Nicky Petrie for half an hour. He made sure that anyone who wanted to gawp had the chance to come into the interview room. Petrie sat there with his head in his hands, not looking up, while a parade of CID and uniforms commented on his shoes, tights and dress.

'I can get you some trousers and a shirt,' Rebus offered.

'I know what you're trying to do,' Petrie said when they were alone. 'Humiliate me all you like, this lady's *not* for talking.' He managed a small defiant smile.

'I'm sure your dad will come riding to the rescue anyway,' Rebus commented, pleased to see some of the colour leave the young man's lips.

'I don't need my father.'

'That's as may be, but we'll need to contact him. Best for us to do it rather than the papers.'

'Papers?'

Rebus barked a laugh. 'Think they'll let something like this pass them by? No, sir, you're going to be cover-boy for a day, Nicky. Congratulations. Bit of pan-stick and a wig, they might even pay you for the privilege.'

'They don't need to know,' Petrie said quietly.

Rebus shrugged. 'Cop-shops are like sieves, Nicky. All these people who've seen you here . . . I can't promise they won't talk.'

'Bastard.'

'If you like, Nicky.' Rebus leaned forward. 'All I want to know is where I can find Damon Mee.'

'Then I can't help you,' Nicky Petrie said, with all the defiance he could muster.

Plan Two: Ama Petrie.

She flew into the station like a whirlwind. Cal Brady was right: she had a soft spot for her little brother.

'Where is he? What have you done with him?'

Rebus looked at her with a façade of utter calm. 'Shouldn't those be *my* questions?'

She didn't seem to understand.

'Damon Mee,' Rebus explained. 'Nicky met him at Gaitano's, took him to the boat where you were having one of your parties. That's the last time he was seen alive, Ms Petrie.'

'It's got nothing to do with Nicky.'

They were seated in the same interview room, Nicky Petrie having been taken down to the cells. It was also the same interview room where Harold Ince had first been questioned. Ince had been sentenced to twelve years, Marshall to eight, the bulk of both sentences to be served at Peterhead. Had Rebus known anyone there, he might have put in a word for Ince. But he didn't know a single damned soul . . .

'What's got nothing to do with Nicky?' he asked.

'It's my fault, not his.'

Rebus understood: she thought Nicky had talked, had somehow incriminated himself. She was underestimating him. The chink in her armour which Cal Brady had detected: she loved her brother too much.

Rebus sat back, knew how to play this. He asked her if she wanted anything to drink. She shook her head violently.

'I want to make a statement,' she blurted out.

'You'll probably want a solicitor, Ms Petrie.'

'Bugger that.' She stopped suddenly. 'Is Nicky here? In this station?'

'Safely in the cells.'

'Safely?' Her voice trembled. 'Poor Nicky . . .' She was dry-eyed but her face was tense.

'Did Damon Mee know Nicky wasn't really a woman?'

'How could he not?'

Rebus shrugged. 'Your brother's pretty convincing.'

She allowed herself a brief smile. 'He always said he should have been the girl and I the boy.'

Rebus knew Nicky had run away from home aged twelve. He'd been running ever since . . .

'So what happened on the boat?'

'We'd all been drinking.' She looked at him. 'You know what parties are like.'

She was trying to win him round to her side. Too late for that, but he nodded anyway.

'Then Nicky brought this piece of rough below decks.'

'Piece of rough?'

'As in rough and ready. I'm not being a snob, Inspector.'

'Of course not. I take it all of you knew Nicky's . . . preferences?'

'The gang of us, yes. A few couples were up dancing. Nicky and this Damon joined them.' Her eyes went unfocused; she was picturing the scene. 'Nicky had his head on Damon's shoulder, and just for a moment our eyes met . . . and he looked so *happy*.' She screwed shut her eyes.

'Then what happened?'

She opened her eyes again, staring at the desk. 'Alfie and Cherie were one of the other couples. Alfie was as drunk as I've ever seen him. For a joke, he leaned over and snatched Nicky's wig. Nicky chased him round the room. And Damon just stood there, like he was thunderstruck. He looked . . . it really seemed hilarious at the time. His face was a picture. Then he ran for the stairs. Nicky saw what was happening and went after him . . .'

'They had a fight?'

She looked at him. 'Is that what he told you?' She smiled. 'Dear Nicky . . . You've seen him, Inspector. He couldn't hurt a fly. No, by the time I came up on deck, this Damon person had Nicky down on the ground. He was strangling the life out of him, at the same time thumping his head against the deck. Lifting it . . . thudding it back down. I grabbed an empty wine bottle, swung it at the side of his head. It didn't knock him cold or anything. The bottle didn't even break, not like in the films. But he let go of Nicky, staggered to his feet.'

'And?'

'And seemed to lose his balance. He fell over the side and into the water. It's funny . . . the deck's not that high above the water line . . . he hardly made a sound as he fell.'

'What did you do?'

'I had to make sure Nicky was all right. I took him back down below. His throat hurt, but I got a brandy down him.'

'I meant, what did you do about Damon?'

'Oh, him . . .' She thought it over. 'Well, by the time I went back up, there was no sign of him. I assumed he'd swum ashore.'

Rebus stared at her. 'Are you quite sure that's what you assumed?'

'To be honest . . . I'm not sure I thought anything at all. He was gone, and he couldn't hurt Nicky, that was all that mattered. That's all that ever matters to me. So you see, whatever Nicky's told you, he only did in order to protect me. I'm the one you should put in the cell. Nicky should go home.'

'Thanks for the advice.'

'You will let him go, won't you?'

He stood up, leaned across the desk towards her. 'I know Damon's family. I've seen the way they've been suffering. Your precious brother doesn't know the half of it.'

She glowered at him. 'And why should he?'

He thought of a thousand answers, knew she'd rebut every one of them. Instead, he told her he'd need a written statement. He'd send someone in to take it. He made for the door.

'And then you'll let Nicky out, won't you, Inspector?'

His one little victory: he left without saying a word.

Epilogue

Later that night, he found himself in Cowgate again, further to the east this time, past the mothballed mortuary, walking towards the building site on Holyrood. Behind it, he could make out a couple of the Greenfield tower-blocks, and behind those Salisbury Crags. The sun had set, but it wasn't quite dark. The twilight could last an age at this time of year. Demolition work had stopped for the day. He couldn't be sure where everything would go, but he knew there'd be a newspaper building, a theme park, and the Parliament building. They'd all be ready for the twenty-first century, or so the predictions went. Taking Scotland into the new millennium. Rebus tried to raise within himself a tiny cheer of hope, but found it stifled by his old cynicism.

No longer twilight now. Darkness had fallen. Shadows seemed to rise all around him as a bell tolled in the distance. The blood that had seeped into stone, the bones that lay twisting in their eternity, the stories and horrors of the city's past and present . . . he knew they'd all come rising in the digger's steel jaws, bubbling to the surface as the city began its slow ascent towards being a nation's capital once again.

Forget it, John, he told himself. It's the Old Town, that's all.

Cary Oakes sat in the visitors' room at Saughton Prison. They hadn't put any cuffs on him, and there was just the one guard. One guard was almost demeaning. Then the door opened and his solicitor walked in. That's what they were called here – solicitors. Cary smiled, bowed his head in greeting. The lawyer was young, looked eager but flustered. First time, probably, but that was OK. Youngsters, working hard to make the grade . . . they'd put in the hours for you, go the extra yard. Cary had nothing against fresh blood.

He waited till the guy was seated and ready, notepad out, pen held in his right hand. Then he began his spiel.

'I'm innocent, man, so help me. And you've got to do that: you've got to help me. Between us, we can prove I didn't do anything.' He leaned forward, rested his elbows on the table. 'It'll make your career. You're my man, I can sense it.'

Gave a big open smile.

Set in Darkness

For my son Kit, with all my hopes, dreams and love

Though my soul may set in darkness
It will rise in perfect light,
I have loved the stars too fondly
To be fearful of the night.

Sarah Williams
'The Old Astronomer to his Pupil'

Part One

The Sense of an Ending

And this long narrow land
Is full of possibility . . .
Deacon Blue, 'Wages Day'

1

Darkness was falling as Rebus accepted the yellow hard hat from his guide.

'This will be the admin block, we think,' the man said. His name was David Gilfillan. He worked for Historic Scotland and was coordinating the archaeological survey of Queensberry House. 'The original building is late seventeenth century. Lord Hatton was its original owner. It was extended at the end of the century, after coming into the ownership of the first Duke of Queensberry. It would have been one of the grandest houses on Canongate, and only a stone's throw from Holyrood.'

All around them, demolition work was taking place. Queensberry House itself would be saved, but the more recent additions either side of it were going. Workmen crouched on roofs, removing slates, tying them into bundles which were lowered by rope to waiting skips. There were enough broken slates underfoot to show that the process was imperfect. Rebus adjusted his hard hat and tried to look interested in what Gilfillan was saying.

Everyone told him that this was a sign, that he was here because the chiefs at the Big House had plans for him. But Rebus knew better. He knew his boss, Detective Chief Superintendent 'Farmer' Watson, had put his name forward because he was hoping to keep Rebus out of trouble and out of his hair. It was as simple as that. And if – *if* – Rebus accepted without complaining and saw the assignment through, then maybe – *maybe* – the Farmer would receive a chastened Rebus back into the fold.

Four o'clock on a December afternoon in Edinburgh; John Rebus with his hands in his raincoat pockets, water seeping up through the leather soles of his shoes. Gilfillan was wearing green wellies. Rebus noticed that DI Derek Linford was wearing an almost identical pair. He'd probably phoned beforehand, checked with the archaeologist what the season's fashion was. Linford was Fettes fast-stream, headed for big things at Lothian and Borders Police HQ. Late twenties, practically deskbound, and glowing from a love of the job. Already there were CID officers – mostly older than him – who were saying it didn't do to get on the wrong side of Derek Linford. Maybe he'd have a long memory; maybe one day he'd be looking down on them all from Room 279 in the Big House.

The Big House: Police HQ on Fettes Avenue; 279: the Chief Constable's office.

Linford had his notebook out, pen clenched between his teeth. He was listening to the lecture. He was *listening*.

'Forty noblemen, seven judges, generals, doctors, bankers . . .' Gilfillan was letting his tour group know how important Canongate had been at one time in the city's history. In doing so, he was pointing towards the near future. The brewery next door to Queensberry House was due for demolition the following spring. The parliament building itself would be built on the cleared site, directly across the road from Holyrood House, the Queen's Edinburgh residence. On the other side of Holyrood Road, facing Queensberry House, work was progressing on Dynamic Earth, a natural history theme park. Next to it, a new HQ for the city's daily newspaper was at present a giant monkey-puzzle of steel girders. And across the road from that, another site was being cleared in preparation for the construction of a hotel and 'prestige apartment block'. Rebus was standing in the midst of one of the biggest building sites in Edinburgh's history.

'You'll probably all know Queensberry House as a hospital,' Gilfillan was saying. Derek Linford was nodding, but then he nodded agreement with almost everything the archaeologist said. 'Where we're standing now was used for car parking.' Rebus looked around at the mud-coloured lorries, each one bearing the simple word DEMOLITION. 'But before it was a hospital it was used as a barracks. This area was the parade ground. We dug down and found evidence of a formal sunken garden. It was probably filled in to make the parade ground.'

In what light was left, Rebus looked at Queensberry House. Its grey harled walls looked unloved. There was grass growing from its gutters. It was huge, yet he couldn't remember having seen it before, though he'd driven past it probably several hundred times in his life.

'My wife used to work here,' another of the group said, 'when it was a hospital.' The informant was Detective Sergeant Joseph Dickie, who was based at Gayfield Square. He'd successfully contrived to miss two out of the first four meetings of the PPLC – the Policing of Parliament Liaison Committee. By some arcane law of bureaucratic semantics, the PPLC was actually a *sub*committee, one of many which had been set up to advise on security matters pertaining to the Scottish Parliament. There were eight members of the PPLC, including one Scottish Office official and a shadowy figure who claimed to be from Scotland Yard, though when Rebus had phoned the Met in London, he'd been unable to trace him. Rebus's bet was that the man – Alec Carmoodie – was MI5. Carmoodie wasn't here today, and neither was Peter Brent, the sharp-faced and sharper-suited Scottish Office representative. Brent, for his sins, sat on several of the subcommittees, and had begged off today's tour with the compelling excuse that he'd been through it twice before when accompanying visiting dignitaries.

Making up the party today were the three final members of the PPLC. DS Ellen Wylie was from C Division HQ in Torphichen Place. It didn't seem to bother her that she was the only woman on the team. She treated it like any other task, raising good points at the meetings and asking questions to which no one seemed to have any answers. DC Grant Hood was from Rebus's own station, St Leonard's. Two of them, because St Leonard's was the closest station to the Holyrood site, and the parliament would be part of their beat. Though Rebus worked in the same office as Hood, he didn't know him well. They'd not often shared the same shift. But Rebus did know the last member of the PPLC, DI Bobby Hogan from D Division in Leith. At the first meeting, Hogan had pulled Rebus to one side.

'What the hell are we doing here?'

'I'm serving time,' Rebus had answered. 'What about you?'

Hogan was scoping out the room. 'Christ, man, look at them. We're Old Testament by comparison.'

Smiling now at the memory, Rebus caught Hogan's eye and winked. Hogan shook his head almost imperceptibly. Rebus knew what he was thinking: waste of time. Almost everything was a waste of time for Bobby Hogan.

'If you'll follow me,' Gilfillan was saying, 'we can take a look indoors.'

Which, to Rebus's mind, really was a waste of time. The committee having been set up, things had to be found for them to do. So here they were wandering through the dank interior of Queensberry House, their way lit irregularly by unsafe-looking strip lights and the torch carried by Gilfillan. As they climbed the stairwell – nobody wanted to use the lift – Rebus found himself paired with Joe Dickie, who asked a question he'd asked before.

'Put in your exes yet?' By which he meant the claim for expenses.

'No,' Rebus admitted.

'Sooner you do, sooner they'll cough up.'

Dickie seemed to spend half his time at their meetings totting up figures on his pad of paper. Rebus had never seen the man write down anything as mundane as a phrase or sentence. Dickie was late thirties, big-framed with a head like an artillery shell stood on end. His black hair was cropped close to the skull and his eyes were as small and rounded as a china doll's. Rebus had tried the comparison out on Bobby Hogan, who'd commented that any doll resembling Joe Dickie would 'give a bairn nightmares'.

'I'm a grown-up,' Hogan had continued, 'and he still scares me.'

Climbing the stairs, Rebus smiled again. Yes, he was glad to have Bobby Hogan around.

'When people think of archaeology,' Gilfillan was saying, 'they almost always see it in terms of digging *down*, but one of our most exciting finds here was in the attic. A new roof was built over the original one, and there are traces of what looks like a tower. We'd have to climb a ladder to get to it, but if anyone's interested . . .?'

'Thank you,' a voice said. Derek Linford: Rebus knew its nasal quality only too well by now.

'Creep,' another voice close to Rebus whispered. It was Bobby Hogan, bringing up the rear. A head turned: Ellen Wylie. She'd heard, and now gave what looked like the hint of a smile. Rebus looked to Hogan, who shrugged, letting him know he thought Wylie was all right.

'How will Queensberry House be linked to the parliament building? Will there be covered walkways?' The questions came from Linford again. He was out in front with Gilfillan. The pair of them had rounded a corner of the stairs, so that Rebus had to strain to hear Gilfillan's hesitant reply.

'I don't know.'

His tone said it all: he was an archaeologist, not an architect. He was here to investigate the site's past rather than its future. He wasn't sure himself why he was giving this tour, except that it had been asked of him. Hogan screwed up his face, letting everyone in the vicinity know his own feelings.

'When will the building be ready?' Grant Hood asked. An easy one: they'd all been briefed. Rebus saw what Hood was doing – trying to console Gilfillan by putting a question he could answer.

'Construction begins in the summer,' Gilfillan obliged. 'Everything should be up and running here by the autumn of 2001.' They were coming out on to a landing. Around them stood open doorways, through which could be glimpsed the old hospital wards. Walls had been gouged at, flooring removed: checks on the fabric of the building. Rebus stared out of a window. Most of the workers looked to be packing up: dangerously dark now to be scrabbling over roofs. There was a summer house down there. It was due to be demolished, too. And a tree, drooping forlornly, surrounded by rubble. It had been planted by the Queen. No way it could be moved or felled until she'd given her permission. According to Gilfillan, permission had now been granted; the tree would go. Maybe formal gardens would be recreated down there, or maybe it would be a staff car park. Nobody knew. 2001 seemed a ways off. Until this site was ready, the parliament would sit in the Church of Scotland Assembly Hall near the top of The Mound. The committee had already been on two tours of the Assembly Hall and its immediate vicinity. Office buildings were being turned over to the parliament, so that the MSPs could have somewhere to work. Bobby Hogan had asked at one meeting why they couldn't just wait for the Holyrood site to be ready before, in his words, 'setting up shop'. Peter Brent, the civil servant, had stared at him aghast.

'Because Scotland needs a parliament *now*.'

'Funny, we've done without for three hundred years . . .'

Brent had been about to object, but Rebus had butted in. 'Bobby, at least they're not trying to rush the job.'

Hogan had smiled, knowing he was talking about the newly opened Museum of Scotland. The Queen had come north for the official opening of the unfinished building. They'd had to hide the scaffolding and paint tins till she'd gone.

Gilfillan was standing beside a retractable ladder, pointing upwards towards a hatch in the ceiling.

'The original roof is just up there,' he said. Derek Linford already had both feet on the ladder's bottom rung. 'You don't need to go all the way,' Gilfillan continued as Linford climbed. 'If I shine the torch up . . .'

But Linford had disappeared into the roof space.

'Lock the hatch and let's make a run for it,' Bobby Hogan said, smiling so they'd assume he was joking.

Ellen Wylie hunched her shoulders. 'There's a real . . . atmosphere in here, isn't there?'

'My wife saw a ghost,' Joe Dickie said. 'Lots of people who worked here did. A woman, she was crying. Used to sit on the end of one of the beds.'

'Maybe she was a patient who died here,' Grant Hood offered.

Gilfillan turned towards them. 'I've heard that story, too. She was the mother of one of the servants. Her son was working here the night the Act of Union was signed. Poor chap got himself murdered.'

Linford called down that he thought he could see where the steps to the tower had been, but nobody was listening.

'Murdered?' Ellen Wylie said.

Gilfillan nodded. His torch threw weird shadows across the walls, illuminating the slow movements of cobwebs. Linford was trying to read some graffiti on the wall.

'There's a year written here . . . 1870, I think.'

'You know Queensberry was the architect of the Act of Union?' Gilfillan was saying. He could see that he had an audience now, for the first time since the tour had begun in the brewery car park next door. 'Back in 1707. This', he scratched a shoe over the bare floorboards, 'is where Great Britain was invented. And the night of the signing, one of the young servants was working in the kitchen. The Duke of Queensberry was Secretary of State. It was his job to lead the negotiations. But he had a son, James Douglas, Earl of Drumlanrig. The story goes, James was off his head . . .'

'What happened?'

Gilfillan looked up through the open hatch. 'All right up there?' he called.

'Fine. Anyone else want to take a look?'

They ignored him. Ellen Wylie repeated her question.

'He ran the servant through with a sword,' Gilfillan said, 'then roasted him in one of the kitchen fireplaces. James was sitting munching away when he was found.'

'Dear God,' Ellen Wylie said.

'You believe this?' Bobby Hogan slid his hands into his pockets.

Gilfillan shrugged. 'It's a matter of record.'

A blast of cold air seemed to rush at them from the roof space. Then a rubber-soled wellington appeared on the ladder, and Derek Linford began his slow, dusty descent. At the bottom, he removed the pen from between his teeth.

'Interesting up there,' he said. 'You really should try it. Could be your first and last chance.'

'Why's that then?' Bobby Hogan asked.

'I very much doubt we'll be letting tourists in here, Bobby,' Linford said. 'Imagine what *that* would do for security.'

Hogan stepped forward so swiftly that Linford flinched. But all Hogan did was lift a cobweb from the young man's shoulder.

'Can't have you heading back to the Big House in less than showroom condition, can we, son?' Hogan said. Linford ignored him, probably feeling that he could well afford to ignore relics like Bobby Hogan, just as Hogan knew he had nothing to fear from Linford: he'd be heading for retirement long before the younger man gained any position of real power and prominence.

'I can't see it as the powerhouse of government,' Ellen Wylie said, examining the water stains on the walls, the flaking plaster. 'Wouldn't they have been better off knocking it down and starting again?'

'It's a listed building,' Gilfillan censured her. Wylie just shrugged. Rebus knew that nevertheless she had accomplished her objective, by deflecting attention away from Linford and Hogan. Gilfillan was off again, delving into the history of the area: the series of wells which had been found beneath the brewery; the slaughterhouse which used to stand near by. As they headed back down the stairs, Hogan held back, tapping his watch, then cupping a hand to his mouth. Rebus nodded: good idea. A drink afterwards. Jenny Ha's was a short stroll away, or there was the Holyrood Tavern on the way back to St Leonard's. As if mind-reading, Gilfillan began talking about the Younger's Brewery.

'Covered twenty-seven acres at one time, produced a quarter of all the beer in Scotland. Mind you, there's been an abbey at Holyrood since early in the twelfth century. Chances are they weren't just drinking well-water.'

Through a landing window, Rebus could see that outside night had fallen prematurely. Scotland in winter: it was dark when you came to work, and dark when you went home again. Well, they'd had their little outing, gleaned nothing from it, and would now be released back to their various stations until the next meeting. It felt like a penance because Rebus's boss had planned it as such. Farmer Watson was on a committee himself: Strategies for Policing in the New Scotland. Everyone called it SPINS. Committee upon committee . . . it felt to Rebus as if they were building a paper tower, enough 'Policy Agendas',

'Reports' and 'Occasional Papers' to completely fill Queensberry House. And the more they talked, the more that got written, the further away from reality they seemed to move. Queensberry House was unreal to him, the idea of a parliament itself the dream of some mad god: 'But Edinburgh is a mad god's dream/Fitful and dark . . .' He'd found the words at the opening to a book about the city. They were from a poem by Hugh MacDiarmid. The book itself had been part of his recent education, trying to understand this home of his.

He took off his hard hat, rubbed his fingers through his hair, wondering just how much protection the yellow plastic would give against a projectile falling several storeys. Gilfillan asked him to put the hat back on until they were back at the site office.

'You might not get into trouble,' the archaeologist said, 'but I would.'

Rebus put the helmet back on, while Hogan tutted and wagged a finger. They were back at ground level, in what Rebus guessed must have been the hospital's reception area. There wasn't much to it. Spools of electric cable sat near the door: the offices would need rewiring. They were going to close the Holyrood/St Mary's junction to facilitate underground cabling. Rebus, who used the route often, wasn't looking forward to the diversions. Too often these days the city seemed nothing but roadworks.

'Well,' Gilfillan was saying, opening his arms, 'that's about it. If there are any questions, I'll do what I can.'

Bobby Hogan coughed into the silence. Rebus saw it as a warning to Linford. When someone had come up from London to address the group on security issues in the Houses of Parliament, Linford had asked so many questions the poor sod had missed his train south. Hogan knew this because he'd been the one who'd driven the Londoner at breakneck speed back to Waverley Station, then had had to entertain him for the rest of the evening before depositing him on the overnight sleeper.

Linford consulted his notebook, six pairs of eyes drilling into him, fingers touching wristwatches.

'Well, in that case—' Gilfillan began.

'Hey! Mr Gilfillan! Are you up there?' The voice was coming from below. Gilfillan walked over to a doorway, called down a flight of steps.

'What is it, Marlene?'

'Come take a look.'

Gilfillan turned to look at his reluctant group. 'Shall we?' He was already heading down. They couldn't very well leave without him. It was stay here, with a bare lightbulb for company, or head down into the basement. Derek Linford led the way.

They came out into a narrow hallway, rooms off to both sides, and other rooms seeming to lead from those. Rebus thought he caught a glimpse of an electrical generator somewhere in the gloom. Voices up ahead and the shadowplay of torches. They walked out of the hallway and into a room lit by a single arc lamp. It was pointing towards a long wall, the bottom half of which had been lined with wooden tongue-and-groove painted the selfsame institutional cream as the plaster walls. Floorboards had been ripped up so that for the most part they were walking on the exposed joists, beneath which sat bare earth. The whole room smelt of damp and mould. Gilfillan and the other archaeologist, the one he'd called Marlene, were crouched in front of this wall, examining the stonework beneath the wood panelling. Two long curves of hewn stone, forming what seemed to Rebus like railway arches in miniature. Gilfillan turned round, looking excited for the first time that day.

'Fireplaces,' he said. 'Two of them. This must have been the kitchen.' He stood up, taking a couple of paces back. 'The floor level's been raised at some point. We're only seeing the top half of them.' He half-turned towards the group, reluctant to take his eyes off the discovery. 'Wonder which one the servant was roasted in . . .'

One of the fireplaces was open, the other closed off by a couple of sections of brown corroding metal.

'What an extraordinary find,' Gilfillan said, beaming at his young co-worker. She grinned back at him. It was nice to see people so happy in their work. Digging up the past, uncovering secrets . . . it struck Rebus that they weren't so unlike detectives.

'Any chance of rustling us up a meal then?' Bobby Hogan said, producing a snort of laughter from Ellen Wylie. But Gilfillan wasn't paying any heed. He was standing by the closed fireplace, prying with his fingertips at the space between stonework and metal. The sheet came away easily, Marlene helping him to lift it off and place it carefully on the floor.

'Wonder when they blocked it off?' Grant Hood asked.

Hogan tapped the metal sheet. 'Doesn't look exactly prehistoric.' Gilfillan and Marlene had lifted away the second sheet. Now everyone was staring at the revealed fireplace. Gilfillan thrust his torch towards it, though the arc lamp gave light enough.

There could be no mistaking the desiccated corpse for anything other than what it was.

2

Siobhan Clarke tugged at the hem of her black dress. Two men, patrolling the perimeter of the dance floor, stopped to watch. She tried them with a glare, but they'd returned to some conversation they were having, half-cupping their free hands to their mouths in an attempt to be heard. Then nods, sips from their pint glasses, and they were moving away, eyes on the other booths. Clarke turned to her companion, who shook her head, indicating that she hadn't known the men. Their booth was a large semicircle, fourteen of them squeezed in around the table. Eight women, six men. Some of the men wore suits, others wore denim jackets but dress shirts. 'No denims. No trainers' was what it said on the sign outside, but the dress code wasn't exactly being enforced. There were too many people in the club. Clarke wondered if it constituted a fire hazard. She turned to her companion.

'Is it always this busy?'

Sandra Carnegie shrugged. 'Seems about normal,' she yelled. She was seated right next to Clarke, but even so was almost rendered unintelligible by the pounding music. Not for the first time, Clarke wondered how you were supposed to meet anyone in a place like this. The men at the table would make eye contact, nod towards the dance floor. If the woman agreed, everyone would have to move so the couple could get out. Then when they danced they seemed to move in their own worlds, barely making eye contact with their partner. It was much the same when a stranger approached the group: eye contact; dance floor nod; then the ritual of the dance itself. Sometimes women danced with other women, shoulders drooped, eyes scanning the other faces. Sometimes a man could be seen dancing alone. Clarke had pointed out faces to Sandra Carnegie, who'd always studied them closely before shaking her head.

It was Singles Night at the Marina Club. Good name for a nightclub sited just the two and a half miles from the coastline. Not that 'Singles Night' meant much. In theory it meant that the music might hark back to the 1980s or '70s, catering for a slightly more mature clientele than some of the other clubs. For Clarke the word singles meant people in their thirties, some of them divorced. But there were lads in tonight who'd probably had to finish their homework before coming out.

Or was she just getting old?

It was her first time at a singles night. She'd tried rehearsing chat lines. If any sleazeball asked her how she liked her eggs in the morning, she was ready to tell him 'Unfertilised', but she'd no idea what she'd say if anyone asked what she did.

I'm a detective constable with Lothian and Borders Police wasn't the ideal opening gambit. She knew that from experience. Maybe that was why lately she'd all but given up trying. All of them around the table knew who she was, why she was here. None of the men had tried chatting her up. There had been words of consolation for Sandra Carnegie, words and hugs, and dark looks at the men in the company, who'd shrivelled visibly. They were *men*, and men were in it together, a conspiracy of bastards. It was a man who had raped Sandra Carnegie, who had turned her from a fun-loving single mum into a victim.

Clarke had persuaded Sandra to turn hunter – that was the way she'd phrased it.

'We've got to turn the tables on him, Sandra. That's my feeling anyway . . . before he does it again.'

Him . . . he . . . But there were two of them. One to carry out the assault, the other to help hold the victim. When the rape had been reported in the newspapers, two more women had come forward with their stories. They'd been assaulted – sexually, physically – but not raped, not insofar as the law defined the crime. The women's stories had been almost identical: all three were members of singles clubs; all three had been at functions organised by their club; all three had been heading home alone.

One man on foot, following them, grabbing them, and another driving the van which pulled up. The assaults took place in the back of the van, its floor covered with material of some kind, maybe a tarpaulin. Kicked out of the van afterwards, usually on the outskirts of the city, with a final warning not to say anything, not to go to the police.

'You go to a singles club, you're asking for what you get.'

The rapist's final words, words which had set Siobhan Clarke thinking, seated in her cramped cupboard of an office; seconded to Sex Crimes. One thing she knew: the crimes were becoming more violent as the attacker grew in confidence. He'd progressed from assault to rape; who knew where he'd want to take it from there? One thing was obvious: he had something about singles clubs. Was he targeting them? Where did he get his information?

She wasn't working Sex Crimes any more, was back at St Leonard's and everyday CID, but she'd been given the chance to work on Sandra Carnegie, to persuade her back into the Marina. Siobhan's reasoning: how would he know his victims belonged to singles clubs unless he'd been in the nightclub? Members of the clubs themselves – there were three in the city – had been questioned, along with those who'd left or been kicked out.

Sandra was grey-faced and drinking Bacardi and Coke. She'd spent most of the evening so far staring at the table-top. Before coming to the Marina, the club had met in a pub. This was how it worked: sometimes they met in the pub and moved on elsewhere; sometimes they stayed put; occasionally some function was arranged – a dance or theatre trip. It was just possible the rapist followed them from the pub, but more likely he started in the dance hall, circling the floor, face hidden behind his drink. Indistinguishable from the dozens of men doing the selfsame thing.

Clarke wondered if it was possible to identify a singles group by sight alone. It would be a fair-sized crowd, mixed sex. But that could make it an office party. There'd be no wedding rings, though . . . and while the age range would be broad, there'd be no one who could be mistaken for the office junior. Clarke had asked Sandra about her group.

'It just gives me some company. I work in an old people's home, don't get the chance to meet anyone my own age. Then there's David. If I want to go out, my mum has to babysit.' David being her eleven-year-old son. 'It's just for company . . . that's all.'

Another woman in the group had said much the same thing, adding that a lot of the men you met at singles groups were 'let's say less than perfect'. But the women were fine: it was that company thing again.

Sitting at the edge of the booth, Clarke had been approached twice so far, turning down both suitors. One of the women had leaned across the table.

'You're fresh blood!' she'd shouted. 'They can always smell that!' Then she'd leaned back and laughed, showing stained teeth and a tongue turned green from the cocktail she was drinking.

'Moira's just jealous,' Sandra had said. 'The only ones who ever ask her up have usually spent all day queuing to renew their bus pass.'

Moira couldn't have heard the remark, but she stared anyway, as if sensing some slight against her.

'I need to go to the toilet,' Sandra said now.

'I'll come with you.'

Sandra nodded her agreement. Clarke had promised: you won't be out of my sight for a second. They lifted their bags from the floor and started pushing their way through the throng.

The loo wasn't much emptier, but at least it was cool, and the door helped muffle the sound system. Clarke felt a dullness in her ears, and her throat was raw from cigarette smoke and shouting. While Sandra queued for a cubicle, Clarke made for the washbasins. She examined herself in the mirror. She didn't normally wear make-up, and was surprised to see her face so changed. The eyeliner and mascara made her eyes look hard rather than alluring. She tugged at one of her shoulder straps. Now that she was standing up, the hem of her dress was at her knees. But when she sat, it threatened to ride up to her stomach. She'd worn it only twice before: a wedding and a dinner party. Couldn't recall the same problem. Was she getting fat in the bum, was that it? She half-turned, tried to see, then turned her attention to her hair. Short: she liked the cut. It made her face longer. A woman bumped against her in the rush for the hand-drier. Loud snorts from one of the cubicles: someone doing a line? Conversations in the toilet queue: off-colour remarks about tonight's talent, who had the nicest bum. Which was preferable: a bulging crotch or a bulging wallet? Sandra had disappeared into one of the cubicles. Clarke folded her arms and waited. Someone stood in front of her.

'Are you the condom attendant or what?'

Laughter from the queue. She saw that she was standing beside the wall dispenser, moved slightly so the woman could drop a couple of coins into the slot. Clarke focused on the woman's right hand. Liver spots, sagging skin. The left hand went to the tray: her wedding finger was still marked from where she'd removed her ring. It was probably in her bag. Her face was machine-tanned, hopeful but hardened by experience. She winked.

'You never know.'

Clarke forced a smile. Back at the station, she'd heard Singles Night at the Marina called all sorts of things: Jurassic Park, Grab-a-Granny. The usual bloke jokes. She found it depressing, but couldn't have said why. She didn't frequent nightclubs, not when she could help it. Even when she'd been younger – school and college years – she'd avoided them. Too noisy, too much smoke and drink and stupidity. But it couldn't just be that. These days, she followed Hibernian football club, and the terraces were full of cigarette smoke and testosterone. But there was a difference between the crowd in a stadium and the crowd at a place like the Marina: not many sexual predators chose to do their hunting in the midst of a football crowd. She felt safe at Easter Road; even attended away matches when she could. Same seat at every home game . . . she knew the faces around her. And afterwards . . . afterwards she melted into the streets, part of the anonymous mass. Nobody 'd ever tried to chat her up. That wasn't why they were there, and she knew it, hugging the knowledge to her on cold winter afternoons when the floodlights were needed from kick-off.

The cubicle bolt slid back and Sandra emerged.

'About bleedin' time,' someone called out. 'Thought you'd a fellah in there with you.'

'Only to wipe my backside on,' Sandra said. The voice – all tough, casual humour – was forced. Sandra started fixing her make-up at the mirror. She'd been crying. There were fresh veins of red in the corners of her eyes.

'All right?' Clarke asked quietly.

'Could be worse, I suppose.' Sandra studied her reflection. 'I could always be pregnant, couldn't I?'

Her rapist had worn a condom, leaving no semen for the labs to analyse. They'd run checks on sex offenders, ruled out a slew of interviewees. Sandra had gone through the picture books, a gallery of misogyny. Just looking at their faces was enough to give some women nightmares. Bedraggled, vacuous features, dull eyes, weak jaws. Some victims who'd gone through the process . . . they'd had unasked questions, questions Clarke thought she could phrase along the lines of: *Look at them, how could we let them do this to us? They're the ones who look weak.*

Yes, weak at the moment of photographing, weak with shame or fatigue or the pretence of submission. But strong at the necessary moment, the crackling moment of hate. The thing was, they worked alone, most of them. The second man, the accomplice . . . Siobhan was curious about him. What did he get out of it?

'Seen anyone you fancy?' Sandra was asking now. Her lipstick trembled slightly as she applied it.

'No.'

'Got someone at home?'

'You know I haven't.'

Sandra was still watching her in the mirror. 'I only know what you've told me.'

'I told you the truth.'

Long conversations, Clarke setting aside the rule book and opening herself to Sandra, answering her questions, stripping away her police self to reveal the person beneath. It had begun as a trick, a ploy to win Sandra over to the scheme. But it had evolved into something more, something real. Clarke had said more than she'd needed to, much more. And now it seemed Sandra hadn't been convinced. Was it that she didn't trust the detective, or was it that Clarke had become part of the problem, just someone else Sandra could never wholly trust? After all, they hadn't known one another until the rape; would never have met if it hadn't happened. Clarke was here at the Marina, looking like Sandra's friend, but that was another trick. They weren't friends; probably would never be friends. A vicious assault had brought them together. In Sandra's eyes, Clarke would always remind her of that night, a night she wanted to forget.

'How long do we have to stay?' she was asking now.

'That's up to you. We can leave any time you like.'

'But if we do, we might miss him.'

'Not your fault, Sandra. He could be anywhere. I just felt we had to give it a try.'

Sandra turned from the mirror. 'Half an hour more.' She glanced at her watch. 'I promised my mum I'd be home by twelve.'

Clarke nodded, followed Sandra back into a darkness punctuated by lightning, as if the light show could somehow earth all the energy in the room.

Back at the booth, Clarke's seat had been taken by a new arrival. Youngish male, fingers running down the condensation on a tall glass of what looked like straight orange juice. The club members seemed to know him.

'Sorry,' he said, getting to his feet as Clarke and Sandra approached. 'I've nicked your seat.' He stared at Clarke, then put out his hand. When Clarke took it, his grip tightened. He wasn't going to let her go.

'Come and dance,' he said, pulling her in the direction of the dance floor. She could do little but follow him, right into the heart of the storm where arms buffeted her and the dancers squealed and roared. He looked back, saw that they were no longer visible from the table, and kept moving, crossing the floor, leading them past one of the bars and into the foyer.

'Where are we going?' Clarke asked. He looked around, seemed satisfied and leaned towards her.

'I know you,' he said.

Suddenly, she knew that his face was familiar to her. She was thinking: criminal, someone I helped put away? She glanced to left and right.

'You work at St Leonard's,' he went on. She stared towards where his hand still held her wrist. Following her gaze, he let go suddenly. 'Sorry,' he said, 'it's just that . . .'

'Who are you?'

He seemed hurt that she didn't know. 'Derek Linford.'

Her eyes narrowed. 'Fettes?' He nodded. The newsletter, that's where she'd seen his face. And maybe in the canteen at HQ. 'What are you doing here?'

'I could ask you the same thing.'

'I'm with Sandra Carnegie.' Thinking: *no, I'm not; I'm out here with you . . . and I promised her . . .*

'Yes, but I don't . . .' His face crumpled. 'Oh, hell, she was raped, wasn't she?' He ran thumb and forefinger down the slope of his nose. 'You're trying for an ID?'

'That's right.' Clarke smiled. 'You're a member?'

'What if I am?' He seemed to expect an answer, but Clarke just shrugged. 'It's not the kind of information I bandy about, DC Clarke.' Pulling rank, warning her off.

'Your secret's safe with me, DI Linford.'

'Ah, speaking of secrets . . .' He looked at her, head tilted slightly.

'They don't know you're CID?' It was his turn to shrug. 'Christ, what have you told them?'

'Does it matter?'

Clarke was thoughtful. 'Hang on a sec, we talked to the club members. I don't remember seeing your name.'

'I only joined last week.'

Clarke frowned. 'So how do we play this?'

Linford rubbed his nose again. 'We've had our dance. We go back to the table. You sit one side, me the other. We really don't need to talk to one another again.'

'Charming.'

He grinned. 'I didn't mean it like that. Of course we can talk.'

'Gee, thanks.'

'In fact, something incredible happened this afternoon.' He took her arm, guided her back into the club. 'Help me get a round of drinks from the bar, and I'll tell you all about it.'

'He's an arse.'

'Maybe so,' Clarke said, 'but he's rather a sweet arse.'

John Rebus sat in his chair, holding the cordless phone to his ear. His chair was by the window. There were no curtains and the shutters were still open. No lights were on in his living room, just a bare sixty-watt bulb in the hall. But the street lamps bathed the room in an orange glow.

'Where did you say you bumped into him?'

'I didn't.' He could hear the smile in her voice.

'All very mysterious.'

'Not compared to your skeleton.'

'It's not a skeleton. Kind of shrivelled, like a mummy.' He gave a short, mirthless laugh. 'The archaeologist, I thought he was going to jump into my arms.'

'So what's the verdict?'

'SOCOs came in, roped the place off. Gates and Curt can't look at Skelly till Monday morning.'

'Skelly?'

Rebus watched a car cruising past, seeking a parking space. 'Bobby Hogan came up with the name. It'll do for now.'

'Nothing on the body?'

'Just what he was wearing: flared jeans, a Stones T-shirt.'

'Lucky us, having an expert on the premises.'

'If you mean a rock dinosaur, I'll take that as a compliment. Yes, it was the cover of *Some Girls*. Album came out in '78.'

'Nothing else to date the body?'

'Nothing in the pockets. No watch or rings.' He checked his own watch: 2 a.m. But she'd known she could call him, had known he'd be awake.

'What's on the hi-fi?' she asked.

'That tape you gave me.'

'The Blue Nile? There goes your dinosaur image. What do you think?'

'I think you're smitten by Mr Smarty-Pants.'

'I do like it when you come over all fatherly.'

'Watch I don't put you over my knee.'

'Careful, Inspector. These days I could have you off the job for saying something like that.'

'Are we going to the game tomorrow?'

'For our sins. I've a spare green and white scarf set aside for you.'

'I must remember to bring my lighter. Two o'clock in Mather's?'

'There'll be a beer waiting for you.'

'Siobhan, whatever it was you were up to tonight . . . ?'

'Yes?'

'Did you get a result?'

'No,' she said, sounding suddenly tired. 'Not even a goalless draw.'

He put the phone down, refilled his whisky glass. 'Refined tonight, John,' he told himself. Oftentimes nowadays he just swigged from the bottle. The weekend stretched ahead of him, one football game the extent of his plans. His living room was wreathed in shadows and cigarette smoke. He kept thinking of selling the flat, finding somewhere with fewer ghosts. Then again, they were the only company he had: dead colleagues, victims, expired relationships. He reached again for the bottle, but it was empty. Stood up and watched the floor sway beneath him. He thought he had a fresh bottle in the carrier bag beneath the window, but the bag was empty and crumpled. He looked out of his window, catching his reflection and its puzzled frown. Had he left a bottle in the car? Had he brought home two bottles or just the one? He thought of a dozen places where he could get a drink, even at two in the morning. The city – his city – was out there waiting for him, waiting to show its dark, shrivelled heart.

'I don't need you,' he said, resting the palms of his hands on the window, as if willing the glass to shatter and take him tumbling with it. A two-storey descent to the street below.

'I don't need you,' he repeated. Then he pushed off from the glass, went to find his coat.

3

Saturday, the clan had lunch at the Witchery.

It was a good restaurant, sited at the top of the Royal Mile. The Castle was a near neighbour. Lots of natural light: it was almost like eating in a conservatory. Roddy had organised it for their mother's 75th. She was a painter, and he reckoned she'd like all the light that poured into the restaurant. But the day was overcast. Squalls of rain drilled at the windows. Low cloud base: standing at the Castle's highest point, you felt you could have touched heaven.

They'd started with a quick walk around the battlements, Mother looking unimpressed. But then she'd first visited the place some seventy years before, had probably been there a hundred times since. And lunch hadn't improved her spirits, though Roddy praised each course, each mouthful of wine.

'You always overdo things!' his mother snapped at him.

To which he said nothing, just stared into his pudding bowl, glancing up eventually to wink at Lorna. When he did so, she was reminded of her brother as a kid, always with that shy, endearing quality – something he mostly reserved for voters and TV interviewers these days.

You always overdo things! Those words hung in the air for a time, as though others at the table wanted to relish them. But then Roddy's wife Seona spoke up.

'I wonder who he gets that from.'

'What did she say? *What did she say?*'

And of course it was Cammo who brokered the peace: 'Now, now, Mother, just because it's your birthday . . .'

'Finish the bloody sentence!'

Cammo sighed, took one of his deep breaths. 'Just because it's your birthday, let's take a walk down towards Holyrood.'

His mother glared at him. She had eyes like a frigate's hull. But then her face cracked into a smile. The others resented Cammo for his ability to bring about this transformation. At that moment, he possessed the powers of a magus.

Six of them at the table. Cammo, the elder son, hair swept back from his forehead, sporting his father's gold cuff links – the one thing the old man had left him in the will. They'd never agreed on politics, Cammo's father a Liberal of the old school. Cammo had joined the Conservative Party while still an undergraduate at St Andrews. Now he had a safe seat in the Home Counties, representing a mainly rural area between Swindon and High Wycombe. He lived in London, loved the nightlife and the sense of being at the core of something. Married, his wife a drunk and serial shopper. They were seldom seen together. He was photographed at balls and parties, always with some new woman on his arm.

That was Cammo.

He'd come north overnight on the sleeper; had complained that the club car hadn't been open – staff shortages.

'Bloody disgrace. You privatise the railways and still can't get a decent whisky and soda.'

'Christ, does anybody still drink soda?'

This was Lorna, back at the house as they prepared to go out to lunch. Lorna had always had the handling of her brother. She was all of eleven months younger than him, had somehow found time in her schedule for this reunion. Lorna was a fashion model – a story she was sticking to despite encroaching age and a shortage of bookings. In her late forties now, she'd been at her earning height in the 1970s. She still got work, cited Lauren Hutton as an influence. She'd dated MPs in her time, just as Cammo had seen fit to 'walk out' with the occasional model. She'd heard stories about him, and was sure he'd heard stories about her. On the rare occasions when they met, they circled one another like bare-knuckle fighters.

Cammo had made a point of choosing whisky and soda as his aperitif.

Then there was baby Roddy, just touching forty. Always the rebel at heart, but somehow lacking the curriculum vitae. Roddy the one-time Scottish Office boffin, now an investment analyst. He was New Labour. Didn't really possess the ammunition when his big brother came in with all ideological guns blazing. But Roddy sat there with quiet, immutable authority, the shells failing to scratch him. One political commentator had called him Scottish Labour's Mr Fixit, because of his ability to brush away the sand from around the party's many landmines and set about defusing them. Others called him Mr Suck-Up, a lazy explanation of his emergence as a prospective MSP. In fact, Roddy had planned today's lunch as a double celebration, since he'd had official notice just that morning that he would be running in Edinburgh West End as Labour's candidate for the Scottish Parliament.

'Bloody hell,' had been Cammo's rolling-eyed reaction as the champagne was being poured.

Roddy had allowed himself a quiet smile, tucking a stray lock of thick black hair back behind his ear. His wife Seona had squeezed his arm in support. Seona was more than the loyal wife; if anything, she was the more politically active of the two, and history teacher at a city comprehensive.

Billary, Cammo often called them, a reference to Bill and Hillary Clinton. He thought most teachers were a short hop from subversives, which hadn't stopped him flirting with Seona on half a dozen separate, usually drunken occasions. When challenged by Lorna, his defence was always the same: 'Indoctrination by seduction. Bloody cults get away with it, why shouldn't the Tory Party?'

Lorna's husband was there, too, though he'd spent half the meal over by the doorway, head tucked in towards a mobile phone. From the back he looked faintly ridiculous: too paunchy for the cream linen suit, the pointy-toed black shoes. And the greying ponytail – Cammo had laughed out loud when introduced to it.

'Gone New Age on us, Hugh? Or is professional wrestling your new forte?'

'Sod off, Cammo.'

Hugh Cordover had been a rock star of sorts back in the 1970s and '80s. These days he was a record producer and band manager, and got less media attention than his brother Richard, an Edinburgh lawyer. He'd met Lorna at the tail-end of her career, when some adviser had assured her she could sing. She'd turned up late and drunk at Hugh's studio. He'd opened the door to her, thrown a glass of water into her face, and ordered her to come back sober. It had taken her the best part of a fortnight. They'd gone to dinner that night, worked in the studio till dawn.

People still recognised Hugh on the street, but they weren't the people worth knowing. These days, Hugh Cordover lived by his holy book, this being a bulging, black leather personal organiser. He had it open in his hand as he paced the restaurant, phone tucked between shoulder and cheek. He was fixing meetings, always meetings. Lorna watched him over the rim of her glass, while her mother demanded that the lights be turned on.

'So damned awful dark in here. Am I supposed to be reminded of the graveyard?'

'Yes, Roddy,' Cammo drawled, 'do something about it, will you? This was your idea after all.' Looking around the premises with all the disdain he could muster. But then the photographers had arrived – one organised by Roddy, one from a glossy magazine – which brought Cordover back to the table, and fixed authentic-seeming smiles to all the members of the Grieve clan.

Roddy Grieve hadn't meant for them to walk the whole length of the Royal Mile. He'd gone so far as to organise a couple of taxis which were waiting for them outside the Holiday Inn. But his mother wouldn't have it.

'If we're going to walk, then for Christ's sake let's walk!' And off she set, her walking stick seven parts affectation to three parts painful necessity, leaving Roddy to pay off the drivers. Cammo leaned towards him.

'You always overdo things.' A pretty good imitation of their mother.

'Bugger off, Cammo.'

'I wish I could, dear brother. But the next train to civilisation's not for some time yet.' Making show of studying his watch. 'Besides, it's Mother's birthday: she'd be devastated if I suddenly departed.'

Which, Roddy couldn't help feeling, was probably true.

'She'll go over on that ankle,' Seona said, watching her mother-in-law moving downhill with that peculiar shuffling gait which attracted all manner of attention. Sometimes, Seona felt that it was affectation, too. Alicia had always had ways and means of drawing the looks of those around her, and of including her offspring in the spectacle. It hadn't been so bad when Allan Grieve had been alive – he'd kept his wife's eccentricities in check. But now that Roddy's father was dead, Alicia had started compensating for years of enforced normality.

Not that the Grieves were a normal family: Roddy had warned Seona about them the first time they'd gone out together. She'd already known, of course – everyone in Scotland knew at least *something* about the Grieves – but had elected to keep her counsel. Roddy wasn't like them, she'd told herself back then. She still said it to herself sometimes, but without the old conviction.

'We could go look at the parliament site,' she suggested as they reached the St Mary's Street junction.

'Good God, whatever for?' Cammo droned predictably.

Alicia pursed her lips, then, saying nothing, turned towards Holyrood Road. Seona tried not to smile: it had been a small but palpable victory. But then who was she fighting?

Cammo held back. The three women were matching each other for pace. Hugh had stopped by a shop window to take yet another call. Cammo fell into step beside Roddy, pleased to note that he was still immeasurably better groomed and dressed than his younger brother.

'I've had another of those notes,' he said, keeping the tone conversational.

'What notes?'

'Christ, didn't I tell you? They come to my parliamentary office. My secretary opens them, poor girl.'

'Hate mail?'

'How many MPs do you know who get fan letters?' Cammo tapped Roddy's shoulder. 'Something you're going to have to live with if you get elected.'

'If,' Roddy repeated with a smile.

'Look, do you want to hear about these bloody death threats or not?'

Roddy stopped in his tracks, but Cammo kept walking. It took Roddy a moment to catch up.

'Death threats?'

Cammo shrugged. 'Not unknown in our line of work.'

'What do they say?'

'Nothing much. Just that I'm "in for it". One of them had a couple of razor blades inside.'

'What do the police say?'

Cammo looked at him. 'So middle-aged, and yet so naïve. The forces of law and order, Roddy – I offer this lesson gratis and for nothing – are like a leaky sieve, especially when there's a drink in it for them and one or more MPs is involved.'

'They'd talk to the media?'

'Bingo.'

'I still don't see . . .'

'The papers would be all over it, and all over me.' Cammo waited for his words to sink in. 'Wouldn't have a life to call my own.'

'But death threats . . .'

'A crank.' Cammo sniffed. 'Not worth mentioning really, except as a warning. My fate could be yours some day, baby bro.'

'If I get elected.' That shy smile again, the shyness masking a real appetite for the fight.

'If ne'er won fair maiden,' Cammo said. Then he shrugged. 'Something like that anyway.' He looked ahead. 'Mother's fairly shifting, isn't she?'

Alicia Grieve had been born Alicia Rankeillor, and it was under this name that she'd found fame – and a certain fortune – as a painter. The particular nature of Edinburgh light had been her subject. Her best-known painting – duplicated on greetings cards, prints and jigsaws – showed a series of jagged beams breaking through a carapace of cloud to pick out the Castle and the Lawnmarket beyond. Allan Grieve, though only a few years her elder, had been her tutor at the School of Art. They'd married young, but hadn't become parents until their careers were well established. Alicia had the sneaking feeling that Allan had always resented her success. He was a great teacher, but lacked the spark of genius as an artist himself. She'd once told him that his paintings were too accurate, that art needed a measure of artifice. He'd squeezed her hand but said nothing until just before his death, when he'd thrown her words back at her.

'You killed me that day, snuffed out any hope I might have still had.' She'd started to protest but he'd hushed her. 'You did me a good turn, you were right. I lacked the vision.'

Sometimes Alicia wished that she'd lacked the vision, too. Not that it would have made her a better, more loving mother. But it might have made her a more generous wife, a more pleasing lover.

Now she lived alone in the huge house in Ravelston, surrounded by the paintings of others – including a dozen of Allan's, smartly framed – and a short walk from the Gallery of Modern Art, where they'd recently held a retrospective of her work. She had contrived an illness to excuse her from attending, then had gone in secret one day, only minutes past opening time when the place was dead, and had been shocked to find that thematic order had been placed on her work, an order she didn't recognise.

'They found a body, you know,' Hugh Cordover was saying.

'Hugh!' Cammo piped up with mock cordiality. 'You're back with us!'

'A body?' Lorna asked.

'It was on the news.'

'I heard it was a skeleton actually,' Seona said.

'Found where?' Alicia asked, pausing to take in the skyline of Salisbury Crags.

'Hidden in a wall in Queensberry House.' Seona pointed to the location. They were standing in front of its gates. They all stared at the building. 'It used to be a hospital.'

'Probably some poor old sod from the waiting list,' Hugh Cordover said, but no one was listening.

4

'Who do you think you are?'

'What?'

'You heard me.' Jayne Lister threw a cushion at her husband's head. 'Those dishes have been sitting since last night.' Her head motioned towards the kitchen. 'You said you were going to do them.'

'I *am* going to do them!'

'When?'

'It's Sunday, day of rest.' He was trying to make a joke of it; didn't want his whole day ruined.

'The whole week's a day of rest as far as you're concerned. What time did you get in last night?'

He tried to see past her to where the TV was playing: some kids' morning show; presenter was a bit of all right. He'd told Nic about her. She was there right now, talking on the telephone, waving a card. Imagine waking up of a morning and finding that beside you in the scratcher.

'Move your arse,' he told his wife.

'You've taken the words out of my mouth.' She turned and pushed the off button. Jerry was off the sofa with a speed which surprised her. He liked the look on her face: startled, and with a little bit of fear mixed in. He pushed her aside, reached for the button, but her hands were in his hair, yanking him back.

'Out with that Nic Hughes till all hours,' she was yelling. 'Think you can come and go as you please, fucking pig!'

He grabbed one of her wrists, squeezed. 'Let go!'

'Think I'm going to put up with it?' She seemed oblivious to the pain. He squeezed harder, wrenching the wrist round. Her grip on his hair tightened. His scalp felt like it was on fire. Threw his head back and caught her just above the nose. That did it. She shrieked and let go, and he half-turned, pushing her hard on to the sofa. Her foot sent the coffee table flying: ashtray, empty cans, Saturday's paper. Whole lot hit the deck. A thumping noise on the ceiling – upstairs neighbours complaining again. Her forehead was reddening where he'd connected.

Christ, she'd given him a headache, too: as if the hangover wasn't enough to be going on with.

He'd done his arithmetic this morning: eight pints and two nips. That tallied with the small change in his pockets. Taxi had cost six quid. Nic had paid for the curry: lamb rogan josh, lovely. Nic had wanted to hit the clubs, but Jerry had said he wasn't in the mood.

'What if *I'm* in the mood, though?' Nic had said. But after the curry he hadn't seemed so keen. Two or three pubs . . . then a taxi for Jerry. Nic had said he'd walk. That was the clever thing about living in the middle of town: no need to worry over transport. Out here in the sticks, transport was always a problem. The buses weren't to be relied on, and he could never remember when they stopped running anyway. Even taxi drivers, you had to lie to them, tell them you were bound for Gatehill. When you reached Gatehill, you could either get out and walk across the playing fields, or you could persuade the driver to take you the final half-mile into the Garibaldi Estate. One time, Jerry had been jumped while crossing the football pitch: four or five of them, and him too drunk to do anything but capitulate. Ever since, he would argue to be taken the distance.

'You really are a bastard,' Jayne was saying, rubbing her brow.

'You started it. I'm lying there with a head like blazes. If you'd just held off a few hours . . .' His voice was soothing. 'I was going to do the dishes, cross my heart. I just need a bit of peace first.' Opening his arms to her. Fact was, the little bout of sparring had given him a hard-on. Maybe Nic was right about sex and violence, about how they were pretty much the same thing.

Jayne pounced to her feet, seemed to have seen straight through him. 'Forget it, pal.' Stalked out of the room. Temper on her . . . and always quick to take the huff. Maybe Nic was right, maybe he really *could* do better. But then look at Nic with his good job and his clothes and everything. Mortgage and money, and still Catriona had left him. Jerry snorted: *left him for someone she met at a singles night! Married woman, and off she trots to a singles night . . . and meets someone!* Life could be cruel, all right; Jerry should be thankful for small mercies. Back on with the telly, lying down on the sofa. His beer can was on the floor, untouched. He lifted it. Cartoons now, but that was all right; he liked cartoons. Didn't have any kids, which was just as well: he was still a bit of a kid at heart himself. The ceiling thumpers upstairs, they had three . . . and had the gall to say *he* was noisy! And there it was on the floor, where it had fallen from the coffee table: the letter from the council. Complaints have reached us . . . powers to deal with problem neighbours . . . blah blah. Was it his fault they built the walls so thin? Bloody things would barely hold a Rawlplug. When the buggers upstairs were trying for kid number four, you felt like you were in the bed with them. One night, when they'd stopped he'd given them a round of applause. Deadly silence after, so he knew they'd heard.

He wondered if maybe that was why Jayne had gone off sex: fear of being heard. One day he'd ask her about it. Either that or he'd make her do it anyway. Make her cry out long and hard so they heard her upstairs, give them something to think about. That wee thing on the telly, he'd bet she was a noisy one. You'd have to clamp your hand over her mouth, but making sure she could still breathe.

Like Nic said, that was the important part.

'You like football then?'

Derek Linford had taken Siobhan's number at the Marina. Saturday, he'd left a message on her machine asking if she fancied a Sunday walk. So here they were in the Botanic Gardens, a crisp afternoon, couples all around, strolling just like them. But talking football.

'I go most Saturdays,' Siobhan confessed.

'I thought there was a winter shutdown or something.' Struggling to show some knowledge of the game.

She smiled at the effort he was making. 'Only for the premier league. Last season, Hibs got knocked down to the first.'

'Oh, right.' They were coming to a signpost. 'If you're cold, we could go to the tropical house.'

She shook her head. 'I'm fine. I don't usually do much on a Sunday.'

'No?'

'Maybe a car boot sale. Mostly, I just stay home.'

'No boyfriend then?' She didn't say anything. 'Sorry I asked.'

She shrugged. 'It's not a sin, is it?'

'Career we're in, how are we supposed to meet people?'

She looked at him. 'Hence the singles club?'

He reddened. 'I suppose so.'

'Don't worry, I'm not about to tell anyone.'

He tried a smile. 'Thanks.'

'You're right anyway,' she went on, 'when *do* we ever meet anyone? Apart from other cops, that is.'

'And villains.'

The way he said it made her suspect he'd not met too many 'villains'. But she nodded anyway.

'I think the tea room'll be open,' he said. 'If you're ready . . . ?'

'Tea and a scone.' She took his arm. 'A perfect Sunday afternoon.'

Except that the family at the table next to them had one hyperactive child and a squealing infant in a pushchair. Linford turned to glower at the infant, as though it would instantly recognise his authority and start behaving.

'What's so funny?' he said, turning back to Clarke.

'Nothing,' she said.

'Must be something.' He started attacking the contents of his coffee cup with a spoon.

She lowered her voice so the family wouldn't hear. 'I was just wondering if you were going to take him into custody.'

'Chance would be a fine thing.' He sounded serious.

They sat in silence for a minute or two, then Linford started telling her about Fettes. When she got a chance, she asked him: 'And what do you like to do when you're not working?'

'Well, there's always a lot of reading to do: textbooks and journals. I keep pretty busy.'

'Sounds fascinating.'

'It is, that's what most people . . .' His voice died away, and he looked at her. 'You were being ironic, right?'

She nodded, smiling. He cleared his throat, got to work with the spoon again.

'Change of subject,' he said at last. 'What's John Rebus like? You work with him at St Leonard's, don't you?'

She was about to say that he hadn't exactly changed the subject, but nodded instead. 'Why do you ask?'

He shrugged. 'The committee, he doesn't seem to take it seriously.'

'Maybe he'd rather be doing something else.'

'From what I've seen of him, that would involve sitting in a pub with a cigarette in his mouth. Got a drink problem, has he?'

She stared at him. 'No,' she said coldly.

He was shaking his head. 'Sorry, shouldn't have asked. Got to stick up for him, haven't you? Same division and all that.'

She bit back a reply. He let the spoon clatter back on to its saucer.

'I'm being an idiot,' he said. The infant was screaming again. 'It's this place . . . Can't think straight.' He risked a look at her. 'Can we go?'

5

Monday morning, Rebus headed for the city mortuary. Normally, when an autopsy was being carried out, he would enter by the side door, which led directly to the viewing area. But the building's air filtering wasn't up to scratch, so all autopsies were now carried out at a hospital, and the mortuary was for storage only. There were none of the distinctive grey Bedford vans in the parking area – unlike most cities, the Edinburgh mortuary picked up every dead body; only later did undertakers enter the equation. He entered by the staff door. There was no one in the 'card room' – so called because employees spent their spare time playing cards there – so he wandered into the storage area. Dougie, who ran the place, was standing there in his white coat, clipboard in hand.

'Dougie,' Rebus said, announcing himself.

Dougie peered at him through wire-rimmed glasses. 'Morning, John.' His eyes twinkled with good humour. He always joked that he worked in the dead centre of Edinburgh.

Rebus twitched his nostrils, letting Dougie know he could smell the faint but noticeable smell.

'Aye,' Dougie said. 'A bad one. Elderly lady, probably dead a week.' He nodded towards the Decomposing Room, where the worst-smelling corpses were stored.

'Well, my one's been dead a sight longer than that.'

Dougie nodded. 'You're too late though. He's already gone.'

'Gone?' Rebus checked his watch.

'Two of my boys took him off to the Western General about an hour ago.'

'I thought the autopsy was scheduled for eleven.'

Dougie shrugged. 'Your man was keen – keen and persuasive. It takes a lot to get the Two Musketeers to change their diaries.'

The Two Musketeers: Dougie's name for Professor Gates and Dr Curt. Rebus frowned.

'My man?'

Dougie looked down at his clipboard, found the name. 'DI Linford.'

When Rebus got to the hospital, the autopsy was in full swing, and with it the double act of Gates and Curt. Professor Gates liked to describe himself as big-boned. Certainly as he leaned over the remains he seemed the antithesis of his colleague, who was tall and gaunt. Curt, Gates' junior by a decade, kept clearing his throat, something newcomers took as a comment on Gates' handiwork. They didn't know about the smoking habit, which was up to thirty a day now. Every moment Curt spent in the autopsy suite was precious time away from his fix. Rebus, whose mind had been on other things during the journey, suddenly craved a cigarette.

'Morning, John,' Gates said, glancing up from his work. Under his rubberised full-length apron he was wearing a crisp white shirt and red-and-yellow striped tie. Somehow his ties always stood out against the grey colours of the suite.

'Been jogging?' Curt asked. Rebus was aware that he was breathing heavily. He ran his hand over his forehead.

'No, I just . . .'

'If he keeps that up,' Gates said, his eyes on Curt, 'he'll be next on the slab.'

'Won't that be fun?' Curt responded. 'Digestive tract full of bridies and beetroot.'

'And the man's so thick-skinned, we'll need hatchets rather than scalpels.' The pair shared a laugh. Not for the first time, Rebus cursed the rule of corroboration, which necessitated two pathologists at each autopsy.

The corpse – literally skin and bone, though some of the skin had been removed already – lay on a shallow stainless-steel trolley, the surface of which was moulded so as to catch any spilled blood. The corpse, however, had dust and cobwebs to spare, but no life fluid. Its skull lay on an angled wooden plinth which, in another context, might have been taken for a curio cheeseboard.

'There's a time and a place for banter, gentlemen.' The voice was Linford's. He was younger than either pathologist, but something about his tone quietened them. Then his eyes were on Rebus. 'Good morning, John.'

Rebus walked over towards him. 'Good of you to tell me about the change of schedule.'

Linford blinked. 'Is there a problem?'

Rebus stared him out. 'No, no problem.' There were others in the room: two hospital technicians, a police photographer, someone from Scene of Crimes, and a suited and queasy-looking man from the Advocate Depute's office. Autopsies were always crowded, everyone either getting on with their work, or else fidgeting nervously.

'I did a bit of boning up over the weekend,' Gates was saying, addressing the room. 'So I can tell you that, judging by the deterioration, our friend here probably died some time in the late nineteen seventies or early eighties.'

'Have his clothes gone for analysis?' Linford asked.

Gates nodded. 'Howdenhall got them this morning.'

'A young man's clothes,' Curt added.

'Or an old one trying to look trendy,' the photographer said.

'Well, the hair shows no signs of grey. Doesn't necessarily mean anything.' Gates looked at the photographer, letting him know his theories weren't welcome. 'The lab will give us a better date of death.'

'How did he die?' This from Linford. Normally Gates would punish such impatience, but he didn't so much as glance at the young DI.

'Skull fracture.' Curt pointed to the area with a pen. 'Could be a post-mortem injury, of course. Might not be the cause of death.' He caught Rebus's eye. 'A lot depends on the Scene of Crime results.'

The SOCO was scribbling into a thick notepad. 'We're working on it.'

Rebus knew what they'd be looking for – murder weapon to start with, and then trace evidence such as blood. Blood had a way of sticking around.

'How did he end up in the fireplace anyway?' he asked.

'Not our problem,' Gates said, smiling towards Curt.

'I take it we're noting this as a suspicious death?' the Fiscal Depute asked, his bass baritone belying the lack of height and brittle frame.

'I'd say so, wouldn't you?' Gates had straightened up, clattering one of his tools back on to its metal tray. It took a moment for Rebus to realise that the pathologist was holding something in his gloved hand. Something shrivelled and the size of a large peach.

'Tough old organ, the heart,' Gates said, examining the specimen.

'You missed the beginning,' Curt explained to Rebus. 'Gash in the skin over the ribcage. Could have been rats . . .'

'Aye,' Gates admitted, 'rats carrying knives.' He showed the organ to his colleague. 'Inch-wide incision. Maybe a kitchen knife, eh?'

'Suspicious death,' the Fiscal Depute muttered to himself, writing it down in his notebook.

'I should have been told,' Rebus hissed. He was in the hospital car park, not about to let Derek Linford drive back to the Big House.

'I know about you, John. You're not a team player.'

'And that was your idea of team playing? Leaving me out?'

'Look, maybe you've got a point. I just don't think it's anything to get het up about.'

'But it's our case, right?'

Linford had opened the driver's door of his shiny new BMW. It was a 3-Series, but would do him for now. 'In what way?'

'The PPLC. We found him.'

'It's not in our brief.'

'Come on. Who else is going to want it? Do you think the parliament really wants an unsolved murder on the premises?'

'A murder from twenty-odd years ago: I hardly think it'll cost them any sleep.'

'Maybe not, but the press won't let it go. Any whiff of scandal, they'll be able to point back to it: Holyrood's murky past, a parliament tainted with blood.'

Linford snorted, but then was thoughtful, finally producing a smile. 'Are you always like this?'

'I think Skelly is ours.'

Linford folded his arms. Rebus knew what he was thinking: the investigation would touch the parliament; it was a route to meeting the movers and shakers. 'How do we play it?'

Rebus rested a hand on the BMW's wing, saw Linford's look and removed it. 'How did he end up there? A couple of decades back, the place was a hospital. I'm guessing you couldn't just walk in, tear down a wall and stuff a body behind it.'

'You think the patients might have noticed?'

It was Rebus's turn to smile. 'It will mean a bit of digging.'

'Your forte, I believe?'

Rebus shook his head. 'I've had enough of all that.'

'What do you mean?'

He meant ghosts, but wasn't about to try to explain. 'What about Grant Hood and Ellen Wylie?' he said instead.

'Will they want it?'

'They won't have any choice. Ever heard the phrase pulling rank?'

Linford nodded thoughtfully, then got into his car, but Rebus's hand stopped him pulling the door closed.

'Just one other thing. Siobhan Clarke is a friend of mine. Anyone makes her unhappy makes *me* unhappy.'

'Don't tell me: I wouldn't like you when you're angry?' Linford smiled again, but coldly this time. 'I get the feeling Siobhan wouldn't thank you for fighting her battles for her. Especially when they're all in your head. Goodbye, John.'

Linford started the engine, then let it idle as he took a call on his mobile. After listening for a few seconds, he stared out at Rebus and slid his window down.

'Where's your car?'

'Two rows back.'

'You'd better follow me then.' Linford terminated the call and tossed the mobile on to his passenger seat.

'Why? What's happened?'

Linford slid both hands around the steering wheel. 'Another body at Queensberry House.' He stared through the windscreen. 'Only a bit fresher this time.'

6

They'd passed the summer house the previous Friday. It was a flimsy wooden affair which had belonged to the hospital and stood inside the grounds, next to Her Majesty's cherry tree. Like the tree, the summer house was for the chop. But for now it was a handy storage area; nothing valuable, there was no lock on the door. And even a lock would have been ineffective, since most of the windows were broken.

This was where the body had been found, lying amidst old paint tins, bags of rubble and broken tools.

'Probably not the way he'd have chosen to go,' Linford muttered, looking around him at the chaos of the site. Uniforms were erecting a cordon around the summer house and its vicinity. Workers in hard hats were being told to disperse. A crowd of them had gathered on the roof of one of the buildings under demolition, from where they had a grandstand view of proceedings. Maybe their fellow workers would join them. Maybe the roof would cave in. Not yet midday and Rebus was conjuring up worst-case scenarios, while praying this would be as bad as it got. The site manager was being interviewed in the security hut, complaining that all the police officers needed to be issued with hard hats. Rebus and Linford had filched a couple from the hut. SOCOs were unpacking the arcana of their craft. A doctor had pronounced death; the call had gone out to the available pathologists. All the building work on Holyrood Road had reduced it to a single lane, controlled by traffic lights. Now, with police cars and vans on the scene (including a grey one from the mortuary, Dougie behind the wheel) queues were forming and tempers fraying. The sound of horns was growing into a chorus, rising into the bruised-looking sky.

'Snow's on the way,' Rebus commented. 'It's cold enough for it.' Yet the previous day had started mild, and even the rain had been like an April shower. Twelve degrees.

'The weather's not exactly a consideration,' Linford snapped. He wanted to get closer to the body, wanted to be inside the summer house, but the *locus* had to be secured. He knew the rules: barging in meant leaving traces.

'Doctor says the back of the skull was cracked open.' He nodded to himself, looked towards Rebus. 'Coincidence?'

Hands in pockets, Rebus shrugged. He was sucking on only his second cigarette of the morning. He knew Linford was tasting something: he was tasting fast-track. Not content with his own momentum, he was seeing a case, a big case. He was seeing himself at its heart, with media attention, the public clamouring for a result. A result he thought *he* could deliver.

'He was running in my constituency,' Linford was saying. 'I've got a flat in Dean Village.'

'Very nice.'

Linford stifled an embarrassed laugh.

'It's okay,' Rebus assured him. 'Times like this, we all tend to talk crap. It fills the spaces.'

Linford nodded.

'Tell me,' Rebus went on, 'just how many murders have you worked?'

'Is this where you pull the old I've-seen-more-corpses-than-you've-had-hot-dinners routine?'

Rebus shrugged again. 'Just interested.'

'I wasn't always at Fettes, you know.' Linford shuffled his feet. 'Christ, I wish they'd get on with it.' The body was still *in situ*, the body of Roddy Grieve. They knew his identity because a gentle search of his pockets had produced a wallet. But they knew, too, because his face was recognisable, even though the light had gone from its eyes. They knew because Roddy Grieve was *somebody*, and seemed so even in death.

He was a Grieve, part of 'the clan', as they'd come to be called. Once, a keen interviewer had gone so far as to name them Scotland's first family. Which was nonsense.

Everyone knew Scotland's first family was the Broons.

'What are you smiling at?'

'Nothing.' Rebus nipped his cigarette and returned it to the packet. He couldn't know for sure whether stubbing it out would have contaminated the crime scene. But he knew the importance of Scene of Crime work. And he felt the sudden pang of desire for a drink, the drink he'd arranged with Bobby Hogan just before Friday's discovery. A long bar-room session of reminiscence and tall tales, with no bodies buried in walls or dumped in summer houses. A drink in some parallel universe where people had stopped being cruel to each other.

And speaking of mental torture, here came Chief Superintendent Farmer Watson. He had Rebus in his sights, and his eyes had narrowed, as though taking aim.

'Don't blame me, sir,' Rebus said, getting his retaliation in first.

'Christ, John, can't you stay out of trouble for one minute?' It was only half a joke. Watson's retirement was a couple of months away. He'd already warned Rebus that he wanted a quiet canter downhill.

Rebus held up his hands in surrender and introduced his boss to Derek Linford.

'Ah, Derek.' The Chief Super held out a hand. 'Heard of you, of course.' The two men shook; kept shaking as they sized one another up.

'Sir,' Rebus interrupted, 'DI Linford and I . . . we feel this should be our case. We're looking at parliamentary security, and this is a prospective MSP who's been killed.'

Watson seemed to ignore him. 'Do we know how he died?'

'Not yet, sir,' Linford was quick to answer. Rebus was impressed at the way he had changed. He was all fawning inferior now, eager to please the Big Chief. It was calculated, of course, but Rebus doubted Watson would notice, or even want to notice.

'Doctor mentioned head trauma,' Linford added. 'Curiously, we're getting a similar result from the body in the fireplace. Skull fracture and stab wound.'

Watson nodded slowly. 'No stab wounds here, though.'

'No, sir,' Rebus said. 'But all the same.'

Watson looked at him. 'You think I'd let you *near* a case like this?'

Rebus shrugged.

'I can show you the fireplace,' Linford told Watson. Rebus wondered if he was trying to defuse the situation. Linford could get the case only through the PPLC, which meant not without Rebus.

'Maybe later, Derek,' the Farmer was saying. 'Nobody's going to bother much about a mouldy old skeleton when we've got Roddy Grieve on our hands.'

'It wasn't that mouldy, sir,' Rebus felt bound to say. 'And it'll still need investigating.'

'Naturally,' Watson snapped. 'But there are priorities, John. Even you've got to see that.' Watson held a hand out, palm upwards. 'Hell, is it starting to snow?'

'Might persuade some of the audience to head indoors,' Rebus said.

The Farmer grunted in agreement. 'Well, if it's going to start snowing, Derek, you might as well show me this fireplace of yours.'

Derek Linford looked as though he'd melt with pleasure, and started leading the Farmer indoors, leaving Rebus out in the cold, where he allowed himself a cigarette and a little smile. Let Linford work on the Farmer . . . that way they might get both cases, a workload to keep Rebus busy through the winter's darkest weeks, and the perfect excuse to ignore Christmas for another year.

7

Identification was a formality, albeit a necessary one. The public entered the mortuary by a door in High School Wynd, and were immediately faced by a door marked Viewing Room. There were chairs for them to sit in. If they chose to wander, they'd come across a desk with a department store mannequin seated behind it. The mannequin was dressed in a white lab coat and had a moustache pencilled below its nose – a rare, if bizarre, example of humour, given the surroundings.

It would be some time before Gates and Curt could get round to doing an autopsy, but, as Dougie reassured Rebus, there was 'plenty of room in the fridge'. There wasn't nearly so much space in the reception area outside the Viewing Room. Roddy Grieve's widow was there. So were his mother and sister. His brother Cammo was flying up from London. An unwritten rule stated that the media kept clear of the mortuary, no matter how juicy the story. But a few of the most rapacious vultures had gathered on the pavement across the road. Rebus, stepping outside for a cigarette, approached them. Two journalists, one photographer. They were young and lean and had little or no respect for old rules. They knew him, shuffled their feet but made no attempt to move.

'I'm going to ask nicely,' Rebus said, shaking a cigarette from its pack. He lit it, then offered the pack around. The three shook their heads. One was fiddling with his mobile phone, checking messages on its tiny screen.

'Anything for us, DI Rebus?' the other reporter asked.

Rebus stared at him, seeing immediately that it was no good appealing to reason.

'Off the record, if you like,' the reporter persisted.

'I don't mind being quoted,' Rebus said quietly. The reporter lifted a tape-recorder from his jacket pocket.

'Bit closer, please.'

The reporter obliged, switched the machine on.

Rebus was careful to enunciate slowly and clearly. After eight or nine words, the reporter flicked the machine off, the look on his face somewhere between a sneer and a grudging smile. Behind him, his colleagues were staring at their shoes.

'Need a spell-check for any of that?' Rebus asked. Then he crossed the road and headed back into the mortuary.

The ID was over, the paperwork complete. The family members looked numb. Even Linford looked a bit shaken: maybe it was another of his acts. Rebus approached the widow.

'We can arrange for a couple of cars . . .'

She sniffed back tears. 'No, that's all right. Thanks anyway.' She blinked, eyes finally focusing on him. 'A taxi should be coming.' The deceased's sister came across, leaving her mother stony-faced and straight-backed on one of the chairs.

'Mum has a funeral home she wants to use, if that's all right with you.' Lorna Cordover was speaking to the widow, but it was Rebus who answered.

'You realise we can't release the body just yet.'

She stared at him with eyes he'd stared at a thousand times in newspapers and magazines. Lorna Grieve: her modelling name. She wasn't yet fifty, but was closing in on it fast. Rebus had first come across her towards the end of the sixties, when she'd have been in her late teens. She'd dated rock stars, was rumoured to have caused the break-up of at least one successful band. She'd been in *Melody Maker* and *NME*. Long straw-blond hair back then, and thin to the point of emaciation. She'd filled out quite a bit, and her hair was shorter, darker. But there was still something about her, even in this place, at this time.

'We're his bloody family,' she snapped.

'Please, Lorna,' her sister-in-law cautioned.

'Well, we are, aren't we? Last thing we need is some jumped-up little squirt with a clipboard telling us—'

'I think maybe you're confusing me with the staff here,' Rebus cut in.

She looked at him again, eyes narrowing. 'Then just who the hell are you?'

'He's the policeman,' Seona Grieve explained. 'He'll be the one who looks into . . .' But she couldn't find the words, and the sentence died softly with an exhalation.

Lorna Grieve snorted, pointed towards Derek Linford, who had seated himself next to the mother, Alicia. He was leaning towards her, his hand touching the back of hers. 'That', Lorna informed them, 'is the officer who'll be investigating Roddy's murder.' She squeezed Seona's shoulder. '*He*'s the one we should be talking to,' she said. Then, with a final glance towards Rebus, 'Not his monkey.'

Rebus watched her move back towards the chairs. Beside him, the widow spoke so softly he didn't catch it.

'Sorry,' she repeated.

He smiled, nodded. There were a dozen platitudes scrawled and waiting in his head. He rubbed a hand across his forehead to erase them.

'You'll want to ask us questions,' she said.

'When you're ready.'

'He didn't have any enemies . . . not really.' She seemed to be speaking to herself. 'That's what they always ask on TV, isn't it?'

'We'll get round to it.' He was watching Lorna Grieve, who was crouched in front of her mother. Linford was looking at her, drinking her in. The main door opened, a head appearing.

'Somebody order a taxi?'

Rebus watched as Derek Linford escorted Alicia Grieve all the way out. It was a shrewd move: not the widow, but the matriarch. Linford knew power when he saw it.

They gave the family a few hours, then drove to Ravelston Dykes.

'What do you reckon then?' Linford asked. From his tone, he might have been asking what Rebus thought of the BMW.

Rebus just shrugged. Between them, they'd managed to sort out a Murder Room at St Leonard's, it being the closest station to the *locus*. Not that it was a murder inquiry yet, but they knew it would be, just as soon as the autopsy was finished. Calls had gone out to Joe Dickie and Bobby Hogan. Rebus had also hooked up with Grant Hood and Ellen Wylie, neither of whom objected to the idea of working together on the Skelly case.

'It'll be a challenge,' both had said, independently of one another. Their bosses would have the final say, but Rebus didn't foresee problems. He'd told Hood and Wylie to get together, thrash out a plan of attack.

'And who do we report to?' Wylie had asked.

'Me,' he'd told her, making sure Linford wasn't in earshot.

The BMW eased down into second as they approached an amber light. Had Rebus been driving, he'd have accelerated, probably just missing red. Maybe not on his own, but with a passenger – he'd have done it to impress. He'd have laid money on Linford doing it, too. The BMW stopped at the lights. Linford applied the handbrake and turned towards him.

'Investment analyst, Labour candidate, high-profile family. What do you think?'

Rebus shrugged again. 'I've seen the newspaper stories, same as you. Some people haven't always liked the way candidates were selected.'

Linford was nodding. 'Maybe some bad blood there?'

'We'll ask. Could just be a mugging gone wrong.'

'Or a liaison.'

Rebus glanced at him. Linford was staring at the lights, fingers poised on the handbrake. 'Maybe the SOCOs will work their magic.'

'Fingerprints and fibres?' Linford sounded sceptical.

'Lot of mud around. Could be we'll find footprints.'

The light turned green. With an empty road ahead, the BMW quickly changed up through its gears.

'The boss has already been on to me,' Linford told his passenger. Rebus knew that by boss he didn't mean anything as middle-management as a chief super. 'The ACC,' Linford explained: Colin Carswell, Assistant Chief Constable (Crime). 'He wanted to bring in a special team, something as high profile as this.'

'Crime Squad?'

It was Linford's turn to shrug. 'Hand picked. I don't know who he had in mind.'

'What did you tell him?'

'I said with me in charge, he didn't have to worry.' Linford couldn't help it, had to turn towards Rebus to enjoy his reaction. Rebus was trying to look unmoved by it all. All his years on the force, he'd probably spoken with the ACC no more than two or three times.

Linford smiled, knew he'd hit some soft, fleshy part beneath Rebus's shell-like exterior.

'Of course,' he went on, 'when I mentioned that DI Rebus would be assisting . . .'

'Assisting?' Rebus bristled, and only now recollected that Linford had also spoken of being in charge.

'He was a bit more dubious,' Linford went on, ignoring the outburst. 'But I told him you'd be fine, said we were working well together. That's what I mean by assisting – you helping me, me helping you.'

'But with you in charge?'

Hearing his own phrase thrown back at him seemed to please Linford: another palpable hit. 'Your own chief super doesn't want you on the case, John. Why is that?'

'None of your business.'

'Everyone knows about you, John. I could say that your reputation precedes you.'

'But it'll be different with you in charge?' Rebus guessed.

Linford shrugged and was silent for a moment, then shifted in his seat. 'While we're enjoying this time together,' he said, 'maybe I should throw in that I'm seeing Siobhan tonight. But don't worry, I'll have her home by eleven.'

Roddy Grieve and his wife had lived together somewhere in Cramond, but Seona Grieve had intimated that she would be with Roddy's mother. Situated at the end of a short narrow street, the huge detached house had a jagged feel to it. Maybe it was to do with the several crow-step gables, or the stone relief thistle set into the wall above the front door. There were no cars in the drive, and curtains had been drawn closed in every window – a sensible precaution: the reporters and cameraman were back, parked kerbside in a silver Audi

80. TV crews were probably on their way. Rebus had no doubt the Grieves would cope with the attention.

Grieve: the resonance of the name hit him for the first time. The grieving Grieves.

Linford rang the doorbell. 'Nice place,' he said.

'I was brought up in something similar,' Rebus told him. Then, after a pause: 'Well, we lived in a cul-de-sac.'

'And there', Linford guessed, 'the comparison ends.'

The door was opened by a man dressed in a camel-hair coat with dark brown lapels. The coat was unbuttoned. Beneath it could be glimpsed a tailored pinstripe suit and white shirt. The shirt was unbuttoned at the neck. In his left hand, the man carried a plain black tie.

'Mr Grieve?' Rebus guessed. He'd seen Cammo Grieve on TV many times. In the flesh he seemed taller and more distinguished, even in his present confused-looking state. His cheeks were red, either from cold or a few airline drinks. A couple of strands of silver and black hair were out of place.

'You the police? Come inside.'

Linford followed Rebus into the hallway. There were paintings and drawings everywhere, not just covering the wood-panelled walls, but resting against the skirting boards, too. Books were piled high on the bottom step of the stone staircase. Several pairs of dusty-looking rubber wellington boots – men's and women's, and all of them black – sat at the foot of an overloaded coat rack. There were walking sticks protruding from an umbrella stand, and umbrellas hooked over the banister. An open jar of honey sat on a telephone table, as did an answering machine. The machine wasn't plugged in, and there was no sign of a phone. Cammo Grieve seemed to take in his surroundings.

'Sorry,' he said. 'In a bit of a . . . well, you understand.' He stroked the stray hairs back into place.

'Of course, sir,' Linford said, his voice deferential.

'A bit of advice, though,' Rebus added, waiting till he had the MP's attention. 'Anyone at all could turn up claiming to be police officers. Make sure you ask for ID before letting them in.'

Cammo Grieve nodded. 'Ah yes, the fourth estate. Bastards for the most part.' He looked at Rebus. 'Off the record.'

Rebus merely nodded; it was Linford who smiled too brightly at the attempted levity.

'I still can't . . .' Grieve's face hardened. 'I trust the police will be working flat-out on this case. If I so much as hear of any corners being cut . . . I know what it's like these days, tightened budgets, all of that. Labour government, you see.'

It was in danger of turning into a speech. Rebus interrupted. 'Well, standing around here isn't exactly helping matters, sir.'

'I'm not sure I like you,' Grieve said, narrowing his eyes. 'What's your name?'

'His name's Monkey Man,' a voice called from a doorway. Lorna Grieve was carrying two glasses of whisky. She handed one to her brother, clinked her own against it before taking a gulp. 'And this one', she said, meaning Linford, 'is the Organ Grinder.'

'I'm DI Rebus,' Rebus informed Cammo Grieve. 'This is DI Linford.'

Linford turned from the wall. He'd been studying one of the framed prints. It was unusual in that it was a series of handwritten lines.

'A poem to our mother,' Lorna Grieve explained. 'From Christopher Murray Grieve. He wasn't any relation, in case you're wondering.'

'Hugh MacDiarmid,' Rebus said, seeing the blank look on Linford's face. The look didn't change.

'The Monkey Man has a brain,' Lorna cooed. Then she noticed the honey. 'Oh, there it is. Mother thought she'd put it down somewhere.' She turned back to Rebus. 'I'll let you into a secret, Monkey Man.' She was standing right in front of him. He stared at lips he had kissed as a young man, tasting printer's ink and cheap paper in his mouth. She smelt of good whisky, a perfume he could savour. Her voice was harsh but her eyes were numb. 'Nobody knows about that poem. He gave it to our mother. No other copy exists.'

'Lorna . . .' Cammo Grieve laid a hand against the back of his sister's neck, but she twisted away from him. 'It's a sin beyond redeeming to stand here drinking while our guests go without.' He ushered them into the morning room. It was wood-panelled like the hall, but boasted only a few small paintings hanging from a picture rail. There were two sofas and two armchairs, a TV and hi-fi. Apart from that, the room was all books, piled on the floor, squeezed into shelves, filling all the spaces between the potted plants on the window sill. With the curtains closed, the lights were on. The ceiling candelabrum could accommodate three bulbs, but only one was working. Rebus lifted a pile of birthday cards from the sofa: someone had decided the celebrations were over.

'How is Mrs Grieve?' Linford asked.

'My mother's resting,' Cammo Grieve said.

'I meant Mr Grieve's . . . um, your brother's . . .'

'He means Seona,' Lorna said, dropping on to one of the sofas.

'Resting also,' Cammo Grieve explained. He walked over to the marble fireplace, gestured towards the grate, which had become a repository for whisky bottles. 'No longer a working fire,' he said, 'but it can still—'

'Put fire in our bellies,' his sister groaned, rolling her eyes. 'Christ, Cammo, that one wore out long ago.'

Red had risen again in her brother's cheeks – anger this time. Maybe he'd been angry when he'd answered the door, too. Lorna Grieve could have that effect on a man, no doubt about it.

'I'll have a Macallan,' Rebus said.

'A man with sharp eyes,' Cammo Grieve said, making it sound like praise. 'And yourself, DI Linford?'

Linford surprised Rebus, asked for a Springbank. Grieve produced tumblers from a small cupboard and poured a couple of decent measures.

'I won't insult you by offering to dilute them.' He handed the drinks over. 'Sit down, why don't you?'

Rebus took one armchair, Linford the other. Cammo Grieve sat on the sofa beside his sister, who squirmed at the intrusion. They drank their drinks and were silent for a moment. Then there was a trilling sound from Cammo's coat pocket. He lifted out a mobile phone and got to his feet, making for the door.

'Hello, yes, sorry about that, but I'm sure you understand . . .' He closed the door after him.

'Well,' Lorna Grieve said, 'what have I done to deserve this?'

'Deserve what, Mrs Cordover?' Linford asked.

She snorted.

'I think, DI Linford,' Rebus said slowly, 'she means what has she done to deserve being left alone here with two complete duds like us. Would that be accurate, Mrs Cordover?'

'It's Grieve, Lorna Grieve.' There was some venom in her eyes, but not enough to kill her prey, merely stun it. But at least she was focused again – focused on Rebus. 'Do we know one another?' she asked.

'I don't think so,' he admitted.

'It's just the way you keep staring at me.'

'And how's that?'

'Like a lot of photographers I've met along the way. Sleazeballs with no film in the camera.'

Rebus hid his smile behind the whisky glass. 'I used to be a big fan of Obscura.'

Her eyes widened a little, and her voice softened. 'Hugh's band?'

Rebus was nodding. 'You were on one of their album sleeves.'

'God, so I was. It seems like a lifetime ago. What was it called . . . ?'

'*Continuous Repercussions*.'

'My God, I think you're right. It was their last record, wasn't it? I never really liked their stuff, you know.'

'Really?'

They were talking now, having a conversation. Linford was on the periphery of Rebus's vision, and if Rebus concentrated on Lorna Grieve, the younger man faded away until he could have been a trick of the light.

'Obscura,' Lorna reminisced. 'That name was Hugh's idea.'

'It's up near the Castle, isn't it, the Camera Obscura?'

'Yes, but I'm not sure Hugh ever went there. He chose the name for another reason. You know Donald Cammell?'

Rebus was stumped.

'He was a film director. He made *Performance*.'

'Yes, of course.'

'He was born there.'

'In the Camera Obscura?'

Lorna nodded, smiled across the room at him with something approaching warmth.

Linford cleared his throat. 'I've been to the Camera Obscura,' he said. 'It's quite amazing, the view.'

There was silence for a moment. Then Lorna Grieve smiled again at Rebus. 'He doesn't have a clue, does he, Monkey Man? Not the slightest clue what we've been talking about.'

Rebus was shaking his head in agreement as Cammo walked back into the room. He'd removed his coat, but not the jacket. Now that Rebus thought of it, the house was none too warm. These big old places, you put in central heating but not double glazing. High ceilings and draughts. Maybe it was time to turn the makeshift drinks cabinet back to its original use.

'Sorry about that,' Cammo said. 'Blair was saddened by the news, apparently.'

Lorna snorted, back to her old self. 'Tony Blair: I'd trust him as far as I could throw him.' She looked at her brother. 'Bet he's never heard of you either. Roddy would have made twice the MP you'll ever be. What's more, at least he had the guts to stand for the *Scottish* parliament, somewhere he felt he could do some good!'

Her voice had risen, and with it the colour in her brother's cheeks.

'Lorna,' he said quietly, 'you're distraught.'

'Don't you dare patronise me!'

The MP looked at his two guests, his smile attempting to reassure them that there was nothing here to worry about, nothing to take to the outside world.

'Lorna, I really think—'

'All the crap this family's been through over the years, it's all down to you!' Lorna was growing hysterical. 'Dad tried his damnedest to hate you!'

'That's enough!'

'And Roddy, poor bastard, actually wanted to *be* you! And everything with Alasdair—'

Cammo Grieve raised his hand to slap his sister. She reared back from him, shrieking. And then there was someone in the doorway, shaking slightly, leaning heavily on a black walking cane. And someone else in the hall, hand clutching at the neck of her dressing-gown.

'Stop this at once!' Alicia Grieve shouted, stamping down hard with her cane. Behind her, Seona Grieve looked almost ghostly, as if alabaster had replaced the blood in her veins.

8

'I didn't even know this place had a restaurant.' Siobhan looked around her. 'You can smell the paint.'

'It's only been open a week,' Derek Linford said, sitting down opposite her. They were in the Tower restaurant at the top of the Museum of Scotland on Chambers Street. There was a terrace outside, but no one was eating alfresco this December night. Their window table gave a view of the Sheriff's Court and the Castle. The rooftops shone with frost. 'I hear it's pretty good,' he added. 'Same owner as the Witchery.'

'Busy enough.' Siobhan was studying the other diners. 'I recognise that woman over there. Doesn't she do restaurant reviews for one of the papers?'

'I never read them.'

She looked at him. 'How did you hear about it?'

'What?'

'This place.'

'Oh.' He was already studying the menu. 'Some guy from Historic Scotland mentioned it.'

She smiled at 'guy', reminded that Linford was her own age, maybe even a year or two younger. His dress sense was so conservative – dark wool suit, white shirt, blue tie – that he seemed older. It might help explain his popularity with the 'high hiedyins' at the Big House. When he'd asked her to dinner, her first instinct had been to refuse. It wasn't as if they'd exactly hit it off in the Botanics. But at the same time she wondered if she could learn anything from him. Her own mentor, Chief Inspector Gill Templer, didn't seem to be helping much – too busy proving to her male colleagues that she was every bit their equal. Which wasn't the truth. Truth was, she was better than most male CIs Siobhan had worked for. But Gill Templer didn't seem to know that.

'Would this be the guy who discovered the body in Queensberry House?'

'That's him,' Linford said. 'See anything you fancy?'

With some men, it would have come out as a chat-up line, trying to hook the expected response from her. But Linford was checking the menu like it was evidence.

'I'm not much of a meat-eater,' she told him. 'Any news on Roddy Grieve?'

The waitress arrived and they ordered. Linford checked that Siobhan wasn't driving before asking for a bottle of white wine.

'Did you walk?' he asked.

She shook her head. 'Taxied it.'

'I should have asked. I could've picked you up.'

'That's all right. You were telling me about Roddy Grieve.'

'God, that sister of his.' Linford shook his head at the memory.

'Lorna? I'd like to meet her.'

'She's a monster.'

'Good-looking monster.' Linford shrugged, as if looks meant nothing to him. 'If I look half as good at her age,' Siobhan went on, 'I'll be doing well.'

He busied himself with his wineglass. Maybe he thought she was fishing for a compliment. Maybe she was.

'She seemed to hit it off with your bodyguard,' he said at last.

'My what?'

'Rebus. The one who doesn't want me seeing you.'

'I'm sure he—'

Linford leaned back suddenly in his chair. 'Oh, let's forget it. Sorry I said anything.'

Siobhan was confused now. She didn't know what kind of signals her dinner partner was giving off. She brushed non-existent crumbs from her red crushed-velvet dress, checked the knees of her black tights for runs that weren't there. With her coat off, her arms and shoulders were bare. Was she making him nervous?

'Is there something wrong?' she asked.

He shook his head, eyes everywhere but on her. 'It's just . . . I've never dated anyone from work before.'

'Dated?'

'You know, gone out for a meal with them. I mean, I've been to official functions, but never . . .' His eyes finally rested on hers. 'Just two people, me and one other. Like this.'

She smiled. 'We're having dinner, Derek, that's all.' She swallowed the sentence back, but too late. *Was* that all they were going to do, have dinner? Was he expecting anything more?

But he seemed to relax a little. 'Bloody strange house, too,' he said, as though his mind had been on the Grieves all along. 'Paintings and newspapers and books spread everywhere. Deceased's mother lives alone, should probably be in a home, someone to look after her.'

'She's a painter, isn't she?'

'Was. Not sure she still is.'

'Her stuff fetches a small fortune. It was in the papers.'

'Bit gaga if you ask me, but then she'd just lost a son. Not really for me to say, is it?' He looked at her to see how he was doing. Her eyes told him to go on. 'Cammo Grieve was there, too.'

'He's supposed to be a rake.'

Linford seemed surprised. 'Bit fat to be a rake.'

'Not a garden rake. You know, a bit of a ladies' man, not to be trusted.'

She was grinning, but he took her at her word. 'Not to be trusted? Hmm.' He went thoughtful again. 'God knows what they were talking about.'

'Who?'

'Rebus and Lorna Grieve.'

'Rock music,' Siobhan stated, leaning back so the waitress could pour the wine.

'Some of the time, yes.' Linford studied her. 'How did you know?'

'She's married to a record producer, and John loves all that. Immediate connection.'

'I can see why you're in CID.'

She shrugged. 'He's probably the only man I know who plays Wishbone Ash on surveillance.'

'Who are Wishbone Ash?'

'Exactly.'

Later, when they'd finished their starters, Siobhan asked again about Roddy Grieve. 'I mean, we are talking suspicious death here, aren't we?'

'Autopsy's not been done yet, but it's a racing certainty. He didn't kill himself and it doesn't look like an accident.'

'Killing a politician.' Siobhan tutted.

'Ah, but he wasn't, was he? He was a financial analyst who just happened to be running for parliament.'

'Making it harder to fathom why he was killed?'

Linford nodded. 'Could be a client with a grudge. Maybe Grieve made some bad investments.'

'Then there are the people he beat to the Labour nomination.'

'Agreed: plenty of infighting there.'

'And there's his family.'

'A way of getting at them.' Linford was still nodding.

'Or he was just in the wrong place, et cetera.'

'Goes to take a look at the parliament site, becomes victim of a mugging gone wrong.' Linford puffed out his cheeks. 'Lots of possible motives.'

'And they all have to be looked at.'

'Yes.' Linford didn't look too happy at the prospect. 'Some hard work ahead. No easy answers.'

It sounded like he was trying to convince himself the whole thing was worth the candle. 'John's reliable, is he? Just between you and me.'

She thought it over, nodded slowly. 'Once he gets his teeth in, he doesn't let go.'

'That's what I'd heard. Doesn't know when to let go.' He made it sound like something less than praise. 'The ACC wants me running the show. How do you think John will take it?'

'I don't know.'

He attempted a laugh. 'It's all right, I won't tell him we've spoken.'

'It's not that,' she said, though partly it was. 'I genuinely don't know.'

Linford looked disappointed in her. 'Doesn't matter,' he said.

But Siobhan knew that it did.

Nic Hughes was driving his friend Jerry through the city streets. Jerry kept asking him where they were headed.

'Christ almighty, Jerry, you're like a broken record.'

'I just like to know.'

'What if I say we're not going anywhere?'

'That's what you said before.'

'And have we reached a destination?' Jerry didn't seem to understand. 'No, we have not.' Nic told him. 'Because we're driving aimlessly, and sometimes that can be fun.'

'Eh?'

'Just shut up, will you?'

Jerry Lister stared from his passenger window. They'd been south as far as the bypass, taken it to the Gyle and headed back towards Queensferry Road. But then instead of heading back into the centre, Nic had forked off towards Muirhouse and Pilton. They saw some guy urinating against a lamp-post and Jerry said to watch; pressed the button so his window slid down, and as they passed he let out a blood-curdling scream, laughing afterwards, checking the result in the rearview. You could hear the guy swearing.

'They're dogs out here, Jerry,' Nic had warned him, as if Jerry needed telling.

Jerry liked Nic's car. It was a shiny black Sierra Cosworth. When they passed a group of lads, Nic sounded the horn, waved as if he knew them. They stared, watching the car, watching its driver watching them.

'Car like this, Jer, those kids would kill for it. I'm not joking, they'd do their granny in just for the chance of a test drive.'

'Better not run out of petrol then.'

Nic looked at him. 'We could take them, pal.' All bravado with some speed in his system and wearing his blue suede jacket. 'You don't think so?' Slowing the car, his foot all the way off the accelerator. 'We could go back there and . . .'

'Just keep driving, eh?'

A few moments of silence after that, Nic caressing the steering wheel round all the roundabouts they came to.

'Are we going to Granton?'

'Do you want to?'

'What's there?' Jerry asked.

'I don't know. You're the one who brought it up.' A sly glance at his friend. 'Ladies of the night, Jer, is that it? You want to try another?' Tongue lolling from his mouth. 'They won't get in the car with two of us, you know. Too sussed for that, the night ladies. Maybe you could hide in the boot. I'd pick one up, take her to the car park . . . There'd be two of us, Jer.'

Jerry Lister licked his lips. 'I thought we'd decided?'

'Decided what?'

Jerry sounding worried. 'You know.'

'Memory's shot, pal.' Nic Hughes tapped his head. 'It's the drink. I drink to forget, and it seems to work.' His face hardened, left hand twisting the gear stick. 'Only I forget all the wrong things.'

Jerry turned to him. 'Let her go, Nic.'

'Easy for you to say.' He bared his teeth as he spoke. There were flecks of white at the corners of his mouth. 'Know what she told me, pal? Know what she said?'

Jerry didn't want to hear. James Bond's car had an ejector seat; all the Cosworth boasted was a sunroof. Jerry looked around anyway, as if seeking the ejector button.

'She said this was a crap car. Said everyone laughed at it.'

'They don't.'

'These kids out here, they'd tear this car up for an hour and then get bored. That's all it would mean to them, which is a hundred per cent more than it meant to Cat.'

Some men got sad, emotional; they cried. Jerry had cried himself once or twice – a few cans of beer in him and watching *Animal Hospital*; and at Christmas when *Bambi* or *The Wizard of Oz* was on. But he'd never seen Nic cry. Instead, Nic turned it all into anger. Even when he was smiling, like now, Jerry knew he was angry, close to blowing. Not everyone knew, but Jerry did.

'Come on, Nic,' he said. 'Let's head into town, do Lothian Road or the Bridges.'

'Maybe you're right,' Nic said at last. He was stopped at lights. A motorbike drew up alongside, revving. Not a big engine, but those things had no weight either. Kid on it, maybe seventeen. His eyes on them, face masked by the crash helmet. Nic's foot went hard on clutch and accelerator, but when the lights changed the bike left them squashed like a hedgehog.

'See that?' Nic asked quietly. 'That's Cat waving me and my crap car bye-bye.'

Back in town they stopped for a breather, burger and chips, ate from the box, standing roadside, leaning against the car. Jerry's jacket was cheap nylon. He had it zipped but was still shivering. Nic had his jacket open, didn't look to be feeling the cold at all. There were kids in the restaurant, girls in their teens sat at a window table. Nic smiled at them, tried to catch their eyes. They sipped milk shakes, ignored him.

'They think they're in control, Jer,' Nic said. 'That's what's so funny about the whole thing. Here we are, standing out here in the cold, but it's *us* that have the power. Their world's forgotten that, but it would take us ten seconds to haul them into *our* world.' He turned to his friend. 'Wouldn't it?'

'If you say so.'

'No, *you've* got to say it. That way, it becomes true.' Nic dropped his burger box on to the pavement. Jerry hadn't finished his, but Nic was getting back into the car, and he knew Jerry didn't like smells in the Cosworth. There was a bin near by. He dropped his meal into it. One minute it's food, the next it's rubbish. The car was already moving as he pulled himself inside.

'We're not going to do one tonight, are we?' The food seemed to have calmed Nic.

'Don't think so, no.'

Jerry relaxed as they cruised Princes Street – wasn't the same since the council had made it one-way for cars. Headed up Lothian Road. Then down into the Grassmarket and up Victoria Street. Big buildings at the top. Jerry had no idea what any of them were. George IV Bridge: he recognised the old Sheriff Court, which was now the High Court, Deacon Brodie's pub opposite. They took a right at the lights, tyres rippling over the setts as they cruised the High Street. Bitter outside, not many people walking. But Nic was pressing a button, lowering the passenger-side window. Jerry saw her: three-quarter-length coat; black stockings; short dark hair. Good height, trim figure. Nic slowed the car beside her.

'Cold night to be out,' he called. She ignored him. 'You can catch a taxi outside the Holiday Inn if you're lucky. It's just down there.'

'I know where it is,' she snapped.

'You English? On holiday?'

'I live here.'

'Just trying to be friendly. We're always accused of being rude to English people.'

'Just piss off, will you?'

Nic pushed the car forwards, then stopped, so he could turn round and see her face properly. She had a scarf around her neck, chin and mouth tucked into it. As she walked past, for all the world as if they didn't exist, Nic caught Jerry's eye and started nodding.

'Lesbian, Jerry,' he confirmed loudly, closing the window and moving off again.

Siobhan didn't know quite why she was walking. But, entering Waverley Station by the back way, seeing it as a shortcut of sorts, she knew why she was shaking.

Lesbian.

Sod them all. The whole lot of them. She'd turned down Derek Linford's offer of a lift. Said she felt like a walk; unsure straight away why she'd said it. They'd parted amicably enough. No handshake or peck on the cheek, that wasn't the Edinburgh way, not on a first dinner-date. Just smiles and a promise to do it again some time: a promise she was pretty sure she'd be breaking. It was strange, taking the lift down from the restaurant through the museum. Workmen were still busy, even at that hour. Cables and ladders, the sound of an electric drill.

'I thought this place was open for business,' Linford had said.

'It is,' she'd told him. 'It's just not ready yet, that's all.'

She'd walked up George IV Bridge, decided to head down the High Street. But that car, those men . . . she'd wanted off that street. A long flight of dark steps, shadows all around, shouts and music from still-open pubs. Then Waverley. She would cut through, back up on to Princes Street, then down Broughton Street, the city's so-called gay village.

Which was where she lived. It was where a lot of people lived.

Lesbian.

Sod them all.

She thought back on the evening, trying to calm herself. Derek had been nervous, but then who was she to talk? The sex crimes secondment, it had put her off men. The register of offenders . . . all those hungry faces . . . the details of their crimes. And then her time with Sandra Carnegie, swapping stories and feelings. One officer who'd worked sex crimes for the best part of four years had warned her: 'It's a passion-basher, puts you right off.' Three tramps had attacked a student, another student had been assaulted on one of the South Side's richest streets. A car cruising past, an attempted chat-up and stinging punchline; small beer by comparison. All the same, she'd remember that name – Jerry – and the shiny black Sierra.

From the pedestrian bridge, she could look down on to the railway tracks and the concourse. Above her was the station's leaky glass roof. When something plummeted, just on the edge of her vision, she thought she was imagining it. She looked across and saw snow falling. No, not snow: big flakes of glass. There was a hole in the roof, and below on one of the platforms someone was yelling. A couple of taxi drivers had opened their doors, were making for the scene.

Another leaper: that's what it was. An area of darkness on the platform: it was like staring into a black hole. But really it was a long coat, the coat the leaper had been wearing. Siobhan made for the steps down to the concourse. Passengers were waiting for the sleeper to London. A woman was crying. One of the taxi drivers had taken off his jacket and laid it over the top half of the body. Siobhan moved forward. The other taxi driver put a hand out to stop her.

'I wouldn't, love,' he said. For a moment she misheard him:

I wouldn't love. I wouldn't love because love makes you weak. I wouldn't love because your job will kill it dead.

'I'm a police officer,' she told him, reaching for her warrant card.

So many people had jumped from North Bridge, the Samaritans had bolted a sign to the parapet. North Bridge connected Old Town Edinburgh to the New Town and passed over the deep gully which housed Waverley Station. By the time Siobhan got there, no one was around. Distant shapes and voices: drinkers heading home. Taxis and cars. If anyone had seen the fall, they hadn't bothered stopping. Siobhan leaned over the parapet, looked down on Waverley's roof. Almost directly below was the hole. Through it, she could glimpse movement on the platform. She'd called for assistance, told them to alert the mortuary. She was off duty; let one of the uniforms – Rebus called them woolly suits – deal with it. From the dead man's clothes, she was assuming he was a tramp. Only you didn't call them tramps these days, did you? Problem was, she couldn't think of the right word. Already in her head she was writing her report. Looking around at the empty street, she realised she could just walk away. Leave it to others. Her foot touched something. A plastic carrier bag. She nudged it and felt resistance. Stooping, she picked it up. It was one of the oversized bags you carried skirts or dresses home in. A Jenners bag, no less. The upmarket department store was a couple of minutes' walk away. She doubted the leaper had ever shopped there. But she guessed his whole life was contained in the bag, so she took it with her back down to Waverley.

She'd dealt with suicides before. People who turned on the gas and sat down next to the fire. Cars left running in locked garages. Pill bottles by the bed, blue lips flecked with white. A CID officer had jumped from Salisbury Crags not so long ago. Plenty of places like that in Edinburgh; no shortage of suicide spots.

'You could go home, you know,' a uniform told her. She nodded. The woman officer smiled. 'So what's keeping you?'

A good question. It was as if she knew, knew there was so little to go home to.

'You're one of DI Rebus's, aren't you?' the uniform asked.

Siobhan glared at her. 'What's that supposed to mean?'

The woman shrugged. 'Sorry I spoke.' Then she turned and walked away. They'd cordoned off the section of platform where the body lay. A doctor had confirmed death, and one of the mortuary vans was getting ready to remove the remains. Station staff were in search of a hose, wanted to get a jet-spray on to the platform. Blood and brains would be washed on to the tracks.

The sleeper passengers had departed, the station readying to close for the night. No taxis now. Siobhan wandered over to the left-luggage lockers. There was a desk there, and a male uniform was emptying the

Jenners bag on to it, picking out each item gingerly, as if dealing with contamination.

'Anything?' Siobhan asked.

'Just what you see.'

There had been no form of ID on the deceased, nothing in his pockets but a handkerchief and some coins. Siobhan studied the items on the table. A polythene bread bag seemed to contain a rudimentary wash-kit. There were a few articles of clothing, an old copy of *Reader's Digest*. A small transistor radio, its back held on with sticking tape. The day's evening paper, folded and crumpled . . .

You're one of DI Rebus's. Meaning what? Meaning she'd grown to be like him: a loner, a drifter? Were there just the two types of cop: John Rebus or Derek Linford? And did she have to choose?

A sandwich wrapped in greaseproof paper; a child's lemonade bottle, half-filled with water. More clothing was appearing from the bag, which was all but empty now. The uniform tipped the remnants out. They looked like things the deceased had collected on his travels: a few pebbles, a cheap ring, shoelaces and buttons. A small, thin cardboard box which, from the faded picture on it, had once contained the radio. Siobhan picked it up and shook it, pulled it open and shook out a little book which at first she took for a passport.

'It's a passbook,' the uniform said. 'Building society.'

'So it'll have a name on it,' Siobhan said.

The uniform opened the book. 'Mr C. Mackie. There's an address in the Grassmarket.'

'And how was Mr Mackie's investment portfolio doing?'

The uniform turned a couple of pages, angling the passbook as if he was having trouble focusing.

'Not bad,' he said at last. 'Just over four hundred grand in credit.'

'Four hundred thousand? Looks like the drinks are on him then.'

But the uniform turned the passbook towards her. She reached out and took it. He hadn't been joking. The tramp being scraped and hosed off platform 11 was worth four hundred thousand pounds.

9

Tuesday, Rebus was back at St Leonard's. Chief Superintendent Watson wanted a meeting with him. When he arrived, Derek Linford was already seated, a mug of oily-looking coffee untouched in one hand.

'Help yourself,' Watson said.

Rebus raised the beaker he was holding. 'Already got some, sir.' Whenever he remembered, he tried to bring half a cup of coffee with him. There was a sign you saw above some bars – 'Do not ask for credit as a refusal can often offend'. The beaker was Rebus's way of not giving offence to his senior officer.

When they were all seated, the Chief Super got straight to the point. '*Everyone*'s interested in this case: reporters, public, government . . .'

'In that order, sir?' Rebus asked.

Watson ignored him. '. . . which means I'm going to be keeping closer tabs on you than usual.' He turned to Linford. 'John here can be like a bull in a china shop. I'm looking to you to be on matador duty.'

Linford smiled. 'As long as the bull's okay about it.' He looked to Rebus, who stayed quiet.

'Reporters are foaming at the mouth. The parliament, the elections . . . dry as dust. Now at last they've got a story.' Watson held up thumb and forefinger. 'Two stories actually. Couldn't be any connection, could there?'

'Between Grieve and the skeleton?' Linford seemed to consider it, glanced towards Rebus who was busy checking the crease in his left trouser leg. 'Shouldn't think so, sir. Not unless Grieve was killed by a ghost.'

Watson wagged a finger. 'That's just the sort of thing the journalists are after. Joking's fine in here, but not outside, understood?'

'Yes, sir.' Linford looked suitably abashed.

'So what have we got?'

'We've conducted preliminary interviews with the family,' Rebus answered. 'Further interviews to follow. Next step is to talk to the deceased's political agent, then maybe to the local Labour Party.'

'No known enemies?'

'Widow didn't seem to think so, sir,' Linford said quickly, leaning forward in his chair. He didn't want Rebus hogging the stage. 'Still, there are things wives don't always know.'

The Chief Super nodded. To Rebus, his face looked even more florid than usual. Run-up to the golden cheerio and he gets landed with this.

'Friends? Business acquaintances?'

Linford nodded back, catching Watson's rhythm. 'We'll speak to them all.'

'Did the autopsy throw up anything?'

'Blow to the base of the skull. It caused immediate haemorrhaging. Seems he died pretty much where he fell. Two more blows after that, producing fractures.'

'These two blows were post-mortem?'

Linford looked to Rebus for confirmation. 'Pathologist seems to think so,' Rebus obliged. 'They were to the top of the skull. Grieve was pretty tall –'

'Six-one,' Linford interrupted.

'– so to render a blow like that, the attacker had to be hellish tall or standing on something.'

'Or Grieve was already prone when the blows arrived,' Watson said, mopping his forehead with a handkerchief. 'Yes, makes sense, I suppose. How the devil did he get in there?'

'Either he climbed the fence,' Linford guessed, 'or else someone had keys. The gates are kept padlocked at night: too much stuff in there worth nicking.'

'There's a security guard,' Rebus continued. 'He says he was there all night, kept a regular patrol, but didn't see anything.'

'What do you think?'

'I think he was kipping in the office. Nice and warm in there. Radio and kettle, all mod cons. Either that or he'd bunked off home.'

'He says he checked the summer house?' Watson asked.

'He says he *thinks* he did.' Linford quoted from memory: ' "I always shine my torch inside, just in case. No reason I wouldn't have that night." '

The Chief Super leaned forward, rested his elbows on the desk. 'What do you think?' He had eyes only for Linford.

'I think we need to concentrate on the motive, sir. Was this a chance encounter? Prospective MSP wants to take a midnight look at his future workplace, happens across someone who decides to bludgeon him to death?' Linford shook his head persuasively, his eyes dodging Rebus, who was glaring, having said almost exactly the same thing to him about an hour before.

'I'm not sure,' Watson said. 'Say someone was in there stealing tools. Grieve interrupts them, so they whack him.'

'And after he's laid out,' Rebus interrupted, 'they hit him twice more for luck?'

Watson grunted, acknowledging the point. 'And the murder weapon?'

'Not recovered yet, sir,' Linford said. 'Lot of building sites around there, places you could conceal something. We've got officers out looking.'

'The contractors are carrying out an inventory,' Rebus added. 'Just in case anything's missing. If your theory about it being a theft is right, maybe the inventory will throw up something.'

'One more thing, sir. Recent scuff marks on the shoes and traces of dirt and dust on the inside legs of Grieve's trousers.'

Watson smiled. 'God bless forensics. What does it mean?'

'Means he probably did climb the fence or the gate.'

'All the same, rule nothing out and everything in. Talk to all the keyholders. *All* of them, understood?'

'Very good, sir,' Linford said.

Rebus just nodded, though no one was paying attention.

'And our friend Skelly?' the Chief Super asked.

'Two other members of the PPLC are on it, sir,' Rebus said.

Watson grunted again, then looked at Linford. 'Something wrong with your coffee, Derek?'

Linford's gaze went to the surface of the drink. 'No, sir, not at all. Just don't like it too hot.'

'And how is it now?'

Linford put the mug to his lips, drained it in two swallows. 'It's very good, sir. Thank you.'

Rebus suddenly had no doubts: Linford would go far in the force.

When the meeting was over, Rebus told Linford he'd catch him up, and knocked again on Watson's door.

'I thought we'd finished?' The Farmer was busy with paperwork.

'I'm being sidelined,' Rebus said, 'and I don't like it.'

'Then do something about it.'

'Such as?'

The Farmer looked up. 'Derek's in charge. Accept the fact.' He paused. 'Either that or ask for a transfer.'

'Wouldn't want to miss your retirement do, sir.'

The Farmer put down his pen. 'This is probably the last case I'll handle, and I can't think of one with a higher profile.'

'You saying you don't trust me with it, sir?'

'You always think you know better, John. That's the problem.'

'All Linford knows are his desk at Fettes and which arses to lick.'

'The ACC says different.' The Farmer sat back in his chair. 'Bit of jealousy there, John? Younger man speeding through the ranks . . . ?'

'Oh aye, I've always been gasping for a promotion.' Rebus turned to leave.

'Just this once, John, play for the team. It's that or the sideline . . .'

Rebus closed the door on his boss's words. Linford was waiting for him at the end of the corridor, mobile pressed to his ear.

'Yes, sir, we're headed there next.' He listened, raised a hand to let Rebus know he'd only be a minute. Rebus ignored him, stalked past and down the stairs. Linford's voice carried down a few moments later.

'I think he'll be fine, sir, but if not . . .'

Rebus dismissed the nightwatchman, but the man stayed in his seat, eyes shifting nervously between Rebus and Linford.

'I said you can go.'

'Go where?' the watchman asked at last, voice trembling. 'This is my office.'

Which was true: the three men were seated in the gatehouse of the parliament site. There was a thick register lying on the table, being pored over by Linford. It listed all the visitors to the site since work had begun. Linford had his notebook out, but hadn't jotted a single name into it.

'I thought you might want to go home,' Rebus told the watchman. 'Shouldn't you be asleep or something?'

'Aye, sure,' the man mumbled. He probably reckoned he wouldn't have the job much longer. Bad PR for the security firm, a body finding its way on to the premises. It was a low-pay job, being a security guard, and the hours tended to suit loners and the desperate. Rebus had told the man that they'd be checking up on him – you found a lot of ex-cons in his line of work. The man had admitted to spending some time at what he called the Windsor Hotel Group, meaning in jail. But he swore no one had asked him for copies of his keys. He wasn't protecting anybody.

'On you go then,' Rebus said. The guard left. Rebus let out a long whistle of breath and stretched his vertebrae. 'Anything?'

'A few suspicious names,' Linford announced. He turned the ledger so Rebus could see. The names were their own, along with Ellen Wylie, Grant Hood, Bobby Hogan and Joe Dickie: the group who'd toured Queensberry House. 'Or how about the Scottish Secretary and the Catalan President?'

Rebus blew his nose. There was a one-bar electric fire in the room, but the heat was having no difficulty escaping through the cracks in the door and window. 'What did you reckon to our nightwatchman?'

Linford closed the register. 'I think if my two-year-old nephew asked for the gate keys, he'd hand them over rather than risk a bite to the ankles.'

Rebus went to the window. It was crusted with dirt. Outside, everyone was busy knocking things down and putting things up. An investigation was like that, too: sometimes you were demolishing an alibi or story, sometimes building up the case, each new piece of information another brick in the often unlovely edifice.

'But is that what happened?' he asked.

'I don't know. Let's see what the background check digs up.'

'I think we're wasting our time. I don't think he knows anything.'

'Oh?'

'I don't even think he was here. Remember how vague he was about the weather that night? He couldn't even be sure which route he took when he patrolled.'

'He's not the brightest of specimens, John. We still have to do the check.'

'Because it's procedure?'

Linford nodded. Outside, something was making a noise: *rugga rugga rugga rugga rugga.*

'Has that thing been going all the time?' Rebus asked.

'What thing?'

'That noise, the cement mixer or whatever it is.'

'I don't know.'

There was a knock at the door. The site manager came in, holding his yellow hard hat by its rim. He wore a yellow oilskin jacket over brown cord trousers. His walking boots were covered in glaur.

'Just a few follow-up questions,' Linford informed him, gesturing for the man to sit.

'I've inventoried the tools,' the site manager said, unfolding a sheet of paper. 'Of course, things *do* go walkabout on any job.'

Rebus looked at Linford. 'You take this one. I need some fresh air.'

He stepped out into the cold and breathed deeply, then searched his pockets for cigarettes. He'd been going off his head in there. Christ, and a drink would go down too well. There was a mobile van parked outside the gates, selling burgers and tea to the construction workers.

'Double malt,' Rebus said to the woman.

'And do you take water with that?'

He smiled. 'Just a tea, thanks. Milk, no sugar.'

'Right, love.' She kept rubbing her hands together between tasks.

'Must get pretty cold, working here.'

'Perishing,' she admitted. 'I could do with a tot now and again myself.'

'What sort of hours are you open?'

'Andy opens at eight, does breakfasts and things. I usually take over at two, so he can hit the cash and carry.'

Rebus checked his watch. 'It's just gone eleven.'

'Sure you don't want anything else? I've just cooked a couple of burgers.'

'Go on then. Just the one.' He patted his midriff.

'You need feeding up, you do,' she told him, winking as she spoke.

Rebus took the tea from her, then the burger. There were sauce bottles on a ledge. He spiralled some brown on to the contents of the roll.

'Andy's not been too good,' she said. 'So it's down to me just now.'

'Nothing serious?' Rebus took a bite of scalding meat and melting onions.

'Just flu, and maybe not even that. You men are all hypochondriacs.'

'Can't blame him for trying, this weather.'

'Don't see me complaining, do you?'

'Women are made of stronger stuff.'

She laughed, rolled her eyes.

'What time do you finish?'

She laughed again. 'You chatting me up?'

He shrugged. 'I might want another of these later.' He held up the burger.

'Well, I'm here till five. But they go quick, come lunchtime.'

'I'll risk it,' Rebus said. It was his turn to wink, as he headed back through the gate. He drank the tea as he walked. When the roof workers started to winch another load of slates down towards the waiting skip, he remembered he wasn't wearing a hard hat. There were some in the gatehouse, but he didn't want to go back there. Instead, he headed into Queensberry House. The stairs down to the basement were unlit. He could hear voices echoing at the end of the hall. Shadows were moving in the old kitchen. When he stepped into the room, Ellen Wylie glanced towards him and nodded a greeting. She was listening to an elderly woman speak. They'd found a chair for her to sit in. It was one of those director's chairs with a canvas seat and back, and it complained every time its occupant moved, which she did often and in animated fashion. Grant Hood was standing by a side wall, taking notes. He was keeping out of the woman's eyeline, so as not to distract her.

'It was always covered in wood,' the woman was saying. 'That's my recollection.' She had one of those high-pitched, authoritative accents.

'This sort of stuff?' Wylie asked. She pointed to a section of tongue-and-groove, still fixed to the wall near the door.

'I believe so, yes.' The woman noticed Rebus, gave him a smile.

'This is Detective Inspector Rebus,' Wylie said.

'Good morning, Inspector. My name is Marcia Templewhite.'

Rebus stepped forward, took her hand for a moment.

'Miss Templewhite worked for the Health Board back in the seventies,' Wylie explained.

'And for many years before that, too,' Miss Templewhite added.

'She remembers some building work,' Wylie went on.

'*Lots* of work,' Miss Templewhite corrected. 'The whole basement was gutted. New heating system, floor repairs, pipework . . . It was quite a guddle, I can tell you. Everything had to be moved upstairs, and then we didn't know where to put it. Went on for weeks.'

'And the wooden sections were removed?' Rebus asked.

'Well, I was just telling . . .'

'DS Wylie,' Wylie reminded her.

'I was just telling DS Wylie, if they'd found these fireplaces, surely they'd have said something?'

'You didn't know about them?'

'Not until DS Wylie told me.'

'But the building work', Grant Hood said, 'coincides fairly well with the skeleton's age.'

'You don't suppose one of the workers could have got himself bricked up?' Miss Templewhite asked.

'I think he'd have been noticed,' Rebus told her. All the same, he knew they'd be asking the builders that very question. 'Who were the contractors?'

Miss Templewhite threw up her hands. 'Contractors, subcontractors . . . I could never really keep up with them.'

Wylie looked at Rebus. 'Miss Templewhite thinks there'll be records somewhere.'

'Oh yes, most definitely.' She looked around her at her surroundings. 'And now Roddy Grieve's dead, too. It was never a lucky place this. Never was, never will be.' She nodded at all three of them, her confident words accompanied by a solemn, knowing face, as if she took no comfort from the truth.

Back at the snack van, he paid for the teas.

'Guilty conscience?' Wylie said, accepting hers. A patrol car had arrived to take Miss Templewhite home. Grant Hood was seeing her safely into the back of it, waving her off.

'Why should I feel guilty?' Rebus asked.

'Story is, it was you that put our names down for this.'

'Who told you that?'

She shrugged. 'Word gets around.'

'Then you should be thanking me,' Rebus said. 'High-profile case like this could make your career.'

'Not as high profile as Roddy Grieve.' She was staring at him.

'Spit it out,' he said. But she shook her head. He handed the spare styrofoam beaker to Grant Hood. 'Seemed like a nice old sort.'

'Grant likes the more mature woman,' Wylie said.

'Get lost, Ellen.'

'Him and his pals go to Grab-a-Granny night at the Marina.'

Rebus looked at Hood, who was blushing. 'That right, Grant?'

Hood just looked at Wylie, concentrated on his tea.

Seemed to Rebus they were getting on okay, felt comfortable enough to talk about their private lives, then to joke about it. 'So,' he said, 'getting back to business . . .' He moved away from the van, where workers were queuing for lunchtime treats of crisps and chocolate bars, their eyes roving towards Ellen Wylie. Wylie and Hood were both wearing hard hats, but didn't look right in them. The line of workers knew they were just visiting. 'What have we got so far?'

'Skelly's gone to some specialist lab down south,' Wylie said. 'They reckon they can give us a more accurate date of death. But meantime the thinking is '79 to '81.'

'And we know building work was going on down there in 1979,' Hood added. 'Which I'd say is our best bet.'

'Based on what?' Rebus asked.

'Based on the fact that if you're going to hide a body down there, you need the means and the opportunity. Most of the time, the basement was off-limits. And who'd dump a body there unless they knew about the fireplace? They knew it was going to be blocked up again, probably thought it would stay that way for a few more hundred years.'

Wylie was nodding agreement. 'Has to be tied in to the refit work.'

'So we need to know which companies were involved, and who was working for them at the time.' The two junior officers shared a look. 'I know, it's a big job. Firms could have gone to the wall. Maybe they're not as good at keeping old paperwork as Miss Templewhite. But they're all we've got.'

'Personnel records will be a nightmare,' Wylie said. 'A lot of the building trade, they take people on for a job, lay them off again afterwards. Builders move on, don't always stay in the business.'

Rebus was nodding. 'You're going to have to depend on goodwill a lot of the time.'

'Meaning what, sir?' Hood asked.

'Meaning you have to be nice and polite. That's why I chose you. Someone like Bobby Hogan or Joe Dickie, they'd go barging in demanding answers. Play it like that, suddenly the person you're talking to could become forgetful. Like the song says, nice and easy does it.' He was looking at Wylie.

Through the gate behind her, he glimpsed the site manager emerging from the gatehouse, slipping his hard hat back on. Linford came out, hard hat in hand, and looked around, seeking Rebus. Saw him and came out of the gate.

'Missing tools?' Rebus asked.

'A few bits and pieces.' Linford nodded across the road. 'Any news from the search parties?' Two groups of uniforms were checking the area for the murder weapon.

'I don't know,' Rebus said. 'I haven't seen them.'

Linford looked at him. 'But you've got time to stop for tea?'

'Just keeping my junior officers happy.'

Linford was still staring. 'You think this is a waste of time, don't you?'

'Yes.'

'Mind if I ask why?' He folded his arms.

'Because it's all arse-backwards,' Rebus said. 'Does it really matter how he got into the site or what he was killed with? We should be looking at the who and why. You're like one of those office managers who worries about paperclips when the case-files are ten feet high on everybody's desk.'

Linford glanced at his watch. 'Bit early in the day for character assassination.' Trying to make a joke of it, aware that others were listening.

'You can interview the site manager as much as you like,' Rebus went on, 'but even if you narrow it down to a missing claw hammer, how much further on will you be? Let's face it, whoever killed Roddy Grieve knew what they were doing. If they'd been caught nicking slates, they might have thumped him, but more likely they'd just have run off. They certainly wouldn't have kept hitting him after he was down. He *knew* his killer, and it wasn't by chance that he was here. It's to do with what he was or who he was. That's what we should be concentrating on.' He paused, aware that the line of workers was watching the performance.

'Here endeth the lesson,' Ellen Wylie said, smiling into her cup.

10

Roddy Grieve's election agent was called Josephine Banks. Sitting in one of the interview rooms at St Leonard's, she explained that she'd known Grieve for about five years.

'We were pretty active in New Labour, right from the start. I did some canvassing for John Smith, too.' Her eyes lost their focus for a moment. 'He's still missed.'

Rebus sat across from her, fingers busy exploring a cheap pen. 'When did you last see Mr Grieve?'

'The day he died. We met in the afternoon. Only five months till the election, there was a lot of work to get through.'

She was five and a half feet tall and carried most of her weight at the stomach and hips. Her face was small and round with the beginnings of a double chin. She'd pulled back her thick black hair and tied it at the nape of her neck. She wore half-moon glasses with Dalmatian-spotted frames.

'You never thought of standing?' Rebus asked.

'What? As an MSP?' She smiled at the suggestion. 'Maybe next time.'

'You've ambitions that way?'

'Of course.'

'So what made you want to help Roddy Grieve, as opposed to any other candidate?'

She wore black mascara and eyeshadow. Her eyes were green. They seemed to sparkle when she moved them.

'I liked him,' she said, 'and I trusted him. He still had ideals, unlike his brother, say.'

'Cammo?'

'Yes.'

'You don't get on?'

'No reason why we should.'

'What about Cammo and Roddy?'

'Oh, they argued politics whenever they could, but that wasn't often. They only met at family occasions, and then they had Alicia and Lorna to stop them.'

'What about Mr Grieve's wife?'

'Which one?'

'Roddy's.'

'Yes, but which one? He had two, you know.'

Rebus was confused momentarily.

'First one didn't last long,' Josephine Banks said, crossing her legs. 'It was a teenage thing.'

Rebus turned his pen the right way round and opened his notebook. 'What was her name?'

'Billie.' She spelled it for him. 'Her maiden name's Collins. But maybe she's remarried.'

'Is she still around?'

'Last I heard she was teaching somewhere in Fife.'

'Did you ever meet her?'

'God no, she was long gone by the time I met Roddy.' She looked at him. 'You know there's a son?'

None of the family had mentioned it. Rebus shook his head. Banks looked disappointed in him.

'His name's Peter. He uses the surname Grief. Ring any bells?'

Rebus was busy writing. 'Should it?'

She shrugged. 'He's in a pop group. The Robinson Crusoes.'

'Never heard of them.'

'Some of your younger colleagues may have.'

'Ouch.' Rebus winced; it made her smile.

'But Peter's almost beyond the pale.'

'Because of what he does?'

'Oh no, not that. I think his grandmother's thrilled to have a pop star in the family.'

'What then?'

'Well, he chooses to make his home in Glasgow.' She paused. 'You *have* spoken to the family, haven't you?' He nodded. 'Only I'd have thought Hugh would have mentioned him.'

'I haven't actually met Mr Cordover yet. He's the band's producer, is he?'

'He's their manager. Dear me, do I have to tell you everything? Hugh's got this thing about young bands now – Vain Shadows, Change and Decay . . .' She smiled at his lack of recognition.

'I'll ask one of my younger colleagues,' he said, causing her to laugh.

He went to the canteen, fetched them coffee. The burger had given him indigestion, so he stopped at his desk and downed a couple of Rennies. At one time, he could have eaten anything, any time of day. But his guts seemed to have taken early retirement. He picked up his phone and called Lorna Grieve, thinking: so far Josephine Banks hadn't mentioned Seona Grieve. She'd managed to sidetrack him by bringing the first Mrs Grieve, Billie Collins, into play. There was no answer at the Cordover residence. He took the drinks back to the interview room. 'There you go, Ms Banks.'

'Thank you.' She looked as if she hadn't moved all the time he'd been away.

'I keep wondering', she said, 'when you'll get round to me. I mean, all this other stuff *is* just a roundabout way of getting there, isn't it?'

'You've lost me.' Rebus took the notebook and pen from his pocket, laid them on the desk.

'Roddy and me,' she said, leaning towards him. 'The affair we were having. Is it time to talk about that now?'

Right hand reaching for the pen, Rebus agreed that it was.

'It's like that in politics.' She paused. 'Well, any profession really. Two people working closely together.' She sipped the coffee. 'Politicians are nothing if not gossips. I think it's down to a lack of self-confidence. Bad-mouthing everyone else is such a simple option.'

'So you weren't actually having an affair?'

She looked at him, smiled. 'Did I give that impression?' Bowed her head slightly in apology. 'What I should have said was, the rumoured affair. And that's as far as it got. You didn't know?'

He shook his head.

'All these interviews . . . I thought someone would have . . .' She straightened in her chair. 'Well, maybe I've misjudged them.'

'You're really the first person we've spoken to.'

'But you've talked to the clan?'

'You mean Mr Grieve's family?'

'Yes.'

'They knew?'

'Seona knew. I'm assuming she didn't keep it to herself.'

'Did Mr Grieve tell her?'

She smiled again. 'Why should he? There wasn't any truth in it. If someone here made a sly reference about you, would you report it to your wife?'

'So how did Mrs Grieve find out?'

'The usual way. Our old friend, Anonymous.'

'A letter?'

'Yes.'

'Just the one?'

'You'll have to ask her.' She placed her beaker on the table. 'You're dying for a cigarette, aren't you?' Rebus looked at her. She nodded towards his pen, which was raised to his mouth. 'You keep doing that,' she said. 'And I wish you wouldn't.'

'Why's that, Ms Banks?'

'Because I'm gasping for one myself.'

Smoking at St Leonard's was restricted to the rear car park. Since this was off-limits to the public, he stood with Josephine Banks on the pavement out front, the pair of them shuffling their feet as they enjoyed their individual fixes.

Nearing the end of his cigarette, perhaps to defer the moment when he would have to finish it, he asked her if she'd any idea who had written the letter.

'Not a clue.'

'It had to be someone who knew you both.'

'Oh, yes. I'm guessing it was someone in the local party. Or maybe a sore loser. The selection process for candidates, it was pretty rough at times.'

'How so?'

'Old Labour versus New. Ancient grievances given fresh momentum.'

'Who stood against Mr Grieve?'

'There were three others: Gwen Mollison, Archie Ure and Sara Bone.'

'Was it a fair fight?'

A mixture of smoke and chilled breath billowed from her mouth. 'As these things go, yes. I mean, there weren't any dirty tricks.'

Something in her tone made him ask: 'But?'

'There was a certain amount of bad feeling when Roddy won the vote. Mostly from Ure. You must have seen it in the papers.'

'Only if it reached the sports pages.'

She looked at him. 'You *are* going to vote?'

He shrugged, examined what was left of his cigarette. 'Why was Archie Ure so upset?'

'Archie's been in the Labour Party for donkey's. And he believes in devolution. Back in '79, he canvassed half of Edinburgh. Then along comes Roddy, snatches his birthright from under his nose. Tell me, did you vote in '79?'

March 1, 1979: the failed devolution referendum. 'I don't remember,' Rebus lied.

'You didn't, did you?' She watched him shrug. 'Whyever not?'

'I wasn't the only one.'

'I'm just curious. It was bitter cold that day, maybe the snow put you off.'

'Are you poking fun at me, Ms Banks?'

She flicked her cigarette stub into the road. 'I wouldn't dare, Inspector.'

1979.

He remembered Rhona, his wife at the time, with her roll of 'Vote Yes' stickers. He kept finding them on his jackets, the car windscreen, even on the flask he sometimes took with him to work. The winter had been hell: dark and freezing and with strikes breaking out all over. The Winter of Discontent, the papers called it, and he wasn't about to disagree. His daughter Sammy was four. When he and Rhona had arguments, they kept their voices down so as not to wake her. His work was a problem: not enough hours in the day. And recently Rhona had been becoming active politically, campaigning for the SNP. For her, devolution meant a step towards independence. For Jim Callaghan and his Labour government, it meant . . . well, Rebus was never sure exactly. A sop to the Nationalists? Or to the nation as a whole? Would it really strengthen the Union?

They argued politics at the kitchen table until Rebus became bored by it all. He would fall on to the sofa and tell Rhona he didn't care. At first she would stand in front of him, blocking his view of the TV screen. Her arguments were cogent as well as passionate.

'I really can't be scunnered,' he'd say when she finished, and she'd start hitting him with a cushion until he wrestled her down on to the carpet, the pair of them laughing.

Maybe it was because he was getting a reaction. Whatever, his intransigence grew. He wore a 'Scotland Says NO' badge home one night. They were at the kitchen table again, eating supper. Rhona looked tired: day job and childcare and out canvassing. She didn't say anything about his badge, even when he unpinned it from his coat and fixed it to his shirt. She just stared at him with deadened eyes, and wouldn't talk the rest of the evening. In bed, she turned her back on him.

'I thought you wanted me to get more political,' he joked. She stayed silent. 'I'm serious,' he said. 'I've thought through the issues like you said, and I've decided to vote No.'

'You do what you want,' she said coldly.

'I will then,' he answered, his eyes on her hunched form.

But on the day, 1 March, he did something worse than voting No. He didn't vote at all. He could blame work, the weather, any number of things. But really, it was to make Rhona suffer. He knew this as he watched the office clock, watched the hands pass the referendum's close. With minutes left, he almost dashed for his car, but told himself it was too late. It was too late.

Felt like hell on the drive home. She wasn't there; was off somewhere to watch ballot boxes being emptied, or with like-minded people in the back room of a pub, awaiting news of exit polls.

The babysitter left him to it. He looked in on Sammy, who was fast asleep, one arm cradling Pa Broon, her favoured teddy bear. It was late when Rhona returned. She was a little bit drunk, and so was he: four cans of Tartan Special in front of the TV. He had the picture on but the sound down, listening to the hi-fi. He was about to tell her that he'd voted No, but knew she'd see through the lie. Instead, he asked how she was feeling.

'Numb,' she said, standing in the doorway, as if reluctant to enter the room. 'But then,' she said, turning back into the hall, 'that's almost an improvement.'

March 1, 1979. The referendum had a clause attached, 40 per cent of the electorate had to vote Yes. The rumour was the Labour government down in London wanted obstacles put in the way of devolution.

They feared that Scottish Westminster MPs would be lost, and that the Conservatives would be gifted a permanent majority in the Commons. Forty per cent had to vote Yes.

It wasn't even close. Thirty-three said Yes, 31 No. The turnout was just under 64 per cent. The result, as one paper put it, was 'a nation divided'. The SNP withdrew their support for the Callaghan government – he called them 'turkeys voting for Christmas' – an election had to be called, and the Conservatives came back into power, led by Margaret Thatcher.

'Your SNP did that,' Rebus told Rhona. 'Now where's your devolution?'

She just shrugged a response, beyond goading. They'd come a long way since the cushion fights on the floor. He turned to his work instead, immersing himself in other people's lives, other people's problems and miseries.

And hadn't voted in an election since.

After Josephine Banks had gone, he returned to the Murder Room. DS 'Hi-Ho' Silvers was making telephone calls. So were a couple of DCs who'd been brought in from other divisions. Chief Inspector Gill Templer was having a confab with the Farmer. A WPC walked past and handed the Farmer a sheaf of telephone messages – so many they were held by a bulldog clip. The Farmer frowned at them, went on listening to Templer. The Farmer's jacket was off and the sleeves of his white shirt were rolled up. All around Rebus people were moving, and computer keyboards were being hammered, and ringing phones were being answered. On his desk were copies of inquiry transcripts, initial interviews with the members of the clan. Cammo Grieve had drawn the short straw, ended up under the inquisitorial gaze of Bobby Hogan and Joe Dickie.

Cammo Grieve: Any idea how long this will take?
Hogan: Sorry, sir. Don't mean to inconvenience you.
Grieve: My brother's been murdered, you know!
Hogan: Why else would we be talking to you, sir?

(Rebus had to smile: Bobby Hogan had a way of saying 'sir' that made it sound like an insult.)

Dickie: You went back down to London on the Saturday, Mr Grieve?
Grieve: First bloody chance I could.
Dickie: You don't get on with your family?
Grieve: None of your bloody business.
Hogan: (To Dickie) Put down that Mr Grieve refused to answer.
Grieve: For Christ's sake!
Hogan: No need to take Our Lord's name in vain, sir.

(Rebus laughed out loud this time. Apart from the usual trinity – weddings, funerals and christenings – he doubted Bobby Hogan had ever seen the inside of a church.)

Grieve: Look, let's just get on with it, shall we?
Dickie: Couldn't agree more, sir.
Grieve: I was back in London Saturday night. You can check with my wife. We spent Sunday together, except when I had some constituency business to discuss with my agent. Couple of friends joined us for dinner. Monday morning, I was on my way to the House when I got the call on my mobile to say Roddy was dead.
Hogan: And how did you feel, sir . . .?

On it went, Cammo Grieve combative, Hogan and Dickie soaking up his hostility like a sponge, hitting back with questions and comments that illustrated their feelings towards him.

As Hogan had commented afterwards – strictly off the record – 'Only time that shite would get a cross from me was if he had fangs.'

Lorna Grieve and her partner had, individually, faced up to the easier pairing of DI Bill Pryde and DS Roy Frazer. Neither had seen Roddy on the Sunday. Lorna had gone to visit friends in North Berwick, while Hugh Cordover had busied himself in his home-based studio, with an engineer and various band members as witnesses.

There were still no sightings of Roddy Grieve on the Sunday night, when he'd supposedly been out for a drink with friends. No friends seemed to have seen him. The implication was: Roddy had enjoyed a secret life, something apart from his marriage. And this, by its very nature, would give the investigation all sorts of problems.

Because no matter how hard you tried, some secrets were bound to stay unrevealed.

11

The building society was on George Street. When Siobhan Clarke had first arrived in Edinburgh, George Street had seemed a windy ghetto of stunning architecture and sluggish business. Half the office space seemed to be empty, with To Let notices strung like pennants from the buildings. Now the street was changing, upmarket shops being joined by a string of bars and restaurants, most of them housed in what had been banks.

That C. Mackie's building society was still trading seemed, under the circumstances, a minor miracle. Clarke sat in the manager's office while he found the relevant paperwork. Mr Robertson was a small, rotund man with a large, polished head and beaming smile. The half-moon glasses gave him the appearance of a Dickensian clerk. Clarke tried not to imagine him in period clothes, but failed. He took her smile as one of approbation – either of his character in general or his efficiency – and sat back down at his modern desk in his modern office. The manila file was slim.

'The C stands for Christopher,' he remarked.

'Mystery solved,' Clarke said, opening her notebook. Mr Robertson beamed at her.

'The account was opened in the March of 1980. The fifteenth, to be precise, a Saturday. I'm afraid I wasn't the manager then.'

'Who was?'

'My predecessor, George Samuels. I wasn't even at this branch, prior to my elevation.'

Clarke flipped through Christopher Mackie's passbook. 'The opening balance was £430,000?'

Robertson checked the figures. 'That is correct. Thereafter, we have a history of occasional minor withdrawals and annual interest.'

'You knew Mr Mackie?'

'No, I don't believe so. I took the liberty of asking the staff.' He ran his fingers down the columns of figures. 'You say he was a tramp?'

'His clothing would suggest he was homeless.'

'Well, I know house prices are extortionate, but all the same . . .'

'With four hundred thousand to spare, he might have found himself something?'

'With that sort of money, he might have found just about anything.' He paused. 'But then there *is* this address in the Grassmarket.'

'I'll be going there later, sir.'

Robertson nodded distractedly. 'One of the staff, our Mrs Briggs. He seemed to deal with her when he made a withdrawal.'

'I'd like to talk to her.'

He nodded again. 'I presumed as much. She's ready for you.'

Clarke looked at her pad. 'Has his address changed at all, while he's been a customer here?'

Robertson peered at the paperwork. 'It would seem not,' he said at last.

'Didn't it seem unusual to you, sir: that amount of money in the one account?'

'We did write to Mr Mackie from time to time, asking if he'd like to discuss other options. Thing is, you can't be too pushy.'

'Or the customer might take umbrage?'

Mr Robertson nodded. 'This is a wealthy place, you know. Mr Mackie wasn't the only one with that kind of cash at his disposal.'

'Thing is, sir, he didn't dispose of it.'

'Which brings me to another point . . .'

'We haven't found anything resembling a will, if that's what you're getting at.'

'And no next of kin?'

'Mr Robertson, I didn't even have a first name till you gave me one.' Clarke closed her notebook. 'I'll talk to Mrs Briggs now, if I may.'

Valerie Briggs was a middle-aged woman who'd recently had her hair restyled. Clarke guessed as much from the way Mrs Briggs kept touching a hand to her head, as if not quite believing the shape and texture.

'The very first time he came in here, it was me he talked to.' A cup of tea had been provided for Mrs Briggs. She looked at it uncertainly: tea in her boss's office was, like her hairstyle, a new and challenging experience. 'Said he wanted to open an account and who should he speak to. So I gave him the form and off he went. Came back with it filled in and asked if he could open the account with cash. I thought he'd made a mistake, put down too many noughts.'

'He had the money with him?'

Mrs Briggs nodded, wide-eyed at the memory. 'Showed me it, all in a smart-looking briefcase.'

'A briefcase?'

'Lovely and shiny it was.'

Siobhan scribbled a note to herself. 'And what happened?' she asked.

'Well, I had to fetch the manager. I mean, that amount of cash . . .' She shivered at the thought.

'This was Mr Samuels?'

'The manager, yes. Lovely man, old George.'

'You keep in touch?'

'Oh, yes.'

'So what happened?'

'Well, George . . . Mr Samuels, that is, took Mr Mackie into the office. The old office.' She nodded at where they were sitting. 'It used to be over by the front door. Don't know why they moved it. And when Mr Mackie came out, that was it, we had a new customer. And every time he came in, he'd wait until I could deal with him.' She shook her head slowly. 'Such a shame to see him go like that.'

'Go?'

'You know, let himself go. I mean, the day he opened the account . . . well, he wasn't dressed to the nines but he was presentable. Suit and what have you. Hair might have needed a wash and trim . . .' She patted her own hair again. '. . . but nicely spoken and everything.'

'Then he started going downhill?'

'Pretty much straight away. I mentioned it to Mr Samuels.'

'What did he say?'

She smiled at the memory, recited the reply: ' "Valerie, dear, there are probably more eccentric rich people out there than normal ones." He had a point, I suppose. But he said something else I remember: "Money brings with it a responsibility some of us are unable to handle." '

'He could have a point.'

'Maybe so, dear, but I told him I'd be willing to take my chances any time he felt like emptying the safe.'

They shared a laugh at this, before Clarke asked Mrs Briggs how she might find Mr Samuels.

'That's an easy one. He's a demon for the bowls. It's like a religion with him.'

'In this weather?'

'Do you give up churchgoing because it's snowing outside?'

It was a good point, and one Clarke was willing to concede in exchange for an address.

She walked past the bowling green and pushed open the door to the social club. She hadn't been to Blackhall before, and the maze of streets had defeated her, twice misleading her back on to the busy Queensferry Road. This was Bungalow Land, an area of the city that seemed to have stepped straight out of the 1930s. It seemed a world away from Broughton Street. Here, you appeared to have left the city. There was precious little commerce, precious few people about. The bowling green had a careworn look, its grass a dull emulsion. The clubhouse behind it was a single-storey affair of brown wooden slats, probably thirty years old and showing its age. She stepped inside to a furnace-blast from the ceiling-mounted heater. There was a bar ahead of her, where an elderly woman was humming some show tune as she dusted the bottles of spirits.

'Bowls?' Clarke called.

'Through the doors, hen.' Nodding in the general direction without losing her beat. Clarke pushed open the double doors and was in a long narrow room. A green baize mat, twelve feet wide and about fifty long, took up most of the available space. A few plastic chairs were scattered around the periphery, but there were no spectators, just the four players, who looked towards the interruption with all the ire they could muster until, noting her sex and youth, their faces melted and backs straightened.

'One of yours, I'll bet,' one man said, nudging his neighbour.

'Away to hell.'

'Jimmy likes them with a bit more meat on their bones,' the third player added.

'And a few more miles on the clock, too,' said player four. They were laughing now, laughing with the confidence of old men, immune from penalty.

'Wouldn't you give your left one to be forty years younger?' The speaker stooped to pick up one of his bowls. The jack had been dispatched to the far end of the carpet. Two bowls sat either side of it.

'Sorry to interrupt your game,' Clarke said, deciding immediately on her approach. 'I'm Detective Constable Clarke.' She showed them her warrant card. 'I'm looking for George Samuels.'

'Told you they'd catch up with you, Dod.'

'It was only a matter of time.'

'I'm George Samuels.' The man who stepped forward was tall and slender and wore a burgundy tie under his sleeveless V-neck jumper. His hand when she shook it had a firm grip and was warm and dry. His hair was snowy white and plentiful, like cotton wadding.

'Mr Samuels, I'm from St Leonard's police station. Would you mind if I had a word?'

'I've been expecting you.' His eyes were the blue of summer water. 'It's about Christopher Mackie, isn't it?' He saw the look of surprise on her face and broke into a smile, pleased that he still had some force in the world.

They sat in a corner of the bar. An elderly couple sat in the other corner: the man had drifted off to sleep and the woman was knitting. A half-pint of beer sat in front of the man, a sherry in front of his companion.

George Samuels had ordered a whisky, doubling its volume with water. He'd signed Clarke in so that she could drink as his guest, but she'd only wanted coffee. Now, after the first sip, she was wishing she hadn't bothered. The catering-sized tin of instant behind the bar should have given her the first clue. The second should have been when the barmaid started chipping away at the contents.

'How did you know?' she asked.

Samuels ran a hand over his forehead. 'I always knew there was something wrong with it . . . with him. You don't just walk into a building society with that amount of money.' He looked up from his drink. 'You don't, do you?'

'I'd like the chance to try,' she said.

He smiled. 'You've been talking to Val Briggs. She said much the same thing. We always joked about it.'

'If you thought there was something odd about it, why take the money?'

He opened his arms. 'If I hadn't, someone else would. This was twenty years ago. We weren't under any obligation to tell the police if something like that happened. That one deposit made me Branch Manager of the Month.'

'Did he say anything about the money?'

Samuels was nodding. There was something Christmasy about his hair; Clarke imagined playing with it, like playing with fresh snow. 'Oh, I asked,' he told her. 'I came straight out.'

'And?' A couple of biscuits had arrived with the coffee. She bit into one. It was soft, felt greasy in her mouth.

'He asked if I needed to know. I said I'd *like* to know, which wasn't quite the same thing. He told me it was from a bank robbery.' Her look pleased him all over again. 'Of course, we both laughed. I mean, he was joking. The notes . . . their serial numbers . . . I'd have known if they'd been stolen.'

Clarke nodded. There was a paste in her mouth. The only way she could swallow it was with the help of a drink, and the only drink available was the coffee. She took a swig, held her breath and swallowed.

'So what else did he say?'

'Oh, he said something about the money coming to him in a will. Him having cashed the cheque to see what that amount of cash looked like.'

'He didn't say where he cashed the cheque?'

Samuels shrugged. 'I'm not sure I'd have believed him, even if he had.'

She looked at him. 'You thought the money was . . . ?'

'Tainted in some way.' He was nodding. 'But no matter what I thought, there he was, offering to place it in an account at *my* branch.'

'No qualms?'

'Not at the time.'

'But you always knew someone would be coming to speak with you about Mr Mackie?'

Another shrug. 'I'm beyond the point of giving excuses, Miss Clarke. But I'm guessing you know where the money came from.'

Clarke shook her head. 'Haven't a clue, sir.'

Samuels sat back in his chair. 'Then why are you here?'

'Mr Mackie committed suicide, sir. Lived like a tramp, then threw himself off North Bridge. I'm trying to find out why.'

Samuels couldn't help. He'd spoken with Mackie only on that one occasion. As Clarke drove back into the city, heading for the Grassmarket, she considered her options. The process took all of three seconds. She had this one slender trail, that was all. To find out the what and why, she had to find out *who* Christopher Mackie had been. She'd already phoned a search request to the records people. He wasn't in any phone book, and, just as she'd suspected, when she arrived at the Grassmarket address she found herself at a hostel for the homeless.

Grassmarket was an odd little world all of its own. Centuries back, they'd held executions here, a fact commemorated by the name of one of the pubs: The Last Drop. Until the 1970s, the area had borne the reputation of being a haven for the destitute and the wandering. But then gentrification became the model. Small specialist shops opened, the bars were spruced up, and tourists began their hesitant, steep descent down Victoria Street and Candlemaker Row.

The hostel wasn't exactly publicising its existence. Two grimy windows and a solid-looking door. Outside, a couple of men were crouched beside the wall. One of them asked if she had a light. She shook her head.

'Probably means you've no fags on you either,' he said, resuming his conversation with his friend.

Clarke turned the door handle, but the door was locked. There was a buzzer on the wall. She pressed it twice and waited. A scrawny young man yanked open the door, took one look at her and retreated back inside, saying to no one in particular, 'Surprise, surprise, it's the polis.' He fell into a chair and got back to the serious business of daytime TV. There were a couple of beaten-up armchairs in the room, plus a long wooden bench and two that looked like bar stools. The TV and a coffee table more or less completed the furnishings. There was a tin ashtray on the table, but the linoleum floor looked to be the more popular destination for stubbed cigarettes. One elderly man was asleep in an armchair, his face speckled with bits of white paper. Clarke was about to investigate, when her meeter and greeter tore a scrap from an old newspaper, moistened it in his mouth, then spat it towards the sleeping figure.

'Two points for the face,' he explained. 'One for the hair or beard.'

'What's your record?'

He grinned, showing a mouth missing half its teeth. 'Eighty-five.'

A door opened at the far end of the room. 'Can I help you?'

Clarke walked over, shook the woman's hand. Behind her, the record-holder made siren noises. 'I'm DC Clarke, St Leonard's police station.'

'Yes?'

'Do you know a man called Christopher Mackie?'

A protective look. 'I might do. What has he done?'

'I'm afraid Mr Mackie's dead. Suicide, it looks like.'

The woman closed her eyes for a second. 'Was he the one who jumped from North Bridge? All it said in the papers was that he was homeless.'

'You knew him then?'

'Let's talk about it in the store.'

Her name was Rachel Drew and she'd been in charge of the hostel for a dozen years.

'Not that it's really a hostel,' she said. 'It's a day centre. But to be honest, when there's no place else for them to go, they do use the front room for bedding down in. I mean, it's winter, what else are you going to do?'

Clarke nodded. The room they sat in was pretty much as Rachel Drew had said: a store. There was a desk and a couple of chairs, but the rest of the space was taken up with boxes of tinned foods. Drew had explained that there was a tiny kitchen annexe, and that she and a couple of helpers rustled up three meals a day.

'It's not *haute cuisine*, but I don't get many complaints.'

Drew was a large, homely woman, maybe mid-forties, with shoulder-length brown hair which looked naturally frizzy. She had dark eyes and a sallow face, but there was warmth and humour in her voice, fighting what Clarke reckoned was near-permanent tiredness.

'What can you tell me about Mr Mackie?'

'He was a lovely, gentle man. Didn't make friends easily, but that was his choice. It took me a long time to get to know him. He was already a feature here when I arrived. I don't mean he was always hanging about the place, but you'd see him regularly.'

'You kept his mail for him?'

Drew nodded. 'There was never much. His DSS cheque was about it . . . Maybe two or three letters a year.'

His building society statements, Clarke guessed. 'How well did you know him?'

'Why do you ask?'

Clarke stared her out. Drew managed a wry smile. 'Sorry, I'm pretty protective about my boys and girls. You're wondering if Chris was suicidal.' She shook her head slowly. 'I wouldn't have said so.'

'When did you last see him?'

'A week or so back.'

'Do you know where he went when he wasn't here?'

'I make it a rule never to ask.'

'Why's that?' Clarke was genuinely interested.

'You never know which question will hit a nerve.'

'He didn't tell you anything about his past?'

'A few stories. He said he'd been in the forces. Another time, he told me he'd been a chef. Said his wife ran off with one of the waiters.'

Clarke caught Drew's tone. 'You didn't believe him?'

Drew sat back in her chair, her face and shoulders framed by tinned goods. Every day she opened some tins and did some cooking, feeding people so the rest of the world could forget about them. 'I get told a lot of stories. I'm a good listener.'

'Did Chris have any close friends?'

'Not here, not that I noticed. But maybe outside . . .' Drew narrowed her eyes. 'Don't get me wrong or anything, but just why the hell are you so interested in a down and out.'

'Because he wasn't. Chris had a building society account. He was in credit to the tune of four hundred thousand pounds.'

'Lucky him,' Drew snorted. Then she saw the look on Clarke's face. 'Oh, Christ, you're serious.' Now she sat forward in her chair, toes on the ground, elbows on her knees. 'Where did he get . . . ?'

'We don't know.'

'Goes some way to explaining your interest. Who gets the money?'

Clarke shrugged. 'Next of kin . . . relatives.'

'Always supposing he has any.'

'Yes.'

'And supposing you can find them.' Drew chewed at her bottom lip. 'You know, there were times when this place was struggling. Christ, we're struggling now. And he never so much as . . .' She laughed suddenly and harshly, clapping her hands together. 'The sneaky little sod. What was he playing at?'

'That's what I'm wondering.'

'If you can't trace his family, where does the money go?'

'I think the Treasury.'

'The government? Christ, there's no justice, is there?'

'Careful who you say that to,' Clarke said with a smile.

Drew was shaking her head and chuckling. 'Four hundred grand. And he jumped and left it all behind.'

'Yes.'

'Knowing you'd find out about it.' Drew stared at Clarke. 'It's like he was setting you a puzzle, isn't it?' She was thoughtful for a moment. 'You should take it to the papers. Once the story's out, the family will come to *you*.'

'Along with every shyster and fraud in the game. That's why I need to find out about him: so I can weed out the con artists.'

'True enough. You've got a head on your shoulders, haven't you?' She exhaled loudly. 'Things I could do with that money.'

'Like hire a cook?'

'I was thinking more of a year in Barbados.'

Clarke smiled again. 'One last thing: I don't suppose you've a picture of Chris?'

Drew raised an eyebrow. 'You know, I think you might be in luck.'

She opened a drawer of the desk and began pulling out sheets of paper and raffle tickets, pens and cassette tapes. Finally she found what she was looking for: a packet of photographs. She flicked through them, picked one out and handed it over.

'Taken last Christmas, but Chris hasn't really changed much since. That's him next to the Bearded Wonder.'

Clarke recognised the sleeping man from the other room. In the photo, he was in his armchair but very much awake, mouth agape in almost a parody of joy. On the arm of the chair sat the man called Christopher Mackie. Medium height, the beginnings of a paunch. Black hair swept back from a prominent forehead. His smile was mischievous, as though he was in on some secret. Yes, and wasn't he just? It was the first time she'd been face to face with him. It felt strange. So far, she'd only known him in death . . .

'Here he is on his own,' Drew said.

The second photo showed Mackie washing a sinkful of dishes. He'd been caught unawares by the photographer, and his face was determined, focused on the job at hand. The flash made his face ghostly white, red dots for eyes.

'Mind if I take these?'

'Go ahead.'

Clarke tucked the pictures into her jacket pocket. 'I'd also appreciate it if you'd keep what I've told you to yourself for the moment.'

'Don't want to be snowed under with cranks?'

'Wouldn't make my job any easier.'

Drew seemed to make her mind up about something. She opened a red plastic card index, flicked through the contents and lifted out one of the cards.

'Chris's personal details,' she said, handing the card over. 'Date of birth and his doctor's name and phone number. Maybe they'll help.'

'Thanks,' Clarke said. She drew a banknote from her pocket. 'This isn't a bribe or anything, I'd just like to put something towards the hostel.'

Drew stared at the money. 'Fair enough,' she said at last, accepting it. 'If it helps your conscience, how can I refuse?'

'I'm a police officer, Ms Drew. The conscience is removed during training.'

'Well,' Rachel Drew said, getting to her feet, 'looks to me like you've maybe grown a new one.'

12

Rebus gave Derek Linford the choice: Roddy Grieve's workplace, or Hugh Cordover's studio. Knowing full well which one Linford would go for.

'I might pick up a few tips for my portfolio while I'm at it,' Linford said, leaving Rebus to head out towards Roslin and the baronial home of Hugh Cordover and Lorna Grieve. Roslin was the home of the ancient and extraordinary Rosslyn Chapel, which in recent years had become the target of a range of millennialist nutters. They said the Ark of the Covenant was buried beneath its floor. Or it was an alien mothership. The village itself was quiet, nondescript. High Manor sat a quarter-mile further on, behind a low stone wall. There were stone gateposts but no gates, just a sign saying 'Private'. It was called High Manor because in his days as a member of Obscura, Hugh had been 'High Chord'. Rebus had one of their albums with him: *Continuous Repercussions*. Lorna was on the sleeve, seated high-priestess style on a throne, diaphanous white dress, a snake coiled around her head. Laser lights shone from her eyes. Around the edges of the album sleeve were rows of hieroglyphs.

He parked his Saab beside a Fiat Punto and a Land-Rover. A couple of other cars stood off to one side: a beaten-up old Merc and an open-topped American classic. He left the album in the car and made for the front door. Lorna Grieve herself opened it. Ice rattled in the glass she was holding.

'My little Monkey Man,' she cooed. 'In here with you. Hugh's down in the bowels. You have to be quiet till he's finished.'

What she meant was that Hugh Cordover was in his studio. It took up the whole lower ground floor of the house. Cordover himself sat in the production suite with an engineer. The equipment around them seemed about to swamp them. Through the thickened window, Rebus could see into the studio proper. Three young men, shoulders slumped with exhaustion. The drummer was pacing behind his kit, a bottle of Jack Daniels hanging from one hand. The guitarist and bassist seemed to be concentrating on the sound from their headphones. Empty beer cans lay strewn around them, along with cigarette packets, wine bottles and guitar strings.

'See what I mean?' Cordover said into a microphone. The musicians nodded. He glanced towards Rebus. 'All right, guys, the police are here to talk to me, so don't go chopping lines in there, okay?'

Sneers, V-signs towards the window. Rock and roll, Rebus thought, had never been so dangerous.

Cordover gave the engineer some instructions, then rose stiffly from his chair. He ran a hand over his unshaven face, shaking his head slowly. Motioned for Rebus to precede him from the production suite.

'Who are they?' Rebus asked.

'The next big thing,' Cordover told him, 'if I get my way. They're called The Crusoes.'

'The Robinson Crusoes?'

'You've heard of them?'

'Someone mentioned you were their manager.'

'Manager, arranger, producer. All-round general father figure.' Cordover pushed open a door. 'This is the Rec Room.'

More mess on the floor. Music magazines lying on chairs. A portable TV, portable hi-fi. A pool table.

'All mod cons,' Cordover said, pulling open the fridge and reaching in for a soft drink. 'Want something?'

Lorna Grieve, seated on a red sofa, closed the newspaper she'd been skimming. 'If I'm any judge of character, my Monkey Man will be wanting something stronger than that.' She rattled her own glass to make the point. She was dressed in a swirling green silk trousersuit. Barefoot, with a red chiffon scarf around her neck.

'A soft drink will be fine actually,' Rebus said, nodding when Cordover brought out two bottles of flavoured mineral water.

'Is it okay to talk here?' Cordover said. 'Or would you prefer upstairs?'

'Mind you,' Lorna added, 'it's no tidier up there than down here.'

'This is fine,' Rebus said, settling himself on one of the chairs. Cordover hauled himself up on to the pool table, legs swinging over the side. His wife rolled her eyes, as if in wonder at his inability to use a chair.

'Which one was Peter Grief?' Rebus asked.

'The bassist,' Cordover answered.

'He knows about his father?'

'Of course he knows,' Lorna Grieve snapped back.

'They were never close,' Cordover added.

'The Monkey Man', Grieve said to her husband, 'is shocked that so soon after Roddy's brutal murder, the pair of you can be back at work as though nothing's happened.'

'Yes,' Cordover shot back. 'So much more useful to hit the bottle.'

'When did I ever need the excuse of a death in the family?' She smiled at Cordover, eyes heavy-lidded. Then, turning to Rebus: 'You've a lot to learn about the clan, Monkey Man.'

'Why do you keep calling him that?' Cordover sounding irritated.

'It's a Rolling Stones song,' Rebus said. He watched Lorna Grieve toast him on this response. Smiled at her, couldn't help himself. She was drinking brandy; even from this distance he could all but taste it.

'I knew Stew,' Cordover said.

'Stew?' Lorna narrowed her eyes.

'Ian Stewart,' Rebus explained. 'The sixth Stone.'

Cordover nodded. 'His face didn't fit the image, so he couldn't be in the band. Played session for them instead.' He turned to Rebus. 'You know he came from Fife? And Stu Sutcliffe was born in Edinburgh.'

'And Jack Bruce was Glaswegian.'

Cordover smiled. 'You know your stuff.'

'I know *some* stuff. For example, I know that Peter's mother is called Billie Collins. Has anyone been in touch with her?'

'Why the hell should we care?' Lorna said. 'She can buy a paper, can't she?'

'I think Peter's spoken with her,' Cordover added.

'Where does she live?'

'St Andrews, I think.' Cordover looked to his wife for confirmation. 'She teaches at a school there.'

'Haugh Academy,' Lorna said. 'Is she a suspect?'

Rebus was writing in his notebook. 'Do you want her to be?' Asked casually, not looking up.

'The more the merrier.'

Cordover leapt from his perch. 'For Christ's sake, Lorna!'

'Oh, yes,' his wife spat back, 'you always did have a soft spot for her. Or should that be a hard spot?' She looked at Rebus. 'Hugh always excused his rutting by saying he was an artist. Only he's never been much of a sack artist, have you, sweetie?'

'Stories, that's all they were.' Cordover was pacing now.

'Speaking of stories,' Rebus said, 'had you heard anything about Josephine Banks?'

Lorna Grieve chuckled, cupped her hands in mock prayer. 'Oh yes, let it be her. That would be *too* perfect.'

'Roddy was a public figure, Inspector,' Cordover said, his eyes on his wife. 'You get all sorts of rumours. It goes with the territory.'

'Does it?' Lorna said. 'How fascinating. And tell me, what rumours have you heard about *me*?'

Cordover stayed silent. Rebus could tell the man had some reply formed, something wounding: *none, which just proves how far you've fallen*. Something like that. But he stayed silent.

It seemed as good a time as any to toss a grenade into the room. 'Who's Alasdair?'

There was silence. Lorna gulped at her drink. Cordover rested against the pool table. Rebus was content to let the silence do his work.

'Lorna's brother,' Cordover said at last. 'Not that I ever knew him.'

'Alasdair was the best of us,' Lorna said quietly. 'That's why he couldn't bear to stay.'

'What happened to him?' Rebus asked.

'He ran off into the wild blue yonder.' She made a sweeping motion with her glass. It was all ice now, nothing left to drink.

'When?'

'Ancient history, Monkey Man. He's in warm climes now, and good luck to him.' She turned towards Rebus, pointed to his left hand. 'No wedding ring. Would I make a good detective, do you think? And you're a drinker, too. You've been eyeing up my glass.' She pouted. 'Or is there something else you're interested in?'

'Please ignore her, Inspector.'

She flung the tumbler at her husband. 'Nobody ignores me! I'm not the has-been here.'

'That's right, the agencies are clamouring at your door. The phone never stops ringing.' The tumbler had missed him; he brushed ice-water from his arm.

Lorna pushed herself off the sofa. Rebus got the idea the pair were used to arguing in public, that they considered it their inalienable right as *artists*.

'Hey, you two.' A voice of reason from the doorway. 'We can't hear ourselves think in there. So much for soundproofing.' It was a drawl, easy, relaxed. Peter Grief reached into the fridge for a bottle of water. 'Besides, it's the rock star who should be having the tantrums, not his aunt and uncle.'

Rebus and Peter Grief sat in the control room. Everyone else was upstairs in the dining room. A baker's van had arrived, bearing trays of sandwiches and patisserie. Rebus had a little paper plate in his hand, just the one triangle of bread on it: chicken tikka filling. Peter Grief was using a finger to remove the cream from a wedge of sponge cake. It was all he'd eaten so far. He'd asked if it was all right to have music on in the background. Music helped him to think.

'Even when it's a rough mix of one of my own songs.'

Which is what they were listening to. Rebus said he considered three-piece bands a rarity. Grief corrected him by mentioning Manic Street Preachers, Massive Attack, Supergrass, and half a dozen others, then added: 'And Cream, of course.'

'Not forgetting Jimi Hendrix.'

Grief bowed his head. 'Noel Redding: not many bassists could keep up with James Marshall.'

Niceties dispensed with, Rebus put down his plate. 'You know why I'm here, Peter?'

'Hugh told me.'

'I'm sorry about your father.'

Grief shrugged. 'Bad career move for a politician. Now if he'd only been in *my* business . . .' It had the sound of a rehearsed line, something to be used over and again as self-protection.

'How old were you when your parents separated?'

'Too young to remember.'

'You were brought up by your mother?'

Grief nodded. 'But they stayed close. You know, "for the sake of the child".'

'Something like that still hurts though, doesn't it?'

Grief glanced up. There was a seam of anger in his voice. 'How would you know?'

'I left my wife. She had to bring up our daughter.'

'And how's your daughter doing?' The anger quickly replaced by curiosity.

'She's okay.' Rebus paused. 'Now, that is. Back then . . . I'm not so sure.'

'You *are* a cop, right? I mean, this isn't some cheap trick to get me discussing my feelings with a counsellor?'

Rebus smiled. 'If I was a counsellor, Peter, my next question would be, "Do you think you need to discuss your feelings?" '

Grief smiled, bowed his head. 'Sometimes I wish I was like Hugh and Lorna.'

'They don't exactly keep things bottled up, do they?'

'Not exactly.' Another smile, dying slowly on his lips. Grief was tall and slender with black hair, possibly dyed, and slicked back from a semi-quiff. His face was long and angular, prominent cheekbones and dark, haunted eyes. He looked right for the part: soiled white T-shirt baggy at the sleeves. Black drainpipe denims and biker boots. Thin leather braids around both wrists and a pentangle hanging from his throat. If Rebus had been casting for bassist in a rock band, he'd have told the other applicants to head for home.

'You know we're trying to figure out who might have wanted to kill your father?'

'Yes.'

'When you spoke with him, did he ever . . . ? Did you get the feeling he had enemies, anyone he was worried about?'

Grief was shaking his head. 'He wouldn't have told me.'

'Who would he have told?'

'Maybe Uncle Cammo.' Grief paused. 'Or Grandma.' His fingers were busy imitating the loudspeaker bass-line. 'I wanted you to hear this song. It's about the last time Dad and I spoke.'

Rebus listened; the rhythm wasn't exactly funereal.

'We had this big falling-out. He thought I was wasting my time, blamed Uncle Hugh for stringing me along.'

Rebus couldn't make out the words. 'So what's the song called?'

'Here's the chorus coming.' Grief began to sing along, and now Rebus could make out the words only too well.

> Your heart could never conceive of beauty,
> Your head could never receive the truth
> And now at last I feel it's my duty
> To deliver the final reproof
> Oh yes, this is the final reproof.

Hugh Cordover and Lorna Grieve walked Rebus out to his car.

'Yes,' Cordover said, 'that's probably their best song.' He carried a cordless phone with him.

'You know it's about his father?'

'I know they argued, and Peter got a song out of it.' Cordover shrugged. 'Does that mean it's about his father? I think you're being a bit too literal, Inspector.'

'Maybe.'

Lorna Grieve was showing no ill-effects from the drink she'd consumed. She examined Rebus's Saab as though it was a museum piece. 'Do they still make these?'

'The new models don't come with gas lamps,' Rebus told her. She smiled at him.

'A sense of humour, how refreshing.'

'Just one more thing . . .' Rebus leaned into the car, came out with the Obscura album.

'My God,' Cordover said. 'You don't see many of these around.'

'Wonder why,' his wife muttered, staring at her photo on the cover.

'I was going to ask if you'd sign it?' Rebus said, bringing out a pen.

Cordover took the pen from him. 'With pleasure. But hang on, do you want me or High Chord?'

Rebus smiled. 'It's got to be High Chord, hasn't it?'

Cordover scrawled the name across the cover and made to hand the album back.

'And the model . . . ?' Rebus asked. She looked at him and he thought she was going to refuse. But then she took the pen and added her name, studying the cover afterwards.

'The hieroglyphs,' Rebus asked, 'any idea what they mean?'

Cordover laughed. 'Not a clue. Some guy I knew, he was into that stuff.' Rebus was noticing that some of the hieroglyphs were actually pentangles, like the pendant Peter Grief had worn.

Lorna laughed. 'Come on, Hugh. You were into that stuff.' She looked at Rebus. 'He still is. Not quite Jimmy Page's league, but it's why we moved to Roslin, to be near the chapel. Bloody New Age mumbo-jumbo, growing a ponytail and everything.'

'I think the Inspector has heard enough character assassination for one day,' Cordover said, his face growing ugly. Then the phone rang, and he turned away to answer it, sounding suddenly excited. His voice took on a transatlantic twang, forgetting all about Lorna, all about Rebus. Leaving the two of them together. She folded her arms.

'He's pathetic, isn't he? What do I see in him?'

'Not for me to say.'

She studied him. 'So was I right? Do you drink?'

'Only socially.'

'You mean as opposed to antisocially?' She laughed. 'I can be social when I want to. It's just that I seldom want to be when Hugh's around.' She glanced back to where her husband was making for the house. He was talking numbers – money or record pressings, Rebus couldn't tell.

'So where do you drink?' she asked.

'A few places.'

'Name them.'

'The Oxford Bar. Swany's. The Malting.'

She wrinkled her nose. 'Why is it I'm seeing bare floorboards and cigarette smoke, swearing and bluster and not many women?'

He couldn't help smiling. 'You know them then?'

'I feel I do. Maybe we'll bump into one another.'

'Maybe.'

'I feel like kissing you. That's probably not allowed, right?'

'Right,' Rebus agreed.

'Maybe I'll do it anyway.' Cordover had disappeared into the house. 'Or would that be classed as assault?'

'Not if no charges were brought.'

She leaned forward, pecked him on the cheek. When she stepped back, Rebus saw a face at a window. Not Cordover: Peter Grief.

'Peter's song,' Rebus said. 'The one about his father. I didn't catch the title.'

' "The Final Reproof",' Lorna Grieve told him. 'As in condemning.'

In his car, Rebus got on his mobile and asked Derek Linford how things had gone at The Exchange.

'Roddy Grieve was whiter than white,' Linford said. 'No bad deals, no cock-ups, no unhappy punters. Also, none of his colleagues were out drinking with him on Sunday night.'

'Which tells us what exactly?'

'I'm not sure.'

'A dead end then?'

'Not quite: I did get a hot tip for an investment. How about you?'

Rebus glanced at the album on the passenger seat. 'I'm not sure what I got, Derek. Talk to you later.' He made another call, this time to a vinyl dealer in the city.

'Paul? It's John Rebus. Obscura's *Continuous Repercussions*, signed by High Chord and Lorna Grieve.' He listened for a moment. 'It's not mint, but it's not bad.' Listened again. 'Get back to me if you can go any higher, eh? Cheers.'

He slowed the car so he could search in the glove compartment, found a Hendrix tape and slotted it home. 'Love or Confusion'. Sometimes, you couldn't be sure what the difference was.

Howdenhall was home to the city's forensic science lab. Rebus wasn't sure why Grant Hood and Ellen Wylie wanted to meet him there. Their message had been vague, hinting at some surprise. Rebus hated surprises. That kiss from Lorna Grieve . . . it hadn't been a surprise exactly, but all the same. And if he hadn't angled his head at the last moment, bottling out of some mouth-to-mouth . . . Jesus, and with Peter Grief watching from the window. Grief: Rebus had meant to ask about the name change. Grieve to Grief; verb to noun. But then he'd been brought up by his mother, so maybe his surname had been Collins. In which case, the change of name was still resonant, the young man laying claim to the missing half of his identity, his missed past.

Howdenhall: full of brainboxes, some of them looking barely out of their teens. People who knew about DNA and computer data. These days at St Leonard's, you didn't roll ink over a suspect's fingers, you merely placed their palm to a computer pad. The prints flashed up on the screen, and Criminal Records came back to you immediately if there was a match. The process still amazed him, even after all these months.

Hood and Wylie were waiting for him in one of the meeting rooms. Howdenhall was still fairly new, and had a clean no-nonsense smell and feel to it. The large oval desk, made up of three movable sections, hadn't had time to get scuffed or scored. The chairs were still comfortably padded. The two junior officers made to get up, but he waved them back down and seated himself across the table from them.

'No ashtray,' he remarked.

'There's no smoking, sir,' Wylie explained.

'I know that well enough. I just keep thinking I'll wake up and it'll all have been a bad dream.' He looked around. 'No coffee or tea either, eh?'

Hood sprang to his feet. 'I can get you . . .'

Rebus shook his head. Still, it was good to see Hood so keen. Two empty polystyrene beakers on the table: he wondered who'd fetched them. Even money on Hood; Wylie at three to one.

'Latest news?' he asked.

'Very little blood in the fireplace,' Wylie said. 'Chances are, Skelly was killed elsewhere.'

'Which means less chance of the SOCOs coming up with anything useful.' Rebus was thoughtful for a moment. 'So why the secrecy?' he asked.

'No secrecy, sir. It's just that when we found out Professor Sendak was going to be here this afternoon for a meeting . . .'

'Seemed too good to miss, sir,' Hood concluded.

'And who's Professor Sendak when he's at home?'

'Glasgow University, sir. Head of Forensic Pathology.'

Rebus raised an eyebrow. 'Glasgow? Listen, if Gates and Curt find out, it's your heads, not mine, okay?'

'We cleared it with the Procurator Fiscal's office.'

'So what can this Sendak do that our own boffins can't?'

There was a knock at the door.

'Maybe we'll let the professor explain,' Hood said, not quite disguising the relief in his voice.

Professor Ross Sendak was approaching sixty, but still boasted a head of thick black hair. The shortest person in the room, he carried himself with weight and confidence, demanding respect. Introductions complete, he settled himself on a chair and spread his hands out on the table.

'You think I can help you,' he stated, 'and perhaps you're right. I'll need the skull brought to Glasgow. Can that be arranged?'

Wylie and Hood shared a look. Rebus cleared his throat.

'I'm afraid the Time Team here haven't had time to brief me, Professor.'

Sendak nodded, took a deep breath. 'Laser technology, Inspector.' He reached into his briefcase, slid out a laptop computer and switched it on. 'Forensic facial reconstruction. Your forensic colleagues here have already ascertained that the decedent's hair was brown. That's a start. What we would do in Glasgow is place the skull on a revolving plinth. We then aim a laser at the skull, feeding the information into a computer, building up details. From these, the facial contours are formed. Other information – the decedent's general physique; his age at date of death – help with the final image.' He turned the computer around so it was facing Rebus. 'And what you get is something like this.'

Rebus had to get up. From where he was sitting, the screen seemed blank. Hood and Wylie did likewise, until all three of them were jockeying for position, the better to make out the face which flickered at them. By moving a few inches to right or left, the image faded, disappeared, but when in focus it was clearly the face of a young man. There was something of the mannequin about it, a deadness to the eyes, the one visible ear not quite right and the hair clearly an afterthought.

'This poor devil rotted on a hillside in the Highlands. He was past normal means of ID by the time he was found. Animals and the elements had taken their toll.'

'But you think this is what he looked like in life?'

'I'd say it's close. Eyes and hairstyle are speculative, but the overall structure of the face is true.'

'Amazing,' Hood said.

'Using the inset screen,' Sendak went on, 'we can reconfigure the face – change hairstyle, add a moustache or beard, even change eye colour. The variations can be printed out and used for a public appeal.' Sendak pointed to the small grey square in the top right corner of the screen. It contained what looked like a children's version of an identikit: the rough outline of a head, plus hats, facial hairstyles, glasses.

Rebus looked to Hood and Wylie. They were looking at him now, seeking his okay.

'So how much is this going to cost?' he asked, turning back to the screen.

'It's not an expensive process,' Sendak said. 'I appreciate that funds are being soaked up by the Grieve case.'

Rebus glanced towards Wylie. 'Someone's been whispering.'

'It's not like we're spending money on anything else,' Wylie argued. Rebus saw anger in her eyes. She was beginning to feel sidelined. Any other time of year, Skelly would have been big news, but not with Roddy Grieve as competition.

In the end, Rebus gave the nod.

Afterwards, there was just time for a coffee. Sendak explained that his Human Identification Centre had helped with war crimes cases in Rwanda and the former Yugoslavia. In fact, he was flying out to The Hague at the end of the week to testify in a war crimes trial.

'Thirty Serb victims buried in a mass grave. We helped identify the victims and prove they were shot at close range.'

'Sort of puts things into perspective, doesn't it?' Rebus said afterwards, eyes on Wylie. Hood was off finding a phone. He needed to talk to the Procurator Fiscal's office again, tell them what was happening.

'You'll have to tell Prof. Gates what's happening,' Rebus went on.

'Yes, sir. Will that be a problem?'

Rebus shook his head. 'I'll have a word. He won't like the fact that Glasgow have got something he hasn't . . . but he'll live with it.' He winked at her. 'After all, we've got everything else.'

13

The Murder Room at St Leonard's was fully operational – computers, civilian support, extra phone lines – with an additional Portakabin parked on the pavement outside Queensberry House. Chief Superintendent Watson was kept busy in a series of meetings with Fettes brass and politicians. He'd lost the head at one of the junior officers, shouting the odds before marching off to his office and slamming the door. Nobody'd seen him like that before. DS Frazer's comment: 'Get Rebus back here, we need to offer a sacrifice.' Joe Dickie had nudged him: 'Any news on overtime?' He had a blank expenses form ready on his desk.

Gill Templer had been put in charge of press briefings. Her background was in liaison work. So far she'd managed to tamp down a couple of the wilder conspiracy theories. ACC Carswell had come to inspect the troops, given the tour by Derek Linford. Space at the station was cramped, and Linford didn't even have his own office. Twelve CID officers were attached to the case, along with a further dozen uniforms. The uniforms were there to search the area around the *locus* and help with door-to-door. Secretarial support came extra, and Linford was still waiting to hear what budget the case would merit. He wasn't stinting, not yet: he reckoned this was a flier, meaning it would justify any amount of staffing and overtime.

All the same, he liked to keep an eye on the money side. It didn't help that he was playing away from home. He ignored the looks and comments, but they got to him all the same. *Fettes bastard . . . thinks he can tell us how to run our station.* It was all about territory. Not that Rebus seemed to mind. Rebus had given him the run of the place, had admitted that Linford was the better administrator. His exact words: 'Derek, to be honest, no one's ever accused me of being able to mind the store.'

Linford made a circuit of the room now: wall charts; staff rotas; crime scene photographs; telephone numbers. Three officers sat silently at their computers, tapping the latest gen into the database. An investigation like this was all about information, its gathering and cross-referencing. Detection lay in making connections, and it could be a painstaking business. He wondered if anyone else in the room felt the same electricity he did. Back to the rota: DS Roy Frazer was in charge of the Holyrood operation, managing the house-to-house inquiries, interviewing the demolition teams and builders. Another DS, George Silvers, was plotting the deceased's final movements. Roddy Grieve had lived in Cramond, had told his wife he was going out for a drink. Nothing unusual in that, and he'd acted naturally. Had taken his mobile with him. Not that there'd been any reason to check up on him. At midnight she'd turned in for the night. Next morning when he wasn't there, she'd begun to worry, but had decided to leave it an hour or two; might be some rational explanation . . . Sleeping it off somewhere.

'Did that often happen?' Silvers had asked.

'Once or twice.'

'And where did he end up sleeping?'

Answer: at his mother's; or on a friend's sofa.

Silvers didn't look like he put much effort into anything. You couldn't imagine him in a hurry. But he gave himself time to form questions and strategies.

Time, too, for the interviewee to start twitching.

Grieve's press officer was a young man called Hamish Hall, and Linford had interviewed him. Playing it back in his head afterwards, Linford reckoned he'd come off second best in the encounter. Hall, in his sharp suit and with a sharp, bright face, had snapped out his answers, as if dismissing the questions. Linford had snapped another question back at him, taking him on rather than playing to his own strengths.

'How did you get on with Mr Grieve?'

'Fine.'

'Never any problems?'

'Never.'

'And Ms Banks?'

'Do you mean how did I get along with her, or how did she get along with Roddy?' Light glinting from the circular chrome frames of his spectacles.

'Both, I suppose.'

'Fine.'

'Yes?'

'That's my answer to both questions: we got along fine.'

'Right.'

And on it went, like machine-gun fire. Hall's background: party man, single-minded, economics degree. Economy his strong point when speaking, too.

'Press agent . . . Is that like a spin doctor?'

A bending of the mouth. 'That's a cheap shot, Inspector Linford.'

'Who else was in Mr Grieve's retinue? I'm assuming there'd be local volunteers . . . ?'

'Not yet. Electioneering proper doesn't start until April. That's when we'd have needed canvassers.'

'You had people in mind?'

'Not my bailiwick. Ask Jo.'

'Jo?'

'Josephine Banks, his election agent. That's what we called her: Jo.' A glance at his watch, loud exhalation.

'So what will you do now, Mr Hall?'

'You mean when I leave here?'

'I mean now your employer's dead.'

'Find another one.' A genuine smile this time. 'There'll be no shortage of takers.'

Linford could see Hall five or ten years down the line, standing just behind some dignitary, maybe even the Prime Minister, murmuring something which the PM would utter aloud mere seconds later. Always in shot; always close to the power.

When the two men stood up, Linford shook Hall's hand warmly, offered him a grin and a cup of tea or coffee.

'Really appreciate . . . sorry to have . . . wish you all the best . . .'

Because you never knew. Five, ten years on, you just never could tell . . .

'Tell me this is a joke.'

Ellen Wylie was examining the dimly lit interior of one of the downstairs interview rooms. It was half-filled with broken equipment: chairs with missing castors; golf-ball typewriters.

'It's been used for storage, as you can see.'

She turned to the desk sergeant, who'd unlocked the door for her and turned on the light. 'I'd never have guessed.'

'So where do we put all this stuff?' Grant Hood asked.

'Maybe you can work around it?' the desk sergeant offered.

'We're working a *murder* inquiry,' Wylie hissed at him. Then she looked around the room again, before turning to her partner. 'And this is how they treat us, Grant.'

'Well, it's all yours,' the desk sergeant said, removing the key from the lock and handing it to Hood. 'Have fun.'

Hood watched him retreat, then held the key up in front of Wylie. 'It's all ours, he says.'

'Can we complain to the management?' Wylie kicked at one of the chairs, whose arm promptly fell off.

'I know the brochure said sea view,' her partner said, 'but with any luck, we won't be spending much time here.'

'Those bastards upstairs have got a coffee-maker,' Wylie said. Then she burst out laughing. 'What am I saying? We haven't even got any phones!'

'Maybe so,' Hood informed her, 'but if I'm not mistaken, we've just cornered the global market in electric typewriters.'

Siobhan Clarke had insisted on somewhere 'a bit fancy' for their drink, and when she told him about her day, Derek Linford thought he understood. Her last couple of working hours had been spent questioning dossers.

'Not easy,' he said. 'You were all right, though?' She looked at him. 'I mean, they didn't bite?'

'No, they were just . . .' She tipped her neck back, inspecting the spectacular ceiling of The Dome Bar and Grill as if expecting the rest of the sentence to be painted there. 'I mean, they weren't even smelly for the most part. But it was the past.' Now she nodded to herself.

'How do you mean?' He was using his swizzle-stick to chase a sliver of lime around his glass.

'I mean the stories, all the tragedies and tiny mishaps and wrong turns that had brought them there. Nobody's *born* homeless, not that I know of.'

'I know what you mean. They needn't be homeless, the majority of them. The support system's out there.' She was looking at him, but he didn't notice. 'I never give them money, it's a sort of principle with me. Some of them probably make more a week than we do. You can make two hundred a day, just begging on Princes Street.' He shook his head slowly, saw the look on her face. 'What?'

She studied her own drink, a large gin and tonic to his lime juice and soda. 'Nothing.'

'What did I say?'

'Maybe it's just . . .'

'Been a rough day?'

She glowered. 'I was going to say, maybe it's just your attitude.'

They sat in silence for a while after that. Not that anyone in The Dome minded. It was the cocktail hour: George Street suits; black two-pieces with matching tights. Everyone focused on their own little group: office blather. Clarke took a long swallow. There was never enough gin; you could order a double and still not feel the kick. At home, she poured half and half, gin to tonic. Lots of ice, and a wedge of lemon rather than something that looked like it had been pared with a razor blade.

'Your accent changes,' Linford said at last. 'Modulates to suit the occasion. It's a clever trick.'

'How do you mean?'

'Well, you've got an English accent, right? But in some company, at the station for example, you manage to bring in some Scots.'

It was true: she knew she did it. She'd been a bit of a mimic even at school and college, knowing she did it so she'd fit in with whoever she was talking to, whichever peer group. Used to be, she could hear herself switching, but not now. The question she'd asked herself was: why the need to change, just to fit in? Was she that desperate, that lonely as a girl?

Was she?

'Where were you born?'

'Liverpool,' she said. 'My parents were lecturers. The week after I was born, they moved to Edinburgh.'

'Mid-seventies?'

'Late sixties, and flattery will get you nowhere.' But she managed a smile. 'We only stayed a couple of years, then it was Nottingham. I got most of my schooling there, finished off in London.'

'Is that where your parents live now?'

'Yes.'

'Lecturers, eh? What do they make of you?'

It was a perceptive question, but she didn't know him well enough to answer it. Just as she'd always let people assume that her New Town flat was a rental. When she'd eventually sold it and got her own mortgage on a place half the size, she'd put the money back into her parents' bank account. She'd never explained to them why she'd done it. They'd only asked the once.

'I came back here to go to college,' she told Linford. 'Fell in love with the city.'

'And chose a career where you'd always see its mucky underwear?'

She chose to ignore this question, too.

'So that makes you a settler . . . one of the New Scots. I think that's what the Nationalists call them. You *will* be voting Scot Nat, I trust?'

'Oh, are you SNP?'

'No.' He laughed. 'I just wondered if you were.'

'It's a pretty underhand way of finding out.'

He shrugged, finished his drink. 'Another?'

She was still studying him, feeling suddenly enervated. All the other drinkers, the nine-to-fives, were winding down, a few drinks before home. Why did people do that? They could get a drink at home, couldn't they? Feet up in front of the telly. Instead of which, they stuck close to their office building and had a drink with their workmates. Was it so hard to let go? Or was home something less than a refuge? You needed a drink before facing it, courage to confront the evening's redundancy? Was that what she was doing here?

'I think I'll head off,' she said suddenly. Her jacket was on the back of her chair. A while back, someone had been stabbed outside this place. She'd worked the case. Just another act of violence, another life wasted.

'Got plans?' He looked expectant, nervous, childlike in his ignorance and egotism. What could she tell him? Belle and Sebastian on the hi-fi; another gin and tonic; the last third of an Isla Dewar novel. Tough competition for any man.

'What are you smiling at?'

'Nothing,' she said.

'Must be something.'

'Women have to have some secrets, Derek.' She had her jacket on now, was wrapping her scarf around her neck.

'I thought a bite to eat,' he blurted out. 'You know, make an evening of it.'

She looked at him. 'I don't think so.' Hoping her tone would alert him to the missing final word: *ever*.

And she walked.

He'd offered to see her home, but she'd declined. Offered to call her a cab, but she lived a stone's throw away. It wasn't even seven thirty, and he was all at once alone. The noise around him was suddenly deafening, skull-crushing. Voices, laughter, chiming glasses. She hadn't asked about his day. Hadn't said much at all, really, except when prompted. His drink looked fake yellow, the colour of children's sweets. Sticky-tasting and souring his stomach, corroding his teeth. He walked to the bar, ordered a whisky. Didn't put any water in it. Looking around, he saw that another couple had already taken his table. Well, that was fine. He didn't stand out so much here at the bar. Could belong to one of the office parties either side of him. But he didn't, and he knew he didn't. He was an outsider in this place, same as in St Leonard's. When you worked as hard as he did, that was what happened: you got the promotions, but lost the intimacy. People steered a course past you, either out of fear or jealousy. The ACC had pulled him aside at the end of the St Leonard's tour.

'You're doing good work, Derek. Keep at it. Few years down the road, who knows? Maybe you'll look back at this one as the inquiry that made your name.' And the ACC had winked and patted his arm.

'Yes, sir. Thank you, sir.'

But then had come the postscript, the ACC readying to leave but half-turning towards him. 'Family men, Derek, that's what the public should see when they look at us. People they can respect, because we're no different from them.'

Family men. He meant wife and kids. Linford had gone straight to his phone and called Siobhan's mobile . . .

Balls to it. He left, nodded to the doorman even though he didn't know him. Out into the horizontal wind, the night seizing him and taking a bite. His lungs complained when he breathed in. Left turn: he'd be home in ten minutes. Left turn, he'd be going home.

He turned right, heading for Queen Street, the top of Leith Walk. The Barony Bar on Broughton Street, he liked it there. Good beer, an old-fashioned place. You wouldn't stand out in a place like that, drinking alone.

And afterwards, it only took him a couple of minutes to find Siobhan Clarke's building. Addresses: no problem in CID. First time they'd met, he'd gone to the office next day, checked up on her. Her flat was on a quiet street, a terrace of four-storey Victorian tenements. Second floor: that was where she lived. 2FL: second floor, left side. He went to the terrace opposite. The main door was unlocked. Climbed the stairs, until he reached the half-landing between second and third floors.

There was a window, looking out on to the street and the flats opposite. Lights burning in her windows, curtains open. Yes, there she was: briefest of glimpses as she walked across the room. Carrying something, reading it: a CD cover? Hard to tell. He wrapped his jacket around him. Temperature wasn't much above freezing. The skylight above had a hole in it; cold gusts assailing him.

But still he watched.

14

'When will his body be released?'

'I'm not sure.'

'It's awful, to have someone die and not be able to bury them.'

Rebus nodded. He was in the sitting room of the house in Ravelston. Derek Linford was seated beside him on the sofa. Alicia Grieve looked small and frail in the armchair opposite. Her daughter-in-law, who'd just been speaking, was perched on the arm. Seona Grieve was dressed in black, but Alicia wore a flowery dress, the splashes of colour contrasting with her ash-grey face. To Rebus, her skin seemed like an elephant's, the way the folds fell from her face and neck.

'You have to understand, Mrs Grieve,' Linford said, his voice pouring like treacle, 'in a case like this, there's a need to keep the body. The pathologist may be called on to—'

Alicia Grieve was rising to her feet. 'I can't listen any more!' she trilled. 'Not here, not now. You're going to have to go.'

Seona helped her up. 'It's all right, Alicia. I'll talk to them. Would you like to go upstairs?'

'The garden . . . I'm going into the garden.'

'Mind you don't slip.'

'I'm not helpless, Seona!'

'Of course not. I'm just saying . . .'

But the old woman was making for the door. She didn't say anything, didn't look back. Closed the door after her. They could hear her feet shuffling away.

Seona slipped into the chair her mother-in-law had vacated. 'Sorry about that.'

'No need to apologise,' Linford said.

'But we *will* need to talk to her,' Rebus cautioned.

'Is that absolutely necessary?'

'I'm afraid so.' He couldn't tell her: because your husband might have confided in his mother; because maybe she knows things we don't.

'How about you, Mrs Grieve?' Linford asked. 'How are you managing?'

'Like an alcoholic,' Seona Grieve said with a sigh.

'Well, a drink often helps—'

'She means', Rebus interrupted, 'she's taking things one day at a time.'

Linford nodded, as though he'd known this all along.

'Incidentally,' Rebus added, 'does anyone in the family have a drink problem?'

Seona Grieve looked at him. 'You mean Lorna?'

He stayed silent.

'Roddy didn't drink much,' she went on. 'The odd glass of red wine, maybe a whisky before dinner. Cammo . . . well, Cammo seems unaffected by drink, unless you know him well. It's not that he slurs or starts singing.'

'What then?'

'His behaviour changes, just ever so slightly.' She looked down at her lap. 'Let's say his morals become hazy.'

'Has he ever . . . ?'

She looked at Rebus. 'He tried once or twice.'

Linford, no subtlety on display, glanced meaningfully towards Rebus. Seona Grieve caught the look and snorted.

'Clutching at straws, Inspector Linford?'

He flinched. 'How do you mean?'

'Crime of passion, Cammo killing Roddy so he can get to me.' She shook her head.

'Are we being too simplistic, Mrs Grieve?'

She considered Rebus's question. Took her time over it. So he lobbed in another.

'You say he didn't drink much, your husband, and yet he went out drinking with friends?'

'Yes.'

'Sometimes stayed out overnight?'

'What are you trying to say?'

'It's just that we can't find anyone who was out drinking with him the night he died.'

Linford checked his notebook. 'So far, we've found one bar in the West End, they think he was there early on in the evening, drinking by himself.'

Seona Grieve didn't have anything to say to that. Rebus sat forward. 'Did Alasdair drink?'

'Alasdair?' Caught unawares. 'What's he got to do with this?'

'Any idea where he might be?'

'Why?'

'I'm wondering if he knows about your husband. Surely he'd want to be here for the funeral.'

'He hasn't phoned . . .' She turned thoughtful again. 'Alicia misses him.'

'Does he ever get in touch?'

'A card now and then: Alicia's birthday, never misses that.'

'But no address?'

'No.'

'Postmarks?'

She shrugged. 'All over, mostly abroad.'

There was something in the way she said it that made Rebus state: 'There's something else.'

'I just . . . I think he gets people to post them for him, when they're on the move.'

'Why would he do that?'

'In case we're trying to find him.'

Rebus sat forward a little further, cutting down the distance between himself and the widow. 'What happened? Why did he leave?'

She shrugged again. 'It was before my time. Roddy was still married to Billie.'

'Had that marriage broken up before you met Mr Grieve?' Linford asked.

Her eyes narrowed. 'What exactly are you implying?'

'To get back to Alasdair,' Rebus said, hoping his tone would dissuade Linford from further queries, 'you've no idea why he left?'

'Roddy talked about him now and again, usually when a card arrived.'

'Cards to him?'

'No, to Alicia.'

Rebus looked around him, but someone had removed Alicia Grieve's birthday cards. 'Did he send one this year?'

'He's always late. It'll arrive in a week or two.' She looked towards the door. 'Poor Alicia. She thinks I'm staying here as a sort of sanctuary.'

'Whereas, in reality, you're looking after her?'

She shook her head. 'Not looking after exactly, but I *am* worried about her. She's grown fragile. This is the only room you've been in. That's because it's practically the only room left that's habitable. The rest, they fill with old papers and magazines – she won't let them be thrown out. All sorts of rubbish, and when the room gets full, she moves into another. This room will go the same way, I suppose.'

'Can't her children do anything?' Linford again.

'She won't let them. Refuses even to have a cleaner. "Everything's in its place for a reason," that's what she says.'

'Maybe she has a point,' Rebus said. Everything in its place – the body in the fireplace; Roddy Grieve in the summer house – for a reason. There had to be an explanation; it was just that they couldn't see it yet. 'Does she still paint?' he asked.

'Not really. She tinkers. Her studio is at the bottom of the garden, that's probably where she's gone.' Seona looked at her watch. 'God, and I need to buy some food . . .'

'You'd heard the rumours about your husband and Josephine Banks?'

The question had come from Linford. Rebus turned towards him, eyes burning, but Linford was concentrating on the widow.

'Someone sent me a letter.' She tugged the sleeve of her blouse down over her watch; suddenly defensive, where before she'd been opening up.

'You trusted your husband?'

'Completely. I know what it's like in politics.'

'Any idea who might have sent the letter?'

'I threw it straight in the bin. We agreed that was the best place for it.'

'How did Ms Banks react?'

'She thought about hiring a detective. We talked her out of it. Anything we did would have made it all seem legitimate. We'd have been playing his game.'

'Whose game?'

'Whoever was spreading the rumour.'

'You're sure it was a he?'

'A question of probability, Inspector Linford. Most of the people in politics are male. It's sad but it's true.'

'I notice', Rebus said, 'there were two women standing against your husband in the selection process.'

'Labour policy.'

'Did you know any of the other candidates?'

'Of course. The Labour Party's one big happy family, Inspector.'

He smiled, as was expected. 'I hear Archie Ure wasn't best pleased with the result.'

'Well, Archie's been in politics a hell of a sight longer than Roddy. He thought it was his birthright.'

Jo Banks had used the selfsame word: birthright.

'And the two women on the shortlist?'

'Young and intelligent . . . they'll get what they want eventually.'

'So what happens now, Mrs Grieve?'

'Now?' She was staring at the pattern in the carpet. 'Archie Ure was the runner-up. I suppose they'll go with him.' Staring hard at the carpet, as if some message were imprinted there.

Linford cleared his throat and turned towards Rebus, indicating that for him the interview was complete. Rebus tried to think of some brilliant final question, but came up empty.

'Just give me back my husband,' Seona Grieve said, leading them into the hall. Alicia was standing there at the foot of the stairs, a china cup in her hand. She'd folded a slice of bread into the cup and squashed it down.

'I wanted something,' she told her daughter-in-law. 'But I'm not sure now why.'

As they left, Roddy Grieve's widow was leading his mother up the stairs like a parent with a sleepy child.

Back at the car, Rebus told Linford: 'You go on ahead.'

'What?'

'I want to stick around, do the Good Samaritan bit.'

'Babysitting?' Linford got in, started the engine. 'Something tells me that's not the whole story.'

'I might have a word with the old woman while I'm at it.'

'Just tell me you're not playing Grab-a-Granny.'

Rebus winked. 'We don't all have young ladies lusting after us.'

The look on Linford's face changed. He put the car into gear and drove off.

A grin spread over Rebus's face. 'Good on you, Siobhan, you went and dumped him.'

He went back up the path, rang the doorbell. Explained to Seona Grieve that he could spare twenty minutes or so if she wanted to pop out. She hesitated.

'It's just milk and bread, Inspector. We can probably manage till—'

'Well, I'm here now, and my driver's gone.' He waved back towards the empty roadway. 'Besides, the way Mrs Grieve is getting through that bread . . .'

He made himself comfy in the sitting room. She told him he was welcome to make tea or coffee, as long as he didn't take milk. 'But fair warning,' she added, 'the kitchen's a bomb-site.'

'I'll be fine,' he said, picking up a Sunday supplement from six months before. He heard the door close – she hadn't bothered telling her mother-in-law, hadn't seen the point. There was a newsagent's a quarter of a mile away. She wouldn't be long. Rebus waited a couple of minutes, then climbed the stairs. Alicia Grieve was standing in her bedroom doorway. She was still dressed, but wore a dressing-gown over her clothes.

'Oh,' she said. 'I thought I heard someone leaving.'

'Nothing wrong with your ears, Mrs Grieve. Seona's just nipped out to the shop.'

'Then why are you still here?' She peered at him. 'You *are* the policeman?'

'That's right.'

She shuffled past him, one hand reaching out to steady herself against the wall. 'I'm looking for something,' she told him. 'It's not in my bedroom.'

He could see into her room through the open door. It was chaotic. Clothes were piled on chairs and the floor, more spilling from the wardrobe and chest of drawers. Books and magazines, paintings stacked against the walls. There was a large patch of damp on the ceiling by the window.

She'd pushed open another door. The patterned carpet inside was faded to an almost uniform grey, where it wasn't threadbare. Rebus followed her in. Was it a living room? An office? Impossible to tell. Cardboard boxes filled with memories and rubbish. Old letters, some not yet opened. Photograph albums spilling loose pictures across the floor. More magazines and newspapers, more paintings. Children's toys and games from ages past. A collection of mirrors on one wall. A wigwam propped up against the far corner, its yellow canvas patched and crumbling. A child's doll, sporting tunic and kilt, lay headless under a chair. Rebus picked it up, found the head resting in an open biscuit tin along with loose dominoes, playing cards, empty cotton reels. He fixed the head back on. The doll's blue eyes looked neither pleased nor displeased.

'What is it you're looking for?'

She looked round. 'What are you doing with Lorna's doll?'

'Its head had come off. I just—'

'No, no, no.' She grabbed the doll from him. 'Its head didn't *come* off, the little madam yanked it off.' Which was what Alicia Grieve did now. 'It was her way of telling us she'd broken with childhood.'

Rebus smiled. 'How old was she?' Expecting to hear nine or ten.

'Twenty-five, twenty-six, something like that.' Her mind was half on her visitor, half on the search.

'What did you think when she took up modelling?'

'I've always supported my children.' It had the sound of a prepared line, a titbit she offered to journalists and the curious.

'How about Cammo and Roddy? Were you political, Mrs Grieve?'

'In my younger days I was. Labour, mostly. Allan was a Liberal, we had many a debate . . .'

'Yet one of your sons is a Tory.'

'Oh, Cammo could always be difficult.'

'And Roddy?'

'Roddy needs to step out from his brother's shadow. You haven't seen the way he runs after Cammo. Always watching, studying him. But Cammo has his own chums. Boys that age can be cruel, can't they?'

She was drifting away from him, the years dancing in her eyes.

'They're grown men now, Alicia.'

'They'll always be boys to me.' She started taking things out of a box, studying each item – binoculars, marmalade jar, football pennant – as though it might reveal itself to her.

'Are you close to Roddy?'

'Roddy's a dear.'

'He talks to you? Comes to you with problems?'

'He's . . .' She broke off, looked confused. 'He's dead, isn't he?' Rebus nodded. 'I told him, warned him often enough. Climbing over railings at his age.' She shook her head. 'Bound to be accidents.'

'He'd done it before? Climbed the railings?'

'Oh yes. It was a shortcut to school, you see.'

Rebus slid his hands into his pockets. She was travelling elsewhere now. 'I did dally with the Nationalists in the fifties. They were a strange lot, maybe they still are. Kilts and Gaelic and a chip on the shoulder. We attended some good parties, though, lots of dancing. Sword and Shield . . .'

Rebus frowned. 'I've heard of that. An offshoot of the Nationalists?'

'It didn't last long. Very little did in those days. An idea would blossom, then you'd have a few drinks and that would be the end of that.'

'Did you know Matthew Vanderhyde?'

'Oh, yes. Everyone knew Matthew. Is he still with us?'

'I see him occasionally. Maybe not as often as I should.'

'Matthew and Allan would argue politics with Chris Grieve . . .' She broke off. 'You know he's not related?' Rebus nodded, remembering the framed poem in the downstairs hall. 'Allan would be doing Chris's portrait, only the man wouldn't sit still. Always moving, flinging out his arms to make a point.' She flung out her own arms in imitation. The marmalade jar was in one hand, a roll of Christmas parcel-tape in the other. 'Edwin Muir was a great foil for him. Then there was dear Naomi Mitchison. Do you know her work?' Rebus was silent, as if speech might break the spell.

'And the painters – Gillies, McTaggart, Maxwell.' She smiled. 'Sparks always flew. We were lucky with the Festival, it brought visitors to the galleries. The Edinburgh School, we called ourselves. It was a different country then, you know. Trapped between one world war and the threat of another. Hard to bring up children with the A-bomb hanging over your head. It affected my work, I think.'

'Were your children interested in art?'

'Lorna dabbled, maybe she still does. But not the boys. Cammo always had his cronies around him, almost like a Praetorian Guard. Roddy liked the company of grown-ups, always so deferential and willing to listen.'

'And Alasdair?'

She angled her head. 'Alasdair was a painter's nightmare, an angelic tearaway. I never captured that. You always knew he was up to something, but you didn't mind because it was Alasdair. Do you see?'

'I think so.' Rebus knew a few young villains like that: charming and cheeky, but always on the make and take. 'He keeps in touch, doesn't he?'

'Oh, yes.'

'Why did he leave home?'

'He wasn't strictly *at* home. He had a flat of his own near the foot of the Canongate. When he'd gone, we found out it was a furnished rental, practically none of it was his. He took a suitcase of clothes, some books, and that was it.'

'He didn't say why he was leaving?'

'No, just phoned out of the blue. Told me he'd be in touch.'

Rebus heard the front door open and close, the words 'I'm back' drifting up the stairs.

'I'd better be going,' he said.

Alicia Grieve looked as though she'd already dismissed him. 'I wish I knew where it was,' she said to herself, replacing the marmalade jar in its box. 'Dear me, if only I knew . . .'

Seona Grieve was halfway up the stairs when he met her.

'Is everything all right?'

'Everything's fine,' he assured her. 'Mrs Grieve's just lost something, that's all.'

Seona stared up towards the landing. 'Inspector, she's lost practically *everything*. It's just that she doesn't know it yet . . .'

15

It was an office much like any other.

Grant Hood and Ellen Wylie shared a look. They'd been expecting a builder's yard – glaur and breeze-blocks, an Alsatian tethered and barking. Wylie even had wellies in the car, just in case. But this was the third floor of a 1960s office block halfway down Leith Walk. Wylie had asked Hood, would it be all right to nip into Valvona and Crolla's after? He'd told her yes, no problem, but wasn't it expensive?

'Quality costs.' That's what she'd said, like an advertising slogan.

They were doing the rounds of Edinburgh's building contractors, starting with the largest and longest established. Phone calls first, and if there was anyone in the firm who could help, then it was time for a visit.

Wylie: 'Maybe John's right when he calls us the Time Team. Never saw myself as an archaeologist.'

'Twenty years, it's hardly prehistory.'

Hood had found that their conversation flowed. No awkward pauses or slips of the tongue. They'd had one disagreement, over whether they were on a dead-end case.

Wylie: 'We should be working the Grieve inquiry. That's where all the attention is.'

Hood: 'But if we get a result here, it's something special, isn't it? And it's all ours.'

Wylie: 'Any leads we get, I'll bet we end up relegated. We're DCs, Grant. That's too low in the league to get any medals that might be going.'

'You like football?'

'I might.'

'Who do you support?'

'You first.'

Hood: 'I've always been Rangers. You?'

Grinning: 'Celtic.'

Sharing a laugh. Then Wylie again: 'What is it they say about opposites attracting?'

A line Grant Hood carried with him as they sat in the waiting room. *Opposites attracting.*

Peter Kirkwall of Kirkwall Construction was in his early thirties and wore an immaculate pinstripe suit. It was impossible to picture him with a shovel in one of his smooth hands, yet there he was in a series of framed photographs around the walls of his office.

'The first one', he said, leading them as if through an exhibition, 'is me at seven, mixing concrete in Dad's yard.' Dad being Jack Kirkwall, who'd founded the company back in the 1950s. He was in some of the photos, too. But the focus was on Peter: Peter bricklaying during a summer break from college; Peter with the plans of one of the city's office blocks, his first Kirkwall project; Peter meeting dignitaries . . . and behind the wheel of a Mercedes CLK . . . and on the day of Jack Kirkwall's retirement.

'If you want it first-hand,' he said, easing into his chair and business both, 'you need to talk to Dad.' He paused. 'Coffee? Tea?' Seemed pleased when they shook their heads: his was a busy schedule.

'We appreciate you taking the trouble, sir,' Wylie said, not above a bit of soft-soap. 'Business good, is it?'

'Phenomenal. What with the Holyrood redevelopment and the Western Approach corridor, Gyle, Wester Hailes, and now the plans for Granton . . .' He shook his head. 'We can hardly keep up. Every week we're making bids on some project or other.' He waved towards where some plans lay on the room's conference table. 'Know how my dad started? He built garages and extensions. Now it looks like we might get a finger in a pie as big as London Docklands.' He rubbed his hands with what looked to Hood like glee.

'But in the seventies, the firm worked on Queensberry House?' Wylie was first with the question. It pulled Kirkwall back down to earth.

'Yes, sorry. Once you get me started, I don't know when to stop.' He cleared his throat, composed himself. 'I did look up our records . . .' Reaching into a drawer, bringing out an old ledger, some notebooks and a card index. 'Late in '78, we were one of the firms renovating the hospital. Not me, of course, I was still at school. And now you've found a skeleton, eh?'

Hood handed over photographs of the two fireplaces. 'The room to the far end of the basement. It was originally the kitchen.'

'And that's where the body was?'

'We estimate it's been there twenty years,' Wylie said, easing into her role: talker to Hood's silent type. 'Which would coincide with the building works.'

'Well, I've had my secretary dig up what she can.' He smiled to let them know the pun was deliberate. Kirkwall – striped shirt, oval glasses, groomed black hair – was, Wylie presumed, trying for the sophisticated look. But there was something uncomfortable and ill-defined about him. She'd seen footballers turned TV pundits: they could wear the clothes but failed to carry the style.

'It's not much, I'm afraid,' Kirkwall was saying, reaching into a drawer. He unrolled the plan so it faced them, weighting its corners with pieces of polished stone. 'I collect one from each job I do,' he explained. 'Get it cleaned and varnished.' Then: 'This is Queensberry House. The blue shaded areas were our project, plus the red lines.'

'It looks like exterior work.'

'It was. Downpipes, cracks in the masonry, and one summer house to be built from scratch. It's like that sometimes with public works, they like to spread the contract around.'

'You obviously weren't greasing enough palms at the council,' Hood muttered.

Kirkwall glared at him.

'So another firm was doing the internal work?' Wylie was studying the plan.

'Firm or firms. I've no record. Like I say, you'd have to ask Dad.'

'Then that's what we'll do, Mr Kirkwall,' Ellen Wylie said.

But first they hit Valvona's, where Wylie did her shopping before asking if Hood fancied a bite to eat. He made show of checking his watch.

'Come on,' she said. 'There's an empty table, and I've been here often enough to know that must be a sign.'

So they ate salad and pizza and shared a bottle of mineral water. Around them, couples were doing the same thing. Hood smiled.

'We don't stick out,' he commented.

She looked at his stomach. 'Well, I don't.'

He sucked in some gut and decided to leave the last slice of pizza. 'You know what I mean,' he said.

Yes, she knew. Being a cop, being around people who knew cops, you always felt they could spot you, and you came to think everyone had the knack.

'Bit of a shock to find you're not a social leper?'

Hood looked at his plate. 'More of a shock to find I can actually leave food.'

Afterwards, they headed out to the house Jack Kirkwall had built for his retirement. It sat in countryside on the edge of South Queensferry, with both bridges visible in the distance. The house was angular with tall windows. When Wylie stated that it was like a scaled-down cathedral, Hood knew what she meant.

Jack Kirkwall welcomed them by insisting that he be remembered to John Rebus.

'You know Inspector Rebus?' Wylie asked.

'He did me a good turn once.' Kirkwall chuckled.

'You might be able to return the favour, sir,' Hood said. 'Depending on how good your memory is.'

'Nothing wrong with the napper,' Kirkwall grumbled.

Wylie shot her partner a warning look. 'What DC Hood meant, Mr Kirkwall, is that we're in the dark and you're our one ray of light.'

Kirkwall perked up, settled into an easy chair and motioned for them to be seated.

The sofa was cream leather and smelt brand new. The lounge was large and bright with inch-thick white shag pile and a whole wall of French windows. To Wylie's eye, there seemed very little of Kirkwall's past on display: no photos or old-looking ornaments or furniture. It was as though, in later life, he had decided to reinvent himself. There was something anonymous about it all. Then Wylie realised: it was a show house. Prospective clients could be shown around, Kirkwall Construction workmanship evident everywhere.

And no place for individual personality.

She wondered if that explained the sad depths to Jack Kirkwall's face. No way was this his idea of retirement: in the choice of fabrics and furnishings she saw the son, Peter.

'Your firm', she said, 'did some work at Queensberry House in 1979.'

'The hospital?' She nodded. 'Started work in '78, finished it in '79. What a hellish time that was.' He peered at them. 'Likely you're too young to remember. That winter there was a rubbish strike, teachers' strike, even the mortuary was on strike.' He snorted at the memory, looked to Hood. Tapping his head, he said: 'See, son? Nothing wrong with the napper. Remember it like it was yesterday. We started in December, finished in March. The eighth, to be precise.'

Wylie smiled. 'That's incredible.'

Kirkwall accepted her praise. He was a big man, broad-shouldered, chisel-jawed. He'd probably never been handsome, but she could imagine him having power and presence.

'Know why I remember?' He shook his head. 'You'll be too young.'

'The referendum?' Hood guessed.

Kirkwall looked deflated. Wylie gave another warning look: they needed him on their side.

'It was March first, wasn't it?' Hood continued.

'Aye, it was. And we won the vote but lost the war.'

'A temporary setback,' Wylie felt bound to add.

He glared at her. 'If you can call twenty years temporary. We had dreams . . .' Wylie thought he was turning wistful, but he surprised her. 'Just think what it would have meant: inward investment, new homes and businesses.'

'A building boom?'

Kirkwall was shaking his head at the thought of so much opportunity wasted.

'The boom's happening now, according to your son,' Wylie said.

'Aye.'

She doubted she'd ever heard so much bitterness in a single syllable. Had Jack Kirkwall gone willingly, or had he been pushed?

'We're interested in the hospital's interior,' Hood said. 'Which firms had the contracts?'

'Roofing was Caspian,' Kirkwall said tonelessly, still lost in thought. 'Scaffolding was Macgregor. Coghill's did a lot of the inside work: replastering, a few new partition walls.'

'Was this in the basement?'

Kirkwall nodded. 'A new laundry room and a boiler.'

'Do you remember any of the original walls being exposed?' Wylie handed over the photo of the fireplaces. 'Like this?' Kirkwall looked, shook his head. 'But the work in the basement was done by a firm called Coghill's?'

Kirkwall nodded again. 'Gone now. Firm went bust.'

'Is Mr Coghill still around?'

Kirkwall shrugged. 'Shouldn't have gone bust really. Good firm. Dean knew his stuff.'

'The building trade's a tough game,' Wylie agreed.

'It's not that.' He looked at her.

'What then?'

'I might be speaking out of turn.' He considered this. 'But at my age, who cares?' Took a deep, noisy breath. 'It's just that, way I heard it, Dean fell foul of Mr Big.'

Wylie and Hood responded as one voice. 'Mr Big?'

The Oxford Bar was busy when Rebus arrived. He'd already had one drink at The Maltings, leaving before the evening influx of students, and two drinks at Swany's on Causewayside. In Swany's he'd bumped into an old colleague, recently retired.

'You look too young,' Rebus had chided him.

'Same age as you, John,' had been the reply.

But Rebus didn't have thirty years in; had joined the force in his mid-twenties. Two or three more years, he could be a gentleman of leisure. Rebus got a round in, then sneaked out into the cold blast of winter. Headlamps piercing the darkness; recent rainfall threatening ice. A fifteen-minute walk home. Across the street, a taxi filling up at the petrol station.

Retirement. The word bouncing around in his skull. Jesus, but what would he do with himself? One man's retirement was another's redundancy. He thought of the Farmer, then waved down the taxi, asked to be taken to the Oxford Bar.

No sign of Doc and Salty, Rebus's usual drinking partners, but plenty of faces he knew. The place was buzzing, bodies crammed in the front room. Football on the TV: a game from down south. A regular called Muir was standing close by the door. He nodded a greeting.

'Your wife has a gallery, doesn't she?' Rebus asked. Muir nodded again. 'Ever sell any stuff by Alicia Rankeillor?'

Muir snorted. 'If only. Rankeillor's stuff, as you call it, fetches tens of thousands. Every city in the western world wants something of hers in its collection – preferably something from the forties or fifties. Even her limited prints fetch a grand or two apiece.' Muir looked up. 'Don't know anyone who wants to sell, do you?'

'I'll let you know.'

The Two Margarets were behind the bar, busy in their confinement. Rebus's IPA arrived, and he ordered a whisky to go with it. Music from the back room. He could just make it out: acoustic guitar, young woman on vocals. But here was his favourite duet: a pint and a dram. He added water to the whisky, removing the edge. A deep swallow, coating his throat. One of the Margarets was back with his change.

'Friend of yours through the back.'

Rebus frowned. 'Singing?'

She smiled, shook her head. 'Up by the cigarette machine.'

He looked. Saw a wall of bodies. The ciggie machine was in an alcove, up three steps and next to the toilets. Fruit machine there, too. But all he could see were men's backs, meaning someone had an audience.

'Who is it?'

Margaret shrugged. 'Said she knew you.'

'Siobhan?'

Another shrug. He craned his neck. A new round was being got in. The backs half-turned. Rebus saw faces he knew: regulars. Glazed smiles and cigarette smoke. And behind them, relaxed, leaning against the fruit machine, Lorna Grieve. A tall drink was raised to her lips. It looked like neat whisky or brandy, three measures at least. She smacked her lips; her eyes met his and she smiled, raising her glass. He smiled back, raised his own glass to her. A sudden flash of memory: as a kid, he'd been coming home from school. Passing a street corner by the sweet shop, a crowd of older boys hemming in a girl from his class. He couldn't see what was going on. Her eyes, suddenly catching his between the heads of two of the boys. Not panicked, but not enjoying herself either . . .

Lorna Grieve touched one of her suitors on the arm, said something to him. His name was Gordon, a Fifer like Rebus. Probably young enough to be her son.

Now she was walking forwards, negotiating the steps. Squeezing through the crowd, touching arms and shoulders and backs; each touch enough to aid her progress.

'Well, well,' she said, 'fancy seeing you here.'

'Yes,' he said, 'just fancy.' He'd finished the whisky. She asked if he wanted another. He shook his head, lifted the pint.

'I don't think I've ever been here,' she said, leaning into the bar. 'I've just been hearing about the old owner, how he wouldn't serve women or people with English accents. I think I might have liked him.'

'He was an acquired taste.'

'The best kind, don't you think?' Her eyes were on him. 'I've been hearing about you, too. I may have to stop calling you Monkey Man.'

'Why's that?'

'Because from what I've been told, not many people make a monkey out of you.'

He smiled. 'Bars are great places for tall stories.'

'There you go, Lorna.' It was Gordon, presenting her with another drink. Armagnac: Rebus had watched Margaret pouring. 'All right, John? You never told us you knew famous people.'

Lorna Grieve accepted the compliment; Rebus stayed quiet.

'And if I'd known there were honeys like you in Edinburgh,' she told Gordon, 'I wouldn't have moved out to the sticks. And I certainly wouldn't have married a grim old beast like Hugh Cordover.'

'Don't knock High Chord,' Gordon said. 'I saw Obscura supporting Barclay James Harvest at the Usher Hall.'

'Were you still at school?'

Gordon considered the question. 'I think I was fourteen.'

Lorna Grieve looked at Rebus. 'We're dinosaurs,' she informed him.

'We were dinosaurs when Gordon here was just primordial soup,' he agreed.

But she wasn't at all like a dinosaur. Her clothes were colourful and flowing, her hair immaculate, and her make-up striking. Surrounded by men in work suits, she was a butterfly in the company of fluttering grey moths.

'What are you doing here?' he asked.

'Drinking.'

'Did you drive in?'

'The band gave me a lift.' She peered at him. 'I didn't just come here to see you, you know.'

'No?'

'Don't flatter yourself.' She brushed invisible flecks from her scarlet jacket. Beneath was an orange silk blouse, and on her legs faded denims, frayed where they touched her ankles. Black suede moccasins on her feet. No jewellery anywhere.

Not even a wedding ring.

'I like new things, that's all,' she was explaining. 'And currently my life is so dreary', looking at her surroundings, 'that this counts as new.'

'Poor you.'

Her glance was arch and wry at the same time. Gordon shuffled his feet and said he'd see her upstairs. She nodded unconvincingly.

'Have you been drinking all day?' he asked.

'Jealous?'

He shrugged. 'I've been there often enough.' He turned so he was facing her. 'How does the Ox measure up?'

Her nose wrinkled. 'It's very *you*,' she said.

'Is that good or bad?'

'I haven't decided yet.' She studied him. 'There's a darkness in you.'

'Probably all the beer.'

'I'm serious. We all come from darkness, you have to remember that, and we sleep during the night to escape the fact. I'll bet you have trouble sleeping at night, don't you?' He didn't say anything. Her face grew less animated. 'We'll all return to darkness one day, when the sun burns out.' A sudden smile lit her eyes. ' "Though my soul may set in darkness, It will rise in perfect light." '

'A poem?' he guessed.

She nodded. 'I forget the rest.'

The door creaked open. Two expectant faces: Grant Hood and Ellen Wylie. Hood looked ready for a drink, but he wasn't coming in. Wylie spotted Rebus, motioned for him to step outside.

'Back in a minute,' he told Lorna Grieve, touching her arm before squeezing his way past the other drinkers. The night air was fresh after the pub fug. Rebus took in several deep gulps.

'Sorry to bother you, sir,' Wylie said.

'You wouldn't be here if there wasn't a good reason.' He slipped his hands into his pockets. There was ice in the gutters now. The narrow street was badly lit. Cars were parked down one side, windscreens rimed with frost. Sudden clouds in the air when the three detectives spoke.

'We went to see Jack Kirkwall,' Hood explained.

'And?'

'You two know each other?' Wylie asked.

'A case few years back.'

Hood and Wylie exchanged a look. 'You tell him,' Hood said. So Wylie told the story, and at the end Rebus was thoughtful.

'He's flattering me,' he said at last.

'He said you'd tell us about Mr Big,' she repeated.

Rebus nodded. 'That's what some in CID called him. Not very original.'

Hood: 'But the name fitted?'

Rebus nodded, moved aside to let a couple into the bar. The singer had started up again: he could hear her through the back room's closed window.

My mind returns, she sang, *to things I should have left behind.*

'His name was Callan, first name Bryce.'

'I thought Big Ger Cafferty ran Edinburgh?'

Rebus nodded. 'But only after Callan retired, moved to the Costa del Sol or somewhere. He's never been away, though.'

Wylie: 'How do you mean?'

'You still hear stories, how a piece of Cafferty's action heads out to Spain. Bryce Callan's almost grown . . .' He sought the word. More lyrics from the back room:

My mind returns, to things best left unsaid.

'Mythical?' Wylie suggested.

He nodded, stared at the window of the barber's shop across the lane. 'Because we never put him away, I suppose.'

'How would Dean Coghill have fallen foul of him?'

Rebus shrugged. 'Protection maybe. There's a lot can go wrong on a building site, and those projects . . . even then they'd be worth thousands. A few days lost could mean everything.'

Hood was nodding. 'So we need to find Coghill.'

'Always supposing he'll speak to us,' Wylie warned.

'Let me do some checking on Bryce Callan,' Rebus said.

The past is here now, insistent, carved from darkness,
So please beware, take care now where you tread . . .

'Meantime,' he went on, 'you better try to get hold of Coghill's employee files. We need to know who was working on the site.'

'And if any of them disappeared,' Hood added.

'I'm assuming you've made a start on MisPer records.'

Wylie and Hood shared a look, said nothing.

'It's shit work,' Rebus acknowledged, 'but it's got to be done. Two of you on it, takes half the time.'

Wylie: 'Can we limit the search to late '78, first three months of '79?'

'To start with, yes.' He looked towards the pub. 'Buy the pair of you a drink?'

Wylie was quick to shake her head. 'I think we'll head for the Cambridge, bit quieter there.'

'Fair enough.'

'In there', nodding towards the door of the Ox, 'looks too much like the broom cupboard we're having to work out of.'

'I'd heard,' Rebus said. Wylie's look was accusatory.

'Sir,' she said, 'the woman in there . . .' Wylie looked down at her feet. 'Was it who I thought it was?'

Rebus nodded. 'Just a coincidence,' he said.

'Of course.' She nodded slowly, began to move off. She still hadn't made eye contact. Hood made to catch up with her. Rebus pushed open the door a crack but waited. Wylie and Hood with their heads together, Hood asking who the woman had been. If the story got around St Leonard's, Rebus would know who'd started it.

And that would be the end of the Time Team.

He woke at 4 a.m. The bedside lamp was still on. The duvet had been kicked to the foot of the bed. The sound of an engine turning over outside. He stumbled to the window, just in time to see a dark shape disappearing into the back of a taxi. He weaved naked into the living room, reaching for handholds, his balance shot. She'd left him a gift: a four-track demo by the Robinson Crusoes. It was titled *Shipwrecked Heart*. Made sense, band having the name they did. 'Final Reproof' was the last song on it. He stuck it on the hi-fi, listened for a minute or two with the volume down low. Empty bottle and two tumblers on the floor by the sofa. There was still half an inch of whisky in one of them. He sniffed it, took it into the kitchen. Poured it down the sink and filled the glass with cold water, gulped it down. Then another, and another after that. No way he was getting away from this one without a hangover, but he'd do his best. Three paracetamol tablets and more water, then another glassful to take through to the bathroom with him. She'd showered: there was a wet towel hanging from the rail. Showered first, then called the taxi. Had he woken her with his snoring? Had she ever been asleep? He ran a bath, looked at himself in the shaving mirror. Slack skin covered his face, looking for somewhere else to go. He bent down, dry-retched into the sink, almost bringing the tablets back up. How much had they drunk? He couldn't begin to count. Had they come back here straight from the Ox? He didn't think so. Back in the bedroom, he searched his pockets for clues. Nothing. But the fifty quid he'd gone out with had been reduced to pennies.

'Dear Christ.' He squeezed shut his eyes. His neck felt stiff; so did his back. In front of the bathroom mirror again he stared into his eyes. 'Did we do it?' he asked himself. The answer came back: definitely maybe. Screwed shut his eyes again. 'Oh, for Christ's sake, John, what have you done?'

Answer: slept with Lorna Grieve. Twenty years ago, he'd have been doing cartwheels. But then twenty years ago, she hadn't been part of a murder inquiry.

He turned off the taps, eased himself into the water and slid down, knees bent, so that his whole head went under. Maybe, he thought, if I just lie here like this it'll all go away. His first mistake on booze had been over thirty years before, outside a school dance.

A bloody long apprenticeship, he thought, coming up for air. Whatever happened now, he felt tied to the Grieves, one more thread of their history.

And if Lorna put the story around, he'd be history, too.

Part Two

Fitful and Dark

16

Jerry had this morning routine, soon as Jayne had gone off to work. Tea, toast and the paper, and then into the living room to play a few records. Old stuff, punk 45s from his teens. Really set him up for the day. There might be thumps from upstairs, but he'd flick the Vs at the ceiling and dance on regardless. He had a few favourites – Generation X, 'Your Generation'; Klark Kent, 'Don't Care'; Spizzenergi, 'Where's Captain Kirk?' Their picture sleeves were dog-eared, and the vinyl was scratched to hell – too many lendings and parties. He still remembered gatecrashing a Ramones gig at the uni: October '78. The Spizz single was May '79: date of purchase scrawled on the back of the sleeve. He was like that back then. He'd time all his singles, make notes. A top five every week – best things he'd heard, not necessarily bought. The Virgin on Frederick Street had been shoplifting heaven for a while. Hadn't been so easy at Bruce's. The guy who ran Bruce's had gone on to manage Simple Minds. Jerry'd seen them when they'd been called Johnny and the Self Abusers.

It all used to matter, to mean something. Weekends, the adrenaline could make you dizzy.

These days, dancing did that for him. He fell on to the sofa. Three records and he was knackered. Rolled himself a joint and switched on the TV, knowing there'd be nothing worth watching. Jayne was working a double shift, wouldn't be home till nine, maybe ten. That gave him twelve hours to wash the dishes. Some days he itched to be working again, sitting in an office maybe with suit and tie on, making decisions and fielding phone calls. Nic said he had a secretary. A *secretary*. Who'd have thought it? He remembered the pair of them at school, kicking a football across the cul-de-sac, pogoing to punk in their bedrooms. Well, Jerry's bedroom mostly. Nic's mum had been funny about visitors; always a frown on her face when she opened her door and saw Jerry standing there. Dead now though, the old cow. Her living room had smelt of the Hamlet cigars Nic's dad smoked. He was the only person Jerry knew who didn't smoke cigarettes, had to be a cigar. Jerry, TV remote busy in his hand, chuckled now at the thought. *Cigars! Who did the old sod think he was?* Nic's dad had worn ties and cardigans . . . Jerry's dad had worn a vest most of the time, and a trouser-belt that came off whenever there was justice to dispense. But Jerry's mum, she'd been a treasure: no way he'd have swapped his parents for Nic's.

'No bloody way,' he said out loud.

He switched off the TV. The joint was down to the hot bit near the roach. He took a last draw and went to flush it down the bog. Not that he was worried about the pigs; it was Jayne didn't like him doing the wacky bac. Way Jerry looked at it, the wacko kept him sane. Government should put the stuff on the National Health, way it kept the likes of him from going off the rails.

He went to the bathroom to have a shave: little treat for Jayne when she came home. Still humming 'Captain Kirk'. Brilliant record, one of the best. He was thinking about Nic, how the two of them had become pals. You could never tell, could you, people you'd end up liking. They'd been in the same class since age five, but it was only when they went up to secondary that they started hanging around together, listening to Alex Harvey and Status Quo, trying to work out which lyrics were about sex. Nic had written a poem, hundreds of lines long, all about an orgy. Jerry had reminded him about it recently, and they'd had a good laugh. That was what it was about, at the end of the day: having a laugh.

He realised he was staring into the bathroom mirror; foam on his face and the razor in his hand. He had bags and lines under his eyes. It was catching up with him. Jayne kept talking about kids and ticking clocks; he kept telling her he'd think about it. Fact was, he didn't fancy himself as a dad, and Nic kept talking about how it ruined a relationship. Guys in the office who hadn't had sex since their nipper was born – months, sometimes years. And the mothers letting themselves go, gravity working against them. Nic would wrinkle his nose in disgust.

'Not a pretty outlook, is it?' Nic would say.

And Jerry would be bound to agree.

After school, Jerry had assumed they'd get jobs in the same place, maybe a factory or something. But Nic had dropped a bombshell: he was staying on an extra year, doing his Highers. It hadn't stopped them seeing one another, but there were all these books in Nic's room now – stuff Jerry couldn't make head or tail of. And after that there was Napier for three years, and more books, essays to hand in. They saw one another some weekends, but almost never through the week – maybe Friday night for a disco or a gig. Iggy Pop . . . Gang of Four . . . the Stones at the Playhouse. Nic hardly ever introduced Jerry to his student pals, unless they met them at a gig. Once or twice they ended up in the pub. Jerry had chatted up one of the girls, then Nic had grabbed him.

'What would Jayne say?'

Because he was seeing Jayne by then. They worked in the same factory: semiconductors. Jerry drove the fork-lift, got really good with it. He'd show off, do circuits around the women. They'd laugh, say he was daft, he'd get someone killed. Then Jayne came along and that was that.

Fifteen years they'd been married. Fifteen years and no kids. How could she expect them to have kids now, with him on the dole? His only letter this morning: dole people wanted him in for an interview. He knew what that meant. They wanted to know what he was doing to find himself a job. Answer: sweet FA. And now Jayne was at him again, 'The clock's ticking, Jerry.' A double meaning there: her body clock, plus the threat that she might walk out if she didn't get what she wanted. She'd done it before, packed her bags and off to her mum's three streets away. Be as well bloody living there anyway . . .

He'd go mad if he stayed in the flat. He wiped the foam from his face and put his shirt back on, grabbed his jacket and was out. Walked the streets, looking for people to talk to, then into the bookies for half an hour, warming himself by the heater, pretending to study form. They knew him in there: highly unlikely he'd place a bet, but he sometimes did, always losing. When the lunchtime paper came in, he took a look. Page three, there was a story about a sexual assault. He read it closely. Nineteen-year-old student, grabbed in the Commonwealth Pool car park. Jerry flung the paper down and headed out to find a phone box.

He had Nic's office number in his pocket, called him there sometimes when he was bored, holding the receiver to the stereo so Nic could hear some song they used to dance to. He got the receptionist and asked for Mr Hughes.

'Nic, man, it's Jerry.'

'Hiya, pal. What can I do you for?'

'Just saw the paper. There was a student attacked last night.'

'The world's a terrible place.'

'Tell me it wasn't you.'

A nervous laugh. 'That's a sick kind of joke, Jerry.'

'Just tell me.'

'Where are you? Got any mates *listening in*?'

The way he said it made Jerry stop. Nic was telling him something, telling him someone could be listening in – maybe the receptionist.

'I'll talk to you later,' Nic said.

'Listen, man, I'm sorry—' But the phone was dead.

Jerry was shaking when he left the phone box. Jogged all the way home, fixed another joint. Put the TV on and sat there, trying to get his heartbeat down. Safer here; wasn't anything could touch him here. This was the only place to be.

Until Jayne got home.

Siobhan Clarke had asked Register House to run a search for Chris Mackie's birth certificate. She'd also begun asking around about

Mackie, concentrating on Grassmarket and the Cowgate, but spreading out to take in the Meadows, Princes Street and Hunter Square.

But this Thursday morning she sat in a doctor's waiting room, surrounded by pale and sickly sufferers, until her name was called and she could put aside the women's magazine with its alien articles on cookery, clothes and kids.

Where, she wondered, was the magazine for her, one that concentrated on Hibs FC, hashed relationships and homicide?

Dr Talbot was in his mid-fifties and wore a weary smile below his half-moon glasses. He already had Chris Mackie's medical records laid out on his desk, but checked that Clarke's own paperwork – death certificate; authorisation – was in order before beckoning for her to move her chair in towards the desk.

It took her a couple of minutes to substantiate that the records only went back as far as 1980. When Mackie had registered with the surgery, he'd given a previous address in London and had stated that his records were held by a Dr Mason in Crouch End. But a letter from Dr Talbot to Dr Mason's address had been returned 'No Such Street'.

'You didn't pursue this?' Clarke asked.

'I'm a doctor, not a detective.'

Mackie's Edinburgh address was the hostel. Date of birth was different from that on Drew's filing-card. Clarke had the uneasy feeling that Mackie had laid a false trail all the way along. She went back to the records. Once or twice a year he'd attended the surgery, usually with some minor complaint: a facial cut turned septic; influenza; a boil requiring to be lanced.

'He was in pretty good health, considering his circumstances,' Dr Talbot said. 'I don't think he drank or smoked, which helped.'

'Drugs?'

The doctor shook his head.

'Is that unusual in someone who's homeless?'

'I've known people with stronger constitutions than Mr Mackie.'

'Yes, but someone homeless, not doing drink or drugs . . .?'

'I'm no expert.'

'But in your opinion . . .?'

'In my opinion, Mr Mackie gave me very little trouble.'

'Thank you, Dr Talbot.'

She left the surgery and headed for the Department of Social Security office, where a Miss Stanley sat her down in a lifeless cubicle usually reserved for claimant interviews.

'Looks like he didn't have a National Insurance number,' she said, going through the file. 'We had to issue an emergency one at the start.'

'When was this?'

It was 1980, of course: the year of Christopher Mackie's invention.

'I wasn't here at the time, but there are some notes from whoever it was interviewed him initially.' Miss Stanley read from these. ' "Filthy, not sure of where he is, no NI number or tax reference." Previous address is given as London.'

Clarke dutifully jotted it all down.

'Does it answer your questions?'

'Pretty much,' she admitted. The night he'd died, that was as close to 'Chris Mackie' as she was going to get. Since then she'd been moving away from him, because he didn't exist. He was a figment, imagined by someone with something to hide.

The who and what she might never discover.

Because Mackie had been clever. Everyone else had said he kept himself clean, but for the DSS he'd camouflaged himself with filth. Why? Because it made his act the more believable: bumbling, forgetful, unhelpful. The sort of person a hard-pressed official would want rid of pronto. No NI number? Never mind, issue an emergency one. Vague address in London? Fine, leave it be. Just sign your name to his claim and get him out of the cubicle.

A call on her mobile to Register House confirmed that there was no birth record of a Christopher Mackie on the date she'd given. She could try the other date she had, or spread the net wider, ask Register House in London . . . But she knew she was chasing shadows. She sat in a cramped café, drinking her drink, staring into space, and wondered if it was time to write up her report and call an end to the hunt.

She could think of half a dozen reasons for doing so.

And just four hundred thousand for not.

Back at her desk, she found over a dozen messages waiting for her. A couple of the names she recognised: local journalists. They'd tried calling three times apiece. She screwed shut her eyes and mouthed a word her grandmother would have clapped her ear for using. Then she headed downstairs to the Coms Room, knowing someone there would have the latest edition of the *News*. Front page: TRAGIC MYSTERY OF MILLIONAIRE TRAMP. As they didn't have a photograph of Mackie, they'd opted for one of the spot where he'd jumped. There wasn't much to the piece: well-known face around city centre . . . bank account well into six figures . . . police trying to establish who might have 'a claim on the cash'.

Siobhan Clarke's worst nightmare.

When she got upstairs, her phone was ringing again. Hi-Ho Silvers came across the floor on his knees, hands held in mock prayer.

'I'm his love child,' he said. 'Give me a DNA test, but for God's sake give me the dosh!'

Laughter in the CID suite. 'It's for yoo-ou,' someone else said, pointing to her phone. Every nutter and chancer in the kingdom would be getting ready. They'd call 999 or Fettes, and to get them off the line, someone would eventually admit that it was a St Leonard's matter.

They all belonged to Siobhan now. They were her children.

So she turned on her heels and left, ignoring the pleas from behind her.

And headed back on to the streets, finding new people to ask about Mackie. She knew she had to be quick: news travelled. Soon they'd all claim to have known him, to have been his best pal, his nephew, his executor. The street people knew her now, called her 'doll' and 'hen'. One old man had even christened her 'Diana, the Huntress'. She was wise to some of the younger beggars, too; not the ones who sold the *Big Issue*, but the ones who sat in doorways, blankets around them. She'd been sheltering from a downpour when one had come into Thin's Bookshop, blanket discarded and a mobile phone to his ear, complaining because his taxi hadn't turned up. He'd seen her, recognised her, but kept the diatribe going.

The foot of the Mound was quiet. Two young guys with ponytails and cross-breeds; the dogs licking themselves while their owners shared a can of headnip.

'Don't know the guy, sorry. Got a fag on you?'

She had learned to carry a packet with her, offered them each a cigarette, smiling when they took two. Then it was back up the Mound. John Rebus had told her something: the steep hill had been constructed from New Town rubble. The man whose idea it had been had owned a business at the top. Construction had meant the demolition of his shop. John Rebus hadn't found the story amusing; he'd told her it was a lesson.

'In what?' she'd asked.

'Scots history,' he'd replied, failing to explain.

She wondered now if it had been a reference to independence, to self-made, self-destructing schemes. It did seem to amuse him that, when pushed, she would defend independence. He wound her up, telling her it was a trick and she was an English spy, sent to undermine the process. Then he'd call her a 'New Scot', a 'settler'. She never knew when he was being serious. People in Edinburgh were like that: obtuse, thrawn. Sometimes she thought he was flirting, that the jibes and jokes were part of some mating ritual made all the more complex because it consisted of baiting the subject rather than wooing them.

She'd known John Rebus for several years now, and still they weren't close friends. Rebus, so far as she could tell, saw none of his colleagues outside work hours, apart from when she invited him to Hibs matches. His only hobby was drinking, and he tended to indulge where few women did, his chosen pubs museum pieces in a gallery marked prehistoric.

He'd been living on and off for years with Dr Patience Aitken, but that seemed to be over, not that he was saying anything about it. At first she'd thought him shy, awkward, but now she wasn't so sure. It seemed more like a strategy, a wilfulness. She couldn't imagine him joining a singles club the way Derek Linford had done. Linford . . .

another of her little mistakes. She hadn't spoken to him since The Dome. He'd left precisely one message on her answerphone: 'Hope you've got over whatever it was.' As if it was her fault! She'd almost called him back, forced an apology, but maybe that was his game: get her to make the move; contact of any kind the prelude to a rematch.

Maybe there was method in John Rebus's madness. Certainly there was a lot to be said for quiet nights in, a video rental, the gin, and a box of Pringle's. Not trying to impress anyone; putting on some music and dancing by yourself. At parties and in clubs there was always that self-consciousness, that sense of being watched and graded by anonymous eyes.

But next morning at the office it would be: 'What did you get up to last night then?' Asked innocently enough, but she never felt comfortable saying more than, 'Not much, how about you?' Because to utter the word alone implied that you were lonely.

Or available. Or had something to hide.

Hunter Square was empty save for a tourist couple poring over a map. The coffee she'd drunk was asking permission to leave, so she headed for the public toilet. When she came out of her cubicle, a woman was standing by the sinks, hunting through a series of carrier bags. Bag lady was an American term, but it suddenly seemed right. The woman's padded jacket was grubby, the stitching loose at the neck and shoulders. Her hair was short and greasy, cheeks red from exposure. She was talking to herself as she found what she'd been looking for: a half-eaten burger, still in its greaseproof wrapper. The woman held the comestible under the hand-dryer and let hot air play on it, turning it in her fingers. Clarke watched in fascination, unsure whether to be appalled or impressed. The woman knew she was being watched, but stuck to her task. When the dryer had finished its cycle, she pushed it on again with her finger. Then she spoke.

'Nosy little beggar, aren't you?' She glanced towards Clarke. 'You laughing at me?'

' "Beggar",' Clarke quoted.

The woman snorted. 'Easy amused then. And I'm no beggar, by the way.'

Clarke took a step forward. 'Wouldn't it heat up quicker if you opened it?'

'Eh?'

'Heat the inside rather than the outside.'

'You saying I'm cack-handed?'

'No, I just . . .'

'I mean, you're the world expert, are you? Lucky for me you just happened to be passing. Got fifty pence on you?'

'Yes, thanks.'

The woman snorted again. 'I make the jokes around here.' She took an exploratory bite of the burger, spoke with her mouth full.

'I didn't catch that,' Clarke said.

The woman swallowed. 'I was asking if you were a lesbian. Men who hang around toilets are poofs, aren't they?'

'You're hanging around a toilet.'

'I'm no lesbian, by the way.' She took another bite.

'Ever come across a guy called Mackie? Chris Mackie?'

'Who's asking?'

Clarke produced her warrant card. 'You know Chris is dead?'

The woman stopped chewing. Tried swallowing but couldn't, ended up coughing the mouthful out on to the floor. She went to one of the sinks, cupped water to her mouth. Clarke followed her.

'He jumped from North Bridge. I'm assuming you knew him?'

The woman was staring into the soap-flecked mirror. The eyes, though dark and knowing, were so much younger and less worn than the face. Clarke placed the woman in her mid-thirties, but knew that on a bad day she could pass for fifty.

'Everybody knew Mackie.'

'Not everybody's reacted the way you just did.'

The woman was still holding her burger. She stared at it, seemed about to ditch it, but finally wrapped it up again and placed it at the top of one of her bags.

'I shouldn't be so surprised,' she said. 'People die all the time.'

'But he was your friend?'

The woman looked at her. 'Gonny buy me a cup of tea?'

Clarke nodded.

The nearest café wouldn't take them. When pressed, the manager pointed to the woman and said she'd caused trouble, trying to beg at the tables. There was another café further along.

'I'm barred there as well,' the woman admitted. So Clarke went in, fetched two beakers of tea and a couple of sticky buns. They sat in Hunter Square, stared at by passengers on the top decks of the passing buses. The woman flicked the Vs from time to time, dissuading the spectators.

'I'm a bad bugger, me,' she confided.

Clarke had her name now: Dezzi. Short for Desiderata. Not her real name: 'Left that behind when I left home.'

'And when was that, Dezzi?'

'I don't remember. A lot of years now, I suppose.'

'You always been in Edinburgh?'

A shake of the head. 'All over. Last summer I ended up on a bus to some commune in Wales. Christ knows how that happened. Got a fag?'

Clarke handed one over. 'Why did you leave home?'

'Like I said, nosy little beggar.'

'All right, what about Chris?'

'I always called him Mackie.'

'What did he call you?'

'Dezzi.' She stared at Clarke. 'Is that you trying to find out my last name?'

Clarke shook her head. 'Cross my heart.'

'Oh aye, a cop's as honest as the day is long.'

'It's true.'

'Only, this time of year the days are awfy short.'

Clarke laughed. 'I walked into that one.' She'd been trying to work out if Dezzi knew about Mackie, knew about the detective who was asking about him. Knew about the story in the *News*. 'So what can you tell me about Mackie?'

'He was my boyfriend, just for a few weeks.' The sudden, unexpected smile lit up her face. 'Wild weeks they were, mind.'

'How wild?'

An arch look. 'Enough to get us arrested. I'm saying no more than that.' She bit into her bun. She was alternating: mouthful of bun, puff on the cigarette.

'Did he tell you anything about himself?'

'He's dead now, what does it matter?'

'It matters to me. Why would he kill himself?'

'Why does anyone?'

'You tell me.'

A slurp of tea. 'Because you give in.'

'Is that what he did, give in?'

'All the shite out here . . .' Dezzi shook her head. 'I tried it once, cut my wrists with a bit of glass. Eight stitches.' She turned one wrist as if to show it, but Clarke couldn't see any scars. 'Couldn't have been serious, could I?'

Clarke was well aware that a great many homeless people were ill; not physically, but mentally. She had a sudden thought: could she trust any stories Dezzi told her?

'When did you last see Mackie?'

'Maybe a couple of weeks back.'

'How did he seem?'

'Fine.' She pushed the last morsel of bun into her mouth. Washed it down with tea, before concentrating on the cigarette.

'Dezzi, did you really know him?'

'What?'

'You haven't told me one thing about him.'

Dezzi prickled. Clarke feared she would walk off. 'If he meant something to you,' Clarke went on, 'help me get to know him.'

'Nobody knew Mackie, not really. Too many defences.'

'But you got past them?'

'I don't think so. He told me a few stories . . . but I think that's all they were.'

'What sort of stories?'

'Oh, all about places he'd been – America, Singapore, Australia. I thought maybe he'd been in the navy or something, but he said he hadn't.'

'Was he well educated?'

'He knew things. I'm positive he'd been to America, not sure about the others. He knew London, though, all the tourist places and the underground stations. When I first met him . . .'

'Yes?' Clarke was shivering; couldn't feel her toes.

'I don't know, I got the feeling he was just passing through. Like, there was somewhere else he could go.'

'But he didn't?'

'No.'

'Are you saying he was homeless by choice rather than necessity?'

'Maybe.' Dezzi's eyes widened a little.

'What is it?'

'I can prove I knew him.'

'How's that?'

'The present he gave me.'

'What present?'

'Only, I didn't have much use for it, so I . . . I gave it to someone.'

'Gave it to someone?'

'Well, sold it. A second-hand shop on Nicolson Street.'

'What was it?'

'A briefcase sort of thing. Didn't hold enough stuff, but it was made of leather.'

Mackie had carried his cash to the building society in a briefcase. 'So now it'll have been sold on to someone else?' Clarke guessed.

But Dezzi was shaking her head. 'The shopkeeper's still got it. I've seen him walking about with it. Leather it was, and the bastard only gave me five quid.'

It wasn't far from Hunter Square to Nicolson Street. The shop was an Aladdin's cave of tat, narrow aisles leading them past teetering pillars of used goods: books, cassettes, music centres, crockery. Vacuum cleaners had been draped with feather boas; picture cards and old comics lay underfoot. Electrical goods and board games and jigsaw puzzles; pots and pans, guitars, music-stands. The shopkeeper, an Asian, didn't seem to recognise Dezzi. Clarke showed her warrant card and asked to see the briefcase.

'Five measly quid he gave me,' Dezzi grumbled. 'Genuine leather.'

The man was reluctant, until Clarke mentioned that St Leonard's was just around the corner. He reached down and placed a scuffed black briefcase on the counter. Clarke asked him to open it. Inside: a newspaper, packed lunch and a thick roll of banknotes. Dezzi seemed to want a closer look, but he snapped shut the case.

'Satisfied?' he asked.

Clarke pointed to a corner of the case where the scuffing was worst. 'What happened?'

'The initials were not my initials. I attempted to erase them.'

Clarke looked more closely. She was wondering if Valerie Briggs could identify the case. 'Do you remember the initials?' she asked Dezzi.

Dezzi shook her head; she was looking, too.

The shop was badly lit. The faintest indents remained.

'ADC?' she guessed.

'I believe so,' the shopkeeper said. Then he wagged a finger at Dezzi. 'And I paid you a fair price.'

'You as good as robbed me, you sod.' She nudged Clarke. 'Stick the handcuffs on him, girl.'

ADC, Clarke was thinking, *was Mackie really ADC?*

Or would it prove another dead end?

Back at St Leonard's, she kicked herself for not checking Mackie's criminal record sooner. August 1997, Christopher Mackie and 'a Ms Desiderata' (she refused to give the police her full name) were apprehended while involved in a 'lewd exhibition' on the steps of a parish church in Bruntsfield.

August: Festival time. Clarke was surprised they hadn't been mistaken for an experimental theatre group.

The arresting officer was a uniform called Rod Harken, and he remembered the incident well.

'She got a fine,' he told Clarke by telephone from Torphichen police station. 'And a few days in clink for refusing to tell us her name.'

'What about her partner?'

'I think he got off with a caution.'

'Why?'

'Because the poor sod was nearly comatose.'

'I still don't get it.'

'Then I'll spell it out. She was straddling him, knickers off and skirt up, trying to haul his pants down. We had to wake him up to take him to the station.' Harken chuckled.

'Were they photographed?'

'You mean on the steps?' Harken was still chuckling.

Clarke heaped more ice into her voice. 'No, I do not mean on the steps. I mean at Torphichen.'

'Oh aye, we took some snaps.'

'Would you still have them?'

'Depends.'

'Well, could you take a look.' Clarke paused. 'Please.'

'Suppose so,' the uniform said grudgingly.

'Thank you.'

She put the phone down. An hour later, the photos arrived by patrol car. The ones of Mackie were better than the hostel pictures. She stared into his unfocused eyes. His hair was thick and dark, brushed back from the forehead. His face was either tanned or weather-beaten. He hadn't shaved for a day or two, but looked no worse than many a summertime backpacker. His eyes looked heavy, as though no amount of sleep could compensate for what they'd seen. Clarke had to smile at the photos of Dezzi: she was grinning like a Cheshire cat, not a care in her world.

Harken had put a note in the envelope: *One other thing. We asked Mackie about the incident and he told us he wasn't a 'sexual beast' any more. Something got lost in the translation and we kept him locked up while we checked if he'd had previous as a sex offender. Turned out he hadn't.*

Her phone rang again. It was the front desk. There was someone downstairs for her.

Her visitor was short and round with a red face. He wore a Prince of Wales check three-piece suit and was mopping his brow with a handkerchief the size of a small tablecloth. The top of his head was bald and shiny, but hair grew copiously to either side, combed back over his ears. He introduced himself as Gerald Sithing.

'I read about Chris Mackie in the newspaper this morning, gave me quite a turn.' His beady eyes were on her, voice high and quavering.

Clarke folded her arms. 'You knew him, sir?'

'Oh, yes. Known him for years.'

'Could you describe him for me?'

Sithing studied her, then clapped his hands. 'Oh, of course. You think I'm a crank.' His laughter was sibilant. 'Come here to claim his fortune.'

'Aren't you?'

He drew himself up, recited a good description of Mackie. Clarke unfolded her arms, scratched her nose. 'In here, please, Mr Sithing.'

There was an interview room just to the side of the front desk. She unlocked it and looked in. Sometimes it was used for storage, but today it was empty. Desk and two chairs. Nothing on the walls. No ashtray or waste bin.

Sithing sat down, looked around as though intrigued by his surroundings. Clarke had gone from scratching her nose to pinching it. She had a headache coming on, felt dead beat.

'How did you come to know Mr Mackie?'

'Complete accident really. Daily constitutional, back then I took it in the Meadows.'

'Back when?'

'Oh, seven, eight years ago. Bright summer's day, so I sat myself down on one of the benches. There was a man already seated there, scruffy . . . you know, gentleman of the road. We got talking. I think I broke the ice, said something about how lovely the day was.'

'And this was Mr Mackie?'

'That's right.'

'Where was he living at the time?'

Sithing laughed again. 'You're still testing me, aren't you?' He wagged a finger like a fat sausage. 'He was in a hostel sort of place, Grassmarket. I met him the very next day, and the day after that. It got to be a routine with us, and one I enjoyed very much.'

'What did you talk about?'

'The world, the mess we've made of it. He was interested in Edinburgh, in all the architectural changes. He was very anti.'

'Anti?'

'You know, against all the new buildings. Maybe in the end it got too much for him.'

'He killed himself in protest at ugly architecture?'

'Despair can come from many quarters.' His tone was admonishing.

'I'm sorry if I sounded . . .'

'Oh, I'm sure it's not your fault. You're just tired.'

'Is it that obvious?'

'And maybe Chris was tired, too. That's the point I was making.'

'Did he ever talk about himself?'

'A little. He told me about the hostel, about people he'd met . . .'

'I meant his past. Did he talk about his life before he went on the street?'

Sithing was shaking his head. 'He was more of a good listener, fascinated by Rosslyn.'

Clarke thought she'd misheard. 'Rosalind?'

'*Rosslyn*. The chapel.'

'What about it?'

Sithing leaned forward. 'My whole life's devoted to the place. You may have heard of the Knights of Rosslyn?'

Clarke was getting a bad feeling. She shook her head. The stems of her eyes ached.

'But you know that in the year 2000, the secret of Rosslyn will reveal itself?'

'Is this some New Age thing?'

Sithing snorted. 'It's very much an *ancient* thing.'

'You believe Rosslyn's some sort of . . . special place?'

'It's the reason Rudolf Hess flew to Scotland. Hitler was obsessed with the Ark of the Covenant.'

'I know. I saw *Raiders of the Lost Ark* three times. You're saying Harrison Ford was looking in the wrong place?'

'Laugh all you like,' Sithing sneered.

'And that's what you talked about with Chris Mackie?'

'He was an acolyte!' Sithing slapped the desk. 'He was a believer.'

Clarke was getting to her feet. 'Did you know he had money?'

'He'd have wanted it to go to the Knights!'

'Did you know anything about him?'

'He gave us a hundred pounds to carry on our researches. Beneath the floor of the chapel, that's where it's buried.'

'What?'

'The portal! The gateway!'

Clarke had the door open. She grabbed Sithing's arm. It felt soft, as if there were no bones beneath the flesh.

'Out,' she commanded.

'The money belongs to the Knights! We were his family!'

'Out.'

He wasn't resisting, not really. She swung him into the revolving door and gave it a push, propelling him out on to St Leonard's Street, where he turned to glare at her. His face was redder than ever. Strands of hair had fallen forwards over his eyes. He began talking again, but she turned away. The desk sergeant was grinning.

'Don't,' she warned.

'I hear my Uncle Chris passed away,' he said, ignoring her raised finger. As she made for the stairs, she could hear his voice. 'He said he'd leave me a little something when he went. Any chance, Siobhan? Come on, just a few quid from my old Uncle Chris!'

Her phone was ringing when she reached it. She picked up the receiver, rubbing at her temples with her free hand.

'What?' she snapped.

'Hello?' A woman's voice.

'You'll be the mystery tramp's sister then?' Clarke slipped into her chair.

'It's Sandra here. Sandra Carnegie.'

The name meant nothing to her for a moment.

'We went to the Marina that night,' the voice explained.

Clarke screwed her eyes shut. 'Oh, hell, yes. Sorry, Sandra.'

'I was just phoning to see if . . .'

'It's been a hellish day, that's all,' Clarke was saying.

'. . . there'd been any progress. Only no one's telling me anything.'

Clarke sighed. 'I'm sorry, Sandra. It's not my case any more. Who's your contact at Sex Crimes?'

Sandra Carnegie mumbled something inaudible.

'I didn't catch that.'

A burst of fury: 'I said you're all the same! You look like you're concerned, but you're not doing anything to catch him! I can't go out now without wondering, is he watching me? Is that him on the bus, or crossing the road?' The anger melting to tears. 'And I thought you . . . that night we . . .'

'I'm sorry, Sandra.'

'Stop saying that! Jesus, just stop, will you?'

'Maybe if I talked to the officers at Sex Crimes . . .' But the phone had gone dead. Siobhan put down the receiver, then lifted it off the hook, sat it on the desktop. She had Sandra's number somewhere, but looking at the chaos of papers on her desk, she knew it might take hours to find.

And her headache was getting worse.

And the frauds and lunatics would keep hammering at her.

And what kind of job was it that could make you feel so bad about yourself . . . ?

17

The kind of morning just made for a long drive: sky a pale wash of blue, thin strings of clouds, almost no traffic and Page/Plant on the radio-cassette. A long drive might help clear his head. The bonus ball: he was missing the morning briefing. Linford could have the stage all to himself.

Rebus headed out of town against the tide of the rush hour. Crawling queues on Queensferry Road, the usual tailback at the Barnton roundabout. Snow on the roofs of some cars: the gritting lorries had been out at dawn. He stopped for petrol and downed two more paracetamol with a can of Irn-Bru. Crossing the Forth Bridge, he saw that they'd put up the Millennium Clock on the Rail Bridge, providing a reminder he didn't need. He remembered a trip to Paris with his ex-wife . . . was it twenty years ago? A similar clock was set up outside the Beaubourg, only it had stopped.

And here he was time travelling, back to the haunt of childhood holidays. When he came off the M90, he was surprised to see he still had over twenty miles to go. Was St Andrews really so isolated? A neighbour had usually given the family a lift: Mum and Dad, and Rebus and his brother. Three of them crushed against each other on the back seat, bags squashed by their knees and legs, beach balls and towels resting on their laps. The trip would take all morning. Neighbours would have waved them off, as though an expedition were being undertaken. Into the dark continent of north-east Fife, final destination a caravan site, where their four-berth rental awaited, smelling of mothballs and gas mantles. At night there'd be the toilet block with its skittering insect life, moths and jenny-long-legs casting huge shadows on the whitewashed walls. Then back to the caravan for games of cards and dominoes, their father usually winning except when their mother persuaded him not to cheat.

Two weeks of summer. It was called the Glasgow Fair Fortnight. He was never sure if 'fair' was as in festival or not raining. He never saw a festival in St Andrews and it seemed to rain often, sometimes for a whole week. Plastic macs and long bleak walks. When the sun broke through, it could still be cold; the brothers turning blue as they splashed in the North Sea, waving at ships on the horizon, the ships their father told them were Russian spies. There was an RAF base near by; the Russians were after their secrets.

As he approached the town, the first thing he saw was the golf course, and heading into the centre he noticed that St Andrews seemed not to have changed. Had time really stood still here? Where were the High Street shoe shops and bargain outlets, the fast-food chains? St Andrews could afford to be without them. He recognised the spot where a toy shop had once stood. It now sold ice cream. A tearoom, an antique emporium . . . and students. Students everywhere, looking bright and cheerful in keeping with the day. He checked his directions. It was a small town, six or seven main streets. Even so, he made a couple of mistakes before driving through an ancient stone archway. He stopped by the side of a cemetery. Across the road were gates which led to a Gothic-style building, looking more like a church than a school. But the sign on the wall was clear enough: Haugh Academy.

He wondered if he needed to lock the car, but did so anyway: too old to change his ways.

Teenage girls were heading into the building. They all wore grey blazers and skirts, crisp white blouses with school ties knotted tight at the throat. A woman was standing in the doorway, donning a long black woollen coat.

'Inspector Rebus?' she asked as he approached. He nodded. 'Billie Collins,' she said, a hand shooting out towards him. Her grip was brisk and firm. As a girl, head bowed, made to pass them, she tutted and gripped her by the shoulder.

'Millie Jenkins, have you finished that homework yet?'

'Yes, Miss Collins.'

'And has Miss McCallister seen it?'

'Yes, Miss Collins.'

'Then along you go.'

The shoulder was released, the girl fairly flew through the door.

'Walk, Millie! No running!' She kept her head turned, checking the girl's progress, then brought her attention back to Rebus.

'The day being a fine one, I thought we might walk.'

Rebus nodded his agreement. He wondered, the day apart, whether there might be some other reason she didn't want him in the school . . .

'I remember this place,' he said.

They'd descended the hill and were crossing a bridge over a burn, harbour and pier to the left of them, sea views ahead. Rebus pointed far to the right, then brought his arm down, lest the teacher scold him: *John Rebus, no pointing!*

'We came here on holiday . . . that caravan site up there.'

'Kinkell Braes,' Billie Collins said.

'That's right. There used to be a putting green just there.' Nodding with his head, a safer option. 'You can still see the outline.'

And the beach falling away just yards below them. The promenade was empty, save for a Labrador being walked by its owner. As the man passed them, he smiled, bowed his head. A typically Scots greeting: more evasion than anything else. The dog's hair hung wetly from its belly, where it had enjoyed a trip into the water. A wind was whipping off the sea, icy-smelling and abrasive. He got the feeling his companion would call it bracing.

'You know,' she said, 'I think you're only the second policeman I've had dealings with since I came here.'

'Not much crime, eh?'

'The usual student boisterousness.'

'What was the other time?'

'I'm sorry?'

'The other policeman.'

'Oh, it was last month. The severed hand.'

Rebus nodded, remembered reading about it. Some student joke, bits going missing from the medical lab, turning up around the town.

'Raisin Day, it's called,' Billie Collins informed him. She was tall, bony. Prominent cheekbones and black brittle-looking hair. Seona Grieve was a teacher, too. Roddy Grieve had married two teachers. Her profile showed a jutting forehead, hooded eyes. Her nose fell to a point. Masculine features married to a strong, deep voice. Low-heeled black shoes, the navy-blue skirt falling way past her knees. Blue woollen jumper with decoration provided by a large Celtic brooch.

'Some sort of initiation?' Rebus asked.

'The third-year students throw out challenges to the first years. There's a lot of dressing up, and far too much drinking.'

'Plus body parts.'

She glanced at him. 'That was a first, so far as I'm aware. An anatomy prank. The hand was found on the school wall. Several of my girls had to be treated for shock.'

'Dear me.'

Their walk had slowed. Rebus gestured towards a bench and they sat a decent distance apart. Billie Collins tugged at the hem of her skirt.

'You came here on holidays, did you say?'

'Most years. Played on the beach down there, went to the castle . . . There was a kind of dungeon there.'

'The bottle dungeon.'

'That's it. And a haunted tower . . .'

'St Rule's. It's just over the cathedral wall.'

'Where my car's parked?' She nodded and he laughed. 'Everything seemed a lot further apart when I was a boy.'

'You'd have sworn St Rule's was a distance from your putting green?' She seemed to consider this. 'Who's to say it wasn't?'

He nodded slowly, almost understanding her. She was saying that the past was a different place, that it could not be revisited. The town had tricked him by seeming unchanged. But *he* had changed: that was what mattered.

She took a deep breath, spread her hands out across her lap. 'You want to talk to me about my past, Inspector, and that's a painful subject. Given the choice, it's something I'd avoid. Few happy memories, and those aren't what interest you anyway.'

'I can appreciate—'

'I wonder if you can, I really do. Roddy and I met when we were too young. Second-year undergraduates, right here. We were happy here, maybe that's why I've been able to stay. But when Roddy got his job in the Scottish Office . . .' She reached into a sleeve for her handkerchief. Not that she was about to cry, but it helped her to work at the cotton with her fingers, her eyes fixed on the embroidered edges. Rebus looked out to sea, imagining spy ships – probably fishing boats, transformed by imagination.

'When Peter was born,' she went on, 'it was at the worst time. Roddy was snowed under at work. We were living at his parents' place. It didn't help that his father was ailing. With my post-natal depression . . . well, it was a kind of living hell.' Now she looked up. In front of her lay the beach, and the Labrador bounding across it to fetch a stick. But she was seeing a different picture altogether. 'Roddy seemed to immerse himself in his work; his way of escaping it all, I suppose.'

And now Rebus had his own pictures: working ever longer hours, keeping clear of the flat. No arguments about politics; no cushion fights. Nothing any more but the knowledge of failure. Sammy had to be protected: the unspoken agreement; the last pact of husband and wife. Until Rhona told him he was a stranger to her, and walked away, taking their daughter . . .

He couldn't recall his own parents ever arguing. Money had always been an issue: every week they put a little aside, saving for the boys' holiday. They scrimped, but Johnny and Mike never went without: patched clothes and hand-me-downs, but hot meals, Christmas treats and the annual holiday. Ice cream and deckchairs, bags of chips on the walk back to the caravan. Games of putting, trips to Craigtoun Park. There was a miniature train there, you sat on it and ended up in some woods with little elfin houses.

It had all seemed so easy, so innocent.

'And the drinking got worse,' she was saying, 'so I ran back here, bringing Peter with me.'

'How bad did the drinking get?'

'He did it in secret. Bottles hidden in his study.'

'Seona says he wasn't much of a drinker.'

'She would, wouldn't she?'

'Protecting his good name?'

Billie Collins sighed. 'I'm not sure I really blame Roddy. It was his family, the way they can suffocate you.' She looked at him. 'All his life, I think he dreamed of parliament. And just when it was within his reach . . .'

Rebus shifted on the bench. 'I've heard he worshipped Cammo.'

'Not quite the right word, but I suppose he did want at least some of what Cammo appeared to have.'

'Meaning?'

'Cammo can be charming and ruthless. Sometimes never more ruthless than when he's being charming to your face. Roddy was attracted to that side of his brother: the ability to scheme.'

'He had more than one brother, though.'

'Oh, you mean Alasdair?'

'Did you know him?'

'I liked Alasdair, but I can't say I blame him for leaving.'

'When did he leave?'

'Late seventies. Seventy-nine, I think.'

'Do you know why he left?'

'Not really. He had a business partner, Frankie or Freddy . . . a name like that. Story was, they went off together.'

'Lovers?'

She shrugged. 'I didn't believe it; nor did Alicia, though I don't think she'd have been against a homosexual in the family.'

'What did Alasdair do?'

'All sorts. He owned a restaurant at one time: Mercurio's on Dundas Street. I should think it's changed names a dozen times since. He was hopeless with the staff. He dabbled in property – I think that was Frankie or Freddy's line of work also – and put money into a couple of bars. As I say, Inspector, all sorts.'

'No arts or politics then?'

She snorted. 'Lord, no. Alasdair was far too down-to-earth.' She paused. 'What has Alasdair got to do with Roddy?'

Rebus slid his hands into his pockets. 'I'm trying to get to know Roddy. Alasdair's just another piece of the puzzle.'

'Bit late to get to know him, isn't it?'

'By getting to know him, it's possible I may see who his enemies were.'

'But we don't always know who our enemies are, do we? The wolf in sheep's clothing, et cetera.'

He nodded agreement, stretched out his legs and crossed them at the ankles. But Billie Collins was getting to her feet. 'We can be at Kinkell Braes in five minutes. Might be interesting for you.'

He doubted it, but as they began to climb the steep path to the caravan site, he remembered something else from his childhood: a hole, deep and manmade, sided with concrete. It had sat to one side of the path, and he'd had to shuffle past it, fearful of falling in. Some sort of sluice? He recalled water trickling through it.

'Christ, it's still here!' He stood looking down. The hole had been fenced off from the path; didn't seem half as deep. But this was definitely the same hole. He looked to Billie Collins. 'This thing scared me half to death when I was a kid. Cliffs to one side and this on the other, I could hardly bring myself to come down this path. I had nightmares about this hole.'

'Hard to believe.' She was thoughtful. 'Or maybe not so hard.' She walked on.

He caught her up. 'How did Peter get on with his father?'

'How do fathers and sons usually get on?'

'Did they see much of one another?'

'I didn't dissuade Peter from visiting Roddy.'

'That doesn't exactly answer my question.'

'It's the only answer I can give.'

'How did Peter react when he heard his father was dead?'

She stopped, swung towards him. 'What is it you're trying to say?'

'Funny, I'm wondering what it is you're trying *not* to say.'

She folded her arms. 'Well, that puts us at somewhat of an impasse, wouldn't you agree?'

'I'm just asking if they got on, that's all. Because Peter's last song about his father is called "The Final Reproof", and that doesn't exactly conjure up harmony and good humour.'

They were at the top of the path. Ahead of them stood the rows of caravans, vacant windows awaiting warmer weather, the arrival of bottled gas and released spirits.

'You spent your holidays here?' Billie Collins asked, looking around. 'Poor you.' She was seeing uniformity and the brutal North Sea, cold facts separated from anecdote.

' "The Final Reproof",' she said to herself. 'It's a powerful line, isn't it?' She looked at him. 'I spent years trying to understand the clan, Inspector. Don't vex yourself. Try something feasible.'

'Such as?'

'Conjure up the past and make it work this time.'

'I might have a round table in my living room,' he said. 'That doesn't necessarily mean I'm Merlin.'

He took the coastal road south to Kirkcaldy. Stopped for lunch in Lundin Links. One of the regulars at the Oxford Bar, his father owned the Old Manor Hotel. Rebus had been promising a visit for a while. He ate East Neuk fish soup followed by the catch of the day: local fish, simply cooked, washed down with mineral water, and tried not to dwell on the past – anyone's past. Afterwards, George gave him the tour. From the main bar, the scenery was stunning: a golf links with the sea and horizon beyond. In a sudden shaft of sunlight, Bass Rock looked like a nugget of white gold.

'Do you play?' George asked.

'What?' Rebus still gazing out of the window.

'Golf.'

Rebus shook his head. 'Tried it when I was a kid. Hopeless.' He managed to turn his head away from the view. 'How can you drink in the Ox with this as the alternative?'

'I only drink at night, John. And after dark, you can't see any of this.'

It was a fair point. Darkness could make you forget what was in front of your face. Darkness would swallow the caravan site, the old putting green, and St Rule's Tower. It would swallow crimes and grieving and remorse. If you gave yourself to the darkness, you might start to make out shapes invisible to others, but without being able to define them: the movement behind a curtain, the shadows in an alleyway.

'See how Bass Rock is shining?' George said.

'Yes.'

'It's the sun reflecting off all the bird shit.' He got up. 'Sit there and I'll fetch us some coffee.'

So Rebus sat by the window, the glorious winter's day set out before him – bird shit and all – while his thoughts churned and churned in the dark. What was waiting for him in Edinburgh? Would Lorna want to see him? When George came back with the coffee, he told Rebus there was a bedroom vacant upstairs.

'Only you look like you could use a few hours off.'

'Christ, man, don't tempt me,' Rebus said. He took his coffee black.

18

The hospital corridors were all rubber-soled efficiency. Nurses darted in and out of doorways. Doctors consulted clipboards as they made their rounds. No beds here, just waiting rooms, examination rooms, offices. Derek Linford disliked hospitals. He'd watched his mother die in one. His father was still alive, but they didn't talk much; the occasional phone call. The first time Derek had owned up to voting Tory, his father had disowned him. That was the kind of man he was: headstrong, full of erroneous grievances. His son had sneered at him: 'How can you be working class? You haven't worked in twenty years.' It was true: disability benefit for a mining accident. A limp that would appear at convenient times, but never when he was on his way to meet old pals at the pub. And Derek's mother, slogging her guts out in a factory until the final illness took her.

Derek Linford had succeeded not in spite of his background but because of it, each rung he climbed another jibe at his father, another way of letting his mother know he was all right. The old man – not so old really; fifty-eight – still lived in the council semi. Linford would drive past it occasionally, slowing to a crawl, not really caring if he was seen. A neighbour might wave, half-recognising the face. Would they pass the news on to his father? *I see young Derek was round the other day. He still keeps in touch then . . . ?* He wondered how his father would react: with a grunt most likely, turning back to his sports pages, his quick crossword. When Derek was a teenager, doing well in all his subjects, his father would make show of asking him for the answers to crossword clues. He'd rack his brains, get them wrong . . . It took Derek a while to realise the old man was making them up. Seven letters, umbrella, c something p. Derek would have a go, then his father would sigh and say something like, 'No, you looper, it's capulet.'

No such word in the dictionary.

Derek's mother hadn't died in this hospital. She'd held his hand, her breathing ragged. She couldn't speak, but her eyes told him she wasn't sorry to go. Worn out, like some machine run to death. And like a machine she'd lacked care, lacked maintenance. The old man standing at the foot of the bed, flowers in his arms: carnations picked from a neighbour's garden. And books he'd brought from the library, books she could no longer read.

Was it any wonder he hated hospitals? Yet in his early days on the force he'd been made to spend long hours in them, waiting for victims and aggressors to be treated, waiting to take statements from patients and staff. Blood and dressings, swollen faces, twisted limbs. He'd watched an ear being stitched, had witnessed grey-white bone protruding from a shattered leg. Crash victims; muggings; rapes.

Was it any wonder?

Finally, he found the family room. It was supposed to be a quiet space for families who were 'awaiting news of a loved one', as the receptionist had put it. But as he pushed open the door, he was assailed by the death rattle of vending machines, a cloud of cigarette smoke, and the glare of daytime TV. Two middle-aged women were puffing away. Their eyes fixed on him for a moment, then returned to the chat show.

'Mrs Ure?'

The women looked up again. 'You don't look like a doctor.'

'I'm not,' he told the speaker. 'Are you Mrs Ure?'

'We're both Mrs Ure. Sisters-in-law.'

'Mrs Archie Ure?'

The other woman, who hadn't spoken yet, stood up. 'That's me.' She saw she was holding a cigarette, stubbed it out.

'My name's Detective Inspector Derek Linford. I'd been hoping to have a word with your husband.'

'Get in the queue,' the sister-in-law said.

'I was sorry to hear . . . Is it serious?'

'He's had trouble with his heart before,' Archie Ure's wife said. 'Never stopped him working for what he believed in.'

Linford nodded. He'd done his reading, knew all about Archie Ure. Head of the council's planning executive, a councillor for more than two decades. He was Old Labour, popular with those who knew him, a thorn in the side of some 'reformers'. A year or so back he'd written several bitter articles for the *Scotsman*, had got into trouble with the party as a result. Chastened, he'd applied for an MSP post, the first to do so. He probably hadn't allowed for the possibility of an upstart like Roddy Grieve beating him for the nomination. He'd worked ceaselessly during the '79 campaign. Twenty years later, his reward was a runner-up spot for a constituency, and the promise of a place near the top of Labour's top-up list.

'Are they operating?' Linford asked.

'Christ, listen to him,' the sister-in-law said, glowering at him. 'How the hell would we know if they're operating? We're only the family, last to be told.' She stood up, too. Linford felt himself shrink back. Big women they were, addicted to Scotland's pantry: cigarettes and lard. Training shoes, elasticated waistbands. Matching YSL tops, probably knock-off if not fake.

'I just wanted to know—'

'What did you want to know?' This from the wife, rising to her friend's ire. She folded her arms. 'What d'you want Archie for?'

To ask questions . . . because he's a possible suspect in a murder. No, he couldn't tell her that. So he shook his head instead. 'It can wait.'

'Is it to do with Roddy Grieve?' she asked. He couldn't answer. 'Bloody thought it might be. *He's* the reason Archie's in here. Tell that slut of a widow of his to remember that. And if my Archie . . . if he . . .' She bowed her head, words choking. An arm went around her shoulder.

'Come on now, Isla. It'll be fine.' The sister-in-law looked at Linford. 'Got what you came for?'

He turned away, but then stopped. 'What did she mean? About Roddy Grieve being to blame?'

'With Grieve dead, it should have been Archie standing.'

'Yes?'

'Only now the widow's put her name forward, and knowing those bastards on the selection committee, she'll be the one. Oh aye, shafted again, Isla. As it was, so shall it be. Shafted all the way to the grave.'

'Frankly, they'd be lunatics not to.'

After the hospital, the wine bar on the High Street came as some relief. Linford sipped his chilled Chardonnay and asked Gwen Mollison why that should be. Mollison was tall with long fair hair, probably mid-thirties. She wore steel-rimmed glasses which magnified her long-lashed eyes, and toyed with her mobile phone as it sat on the table between them, just next to a bulging Filofax. She kept looking around, as though expecting to be able to greet a friend or acquaintance. Here, Linford had done his reading, too. Mollison was number three in the council's housing department. She didn't quite have Roddy Grieve's pedigree, or Archie Ure's longevity, which was why she'd lost to them, but great things were expected of her. Good working-class roots; New Labour to her core. She spoke well in public, presented well. Today she was wearing a cream linen trouser suit, maybe Armani. Linford recognised a kindred spirit and had laid his own mobile a foot and a half from hers.

'It's a PR coup,' Mollison explained. She had a glass of Zinfandel in front of her, but had asked for mineral water as an accompaniment, and had concentrated on that so far. Linford appreciated the tactic: you were a drinker, not an abstainer, but somehow you contrived to drink only water.

'I mean,' Mollison went on, 'the sympathy vote's out there. And Seona has friends in the party: she's been every bit as active as Roddy ever was.'

'Do you know her?'

Mollison shook her head – not in answer to the question but to dismiss it as irrelevant. 'I don't think the party would have gone to her; might've looked like bad taste. But when she phoned them, they weren't slow to see the possibilities.' She angled her phone, testing the signal strength. There was jazz music in the background. Only half a dozen other people in the place: mid-afternoon hiatus. Linford had skipped lunch. He'd finished one bowl of rice crackers; they weren't about to bring another.

'Are you disappointed?' he asked.

Mollison shrugged. 'There'll be other chances.' So confident; so controlled. No telling where she'd be in a few years. Linford had already handed over one of his business cards, the good ones, embossed. He'd added his home phone number on the back, smiled at her: 'Just in case.' A little later, she'd caught him stifling a yawn, had asked if she was boring him.

'Just a late night,' he'd explained.

'It's Archie I feel sorry for,' she went on now. 'This might've been his last chance.'

'But he's going on the regional list, isn't he?'

'Well, they have to, or else it looks like they're snubbing him. But you don't understand, that list is weighted against whichever party gets most first-past-the-post seats.'

'I think you've lost me.'

'Even if Archie was top of the list, he probably wouldn't get in.'

Linford mulled that over; decided he still didn't get it. 'You're being very magnanimous,' he said instead.

'Am I?' She smiled at him. 'You don't understand politics. If I'm graceful in defeat, that counts for me next time. You have to learn to lose.' She shrugged again. Padded shoulders, giving some bulk to her thin frame. 'Anyway, shouldn't we be talking about Roddy Grieve?'

Linford smiled. 'You're not a suspect, Ms Mollison.'

'That's good to hear.'

'Not unless *Mrs* Grieve meets with some accident.'

Mollison laughed, a sudden trill which had the other drinkers looking at them. She clamped a hand over her mouth, took it away. 'God, I shouldn't laugh, should I? What if something did happen to her?'

'Such as?'

'I don't know . . . Say she gets hit by a car.'

'Then I'll want to talk to you again.' He opened his notebook, reached for his pen. It was a Mont Blanc; she'd commented on it earlier, looking impressed. 'Maybe I should take down your number,' he said with a smile.

The final candidate on the shortlist, Sara Bone, was a social worker in south Edinburgh. He caught up with her at a daycare centre for the elderly. They sat in the conservatory, surrounded by potted plants wilting from neglect. Linford said as much.

'Quite the opposite,' she informed him. 'They're suffering from over-attention. Everybody thinks they need a drop of water. Too much is as bad as not enough.'

She was a small woman – a shade over five feet – with a mother's face framed by a youthful haircut, short and feathered.

'Horrible,' was what she said when he asked her about Roddy Grieve's death. 'The world just seems to get worse and worse.'

'Could an MSP do anything to help?'

'I'd hope so,' she said.

'But now you're not going to get the chance?'

'Much to the relief of my clients.' She nodded towards the building's interior. 'They were all saying how much they would miss me.'

'It's nice to be wanted,' Linford said, feeling that he was wasting his time with this woman . . .

He called Rebus. The two met at Cramond. The normally leafy suburb had a grey, pinched look to it: winter wasn't welcome here. They stood on the pavement by Linford's BMW. Rebus, having listened to Linford's report, was thoughtful.

'How about you?' Linford asked. 'How was St Andrews?'

'Fine. I took a walk down by the seashore.'

'And?'

'And what?'

'And did you talk to Billie Collins?'

'That's why I was there.'

'And?'

'And she shed about as much light as an asbestos candle.'

Linford stared at him. 'You wouldn't tell me anyway, would you? She could confess, and I'd be the last to know.'

'It's how I work.'

'Keeping things to yourself?' Linford's voice was rising.

'You're awfully tense, Derek. Not been getting any lately?'

Linford's face flushed. 'Sod you.'

'Come on, you can do better than that.'

'I don't need to. You're not worth it.'

'Now that's a comeback.'

Rebus lit a cigarette, smoked in the uncompanionable silence. He could still see St Andrews as it had been to him nearly half a century before. He knew it represented something extraordinary, but couldn't have said what. The words didn't quite exist. It was as though loss and permanence had mingled and become some new entity, the one tasting of the other.

'Should we talk to her?'

Rebus sighed, sucked again on the cigarette. The smoke was blowing back into Linford's face. The wind, Rebus thought, is on my side. 'I suppose so,' he said at last. 'Now we're here.'

'It's good to hear such enthusiasm. I'm sure our respective bosses would be thrilled.'

'Oh, I've always cared what the brass think.' He looked at Linford. 'You don't get it, do you? I'm the best thing that could have happened to you.' Linford hooted. 'Think about it,' Rebus went on. 'Case solved, you take the credit. Case unsolved, you lay the blame on me. Either way, your boss and mine will go for it. You're their blue-eyed boy.' He flicked the cigarette on to the road. 'Every time I refuse to share information with you, you should make a note. Gives you ammo for later. Every time I piss you off or head off on my own tangent, same thing.'

'Why are you telling me this? Does pariah status give you some kind of thrill?'

'I'm not the pariah here, son. Think about it.' Rebus unbuttoned his jacket, affected a Wild West drawl. 'Now let's go visit the widow lady.'

Left Linford lurching in his wake.

The door was opened by Hamish Hall, Roddy Grieve's press officer.

'Oh, hello again,' he said, ushering them inside. It was a neat semi-detached, brick-built and of 1930s vintage. Lots of doors seemed to lead off the entrance hall. Hamish squeezed past them and they followed, through the dining room and into a recent addition, a conservatory, much smarter, Linford noted, than the one out at the daycare centre. An electric fan-heater was humming briskly in one corner. Cane furniture, including a glass-topped table, and seated at the table Seona Grieve and Jo Banks, a mound of paperwork before them. The few pot plants looked expertly tended.

'Oh, hello,' Seona Grieve said.

'Coffee?' Hamish asked. Both detectives nodded, and he headed into the kitchen.

'Sit down if you can find a space,' Seona Grieve said. Jo Banks got up and scooped newspapers and folders from a couple of the chairs. Rebus picked up one folder, examined it: *In Prospect – A Briefing Pack on the Scottish Parliament for Prospective Candidates*. Notes had been scribbled in most of the margins; Roddy Grieve's writing, most probably.

'And to what do we owe this pleasure?' Seona Grieve asked.

'Just a few follow-up questions,' Linford told her, easing his notebook out of his pocket.

'We heard you were stepping into your husband's shoes,' Rebus added.

'My feet are much smaller than Roddy's,' the widow said.

'Maybe so,' Rebus went on, 'but we've not got a motive yet for his death. DI Linford here thinks maybe you've just supplied us with one.'

Linford looked ready to remonstrate, but Jo Banks beat him to it. 'You think Seona would kill Roddy, just to become an MSP? That's ludicrous!'

'Is it?' Rebus scratched his nose. 'I don't know, I tend to agree with DI Linford. It *is* a motive. Had you thought of running before?'

Seona Grieve straightened her back. 'You mean before Roddy was killed?'

'Yes.'

She thought about it, then nodded. 'I suppose I had, yes.'

'What stopped you?'

'I'm not sure.'

'This is totally out of order,' Jo Banks said. Seona Grieve touched her arm.

'It's all right, Jo. Best just put their minds at rest.' She glared at Rebus. 'It was when I realised that one of them, Ure, Mollison or Bone, would take Roddy's place . . . I thought: I could do it, maybe better than any of them, so why not ask?'

'Good for you,' Jo Banks said. 'It's in memory of Roddy. It's what he would have wanted.'

They had the sound of words used previously. Rebus wondered: maybe Jo Banks had come to the widow with the idea. Just maybe . . .

'I can see your point, Inspector,' Seona Grieve informed Rebus. 'But if I'd wanted to, I could have stood. Roddy wouldn't have minded. I didn't need him dead for me to stand.'

'And yet he's dead, and here you are.'

'Here I am,' she agreed.

'With the whole of the party behind her,' Jo Banks cautioned. 'So if you're thinking of making any accusations . . .'

'They just want to find Roddy's killer,' Seona Grieve told her. 'Isn't that right, Inspector?'

Rebus nodded.

'Then we're still on the same side, aren't we?'

Rebus nodded again, but judging from the look on Jo Banks' face, he wasn't so sure she'd agree.

By the time Hamish arrived with a tray bearing coffee pot and cups, Seona Grieve was asking for a progress report and Linford was hauling out the usual flannel about 'pursuing leads' and 'inquiries still to make'. None of which looked to be convincing the two women, despite the effort he was putting in. Seona Grieve met Rebus's eyes and inclined her head a little, telling him she knew what he was thinking. Then she turned to Linford, interrupting him.

'It's an American phrase, I think. Never kid a kidder . . . Or is it never shit a shitter?' She looked to Hamish as if for help, but he merely shrugged and went on handing out the coffees. 'Sounds to me, DI Linford, as though you've made precious little progress.'

'Clutching at straws, more like,' Jo Banks muttered.

'We still have every confidence . . .' Linford began.

'Oh, I can see that. I can see you're positively brimming with the stuff. Because that's what's got you where you are today. I'm a teacher, DI Linford. I've seen plenty of boys like you. They leave school and feel it in their bones that they can do anything they set their minds to. With most of them, it doesn't last long. But you . . .' She wagged a finger, then turned towards Rebus, who was blowing on the scalding coffee. 'DI Rebus, on the other hand . . .'

'What?' The question coming from Linford.

'DI Rebus has no confidence in anything very much any more. An accurate assessment?' Rebus blew on the coffee, said nothing. 'DI Rebus is jaded and cynical about most things. *Weltschmerz*, do you know that word, Inspector?'

'I think I ate some last time I was abroad,' Rebus said.

She smiled at him; a smile without happiness. 'World-weariness.'

'Pessimism,' Hamish agreed.

'You won't be voting, will you, Inspector?' Seona Grieve asked. 'Because you don't see the point.'

'I'm all for job creation schemes,' Rebus said. Jo Banks let out a hiss of air; Hamish snorted good-naturedly. 'But there's something I can't figure out. If I've got a problem, who do I go to – my MSP, my list MSP, or my MP? Maybe my MEP or councillor? That's what I mean about job creation.'

'Then why am I doing this?' Seona Grieve said quietly, her hands in her lap. Jo Banks reached out and touched her hand.

'Because it makes sense,' she said.

When Seona Grieve looked up at Rebus, there were tears in her eyes. Rebus looked away.

'This may not seem like the time,' he said, 'but you told us your husband didn't drink. I believe at one time his drinking may have been a problem.'

'For heaven's sake,' Jo Banks hissed.

Seona Grieve blew her nose, sniffed. 'You've been talking to Billie.'

'Yes,' he acknowledged.

'Trying to blacken a dead man's name,' Jo Banks muttered.

Rebus looked at her. 'See, there's a problem, Ms Banks. We don't know what Roddy Grieve was doing in the hours prior to his death. So far we've a sighting of him in one pub, just the one, drinking on his own. We need to know if that's the kind of man he was: a solitary drinker. Then maybe we can stop wasting our time trying to locate the friends we've been told he would be out drinking with.'

'It's all right, Jo,' Seona Grieve said quietly. Then, to Rebus: 'He said he felt he sometimes had to get out of himself.'

'Where would he have gone?'

She shook her head. 'He never said.'

'The times he stayed out all night . . .?'

'I think maybe he went to hotels, or slept in the car.'

Rebus nodded, and she seemed to read his thoughts. 'Maybe he wasn't alone in doing that, Inspector?'

'Maybe,' he conceded. Some mornings, he'd woken in his car and didn't even know where he was . . . country roads, the middle of nowhere . . . 'Is there anything else we should know?'

She shook her head slowly.

'I'm sorry,' he said. 'I really am. I'm sorry.'

Rebus laid his coffee cup on the table, got up, and left the room.

By the time Linford caught up with him, Rebus was seated in his Saab, window down, smoking. Linford leaned down so their faces were almost touching. Rebus blew some smoke past his ear.

'So what do you think?' Linford asked.

Rebus considered his answer. Late afternoon; light had died from the sky. 'I think we're in the dark,' he said, 'swiping at things we think might be bats.'

'What does that mean?' The young man sounding genuinely annoyed.

'It means we'll never understand one another,' Rebus answered, starting his engine.

Linford stood at the kerbside, watching the Saab move off. He reached into his pocket for his mobile, put in a call to ACC Carswell at Fettes. He had the words formed and waiting in his head: *I think maybe Rebus is going to be a problem after all*. But as he waited to be put through, he had another thought: in saying as much to Carswell, he'd be admitting defeat, showing weakness. Carswell might understand, but that didn't mean he wouldn't see it as such: defeat; weakness. Linford cut the call, switched the phone off. This was his problem. It was up to him to think of a way round it.

19

Dean Coghill was dead. His building firm had been wound up, the company office now a design consultancy, the builders' yard turned into a three-storey block of flats. Hood and Wylie eventually tracked down an address for Coghill's widow.

'All these dead guys . . .' Grant Hood had commented.

Ellen Wylie's reply: 'The male of the species doesn't live as long as the female.'

They couldn't get a phone number for the widow, so went to the last known address.

'Probably died or retired to Benidorm,' Wylie said.

'Is there a difference then?'

Wylie smiled, brought the car in to the kerbside and pulled on the handbrake. Hood opened his door a fraction and peered down.

'No,' he said, 'this is fine. I can walk to the kerb from here.'

Wylie gave his arm a thump. He suspected it would bruise.

Meg Coghill was a short, spry woman in her early seventies. Though it didn't look like she was going out or ready for visitors, she was dressed immaculately and had made up her face. As she led them into the sitting room, there were noises from the kitchen.

'My cleaner,' Mrs Coghill explained. Hood felt like asking if she always dressed up for the cleaner, but thought he probably knew the answer already.

'Do you want a cup of tea or something?'

'No, thank you, Mrs Coghill.' Ellen Wylie sat on the sofa. Hood remained standing, while Mrs Coghill sank into an armchair big enough to accommodate someone three times her size. Hood was looking at some framed photographs on a wall unit.

'Is this Mr Coghill?'

'That's Dean. I still miss him, you know.'

Hood guessed that the chair the widow now sat in had been her husband's. The photos showed a bear of a man, thick arms and neck, back held straight, the chest prominent and gut sucked in. His face told you he'd be fair as long as you didn't muck him around. Cropped silver hair. Jewellery around his neck and on his left wrist, a fat Rolex on the right.

'When did he pass away?' Wylie was asking, her voice trained in dealing with the bereaved.

'Best part of a decade ago.'

'Was it a medical condition?'

'He'd had problems with his heart before. Hospitals, specialists. He couldn't slow down, you see. Had to keep working.'

Wylie nodded slowly. 'It's hard for some people.'

'Were there any partners in the business, Mrs Coghill?' Hood had rested his backside on the arm of the sofa.

'No.' Mrs Coghill paused. 'Dean had hopes for Alexander.'

Hood turned to look again at the photos: family groups, a boy and girl from their pre-teens through to their twenties. 'Your son?' he asked.

'But Alex had other ideas. He's in America, married. He works in a car showroom, only over there they call them automobiles.'

'Mrs Coghill,' Wylie said, 'did your husband know a man called Bryce Callan?'

'Is that why you're here?'

'You know the name then?'

'He was some kind of gangster, wasn't he?'

'He had that reputation, certainly.'

Meg Coghill got up, fussed with some ornaments on the mantelpiece. Little china animals: cats playing with balls of wool; spaniels with floppy ears.

'Is there something you want to tell us, Mrs Coghill?' Hood spoke quietly, his eyes meeting Wylie's.

'It's too late now, isn't it?' There was a tremor in Meg Coghill's voice. She kept her back to her visitors. Wylie wondered if she took any tablets for nerves.

'You tell us, Mrs Coghill,' she suggested.

The widow's hands kept busy with the ornaments as she spoke.

'Bryce Callan was a thug, wasn't he? You paid up, or you got in trouble. Tools would disappear, or the tyres on the van would be slashed. The job you were working on might end up vandalised, only they weren't just vandals, they were Bryce Callan's men.'

'Your husband paid protection to Bryce Callan?'

She turned towards them. 'You didn't know my Dean. He was the only one who stood up to Callan. And I think it killed him. All the extra work and worry . . . Bryce Callan as good as stuck his hand into Dean's chest and squeezed his heart dry.'

'Your husband told you this?'

'Lord, no. He never said a word, liked to keep me separate from anything to do with the business. Family on one hand, work on the other, he'd say. That's why he needed an office, didn't want work coming home with him.'

'He wanted his family kept separate,' Wylie said, 'yet he thought maybe Alex would help in the business?'

'That was in the early days, before Callan.'

'Mrs Coghill, you heard about the body in the fireplace at Queensberry House?'

'Yes.'

'Your husband's firm worked there twenty years ago. Would there be any records, or anyone who worked for your husband that we could talk to?'

'You think it has something to do with Callan?'

'The first thing we need', Hood said, 'is to identify the body.'

'Do you remember your husband working there, Mrs Coghill?' Wylie asked. 'Maybe he mentioned someone disappearing from the job. . . ?'

When Mrs Coghill started shaking her head, Wylie looked to Hood, who smiled. Yes, that would have been too easy. She got the feeling this would be one of those cases where you never got a lucky break.

'His business came here in the end,' Mrs Coghill said. 'Maybe that will help you.'

And when Ellen Wylie asked what she meant, Meg Coghill said it might be easier if she showed them.

'I can't drive,' the widow explained. 'I sold Dean's cars. He had two of them, one for work and one for pleasure.' She smiled at some private memory. They were walking across the mono-blocked drive in front of the house. It was an elongated bungalow on Frogston Road, with views to the snowcapped Pentland Hills to the south.

'He had his men build this double garage,' Mrs Coghill went on. 'They extended the house, too, added a couple of rooms to either side of the original.'

The two CID officers nodded, still unsure why they were headed for the twin garage. There was a door to the side. Mrs Coghill unlocked it and reached in to turn on a light. The large space had been almost completely filled with tea chests, office furniture and tools. There were pickaxes and crowbars, hammers and boxes filled with screws and nails. Industrial drills, a couple of pneumatics, even steel pails splashed with mortar. Mrs Coghill rested her hand on one of the tea chests.

'All the paperwork. There's a filing-cabinet somewhere, too . . .'

'Under that blanket maybe?' Wylie suggested, pointing towards the far corner.

'If you want to know anything about Queensberry House, it'll be here somewhere.'

Wylie and Hood shared a look. Hood puffed out his cheeks.

'Another job for the Time Team,' Ellen Wylie said.

Hood nodded, looked around. 'Any heating in here, Mrs Coghill?'

'I could bring you out an electric fire.'

'Show me where it is,' Hood said, 'I'll fetch it.'

'And something tells me you wouldn't say no to that cup of tea now,' said Mrs Coghill, seeming delighted by the thought of their company.

Siobhan Clarke sat at her desk with 'Supertramp''s effects spread before her. To wit: the contents of his carrier bag, his building society passbook, the briefcase (which its most recent owner hadn't given up without a fight) and the photographs. She also had a pile of crank letters and telephone messages, including three from Gerald Sithing.

It was one of the tabloids who had coined the name Supertramp. They'd also dragged up the sex-on-church-steps story, with an archive photo of Dezzi. Siobhan knew the vultures would be out there, trying to track Dezzi down for an interview, for some juicy morsel. Maybe Dezzi would tell them about the briefcase. It wouldn't be chequebook journalism – she doubted Dezzi had a bank account. Call it cashpoint journalism then. Maybe they'd talk to Rachel Drew, too. She wouldn't say no to a cheque. A few more titbits for the readers and gold-diggers.

And as long as the story ran, the letters and calls would keep coming.

She rose from the desk, pushed at her spine until the vertebrae clicked. It was gone six, and the office was empty. She'd had to move desks – the Grieve murder had taken priority – and was squeezed into a corner of the long, narrow room. No window near by. Mind you, Hood and Wylie had it even worse: no natural light at all in the shoebox they'd been given. The Chief Super had been blunt with her this afternoon: take a few more days, but if there was no ID on Supertramp by then, that was an end of it. The cash went to the Treasury; the suicide, Mackie's whole prehistory, would remain unexplained.

'We've got real work to be getting on with,' her boss had said. He looked like a candidate for a stroke. 'Dossers kill themselves every day.'

'No suspicious circumstances, sir?' she'd dared to ask.

'The money doesn't make for suspicious circumstances, Siobhan. It's a mystery, that's all. Life's full of them.'

'Yes, sir.'

'You've been too close to John Rebus for too long.'

She'd looked up, frowning. 'Meaning?'

'Meaning you're looking for something here that probably doesn't exist.'

'The money exists. He walked into a building society, all of it in cash. Next thing he's living as a down and out.'

'A rich eccentric; money does strange things to some people.'

'He erased his past. It's like he was in hiding.'

'You think the money was stolen? Then why didn't he spend it?'

'That's just one other question, sir.'

A sigh; a scratch of the nose. 'A few more days, Siobhan. All right?'

She'd nodded. 'Yes, sir,' she'd said . . .

'Evening all.'

John Rebus was standing in the doorway.

She glanced at her watch. 'How long have you been there?'

'How long have you been staring at that wall?'

She realised she was halfway down the office, and had been gazing at photos of the Grieve *locus*. 'I was dreaming. What are you doing here?'

'Working, same as you.' He came into the office, leaned against one of the desks with his arms folded.

You've been too close to John Rebus for too long.

'How's the Grieve case?' she asked.

He shrugged. 'Shouldn't your first question be "How's Derek?"'

She half-turned from him, cheeks reddening slightly.

'Sorry,' he said. 'That was bad taste, even for me.'

'We just didn't hit it off,' she told him.

'I'm having the selfsame problem.'

She turned to him. 'Is Derek the problem though, or is it you?'

He feigned a pained look, then winked and walked up the central aisle between the rows of desks. 'Is this your man's stuff?' he asked. She followed him back to her desk. She could smell whisky.

'They're calling him Supertramp.'

'Who are?'

'The media.'

He was smiling. She asked him why.

'Supertramp: I saw them in concert once. Usher Hall, I think it was.'

'Before my time.'

'So what's the story with Mr Supertramp anyway?'

'He had all this money he either couldn't spend or didn't want to. He took on a new identity. My theory is that he was hiding.'

'Maybe.' He was rifling through the scraps on the desk. She folded her arms, gave him a hard look which he failed to notice. He opened the bread bag and shook out the contents: disposable razor, a sliver of soap, toothbrush. 'An organised mind,' he said. 'Makes himself a washbag. Doesn't like being dirty.'

'It's like he was acting the part,' she said.

He caught her tone, looked up. 'What is it?' he asked.

'Nothing.' She couldn't say the words: *my* case, *my* pitch.

Rebus lifted the arrest photograph. 'What did he do?' She told him and he laughed.

'I've tracked him back as far as 1980. That was when "Chris Mackie" was born.'

'You should talk to Hood and Wylie. They're checking MisPers from '78 and '79.'

'Maybe I'll do that.'

'You sound tired. What if I offered to buy you dinner?'

'And we talk shop all through the meal? Yes, that would be a real break from routine.'

'I happen to have a wide range of conversational topics.'

'Name three.'

'Pubs, progressive rock, and . . .'

'And you're struggling.'

'Scottish history: I've been reading up on it lately.'

'How thrilling. Besides, pubs are where you have conversations; they're not what you talk about.'

'*I* talk about them.'

'That's because you're obsessed.'

He was sorting through her messages. 'Who's G. Sithing?'

She rolled her eyes. 'His first name's Gerald. He came to see me this morning: the first of many, no doubt.'

'He's keen to talk to you.'

'Once was enough.'

'Woodwork creaks and out come the freaks, eh?'

'I've a feeling that's a line from a song.'

'Not a song, a *classic*. So who is he?'

'He runs some bunch of nutters called the Knights of Rosslyn.'

'As in Rosslyn Chapel?'

'The same. He says Supertramp was a member.'

'Sounds unlikely.'

'Oh, I think they knew one another. I just can't see Mackie leaving all that money to Mr Sithing.'

'So who are these Knights of Rosslyn?'

'They think there's something beneath the chapel floor. Come the millennium, up it pops and they're in the vanguard.'

'I was out there the other day.'

'I didn't know you were interested.'

'I'm not. But Lorna Grieve lives out that way.' Rebus had turned his attention to the newspaper which had been in Mackie's carrier. 'Was this folded like this?'

The newspaper looked filthy, as though it had been fished out of a bin. It had been opened to an inside page, and folded into quarters.

'I think so,' she said. 'Yes, it was crumpled like that.'

'Not crumpled, Siobhan. Look what story it's open at.'

She looked: a follow-up article on the 'body in the fireplace'. She took the paper from Rebus and unfolded it. 'Could be one of these other stories.'

'Which one: traffic congestion or the doctor who's prescribing Viagra?'

'Don't forget the advert for New Year in County Kerry.' She gnawed her bottom lip, turned to the paper's front page: the lead was Roddy Grieve's murder. 'Are you seeing something I'm not?' Thinking of the Chief Super's words: *you're looking for something here that probably doesn't exist*.

'Seems to me maybe Supertramp had some interest in Skelly. You should ask the people who knew him.'

Rachel Drew at the hostel; Dezzi, heating burgers by hand-dryer; Gerald Sithing. Siobhan managed not to look thrilled by Rebus's suggestion.

'We've a body in Queensberry House,' Rebus said, 'dates back to late '78 or early '79. A year later, Supertramp is born.' He held up a finger on his right hand. 'Supertramp suddenly decides to top himself, having read in the paper about the find in the fireplace.' He held up a finger on his left hand, touched the two together.

'Careful,' Siobhan said, 'that means something rude in several countries.'

'You don't see a connection?' He sounded disappointed.

'Sorry to play Scully to your Mulder, but couldn't it be that you're seeing connections here because nothing's happening in your own case?'

'Which translated means: get your nose out of my business, Rebus?'

'No, it's just that I . . .' She rubbed at her forehead. 'I only know one thing.'

'What's that?'

'I haven't eaten since breakfast.' She looked at him. 'The dinner offer still stand?'

20

They ate at Pataka's on Causewayside. She asked how his daughter was doing. Sammy was down south, some specialist physiotherapy place. Rebus told her there wasn't much news.

'She'll get over it though?'

Meaning the hit and run which had left Sammy in a wheelchair. Rebus nodded; didn't say anything for fear of tempting fate.

'And how's Patience?'

Rebus helped himself to more tarka dal, though he'd eaten way too much as it was. Siobhan repeated the question.

'Nosy little beggar, aren't you?'

She smiled: Dezzi had said the selfsame thing. 'Sorry, I thought maybe at your age it was just that your hearing was going.'

'Oh, I heard you all right.' He lifted a forkful of ginger murgh, but put it down again untouched.

'Me, too,' Siobhan said. 'I always eat too much in Indian restaurants.'

'I always eat too much all the time.'

'So the pair of you have split up then?' Siobhan hid behind her glass of wine.

'We parted amicably.'

'I'm sorry.'

'How did you want us to part?'

'No, I just . . . the two of you seemed . . .' She looked down at her plate. 'Sorry, I'm talking rubbish here. I only met her four or five times, and here I am pontificating.'

'You don't look much like a pontiff.'

'Bless you for that.' She glanced at her watch. 'Not bad: eighteen minutes without shop talk.'

'Is that a new record?' He finished his beer. 'I notice we haven't been talking much about *your* private life. Seen anything of Brian Holmes?'

She shook her head, made show of looking around the restaurant. Three other couples in the place, and one family of four. Ethnic music kept low enough that it didn't intrude but ensured a conversation stayed private.

'I saw him a couple of times after he left the force. Then we lost touch.' She shrugged.

'Last I heard,' Rebus said, 'he was in Australia; thinking of staying there.' He pushed some of the food around his plate. 'You don't think it's worth asking around about Supertramp and Queensberry House?'

Siobhan mimicked the noise of a buzzer as she checked her watch again. 'Twenty minutes dead. You've let the side down, John.'

'Come on.'

She sat back. 'You're probably right. Thing is, the boss has only given me a couple more days.'

'Well, what other leads have you got?'

'None,' she admitted. 'Just a slew of cranks and gold-diggers to put out of the frame.'

Their waiter materialised and asked if they wanted any more drinks. Rebus looked at Siobhan. 'I'm driving,' he told her. 'You go ahead.'

'In that case I'll have another glass of white.'

'And another pint for me,' Rebus said, handing the waiter his empty glass. Then, to Siobhan: 'It's only my second. My vision doesn't start blurring till four or five.'

'But you were drinking earlier; I could smell it.'

'So much for the extra-strong mints,' Rebus muttered.

'How long till it starts affecting your job.'

His eyes smouldered. '*Et tu*, Siobhan?'

'Just wondering,' she said, not about to apologise for the question.

He shrugged. 'I could stop drinking tomorrow.'

'But you won't.'

'No, I won't. And I won't stop smoking either, or swearing, or cheating at crosswords.'

'You cheat at crosswords?'

'Doesn't everybody?' He watched as one of the couples got up to leave. They left the restaurant hand in hand. 'Funny,' he said.

'What?'

'Lorna Grieve's husband, he has an interest in Rosslyn, too.'

Siobhan snorted. 'Speaking of changing the subject . . .'

'They bought a house in the village,' Rebus went on, 'that's how serious he is.'

'So?'

'He might know your Mr Sithing. He could even be a member of the Knights.'

'So?'

'So you're beginning to sound like a record with the needle stuck.' He stared at her until, suitably chastened, she mouthed the word 'sorry' before taking another glug of wine. 'An interest in Rosslyn connects your Supertramp to my murder case. And Mr Supertramp also might have had an interest in Queensberry House.'

'You're turning three cases into one?'

'I'm just saying there are—'

'Connections, I know. The old six degrees of separation.'

'The old what?'

She looked at him. 'Okay, maybe it was after your time. It's to do with how anyone on the planet is connected to anyone else by only six links.' She paused. 'I think that's right anyway.'

As her second glass of wine arrived, she drained the first.

'It's at least got to be worth talking to Sithing.'

She wrinkled her nose. 'I didn't like him.'

'I'll sit in with you, if you like.'

'You *are* trying to hijack my case.' She smiled to let him know she was joking. But inside, she wasn't so sure.

After their meal, Rebus asked if she fancied a nightcap in Swany's, but she shook her head.

'I wouldn't want to lead you into temptation,' she said.

'I'll give you a lift home then.' Rebus, heading for the Saab, gave a valedictory wave towards the pub's bright lights. Sleet was blowing horizontally down Causewayside. They got into the car and he started the engine, making sure the heating was on full.

'Did you notice the weather today?' Siobhan asked.

'What about it?'

'Well, it was cold, raining, windy and sunny – all at the same time. It was like four seasons in one.'

'You can't say you don't get your money's worth in Edinburgh. Here, hang on a sec.' He reached over to open the glove compartment, saw Siobhan stiffen her body, thinking he was going to touch her. He smiled, found the tape he was looking for.

'Little treat for you,' he said, pushing the tape home. She'd flinched; she'd thought he was making a move on her. Jesus. She wasn't much older than Sammy.

'What is it?' she asked. He had the idea she was blushing; hard to tell in the semi-dark interior. He handed her the case. '*Crime of the Century*,' she recited.

'Supertramp's finest moment,' he explained.

'You like all this old music, don't you?'

'And that Blue Nile tape you made for me. I might be a dinosaur in many respects, but I'm open-minded about rock.'

They headed for the New Town. Divided city, Rebus was thinking. Divided between the Old Town to the south and the New Town to the north. And divided again between the east end (Hibs FC) and west (Hearts). A city which seemed defined by its past as much as by its present, and only now, with the parliament coming, looking towards the future.

'*Crime of the Century*,' Siobhan repeated. 'Which one, do you think – your dead MSP or my mystery suicide?'

'Don't forget the body in the fireplace. Where's your flat again?'

'Just off Broughton Street.'

As they drove, they watched the buildings and the pedestrians, were aware of other cars drawing level with them at traffic lights. Cop instinct: always on the lookout. Most people just got on with their lives, but a detective's life was made up of other people's lives. The city seemed quiet enough. Not yet late enough for drunks, and the weather was keeping people off the streets.

'You have to worry about the homeless, this time of year,' Siobhan said.

'You should take a look at the cells on the run-up to Christmas. The woolly suits take in as many as they can.'

She looked at him. 'I didn't know that.'

'You've never worked Christmas.'

'They arrest them?'

Rebus shook his head. 'Ask to be locked up. That way there's a hot meal for them right through to New Year. Then we let them out again.'

She leaned back against the headrest. 'God, Christmas.'

'Do I detect a hint of humbug?'

'My parents always want me to go back home.'

'Tell them you're working.'

'That would be dishonest. What are you doing anyway?'

'For Christmas?' He thought about it. 'If they want me for a shift at St Leonard's, I'll probably clock in. It's a good laugh at the station, Christmas Day.'

She looked at him but didn't say anything, until she told him her street was next left. There were no parking spaces outside her building. Rebus drew up alongside a gleaming black 4×4.

'That's not yours, is it?'

'Hardly.'

He peered up at the flats. 'Nice street though.'

'Do you want some coffee?'

He thought it over, remembering the way she'd flinched: did it say something about what she thought of him, or about Siobhan herself? 'Why not?' he said at last.

'There's a parking space further back.'

So Rebus reversed fifty yards and parked kerbside. Her flat was two floors up. No clutter; everything in its place. It was what he'd have expected, and he was pleased he'd been right. Framed prints on the walls, adverts for art exhibitions. A rack of CDs and a decent hi-fi system. Several shelves of videos: comedies mostly, Steve Martin, Billy Crystal. Books: Kerouac, Kesey, Camus. Lots of law texts. There was a functional-looking green two-seat sofa, plus a couple of unmatching chairs. From the window, he looked on to an identical tenement, curtains closed, windows darkened. He wondered if Siobhan wanted her curtains left open.

She'd gone straight into the kitchen to put the kettle on. His tour of the living room complete, he went to find her. Past two bedrooms, doors open. Clatter of mugs and teaspoons. She was opening the fridge as he came in.

'We should talk about Sithing,' Rebus said. 'How best to tackle him.' Siobhan swore. 'What is it?'

'Out of milk,' she said. 'I thought I'd one of those UHT packets in the cupboard.'

'I'll take it black.'

She turned to the worktop. 'Fine.' Opened a storage jar, peered in. 'Except I'm out of coffee, too.'

Rebus laughed. 'Do much entertaining, do you?'

'Just haven't managed a supermarket run this week.'

'No problem. There's a chippie on Broughton Street. Coffee and milk both, if we're lucky.'

'Let me give you some money.' She was looking for her bag.

'My treat,' he said, heading for the door.

When he was gone, Siobhan rested her head against the cupboard door. She'd hidden the coffee right at the back. She just needed a minute or two. It was so seldom she brought people back here, and John Rebus's first visit. A minute or two to herself, that was all she wanted. In the car, when he'd reached towards her . . . what was he going to think about that? She'd thought he was making a move; not that he ever had before, so why had she flinched? Most of the men she worked with, there was innuendo, the occasional blue joke – looking for her to react. But never John Rebus. She knew he was flawed, had problems, but still he'd brought a certain solidity to her life. He was someone she felt she could trust, come hell or high water.

Something she didn't want to lose.

She turned the kitchen light off, walked into the living room, stood at her window and stared out at the night. Then turned and started doing some tidying.

Rebus buttoned up his jacket, glad to be outdoors. Siobhan hadn't been happy about him being there, that was obvious. He'd felt the same way: uncomfortable. Try to keep your work and social life separate. It was hard in the force: you drank together, telling stories outsiders wouldn't understand. The bond went deeper than desk and office, patrol car and local beat.

But tonight, he felt, was different. And after all, he didn't like visitors either; had never encouraged Siobhan or anyone else to visit his home. Maybe she was more like him than he realised. Maybe that was what made her nervous.

He didn't think he was going to go back. Head home, phone and apologise. He unlocked the car, but didn't start the engine straight away: left the keys hanging from the ignition. Lit a cigarette instead. Maybe he'd fetch the milk and coffee, leave them at her door before heading off. That would be the decent thing. But the main door to the building was locked. He'd have to buzz her to be let in. Leave the stuff on the pavement . . . ?

Just go home.

He heard a sudden noise, watched as someone left the tenement opposite Siobhan's. Sort of jogging their way along the pavement, but then taking the first left into an alley, where they stopped. A jet of urine hitting the wall, steam rising into the frosted air. Rebus sitting in darkness, watching. Someone on their way out, caught short? Maybe a blocked toilet at home . . . ? The man was zipping himself up, jogging back the way he'd come. Rebus caught a glimpse of the face as the man passed beneath a street lamp. Back to the tenement, door opening and closing.

Rebus kept smoking his cigarette, a vertical frown-line appearing in the centre of his brow.

He stubbed the cigarette into his ashtray, removed his keys from the ignition. Opened and closed his door quietly, leaving it unlocked. Crossed the street practically on tiptoe, keeping out of the light. A taxi passed by at speed, Rebus hugging the rails in front of the tenement. Reached the main door. This one, unlike Siobhan's, was unlocked. The block looked less cared-for, the stairwell needing a coat of paint. Faint smell of cat piss. Rebus closed the door slowly, another taxi masking any noise. Made his way to the foot of the stairs and listened. He could hear a television playing somewhere, or maybe it was a radio. He looked at the stone steps, knew he couldn't walk up them without making a noise. His shoes would sound like sandpaper on wood, echoing up four storeys. Shoes off? Not a chance. Besides, he wasn't sure an element of surprise was strictly necessary.

He began to climb.

Reached the first-floor landing. Started up to the second.

Now footsteps could be heard coming down. A man with the collar of his raincoat turned up, face all but obscured. Hands deep in pockets. A grunt, but no eye contact as he made to pass Rebus.

'Hello there, Derek.'

Derek Linford was two steps further on before he seemed to realise. He stopped, turned.

'Thought you lived in Dean Village,' Rebus said.

'I was just visiting a friend.'

'Oh aye? Who's that then?'

'Christie, next floor up.' Said too quickly.

'First name?' Rebus asked, smiling a humourless smile.

'What do you want?' Climbing back up one step, not liking the fact that Rebus was standing so far above him. 'What are you doing here?'

'This Christie, got a blocked toilet or what?'

Now Linford realised. He tried to think of something to say.

'Save it,' Rebus advised him. 'We both know what's going on here. You're a peeping Tom.'

'That's a lie.'

Rebus tutted. 'Try a bit more conviction next time.' He paused. 'Otherwise a conviction's just what you're going to get.'

'And what about you, eh?' Sneering. 'A quickie, was it? I notice it didn't take you long.'

'If you'd been noticing anything, you'd have seen me get into my car.' Rebus shook his head. 'How long's this been going on? Don't you think the neighbours will suss eventually? Strange man shuffling up and down the stairs at all hours . . .?'

Rebus went down a step to meet Linford at eye level.

'Go away now,' he said quietly. 'And don't come back. If you do, first thing I do is tell Siobhan. And after her, your boss at Fettes. They might like pretty boys there, but they don't go big on perverts.'

'It would be your word against mine.'

Rebus shrugged. 'What have I got to lose? You, on the other hand . . .' He let the sentence drift away. 'One more thing: it's my case now. I want you to stay out of the way; do you understand?'

'The brass won't go for it,' Linford scoffed. 'Without me, they'll take it away from you.'

'Will they?'

'Bet on it.' Derek Linford turned and started down the stairs. Rebus watched him leave, then climbed to the next landing. From the window, he could see Siobhan's living room and one of her bedrooms. Her curtains still weren't closed. She was seated on her sofa, chin resting on one hand, staring into space. She looked utterly miserable, and somehow he didn't think coffee was the answer.

He called her from his mobile as he headed home. She didn't sound too upset. Back at his own flat, he collapsed into the chair with a single measure of Bunnahabhain. 'Westering home', it said on the bottle, and they'd quoted from the ballad: *Light in the eye, and it's goodbye to care*. Yes, he'd known malts that could do that. But it was a sham relief. He got up, added a dribble of water to the drink and put some music on the hi-fi: Siobhan's tape of the Blue Nile. There were messages on his answerphone.

Ellen Wylie: progress report, and reminding him he'd said he'd find out about Bryce Callan.

Cammo Grieve: wanting a meeting; suggesting time and place. 'If it's at all convenient, don't bother getting back to me. I'll see you there.'

Bryce Callan was long gone. Rebus checked his watch. He knew someone he could talk to. Wasn't sure it would help, but he'd made the offer to Wylie and Hood. It didn't do to go crapping on the junior officers.

Remembering how he'd just dumped a bucketload on Derek Linford, Rebus grew thoughtful.

Another ten minutes of the Blue Nile – 'Walk Across the Roofops', 'Tinseltown in the Rain' – and he decided it was time to take his own walk. Not across the rooftops, but down to his car. He was heading for the badlands of Gorgie.

Gorgie was the centre of Big Ger Cafferty's operations. Cafferty had been Edinburgh's biggest player until Rebus had put him in Barlinnie Prison. But Cafferty's empire still existed, maybe even flourished, under the control of a man called the Weasel. Rebus knew that the Weasel operated out of a private cab company in Gorgie. The place had been torched a while back, but had risen from the ashes. There was a small front office, with a compound behind. But the Weasel did his business upstairs, in a room few people knew about. It was nearly ten by the time Rebus got there. He parked the car and left it unlocked: this was probably the safest place in the city.

The front office comprised a counter, with chair and telephone behind, and a bench-seat in front. The bench-seat was where you sat if you were waiting for your cab. The man seated behind the counter eyed Rebus as he walked in. He was on the phone, taking details of a morning booking: Tollcross to the airport. Rebus sat on the bench and picked up a copy of the evening paper from the day before. Fake wood panelling surrounded him. The floor was linoleum. The man finished his call.

'Can I help you?' he asked.

He had black hair so badly cut it looked like an ill-fitting wig, and a nose which hadn't so much been broken in the past as thoroughly dismantled. His eyes were narrow, almond-shaped, and his teeth were crooked where they existed at all.

Rebus took a look around. 'Thought the insurance money might have bought better than this.'

'Eh?'

'I mean it's no better than what was here before Tommy Telford torched the place.'

The eyes became little more than slits. 'What do you want?'

'I want to see the Weasel.'

'Who?'

'Look, if he's not upstairs, just say so. But make sure you're not lying, because I get the feeling I'll be able to tell, and I won't be very happy.' He flipped open his warrant card, then stood up and held it towards the security camera in the far corner. A wall-mounted speaker crackled into life.

'Henry, send Mr Rebus up.'

There were two doors at the top of the stairs, but only one was open. It led to a small, neat office. Fax machine and photocopier, one desk with a laptop and surveillance screen on it, and at the second desk the Weasel. He still looked insignificant, but he was the power in this part of Edinburgh until Big Ger came home. Thinning hair greased back from a protruding forehead; a jawline that was all bones; narrow mouth, so that his face seemed to come to a point.

'Take a seat,' the Weasel said.

'I'll stand,' Rebus answered. He made to close the door.

'Leave it open.'

Rebus took his hand off the door handle, thought for a moment – the room was stuffy, mixed body odours – then crossed the narrow landing to the other door. He knocked three times. 'All right in there, lads?' Pushed the door open. Three of the Weasel's men were standing just inside. 'This won't take long,' he told them, closing the door again. Then he closed the Weasel's door, too, so that it was just the two of them.

Now he sat down. Spotted the carrier bags by one wall, whisky bottles peeping out.

'Sorry to spoil the party,' he said.

'What can I do for you, Rebus?' The Weasel's hands were resting on the arms of his chair, as though he might be about to spring to his feet.

'Were you here in the late seventies? I know your boss was. But he was small beer then: playing a few little games, bedding himself in. Were you with him that far back?'

'What do you want to know?'

'I thought I'd just told you. Bryce Callan was running things then. Don't tell me you didn't know Bryce?'

'I know the name.'

'Cafferty was his muscle for a while.' Rebus cocked his head. 'Any of this jarring your memory? See, I thought I could ask you, save a trip to the Bar-L and me wasting your boss's time.'

'Ask me what?' The hands came off the chair arms. He was relaxing, now that he knew Rebus's subject was ancient history rather than current affairs. But Rebus knew that one false move on his part and the Weasel would squeal, bringing his minders charging in and ensuring Rebus a visit to A&E at the very least.

'I want to know about Bryce Callan. Did he have a spot of bother with a builder called Dean Coghill?'

'Dean Coghill?' The Weasel frowned. 'Never heard of him.'

'Sure?'

The Weasel nodded.

'I heard Callan had been giving him grief.'

'This was twenty years ago?' The Weasel waited till Rebus nodded. 'Then what the hell's it got to do with me? Why should I tell you anything?'

'Because you like me?'

The Weasel snorted. But now his face changed. Rebus turned to look at the monitor, but too late; he'd missed whatever the Weasel had seen. Heavy footsteps, taking the stairs with effort. The door swung open. The Weasel was on his feet, moving from behind the desk. And Rebus was on his feet, too.

'Strawman!' The voice booming. Big Ger Cafferty filled the doorway.

He was wearing a blue silk suit, crisp white shirt open a couple of buttons at the neck. 'Just to make my day complete.'

Rebus just stood there, speechless for maybe the second or third time in his life. Cafferty entered the room, so that it suddenly became crowded. He brushed past Rebus, moving with the slow agility of a predator. His skin was as pale and creased as a white rhino's, his hair silver. His bullet-shaped head seemed to disappear into the neck of his shirt as he leaned down, his back to Rebus. When he straightened, he was holding one of the whisky bottles.

'Come on,' he told Rebus, 'you and me are going for a wee ride.' Then he gripped Rebus's arm and steered him to the door.

And Rebus, still numb, did what he was told.

Strawman: Cafferty's nickname for Rebus.

The car was a black 7-Series BMW. Driver in the front, and someone equally large in the passenger seat, which left Rebus and Cafferty in the back.

'Where are we going?'

'Don't panic, Strawman.' Cafferty took a slug of whisky, passed the bottle over, and exhaled noisily. The windows were down a fraction, and cold air slapped at Rebus's ears. 'Bit of a mystery tour, that's all.' Cafferty gazed from his window. 'I've been away a while. I hear the place has changed. Morrison Street and the Western Approach Road,' he told the driver, 'then maybe Holyrood and down to Leith.' He turned to his passenger. 'Regeneration: music to my ears.'

'Don't forget the new museum.'

Cafferty stared at him. 'Why would I be interested in that?' He held out his hand for the bottle. Rebus took a swig and passed it across.

'I get the horrible feeling your being here is legit,' Rebus said at last.

Cafferty just winked.

'How did you swing it?'

'To be honest with you, Strawman, I think the governor didn't like it that I was running the show. I mean, that's what *he's* paid to do, and his own officers were giving Big Ger more respect than they gave him.' He laughed. 'The governor decided I'd be less of a grievance out here.'

Rebus looked at him. 'I don't think so,' he said.

'Well, maybe you're right. I dare say good behaviour and the inoperable cancer swung it for me.' He looked at Rebus. 'You still don't believe me?'

'I want to.'

Cafferty laughed again. 'Knew I could depend on you for sympathy.' He tapped the magazine pouch in front of him. 'The big brown envelope,' he said. 'My X-rays from the hospital.'

Rebus reached across, pulled them out, held them up one at a time to his window.

'The darkish area's the one you're looking for.'

But what he was looking for was Cafferty's name. He found it at the bottom corner of each of the X-rays. Morris Gerald Cafferty. Rebus slid the sheets back into the envelope. It all looked official enough: hospital in Glasgow; radiology department. He handed the envelope to Cafferty.

'I'm sorry,' he said.

Cafferty chuckled quietly, then slapped the front-seat passenger on the shoulder. 'It's not often you'll hear that, Rab: an apology from the Strawman!'

Rab half-turned. Curly black hair with long sideburns.

'Rab got out the week before me,' Cafferty said. 'Best pals inside, we were.' He grabbed Rab's shoulder again. 'One minute you're in the Bar-L, the next you're in a Beamer. Said I'd look after you, didn't I?' Cafferty winked at Rebus. 'Saw me through a few scrapes did Rab.' He rested against the back of his seat, took another gulp of whisky. 'City's certainly changed, Strawman.' His eyes fixed on the passing scene. 'Lots of things have changed.'

'But not you?'

'Prison changes a man, surely you've heard that? In my case, it brought on the big C.' He snorted.

'How long do they say . . . ?'

'Now don't you go getting all maudlin on me. Here.' He passed over the bottle, then pushed the X-rays back into the seat pocket. 'We're going to forget all about these. It's good to be out, and I don't care what got me here. I'm here, and that's that.' He went back to his window-gazing. 'I hear tell there's building work going on all over.'

'See for yourself.'

'I intend to.' He paused. 'You know, it's very nice, just the two of us here, sharing a drink and catching up on old times . . . but what the hell were you doing in my office in the first place?'

'I was asking the Weasel about Bryce Callan.'

'Now there's a name from the crypt.'

'Not quite: he's out in Spain, isn't he?'

'Is he?'

'I must have misheard. I thought you still passed a little percentage on to him.'

'And why would I do that? He's got family, hasn't he? Let them look after him.' Cafferty shifted in his seat, as though made physically uncomfortable by the mere mention of Bryce Callan.

'I don't want to spoil the party,' Rebus said.

'Good.'

'So if you'll tell me what I want to know, we can drop the subject.'

'Christ, man, were you always this irritating?'

'I've been taking lessons while you were away.'

'Your teacher deserves a fucking bonus. Well, if you've a bone stuck in your craw, spit it out.'

'A builder called Dean Coghill.'

Cafferty nodded. 'I knew the man.'

'A body turned up in a fireplace at Queensberry House.'

'The old hospital?'

'They're turning it into part of the parliament.' Rebus was watching Cafferty carefully. His body felt tired, but his mind was fizzing, still getting over the shock. 'This body had been there twenty-odd years. Turns out there was building work going on in '78 and '79.'

'And Coghill's firm was involved?' Cafferty was nodding. 'Fair play, I can see what you're on about. But what's it got to do with Bryce Callan?'

'It's just that I hear Callan and Coghill might have crossed swords.'

'If they had, Coghill would have gone home minus a couple of hands. Why don't you ask Coghill himself?'

'He's dead.' Cafferty looked round. 'Natural causes,' Rebus assured him.

'People come and go, Strawman. But you're always trying to dig up the corpses. One foot in the past and one in the grave.'

'I can promise you one thing, Cafferty.'

'And what's that?'

'When they bury you, I won't come round after with a shovel. Yours is one corpse I'll be happy to leave rotting.'

Rab turned his head slowly, fixing soulless eyes on Rebus.

'Now you've upset him, Strawman.' Cafferty patted his henchman's shoulder. 'And I know I should take offence myself.' His eyes bored into Rebus's. 'Maybe another time, eh?' He leaned forward. 'Pull over!' he barked. The driver brought them to an immediate skidding halt.

Rebus didn't need to be told. He opened his door, found himself on West Port. The car sped off again, acceleration pulling the door shut. Headed for the Grassmarket . . . and Holyrood after that. Cafferty had said he wanted to see Holyrood, centre of the changing city. Rebus rubbed at his eyes. Cafferty, re-entering his life now of all times. He reminded himself that he didn't believe in coincidence. He lit a cigarette and started in the direction of Lauriston Place. He could cut through the Meadows and be home in fifteen minutes.

But his car was back in Gorgie. Hell, it could stay there till tomorrow; best of British to whoever wanted to steal it.

When he reached Arden Street, however, there it was, waiting for him, double parked and with a note asking him to shift it so the note's author could move his own blocked car. Rebus tried the driver's door. It wasn't locked. No keys: they were in his coat pocket.

Cafferty's men had done it.

They'd done it simply to show that they could.

He headed upstairs, poured himself a malt and sat on the edge of his bed. He'd checked his phone: no messages. Lorna hadn't tried to get in touch. He felt relief, tinged with disappointment. He stared at the bedclothes. Bits and pieces kept coming back to him, making no particular order. And now his nemesis was back in town, ready to reclaim its streets as his own. Rebus went back to his door and put the chain on. He was halfway down the hall when he stopped.

'What are you doing, man?'

He walked back, slid the chain off again. Cafferty would have no intention of going quietly. Doubtless there were scores to be settled. Rebus didn't doubt that he was one of them, which was fine by him.

When Cafferty came, Rebus would be waiting . . .

21

'It'd be easier with the door open,' Ellen Wylie said. She meant that they'd have more room to move, and more light to work by.

'We'd freeze,' Grant Hood reminded her. 'I've lost all feeling in my fingers as it is.'

They were inside the garage at the Coghill house. Another grey winter's morning, bringing chill gusts which shook the metal up-and-over door. The ceiling light was dusty and dim, and only one small frosted window gave any natural light. Wylie held a pocket torch between her teeth as she searched. Hood had brought a plug-in lamp with him, the kind mechanics used in their work bays. But its light was too piercing, and it was awkward to manoeuvre. It sat clipped to a shelf, doing its best to throw shadows over most of the interior.

Wylie thought she'd come prepared: not just the torch, but flasks of hot soup and tea. She was wearing two pairs of wool socks under a pair of walking boots. Her chin was tucked into a scarf. The hood of her olive-green duffel coat was covering her head. Her ears were cold. Her knees were cold. The one-bar electric heater worked to a radius of about six inches.

'We'd get done a lot quicker with the door open,' she argued.

'Can't you hear the wind? Everything would be blown halfway to the Pentlands.'

Mrs Coghill had brought them out a pot of coffee and some biscuits. She seemed worried about them. Loo-breaks came as their only relief. Stepping into the centrally heated house, there was a strong temptation to stay put. Grant had commented on the length of Ellen's last trip to the house. She'd snapped back that she didn't know she was being timed.

Then they'd drifted into this argument about the garage door.

'Anything?' he said now, for about the twentieth time.

'You'll be the first to know,' she replied through gritted teeth. It was no good just ignoring his question: he'd go on asking, same as last time.

'This stuff's all way too recent,' he complained, slapping a pile of paperwork down on to one of the tea chests. Unbalanced, the papers cascaded to the floor.

'Well, that's one way to organise a search,' Wylie muttered. If they put the stuff outside when they'd finished with it, they'd have room to work in, and they'd know which files had been checked . . . And it would all blow away.

'I'm no expert,' Wylie said at last, stopping to pour out some tea from the flask, 'but Coghill's business affairs look pretty disorganised, if this lot's anything to go by.'

'He got in trouble over his VAT returns,' Hood commented.

'And all the casual labour he employed.'

'Doesn't make our job any easier.' Hood came over, accepted a cup from her with a nod of thanks. There was a knock, and someone came in.

'Any left in that?' Rebus asked, nodding towards the flask.

'Half a cup,' Wylie said. Rebus looked at the coffee cups, lifted the cleanest one and held it out while she poured.

'How's it going?' he asked.

Hood made a point of closing the door. 'You mean apart from the wind-chill factor?'

'Cold's healthy,' Rebus said. 'Good for you.' He'd moved to within six inches of the heater.

'It's slow going,' Wylie said. 'Coghill's biggest problem was he was a one-man band. Tried to run the whole business himself.'

'Now if only he'd employed a nice personnel manager . . .'

Wylie finished the thought: 'We might have what we're looking for by now.'

'Maybe he chucked stuff out,' Rebus said. 'How far back have you found records for?'

'He didn't throw *anything* out, sir: that's the real problem here. He kept every scrap of paper.' She waved a letter at him. It was on paper headed Coghill Builders. He took it from her. The estimate for construction of a one-car garage at an address in Joppa. The estimate was in pounds, shillings and pence. The date was July 1969.

'We're looking for one year out of thirty,' Wylie said. She drained the tea, screwed the cup back on to the Thermos. 'A needle in a bloody haystack.'

Rebus drained his cup. 'Well, sooner I let you get back to it . . .' He checked his watch.

'If you're at a loose end, sir, we can always use another pair of hands.'

Rebus looked at Wylie. She wasn't smiling. 'Another appointment,' he told her. 'Just thought I'd drop by.'

'Much appreciated, sir,' Hood said, catching something of his partner's tone. They went back to work, watched Rebus leave.

Wylie heard an engine start, and flung down her sheaf of papers. 'Do you believe that? Swans in, finishes off the tea, and swans out again.

And if we'd found anything, he'd have been off back to the station with it to bag the glory.'

Hood was staring at the door. 'Think so?'

She looked at him. 'Don't you?'

He shrugged. 'Not his style,' he said.

'Then why did he come?'

Hood was still looking at the door. 'Because he can't let go.'

'Another way of saying he doesn't trust us.'

Hood was shaking his head. He picked up another box-file. 'Seventy-one,' he said, looking at it. 'Year I was born.'

'I hope you don't mind the choice of meeting place,' Cammo Grieve said, picking his way over lengths of scaffolding which had either just come down or were just going up.

'No problem,' Rebus said.

'Only I wanted the excuse for a poke around here.'

Here being the temporary home of the Scottish Parliament in the General Assembly building at the top of The Mound. The builders were hard at work. Black metal lighting gantreys had already appeared amidst the wooden ceiling beams. Gyproc walls were being cut to shape, their skeletal wooden frames standing ready to receive them. A new floor was being laid on top of the existing one. It rose amphi-theatre-style in a graduated semicircle. The desks and chairs hadn't arrived yet. In the courtyard outside, the statue of John Knox had been boxed in – some said for safekeeping, some so that he could not show his disgust at the renovations to the Church of Scotland's supreme court.

'I hear Glasgow had a building ready and waiting to accommodate the parliament,' Grieve said. He tutted, smiling. 'As if Edinburgh would let them get away with that. All the same . . .' He looked around. 'Shame they couldn't just wait for the permanent site to be ready.'

'We can't wait that long, apparently,' Rebus said.

'Only because Dewar has a bee in his bonnet. Look at the way he banjaxed Calton Hill as a site, all because he worried it was a "Nationalist symbol". Bloody man's an eejit.'

'I'd have preferred Leith myself,' Rebus said.

Grieve looked interested. 'Why's that then?'

'Traffic's bad enough in the city as it is. Besides,' Rebus went on, 'it would have saved the working girls having to tramp all the way to Holyrood to ply their trade.'

Cammo Grieve's laughter seemed to fill the hall. Around them, carpenters were sawing and hammering. Someone had plugged a radio in. Tinny pop tunes, a couple of the workmen whistling along. Someone hit his thumb with a hammer. His blasphemies echoed off the walls.

Cammo Grieve glanced towards Rebus. 'You don't have a very high opinion of my calling, do you, Inspector?'

'Oh, I think politicians have their uses.'

Grieve laughed again. 'Something tells me I better not ask what those uses might be.'

'You're learning, Mr Grieve.'

They walked on. Rebus, remembering snippets of information from his PPLC tours of the site, kept up a commentary for the English-based MP.

'So this will just be the debating hall?' Grieve said.

'That's right. There are six other buildings, most of them council-owned. Corporate services in one, MSPs and their staff in another. I forget the rest.'

'Committee rooms?'

Rebus nodded. 'Other side of George IV Bridge from the MSP offices. There's a tunnel connecting the two.'

'A tunnel?'

'Saves them crossing the road. We wouldn't want accidents.'

Grieve smiled. Rebus, despite himself, was warming to the man.

'There'll be a media centre, too,' Grieve suggested.

Rebus nodded. 'On the Lawnmarket.'

'Bloody media.'

'Are they still camping outside your mother's house?'

'Yes. Every time I visit, I have to field the same questions.' He looked at Rebus; all the humour had leaked from his features, leaving them pale and tired.

'Have you still no idea who killed Roddy?'

'You know what I'll say, sir.'

'Oh yes: inquiries are proceeding . . . all that guff.'

'It might be guff, but it's also true.'

Cammo Grieve plunged his hands deep into the pockets of his black Crombie-style coat. He looked old and somehow unfulfilled; shared something of Hugh Cordover's solemn disenchantment with life. As crisply dressed as he was, his skin and shoulders were slack. The mandatory white hard hat bothered him; he kept trying to make it fit properly. Rebus had the impression of an ill-fitting life.

They had climbed the stairs to the gallery. Grieve dusted off one of the benches and sat down, arranging his coat around him. Below, in the middle of the amphitheatre, two men were studying plans and pointing in different directions with their fingers.

'A portent?' Grieve asked.

The plan was spread out on a workbench, weighted each end with coffee mugs.

'What can you smell?' Rebus asked, settling himself next to the MP.

Grieve sniffed the air. 'Sawdust.'

'One man's sawdust is another's new wood. That's what I smell.'

'Where I see portents, you see a fresh start?' Grieve looked appraisingly at Rebus, who just shrugged. 'Point taken. Sometimes it's too easy to read meanings into things.' Coils of electric cable sat near them. Grieve rested his feet on one, as though on a footstool. He took off the hard hat and laid it beside him, smoothing his hair back into place.

'We can start any time you're ready,' Rebus said.

'Start what?'

'There's something you want to tell me.'

'Is there? What makes you so sure?'

'If you brought me here as a tour guide, I'll be less than chuffed.'

'Well, yes, there was something, only now I'm not so sure it's relevant.' Grieve stared up at the glass windows in the roof. 'I was getting these letters. I mean, MPs get all sorts of cranks writing to them, so I wasn't too bothered. But I did mention them to Roddy. I suppose I was warning him what he was getting into. As an MSP, he'd probably have to put up with the selfsame thing.'

'He hadn't been getting any then?'

'Well, he didn't *say* he had. But there was something . . . When I told him, I got the feeling he already knew about them.'

'What did these letters say?'

'The ones to me? Just that I'd die for being a Tory bastard. There'd be razor blades enclosed, presumably in case I ever felt suicidal.'

'Anonymous, of course?'

'Of course. Various postmarks. Whoever he is, he travels.'

'What did the police say?'

'I didn't tell them.'

'So who knows about them, apart from your brother?'

'My secretary. She opens all my mail.'

'You still have them?'

'No, they were binned the same day. Thing is, I contacted my office, and none have been received since Roddy's death.'

'Respect for the bereaved?'

Cammo Grieve looked sceptical. 'I'd've thought the bastard would want to gloat.'

'I know what you're thinking,' Rebus said. 'You're wondering if the letter writer has something against the whole family, maybe got at Roddy because he or she couldn't get at you.'

'It has to be he surely?'

'Not necessarily.' Rebus was thoughtful. 'If any more letters arrive, let me know. And hang on to them this time.'

'Understood.' He got to his feet. 'I'm off down to London again this afternoon. If you need me, you have the office number.'

'Yes, thanks.' Rebus showed no sign of moving.

'Well, goodbye then, Inspector. And good luck.'

'Goodbye, Mr Grieve. Mind how you go.'

Cammo Grieve stopped for a moment, but then carried on down the stairs. Rebus sat, staring into space, letting the sounds of hammer and saw wash over him.

Back at St Leonard's, he made a couple of phone calls. As he sat at his desk with the receiver at his ear, he sorted through the various messages left for him. Linford communicated only by notes now, and the latest said he was out interviewing people who'd been walking along Holyrood Road on the night of the murder. Hi-Ho Silvers, in his dogged way, had now identified four pubs where Roddy Grieve had been drinking – all alone – on the night he was killed. Two were in the West End, one was in Lawnmarket, and the last was the Holyrood Tavern. There was now a list of Tavern regulars, and these were the men and women Linford was canvassing. Almost certainly a waste of time, but then what was Rebus doing that was so crucial, so wonderful? Following-up hunches.

'Is that Mr Grieve's secretary?' he asked into the mouthpiece. He went on to ask her about the hate mail. From her voice, he had an impression of youth – mid-twenties to early thirties. From what she said, he pictured her as faithful to her boss. But her story didn't sound rehearsed; no reason to think that it was.

Just a hunch.

Next, he spoke to Seona Grieve. He caught her on her mobile. She sounded flustered, and he said as much.

'Not much time to put a campaign together,' she said. 'And my school's not too happy about it. They thought I was taking a bit of time off for bereavement, and now I'm telling them I might not be back ever.'

'If you get elected.'

'Well, yes, there is just that one tiny hurdle.'

She'd mentioned the word bereavement, but she didn't sound recently bereaved. No time to mourn. Maybe it was a good thing, take her mind off the murder. Linford had wondered if Seona Grieve had a motive: kill her husband, step into his shoes, fast-track to parliament. Rebus couldn't see it.

But then right now he couldn't see very much.

'So if this isn't just a social call, Inspector . . . ?'

'Sorry, yes. I was just wondering if your husband ever received any crank letters.'

There was silence for a moment. 'No, not that I'm aware of.'

'Did he tell you that his brother had been receiving them?'

'Really? No, Roddy never mentioned it. Did Cammo tell him?'

'Apparently.'

'Well, it's news to me. Don't you think I might have mentioned it to you before now?'

'You might.'

She was irritated now, sensing that something was being insinuated, but not sure what. 'If there's nothing else, Inspector . . . ?'

'No, just you carry on, Mrs Grieve. Sorry to have bothered you.' He wasn't, of course, and didn't sound it.

She caught the hint. 'Look, I do appreciate what you're doing, all the trouble you're taking.' Suddenly it was a politician's voice, high on effects and low on sincerity. 'And of course you should phone me whenever there's something – anything – that you think I can help with.'

'That's very kind of you, Mrs Grieve.'

She made an effort to ignore the irony in his voice. 'Now, if you've no more questions at this point . . .?'

Rebus didn't say anything; just put the phone down.

In the office next door, he found Siobhan. She had her receiver tucked between chin and shoulder while she wrote something down.

'Thank you,' she said. 'I really do appreciate it. I'll see you then.' She glanced up at Rebus. 'And I'll have a colleague with me, if that's all right.' She listened. 'All right, Mr Sithing. Goodbye.'

The receiver fell from her shoulder, clattered home. Rebus looked at the apparatus.

'That's a good trick,' he said.

'It's taken a while to perfect. Tell me it's lunchtime.'

'And I'm buying.' She got her jacket from the back of the chair and slid her arms into it. 'Sithing?' he asked.

'Later this afternoon, if that suits you.' He nodded. 'He's out at the chapel. I said we'd meet him there.'

'How much grovelling did he make you do?'

She smiled, remembering how she'd practically dragged Sithing out of St Leonard's. 'Plenty,' she said. 'But I've got one hell of a carrot.'

'The four hundred thou?'

She nodded. 'So where are you taking me?'

'Well, there's this delightful little place up in Fife . . .'

She smiled. 'Or the canteen does filled rolls.'

'It's a tough choice, but then life's full of them.'

'Fife's too far a drive anyway. Maybe next time.'

'Next time it is,' Rebus said.

They sat at the table in Mrs Coghill's kitchen. Starter was the flask of soup, but for the main course Mrs Coghill had prepared macaroni cheese. They'd been about to demur politely until she'd lifted it from the oven, bubbling and with a crisp golden crust of breadcrumbs.

'Well, maybe just a smidge.'

Having served them, she left them to it, saying she'd already eaten. 'I don't have much of an appetite these days, but a young pair like you . . .' She'd nodded towards the dish. 'I'll expect that to be empty next time I see it.'

Grant Hood leaned his chair back on two legs and stretched his arms. He'd managed two helpings. There was plenty still left.

Ellen Wylie lifted the serving spoon, gesturing with it towards him.

'God, no,' he said. 'It's all yours.'

'I couldn't,' she said. 'In fact, I'm not sure I can stand up, so it better be you that makes the coffee.'

'Hint taken.' He poured water into the kettle. Outside the window, the sky had darkened. The kitchen lights were on. Leaves and crisp packets were flying past. 'Hellish day,' he commented.

Wylie wasn't listening. She'd opened the black box-file, the one she'd found just before lunch. Business transactions from 6 April 1978 to 5 April 1979. Dean Coghill's tax year. She took out half the documents, slid them across the table. The rest she kept for herself. Hood cleared the plates into the sink, placing the casserole back in the oven. Then he sat down and, waiting for the kettle to boil, picked up the first sheet of paper.

Half an hour later, they got their break. A list of personnel signed up to work at Queensberry House. Eight names. Wylie jotted them into her notebook.

'All we need to do now is track them down and talk to each of them.'

'You make it sound so easy.'

Wylie slid the list towards him. 'Some of them are bound to be still in the building trade.'

Hood read the names. The first seven were typed, the eighth added in pencil. 'Does that say Hutton?' he asked.

'The last one?' Wylie checked her notebook. 'Hutton or Hatton, first name's either Benny or Barry.'

'So we talk to every building firm in Edinburgh? Try out these names on them?'

'It's either that or the phone book.'

The kettle clicked off. Hood went to see if Mrs Coghill wanted a cup. He came back with a copy of Yellow Pages, opened it at the section headed 'Builders'.

'Read the names off to me,' he said. 'We might strike lucky.'

The third name they tried, Hood said, 'Bingo,' his finger stabbing at a display ad. The name on the sheet was John Hicks, and he'd just found J. Hicks. ' "Extensions, Renovations, Conversions",' he recited. 'Got to be worth a call.'

So Wylie got on her mobile, and they celebrated with coffee.

John Hicks' business premises were in Bruntsfield, and the man himself was working on a job in Glengyle Terrace, just off The Links. It was a garden flat, and he was busy converting the large back bedroom into two smaller units.

'Ups the rental income,' he explained. 'Some people don't seem to mind living in a rabbit hutch.'

'Or haven't got the money for anything else.'

'True enough, love.' Hicks was in his late fifties, small and wiry with a tanned dome of a head and thick black eyebrows. His eyes twinkled with humour. 'Way things are in Edinburgh,' he said, 'there won't be a decent building left that hasn't been subdivided.'

'Good for business,' Hood said.

'Oh, I'm not complaining.' He winked at them. 'You said on the phone it was to do with Dean Coghill?'

Somewhere in the flat, a door banged.

'Students,' Hicks explained. 'It pisses them off I'm here at eight, and hammering till four or five.' He picked up his hammer and thumped it a couple of times against a length of two-by-four. Wylie held out the list towards him. He peered at it, took it from her and whistled.

'Now this takes me back,' he said.

'We need to know about the others.'

He looked up. 'Why?'

'Did you read about the body found in Queensberry House?' Hicks nodded. 'It was put there late '78, early '79.'

Hicks nodded again. 'While we were working there. You think one of us . . .?'

'We're just following a line of inquiry, sir. Do you remember the fireplace being open?'

'Oh, yes. We were supposed to be putting in a damp-proof course. Pulled the wall open and there it was.'

'When was it closed up again?'

Hicks shrugged. 'I don't remember. Before we finished the job, but I don't actually recall it happening.'

'Who closed it up?'

'No idea.'

'Can you tell us anything about the other men on this list?'

He looked at it again. 'Well, Bert and Terry, the three of us worked together on a lot of jobs. Eddie and Tam were part-timers, cash in hand. Let's see . . . Harry Connors, he was a bit older, worked with Dean for donkey's. Died a couple of years later. Dod McCarthy moved to Australia.'

'Nobody walked off the job?' Wylie asked.

He shook his head. 'No, we were all present and accounted for at job's end, if that's what you're getting at.' Wylie and Hood shared a look: another theory blown out the water.

Hicks was still studying the list.

'There's one name you haven't mentioned yet,' Hood reminded him.

'Benny Hatton,' Wylie added.

'Barry Hutton,' Hicks corrected her. 'Well, Barry was just with us for a couple of jobs. Bit of a favour to his uncle, or something.'

'But there's something about him?'

'No, not really. It's just, you know . . .'

'What, sir?'

'Well, Barry's made it big, hasn't he? Out of all of us, he's the one who's got to the top.'

Wylie and Hood looked blank.

'You don't know him?' Hicks seemed surprised. 'Hutton Developments.'

Wylie's eyes widened. 'That's *this* Barry Hutton?' She looked to Hood. 'He's a land developer,' she explained.

'One of the biggest,' Hicks added. 'You can never tell with people, eh? When I knew Barry, well, he was nothing really.'

'Mr Hicks,' Hood said, 'you were saying something about his uncle?'

'Well, Barry didn't have much experience in the building game. Seemed to me his uncle must have put a word in with Dean, give the boy a bit of a start.'

'His uncle being . . . ?'

Hicks looked at them again; he couldn't believe they didn't know this either.

'Bryce Callan,' he explained, whacking his hammer against the two-by-four again. 'Barry belongs to Bryce's sister. Friends in high places, eh? No wonder the kid's got where he has.'

22

Rebus took the call on his mobile as Siobhan drove them out to Roslin. When he'd finished, he half-turned in his seat.

'That was Grant Hood. The body in the fireplace; one of the labourers working there at the time was Bryce Callan's nephew. His name's—'

'Barry Hutton,' she interrupted.

'You've heard of him?'

'He's in his thirties, single and a millionaire; of course I've heard of him. I was out with a singles group one night.' She glanced at him. 'Working, I might add. But a couple of the women were talking about eligible bachelors. There was some magazine piece on him. Good-looking, by all accounts.' She looked at Rebus again. 'But he's legit, isn't he? I mean, he runs his own business, nothing to do with his uncle.'

'No.' But Rebus was thoughtful all the same. What was it Cafferty had said about Bryce Callan? *Let his family look after him*, something like that.

As they drove into Roslin and approached Rosslyn Chapel, Siobhan asked why they had different spellings.

'Just another of the chapel's unfathomable mysteries,' Rebus told her. 'Probably with some conspiracy at the bottom of it all.'

'I wanted you to see it,' Gerald Sithing said as he met them in the car park. He was wearing a knee-length blue plastic mac over a tweed jacket and baggy brown cords. The mac made swishing sounds as he moved. He shook Rebus's hand, but kept his distance from Siobhan.

The chapel's exterior didn't look promising, covered as it was by a corrugated structure.

'That's only until the walls dry out,' Sithing explained. 'Then the repairs can be done.'

He led them inside. Prepared as she was, Siobhan Clarke still gave an audible gasp. The interior was as ornate as any cathedral's, its scale serving to heighten the effect of the stonework. The vaulted ceiling boasted carvings of different kinds of flowers. There were intricate pillars and stained-glass windows. The place was chilled, its doors standing open. Green discoloration on the ceiling showed there was a problem with damp.

Rebus stood in the centre aisle and tapped his foot on the stone floor. 'This is where the spaceship is, eh? Under here.'

Sithing wagged a finger, too excited by his surroundings to be annoyed. 'The Ark of the Covenant, the body of Christ . . . yes, I know all the stories. But there are Templar artefacts everywhere you look. Shields and inscriptions . . . some of the carvings. The tomb of William St Clair; he died in Spain in the fourteenth century. He was transporting Robert the Bruce's heart to the Holy Land.'

'Wouldn't it have been easier posting it? Might have got there by now.'

'The Templars', Sithing said patiently, 'were the military wing of the Prieuré de Sion, whose purpose was to find the treasure from the Temple of Solomon.'

'Hence the name?' Siobhan guessed. 'There's a village called Temple near here, isn't there?'

'With a ruined Templar church,' Sithing added quickly. 'Some say that Rosslyn Chapel is a replica of the Temple of Solomon. The Templars came to Scotland to escape persecution in the fourteenth century.'

'When was it built?' Siobhan couldn't take her eyes off the treasures around her.

'Fourteen forty-six, that's when the foundations were laid. It took forty years to complete.'

'Sounds like some builders I know,' Rebus said.

'Can't you feel it?' Sithing was staring at Rebus. 'Right at the core of your cynical heart, can't you feel *something*?'

'It's just indigestion, thanks for asking.' Rebus rubbed his chest. Sithing turned to Siobhan. 'But you can feel it, I know you can.'

'It's an amazing place, I'll grant you that.'

'You could spend a lifetime studying it, and still you wouldn't have learned half its secrets.'

'Who's this ugly mug?' Siobhan pointed to a gargoyle's head.

'That's the Green Man.'

She turned to him. 'Isn't he a pagan symbol?'

'That's the whole point!' Sithing yelped excitedly. He bounded over to her. 'The chapel is almost pantheistic. Not just Christianity, but all belief systems.'

Siobhan nodded.

Rebus shook his head. 'Earth to DC Clarke. Earth to DC Clarke.'

She made a face at him.

'And those carvings on the roof,' Sithing was saying, 'plants from the New World.' He paused for effect. 'Carved a century before Columbus landed in America!'

'Fascinating as this all is, sir,' Rebus said tiredly, 'it isn't why we're here.'

Siobhan pulled her gaze away from the Green Man. 'That's right, Mr Sithing. I told your story to Inspector Rebus, and he felt we should talk.'

'About Chris Mackie?'

'Yes.'

'So you accept I knew him?' He waited till Siobhan nodded. 'And you accept he'd have wanted the Knights to have some sort of financial consideration from his estate?'

'That's not really for us to decide, Mr Sithing,' Rebus said. 'It'll be a case for the lawyers.' He paused. 'But we can always put in a friendly word.' He ignored Siobhan's look, nodded slowly so that Gerald Sithing wouldn't mistake the implication.

'I see,' Sithing said. He sat down on one of the chairs laid out for the congregation. 'What is it you want to know?' he asked quietly. Rebus sat on a chair across the aisle.

'Did Mr Mackie seem at all interested in the Grieve family?'

For a moment, Sithing didn't seem to have understood the question, then he asked, 'How did you know?' And Rebus knew they'd struck gold.

'Is Hugh Cordover a member of your group?'

'Yes,' Sithing said, his eyes widening, as though in the presence of a magus.

'Did Chris Mackie ever come here?'

Sithing shook his head. 'I asked him many times, but he always said no.'

'Didn't that seem strange? I mean, you say he was interested in Rosslyn.'

'I assumed he disliked travelling.'

'So you met him in The Meadows, and talked about . . . ?'

'Lots of things.'

'Among them, the Grieve family?'

Siobhan, aware that she was being excluded, sat herself in the row in front of Sithing, half-facing him.

'Who brought up the Grieves first?' she asked.

Sithing said he wasn't sure.

'My guess is', Rebus said, 'you were telling him about the Knights, and you mentioned Hugh Cordover.'

'Maybe,' Sithing admitted. Then he looked up. 'Actually, that's just how it happened!' His gaze went to Rebus again: magus status confirmed.

Siobhan, even though it was her case, decided to keep quiet. Rebus quite clearly had Gerald Sithing in a kind of trance.

'You mentioned Cordover,' Rebus stated, 'and Mackie wanted to know more?'

'He'd been a fan of the band, said he knew their music. I think he even hummed me one of their songs, not that I was familiar with it. He asked a few questions, I answered where I could.'

'And thereafter, when you met . . . ?'

'He would ask how Hugh and Lorna were.'

'Did he ask about anyone else?'

'They're never out of the news, are they? I told him what stories I had.'

'Ever wonder why he was so interested in the Grieves, Mr Sithing?'

'Please, call me Gerald. Did you know, there's an aura around you, Inspector? I'm sure of it.'

'Probably just my aftershave.' Siobhan snorted, but he ignored her. 'Didn't it seem to you that he was more interested in Hugh Cordover and his family than he was in the Knights of Rosslyn?'

'Oh no, I'm sure that wasn't the case.'

Rebus leaned forward. 'Look into your heart, Gerald,' he intoned.

Sithing did so, swallowed noisily. 'Maybe you're right. Yes, maybe you are. But tell me, why was he so interested in the Grieves?'

Rebus stood up, leaned down over Sithing. 'Now how the hell would I know that?' he said.

Back in the car, Siobhan smiled as she mimicked him. ' "Look into your heart, Gerald." '

'Rum old bugger, wasn't he?' Rebus had the window down, so Siobhan would let him smoke.

'So what have we got?'

'We've got Supertramp feigning an interest in the Knights of Rosslyn while pumping information about the clan. We've got him interested in Hugh Cordover, but unwilling to come down to the chapel. Why? Because he didn't want to meet Cordover.'

'Because Cordover knew him?' Siobhan guessed.

'It's a possibility.'

'So are we any nearer finding out who he was?'

'Maybe. Supertramp's interested in the Grieves *and* in Skelly. Roddy Grieve dies in the grounds of Queensberry House, shortly after Skelly's been uncovered. Around the same time, Supertramp takes the high dive.'

'You want to roll three cases into one?'

Rebus shook his head. 'We don't have enough; the Farmer would never go for it. He'd certainly never let me run it the way it needs to be run.'

'Speaking of which . . .' Siobhan changed up through the gears as she left the village behind. 'Where's your sidekick?'

'You mean Linford?' Rebus shrugged. 'Doing interviews.'

Siobhan looked sceptical. 'Leaving you to your own devices?'

'Derek Linford knows what's good for him,' Rebus said, flicking his cigarette out across the blood-bruised sky.

They had a war meeting: Rebus and Siobhan, Wylie and Hood. The back room at the Oxford Bar. They took the table at the far end, so there'd be no one near enough to overhear the conversation.

'I'm seeing links between the three cases,' Rebus said, having gone through his reasons. 'Tell me now if you think I'm wrong.'

'I'm not saying you're wrong, sir,' Wylie piped up, 'but where's the evidence?'

Rebus nodded. The beer in front of him was almost untouched. In deference to the non-smokers, his cigarette packet was still in its Cellophane. 'Exactly,' he said. 'That's why I want us to ca'canny. At this stage, we need to be aware of each other. That way, when the connections come, we'll see them straight off.'

'What do I tell CI Templer?' Siobhan asked. Gill Templer, Siobhan's boss, the name resonant now.

'You keep her up to snuff. The Chief Super, too, if it comes to that.'

'He's going to close the case on me,' she complained.

'We'll persuade him otherwise,' Rebus promised. 'Now drink up, the next round's on me.'

While Rebus went to the bar, Siobhan stepped outside to call home and check her answering machine messages. There were two of them, both from Derek Linford, making apologies and asking to see her.

'Took you long enough,' she muttered to herself. He'd left his home phone number, but she was only half listening.

Left alone at the table, Wylie and Hood drank in silence for a few moments. Wylie spoke first.

'What do you reckon?'

Hood shook his head. 'The DI has a rep for going out on a limb. Do we want to be out there with him?'

'I don't see it, to be honest with you. What's our case – or Siobhan's, come to that – got to do with this dead MSP?'

'What are you thinking?'

'I think he might be trying to hijack our cases because his own one's hit a wall.'

Hood shook his head. 'I've told you, he's not like that.'

Wylie was thoughtful. 'Mind you, if he's right then we've got a bigger case than we thought.' Her mouth twisted into a smile. 'And if he's wrong, it's not us who'll get carpeted, is it?'

Rebus was coming back with the drinks. Gin, lime and soda for Wylie, half of lager for Hood. He went back to the bar and returned with a whisky for himself, Coke for Siobhan.

'*Slainte*,' he said, as Siobhan settled next to him on the narrow banquette.

'So what's the plan?' Wylie asked.

'You don't need me to tell you,' Rebus said. 'You follow procedure.'

'Talk to Barry Hutton?' Hood guessed.

Rebus nodded. 'You might want to do a little digging, too, just in case there's something about him we should know.'

'And Supertramp?' Siobhan asked.

Rebus turned to her. 'Well, as it happens, I've an idea . . .'

Someone put their head round the corner, as if checking who was in the bar. Rebus recognised the face: Gordon, one of the regulars. He was still in his work suit; probably been out with the office. He saw Rebus, seemed about to retreat but then decided on another course of action. Approached the table, hands in the pockets of his overcoat. Rebus could tell immediately that he'd been celebrating.

'You jammy bastard,' Gordon said. 'You got off with Lorna that night, didn't you?' He was getting ready to make a joke of it: something to embarrass Rebus in front of his friends. 'Sixties supermodel, and you're the best she can do.' He shook his head, missing the look on Rebus's face.

'Thanks, Gordon,' Rebus said. The tone alerted the younger man, who looked at his fellow drinker and slapped his hand to his mouth.

'Sorry I spoke,' he mumbled, heading back towards the bar. Rebus looked at the faces around the table. They all suddenly seemed very interested in their drinks.

'You'll have to excuse Gordon,' he told them. 'Sometimes he gets the wrong end of the stick.'

'I take it he meant Lorna Grieve?' Siobhan said. 'Does she drink in here often?'

Rebus gave her a look; refused to answer.

'She's the sister of the murder victim,' Siobhan went on, her voice low.

'She came in here one night, that's all.' But Rebus knew he was fidgeting too much. He glanced towards Wylie and Hood, remembered that they'd seen her in the Ox that night. He picked up his whisky, found he'd already finished it. 'Gordon doesn't know what he's talking about,' he muttered. Even to his ears, it sounded limp.

23

There were those who said that Edinburgh was an invisible city, hiding its true feelings and intentions, its citizens outwardly respectable, its streets appearing frozen in time. You could visit the place and come away with little sense of having understood what drove it. This was the city of Deacon Brodie, where bridled passions were given free play only at night. The city of John Knox, his rectitude stern and indomitable. You might need half a million pounds to buy one of the better houses, yet outward show was frowned upon; a city of Saabs and Volvos rather than Bentleys and Ferraris. Glaswegians – who considered themselves more passionate, more Celtic – thought Edinburgh staid and conventional to the point of prissiness.

Hidden city. The historical proof: when invading armies advanced, the populace made themselves scarce in the caves and tunnels below the Old Town. Their homes might be ransacked, but the soldiers would leave eventually – it was hard to enjoy victory without the evidence of the vanquished – and the locals would come back into the light to begin the work of rebuilding.

Out of the darkness and into the light.

The Presbyterian ethos swept idolatry from the churches, but left them strangely empty and echoing, filling them with congregations who'd been told that from birth they were doomed. All of this filtering down through the consciousness of the years. The citizens of Edinburgh made good bankers and lawyers perhaps precisely because they held their emotions in check, and were good at keeping secrets. Slowly, the city gained a reputation as a financial centre. At one time, Charlotte Square, where many of the banking and insurance institutions had made their headquarters, was reckoned to be the richest such street in Europe. But now, with the need for purpose-built offices and car-parking facilities, the banks and insurance companies were regrouping in the area around Morrison Street and the Western Approach Road. This was Edinburgh's new financial district, a maze of concrete and glass with the arena-like International Convention Centre at its hub.

Everyone seemed to agree that until the arrival of these new buildings, the area had been a waste ground, an eyesore. But opinion was divided over just how user-unfriendly the maze now was. It was as if humans had been dropped from the planning equation, the buildings existing only to serve themselves. Nobody walked around the financial district for the pleasure of the architecture.

Nobody walked around the financial district at all.

Except, this Monday morning, for Ellen Wylie and Grant Hood. They'd made the mistake of parking too early, in a convenient car park on Morrison Street. Hood's reasoning: the place had to be near by. But the anonymity of the buildings and the fact that walkways were closed due to ongoing construction work meant that they ended up lost somewhere behind the Sheraton on Lothian Road. In the end, Wylie got on her mobile and had a receptionist direct them, until they found themselves entering a twelve-storey building of grey smoked glass and pink facing-stone. The receptionist was smiling as they marched across the floor towards her.

'And here you are,' she said, putting down the phone.

'And here we are,' Wylie agreed, bristling.

Workmen were still busy in Hutton Tower. Electricians in blue overalls fringed with tool belts; painters in white overalls spotted with greys and yellows, whistling as they rested their tins on the floor, awaiting the lift.

'It'll be fine when it's finished,' Hood told the receptionist.

'Top floor,' she said. 'Mr Graham's expecting you.'

They shared their lift with a grey-suited executive, his arms wrestling squid-like with paperwork. He got out three floors below them, almost colliding with a sparky positioning a ladder under some ceiling cables. But when the lift doors opened on the twelfth floor, they entered a calm reception area, with an elegant woman rising from behind her desk to greet them and direct them the eight feet to where two chairs awaited in front of a polished coffee table, arranged with the morning papers.

'Mr Graham will be with you in a moment. Can I get you anything: tea, coffee?'

'It was actually Mr Hutton we were wanting to see,' Wylie said. The woman just kept smiling.

'Mr Graham won't keep you,' she said, turning back to her desk.

'Oh, good,' Hood said, lifting one of the papers. 'My *Financial Times* didn't turn up this morning.'

Wylie looked both ways along the narrow corridor, which disappeared round corners at either end. She got the feeling the corridor made a circuit of this floor of the building, and that the floors below would be identical. There were doors either side, leading either to a window view or to interior space. The windowed offices would be coveted. Working as she presently did from a windowless box in St Leonard's, she herself coveted anything big enough to swing a cat in, even if the cat suffered minor concussion.

A man had rounded the far corner. He was tall, well built, young. His short black hair was professionally styled and gelled, his suit dark grey, immaculately tailored. He wore oval glasses and a gold Rolex. When he introduced himself as John Graham, and put his hand out to shake, Wylie saw a gold cuff link at the end of his pale lemon shirt. It was one of those collarless affairs that wouldn't support a tie. She'd met men before who'd had about them the sheen of success, but for this one she almost needed Ray-Bans.

'We were hoping to speak to Mr Hutton,' Grant Hood said.

'Yes, of course. But you'll appreciate that Barry's an incredibly busy man.' He glanced at his watch. 'He's in a meeting as I speak, and we wondered if perhaps I could be of assistance. Perhaps if we go through what it is you need, I can transmit that to Barry.'

Wylie was about to say that it sounded like a long-winded way of 'assisting', but Graham was already leading them down the corridor, calling back to the receptionist that his calls were to be held for the next fifteen minutes. Wylie shared a look with Hood: *big of him*. Hood's mouth twitched, telling her there was nothing to be gained by riling the emissary – not just yet, at any rate.

'This is the boardroom,' Graham said, leading them into an L-shaped room at one corner of the building. A large rectangular desk filled most of the space. Water glasses, pencils and notepads were laid out, ready for the next meeting. A large marker-board stood unsullied at the head of the table. At the far end, a sofa faced a widescreen TV and video. But what impressed most was the view – east towards the castle, and north towards Princes Street and the New Town, with the Fife coastline just visible beyond.

'Enjoy it while you can,' Graham told them. 'There's a plan to build an even taller tower right next door.'

'A Hutton development?' Wylie guessed.

'Of course,' Graham said. He'd motioned for them to sit, having taken the chair at the top of the table. He brushed non-existent specks from one trouser leg. 'So, if you'd care to give me the background?'

'It's simple enough, sir,' Grant Hood said, pulling his chair in. 'DS Wylie and myself are carrying out a murder inquiry.' Graham raised an eyebrow, and pressed his hands together. 'As part of that inquiry, we need to talk to your boss.'

'Would you care to elaborate?'

Wylie took over. 'Not really, sir. You see, in a case like this, we don't really have the time. We came here out of common courtesy. If Mr Hutton won't see us, then we'll just have to take him down to the station.' She shrugged, her piece said.

Hood glanced at her, then back to Graham. 'What DS Wylie says is correct, sir. We have the powers to question Mr Hutton whether he likes it or not.'

'I can assure you, it's nothing like that.' Graham held both hands up in a pacifying gesture. 'But he does happen to be in a meeting, and these things can take time.'

'We did phone ahead to warn we were coming.'

'And we do appreciate that, DS Wylie. But something came up. This is a multimillion-pound business, and the unexpected does arise from time to time. Decisions sometimes have to be made immediately; millions can depend on it. You do see that, don't you?'

'Yes, sir, but as *you* can see, there's nothing you can help us with,' Wylie said. 'You weren't working for a man called Dean Coghill in 1978, were you? I'd guess that twenty years ago, you were still busy in the school playground, trying to look up girls' skirts and comparing plook collections with your pals. So if Mr Hutton would deign to join us . . .' She nodded towards a camera in the corner of the ceiling. 'We'd be very grateful.'

Hood began to apologise for his partner's behaviour. Graham's cheeks had coloured, and he didn't seem to have an answer. Then a voice broke in, coming from a loudspeaker somewhere.

'Show the officers the way.'

Graham rose to his feet, avoiding their eyes. 'If you'll follow me,' he said.

He took them into the corridor, pointed along it. 'Second door on the left.' Then he turned and walked away; his small victory over them.

'Think this corridor's bugged, too?' Wylie asked in an undertone.

'Who knows?'

'He got a fright, didn't he? Wasn't expecting the one in the skirt to play tough.' Hood watched a grin spread across her face. 'And as for you . . .'

'What about me?'

She looked at him. 'Apologising on my behalf.'

'That's what the "good" cop does.'

They knocked at the door, then opened it unasked. An anteroom, with a secretary already rising from her desk. She opened the inner door, and they entered Barry Hutton's office.

The man himself was standing just inside, legs slightly apart and hands behind his back.

'I thought you were a bit rough on John.' He shook Wylie's hand. 'All the same, I admire your style. If you want something, don't let anyone stand in your way.'

It wasn't that big an office, but the walls dripped modern art, and there was a bar in one corner, which is where Hutton was headed.

'Can I get you something?' He pulled a bottle of Lucozade out of the fridge. They shook their heads. He twisted the cap off the bottle and took a swallow. 'I'm addicted,' he said. 'Used to be, when I was a kid you only ever got the stuff when you were ill. Do you remember that? Come on, let's sit here.'

He led them to a cream leather sofa, and took the matching chair opposite. The portable TV in front of them was actually a monitor. It was still showing a view of the boardroom table.

'Cute, isn't it?' Hutton said. He picked up a remote. 'Look, I can move it around, zoom in on faces . . .'

'And it has sound, too?' Wylie guessed. 'So you know what we want to talk to you about.'

'Something about a murder?' Hutton took another swig of his addiction. 'I heard Dean Coghill was dead, but that was natural causes, wasn't it?'

'Queensberry House,' Grant Hood stated.

'Oh, right: the body behind the wall?'

'In a room renovated by Dean Coghill's team between 1978 and '79.'

'And?'

'And that's when the body got walled up.'

Hutton looked from one officer to the other. 'You're kidding?'

Wylie unfolded the list of people who'd worked in the building. 'Recognise these names, sir?'

Hutton ended up smiling. 'Brings back memories.'

'None of them went missing?'

The smile vanished. 'No.'

'Was anyone else working there, casual labour maybe?'

'Not that I remember. Not unless you're counting me.'

'We did notice your name was a late addition.'

Hutton nodded. He was short, maybe five-eight, skinny but with a developing paunch and jowls. His black suit was shiny new, and all three buttons were done up. His black brogues gleamed, the leather not yet broken in. He had small, dark, deep-set eyes, his brown hair cut above the ears but with prominent sideburns. Wylie knew she wouldn't pick him out in a crowd as being especially rich or influential.

'Work experience. I fancied the building trade. Looks like I made the right decision.' His smile invited them to join in his good fortune. Neither detective did so.

'Do you ever have any dealings with Peter Kirkwall?' Wylie asked.

'He's a builder, I'm a developer. Different game.'

'That doesn't quite answer the question.'

Hutton smiled again. 'I'm wondering why you asked it.'

'Just that we talked to him, too. His office was full of plans, photos of his projects . . .'

'And mine isn't? Maybe Peter's got an ego, and I haven't.'

'You do know him then?'

Hutton acknowledged as much with a shrug. 'I've used his firm occasionally. What's that got to do with your body?'

'Nothing,' Wylie conceded. 'Just curious.' All the same, she sensed she'd touched a nerve.

'So,' Grant Hood said, 'getting back to Queensberry House . . .'

'What can I tell you? I was eighteen, nineteen. They had me mixing concrete, all the unskilled jobs. It's called learning from the floor up.'

'You remember that room, though? The fireplaces?'

Hutton nodded. 'Putting in a DPC, yes. I was there when we opened the wall.'

'Was anyone told about the fireplaces?'

'To be honest, I don't think so.'

'Why not?'

'Well, Dean had the feeling they'd want to send in the historians, which would knock our schedule on the head. Something about not getting paid till the work was complete. If we were hanging around waiting for them to do their stuff, it'd be time lost.'

'So you just covered it up again?'

'Must've done. I came to work one morning, and the wall was back up.'

'Do you know who did it?'

'Dean himself maybe, or Harry Connors. Harry was pretty close to Dean, like a right-hand man.' He nodded. 'I see what you're getting at, though: whoever covered that fireplace over had to know there was a body inside.'

'Any theories?' Wylie asked. Hutton shook his head. 'You must have read about the case in the papers, Mr Hutton. Any reason you didn't come forward?'

'I didn't know the body dated from back then. That fireplace could have been opened and closed again a dozen times since we worked there.'

'Any other reason?'

Hutton looked at her. 'I'm a businessman. Any stories about me get into the press, it can affect how I'm seen in the business community.'

'In other words, not all publicity is good publicity?' Hood asked.

Hutton smiled at him. 'Got it in one.'

'Before we get too cosy,' Wylie interrupted, 'can I just ask how you got your job with Mr Coghill's firm.'

'I applied, same as everyone else.'

'Really?'

Hutton frowned. 'What do you mean?'

'I was just wondering if maybe your uncle put in a word, or maybe more than a word.'

Hutton rolled his eyes. 'I wondered when this would come up. Look, my mum happens to be Bryce Callan's sister, okay? It doesn't make me a criminal.'

'Are you saying your uncle's a criminal?' Wylie asked.

Hutton looked disappointed in her. 'Don't get glib. We all know what the police think of my uncle. All the rumours and insinuations. But nothing's ever been proved, has it? Never even been to a court of law. What does that say, eh? To me, it says you're wrong. It says I've worked to get where I am. Taxes, VAT and the rest: I'm cleaner than anybody. And the idea that you can walk in here and start—'

'I think we get the picture, Mr Hutton,' Hood interrupted. 'Sorry if you thought we were suggesting anything. This is a murder inquiry, which means every angle ends up being considered, no matter how insignificant.'

Hutton stared at Hood, trying to read something into that last word.

'When did you leave Mr Coghill's firm?' Wylie asked.

Hutton had to think about it. 'April, May, something like that.'

'Of '79?' Hutton nodded. 'And you joined . . . ?'

'October, '78.'

'Just the six months then? Not very long.'

'I had a better offer.'

'And what was that, sir?' Hood asked.

'I've got nothing to hide!' Hutton spat.

'We appreciate that, sir,' Wylie said, her voice soothing.

Hutton calmed quickly. 'I went to work for my uncle.'

'For Bryce Callan?' Hutton nodded.

'Doing what?' Hood asked.

Hutton took his time finishing the bottle. 'Some land development thing of his.'

'That was your big break then?' Wylie asked.

'It's how I got started, yes. But as soon as I could, I branched off on my own.'

'Yes, sir, of course.' Hood's tone said: *I've worked to get where I am*; but with a helping hand the size of a football field.

As they were leaving, Wylie asked one more question. 'This must be an exciting time for you?'

'We've got plenty of ideas.'

'Sites around Holyrood?'

'The parliament's just the beginning. Out-of-town shopping, marina developments. It's astonishing how much of Edinburgh is still underdeveloped. And not just Edinburgh. I've got projects in Glasgow, Aberdeen, Dundee . . .'

'And there are enough clients?' Hood asked.

Hutton laughed. 'They're queuing up, pal. All we need is less red tape.'

Wylie nodded. 'Planning permission?'

At mention of the words, Hutton made the sign of the cross with the index fingers of both hands. 'The curse of the developer.'

But he could afford a final laugh as he closed his office door on them.

24

'Fair warning,' Rebus said as they walked up the drive, 'the mother's a bit fragile.'

'Understood,' Siobhan Clarke replied. 'So you'll be your usual charming self?'

'It's Lorna Grieve we want to talk to,' he reminded her. Then he nodded towards the Fiat Punto parked to the right of the front door. 'That's her car.' He'd called High Manor, spoken with Hugh Cordover, listening intently for any new or accusing tone, but all Cordover had done was tell him Lorna was in Edinburgh.

'I'm still not sure this is a good idea,' Siobhan was saying.

'Look,' he said, 'I've told you—'

'John, you can't go getting involved with—'

He grabbed her by the shoulder, turned her so she was facing him. 'I'm not involved!'

'You didn't sleep with her?' Siobhan was trying to keep her voice down.

'What does it matter if I did?'

'We're working a murder case. We're about to question her.'

'I'd never have guessed.'

She stared at him. 'You're hurting my shoulder.'

He released his grip, mumbled an apology.

They rang the doorbell and waited. 'How was your weekend?' Rebus asked. She just glared at him. 'Look,' he said, 'if we go in there spitting at one another, we're not going to get very far.'

She seemed to consider this. 'Hibs won again,' she said at last. 'What did you get up to?'

'I went into the office, can't say I achieved much.'

Alicia Grieve answered the door. She looked older than when Rebus had last seen her, as if she'd lived too long already and was realising the fact. Age could dupe you like that, almost its cruellest trick. You lost a loved one, and time seemed to go into fast forward, so that you withered, sometimes even died. Rebus had seen it before: fit spouses dying in their sleep only days or weeks after burying their partner. It was as if a switch had been flicked, voluntary or involuntary, you could never tell.

'Mrs Grieve,' he said. 'Remember me? DI Rebus?'

'Yes, of course.' Her voice was reedy, parched. 'And who is this?'

'DC Clarke,' Siobhan said by way of introduction. She was smiling the smile of youth when faced with the aged: sympathetic yet not quite understanding. Rebus realised that he was closer to Alicia Grieve's age than Siobhan's. He had to push that thought away.

'Can we bury Roddy? Is that why you've come?' She didn't sound hopeful; she would accept whatever they had to tell her. That was her role now in what was left of the world.

'I'm sorry, Mrs Grieve,' Rebus said. 'Just a little longer.'

She mimicked the final phrase, and added: 'Time is elastic, don't you find?'

'We're actually here to see Mrs Cordover,' Siobhan stressed, trying to draw the woman back from wherever she was headed.

'Lorna,' Rebus added.

'Is she here?' Alicia Grieve asked.

A voice from the interior: 'Of course I'm here, Mother. We were talking not two minutes ago.'

Mrs Grieve stood aside, letting them in. Lorna Grieve stood in the doorway of one of the rooms, a cardboard box in her arms.

'Hello again,' she said to Rebus, ignoring Siobhan.

'Could we have a word, do you think?' Rebus asked. He wasn't quite looking at her. She became amused, nodded towards the room she'd just left.

'I'm trying to tidy some of this crap away.'

Mrs Grieve's fingers touched the back of Rebus's hand. They were as cold as a slab. 'She wants to sell my paintings. She needs the money.'

Rebus looked to Lorna, who was shaking her head.

'I want them cleaned and reframed, that's all.'

'She'll sell them,' Mrs Grieve warned. 'I know that's what she's up to.'

'Mother, for Christ's sake. I don't need money.'

'Your husband needs it. He has debts and only the last vestige of anything resembling a career.'

'Thanks for the vote of confidence,' Lorna muttered.

'Don't you get cheeky with me, my girl!' Mrs Grieve's voice was trembling. Her fingers still held Rebus's hand. They were talons; fleshless claws.

Lorna sighed. 'What do you two want anyway? I hope you're here to arrest me; anything would be better than this.'

'You can always go home!' her mother shrieked.

'And leave you here to wallow in self-pity? Oh no, Mummy dearest, we can't have that.'

'Seona looks after me.'

'Seona's too busy with her political career,' Lorna spat. 'She doesn't need you now. She's found a more useful cause.'

'You're a monster.'

'Which must make you Dr Frankenstein, I presume?'

'Vile body.'

'Yes, on you go. You'll be telling us you knew him next.' She turned to Rebus and Siobhan. 'Evelyn Waugh,' she explained. '*Vile Bodies*.'

'Putrid. You threw yourself at every man you ever met.'

'I still do,' Lorna snarled. She didn't so much as glance at Rebus. 'While you only ever threw yourself at Father, because you knew he'd be useful to you. And once your reputation was established, that was, in a phrase, the end of the affair.'

'How dare you.' Cold rage, the rage of a much younger woman.

Siobhan was touching Rebus's sleeve, edging back towards the door. Lorna saw what she was doing. 'Oh look, we're frightening off the filth! Isn't that precious, Mother? Did you realise we possessed such power?' She started to laugh. A few moments later, Alicia Grieve joined her.

Rebus's thought: it's a fucking mad house. Then he realised that this was normal behaviour for mother and daughter: fighting and spitting the prelude to catharsis. They'd been in the public's eye so long, they'd become actors in their own melodrama; played out their quarrels as though each one had measure and meaning.

Scenes from family life.

Bloody hell.

Lorna was wiping an imaginary tear from her eye, still cradling the paintings. 'I'll put these back,' she said.

'No,' said her mother, 'leave them in the hall with the others.' She pointed to where a dozen or so framed paintings sat against the wall. 'You're right, we'll have them looked at: cleaned up, maybe a few new frames.'

'We should get an insurance quote while we're at it.' Her mother was about to interrupt, so Lorna went on quickly. 'That's not so I can sell them. But if they were stolen . . .'

Alicia seemed about to argue, but sucked in a deep breath and just nodded. The paintings were laid with the others. Lorna stood up again, brushing her hands free of dust.

'Must be forty years since you painted some of these.'

'You're probably right. Maybe even longer.' Alicia nodded. 'But they'll survive long after I'm gone. It's just that they won't mean the same.'

'How's that?' Siobhan felt compelled to ask.

Alicia looked at her. 'They mean things to me which they never can to anyone else.'

'That's why they're here,' Lorna explained, 'rather than on some collector's walls.'

Alicia Grieve nodded. 'Meaning is precious. The personal is all we have; without it, we're animals, pure and simple.' She suddenly perked up, her hand dropping from Rebus's. 'Tea,' she barked, clapping her hands together. 'We must all have some tea.'

Rebus was wondering if there was any chance of a tot of whisky on the side.

They sat in the sitting room, making small talk while Lorna coped in the kitchen. She brought in a tray, started pouring.

'I'm bound to have forgotten something,' she said. 'Tea's not my strong point.' She looked at Rebus as she spoke, but he was focused on the fireplace. 'Something stronger, Inspector? I seem to remember you enjoy a malt.'

'No, I'm fine, thank you,' he felt compelled to say.

'Sugar,' Lorna said, studying the tray. 'Told you.' She made for the door, but Rebus and Siobhan announced that neither of them took it, so she returned to her seat. There were crumbly digestives on a plate. They turned down the offer, but Alicia took one, dunking it into her tea, where it broke into pieces. They ignored her as she fished the morsels out, popping them into her mouth.

'So,' Lorna said at last, 'what brings you to Happy Acres?'

'It might be something or nothing,' Rebus said. 'DC Clarke has been investigating the suicide of a homeless person. It looks like he was very interested in your family.'

'Oh?'

'And the fact of his suicide, so soon after the murder . . .'

Lorna sat forward in her chair. She was looking at Siobhan. 'This wouldn't be the millionaire tramp by any chance?'

Siobhan nodded. 'Though he wasn't quite a millionaire.'

Lorna turned to her mother. 'You remember me telling you?'

Her mother nodded, but appeared not to have been listening. Lorna turned back to Siobhan. 'But what's it got to do with us?'

'Maybe nothing,' Siobhan conceded. 'The deceased was calling himself Chris Mackie. Does that name mean anything?'

Lorna thought hard, then shook her head.

'We have some photos,' Siobhan said, handing them over. She glanced at Rebus.

Lorna studied the photos. 'Grim-looking creature, isn't he?'

Siobhan was still looking at Rebus, willing him to ask the question.

'Mrs Cordover,' he said, 'there's no easy way to ask this.'

She looked at him. 'Ask what?'

Rebus took a deep breath. 'He's a lot older . . . been living rough.' He dived in. 'It couldn't be Alasdair, could it?'

'*Alasdair?*' Lorna took another look at the top photo. 'What the hell are you talking about?' She looked towards her mother, who seemed to have turned whiter than ever. 'Alasdair's got fair hair, nothing like this.' Alicia's hand was reaching out, but Lorna passed the photos back to Siobhan. 'What are you trying to do? This man's nothing like Alasdair, nothing like him at all.'

'People can change in twenty years,' Rebus said quietly.

'People can change overnight,' she retorted coldly, 'but that's not my brother. What made you think it was?'

Rebus shrugged. 'A hunch.'

'I'll show you Alasdair,' Alicia Grieve said, rising to her feet. She put her cup down on the table. 'Come with me, and I'll show you him.'

They followed her into the kitchen. The glass-fronted china cabinet was full, and piles of clean crockery covered the worktops, awaiting space that would never be there. The sink was full of dirty dishes. An ironing board was piled with clothes. A radio was playing softly: some classical station.

'Bruckner,' Alicia said, unlocking the back door. 'They always seem to be playing Bruckner.'

'Her studio,' Lorna explained as they followed Alicia into the garden. It was overgrown now, untended, but the notion of the garden it had once been was still there. A free-standing swing, its pipework corroded. A stone urn, waiting to be put upright on its plinth. The leaves on the lawn had turned to mulch, making progress difficult. And at the far end of the garden, a stone outhouse.

'The servants' quarters?' Rebus guessed.

'I suppose so,' Lorna said. 'It was our secret place when we were kids. Then Mother turned it into a studio, and we were locked out.' She was watching her mother lead the way, the old woman's back stooped. 'Time was, Father and she painted in the same room – his studio's in the attic.' She pointed back to two skylights in the roof. 'Then Mother decided she needed her own space, her own light. She was locking him out of her life, too.' She looked at Rebus. 'It wasn't easy, growing up a Grieve.'

He almost thought she'd said *growing up aggrieved.*

Alicia took a key from her cardigan pocket, unlocked the door to her studio. It was just one room inside, the stone walls whitewashed and spattered with paint. Paint on the floor, too. Three easels of different sizes. Threads of cobweb hanging from the ceiling. And against one wall, a series of portraits, head and neck only, the canvasses of varying size. The same man, caught at different stages of his life.

'Good God,' Lorna gasped, 'it's Alasdair.' She started sorting through the portraits; there were over a dozen.

'I imagine him growing, ageing,' Alicia said quietly. 'I see him in my mind and then I paint him.'

Fair-haired, sad-eyed. A troubled man, despite the smiles the artist had given him. And nothing at all like Chris Mackie.

'You never said anything.' Lorna had picked up one of the paintings to study it more closely. Her finger brushed the shadowing of cheekbones.

'You'd have been jealous,' her mother said. 'No good denying it.' She turned to Rebus. 'Alasdair was my favourite, you see. And when he ran away . . .' She looked at her own work. 'Maybe this was my way of explaining it.' When she turned back, she saw that Siobhan was still holding the photographs. 'May I?' She took them, held them up to her face.

Recognition lit up her eyes. 'Where is he?'

'You know him?' Siobhan asked.

'I need to know where he is.'

Lorna had put down the portrait. 'He killed himself, Mother. The tramp who left all the money.'

'Who is he, Mrs Grieve?' Rebus asked.

Alicia's hands were shaking as she went through the photos again. 'I've been so wanting to talk to him.' There were tears in her eyes. She wiped them with her wrist. Rebus had taken a step forward.

'Who is it, Alicia? Who's the man in the photographs?'

She looked at him. 'His name's Frederick Hastings.'

'Freddy?' Lorna came over to look. She pried the police photo from her mother's fingers.

'Well?' Rebus asked.

'I suppose it could be. It's twenty years since I last laid eyes on him.'

'But who was he?' Siobhan asked.

Suddenly Rebus remembered. 'Alasdair's business partner?'

Lorna was nodding.

Rebus turned to Siobhan. She looked puzzled.

'You say he's dead?' Alicia asked. Rebus nodded. 'He'd have known where Alasdair is. Those two were inseparable. Maybe there's an address amongst his belongings.'

Lorna was looking at the other photos, the ones of 'Chris Mackie' at the hostel. 'Freddy Hastings a tramp.' Her laughter was a sudden explosion in the room.

'I don't think there was any address,' Siobhan was telling Alicia Grieve. 'I've been through his effects several times.'

'Maybe we'd best go back to the house,' Rebus announced. Suddenly, he had a lot more questions to ask.

Lorna made another pot of tea, but this time fixed herself a drink, half-and-half whisky and spring water. She'd made the offer, but Rebus had turned it down. Her eyes were on him as she took the first sip.

Siobhan had her notebook out, pen ready.

Lorna exhaled; the fumes wafted all the way to where Rebus was sitting. 'We thought they'd gone off together,' she began.

'Utter nonsense,' her mother interrupted.

'Okay, *you* didn't think they were gay.'

'They disappeared at the same time?' Siobhan asked.

'Looked like. After Alasdair had been gone a few days, we tried contacting Freddy. No sign of him.'

'Was he reported as a missing person?'

Lorna shrugged. 'Not by me.'

'Family?'

'I don't think he had any.' She looked to her mother for confirmation.

'He was an only child,' Alicia said. 'Parents died within a year of one another.'

'Left him some money, most of which I thought he'd lost.'

'They *both* lost money,' Alicia added. 'That's why Alasdair ran off, Inspector. Bad debts. He was too proud to ask for help.'

'But not too proud to clear off,' Lorna couldn't help saying. Her mother fixed her with a glare.

'When was this?' Rebus asked.

'Some time in '79.' Lorna looked to her mother for confirmation.

'Halfway through March,' the old woman said.

Rebus and Siobhan locked eyes. March '79: Skelly.

'What sort of business did they have?' Siobhan asked, keeping her voice under control.

'Their last foray was into property.' Lorna shrugged again. 'I don't know much more than that. Probably bought places they couldn't sell on.'

'Land development?' Rebus guessed. 'Would that be it?'

'I don't know.'

Rebus turned to Alicia, who shook her head. 'Alasdair was very private in some ways. He wanted us to think he was so capable . . . so self-sufficient.'

Lorna got up to refill her glass. 'My mother's way of saying he was hopeless at most things.'

'Unlike you, I suppose,' Alicia snapped.

'If they ran off because they were in debt,' Siobhan said, 'how come Mr Hastings had nearly half a million pounds in a briefcase a year or so on?'

'You're the detectives, you tell us.' Lorna sat down again.

Rebus was thoughtful. 'All this stuff about the two men's business failings, is there anything to back it up, or is it another clan myth?'

'What are you suggesting?'

'It's just that we could do with a few solid facts in this case.'

'What case?' The alcohol was kicking in; Lorna's voice had turned combative, her cheeks tinged with red. 'You're supposed to be investigating Roddy's murder, not Freddy's suicide.'

'The Inspector thinks they may be linked,' Alicia said, nodding at her own deduction.

'What makes you say that, Mrs Grieve?' Rebus asked.

'Freddy was interested in us, you say. Do you think he could have killed Roddy?'

'Why would he do that?'

'I don't know. Something to do with the money, perhaps.'

'Did Roddy and Freddy know one another?'

'They met a few times, when Alasdair brought Freddy to the house. Maybe other times, too.'

'So if Roddy met Freddy again after twenty years, you think he'd have recognised him?'

'Probably.'

'I didn't,' Lorna said, 'when you showed me the photos.'

Rebus looked at her. 'No, you didn't.' He was thinking: *or did you*? Why had she handed the photos back to Siobhan rather than passing them to her mother?

'Did Mr Hastings have an office?'

Alicia nodded. 'In Canongate, not far from Alasdair's flat.'

'Can you remember the address?'

She recited it, seeming pleased that she still had the ability.

'And his home?' Siobhan was writing in her notebook.

'A flat in the New Town,' Lorna said. But again it was her mother who gave the address.

The hotel's downstairs dining room was quiet at lunchtime. Diners either preferred the bistro-style restaurant on the ground floor or else didn't know of this second restaurant's existence. The décor was minimalist, oriental, and the elegantly set tables had plenty of space between them. A discreet place for a conversation. Cafferty got to his feet, shook Barry Hutton's hand.

'Uncle Ger, sorry I'm late.'

Cafferty shrugged, while a flunky helped Hutton into his chair. 'Long time since anyone called me that,' he said with a smile. 'It's not like it's true.'

'It's what I always called you.'

Cafferty nodded, examining the well-dressed young man before him. 'But look at you now, Barry. Doing so well for yourself.'

It was Hutton's turn to shrug. Menus were being handed out.

'Any drinks, gentlemen?' the waiter asked.

'Calls for champagne, I think,' Cafferty said. He winked at Hutton. 'And this is on me, so no arguing.'

'I wasn't about to. It's just that I'll stick to water, if that's all right.'

The smile stuck to Cafferty's face. 'Whatever you want, Barry.'

Hutton turned to the waiter. 'Vittel, if you have it. Evian otherwise.'

The waiter bowed his head, turned to Cafferty. 'And will you still be requiring the champagne, sir?'

'Didn't hear me say otherwise, did you?'

The waiter made his little bow again and headed off.

'Vittel, Evian . . .' Cafferty chuckled and shook his head. 'Christ, if Bryce could see you now.' Hutton was busy adjusting his shirt cuffs. 'Rough morning, was it?'

Hutton looked up, and Cafferty knew something had happened. But the younger man was shaking his head. 'I don't drink at lunchtime, that's all.'

'Then you'll have to let me buy you dinner.'

Hutton looked around the restaurant. There were only two other diners in the place, seated at a far corner and deep in what looked like a business conversation. Hutton studied the faces, but didn't recognise them. He turned back to his host.

'You're staying here?'

Cafferty nodded.

'Did you sell the house?'

Cafferty nodded again.

'And made a fair bit on it, I'd guess.' Hutton looked at him.

'Money's not everything though, is it, Barry? That's one thing I've learned.'

'You mean good health? Happiness?'

Cafferty pressed his palms together. 'You're young still. Wait a few years and maybe you'll see what I mean.'

Hutton nodded, not really sure what the older man was getting at. 'You got out pretty early,' he commented.

'Time off for good behaviour.' Cafferty sat back as one waiter produced a basket of bread rolls, and another asked if he wanted the champagne chilled or served slightly cool.

'Chilled,' Cafferty said, looking at his guest. 'So, Barry, business is good, eh? That's what I hear.'

'I'm not complaining.'

'And how's your uncle?'

'Fine, as far as I know.'

'You ever see him?'

'He won't set foot back here.'

'I know that. I thought maybe you headed out there. Holidays and stuff.'

'I can't remember my last holiday.'

'All work and no play, Barry,' Cafferty counselled.

Hutton looked at him. 'It's not all work.'

'Glad to hear it.'

Their food order was taken, and the drinks arrived. They toasted one another, Hutton refusing the offer of 'just one wee glass'. He took his water neat: no ice, no lemon.

'What about you?' he asked at last. 'Not many people come straight from the Bar-L to a place like this.'

'Let's just say I'm comfortable,' Cafferty said with a wink.

'Of course, you kept a lot of your business interests going while you were away?'

Cafferty heard the quotation marks around business interests. He nodded slowly. 'Lot of people would be disappointed if I hadn't.'

'I don't doubt it.' Hutton tore open one of the tiny, glazed rolls.

'Which brings me to our little lunch here,' Cafferty went on.

'A business lunch then?' Hutton asked. When Cafferty nodded, he felt a little more comfortable. It wasn't just a meal any more; he wasn't wasting his time.

25

Jerry's face recoiled from the slap. He was getting used to slaps recently. But this wasn't Jayne.

This was Nic.

He felt his cheek beginning to sting, knew the imprint of a hand would be forming there, pinkish red against his pale skin. Nic's hand would be stinging, too: small consolation.

They were in Nic's Cosworth. Jerry had just got in. It had been Nic who'd called – Monday night – and Jerry had jumped at the chance of escape. Jayne was in front of the telly, arms folded, eyes drooping. They'd eaten their tea watching the news: sausage, beans and egg. No chips: the freezer was bare, and neither of them felt like taking the trip to the chip shop. That was when the argument had started.

Ya useless lump of . . .

It's you needs to get off your fat arse, no' me . . .

Then the phone call. The phone was Jayne's side of the couch, but she ignored it.

'Two guesses who that'll be,' was all she said. He was hoping she'd be wrong, that it would be her mum. Then he could say, 'That's you quietened,' as he handed over the receiver.

Because if it was Nic . . . Nic on a Monday night, he never usually went out Mondays . . . that could probably mean only one thing.

And now here they were together in the car, and Nic was having a go at him.

'See that stunt you pulled, you ever do something as stupid as that again . . .'

'What stunt?'

'Phoning me at work, ya donkey!'

Jerry thought he was in for another slap, but Nic punched him in the side instead. Not too hard: he was calming down a bit.

'I wasn't thinking.'

Nic snorted. 'When did you ever?' The engine was already turning over. He slammed the car into gear and got a squeal from the tyres as they sped off. No indicator or mirror; a car behind tooted its horn three or four times. Nic checked the rearview, saw an old guy, all by himself. So he gave him the finger and a mouthful of abuse.

When did you ever?

Jerry's mind was working back, forming answers. Hadn't *he* been the one who'd done most of the shoplifting? And the one who bought them their booze when they were under age, because he was that bit taller and older-looking than Nic. Nic: smooth, shiny face, still like a kid's even now; thick dark hair always cut and styled. Nic was the one the girls went for, Jerry hanging back to see if any of them would find him worth talking to.

Nic at college, telling Jerry stories of shagging marathons. Even then, even back then there'd been glimpses: *she didn't fancy that, so I slapped her till she did . . . had her wrists held in one hand and I was pumping away like.*

It was as if the world deserved his violence, and would accept it because in every other way he was just fine, just perfect. The night Nic had met Catriona . . . he'd given Jerry a slap that night, too. They'd been to a couple of bars – Madogs, trendy but pricey, Princess Margaret was supposed to've drunk there, and the Shakespeare, next to the Usher Hall. That's where they'd met Cat and her friends, who were off to see some play at the Lyceum, something to do with horses. Nic knew one of the girls, introduced himself to the group, Jerry mute but keen beside him. And Nic had got talking to this other girl, Cat, short for Catriona. Not a bad looker, but not the best of the bunch either.

'Are you at Napier?' someone asked Jerry.

'Naw,' he said, 'I'm in the electronics business.' That was his line. They were supposed to think he was a games designer, maybe ran his own software company. But it never seemed to work. They asked questions he couldn't answer, until he laughed and admitted he drove a fork-lift. There were smiles at the news, but not much more in the way of conversation.

When the group headed off to their play, Nic nudged Jerry. 'Solid gold, pal,' he said. 'Cat's meeting me after for a drink.'

'Like her then?'

'She's all right.' A wary look. 'She is, eh?'

'Oh aye, she's rare.'

Another nudge. 'And she's related to Bryce Callan. That's her surname: Callan.'

'So?'

Nic going wide-eyed. 'Never heard of Bryce Callan? Fuck me, Jerry, he runs the place.'

Jerry looking around the pub. 'This place?'

'Ya tube, he runs *Edinburgh*.'

Jerry nodding, even though he still didn't understand.

Later, a few more boozers down the road, he'd asked if he could go with Nic when he met Catriona.

'Don't be wet.'

'What am I supposed to do then?'

They were walking along the pavement, and Nic had stopped suddenly, facing him, his eyes glowering.

'I'll tell you what would be a start – you growing up. Everything's changed, we're not kids now.'

'I know that. I'm the one with the job, the one that's getting married.'

And Nic had slapped him. Not hard, but the act itself shocking Jerry rigid.

'Time to grow up, pal. You might have a job but everywhere I take you, you just stand there like a drink of fucking water.' Grabbing Jerry's face. 'Study me, Jer, watch how I do things. You might start growing up.'

Growing up.

Jerry wondered if this was what growing up brought you to: the two of them, in the Cosworth, and, it being a Monday night, out on the hunt. There were Monday-night singles clubs, usually catering to a slightly older clientele. Not that Nic minded what age the women were. He just wanted one of them. Jerry risked a glance at his friend. So good-looking . . . why did he need to do it this way? What was his problem?

But Jerry knew the answer to that. Cat was the problem. The problem of Cat was there at every bloody turn.

'Where we going then?' he asked.

'The van's parked in Lochrin Place.' Nic's voice was cold. Jerry was feeling the boak again in his stomach, like he was breathing bile. But the thing was . . . once they got started, he knew it would be joined by a completely different feeling: he'd get excited, same as Nic. Hunters, the pair of them.

'Treat it like a game,' Nic had said the first time.

Treat it like a game.

And his heart would beat faster, groin tingling. With the gloves and the ski mask, and sitting in the Bedford van, he was a different person. Not Jerry Lister any more, but someone out of a comic book or a film, someone stronger and scarier. Someone you had to fear. It was almost enough to tamp down the dry boak. Almost.

The van belonged to a guy Nic knew. Nic told the bloke he needed it now and again for a bit of moonlighting, helping a friend shift second-hand stuff around. The bloke took two tenners from him and didn't want any other details. Nic had these licence plates, got them from a scrapyard. He'd fix them on with wire, covering the real plates. The van was rusty, a dull white respray. It didn't stand out at all, not when the streets were dark and cold and you were hurrying home, maybe a bit the worse for wear.

The worse for wear was what Nic wanted. They'd park near the nightclub, pay their money and go in. Plenty of guys turning up in pairs, nothing suspicious about them, nothing to mark them out from anyone else. Then Nic would pick out the tables with parties at them. He seemed to be able to tell which ones were singles clubs. One time, he'd even got one of the women up for a dance. Jerry had asked him afterwards, wasn't that risky?

'What's life without a bit of risk?'

Tonight, they drove around a bit first. Nic knew the club would be at its best come ten o'clock. The post-pub drunks wouldn't have arrived yet, but the singles clubs would be in full swing. Most of them had work in the morning, couldn't make too late a night of it. They'd stay till eleven, maybe, then start heading home. And by then, Nic would have picked one or two. He always had a reserve, just in case. Some nights it didn't work out; the women all headed off together or with partners, none of them branching off on her own.

Other nights, it worked to perfection.

Jerry stood at the edge of the dance floor, lager in hand. Already he could feel the surge in him, the dark excited tide. But he was twitchy, too, never knew when some friend of his or Jayne's would come wandering up. *Jayne know you're here, does she*? No, she didn't. Didn't even ask any more. He'd get home at one or two in the morning, and she'd be asleep. Even if he woke her up coming in, she wouldn't say much.

'Hammered again?' Something like that.

He'd go back through to the living room, sit there with the remote in his hand, staring at the TV without switching it on. Sitting in the dark, where nobody could see him, nobody point an accusing finger.

It was you, it was you, it was you.

Not true. It was Nic. It was always Nic.

He stood by the dance floor and held his drink in a hand just barely shaking. And inside he was praying: *Don't let us get lucky tonight!*

But then Nic was coming towards him, a weird gleam in his eyes.

'I don't believe it, Jer. I *do not* believe it!'

'Calm down, man. What's up?'

Nic was running his hands through his hair. '*She's* here!'

'Who?' Looking around, wondering if anyone was listening. No chance: the music was just this side of the pain barrier. Orbital, it sounded like. Jerry kept up with the latest bands.

Nic was shaking his head. 'She didn't see me.' His mind was working now. 'We could do this.' Looking at Jerry. 'We could *do* this.'

'Aw, Jesus, it's not Cat, is it?'

'Don't be dense. It's that slut Yvonne!'

'Yvonne?'

'The one Cat was with that night. The one who took her along.'

Jerry was shaking his head. 'No way. No way, man.'

'But it's perfect!'

'Perfect's just what it isn't, Nic. It's suicide.'

'She could be the last one, Jerry. Think about it.' Nic checked his watch. 'We'll stick around a while, see if she hooks up with anyone.' He slapped Jerry's shoulder. 'I'm telling you, Jer, this'll be wild.'

That's what I'm afraid of, Jerry felt like saying.

Cat had this friend Yvonne who'd split up from her husband. Yvonne had joined a singles club. And one night she'd persuaded Cat to go with her. Jerry wasn't too good on the background. He didn't know why Cat had agreed. Had to mean her own marriage was rocky, but Nic had never said anything. Only things he ever said were along the lines of 'She betrayed me, Jer,' and 'I never saw it coming.' They'd gone to a nightclub – not this one, but a Thursday nighter, same sort of crowd – and one of the singles guys had taken Cat up for a dance, then another. And that was that. Basically, she'd gone off with him.

And now Nic saw his chance for revenge, not on Cat – no way he could touch her; Christ, her uncle was Bryce Callan, her cousin was Barry Hutton – but on her friend Yvonne.

When Nic came over again and nudged him, Jerry knew the singles group was preparing to leave. He finished his pint and followed Nic out of the club. The van was a hundred yards away. What happened was: Nic followed on foot, Jerry driving. Then Nic would find his spot, make a grab, and Jerry would pull up alongside, haul open the back doors. Then it was back on the road till they found a deserted spot, Nic in the back holding down the woman, Jerry taking care not to run any red lights or pull out in front of cop cars. The gloves and ski masks were in the glove box.

Nic unlocked the van, stared at Jerry.

'It's got to be you on foot tonight.'

'What?'

'Yvonne knows me. If she hears something, turns her head, she'd see it was me.'

'Put the mask on then.'

'You thick? Following a woman down the road with a ski mask on?'

'I'm not doing it.'

Nic's teeth were gritted in sudden anger. 'Help me out here!'

'No way, man.' Shaking his head.

Nic made an effort to calm himself. 'Look, maybe she won't be on her own anyway. I'm just asking—'

'And I'm saying no. Whole thing's way too risky, I don't care what you say.' Jerry was moving backwards away from the van.

'Where you going?'

'I need some fresh air.'

'Don't be like that. Christ, Jer, when are you going to grow up?'

'No way.' It was all Jerry could think of to say. Then he turned and ran.

26

Rebus walked from room to room in his flat, waiting for the grill to heat up. Toasted cheese: that most solitary of meals. You never saw it on menus, never invited friends round to share a few slices. It was what you ate when you were alone. A trip to the cupboard revealing a few final slices of bread; marge and cheese in the fridge. You wanted a hot meal this winter evening.

Toasted cheese.

He went back into the kitchen, put the bread under the grill, started slicing the slick wedge of orange Cheddar. A refrain came into his head, something from an old Fringe revue show:

Scottish Cheddar, it's our kind of cheese,
Scottish Cheddar, orange, full of grease . . .

Back into the living room, early Bowie on the hi-fi. 'The Man Who Sold the World.' Life was all about commerce, no doubt about it, daily transactions with friends, enemies and strangers, each one providing a winner and a loser, a sense of something lost or gained. You might not be selling the world, but everyone was selling something, some idea of themselves. When Bowie sang of passing someone on the stairs, Rebus thought again of Derek Linford, caught on the tenement stairwell: voyeur, or just insecure? Rebus himself had done some crazy things in his younger days. One girl, when she'd chucked him he'd phoned her parents to say she was pregnant. Christ, they hadn't even had sex together. He stood beside the window, gazing out at the flats across the way, some still with curtains or shutters open. All those other lives. Opposite him lived a family with two kids, boy and girl. He'd been watching them for so long that one Saturday morning, bumping into them outside the newsagent's, he'd said hello. The kids, no parents to protect them, had edged past him, eyes wary, while he tried to explain that he was one of their neighbours.

Never talk to strangers: it was advice he'd have given them himself. He might be their neighbour, but he was also a stranger. People on the pavement had looked at him oddly, standing there with his bag of rolls, his newspaper and milk, while two kids walked backwards away from him, and him calling out: 'I live across the road from you! You must have seen me!'

Of course, they hadn't seen him. Their minds were elsewhere, fixed on a world entirely separate from his. And from then on, maybe they called him the 'creepy neighbour', the man who lived on his own.

Sell the world? He couldn't even sell himself.

But that was Edinburgh for you. Reserved, self-contained, the kind of place where you might never talk to the person next door. Rebus's stairwell of six flats boasted only three owner-occupiers; the other three were let to students. He couldn't have said who owned them until the statutory notice had come round for roof repairs. Absentee landlords. One of them lived in Hong Kong or somewhere, and the lack of his signature had led the council to make their own estimate of repairs – ten times the original – and pass the work on to a favoured firm.

Not too long ago, one stairwell resident out Dalry way had had a contract taken out on him by someone else in the tenement because he wouldn't sign his name to a repair estimate. That was Edinburgh for you: reserved, self-contained, and lethal when crossed.

Bowie was singing 'Changes' now. Black Sabbath had a song with the same title, a ballad of sorts. Ozzy Osbourne singing, '*I'm going through changes*'. Me too, pal, Rebus felt like telling him.

Back into the kitchen: turning the toast and arranging the cheese slices, then back under the grill. He put the kettle on.

Changes: like with his drinking. A hundred pubs he could name in Edinburgh, yet here he was at home, no beer in the cupboard, and just the one bottle of malt whisky on top of the fridge, half of it gone. He would allow himself a single glass before bed, maybe top it up with water. Then under the duvet with a book. He had all these Edinburgh histories to get through, though he'd already given up on Sir Walter Scott's *Journals*. Plenty of pubs in the city named after Scott's works; probably more than he realised, seeing as how he hadn't read any of the novels.

Smoke from the grill told him the edges of the toast were burning. He tossed both slices on to a plate, took it back through to his chair. The TV was on with the sound muted. His chair was by the window, cordless phone and TV remote on the floor next to it. Some nights the ghosts came, settling themselves on the sofa or cross-legged on the floor. Not enough to fill the room, but more than he'd have liked. Villains, dead colleagues. And now Cafferty was back in his life, as if resurrected. Rebus, chewing, looked to the ceiling, asking God what he'd done to deserve it all. He liked a bit of a laugh, God, even if it was the laughter of cruelty.

Toasted cheese: sometimes at weekends, when Rebus's father had been alive and the son had headed back to Fife to visit, the old boy would be sitting at the table, munching the selfsame meal, washing down each mouthful with swilled tea. When Rebus had been a kid, they'd eaten as a family in the kitchen, bringing out the fold-down table. But in later years, Rebus senior had hauled the table into the living room, so he could eat near the fire and the television. A two-bar electric heater warming his back. There was a Calor gas heater, too. It always steamed up the windows. And then overnight in winter the condensation would freeze, so you had to scrape it off in the morning, or mop it with the kitchen flannel once the heating got going.

A grunt from his father, Rebus settling into what had been his mother's chair. He would say he'd eaten; no intention of joining his father at the table set for one. His mother had always laid a tablecloth, his father never did. Same plates and cutlery, but that one telling difference.

And now, Rebus thought, I don't even use a table.

The ghosts of his parents never visited. Maybe they were at rest, unlike the others. No ghosts tonight, though, just shadows cast by the television screen, street light and the halogen glow of passing cars, the world presented not in terms of colour so much as of light and shade. And Cafferty's shadow looming larger than any. What was he up to? When would he make his move, his real move, the last one of whatever game he was playing?

Christ, he wanted a drink. But he wouldn't have one just yet – to prove it to himself. Siobhan was right about him; he'd made a big mistake with Lorna Grieve. He didn't think it was just the drink to blame – he'd been under the spell of the past, a past of album covers and newspaper photos – but it had played its part. Siobhan had asked when the booze would start affecting his work. He could have told her: it already has.

He picked up his phone, thought about calling Sammy. Then he checked his watch, angling it towards the window. Gone ten. No, it was too late; it was always too late by the time he remembered. And then she'd end up calling him, and he'd apologise, and she'd say he should call anyway, no matter how late. Even so . . . he told himself it was too late. There'd be someone in the room next to hers, what if his call woke them up? And Sammy needed her sleep; it was rigorous, all the stuff she was doing: the tests, the exercises. She'd told him she was 'getting there', her way of saying that progress was slow.

Slow progress: he knew all about it. But things were moving now, definitely moving. He felt as if he was in the driving seat, but blindfolded, taking directions from anyone in the car. There were probably lots of Give Way and No Entry signs ahead on the route, but he was pretty good at ignoring those. Problem was, the car had no seat belts, and Rebus's instinct was always to go faster.

He got up, swapped Bowie for Tom Waits. *Blue Valentine*, recorded just before he went 'junkyard'. Bluesy and seamy and seamless. Waits knew the soul's rotten marrow: the vocals might be an affectation, but the lyrics were from the heart. Rebus had seen him in concert, the actorliness all too apparent, the words still failing to ring false. Selling a version of himself, something packaged for public consumption. Pop stars and politicians did it all the time. These days the successful politicians lacked opinion and colour. They were ventriloquists' dummies, their clothes chosen for them by others, colour-coordinated and 'on message'. He wondered if Seona Grieve would be any different; somehow doubted it. The renegades never found progress easy, and he felt Seona Grieve was too ambitious to take that road. No blindfold for her, just careful hard work in between the mourning. He'd joked with Linford about the widow's motives. Motive, means and opportunity: the Holy Trinity of murder. Rebus's real problem was with the means: he didn't see Seona Grieve as the clawhammer type. But then, if she was being clever, that's exactly the weapon she'd have used: something people would find hard to associate with her.

While Linford had stuck to the main road, following the signposts marked Investigative Procedure, Rebus had managed to find himself on a rutted track. What if the suicide of Freddy Hastings was unconnected to Roddy Grieve? Maybe it was even unconnected to the find in Queensberry House. Was he really chasing shadows, every bit as worthwhile as following the trail of headlamp shadows across his ceiling? His phone rang just as a track ended, startling him.

'It's me,' Siobhan Clarke said. 'I think somebody's spying on me.'

Rebus rang her buzzer. She checked it was him before letting him into the stairwell. Her door was open by the time he reached her floor.

'What's happened?' he asked. She led him into the living room, looking a lot calmer than he felt. There was a bottle of wine on the coffee table: a third of it gone, a little left in the single glass. She'd eaten Indian food: he could smell it. But there were no signs of dishes, everything tidied away.

'I've been getting these calls.'

'What sort of calls?'

'Hang-ups. Two or three times a day. If I'm not in, the answering machine picks them up. Whoever's calling, they wait till the thing's recording before putting the phone down.'

'And if you're here?'

'Same thing: the line goes dead. I tried 1471, but they always withhold their number. And then tonight . . .'

'What?'

'I just got this feeling I was being watched.' She nodded towards her window. 'From across there.'

He looked to where she'd closed her curtains. He walked over and opened them, stared out at the tenement opposite. 'Wait here,' he said.

'I could have confronted them myself,' she said, 'but . . .'

'I won't be a tick.'

She stood by her window, arms folded. Heard the main door close, watched Rebus cross the road. He'd been out of breath. Was he just out of condition, or had he arrived in such a rush? Maybe afraid for her . . . She wondered now why she'd called him. Gayfield Square was five minutes away; any officer from there would have responded. Or she could have investigated for herself. It wasn't that she was scared. But things like this . . . creeping feelings . . . once they were shared, they tended to evaporate. He'd pushed open the main door, gone straight in. She saw him pass the first-floor window, and now he was at the second. Standing there, then pressing himself to the glass and waving to let her know it was okay. Up a further flight, checking no one was hiding there, and straight back down again.

By the time he arrived back, he was breathing harder than ever. 'I know,' he said, falling on to her sofa, 'I should join a gym.' He reached into his pocket for his cigarettes, then remembered that she wouldn't let him smoke, not here. She'd fetched a tall-stemmed glass from the kitchen.

'Least I can do,' she said, pouring in some red.

'Cheers.' He took a long swallow, exhaled. 'This your first bottle tonight?' Trying to make a joke of it.

'I'm not seeing things,' she said. She was kneeling by the coffee table, turning the glass in her hand.

'It's just that when you're on your own . . . I don't mean you personally, it goes for me, too.'

'What does? Imagining things?' There was a hint of colour to either cheekbone. 'How come you knew?'

He looked at her. 'Knew what?'

'Tell me you've not been watching me.'

His mouth opened, but he couldn't find the words.

'You pushed open the door,' she explained. 'Didn't check to see if it was locked or anything. Because you already knew it wasn't. Then you stopped two floors up. Just taking a breather?' She widened her eyes. 'That was where he was watching from. Not the tenement either side, and *that* landing.'

Rebus cast his eyes down into his drink. 'It wasn't me,' he said.

'But you know who it is.' She paused. 'Is it Derek?' His silence was answer enough. She bounded to her feet, began pacing. 'When I get my hands on him . . .'

'Look, Siobhan—'

She turned on him. 'How did you know?'

So then he had to explain it, and as he finished she reached for her phone, punched in Linford's number. When the call was answered, she cut the connection. She was the one breathing hard now.

'Can I ask a question?' Rebus asked.

'What?'

'Did you put 141 first?' She looked at him blankly. 'That's the prefix if you don't want the caller knowing your number.'

She was still wincing when the phone rang.

'I'm not answering,' she said.

'It might not be Derek.'

'Let the machine take it.'

Seven rings, and the machine clicked into life. Her message first, then the sound of a receiver being replaced.

'Bastard!' she hissed. She picked up her receiver again, hit 1471, listened and slammed the phone down.

'Number withheld?' Rebus guessed.

'What's he playing at, John?'

'He's been jilted, Siobhan. We can turn strange when that happens.'

'You sound like you're on his side.'

'No way. I'm just trying to explain it.'

'Someone jilts you, you start stalking them?' She picked up her wineglass, took gulps from it as she paced. Then she noticed the curtains were still open, hurried over and closed them.

'Come and sit down,' Rebus said. 'We'll talk to him in the morning.'

She ran out of floor eventually, dropped on to the sofa next to him. He tried pouring more wine into her glass, but she didn't want any.

'Shame to waste it,' he said.

'You have it.'

'I don't want it.' She stared at him, and he offered a smile. 'I've spent half of this evening avoiding going out for a drink,' he explained.

'Why?'

He just shrugged, and she took the bottle from him. 'Then let's put it out of harm's way.'

When he caught up with her, she was pouring the contents down the kitchen sink.

'Bit radical,' he said. 'The fridge would have done.'

'You don't chill red wine.'

'You know what I mean, though.' He saw the clean dishes on the draining board. Her supper things had already been washed up. The kitchen was white-tiled and spotless. 'We're chalk and cheese,' he said.

'How's that?'

'I only wash up when I run out of mugs.'

She smiled. 'I've always wanted to be a hygiene slut.'

'But?'

She shrugged, surveying the room. 'Must be my upbringing or something. I suppose some people would call me neurotically tidy.'

'They just call me a slob,' Rebus said.

He watched her rinse the bottle and place it beside a few others which, along with empty jars, sat in an orange-box beside the swingbin.

'Don't tell me,' he said: 'recycling?'

She nodded, laughed. Then her face crumpled into seriousness. 'Jesus, John, I only went out with him three times.'

'Sometimes that's all it takes.'

'You know where I met him?'

'You wouldn't tell me, remember?'

'I'll tell you now: it was at a singles club.'

'That night you were out with the rape victim?'

'He goes to this singles club. They don't know he's a cop.'

'Well, it shows he has trouble meeting women.'

'He meets them every day, John.' She paused. 'I don't know, maybe it shows something else.'

'What?'

'I'm not sure. A different side to him.' She leaned back against the sink, folded her arms. 'Remember what you said?'

'I say so many memorable things.'

'You said about jilted guys, what they do sometimes.'

'You think Linford's been jilted one time too many?'

'Maybe.' She was thoughtful. 'But I was thinking more of the rapist, why he seems to focus on singles nights.'

Rebus was concentrating now. 'He went along to one, got the cold shoulder?'

'Or his wife or girlfriend went to one . . .'

Rebus was nodding. 'And got a nice warm shoulder?'

Siobhan was nodding, too. 'It's not my case, of course . . .'

'But whoever's running it, Siobhan, they'll have been asking around all the singles clubs.'

'Yes, but they won't have been asking the female members about jealous partners.'

'Good point. Another job for the morning.'

'Yes,' she said, turning to fill the kettle, 'just as soon as I've had a word with dear old Derek.'

'And if he denies it?'

'I've got corroboration, John.' She looked at him over her shoulder. 'I've got you.'

'No, you've got me and a few suspicions of your own. Not exactly the same thing.'

'What are you getting at?'

'People know Linford and me haven't been getting on like a house on fire. Now I come along and say I've seen him playing peeping Tom. You don't know Fettes, Siobhan.'

'They look after their own?'

'Maybe, maybe not. But they definitely would think more than twice about taking the word of John Rebus over that of a future chief constable.'

'Is that why you wouldn't tell me about Linford?'

'Maybe.'

She turned away from him again. 'How do you want your coffee?'

'Black.'

Derek Linford's flat looked down on to Dean Valley and the Water of Leith. He'd got a good deal on the mortgage – playing the Fettes card for all it was worth – but even so he was making hefty repayments. And with the BMW on top. He had so much to lose.

He'd stripped off his coat and his shirt, sweating after the drive home. She'd seen him at the window, then made a phone call. And he'd run for it, driving like a maniac, taking the stairs to his own flat two at a time . . . and his own phone was ringing. He'd snatched at it, thinking: it's Siobhan! She's seen someone and decided to call me, wanting my help! But the phone had gone dead, and when he'd checked, it *had* been her on the phone. He'd called straight back and she hadn't answered.

Standing shaking by his window, ignoring the rooftop view . . . *She knows it was me!* It was all he could think of. She wouldn't have been calling him for help; she'd have called Rebus. And of course Rebus had told her. Of course he had.

'She knows,' he said aloud. 'She knows, she knows, she knows.'

He walked across the living room, turned and walked back. His right fist was slapping into his open left hand.

He had so much to lose.

'No,' he said, shaking his head, getting his breathing back under control. He wasn't going to lose any of this. Not for anyone or anything. This was all he had to show for the years of work, the long nights, the weekends, the courses and the studying.

'No,' he said again. 'Nobody's taking this away.'

Not if he could help it.

Not without one hell of a fight.

They rang up to Cafferty's room, told him there was a problem in the bar. He got dressed, went down there, and found Rab being pinned to the floor by two of the barmen and a couple of customers. Another man was seated on the floor near by, legs splayed, his nose bust open but holding his ear, blood seeping out between the fingers. He was yelling out for someone to call the police, while his girlfriend knelt beside him.

Cafferty looked at him. 'What you need is an ambulance,' he said.

'Bastard bit my ear!'

Cafferty crouched in front of the man, held two fifties out, and then tucked them into the man's breast pocket. 'An ambulance,' he repeated. The girlfriend took the hint, got up to find the phone. Then Cafferty walked over to Rab, squatted down and took hold of him by the hair.

'Rab,' he said, 'what the fuck are you doing?'

'I was just enjoying masel, Big Ger.' There was a smear of blood on his lips; blood from the wounded man's ear.

'No fun for anyone else,' Cafferty told him.

'What's life if ye can't enjoy yirsel?'

Cafferty stared at him but didn't answer. 'See when you go getting like this,' he said quietly, 'I don't know what I'm going to do with you.'

'Does it matter?' Rab said.

Cafferty didn't answer this either. He told the men they could let go, and they did, cautiously. Rab didn't seem inclined to get up. 'Maybe you could help him,' Cafferty told the men. He had a bundle of notes out, peeled off several and handed them round.

'For your help, and to keep this on the q.t.' The bar hadn't been damaged, but he insisted on paying up anyway. 'Sometimes it takes a while for the damage to show,' he told the barman. Then he bought a round of drinks and clapped a hand on Rab's neck.

'Time you were in bed, son.' Rab's room key was on the bar. The staff all knew he was with Big Ger. 'Next time you want a rammy, try playing away from home, eh?'

'Sorry, Big Ger.'

'Got to look out for one another, eh, Rab? Sometimes that means using the brain as well as the brawn.'

'I'll be fine, Big Ger. Sorry again.'

'Off you go now. There's a mirror in the lift, so don't you go swinging a punch at it.'

Rab tried to smile. He looked sleepy after all the excitement. Cafferty watched him slouch out of the bar. He felt like a drink, but not here, not with these people. Leave them be, let them get it out of their systems with gossip and retelling. There was a minibar in his room, and that would do him for tonight. He apologised with a wave of his arms, then followed Rab to the lift, stood with him in its close confines all the way to the third floor. It was like being back in a cell. Rab's eyes were closed. He was leaning against the mirror. Cafferty kept his eyes on him and didn't blink once.

Does it matter? That had been Rab's question. Cafferty was beginning to wonder.

27

As Rebus walked into St Leonard's next morning, two uniforms were discussing a film from the previous night's TV.

'*When Harry Met Sally*, you must've seen it, sir.'

'Not last night. Some of us have got better things to do.'

'We're just talking about whether men can be friends with women without wanting to sleep with them. That's the plot, you see.'

'I reckon,' the second uniform said, 'as soon as a bloke claps eyes on a woman, first thing he wonders is what she'd be like in the scratcher.'

Rebus could hear raised voices in the CID suite. 'If you'll excuse me, gents, more urgent business . . .'

'Lovers' tiff,' one of the uniforms said.

Rebus turned back towards him. 'Pal, you couldn't be further from the truth.'

Siobhan had Derek Linford backed into a corner of the room. She also had an audience: DI Bill Pryde, DS Roy Frazer and DS George Hi-Ho Silvers. They were seated at their desks, enjoying the spectacle. Rebus gave all three a withering glance as he waded in. Siobhan had Linford by the throat, her face close to his – by dint of standing on tiptoe. He had paperwork in one hand, turned into a crumpled wad by the involuntary tightening of his fist. He was holding his other hand up in a gesture of surrender.

'And if you so much as *think* my telephone number, never mind calling it,' Siobhan was yelling, 'I'll twist your balls so hard they'll drop off!'

From behind, Rebus brought his hands down hard on hers, pulling them off Linford. Her head snapped round, face flushed with anger. Linford was coughing.

'This what you call a word?' Rebus asked her.

'Knew you'd be involved somewhere,' Linford spat.

Siobhan turned back to him. 'This is you and me, arsehole, nobody else!'

'Think you're God's gift, don't you?'

Rebus: 'Shut up, Linford. Don't make it any worse than you have.'

'I haven't done anything.'

Siobhan tried pulling away from Rebus. 'You fucking snake!'

And then a voice behind them, booming with authority: 'What the hell's going on here?' All three looked towards the open doorway. Chief Superintendent Watson was standing there. And he had a visitor: Colin Carswell, the Assistant Chief Constable.

Rebus was the last to be 'invited' to give the Chief Super his side of the story. There were just the two of them in the office. The Farmer – nicknamed for his ruddy-coloured face and north-east agricultural background – sat with hands pressed together, a sharpened pencil resting between them.

'Am I supposed to fall on that?' Rebus asked, pointing to the pencil. 'Ritual hara-kiri?'

'You're supposed to tell me what was happening back there. The one day the ACC comes calling . . .'

'He'll be taking Linford's side, of course?'

The Farmer glared at him. 'Don't start. Just give me your version, for what it's worth.'

'What's the point? I know what the other two will have told you.'

'What exactly?'

'Siobhan will have told the truth, and Linford will have come up with a pack of lies to save his arse.' Rebus shrugged as the Farmer's face grew darker.

'Humour me,' he said.

'Siobhan went out a couple of times with Linford,' Rebus recited. 'Nothing serious. Then she sent him packing. I was round her place one evening discussing her case. Came out and was sitting in my car, saw someone from the opposite tenement come out, go for a pee round the corner, and head back again. I went to investigate, and it was Linford, spying on her from the tenement stairwell. Then last night, she phones me, says she thinks she's being watched. So I told her about Linford.'

'Why didn't you tell her before?'

'Didn't want to upset her. Besides, I thought I'd scared him off.' Rebus shrugged again. 'I'm obviously not the hard case I think I am.'

The Farmer leaned back in his chair. 'And what does Linford say?'

'I'm betting he's told you it's a pile of shite concocted by DI John Rebus. Siobhan was mistaken, I made up this story, and she swallowed it.'

'And why would you do that?'

'So he'd push off and let me work the case the way I want to work it.'

The Farmer looked down at the pencil he was still holding. 'Actually, that's not the reason he gave.'

'What then?'

'He says you want Siobhan for yourself.'

Rebus screwed his face into a sneer. 'Well, that's his fantasy, not mine.'

'No?'

'Absolutely not.'

'I can't let this go, you know. Not with Carswell as witness.'

'Yes, sir.'

'What do you think I should do?'

'If it were me, sir, pack Linford off back to Fettes where he can continue to be their desk-bound blue-eyed boy, far from the hurly-burly of actual policing.'

'Mr Linford doesn't want that.'

Rebus couldn't help reacting. 'He wants to stay here?' The Farmer nodded. 'Why?'

'He says he holds no grudge. Puts it down to the "hothouse conditions" on the case.'

'I don't get it.'

'Frankly, neither do I.' The Farmer rose, made for his coffee machine. Pointedly, he poured just the one mug. Rebus tried not to let his relief show. 'If I was him, I'd want to be shot of the lot of you.' The Farmer paused, sat down again. 'But what DI Linford wants, DI Linford gets.'

'It's going to be ugly.'

'Why?'

'Seen the CID suite lately? We're swamped. Hard enough to keep Siobhan and him apart under normal conditions, but the cases we're working on could be connected.'

'So DS Clarke tells me.'

'She said you were thinking of pulling the Supertramp inquiry.'

'There never really was an inquiry. But I was as curious as the next man about that four hundred thou. To be honest, I didn't give her much chance.'

'She's a good detective, sir.'

Watson nodded. 'Despite the role model,' he said.

'Look,' Rebus said, 'I know the score here. You're coasting to retirement, would rather this was someone else's shit-pile.'

'Rebus, don't think you can—'

'Linford belongs to Carswell, so you're not about to rub his nose in it. That just leaves the rest of us.'

'Careful what you're saying.'

'I'm not saying anything you don't know yourself.'

The Farmer rose to his feet, rested his knuckles on the desk and leaned towards Rebus. 'And what about you? Building your own private little police force – meetings in the Oxford Bar, running around like it's *you* that runs this station.'

'I'm trying to solve a case.'

'And get into Clarke's knickers at the same time?'

Rebus jumped to his feet. Their faces were inches apart. Neither man said anything, as if the next word could prove a hair-trigger. The

Farmer's phone started ringing. He moved a hand, picked it up and held it to his ear.

'Yes?' he said. Rebus was so close, he could hear Gill Templer in the earpiece:

'Press briefing, sir. You want to see my notes?'

'Bring them in, Gill.'

Rebus pushed away from the desk. He heard the Farmer calling behind him:

'Had we finished, Inspector?'

'I think so, sir.' Managed to close the door without slamming it.

And went to find Linford. Not in the office. He was told that Siobhan was in the ladies' loo, being calmed by a WPC. Canteen? No. The front desk said he'd left the station five minutes earlier. Rebus looked at his watch: it wasn't opening time yet. Linford's BMW wasn't in the car park. He stood on the pavement, took out his mobile, and called Linford's.

'Yes?'

'Where the hell are you?'

'Parked in the Engine Shed car park.'

Rebus turned and looked down St Leonard's Lane: the Engine Shed was at the end. 'What are you doing there?'

'Some thinking.'

'Don't strain yourself.' Rebus was walking along the lane.

'Great. I really appreciate you calling my mobile to hurl insults at me.'

'Always happy to oblige.' He turned into the car park. And there was the Beamer, parked in a disabled spot beside the front door. Rebus switched off his phone and opened the passenger door, got in.

'What an unexpected pleasure,' Linford said, putting his own phone away and resting his hands on the steering wheel, eyes focused on the windshield.

'I like surprises myself,' Rebus said. 'Like being told by my chief super that I'm chasing DC Clarke.'

'Well, aren't you?'

'You know bloody fine I'm not.'

'You seem to be round her flat often enough.'

'Yeah, with you peeking in the windows.'

'Look, okay, when she dumped me I got a bit . . . It doesn't happen to me very often.'

'Being chucked? I find that hard to believe.'

Linford gave the ghost of a smile. 'Believe what you like.'

'You lied to Watson.'

Linford turned to him. 'You'd have done the same in my shoes. That was my career on the line, right there!'

'Should have thought of that first.'

'Easy to say now,' Linford said quietly. He bit his bottom lip. 'What if

I apologise to Siobhan? Went off the rails a bit . . . won't happen again . . . that sort of thing?'

'Better put it in writing.'

'In case I make a mess of it?'

Rebus shook his head. 'It's hard to apologise when there's one hand round your throat and another round your balls.'

'Christ, man, I thought a blood vessel was going to burst.'

Rebus was stony faced. 'You could always have fought back.'

'That would have looked good, three other men in the room watching.'

Rebus studied him. 'You're bloody smooth, aren't you? Every step calculated before you take it.'

'Watching Siobhan wasn't calculated.'

'No, I don't suppose it was.' But, despite his words, Rebus wasn't so sure.

Linford turned in his seat, reached for something in the back. Papers: the same crushed bundle he'd been holding in the CID suite.

'Do you think we can talk shop for a minute?'

'Maybe.'

'I know you've been sidetracking me, running your own show and not letting me in. Fine, that's your decision. But all the interviews I've done, there might just be a nugget . . .' He handed the lot over to Rebus. Pages and pages of meticulous interview notes. The Holyrood Tavern, Jennie Ha's . . . and not just pubs but flats and businesses in the vicinity of Queensberry House. Cheekily, he'd even gone asking at Holyrood Palace.

'You've been busy,' Rebus grudgingly admitted.

'Shoe leather: it's an old standby, but sometimes it works.'

'So where's the nugget? Or do I have to sift this lot and be impressed by the number of rocks and stones along the way?'

Linford smiled. 'I saved the best for last.'

Meaning the last few pages, stapled together. Two interviews with the same man, conducted over a single day. One casual chat in the Holyrood Tavern itself, the other conducted at St Leonard's, with Hi-Ho Silvers in tow.

The interviewee's name was Bob Cowan and he gave his address as Royal Park Terrace. He was a university lecturer, Economic and Social History. Once a week, he met a friend for a drink at the Holyrood Tavern. The friend lived in the Grassmarket, and the Tavern made for a convenient halfway house. Cowan enjoyed his walk back through Holyrood Park, past St Margaret's Loch with its colony of swans.

> *The moon was nearly full that night* – the night Roddy Grieve met his end – *and I left the Tavern about quarter to midnight. Most nights, I never meet a soul on that walk. Precious few dwellings around there. I suppose some people would get a bit nervous. I mean, you read all sorts of stories. But I've never had*

any bother the three years I've been making that trip. Now, this may not be relevant. I thought about it hard for days after the murder, and I was inclined to think that it wasn't. I saw the photos of Mr Grieve, and neither of these two men looked like him, in my opinion. Of course, I could be mistaken. And though the night was pretty bright, plenty of stars out, a good clear sky, I really only got a good view of one of the men. They were standing across the road from Queensberry House. I'd say directly opposite its gates. They looked like they were waiting for someone. That was what attracted my attention. I mean, that time of night, down there with all the roadworks and construction? A strange choice for a meeting. I remember speculating as I walked home. The usual things: maybe the third man had nipped off somewhere to pee; or it could be some sort of sexual encounter; or they could be about to break into the construction site . . .

An interjection from Linford:

You really should have come forward with this at the time, Mr Cowan.

Then back to Cowan's story:

Oh, I suppose so, but you're always worried you'll get everyone excited about nothing. And these men, they didn't really look suspicious. I mean, they weren't wearing masks or carrying bags marked Swag. They were just two men who were chatting. Could have been friends who'd bumped into one another. Do you see what I mean? Both dressed quite normally, casually: denims, I think, and dark jackets, maybe training shoes. The one I got the closest look at had close-cropped hair, either dark brown or black. These big sallow eyes, like a basset-hound. Cheeks to match, and a downtrodden sort of scowl to his mouth, as if he'd just heard something that hadn't pleased him. He was big, had to be over six feet tall. Broad shoulders. Do you think he had something to do with it? My God, maybe I was the last person to see the killer . . .

'What do you think?' Linford asked.

Rebus was sifting through the other interviews.

'I know,' Linford said, 'it doesn't look like much.'

'Actually, it looks pretty good.' Linford seemed surprised by the comment. 'Problem is, there's not enough of it. Big guy, broad-shouldered . . . could be a hundred people who fit.'

Linford nodded; he'd thought this through. 'But if we can get a photofit . . . Cowan says he's willing.'

'And then what?'

'Pubs in the area, maybe he's local. Plus, a description like that, wouldn't surprise me if he was a brickie.'

'One of the construction workers?'

Linford shrugged. 'Once we've got a photofit . . .'

Rebus made to hand the sheaf of interviews back. 'Got to be worth a go. Congratulations.'

Linford preened visibly, reminding Rebus why he'd started hating him in the first place. The mildest praise and the man forgot everything else.

'And meantime,' Linford said, 'you go your own way?'

'That's right.'

'And I'm kept out of the picture?'

'Right now, Linford, that's the best place for you, believe me.'

Linford nodded his agreement. 'So what do I do now?' Rebus pushed open the passenger door.

'Stay away from St Leonard's till you've got that letter written. Make sure Siobhan gets it by the end of play today – but not before this afternoon; she needs time to cool off. Tomorrow, maybe it'll be safe to show your face. With the stress on maybe.'

It was enough for Linford. He wanted to shake Rebus's hand. But Rebus closed the door. No way he was shaking the bastard's hand: he'd turned up a nugget, not transformed base metals into gold. And Rebus still didn't trust him, got the feeling he'd turn in his grandmother for a sniff of promotion. The question was: what would he do if he thought his job was under threat?

A bleak occasion; a bleak spot.

Siobhan was there with Rebus. A woolly suit was in attendance, too: the WPC who'd been on the scene the night 'Mackie' had jumped, the one who'd said, *You're one of Rebus's, aren't you*? A minister was present, and a couple of faces Siobhan recognised from the Grassmarket: they'd nodded a greeting towards her. She hoped they wouldn't want cigarettes today; she'd none with her. Dezzi was there, too, sobbing into a wad of pink toilet paper. She'd found some scraps of black clothing: a gypsy-style skirt, long lace shawl torn almost to streamers. Black shoes, too, a different style on either foot.

No sign of Rachel Drew; maybe she hadn't heard.

So you couldn't have called the graveside busy. Crows were calling near by, threatening to drown out the minister's few and hasty words. One of the Grassmarket pair had to keep nudging his pal, who looked like nodding off. Every time the minister said the name Freddy Hastings, Dezzi mouthed the word Chris. When it was finished, Siobhan turned on her heels and walked quickly away. She didn't want to talk to anyone, had come only from a sense of duty, something no one would thank her for.

Back at the cars, she looked at Rebus for the first time.

'What did the Farmer say to you?' she asked. 'He's taking Linford's word against ours, isn't he?' When Rebus didn't answer, she got into her car, turned the ignition and was gone. Standing by his own car, yet to unlock it, Rebus thought he had seen the beginnings of tears in her eyes.

The yellow JCB digger was going in, clawing rubble from the base. With the tenement's innards showing, the whole scene had a voyeuristic quality, yet at the same time Rebus noticed that some bystanders couldn't look. It was as if a pathologist had gone to work, exposing the body's secrets. These had been people's homes: doors they'd painted and repainted; wallpaper carefully chosen. Perhaps some young couple – newly-weds – had done the skirting boards, getting gloss on their overalls but not really caring. Light fittings, electrical sockets, switches . . . tumbling into a heap or hanging by threads of cable. And even more furtive elements of the structure: roof beams, plumbing, gaping wounds which had once been chimneys. A roaring fire at Christmas time . . . tree decorated in the corner.

The vultures had been at work: few of the better doors remained. Fireplaces had been removed, as had cisterns, wash-hand basins, baths. Water tanks and radiators . . . the scavengers would turn a profit from them. But what fascinated Rebus were the layers. Paint hidden by paint, wallpaper by wallpaper. A striped confection could be peeled to reveal hints of pale pink peony roses, and beneath that layer yet another, red-coated horsemen. A kitchen had been added to one flat, and the original kitchenette papered over. When the paper was ripped away, the original black and white tiles were revealed. Skips were being filled and loaded on to lorries, taking them to landfills outside the city where the jigsaw pieces would be covered over, a final layer for future archaeologists to scrape away.

Rebus lit a cigarette, narrowing his eyes against gusts of powder and grit. 'Looks like we're a bit on the late side.'

He was standing with Siobhan outside what had been the building containing Freddy Hastings' office. She was calm now, seemed to have put Linford out of her mind as she watched the demolition. Hastings' office had been on the ground floor, with flats above. There was no sign of it now. Once levelled, contractors would commence putting up a new structure, an 'apartment complex' only a stone's throw from the new parliament.

'Someone on the council might know,' Siobhan offered. Rebus nodded: she meant, might know what had happened to the contents of Hastings' office. 'You don't look very hopeful,' she added.

'It's not in my nature,' Rebus said, inhaling the smoke, and with it a mixture of plaster dust and other people's lives.

They drove to the City Chambers on the High Street, where an official was eventually able to provide the name of a solicitor. The solicitor was based in Stockbridge. On the way there, they stopped off at what had been Hastings' home, but the present owners didn't know anything about him. They'd bought from an antique dealer who, they thought, had bought from a football player. 1979 was ancient history; New Town flats could change hands every three or four years. Young professionals bought them, one eye on the investment potential. Then they had kids, and the stairs became a chore, or they bemoaned the lack of a garden. They sold up, moved on to something bigger.

The solicitor was young, too, and knew nothing of Frederick Hastings. But he got on the phone to one of the senior partners, who was in a meeting elsewhere. A time was arranged. Rebus and Siobhan debated over whether to return to the office. She suggested a walk along the Dean Valley, but Rebus, remembering that Linford lived in Dean Village, made the excuse that his heart wasn't up to the exertion required.

Siobhan: 'I suppose you want to find a pub.'

Rebus: 'There's a good one actually, just at the corner of St Stephen's Street.'

In the end, they walked to a café on Raeburn Place. Siobhan ordered tea, Rebus decaf. A waitress apologised for the fact that they were seated in a no smoking establishment. With a sigh, Rebus put the packet away.

'You know,' he said, 'life used to be so simple.'

She nodded agreement. 'You lived in a cave, clubbed your food to death . . .'

'And little girls went to charm schools. Now, you've all got degrees from the University of Sarcasm.'

'Three words,' she said: 'pot, kettle and black.'

Their drinks came. Siobhan checked that she had no messages on her mobile.

'Okay,' Rebus said, 'it'll have to be me who asks it.'

'Asks what?'

'What are you going to do about Linford?'

'Do I know anyone called that?'

'Fair enough.' Rebus went back to drinking his coffee.

Siobhan poured some tea into her cup and lifted it with both hands. 'Did you talk to him?' she asked. Rebus nodded slowly. 'Thought so. You were spotted running out after him.'

'He told the Farmer a lie about me.'

'I know. The chief mentioned it.'

'What did you tell him?'

'The truth,' she said. They were silent, raising their cups and drinking, lowering them again as though synchronised. Rebus was nodding again, though he didn't really know why. Siobhan cracked first. 'So what did you say to Linford?'

'He's going to send you an apology.'

'That's big of him.' She paused. 'You think he means it?'

'I think he regrets what he did.'

'Only because it might have affected his glorious career.'

'You could be right. All the same . . .'

'You think I should let it drop?'

'Not exactly. But Linford's got his own leads to follow. With any luck, they'll keep him out of your way.' He looked at her. 'I think he's scared of you.'

She snorted. 'He should be.' She lifted her cup again. 'But fair enough, if he keeps out of my way, I'll keep out of his.'

'Sounds good.'

'You think the trail's gone cold, don't you?'

'Hastings?' She nodded. 'I'm not sure,' he said. 'It's amazing what you can turn up in Edinburgh.'

Blair Martine was waiting for them when they returned to the solicitors' offices. He was rotund and elderly, with a chalk-stripe suit and silver watch-chain.

'I always wondered', he said, 'whether Freddy Hastings would come back to haunt me.' In front of him on the desk sat a ten-inch-thick bundle of manila folders and envelopes, tied together with parcel string. His fingers brushed the topmost folder, came away dusty.

'How do you mean, sir?'

'Well, it was never a case for you lot, but it was a mystery all the same. He just upped and left.'

'Creditors at his heels,' Rebus added.

Martine looked sceptical. He'd obviously lunched very well, his cheeks suffused with contentment, waistcoat straining. When he leaned back in his chair, Rebus feared the buttons would pop slapstick-style.

'Freddy was not without resources,' Martine said. 'That's not to say he didn't make some bad investments; he did. But all the same . . .' He tapped the files again. Rebus was champing at the bit to be let loose on them, but knew Martine would plead client confidentiality.

'And he did leave a number of creditors,' Martine went on. 'But none of them so very significant. We had to arrange for his flat to be sold. It fetched a fair price, not quite what it might have done.'

'Enough to see off these creditors?' Siobhan asked.

'Yes, and my firm's own fees. Costly business, when someone disappears.' He paused. There was a trick hiding beneath his cuff-linked sleeve. Rebus and Siobhan stayed silent; they could see he was bursting to play it. Martine leaned forward, elbows on the desk.

'I did keep a little aside,' he said conspiratorially, 'to defray the storage costs.'

'Storage?' Siobhan echoed.

The lawyer shrugged. 'I did think Freddy might walk back into my life some day. I just never expected it to be posthumous.' He sighed. 'When is the funeral, incidentally?'

'We've just been to it,' Siobhan told him. She didn't add: with half a dozen mourners. A speedy burial, no personal eulogy from the minister. It could have been called a pauper's funeral, only Supertramp had been no pauper.

'So what exactly is it that's in storage?' Rebus asked.

'Effects from his flat: everything from pens and pencils to a rather fine Persian carpet.'

'Had your eye on that, did you?'

The lawyer glared at Rebus. 'Plus the contents of his office.'

Rebus's back stiffened visibly. 'And where', he asked, 'might we find this storage facility?'

The answer was: on a bleak stretch of road round the northern perimeter of the city. Edinburgh, being coastal, was bounded on its northern and eastern sides by the Firth of Forth. Developers and the council had big plans for Granton, at the city's northernmost extreme.

'Active imagination required,' Rebus said as they drove.

Meaning: Granton at present was an unassuming, in places ugly and brutal, region of harsh sea-wall views, grey industrial buildings and redundancy. Broken factory windows, spray paint, sooty lorries. People like Sir Terence Conran had taken one look at the place and visualised a future of retail and leisure developments, Docklands-style warehouse apartments. They foresaw moneyed people moving in, jobs and homes, a whole new lifestyle.

'Any redeeming features?' Siobhan asked.

Rebus thought for a moment. 'The Starbank's not a bad boozer,' he said. She looked at him. 'You're right,' he conceded. 'That's more Newhaven than Granton.'

Seismic Storage, the premises were called. Three long rows of concrete bunkers, each one roughly three-quarters the size of a normal garage.

'Seismic,' the owner, Gerry Reagan explained, 'in that they'll survive an earthquake.'

'A real worry around here, earthquakes,' Rebus commented.

Reagan smiled. He was leading them down one of the rows. The weather was closing in, clouds gathering and a fierce wind blowing off the estuary. 'The Castle's built on a volcano,' he said. 'And do you remember those tremors a while back in Portobello?'

'Wasn't that mine workings?' Siobhan asked.

'Whatever,' Reagan said. There was constant humour in his eyes, topped off with bushy grey eyebrows. He wore metal-rimmed glasses on a chain around his neck. 'Thing is, my customers know their stuff'll be safe till kingdom come.'

'What sort of customers do you get?' Siobhan asked.

'All sorts: old folk who've moved into sheltered accommodation, no space for all their furniture. People flitting, either on their way here or heading south. Sometimes they sell up before their new place is ready. I've one or two collectors' cars, too.'

'Do they fit?' Rebus asked.

'It's snug,' Reagan conceded. 'One of them, we had to remove the bumpers. This is it.'

They'd come armed with a letter of authorisation from Blair

Martine, which Reagan now held in his hand, along with a key to unlock the up-and-over door.

'Unit thirteen,' he said, double-checking he was in the right place. Then he stooped to unlock the door, yanking it open.

As Martine had explained, Hastings' effects had first been stored in a warehouse. But then the warehouse had undergone conversion, forcing the lawyer to make other arrangements: 'I swear, him going off like that gave me more headaches than a dozen contested estates.' The effects had ended up at Seismic Storage only three years before, and Martine couldn't swear that everything was intact. He'd also told them that he hadn't known Hastings well – a few social occasions: dinners, parties. And that he'd had no dealings with Alasdair Grieve.

Siobhan's question afterwards: 'So if money wasn't why they left, what was?'

Rebus's response: 'Freddy didn't leave.'

'He left and came back,' Siobhan corrected. 'And Alasdair? Is it his body in the fireplace?'

Rebus had let that one go unanswered.

Now, as Reagan opened the door to its fullest extent, they saw that the place was a ready-made bric-a-brac shop, lacking only the cash register.

'Nice, neat job we made of it,' Reagan said, admiring his self-storage handiwork.

'Oh, dear heavens,' Siobhan gasped. Rebus was already punching numbers into his mobile phone.

'Who are you calling?' she asked.

He said nothing, straightening up when the call was answered. 'Grant? Is Wylie with you?' He grinned wickedly. 'Get a pen in your mitt, I'll give you directions. Little job here that's just perfect for the Time Team.'

Linford was back at Fettes, seated in ACC Carswell's office. He sipped his tea – china cup and saucer – while Carswell took a call. When the call was finished, Carswell lifted his own cup, held it to his lips and blew.

'Bit of a mess at St Leonard's, Derek.'

'Yes, sir.'

'I told Watson to his face, if he's got no control over his officers . . .'

'With respect, sir, a case like this one, tempers are bound to flare.'

Carswell nodded. 'I admire you for that, Derek.'

'Sir?'

'You're not the kind to drop fellow officers in the soup, even when they're at fault.'

'I'm sure I was partly to blame, sir. Nobody likes it when someone comes into an inquiry from outside.'

'So you become the scapegoat?'

'Not exactly, sir.' Linford was looking at his cup. Small blobs of oil dotted the surface. He wasn't sure if the tea, the water or the milk was to blame.

'We could transfer the investigation here,' Carswell was saying. 'Lock, stock and barrel if need be. Use Crime Squad officers to—'

'With respect, sir, it's late on in the investigation to start over from scratch. We'd lose a lot of time.' He paused. 'And it would send the budget rocketing.'

Carswell was known to like a nice, tidy budget. He frowned, took a sip from his cup. 'Don't want that,' he said. 'Not if we can help it.' He stared across the desk at Linford. 'You want to stay put, that's what you're telling me?'

'I think I can win them over, sir.'

'Well, you're braver than most, Derek.'

'Most of the team are absolutely fine,' Linford went on. 'It's just a couple . . .' He broke off, lifted his cup again.

Carswell looked at the notes he'd made for himself back in St Leonard's. 'Would that be DI Rebus and DC Clarke, by any chance?'

Linford said nothing; made sure his eyes didn't meet Carswell's.

'No one's irreplaceable, Derek,' the ACC said quietly. 'Believe me, no one.'

28

'It's *déjà vu* all over again,' Wylie said, as she and Hood inspected the contents. The concrete store was full almost to its roof. Desks, tables, chairs, rugs. Cardboard boxes, framed prints, a stereo system.

'This'll take days,' Hood complained. And with no Mrs Coghill to make coffee, no inviting kitchen. Just this bleak wasteland, the wind forcing tears from his eyes, rain threatening.

'Nonsense,' Rebus said. 'We're looking for paperwork. All the big items, we just put to one side. The interesting-looking stuff goes into the back of the car. We'll work shifts of two.'

Wylie looked at him. 'Meaning?'

'Meaning two clearing out the junk, and two sorting through all the papers. We'll take the stuff back to St Leonard's.'

'Fettes is closer,' Wylie reminded him.

He nodded. But Fettes was Linford's home turf. It was as though Siobhan could read his mind.

'That's even closer,' she said, nodding towards the glorified Portakabin which acted as Gerry Reagan's office.

Rebus nodded. 'I'll go square it with him.'

Grant Hood carried a portable TV out of the garage and placed it on the ground. 'Ask him if he's got a tarp, too.' He looked up. 'Rain's not far off.'

Half an hour later, the first showers blew in off the Forth, jabbing their faces and hands with needles of cold, and bringing a thick haar which seemed to cut them off from the world. Reagan had provided a large sheet of thick translucent polythene, which was going to blow away given half a chance. They'd fixed down three of its corners with bricks, leaving one open, flapping entrance. Then Reagan had a better idea: the garage two along was currently out of use. So the three of them – Hood, Wylie and Siobhan Clarke – carried the goods along to this new site while Reagan attempted to fold up his polythene sheet.

'What's the boss up to?' Hood asked Reagan.

Slitting his eyes against the rain, Reagan peered back towards his office, its lit windows like beacons of warmth and shelter against the darkening afternoon. 'Setting up the command post, that's what he told me.'

Hood and Wylie exchanged a look. 'And did that involve a kettle and a seat by the heater?' Wylie asked.

Reagan laughed.

'He said shifts,' Siobhan reminded them. 'You'll get your turn.' All the same, she wished they'd find some files or something, so she, too, would have an excuse to visit the Portakabin.

'I knock off at five,' Reagan said. 'No point staying here in the dark.'

'Any lamps we could use?' Siobhan asked. Wylie and Hood looked disappointed: a five o'clock homer sounded good to them. Reagan was looking doubtful, but for different reasons.

'We'd lock up after us,' Siobhan reassured him. 'Set the alarms or whatever.'

'I'm not sure my insurance company would be happy.'

'When are they ever?'

He laughed again, rubbed his head. 'I could stick around till six, I suppose.'

She nodded. 'Six it is then.'

Soon afterwards, they started finding the box-files. Reagan had produced a wheelbarrow, with the folded-up sheet of polythene covering its base. They loaded the files into the barrow, and Siobhan wheeled it towards the office. She pushed open the door and saw that Rebus was just finishing clearing one of the room's two desks. He'd piled all the stuff on the floor in a corner.

'Reagan said we could use this one,' he told her. He pointed to a door. 'There's a chemical toilet through there. Plus sink and kettle. Boil the water before you drink it.' She noticed there was a mug of coffee on the chair by Rebus.

'I think we could all do with a cup,' she said. She found a socket and plugged in her mobile phone, letting it charge while she filled the kettle and switched it on. Rebus went outside and started bringing the box-files in.

'It's getting pretty dark,' she said.

'How are you coping?'

'There's a light inside the garage. That's pretty much it. Mr Reagan says he can stay till six.'

Rebus checked his watch. 'So be it.'

'Just one thing,' she reminded him, 'this is the Grieve case we're working on now, right?'

He looked at her. 'We can probably swing overtime, if that's what you're thinking.'

'Might help pay for the Christmas shopping . . . if I ever get time to do any.'

'Christmas?'

'You know, festive time of year, coming up fast.'

He looked at her. 'You can just switch off like that?'

'I don't think you have to be obsessed to make a good detective.'

He went back outside, gathered more files into his arms. In the distance, he could see the three figures working in the mist – Wylie, Hood, Reagan – while their shadows danced on the pitted surface of the compound. The scene seemed timeless to him. Humans had been working like this, moving things in sub-zero gloom, for thousands of years. And to what end? So much of the past simply disappeared. But it was their job to make sure past crimes did not go unpunished, whether they be committed the day before or two decades before. Not because justice or the lawmakers demanded it, but for all the silent victims, the haunted souls. And for their own satisfaction, too. Because in trapping the guilty, they atoned for their own sins of commission and omission. How in God's name could you switch that all off for the sake of swapping some presents . . . ?

Siobhan came out to help, broke the spell. She cupped hands to her mouth and called out that she was making coffee. Cheers and clapping. The scene no longer timeless but discrete, the figures turned into personalities. Reagan thumping his gloved hands together, bouncing on his toes, glad to be part of this adventure: something to stave off the daily loneliness of his job. Hood whooping, but not breaking stride as he moved chairs from one unit to the other: the work ethic strong in him. Wylie raising her hand, announcing that she took two sugars: making sure she got what she wanted.

'Strange job, isn't it?' Siobhan commented.

'Yes,' he agreed. But she meant Reagan's.

'Every day stuck out here on your own, all these concrete boxes full of secrets and other people's stuff. Aren't you curious what else we'd find if we opened a few doors?'

Rebus smiled. 'Why do you think he's so keen to help out?'

'Because he's a generous soul?' Siobhan guessed.

'Or he doesn't want us snooping.' She looked at him. 'Reason I was indoors so long, I thought I'd take a look at his client list.'

'And?'

'Couple of names I recognised: fences who live in Pilton and Muirhouse.'

'Just along the road.' Rebus nodded. 'No way we can search without a warrant.'

'All the same, a useful piece of ammo should Mr Reagan start proving uncooperative.' He glanced at her. 'And something to bear in mind next time we pull either of them in on a charge: no point getting a search warrant for a flat in Muirhouse when the stuff's sitting in self-storage.'

They took a break, huddling in the office. Four of them: Hood said he wanted to keep going; Wylie could take his coffee out to him when she'd finished hers.

'Boy wouldn't go down well with the unions,' was Reagan's comment.

The heater was Calor gas, all three elements lit. Not much

insulation in the cabin. The long narrow window to the front wore a film of condensation, with occasional beads breaking free to trickle downwards, gathering on the sill. There was one overhead bulb, and a desk lamp. The room was fuggy and yellow-bathed. Reagan accepted a cigarette from Rebus, the two men forming a huddle while the non-smoking women edged away.

'New Year resolution,' Reagan said, examining the tip of the cigarette. 'I'm giving them up.'

'Reckon you'll make it?'

The man shrugged. 'Might do, all the practice I get – two or three times a year I try calling a halt.'

'Practice makes perfect,' Rebus admitted.

'How long do you reckon this'll all take?' Reagan asked.

'We appreciate your cooperation, sir.' Said in the voice of someone who had suddenly become an official, all cigarette-sharing *bonhomie* erased. Reagan got the point: this policeman could make a nuisance of himself given the motivation. Then the door flew open and Grant Hood staggered in. He was carrying a computer screen and keyboard, pushed his way past them and dropped it on to the cleared desk.

'What do you think?' he asked, getting his breath.

'Looks ancient,' Siobhan commented.

'Not much use without the hard drive,' Ellen Wylie added.

Hood grinned. It was the answer he'd been waiting for. He reached beneath his coat, to where something was tucked into his waistband. 'Hard disks like we have weren't around back then. Slot on the side is for floppies.' He pulled out half a dozen cardboard squares, circular holes in them like old novelty records. 'Nine-inch floppies,' he said, waving them in front of him. With his free hand, he patted the keyboard. 'Probably a DOS-based WP package. Which, if that doesn't say much to any of you, means I'm going to be stuck in here.' He put down the floppies and rubbed his hands in front of the flames. 'While you lot are out there seeing if you can find any more disks.'

By the end of play, they'd emptied half the garage, and a lot of what was left looked like furniture. Rebus took three box-files away with him, thinking he'd make an evening of it at St Leonard's. The station was quiet. This time of year, pickpockets and shoplifting were the major concerns: crowds in the Princes Street stores, wallets and purses bulging. You got muggings at cash machines, too. And depression: some said it was the short bursts of daylight and longer stretches of dark. People drank themselves angry, drank until they unravelled. Bust-ups, windows smashed – bus shelters; phone boxes; shops and pubs. They took knives to their loved ones, slashed at their own wrists. SAD: Seasonal Affective Disorder.

More work for Rebus and his colleagues. More work for the A&E departments, the social workers, the courts and prisons. Paperwork mounting as the Christmas cards started to arrive. Rebus had long since given up writing cards, but people persisted in sending them to him: family, colleagues, a few of his drinking cronies.

Father Conor Leary always sent one. But Leary was still convalescing, and Rebus hadn't been to see him for a while. Hospital beds reminded him of his daughter Sammy, unconscious after the hit-and-run which had put her in a wheelchair. In Rebus's experience, Christmas was about sham get-togethers, about pretending that all was well with the world. A celebration of one man's birth, carried out with tinsel and trappings, and conducted in a haze of white lies and alcohol.

Or maybe it was just him.

There was no sense of urgency as he studied each page from the box. He kept taking coffee and cigarette breaks, stepping outside, lighting up in the car park at the rear of the station. Business correspondence: deadly dull. Newspaper clippings: commercial properties for sale and rent, some of them circled, some with double question marks in the margin. Once Rebus had identified Freddy Hastings' handwriting, he was able to tell that it was a one-man operation, no other hand at work. No secretary. And where did Alasdair Grieve fit in? Meetings: Alasdair was always mentioned at the meetings; business lunches. Maybe he was a meeter and greeter, his surname lending a certain something to the operation. Cammo's brother, Lorna's brother, Alicia's son – someone prospective clients would want to dine with.

Back inside to warm his feet and dig into the box, retrieving another batch of documents. And then another cup of coffee, a wander downstairs to talk to the night shift in the Comms Room. Break-ins, fist fights, family quarrels. Cars stolen, vandalised. Burglar alarms tripped. A missing person reported. A patient who'd absconded from his hospital ward, dressed only in pyjamas. Car smashes: black ice on the roads. One alleged rape; one serious assault.

'Quiet night,' the duty officer said.

Camaraderie on the night shift. One officer shared his sandwich snack with Rebus. 'I always seem to make one more than I need.' Salami and lettuce on wholemeal bread. A carton of orange juice if Rebus wanted one, but he shook his head.

'This is fine,' he said.

Back at his desk, he jotted notes based on his findings, flagging some of the pages by dint of fixing Post-it notes to them. Looked at the office clock and saw it was almost midnight. Reached into his pocket and checked his cigarette packet: just the one left. That decided it. He locked the files in a drawer, put his coat on, and headed out. Cut through to Nicolson Street. There were all-night shops there, three or four of them. Cigarettes and a snack on his shopping list; maybe something for tomorrow's breakfast. The street was noisy. A group of teenagers screaming for a non-existent taxi; people weaving home, cartons of carry-out food held close to them, faces bathing in steam. Underfoot: greasy wrappings, dropped gobbets of tomato and onion, squashed chips. An ambulance sped past, blue light flashing but sirenless, eerily silent amidst the street's cacophony. Conversations turned high decibel by drink. And older groups, too, well dressed, heading home from a night at the Festival Theatre or Queen's Hall.

Clusters of young people, standing in doorways and the corners of buildings. Voices low, eyes scanning. Rebus saw crime where none existed; or perhaps it was that he was attuned to the *possibility* of crime. Had the midnight revels always been this harsh and alarming? He didn't think so. The city was changing for the worse, and no amount of imaginative construction in glass and concrete could hide the fact. The old city was dying, wounded by these roars, this new paradigm of . . . not lawlessness exactly, but certainly lack of respect: for surroundings, neighbours, self.

The fear was all too apparent in the tense faces of the elders, their theatre programmes tightly rolled. But there was something mixed in with the fear: sadness and impotence. They couldn't hope to change this scene; they could only hope to survive it. And back home they would collapse on the sofa, door locked and bolted, curtains or shutters closed tight. Tea would be poured into the pot, biscuits nibbled as they stared at the wallpaper and dreamed of the past.

There was a scrum outside Rebus's chosen shop. Cars had drawn up kerbside, music blaring from within. Two dogs were attempting to copulate, cheered on by their youthful owners as girls squealed and looked away. Rebus went inside, the glare forcing his eyes closed for a moment. A pack of lorne sausage, four rolls. Then up to the counter for cigarettes. A white poly bag to take his purchases home. Home meant turning right, but he turned left.

He needed to pee, that was all, and the Royal Oak was near by. Just off the main drag, the place never seemed to close. Thing was, he could use their toilet without entering the bar, so it wasn't as if he was going there to drink. You walked through the doorway, and the bar was straight ahead through another door, but if you headed down the stairs, that's where the toilets were. The toilets, plus another, quieter bar. The upstairs bar at the Oak was famous. Open late, and always, it seemed, with live music. Locals would sing the old songs, but then some Spanish flamenco guitarist might do his piece, followed by a guy with an Asian face and Scots inflections playing the blues.

You never could tell.

As Rebus made for the stairs, he looked in through the window. The pub was tiny, and packed this night with gleaming faces: old folkies and hardened drinkers, the curious and the captivated. Someone was singing unaccompanied. Rebus saw fiddles and an accordion, but resting while their owners concentrated on the rich baritone voice. The singer was standing in the corner. Rebus couldn't see him, but that's where all eyes were focused. The words were by Burns:

What force or guile could not subdue,
Through many warlike ages,
Is wrought now by a coward few,
For hireling traitors' wages . . .

Rebus was halfway down when he stopped. He'd recognised one of the faces. Back up he went, his face a bit closer to the window this time. Yes, seated next to the piano: Cafferty's pal, the one from the Bar-L. What was his name? Rab, that was it. Sweating, hair slick. His face was jaundiced, eyes dull. His fist was wrapped around what Rebus took to be a vodka and orange.

And then the singer took a step forward, and now Rebus saw who it was.

Cafferty.

The English steel we could disdain,
Secure in valour's station,
But English gold has been our bane –
Such a parcel of rogues in a nation . . .

As the verse ended, Cafferty glanced towards the window. He was smiling grimly as Rebus pushed open the door, starting the final verse as Rebus made his way to the bar. Rab was watching, trying to place him perhaps. One of the barmaids took Rebus's order: a half of Eighty and a whisky. There was no conversation in the bar, respectful silence and even a tear in one patriot's eye as she sat on her stool with her brandy and Coke raised to her lips, her ragged boyfriend stroking her shoulders from behind.

When the song finished, there was applause, a few whistles and cheers. Cafferty bowed his head, lifted his whisky glass and toasted the room. As the clapping subsided, the accordionist took it as his cue to commence. Cafferty accepted a few compliments as he made his way to the piano, where he leaned down to mutter something in Rab's ear. Then, as Rebus had known he would, he came over to the bar.

'Something to ponder, come the election,' Cafferty said.

'Plenty of rogues in Scotland,' Rebus said. 'I can't see how independence would mean less of them.'

Cafferty wasn't going to rise to it. Instead, he toasted him, emptied his glass, and ordered another. 'And one for my friend Strawman.'

'I've got one,' Rebus said.

'Be nice to me, Strawman. I'm celebrating coming home.' Cafferty eased a folded newspaper out of his pocket, placed it on the bar top. It was folded at the commercial property section.

'In the market?' Rebus asked.

'I might be,' Cafferty said with a wink.

'What for?'

'I hear there's a killing to be made, way the Old Town is now.'

Rebus nodded towards the piano, where Rab had angled his chair, the better to watch the bar. 'He's not just on the booze, is he? What is it, jellies?'

Cafferty looked over towards his minder. 'Place like the Bar-L, you take whatever you need. Mind you,' he smiled, 'I've been in cells bigger than this.'

Two glasses of malt had arrived. Cafferty added a dribble of water to his, while Rebus watched. Rab seemed to him such an unlikely companion – doubtless fine in a place like the Bar-L; you'd need muscle there. But out here, back on his home ground where he had all the men he needed, what was it tied Cafferty to Rab, Rab to Cafferty? Had something happened in jail . . . or was something happening out here? Cafferty was holding the jug above Rebus's glass, awaiting a reaction. Rebus nodded eventually, and when the pouring was done raised the glass.

'Cheers,' he said.

'*Slainte.*' Cafferty took a sip, let it roll around his mouth.

'You seem surprisingly chipper,' Rebus told him, lighting a cigarette.

'What good's a long face going to do?'

'You mean apart from cheering me up?'

'Ah, you're a hard man. I sometimes wonder if you're not harder than me even.'

'Want to put it to the test?'

Cafferty laughed. 'In my current condition? And you with a face like thunder?' He shook his head. 'Another time maybe.'

They stood in silence, Cafferty applauding when the accordionist finished. 'He's French, you know. Barely a word of English.' Then, to the musician: '*Encore! Encore, mon ami!*'

The accordionist acknowledged this with a bow. He was seated at one of the tables, a guitarist beside him tuning up for the next slot. When he began to play again, something a little more sombre this time, Cafferty turned to Rebus.

'Funny, you bringing up Bryce Callan the other day.'

'Why?'

'Just that I'd been meaning to call Barry, see how old Bryce was doing.'

'And what did Barry say?'

Cafferty looked down into his drink. 'He didn't say anything. I got as far as some dogsbody, who told me he'd pass my message on.' His face was dark, but he laughed anyway. 'Wee Barry still hasn't got back.'

'Wee Barry is a big player these days, Cafferty. Maybe he can't afford to be seen with you.'

'Aye, well, good luck to him, but he'll never be a quarter the man his uncle was.' He drained his glass; Rebus felt obliged to order refills. Between times, he drained his half-pint and the blended whisky which had accompanied it, so he could now concentrate on the malt. Why the hell was Cafferty telling him all this?

'Maybe Bryce did the right thing,' Cafferty said, as their drinks came. 'Getting out like that, retiring to the sun.'

Rebus added water to both glasses. 'You thinking of following him?'

'I might at that. I've never been abroad.'

'Never?'

Cafferty shook his head. 'The ferry to Skye, that was enough for me.'

'There's a bridge these days.'

Cafferty scowled. 'Wherever they find romance, they replace it.'

Privately, Rebus didn't disagree, but he was damned if Cafferty was going to know that. 'The bridge is a lot handier,' he said instead.

Cafferty's scowl looked even more pained. But it wasn't that . . . he was in real pain. He bent forward, hand going to his stomach. Put down his drink and fumbled in his pocket for some tablets. He was wearing a dark woollen blazer with a black polo neck beneath. He shook two tablets out, washed them down with water poured into an empty glass.

'You okay?' Rebus asked, trying not to sound too concerned.

Cafferty caught his breath at last, patted Rebus's forearm as though reassuring a friend.

'Bit of indigestion, that's all.' He picked up his drink again. 'We're all on the way out, eh, Strawman? Barry could have gone the way of his uncle, but instead he's a businessman. And you . . . I'll bet most of your CID colleagues are younger, college-educated. The old ways don't work any more, that's what they'll tell you.' He opened his arms. 'If I'm a liar, let me hear it.'

Rebus stared at him, then looked down. 'You're not a liar.'

Cafferty seemed pleased to have found common ground. 'You can't be too far off retirement.'

'I've a few years in me yet.'

Cafferty raised his hands in surrender. 'The phrase more's the pity never entered my mind.'

And this time when he laughed, Rebus almost joined in. Another round of whiskies was ordered. This time, Cafferty added a vodka and fresh, which he took over to Rab. When he came back, Rebus asked again about the bodyguard.

'Only, the way he looks tonight, I'm not sure he'd be much use to you.'

'He'd do fine in a clinch, don't you worry.'

'I'm not worried. I'm just thinking this may be the best chance I ever get to take a pop at you.'

'Take a pop at me? Christ, man, state I'm in, if you sneezed I'd be in a thousand pieces on the floor. Now come on, have another.'

Rebus shook his head. 'I've got work to do.'

'At this hour?' Cafferty's voice had risen so much, other drinkers were looking at him. Not that he was paying them any heed. 'No crows to scare off this time of night, Strawman.' He laughed again. 'Not too many of these old howffs left, eh? It's all theme pubs now. Do you remember the Castle o' Cloves?'

Rebus shook his head.

'Best pub there was. I drank there often. And now . . . well, down it came. They built a DIY store where it stood. Just up the road from your cop shop.'

Rebus nodded. 'I know the spot.'

'All changing,' Cafferty said. 'Maybe you'd be better out of the game, after all.' He lifted the glass to his lips. 'Just a thought, mind.' He finished the drink.

Rebus took a deep breath. 'Ah-choo!' Making show of sneezing across Cafferty's chest, then studying his handiwork. His eyes met Cafferty's. If looks were weapons, they'd have cleared the pub. 'You lied to me,' Rebus said quietly, walking away from the bar as the guitarist finally got his instrument in tune.

'You'll go to your grave a gobshite!' Cafferty yelled, brushing flecks of saliva from his polo neck. His voice stilled the music for a moment. 'Hear me, Strawman? I'll be dancing on your bastard coffin!'

Rebus let the door close behind him, inhaled the street's smoke-free air. Noises off: more kids heading home. He rested his head against a wall, a cold compress for his burning thoughts.

I'll be dancing on your coffin.

Strange words to come from a dying man. Rebus walked: down Nicolson Street to the Bridges, and from there down into the Cowgate. He stopped near the mortuary, smoked a cigarette. He still had his bag with him: rolls and sausage. He felt like he'd never be hungry again. His stomach was too full of bile. He sat on a wall.

I'll be dancing on your coffin.

A jig it would be, unrestrained and awkward, but a jig all the same.

Back up Infirmary Street. Back along to the Royal Oak. He kept back from the windows this time. No music: just a man's voice.

How slow ye move, ye heavy hours,
The joyless day how dreary.
It wasna sae ye glinted by,
When I was wi' my dearie . . .

Cafferty again; another of Burns' songs. His voice full of pain and pleasure, pulsing with life. And Rab, seated by the piano, eyes almost closed, breathing laboured. Two men fresh minted from the Bar-L. One dying in full voice; the other wasted on freedom.

It was wrong. It was very, very wrong.

Rebus felt it in his own doomed heart.

Part Three

Beyond This Mist

Yet frost under sunlight can sparkle like hope
even while muscles cramp, and the freezing damp
can whisper 'let the bottle rest for once.
There are warm mysteries beyond this mist.'

Angus Calder, 'Love Poem'

29

Jerry walked into the dole office frozen and soaked. There hadn't been any shaving foam left in the can, so he'd had to use ordinary soap, and then his last razor was in the bath, where Jayne had blunted it shaving her legs. Cue the morning's first argument. He'd nicked himself a couple of times; one of the spots wouldn't stop bleeding. And now his face was stinging from the sudden sleet, and of course as soon as he got in through the dole office door, didn't the cloud break and the sun come out?

It was a cruel city, this.

And then it turned out, after he'd waited half an hour, that his appointment wasn't at the dole office at all, but with the DSS, which was another half-hour's walk. He almost gave up and headed home, but something stopped him. Home: was that what it was? How come these days it felt like a prison, a place where his gaoler wife could nag and grind him down?

So he made for the DSS office, and they told him he was an hour late, and he started explaining but nobody was listening.

'Take a seat. I'll see what we can do.'

So he sat down with the wheezing masses, next to an old guy with a blood-curdling cough who spat on the floor when he'd finished. Jerry moved seats. The sun had dried out his jacket, but his shirt beneath was still damp, and he was shivering. Maybe he was coming down with something. Three-quarters of an hour he sat there. Other people came and went. Twice he went up to the desk, where the same woman said they were trying to find him 'a slot'. Her mouth looked like a slot, thin and disapproving. He sat back down.

Where else was there for him to go? He thought of working in an office like Nic's, nice and warm and with coffee on tap, watching the short skirts swish past his desk, one of them leaning over the photocopier. Christ, wouldn't that be heaven? Nic was probably heading off to lunch now, out to some swank place with crisp white tablecloths. Business lunches and business drinks and deals done with a handshake. Anybody could do a job like that. But then not everybody married the boss's cousin.

Nic had phoned him last night, started given him a roasting for bottling out, running off into the night like that, but making a joke of it in the end. Jerry had caught an inkling of something: Nic was afraid of him. And then it had struck him why: Jerry could tell the cops, spill the beans. Nic *had* to keep him sweet, that was why he turned the episode into a joke, ended with the words, 'I forgive you. After all, we go back a long way, eh? The two of us against the world.'

Except that right now, it felt like Jerry was all on his own against the world, stuck here in this smelly hole, no one to help him. He was thinking back: *two of us against the world*, when had that ever been true? When had they ever been equals, partners? *What in God's name did they see in one another?* He thought maybe he had an answer for that now, too. It was a way of cheating time, because when they were together they were the same kids they'd always been. And so the things they did . . . they really *were* a game, albeit a deadly serious one.

Someone left their paper behind when they went in for their interview. Christ, and the guy had turned up twenty minutes after Jerry, yet here the bastard was, waltzing into a cubicle ahead of him! Jerry slid over, picked up the tabloid, but didn't open it. There was that bile in his gut again, that fear of what stories he might find inside: rapes, assaults, not knowing if Nic was responsible. Who knew what Nic was doing behind his back, all the nights they didn't meet? And all the other stories, too: newly-weds, happy marriages, stormy relationships, sex problems, babies being born to famous mums. Everything bounced back on his own life, and all it did was make him feel worse.

Jayne: *clock's ticking*.

Nic: *time you grew up*.

The minute hand on the clock above the desk moved another notch. Clock-watching: wasn't that something you did in offices, when you weren't watching the skirts swish past? Who was to say Nic had it so good? He'd been working for Barry Hutton's company these past eight years, hadn't seen much in the way of promotion.

'Sometimes,' he'd complained to Jerry, 'that family thing can backfire on you. Barry daren't promote me or everyone'll just say it's for who I am, not what I do. Do you see?'

And then, when Cat had left him: 'That bastard Hutton's just looking to get rid of me. Now Cat's done a runner, he sees me as an embarrassment. See what she's done to me, Jerry? The cow's as good as lost me my job. Her and her bastard cousin!'

Fuming, seething, raging.

And this from a guy who lived in a £200,000 house and had a job and car! Who was it really needed to grow up? Jerry wondered about this more and more.

'He'll ditch me, Jer, soon as he gets half a chance.'

'Jayne says she's going to ditch me, too.'

But Nic hadn't wanted to hear about Jayne. His only comment: 'They're all as bad as each other, swear to God, pal.'

All as bad as each other.

He stomped back to the desk. What was he? A dummy or what? Wasn't he married, settled? Didn't he deserve a bit of respect?

Didn't he deserve that at the very least, and maybe something more besides?

The woman was there. She'd fetched herself a mug of coffee. Jerry's throat felt dry; couldn't stop shivering.

'Look,' he said, 'are you taking the piss or what?'

She had these glasses on, thick black frames. There were lipstick smears on the rim of the mug. Her hair looked dyed, and she was getting on for fat. Middle-aged, going to seed. But at the moment, she was in a position of power, and no way she was letting him interfere with that. She gave a cold smile, blinked so he saw her blue eyeshadow.

'Mr Lister, if you'll try to stay calm . . .'

Necklace hanging around her neck, all mixed in with the creases of loose skin. Big bust on her, too. Jesus, he'd never seen a chest like it.

'Mr Lister.' Trying to drag his attention back to her face. But he was transfixed, his hands gripping the edge of the desk. He saw her in the back of the van, saw himself giving her a good punch in that lipsticked mouth, ripping at the blouse, necklace sent flying.

'Mr Lister!'

She was getting to her feet. He'd been leaning further and further across the desk. And now members of staff were closing in, alerted by her yell.

'Jesus,' he said. Couldn't think of anything else to say; his whole body was shaking, head spinning. He tried to clear his head, wipe the blood from the pictures there. He was eye to eye with her for a second, and he felt she could see what he'd been thinking, every vivid frame of it.

'Oh, Jesus.'

Two big blokes coming at him; that was all he needed, get arrested. He shoved his way out of there, back into the outside world where the sun was drying the streets and everything looked eerily normal.

'What's happening?' he said. He found he was crying, couldn't stop himself. Stumbled blearily along the street, holding the wall for support. He just kept walking, breaking into a sweat eventually. It took him the best part of three hours.

He'd walked clean across town.

Grey morning. Rebus waited for the rush hour to pass before setting out.

Glasgow's Barlinnie Prison lay just off the M8 motorway. If you knew what you were looking for, you could see it in the near distance as you drove between Edinburgh and Glasgow. It sat on the edge of the

Riddrie housing scheme, unsignposted until you got really close. At visiting time, you could follow the cars and pedestrians. Tattooed men in their fifties, wiry and sunken-cheeked, off to visit pals who'd got caught. Stressed mothers, kids in tow. Quiet relatives, not quite sure how things had come to this.

All of them bound for HMP Barlinnie.

The Victorian blocks sat behind high stone walls, but the reception area itself was modern. Workmen were busy on the finishing touches. A member of staff was checking visitors for drug contamination. You swiped the magic glove over them, and it came up positive if they'd recently been in contact with drugs. Positive meant no open visit: you could still go in, but only with a glass wall between you and the prisoner. Bags were being checked, and then placed inside lockers, to be retrieved on the way out. Rebus knew that the visiting area had been revamped, too, with smart new seating arrangements and even a play area for the kids.

But inside the jail, it would be the same old wings. Slopping-out was still a fact of life, and the smell permeated the interiors. There were two new wings, but restricted to sex offenders and drug users. It rankled with the 'pros', the career criminals who didn't think scum like that deserved to live, never mind the special treatment.

Another new addition was the cubicles for agent interviews. This was where lawyers met their clients: glass-fronted but allowing for privacy. The Assistant Governor, Bill Nairn, seemed pleased with the renovations as he showed Rebus around. He even took Rebus into one of the cubicles, the two men sitting down opposite one another.

'Far cry from the old days, eh?' Nairn beamed.

Rebus nodded. 'I've stayed in tattier hotels.' The two men knew one another of old: Nairn had worked for the Procurator Fiscal's office in Edinburgh, and then in the city's Saughton Prison, before the promotion to the Bar-L.

'Cafferty doesn't know what he's missing,' Rebus added.

Nairn shifted in his seat. 'Look, John, I know it grates when we let one back out . . .'

'It's not that, it's *why* he's out.'

'The man's got cancer.'

'And the Guinness boss had Alzheimer's.'

Nairn stared at him. 'What are you saying?'

'I'm saying Cafferty looks pretty chirpy.'

Nairn shook his head. 'He's ill, John. You know it and I know it.'

'I know he said you wanted rid of him.' Nairn looked at him blankly. 'Because he was in danger of running the show.'

Now Nairn smiled. 'John, you've seen this place. Every door's kept locked. No easy access. Think how hard it would be for one man to run all five wings.'

'They mix though, don't they? Wood-shop, textiles, chapel . . . I've seen them wandering around outside.'

'You've seen the trusties, and always with a guard. Cafferty didn't have that level of freedom.'

'He didn't run the show?'

'No.'

'Then who does?' Nairn shook his head. 'Come on, Bill. You get drugs in here, moneylending, gang fights. You've got a scrap contract to strip anything valuable out of old wiring: don't tell me none of that stuff's been sharpened and used for a stabbing.'

'Isolated cases, John. I'm not going to deny it: drugs are the big problem here. But it's still petty stuff. And it wasn't Cafferty's bailiwick.'

'Then whose was it?'

'I'm telling you, it's not organised that way.'

Rebus leaned back in his chair, studied his surroundings: clean paint and new carpets. 'Know what, Bill? You can change the surface, but it'll take more than that to change the culture.'

'It's a start, though,' Nairn said determinedly.

Rebus scratched his nose. 'Any chance I can see Cafferty's medical records?'

'No.'

'Then can you take a look for me? Put my mind at rest.'

'X-rays don't lie, John. The hospitals here are pretty hot on cancer. It's always been a west coast growth industry.'

Rebus smiled, as was expected. A solicitor was entering the cubicle next door. The prisoner followed a few moments later. He looked young, bewildered. Remand, probably; up to court later in the day. Yet to be found guilty, but already tasting the low life.

'What was he like?' Rebus asked.

Nairn's pager had sounded. He was fumbling to switch it off. 'Cafferty?' Looking towards where the pager was clipped to his belt. 'He wasn't too bad. You know how it is with career villains: serve their time, just part and parcel of the job, like a temporary relocation.'

'You think he's changed?'

Nairn shrugged. 'Man's older.' He paused. 'I'm assuming power's shifted in Edinburgh while he's been away.'

'Not so you'd notice.'

'He's back to his old ways, then?'

'He's not ready for the Costa del Sol just yet.'

Nairn smiled. 'Bryce Callan, now there's a name from the vaults. Never did manage to lock him up, did we?'

'Not for want of trying.'

'John . . .' Nairn looked down at his hands, which rested on the table top. 'You used to come and visit Cafferty.'

'So?'

'So it's more than just the usual cop/villain thing with you two, isn't it?'

'How do you mean, Bill?'

'I'm just saying . . .' He sighed. 'I'm not sure what I'm saying.'

'You're saying I'm too close to Cafferty? Maybe obsessed, not objective?' Rebus was remembering Siobhan's words: you didn't need to be obsessed to be a good cop. Nairn looked about to argue. 'I agree a hundred per cent,' Rebus went on. 'Sometimes I feel closer to that bastard than I do . . .' He bit off the ending: *to my own family*. Frankly, most of the time it felt like no contest. 'That's why I'd rather he was in here.'

'Out of sight, out of mind?'

Rebus leaned forward, looked around. 'Strictly between us?' Nairn nodded. 'I'm scared what'll happen, Bill.'

Nairn held his gaze. 'He's planning to have a go at you?'

'If what you say is true, what's he got to lose?'

Nairn was thoughtful. 'What about you?'

'Me?'

'Say he's going to die, natural causes. Doesn't that cheat you? No chance of *you* trying to get at *him*? One final victory.'

One final victory.

'Bill,' Rebus chastised, 'do I look the sort to you who'd have any truck with that?'

The two men smiled. Next door, the prisoner's voice was rising.

'But ah havnae done nuthin'!'

Nairn tutted. 'Double negatives,' he said.

'Thought these booths were soundproofed?' Rebus said. Nairn's shrug told him they'd done their best. Then Rebus had a thought. 'What about someone called Rab, released about the same time as Cafferty?'

Nairn nodded. 'Rab Hill.'

'Rab was Cafferty's bodyguard?'

'I wouldn't go that far. They were only on the same wing for four, five months.'

Rebus frowned. 'Way Cafferty tells it, they were best pals.'

Nairn shrugged. 'Prison makes for strange alliances.'

'Rab's not coping too well with the outside world.'

'No? You'll excuse me if my heart doesn't bleed.'

The voice from next door again: 'How many times dae ah huv tae tell ye?'

Rebus got to his feet. *Strange alliances* he was thinking. Cafferty and Rab Hill. 'How did it come about, Cafferty's cancer?'

'How do you mean?'

'How was it diagnosed?'

'Usual way. He hadn't been feeling too hot. Took him in for tests, and bingo.'

'Just do me one favour, Bill. Look at our friend Rab. Medical records, whatever you've got. Will you do that for me?'

'Know something, John? You're harder work than half my prisoners.'

'Then pray a jury never finds me guilty.'

Bill Nairn was about to laugh that off, until he saw the look in Rebus's eyes.

By the time he got to Seismic Storage, Ellen Wylie and Siobhan Clarke had finished emptying the container. On the spare desk in Reagan's office sat eight columns of paperwork. The women were warming themselves by the heater, mugs of tea in their hands.

'What now, sir?' Wylie asked.

'St Leonard's,' Rebus said. 'That interview room you were using as an office, we'll take them there.'

'So no one else can see them?' Siobhan guessed.

Rebus looked at her. Her face was pink with cold, nose shiny. She was wearing ankle boots with socks over black woollen tights; a pale grey scarf accentuating the colour in her cheeks.

'Have you got two cars?' Rebus asked. The women agreed that they had. 'Load them up, and I'll see you back at base, okay?'

He left them to it, drove to the South Side and was smoking a cigarette in the car park when the Chief Super arrived in his Peugeot 406.

'Mind if I have a word, sir?' Rebus asked, in place of any greeting.

'Out here or in the warm?' Farmer Watson hoisted his briefcase, checked his watch. 'I've a noon appointment.'

'This'll only take a minute.'

'Fair enough. My office, soon as you've finished out here.'

The Farmer went in, closed the door. Rebus nipped his cigarette, tossed it, and followed.

Watson was firing up the coffee-maker when Rebus knocked at his open door. He glanced up, nodded for Rebus to enter. 'You look rough, Inspector.'

'I was working late.'

'What on?'

'The Grieve case.'

The Farmer looked at him again. 'Is that true?'

'Yes, sir.'

'Only, from what I hear, you're involving yourself in everything but.'

'I think the cases tie up.'

With the machine on, the Farmer retreated behind his desk. He sat down and motioned for Rebus to do the same, but Rebus stayed standing.

'Progress?'

'Getting there, sir.'

'And DI Linford?'

'He's working his own leads.'

'But the two of you are in contact?'

'Absolutely, sir.'

'And Siobhan's keeping out of his way?'

'He's keeping out of *hers*.'

The Chief Super seemed dissatisfied. 'I'm getting no end of flak.'

'From Fettes?'

'And beyond. Someone from the Scottish Secretary's office was on to me first thing this morning, wanting results.'

'Hard to run an election campaign', Rebus guessed, 'with a murder inquiry ongoing.'

The Farmer stared at him coldly. 'Almost his exact words.' His eyes narrowed a fraction. 'So what's on your mind?'

Now Rebus sat down, leaning forward, elbows on knees. 'It's Cafferty, sir.'

'Cafferty?' Whatever he'd been expecting, Watson hadn't been expecting this. 'What about him?'

'He's out of the Bar-L and back here.'

'So I've heard.'

'I want a watch kept on him.' There was silence in the room as Rebus waited in vain for the Chief Super to comment. 'I think we need to know what he's up to.'

'You know we can't do that without good reason.'

'His rep's not enough?'

'Lawyers and the media would have a field day. Besides, you know how stretched we are.'

'We'll be more stretched once Cafferty gets started.'

'Started on what?'

'I bumped into him last night.' He saw the look on his chief's face. 'Completely by accident. Thing was, he'd been browsing the *Scotsman*'s commercial property section.'

'So?'

'So what's he after?'

'Turning a profit, maybe.'

'That's more or less what he said.'

'Well then?'

Only it wasn't the way he'd put it: *a killing to be made* . . .

'Look,' the Farmer rubbed his temples, 'let's just get on with the work at hand. Clear up the Grieve case and I'll think about Cafferty. Deal?'

Rebus nodded distractedly. The door was still ajar. A knock came, and a uniform appeared round it. 'Visitor for DI Rebus.'

'Who is it?'

'She didn't say, sir. Just told me to tell you she'd not brought any peanuts. Said you'd understand.'

Rebus understood.

30

Lorna Grieve was in the waiting area. He unlocked the interview room, then remembered that Freddy Hastings' stuff was piled up in there. So he told her there was a change of plan, led her across the road to the Maltings.

'You have to be drunk before you can talk to me?' she teased. She was dressed to the tens: tight red leather trousers tucked into knee-high black boots; a black silk blouse with plunging neckline, black suede jacket open over it. More than enough make-up, and her hair freshly styled. She was carrying shopping bags from a couple of boutiques.

Rebus ordered fresh orange and lemonade for himself. She seemed to think her words had forced him into it, rose to the occasion by asking for a Bloody Mary.

'Mary, Queen of Scots, isn't it?' she said. 'Head chopped off, that's the bloody part.'

'I wouldn't know.'

'Never drunk one? Perfect pick-me-up.' She waited for a joke, but he didn't offer one. Nodded when the barmaid asked if she wanted Lea and Perrin's. They sat at a table inlaid with squares. She admired the pattern.

'It's so people can play chess,' Rebus explained.

'Loathsome game. Takes for ever, and at the end it all falls apart. No sense of climax.' Another pause. Again, Rebus wasn't biting.

'Cheers,' he said.

'First one today.' She took a gulp of her drink. Rebus doubted her veracity: he considered himself something of an expert, and would say she'd had at least a couple of belts already.

'So what can I do for you?' The commerce of the everyday: people wanting things from people. Sometimes it was an exchange, sometimes not.

'I want to know what's happening.'

'Happening?'

'The murder inquiry: we're being kept in the dark.'

'I don't think that's true.'

She lit a cigarette; didn't offer him one. 'Well, *is* anything happening?'

'We'll let you know as soon as we can.'

She straightened her back. 'That's not good enough.'

'I'm sorry.'

She narrowed her eyes. 'No, you're not. The family should be told—'

'In point of fact, it's the widow we'd talk to first.'

'Seona? You'll have to get in the queue. She's a media darling now, you know. Papers, TV . . . falling over themselves for a photo of the "brave widow", carrying on where her husband left off.' She modulated her voice, imitating Seona Grieve: '"It's what Roddy would have wanted." Like hell it is.'

'How do you mean?'

'Roddy may have seemed the quiet type, but there was steel in him, too. His wife running for MSP? He wouldn't have wanted that. It turns *her* into the martyr rather than him. He's already being forgotten about, except when she dusts off the corpse in the great cause of publicity!'

There were only the two of them in the bar; all the same, the barmaid gave a warning look.

'Easy,' Rebus said.

Her eyes were liquid with tears. Rebus got the feeling they weren't for anyone but Lorna herself: the lost one, the forgotten one. 'I've got the right to know what's going on.' Her eyes were clearing as she looked at him. 'Special rights,' she said in a low voice.

'Look,' he said, 'what happened that night—'

'I don't want to hear it.' She shook her head, steadied herself with another gulp of Bloody Mary, reducing it to ice.

'Whatever you're going through, if I can help I will, but don't resort to blackm—'

She was on her feet. 'I don't know why I came.'

He stood up, grabbed her hands. 'What have you taken, Lorna?'

'Just some . . . My doctor prescribed them. Not supposed to mix with alcohol.' Her eyes were everywhere but on him. 'That's all it is.'

'I'll get a patrol car to run you—'

'No, no, I'll find a cab. Don't worry.' She modelled a smile for him. 'Don't worry,' she repeated.

He picked her bags up for her; she seemed to have forgotten they were there. 'Lorna,' he said, 'have you ever met a man called Gerald Sithing?'

'I don't know. Who is he?'

'I think Hugh knows him. He runs a group called the Knights of Rosslyn.'

'Hugh keeps that side of his life separate. He knows I'd laugh at him.' She was on the verge of laughing now; she was on the verge of more than laughter. Rebus led her from the bar.

'Why do you ask?' she said.

'Doesn't matter.' He saw Grant Hood waving from across the road. In the distance, Siobhan Clarke and Ellen Wylie were unloading their cars. Hood dodged the traffic.

'What's up?' Rebus asked.

'The reconstruction,' Hood told him breathlessly. 'We've got a printout.'

Rebus nodded thoughtfully, then looked towards Lorna Grieve. 'Maybe you should see this,' he said.

So they went into St Leonard's and took her to an empty office. Hood fetched the computer graphic while Rebus provided tea. She wanted two sugars; he added a third, watched her drink.

'What's the mystery?' she asked.

'It's a face,' he explained slowly, studying her. 'The university in Glasgow put it together for us from a skull.'

'Queensberry House?' she guessed, amused by his look of surprise. 'Not all the brain cells have emigrated to a better place. Why do you want me to see it?' Then that, too, came to her. 'You think it might be Alasdair?' She started shaking; Rebus realised his mistake.

'Maybe it'd be better if—'

Rising to her feet, she knocked the tea on to the floor, but seemed not to notice. 'Why? What would Alasdair be doing . . . ? He sends postcards.'

Rebus was cursing himself for being an insensitive bastard, short-sighted, unsubtle, twisted.

And then Grant Hood was in the doorway, brandishing the picture. She snatched it from him, stared at it intently, then burst out laughing.

'It's nothing like him,' she said. 'You bloody imbecile.'

Imbecile: he hadn't got to that one yet. He took the sheet from her. It was a good likeness of someone, but he had to agree: judging by the paintings in Alicia Grieve's studio, this was not her son. The face was a completely different shape, hair a different colour . . . cheekbones, chin, forehead . . . No, whoever it was in the fireplace, it wasn't Alasdair Grieve.

That would have been too simple. Rebus's life had never been simple; no reason to suppose it would start now.

Wylie was in the doorway, too, alerted by the laughter: not a regular sound in a police station.

'He thought it was Alasdair,' Lorna Grieve was saying, pointing at Rebus. 'He told me my brother was dead! As if one wasn't enough.' There was poison in her eyes. 'Well, you've had your little laugh, and I hope you're happy.' She stormed out of the office and down the corridor.

'Go after her,' Rebus told Wylie. 'Make sure she finds the way out. And here . . .' He stooped down, retrieved the shopping bags. 'Give her these.'

She stared at him for a moment.

'Go!' he yelled.

'I hear and obey,' Ellen Wylie muttered. After she'd gone, Rebus slumped back down on his chair, rubbed both hands through his hair. Grant Hood was watching him.

'Not looking for tips, I hope,' Rebus told him.

'No, sir.'

'Because if you are, here's the best I can offer: study what I do, and then strive to do the exact fucking opposite. That way, you might make something of yourself.' He dragged his hands down his face, stared at the picture.

'Who the hell are you?' he asked. For some reason, he knew Skelly was the key, not just to Hastings' suicide and the four hundred grand, but to Roddy Grieve's murder, too . . . and maybe a lot more besides.

They sat in the cramped interview room, door closed to passers-by. People in the station were beginning to talk about them, calling them 'the Manson family', 'the Lodge', 'the swingers' club'. Hood was seated in the corner. He had the computer set up. Its screen was weird: black background, orange writing. He'd warned that the disks might be corrupted. Rebus, Wylie and Clarke sat round the centre table, box-files at their feet, the computer-generated image of the Queensberry House victim in front of them.

'You know what we have to do?' Rebus told them. Wylie and Clarke shared a look, sceptical of that 'we'.

'MisPers,' Wylie guessed. 'Back into the files and try to match this with one of the photos.'

Rebus nodded; Wylie shook her head. He turned to Hood: 'Any problems?'

'Seems to be running fine,' Hood said, hammering keys two-fingered. 'Printer connection's a problem. None of the ones we've got will fit. Might have to scour the second-hand shops.'

'So what's on the disks?' Siobhan Clarke asked.

He looked at her. 'Give me a chance.' And got back to work. Ellen Wylie lifted the first box-file on to the table and opened it. Rebus hoisted up three more, patted them.

'I've already done these,' he said. The others looked at him. 'Late night,' he said, winking.

Just so they knew he wasn't slacking.

Lunch consisted of sandwiches. By the time they broke at three for coffee, Hood was beginning to get somewhere with the disks.

'The good news', he said, unwrapping a chocolate bar, 'is that the computer was a late addition to Hastings' office.'

'How do you work that out?'

'The stuff on the disks, it's all dated '78, early '79.'

'My box-file goes back to '75,' Siobhan Clarke complained.

'*Wish You Were Here*,' Rebus said. 'Pink Floyd. September, I think it was. Much underrated.'

'Thank you, Professor,' Wylie said.

'You lot were still at nursery, I presume?'

'I'd really like to print this stuff out,' Grant Hood mused. 'Maybe if I phoned around the computer shops . . .'

'What sort of stuff are we talking about?' Rebus asked.

'Bids on land. You know, gap sites, all that.'

'Where?'

'Calton Road, Abbey Mount, Hillside . . .'

'What was he planning to do with them?'

'Doesn't say.'

'He wanted *all* of them?'

'Looks that way.'

'That's a lot of property,' Wylie commented.

'Well, a lot of building sites anyway.'

Rebus left the room, came back with an *A–Z*. He circled Calton Road, Abbey Mount and Hillside Crescent. 'Tell me he had plans for Greenside,' he said. Hood sat back down at the computer. They waited.

'Yep,' he said. 'How did you know?'

'Take a look. He was drawing a circle around Calton Hill.'

'Why would he do that?' Wylie asked.

'1979,' Rebus stated. 'The devolution referendum.'

'With the parliament sited there?' Siobhan guessed.

Rebus nodded. 'The old Royal High School.'

Wylie was seeing it now. 'With the parliament there, all that land would have been worth a fortune.'

'He took a gamble on Scotland voting Yes,' Siobhan said. 'And he lost.'

'I wonder,' Rebus said. 'Did he have the money in the first place? Even back in the seventies – which is prehistory for you lot – those areas weren't exactly cheap.'

'What if he didn't have the money?' Hood asked.

It was Ellen Wylie who answered: 'Then someone else did.'

They knew what they were after now: financial records; clues that someone other than Hastings and Alasdair Grieve had been a partner in the business. They stayed late, Rebus reminding them that they could head home if they liked. But they were working as a team – uncomplaining, focused – and no one was about to break the spell. He got the feeling it had nothing to do with overtime. Out in the corridor, taking a breather, he found himself alone with Ellen Wylie.

'Still feel hard-done-by?' he asked.

She stopped, looked at him. 'How do you mean?'

'You thought I was using the pair of you; just wondering if that's still how you feel.'

'Keep wondering,' she said, moving off.

At seven o'clock, he treated them to dinner at Howie's Restaurant.

They discussed the case, progress and theories. Siobhan asked when the devolution vote had taken place.

'March first,' Rebus told her.

'And Skelly was killed early in '79. Could it have happened straight after the election?'

Rebus shrugged.

'They finished in the basement at Queensberry House on March eighth,' Wylie said. 'A week or so later, Freddy Hastings and Alasdair Grieve do a runner.'

'As far as we know,' Rebus added.

Hood, cutting into his gammon, just nodded. Rebus, big spender, had splashed out on a bottle of the house white, but they weren't making inroads. Siobhan was sticking to water; Wylie had taken a glass of wine but had yet to touch it. Hood had finished his glass but refused a refill.

'Why is it I'm seeing Bryce Callan?' Rebus said.

There was silence around the table for a moment, then Siobhan: 'Because you want to?'

'What would have happened to the land?' Rebus asked.

Hood: 'It would have been developed.'

'And what does Callan's nephew do?'

Clarke: 'He's a developer. But back then he was a labourer.'

'Learning the ropes.' Rebus swallowed some wine. 'Land around Holyrood, any idea what it's worth now they're building the parliament there rather than Calton Hill or Leith?'

'More than it was,' Wylie guessed.

Rebus was nodding. 'And now Barry Hutton's eyeing up Granton, the Gyle, God knows where else.'

'Because that's his job.'

Rebus was still nodding. 'Bit easier if you've got something your competitors haven't.'

Hood: 'You mean strongarm tactics?'

Rebus shook his head. 'I mean friends in the right places.'

'AD Holdings,' Hood said, tapping the screen. Rebus stood over him, eyes squinting at the orange letters. Hood pinched the bridge of his nose, squeezed his own eyes shut, then opened them and shook his head briskly, as if to shake off cobwebs.

'Long night,' Rebus agreed. It was nearly ten; they were on the verge of calling a halt. A lot of good work done, but still – as Rebus had been the first to pun – nothing concrete.

And now this.

'AD Holdings,' Hood repeated. 'Seems that's who they were in bed with.'

Wylie had the phone book open. 'Not in here.'

'Probably gone bust,' Siobhan guessed. 'If they ever existed.'

Rebus was smiling. 'Bryce Callan's initials?'

'BC,' Hood supplied. Then he got it: 'BC, AD.'

'A little private joke. AD was going to be BC's future.' Rebus had already been busy on the phone, asking a couple of retired colleagues about Bryce Callan. He'd sold up late in '79. Some of what he'd sold had gone to the upstart Morris Gerald Cafferty. Cafferty had started on the west coast, 1960s muscle for loan sharks. Drifted down to London for a time, post-Krays and Richardson. Made his name and learned his trade.

'There's always an apprenticeship, John,' Rebus had been told. 'These guys don't come fully formed from the womb. And if they don't learn, we put them away . . . and we keep on putting them away.'

But Cafferty had learned fast and well. By the time he'd reached Edinburgh, associated with Bryce Callan's operation, and then branching out on his own, he'd shown a propensity for not making mistakes.

Until he'd met John Rebus.

And now he was back, and Callan, his old employer, was tied to the case. Rebus tried to make a connection, but couldn't.

Bottom line: late in '79, Callan threw in the towel. Or, put another way, headed overseas to where Britain's extradition laws didn't apply. Because he'd had enough? Or had his fingers burned? Or because he was worried about something . . . some crime that could come straight back to him?

'It's Bryce Callan,' Rebus said now, 'it's got to be.'

'Which just leaves the one little problem,' Siobhan reminded him.

Yes: proving it.

31

It took them the best part of the next day, Thursday, to set everything up. Trawls through company records; phone calls. Rebus spent over an hour talking to Pauline Carnett, his contact at the National Criminal Intelligence Service, then another hour talking to a retired chief superintendent who had spent eight fruitless years in the 1970s pursuing Bryce Callan. When Pauline Carnett called him back, after she'd spoken to Scotland Yard and Interpol, she had a Spanish telephone number. 950 code: Almeria.

'I once went there on holiday,' Grant Hood said. 'Too many tourists; we ended up trekking into the Sierra Nevadas.'

'We?' Ellen Wylie said, raising an eyebrow.

'Me and a mate,' Hood mumbled, his neck reddening. Wylie and Siobhan shared a wink and a smile.

They would have to make the call from the Chief Super's office: his was the only one with a speaker phone. Besides, international calls were blocked in the rest of the station. Chief Superintendent Watson would be present, but that didn't leave much room. It was decided that the three junior officers would be kept out, but a recording made.

If the interviewee agreed.

Rebus sent Siobhan Clarke and Ellen Wylie in to negotiate with the Farmer. His first two questions to them: 'Where's DI Linford? What's his take on this?'

Rebus had briefed them; they'd talked their way around Linford, pressed their case again until the Farmer, worn down, nodded his agreement.

With everything set up, Rebus sat in the Chief Super's chair and hit the buttons. The Chief Super himself was seated across the desk, in the chair Rebus usually occupied.

'Try not to get used to it,' had been the Farmer's comment.

The phone was picked up at the other end; Rebus hit the record button. A woman's voice: Spanish.

'Could I speak to Mr Bryce Callan, please?'

More Spanish. Rebus repeated the name. Eventually the woman

went away. 'Housekeeper?' Rebus guessed. The Farmer just shrugged. Now someone else was picking up the receiver.

'Yes? Who's this?' Annoyed. Maybe a siesta interrupted.

'Is that Bryce Callan?'

'I asked first.' The voice deep, guttural: no trace that he was losing his Scottish inflections.

'I'm Detective Inspector John Rebus, Lothian and Borders Police. I'd like to speak to Mr Bryce Callan.'

'Fucking good manners you lot have got these days.'

'That'll be the customer relations training.'

Callan let out a wheezy laugh, rolling it into a cough. Catarrh: smoker. Rebus made to light a cigarette of his own. The Farmer was frowning, but Rebus ignored him. Two smokers having a chat: instant rapport.

'So what can you do me for?' Callan asked.

Rebus kept his tone light. 'Is it okay if I record this, Mr Callan? Just so I've got a record.'

'You might have one, son, but my sheet's clean. No criminal convictions.'

'I'm aware of that, Mr Callan.'

'So what's this about?'

'It's about a company called AD Holdings.' Rebus glanced at the sheets of paper spread out on the desk. They'd done their work: could prove the company was part of Callan's little empire.

There was a pause on the line.

'Mr Callan? You still there?' The Farmer was off his chair, drawing the waste bin over so Rebus could flick his ash into it. Then he went to open a window.

'I'm here,' Callan said. 'Call me back in an hour.'

'I'd really appreciate it if we could . . .' Rebus realised he was talking to the dialling tone. He cut the call.

'Bugger,' he said. 'Now he's got time to fix a story.'

'He doesn't have to talk to us at all,' Farmer Watson reminded him.

Rebus nodded.

'And now he's gone, you can put that bloody thing out,' the Farmer added. Rebus stubbed his cigarette against the side of the bin.

They were waiting for him in the corridor, expectant faces collapsing as he shook his head.

'He said to call back in an hour.' He checked his watch.

'He'll have a story by then,' Siobhan Clarke said.

'What do you want me to do?' Rebus snapped.

'Sorry, sir.'

'Ach, it's not your fault.'

'He's given himself an hour,' Wylie said, 'but that means we've got an hour, too. Make a few more calls, keep going through Hastings' paperwork . . .' She shrugged. 'Who knows?'

Rebus nodded his approval. She was right: anything was better than waiting. So they went back to work, fuelled by tins of soft drinks and background music courtesy of a cassette machine provided by Grant Hood. Instrumental stuff – jazz, classical. Rebus had been dubious at first, but it did help stave off the boredom. Farmer's orders: keep the volume down.

Siobhan Clarke agreed: 'If it got out that I listened to jazz, I'd never be able to show my face.'

An hour later, it was back upstairs to the Farmer's office. Rebus left the door open this time; felt it was the least they deserved. Watson didn't seem to notice. Called again, and this time it rang and rang. Callan wasn't going to answer; of course he wasn't.

But he did. No housekeeper this time, and straight to the point. 'You got a conference facility?'

The Chief Super nodded. 'Yes,' Rebus said.

Callan gave him a number to ring: Glasgow code. The name was C. Arthur Milligan – Rebus knew him as 'the Big C', a nickname he shared, seemingly happily, with cancer. And Milligan was like cancer to police officers and the Procurator Fiscal's office. He was one of the really big defence solicitors, worked a lot with the advocate Richie Cordover, Hugh's brother. If you had Big C by your side, and Cordover defending you in court, you had the sharpest edge there was.

At a price.

The Farmer was showing Rebus how to work the conference call. Milligan's voice: 'Yes, Inspector Rebus, can you hear me?'

'Loud and clear, sir.'

'Hiya, Big C,' Callan said. 'I'm hearing you, too.'

'Good afternoon, Bryce. How's the weather out there?'

'God knows. I'm stuck indoors because of this arsehole.'

Meaning Rebus. 'Look, Mr Callan, I really do appreciate—'

Milligan interrupted. 'I believe you wish to record your conversation with my client. Who else is present?'

Rebus identified the Chief Super, didn't bother mentioning the others. Milligan and Callan had a discussion about the taping. At last, it was agreed the recording could begin. Rebus hit the button.

'That's us,' he said. 'Now if I could just—'

Milligan again: 'If I could just say at the outset, Inspector, that my client is under no obligation of any kind to answer what questions you may have.'

'I appreciate that, sir.' Trying to keep his voice level.

'And he's only talking to you out of a sense of public duty, even though the United Kingdom is no longer his chosen country of residence.'

'Yes, sir, and I'm very grateful.'

'Are you charging him with anything?'

'Absolutely not. This is for information only.'

'And this tape wouldn't be produced in a court of law?'

'I shouldn't think so, sir.' Choosing his words carefully.

'But you can't be definite?'

'I can only speak for myself, sir.'

There was a pause. 'Bryce?' Milligan asked.

'Fire away,' Bryce Callan said.

Milligan: 'Fire away, Inspector.'

Rebus took a moment to compose himself, looking at the documents on the desk as he fished his cigarette out of the bin and relit it.

'What are you smoking?' Callan asked.

'Embassy.'

'Tuppence a bloody packet out here. I stick to cigars these days. Now get on with it.'

'AD Holdings, Mr Callan.'

'What about them?'

'Your company, I believe.'

'Nope. I had a few shares, but that's as far as it went.'

Eyes were on Rebus from the doorway: *we know that's a lie*. But Rebus didn't want to catch Callan out, not this early on. 'AD were buying up parcels of land around Calton Hill, using another business as a front. Two men: Freddy Hastings and Alasdair Grieve. Ever meet either of them?'

'You're going back how far?'

'Late 1970s.'

'Bloody hell, lot of water been passed since then.'

Rebus repeated the two names.

'If you'd care to tell my client what this is about, Inspector,' Milligan said, sounding curious himself.

'Yes, sir. It's a question of a sum of money.'

'Money?' Now Callan was hooked, too.

'Yes, sir, quite a lot of money. We're trying to find a home for it.'

Stares from the doorway: he hadn't told them how he'd play it.

Callan was laughing. 'Well, look no further, chum.'

'How much money?' the lawyer asked.

'Even more than Mr Callan will be paying you for your services this afternoon,' Rebus told him. More laughter from Callan, and a warning look from the Farmer: it didn't do to wind up people like the Big C unnecessarily. Rebus concentrated on his cigarette. 'Four hundred thousand pounds,' he said at last.

'A not inconsiderable sum,' Milligan admitted.

'We think Mr Callan might be able to claim it,' Rebus told him.

'How?' Callan sounding cagey; wary of traps.

'It belonged to a man called Freddy Hastings,' Rebus explained. 'Belonged in the sense that he carried it around with him in a briefcase. At one time, Mr Hastings was a property developer, working with AD Holdings to buy land near Calton Hill. This was in late '78 and early '79, prior to the referendum.'

Milligan: 'And if there had been a Yes result, the land would have been worth a fortune?'

Rebus: 'Possibly.'

'What does this have to do with my client?'

'In later years, Mr Hastings lived as a down and out.'

'With all that money?'

'We can only speculate why he didn't spend it. Maybe he was holding it for someone. Maybe he was afraid.'

'Or off his rocker,' Callan added. But the remark was bravado; Rebus could tell he was thinking about things.

'The point is, AD Holdings, of which we believe Mr Callan was prime mover, was using Hastings to make bids on all this land.'

'And you think Hastings just pocketed the money?'

'It's one theory.'

'So the money would belong to AD Holdings?'

'It's possible. Mr Hastings left no family, no will. The Treasury will claim it if no one else does.'

'That would be a shame,' Milligan said. 'What do you say, Bryce?'

'I've already told him, I only had a few shares in AD.'

'You wish to add to that? Perhaps elucidate?'

'Well, it might have been more than a few shares, now you mention it.'

Rebus: 'You had dealings with Mr Hastings?'

'Yes.'

'Using his company as a front for buying land and property?'

'Maybe.'

'Why?'

'Why what?'

'You already had a company – AD Holdings. In fact, you had dozens of companies.'

'I'll take your word for it.'

'So why did you need to hide behind Hastings?'

'Work it out for yourself.'

'I'd rather you told me.'

Milligan interrupted: 'And why is that, Inspector?'

'Mr Milligan, we need to be clear about whether Mr Callan here and Freddy Hastings did business together. We need some sort of proof that the money could conceivably have belonged to Mr Callan.'

Milligan was thoughtful. 'Bryce?' he said.

'As it happens, he *did* take money off me, and then scarpered.'

Rebus paused. 'You notified the police, of course?'

Callan laughed. 'Of course.'

'Why not?'

'Same reason I used Hastings as a go-between. Filth were trying to drag my good name down, all sorts of lies and accusations. I wasn't just buying land.'

'You were going to build on it?'

'Houses, clubs, bars . . .'

'And you'd have needed planning permission, which Mr Hastings, with his credentials, might have found easier to come by.'

'See? You've worked it out all by yourself.'

'How much did Hastings take?'

'Best part of half a mil.'

'You must have been . . . displeased.'

'I was raging. But he'd disappeared.'

Rebus looked towards the doorway. It explained why Hastings had changed identity so radically. It explained the money, but not why he hadn't spent it.

'What about Hastings' partner?'

'Did a runner at the same time, didn't he?'

'He doesn't seem to have got any of the money.'

'You'd have to talk to him about that.'

Milligan interrupted again. 'Bryce, any chance you've got paperwork proving any of this? It would help validate any claim.'

'I might have,' Callan conceded.

'Forgeries won't count,' Rebus warned. Callan tutted. Now Rebus sat forward in his chair. 'But thanks for clearing that up. It brings me to a connected series of questions, if you don't mind?'

'Go ahead,' Callan said breezily.

Milligan: 'I think perhaps we should—'

But Rebus was off and running. 'I don't think I said how Mr Hastings died: he committed suicide.'

'Not before time,' Callan snapped.

'He did so shortly after the prospective MSP Roddy Grieve was murdered. That's Alasdair's brother, Mr Callan.'

'So?'

'And also shortly after the discovery of a corpse in one of the old fireplaces at Queensberry House. You'll remember that, Mr Callan?'

'What do you mean?'

'I just mean, maybe your nephew Barry told you about Queensberry House.' Rebus picked up a sheet of paper, checked the facts. 'He was working there early in 1979, around the time of the devolution vote. That's when you found out that all the land you'd been buying up wasn't going to be a gold mine after all. It's also probably when you learned that Hastings had been skimming. Either that or he'd just kept all the loot on one of the deals and pretended to you it had gone through. You'd only find out later that it hadn't, and by then he'd have done a runner.'

'What's that got to do with Barry?'

'He was working for Dean Coghill.' Rebus picked up another sheet. Milligan was trying to interrupt, but no way Rebus was letting him. Ellen Wylie was bouncing on her toes, willing him on. 'I think you were putting pressure on Coghill. You got him to take on Barry. Barry was working for you at the time. I think you put Barry in there to screw things up for Coghill. It was like an apprenticeship.'

Callan – Rebus could imagine his face suffused with blood: 'Here, Milligan, you going to let him talk to me like this?'

Milligan; not Big C; not pal or chum. Oh yes, Callan was fizzing.

Rebus talked right across the pair of them. 'See, the body went into the fireplace same time your boy Barry was there, same time you were finding out that Hastings and Grieve had ripped you off. So my question to you, Mr Callan, is: whose body is it? And why did you have him killed?'

Silence, and then the explosion: Callan screaming; Milligan threatening.

'You lousy conniving—'

'Must strongly object to the—'

'Come on the phone with a load of shit about four hundred grand—'

'Unwarranted attack on someone with no criminal record in this or any other country, a man whose reputation—'

'I swear to God, if I was there you'd need to slap me in chains to stop me smacking you one!'

'I'm waiting,' Rebus said, 'any time you want to hop on a plane.'

'Just you watch me.'

Milligan: 'Now, Bryce, don't let this appalling situation goad you into . . . Isn't there a senior officer present?' Milligan checked his notes. 'Chief Superintendent Watson, isn't it? Chief Superintendent, I must protest in the strongest terms about these underhand tactics, entrapping my client with tales of an unclaimed fortune . . .'

'The story's true,' Watson said into the speaker phone. 'The money's here. But it seems to be part of a wider mystery, and one which Mr Callan could help clear up by flying back here for a proper interview.'

'Any recording made today is, of course, inadmissible in a court of law,' Milligan said.

'Really? Well,' the Farmer said, 'I leave questions like that to the Fiscal's office. Meantime, am I right in thinking that your client has yet to deny anything?'

Callan: 'Deny? What do I need to deny? You can't touch me, you bastards!'

Rebus imagined him on his feet, face turned a colour no hours of tanning would ever match, gripping the receiver in his fist, strangling the tormentor it had become.

'You admit it then?' Watson asked, his voice all naïve sincerity. He winked towards the doorway as he spoke. If Rebus didn't know better, he'd say the man was beginning to enjoy himself.

'Piss off!' Callan growled.

'I think you can take that as a denial,' Milligan said tonelessly.

'I think you're probably right,' Watson agreed.

'Away to hell, the lot of you!' Callan yelled. There was a click on the line.

'I think Mr Callan has left us,' Rebus said. 'Are you still there, Mr Milligan?'

'I'm here, and I really do feel the need to protest in the strongest—'

Rebus cut the connection. 'I think we just lost him,' he told the room. There were whoops from the doorway. Rebus got up. Watson reclaimed his chair.

'Let's not get too carried away,' he said as Rebus switched off the tape-recorder. 'Pieces are beginning to fit, but we still don't know who did the killing, or even who was killed. Without those two pieces, all the fun we've just had with Bryce Callan counts for nothing.'

'All the same, sir . . .' Grant Hood was grinning.

Watson nodded. 'All the same, DI Rebus showed us the way to that man's black heart.' He looked at Rebus, who was shaking his head.

'I didn't get enough.' He hit the rewind button. 'I'm not sure I got anything.'

'We know what we're dealing with, and that's half the battle,' Wylie said.

'We should bring in Hutton,' Siobhan Clarke added. 'It seems to revolve around him, and at least *he's* here.'

'All he has to do is deny it,' Watson reminded her. 'He's not a man without influence. Drag him in here, it would reflect badly on us.'

'Can't have that,' Clarke grumbled.

Rebus looked to his boss. 'Sir, it's my shout. Any chance you can join us?'

The Farmer glanced at his watch. 'Just the one then,' he said. 'And a packet of mints for the car home – my wife can smell alcohol on my breath at twenty paces.'

Rebus brought the drinks to the table, Hood helping. Wylie just wanted cola from the gun. Hood himself was on a pint of Eighty. For Rebus: a half and a 'hauf'. A single malt for the Farmer, and red wine for Siobhan Clarke. They toasted each other.

'To teamwork,' Wylie said.

The Farmer cleared his throat. 'Speaking of which, shouldn't Derek be here?'

Rebus filled the silence. 'DI Linford is following up a line of inquiry of his own: a description of Grieve's possible murderer.'

The Chief Super met his eyes. 'Teamwork should mean just that.'

'You don't have to tell me, sir,' Rebus said. 'I'm usually the one out in the cold.'

'Because that's where you've wanted to be,' the Chief Super reminded him. 'Not because we wouldn't let you in.'

'Point taken, sir,' Rebus said quietly.

Clarke put down her glass. 'It's my fault really, sir, blowing up the way I did. I think John just thought there'd be less tension if DI Linford was kept at a distance.'

'I know that, Siobhan,' Watson said. 'But I also want Derek appraised of what's been going on.'

'I'll talk to him, sir,' Rebus said.

'Good.' They sat in silence for a minute. 'Sorry if I put a damper on things,' the Farmer said at last. Then he drained his glass and said he'd better be off. 'Just get my round in first.' They assured him he didn't need to, that it wasn't expected, but he got the round in anyway. When he'd gone, they could feel themselves relax. Maybe it was the alcohol.

Maybe.

Hood brought draughts over from the bar, and commenced a game against Clarke. Rebus said he never played.

'I'm a bad loser, that's my problem.'

'What I hate is a bad winner,' Clarke said, 'the kind that rubs your nose in it.'

'Don't worry,' Hood said, 'I'll be gentle with you.'

The lad was definitely coming out of himself, Rebus thought. Then he watched as Siobhan Clarke took her opponent apart, getting a crown while her own top row was still covered.

'This is brutal,' Wylie said, comforting Hood by ruffling his hair. When a second game was set up, Wylie and Hood swapped places. Hood sat across from Rebus now, and drained his first pint, replacing it with the one the Chief Super had bought.

'Cheers,' he said, taking a sip. Rebus raised his glass to him. 'I can't drink whisky,' Hood confided. 'Gives me blazing hangovers.'

'Me, too, sometimes.'

'Then why do you drink it?'

'The pleasure before the pain: it's a Calvinist thing.' Hood looked at him blankly. 'Never mind,' Rebus told him.

'He had it all wrong, you know,' Siobhan Clarke said, as Wylie concentrated on her next move.

'Who did?'

'Callan. Using a front company so the plans stood a better chance of going through. There was an easier route.'

Wylie glanced over towards the men. 'Wonder if she's going to tell us?'

'I think she wants us to guess first,' Rebus said.

Wylie jumped one of Clarke's draughts; Clarke retaliated. 'Simple really,' she said. 'Why not just pay off the planners?'

'Bribe the council?' Hood smiled at the thought.

'Bloody hell,' Rebus said, staring into his drink. 'Maybe that's it . . .'

A comment he refused to explain, even when they threatened to make him play draughts.

'I'll never crack,' he said, making light of it. But inside, his mind was buzzing with new possibilities and permutations, some of them including Cafferty's face. He sat there wondering what the hell he could do about them . . .

32

Rebus and Derek Linford, the canteen at Fettes police HQ, Friday morning. Rebus nodded towards familiar faces: Claverhouse and Ormiston, Scottish Crime Squad, tucking into bacon rolls. Linford glanced in their direction.

'You know them?'

'I'm not in the habit of nodding at strangers.'

Linford looked at the slice of toast cooling on his plate. 'How's Siobhan?'

'All the better for not seeing you.'

'She got my note?'

Rebus drained his cup. 'She hasn't said anything.'

'Is that a good sign?'

Rebus shrugged. 'Look, you're not suddenly going to be pals again. She could have reported you as a stalker, for Christ's sake. How would that have gone down in Room 279?' Rebus pointed upstairs with his thumb.

Linford's shoulders slumped. Rebus got up, fetched a fresh cup of coffee. 'Anyway,' he said, 'there's some news.' He went on to explain about the links between Freddy Hastings and Bryce Callan. The tension came back into Linford's shoulders. He was forgetting about Siobhan Clarke.

'So how does Roddy Grieve enter the equation?' he asked.

'That's what we don't know,' Rebus admitted. 'Revenge for the way his brother ripped off Callan?'

'And Callan waits twenty years?'

'I know, I can't see it either.'

Linford stared at him. 'But there's something, isn't there? Something you're not telling me?'

Rebus shook his head. 'But do yourself a favour: look into Barry Hutton. If it *was* Callan, he had to have someone here.'

'And Barry fits the bill?'

'He's his nephew.'

'Any evidence he's not just the Rotarian businessman?'

Rebus gestured towards Claverhouse and Ormiston. 'Ask Crime Squad, maybe they'll know.'

'From what little I know of Hutton, he doesn't fit the witness description of the man on Holyrood Road.'

'He has employees, doesn't he?'

'Chief Superintendent Watson's already warned that Hutton has "friends": how do I go snooping without raising hackles?'

Rebus looked at him. 'You don't.'

'I don't go snooping?' Linford seemed confused.

Rebus shook his head. 'You don't *not* raise hackles. Look, Linford, we're cops. Sometimes you have to step out from behind the desk and get in people's faces.' Linford didn't look convinced. 'You think I'm setting you up for something?'

'Are you?'

'Would I admit it if I was?'

'I suppose not. I'm just wondering if this is some sort of . . . test.'

Rebus stood up, coffee untouched. 'You're getting a suspicious mind. That's good, goes with the territory.'

'And what territory is that?'

But Rebus just winked, walked away with hands in pockets. Linford sat there, drumming his fingers on the table, then pushed his toast away and got up, too, walked over to where the two Crime Squad detectives were sitting.

'Mind if I join you?'

Claverhouse gestured to the spare chair. 'Any friend of John Rebus's . . .'

'. . . is probably after some bloody big favour,' Ormiston said, completing his colleague's thought.

Linford sat in his BMW in the only spare bay at the front of Hutton Tower. Lunchtime: workers were streaming out of the building, returning later with sandwich bags, cans of soft drink. Some stood on the steps, smoking the cigarettes they couldn't smoke indoors. It hadn't been easy to find the place: he'd driven through a building site, the road surface not yet finished. A wooden board – CAR PARK FOR REGISTERED PERSONNEL ONLY. But one free space, which he accepted gladly.

He'd got out of the BMW, checking the wheels were intact after the rutted and pitted roadway. Sprays of grey mud radiating from his wheel arches. Car wash at day's end. Back in the driving seat, watching the parade of sandwiches, baps and fresh fruit, he regretted not eating that breakfast toast. Claverhouse and Ormiston had whisked him upstairs, but their search on Hutton had drawn a blank other than some parking fines and the fact that his mother's brother was one Bryce Edwin Callan.

Rebus had said, in effect, that there was no subtle way to go about this, that he would have to announce himself and his intentions. He had no good reason to walk into the building and demand a line-up of every member of staff. Even if Hutton had nothing to hide, Linford couldn't see him agreeing. He'd want to know why, and when told would refuse the request outright and be on the phone to his lawyer, the newspapers, civil rights . . . And now that Linford thought about it, wasn't this looking more and more like a wild-goose chase dreamed up by Rebus – or maybe even Siobhan – to punish him? If he walked into trouble, *they'd* be the ones to profit from it.

All the same . . .

All the same, didn't he deserve it? And if he went along, might he be forgiven? Not that he was about to walk into the building, but surveillance . . . studying each employee as they left the building. It was worth an afternoon. And if Hutton himself should leave, he would follow, because if Grieve's murderer didn't work here, there was always the chance that he'd meet up with Hutton anyway.

A contract killing . . . revenge. No, he still didn't see it. Roddy Grieve hadn't been killed for anything in his personal or professional life – not that Linford could find. Admittedly, his family was barmy, but that in itself didn't constitute a motive. So why had he died? Had he been in the wrong place at the wrong time, seen something he shouldn't have? Or was it to do with the person he was about to become rather than the person he was? Someone hadn't wanted him as an MSP. The wife came to mind again; again he dismissed her. You didn't kill your spouse just so you could stand for parliament.

Linford rubbed his temples. The smokers on the steps were throwing him looks, wondering who he was. Eventually, they might tell Security, and that would be that. But now a car was approaching, stopping. Its driver sounded his horn, gesturing towards Linford. And now he was getting out, stomping towards the BMW. Linford slid his window down.

'That's my space you're in, so if you wouldn't mind . . .?'

Linford looked around. 'I don't see any signs.'

'This is staff parking.' A glance at a wristwatch. 'And I'm late for a meeting.'

Linford looked towards where another driver was getting into his car. 'Space there for you.'

'You deaf or what?' Angry face, jaw jutting and tensed. A man looking for a fight.

Linford was just about ready. 'So you'd rather argue with me than get to your meeting?' He looked to where the other car was leaving. 'Nice spot over there.'

'That's Harley. He takes his lunch hour at the gym. I'll be in the meeting when he gets back, and that's *his* space. Which is why *you* move your junk heap.'

'This from a man who drives a Sierra Cosworth.'

'Wrong answer.' The man yanked Linford's door open.

'The assault charge is going to look bloody good on your CV.'

'You'll have fun trying to make a complaint through broken teeth.'

'And you'll be in the cells for assaulting a police officer.'

The man stopped, his jaw retreating a fraction. His Adam's apple was prominent when he swallowed. Linford took the opportunity to reach into his jacket, showing his warrant card.

'So now you know who I am,' Linford said. 'But I didn't catch your name . . .?'

'Look, I'm sorry.' The man had turned from fire to sun, his grin trying for embarrassed apology. 'I didn't mean to . . .'

Linford was taking out his notebook, enjoying the sudden reversal. 'I've heard of road rage, but parking rage is a new one on me. They might have to rewrite the rule book for you, pal.' He peered out at the Sierra, took down its registration. 'Don't worry about your name.' He tapped the notebook. 'I can get it from this.'

'My name's Nic Hughes.'

'Well, Mr Hughes, do you think you're calm enough now to talk about this?'

'No problem, it's just that I was in a hurry.' He nodded towards the building. 'You've got some business with . . . ?'

'That's not something I can discuss, sir.'

'Course not, no, it's just that I was . . .' The sentence trailed off.

'You'd best get to your meeting.' The revolving door was moving, Barry Hutton coming out, buttoning his suit. Linford knew him from newspaper photos. 'I was just off anyway, as it happens.' Linford beamed at Hughes, then reached for the ignition. 'Spot's all yours.' Hughes stepped back. Hutton, unlocking his own car – a red Ferrari – saw him.

'Fuck's sake, Nic, you're supposed to be upstairs.'

'Right away, Barry.'

'Right away's not good enough, arsehole!'

And now Hutton was looking at Linford, frowning. He tutted. 'Letting someone use your space, Nic? You're not the man I thought you were.' Grinning, Hutton got into the Ferrari, but then got out again, came over to the BMW.

Linford thinking: *I've blown it; he knows my face now, knows my car. Following him is going to be a nightmare . . . 'You don't* not *raise hackles . . . Get in people's faces.'* Well, he'd got in the Cosworth driver's face, and here was his reward, Barry Hutton standing in front of the BMW, pointing towards him.

'You're a cop, aren't you? Don't ask me how it is you lot stick out, even in a motor like that. Look, I told the other two, and that's all I'm saying, right?'

Linford nodded slowly. The 'other two': Wylie and Hood. Linford had read their report.

'Good,' Hutton said, turning on his heels. Linford and Hughes watched as the Ferrari's engine fired, that low rumble like money in the bank. Hutton kicked up dust as he raced out of the car park.

Hughes was staring at Linford. Linford stared back. 'Do something for you?' he said.

'What's going on?' The man had trouble getting the words out.

Linford shook his head, smallest of victories, and put the Beamer into gear. Crawled out of the car park, wondering if it was worth trying to catch up with Hutton. Saw Hughes in his rearview. Something not right about the man. The warrant card hadn't just pacified him, it had freaked him out.

Something to hide? It was funny how even church ministers could break into a sweat when there was a copper in front of them. But this guy . . . No, he looked nothing like the description. All the same . . . all the same . . .

At the lights on Lothian Road, Barry Hutton was three cars in front. Linford decided he'd nothing to lose.

33

Big Ger Cafferty was on his own, parked outside Rebus's flat in a metallic-grey Jaguar XK8. Rebus, locking his own car, pretended he hadn't seen him. He walked towards the tenement door, hearing the electric hum of the Jag's window sliding down.

'Thought we might take another drive,' Cafferty called.

Rebus ignored him, unlocked the door, and went into the stairwell. As the door closed behind him, he stood there, debating with himself. Then he opened the door again. Cafferty was out of the car, leaning against it.

'Like the new motor?'

'You bought it?'

'You think I stole it?' Cafferty laughed.

Rebus shook his head. 'I just thought you might have been better off hiring, seeing how you're on the way out.'

'All the more reason for indulging myself while I'm here.'

Rebus looked around. 'Where's Rab?'

'Didn't think I'd need him.'

'I don't know whether to be flattered or insulted.'

Cafferty frowned. 'By what?'

'You coming here without a minder.'

'You said it yourself the other night: that was the time to take a pop at me. Now how about that drive?'

'How good a driver are you?'

Cafferty laughed again. 'It's true I'm a bit rusty. I just thought it might be more private.'

'For what?'

'Our little chat about Bryce Callan.'

They headed east, through the one-time slums of Craigmillar and Niddrie, now falling to the bulldozers.

'I've always thought', Cafferty said, 'that this should be the ideal spot. Views to Arthur's Seat, and Craigmillar Castle behind you. Yuppies would think they'd died and gone to heaven.'

'I don't think we say yuppies any more.'

Cafferty looked at him. 'I've been away a while.'

'True.'

'I see the old cop shop's gone.'

'Just moved around the corner.'

'And great God, all these new shopping centres.'

Rebus explained that it was called The Fort. Nothing to do with Craigmillar's old police station, whose nickname had been Fort Apache. They were past Niddrie now, following signs to Musselburgh.

'The place is changing so fast,' Cafferty mused.

'And I'm ageing fast just sitting here. Any chance of you getting to the point?'

Cafferty glanced in his direction. 'I've been making the point all along, it's just you've not been listening.'

'What is it you want to tell me about Callan?'

'Just that he called me.'

'He knows you're out, then?'

'Mr Callan, like many a wealthy expat, likes to keep abreast of Scottish current affairs.' Cafferty glanced at him again. 'Nervous, are you?'

'Why do you ask?'

'Your hand's on the door handle, like you're ready to bale out.'

Rebus moved his hand. 'You're setting me up for something.'

'Am I?'

'And I'd bet three months' salary there's nothing wrong with you.'

Cafferty kept his eyes on the road. 'So prove it.'

'Don't worry.'

'Me? What have I got to worry about? It's you that's the nervous one, remember.' They were silent for a moment. Cafferty slid his hands around the steering wheel. 'Nice car, though, isn't it?'

'And doubtless purchased with the honest sweat of your brow.'

'Others do my sweating for me. That's what makes a successful businessman.'

'Which brings us to Bryce Callan. You couldn't even get to speak to his nephew, and suddenly he calls you out of the blue?'

'He knows I know you.'

'And?'

'And he wanted to know what I knew. You haven't made yourself a friend there, Strawman.'

'Inside, I'm crying.'

'You think he's mixed up in these murders?'

'Are you here to tell me he isn't?'

Cafferty shook his head. 'I'm here to tell you that his nephew's the one you should be looking at.'

Rebus digested this.

'Why?' he asked at last.

Cafferty just shrugged.

'Does this come from Callan?'

'Indirectly.'

Rebus snorted. 'I don't get it. Why would Callan dump Barry Hutton in it?' Cafferty shrugged again. 'It's a funny thing . . .' Rebus went on.

'What?'

Rebus stared out of his window. 'Here we are coming into Musselburgh. Know what its nickname is?'

'I forget.'

'The Honest Toun.'

'What's funny about that?'

'Just that you've brought me here to feed me a load of shite. It's *you* that wants to see Hutton get burned.' He stared at Cafferty. 'I wonder why that should be?'

The sudden anger in Cafferty's face seemed to give off a heat all of its own. 'You're mad, do you know that? You'd ignore any crime sitting in your path, sidestep it just so you could give *me* a bloody nose. That's the truth, isn't it, Strawman? You don't want anyone else; you just want Morris Gerald Cafferty.'

'Don't flatter yourself.'

'I'm trying to do you a favour here. Get you a bit of glory *and* maybe keep Bryce Callan from killing you.'

'So when did you become the UN peacekeeper?'

'Look . . .' Cafferty sighed; some of the blood had left his cheeks. 'Okay, maybe there *is* something in it for me.'

'What?'

'All you need to know is there's more in it for John Rebus.' Cafferty was indicating, bringing the car to a halt kerbside on the High Street. Rebus looked around; saw just the one landmark.

'Luca's?' In summer, the café had queues out the door. But this was winter. Mid-afternoon and the lights were on inside.

'Used to be the best ice cream around,' Cafferty was saying, undoing his seat belt. 'I want to see if it still is.'

He bought two vanilla cones, brought them outside. Rebus was pinching his nose, shaking his head incredulously.

'One minute Callan's putting a contract on me, the next we're eating ice cream.'

'It's the small things you savour in this life, ever noticed that?' Cafferty had already started on his cone. 'Now if there was racing on, we could have had a flutter.' Musselburgh Racecourse: the Honest Toun's other attraction.

Rebus tasted the ice cream. 'Give me something on Hutton,' he said, 'something I can use.'

Cafferty thought for a moment. 'Council junkets,' he said. 'Everyone in Hutton's line of work needs friends.' He paused. 'The city might be changing, but it still works the same old way.'

Barry Hutton went shopping: parked his car in the St James Centre and hit a computer shop, John Lewis department store, and then out on to Princes Street and the short walk to Jenners. He bought clothes, while Derek Linford pretended to study a range of neckties. The shops were all busy enough; Linford knew he hadn't been spotted. He'd never done surveillance before, but knew the theory. He bought one of the ties – pale orange and green stripes – and swapped it for his own plain maroon.

The man Hutton had seen in the company car park had worn the maroon tie: different tie, different man.

Across the road to the Balmoral Hotel, afternoon tea with a man and a woman: business, briefcases open. Then back to the car park and the crawl to Waverley Bridge, traffic building as the rush hour neared. Hutton parked on Market Street, made for the rear entrance to the Carlton Highland Hotel. He was carrying a sports holdall. Linford made the deduction: health club. He knew the hotel had one – he'd almost joined it, but the fees had put him off. His thinking at the time: way to meet people, the city's movers and shakers. But at a price.

He bided his time. There was a bottle of water in the glove compartment, but he knew he daren't drink anything – just his luck to be off having a pee when Hutton came out. Ditto eating. His stomach was growling; café just along the road . . . He searched the glove compartment again, came up with a stick of chewing gum.

'*Bon appetit*,' he said to himself, unwrapping it.

Hutton spent an hour in the club. Linford was keeping a record of his movements, and duly noted the time to the minute. He was alone when he came out, his hair damp from the shower, holdall swinging. He had that sheen, that scrubbed confidence which came with a workout. Back into his car, and heading towards Abbeyhill. Linford checked his mobile phone. The battery was dead. He plugged it into the cigar lighter, got it charging. He wondered about calling Rebus, but to say what exactly? To ask his consent? *You're doing the right thing; keep at it*. The action of a weak man.

He wasn't weak. And here was the proof.

They were on Easter Road now, Hutton busy on his own mobile. The whole trip he'd been carrying on conversations, hardly ever glancing in rearview or side mirrors. Not that it would have mattered – Linford was three cars back.

But then suddenly they were in Leith, taking side roads. Linford hung back, hoping someone would overtake, but there was nobody there, nobody but the suspect and him. Left and right, the roads getting narrower, tenements either side of them, front doors opening directly on to the pavement. Children's playgrounds, broken glass sparkling in the headlights. Dusk. Hutton pulling over suddenly. Down by the docks, Linford guessed. He didn't know this part of town at all; tried to avoid it: schemes and hard-man dives. Weapons of choice: the bottle and the kitchen knife. The assaults tended to be on friends and 'loved ones'.

Hutton had parked outside one of the hard-man dives: a tiny pub, with narrow curtained windows seven feet off the ground. Solid-looking door: you'd think the place was locked. But Hutton knew better, pushed open the door and walked straight in. He left his holdall on the Ferrari's front seat, shopping bags in the back, the whole lot in full view.

Stupid or confident. Linford would bet the latter. He thought of the Leith pub in *Trainspotting*, the American tourist asking for the toilet, the schemies following him in, divvying the spoils after. That was this kind of pub. The place didn't even have a name, just a sign outside advertising Tennent's Lager. Linford checked his watch, entered the details in his log. A textbook surveillance. He checked his phone for messages. There weren't any. He knew the singles club was having a night out, starting at nine. He wasn't sure whether to go or not. Maybe Siobhan would be there again – it wasn't her case now but you never knew. He hadn't heard any stories about him being at the club that night, so probably Siobhan had kept her word, not said anything to anyone. That was good of her, considering . . . He'd given her the ammo, and after what he'd done, she still hadn't used it.

Then again, what *had* he done? Loitered outside her flat like a lovelorn teenager. Not such a heinous crime, was it? It had only been the three times. Even if Rebus hadn't found him . . . well, he'd have given up soon enough, and that would have been an end of it. It was down to Rebus really, wasn't it? Landing him in it with Siobhan, leaving him marginalised at work. Christ, yes, exactly what Rebus had wanted all along. One in the eye for the Fettes fast-stream. He could rise to chief constable and it would be there, hanging over him. Rebus would be retired, of course, maybe even have drunk himself to death, but Siobhan would be around, unless she went off to get married, have kids.

Always with the power to hurt him.

He didn't know what to do about that. The ACC had told him, no one's irreplaceable.

He passed the time reading whatever was in the car: owner's manual, service log, some leaflets from the passenger-side pocket: tourist attractions; old grocery lists . . . He was poring over his map book, looking at how much of Scotland he didn't know, when his phone sounded, shocking him with its sudden shrill cry. He picked it up, fumbled to switch it on.

'It's Rebus,' the voice said.

'Something happened?'

'No, it's just . . . nobody'd seen you this afternoon.'

'And you were worried?'

'Let's say I was curious.'

'I'm following Hutton. He's in a pub down in Leith. Been in there . . .' He checked his watch. 'An hour and a quarter.'

'Which pub?'

'No name above the door.'

'Which street?'

Linford realised that he didn't know. He looked around, saw nothing to help him.

'How well do you know Leith?' Rebus asked. Linford felt his confidence ebb.

'Well enough,' he said.

'So are you North Leith or South? Port? Seafield? What?'

'Near the port,' Linford spluttered.

'Can you see any water?'

'Look, I've been on his tail all afternoon. He did some shopping, had a business meeting, went to his health club . . .'

Rebus wasn't listening. 'He's got a pedigree, whether he's straight or not.'

'How do you mean?'

'I mean he used to work for his uncle. He probably knows more about this sort of thing than you do.'

'Look, I don't need you to tell me about—'

'Hello? Anyone home? What do you do when you need a pee?'

'I don't.'

'Or something to eat?'

'Ditto.'

'I said you should look at people who work for him. I didn't mean like this.'

'Don't tell me how to do my job!'

'Just don't go into that pub, okay? I've half an idea where you are, I'll come down there.'

'There's no need.'

'Try and stop me.'

'Look, this is *my*—' But Linford's caller had gone.

He cursed silently, tried calling Rebus back. 'I'm sorry,' said the recording, 'but the phone you have called may be switched off . . .'

Linford cursed again.

Did he want Rebus here, sharing his inquiry, sticking his nose in? *Meddling?* Soon as he arrived, he'd be told where he could go.

The pub door rattled open. All the time Hutton had been inside – one hour and twenty minutes – no one else had gone in or come out. But now here he was, emerging, bathed in light from the open door. And there was another man with him. They stood chatting in the doorway, Linford, parked across the road and down a ways, peering at this new figure. He ticked off the Holyrood description in his mind, came up with a close match.

Denims, dark bomber jacket, white trainers. Black cropped hair. Big round eyes and a permanent-looking scowl.

Hutton punched the man's shoulder. The man didn't seem too happy about what was being said. He put out a hand for Hutton to shake, but Hutton wasn't having any of it. Went and unlocked his Ferrari, started the engine and headed off. The man looked like he was going to turn back into the pub. Linford had a new scenario now: in he walks with Rebus as back-up, takes the man in for questioning. Not a bad day's work.

But the man was just shouting his goodbyes to someone. Then he headed off on foot. Linford didn't think twice, slid from his car, made to lock it, then remembered the little squeak of acknowledgement which the alarm made. Left it unlocked.

Forgot to take his mobile.

The man seemed drunk, weaving slightly, arms hanging loose. He went into another pub, came out again scant minutes later, stood by the doorway lighting a cigarette. Then back on his travels, stopping to talk to someone he seemed to know, then slowing as he fished a mobile phone out of his jacket and took a call. Linford patted his own pockets, realised the mobile was back in his car. He'd no idea where they were, tried memorising the few street names on show. Another pub: three minutes and out again. A short cut down a lane. Linford waited till the suspect had turned left out of the lane before entering it himself, sprinting to the other end. A housing scheme now, high fences and curtained windows, sounds of TVs and kids playing. Dark passageways smelling faintly of urine. Graffiti: Easy, Provos, Hibs. More walkways, the man pausing now, knocking at a door. Linford sticking to the shadows. The door opened and the man stepped quickly inside.

Linford didn't think it was a last stop. No keys, so probably not his home. He checked the time again, but had left his notebook back in the car, lying on the seat with the mobile. The BMW unlocked. He gnawed at his bottom lip, looked around at the concrete maze. Could he find his way back to the pub? Would his pride and joy be there if he did?

But Rebus was on his way, wasn't he? He'd work out what had happened, keep guard till Linford came back. He took a couple of steps further back into the darkness, plunged his hands into his pockets. Bloody freezing.

When the blow came, it came silently and from behind. He was unconscious before he hit the ground.

34

Jayne had gone and done it this time. She wasn't at her mum's. The old crone told him: 'Just said to tell you she was going to a friend's, and don't bother asking which one because she said it was better I didn't know.' She had her arms folded, filling the doorway of her semi-detached.

'Well, thanks for helping me save my marriage,' Jerry replied, heading back down the garden path. Her dog was sitting by the gate. Nice little thing, name of Eric. Jerry gave it a kick up its arse and opened the gate. He was laughing as Jayne's mum swore at him above Eric's yelps and howls.

Back at the flat, he went on another recce, see if she'd left any clues for him to find. No note, and at least half her clothes had gone. She hadn't been in a temper. Evidence of this: one of his boxes of 45s was sitting on the floor, a pair of scissors next to it, but she hadn't touched the records. Maybe a peace offering of sorts? Couple of things knocked off shelves, but put that down to her being in a hurry. He looked in the fridge: cheese, marge, milk. No beer. Nothing to drink in any of the cupboards either. He emptied his pockets on to the couch. Three quid and some change. Christ almighty, and when was the next giro due? Best part of a week away, was it? Friday night, and all he had was three quid. He searched drawers and down the back of the couch and under the bed. A grand total haul of a further eighty pence.

And the bills, staring at him from the noticeboard in the kitchen: gas, electric, council tax. Plus, somewhere, the rent and telephone. Phone bill had only come in that morning, Jerry asking Jayne why she had to spend three hours a week on the blower to her mum who only lived round the corner?

He went back through to the living room, dug out 'Stranded' by The Saints. B-side was even faster – 'No Time'. Jerry had all the time in the world; thing was, he felt utterly stranded.

The Stranglers next, 'Grip', and he wondered if he would strangle Jayne for putting him through this.

'Get a grip,' he told himself.

Made a cup of tea and tried working out his options, but his mind wasn't up to thinking. So he slumped back on to the sofa. At least he could play his music now, any time he liked. She'd taken her tapes with her – Eurythmics, Celine Dion, Phil Collins. Good riddance, the lot of them. He went along three doors to Tofu's pad and asked if he had any blow. Tofu offered to sell him a quarter.

'I just need enough for a joint. I'll give it back.'

'What? After you've smoked it?'

'I mean I'll owe you it.'

'Yeah, you will. Like you still owe me for last Wednesday.'

'Come on, Tofu, just one measly hit.'

'Sorry, pal, no more tick from Tofu.'

Jerry jabbed a finger at him. 'I'll remember this. Don't think I won't.'

'Aye, sure thing, Jer.' Tofu closed the door. Jerry heard the chain rattle back across it.

Inside the flat again. Feeling itchy now, wanting some *action*. Where were your friends when you needed them? Nic . . . he could phone Nic. Tap him for a loan if nothing else. Christ, with the stuff Jerry knew, he had Nic over a barrel. Make the loan more of a weekly retainer. He checked the clock on the video. Gone five. Would Nic be at work, or maybe at home? He tried both numbers: no luck. Maybe he was out on the pull, a few drinks in the wine bar with some of the short skirts from the office. No place in that picture for his old comrade-in-arms. The only thing Jerry was useful for was as a punchbag, somebody to make Nic look good because *he* looked bad.

A stooge, plain and simple. They were all laughing at him: Jayne, her mum, Nic. Even the woman at the DSS. And Tofu . . . he could almost *hear* that bastard's laughter, sitting snug in his padlocked flat with his bags of grass and nuggets of hash, bit of music on the hi-fi and money in his pocket. Jerry picked up the coins one by one from around him on the couch and tossed them at the blank TV screen.

Until the doorbell rang. Jayne, had to be! Okay, he had to pull himself together, act casual. Maybe be a bit huffy with her, but grown-up about it. Things happened sometimes, and it was down to those involved to . . . More ringing. Hang on, she'd have her keys, wouldn't she? And now the banging of a fist on the door. Who did they owe money to? Were they taking away the TV? The video? There was precious little else.

He stood in the hallway, holding his breath.

'I can see you, you tosser!'

A pair of eyes at the letter box. Nic's voice. Jerry started moving forward.

'Nic, man, I was just trying to get you.'

He unsnibbed the door and it flew inwards, driving him backwards and on to his arse. He was pulling himself upright when Nic gave him another push that sent him sprawling. Then the door slammed shut.

'Bad move, Jerry, really, *really* bad move.'

'What're you talking about? What've I done this time?'

Nic was sweating profusely. His eyes were darker and colder than ever before, and his voice was like a chisel.

'I never should've told you,' he hissed.

Jerry was back up on his feet. He slid along the wall and into the living room. 'Told me what?'

'That Barry wanted me out.'

'What?' This wasn't making sense to Jerry; he was panicking that it was his fault, that it would make sense if only he'd concentrate.

'It wasn't enough to grass me to the pigs—'

'Whoah, hold on—'

'No, *you* hold on, Jerry. Because when I'm finished with you . . .'

'I didn't do anything!'

'Grassed me up *and* told them where I work.'

'I never!'

'They've been talking to Barry about me! There was one sitting in the car park this afternoon! He'd been there for hours, sitting in *my* space! Now why else would he be there, eh?'

Jerry was shaking. 'Loads of reasons.'

Nic shook his head. 'No, Jer, just the one. And you're so fucking stupid you think I won't take you with me.'

'Christ's sake, man.'

Nic had brought something from his pocket. A knife. A bloody great carving knife! And Jerry noticed that he was wearing gloves, too.

'I swear to God, man.'

'Shut up.'

'Why would I *do* that, Nic? Think for a minute!'

'Your bottle's gone. I can see you shaking from here.' Nic laughed. 'I knew you were weak, but not this bad.'

'Look, man, Jayne's gone and I—'

'Jayne's the last thing you have to worry about.' There were thumps on the ceiling. Nic glanced up. '*Shut it!*'

Jerry saw a half-chance, dived through the doorway and into the kitchen. The sink was full of dishes. He plunged a hand in, pulled out forks, teaspoons. Nic was on him. Jerry chucked the lot at him. He was screaming now.

'Call the police! You upstairs, get on to the cops!'

Nic swung with the knife, caught Jerry on his right hand. Now a current of blood flowed down his wrist, mixing with the dishwater. Jerry cried out in pain, lashed out with a foot, caught Nic smack on the kneecap. Nic lunged again, and Jerry pushed past him, back into the living room. Tripped and fell. Fell over the box of 45s, scattering them. Nic was coming, his feet grinding one of the records into the floor.

'Bastard,' he was saying. 'You won't be saying a word against me.'

'Nic, man, you've lost it!'

'It wasn't enough, Cat leaving me, you had to rub my nose in it. Well, pal, it's *you* that's the rapist here. I just drove the van. That's what I'll tell them.' There was a sick grin on his face. 'We got into a fight, it was self-defence. That's what I'll say. See, I'm the one with the brains here, Jerry-fucking-nobody. The job, the mortgage, the car. And *I'm* the one they'll believe.' He raised the knife, and Jerry lunged. Nic sort of wheezed, and froze for a second, mouth agape, then angling his chin to stare down at where the scissors protruded from his chest.

'What were you saying about brains, man?' Jerry said, rising to his feet as Nic slumped face forwards on to the floor.

He sat back down on the couch, Nic's body twitching once or twice and then falling still. Jerry ran his hands through his hair. He examined his cut. It was a deep wound, and about three inches long. Hospital job, stitches. He knelt down, searched Nic's pockets and came up with the keys to the Cosworth. Nic had never let him drive it, never once offered.

Now, at last, he had a choice. Sit here and wait it out? Get his story straight for the cops? Self-defence was the truth of it. Maybe the neighbours would tell what they'd heard. But the cops . . . the cops knew Nic was the rapist. And they also knew there were two men involved.

Stood to reason it was him: Nic's pal from way back, the underachiever, Nic's killer. They'd get witnesses who'd identify him from the nightclubs. Maybe there were clues in the van.

Not such a difficult choice then, in the end. He tossed the keys, caught them, and headed out of the flat. Left the door wide open. Pigs would only kick it in otherwise.

He wondered if Nic would have thought of that.

35

Rebus was renewing his old acquaintance with the rougher end of the Leith pub scene. Not for him the charming, rejuvenated taverns of The Shore or the gleaming Victorian hostelries to be found on Great Junction Street and Bernard Street. For the nameless howffs, the spit 'n' sawdusts, you had to look slightly further afield, charting streets which few Scottish Office brogues from the HQ down the road ever trod. He had drawn up a shortlist of four – drew a blank with the first two. But at the third, saw Linford's BMW parked eighty yards away, under a busted street light: smart enough to park where he wouldn't easily be spotted. Then again, every second street light was busted.

Rebus tucked his Saab behind the BMW. He flashed his lights: no response. Got out of his car and lit a cigarette. That's all he was: a local lighting a cigarette. But his eyes were busy. The street was quiet. There was light in the high windows of Bellman's Bar – its name from years back. What it was called now was anybody's guess. Probably nobody who drank there knew, or cared.

He walked past the BMW, glancing inside. Something on the passenger seat: mobile phone. Linford couldn't be far. Taking that piss maybe, the one he'd said he wouldn't need. Rebus smiled and shook his head, then saw that the BMW's doors weren't locked. He tried the driver's side. By the interior light he could see Linford's notebook. He reached for it, started reading, but the light went off. So he slipped into the driver's seat, closed the door, and flipped the light back on again. Meticulous in every detail, but that didn't count for anything if you were spotted. Rebus went back outside, inspected the few parked cars. They were ageing and ordinary, the kind that passed each MOT with a backhander to a friendly mechanic. He wouldn't place Barry Hutton as the owner of any of them. Yet Hutton had driven here. Did that mean he'd left?

Did that mean Linford had missed him?

Suddenly, this began to seem like the best-case scenario. Rebus started to think of others, not half as appealing. He walked back to the Saab and called in, got St Leonard's to check any activity in Leith. They got back to him pronto: quiet night so far. He sat there, smoking three or four cigarettes, killing the packet. Then he walked over to Bellman's and pushed open the door.

Smoky inside. No music or TV. Just half a dozen men, all standing at the bar, all staring at him. No Barry Hutton; no Linford. Rebus was taking coins from his pocket as he approached.

'Cigarette machine?' he asked.

'Havenae got one.' The man behind the bar was practising a scowl. Rebus blinked sleepily.

'Any packs behind the bar?'

'Naw.'

He turned to look at the drinkers. 'Any of you guys sell me some?'

'A pound each,' came the lightning response. Rebus snorted.

'That's criminal,' he said.

'Then fuck off and buy them somewhere else.'

Rebus took his time studying the faces, then the bar's blunt décor: three tables, a linoleum floor the colour of ox blood, wood panelling on the walls. Pictures of yesteryear's page three girls. A dartboard gathering cobwebs. He couldn't see any toilets. There were only four optics behind the bar, and two taps: lager or export.

'Must do a roaring trade,' he commented.

'I didn't know you'd booked a floor show tonight, Shug,' one drinker said to the barman.

'The floor's where he'll end up,' the barman said.

'Easy, boys, easy.' Rebus held up his hands in appeasement, started backing away. 'I'll be sure to tell Barry that this is what you call hospitality.'

They weren't falling for it, stayed silent until Shug the barman spoke. 'Barry who?' he said.

Rebus shrugged, turned and walked out.

It was another five minutes before he got the call. Derek Linford: already on his way to the Infirmary.

Rebus paced the corridor: didn't like hospitals; liked this one less than most. This was where they'd brought Sammy after the hit and run.

At just after eleven, Ormiston appeared. Police officer attacked, Fettes and Crime Squad always took an interest.

'How is he?' Rebus asked. He wasn't alone: Siobhan was seated with a can of Fanta, looking shell-shocked. More officers had looked in – including the Farmer and Linford's boss from Fettes, the latter pointedly ignoring Rebus and Siobhan.

'Not good,' Ormiston said, searching in his pockets for change for the coffee machine. Siobhan asked him what he needed, handed over some coins.

'Did he say what happened?'

'Doctors didn't want him talking.'

'But did he tell you?'

Ormiston straightened up, plastic cup in hand. 'He got whacked from the back, and a few kicks for good measure. Best part of a broken jaw, I'd say.'

'So he probably wasn't in a chatty mood,' Siobhan said, looking at Rebus.

'They've pumped him full of drugs anyway,' Ormiston said, blowing on the liquid in his cup and eyeing it speculatively. 'Is this coffee or soup, would you say?'

Siobhan shrugged.

'He did write something down,' Ormiston said at last. 'Bugger seemed keen enough about that.'

'What did it say?' Siobhan asked.

Ormiston glanced towards Rebus. 'I might be paraphrasing, but it was along the lines of: Rebus knew I was there.'

'What?' Rebus's face was like stone. Ormiston repeated the words for him.

Siobhan looked from one man to the other. 'Meaning what?'

'Meaning,' Rebus said, slumping into a chair, 'he thinks I did it. Nobody else knew where he was.'

'But it had to be whoever he was following,' Siobhan argued. 'Stands to reason.'

'Not Derek Linford's reason.' Rebus looked up at her. 'I phoned him, said I was on my way down. Could be I set him up, grassed him to whoever was in the bar. Or could be I was the one who whacked him.' He looked to Ormiston for confirmation. 'That how you see it, Ormie?'

Ormiston said nothing.

'But why would you . . . ?' Siobhan's question trailed off as she saw the answer. Rebus nodded, letting her know she was right. Revenge . . . jealousy . . . because of what Linford had done to Siobhan.

That was Linford's thinking. The way he saw the world, it made perfect sense.

To Linford's mind, it was perfect.

Siobhan was sitting outside the hospital in her car, debating whether to visit the patient or not, when she heard the call on her radio.

Be on the lookout for a black Ford Sierra Cosworth, driver may be Jerry Lister, wanted for questioning concerning a major incident, code six.

Code six? The codes were always changing – all except code twenty-one, officer requiring assistance. Right now a code six was suspicious death – usually meaning homicide. She called in, was told that the victim's name was Nicholas Hughes. He'd been stabbed to death with a pair of scissors, his body found by Lister's wife on her return home. The woman was now being treated for shock. Siobhan was thinking back to that night, the night she'd taken the short cut through Waverley. She'd taken it because of the two men in the black Sierra, one of them saying to the other, *Lesbian, Jerry*, and now a man called Jerry was on the run in a black Sierra.

She'd tried to get away, and in doing so had ended up involved with a tramp's suicide.

The more she thought about it, the more she couldn't help wondering . . .

36

The Farmer was apoplectic.

'Whose idea was it for him to be tailing Barry Hutton in the first place?'

'DI Linford was using his own initiative, sir.'

'Then how come I see your grubby little prints all over this?'

Saturday morning, they were seated in the Farmer's office. Rebus was edgy to start with: he had a pitch to sell, and couldn't see his boss going for it.

'You've seen his note,' the Farmer continued. ' "Rebus knew". How the hell do you think that looks?'

There was so much tension in Rebus's jaw, his cheeks were aching. 'What does the ACC say?'

'He wants an inquiry. You'll be suspended, of course.'

'Should keep me out of your way till retirement.'

The Chief Super slammed both hands against his desk, too angry to speak. Rebus took his chance.

'We've got a description of the guy seen hanging around Holyrood the night Grieve was murdered. Add to this the fact that he drinks in Bellman's, and there's a good chance we can nab him. Bellman's won't give us anything; it's the sort of pub where they look after their own. But I've got snitches in Leith. We're looking for a hard man, someone who uses that pub almost as an office. With a few officers, I think I can—'

'He says *you* did it.'

'I know he does, sir. But with respect—'

'How would it look if I put you in charge of the investigation?' The Farmer suddenly looked tired, beaten half to death by the job.

'I'm not asking to be put in charge,' Rebus said. 'I'm asking you to let me go to Leith, ask some questions, that's all. A chance to clear my own name if nothing else.'

Watson leaned back in his chair. 'Fettes are going ape-shit as it is. Linford was one of theirs. And Barry Hutton under unauthorised surveillance – know what that would do to any case against him? The Procurator Fiscal will have a seizure.'

'We need evidence. That's why we need someone in Leith with a few contacts.'

'What about Bobby Hogan? He's Leith based.'

Rebus nodded. 'And I'd want him there.'

'But you want to be there, too?' Rebus stayed silent. 'And we both know you'll go there anyway, no matter what I say.'

'Better to have it official, sir.'

The Farmer ran a hand over the dome of his head.

'Sooner the better, sir,' Rebus prompted.

The Chief Super started shaking his head, his eyes on Rebus. 'No,' he said, 'I don't want you down there, Inspector. It's just not something I can sanction, bearing in mind the flak from headquarters.'

Rebus stood up. 'Understood, sir. I don't have permission to go down to Leith and ask my informants about the attack on DI Linford?'

'That's right, Inspector, you don't. You're awaiting suspension; I want you close by when word comes through.'

'Thank you, sir.' He headed for the door.

'I mean it. You don't leave St Leonard's, Inspector.'

Rebus nodded his understanding. The Murder Room was quiet when he reached it. Roy Frazer was reading a paper. 'Finished with this?' Rebus asked, picking up another. Frazer nodded. 'Chicken *phal*,' Rebus explained, rubbing his stomach. 'Hold all my calls and let everyone know the shunkie's off-limits.'

Frazer nodded and smiled. Saturday morning on the bog with the paper: everyone had done it at one time.

So Rebus headed out of the station and into the car park, jumped into his Saab and got on the mobile to Bobby Hogan.

'I'm ahead of you, pal,' Hogan said.

'How far?'

'Sitting outside Bellman's waiting for it to open.'

'Waste of time. See if you can track down some of your contacts.' Rebus flipped open his notebook, read the description of the Holyrood man to Hogan as he drove.

'A hard man who likes rough pubs,' Hogan mused when he'd finished. 'Now where the hell would we find anyone like that in Leith these days?'

Rebus knew a few places. It was 11 a.m., opening time. Grey overcast morning. The cloud hung so low over Arthur's Seat, you could pick out the rock only in shifting patches. Just like this case, Rebus was thinking. Bits of it visible at any one time, but the whole edifice ultimately hidden.

Leith was quiet, the day keeping people indoors. He drove past carpet shops, tattoo parlours, pawnbrokers. Laundrettes and social security offices: the latter were locked for the weekend. Most days, they'd be doing more business than the local stores. Parked his car in an alley and made sure it was locked before leaving it. At twelve minutes past opening, he was in his first pub. They were serving coffee, so he had a mug, same as the barman was drinking. Two ancient regulars watched morning television and smoked diligently: this was their day job, and they approached it with the seriousness of ritual. Rebus didn't get much out of the barman, not so much as a free refill. It was time to move on.

His mobile went off while he was walking. It was Bill Nairn.

'Working weekends, Bill?' Rebus said. 'How's the overtime?'

'The Bar-L never closes, John. I did what you asked, checked out our friend Rab Hill.'

'And?' Rebus had stopped walking. A few shoppers moved around him. They were mostly elderly, feet hardly clearing the pavement. No cars to take them to the retail parks; no energy to take the bus uptown.

'Not much really. Released on his due date. Said he was moving through to Edinburgh. He's seen his parole officer there . . .'

'Illnesses, Bill?'

'Well, yes, he did complain of a dicky stomach. Didn't seem to clear up, so he had some tests. They were all clear.'

'Same hospital as Cafferty?'

'Yes, but I really don't see . . .'

'What's his Edinburgh address?'

Nairn repeated the details: it was a hotel on Princes Street. 'Nice,' Rebus said. Then he took down the parole officer's details, too. 'Cheers, Bill. I'll talk to you later.'

The second bar was smoky, its carpet tacky with the previous night's spillage. Three men stood drinking nips, sleeves rolled up to show off their tattoos. They examined him as he entered, seemed not to find his presence objectionable enough to arouse comment. Later in the day, with sobriety a dull memory, things would be different. Rebus knew the barman, sat down at a corner table with a half-pint of Eighty and smoked a cigarette. When the barman came to empty the ashtray of its single dowp, it gave time for a couple of muted questions. The barman replied with little twitches of the head: negative. He either didn't know or wasn't saying. Fair enough. Rebus knew when he could push a bit harder, and this was not one of those times.

He knew as he left that the drinkers would be talking about him. They'd smelt cop on him, and would want to know what he'd been after. The barman would tell them: no harm in that. By now it would be common knowledge – and when one of their own was attacked, the police always went in quickly and with prejudice. Leith would be expecting little else.

Outside, he got on the phone again, called the hotel and asked to be put through to Robert Hill's room.

'I'm sorry, sir. Mr Hill's not answering.'

Rebus cut the call.

Pub three: a relief barman, and no faces Rebus recognised. He didn't even stay for a drink. Two cafés after that, Formica tables pockmarked with cigarette burns, the vinegary haze of brown sauce and chip fat. And then a third café, a place the men from the docks came to for huge doses of reviving cholesterol, as if it were more doctor's surgery than eating place.

And seated at one of the tables, scooping up runny egg with a fork, someone Rebus knew.

His name was Big Po. Sometime doorman for pubs and clubs of the parish, Po's past included a long stint in the merchant navy. His fists were nicked and scarred, face weathered where it wasn't hidden by a thick brown beard. He was massive, and watching him squashed in at the table was like watching a normal-sized adult seated in a primary-school classroom. Rebus had the impression that the whole world had been built on a scale out of kilter with Big Po's needs.

'Jesus,' the man roared as Rebus approached, 'it's been a lifetime and a half!' Flecks of saliva and egg peppered the air. Heads were turning, but didn't stay turned long. No one wanted Big Po accusing them of nosing into his business. Rebus took the proffered hand and prepared for the worst. Sure enough, it was like a car going through a crusher. He flexed his fingers afterwards, checking for fractures, and pulled out the chair opposite the man mountain.

'What'll you have?' Po asked.

'Just coffee.'

'That counts as blasphemy in here. This is the blessed church of St Eck the Chef.' Po nodded towards where a fat, elderly man was wiping his hands on a cook's apron and nodding towards him. 'Best fry-up in Edinburgh,' Po roared, 'is that right, Eck?'

Eck nodded again, then got back to his skillet. He looked the nervous sort, and with Big Po on the premises, who could blame him?

When a middle-aged waitress came out from behind the counter, Rebus ordered his coffee. Big Po was still busy with his fork and egg yolk.

'Be easier with a spoon,' Rebus suggested.

'I like a challenge.'

'Well, could be I've another for you.' Rebus paused while the coffee arrived. It was in a see-through Pyrex cup with matching saucer. In some cafés, they were becoming trendy again, but Rebus had the feeling this was an original. He hadn't asked for milk, but it was already added, with bubbles of white froth breaking on the surface. He took a sip. It was hot and didn't taste of coffee.

'So tell me what's on your mind,' Big Po said.

Rebus gave him the background. Po listened as he ate, finishing with a mopping-up operation involving the addition to the bare greasy plate of a liberal squirt of brown sauce, and two further slices of toast. Afterwards, Big Po tried sitting back, but there wasn't really the room. He slurped at his mug of dark brown tea and tried to turn his bear growl into something mere mortals might recognise as an undertone.

'Gordie's the man to talk to about Bellman's; used to drink there till they barred him.'

'Barred from Bellman's? What did he do, machine-gun the place or ask for a gin and tonic?'

Big Po snorted. 'I think he was shagging Houton's missus.'

'Houton being the owner?'

Po nodded. 'Big bad bastard.' Which meant a lot, coming from him.

'Is Gordie a first or last name?'

'Gordie Burns, drinks in the Weir O'.'

Meaning the Weir O' Hermiston, on the shore road out towards Portobello. 'How will I know him?' Rebus asked.

Po reached into his blue nylon windcheater, brought out a mobile phone. 'I'll give him a call, make sure he's there.'

As he did so, knowing the number by heart, Rebus stared out of the steamed-up window. At call's end, he thanked Po and stood up.

'Not finishing your coffee?'

Rebus shook his head. 'But this is on me.' He walked up to the counter, handed over a fiver. Three fifty for the fry-up, cheapest coronary in town. On his way back past Big Po's table, he patted the man's shoulder, slid a twenty into the windcheater's breast zip-up pocket.

'God bless you, young sir,' Big Po boomed. Rebus couldn't have sworn to it, but as he closed the door behind him he got the feeling the big man was ordering another breakfast.

The Weir O' was a civilised sort of pub: car park out front, and a chalkboard advertising a range of 'home cooked fayre'. As Rebus stepped up to the bar and ordered a whisky, a drinker, two along, started finishing up. By the time Rebus's drink arrived, the man was leaving, telling his companion that he'd be back in a wee while. Rebus took a minute or two to savour his own drink, then made for the door. The man was waiting for him around the corner, where the view was of disused warehouses and slag heaps.

'Gordie?' Rebus asked.

The man nodded. He was tall and gangly, late thirties with a long, sad face and thinning, ill-cut hair. Rebus made to hand him a twenty. Gordie paused just long enough to let Rebus know he had some pride, then pocketed the note.

'Make it quick,' he said, eyes darting from side to side. Traffic was thundering past, lorries mostly, travelling too quickly to take note of the two men.

Rebus kept it brief: description; pub; attack.

'Sounds like Mick Lorimer,' Gordie said, turning to walk away.

'Whoah,' Rebus said. 'What about an address or something?'

'Mick Lorimer,' Gordie repeated, heading back into the pub.

John Michael Lorimer: known as Mick. Previouses for assault, entering lockfast premises, housebreaking. Bobby Hogan knew him, which was why they took Lorimer to Leith cop shop, let him sweat there for a little while before starting the questioning.

'We're not going to get much out of this one,' Hogan warned. 'Vocabulary of about a dozen words, half of which would make your granny shriek.'

And he'd been waiting for them, seated quietly in his two-storey house just off Easter Road. A 'friend' had let them in, and Lorimer had been in a chair in the living room, newspaper open on his lap. He'd said almost nothing, not even bothering to ask them why they were there, why they were asking him to go down to the station with them. Rebus had taken an address from the girlfriend. It was on the housing scheme where Linford had been attacked. Which was fair enough: even if they proved it was Lorimer Linford had been following, he now had an alibi – went to his girlfriend's, didn't leave the flat all night.

Convenient and cost-effective; no way she'd suddenly change her story, not if she knew what was good for her. From her washed-out eyes and slow movements, Rebus would guess she'd had a pretty good education at the hands of Mick Lorimer.

'Are we wasting our time, then?' Rebus asked. Bobby Hogan just shrugged. He'd been on the force as long as Rebus; both men knew the score. Getting them into custody was just the opening bell of the bout, and most times the fight seemed fixed.

'We've got the line-ups anyway,' Hogan said, pushing open the door to the interview room.

Leith police station wasn't modern, not like St Leonard's. It was a solid late-Victorian design, reminding Rebus of his old school. Cold stone walls covered with maybe their twentieth layer of paint, and lots of exposed pipework. The interview rooms were like prison cells, sparse and dulling the senses. Seated at the table, Lorimer looked as much at home as he had in his own living room.

'Solicitor,' he said as the two detectives entered.

'Think you need one?' Hogan asked.

'Solicitor,' Lorimer repeated.

Hogan looked to Rebus. 'Like a broken record, isn't he?'

'Stuck in the wrong groove.'

Hogan turned back to Lorimer. 'We get you for six hours to ourselves without as much as a whiff of legal advice. That's what the law says.' He slipped his hands into his trouser pockets. All he was doing, the gesture said, was having a bit of a chat with a friend. 'Mick here', he told Rebus, 'used to be one of Tommy Telford's doormen, did you know that?'

'I didn't,' Rebus lied.

'Had to make himself scarce when Tommy's little empire blew up.'

Rebus was nodding now. 'Big Ger Cafferty,' he said.

'We all know Big Ger wasn't happy about Tommy and his gang.' A meaningful look towards Lorimer. 'Or with anyone connected to them.'

Rebus was standing in front of the table now. He leaned down so that his hands rested on the back of the empty chair. 'Big Ger's out. Did you know that, Mick?'

Lorimer didn't so much as blink.

'Large as life and back in Edinburgh,' Rebus went on. 'Maybe I could put you in touch with him . . . ?'

'Six hours,' Lorimer said. 'Nae bother.'

Rebus glanced towards Hogan: so much for that.

They took a break, stood outside smoking cigarettes.

Rebus was thinking aloud. 'Say Lorimer killed Roddy Grieve. Putting aside the question of why, we think Barry Hutton was behind it.' Hogan was nodding. 'Two questions really: first, was Grieve meant to die?'

'Wouldn't put it past Lorimer to get a bit overzealous. He's one of those guys, gets the red mist once he gets started.'

'Second,' Rebus went on, 'was Grieve meant to be found? Wouldn't they try hiding the body?'

Hogan shrugged. 'That's Lorimer again; hard as nails but not half as sharp.'

Rebus looked at him. 'So say he cocked up: how come he's not been punished?'

Now Hogan smiled. 'Punish Mick Lorimer? You'd need a big army. Either that or you'd want to lull him, get him when his guard was down.'

Which reminded Rebus . . . He called the hotel again. There was still no sign of Rab Hill. Maybe face to face would be better. He needed Hill on his side. Hill was the proof, which was why Cafferty was keeping him close.

If Rebus could get to Rab Hill, he could put Cafferty away again. There was almost nothing he wanted more in the world.

'It'd be like Christmas,' he said aloud. Hogan asked him to explain, but Rebus just shook his head.

Mr Cowan, who'd given them the description of the man on Holyrood Road, took his time over the line-up, but picked out Lorimer eventually. While the prisoner went back to his cell, the others were led away to be given tea and biscuits until their second appearance. They were students mostly.

'I get them from the rugby team,' Hogan explained. 'When I need a few bruisers. Half of them are training to be doctors and lawyers.'

But Rebus wasn't listening. The two men were standing outside the station's front door, enjoying a cigarette. And now an ambulance had drawn up, and its back doors were being opened, a ramp lowered. Derek Linford, face heavily bruised, head bandaged and with a surgical collar around his neck. He was in a wheelchair, and as the orderly pushed him closer, Rebus could see wiring around his jaw. His pupils had a drugged blankness to them, but when he spotted Rebus his vision cleared a little, his eyes narrowing. Rebus shook his head slowly, a mixture of sympathy and denial. Linford looked away, trying for a measure of dignity as his wheelchair was turned, the better to get it up the steps.

Hogan flicked his cigarette on to the road, just in front of the ambulance. 'You staying out of it?' he asked. Rebus nodded.

'Think I'd better, don't you?'

He'd smoked two more cigarettes before Hogan reappeared.

'Well,' he said, 'he gave us the nod: Mick Lorimer.'

'Can he talk?'

Hogan shook his head. 'Mouth's full of metal. All he did was nod when I gave him the number.'

'What does Lorimer's lawyer say?'

'Not too happy. He was asking what medicines DI Linford had taken.'

'Are you charging Lorimer?'

'Oh, I think so. We'll try assault to start with.'

'Will it get far?'

Hogan blew out his cheeks. 'Between you and me? Probably not. Lorimer's not denying being the man Linford followed. Problem with that is, it opens a whole other can of worms.'

'Unauthorised surveillance?'

Hogan nodded. 'Defence would have a field day in court. I'll talk to the girlfriend again. Maybe there's a grudge there . . .'

'She won't talk,' Rebus said with some confidence. 'They never do.'

Siobhan went to the hospital. Derek Linford was propped up with four pillows at his back. A plastic jug of water and tabloid newspaper for company.

'Brought a couple of magazines,' she said. 'Didn't know what you liked.' She laid the carrier bag on the bed, found a chair near by and brought it over. 'They said you can't talk, but I thought I'd come anyway.' She smiled. 'I won't ask how you're feeling: no point really. I just wanted you to know, it wasn't John's fault. He'd never do something like that . . . or let something like that happen to someone. He's not that subtle.' She wasn't looking at him. Her fingers played with the handles on the carrier bag. 'What happened between us . . . between you and me . . . it was my fault, I see that now. I mean, mine as much as yours. It's not going to help anyone if you . . .' She happened to glance up, saw the fire and mistrust in his eyes.

'If you . . .' But the words died in her mouth. She'd rehearsed a little speech, but could see now how little difference it would make.

'The only person you can blame is the person who did this to you.' She glanced up again, then looked away. 'I'm wondering if that loathing is for me or for John.'

She watched him slowly reach for his tabloid, bringing it down on to the bedcover. There was a biro attached to it. He unclipped it and drew something on the paper's front page. She stood up to get a better look, angling her neck. It was a rough circle, as big as he could make it, and it stood, she quickly realised, for the world, for everything, the whole damned lot.

The subject of his loathing.

'I missed a Hibs match to come here,' she told him. 'That's how important this is to me.' He just glared. 'Okay, bad joke,' she said. 'I'd have come anyway.' But he was closing his eyes now, as if tired of listening.

She gave it a couple more minutes, then walked out. Back in her car, she remembered a call she had to make: the slip of paper with the number was in her pocket. It had only taken her twenty minutes to find it amongst the paperwork on her desk.

'Sandra?'

'Yes.'

'I thought you might be out shopping or something. It's Siobhan Clarke.'

'Oh.' Sandra Carnegie didn't sound exactly pleased to hear her.

'We think the man who attacked you has ended up getting himself killed.'

'What happened?'

'He was stabbed.'

'Good. Give whoever did it a medal.'

'Looks like it was his accomplice. He got a sudden attack of conscience. We caught him heading for Newcastle down the A1. He's told us everything.'

'Will you do him for murder?'

'We'll do him for everything we can.'

'Does that mean I'll have to testify?'

'Maybe. But it's great news, isn't it?'

'Yeah, great. Thanks for letting me know.'

The phone went dead in Siobhan's hand. She made an exasperated sound. Her one planned victory of the day snatched away.

'Go away,' Rebus said.

'Thanks, I will.' Siobhan pulled out the chair and sat down opposite him, shrugged her arms out of her coat. She'd already bought her drink: fresh orange topped up with lemonade. They were in the back room of the Ox. The front room was busy: Saturday early evening, the football crowd. But the back room was quiet. The TV wasn't on. A lone drinker over by the fire was reading the *Irish Times*. Rebus was drinking whisky: no empties on the table, but all that meant was he was taking his glass back for a refill each time.

'I thought you were cutting down,' Siobhan said. He just glared at her. 'Sorry,' she said, 'I forgot whisky's the answer to the world's problems.'

'It's no dafter than yogic flying.' He raised the glass to his mouth, paused. 'What do you want anyway?' Tipped the glass and let the warmth trickle into his mouth.

'I went to see Derek.'

'How is he?'

'Not talking.'

'Poor bastard can't, can he?'

'It's more than that.'

He nodded slowly. 'I know. And who's to say he's not right?'

Her frown brought a little vertical crease to the middle of her forehead. 'How do you mean?'

'It was me told him to go chasing Hutton's men. In effect, I was telling him to tag a murderer.'

'But you weren't expecting him to—'

'How do you know? Maybe I *did* want the bugger hurt.'

'Why?'

Rebus shrugged. 'To teach him something.'

Siobhan wanted to ask what: humility? Or as punishment for his voyeurism? She drank her drink instead.

'But you don't know for sure?' she said at last.

Rebus made to light a cigarette, then thought better of it.

'Don't mind me,' she said.

But he shook his head, slid the cigarette back into its packet. 'Too many today as it is. Besides, I'm outnumbered.' Nodding towards the *Irish Times*. 'Hayden there doesn't smoke either.'

Hearing his name, the man smiled across, called out, 'For which relief, much thanks,' and went back to his reading.

'So what now?' Siobhan asked. 'Have they suspended you yet?'

'They have to catch me first.' Rebus began playing with the ashtray. 'I've been thinking about cannibals,' he said. 'Queensberry's son.'

'What about him?'

'I was wondering whether there are still cannibals out there, maybe more than we think.'

'Not literally?'

He shook his head. 'We talk about getting a roasting, chewing someone up, eating them for breakfast. We say it's a dog-eat-dog world, but really we're talking about ourselves.'

'Communion,' Siobhan added. 'The body of Christ.'

He smiled. 'I've always wondered about that. I couldn't do it, that wafer turning to flesh.'

'And drinking the blood . . . that makes us vampires as well.'

Rebus's smile broadened, but his eyes said that his thoughts were elsewhere.

'I'll tell you a strange coincidence,' she said. She went on to tell him about the night at Waverley, the black Sierra and the singles club rapist.

He nodded at the story. 'And I'll tell you a stranger one: that Sierra's licence number was found in Derek Linford's notebook.'

'How come?'

'Because Nicholas Hughes worked for Barry Hutton's company.' Siobhan made to form a question, but Rebus anticipated it. 'Looks like complete coincidence at this stage.'

Siobhan sat back and was thoughtful for a moment. 'Know what we need?' she said at last. 'I mean in the Grieve case. We need corroboration, witnesses. We need someone who'll talk to us.'

'Better get the Ouija board out then.'

'You still think Alasdair's dead?' Waited till he'd shrugged. 'I don't. If he was six feet under, we'd know about it.' She broke off, watching Rebus's face clear suddenly. 'What did I say?'

He was looking at her. 'We want to talk to Alasdair, right?'

'Right,' she agreed.

'Then all we have to do is issue the invitation.'

She was puzzled now. 'What sort of invitation?'

He drained his glass, got to his feet. 'You better do the driving. Knowing my luck recently, I'd wrap us round a lamp-post.'

'What invitation?' she repeated, struggling to get her arms into the sleeves of her coat.

But Rebus was already on his way. As she passed the man with the newspaper, he raised his glass and wished her good luck.

His tone implied that she'd need it.

'You know him then,' she complained, heading for the outside world.

37

The funeral of Roderick David Rankeillor Grieve took place on an afternoon of steady sleet. Rebus was at the church. He stood towards the back, hymnary open but not singing. Despite the short notice, the place was packed: family members from all over Scotland, plus establishment figures – politicians, media, people from the banking world. There were representatives from the Labour hierarchy in London, playing with their cuff links and checking their silent pagers, eyes darting around for faces they ought to know.

At the church gates, members of the public had gathered, ghouls on the lookout for anyone worth an autograph. Photographers, too, with deadlines to meet, wiping beads of water from zoom lenses. Two TV crews – BBC and independent – had set up their vans. There was a protocol to be observed: invitees only in the churchyard. Police were patrolling the perimeter. With so many public figures around, security was always going to be an issue. Siobhan Clarke was out there somewhere, mingling with the public, scrutinising them without seeming to.

The service seemed long to Rebus. There wasn't just the local minister: the dignitaries had to make their speeches, too. Protocol again. And, filling the front pews, the immediate family. Peter Grief had been asked if he'd sit with his aunts and uncles, but preferred to be with his mother, two rows back. Rebus spotted Jo Banks and Hamish Hall, five rows ahead of his own. Colin Carswell, the Assistant Chief Constable, was wearing his best uniform, looking slightly piqued that there wasn't room for him in the row in front, where so many distinguished invitees had crammed themselves that they had to rise and sit in single, fluid movements.

Speech after speech, the centre aisle decked with wreaths. Roddy Grieve's old headmaster had spoken haltingly and softly, so that each clearing of the throat from the pews drowned out half a sentence. The coffin, dark polished oak, gleaming brass handles, was resting on a trestle. The hearse had been a venerable Rolls-Royce. Limos clogged the narrow streets around the church, some of the cars sporting national flags – representatives from the various Edinburgh consulates. Out on the path, Cammo Grieve had given Rebus a half-twist of his mouth, a sombre smile of greeting. He'd done most of the organising, drawing up lists of names, liaising with officials. After the interment, there was to be a finger buffet at a hotel in the West End. Fewer invitees to this function: family and close friends. There'd be a police presence – security again – but provided by the Scottish Crime Squad.

As another hymn got under way, Rebus slipped from the back of the congregation and out into the churchyard. The burial site was eighty yards away, a family plot containing the deceased's father and one set of grandparents. The hole had already been dug, its edges covered with lengths of green baize. There was melt water in the bottom of the grave. The mound of earth and clay sat ready to one side. Rebus smoked a cigarette, paced the area. Then when he'd finished, he didn't know what to do with the dowp: nicked it and popped it back into the packet.

He heard the church doors opening, the organ music swelling. Walked away from the graveside and took up position at a nearby grouping of poplars. Half an hour later it was all over. Howls and handkerchiefs, black ties and lost looks. As the mourners filtered away, their emotions went with them. What was left was industry, as the diggers got busy filling in the hole. Car doors, engines revving. The scene was cleared in minutes. The churchyard was just that again: no voices or cries, just a crow's defiant call and the crisp working of shovels.

Rebus moved further away, towards the rear of the church building, but keeping the graveside in view. Trees and headstones camouflaging him. The headstones were worn almost smooth. He got the feeling very few these days were privileged to have their resting place here. There was a much larger purpose-built cemetery across the road. He picked out a few names – Warriston, Lockhart, Milroy – and read evidence of infant mortality. Hellish to lose a son or daughter. Now Alicia Grieve had lost two.

An hour he waited, feet growing icy as the damp penetrated his shoe soles. The sleet wasn't letting up, the sky a hard grey shell, muffling the life beneath. He didn't smoke; smoke might draw attention. Even kept his breathing slow and regular, each exhalation a billowing indication of life. Just a man coming to terms with mortality, graveyard memories of past family, past friends. Rebus had ghosts in his life: they came hesitantly these days, not sure how welcome they'd be. Came to him as he sat in darkness, incidental music playing. Came to him on the long nights when he had no company, a gathering of souls and gestures, movement without voice. Roddy Grieve might join them some day, but Rebus doubted it. He hadn't known the man in life, and had little to share with his shade.

He'd spent all day Sunday in pursuit of Rab Hill. At the hotel, they admitted that Mr Hill had checked out the previous evening. A bit of pressing, and Rebus was informed that Mr Hill hadn't been seen for a day or two beforehand. Then Mr Cafferty had explained that his friend had been called away. He'd settled the account, keeping his own room open, date of departure uncertain. Cafferty was the last person Rebus wanted to talk to about Hill. He'd been shown the bedroom – nothing had been left behind. As staff said, Mr Hill had brought only the one canvas duffel bag with him. Nobody'd seen him leave.

Rebus's next stop had been Hill's parole officer. It had taken him a couple of hours to track down her home phone number, and she'd been none too pleased to have her Sunday disturbed.

'Surely it can wait till tomorrow.'

Rebus was beginning to doubt it. Eventually she'd given him what she could. Robert Hill had attended two interviews with her. He wasn't due to see her again until the following Thursday.

'I think you'll find he misses that appointment,' Rebus told her, putting down the receiver.

He'd spent his Sunday evening parked outside the hotel; no sign of either Cafferty or Hill. Monday and Tuesday he'd been back at St Leonard's, while his future was debated by people so far up the ladder they were little more than names to him. In the end, he was kept on the case. Linford hadn't been able to offer any real evidence to support his claim, but Rebus got the feeling it was more to do with PR. Gill Templer, the rumour went, had argued that the last thing the force needed was more bad publicity, and pulling a well-known officer from a high-profile inquiry would have the media vultures hovering.

Her approach had gone straight to the deepest fears of the High Hiedyins. Only Carswell, the story went, voted for Rebus's suspension.

Rebus still had to thank her.

He looked up now and saw a cream trench coat moving across the grass towards the grave, hands deep in pockets, head bowed. Moving briskly, and with definite purpose. Rebus started moving, too, eyes never leaving the figure. A man, tall, thick hair slightly tousled, giving an impression of boyishness. He was standing graveside as Rebus approached. The diggers were still working, nearly done now. The headstone would come later. Rebus felt slightly dizzy, the way gamblers sometimes did when long odds romped home. Three feet behind the figure now . . . Rebus stopped, cleared his throat. The man's head half-turned. His back straightened. He began to walk away, Rebus following.

'I'd like you to come with me,' he said quietly, his performance watched by the gravediggers. The man said nothing, kept moving.

Rebus repeated the request, this time adding: 'There's another grave you should see.'

The man slowed, but didn't stop.

'I'm a police officer, if that's what you're worried about. You can check my warrant card.'

The man had stopped on the path, only a yard or two inside the gate. Rebus moved around in front of him, seeing the full face for the first time. Sagging flesh, but suntanned. Eyes which spoke of experience and humour and – above all – fear. A cleft chin, showing flecks of grey stubble. Weary from travel, mistrustful of this stranger, this strange land.

'I'm Detective Inspector Rebus,' Rebus said, holding up the warrant card.

'Whose grave?' It was said almost in a whisper, no sign of native accent.

'Freddy's,' Rebus said.

Freddy Hastings had been buried in a barren spot in a sprawling cemetery on the other side of the city. No marker had been erected, so that they stood by an anonymous soft hillock, the bare earth covered patchily with sections of turf.

'There weren't many turned out for this one,' Rebus said. 'Couple of fellow officers, old flame, couple of winos.'

'I don't understand. How did he die?'

'He killed himself. Saw something in the paper, and decided, God knows why, that he'd had enough of hiding.'

'The money . . .'

'Oh, he spent some of it at first, but after that . . . Something made him leave it untouched, for the most part. Maybe he was waiting for you to show up. Maybe it was just the guilt.'

The man didn't say anything. His eyes were glassy with tears. He reached into his pocket for a handkerchief and wiped at his face, shivering as he replaced it.

'Bit parky this far north, eh?' Rebus said. 'Where have you been living?'

'The Caribbean. I run a bar there.'

'Bit of a ways from Edinburgh.'

He turned towards Rebus. 'How did you find me?'

'I didn't have to: *you* found *me*. All the same, the paintings helped.'

'Paintings?'

'Your mother, Mr Grieve. She's been putting you on canvas ever since you left.'

Alasdair Grieve wasn't sure if he wanted to see his family.

'At this time,' he argued, 'it might be too much.'

Rebus nodded. They were seated in an interview room at St Leonard's. Siobhan Clarke was there, too.

'Don't suppose', Rebus said, 'you want your visit here trumpeted from the Castle ramparts?'

'No,' Grieve agreed.

'Incidentally, what name do you go by these days?'

'My passport says Anthony Keillor.'

Rebus wrote the name down. 'I won't ask where you got the passport.'

'I wouldn't tell you if you did.'

'Couldn't shrug off every link with the past, though, could you? Keillor, short for Rankeillor.'

Grieve stared. 'You know my family.'

Rebus shrugged. 'When did you find out about Roddy?'

'A few days after it happened. I thought of coming back then, but didn't know what good it would do. Then I saw the funeral announcement.'

'I wouldn't have thought it would make the Caribbean papers.'

'The Internet, Inspector. The *Scotsman* online.'

Rebus nodded. 'And you thought you'd take the chance?'

'I always liked Roddy . . . thought it was the least I could do.'

'Despite the risks?'

'It was twenty years ago, Inspector. Hard to know after that length of time . . .'

'Just as well it was me at that graveside and not Barry Hutton.'

The name brought back all sorts of memories. Rebus watched them pass across Alasdair Grieve's face. 'That bastard,' Grieve said at last. 'Is he still around?'

'Land developer of the parish.'

Grieve scowled, muttered the word 'Christ'.

'So,' Rebus said, leaning forward, resting his elbows on the table, 'I think maybe it's time you told us who the body in the fireplace belongs to.'

Grieve stared at him again. 'The what?'

When Rebus had explained, Grieve started to nod.

'Hutton must have put the body there. He was working at Queensberry House, keeping an eye on Dean Coghill for his uncle.'

'Bryce Callan?'

'The same. Callan was grooming Barry. Looks like he did a good job of it, too.'

'And you were in cahoots with Callan?'

'I wouldn't call it that.' Grieve half rose from the table, then stopped. 'Do you mind? I get a bit claustrophobic.'

Grieve began pacing what floor space there was. Siobhan was standing by the door. She smiled reassuringly at him. Rebus handed him a photo – the computer-generated face from the fireplace.

'How much do you know?' Grieve asked Rebus.

'Quite a bit. Callan was buying up lots of land around Calton Hill, presumably with both eyes on a new parliament. But he didn't want the planners knowing it was him, so he used Freddy and you as a front.'

Grieve was nodding. 'Bryce had a contact in the council, someone in the planning department.' Rebus and Siobhan exchanged a look. 'He'd given Bryce a promise on the parliament site.'

'Bloody risky, though: it was all down to how the vote went in the first place.'

'Yes, but that looked solid at first. It was only later the fix went in, the government making damned sure it wouldn't happen.'

'So, Callan had all this land and now nothing was going to happen to make it worth anything?'

'The land was still worth something. But he blamed us for everything.' Grieve laughed. 'As if *we'd* rigged the election!'

'And?'

'Well . . . Freddy had been playing silly buggers with the figures, telling Callan we'd had to pay more for the land than was the case. Callan found out, wanted the difference back plus the money he'd paid as a fee for fronting the whole thing.'

'He sent someone round?' Rebus guessed.

'A man called Mackie.' Grieve tapped the photo. 'One of his thugs, a real piece of work.' He rubbed at his temples. 'Christ, you don't know how strange it feels, saying all this at last . . .'

'Mackie?' Rebus prompted. 'First name Chris?'

'No, not Chris: Alan or Alex . . . something like that. Why?'

'It's the name Freddy took for himself.' Guilt again? Rebus wondered. 'So how did Mackie end up dead?'

'He was there to scare us into paying, and he could be *very* scary. Freddy just got lucky. There was a knife he kept in his drawer, a sort of letter opener. Took it with him that night for protection. We were supposed to be meeting Callan, sort it all out. Car park off the Cowgate, late night . . . the pair of us were scared shitless.'

'But you went anyway?'

'We'd discussed doing a runner . . . but, yes, we went anyway. Hard to turn down Bryce Callan. Only Bryce wasn't there. It was this guy Mackie. He gave me a couple of whacks on the head – one of my ears still doesn't work properly. Then he turned on Freddy. He had this gun, hit me with the butt. I think Freddy was going to get worse . . . I'm sure of it. He was the one in charge, Callan knew that. It was self-defence, I'd swear to it. All the same, I don't think he meant to kill Mackie, just . . .' He shrugged. 'Just stop him, I suppose.'

'Stabbed him through the heart,' Rebus commented.

'Yes,' Grieve agreed. 'We could see straight off he was dead.'

'What did you do?'

'Dumped him back in his car and ran for it. We knew we had to split up, knew Callan would have to kill us now, no two ways about it.'

'And the money?'

'I told Freddy I didn't want anything to do with it. He said we should meet, a year to the day, a bar on Frederick Street.'

'You didn't make the meet?'

Grieve shook his head. 'I was someone else by then, somewhere I was getting to know and like.'

Freddy had travelled, too, Siobhan was thinking: all the places he'd told Dezzi about.

But a year to the day, when Alasdair didn't show, Freddy Hastings had walked into the building society on George Street, just round the corner from Frederick Street, and opened an account in the name of C. Mackie . . .

'There was a briefcase,' Siobhan asked.

Grieve looked at her. 'God, yes. It belonged to Dean Coghill.'

'The letters on it were ADC.'

'I think Dean's his second name, but he liked it better than the first. Barry Hutton brought us one lot of cash in that briefcase, boasted how he'd taken it from Coghill; "Because I can, and there's nothing he can do about it." ' He shook his head.

'Mr Coghill's dead,' Siobhan said.

'Chalk up another victim to Bryce Callan.'

And though Coghill had died of natural causes, Rebus knew exactly what Grieve meant.

Rebus and Siobhan, a powwow in the CID suite.

'What've we got?' she asked.

'Lots of bits,' he acknowledged. 'We've got Barry Hutton heading out to check on Mackie, finding the body. Not far from Queensberry House, so he takes the body there, walls it in. Chances were, it wouldn't be found for centuries.'

'Why?'

'Couldn't have the police asking questions, I suppose.'

'How come no one called Mackie ended up posted a MisPer?'

'Mackie belongs to Bryce Callan, no one to mourn him or post him missing.'

'And Freddy Hastings kills himself when he reads the story in the paper?'

Rebus nodded. 'The whole thing's coming back again, and he can't deal with it.'

'I'm not sure I understand him.'

'Who?'

'Freddy. What made him do what he did, living like that . . .'

'There's a slightly more pressing concern,' Rebus told her. 'Callan and Hutton are getting away with this.'

Siobhan was leaning against her desk. She folded her arms. 'Well, in the end, what did they *do*? They didn't kill Mackie, they didn't push Freddy Hastings off North Bridge.'

'But they made it all happen.'

'And now Callan's a tax exile, and Barry Hutton's a reformed character.' She waited for him to say something, but he didn't. 'You don't think so?' Then she remembered what Alasdair Grieve had said in the interview room.

'A contact in the council,' she quoted.

'Someone in the planning department,' Rebus quoted back.

38

It took them a week to get everything together, the team working flat out. Derek Linford was convalescing at home, drinking his meals through a straw. As someone commented, 'Every time an officer takes a kicking, the brass has to reward them.' The feeling was Linford would be going on a promotion shortlist. Meantime, Alasdair Grieve was acting the tourist. He'd got himself a room at a bed and breakfast on Minto Street. They weren't letting him leave the country, not quite yet. He'd surrendered his passport, and had to report each day to St Leonard's. The Farmer didn't think they'd be charging him with anything, but as the witness to a fatal assault, a case-file would have to be prepared. Rebus's unofficial contract with Grieve: stay put, and your family needn't know you're back.

The team compiled their case. Not just the Roddy Grieve team, but Siobhan and Wylie and Hood, Wylie making sure she had a desk by a window: her reward, she said, for all the hours in the interview room.

They had help from further afield, too – NCIS, Crime Squad, the Big House. And when they were ready, there was still work to be done. A doctor had to be arranged, the suspect contacted and informed that a solicitor might be a good idea. He would know they'd been asking questions; even in his state, he'd have to know – friends tipping him the wink. Again, Carswell argued against Rebus's involvement; again, he was voted down, but only just.

When Rebus and Siobhan turned up at the detached, walled house on Queensferry Road, there were three cars in the driveway: both doctor and solicitor had already arrived. It was a big house, 1930s vintage, but next to the main artery between the city and Fife. That would knock £50k from the value, easy; even so, it had to be worth a third of a million. Not bad for a 'toon cooncillor'.

Archie Ure was in bed, but not in his bedroom. To avoid the stairs, a single bed had been erected in the dining room. The dining table now sat out in the hall, six formal chairs upended and resting on its polished surface. The room was redolent of illness: that stuffy, fusty smell of sweat and unbrushed teeth. The patient sat up, breathing noisily. The doctor had just finished his examination. Ure was hooked up to a heart monitor, his pyjama top unbuttoned, thin black wires disappearing beneath circles of flesh-toned tape. His chest was near hairless, falling with each laboured exhalation like a punctured bellows.

Ure's solicitor was a man called Cameron Whyte, a short, meticulous-looking individual who, according to Ure's wife, had been a family friend for the past three decades. He was seated on a chair at the bedside, briefcase on his knees and a fresh pad of A4 lined paper resting atop it. Introductions had to be made. Rebus did not shake Archie Ure's hand, but did ask how he was feeling.

'Bloody fine till all this nonsense,' was the gruff response.

'We'll try to be as quick as we can,' Rebus said.

Ure grunted. Cameron Whyte went on to ask some preliminary questions, while Rebus opened one of the two cases he was carrying and brought out the cassette machine. It was a cumbersome piece of kit, but would record two copies of the interview and time-stamp each one. Rebus went over the procedure with Whyte, who watched carefully as Rebus set the date and time, then broke open two fresh tapes. There were problems with the flex, which just barely stretched from the wall socket, and then with the double-headed microphone, whose lead just made it to the bed. Rebus shifted his own chair, so that he was seated in a claustrophobic triangle with lawyer and patient, the mike resting on top of the duvet. The whole process had taken the best part of twenty minutes. Not that Rebus was hurrying: he was hoping the wait might bore Mrs Ure into retreating. She did disappear at one point, returning with a tray containing teacups and pot. Pointedly, she poured for the doctor and lawyer, but told the police officers to 'serve yourselves'. Siobhan did so smilingly, before moving back to stand by the door, there being no chair for her – and little enough room for one. The doctor was seated at the far side of the bed, beside the heart monitor. He was young, sandy-haired, and seemed bemused by the whole scene being acted out before him.

Mrs Ure, unable to get next to her husband, stood by the solicitor's shoulder, making him twitch with discomfort. The room grew hotter, stuffier. There was condensation on the window. They were at the rear of the house, with a view on to a sweeping expanse of lawn, ringed by trees and bushes. A bird table had been fixed into the ground near the window, tits and sparrows visiting from time to time, peering into the room, dismayed by the quality of service.

'I could die of boredom,' Archie Ure commented, sipping apple juice.

'Sorry about that,' Rebus said. 'I'll see what I can do to help.' He was opening his second case, pulling out a fat manila folder. Ure seemed momentarily transfixed by its sheer weight, but Rebus pulled out a single sheet and laid it on top, creating a makeshift desk much like the lawyer's.

'I think we can start,' Rebus said. Siobhan crouched on the floor and activated the recorder. Nodded to let him know both tapes were rolling. Rebus identified himself for the record, then asked the others present to do likewise.

'Mr Ure,' he said, 'do you know a man called Barry Hutton?'

It was one question Ure had been expecting. 'He's a property developer,' he said.

'How well do you know him?'

Ure took another sip of juice. 'I run the council's planning department. Mr Hutton always has schemes coming before us.'

'How long have you been head of planning?'

'Eight years.'

'And before that?'

'How do you mean?'

'I mean, what positions did you fill.'

'I've been a councillor for the best part of twenty-five years; not many posts I haven't filled at one time or another.'

'But mostly planning?'

'Why bother asking? You already know.'

'Do I?'

Ure's face twisted. 'Quarter of a century, you make a few friends.'

'And your friends tell you we've been asking questions?'

Ure nodded, went back to his drink.

'Mr Ure nods,' Rebus said, for the benefit of the tape. Ure looked up at him. There was a measure of loathing there, but something in the man was prepared to enjoy this game, because that's what it was to him: a game. Nothing they could pin on him; no need to say anything incriminating.

'You were on the planning board in the late seventies,' Rebus went on.

''Seventy-eight to '83,' Ure agreed.

'You must have come across Bryce Callan?'

'Not really.'

'What does that mean?'

'It means I know his name.' Both Ure and Rebus watched the lawyer scratch a note on his pad. Rebus noticed he was using a fountain pen, his letters tall and slanting. 'I don't recall his name ever cropping up on a planning application.'

'How about Freddy Hastings?'

Ure nodded slowly: he'd known this name would come up, too. 'Freddy was around for a few years. Bit of a wide boy, liked to gamble. All the best developers do.'

'And was Freddy a good gambler?'

'He didn't last long, if that's what you're getting at.'

Rebus opened the file, pretending to check something. 'Did you know Barry Hutton back then, Mr Ure?'

'No.'

'I believe he was dipping a toe in the water at that time.'

'Maybe so, but I wasn't on the beach.' Ure wheezed out a laugh at his joke. His wife stretched an arm across the solicitor, touched her husband's hand. He patted hers. Cameron Whyte looked trapped. He'd had to stop scratching on his pad, seemed relieved when Mrs Ure withdrew the arm.

'Not even selling the ice creams?' Rebus asked. Both Ures, husband and wife, glared at him.

'No need to be glib, Inspector,' the lawyer drawled.

'I apologise,' Rebus said. 'Only it wasn't cones you were selling, was it, Mr Ure? It was information. As a result of which, to coin a phrase, you ended up with the lolly.' Behind him, he could hear Siobhan choke back a laugh.

'That's a strong accusation, Inspector,' Cameron Whyte said.

Ure turned his head towards his lawyer. 'Do I need to deny that, Cam, or do I just wait for him to fail to prove it?'

'I'm not sure I *can* prove it,' Rebus admitted guilelessly. 'I mean, we know someone in the council tipped off Bryce Callan about the parliament site, and probably about land in the area that could be available for purchase. We know someone smoothed the way for a lot of plans put forward by Freddy Hastings.' Rebus fixed eyes with Ure. 'Mr Hastings' business partner of the time, Alasdair Grieve, has given us a full statement.' Rebus searched in the folder again, read from a transcript: 'We were told there wouldn't be any problems with consents. Callan had that under control. Someone in planning was making sure.'

Cameron Whyte looked up. 'I'm sorry, Inspector, maybe my ears aren't what they were, but I failed to hear my client's name mentioned there.'

'Your ears are fine, sir. Alasdair Grieve never knew the mole's name. Six people on the planning committee at that time: could have been any one of them.'

'And presumably,' the lawyer went on, 'other members of council staff had access to such information?'

'Perhaps.'

'Everyone from the Lord Provost down to the typing pool?'

'I wouldn't know, sir.'

'But you *should* know, Inspector, otherwise such flimsy allegations could get you into serious trouble.'

'I don't think Mr Ure will want to sue,' Rebus said. He kept stealing glances at the heart monitor. It wasn't as good as a lie detector, but Ure's rate had leapt in the past couple of minutes. Rebus again made a show of glancing at his notes.

'A general question,' he said, again fixing eyes with Ure. 'Planning decisions can make people millions of pounds, can't they? I don't mean the councillors themselves, or whoever else is responsible for taking the decisions . . . but the builders and developers, anyone who owns land or property near the development site?'

'Sometimes, yes,' Ure conceded.

'So these people, they need to be on good terms with the decision-makers?'

'We're under constant scrutiny,' Ure said. 'I know *you* think we're probably all bent, but even if someone wanted to take a backhander, chances are they'd be found out.'

'Which means there's a chance they wouldn't?'

'They'd be a fool to try.'

'Plenty of fools around, if the price is right.' Rebus glanced back down at his notes. 'You moved into this house in 1980, is that right, Mr Ure?'

It was Whyte who answered. 'Look, Inspector, I don't know what you're insinuating—'

'August 1980,' Ure interrupted. 'Money from my wife's late mother.'

Rebus was ready. 'You sold her house to pay for this one?'

Ure was immediately suspicious. 'That's right.'

'But she had a two-bedroom cottage in Dumfriesshire, Mr Ure. Hardly comparable to Queensferry Road.'

Ure was silent for a moment. Rebus knew what he was thinking. He was thinking: if they've dug that far back, what else do they know?

'You're an evil man!' Mrs Ure snapped. 'Archie's just had a heart attack, and you're trying to kill him off!'

'Don't fret, love,' Archie Ure said, trying to reach out for her.

'Again, Inspector,' Cameron Whyte was saying, 'I must protest at this line of questioning.'

Rebus turned to Siobhan. 'Any more tea in that pot?' Ignoring the flurry of voices; the doctor getting out of his chair, concerned at his patient's state of agitation. Siobhan poured. Rebus nodded his thanks. He turned back to them again.

'Sorry,' he said, 'I missed all that. Point I was going to make is that if there's money to be made on projects in Edinburgh, how much more power would someone have if they were in charge of planning for the whole of Scotland?' He sat back, sipped the tea, waited.

'I don't follow,' the lawyer said.

'Well, the question was really for Mr Ure.' Rebus looked at Ure, who cleared his throat before speaking.

'I've already said, at council level there are all sorts of checks and scrutinies. At national level, they'd be multiplied tenfold.'

'Doesn't quite answer the question,' Rebus commented affably. He shifted in his chair. 'You were runner-up to Roddy Grieve in the ballot, weren't you?'

'So?'

'With Mr Grieve dead, you should have taken his place.'

'If *she* hadn't stuck her oar in,' Mrs Ure spat.

Rebus looked at her. 'I'm assuming that by "she" you mean Seona Grieve?'

'That's enough, Isla,' her husband said. Then, to Rebus: 'Say your piece.'

Rebus shrugged. 'It's just that by rights, with the candidate out of the way, the nomination should have been yours. No wonder you got a shock when Seona Grieve stepped forward.'

'Shock? It nearly killed him. And now you come in here, stirring it—'

'I said be quiet, woman!' Ure had turned on to one side, leaning on an elbow, the better to confront his wife. The beeping of the heart monitor seemed louder to Rebus. The patient was being coaxed on to his back by his doctor. One of the wires had come loose.

'Leave me alone, man,' Ure complained. His wife had folded her arms, her mouth and eyes reduced to narrow, angry fissures. Ure took another sip of juice, lay his head back against the pillows. His eyes were focused on the ceiling.

'Just say your piece,' he repeated.

Rebus all of a sudden felt a pang of pity for the man, a bond that recognised their common mortality, their pasts paved with guilt. The only enemy Archie Ure had now was death itself, and such self-knowledge could change a man.

'It's a supposition really,' Rebus said quietly. He was shutting them all out; it was just him and the man in the bed now. 'But say a developer had someone in the council he could trust to make the right decision. And say this councillor was thinking of running for parliament. Well, if they got in . . . with all that experience behind them – over twenty years mostly spent in city planning – they'd be odds-on for a similar post. Planning supremo for the new Scotland. That's a lot of power to wield. The power to say aye or nay to projects worth billions. All that knowledge, too: which areas are going to get redevelopment grants; where this factory or that housing development is going to be sited . . . Got to be worth something to a developer. Almost worth killing for . . .'

'Inspector,' Cameron Whyte warned. But Rebus had pulled his chair as close to the bed as he could get it. Just him and Ure now.

'See, twenty years ago, I think you were Bryce Callan's mole. And when Bryce moved away, he handed you on to his nephew. We've checked: Barry Hutton hit a golden streak early on in the game. You said it yourself, a good developer is a gambler. But everyone knows the only way to beat the house is if you cheat. Barry Hutton was cheating, and you were his edge, Mr Ure. Barry had high hopes for you, and then Roddy Grieve ended up selected in your place. Barry couldn't have that. He decided to have Roddy Grieve followed. Maybe only so he could be "persuaded", but Mick Lorimer went too far.' Rebus paused. 'That's the name of the man who killed Roddy Grieve: Lorimer. Hutton hired him; we know that.' He could feel Siobhan shifting uneasily behind him – the tape running, catching him saying something they couldn't yet prove.

'Roddy Grieve was drunk. He'd just been selected and wanted a look at his future. I think Lorimer watched Roddy Grieve climb the fence into the parliament site and then followed him. And suddenly, with

Grieve out of the way, it was your show again.' Now Rebus narrowed his eyes thoughtfully. 'What I can't figure out is the heart attack: was it because you realised a man had been murdered, or was it when Seona Grieve stepped into her husband's shoes, depriving you all over again?'

'What do you want?' Ure's voice was hoarse.

'There's no evidence, Archie,' the lawyer was saying.

Rebus blinked, his eyes never leaving Ure's. 'What Mr Whyte says is not quite true. I think we've got enough to present in court, but not everyone would agree. We need just that little bit more. And I think you want it, too. Call it a legacy.' His voice was almost a whisper now; he hoped the recorder was catching it. 'After all the shit, a clean break of sorts.'

Silence in the room, except for the monitor, its bleeping slower now. Archie Ure raised himself up so he was sitting unsupported. He crooked a finger, beckoning Rebus closer. Rebus half rose from his chair. A whisper in his ear: it wouldn't make the tape. All the same, he needed to hear . . .

Ure's breathing sounded even more laboured this close, hot rasps against Rebus's neck. Grey bristles on the man's cheeks and throat. Hair oily. When washed, it would be soft and fluffy like a baby's. Talcum powder, that sweet masking smell: his wife probably used it on him, stopping bed sores.

Lips close to his ear, grazing it at one point. Then the words, louder than a whisper, words everyone was meant to hear.

'Nice fucking try.'

And then wheezing laughter, rising in volume, filling the room with sudden, violent energy, drowning out the doctor's advice, the machine's staccato arrhythmia, the wife's pleas. The lawyer's glasses were knocked flying as she lunged at her husband, sensing something. As Whyte leaned down to retrieve them, Isla Ure half clambered across his back. The doctor was studying the machine, pushing Archie Ure back down on to the bed. Rebus stood back. The laughter was for him. The defiance was for him. The red-veined eyes, bulging from their sockets, were for him. All that was demanded of Rebus was that he play the part of spectator.

For now the laughter had a choked, rending sound to it, disappearing in a white noise of gargled froth as the face turned puce, the chest falling and refusing to rise. Isla Ure shrieking now.

'Not again, Christ! Not again!'

Cameron Whyte was rising to his feet, glasses back in place. His teacup had been knocked over, a brown stain spreading across the pale pink carpet. The doctor was speaking, Siobhan springing forward to help: she'd had the training. So had Rebus, come to that, but something held him back: the audience didn't clamber on to the stage. The performance had to belong to the actor.

While the doctor issued instructions, he was sliding his body atop his patient, readying himself for CPR. Siobhan was ready to administer mouth-to-mouth. Pyjama shirt wide open, fists flattened one on the other, right at the centre of the chest . . .

The doctor started, Siobhan counting for him.

'One, two, three, four . . . one, two, three.' She pinched the nose, blew into the mouth. Then the doctor started pushing again, almost lifting himself off the bed with the effort.

'You'll break his ribs!'

Isla Ure was sobbing, knuckles to her mouth. Siobhan's mouth locked on to the dying man's. Breath of life.

'Come on, Archie, come on!' the doctor roared, as if decibels could counter death. Rebus knew, or feared he knew: if you wished for death, it came for you all too easily. Every step you took, it shadowed your thoughts, waiting for that invitation. It sensed despair, and tiredness and resignation. He could almost sense it in the room. Archie Ure had willed death upon himself, consumed it readily and with that final relished bellow, because it was the only possible victory.

Rebus couldn't despise him for it.

'Come on, come on!'

'. . . three, four . . . one, two . . .'

The lawyer stood pale-faced, one arm missing from his glasses, snapped underfoot. And Isla Ure, head down by her husband's ear, voice cracked to the point of unintelligibility.

'Allu . . . archmon . . . allu-yoosweess . . .'

For all the noise, the sweeping chaos of the room, it was an echo of laughter which filled Rebus's ears. The final, stripped-down laughter of Archie Ure. His eyes gazed past the bed, caught movement behind the window. The bird table, a robin clinging to its underside, head turned towards the human pantomime within. First robin he'd seen this winter. Someone had told him once they weren't seasonal, but if that were the case, then why did you only ever see them in the cold months?

One more question to add to the list.

Two, three minutes had passed. The doctor was tiring. He checked for a pulse in the throat, then put his ear to the chest cavity. The wires were hanging dislodged. The monitor making no sound at all; just three red LED letters where numbers had previously been:

ERR

Now flashing to a new message:

RESET

The doctor slid his feet off the bed and on to the floor. Cameron Whyte had picked up the teacup. His spectacles sat at the wrong angle on his face. The doctor was pushing his hair back from his forehead, sweat gleaming in his eyelashes and dripping from his nose. Siobhan Clarke's lips looked dry and pale, as if some of the life had been sucked from them. Isla Ure was lying across her husband's face, shoulders juddering. The robin had flown off, its spirit unfettered by doubt.

John Rebus bent down, retrieved the microphone from the floor. 'Interview ends at . . .' He checked his watch. 'Eleven thirty-eight a.m.'

Eyes turned to him. When he stopped the tapes, it was as if he'd switched off Archie Ure's life-support.

39

Fettes HQ, the office of the Assistant Chief Constable. Colin Carswell, the ACC (Crime), listened to the jumble of noises which made up the last five minutes of the recording.

You had to be there, Rebus felt like telling him. He identified: the moment when Ure sat up, beckoning him closer . . . the moment flecks of foam had appeared at the corners of his twisted mouth . . . the sound of the doctor climbing on to the bed . . . and that dull static was the mike hitting the floor. From then on, everything was muffled. Rebus turned the bass down, upped the treble and volume. Even so, most of the sounds were indistinct.

Carswell had the two reports – Rebus's and Siobhan Clarke's – on the desk in front of him. He'd moistened his thumb before perusing them, lifting each page by a corner. Between them, they'd put together a second-by-second account of Archie Ure's demise, their timings matched to the tape.

There was one other copy of the tape, of course. It had been handed over to Cameron Whyte. Whyte said that Ure's widow was considering a claim against the police. That's why they were here in the ACC's office. Not just Rebus, but Siobhan and the Farmer, too.

More static: that was the mike being picked up. *Interview ends at . . . eleven thirty-eight a.m.*

Rebus stopped the tape. Carswell had listened to it twice now. After the first listen, he'd asked a couple of questions. Now he sat back, hands pressed together in front of his nose and lips. The Farmer made to mimic him, saw what he was doing and lowered his hands, pressing them between his legs instead. Then, seeing this as an unflattering pose to strike, he removed them quickly, laid them on his knees.

'Prominent local politician dies under police questioning,' Carswell commented. He might have been repeating a newspaper headline, but in fact so far they'd managed to keep the truth away from the newshounds. The lawyer had seen the sense of it, and had prevailed with the widow: a headline like that, and people would begin asking questions. Why had police wanted to talk to the recent heart-attack victim? She had enough to cope with without all that.

And she had concurred, while at the same time urging Whyte to 'sue the bastards for every penny'.

Words which acted like a frozen sword to the spines of the High Hiedyins at the Big House. So, just as Cameron Whyte and his team were doubtless poring over the tape, looking to build their case, the lawyers for Lothian and Borders Police were already seated in a room along the corridor, ready to take delivery of the evidence.

'A fatal error of judgement, Chief Superintendent,' Carswell was telling the Farmer. 'Sending someone like Rebus into a situation like that. I had my doubts all along, of course, and now I find myself vindicated.' He looked at Rebus. 'I wish I could take some pleasure in that.' He paused. 'A fatal error,' he repeated.

Fatal error, Rebus was thinking. ERR RESET.

'With respect, sir,' the Farmer said, 'we could hardly be expected to know . . .'

'Sending someone like Rebus to interview a sick man is tantamount to unlawful killing.'

Rebus clenched his jaw, but it was Siobhan who spoke. 'Sir, Inspector Rebus has been invaluable to this investigation throughout.'

'Then how come one of our best officers ends up with his face wired together? How come a long-time Labour councillor is in one of the fridges at the Cowgate? How come we don't have a single solitary conviction? And bloody unlikely to get one now.' Carswell pointed to the tape machine. 'Ure was as good a shout at it as we were going to get.'

'There was nothing wrong with the line of questioning,' the Farmer said quietly. He looked like he wanted to go sit hunched in a corner till gold-watch day.

'Without Ure, there's no case,' Carswell persisted, his attention focused on Rebus. 'Not unless you think Barry Hutton will crack under your rapier-like assault.'

'Give me a rapier and let's see.'

Carswell threw him a furious look. The Farmer started apologising.

'Look, sir,' Rebus interrupted, eyes fixed on the ACC, 'I feel as badly about this as anyone. But we didn't kill Archie Ure.'

'Then what did?'

'Maybe a guilty conscience?' Siobhan offered.

Carswell leapt to his feet. 'This whole investigation has been a farce from the start.' He was pointing at Rebus. 'I hold *you* responsible, and so help me I'll make sure you pay for it.' He turned to the Farmer. 'And as for you, Chief Superintendent . . . well, it's not a very pretty end to your career, is it?'

'No, sir. But with respect, sir . . .'

Rebus could see a change in Watson's demeanour.

'What?' Carswell asked.

'Nobody asked your blue-eyed boy to keep tabs on Hutton. No one told him to head off into a Leith housing scheme in pursuit of a possible murder suspect. Those were *his* decisions and they got him where he is now.' The Farmer paused. 'I think you're putting up a smokescreen so everyone will conveniently forget those facts. The officers here . . .' the Farmer looked at them, '*my* officers . . . also have your protégé pegged as a peeper. Something else you've conveniently ignored.'

'Careful now . . .' Carswell's eyes were boring into the Farmer.

'I think that time's past, don't you?' The Farmer pointed to the tape machine. 'Same as you, I've listened to that tape, and I can't see a damned thing wrong with DI Rebus's methods or his line of questioning.' He stood up, face to face with Carswell. 'You want to make something of it, fine. I'll be waiting.' He started heading for the door. 'After all, what have I got to lose?'

Carswell told them to get the hell out, but it was too late: they were already gone.

Down in the canteen, they left the food on their plates, pushed it around, feeling numb, and didn't talk very much. Rebus turned to the Farmer.

'What happened there?'

The Chief Super shrugged, tried to smile. The fight had gone out of him again; he looked exhausted. 'I just got fed up, simple as that. Thirty years I've been on the force . . .' He shook his head. 'Maybe I've just had a bellyful of the Carswells. Thirty years, and he thinks he can talk to me like that.' He looked at the pair of them, tried out a smile.

'I liked your parting shot,' Rebus said: ' "What have I got to lose?" '

'Thought you might,' the Farmer said. 'You've used it on me often enough.' Then he went to fetch three more coffees – not that they'd finished the first ones; he just needed to be moving – and Siobhan leaned back in her chair.

'What do you think?' she asked.

'Golgotha via Calvary,' he said. 'And don't bother looking for the return portion.'

'Not that you like to exaggerate.'

'Know what really sticks in my craw? We might be crucified for this, and that bastard Linford's going to get a peg up.'

'At least we can eat solids.' She tossed the fork on to her plate.

40

'Why here?' Rebus said.

He was walking across a frozen lawn in Warriston Crematorium's garden of remembrance. Big Ger Cafferty was wearing a black leather flying-jacket with fur collar, zipped to the chin.

'Remember, you came on a run with me once, years back?'

'Duddingston Loch.' Rebus was nodding. 'I remember.'

'But do you remember what I told you?'

Rebus thought for a moment. 'You said we're a cruel race, and at the same time we like pain.'

'We thrive on defeat, Strawman. And this parliament will put us in charge of our own destinies for the first time in three centuries.'

'So?'

'So it's maybe a time for looking forward, not back.' Cafferty stopped. His breath came out as a grey vapour. 'But you . . . you just can't leave the past alone, can you?'

'You brought me to a garden of remembrance to tell me I'm living in the past?'

Cafferty shrugged. 'We all have to live with the past; doesn't mean we have to live *in* it.'

'Is this a message from Bryce Callan?'

Cafferty looked at him. 'I know you're going after Barry Hutton. Think you'll get a result?'

'It's been known to happen.'

Cafferty chuckled. 'Something I know to my cost.' He started walking again. The only things visible in the flower beds were roses, their branches clipped back, looking brittle and stunted but with the promise of renewal hibernating within. *That's us*, Rebus thought, *thorns and all*. 'Morag died a year back,' Cafferty was saying. Morag: his wife.

'Yes, I heard.'

'They said I could go to the funeral.' Cafferty kicked at a stone, sent it flying into a flower bed. 'I didn't go. The guys in the Bar-L, they thought that made me hard.' A wry smile. 'What do you think?'

'You were scared.'

'Maybe I was at that.' He looked at Rebus again. 'Bryce Callan isn't as forgiving as I am, Strawman. You managed to put me away, and you're still walking around. But now Bryce knows you're after Barry, he's got to have you put out of the game.'

'Then he goes away, too.'

'He's not that stupid. Remember: where there's no body, there's no crime.'

'I'll just disappear?'

Cafferty was nodding. 'Whether you get your precious result or not.' He stopped walking. 'Is that what you want?'

Rebus stopped, looked around as if enjoying the view for the last time. 'What's it to you?'

'Maybe I like having you around.'

'Why?'

'Who else cares about me?' Cafferty chuckled again. In the distance, Rebus could see Cafferty's car – the grey Jag – the Weasel standing beside it, not quite daring to rest against its paintwork. Shuffling his feet in an effort to defrost them.

'Speaking of no body, no crime . . . where's Rab Hill?'

Cafferty looked at him. 'Yes, I heard you'd been asking.'

'It's Rab that has cancer, not you. He went for tests, came back with the news and told his good friend.' Rebus paused. 'You switched X-rays somehow.'

'NHS,' Cafferty said. 'Don't pay those doctors half what they're worth.'

'I'm going to prove it, you know that.'

'You're a cop with a vendetta. Not much a poor citizen like me can do about that.'

'Maybe I could ease up a little,' Rebus said.

'In return for . . .?'

'Testify against Bryce Callan. You were there in '79, you know what was going on.'

Cafferty shook his head. 'That's not the way to play it.'

Rebus stared at him. 'Then what is?'

Cafferty ignored the question. 'It's a cold place this, isn't it?' he said instead. 'When they bury me, I want it to be somewhere warm.'

'You'll be going somewhere warm,' Rebus told him. 'Might even be a bit *too* warm.'

'And you're on the side of the angels, eh?' They were heading for the car now. Rebus stopped; his Saab was parked the other side of the chapel. Cafferty didn't check; he half waved and kept on walking. 'Next funeral I go to will probably be yours, Strawman. Anything you want put on your headstone?'

'How about "Died peacefully in his sleep, aged ninety"?'

Cafferty laughed with the confidence of the immortal.

Rebus turned, retraced his steps. He was out in the open, and his shoulders jerked when he heard a sharp report, but it was only the

Weasel slamming shut the door of the Jag. Rebus walked round to the front of the chapel, opened the door and stepped inside. There was an ante-room, a big book of remembrance open on a marble-topped table. A red silk marker kept it open at the day's date on the previous year: eight names, meaning eight cremations that day, eight grieving families who might or might not turn up to pay their respects. No . . . that wasn't right. Not the date of cremation . . . these were dates of death. He kept the place but started at the back of the book, letting the as-yet-empty sheets slide through his fingers. There'd be names in there eventually. If Cafferty was right, his wouldn't be among them: he'd just disappear. He didn't know how he felt about that. Didn't feel anything really. Today's date: no names entered as yet. But cars had been pulling away as he'd been arriving, a teenager peering out at him from the back seat of a limousine, black tie knotted awkwardly at the throat.

Yesterday: no names; too soon. Day before that: none. Then it was back to the weekend. Friday: nine names – the cremations had probably taken place yesterday. Rebus looked down the list, neat entries made in black ink by someone with a gift for calligraphy. Fountain pen: thick downstrokes, tapering flicks. Dates of birth, maiden names . . .

Bingo.

Robert Wallace Hill. Known as Rab.

He'd died the previous Friday. The funeral had probably taken place yesterday, the ashes scattered over the garden of remembrance: the reason Cafferty had come here, paying his respects to the man who'd been his ticket out of jail. Rab, his body riddled with cancer. Rebus saw it all now. Rab, with his release date coming, the cancer a cruel blow. Taking the news back to the Bar-L, confiding in Cafferty, who'd feigned illness, gone for tests himself, arranging the switch of records, some bribe or threat to a doctor. Rab pumped full of painkillers, his release date almost coinciding with Cafferty's. Doubtless paid well: money for a decent send-off, an envelope thick with banknotes finding its way to any family left behind.

Rebus somehow doubted Cafferty would return to the chapel a year down the line. He'd have more important things on his mind. He'd be back in business. And Rab? Well, hadn't Cafferty said it himself: *a time for looking forward, not back*. Christmas was on its way. 1999 would bring the Scottish Parliament back to Edinburgh. In the spring, they'd flatten the old brewery, start constructing the glass boxes which would eventually house the MSPs. Glass walls: the theme was openness, accountability. Okay, till then they'd be meeting in a church hall on The Mound, but even so . . .

Even so. So what?

'And then you die,' he muttered to himself, turning to leave the chapel.

He got on his mobile to the mortuary, asked Dougie who'd done the autopsy on Rab Hill. The answer: Curt and Stevenson. He thanked Dougie, punched in Curt's number. He was thinking of Rab's body: ashes now. *Where there's no body, there's no crime*. But there'd be the autopsy report, and when it showed up the cancer, Rebus would have evidence enough to have Cafferty re-examined.

'It was an overdose,' Curt explained. 'He'd been a user in prison, got a bit too greedy when he came out.'

'But when you opened him up, what else did you find?' Rebus was holding the phone so tightly, his wrist was hurting.

'Family were against it, John.'

Rebus blinked. 'A young man . . . suspicious death.'

'Some religious thing . . . church I'd never heard of. Their lawyer put it in writing.'

I'll bet he did, Rebus thought. 'There was no autopsy?'

'We did as much as we could. Chemical tests were clear enough . . .'

Rebus cut the call, screwed shut his eyes. A few flakes of snow fell on his lashes. He was slow to blink them away.

No body, no evidence. He shivered suddenly, remembering Cafferty's words: *Yes, I heard you'd been asking*. Asking about Rab Hill. Cafferty had known . . . known that Rebus knew. So easy to administer an overdose to a sick man. So easy for someone like Cafferty, someone with so much to lose.

41

The few days running up to Hogmanay were a nightmare. Lorna had sold her story to a tabloid – Model's Night-Time Romp With Murder Case Cop. Rebus's name hadn't been mentioned . . . not yet.

It was a move which might ostracise her from husband and family alike, but Rebus could see why she'd done it. There was a middle-page spread, showing her to her best in diaphanous clothing, face and hair done to the nines. Maybe it was the relaunch she thought she needed. Maybe it was a case of using what she had.

A moment's notoriety.

Rebus could see his career crumbling before him. To keep herself in the news, she'd have to name names, and Carswell would pounce. So Rebus went to see Alasdair, and made him a proposition. Alasdair phoned his sister at High Manor, talked her round. They were on the phone forty minutes, at the end of which Rebus handed Alasdair's passport back and wished him good luck. He'd even driven him out to the airport. Grieve's parting words to him: 'Home in time for New Year.' A handshake and a brief wave of farewell. Rebus had felt obliged to warn that they might need him back to give testimony. Grieve had nodded, knowing he could always refuse. Either that or keep moving . . .

Rebus wasn't working on Hogmanay. A trade-off because he'd been on call over Christmas. The town had been quiet, which hadn't stopped the cells filling up. Sammy had sent him a present: the CD edition of the Beatles' *White Album*. She was staying down south, visiting her mum. Siobhan had left her present to him in his desk drawer: a history of Hibernian FC. He flicked through it during the dead hours, hours when he'd no need to be at the station. When he wasn't reading about the Hibs, he was poring over case-notes, trying to restructure them into something more acceptable to the Procurator Fiscal. He'd had a series of meetings with various advocates depute. So far, they were of the opinion that the only person they could try with any hope of securing a conviction was Alasdair Grieve: accessory to . . . fleeing the scene of . . .

Another good reason for putting Grieve on the plane.

And now it was Hogmanay, and everyone was talking about how bad the television had been. Princes Street would fill tonight, maybe two hundred thousand revellers. The Pretenders were playing, almost reason enough to go along, but he knew he'd stay home. He wasn't risking the Ox: too close to the mayhem, and getting there would be difficult. Barriers had been erected, ringing the city centre. So he'd headed to Swany's instead.

When he was a kid, all the mothers would be out bleaching their front steps, busy house cleaning: you had to see the New Year in with a clean house. There'd be sandwiches and stovies for the drinkers. Chimes at midnight: someone tall and dark waiting outside, carrying bottle and lump of coal, plus something to eat. Welcoming the New Year with a knock at the door. Songs and 'doing a turn'. One of his uncles had played harmonica, an aunt might sing with a tear in her eye, a catch in her throat. Tables groaning with black bun and shortie, Madeira cake, crisps and peanuts. Juice in the kitchen for the kids, maybe homemade ginger beer. Steak pie sitting in the oven, waiting to be cooked for lunch. Strangers would see a light on, knock and be welcomed in. Anyone was welcome into your home, on that night if no other.

And if no one came . . . then you sat and waited. You didn't go out until you'd been 'first-footed': it was bad luck. One aunt had sat alone for a couple of days; everyone thought she was at her daughter's. Elsewhere: songs in the street, handshakes, drunken reminiscence and prayers for a better year to come.

The old days. And now Rebus was old himself, heading home from Swany's at eleven. He'd see the New Year in alone, and would go out tomorrow even though he'd had no first foot. Maybe he'd walk under a ladder, too, and step on every crack in the pavement.

Just to show that he could.

His car was parked one street over from Arden Street – no spaces available near his flat. He unlocked the boot and extracted his carry-out: a bottle of Macallan, six bottles of Belhaven Best, paprika crisps, dry roasted peanuts. There was a pizza in the freezer, and some sliced tongue in the fridge. Enough to see him through. He'd been saving the *White Album*; could think of worse ways to see in the New Year.

One of them was standing by his tenement door: Cafferty.

'Would you look at us?' Cafferty said, opening his arms. 'Both on our ownios, this of all nights!'

'Speak for yourself.'

'Oh, right,' Cafferty said, nodding, 'you're hosting the social event of the year – I'd forgotten. A bevvy of beauties are on their way as I speak, scented and mini-skirted.' He paused. 'Merry Christmas, by the way.' He tried handing something to Rebus, who wasn't of a mind to take it. Something small and shiny . . .

'Twenty fags?'

Cafferty shrugged. 'An impulse buy.'

Rebus had three packets waiting for him upstairs. 'Keep them,' he said. 'Maybe I'll get lucky and you'll get cancer.'

Cafferty tutted. His face seemed huge, moon-like in the sodium light. 'I thought we'd take a drive.'

Rebus stared at him. 'A drive?'

'Where d'you fancy: Queensferry, Portobello . . . ?'

'What's so urgent?' Rebus put his carrier bags down; they clinked musically as they came to rest.

'Bryce Callan.'

'What about him?'

'You don't have a case, do you?' Rebus didn't respond. 'Won't get one either. And I haven't noticed any worry lines on Barry Hutton's brow.'

'So?'

'So maybe I can help.'

Rebus shuffled his feet. 'And why would you do that?'

'I might have my reasons.'

'Reasons you didn't have ten days ago when I asked?'

'Maybe you didn't ask nicely enough.'

'Then I've got some bad news: my manners haven't improved with age.'

Cafferty smiled. 'Just a drive, Strawman. You can do your drinking, and fill me in on the case.'

Rebus narrowed his eyes. 'Land developer,' he mused. 'It would be branching out, wouldn't it?'

'Easier to do if you can take over an existing business,' Cafferty admitted.

'Barry Hutton's business? I put him away, you step in. I can't see Bryce being too happy.'

'My problem.' Cafferty winked. 'Let's go for that drive. Stick a note on the door, let the glamour models know the party's shifted back an hour.'

'They won't be happy. You know what models are like.'

'Overpaid and underfed, you mean? Would that be the opposite of yourself, DI Rebus?'

'Ha ha.'

'Careful now,' Cafferty warned. 'This time of the season, a split side can take ages to heal.'

Somehow, they'd been moving while they talked, and Rebus was surprised to find that he'd picked up his carrier bags, too. Now they stood by the Jag. Cafferty yanked open the driver's door, slid in behind the steering wheel in a single, practised movement. Rebus stood there a moment longer. Hogmanay, last day of the year: a day for paying debts, balancing the books . . . a day for finishing things.

He made to get in.

'Sling the booze in the back,' Cafferty suggested. 'I've a hip flask in the glove compartment, twenty-five-year-old Armagnac. Wait till you taste this stuff. I'm telling you, it would turn a heathen into John the fucking Baptist.'

But Rebus had extracted the Macallan from one of his bags. 'I'll stick to my own,' he said.

'Not a bad drop either.' Cafferty was making a great effort not to be offended. 'Make sure you waft some of it my way, so I can at least inhale.' He turned the ignition. The Jaguar purred like the cat it resembled. And suddenly they were moving, looking to the outside world like nothing more suspicious than two friends out for a jaunt. South to the Grange, and further south to Blackford Hill, then east towards the coast. And Rebus talked, as much for his own benefit as Cafferty's. About the pact two business friends had made with a devil called Bryce Callan, a pact which would lead to a killing. About how the killer waited in vain for his friend to return, living rough – a disguise against detection, or a route to penitence? Past lessons learned by Barry Hutton, now a successful businessman, seeing an opportunity for fresh riches and increased fame: replaying that game from twenty years before, determined that his man on the council would become his player in parliament . . .

At the end of the story Cafferty seemed thoughtful, then said, 'So it's tainted before it begins?'

'Maybe,' Rebus replied, putting the bottle back to his mouth. Portobello: that's where they looked to be headed, maybe park by the harbour and sit with windows open. But Cafferty headed on to Seafield Road and started driving towards Leith.

'There's some land up this way I'm thinking of buying,' he explained. 'Got some plans drawn up, builder called Peter Kirkwall did the costings.'

'For what?'

'Leisure complex – restaurant, maybe a cinema or health club. Some luxury flats parked on top.'

'Kirkwall works with Barry Hutton.'

'I know.'

'Hutton's sure to find out.'

Cafferty shrugged. 'Something I just have to live with.' He gave a smile Rebus couldn't read. 'I heard about this plot of land next to where they're building the parliament. It sold for three-quarters of a million four years ago. Know what its price is now? Four million. How's that for a yield?'

Rebus pushed the cork back into the bottle. This stretch of road was all car dealers, wasteland behind, and then the sea. They headed up a narrow, unlit lane, its surface uneven. A large metal fence at the far end. Cafferty stopped the Jag, got out and took a key to the padlock, pulled the heavy metal chain free and pushed the gates open with his foot.

'What's there to see?' Rebus asked, uneasy now, as Cafferty got back into the driving seat. He could run, but it was a long way to civilisation, and he was dead beat. Besides, he was done running.

'It's all warehouses just now. If you coughed too loud, they'd collapse. Easy enough to bulldoze, and there's a quarter-mile of seafront to play with.'

They drove through the gates.

'A quiet place for a chat,' Cafferty said.

But they weren't here to chat; Rebus knew that now. He turned his head, saw that another car was following them into the compound. It was a red Ferrari. Rebus turned back to Cafferty.

'What's going on?'

'Business,' Cafferty said coldly, 'that's all.' He stopped the Jag, pulled on the handbrake. 'Out,' he ordered. Rebus didn't move. Cafferty got out of the car, left his door open. The other car had pulled up alongside. Both sets of headlamps stayed on dipped, illuminating the cracked concrete surface of the compound. Rebus focused on one of the weeds, its jagged shadow crawling up the wall of one of the warehouses. Rebus's door was pulled open. Hands grabbed at him. He heard a soft click as his seat belt was unlocked, and then he was being dragged out, thrown on to the cold ground. He took his time looking up. Three figures, silhouetted against the headlamps, breath billowing from their dark faces. Cafferty and two others. Rebus started getting to his feet. The single malt had fallen from the car, smashed on the concrete. He wished he'd taken one more hit of it while he had the chance.

A boot to the chest had enough force to send him on to his backside. He put his hands out behind him, steadying himself, so that he was unprotected when the next blow came. To the face this time, connecting with his chin, cracking his head back. He felt the snap as bones in his neck uttered a complaint.

'Can't take a warning,' a voice said: not Cafferty's. A thin man, younger. Rebus narrowed his eyes, shielded them with a hand as though peering into the sun.

'It's Barry Hutton, isn't it?' Rebus asked.

'Pick him up,' was the barked response. The third man – Hutton's man – pulled Rebus to his feet as though he were made of cardboard, held him from behind.

'Gonny teach you,' Hutton hissed. Rebus could make out the features now: face tight with anger, mouth downturned, nose pinched. He was wearing black leather driving gloves. A question – absurd under the circumstances – flashed through Rebus's mind: *wonder if they were a Christmas present?*

Hutton hit him with a fist, connecting with Rebus's left cheek. Rebus rode the blow, but still felt it. As he turned his face, he caught a glimpse of the man pinning him from behind. It wasn't Mick Lorimer.

'Lorimer isn't with you tonight, then?' Rebus asked. Blood was pooling in his mouth. He swallowed it. 'Were you there the night he killed Roddy Grieve?'

'Mick just doesn't know when to stop,' Hutton said. 'I wanted the bastard warned off, not on a slab.'

'You just can't get the staff these days.' He felt the grip around his chest tighten, forcing the breath from his lungs.

'No, but there always seems to be a smart-arsed cop around when you least need it.' Another blow, this time bursting Rebus's nose open. Tears pounded from his eyes. He tried blinking them away. Oh, Jesus Christ, that hurt.

'Thanks, Uncle Ger,' Hutton was saying. 'That's one I owe you.'

'What else are partners for?' Cafferty said. He took a step forward, and now Rebus could see his face clearly. It was dead of any emotion. 'You wouldn't have been this careless, Strawman, not five years back.' He stepped back again.

'You're right,' Rebus said. 'Maybe after tonight I'll retire.'

'You'll do that all right,' Hutton said. 'A nice long rest.'

'Where'll you put him?' Cafferty asked.

'Plenty of sites we're working on. A nice big hole and half a ton of concrete.'

Rebus wrestled, but the grip was fierce. He raised a foot, stomped hard, but his captor was wearing steel toecaps. The grip tightened, like a thick metal band, crushing him. He let out a groan.

'But first, a bit more fun,' Hutton was saying. He came close, so his face was inches from Rebus's. Then Rebus felt pain explode behind his eyeballs as Hutton's knee thudded into his groin. Bile rose in his throat, the whisky seeking the quickest exit route. The grip loosened, fell away, and he dropped to his knees. Mist in front of his eyes, thick as haar, the sea singing in his ears. He wiped his hand across his face, clearing his vision. Fire was spreading out from his groin. Whisky fumes at the back of his throat. When he tried breathing through his nose, huge bubbles of blood expanded and popped. The next blow caught him on the temple. A kick this time, sending him rolling across concrete to end hunched foetus-like on the ground. He knew he should get up, take the fight to them. Nothing to lose. Go down kicking and scratching, punching and spitting. Hutton was crouching in front of him, pulling his head up by the hair.

There were explosions in the distance: the fireworks at the Castle, meaning it was midnight. The sky was lit with coloured blooms, blood-red, aching yellow.

'You'll stay hidden a sight longer than twenty years, believe me,' Hutton was saying. Cafferty was standing just behind him, holding something. Light from the fireworks glinted from it. A knife, blade had to be eight or nine inches. Cafferty was going to do it himself. A determined grip on the handle. This was the moment they'd been coming to, ever since the Weasel's office. Rebus almost welcomed it: Cafferty rather than the young thug. Hutton had camouflaged his criminality well, the veneer thick and brightly polished. Rebus would take Cafferty every time . . .

But now the sea was washing over all of it, washing Rebus, cleaning him with its flow of noise, building in his ears to a deafening roar, the shadows and light blurring, becoming one . . .

Fade to grey.

42

He woke up.

Frozen, aching, as if he'd spent the night in a sepulchre. His eyes were crusted. He prised them open. Cars all around him. Couldn't stop shivering, body temperature dangerously low. He rose shakily to his feet, held on to one of the cars for support. Garage forecourt; had to be Seafield Road. He broke the crust of blood in his nostrils, started breathing fast. Get that blood pumping round his body. His shirt and jacket were spattered with blood, but no wounds, no sign that he'd been stabbed or slashed.

What the hell is this?

It wasn't light yet. He angled his watch to the nearest street lamp: three thirty. Started patting his pockets, found his mobile and entered the access code. Got the night shift at St Leonard's.

Is this heaven or hell?

'I need a car,' he said. 'Seafield Road, the Volvo concession.'

He ran on the spot while he waited, patting himself with aching arms. Still couldn't stop shivering. The patrol car took ten minutes, two uniforms emerging from it.

'Christ, look at you,' one of them said.

Rebus stumbled into the back seat. 'That heating on full blast?' he asked.

The uniforms got into the front, closed their doors. 'What happened to you?' the passenger asked.

Rebus thought the question over. 'I'm not sure,' he said at last.

'Happy New Year anyway, sir,' the driver said.

'Happy New Year,' the passenger added.

Rebus tried to form the words; couldn't. Slouched down in the seat instead and concentrated on staying alive.

He took a team back to the compound. The concrete surface was like a skating rink.

'What's happened here?' Siobhan Clarke asked.

'Wasn't like this,' Rebus answered, fighting to keep his balance. The hospital had been reluctant to let him go. But his nose wasn't broken, and though he might be seeing some blood in his urine, there wasn't any sign of internal injury or infection. It was one of the nurses who'd made the comment: 'Lot of blood for a busted nose.' She was studying his clothes at the time. It had made him think: lacerations and grazes to the face, a cut on the inside of the cheek and a bloody nose. He had spatters of blood all over him. Saw the knife again, Cafferty standing behind Barry Hutton . . .

And now, standing pretty much where he'd been only ten hours before . . . nothing except the sheet of ice.

'It's been hosed down,' he said.

'What?'

'They hosed away the blood.'

He began to walk back towards the car.

Barry Hutton wasn't home. His girlfriend hadn't seen him since the previous evening. His car was parked outside his office block, locked and with the alarm set, no sign of the keys. No sign of Barry Hutton either.

They found Cafferty at the hotel. He was enjoying morning coffee in the lounge. Hutton's man – now Cafferty's, if he hadn't been all along – was reading a paper at a neighbouring table.

'I've just found out what they're charging come the millennium,' Cafferty said of the hotel. 'Shysters, the lot of them. Wrong line of work, you and me.'

Rebus sat down opposite his nemesis. Siobhan Clarke introduced herself, stayed standing.

'Two of you,' Cafferty mused. 'That means corroboration.'

Rebus turned to Siobhan. 'Go wait outside.' She didn't move. 'Please.' She hesitated, then turned and stomped off.

'A fiery one that.' Cafferty laughed, sitting forward, face suddenly showing concern. 'How are you, Strawman? Thought I was going to lose you there.'

'Where's Hutton?'

'Christ, man, how should I know?'

Rebus turned to the bodyguard. 'Go to Warriston Crem, check the name Robert Hill. Cafferty's minders tend to live short lives.' The man stared at him blankly.

'Has Barry not turned up, then?' Cafferty was feigning amazement.

'You killed him. Now you step into his shoes.' Rebus paused. 'Which was the plan all along?'

Cafferty just smiled.

'What's Bryce Callan going to say?' Rebus watched the smile broaden still further. He began nodding. 'Bryce okayed it? This was where it was always headed?'

Cafferty spoke in an undertone. 'You can't go around bumping off people like Roddy Grieve. It's bad for everyone.'

'But you *can* murder Barry Hutton?'

'I saved your neck, Strawman. You owe me.'

Rebus pointed a finger. 'You took me there. You set the whole trap, and Hutton walked into it.'

'You both walked into it.' Cafferty was almost preening. Rebus wanted to stick a fist in his face, and Cafferty knew it. He looked around at the elegant surroundings. Chintz and antimacassars, chandeliers and sound-deadening carpets. 'Wouldn't do, really now, would it?'

'I've been thrown out of better places than this.' Rebus glowered. 'Where is he?'

Cafferty sat back. 'You know the story about the Old Town? Reason it's so narrow and steep, there's some big serpent buried under it.' He waited for Rebus to get it; decided to supply the punchline himself. 'Room for more than one snake under the Old Town, Strawman.'

The Old Town: the building works around Holyrood – Queensberry House, Dynamic Earth, *Scotsman* offices . . . hotels and apartments. So many building sites. Lots of good, deep holes, filling with concrete . . .

'We'll look for him,' Rebus said. Cafferty's words in the garden of remembrance: *where there's no body, there's no crime.*

Cafferty shrugged. 'You do that. And be sure to hand your clothes in as evidence. Maybe his blood's mixed in there with yours. Maybe it'll be *you* who has to do some explaining. Me, I was here all evening.' He waved an arm casually. 'Ask around. It was a hell of a party, a hell of a night. By next Hogmanay . . . well, who knows what we'll all be doing? We'll have our parliament by then, and this . . . this will all be history.'

'I don't care how long it takes,' Rebus warned. But Cafferty just laughed. He was back, and in charge of *his* Edinburgh, and that was all that mattered . . .

Acknowledgements

I'd like to thank the following: Historic Scotland, for providing a tour of Queensberry House; The Scottish Office Constitution Group; Professor Anthony Busuttil, University of Edinburgh; the staff at Edinburgh Mortuary; staff at St Leonard's police station and Lothian and Borders Police HQ; the Old Manor Hotel, Lundin Links (especially Alistair Clark and George Clark).

The following books and guides were helpful: 'Who's Who in the Scottish Parliament' (a supplement provided with *Scotland on Sunday*, the issue of 16 May 1999); *Crime and Criminal Justice in Scotland* by Peter Young (Stationery Office, 1997); *A Guide to the Scottish Parliament* edited by Gerry Hassan (Stationery Office, 1999); *The Battle for Scotland* by Andrew Marr (Penguin, 1992).

The lyrics to 'Wages Day' are by Ricky Ross. The track can be found on the Deacon Blue albums *Raintown* and *Our Town: the Greatest Hits*.

I'd also like to thank Angus Calder for permission to quote from his poem 'Love Poem', and Alison Hendon, who brought another poem to my attention and gifted me the title of this book.

For further information on the remarkable Rosslyn Chapel, visit its website at www.ROSSLYNCHAPEL.org.uk

The Falls

To Allan and Euan, who set the ball rolling

Not my accent – I didn't lose that so much as wipe it off my shoe, as soon as I started to live in England – but rather my own temperament, the prototypically Scottish part of my character that was chippy, aggressive, mean, morbid and, despite my best endeavours, persistently deist. I was, and always would be, a lousy escapee from the unnatural history museum . . .

Philip Kerr, 'The Unnatural History Museum'

1

'You think I killed her, don't you?'

He sat well forward on the sofa, head slumped in towards his chest. His hair was lank, long-fringed. Both knees worked like pistons, the heels of his grubby trainers never meeting the floor.

'You on anything, David?' Rebus asked.

The young man looked up. His eyes were bloodshot, dark-rimmed. A lean, angular face, bristles on the unshaved chin. His name was David Costello. Not Dave or Davy: David, he'd made that clear. Names, labels, classification: all very important. The media had varied its descriptions of him. He was 'the boyfriend', 'the tragic boyfriend', 'the missing student's boyfriend'. He was 'David Costello, 22' or 'fellow student David Costello, in his early twenties'. He 'shared a flat with Ms Balfour' or was 'a frequent visitor' to the 'disappearance riddle flat'.

Nor was the flat just a flat. It was 'the flat in Edinburgh's fashionable New Town', the 'quarter-million flat owned by Ms Balfour's parents'. John and Jacqueline Balfour were 'the numbed family', 'the shocked banker and his wife'. Their daughter was 'Philippa, 20, a student of art history at the University of Edinburgh'. She was 'pretty', 'vivacious', 'carefree', 'full of life'.

And now she was missing.

Detective Inspector John Rebus shifted position, from in front of the marble fireplace to slightly to one side of it. David Costello's eyes followed the move.

'The doctor gave me some pills,' he said, finally answering the question.

'Did you take them?' Rebus asked.

The young man shook his head slowly, eyes still on Rebus.

'Don't blame you,' Rebus said, sliding his hands into his pockets. 'Knock you out for a few hours, but they don't change anything.'

It was two days since Philippa – known to friends and family as 'Flip' – had gone missing. Two days wasn't long, but her disappearance was out of character. Friends had called the flat at around seven in the evening to confirm that Flip would be meeting up with them within the hour at a bar on the South Side. It was one of those small, trendy places which had sprung up around the university, catering to an economic boom and the need for dim lighting and overpriced flavoured vodkas. Rebus knew this because he'd walked past it a couple of times on his way to and from his place of work. There was an old-fashioned pub practically next door, with vodka mixers at a pound-fifty. No trendy chairs though, and serving staff who knew their way around a brawl but not a cocktail list.

Seven, seven-fifteen, she probably left the flat. Tina, Trist, Camille and Albie were already on their second round of drinks. Rebus had consulted the files to confirm those names. Trist was short for Tristram, and Albie was Albert. Trist was with Tina; Albie was with Camille. Flip should have been with David, but David, she explained on the phone, wouldn't be joining them.

'Another bust-up,' she'd said, not sounding too concerned.

She'd set the flat's alarm before leaving. That was another first for Rebus – student digs with an alarm. And she'd done the mortise lock as well as the Yale, leaving the flat secure. Down a single flight of stairs and out into the warm night air. A steep hill separated her from Princes Street. Another climb from there would take her to the Old Town, the South Side. No way she'd be walking. But records from her home telephone and mobile had failed to find a match for any taxi firm in the city. So if she'd taken one, she'd hailed it on the street.

If she'd got as far as hailing one.

'I didn't, you know,' David Costello said.

'Didn't what, sir?'

'Didn't kill her.'

'Nobody's saying you did.'

'No?' He looked up again, directly into Rebus's eyes.

'No,' Rebus assured him, that being his job after all.

'The search warrant . . .' Costello began.

'It's standard, any case of this kind,' Rebus explained. It was, too: suspicious disappearance, you checked all the places the person might be. You went by the book: all the paperwork signed, clearance given. You searched the boyfriend's flat. Rebus could have added: *we do it because nine times out of ten, it's someone the victim knows*. Not a stranger, plucking prey from the night. It was your loved ones who killed you: spouse, lover, son or daughter. It was your uncle, your closest friend, the one person you trusted. They'd been cheating on you, or you'd cheated them. You knew something, you had something. They were jealous, spurned, needed money.

If Flip Balfour was dead, her body would turn up soon; if she was alive and didn't want to be found, then the job would be more difficult. Her parents had appeared on TV, pleading with her to make contact. Police were at the family home, intercepting calls in case any ransom demand should arrive. Police were wandering through David Costello's flat on the Canongate, hoping to turn up something. And police were here – in Flip Balfour's flat. They were 'babysitting' David

Costello – stopping the media from getting too close. This was what the young man had been told, and it was partly true.

Flip's flat had been searched the previous day. Costello had keys, even to the alarm system. The phone call to Costello's own flat had come at ten p.m.: Trist, asking if he'd heard from Flip, only she'd been on her way to Shapiro's and hadn't turned up.

'She's not with you, is she?'

'I'm the last person she'd come to,' Costello had complained.

'Heard you'd fallen out. What is it this time?' Trist's voice had been slurred, ever-so-slightly amused. Costello hadn't answered him. He'd cut the call and tried Flip's mobile, got her answering service, left a message asking her to phone him. Police had listened to the recording, concentrating on nuance, trying to read falseness into each word or phrase. Trist had phoned Costello again at midnight. The group had been to Flip's flat: no one home. They'd been ringing round, but none of her friends seemed to know anything. They waited until Costello himself arrived at the flat, unlocking it. No sign of Flip inside.

In their minds, she was already a Missing Person, what police called a 'MisPer', but they'd waited till next morning before calling Flip's mother at the family home in East Lothian. Mrs Balfour had wasted no time, dialling 999 immediately. After receiving what she felt was short shrift from the police switchboard, she'd called her husband at his London office. John Balfour was the senior partner in a private bank, and if the Chief Constable of Lothian and Borders Police wasn't a client, someone certainly was: within an hour, officers were on the case – orders from the Big House, meaning Force HQ in Fettes Avenue.

David Costello had unlocked the flat for the two CID men. Within, they found no signs of a disturbance, no clues as to Philippa Balfour's whereabouts, fate, or state of mind. It was a tidy flat: stripped floors, fresh paint on the walls. (The decorator was being interviewed, too.) The drawing room was large, with twin windows rising from floor level. There were two bedrooms, one turned into a study. The designer kitchen was smaller than the pine-panelled bathroom. There was a lot of David Costello's stuff in the bedroom. Someone had piled his clothes on a chair, then placed some books and CDs on top, crowning the structure with a wash-bag.

When asked, Costello could only assume it was Flip's work. His words: 'We'd had a falling-out. This was probably her way of dealing with it.' Yes, they'd had arguments before, but no, she'd never piled up all his stuff, not that he could remember.

John Balfour had travelled to Scotland by private jet – loaned him by an understanding client – and was at the New Town flat almost before the police.

'Well?' had been his first question. Costello himself offered an answer: 'I'm sorry.'

Much had been read into those words by CID officers, discussing the case in private. An argument with your girlfriend turns nasty; next you know, she's dead; you hide the body but, confronted by her father, innate breeding takes over and you blurt out a semi-confession.

I'm sorry.

So many ways to read those two short words. Sorry we argued; sorry you've been troubled; sorry this has happened; sorry I didn't look after her; sorry for what I've done . . .

And now David Costello's parents were in town, too. They'd taken two rooms at one of the best hotels. They lived on the outskirts of Dublin. The father, Thomas, was described as 'independently wealthy', while the mother, Theresa, worked as an interior designer.

Two rooms: there'd been some discussion back at St Leonard's as to why they'd need two rooms. But then, when David was their only son, why did they bother to live in an eight-bedroom house?

There'd been even more discussion about what St Leonard's was doing in a New Town case. The nearest cop shop to the flat was Gayfield Square, but additional officers had been drafted in from Leith, St Leonard's and Torphichen.

'Someone's been pulling strings,' was the universal view. 'Drop everything, some posh bit's done a runner.'

Privately, Rebus didn't disagree.

'Do you want anything?' he said now. 'Tea? Coffee?'

Costello shook his head.

'Mind if I . . . ?'

Costello looked at him, seeming not to understand. Then realisation dawned. 'Go ahead,' he said. 'The kitchen's . . .' He started to gesture.

'I know where it is, thanks,' Rebus said. He closed the door after him and stood for a moment in the hallway, glad to be out of the stifling drawing room. His temples throbbed and the nerves behind his eyes felt stretched. There were sounds coming from the study. Rebus stuck his head round the door.

'I'm putting the kettle on.'

'Good idea.' Detective Constable Siobhan Clarke didn't take her eyes from the computer screen.

'Anything?'

'Tea, please.'

'I meant—'

'Nothing yet. Letters to friends, some of her essays. I've got about a thousand e-mails to go through. Her password would help.'

'Mr Costello says she never told him.'

Clarke cleared her throat.

'What does that mean?' Rebus asked.

'It means my throat's tickly,' Clarke said. 'Just milk in mine, thanks.'

Rebus left her and went into the kitchen, filled the kettle and searched for mugs and tea-bags.

'When can I go home?'

Rebus turned to where Costello was standing in the hall.

'Might be better if you didn't,' Rebus told him. 'Reporters and cameras . . . they'll keep on at you, phoning day and night.'

'I'll take the phone off the hook.'

'Be like being a prisoner.' Rebus watched the young man shrug. He said something Rebus didn't catch.

'Sorry?'

'I can't stay here,' Costello repeated.

'Why not?'

'I don't know . . . it's just . . .' He shrugged again, ran his hands through his hair, pulling it back from his forehead. 'Flip should be here. It's almost too much. I keep remembering that the last time we were here together, we were having a row.'

'What was it about?'

Costello laughed hollowly. 'I can't even remember.'

'This was the day she disappeared?'

'The afternoon, yes. I stormed out.'

'You argue a lot then?' Rebus tried to make the question sound casual.

Costello just stood there, staring into space, head shaking slowly. Rebus turned away, separated two Darjeeling tea-bags and dropped them into the mugs. Was Costello unravelling? Was Siobhan Clarke listening from behind the study door? They were babysitting Costello, yes, part of a team running three eight-hour shifts, but they'd brought him here for another reason, too. Ostensibly, he was on hand to explain names that occurred in Philippa Balfour's correspondence. But Rebus had wanted him there because just maybe it was the scene of the crime. And just maybe David Costello had something to hide. The betting at St Leonard's was even money; you could get two-to-one at Torphichen, while Gayfield had him odds-on favourite.

'Your parents said you could move into their hotel,' Rebus said. He turned to face Costello. 'They've booked two rooms, so one's probably going spare.'

Costello didn't take the bait. He watched the detective for a few seconds more, then turned away, putting his head around the study door.

'Have you found what you're looking for?' he asked.

'It could take some time, David,' Siobhan said. 'Best just to let us get on with it.'

'You won't find any answers in there.' He meant the computer screen. When she didn't answer, he straightened a little and angled his head. 'You're some sort of expert, are you?'

'It's something that has to be done.' Her voice was quiet, as though she didn't want it to carry beyond the room.

He seemed about to add something, but thought better of it, and stalked back towards the drawing room instead. Rebus took Clarke's tea through.

'Now that's class,' she said, examining the tea-bag floating in the mug.

'Wasn't sure how strong you'd want it,' Rebus explained. 'What did you think?'

She considered for a moment. 'Seems genuine enough.'

'Maybe you're just a sucker for a pretty face.'

She snorted, fished the tea-bag out and tipped it into the waste-bin. 'Maybe,' she said. 'So what's *your* thinking?'

'Press conference tomorrow,' Rebus reminded her. 'Reckon we can persuade Mr Costello to make a public appeal?'

Two detectives from Gayfield Square had the evening shift. Rebus headed home and started to fill a bath. He felt like a long soak, and squeezed some washing-up liquid under the hot tap, remembering it was something his parents had done for him when he was a kid. You came in muddy from the football pitch, and it was a hot bath with washing-up liquid. It wasn't that the family couldn't afford bubble-bath: 'It's just washing liquid at a posh price,' his mother had said.

Philippa Balfour's bathroom had boasted over a dozen different 'balms', 'bathing lotions' and 'foaming oils'. Rebus did his own stock-take: razor, shaving cream, toothpaste and a single toothbrush, plus a bar of soap. In the medicine cabinet: sticking plasters, paracetamol and a packet of condoms. He looked in the packet – one left. The sell-by was the previous summer. When he closed the cabinet, he met the gaze of his reflection. Grey-faced, hair streaked grey, too. Jowly, even when he stuck out his chin. Tried smiling, saw teeth which had missed their last two appointments. His dentist was threatening to strike him from his list.

'Get in line, pal,' Rebus muttered, turning away from the mirror before undressing.

The retirement party for Detective Chief Superintendent 'Farmer' Watson had commenced at six. It was actually the third or fourth party of its kind, but was to be the last – and the only official gathering. The Police Club on Leith Walk had been decked out with streamers, balloons and a huge banner which read FROM UNDER ARREST TO A WELL-DESERVED REST. Someone had dumped a bale of straw on the dance-floor, completing the farmyard scene with an inflatable pig and sheep. The bar was doing roaring business when Rebus arrived. He'd passed a trio of departing Big House brass on his way in. Checked his watch: six-forty. They'd given the retiring DCS forty minutes of their valuable time.

There'd been a presentation earlier in the day at St Leonard's. Rebus had missed it; he'd been babysitting at the time. But he'd heard about the speech made by Assistant Chief Constable Colin Carswell. Several officers from the Farmer's previous postings – some now retired themselves – were on hand to say a few words. They'd stuck around for the evening's proceedings, and looked to have been drinking the afternoon away: ties discarded or hanging limply askew, faces shiny with alcoholic heat. One man was singing, his voice battling the music from the ceiling-mounted loudspeakers.

'What can I get you, John?' the Farmer said, leaving his table to join Rebus at the bar.

'Maybe a small whisky, sir.'

'Half-bottle of malt over here when you've a minute!' the Farmer roared at the barman, who was busy topping up pints of lager. The Farmer's eyes narrowed as he focused on Rebus. 'Did you see those buggers from the Big House?'

'Passed them as I came in.'

'Bloody orange juices all round, then a quick handshake before home.' The Farmer was concentrating on not slurring his words, overcompensating as a result. 'Never really understood the phrase "biscuit-ersed" before, but that's what those lot were: biscuit-ersed to a man!'

Rebus smiled, told the barman to make it an Ardbeg.

'A bloody double, mind,' the Farmer ordered.

'Been enjoying a drink yourself, sir?' Rebus asked.

The Farmer blew out his cheeks. 'Few old pals came to see me off.' He nodded in the direction of the table. Rebus looked, too. He saw a posse of drunks. Beyond them stood tables spread with a buffet: sandwiches, sausage rolls, crisps and peanuts. He saw faces he knew from all the Lothian and Borders Divisional HQs. Macari, Allder, Shug Davidson, Roy Frazer. Bill Pryde was in conversation with Bobby Hogan. Grant Hood was standing next to a couple of Crime Squad officers called Claverhouse and Ormiston, and trying not to look as though he was sucking up to them. George 'Hi-Ho' Silvers was finding that DC Phyllida Hawes and DS Ellen Wylie weren't about to fall for his chat-up lines. Jane Barbour from the Big House was exchanging gossip with Siobhan Clarke, who'd at one time been attached to Barbour's Sex Offences Unit.

'If anyone knew about this,' Rebus said, 'the bad guys would have a field day. Who's left to mind the store?'

The Farmer laughed. 'It's a skeleton crew at St Leonard's, all right.'

'Good turn-out. Wonder if I'd get as many at mine.'

'More, I'd bet.' The Farmer leaned close. 'The brass would all be there for a start, just to make sure they weren't dreaming.'

It was Rebus's turn to smile. He lifted his glass, toasted his boss. They both savoured their drinks, then the Farmer smacked his lips.

'How long d'you think?' he asked.

Rebus shrugged. 'I've not got my thirty yet.'

'Can't be long though, can it?'

'I'm not counting.' But he was lying: most weeks he thought about it. 'Thirty' meant thirty years of service. That was when your pension hit the max. It was what a lot of officers lived for: retirement in their fifties and a cottage by the sea.

'Here's a story I don't often tell,' the Farmer said. 'My first week on the force, they had me working the front desk, graveyard shift. This young lad – not even in his teens – comes in, walks straight up to the desk. "I've broke my wee sister," he says.' The Farmer's eyes were staring into space. 'I can see him now, the way he looked, the exact words . . . "I've broke my wee sister." I hadn't a clue what he meant. Turned out he'd pushed her down the stairs, killed her.' He paused, took another gulp of whisky. 'My first week on the force. Know what my sergeant said? "It can only get better." ' He forced a smile. 'I've never been sure he was right . . .' Suddenly his arms went into the air, the smile broadening into a grin. 'Here she is! Here she is! Just when I thought I was being stood up.'

His embrace almost swamped DCI Gill Templer. The Farmer planted a kiss on her cheek. 'You're not the floor-show by any chance?' he asked. Then he mimed a slap to his forehead. 'Sexist language – are you going to report me?'

'I'll let it go this time,' Gill said, 'in exchange for a drink.'

'My shout,' Rebus said. 'What'll you have?'

'Long vodka.'

Bobby Hogan was yelling for the Farmer to go settle an argument.

'Duty calls,' the Farmer said by way of an apology, before heading unsteadily across the floor.

'His party piece?' Gill guessed.

Rebus shrugged. The Farmer's speciality was naming all the books of the Bible. His record was just under a minute; no way would it be challenged tonight.

'Long vodka,' Rebus told the barman. He raised his whisky glass. 'And a couple more of these.' He saw Gill's look. 'One's for the Farmer,' he explained.

'Of course.' She was smiling, but the smile didn't reach her eyes.

'Fixed a date for your own bash?' Rebus asked.

'Which one is that?'

'I just thought, first female DCS in Scotland . . . got to be worth a night out, hasn't it?'

'I drank a Babycham when I heard.' She watched the barman dribble angostura into her glass. 'How's the Balfour case?'

Rebus looked at her. 'Is this my new Chief Super asking?'

'John . . .'

Funny how that single word could say so much. Rebus wasn't sure he caught all the nuances, but he caught enough.

John, don't push this.

John, I know there's a history between us, but that's long dead.

Gill Templer had worked her arse off to get where she was now, but she was also under the microscope – plenty of people would want her to fail, including some she probably counted as friends.

Rebus just nodded and paid for the drinks, tipping one of the whiskies into the other glass.

'Saving him from himself,' he said, nodding towards the Farmer, who was already on to the New Testament.

'Always the willing martyr,' Gill said.

A cheer went up as the Farmer's recitation finished. Someone said it was a new record, but Rebus knew it wasn't. It was just another gesture, another version of the gold watch or mantel-clock. The malt tasted of seaweed and peat, but Rebus knew that whenever he drank Ardbeg from now on, he'd think of a small boy walking through the doors of a police station . . .

Siobhan Clarke was making her way across the room.

'Congratulations,' she said.

The two women shook hands.

'Thanks, Siobhan,' Gill said. 'Maybe it'll be you one day.'

'Why not?' Siobhan agreed. 'Glass ceiling's what truncheons are for.' She punched her fist into the air above her head.

'Need a drink, Siobhan?' Rebus asked.

The two women shared a look. 'About all they're good for,' Siobhan said with a wink. Rebus left the pair of them laughing.

The karaoke started at nine. Rebus went to the toilets and felt the sweat cooling on his back. His tie was already off and in his pocket. His jacket was slung over one of the chairs near the bar. Personnel at the party changed as some headed off, either to prepare for the night shift or because their mobile or pager had news for them. Others arrived, having been home to change out of work clothes. A female officer from the St Leonard's comms room had turned up in a short skirt, the first time Rebus had seen her legs. A rowdy quartet from one of the Farmer's postings in West Lothian arrived bearing photos of the Farmer from a quarter-century before. They'd slipped a few doctored prints into the mix, grafting the Farmer's head on to beefcake bodies, some of them in positions which went several leagues beyond compromising.

Rebus washed his hands, splashing some of the water on to his face and the back of his neck. Then of course there was only an electric hand-drier, so he had to use his handkerchief as a towel. Which was when Bobby Hogan walked in.

'See you're bottling it too,' Hogan said, making for the urinals.

'Ever heard me sing, Bobby?'

'We should do a duet: "There's a Hole in My Bucket".'

'We'd be about the only buggers who knew it.'

Hogan chuckled. 'Remember when it was us that were the young turks?'

'Long dead,' Rebus said, half to himself. Hogan thought he'd misheard, but Rebus just shook his head.

'So who's next for the golden cheery-bye?' Hogan asked, ready to head out again.

'Not me,' Rebus stated.

'No?'

Rebus was wiping at his neck again. 'I can't retire, Bobby. It would kill me.'

Hogan snorted. 'Same here. But then the job's killing me too.' The two men studied one another, then Hogan winked and yanked open the door. They walked back out into the heat and noise, Hogan opening his arms wide to greet an old friend. One of the Farmer's cronies pushed a glass towards Rebus.

'Ardbeg, right?'

Rebus nodded, sucked at where some had spilled on to the back of his hand, then, picturing a small boy with news to impart, raised the glass and downed it.

He took the set of keys from his pocket and unlocked the main door of the tenement block. The keys were shiny new, cut just that day. His shoulder rubbed against the wall as he headed for the stairs, and he kept a tight grip on the banister as he climbed. The second and third shiny keys unlocked the door to Philippa Balfour's flat.

There was no one inside, and the alarm hadn't been set. He switched on the lights. The loose rug underfoot seemed to want to wrap itself around his ankles, and he had to fight his way loose, holding on to the wall. The rooms were just as he'd left them, except that the computer was now missing from its desk, having been transferred to the station, where Siobhan was certain someone from Balfour's Internet service provider could help bypass the password.

In the bedroom, someone had removed the neat pile of David Costello's clothes from the chair. Rebus presumed the culprit to be Costello himself. He wouldn't have done so without permission – nothing left the flat unless okayed by the bosses. Forensics would have checked the clothes first, maybe taken samples from them. Already there were rumours of belt-tightening. A case like this, the cost could spiral skywards like smoke.

In the kitchen, Rebus poured himself a big glass of water and went through to sit in the drawing room, pretty much where David Costello had sat. A little of the water dribbled down his chin. The paintings on the walls – framed abstracts – were playing tricks, moving with him as he moved his eyes. He bent down to place the empty glass on the floor, and ended up on his hands and knees. Some bastard had spiked the drinks, only explanation. He turned and sat down, closed his eyes for a moment. MisPers: sometimes you worried in vain; they either turned up, or didn't want to be found. So many of them . . . photos and descriptions were always passing through the office, the faces slightly out of focus as though they were in the process of becoming ghosts. He blinked open his eyes and raised them to the ceiling, with its ornate cornicing. Big flats, the New Town had, but Rebus preferred it where he lived: more shops, not quite so smug . . .

The Ardbeg, it had to've been spiked. He probably wouldn't drink it again. It would come with its own ghost. He wondered what had happened to the boy: had it been accident or design? The boy would be a parent himself these days, maybe even a grandparent. Did he still dream about the sister he'd killed? Did he remember the young, nervous uniform standing behind the reception desk? Rebus ran his hands over the floor. It was bare wood, sanded and sealed. They hadn't taken the boards up, not yet. He felt for a gap between two planks and dug his nails in, but couldn't get any purchase. Somehow he knocked the glass and it started rolling, the noise filling the room. Rebus watched it until it stopped in the doorway, progress blocked by a pair of feet.

'What in the hell's going on?'

Rebus stood up. The man in front of him was in his mid-forties, hands in the pockets of a three-quarter-length black woollen overcoat. The man opened his stance a little, filling the doorway.

'Who are you?' Rebus asked.

The man slid a hand from his pocket, angled it towards his ear. He was holding a mobile phone. 'I'm calling the police,' he said.

'I'm a police officer.' Rebus reached into his own pocket, brought out his warrant card. 'DI Rebus.'

The man studied the card and handed it back. 'I'm John Balfour,' he said, his voice losing a little of its edge. Rebus nodded; he'd already figured as much.

'Sorry if I . . .' Rebus didn't finish the sentence. As he put the warrant card away, his left knee unlocked for a second.

'You've been drinking,' Balfour said.

'Sorry, yes. Retirement do. Not on duty or anything, if that's what you mean.'

'Then might I ask what you're doing in my daughter's flat?'

'You might,' Rebus agreed. He looked around. 'Just wanted to . . . well, I suppose I . . .' But he couldn't find the words.

'Will you leave, please?'

Rebus bowed his head a little. 'Of course.' Balfour moved so that Rebus could pass him without any contact. Rebus stopped in the hallway, half turned, ready with a further apology, but Philippa Balfour's father had walked over to the drawing-room window and was staring out at the night, hands gripping the shutters at either side.

He walked downstairs quietly, halfway sober now, closed the main door after him, not looking back, not looking up at the first-floor window. The streets were deserted, pavements glistening from an earlier downpour, street light reflected in them. Rebus's shoes were the only noise to be heard as he started the climb back up the slope: Queen Street, George Street, Princes Street, and then North Bridge. People were heading home from pubs, seeking taxis and lost friends.

Rebus took a left at the Tron Kirk and headed down the Canongate. A patrol car was parked kerbside, two bodies inside: one awake, the other asleep. They were detective constables from Gayfield, and had either drawn the short straw or were disliked by their boss: no other way to explain this thankless night-shift. Rebus was just another passer-by to the one who was awake. He had a newspaper folded in front of him, angled towards what light there was. When Rebus thumped the roof of the patrol car, the paper flew, landing on the head of the sleeper, who jerked awake and clawed at the smothering sheets.

As the passenger-side window was wound down, Rebus leaned on the sill. 'Your one o'clock alarm call, gentlemen.'

'I nearly shat myself,' the passenger said, trying to gather up his newspaper. His name was Pat Connolly, and he'd spent his first few years in CID waging a campaign against the nickname 'Paddy'. His colleague was Tommy Daniels, who seemed at ease – as he did in all things – with his own nickname of 'Distant'. Tommy to Tom-Tom to Distant Drums to Distant was the logic behind the name, but it also said much about the young man's character. Having been so rudely awakened from sleep, upon seeing and recognising Rebus all he'd done was roll his eyes.

'Could've fetched us a coffee,' Connolly was complaining.

'Could have,' Rebus agreed. 'Or maybe a dictionary.' He glanced towards the newspaper crossword. Less than a quarter of the grid had been filled in, while the puzzle itself was ringed by doodles and unsolved anagrams. 'Quiet night?'

'Apart from foreigners asking directions,' Connolly said. Rebus smiled and looked up and down the street. This was the heart of tourist Edinburgh. A hotel up by the traffic lights, a knitwear shop across the road. Fancy gifts and shortbread and whisky decanters. A kiltmaker's only fifty yards away. John Knox's house, hunched against its neighbours, half hidden in scowling shadow. At one time, the Old Town had been all there was of Edinburgh: a narrow spine running from the Castle to Holyrood, steep vennels leading off like crooked ribs. Then, as the place became ever more crowded and insanitary, the New Town had been built, its Georgian elegance a calculated snub to the Old Town and those who couldn't afford to move. Rebus found it interesting that while Philippa Balfour had chosen the New Town, David Costello had elected to live in the heart of the Old.

'Is he home?' he said now.

'Would we be here if he wasn't?' Connolly's eyes were on his partner, who was pouring tomato soup from a thermos. Distant sniffed the liquid hesitantly, then took a quick gulp. 'Actually, you could be the very man we want.'

Rebus looked at him. 'Oh aye?'

'Settle an argument. Deacon Blue, *Wages Day* – first album or second?'

Rebus smiled. 'It *has* been a quiet night.' Then, after a moment's reflection: 'Second.'

'Ten notes you owe me,' Connolly told Distant.

'Mind if I ask one?' Rebus had crouched down, felt his knees crack with the effort.

'Fire away,' Connolly said.

'What do you do if you need a pee?'

Connolly smiled. 'If Distant's asleep, I just use his thermos.'

The mouthful of soup almost exploded from Distant's nostrils. Rebus straightened up, feeling the blood pound in his ears: weather warning, force-ten hangover on its way.

'You going in?' Connolly asked. Rebus looked at the tenement again.

'Thinking about it.'

'We'd have to make a note.'

Rebus nodded. 'I know.'

'Just come from the Farmer's leaving do?'

Rebus turned towards the car. 'What's your point?'

'Well, you've had a drink, haven't you? Might not be the best time for a house call . . . sir.'

'You're probably right . . . Paddy,' Rebus said, making for the door.

'Remember what you asked me?'

Rebus had accepted a black coffee from David Costello. Popped two paracetamol from their foil shroud and washed them down. Middle of the night, but Costello hadn't been asleep. Black T-shirt, black jeans, bare feet. He'd made an off-licence run at some point: the bag was lying on the floor, the half-bottle of Bell's sitting not far from it, top missing but only a couple of decent measures down. Not a drinker then, Rebus surmised. It was a non-drinker's idea of how you handled a crisis – you drank whisky, but had to buy some first, and no point lashing out on a whole bottle. A couple of drinks would do you.

The living room was small, the flat itself reached from a turreted stairwell, winding ever upwards, the stone steps worn concave. Tiny windows. They'd planned this building in a century where heat was a luxury. The smaller the windows, the less heat you lost.

The living room was separated from the kitchen only by a step and what looked like partition walls. An open doorway, double-width. Signs that Costello liked to cook: pots and pans hanging from butcher's hooks. The living area was all books and CDs. Rebus had trawled the latter: John Martyn, Nick Drake, Joni Mitchell. Laid-back but cerebral. The books looked like stuff from Costello's English Literature course.

Costello was seated on a red futon; Rebus had chosen one of two straight-backed wooden chairs. They looked like the stuff he saw on Causewayside, placed outside shops for which the description 'antique' encompassed school desks from the sixties and green filing cabinets salvaged from office refits.

Costello ran his hand through his hair, didn't say anything.

'You asked if I thought you did it,' Rebus said, answering his own question.

'Did what?'

'Killed Flip. I think that's how you phrased it: "You think I killed her, don't you?"'

Costello nodded. 'It's so obvious, isn't it? We'd fallen out. I accept that you have to regard me as a suspect.'

'David, right now you're the *only* suspect.'

'You really think something's happened to her?'

'What do you think?'

Costello shook his head. 'I've done nothing but rack my brains since this all started.'

They sat in silence for a few moments.

'What are you doing here?' Costello asked suddenly.

'As I said, it's on my way home. You like the Old Town?'

'Yes.'

'Bit different from the New. You didn't want to move nearer Flip?'

'What are you trying to say?'

Rebus shrugged. 'Maybe it says something about the pair of you, the parts of town you prefer.'

Costello laughed drily. 'You Scots can be so reductive.'

'How's that?'

'Old Town versus New, Catholic/Protestant, east coast/west . . . Things can be a mite more complicated than that.'

'Attraction of opposites, that's all I was getting at.' There was another silence between them. Rebus scanned the room.

'Didn't make a mess then?'

'Who?'

'The search party.'

'Could have been worse.'

Rebus took a sip of coffee, pretended to savour it. 'You wouldn't have left the body here though, would you? I mean, only perverts do that sort of thing.' Costello looked at him. 'Sorry, I'm being . . . I mean, it's just theoretical. I'm not trying to say anything. But the forensics, they weren't looking for a body. They deal in things you and me can't even see. Flecks of blood, fibres, a single hair.' Rebus shook his head slowly. 'Juries eat that stuff up. The old idea of policing, it's going out the window.' He put down the gloss-black mug, reached into a pocket for his cigarette packet. 'Mind if I . . . ?'

Costello hesitated. 'Actually, I'll take one from you if that's all right.'

'Be my guest.' Rebus took one out of the packet, lit it, then tossed both packet and lighter to the younger man. 'Roll yourself a joint if you like,' he added. 'I mean, if that's your thing.'

'It's not.'

'Student life must be a bit different these days.'

Costello exhaled, studying the cigarette as if it was something alien to him. 'I'd assume it is,' he said.

Rebus smiled. Just two grown-ups having a smoke and a chat. The wee sma' hours and all that. A time for honesty, the outside world asleep, no one eavesdropping. He got up and walked over to the bookshelves. 'How did you and Flip meet?' he asked, picking a book at random and flipping through it.

'Dinner party. We clicked straight away. Next morning, after breakfast, we took a walk through Warriston Cemetery. That was when I first felt that I loved her . . . I mean, that it wasn't just going to be a one-night stand.'

'You like films?' Rebus said. He was noticing that one shelf seemed to be all books about movies.

Costello looked over towards him. 'I'd like to try writing a script some day.'

'Good for you.' Rebus had opened another book. It seemed to be a sequence of poems about Alfred Hitchcock. 'You didn't go to the hotel?' he asked after a pause.

'No.'

'But you've seen your parents?'

'Yes.' Costello took another draw, sucking the life from the cigarette. He realised he'd no ashtray and looked around for something suitable: candle-holders, one for Rebus and one for him. Turning from the bookshelves, Rebus's foot brushed something: a metal toy soldier, no more than an inch high. He stooped to pick it up. The musket had been snapped off, the head twisted over to one side. He didn't think he was responsible. Rebus placed it quietly on a shelf before sitting down again.

'Did they cancel the other room then?' he asked.

'They sleep in separate rooms, Inspector.' Costello looked up from where he'd been tidying the tip of the cigarette against the rim of the makeshift ashtray. 'Not a crime, is it?'

'I'm not best placed to judge. My wife left me more years ago than I can remember.'

'I'll bet you *do* remember.'

Rebus smiled again. 'Guilty.'

Costello rested his head against the back of the futon, stifled a yawn.

'I should go,' Rebus said.

'Finish your coffee at least.'

Rebus had already finished it, but nodded anyway, not about to leave unless pushed out. 'Maybe she'll turn up. People do things sometimes, don't they? Take a notion to head for the hills.'

'Flip was hardly the hill-heading type.'

'But she could have had a mind to take off somewhere.'

Costello shook his head. 'She knew they were waiting for her in the bar. She wouldn't have forgotten that.'

'No? Say she'd just met someone else . . . you know, an impulse thing, like in that advert.'

'Someone else?'

'It's possible, isn't it?'

Costello's eyes darkened. 'I don't know. It was one of the things I thought about – whether she'd met someone else.'

'You dismissed it?'

'Yes.'

'Why?'

'Because something like that, she'd have told me. That's the way Flip is: doesn't matter if it's a grand's worth of designer dress or a Concorde flight courtesy of her parents, she can't keep it to herself.'

'Likes attention?'

'Don't we all, from time to time?'

'She wouldn't pull a stunt, would she, just to get us all looking for her?'

'Fake her own disappearance?' Costello shook his head, then stifled another yawn. 'Maybe I should get some sleep.'

'What time's the press conference?'

'Early afternoon. Something to do with catching the main news bulletins.'

Rebus nodded. 'Don't be nervous out there, just be yourself.'

Costello stubbed out his cigarette. 'Who else could I be?' He made to hand the packet and lighter back to Rebus.

'Keep them. Never know when you might feel the need.' He got to his feet. The blood was beating in his skull now, despite the paracetamol. *That's the way Flip is:* Costello had spoken of her in the present tense – a casual remark, or something more calculated? Costello stood up too, now, and he was smiling, though without much humour.

'You never did answer that question, did you?' he said.

'I'm keeping an open mind, Mr Costello.'

'Are you now?' Costello slipped his hands into his pockets. 'Will I see you at the press conference?'

'Could be.'

'And will you be on the lookout for slips of the tongue? Something like your forensic bods?' Costello's eyes narrowed. 'I may be the only suspect, but I'm not stupid.'

'Then you'll appreciate we're on the same side . . . unless you know differently?'

'Why did you come here tonight? You're not on duty, are you?'

Rebus took a step closer. 'Know what they used to think, Mr Costello? They thought murder victims kept an imprint of their killer on their eyeballs – last thing they ever saw. Some killers, they gouged out the eyes after death.'

'But we're not so naïve these days, Inspector, are we? You can't hope to know someone, to get the measure of them, just from eye contact.'

Costello leaned in towards Rebus, his eyes widening slightly. 'Take a good long look, because the exhibit's about to close.'

Rebus met the gaze, returned it. Costello was the first to blink, breaking the spell. Then he turned away and told Rebus to leave. As Rebus made for the door, Costello called out to him. He was wiping the cigarette packet with a handkerchief. He did the same with the lighter, then tossed both items towards Rebus. They fell at his feet.

'I think your need's probably greater than mine.'

Rebus stooped to pick them up. 'Why the handkerchief?'

'Can't be too careful,' Costello said. 'Evidence can turn up in the strangest places.'

Rebus straightened, decided against saying anything. At the door, Costello called out goodnight to him. Rebus was halfway down the stairwell before he returned the sentiment. He was thinking about the way Costello had wiped both lighter and packet. All the years he'd been on the force, he'd never seen a suspect do anything like that. It had meant Costello was expecting to be set up.

Or, perhaps, that was what it was intended to look like. But it had shown Rebus a side of the young man that was cool and calculating. It showed someone who was capable of thinking ahead . . .

2

It was one of those cool, crepuscular days that could have belonged to any of at least three Scottish seasons; a sky like slate roofing and a wind that Rebus's father would have called 'snell'. His father had told a story once – many times actually – about walking into a grocer's in Lochgelly one freezing winter's morning. The grocer had been standing by the electric fire. Rebus's father had pointed to the cold cabinet and asked, 'Is that your Ayrshire bacon?' to which the grocer had replied, 'No, it's my hands I'm heating.' He'd sworn it was a true story, and Rebus – maybe seven or eight years old – had believed him at the time. But now it seemed an old chestnut of a joke, something he'd heard elsewhere and twisted to his own use.

'Not often I see you smiling,' his *barista* said as she made him a double *latte*. Those were her words: *barista, latte*. The first time she'd described her job, she'd pronounced it 'barrister', which had led a confused Rebus to ask if she was moonlighting. She worked from a converted police-box at the corner of the Meadows, and Rebus stopped there most mornings on his way to work. 'Milky coffee' was his order, which she always corrected to '*latte*'. Then he'd add 'double shot'. He didn't need to – she knew the order by heart – but he liked the feel of the words.

'Smiling's not illegal, is it?' he said now, as she spooned froth on to the coffee.

'You'd know better than me.'

'And your boss would know better than either of us.' Rebus paid up, punted the change into the marge tub left for tips, and headed for St Leonard's. He didn't think she knew he was a cop: *you'd know better than me* . . . it had been said casually, no meaning behind it other than to continue their banter. In turn, he'd made his remark about her boss because the owner of the chain of kiosks had once been a solicitor. But she hadn't seemed to understand.

At St Leonard's, Rebus stayed in his car, enjoying a last cigarette with his drink. A couple of vans sat at the station's back door, waiting for anyone who was being taken to court. Rebus had given evidence in a case a few days ago. He kept meaning to find out what the result had been. When the station door opened, he expected to see the custody line, but it was Siobhan Clarke. She saw his car and smiled, shaking her head at the inevitability of the scene. As she came forwards, Rebus lowered the window.

'The condemned man ate a hearty breakfast,' she said.

'And a good morning to you too.'

'Boss wants to see you.'

'He sent the right sniffer dog.'

Siobhan didn't say anything, just smiled to herself as Rebus got out of the car. They were halfway across the car park before he heard the words: 'It's not a "he" any more.' He stopped in his tracks.

'I'd forgotten,' he admitted.

'How's the hangover, by the way? Anything else you might have managed to forget?'

As she opened the door for him, he had the sudden image of a gamekeeper opening a trap.

The Farmer's photos and coffee machine had gone, and there were some Good Luck cards on top of the filing cabinet, but otherwise the room was just as before, down to the paperwork in the in-tray and the solitary potted cactus on the windowsill. Gill Templer looked uncomfortable in the Farmer's chair, his daily bulk having moulded it in ways which would never fit her slimmer proportions.

'Sit down, John.' Then, when he was halfway on to the seat: 'And tell me what last night was all about.' Elbows on the desk, she placed the tips of her fingers together. It was something the Farmer had often done when trying to hide irritation or impatience. She'd either picked it up from him, or it was a perk of her new seniority.

'Last night?'

'Philippa Balfour's flat. Her father found you there.' She looked up. 'Apparently you'd been drinking.'

'Hadn't we all?'

'Not as much as some.' Her eyes moved down again to the sheet of paper on her desk. 'Mr Balfour's wondering what you were up to. Frankly, I'm more than a little curious myself.'

'I was on my way home . . .'

'Leith Walk to Marchmont? Via the New Town? Sounds like you got bad directions.'

Rebus realised that he was still holding his beaker of coffee. He placed it on the floor, taking his time. 'It's just something I do,' he said at last. 'When things are quiet, I like to go back.'

'Why?'

'In case anything's been missed.'

She seemed to consider this. 'I'm not sure that's the whole story.'

He shrugged, said nothing. Her eyes were on the sheet again.

'And then you decided to pay Ms Balfour's boyfriend a call. How wise was that?'

'That really was on the way home. I stopped to talk to Connolly and Daniels. Mr Costello's light was on; I thought I'd make sure he was all right.'

'The caring copper.' She paused. 'That's presumably why Mr Costello felt it necessary to mention your visit to his solicitor?'

'I don't know why he did that.' Rebus shifted a little on the hard chair; disguised it by reaching for his coffee.

'His lawyer's talking about "harassment". We might have to pull the surveillance.' Her eyes were fixed on him.

'Look, Gill,' he said, 'you and me, we've known each other for donkey's. It's no secret how I work. I'm sure DCS Watson quoted scripture on the subject.'

'That was then, John.'

'Meaning what?'

'How much did you have to drink last night?'

'More than I should have, but it wasn't my fault.' He watched as Gill raised an eyebrow. 'I'm positive someone slipped me a Mickey Finn.'

'I want you to see a doctor.'

'Christ Almighty . . .'

'Your drinking, your diet, your general health . . . I want you to take a medical, and whatever the doctor says is necessary, I want you to abide by it.'

'Alfalfa and carrot juice?'

'You'll see a doctor, John.' It was a statement. Rebus just snorted and drained his coffee, then held up the beaker.

'Half-fat milk.'

She almost smiled. 'It's a start, I suppose.'

'Look, Gill . . .' He got up, tipped the beaker into the otherwise pristine waste-bin. 'My drinking's not a problem. It doesn't interfere with my work.'

'It did last night.'

He shook his head, but her face had hardened. Finally she took a deep breath. 'Just before you left the club . . . you remember that?'

'Sure.' He hadn't sat down; was standing in front of her desk, hands by his sides.

'You remember what you said to me?' His face told her all she needed to know. 'You wanted me to go home with you.'

'I'm sorry.' He was trying to remember, but nothing was coming. He couldn't remember leaving the club at all . . .

'On you go, John. I'll make that appointment for you.'

He turned, pulled open the door. He was halfway out when she called him back.

'I lied,' she said with a smile. 'You didn't say anything. Going to wish me well in the new job?'

Rebus tried for a sneer but couldn't quite manage one. Gill held her smile until he'd slammed shut the door; after he'd gone, it fell away again. Watson had given her chapter and verse all right, but nothing she hadn't already known: *Enjoys his drink a bit too much, maybe, but he's a good cop, Gill. He just likes to pretend he can do without the rest of us* . . . Maybe that was true, as far as it went, but maybe, too, the time was coming fast when John Rebus would have to learn that *they* could do without *him*.

It was easy to spot the crew from the leaving do: local chemists had probably sold out of aspirin, vitamin C and patented hangover cures. Dehydration seemed a major factor. Rebus had seldom seen so many bottles of Irn-Bru, Lucozade and Coke in the grip of so many pallid hands. The sobersides – who'd either not been to the party or who'd stuck to soft drinks – were gloating, whistling shrilly and slamming drawers and cupboards wherever possible. The main incident room for the Philippa Balfour inquiry was based at Gayfield Square – much closer to her flat – but with so many officers involved, space was an issue, so a corner of the CID room at St Leonard's had been set aside. Siobhan was there now, busy at her terminal. A spare hard disk sat on the floor, and Rebus realised that she was using Balfour's computer. She held a telephone receiver between cheek and shoulder, and typed as she talked.

'No luck there either,' Rebus heard her say.

He was sharing his own desk with three other officers, and it showed. He brushed the remnants from a bag of crisps on to the floor and deposited two empty Fanta cans in the nearest bin. When the phone rang he picked it up, but it was just the local evening paper trying to pull a flanker.

'Talk to Press Liaison,' Rebus told the journalist.

'Give me a break.'

Rebus was thoughtful. Liaison had been Gill Templer's speciality. He glanced across towards Siobhan Clarke. 'Who's in charge of PL anyway?'

'DS Ellen Wylie,' the journalist said.

Rebus said thanks and cut the connection. Liaison would have been a step up for Siobhan, especially on a high-profile case. Ellen Wylie was a good officer based at Torphichen. As a liaison specialist, Gill Templer would have been asked for advice on the appointment, maybe even made the decision herself. She'd chosen Ellen Wylie. He wondered if there was anything in it.

He rose from the desk and studied the paperwork now pinned to the wall behind him. Duty rosters, faxes, lists of contact numbers and addresses. Two photos of the missing woman. One of them had been released to the press, and it was duplicated in a dozen news stories, clipped and displayed. Soon, if she wasn't found safe and well, space would be at a premium on the wall, and those news stories would be discarded. They were repetitious, inaccurate, sensationalised. Rebus lingered on one phrase: *the tragic boyfriend*. He checked his watch: five hours until the news conference.

With Gill Templer promoted, they were down a DCI at St Leonard's. Detective Inspector Bill Pryde wanted the job, and was trying to stamp his authority on the Balfour case. Rebus, newly arrived at the Gayfield Square incident room, could only stand and marvel. Pryde had smartened himself up – the suit looked brand new, the shirt laundered, the tie expensive. The black brogues were immaculately polished and, if Rebus wasn't mistaken, Pryde had been to the barber's, too. Not that there was too much to trim, but Pryde had made the effort. He'd been put in charge of assignments, which meant putting teams out on the street for the daily drudgery of doorsteppings and interviews. Neighbours were being questioned – sometimes for the second or third time – as were friends, students and university staff. Flights and ferry crossings were being checked, the official photograph faxed to train operators, bus companies and police forces outwith the Lothian and Borders area. It would be someone's job to collate information on fresh corpses throughout Scotland, while another team would focus on hospital admissions. Then there were the city's taxi and car hire firms . . . It all took time and effort. These comprised the public face of the inquiry, but behind the scenes other questions would be asked of the MisPer's immediate family and circle of friends. Rebus doubted the background checks would amount to anything, not this time round.

At last, Pryde finished giving instructions to the group of officers around him. As they melted away, he caught sight of Rebus and gave a huge wink, rubbing his hand over his forehead as he approached.

'Got to be careful,' Rebus said. 'Power corrupts, and all that.'

'Forgive me,' Pryde said, dropping his voice, 'but I'm getting a real buzz.'

'That's because you can do it, Bill. It's just taken the Big House twenty years to recognise the fact.'

Pryde nodded. 'Rumour is, you turned down DCI a while back.'

Rebus snorted. 'Rumours, Bill. Like the Fleetwood Mac album, best left unplayed.'

The room was a choreography of movement, each participant now working on his or her allotted task. Some were donning coats, picking up keys and notebooks. Others rolled their sleeves as they got comfortable at their computers or telephones. New chairs had appeared from some darkened corner of the budget. Pale blue swivel jobs: those who'd managed to grab one were on the defensive, sliding across the floor on castors rather than getting up to walk, lest someone else snatch the prized possession in the interim.

'We're done with babysitting the boyfriend,' Pryde said. 'Orders from the new boss.'

'I heard.'

'Pressure from the family,' Pryde added.

'Won't do any harm to the operation budget,' Rebus commented, straightening up. 'So is there work for me today, Bill?'

Pryde flicked through the sheets of paper on his clipboard. 'Thirty-seven phone calls from the public,' he said.

Rebus held up his hands. 'Don't look at me. Cranks and desperadoes are for the L-plates, surely?'

Pryde smiled. 'Already allocated,' he admitted, nodding towards where two DCs, recently promoted out of uniform, were looking dismayed at the workload. Cold calls constituted the most thankless task around. Any high-profile case threw up its share of fake confessions and false leads. Some people craved attention, even if it meant becoming a suspect in a police investigation. Rebus knew of several such offenders in Edinburgh.

'Craw Shand?' he guessed.

Pryde tapped the sheet of paper. 'Three times so far, ready to admit to the murder.'

'Bring him in,' Rebus said. 'It's the only way to get rid of him.'

Pryde brought his free hand to the knot in his tie, as if checking for defects. 'Neighbours?' he suggested.

Rebus nodded. 'Neighbours it is,' he said.

He gathered together the notes from initial interviews. Other officers had been assigned the far side of the street, leaving Rebus and three others – working teams of two – to cover the flats either side of Philippa Balfour's. Thirty-five in total, three of them empty, leaving thirty-two. Sixteen addresses per team, maybe fifteen minutes at each . . . four hours total.

Rebus's partner for the day, DC Phyllida Hawes, had done the arithmetic for him as they climbed the steps of the first tenement. Actually, Rebus wasn't sure you could call them 'tenements', not down in the New Town, with its wealth of Georgian architecture, its art galleries and antique emporia. He asked Hawes for advice.

'Blocks of flats?' she suggested, raising a smile. There were one or two flats per landing, some adorned with brass nameplates, others ceramic. A few went so low as to boast just a piece of sellotaped card or paper.

'Not sure the Cockburn Association would approve,' Hawes remarked.

Three or four names listed on the bit of card: students, Rebus guessed, from backgrounds less generous than Philippa Balfour's.

The landings themselves were bright and cared for: welcome mats and tubs of flowers. Hanging baskets had been placed over banisters. The walls looked newly painted, the stairs swept. The first stairwell went like clockwork: two flats with nobody home, cards dropped through either letterbox; fifteen minutes in each of the other flats – 'just a few back-up questions . . . see if you've thought of anything to add . . .' The householders had shaken their heads, had professed themselves still shocked. Such a quiet little street.

There was a main door flat at ground level, a much grander affair, with a black-and-white-chequered marble entrance hall, Doric columns either side. The occupier was renting it long term, worked in 'the financial sector'. Rebus saw a pattern emerging: graphic designer; training consultant; events organiser . . . and now the financial sector.

'Does no one have real jobs any more?' he asked Hawes.

'These are the real jobs,' she told him. They were back on the pavement, Rebus enjoying a cigarette. He noticed her staring at it.

'Want one?'

She shook her head. 'Three years I've managed so far.'

'Good for you.' Rebus looked up and down the street. 'If this was a net curtain kind of place, they'd be twitching right now.'

'If they had net curtains, you wouldn't be able to peer in and see what you're missing.'

Rebus held the smoke, let it billow out through his nostrils. 'See, when I was younger, there was always something rakish about the New Town. Kaftans and wacky baccy, parties and ne'er-do-wells.'

'Not much space left for them these days,' Hawes agreed. 'Where do you live?'

'Marchmont,' he told her. 'You?'

'Livingston. It was all I could afford at the time.'

'Bought mine years back, two wages coming in . . .'

She looked at him. 'No need to apologise.'

'Prices weren't as crazy back then, that's all I meant.' He was trying not to sound defensive. It was that meeting with Gill: the little joke she'd made, just to unsettle him. And the way his visit to Costello had KO'd the surveillance . . . Maybe it was time to talk to someone about the drinking . . . He flicked the stub of his cigarette on to the roadway. The surface was made of shiny rectangular stones called setts. When he'd first arrived in the city he'd made the mistake of calling them cobbles; a local had put him right.

'Next call,' he said now, 'if we're offered tea, we take it.'

Hawes nodded. She was in her late thirties or early forties, hair brown and shoulder-length. Her face was freckled and fleshed-out, as though she'd never quite lost her puppy fat. Grey trouser-suit and an emerald blouse, pinned at the neck with a silver Celtic brooch. Rebus could imagine her at a ceilidh, being spun during Strip the Willow, her face bearing the same concentration she brought to her work.

Below the main door flat, down a curving set of external steps, was the 'garden flat', so called because the garden at the back of the building came with it. At the front, the stone slabs were covered in more tubs of flowers. There were two windows, with two more at ground level – the place boasted a sub-basement. A pair of wooden doors was set into the wall opposite the entrance. They would lead into cellars beneath the pavement. Though they would have been checked before, Rebus tried opening them both, but they were locked. Hawes checked her notes.

'Grant Hood and George Silvers got there before you,' she said.

'But were the doors locked or unlocked?'

'I unlocked them,' a voice called out. They turned to see an elderly woman standing just inside the flat's front door. 'Would you like the keys?'

'Yes please, madam,' Phyllida Hawes said. When the woman had turned back into the flat, she turned to Rebus and made a T shape with the index finger of either hand. Rebus held both his thumbs up in reply.

Mrs Jardine's flat was a chintz museum, a home for china waifs and strays. The throw which covered the back of her sofa must have taken weeks to crochet. She apologised for the array of tin cans and metal pots which all but covered the floor of her conservatory – 'never seem to get round to fixing the roof'. Rebus had suggested they take their tea there: every time he turned round in the living room he feared he was about to send some ornament flying. When the rain started, however, their conversation was punctuated by drips and dollops, and the splashes from the pot nearest Rebus threatened to give him the same sort of soaking he'd have had outside.

'I didn't know the lassie,' Mrs Jardine said ruefully. 'Maybe if I got out a bit more I'd have seen her.'

Hawes was staring out of the window. 'You manage to keep your garden neat,' she said. This was an understatement: the long, narrow garden, slivers of lawn and flowerbed either side of a meandering path, was immaculate.

'My gardener,' Mrs Jardine said.

Hawes studied the notes from the previous interview, then shook her head almost imperceptibly: Silvers and Hood hadn't mentioned a gardener.

'Could we have his name, Mrs Jardine?' Rebus asked, his voice casually polite. Still, the old woman looked at him with concern. Rebus offered her a smile and one of her own drop scones. 'It's just that I might need a gardener myself,' he lied.

The last thing they did was check the cellars. An ancient hot-water tank in one, nothing but mould in the other. They waved Mrs Jardine goodbye and thanked her for her hospitality.

'All right for some,' Grant Hood said. He was waiting for them on the pavement, collar up against the rain. 'So far we've not been offered as much as the time of day.' His partner was Distant Daniels. Rebus nodded a greeting.

'What's up, Tommy? Working a double shift?'

Daniels shrugged. 'Did a swap.' He tried to suppress a yawn. Hawes was tapping her sheaf of notes.

'You,' she told Hood, 'didn't do your job.'

'Eh?'

'Mrs Jardine has a gardener,' Rebus explained.

'We'll be talking to the bin-men next,' Hood said.

'We already have,' Hawes reminded him. 'And been through the bins, too.'

The two of them looked to be squaring up. Rebus considered brokering the peace – he was St Leonard's, same as Hood: he should be sticking up for him – but lit another cigarette instead. Hood's cheeks had reddened. He was a DC, same rank as Hawes, but she had more years behind her. Sometimes you couldn't argue with experience, which wasn't stopping Hood from trying.

'This isn't helping Philippa Balfour,' Distant Daniels said at last, stopping the confab dead.

'Well said, son,' Rebus added. It was true: big inquiries could blind you to the single essential truth. You became a tiny cog in the machine, and as such you made demands in order to assure yourself of your importance. The ownership of chairs became an issue, because it was an easy argument, something that could be resolved quickly either way. Unlike the case itself, the case which was growing almost exponentially, making you seem ever smaller, until you lost sight of that single essential truth – what Rebus's mentor Lawson Geddes had called 'the SET' – which was that a person or persons needed your help. A crime had to be solved, the guilty brought to justice: it was good to be reminded sometimes.

They split up amicably in the end, Hood noting the gardener's details and promising to talk to him. After which there was nothing else to do but start climbing stairs again. They'd spent the best part of half an hour at Mrs Jardine's; already Hawes' calculations were unravelling, proving another truism: inquiries ate up time, as if the days went into fast forward and you couldn't show how the hours had been spent, were hard pressed to explain your exhaustion, knowing only the frustration of something left incomplete.

Two more no-one-homes, and then, on the first landing, the door was opened by a face Rebus recognised but couldn't place.

'It's about Philippa Balfour's disappearance,' Hawes was explaining. 'I believe two of my colleagues spoke to you earlier. This is just by way of a follow-up.'

'Yes, of course.' The gloss-black door opened a little wider. The man looked at Rebus and smiled. 'You're having trouble placing me, but I remember you.' The smile widened. 'You always remember the virgins, don't you?'

As they were shown down the hall, the man introduced himself as Donald Devlin, and Rebus knew him. The first autopsy Rebus had ever attended as a CID officer, Devlin had done the cutting. He'd been Professor of Forensic Medicine at the university, and the city's chief pathologist at the time. Sandy Gates had been his assistant. Now, Gates was Professor of Forensic Medicine, with Dr Curt as his 'junior'. On the walls of the hallway were framed photos of Devlin receiving various prizes and awards.

'The name's not coming to me,' Devlin said, gesturing for the two officers to precede him into a cluttered drawing room.

'DI Rebus.'

'It would have been Detective Constable back then?' Devlin guessed. Rebus nodded.

'Moving out, sir?' Hawes asked, looking around her at the profusion of boxes and black bin-liners. Rebus looked too. Tottering towers of paperwork, drawers which had been wrenched from their chests and now threatened to spill mementoes across the carpet. Devlin chuckled. He was a short, portly man, probably in his mid-seventies. His grey cardigan had lost most of its shape and half its buttons, and his charcoal trousers were held up with braces. His face was puffy and red-veined, his eyes small blue dots behind a pair of metal-framed spectacles.

'In a manner of speaking, I suppose,' he said, pushing a few strands of hair back into some semblance of order across the expanse of his domed scalp. 'Let's just say that if the Grim Reaper is the *ne plus ultra* of removers, then I'm acting as his unpaid assistant.'

Rebus recalled that Devlin had always spoken like this, never settling for six words where a dozen would do, and tossing the odd spanner into the dictionary. It had been a nightmare trying to take notes while Devlin worked an autopsy.

'You're moving into a home?' Hawes guessed. The old man chuckled again.

'Not quite ready for the heave-ho yet, alas. No, all I'm doing is dispensing with a few unwanted items, making it easier for those family members who'll wish to pick over the carcass of my estate after I've shuffled off.'

'Saving them the trouble of throwing it all out?'

Devlin looked at Rebus. 'A correct and concise summary of affairs,' he noted approvingly.

Hawes had reached into a box for a leatherbound book. 'You're binning all of it?'

'By no means,' Devlin tutted. 'The volume in your hand, for example, an early edition of Donaldson's anatomical sketches, I intend to offer to the College of Surgeons.'

'You still see Professor Gates?' Rebus asked.

'Oh, Sandy and I enjoy the occasional tincture. He'll be retiring himself soon enough, I don't doubt, making way for the young. We fool ourselves that this makes life cyclical, but of course it's anything but, unless you happen to practise Buddhism.' He smiled at what he saw as this little joke.

'Just because you're a Buddhist doesn't mean you'll come back again though, does it?' Rebus said, delighting the old man further. Rebus was staring at a framed news report on the wall to the right of the fireplace: a murder conviction dated 1957. 'Your first case?' he guessed.

'Actually, yes. A young bride bludgeoned to death by her husband. They were in the city on honeymoon.'

'Must cheer the place up,' Hawes commented.

'My wife thought it macabre too,' Devlin admitted. 'After she died, I put it back up.'

'Well,' Hawes said, dropping the book back into its box and looking in vain for somewhere to sit, 'sooner we're finished, the sooner you can get back to your clear-out.'

'A pragmatist: good to see.' Devlin seemed content to let the three of them stand there, in the middle of a large and threadbare Persian carpet, almost afraid to move for fear that a domino effect would ensue.

'Is there any order, sir?' Rebus asked. 'Or can we move a couple of boxes on to the floor?'

'Better to take our tête-à-tête into the dining room, I think.'

Rebus nodded and made to follow, his gaze drifting to an engraved invitation on the marble mantelpiece. It was from the Royal College of Surgeons, something to do with a dinner at Surgeons' Hall. 'Black/white tie and decorations' it said along the bottom. The only decorations *he* had were in a box in his hall cupboard. They went up every Christmas, if he could be bothered.

The dining room was dominated by a long wooden table and six unupholstered, straight-backed chairs. There was a serving-hatch – what Rebus's family would have called a 'bowley-hole' – through to the kitchen, and a dark-stained sideboard spread with a dusty array of glassware and silver. The few framed pictures looked like early examples of photography: posed studio shots of Venetian boat-life, maybe scenes from Shakespeare. The tall sash window looked out on to gardens at the rear of the building. Down below, Rebus could see that Mrs Jardine's gardener had shaped her plot – either by accident or design – so that from above it resembled a question mark.

On the table lay a half-finished jigsaw: central Edinburgh photographed from above. 'Any and all help,' Devlin said, waving a hand expansively over the puzzle, 'will be most gratefully received.'

'Looks like a lot of pieces,' Rebus said.

'Just the two thousand.'

Hawes, who had at last introduced herself to Devlin, was having trouble getting comfortable on her chair. She asked how long Devlin had been retired.

'Twelve . . . no, fourteen years. Fourteen years . . .' He shook his head, marvelling at time's ability to speed up even as the heartbeat slowed.

Hawes looked at her notes. 'At the first interview, you said you'd been home that evening.'

'That's right.'

'And you didn't see Philippa Balfour?'

'Your information is correct thus far.'

Rebus, deciding against the chairs, leaned back, putting his weight on the windowsill, and folded his arms.

'But you knew Ms Balfour?' he asked.

'We'd exchanged pleasantries, yes.'

'She's been your neighbour for the best part of a year,' Rebus said.

'You'll recall that this is Edinburgh, DI Rebus. I've lived in this apartment nearly three decades – I moved in when my wife passed away. It takes time to get to know one's neighbours. Often, I'm afraid, they move on before one has had the opportunity.' He shrugged. 'After a while, one ceases trying.'

'That's pretty sad,' Hawes said.

'And you live where . . . ?'

'If I could just,' Rebus interrupted, 'bring us back to the matter in hand.' He'd moved off the windowsill, hands now resting on the tabletop. His eyes were on the loose pieces of the jigsaw.

'Of course,' Devlin said.

'You were in all evening, and didn't hear anything untoward?'

Devlin glanced up, perhaps appreciative of Rebus's final word. 'Nothing,' he said after a pause.

'Or see anything?'

'Ditto.'

Hawes wasn't just looking uncomfortable now; she was clearly irritated by these responses. Rebus sat down across from her, trying for eye contact, but she was ready with a question of her own.

'Have you ever had a falling-out with Ms Balfour, sir?'

'What is there to fall out about?'

'Nothing now,' Hawes stated coldly.

Devlin gave her a look and turned towards Rebus. 'I see you're interested in the table, Inspector.'

Rebus realised that he'd been running his fingers along the grain of the wood.

'It's nineteenth-century,' Devlin went on, 'crafted by a fellow anatomist.' He glanced towards Hawes, then back to Rebus again. 'There *was* something I remembered . . . probably nothing important.'

'Yes, sir?'

'A man standing outside.'

Rebus knew that Hawes was about to say something, so beat her to it. 'When was this?'

'A couple of days before she vanished, and the day before that, too.' Devlin shrugged, all too aware of the effect his words were having. Hawes had reddened; she was dying to scream out something like *when were you going to tell us?* Rebus kept his voice level.

'On the pavement outside?'

'That's right.'

'Did you get a good look at him?'

Another shrug. 'In his twenties, short dark hair . . . not cropped, just neat.'

'Not a neighbour?'

'It's always possible. I'm merely telling you what I saw. He seemed to be waiting for someone or something. I recall him checking his watch.'

'Her boyfriend maybe?'

'Oh no, I know David.'

'You do?' Rebus asked. He was still casually scanning the jigsaw.

'To talk to, yes. We met a few times in the stairwell. Nice young chap . . .'

'How was he dressed?' Hawes asked.

'Who? David?'

'The man you saw.'

Devlin seemed almost to relish the glare which accompanied her words. 'Jacket and trousers,' he said, glancing down at his cardigan. 'I can't be more specific, never having been a follower of fashion.'

Which was true: fourteen years ago, he'd worn similar cardigans under his green surgeon's smock, along with bow-ties which were always askew. You could never forget your first autopsy: those sights, smells and sounds which were to become familiar. The scrape of metal on bone, or the whispering of a scalpel as it parted flesh. Some pathologists carried a cruel sense of humour and would put on an especially graphic performance for any 'virgins'. But never Devlin; he'd always focused on the corpse, as if the two of them were alone in the room, that intimate final act of filleting carried out with a decorum bordering on ritual.

'Do you think,' Rebus asked, 'that if you thought about it, maybe let your mind drift back, you could come up with a fuller description?'

'I rather doubt it, but of course if you think it important . . .'

'Early days, sir. You know yourself, we can't rule anything out.'

'Of course, of course.'

Rebus was treating Devlin as a fellow professional . . . and it was working.

'We might even try to put together a photofit,' Rebus went on. 'That way, if it turns out to be a neighbour or someone anyone knows, we can eliminate him straight away.'

'Seems reasonable,' Devlin agreed.

Rebus got on his mobile to Gayfield and made an appointment for the next morning. Afterwards, he asked if Devlin would need a car.

'Should manage to find my own way. Not utterly decrepit just yet, you know.' But he got to his feet slowly, his joints seemingly stiff as he showed the two detectives out.

'Thanks again, sir,' Rebus said, shaking his hand.

Devlin just nodded, avoiding eye contact with Hawes, who wasn't about to offer him her own thanks. As they made their way up to the next landing, she muttered something Rebus didn't catch.

'Sorry?'

'I said: bloody men.' She paused. 'Present company excluded.' Rebus didn't say anything, prepared to let her get it off her chest. 'Do you suppose for one second,' she went on, 'that if it had been two female officers down there, he'd have said anything?'

'I think that would depend how he was handled.'

Hawes glared at him, seeking levity that wasn't there.

'Part of our job,' Rebus went on, 'is pretending we like everyone, pretending we're interested in everything they have to say.'

'He just—'

'Got on your nerves? Mine too. Bit pompous, but that's just his way; you can't let it show. You're right: I'm not sure he'd have told us anything. He'd dismissed it as irrelevant. But then he opened up, just to put *you* in your place.' Rebus smiled. 'Good work. It's not often I get to play "good cop" around here.'

'It wasn't just that he got on my nerves,' Hawes conceded.

'What then?'

'He gave me the creeps.'

Rebus looked at her. 'Not the same thing?'

She shook her head. 'The old-pal act he played with you, that irritated me a bit, because I wasn't part of it. But the newspaper clipping . . .'

'The one on the wall?'

She nodded. '*That* gave me the creeps.'

'He's a pathologist,' Rebus explained. 'They've thicker skins than most of us.'

She thought about this, and allowed herself a little smile.

'What?' Rebus asked.

'Oh, nothing,' she said. 'It's just that, as I was getting up to leave, I couldn't help noticing a piece of the jigsaw on the floor under the table . . .'

'Where it still sits?' Rebus guessed, smiling too now. 'With that kind of eye for detail, we'll make a detective of you yet . . .'

He pressed the next door-buzzer, and it was back to work.

The news conference took place at the Big House, with a live feed to the inquiry room at Gayfield Square. Someone was trying to clean fingerprints and smears from the TV monitor with a handkerchief, while others tilted the blinds against the afternoon's sudden burst of sunshine. With the chairs all filled, officers were sitting two and three to a desk. A few of them were taking a late lunch: sandwiches and bananas. There were mugs of tea and coffee, cans of juice. The conversation was muted. Whoever was in charge of the police camera at the Big House, they were coming in for some stick.

'Like my eight-year-old with the video-cam . . .'

'Seen *Blair Witch* a couple times too many . . .'

It was true that the camera seemed to be swooping and diving, picking out bodies at waist height, rows of feet, and the backs of chairs.

'Show's not started yet,' a wiser head counselled. It was true: the other cameras, the ones from TV, were still being set up, the invited audience – journalists clutching mobile phones to their ears – still settling. Hard to make out anything that was being said. Rebus stood at the back of the room. A bit too far from the TV, but he wasn't about to move. Bill Pryde stood next to him, clearly exhausted and just as clearly trying not to show it. His clipboard had become a comforter, and he held it close to his chest, now and then pulling back to look at it, as though fresh instructions might magically have appeared. With the blinds closed, thin beams of light pierced the room, highlighting motes of dust which would otherwise have remained invisible. Rebus was reminded of cinema trips in childhood, the sense of expectation as the projector came to life and the show began.

On the TV, the crowd was settling. Rebus knew the room – a soulless space used for seminars and occasions such as this. One long table sat at the end, a makeshift screen behind it displaying the Lothian and Borders badge. The police video-cam swung round as a door opened and a file of bodies trooped into the room, quieting the hubbub. Rebus could hear the sudden whirr of camera motors. Flashes of illumination. Ellen Wylie first, then Gill Templer, followed by David Costello and John Balfour.

'Guilty!' someone in front of Rebus called out as the camera zoomed in on Costello's face.

The group sat down in front of a sudden array of microphones. The camera stayed with Costello, panning back a little to take in his upper body, but it was Wylie's voice that came over the loudspeaker, preceded by a nervous clearing of the throat.

'Good afternoon, ladies and gentlemen, and thank you for joining us. I'll just go over the format and some of the rules, before we get started . . .'

Siobhan was over to Rebus's left. She was sitting on a desk alongside Grant Hood. Hood was staring at the floor. Maybe he was concentrating on Wylie's voice: Rebus remembered that the pair of them had worked closely together on the Grieve case a few months before. Siobhan was watching the screen, but her gaze kept wandering elsewhere. She held a bottle of water, and her fingers were busy picking off the label.

She wanted that job, Rebus thought to himself. And now she was hurting. He willed her to turn his way, so he could offer something – a smile or shrug, or just a nod of understanding. But her eyes were back on the screen again. Wylie had finished her spiel, and it was Gill Templer's turn. She was summarising and updating the details of the case. She sounded confident, an old hand at news conferences. Rebus could hear Wylie clearing her throat again in the background. It seemed to be putting Gill off.

The camera, however, showed no interest in the two CID officers. It was there to concentrate on David Costello, and – to a far lesser extent – Philippa Balfour's father. The two men sat next to one another, and the camera moved slowly between them. Quick shots of Balfour, then back to Costello. The auto-focus was fine until the cameraman decided to zoom in or out. Then, the picture took a few seconds to clear.

'Guilty,' the voice repeated.

'Want a bet?' someone else called back.

'Let's have a bit of shush,' Bill Pryde barked. The room fell silent. Rebus gave him a round of mimed applause, but Pryde was looking at his clipboard again, then back to the screen, where David Costello was beginning to speak. He hadn't shaved, and looked to be in the same clothes as the previous night. He'd unfolded and flattened a sheet of paper against the table-top. But when he spoke, he didn't glance down at what he'd written. His eyes flitted between cameras, never sure where he should be looking. His voice was dry and thin.

'We don't know what happened to Flip, and we desperately want to know. All of us, her friends, her family . . .' he glanced towards John Balfour '. . . all those who know and love her, we need to know. Flip, if you're watching this, please get in touch with one of us. Just so we know you're . . . you've not come to any harm. We're worried sick.' His eyes were shining with the onset of tears. He stopped for a second, bowed his head, then drew himself straight again. He picked up the sheet of paper but couldn't see anything there that hadn't been said. He half turned, as if seeking guidance from the others. John Balfour put his hand out to squeeze the younger man's shoulder, then Balfour himself started speaking, his voice booming as if the microphones might somehow be defective.

'If anyone's holding my daughter, please get in touch. Flip has the number for my private mobile phone. I can be reached at any time, day or night. I'd like to talk with you, whoever you are, why ever you've done what you've done. And if anyone knows Flip's whereabouts, there'll be a number onscreen at the end of this broadcast. I just need to know Flip's alive and well. To people watching this at home, please take a second to study Flip's photograph.' A further clicking of cameras as he held up the photo. He turned slowly so every camera could capture the moment. 'Her name's Philippa Balfour and she's just twenty. She's my daughter. If you've seen her, or even just think you may have, please get in touch. Thank you.'

The reporters were ready with their questions, but David Costello was already on his feet and making for the exit.

It was Wylie's voice again: 'Not appropriate at this time . . . I'd like to thank you for your continuing support . . .' But the questions battered against her. Meantime the video-cam was back on John Balfour. He looked quite composed, hands clasped on the table in front of him, unblinking as the flash-guns threw his shadow on to the wall behind.

'No, I really don't . . .'

'Mr Costello!' the journalists were yelling. 'Could we just ask . . .?'

'DS Wylie,' another voice barked, 'can you tell us something about possible motives for the abduction?'

'We don't have any motives yet.' Wylie was sounding flustered.

'But you accept that it *is* an abduction?'

'I don't . . . no, that's not what I meant.'

The screen showed John Balfour trying to answer someone else's question. The ranks of reporters had become a scrum.

'Then what *did* you mean, DS Wylie?'

'I just . . . I didn't say anything about . . .'

And then Ellen Wylie's voice was replaced by Gill Templer's. The voice of authority. The reporters knew her of old, just as she knew them.

'Steve,' she said, 'you know only too well that we can't speculate on details like that. If you want to make up lies just to sell a few more papers, that's your concern, but it's hardly respectful to Philippa Balfour's family and friends.'

Further questions were handled by Gill, who insisted on some calm beforehand. Although Rebus couldn't see her, he imagined Ellen Wylie would be shrinking visibly. Siobhan was moving her feet up and down, as though all of a sudden some adrenalin had kicked in. Balfour interrupted Gill to say that he'd like to respond to a couple of the points raised. He did so, calmly and effectively, and then the conference started to break up.

'A cool customer,' Pryde said, before moving off to regroup his troops. It was time to get back to the real work again.

Grant Hood approached. 'Remind me,' he said. 'Which station was giving the longest odds on the boyfriend?'

'Torphichen,' Rebus told him.

'Then that's where my money's going.' He looked to Rebus for a reaction, but didn't get one. 'Come on, sir,' he went on, 'it was written all over his face!'

Rebus thought back to his night-time meeting with Costello . . . the story of the eyeballs and how Costello had come up close. *Take a good long look . . .*

Hood was shaking his head as he made to pass Rebus. The blinds had been opened, the brief interlude of sun now ended as thick grey clouds rolled back over the city. The tape of Costello's performance would go to the psychologists. They'd be looking for a glimmer of something, a short outburst of bright illumination. He wasn't sure they'd find it. Siobhan was standing in front of him.

'Interesting, wasn't it?' she said.

'I don't think Wylie's cut out for liaison,' Rebus answered.

'She shouldn't have been there. A case like this for her first outing . . . she was as good as thrown to the lions.'

'You didn't enjoy it?' he asked slyly.

She stared at him. 'I don't like blood sports.' She made to move away, but hesitated. 'What did you think, really?'

'I thought you were right about it being interesting. Singularly interesting.'

She smiled. 'You caught that too?'

He nodded. 'Costello kept saying "we", while her father used "I".'

'As if Flip's mother didn't matter.'

Rebus was thoughtful. 'It might mean nothing more than that Mr Balfour has an inflated sense of his own importance.' He paused. 'Now wouldn't that be a first in a merchant banker? How's the computer stuff going?'

She smiled – 'computer stuff' just about summed up Rebus's knowledge of hard disks and the like. 'I got past her password.'

'Meaning?'

'Meaning I can check her most recent e-mails . . . soon as I get back to my desk.'

'No way to access the older ones?'

'Already done. Of course, there's no way of telling what's been deleted.' She was thoughtful. 'At least I don't think there is.'

'They're not stored somewhere on the . . . mainframe?'

She laughed. 'You're thinking of sixties spy films, computers taking up whole rooms.'

'Sorry.'

'Don't worry. You're doing okay for someone who thinks LOL means Loyal Orange Lodge.'

They'd moved out of the office and into the corridor. 'I'm heading back to St Leonard's. Need a lift?'

She shook her head. 'Got my car with me.'

'Fair enough.'

'It looks like we're getting hooked up to HOLMES.'

This was one piece of new technology Rebus did know something about: the Home Office Large Major Enquiry System. It was a software system that collated information and speeded up the whole process of gathering and sifting. Its application meant that Philippa Balfour's disappearance was now the priority case in the city.

'Won't it be funny if she traipses back from an unannounced shopping spree?' Rebus mused.

'It would be a relief,' Siobhan said solemnly. 'But I don't think that's going to happen, do you?'

'No,' Rebus said quietly. Then he went to find himself something to eat on the way back to base.

Back at his desk, he went through the files again, concentrating on family background. John Balfour was the third generation of a banking family. The business had started in Edinburgh's Charlotte Square in the early 1900s. Philippa's great-grandfather had handed the running of the bank to her grandfather in the 1940s, and he hadn't taken a back seat until the 1980s, when John Balfour had taken over. Almost the first thing Philippa's father had done was open a London office, concentrating his efforts there. Philippa had gone to a private school in Chelsea. The family relocated north in the late eighties after the death of John's father, Philippa changing to a school in Edinburgh. Their home, Junipers, was a baronial mansion in sixteen acres of countryside somewhere between Gullane and Haddington. Rebus wondered how Balfour's wife Jacqueline felt. Eleven bedrooms, five public rooms . . . and her husband down in London a minimum of four days each week. The Edinburgh office, still in its original premises in Charlotte Square, was run by an old friend of John Balfour's called Ranald Marr. The two had met at university in Edinburgh, heading off together to the States for their MBAs. Rebus had called Balfour a merchant banker, but Balfour's was really a small private bank geared to the needs of its client list, a wealthy elite requiring investment advice, portfolio management, and the kudos of a leatherbound Balfour's chequebook.

When Balfour himself had been interviewed, the emphasis had been on the possibility of a kidnapping for profit. Not just the family phone, but those in the Edinburgh and London offices were being monitored. Mail was being intercepted in case any ransom demand arrived that way: the fewer fingerprints they had to deal with, the better. But as yet, all they'd had were a few crank notes. Another possibility was a deal gone sour: revenge the motive. But Balfour was adamant that he had no enemies. All the same, he'd denied the team access to his bank's client base.

'These people trust me. Without that trust, the bank's finished.'

'Sir, with respect, your daughter's well-being might depend . . .'

'I'm perfectly aware of that!'

After which the interview had never lost its edge of antagonism.

The bottom line: Balfour's was conservatively estimated to be worth around a hundred and thirty million, with John Balfour's personal wealth comprising maybe five per cent of the whole. Six and a half million reasons for a professional abduction. But wouldn't a professional have made contact by now? Rebus wasn't sure.

Jacqueline Balfour had been born Jacqueline Gil-Martin, her father a diplomat and landowner, the family estate a chunk of Perthshire comprising nearly nine hundred acres. The father was dead now, and the mother had moved into a cottage on the estate. The land itself was managed by Balfour's Bank, and the main house, Laverock Lodge, had become a setting for conferences and other large gatherings. A TV drama had been filmed there apparently, though the show's title meant nothing to Rebus. Jacqueline hadn't bothered with university, busying herself instead with a variety of jobs, mainly as a personal assistant to some businessman or other. She'd been running the Laverock estate when she'd met John Balfour, on a trip to her father's bank in Edinburgh. They'd married a year later, and Philippa had been born two years after that.

Just the one child. John Balfour himself was an only child, but

Jacqueline had two sisters and a brother, none of them currently living in Scotland. The brother had followed in his father's footsteps and was on a Washington posting with the Foreign Office. It struck Rebus that the Balfour dynasty was in trouble. He couldn't see Philippa rushing to join Daddy's bank, and wondered why the couple hadn't tried for a son.

None of which, in all probability, was pertinent to the inquiry. All the same, it was what Rebus enjoyed about the job: constructing a web of relationships, peering into other people's lives, wondering and questioning . . .

He turned to the notes on David Costello. Dublin-born and educated, the family moving just south of the city to Dalkey in the early nineties. The father, Thomas Costello, didn't seem to have turned a day's work in his life, his needs supplied by a trust fund set up by his father, a land developer. David's grandfather owned several prime sites in the centre of Dublin, and made a comfortable living from them. He owned half a dozen racehorses, too, and spent all his time these days concentrating on that side of things.

David's mother, Theresa, was something else again. Her background could at best be called lower middle class, mother a nurse, father a teacher. Theresa had gone to art school but dropped out and got a job instead, providing for the family when her mother got cancer and her father fell apart. She worked behind the counter in a department store, then moved to window-dressing, and from there to interior design – for shops at first, and then for wealthy individuals. Which was how she met Thomas Costello. By the time they married, both her parents were dead. Theresa probably didn't need to work, but she worked anyway, building up her one-woman company until it had grown into a business with a turnover in the low millions and a workforce of five, not including herself. There were overseas clients, and the list was still growing. She was fifty-one now, and showing no signs of slacking, while her husband, a year her junior, remained the man about town. Press clippings from the Irish news showed him at racing events, garden parties and the like. In none of the photos did he appear with Theresa. Separate rooms in their Edinburgh hotel . . . As their son said, it was hardly a crime.

David had been late going to university, having taken a year out to travel the world. He was now in the third year of his MA degree in English Language and Literature. Rebus remembered the books in his living room: Milton, Wordsworth, Hardy . . .

'Enjoying the view, John?'

Rebus opened his eyes. 'Deep in thought, George.'

'You weren't dropping off, then?'

Rebus glared at him. 'Far from it.'

As Hi-Ho Silvers moved away, Siobhan came and rested against the side of Rebus's desk.

'So how deep in thought were you?'

'I was wondering if Rabbie Burns could have murdered one of his lovers.' She just stared at him. 'Or whether someone who reads poetry could.'

'Don't see why not. Didn't some death-camp commander listen to Mozart of an evening?'

'Now there's a cheery thought.'

'Always here to make your day that little bit brighter. Now what about doing me a favour?'

'How can I refuse?'

She handed him a sheet of paper. 'Tell me what you think that means.'

Subj: Hellbank
Date: 5/9
From: Quizmaster@PaganOmerta.com
To: Flipside1223@HXRmail.com

Did you survive Hellbank? Time running out. Stricture awaits your call.
QuiM

Rebus looked up at her. 'Going to give me a clue?'

She took back the sheet of paper. 'It's an e-mail printout. Philippa had a couple of dozen messages waiting for her, dating back to the day she went missing. All of them except this one are addressed to her other name.'

'Her other name?'

'ISPs—' she paused – 'Internet service providers will usually allow you a range of log-on names, as many as five or six.'

'Why?'

'So you can be . . . different people, I suppose. Flipside 1223 is a sort of alias. Her other e-mails all went to Flip-dot-Balfour.'

'So what does it mean?'

Siobhan expelled air. 'That's what I'm wondering. Maybe it means she had a side we don't know about. There's not a single saved message from her or to her in the name of Flipside 1223. So either she's been erasing them as she goes, or else this got to her by mistake.'

'Doesn't look like coincidence, does it, though?' Rebus said. 'Her nickname's Flip.'

Siobhan was nodding. 'Hellbank, Stricture, Pagan Omerta . . .'

'Omerta's the mafia code of silence,' Rebus stated.

'And Quizmaster,' Siobhan said. 'Signs herself or himself QuiM. Little touch of juvenile humour there.'

Rebus looked at the message again. 'Beats me, Siobhan. What do you want to do?'

'I'd like to track down whoever sent this, but that's not going to be easy. Only way I can think of is to reply.'

'Let whoever it is know that Philippa's gone missing?'

Siobhan lowered her voice. 'I was thinking more along the lines of *her* replying.'

Rebus was thoughtful. 'Think it would work? What would you say?'

'I haven't decided.' The way she folded her arms, Rebus knew she was going to do it anyway.

'Run it past DCS Templer when she gets in,' he cautioned. Siobhan nodded and made to leave, but he called her back. 'You went to uni. Tell me, did you ever mix with the likes of Philippa Balfour?'

She snorted. 'That's another world. No tutorials or lectures for them. Some of them I only ever saw in the exam hall. And you know what?'

'What?'

'The sods always passed . . .'

That evening, Gill Templer hosted a celebratory gathering at the Palm Court in the Balmoral Hotel. A tuxedoed pianist was playing in the opposite corner. A bottle of champagne sat in an ice-bucket. Bowls of nibbles had been brought to the table.

'Remember to leave space for supper,' Gill told her guests. A table in Hadrian's had been booked for eight-thirty. It had just gone half past seven, and the last arrival was coming through the door.

Slipping off her coat, Siobhan apologised. A waiter appeared and took the coat from her. Another waiter was already pouring champagne into her glass.

'Cheers,' she said, sitting down and lifting the glass. 'And congratulations.'

Gill Templer lifted her own glass and allowed herself a smile. 'I think I deserve it,' she said, to enthusiastic agreement.

Siobhan already knew two of the guests. Both were fiscals depute, and Siobhan had worked with them on several prosecutions. Harriet Brough was in her late forties, her black hair permed (and maybe even dyed, too), her figure hidden behind layers of tweed and thick cotton. Diana Metcalf was early forties, with short ash-blonde hair and sunken eyes which, rather than masking, she exaggerated with dark eye-shadow. She always wore brightly coloured clothes, which helped to heighten still further her waif-like, undernourished look.

'And this is Siobhan Clarke,' Gill was telling the last member of the party. 'A detective constable in my station.' The way she said 'my station', it was as if she'd taken on ownership of the place, which, Siobhan supposed, wasn't so far from the truth. 'Siobhan, this is Jean Burchill. Jean works at the museum.'

'Oh? Which one?'

'The Museum of Scotland,' Burchill answered. 'Have you ever been?'

'I had a meal in The Tower once,' Siobhan said.

'Not quite the same thing.' Burchill's voice trailed off.

'No, what I meant was . . .' Siobhan tried to find a diplomatic way of putting it. 'I had a meal there just after it opened. The guy I was with . . . well, bad experience. It put me off going back.'

'Understood,' Harriet Brough said, as though every mishap in life could be explained by reference to the opposite sex.

'Well,' Gill said, 'it's women only tonight, so we can all relax.'

'Unless we hit a nightclub later,' Diana Metcalf said, her eyes glinting.

Gill caught Siobhan's eye. 'Did you send that e-mail?' she asked.

Jean Burchill tutted. 'No shop talk, please.'

The fiscals agreed noisily, but Siobhan nodded anyway, to let Gill know the message had gone out. Whether anyone would be fooled by it was another matter. It was why she'd been late getting here. She'd spent too long going over Philippa's e-mails, all the ones she'd sent to friends, trying to work out what sort of tone might be convincing, what words to use and how to order them. She'd gone through over a dozen drafts before deciding to keep it simple. But then some of Philippa's e-mails were like long chatty letters: what if her previous messages to Quizmaster had been the same? How would he or she react to this curt, out-of-character reply? *Problem. Need to talk to you. Flipside.* And then a telephone number, the number for Siobhan's own mobile.

'I saw the press conference on TV tonight,' Diana Metcalf said.

Jean Burchill groaned. 'What did I just say?'

Metcalf turned to her with those big, dark, wary eyes. 'This isn't shop, Jean. Everyone's talking about it.' Then she turned to Gill. 'I don't think it was the boyfriend, do you?'

Gill just shrugged.

'See?' Burchill said. 'Gill doesn't want to talk about it.'

'More likely the father,' Harriet Brough said. 'My brother was at school with him. A very cold fish.' She spoke with a confidence and authority that revealed her upbringing. She'd probably wanted to be a lawyer from nursery school on, Siobhan guessed. 'Where was the mother?' Brough now demanded of Gill.

'Couldn't face it,' Gill answered. 'We did ask her.'

'She couldn't have made a worse job than those two,' Brough stated, picking cashews out of the bowl nearest her.

Gill looked suddenly tired. Siobhan decided on a change of subject and asked Jean Burchill what she did at the museum.

'I'm a senior curator,' Burchill explained. 'My main specialism is eighteenth- and nineteenth-century.'

'Her main specialism,' Harriet Brough interrupted, 'is death.'

Burchill smiled. 'It's true I put together the exhibits on belief and—'

'What's truer,' Brough cut in, her eyes on Siobhan, 'is that she puts together old coffins and pictures of dead Victorian babies. Gives me the collywobbles whenever I happen to be on whichever floor it is.'

'The fourth,' Burchill said quietly. She was, Siobhan decided, very pretty. Small and slender, with straight brown hair hanging in a pageboy cut. Her chin was dimpled, her cheeks well defined and tinged pink, even in the discreet lighting of the Palm Court. She wore no make-up that Siobhan could see, nor did she need any. She was all muted, pastel shades: jacket and trousers which had probably been called 'taupe' in the shop; grey cashmere sweater beneath the jacket, and a russet pashmina fixed at the shoulder with a Rennie Mackintosh brooch. Late forties again. It struck Siobhan that *she* was the youngest person here by probably fifteen years.

'Jean and I were at school together,' Gill explained. 'Then we lost touch and bumped into one another just four or five years back.'

Burchill smiled at the memory.

'Wouldn't want to meet anyone I was at school with,' Harriet Brough said through a mouthful of nuts. 'Arseholes, the lot of them.'

'More champagne, ladies?' the waiter said, lifting the bottle from its ice-bucket.

'About bloody time,' Brough snapped.

Between dessert and coffee, Siobhan headed to the loo. Walking back along the corridor to the brasserie, she met Gill.

'Great minds,' Gill said with a smile.

'It was a lovely meal, Gill. Are you sure I can't . . . ?'

Gill touched her arm. 'My treat. It's not every day I have something worth celebrating.' The smile melted from her lips. 'You think your e-mail will work?' Siobhan just shrugged, and Gill nodded, accepting the assessment. 'What did you reckon to the press conference?'

'The usual jungle.'

'Sometimes it works,' Gill mused. She'd had three glasses of wine on top of the champagne, but the only sign that she wasn't stone-cold sober was a slight tilt to her head and heaviness to her eyelids.

'Can I say something?' Siobhan asked.

'We're off duty, Siobhan. Say what you like.'

'You shouldn't have given it to Ellen Wylie.'

Gill fixed her with a stare. 'It should have been you, eh?'

'That's not what I mean. But to give someone that as their first liaison job . . .'

'You'd have done it better?'

'I'm not *saying* that.'

'Then what are you saying?'

'I'm saying it was a jungle and you threw her in there without a map.'

'Careful, Siobhan.' Gill's voice had lost all its warmth. She considered for a moment, then sniffed. When she spoke, her eyes surveyed the hallway. 'Ellen Wylie's been bending my ear for months. She wanted liaison, and as soon as I could, I gave it to her. I wanted to see if she was as good as she thinks she is.' Now her eyes met Siobhan's. Their faces were close enough for Siobhan to smell the wine. 'She fell short.'

'How did that feel?'

Gill held up a finger. 'Don't push this, Siobhan. I've enough on my plate as it is.' It seemed she was about to say something more, but she merely wagged the finger and forced a smile. 'We'll talk later,' she said, sliding past Siobhan and pushing open the door to the loos. Then she paused. 'Ellen's no longer liaison officer. I *was* thinking of asking you . . .' The door closed behind her.

'Don't do me any favours,' Siobhan said, but she said it to the same closed door. It was as if Gill had hardened overnight, the humiliation of Ellen Wylie an early show of strength. The thing was . . . Siobhan *did* want liaison, but at the same time she felt disgusted with herself, because she'd enjoyed watching the press conference. She'd enjoyed Ellen Wylie's defeat.

When Gill emerged from the toilets, Siobhan was sitting on a chair in the corridor. Gill stood over her, gazing down.

'The spectre at the feast,' she commented, turning away.

3

'I was expecting some pavement artist,' Donald Devlin said. To Rebus's eyes, he was wearing the exact same clothes as when they'd last met. The retired pathologist was seated at a desk beside a computer and the only detective at Gayfield Square who seemed to know how to use the Facemaker programme. Facemaker was a database of eyes, ears, noses and lips, consolidated by special effects which could morph the details. Rebus got an idea of how the Farmer's old colleagues had been able to graft his features on to beefcake torsos.

'Things have moved on a little,' was all Rebus said, in reply to Devlin's comment. He was drinking coffee from a local café; not up to his *barista*'s standards, but better than the stuff from the station's vending machine. He'd had a broken night, waking up sweating and shaking in his living-room chair. Bad dreams and night sweats. Whatever any doctor could tell him, he knew his heart was okay – he could feel it pumping, doing its work.

Now, the coffee was just barely stopping him from yawning. The detective at the computer had finished the draft and was printing it out.

'There's *something* . . . something not quite right,' Devlin said, not for the first time. Rebus took a look. It was a face, anonymous and forgettable. 'It could almost be female,' Devlin went on. 'And I'm pretty sure *he* was not a *she*.'

'How about this?' the detective asked, clicking the mouse. Onscreen, the face developed a full, bushy beard.

'Oh, but that's absurd,' Devlin complained.

'DC Tibbet's idea of humour, Professor,' Rebus apologised.

'I *am* doing my best, you know.'

'We appreciate that, sir. Lose the beard, Tibbet.'

Tibbet lost the beard.

'You're sure it couldn't have been David Costello?' Rebus asked.

'I *know* David. It wasn't him.'

'How well do you know him?'

Devlin blinked. 'We spoke several times. Met one another on the stairs one day, and I asked him about the books he was carrying. Milton, *Paradise Lost*. We started a discussion.'

'Fascinating, sir.'

'It was, believe me. The laddie's got a brain on him.'

Rebus was thoughtful. 'Think he could kill someone, Professor?'

'Kill someone? *David?*' Devlin laughed. 'I doubt he'd find it quite cerebral enough, Inspector.' He paused. 'Is he still a suspect?'

'You know what it's like with police work, Professor. The world's guilty until proven otherwise.'

'I thought it was the other way round: innocent until proven guilty.'

'I think you're confusing us with lawyers, sir. You say you didn't really know Philippa?'

'Again, we passed on the stairs. The difference between David and her is that she never seemed to want to stop.'

'Bit stuck-up, was she?'

'I don't know that I would say that. She was, however, raised in a somewhat rarefied atmosphere, wouldn't you think?' He grew thoughtful. 'I bank with Balfour's, actually.'

'Have you met her father then?'

Devlin's eyes twinkled. 'Good Lord, no. I'm hardly one of their more important clients.'

'I meant to ask,' Rebus said. 'How's your jigsaw coming along?'

'Slowly. But then that's the inherent pleasure of the thing, isn't it?'

'I've never been one for jigsaws.'

'But you like your puzzles. I spoke to Sandy Gates last night, he was telling me all about you.'

'That must have done BT's profits a power of good.'

They shared a smile and got back to work.

At the end of an hour, Devlin decided that a previous incarnation had been closer. Thankfully, Tibbet had stored each and every version.

'Yes,' Devlin said. 'It's far from perfect, but I suppose it's satisfactory . . .' He made to rise from his chair.

'While you're here, sir . . .' Rebus was reaching into a drawer. He pulled out a fat dossier of photographs. 'Some pictures we'd like you to look at.'

'Pictures?'

'Photos of Ms Balfour's neighbours, friends from university.'

Devlin was nodding slowly, but with no show of enthusiasm. 'The process of elimination?'

'If you feel you're up to it, Professor.'

Devlin sighed. 'Perhaps some weak tea to aid concentration . . . ?'

'I think we can manage weak tea.' Rebus looked over to Tibbet, who was busy with his mouse. As Rebus got closer, he saw a face on the screen. It was a pretty good resemblance of Devlin's own, save for the addition of horns. 'DC Tibbet will fetch it,' Rebus said.

Tibbet made sure to save the image before rising from his chair . . .

By the time Rebus got back to St Leonard's, news was coming in of another thinly veiled search, this time of the lock-up on Calton Road where David Costello garaged his MG sports car. The forensic unit from Howdenhall had been in, finding nothing of apparent consequence. They already knew Flip Balfour's prints would be all over the car. No surprise either that some of her belongings – a lipstick, a pair of sunglasses – were in the glove compartment. The garage itself was clean.

'No chest freezer with a padlock on it?' Rebus guessed. 'No trapdoor leading to the torture dungeon?'

Distant Daniels shook his head. He was playing errand boy, transferring paperwork between Gayfield and St Leonard's. 'A student with an MG,' he commented, shaking his head again.

'Never mind the car,' Rebus told him. 'That lock-up probably cost more than your flat.'

'Christ, you could be right.' The smile they shared was sour. Everyone was busy: highlights of yesterday's news conference – with Ellen Wylie's performance edited out – had been broadcast on the nightly news. Now, sightings of the missing student were being followed up, meaning lots of phone calls . . .

'DI Rebus?' Rebus turned towards the voice. 'My office.'

And it *was* her office. Already, she was making it her own. Either the bunch of flowers on the filing cabinet had freshened the air, or she'd used something out of a can. The Farmer's chair had gone, too, replaced by a more utilitarian model. Where the Farmer had often slouched, Gill sat straight-backed, as if poised to rise to her feet. She held a piece of paper out, so that Rebus had to get out of the visitor's chair to reach it.

'A place called Falls,' she said. 'Do you know it?' He shook his head slowly. 'Me neither,' she confided.

Rebus was busy reading the note. It was a telephone message. A doll had been found in Falls.

'A doll?' he said.

She nodded. 'I want you to go take a look.'

Rebus burst out laughing. 'You're having me on.' But when he looked up, her face was blank. 'Is this my punishment?'

'For what?'

'I don't know. Maybe for being drunk in front of John Balfour.'

'I'm not that petty.'

'I'm beginning to wonder.'

She stared at him. 'Go on, I'm listening.'

'Ellen Wylie.'

'What about her?'

'She didn't deserve it.'

'You're a fan of hers then?'

'She didn't deserve it.'

She cocked a hand to her ear. 'Is there an echo in here?'

'I'll keep saying it till you start listening.'

There was silence in the room as they held one another's stare. When the phone rang, Gill seemed inclined not to answer. Eventually she reached out a hand, eyes still locked on Rebus.

'Yes?' She listened for a moment. 'Yes, sir. I'll be there.' She broke eye contact to put the phone down, sighed heavily. 'I have to go,' she told Rebus. 'I've a meeting with the ACC. Just go to Falls, will you?'

'Wouldn't want to get under your feet.'

'The doll was in a coffin, John.' She sounded tired all of a sudden.

'A kids' prank,' he said.

'Maybe.'

He checked the note again. 'It says here Falls is East Lothian. Let Haddington or somewhere take it.'

'I want *you* to take it.'

'You're not serious. It's a joke, right? Like telling me I tried chatting you up? Like telling me I was to see a doctor?'

She shook her head. 'Falls isn't just in East Lothian, John. It's where the Balfours live.' She gave him time for this to sink in. 'And you'll be getting that appointment any day . . .'

He drove out of Edinburgh along the A1. Traffic was light, the sun low and bright. East Lothian to him meant golf links and rocky beaches, flat farming land and commuter towns, fiercely protective of their own identities. The area had its share of secrets – caravan parks where Glasgow criminals came to hide – but it was essentially a calm place, a destination for day-trippers, or somewhere you might detour through on the route south to England. Towns such as Haddington, Gullane and North Berwick always seemed to him reserved, prosperous enclaves, their small shops supported by local communities which looked askance at the retail-park culture of the nearby capital. Yet Edinburgh was exerting its influence: house prices in the city were forcing more people further out, while the green belt found itself eroded by housing and shopping developments. Rebus's own police station was on one of the main arteries into town from the south and east, and over the past ten years or so he'd noticed the increase of rush-hour traffic, the slow, pitiless convoy of commuters.

Falls wasn't easy to find. Trusting to instinct rather than his map-book, he managed to miss a turning and ended up in Drem. While there, he stopped long enough to buy two bags of crisps and a can of Irn-Bru, had a bit of a picnic right there in the car, his window down. He still thought he was out here to prove a point, the point being to put him in his place. And as far as his new Detective Chief Super was concerned, that place was some distant outpost called Falls. Snack finished, he found himself whistling a tune he only half remembered. Some song about living beside a waterfall. He got the feeling it was something Siobhan had taped for him, part of his education in post-seventies music. Drem was just a single main street, and that street was quiet around him. The odd passing car or lorry, but no one on the pavement. The shopkeeper had tried engaging him in conversation, but Rebus hadn't had anything to add to her remarks about the weather, and he hadn't been about to ask directions to Falls. He didn't want to look like a bloody tourist.

He got the map-book out instead. Falls barely registered as a dot. He wondered how the place had come by its name. Knowing how things went, he wouldn't be surprised to find that it had some obscure local pronunciation: Fails or Fallis, something like that. It took him only another ten minutes along winding roads, dipping and rising like a gentle roller-coaster, before he found the place. It would have taken less than ten minutes, too, had a combination of blind summits and slow-moving tractor not reduced his progress to a second-gear crawl.

Falls wasn't quite what he'd been expecting. At its centre was a short stretch of main road with houses either side. Nice detached houses with well-tended gardens, and a row of cottages which fronted the narrow pavement. One of the cottages had a wooden sign outside with the word Pottery painted neatly on it. But towards the end of the village – more of a hamlet actually – was what looked suspiciously like a 1930s council estate, grey semis with broken fences, tricycles sitting in the middle of the road. A patch of grass separated this estate from the main road, and two kids were kicking a ball back and forth between them, with little enthusiasm. As Rebus drove past, their eyes turned to study him, as though he were some rare species.

Then, as suddenly as he'd entered the village, he was out into countryside again. He stopped by the verge. Ahead in the distance he could see what looked like a petrol station. He couldn't tell if it was still a going concern. The tractor he'd overtaken earlier came past him now, then slowed so it could make a turn into a half-ploughed field. The driver didn't pay Rebus any heed. He came to a juddering halt and eased himself from the cab. Rebus could hear a radio blaring inside.

Rebus opened his car door, slamming it shut after him. The farmhand still hadn't paid him any attention. Rebus rested his palms against the waist-high stone wall.

'Morning,' he said.

'Morning.' The man was tinkering with the machinery at the back of his tractor.

'I'm a police officer. Do you know where I could find Beverly Dodds?'

'At home probably.'

'And where's home?'

'See the cottage with the pottery sign?'

'Yes.'

'That's her.' The man's voice was neutral. He still hadn't so much as glanced in Rebus's direction, concentrating instead on the blades of his plough. He was thick-set, with black curly hair and a black beard framing a face that was all creases and curves. For a second, Rebus was reminded of cartoon drawings from the comics of his childhood, strange faces that could be viewed either way up and still make sense. 'To do with that bloody doll, is it?'

'Yes.'

'Piece of bloody nonsense, going to you lot about that.'

'You don't think it has anything to do with Ms Balfour's disappearance?'

'Course it hasn't. Kids from Meadowside, that's all it is.'

'You're probably right. Meadowside's that patch of houses, is it?' Rebus nodded back towards the village. He couldn't see the boys – they, along with Falls, were hidden around a bend – but he thought he could hear the distant thud of the football.

The farmhand nodded agreement. 'Like I said, waste of time. Still, it's yours to waste, I suppose . . . and my taxes paying for it.'

'Do you know the family?'

'Which one?'

'The Balfours.'

The farmhand nodded again. 'They own this land . . . some of it, any road.'

Rebus looked around, realising for the first time that there wasn't a single dwelling or building in sight, other than the petrol station. 'I thought they just had the house and grounds.'

Now the farmhand shook his head.

'Where is their place, by the way?'

For the first time, the man locked eyes with Rebus. Satisfied with whatever checks he'd been making, he was cleaning his hands by rubbing them down his faded denims. 'The track the other end of town,' he said. 'About a mile up that way, big gates, you can't miss them. The falls are up there too, about halfway.'

'Falls?'

'The waterfall. You'll want to see it, won't you?'

Behind the farmhand, the land rose gently. Hard to imagine any point nearby high enough for a waterfall.

'Wouldn't want to waste your tax money on sightseeing,' Rebus said with a smile.

'It's not sightseeing though, is it?'

'What is it then?'

'The scene of the bloody crime.' Exasperation had crept into the man's voice. 'Don't they tell you anything back in Edinburgh . . . ?'

A narrow lane wound uphill out of the village. Anybody passing through would probably assume, as Rebus had, that it was leading to a dead end, maybe turning into somebody's driveway. But it opened out a little eventually, and at that point Rebus pulled the Saab up on to the verge. There was a stile, as the local had explained. Rebus locked his car – city instinct, hard to resist – and climbed over, into a field where cows were grazing. They showed about as much interest in him as the farmhand had. He could smell them, hear their snorts and munching. He did his best to avoid the cow-pats as he walked towards a line of nearby trees. The trees indicated the route of the stream. This was where the waterfall could be found. It was also where, the previous morning, Beverly Dodds had found a tiny coffin, and within it a doll. When he found the waterfall from which Falls had derived its name, he laughed out loud. The water dropped a full four feet.

'Not exactly Niagara, are you?' Rebus crouched down at the foot of the waterfall. He couldn't be sure exactly where the doll had been lying, but he looked around anyway. It was a scenic spot, probably popular with the locals. A couple of beer cans and some chocolate wrappers had found their way here. He stood up and surveyed the land. Scenic and isolated: no habitations in sight. He doubted anyone had seen whoever placed the doll here, always supposing it hadn't been washed down from above. Not that there *was* much above. The burn could be traced in its meandering route down the hillside. He doubted there was anything up there except wilderness. His map didn't even show the burn, and there'd be no dwellings up there, just hills where you could walk for days without seeing another human soul. He wondered where the Balfours' house was, then found himself shaking his head. What did it matter? It wasn't dolls he was chasing out here, coffin or no coffin . . . it was wild geese.

He crouched down again, rested a hand in the water, palm up. It was cold and clear. He scooped some up, watched it trickle through his fingers.

'I wouldn't drink any,' a voice called. He looked up into the light, saw a woman emerging from the line of trees. She wore a long muslin dress over her thin frame. With the sun behind her, the outline of her figure was discernible beneath the cloth. As she came forward, she ran a hand behind her head to pull back long curly blonde hair, taking it out of her eyes. 'The farmers,' she explained. 'All the chemicals they use run off the soil and into the streams. Organo-phosphates and who knows what.' She seemed to tremble at the thought.

'I never touch the stuff,' Rebus said, drying his hand on his sleeve as he stood up. 'Are you Ms Dodds?'

'Everybody calls me Bev.' She stuck out a skeletal hand which itself was at the end of a tapering arm. Like chicken bones, Rebus thought, making sure not to squeeze too hard.

'DI Rebus,' he said. 'How did you know I was here?'

'I saw your car. I was watching from my window. When you drove up the lane, I just knew instinctively.' She bounced on her toes, pleased to have been proved right. She reminded Rebus of a teenager, but her face told a different story: laughter lines around the eyes; the skin of the cheekbones sagging. She had to be in her early fifties, albeit with the zest of someone far younger.

'You walked?'

'Oh yes,' she said, looking down at her open-toed sandals. 'I was surprised you didn't come to me first.'

'I just wanted a look around. Where exactly was it you found this doll?'

She pointed towards the fall of water. 'Right at the foot, sitting on the bank. It was completely dry.'

'Why do you say that?'

'Because I know you'll have been wondering if it floated downstream.'

Rebus didn't let on that he'd been thinking exactly this, but she seemed to sense it anyway and bounced on her toes again.

'And it was out in the open,' she went on. 'I don't think it could have been left there by accident. They'd have noticed and come back for it.'

'Ever considered a career in the police, Ms Dodds?'

She tutted. 'Please, call me Bev.' She didn't answer his question, but he could see she was pleased by it.

'I don't suppose you brought it with you?'

She shook her head, which sent her hair tumbling, so that she had to draw it back again. 'It's down in the cottage.'

He nodded. 'Lived here long, Bev?'

She smiled. 'Haven't quite got the accent yet, have I.'

'You've a way to go,' he admitted.

'I was born in Bristol, spent more years than I care to remember in London. Divorce sent me scampering, and this is where I ran out of breath.'

'How long ago was that?'

'Five, six years. They still call my home "the Swanston cottage".'

'The family who lived there before you?'

She nodded. 'Falls is that kind of place, Inspector. Why are you smiling?'

'I wasn't sure how it would be pronounced.'

She seemed to understand. 'Funny, isn't it? I mean, there's just the one little waterfall, so why "Falls"? Nobody seems to know.' She paused. 'It was a mining village.'

His forehead furrowed. 'Coal mines? Here?'

She stretched out her arm towards the north. 'A mile or so that way. Little came of it. This was back in the thirties.'

'Which was when they built Meadowside?'

She nodded.

'But there's no mining now?'

'Not for forty years. I think most of Meadowside is unemployed. That patch of scrubland, it's not the meadow in question, you know. When they built the first houses there was a proper meadow there, but then they needed more houses . . . and they built right on top of it.' She shivered again, and changed the subject. 'Think you can get your car turned?'

He nodded.

'Well, take your time,' she said, beginning to move away. 'I'll head back and make some tea. See you at Wheel Cottage, Inspector.'

'Wheel,' she explained, pouring water into the teapot, for her potter's wheel.

'It began as therapy,' she went on. 'After the break-up.' She paused for a moment. 'But I found out I was actually quite good at it. I think that surprised quite a number of my old friends.' The way she said these last two words made Rebus think that these friends had no place in her new life. 'So maybe "wheel" stands for the wheel of life too,' she added, lifting the tray and leading him into what she called her 'parlour'.

It was a small, low-ceilinged room with bright patterns everywhere. There were several examples of what he took to be Beverly Dodds's work: glazed blue earthenware shaped into dishes and vases. He made sure she noticed him noticing them.

'Mostly early stuff,' she said, trying for a dismissive tone. 'I keep them for sentimental reasons.' Bangles and bracelets slid down her wrists as she pushed her hair back again.

'They're very good,' he told her. She poured the tea and handed him a robust cup and saucer of the same blue colouring. He looked around the room but couldn't see any sign of a coffin or doll.

'In my workshop,' she said, seeming to read his mind again. 'I can fetch it, if you like.'

'Please,' he said. So she got up and left the room. Rebus was feeling claustrophobic. The tea wasn't tea at all but some herbal alternative. He considered pouring it into one of the vases, but pulled out his mobile instead, intending to check for messages. The screen was blank, no signal showing. The thick stone walls perhaps; either that or Falls was in a dead zone. He'd known it happen in East Lothian. There was just the one small bookcase in the room: arts and crafts mostly, and a couple of volumes on 'Wiccan'. Rebus picked one up, started to flip through it.

'White magic,' the voice behind him said. 'A belief in the power of Nature.'

Rebus put the book back and turned towards her.

'Here we are,' she said. She was carrying the coffin as though part of some solemn procession. Rebus took a step forward and she held it at arm's length towards him. He lifted it gently from her, as he felt was expected, and at the same time a thought hurtled through his brain: *she's unhinged . . . this is all her doing!* But his attention was diverted to the coffin itself. It was made of a dark wood, aged oak maybe, and held together with black nails, akin to carpet tacks. The wooden panels had been measured and sawn, the cut edges sandpapered but otherwise untreated. The whole thing was about eight inches long. It wasn't the work of a professional carpenter; even Rebus, who wouldn't know an awl from his elbow, could tell that. And then she lifted off the lid for him. Her eyes were wide and unblinking, fixed on his, awaiting his response.

'It was nailed shut,' she explained. 'I prised it open.'

Inside, the small wooden doll lay with arms flat by its sides, its face rounded but blank, dressed in scraps of muslin. It had been carved, but with little artistry, deep grooves in the surface where the chisel had done its work. Rebus tried lifting it out of its box, but his fingers were too clumsy, the space between doll and coffin sides too tight. So he turned the container upside down and the doll slid into his palm. His first thought was to compare the cloth wraparound to the various materials on show in the parlour, but there were no obvious matches.

'The cloth's quite new and clean,' she was whispering. He nodded. The coffin hadn't been outdoors long. It hadn't had time to stain or suffer damp.

'I've seen some strange things, Bev . . .' Rebus said, his voice trailing off. 'Nothing else at the scene? Nothing unusual?'

She shook her head slowly. 'I walk up that way every week. This,' touching the coffin, 'was the only thing out of place.'

'Footprints . . . ?' Rebus started, but he broke off. It was asking too much of her. But she was ready with an answer.

'None that I could see.' She tore her eyes away from the coffin and towards him again. 'I *did* look, because I knew it couldn't just have appeared out of thin air.'

'Is there anyone in the village who's keen on woodwork? Maybe a joiner . . . ?'

'Nearest joiner is Haddington. Offhand, I don't know anyone who's . . . I mean, who in their right mind would do something like *this*?'

Rebus smiled. 'I bet you've thought about it though.'

She smiled back. 'I've thought of little else, Inspector. I mean, in general maybe I'd shrug something like this off, but with what's happened to the Balfour girl . . .'

'We don't know anything's happened,' Rebus felt bound to say.

'Surely it's connected though?'

'Doesn't mean it's not a crank.' He kept his eyes on hers as he spoke. 'In my experience, every village has its resident oddball.'

'Are you saying that I—' She broke off at the sound of a car drawing up outside. 'Oh,' she said, getting to her feet, 'that'll be the reporter.'

Rebus followed her to the window. A young man was emerging from the driver's side of a red Ford Focus. In the passenger seat, a photographer was fixing a lens on to his camera. The driver stretched and rolled his shoulders, as though at the end of a long journey.

'They were here before,' Bev was explaining. 'When the Balfour girl first went missing. Left me a card, and when this happened . . .' Rebus was following her into the narrow hall as she made for the front door.

'That wasn't the cleverest move, Ms Dodds.' Rebus was trying to keep his anger in check.

Hand on the doorhandle, she half turned towards him. 'At least *they* didn't accuse me of being a crank, Inspector.'

He wanted to say, *but they will*, but the damage was already done.

The reporter's name was Steve Holly, and he worked for the

Edinburgh office of a Glasgow tabloid. He was young, early twenties, which was good: maybe he'd take a telling. If they'd sent one of the old pros out, Rebus wouldn't even have bothered trying.

Holly was short and a bit overweight, his hair gelled into a jagged line, reminding Rebus of the single strand of barbed wire you got at the top of a farmer's fence. He had a notebook and pen in one hand, and shook Rebus's with the other.

'Don't think we've met,' he said, in a way that made Rebus suspect his name was not unknown to the reporter. 'This is Tony, my glamorous assistant.' The photographer snorted. He was hefting a camera bag over one shoulder. 'What we thought, Bev, is if we take you to the waterfall, have you picking the coffin up off the ground.'

'Yes, of course.'

'Saves the hassle of setting up an interior shot,' Holly went on. 'Not that Tony would mind. But stick him in a room and he comes over all creative and arty.'

'Oh?' She looked appraisingly at the photographer. Rebus repressed a smile: the words 'creative' and 'arty' had different connotations for the reporter and Bev. But Holly was quick to pick up on it, too. 'I could send him back later, if you like. Do a nice portrait of you, maybe in your studio.'

'It's hardly a studio,' Bev countered, stroking a finger down her neck, enjoying the thought. 'Just the spare bedroom with my wheel and some drawings. I pinned white sheets to the walls to help with the light.'

'Speaking of light,' Holly broke in, staring at the sky meaningfully, 'we'd better get a move on, eh?'

'Perfect just now,' the photographer explained to Bev. 'Won't stay that way for long.'

Bev looked up too, nodding agreement, one artist to another. Rebus had to admit: Holly was good.

'Do you want to stay here, mind the fort?' he was now asking Rebus. 'We'll only be fifteen minutes.'

'I've got to get back to Edinburgh. Any chance I can have your number, Mr Holly?'

'Should have my card somewhere.' The reporter began searching his pockets, produced a wallet and from it a business card.

'Thanks,' Rebus said, taking it. 'And if I could have a quick word . . . ?'

As he led Holly a few steps away, he saw that Bev was standing close beside the photographer, asking him if her clothes were suitable. He got the feeling she missed the presence of another artist in the village. Rebus turned his back on them, the better to mask what he was about to say.

'Have you seen this doll thing?' Holly was asking. Rebus nodded. Holly wrinkled his nose. 'Reckon we're wasting our time?' His tone was matey, inviting the truth.

'Almost certainly,' Rebus said, not believing it, and knowing that once Holly saw the bizarre carving he wouldn't believe it either. 'It's a day out of the city anyway,' Rebus went on, forcing levity into his tone.

'Can't stand the countryside,' Holly admitted. 'Too far from the carbon monoxide for my liking. Surprised they sent a DI . . .'

'We have to treat each lead seriously.'

'Sure you do, I understand that. I'd still have sent a DC or DS, tops.'

'Like I say—' But Holly was turning away from him, ready to get back to work. Rebus gripped his arm. 'You know that if this *does* turn out to be evidence, we could want it kept quiet?'

Holly nodded perfunctorily and tried for an American accent. 'Get your people to speak to my people.' He released his arm and turned back to Bev and the photographer. 'Here, Bev, that what you're wearing? I just thought, nice day like this, maybe you'd be comfier in a shorter skirt . . .'

Rebus drove back up the lane, not stopping by the stile this time, keeping going, wondering what else he might find. A half-mile further along, a wide driveway surfaced with pink chippings ended abruptly in a set of tall wrought-iron gates. Rebus pulled over and got out of the car. The gates were padlocked shut. Beyond them he could see the driveway curve through a forest, the trees blocking any view of a house. There were no signs, but he knew this had to be Junipers. High stone walls either side of the gates, but eventually tapering down to a more manageable height. Rebus left his car, walked a hundred yards down the main road, then hoisted himself over the wall and into the trees.

He got the feeling that if he tried a short cut, he could end up wandering the woods for hours, so he made for the driveway and hoped that around the curve he wouldn't find another, and another after that.

Which was precisely what he did find. He wondered idly about deliveries: how did the postman get on? Probably not something that concerned a man like John Balfour. He'd walked a full five minutes before the house came into view. Its walls had aged the colour of slate, an elongated two-storey Gothic confection with turrets either end. Rebus didn't bother getting too close, couldn't even be sure there'd be anyone home. He supposed there'd be security of some kind – maybe a police officer manning the phone – but if so it was low-key. The house looked on to a spread of manicured lawn, flowerbeds either side. There was what looked like a paddock beyond the far end of the main building. No cars or garages, probably out of sight around the back. He couldn't imagine anyone actually being happy in such a dour setting. The house almost seemed to have a frown on it, a warning against gaiety and ill manners. He wondered if Philippa's mother felt like an exhibit in some locked museum. Then he caught sight of a face at an upstairs window, but as soon as he saw it, it vanished again. Some apparition maybe, but a minute later the front door was hauled open and a woman came running down the steps and on to the gravel driveway. She was heading towards him, wild hair obscuring her face. When she tripped and fell, he ran forwards to help her, but she saw him coming and got quickly to her feet, ignoring her skinned knees and the chippings still sticking to them. A cordless phone had slipped from her hand. She picked it up.

'Stay away!' she shrieked. When she pushed the hair away from her face, he saw that it was Jacqueline Balfour. As soon as the words were out, she seemed to regret them, and put up two pacifying hands. 'Look, I'm sorry. Just . . . just tell us what it is you want.'

And then he realised, realised that this stricken woman standing before him thought he was her daughter's abductor.

'Mrs Balfour,' he said, raising his own hands, palms out towards her, 'I'm a police officer.'

She had stopped crying finally, the pair of them seated on the front step, as if she were unwilling to let the house take possession of her again. She kept saying she was sorry, and Rebus kept saying he was the one who should be apologising.

'I just didn't think,' he said. 'I mean, I didn't think anyone would be home.'

Nor was she alone. A WPC had come to the door, but had been ordered firmly by Jacqueline Balfour to 'just go away'. Rebus had asked if she wanted him to go too, but she'd shaken her head.

'Is there something you've come to tell me?' she asked, handing back his dampened handkerchief. Tears: tears he'd caused. He told her to keep it, and she folded it neatly, then unfolded it and started the process again. She still hadn't seemed to notice the damage to her knees. Her skirt was tucked between them as she sat.

'No news,' he said quietly. Then, seeing all hope drain from her: 'There might be a lead down in the village.'

'The village?'

'Falls.'

'What sort of lead?'

Suddenly he wished he'd never started. 'I can't really say just now.' An old fallback and one that wouldn't work here. All she had to do was say something to her husband, and he'd be on the phone, demanding to know. And even if he didn't, or if he hid the news of the strange find from her, the media would hardly be so tactful . . .

'Did Philippa collect dolls?' Rebus asked now.

'Dolls?' She was playing with the cordless phone again, turning it in her hand.

'It's just that someone found one, down by the waterfall.'

She shook her head. 'No dolls,' she said quietly, as if feeling that somehow there should have been dolls in Philippa's life, and that their absence reflected badly on her as a mother.

'It's probably nothing,' Rebus said.

'Probably,' she agreed, filling the pause.

'Is Mr Balfour at home?'

'He'll be back later. He's in Edinburgh.' She stared at the phone. 'No one's going to call, are they? John's business friends, they've all been told to keep the line clear. Same thing with family. Keep the line clear in case *they* phone. But they won't, I know they won't.'

'You don't think she's been kidnapped, Mrs Balfour?'

She shook her head.

'What then?'

She stared at him, her eyes red-veined from crying, and shadowed underneath from lack of sleep. 'She's dead.' It came out almost in a whisper. 'You think so too, don't you?'

'It's far too early to be thinking that. I've known MisPers turn up weeks or months later.'

'Weeks or months? I can't bear the thought. I'd rather know . . . one way or the other.'

'When was the last time you saw her?'

'About ten days ago. We went shopping in Edinburgh, just the usual places. Not really meaning to buy anything. We had a bite to eat.'

'Did she come to the house often?'

Jacqueline Balfour shook her head. 'He poisoned her.'

'Sorry?'

'David Costello. He poisoned her memories, made her think she could remember things, things which never happened. That last time we met . . . Flip kept asking about her childhood. She said it had been miserable for her, that we'd ignored her, hadn't wanted her. Utter rubbish.'

'And David Costello put these ideas in her head?'

She straightened her back, took a deep breath and released it. 'That's my belief.'

Rebus was thoughtful. 'Why would he do something like that?'

'Because of who he is.' She left the statement hanging in the air. The ringing of the phone was a sudden cacophony. She fumbled to find the right button to press.

'Hello?'

Then her face relaxed a little. 'Hello, darling, what time will you be home . . . ?'

Rebus waited till the call was finished. He was thinking of the press conference, the way John Balfour had said 'I' rather than 'we', as if his wife had no feelings, no existence . . .

'That was John,' she said. Rebus nodded.

'He's in London a lot, isn't he? Doesn't it get lonely out here?'

She looked at him. 'I do have friends, you know.'

'I wasn't suggesting otherwise. You probably go into Edinburgh a lot.'

'Once or twice a week, yes.'

'Do you see much of your husband's business partner?'

She looked at him again. 'Ranald? He and his wife are probably our best friends . . . Why do you ask?'

Rebus made show of scratching his head. 'I don't know. Just making conversation, I suppose.'

'Well don't.'

'Don't make conversation?'

'I don't like it. I feel like everyone's trying to trap me. It's like at business parties, John's always warning me not to give anything away, you never know who's fishing for some info on the bank.'

'We're not competitors here, Mrs Balfour.'

She bowed her head a little. 'Of course not. I apologise. It's just . . .'

'No need for apologies,' Rebus said, getting to his feet. 'This is your home, your rules. Wouldn't you say?'

'Well, when you put it like that . . .' She seemed to brighten a little. All the same, Rebus reckoned that whenever Jacqueline Balfour's husband was at home, it was *his* rules they played by . . .

Inside the house, he found two colleagues sitting comfortably in the lounge. The WPC introduced herself as Nicola Campbell. The other officer was CID based at Fettes HQ. His name was Eric Bain, more usually called 'Brains'. Bain was seated at a desk upon which sat a land-line telephone, notebook and pen, and a recording machine, along with a mobile phone connected to a laptop. Having established that the current caller was Mr Balfour, Bain had slid the headphones back down around his neck. He was drinking strawberry yoghurt straight from the pot, and nodded a greeting at Rebus.

'Cushy number,' Rebus said, admiring the surroundings.

'If you don't mind the crushing boredom,' Campbell admitted.

'What's the deal with the laptop?'

'It connects Brains to his nerdy friends.'

Bain wagged a finger at her. 'It's part of the TT technology: tracking and tracing.' Concentrating on the last vestiges of his snack, he didn't see Campbell mouth the word 'nerd' at Rebus.

'Which would be great,' Rebus said, 'if there was anything worth the effort.'

Bain nodded. 'Lots of sympathy calls to start with, friends and family. Impressively low number of crackpots. Not being listed in the book probably helps.'

'Just remember,' Rebus warned, 'the person we're looking for might be a crackpot too.'

'Probably no shortage of nutters around here,' Campbell said, crossing her legs. She was seated on one of the room's three sofas, copies of *Caledonia* and *Scottish Field* spread out in front of her. There were other magazines on a table behind her sofa. Rebus got the feeling they belonged to the house, and that she'd read each and every one of them at least once.

'How do you mean?' he asked.

'Been through the village yet? Albinos in the trees picking at banjos?'

Rebus smiled. Bain looked puzzled. 'I didn't see any,' he said.

Campbell's look said it all: *that's because in some parallel world, you're up in the trees with them . . .*

'Tell me something,' Rebus said, 'at the press conference, Mr Balfour mentioned his mobile phone . . .'

'Shouldn't have done that,' Bain said, shaking his head. 'We'd asked him not to.'

'Not so easy to trace a mobile call?'

'They're more flexible than land-lines, aren't they?'

'But still traceable?'

'Up to a point. Lot of dodgy mobiles out there. We could trace one to an account, only to find it'd been nicked the previous week.'

Campbell suppressed a yawn. 'You see how it is?' she told Rebus. 'Thrill after thrill after thrill . . .'

He took his time heading back into town, aware of traffic picking up in the opposite direction. The rush hour was starting, executive cars streaming back into the countryside. He knew of people who commuted to and from Edinburgh every day now from as far afield as the Borders, Fife and Glasgow. They all said housing was to blame. A three-bedroom semi in a nice part of the city could cost £250,000 or more. For that money, you could buy a big detached place in West Lothian, or half a street in Cowdenbeath. On the other hand, Rebus had had cold callers to his flat in Marchmont. He'd had letters addressed to 'The Occupier' from desperate buyers. Because that was the other thing about Edinburgh: no matter how high the prices seemed to go, there were always buyers. In Marchmont it was often landlords, looking for something to add to their portfolio, or parents whose kids wanted a flat near the university. Rebus had lived in his tenement twenty-odd years, and had seen the area change. Fewer families and old people, more students and young, childless couples. The groups didn't seem to mix. People who'd lived in Marchmont all their lives watched their children move away, unable to afford a place nearby. Rebus didn't know anyone in his tenement now, or the ones either side of him. As far as he could tell, he was the only owner-occupier left. More worrying still, he seemed to be the oldest person there. And still the letters and offers came, and the prices kept rising.

Which was why he was moving out. Not that he'd found a place to buy yet. Maybe he'd go back into the rental market, that way he had freedom of choice: a year in a country cottage, then a year by the seaside, and a year or two above a pub . . . The flat was too big for him, he knew that. Nobody ever stayed in the spare bedrooms, and many nights he slept on the chair in the living room. A studio flat would be big enough for him; everything else was excess.

Volvos, BMWs, sporty Audis . . . they were all passing him on their way home. Rebus was wondering if he wanted to commute. From Marchmont he could walk to work. It took about fifteen minutes, the only exercise he ever got. He wouldn't fancy the drive every day between Falls and the city. The streets had been quiet when he'd been there, but he guessed tonight the narrow main road would be lined with cars.

When he started looking for a parking space in Marchmont, however, he was reminded of another reason for moving out. In the end, he left the Saab on a yellow line, and went into the nearest shop for an evening paper, milk, rolls and bacon. He'd called into the station, asked if he was needed: he wasn't. Back in his flat, he took a can of beer from the fridge and settled into his chair by the living-room window. The kitchen was more of a mess than usual: some of the hall stuff was in there while the rewiring went on. He didn't know when the electrics had last been done. He didn't think they'd been touched since he bought the place. After the rewiring, he had a painter booked to slap on some magnolia, freshen the place up. He'd been told not to make too many renovations: whoever bought the place would probably just do it all over again anyway. Rewiring and decorating: he'd stop at that. The Property Centre had said it was impossible to tell how much he'd get for the place. In Edinburgh, you put your home on the market for 'offers over', but that premium could reach thirty or forty per cent. A conservative estimate valued his Arden Street shell at £125,000 to £140,000. There was no mortgage outstanding. It was cash in the bank.

'You could retire on that,' Siobhan had told him. Well, maybe. He'd have to split it with his ex-wife, he supposed, even though he'd written her a cheque for her share of the place soon after they'd split up. And he could slip some money to Sammy, his daughter. Sammy was another reason for selling, or so he told himself. After her accident, she was finally out of the wheelchair but still used a pair of sticks. Two flights of tenement stairs were beyond her . . . not that she'd been a regular visitor even before the hit-and-run.

He didn't have many visitors, was not a good host. When his ex, Rhona, had moved out, he'd never got round to filling the gaps she'd left. Someone had once described the flat as 'a cave', and there was some truth in this. It provided a form of shelter for him, and that was about all he asked of it. The students next door were playing something semi-raucous. It sounded like bad Hawkwind from twenty years before, which probably meant it was by some fashionable new band. He looked through his own collection, came up with the tape Siobhan had made, and put it on. The Mutton Birds: three songs from one of their albums. They came from New Zealand, somewhere like that, and one of the instruments had been recorded here in Edinburgh. That was about as much as she could tell him about them. The second song was 'The Falls'.

He sat back down again. There was a bottle on the floor: Talisker, a clean, honed taste. Glass beside it, so he poured, toasted the reflection in the window, leaned back and closed his eyes. He wasn't having this room redecorated. He'd done it himself not that long back, his old friend and ally Jack Morton helping. Jack was dead now, one of too many ghosts. Rebus wondered if he'd leave them behind when he moved. Somehow he doubted it, and deep down, he would miss them anyway.

The music was all about loss and redemption. Places changing and people with them, dreams shifting ever further beyond reach. Rebus didn't think he'd be sorry to see the back of Arden Street. It was time for a change.

4

On her way into work next morning, Siobhan thought of nothing but Quizmaster. Nobody had called her mobile, so she was thinking up another message to send him. Him or her. She knew she had to keep an open mind, but couldn't help thinking of Quizmaster as 'him'. 'Stricture', 'Hellbank' . . . they seemed masculine to her. And the whole idea of some game being played by computer . . . it all sounded so blokeish, sad anoraks stuck in their bedrooms. Her first message – *Problem. Need to talk to you. Flipside* – seemed not to have worked. Today, she was going to end the pretence. She would e-mail him as herself, and explain Flip's disappearance, asking him to get in touch. She'd kept the mobile phone beside her all night, waking every hour or so and checking to see that she hadn't slept through a call. But no calls came. Finally, as dawn approached, she'd got dressed and gone for a walk. Her flat was just off Broughton Street, in an area undergoing rapid gentrification: not as pricey as the New Town which it neighboured, but close to the city centre. Half her street seemed to be taken up with skips, and she knew that by mid-morning builders' vans would be struggling to find a parking space.

She broke the walk with breakfast at an early opener: beans on toast and a mug of tea so strong she feared for tannin poisoning. At the top of Calton Hill, she stopped to watch the city gearing up for another day. Down by Leith, a container ship was sitting off the coast. The Pentland Hills to the south wore their covering of low cloud like a welcoming duvet. There wasn't much traffic yet on Princes Street: buses and taxis mostly. She liked Edinburgh best at this time of day, before routine set in. The Balmoral Hotel was one of the closest landmarks. She thought back to the party Gill Templer had hosted there . . . how Gill had talked of having a lot on her plate. Siobhan wondered if she'd meant the case itself or her new promotion. Thing about the promotion was, John Rebus came with it. He was Gill's problem now rather than the Farmer's. Word in the office was, John had already got into a spot of bother: found drunk inside the MisPer's flat. In the past, people had warned Siobhan that she was growing too much like Rebus, picking up his faults as well as his strengths. She didn't think that was true.

No, that wasn't true . . .

Her walk downhill took her on to Waterloo Place. A right turn, she'd be home in five minutes. A left, and she could be at work in ten. She turned left on to North Bridge, kept walking.

St Leonard's was quiet. The CID suite had a musty smell: too many bodies each day spending too long cooped up there. She opened a couple of windows, made herself a mug of weak coffee, and sat down at her desk. When she checked, there were no messages on Flip's computer. She decided to keep the line open while she composed her new e-mail. But after only a couple of lines, a message told her she had post. It was from Quizmaster, a simple *Good morning*. She hit reply and asked, *How did you know I was here?* The response was immediate.

That's something Flipside wouldn't have to ask. Who are you?

Siobhan typed so quickly, she didn't correct her errors. *I'm a police officer, baesd in Edinburgh. We're investgating Philippa Balfour's disappearance.* She waited a full minute for his reply.

Who?

Flipside, she typed.

She never told me her real name. That's one of the rules.

The rules of the game? Siobhan typed.

Yes. Did she live in Edinburgh?

She was a student here. Can we talk? You've got my mobile number.

Again, the wait seemed interminable.

I prefer this.

Okay, Siobhan typed, *can you tell me about Hellbank?*

You'd have to play the game. Give me a name to call you.

My name's Siobhan Clarke. I'm a detective constable with Lothian and Borders Police.

I get the feeling that's your real name, Siobhan. You've broken one of the first rules. How do you pronounce it?

Siobhan could feel the blood rising to her face. *It's not a game, Quizmaster.*

But that's exactly what it is. How do you pronounce your name?

Shi-vawn.

There was a longer pause, and she was about to re-send the message when his response came.

To answer your question, Hellbank is one level of the game.

Flipside was playing a game?

Yes. Stricture is the next level.

What sort of game? Could she have got into trouble?

Later.

Siobhan stared at the word. *What do you mean?*

We'll talk later.

I need your cooperation.

Then learn patience. I could shut down right now and you'd never find me, do you accept that?

Yes. Siobhan was about ready to punch the screen.

Later.

Later, she typed.

And that was it. No further messages. He'd gone off-line, or was still there but wouldn't respond. And all she could do was wait. Or was it? She logged on to the Internet and tried all the search engines she could find, asking them for sites related to Quizmaster and PaganOmerta. She came up with dozens of Quizmasters, but got the feeling none of them was hers. PaganOmerta was a blank, though separating the words gave her hundreds of sites, almost all of them trying to sell her a new-age religion. When she tried PaganOmerta.com there was nothing there. It was an address rather than a site. She made more coffee. The rest of the shift was drifting in. A couple of people said hello, but she wasn't listening. She'd had another idea. She sat back down at her desk with the phone book and a copy of Yellow Pages, drew her notebook towards her and picked up a pen.

She tried computer retailers first, until finally someone directed her towards a comic shop on South Bridge. To Siobhan, comics meant things like the *Beano* and *Dandy*, though she'd once had a boyfriend whose obsession with *2000AD* was at least partly responsible for their break-up. But this shop was a revelation. There were thousands of titles, along with sci-fi books, T-shirts and other merchandise. At the counter, a teenage assistant was arguing the merits of John Constantine with two schoolboys. She'd no way of knowing whether Constantine was a comic character or a writer or artist. Eventually the boys noticed her standing right behind them. They stopped being excited, turned back into awkward, gangling twelve-year-olds. Maybe they weren't used to women listening in. She didn't suppose they were used to women at all.

'I heard you talking,' she said. 'Thought maybe you could help me with something.' None of the three said anything. The teenage assistant was rubbing at a patch of acne on his cheek. 'You ever play games on the Internet?'

'You mean like Dreamcast?' She looked blank. 'It's Sony,' the assistant clarified.

'I mean games where there's someone in charge, and they contact you by e-mail, set you challenges.'

'Role-playing.' One of the schoolboys nodded, looking to the others for confirmation.

'Have you ever played one?' Siobhan asked him.

'No,' he admitted. None of them had.

'There's a games shop about halfway down Leith Walk,' the assistant said. 'It's D & D but they might be able to help.'

'D & D?'

'Sword and sorcery, dungeons and dragons.'

'Does this shop have a name?' Siobhan asked.

'Gandalf's,' they chorused.

Gandalf's was a piece of narrow frontage squeezed unpromisingly between a tattoo parlour and a chip shop. Even less promisingly, its filthy window was covered with a metal grille held in place with padlocks. But when she tried the door, it opened, setting off a set of wind chimes hanging just inside. Gandalf's had obviously been something else – maybe a second-hand bookshop – and a change of use hadn't been accompanied by any sort of makeover. The shelves held an assortment of board games and playing pieces – the pieces themselves looking like unpainted toy soldiers. Posters on the walls depicted cartoon Armageddons. There were instruction books, their edges curling, and in the centre of the room four chairs and a foldaway table, on which sat a playing-board. There was no sales counter and no till. A door at the back of the shop creaked open and a man in his early fifties appeared. He had a grey beard and ponytail, and a distended stomach clad in a Grateful Dead T-shirt.

'You look official,' he said glumly.

'CID,' Siobhan said, showing him her warrant card.

'Rent's only eight weeks late,' he grumbled. As he shuffled towards the board, she saw that he was wearing leather open-toed sandals. Like their owner, they had a good few miles on them. He was studying the placement of pieces on the board. 'You move anything?' he asked suddenly.

'No.'

'You sure?'

'Sure.'

He smiled. 'Then Anthony's fucked, pardon my French.' He looked at his watch. 'They'll be here in an hour.'

'Who's they?'

'The gamers. I had to shut up shop last night before they had a chance to finish. Anthony must've been flustered, trying to finish Will off.'

Siobhan looked at the board. She couldn't see any grand design to the way the playing pieces were arranged. The beardie-weirdie tapped the cards laid out beside the board.

'These are what matters,' he said irritably.

'Oh,' Siobhan said. 'Afraid I'm no expert.'

'You wouldn't be.'

'What does that mean?'

'Nothing, I'm sure.'

But she was pretty sure she knew what he meant. This was a private club, males only, and every bit as exclusive as any other bastion.

'I don't think you can help me,' Siobhan admitted, looking around.

She was resisting the urge to scratch herself. 'I'm interested in something slightly more high-tech.'

He bristled at this. 'What do you mean?'

'Role-playing by computer.'

'Interactive?' His eyes widened. She nodded and he checked his watch again, then shuffled past her to the door and locked it. She went on the defensive, but he merely shuffled past her again on his way to the far door. 'Down here,' he said, and Siobhan, feeling a bit like Alice at the mouth of the tunnel, eventually followed.

Down four or five steps, she came into a dank, windowless room, only partially lit. There were boxes piled high – more games and accessories, she guessed – plus a sink with kettle and mugs on the draining-board. But on a table in one corner sat what looked like a state-of-the-art computer, its large screen as thin as a laptop's. She asked her guide what his name was.

'Gandalf,' he blithely replied.

'I meant your real name.'

'I know you did. But in here, that *is* my real name.' He sat down at the computer and started work, talking as he moved the mouse. It took her a moment to realise that the mouse was cordless.

'There are lots of games on the Net,' he was saying. 'You join a group of people to fight either against the program or against other teams. There are leagues.' He tapped the screen. 'See? This is a Doom league.' He glanced at her. 'You know what Doom is?'

'A computer game.'

He nodded. 'But here, you're working in cooperation with others and against a common foe.'

Her eyes ran down the team names. 'How anonymous is it?' she asked.

'How do you mean?'

'I mean, does each player know who his team-mate is, or who's on the opposing team?'

He stroked his beard. 'At most, they'd have a *nom de guerre*.'

Siobhan thought of Philippa, with her secret e-mail name. 'And people can have lots of names, right?'

'Oh yes,' he said. 'You can amass dozens of names. People who've spoken to you a hundred times . . . they come back under a new name, and you don't realise you already know them.'

'So they can lie about themselves?'

'If you want to call it that. This is the *virtual* world. Nothing's "real" as such. So people are free to invent virtual lives for themselves.'

'A case I'm working on, there's a game involved.'

'Which game?'

'I don't know. But it's got levels called Hellbank and Stricture. Someone called Quizmaster seems to be in charge.'

He was stroking his beard again. Since sitting at the computer, he'd donned a pair of metal-rimmed glasses. The screen was reflected in the lenses, hiding his eyes. 'I don't know it,' he said at last.

'What does it sound like to you?'

'It sounds like SIRPS: Simple Role-Play Scenario. Quizmaster sets tasks or questions, could be to one player or dozens.'

'You mean teams?'

He shrugged. 'Hard to know. What's the website?'

'I don't know.'

He looked at her. 'You don't know very much, do you?'

'No,' she admitted.

He sighed. 'How serious is the case?'

'A young woman's gone missing. She was playing the game.'

'And you don't know if the two are connected?'

'No.'

He rested his hands on his stomach. 'I'll ask around,' he said. 'See if we can track down Quizmaster for you.'

'Even if I had an idea what the game involved . . .'

He nodded, and Siobhan remembered her dialogue with Quizmaster. She'd asked about Hellbank. And his reply?

You'd have to play the game . . .

She knew that requisitioning a laptop would take time. Even then, it wouldn't be hooked up to the Net. So on her way back to the station she stopped off at one of the computer shops.

'Cheapest one we do is around nine hundred quid,' the saleswoman informed her.

Siobhan flinched. 'And how long before I could be online?'

The saleswoman shrugged. 'Depends on your server,' she said.

So Siobhan thanked her and left. She knew she could always use Philippa Balfour's computer, but she didn't want to, for all sorts of reasons. Then she had a brainwave and got on her mobile instead. 'Grant? It's Siobhan. I need a favour . . .'

DC Grant Hood had bought his laptop for the same reason he'd bought a mini-disc player, DVD and digital camera. It was *stuff*, and stuff was what you bought to impress people. Sure enough, each time he brought a new gadget into St Leonard's he was the centre of attention for five or ten minutes – or rather, the *stuff* was. But Siobhan had noticed that Grant was always keen to lend these bits of high-tech to anyone who asked. He didn't use them himself, or if he did he tired of them after a few weeks. Maybe he never got past the owner's manuals: the one with the camera had been chunkier than the apparatus itself.

So Grant had been only too happy to make a trip home, returning with the laptop. Siobhan had already explained that she would need to use it for e-mails.

'It's up and ready,' Grant had told her.

'I'll need your e-mail address and pass name.'

'But that means you can access *my* e-mails,' he realised.

'And tell me, Grant, how many e-mails do you get a week?'

'Some,' he said, sounding defensive.

'Don't worry. I'll save them for you . . . and I promise not to peek.'

'Then there's the matter of my fee,' Grant said.

She looked at him. 'Your fee?'

'Yet to be discussed.' His face broke into a grin.

She folded her arms. 'So what is it?'

'I don't know,' he told her. 'I'll have to think . . .'

Transaction complete, she headed back to her desk. She already had a connector which would link her mobile phone to the laptop. But first she checked Philippa's computer: no messages, nothing from Quizmaster. Getting online with Grant's machine took her only a few minutes. Once there, she sent a note to Quizmaster, giving him Grant's e-mail address:

Maybe I want to play the game. Over to you. Siobhan.

Having sent the message, she left the line open. It would cost her a small fortune when her next mobile bill appeared, but she pushed that thought aside. For now, the game itself was the only lead she had. Even if she had no intention of playing, she still wanted to know more about it. She could see Grant, the other side of the room. He was talking to a couple of other officers. They kept glancing in her direction.

Let them, she thought.

Rebus was at Gayfield Square, and nothing was happening. Which was to say, the place was a flurry of activity, but all the sound and fury couldn't hope to hide a creeping sense of desperation. The ACC himself had put in an appearance and been briefed by both Gill Templer and Bill Pryde. He'd made it plain that what they needed was 'a swift conclusion'. Both Templer and Pryde had used the phrase a little later, which was how Rebus knew.

'DI Rebus?' One of the woolly-suits was standing in front of him. 'Boss says she'd like a word.'

When he walked in, she told him to close the door. The place was cramped and smelled of other people's sweat. Space being at a premium, Gill was sharing this space with two other detectives, working in shifts.

'Maybe we should start commandeering the cells,' she said, collecting up mugs from the desk and failing to find anywhere better for them. 'Could hardly be worse than this.'

'Don't go to any trouble,' Rebus said. 'I'm not staying.'

'That's right, you're not.' She put the mugs on the floor, and almost immediately kicked one of them over. Ignoring the spill, she sat down. Rebus stayed standing, as was obligatory, there being no other chairs in the room today. 'How did you get on in Falls?'

'I came to a swift conclusion.'

She glared at him. 'Which was?'

'That it'll make a good story for the tabloids.'

Gill nodded. 'I saw something in the evening paper last night.'

'The woman who found the doll – or says she did – she's been talking.'

'"Or says she did"?'

He just shrugged.

'You think she might be behind it?'

Rebus slipped his hands into his pockets. 'Who knows?'

'Someone thinks they might. A friend of mine called Jean Burchill. I think you should talk to her.'

'Who is she?'

'She's a curator at the Museum of Scotland.'

'And she knows something about this doll?'

'She might do.' Gill paused. 'According to Jean, this is far from the first.'

Rebus admitted to his guide that he'd never been inside the museum before.

'The old museum, I used to take my daughter there when she was a kid.'

Jean Burchill tutted. 'But this is quite another thing, Inspector. It's all about who we are, our history and culture.'

'No stuffed animals and totem poles?'

She smiled. 'Not that I can think of.' They were walking through the ground floor's exhibit area, having left the huge whitewashed entrance hall behind. They stopped at a small lift, and Burchill turned to face him, her eyes running the length of his body. 'Gill's talked about you,' she said. Then the lift doors opened and she got in, Rebus following.

'Nothing but good, I hope.' He tried hard for levity. Burchill just looked at him again and smiled her little smile. Despite her age, she reminded him of a schoolgirl: that mixture of the shy and the knowing, the prim and the curious.

'Fourth floor,' she told him, and when the lift doors opened again, they walked out into a narrow corridor filled with shadows and images of death. 'The section on beliefs,' she said, her voice barely audible. 'Witchcraft and grave-robbers and burials.' A black coach waited to take its next cargo to some Victorian graveyard, while nearby sat a large iron coffin. Rebus couldn't help reaching out to touch it.

'It's a mortsafe,' she said, then, seeing his lack of comprehension: 'The families of the deceased would lock the coffin inside a mortsafe for the first six months to deter the resurrectionists.'

'Meaning body-snatchers?' Now this was a piece of history he knew. 'Like Burke and Hare? Digging up corpses and selling them to the university?'

She peered at him like a teacher with a stubborn pupil. 'Burke and

Hare didn't dig up anything. That's the whole point of their story: they killed people, then sold the bodies to the anatomists.'

'Right,' Rebus said.

They passed funeral weeds, and photos of dead babies, and stopped at the furthest glass case.

'Here we are,' Burchill said. 'The Arthur's Seat coffins.'

Rebus looked. There were eight coffins in all. They were five or six inches long, well made, with nails studded into their lids. Inside the coffins were little wooden dolls, some wearing clothes. Rebus stared at a green and white check.

'Hibs fan,' he said.

'At one time they were all dressed. But the cloth perished.' She pointed to a photograph in the case. 'In eighteen thirty-six, some children playing on Arthur's Seat found the concealed mouth of a cave. Inside were seventeen little coffins, of which only these eight survive.'

'They must have got a fright.' Rebus was staring at the photograph, trying to place where on the massive slopes of the hill it might be.

'Analysis of the materials suggests they were made in the eighteen thirties.'

Rebus nodded. The information was printed on a series of cards attached to the display. Newspapers of the time suggested that the dolls were used by witches casting death spells on certain individuals. Another popular theory was that they were put there by sailors as good-luck charms prior to sea voyages.

'Sailors on Arthur's Seat,' Rebus mused. 'Now there's something you don't see every day.'

'Do I detect some homophobic connotation, Inspector?'

He shook his head. 'It's just a long way from the docks, that's all.'

She looked at him, but his face didn't betray anything.

Rebus was studying the coffins again. Were he a betting man, he'd see short odds on a connection between these objects and the one found in Falls. Whoever had made and placed the coffin by the waterfall knew about the museum exhibit, and had for some reason decided to copy it. Rebus looked around at the various sombre displays of mortality.

'You put this lot together?'

She nodded.

'Must make for a popular topic at parties.'

'You'd be surprised,' she said quietly. 'When it comes down to it, aren't we all curious about the things we fear?'

Downstairs in the old museum, they sat on a bench carved to resemble a whale's ribcage. There were fish in a water feature nearby, kids almost reaching in to touch them, but then pulling back at the last moment, giggling and squeezing their hands: that mix again of the curious and the fearful.

At the end of the great hall, a huge clock had been erected, its complex mechanism comprising models of skeletons and gargoyles. A naked carving of a woman seemed to be wrapped in barbed wire. Rebus got the feeling there might be other scenes of torture just beyond his vision.

'Our Millennium Clock,' Jean Burchill explained. She checked her watch. 'Ten minutes before it strikes again.'

'Interesting design,' Rebus said. 'A clock full of suffering.'

She looked at him. 'Not everyone notices straight away . . .'

Rebus just shrugged. 'Upstairs,' he said, 'the display said something about the dolls connecting to Burke and Hare?'

She nodded. 'A mock burial for the victims. We think they may have sold as many as seventeen bodies for dissection. It was a horrible crime. You see, a dissected body cannot rise up again on the day of the Last Judgment.'

'Not without its guts spilling out,' Rebus agreed.

She ignored him. 'Burke and Hare were arrested and tried. Hare testified against his friend, and only William Burke went to the gallows. Guess what happened to his body afterwards?'

That was an easy one. 'Dissection?' Rebus guessed.

She nodded. 'His body was taken to Old College, the same route most if not all of his victims were taken, and used by an anatomy class. This was in January eighteen twenty-nine.'

'And the coffins date from the early eighteen thirties.' Rebus was thoughtful. Hadn't someone once boasted to him about owning a souvenir made from Burke's skin? 'What happened to the body afterwards?' he asked.

Jean Burchill looked at him. 'There's a pocket-book in the museum at Surgeons' Hall.'

'Made from Burke's skin?'

She nodded again. 'I feel sorry for Burke actually. He seems to have been a genial man. An economic migrant. Poverty and chance led to his first sale. A visitor to his home died owing money. Burke knew that there was a crisis in Edinburgh, a successful medical faculty with not enough bodies to go round.'

'Were people living long lives then?'

'Far from it. But as I told you, a dissected corpse could not enter heaven. The only bodies available to medical students belonged to executed criminals. The Anatomy Act of eighteen thirty-two put an end to the need to rob graves . . .'

Her voice had died away. She seemed momentarily lost to the present as she considered Edinburgh's blood-soaked past. Rebus was there with her. Resurrectionists and wallets made of human skin . . . witchcraft and hangings. Next to the coffins on the fourth floor he'd seen a variety of witch's accoutrements: configurations of bones; shrivelled animal hearts with nails protruding.

'Some place this, eh?'

He meant Edinburgh, but she considered her surroundings. 'Ever since I was a child,' she said, 'I've felt more at peace here than anywhere else in the city. You might think my work morbid, Inspector, but fewer would be reconciled to the work *you* do.'

'Fair shout,' he agreed.

'The coffins interest me because they *are* such a mystery. In a museum, we live by the rules of identification and classification. Dates and provenance may be uncertain, but we almost always know what we're dealing with: a casket, a key, the remains of a Roman burial site.'

'But with the coffins, you can't be sure what they mean.'

She smiled. 'Exactly. That makes them frustrating for a curator.'

'I know the feeling,' he said. 'It's like me with a case. If it can't be solved, it nips my head.'

'You keep mulling it over . . . coming up with new theories . . .'

'Or new suspects, yes.'

Now they looked at one another. 'Maybe we've more in common than I thought,' Jean Burchill said.

'Maybe we have,' he admitted.

The clock had begun to sound, though its minute hand had yet to reach twelve. Visitors were summoned to it, the children's mouths falling open as the various mechanisms brought the garish figures to life. Bells clanged and ominous organ music started playing. The pendulum was a polished mirror. Looking at it, Rebus caught glimpses of himself, and behind him the whole museum, each spectator captured.

'Worth a closer look,' Jean Burchill told him. They got up and began to move forwards, joining the congregation. Rebus thought he recognised wooden carvings of Hitler and Stalin. They were operating a jagged-toothed saw.

'There's something else,' Jean Burchill was saying. 'There've been other dolls, other places.'

'What?' He tore his eyes away from the clock.

'Best thing is if I send you what I've got . . .'

Rebus spent the rest of that Friday waiting for his shift to end. Photos of David Costello's garage had been placed on one of the walls, joining the haphazard jigsaw there. His MG was a dark blue soft-top. The forensic boffins hadn't had permission to remove traces from the vehicle and its tyres, but that hadn't stopped them taking a good look. The car hadn't been washed of late. If it had been, they'd have been asking David Costello why. More photos of Philippa's friends and acquaintances had been gathered and shown to Professor Devlin. A couple of prints of the boyfriend had been slipped in, which had caused Devlin to complain about 'tactics beneath contempt'.

Five days since that Sunday night, five days since she'd disappeared. The more Rebus stared at the jigsaw on the wall, the less he saw. He thought again of the Millennium Clock, which was just the opposite:

the more he'd looked at it, the more he'd seen – small figures suddenly picked out from the moving whole. He saw it now as a monument to the lost and forgotten. In its way, the wall display – the photos, faxes, rotas and drawings – comprised a monument too. But eventually, whatever happened, this monument would be dismantled and relegated to some box in a storeroom somewhere, its life limited to the length of the search.

He'd been here before: other times, other cases, not all of them solved to anyone's satisfaction. You tried not to care, tried to maintain objectivity, just as the training seminars told you to, but it was hard. The Farmer still remembered a young boy from his first week on the force, and Rebus had his memories, too. Which was why, at day's end, he went home, showered and changed, and sat in his chair for an hour with a glass of Laphroaig and the Rolling Stones for company: *Beggars Banquet* tonight, and more than one glass of Laphroaig actually. Carpets from the hall and bedrooms were rolled up either side of him. Mattresses and wardrobes, chests of drawers . . . the room was like a scrapyard. But there was a clear path from the door to his chair, and from his chair to the hi-fi, and that was all he needed.

After the Stones, he still had half a glass of malt to finish, so put on another album. Bob Dylan's *Desire*, and the track 'Hurricane', a tale of injustice and wrongful accusation. He knew it happened: sometimes wilfully, sometimes by accident. He'd worked cases where the evidence seemed to be pointing conclusively to an individual, only for someone else to come forward and confess. And in the past – the distant past – maybe one or two criminals had been 'fitted up', to get them off the street, or to satisfy the public's need for a conviction. There were times when you were sure you knew who the culprit was, but were never going to be able to prove it to the Procurator Fiscal's satisfaction. One or two cops down the years had crossed the line.

He toasted them, catching his reflection in the living-room window. So he raised a toast to himself, too, then picked up the phone and called for a cab.

Destination: pubs.

In the Oxford Bar, he got talking to one of the regulars, happened to mention his trip to Falls.

'I'd never heard of it before,' he confided.

'Oh aye,' his companion stated, 'I know Falls. Isn't that where Wee Billy comes from?'

Wee Billy was another regular. A search confirmed that he wasn't in the bar as yet, but he walked in twenty minutes later, still wearing his chef's uniform from a restaurant around the corner. He wiped sweat from his eyes as he squeezed up to the bar.

'That you done?' someone asked him.

'Fag break,' he said, glancing at his watch. 'Pint of lager, please, Margaret.'

As the barmaid poured, Rebus asked for a refill and said that both drinks were on him.

'Cheers, John,' Billy said, unused to such largesse. 'How's tricks?'

'I was out at Falls yesterday. Is it right you grew up there?'

'Aye, that's right. Haven't been back in years, mind.'

'You didn't know the Balfours then?'

Billy shook his head. 'After my time. I was already in college when they moved back. Thanks, Margaret.' He lifted the pint. 'Your health, John.'

Rebus handed the cash over and raised his own pint, watching Billy demolish half the drink in three needy gulps.

'Jesus, that's better.'

'Hard shift?' Rebus guessed.

'No more so than usual. You working the Balfour case then?'

'Along with every other cop in the city.'

'What did you reckon to Falls?'

'Not big.'

Billy smiled, reached into his pocket for cigarette papers and tobacco. 'Expect it's changed a bit since I lived there.'

'Were you a Meadowside boy?'

'How did you know?' Billy lit his roll-up.

'A lucky guess.'

'Mining stock, that's me. Grandad worked all his days down the pit. Dad started off the same, but they made him redundant.'

'I grew up in a mining town myself,' Rebus said.

'Then you'll know what it's like when the pits close. Meadowside was fine until then.' Billy was staring at the optics, remembering his youth.

'The place is still there,' Rebus told him.

'Oh aye, but not the same . . . couldn't be the same. All the mums out scrubbing their steps, getting them whiter than white. Dads cutting the grass. Always popping into the other semis for a gossip or a loan of something.' He paused, ordered them up a couple of refills. 'Last I heard, Falls was all yuppies. Anything out of Meadowside's too dear for the locals to buy. Kids grow up and move away – like I did. Anyone say anything to you about the quarry?'

Rebus shook his head, content to listen.

'This was maybe two, three years back. There was talk of opening a quarry just outside the village. Plenty of jobs, all that. But suddenly this petition appeared – not that anyone on Meadowside had signed it, or been asked to sign it, come to that. Next thing, the quarry wasn't coming.'

'The yuppies?'

'Or whatever you want to call them. Plenty of clout, see. Maybe Mr Balfour had a hand in it too, for all I know. Falls . . .' He shook his head. 'It's not the place it was, John.' He finished his roll-up and stubbed it into the ashtray. Then he thought of something. 'Here, you like your music, don't you?'

'Depends what kind.'

'Lou Reed. He's coming to the Playhouse. I've two tickets going spare.'

'I'll think about it, Billy. Got time for another?' He nodded towards the dregs in Billy's glass.

The chef checked his watch again. 'Got to get back. Maybe next time, eh?'

'Next time,' Rebus agreed.

'And let me know about those tickets.'

Rebus nodded, watched Billy push his way back towards the door and out into the night. Lou Reed: there was a name from the past. 'Walk on the Wild Side', one of Rebus's all-time favourites. And a bass-line played by the same guy who wrote 'Grandad' for that *Dad's Army* actor. Sometimes there was such a thing as too much information.

'Another, John?' the barmaid asked.

He shook his head. 'I can hear the call of the wild side,' he said, pushing off from his stool and towards the door.

5

Saturday he went to the football with Siobhan. Easter Road was bathed in sunshine, the players throwing long shadows across the pitch. For a while, Rebus found himself following this shadow-play rather than the game itself: black puppet shapes, not quite human, playing something that wasn't quite football. The ground was full, as only happened with local derbies and when Glasgow came to town. Today it was Rangers. Siobhan had a season ticket. Rebus was in the seat next to her, thanks to another season-ticket holder who couldn't make it.

'Friend of yours?' Rebus asked her.

'Bumped into him once or twice in the pub after the match.'

'Nice guy?'

'Nice *family* guy.' She laughed. 'When are you going to stop trying to marry me off?'

'I was only asking,' he said with a grin. He'd noticed that TV cameras were covering the game. They would concentrate on the players, the spectators a background blur or piece of half-time filler. But it was the fans who really interested Rebus. He wondered what stories they could tell, what lives they'd led. He wasn't alone: around him other spectators seemed equally interested in the antics of the crowd rather than anything happening on the pitch. But Siobhan, knuckles white as she clenched either end of her supporter's scarf, brought the same concentration to the game as she did to police work, yelling out advice to the players, arguing each refereeing decision with fans nearby. The man on Rebus's other side was equally fevered. He was overweight, red-faced and sweating. To Rebus's eyes, he seemed on the verge of a coronary. He'd mutter to himself, the noise growing in intensity until there was a final defiant hurl of abuse, after which he'd look around, smile sheepishly, and begin the whole process again.

'Easy . . . take it easy, son,' he was now telling one of the players.

'Anything happening your end of the case?' Rebus asked Siobhan.

'Day off, John.' Her eyes never left the pitch.

'I know, I was just asking . . .'

'Easy now . . . go on, son, on you go.' The sweating man was gripping the back of the seat in front of him.

'We can have a drink after,' Siobhan said.

'Try and stop me,' Rebus told her.

'That's it, son, that's the way!' The voice growing the way a wave would. Rebus took out another cigarette. The day might be bright, but it wasn't warm. The wind was whipping in from the North Sea, the gulls overhead working hard to stay airborne.

'Go on now!' the man was yelling. *'Go on! Get right into that fat Hun bastard!'*

Then the look around, the sheepish grin. Rebus got his cigarette lit at last and offered one to the man, who shook his head.

'It relieves stress, you know, the shouting.'

'Might relieve yours, pal,' Rebus said, but anything after that was drowned out as Siobhan joined a few thousand others in rising up to scream their reasoned and objective judgement concerning some infringement Rebus – along with the referee – had missed.

Her usual pub was heaving. Even so, people were still piling in. Rebus took one look and suggested somewhere else. 'It's a five-minute walk, and it's got to be quieter.'

'Okay then,' she said, but her tone was one of disappointment. The after-match drink was a time for analysis, and she knew Rebus's abilities in this field were somewhat lacking.

'And tuck that scarf away,' he ordered. 'Never know where you'll bump into a blue-nose.'

'Not down here,' she said confidently. She was probably right. The police presence outside the stadium had been large and knowledgeable, channelling Hibs fans down Easter Road while the visitors from Glasgow were dispatched back up the hill towards the bus and railway stations. Siobhan followed Rebus as he cut through Lorne Street and came out on Leith Walk, where weary shoppers were struggling home. The pub he had in mind was an anonymous affair with bevelled windows and an oxblood carpet pocked with cigarette burns and blackened gum. Game-show applause crackled from the TV, while two old-timers carried out a swearing competition in the corner.

'You sure know how to treat a lady,' Siobhan complained.

'And would the lady like a Bacardi Breezer? Maybe a Moscow Mule.'

'Pint of lager,' Siobhan said defiantly. Rebus ordered himself a pint of Eighty with a malt on the side. As they took their seats, Siobhan told him he seemed to know every bad pub in the city.

'Thanks,' he said without a trace of irony. 'So,' he lifted his glass, 'what's the news on Philippa Balfour's computer?'

'There's a game she was playing. I don't know much about it. It's run by someone called Quizmaster. I've made contact with him.'

'And?'

'And,' she sighed, 'I'm waiting for him to get back to me. So far I've sent a dozen e-mails and no joy.'

'Any other way we can track him down?'

'Not that I know of.'

'What about the game?'

'I don't know the first thing about it,' she admitted, attacking her drink. 'Gill's beginning to think it's a dead end. She's got me interviewing students instead.'

'That's because you've been to college.'

'I know. If Gill's got a flaw, it's that she's literal-minded.'

'She speaks very highly of you,' Rebus said archly, gaining him a punch on the arm.

Siobhan's face changed as she picked up her glass again. 'She offered me the liaison post.'

'I thought she might. Are you going to take it?' He watched her shake her head. 'Because of what happened to Ellen Wylie?'

'Not really.'

'Then why?'

She shrugged. 'Not ready for it, maybe.'

'You're ready,' he stated.

'It's not real police work though, is it?'

'What it is, Siobhan, is a step up.'

She looked down at her drink. 'I know.'

'Who's doing the job meantime?'

'I think Gill is.' She paused. 'We're going to find Flip's body, aren't we?'

'Maybe.'

She looked at him. 'You think she's still alive?'

'No,' he said bleakly, 'I don't.'

That night he hit a few more bars, sticking close to home at first, then hailing a taxi outside Swany's and asking to be taken to Young Street. He made to light up but the driver asked him not to, and he noticed the No Smoking signs.

Some detective I am, he told himself. He'd spent as much time as possible away from the flat. The rewiring had come to a halt Friday at five o'clock with half the floorboards still up and runs of cable straggling everywhere. Skirting-boards had been uprooted, exposing the bare wall behind. The sparkies had left their tools – 'be safe enough here', they'd quipped, knowing his profession. They'd said they might manage Saturday morning, but they hadn't. So that was him for the weekend, stumbling over lengths of wire and every second floorboard either missing or loose. He'd eaten breakfast in a café, lunch in a pub, and was now harbouring lubricious thoughts of a haggis supper with a smoked sausage on the side. But first, the Oxford Bar.

He'd asked Siobhan what her own plans were.

'A hot bath and a good book,' she'd told him. She'd been lying. He knew this because Grant Hood had told half the station he was taking her on a date, his reward for lending her his laptop. Not that Rebus had said anything to her: if she didn't want him to know, that was fair enough. But knowing, he hadn't bothered trying to tempt her with an Indian meal or a film. Only when they were parting outside the pub on Leith Walk had it struck him that maybe this had been bad manners on his part. Two people with no apparent plans for Saturday night: wouldn't it have been natural for him to ask her out? Would she now be offended?

'Life's too short,' he told himself, paying off the taxi. Heading into the pub, seeing the familiar faces, those words stayed with him. He asked Harry the barman for the phone book.

'It's over there,' Harry answered, obliging as ever.

Rebus flipped through but couldn't find the number he wanted. Then he remembered she'd given him her business card. He found it in his pocket. Her home number had been added in pencil. He stepped back outdoors again and fired up his mobile. No wedding ring, he was sure of that . . . The phone was ringing. Saturday night, she was probably . . .

'Hello?'

'Ms Burchill? It's John Rebus here. Sorry to call you on a Saturday night.'

'That's all right. Is something the matter?'

'No, no . . . I just wondered if maybe we could meet. It was all very mysterious, what you said about there being other dolls.'

She laughed. 'You want to meet *now*?'

'Well, I was thinking maybe tomorrow. I know it's the day of rest and all, but we could maybe mix business with pleasure.' He winced as the words came out. He should have thought it all through first: what he was going to say, how he was going to say it.

'And how could we do that?' she asked, sounding amused. He could hear music in the background: something classical.

'Lunch?' he suggested.

'Where?'

Where indeed. He couldn't remember the last time he'd taken someone to lunch. He wanted somewhere impressive, somewhere . . .

'I'm guessing,' she said, 'that you like a fry-up on a Sunday.' It was almost as if she could feel his discomfort and wanted to help.

'Am I so transparent?'

'Quite the opposite. You're a flesh-and-blood Scottish male. I, on the other hand, like something simple, fresh and wholesome.'

Rebus laughed. 'The word "incompatible" springs to mind.'

'Maybe not. Where do you live?'

'Marchmont.'

'Then we'll go to Fenwick's,' she stated. 'It's perfect.'

'Great,' he said. 'Half-twelve?'

'I look forward to it. Goodnight, Inspector.'

'I hope you're not going to call me Inspector all the way through lunch.'

In the silence that followed, he thought he could hear her smiling.

'See you tomorrow, John.'

'Enjoy the rest of your . . .' But the connection was dead. He went back inside the pub and grabbed the phone book again. Fenwick's: Salisbury Place. Less than a twenty-minute walk from his flat. He must have driven past it a dozen times. It was fifty yards from Sammy's accident, fifty yards from where a killer had tried to stick a knife in him. He would make the effort tomorrow, push those memories aside.

'Same again, Harry,' he said, bouncing on his toes.

'You'll wait your turn like everyone else,' Harry growled at him. It didn't matter to Rebus; didn't bother him at all.

He was ten minutes early.

She walked in only five minutes later, so she was early too. 'Nice place,' he told her.

'Isn't it?' She was wearing a black two-piece over a grey silk blouse. A blood-red brooch sparkled just above her left breast.

'Do you live nearby?' he asked.

'Not exactly: Portobello.'

'But that's miles away! You should have said.'

'Why? I like this place.'

'You eat out a lot?' He was still trying to digest the fact that she'd come all the way into Edinburgh for lunch.

'Whenever I can. One of the perks of my PhD is that I call myself "Dr Burchill" whenever I'm making a booking.'

Rebus looked around. Only one other table was occupied: down near the front, a family party by the look of it. Two kids, six adults.

'I didn't bother booking for today. It's never too busy at lunchtime. Now, what shall we have . . .?'

He thought about a starter and a main course, but she seemed to know that really he wanted the fry-up, so that was what he ordered. She went for soup and duck. They decided to order coffee and wine at the same time.

'Very brunchy,' she said. 'Very Sunday somehow.'

He couldn't help but agree. She told him he could smoke if he liked, but he declined. There were three smokers at the family table, but the craving was still a little way off.

They talked about Gill Templer to start with, finding common ground. Her questions were canny and probing.

'Gill can be a bit driven, wouldn't you say?'

'She does what she has to.'

'The pair of you had a fling a while back, didn't you?'

His eyes widened. 'She told you that?'

'No.' Jean paused, flattened her napkin against her lap. 'But I guessed it from the way she used to speak about you.'

'Used to?'

She smiled. 'It *was* a long time ago, wasn't it?'

'Prehistoric,' he was forced to agree. 'What about you?'

'I hope I'm not prehistoric.'

He smiled. 'I meant, tell me something about yourself.'

'I was born in Elgin, parents both teachers. Went to Glasgow University. Dabbled in archaeology. Doctorate from Durham University, then post-doctoral studies abroad – the USA and Canada – looking at nineteenth-century migrants. I got a job as a curator in Vancouver, then came back here when the opportunity arose. The old museum for the best part of twelve years, and now the new one.' She shrugged. 'That's about it.'

'How do you know Gill?'

'We were at school together for a couple of years, best mates. Lost touch for a while . . .'

'You never married?'

She looked down at her plate. 'For a while, yes, in Canada. He died young.'

'I'm sorry.'

'Bill drank himself to death, not that his family would ever believe it. I think that's why I came back to Scotland.'

'Because he died?'

She shook her head. 'If I'd stayed, it would have meant participating in the myth they were busy establishing.'

Rebus thought he understood.

'You've got a daughter, haven't you?' she said suddenly, keen to change the subject.

'Samantha. She's . . . in her twenties now.'

Jean laughed. 'You don't know how old exactly though?'

He tried a smile. 'It's not that. I was going to say that she's disabled. Probably not something you want to know.'

'Oh.' She was silent for a moment, then looked up at him. 'But it's important to you, or it wouldn't have been the first thing you thought of.'

'True. Except that she's getting back on her feet again. Using one of those Zimmer frames old people use.'

'That's good,' she said.

He nodded. He didn't want to go into the whole story, but she wasn't going to ask him anyway.

'How's the soup?'

'It's good.'

They sat in silence for a minute or two, then she asked him about police work. Her questions had reverted to the kind you asked of a new acquaintance. Usually Rebus felt awkward talking about the job. He wasn't sure people were really interested. Even if they were, he knew they didn't want to hear the unexpurgated version: the suicides and autopsies; the petty grudges and black moods that led people to the cells. Domestics and stabbings, Saturday nights gone wrong, professional thugs and addicts. When he spoke, he was always afraid his voice would betray his passion for the job. He might be dubious about methods and eventual outcomes, but he still got a thrill from the work itself. Someone like Jean Burchill, he felt, could peer beneath the surface of this and watch other things swim into focus. She would realise that his enjoyment of the job was essentially voyeuristic and cowardly. He concentrated on the minutiae of other people's lives, other people's problems, to stop him examining his own frailties and failings.

'Are you planning to smoke that thing?' Jean sounded amused. Rebus looked down and saw that a cigarette had appeared in his hand. He laughed, took the packet from his pocket and slid the cigarette back in.

'I really don't mind,' Jean told him.

'Didn't realise I'd done it,' he said. Then, to hide his embarrassment: 'You were going to tell me about these other dolls.'

'After we've eaten,' she said firmly.

But after they'd eaten, she asked for the bill. They went halves on it, and found themselves outside, the afternoon sun doing its best to remove the chill from the day. 'Let's walk,' she said, sliding her arm through his.

'Where to?'

'The Meadows?' she suggested. So that was where they went.

The sun had brought people out to the tree-lined playing field. Frisbees were being thrown, while joggers and cyclists sped past. Some teenagers were lying with their T-shirts off, cans of cider beside them. Jean was painting some of the area's history for him.

'I think there was a pond here,' she said. 'There were certainly stone quarries in Bruntsfield, and Marchmont itself was a farm.'

'More like a zoo these days,' he said.

She threw him a glance. 'You work hard on your cynicism, don't you?'

'It gets rusty otherwise.'

At Jawbone Walk she decided they should cross the road and start up Marchmont Road. 'So where exactly is it you live?' she asked.

'Arden Street. Just off Warrender Park Road.'

'Not far then.'

He smiled, trying for eye contact. 'Are you angling for an invitation?'

'To be honest, yes.'

'The place is a tip.'

'I'd be disappointed if it were anything else. But my bladder says it'll settle for what's available . . .'

He was desperately tidying the living room when he heard the toilet flush. He looked around and shook his head. It was like picking up a duster after a bomb-strike: futile. So instead he went back into the kitchen and spooned coffee into two mugs. The milk in the fridge was Thursday's, but usable. She was standing in the doorway, watching him.

'Thank God I have an excuse for all the mess,' he said.

'I had my place rewired a few years back,' she commiserated. 'At the time, I was thinking of selling.' When he looked up, she saw she'd hit a chord.

'I'm putting it on the market,' he admitted.

'Any particular reason?'

Ghosts, he could have told her, but he just shrugged instead.

'A fresh start?' she guessed.

'Maybe. Do you take sugar?' He handed her the mug. She studied its milky surface.

'I don't even take milk,' she told him.

'Christ, sorry.' He tried taking the mug from her, but she resisted. 'This'll be fine,' she said. Then she laughed. 'Some detective. You just watched me drink two cups of coffee in the restaurant.'

'And never noticed,' Rebus agreed, nodding.

'Is there space to sit down in the living room? Now that we've got to know one another a little, it's time to show you the dolls.'

He cleared an area of the dining table. She placed her shoulder-bag on the floor and pulled out a folder.

'Thing is,' she said, 'I know this may sound barmy to some people. So I'm hoping you'll keep an open mind. Maybe that's why I wanted to know you a bit better . . .'

She handed over the folder and he pulled out a sheaf of press cuttings. While she spoke, he started arranging them before him on the table.

'I came across the first one when someone wrote a letter to the Museum. This was a couple of years back.' He held up the letter and she nodded. 'A Mrs Anderson in Perth. She'd heard the story of the Arthur's Seat coffins and wanted me to know that something similar had happened near Huntingtower.'

The clipping attached to the letter was from the *Courier*. 'Mysterious Find Near Local Hotel': a coffin-shaped wooden box with a scrap of cloth nearby. Found beneath some leaves in a copse when a dog had been out for its daily walk. The owner had taken the box to the hotel, thinking maybe it was some sort of toy. But no explanation had been found. The year was 1995.

'The woman, Mrs Anderson,' Jean was saying, 'was interested in local history. That's why she kept the cutting.'

'No doll?'

Jean shook her head. 'Could be some animal ran off with it.'

'Could be,' Rebus agreed. He turned to the second cutting. It was dated 1982 and was from a Glasgow evening paper: 'Church Condemns Sick Joke Find'.

'It was Mrs Anderson herself told me about this one,' Jean explained. 'A churchyard, next to one of the gravestones. A little wooden coffin, this time with a doll inside, basically a wooden clothes-peg with a ribbon around it.'

Rebus looked at the photo printed in the paper. 'It looks cruder, balsa wood or something.'

She nodded. 'I thought it was quite a coincidence. Ever since, I've been on the lookout for more examples.'

He separated the two final cuttings. 'And finding them, I see.'

'I tour the country, giving talks on behalf of the Museum. Each time, I ask if anyone's heard of such a thing.'

'You struck lucky?'

'Twice so far. Nineteen seventy-seven in Nairn, nineteen seventy-two in Dunfermline.'

Two more mystery finds. In Nairn, the coffin had been found on the beach; in Dunfermline, in the town's glen. One with a doll in it, one without. Again, an animal or child could have made off with the contents.

'What do you make of it?' he asked.

'Shouldn't that be *my* question?' He didn't answer, sifted back through the reports. 'Could there be a link with what you found in Falls?'

'I don't know.' He looked up at her. 'Why don't we find out?'

Sunday traffic slowed them down, though most of the cars were heading back into the city after a day in the country.

'Do you think there could be more?' he asked.

'It's possible. But the local history groups, they pick up on oddities like that – and they've got long memories, too. It's a close network. People know I'm interested.' She rested her head against the passenger-side window. 'I think I'd have heard.'

As they passed the road sign welcoming them to Falls, she smiled. 'Twinned with Angoisse,' she said.

'Sorry?'

'The sign back there, Falls is twinned with some place called Angoisse. It must be in France.'

'How do you work that out?'

'Well, there was a picture of the French flag next to the name.'

'I suppose that would help.'

'But it's a French word, too: *angoisse*. It means "anguish". Imagine that: a town called anguish . . .'

There were cars parked either side of the main road, making for a bottleneck. Rebus didn't think he'd find a space, so turned into the lane and parked there. As they walked down to Bev Dodds's cottage, they passed a couple of locals washing their cars. The men were middle-aged and casually dressed – cords and V-necks – but wore the clothes like a uniform. Rebus would bet that midweek, they were seldom without a suit and tie. He thought of Wee Billy's memories: mums scrubbing their front steps. And here was the contemporary equivalent. One of the men said 'hello' and the other 'good afternoon'. Rebus nodded and knocked on Bev Dodds's door.

'I think you'll find she's taking her constitutional,' one man said.

'Shouldn't be long,' added the other.

Neither had stopped work on his car. Rebus wondered if they were in some sort of race; not that they were rushing, but there seemed an element of competition, their concentration intense.

'Looking to buy some pottery?' the first asked, as he got to work on the front grille of his BMW.

'Actually, I wanted a look at the doll,' Rebus said, sliding his hands into his pockets.

'Don't think that's likely. She's signed some sort of exclusive with one of your rivals.'

'I'm a police officer,' Rebus stated.

The Rover owner snorted at his neighbour's mistake. 'That might make a difference,' he said, laughing.

'Odd sort of thing to happen,' Rebus said conversationally.

'No shortage of those around here.'

'How do you mean?'

The BMW driver rinsed out his sponge. 'We had a spate of thefts a few months back, then someone daubed the door of the church.'

'Kids from the estate,' the Rover driver interrupted.

'Maybe,' his neighbour conceded. 'But it's funny it never happened before. Then the Balfour girl goes missing . . .'

'Do either of you know the family?'

'Seen them around,' the Rover driver conceded.

'They held a tea party two months back. Opened the house. It was for some charity, I forget which. They seemed very pleasant, John and Jacqueline.' The BMW driver glanced at his neighbour as he spoke the names. Rebus saw it as yet another element of the game their lives had become.

'What about the daughter?' Rebus asked.

'Always seemed a bit distant,' the Rover driver said hurriedly, not about to be left out. 'Hard to strike up a conversation with her.'

'She spoke to me,' his rival announced. 'We had quite a chin-wag once about her university course.'

The Rover driver glared at him. Rebus could foresee a duel: dampened chamoises at twenty paces. 'What about Ms Dodds?' he asked. 'Good neighbour, is she?'

'Bloody awful pottery,' was the only comment.

'This doll thing's probably been good for business though.'

'I don't doubt it,' the BMW owner said. 'If she has any sense, she'll capitalise on it.'

'Promotion's the life-blood of any new business,' his neighbour added. Rebus got the feeling they knew what they were talking about.

'Small concession might do wonders,' BMW man mused. 'Teas, home baking . . .' Both men had stopped working, growing thoughtful.

'I thought that was your car in the lane,' Bev Dodds said, striding towards the group.

While tea was being made, Jean asked if she could see some of the pottery. An extension at the back of the cottage housed both the kitchen and the spare bedroom, which had become a studio. Jean praised the various bowls and plates, but Rebus could tell she didn't like them. Then, as Bev Dodds was sliding the various bangles and bracelets up her arms again, Jean praised those, too.

'I make them,' Bev Dodds said.

'Do you?' Jean sounded delighted.

Dodds put her arm out so she could take a closer look. 'Local stones. I wash them and varnish them. I think they act a little like crystals.'

'Positive energy?' Jean guessed. Rebus could no longer tell if she was genuinely interested or just faking it. 'Could I buy one, do you think?'

'Of course,' Dodds said delightedly. Her hair was windswept, cheeks red from the walk she'd just taken. She slid one of the bracelets from her wrist. 'How about this? It's one of my favourites, and just ten pounds.'

Jean paused at mention of the price, but then smiled and handed over a ten-pound note, which Dodds tucked into her pocket.

'Ms Burchill works at the museum,' Rebus said.

'Really?'

'I'm a curator.' Jean had slipped the bracelet on to her wrist.

'What a wonderful job. Whenever I'm in town, I try to make time for a visit.'

'Have you heard of the Arthur's Seat coffins?' Rebus asked.

'Steve told me about them,' Dodds said. Rebus presumed she meant Steve Holly, the reporter.

'Ms Burchill has an interest in them,' Rebus said. 'She'd like to see the doll you found.'

'Of course.' She slid open one of the drawers and brought out the coffin. Jean handled it with care, placing it on the kitchen table before examining it.

'It's quite well made,' she said. 'More like the Arthur's Seat coffins than those others.'

'"Others"?' Bev Dodds asked.

'Is it a copy of one of them?' Rebus asked, ignoring this.

'Not an exact copy, no,' Jean said. 'Different nails, and constructed slightly differently, too.'

'By someone who'd seen the museum exhibit?'

'It's possible. You can buy a postcard of the coffins in the museum shop.'

Rebus looked at Jean. 'Has anyone shown interest in the exhibit recently?'

'How would I know that?'

'Maybe a researcher or someone?'

She shook her head. 'There was a doctoral student last year . . . but she went back to Toronto.'

'Is there some connection here?' Bev Dodds asked, wide-eyed. 'Something between the museum and the abduction?'

'We don't know that anyone's been abducted,' Rebus cautioned her.

'All the same . . .'

'Ms Dodds . . . Bev . . .' Rebus fixed her with his eyes. 'It's important that this conversation stays confidential.'

When she nodded understanding, Rebus knew that within minutes of them leaving, she'd be on the phone to Steve Holly. He left his tea unfinished.

'We'd better be off.' Jean took the hint, and placed her own cup on the draining-board. 'That was lovely, thanks.'

'You're welcome. And thank you for buying the bracelet. My third sale today.'

As they walked back up the lane, two cars passed them. Day-trippers, Rebus guessed, on their way to the waterfall. And afterwards, maybe they'd stop by the pottery, asking to see the famous coffin. They'd probably buy something too . . .

'What are you thinking?' Jean asked, getting into the car and studying the bracelet, holding it up to the light.

'Nothing,' Rebus lied. He decided to drive through the village. The Rover and BMW stood drying in the late-afternoon sun. A young couple with two kids stood outside Bev Dodds's cottage. The father had a video camera in his hand. Rebus gave way to four or five cars, then continued along the road to Meadowside. Three boys – maybe including the two from his previous visit – were playing football on the grass. Rebus stopped and wound down his window, calling out to them. They looked at him, but weren't about to interrupt their game. He told Jean he'd only be a second, and got out of the car.

'Hello there,' he told the boys.

'Who are you?' The questioner was skinny, ribs protruding, and thin arms ending in bunched fists. His hair had been shorn to the scalp, and as he squinted into the light he managed to be four-feet-six of aggression and mistrust.

'I'm the police,' Rebus said.

'We haven't done nothing.'

'Congratulations.'

The boy kicked the ball hard. It thundered into the upper thigh of one of the other players, leading the third to start laughing.

'I was wondering if you knew anything about this spate of thefts I've been hearing about.'

The boy looked at him. 'Get a grip,' he said.

'With pleasure, son. What'll it be, your neck or your balls?' The boy tried for a sneer. 'Maybe you can tell me something about the church getting vandalised?'

'No,' he said.

'No?' Rebus sounded surprised. 'Okay then, last shot . . . what about this wee coffin that's been found?'

'What about it?'

'Have you seen it?'

The boy shook his head. 'Tell him to sod off, Chick,' one of his friends advised.

'Chick?' Rebus nodded, to let the boy know he was filing the information away.

'Never saw the coffin,' Chick said. 'No way I'm going to knock on *her* door.'

'Why not?'

'Because she's well fucking weird.' Chick laughed.

'Weird how?'

Chick was losing patience. Somehow he'd been duped into having a conversation. 'Weird like the rest of them.'

'They're all a bunch of tampons,' his pal said, coming to rescue him. 'Let's go, Chick.' They ran off, collecting the third boy and the ball on their way. Rebus watched for a moment, but Chick didn't look back. As he returned to the car, he saw that Jean's window was down.

'Okay,' he said, 'so I'm not the world's best at asking questions of schoolkids.'

She smiled. 'What did he mean about tampons?'

Rebus turned the ignition and glanced at her. 'He meant they're all stuck-up.' He didn't add the final word, didn't need to. Jean knew exactly what he meant . . .

Late that Sunday night, he found himself on the pavement outside Philippa Balfour's flat. He still had the set of keys in his pocket, but wasn't going inside, not after what happened last time. Someone had closed the shutters in her living room and bedroom. No light was being allowed into the flat, none at all.

It was one week since her disappearance, and a reconstruction was under way. A WPC with a passing resemblance to the missing student had been dressed in clothes similar to the ones Flip might have been wearing that evening. A recently bought Versace T-shirt was missing from Flip's wardrobe, so the WPC was wearing one just like it. She would walk out of the tenement and be photographed by the waiting newsmen. Then she'd walk briskly to the end of the street, where she'd step into a waiting taxi cab, commandeered for the purpose. She'd get out again and start climbing the hill towards the city centre. There would be photographers with her all the way, and uniformed officers stopping pedestrians and drivers, clipboards ready, questions prepared. The WPC would travel all the way to the bar on the South Side . . .

Two TV crews – BBC and Scottish – were readying to film the reconstruction. News programmes would show snippets of it.

It was an exercise, a way of showing that the police were doing *something*.

That was all.

Gill Templer, catching Rebus's eye from the other side of the street, seemed to acknowledge as much with a shrug. Then she went back to her conversation with Assistant Chief Constable Colin Carswell. The ACC seemed to have a few points he wished to get across. Rebus didn't doubt that the words 'a swift conclusion' would figure at least once. From past experience, he knew that when Gill Templer was irritated, she tended to play with a string of pearls she sometimes wore. They were around her neck now, and she had slipped a finger beneath them, running it back and forth. Rebus thought of all Bev Dodds's bracelets, and what the kid called Chick had said: *well fucking weird* . . . Books of Wiccan in her living room, only she didn't call it that, called it her 'parlour' instead. A Stones song popped into his head: 'Spider and the Fly', B-side to 'Satisfaction'. He saw Bev Dodds as a spider, her parlour a web. For some reason the image, though fanciful, stuck with him . . .

6

On Monday morning, Rebus took Jean's press cuttings in to work. Waiting for him on his desk were three messages from Steve Holly and a note in Gill Templer's handwriting, informing him of a doctor's appointment at eleven o'clock. He went to her office to plead his case, but a sheet of paper on her door stated that she would be spending the day at Gayfield Square. Rebus went back to his chair, grabbed his cigarettes and lighter, and headed for the car park. He'd just got one lit when Siobhan Clarke arrived.

'Any luck?' he asked her. Siobhan lifted the laptop she was carrying.

'Last night,' she told him.

'What happened?'

She looked at his cigarette. 'Soon as you finish that foul thing, come upstairs and I'll show you.'

The door swung shut behind her. Rebus stared at the cigarette, took one last puff, and flicked it on to the ground.

By the time he got to the CID room, Siobhan had set up the laptop. An officer called over that there was a Steve Holly on the line. Rebus shook his head. He knew damned well what Holly wanted: Bev Dodds had told him about the trip to Falls. He held up a finger, asking Siobhan to wait a second, then got on the phone to the museum.

'Jean Burchill's office, please,' he said. Then he waited.

'Hello?' It was her voice.

'Jean? John Rebus here.'

'John, I was just thinking of calling you.'

'Don't tell me: you're being hassled?'

'Well, not exactly hassled . . .'

'A reporter called Steve Holly, wanting to talk about the dolls?'

'He's been on to you too, then?'

'Best advice I can give, Jean: don't say anything. Refuse his calls, and if he does get through, tell him you've nothing to say. No matter how hard he pushes . . .'

'Understood. Did Bev Dodds blab?'

'My fault, I should've known she would.'

'I can look after myself, John, don't worry.'

They said their goodbyes and he put down the receiver, took the short walk to Siobhan's desk and read the message on the laptop's screen.

This game is not a game. It's a quest. You'll need strength and endurance, not to mention intelligence. But your prize will be great. Do you still wish to play?

'I sent back an e-mail saying I was interested, but asking how long the game would take.' Siobhan was moving her finger across the keypad. 'He told me it could take a few days, or a few weeks. So then I asked if I could start with Hellbank. He came back straight away, telling me Hellbank was the fourth level, and I'd have to play the whole thing. I said okay. At midnight, this arrived.'

There was another message on the screen. 'He's used a different address,' Siobhan said. 'God knows how many he's got.'

'Making him difficult to track down?' Rebus guessed. Then he read:

How can I be sure you are who you say you are?

'He means my e-mail address,' Siobhan explained. 'I was using Philippa's before; now I'm using Grant's.'

'What did you tell him?'

'I told him he'd have to trust me; either that or we could always meet.'

'And was he keen?'

She smiled. 'Not overly. But he did send me this.' She hit another button.

Seven fins high is king. This queen dines well before the bust.

'Is that it?'

Siobhan nodded. 'I asked if he could give me a clue. All he did was send me the message again.'

'Presumably because it *is* the clue.'

She ran a hand through her hair. 'I was up half the night. I don't suppose it means anything to you?'

He shook his head. 'You need someone who likes puzzles. Doesn't young Grant do cryptic crosswords?'

'Does he?' Siobhan looked across the room to where Grant Hood was making a phone call.

'Why don't you go and ask?'

When Hood came off the phone, Siobhan was waiting. 'How's the laptop?' he asked.

'Fine.' She handed him a sheet of paper. 'I hear you like a puzzle.'

He took the sheet, but didn't look at it. 'Saturday night?' he asked.

She nodded. 'Saturday night was fine.'

And it had been, too: a couple of drinks and then dinner at a decent, small restaurant in the New Town. They'd talked shop mostly, having not much else in common, but it was good to have a laugh, relive a few stories. He'd been quite the gentleman, walking her home afterwards. She hadn't asked him up for coffee. He'd said he'd find a cab on Broughton Street.

Now, Grant nodded back and smiled. 'Fine' was good enough for him. Then he looked at the sheet. '"Seven fins high is king",' he read aloud. 'What's it mean?'

'I was hoping maybe you'd tell me.'

He studied the message again. 'Could be an anagram. Unlikely though: not enough vowels, it's all i's and e's. "Before the bust" – drugs bust maybe?' Siobhan just shrugged. 'Maybe it would help if you told me a bit about it,' Hood said.

Siobhan nodded. 'Over a coffee, if you like,' she said.

Back at his desk, Rebus watched them leave the room, then picked up the first of the cuttings. There was a conversation going on nearby, something about another press conference. The consensus was, if DCS Templer wanted you to front it, it meant she had the knives out. Rebus's eyes narrowed. There was a sentence he must have missed first time round. It was the 1995 clipping: Huntingtower Hotel near Perth, a dog finding the coffin and scrap of cloth. Three-quarters of the way through the story, an anonymous member of the hotel staff was quoted as saying, 'If we're not careful, Huntingtower's going to get itself a reputation.' Rebus wondered what was meant by that. He picked up the phone, thinking maybe Jean Burchill would know. But he didn't make the call, didn't want her to think he was . . . well, what exactly? He'd enjoyed yesterday, and thought she had too. He'd dropped her at her home in Portobello, but had declined the offer of coffee.

'I've taken up too much of your day as it is,' he'd said. She hadn't denied it.

'Maybe another time then,' was all she'd said.

Driving back to Marchmont, he'd felt that something had been lost between them. He'd almost called her that evening, but had switched on the TV instead, losing himself in a nature programme, unable afterwards to recall anything about it. Until he'd remembered about the reconstruction and headed out to watch it . . .

His hand was still resting on the receiver. He picked it up and got a number for the Huntingtower Hotel, asked to speak to the manager.

'I'm sorry,' the receptionist said. 'He's in a meeting at the moment. Can I take a message?'

Rebus explained who he was. 'I want to speak to someone who was working at the hotel in nineteen ninety-five.'

'What's their name?'

He smiled at her mistake. 'No, I mean, anyone will do.'

'Well, I've been here since ninety-three.'

'Then you might remember the little coffin that was found.'

'Vaguely, yes.'

'Only I've got a cutting from a newspaper at the time. It says that the hotel might be getting a reputation.'

'Yes.'

'And why would that have been?'

'I'm not sure. Maybe it was that American tourist.'

'Which one?'

'The one who disappeared.'

He didn't say anything for a moment, and when he did it was to ask her to repeat what she'd just said.

Rebus went to the National Library annexe on Causewayside. It wasn't much more than a five-minute walk from St Leonard's. When he'd shown his ID and explained what he needed, he was taken to a desk where a microfilm reader sat. This was a large illuminated screen above two spools. The film was placed on one spool and would be wound on to the empty one. Rebus had used the machine before, back when newspapers had been stored at the main building on George IV Bridge. He'd told the staff that today's was 'a rush job'. Even so, he sat for the best part of twenty minutes before a librarian arrived with the film boxes. The *Courier* was Dundee's daily paper. Rebus's own family had taken it. He remembered that up until recently it had retained the look of a broadsheet from a previous era, with column-wide ads covering its front page. No news, no photos. The story went that when the *Titanic* sank, the headline in the *Courier* had been 'Dundee Man Lost at Sea'. Not that the paper was parochial or anything.

Rebus had the Huntingtower cutting with him, and wound the tape forward until he was four weeks shy of its appearance. There, on an inside page, was the headline 'Tourist's Disappearance a Mystery, Say Police'. The woman's name was Betty-Anne Jesperson. She was thirty-eight and married. She'd been a member of a tour party from the USA. The tour was called 'The Mystical Highlands of Scotland'. The photograph of Betty-Anne came from her passport. It showed a heavy-set woman with dark permed hair and thick-rimmed glasses. Her husband, Garry, said she was in the habit of waking early and going for a pre-breakfast walk. No one in the hotel had seen her depart. The countryside was searched, and police went into Perth town centre armed with copies of the photograph. But as Rebus wound the film forward a week, the story was cut down to half a dozen paragraphs. A further week along, and there was just a single paragraph. The story was in the process of vanishing as completely as Betty-Anne had.

According to the hotel receptionist, Garry Jesperson had made several trips back to the area in that first year, with a further month-long trip the year after. But then the last she'd heard, Garry had met someone else and moved from New Jersey to Baltimore.

Rebus copied the details into his notebook, then sat tapping at the page he'd just written on until one of the browsers cleared their throat, warning him that he'd started to make too much noise.

Back at the main desk, he put in a request for more papers: the *Dunfermline Press, Glasgow Herald* and *Inverness Courier*. Only the *Herald* was on microfilm, so he started with that. Nineteen eighty-two, the doll in the churchyard . . . Van Morrison had released *Beautiful*

Vision early in '82. Rebus found himself humming 'Dweller on the Threshold', then stopped when he remembered where he was. Nineteen eighty-two, he'd been a detective sergeant, working cases with another DS called Jack Morton. They'd been based at Great London Road, back before the station had caught fire. When the *Herald* film arrived, he spooled it and got to work, the days and weeks a blur across his screen. All the officers above him at Great London Road, they were either dead or retired. He hadn't kept in touch with any of them. And now the Farmer was gone too. Soon, whether he liked it or not, it would be his turn. He didn't think he'd go quietly. They'd have to pull him screaming and kicking . . .

The churchyard doll had been found in May. He started at the beginning of April. Problem was, Glasgow was a big city, more crime than a place like Perth. He wasn't sure he'd know if and when he found something. And if it was a missing person, would it even make the paper? Thousands of people disappeared each year. Some of them left without being noticed: the homeless, the ones with no family or friends. This was a country where a corpse could sit in a chair by the fire until the smell alerted the neighbours.

By the time he'd searched April, he had no reported MisPers, but six deaths, two of them women. One was a stabbing after a party. A man, it was stated, was helping police with their inquiries. Rebus guessed the boyfriend. He was pretty sure that if he read on, he'd find the case coming to court. The second death was a drowning. A stretch of river Rebus had never heard of: White Cart Water, the body found by its banks on the southern border of Rosshall Park. The victim was Hazel Gibbs, aged twenty-two. Her husband had walked out, leaving her with two kids. Friends said she'd been depressed. She'd been seen out drinking the previous day, while the kids fended for themselves.

Rebus walked outside and got on his mobile, punching in the number for Bobby Hogan at Leith CID.

'Bobby, it's John. You know a bit about Glasgow, don't you?'

'A bit.'

'Ever heard of White Cart Water?'

'Can't say I have.'

'What about Rosshall Park?'

'Sorry.'

'Got any contacts out west?'

'I could make a phone call.'

'Do that, will you?' Rebus repeated the names and ended the call. He smoked a cigarette, staring across at a new pub on the opposite corner. He knew one drink wouldn't do him any harm. Then he remembered that he was supposed to be seeing the doctor. Hell, it would have to wait. He could always make another appointment. When, at cigarette's end, Hogan hadn't called back, Rebus returned to his desk and started going through the editions for May '82. When his mobile sounded, the staff and readers gave a look of collective horror. Rebus cursed and put the phone to his ear, getting up from his seat to head outside again.

'It's me,' Hogan said.

'Go ahead,' Rebus whispered, moving towards the exit.

'Rosshall Park's in Pollok, south-west of the city centre. White Cart Water runs along the top of it.'

Rebus stopped in his tracks. 'You sure?' His voice was no longer a whisper.

'It's what I'm told.'

Rebus was back at his desk. The *Herald* cutting was just below the one from the *Courier*. He eased it out, just to be sure.

'Thanks, Bobby,' he said, ending the call. People around him were making exasperated noises, but he didn't pay them any heed. 'Church Condemns Sick Joke Find': the coffin found in the churchyard. The church itself located on Potterhill Road.

In Pollok.

'I don't suppose you'd care to explain yourself,' Gill Templer said.

Rebus had driven to Gayfield Square and asked her for five minutes. They were back in the same stale office.

'That's just what I want to do,' Rebus told her. He placed a hand to his forehead. His face felt like it was burning.

'You were supposed to be attending a doctor's appointment.'

'Something came up. Christ, you're not going to believe it.'

She stabbed a finger at the tabloid newspaper open on her desk. 'Any idea how Steve Holly got hold of this?'

Rebus turned the paper so it was facing him. Holly couldn't have had much time, but he'd patched together a story which managed to mention the Arthur's Seat coffins, a 'local expert from the Museum of Scotland', the Falls coffin, and the 'persistent rumour that more coffins exist'.

'What does he mean, "more coffins"?' Gill asked.

'That's what I'm trying to tell you.' So he told her, laid the whole thing out before her. In the musty, leatherbound sets of *Dunfermline Presses* and *Inverness Couriers* he'd found exactly what he'd known and dreaded he would find. In July 1977, a scant week before the Nairn beach coffin had been found, the body of Paula Gearing had been washed ashore four miles further along the coast. Her death could not be explained, and was put down to 'misadventure'. In October 1972, three weeks before the finding of the coffin in Dunfermline Glen, a teenage girl had been reported missing. Caroline Farmer was a fourth-year student at Dunfermline High. She'd recently been jilted by a long-term boyfriend, and the best guess was that this had led her to leave home. Her family said they wouldn't rest until they'd heard from her. Rebus doubted they ever had . . .

Gill Templer listened to his story without comment. When he'd finished, she looked at the cuttings and the notes he'd taken in the library. Finally, she looked up at him.

'It's thin, John.'

Rebus jumped from his seat. He needed to be moving, but the room didn't have enough space. 'Gill, it's . . . there's something there.'

'A killer who leaves coffins near the scene?' She shook her head slowly. 'I just can't see it. You've got two bodies, no signs of foul play, and two disappearances. Doesn't exactly make a pattern.'

'Three disappearances including Philippa Balfour.'

'And there's another thing: the Falls coffin turned up less than a week after she went AWOL. No pattern again.'

'You think I'm seeing things?'

'Maybe.'

'Can I at least follow it through?'

'John . . .'

'Just one, maybe two more officers. Give us a few days to see if we can convince you.'

'We're stretched as it is.'

'Stretched doing what? We're whistling in the dark till she comes back, phones home or turns up dead. Give me two people.'

She shook her head slowly. 'You can have one. And three or four days, tops. Understood?'

Rebus nodded.

'And John? Go see the doctor, or I'm reeling you back in. Understood?'

'Understood. Who will I be working with?'

Templer was thoughtful. 'Who do you want?'

'Give me Ellen Wylie.'

She stared at him. 'Any particular reason why?'

He shrugged. 'She'll never make it as a TV presenter, but she's a good cop.'

Templer was still staring. 'Okay,' she said at last. 'Go ahead.'

'And is there any chance you can keep Steve Holly away from us?'

'I can try.' She tapped the newspaper. 'I'm assuming the "local expert" is Jean?' She waited till he'd nodded, then she sighed. 'I should have known better, bringing the two of you together . . .' She started rubbing at her forehead. It was something the Farmer had done, too, whenever he got what he called his 'Rebus heads' . . .

'What exactly are we looking for?' Ellen Wylie asked. She'd been summoned to St Leonard's, and didn't look thrilled at the prospect of working a two-hander with Rebus.

'The first thing,' he told her, 'is to cover our backsides, and that means checking that the MisPers never turned up.'

'Talking to the families?' she guessed, writing a note to herself on her pad.

'Right. As for the two bodies, we need to take another look at the PM results, see if there's anything the pathologists could have missed.'

'Nineteen seventy-seven and eighty-two? You think the records won't have been ditched?'

'I hope not. In any case, some of those pathologists have long memories.'

She made another note. 'I'll ask again: what are we looking for? You think there's a possibility of proving these women and the coffins are related?'

'I don't know.' But he knew what she meant: it was one thing to believe something, quite another to be able to prove it, especially in a court of law.

'It might set my mind at rest,' he said at last.

'And all of this started with some coffins on Arthur's Seat?' He nodded, his own enthusiasm making no impact on her scepticism.

'Look,' he said, 'if I'm seeing things, you'll get your chance to tell me. But first we do a bit of digging.'

She shrugged, made a show of jotting another note on to her pad. 'Did you ask for me, or were you given me?'

'I asked.'

'And DCS Templer said okay?'

Rebus nodded again. 'Is there a problem?'

'I don't know.' She gave the question serious consideration. 'Probably not.'

'Okay,' he said. 'Then let's get started.'

It took him the best part of two hours to type up everything he had. What he wanted was a 'bible' they could work from. He had dates and page references for each of the newspaper stories, and had arranged with the library for copies to be made. Wylie meantime was busy on the phone, begging favours from police stations in Glasgow, Perth, Dunfermline and Nairn. She wanted case notes if any still existed, plus pathologists' names. Whenever she laughed, Rebus knew what had just been said to her: 'You don't ask for bloody much, do you?' Hammering away at his keyboard, he listened to her work. She knew when to be coy, when to get tough, and when to flirt. Her voice never betrayed the set features of her face as repetition made her weary.

'Thank you,' she said for the umpteenth time, dropping the receiver into its cradle. She scribbled a note on her pad, checked the time and wrote that down too. She was thorough, all right. 'A promise is one thing,' she said more than once.

'It's better than nothing.'

'As long as they come through.' Then she lifted the handset again, took another deep breath, and made the next call.

Rebus was intrigued by the long gaps in the chronology: 1972, 1977, 1982, 1995. Five years, five years, thirteen years. And now, just maybe, another five-year gap. The fives made for a nice pattern, but it was immediately broken by that silence between '82 and '95. There were all sorts of explanations: the man, whoever he was, could have been away somewhere, maybe in prison. Who was to say the coffins had only been left dotted around Scotland? It might be worth putting out a more general search, see if any other forces had come across the phenomenon. If he'd done a stretch in prison, well, records could be checked. Thirteen years was a long one: had to be murder, most probably.

There was another possibility, of course: that he hadn't been anywhere. That he'd gone on with his spree right here, but somehow hadn't bothered with the coffins, or they hadn't ever been found. A little wooden box . . . a dog would chew it to pulp; a kid might take it home; someone might bin it, the better to be rid of the sick joke. Rebus knew that a public appeal would be one way of finding out, but he couldn't see Templer going for it. She would need convincing first.

'Nothing?' he asked as Wylie put down the phone.

'No one's answering. Maybe word's gone round about the crazy cop from Edinburgh.'

Rebus crumpled a sheet of paper and tossed it overarm towards the bin. 'I think maybe we're getting a bit stir-crazy,' he said. 'Let's take a break.'

Wylie was heading off to the baker's for a jam doughnut. Rebus decided he'd just take a walk. The streets around St Leonard's didn't offer a great deal of choice. Tenements and housing schemes, or Holyrood Road with its speeding traffic and backdrop of Salisbury Crags. Rebus decided to head into the warren of narrow passages between St Leonard's and Nicolson Street. He nipped into a newsagent's and bought a can of Irn-Bru, sipping from it as he walked. They said the stuff was perfect for hangovers, but he was using it to fend off the craving for a proper drink, a pint and a nip, somewhere smoky with the horses on TV . . . The Southsider was a possibility, but he crossed the road to avoid it. There were kids playing on the pavements, Asians mostly. School was over for the day and here they were with their energy, their imagination. He wondered if maybe his own imagination was putting in some overtime today . . . It was the final possibility: that he was seeing connections where none existed. He got out his mobile and a scrap of paper with a number on it.

When the call was answered, he asked to be put through to Jean Burchill.

'Jean?' He stopped walking. 'It's John Rebus. We might have struck gold with your little coffins.' He listened for a moment. 'I can't tell you about it right now.' He looked around. 'I'm on my way to a meeting. Are you busy tonight?' He listened again. 'That's a pity. Would you be up for a nightcap?' He brightened. 'Ten o'clock? Portobello or in town?' Another pause. 'Yes, town makes sense if you've been in a meeting. I'll drive you home after. Ten at the museum then? Okay, bye.'

He looked around. He was in Hill Square, and there was a sign on the railings nearest him. Now he knew where he was: at the back of Surgeons' Hall. The anonymous door in front of him was the entrance to something called the Sir Jules Thorn Exhibition of the History of Surgery. He checked his watch against the opening times. He had about ten minutes. What the hell, he thought, pushing the door and going inside.

He found himself in an ordinary tenement stairwell. Climbing one flight brought him to a narrow landing with two doors facing. They looked like they led to private flats, so he climbed a further flight. As he passed the museum threshold an alarm sounded, alerting a member of staff that there was a new visitor.

'Have you been here before?' she asked. He shook his head. 'Well, modern-day is upstairs, and just off to the left is the dental display . . .' He thanked her and she left him to it. There was no one else around, no one Rebus could see. He lasted half a minute in the dentistry room. It didn't seem to him that the technology had moved so very far in a couple of centuries. The main museum display took up two floors, and was well presented. The exhibits were behind glass, well lit for the most part. He stood in front of an apothecary's shop, then moved to a full-size dummy of the physician Joseph Lister, examining his list of accomplishments, chief among them the introduction of carbolic spray and sterile catgut. A little further along, he came across the case containing the wallet made from Burke's skin. It reminded him of a small leatherbound Bible an uncle had gifted him one childhood birthday. Beside it was a plaster cast of Burke's head – the marks of the hangman's noose still visible – and one of an accomplice, John Brogan, who had helped transport the corpses. While Burke looked peaceful, hair groomed, face at rest, Brogan looked to have suffered torments, the skin pulled back from his lower jaw, skull bulbous and pink.

Next along was a portrait of the anatomist Knox, recipient of the still-warm cadavers.

'Poor Knox,' a voice behind him said. Rebus looked around. An elderly man, dressed in full evening attire – bow-tie, cummerbund and patent shoes. It took Rebus a second to place him: Professor Devlin, Flip's neighbour. Devlin shuffled forward, staring at the exhibits. 'There's been a lot of discussion about how much he knew.'

'You mean, whether he knew Burke and Hare were killers?'

Devlin nodded. 'For myself, I think there's no doubt he knew. At the time, most bodies worked on by the anatomists were cold indeed. They were brought to Edinburgh from all over Britain – some came by way of the Union Canal. The resurrectionists – body-snatchers – pickled them in whisky for transportation. It was a lucrative trade.'

'But did the whisky get drunk afterwards?'

Devlin chuckled. 'Economics would dictate that it did,' he said. 'Ironically, both Burke and Hare came to Scotland as economic migrants. Their job was to help build the Union Canal.' Rebus recalled

Jean saying something similar. Devlin paused, tucked a finger into his cummerbund. 'But poor Knox . . . the man was possessed of a kind of genius. It was never proven that he was complicit in the murders. But the Church was against him, that was the problem. The human body was a temple, remember. Many of the clergy were against exploration – they saw it as desecration. They raised the rabble against Knox.'

'What happened to him?'

'He died of apoplexy, according to the literature. Hare, who had turned King's evidence, had to flee Scotland. Even then he wasn't safe. He was attacked with lime, and ended his days blind and begging on the streets of London. I believe there's a pub called the Blind Beggar somewhere in London, but whether it has any connection . . .'

'Sixteen murders,' Rebus said, 'in an area as confined as the West Port.'

'We can't imagine it happening these days, can we?'

'But these days we've got forensics, pathology . . .'

Devlin unhooked the finger from his cummerbund and wagged it before him. 'Exactly,' he said. 'And we'd have had no pathological studies at all had it not been for the resurrectionists and the likes of Messrs Burke and Hare!'

'Is that why you're here? Paying homage?'

'Perhaps,' Devlin said. Then he checked his watch. 'There's a dinner upstairs at seven. I thought I'd arrive early and spend some time amongst the exhibits.'

Rebus recalled the invitation on Devlin's mantelpiece: *black tie and decorations* . . .

'I'm sorry, Professor Devlin,' the curator called. 'It's time I was locking up.'

'That's okay, Maggie,' Devlin called back. Then, to Rebus: 'Would you like to see the rest of the place?'

Rebus thought of Ellen Wylie, probably back at her desk by now. 'I should really . . .'

'Come on, come on,' Devlin insisted. 'You can't visit Surgeons' Hall and miss out on the Black Museum . . .'

The curator had to let them through a couple of locked doors, after which they entered the main body of the building. The corridors were hushed and lined with portraits of medical men. Devlin pointed out the library, then stopped in a marble-floored circular hall, pointing upwards. 'That's where we'll be eating. Lots of Profs and Docs all dressed to the nines and feasting on rubber chicken.'

Rebus looked up. The ceiling was topped with a glass cupola. There was a circular railing on the first floor, with a doorway just visible beyond. 'What's the occasion?'

'Lord alone knows. I just bung them a cheque whenever an invite arrives.'

'Will Gates and Curt be there?'

'Probably. You know Sandy Gates has trouble turning down a square meal.'

Rebus was studying the inside of the large main doors. He'd seen them before, but only ever from the other side, while driving or walking down Nicolson Street. He didn't think he'd ever seen them open, and said as much to his guide.

'They'll be open this evening,' Devlin told him. 'Guests march in and straight up the stairs. Come on, this way.'

Along more corridors and up some steps. 'Probably won't be locked,' Devlin said, as they approached another imposing set of doors. 'The dinner guests like a stroll after their meal. Most of them end up here.' He tried the doorhandle. He was right; the door opened and they entered a large exhibition hall.

'The Black Museum,' Devlin said, gesturing with his arms.

'I've heard of it,' Rebus said. 'Never had cause to visit.'

'Off limits to the public,' Devlin explained. 'Never been sure why. The College could make itself a bit of money, open it as a tourist attraction.'

Its given name was Playfair Hall, and it wasn't, to Rebus's eye, as grisly as its nickname suggested. It seemed to consist of old surgical tools, looking more fit for a torture chamber than an operating theatre. There were lots of bones and body parts and things floating in hazy jars. A further narrow staircase took them up to a landing, where more jars awaited them.

'Pity the poor bugger whose job is keeping the formaldehyde topped up,' Devlin said, panting from the exertion.

Rebus stared at the contents of one glass cylinder. The face of an infant stared back at him, but it looked distorted somehow. Then he realised that it sat atop two distinct bodies. Siamese twins, joined at the head, parts of either face forming a singular whole. Rebus, who'd seen his fair share of horror, was held in grim fascination. But there were other exhibits to explore: further deformed foetuses. Paintings, too, mostly from the nineteenth century: soldiers with bits blown off them by cannonball or musket.

'This is my favourite,' Devlin said. Surrounded by obscene images, he had found a still point, the portrait of a young man, almost smiling for the artist. Rebus read the inscription.

'"Dr Kennet Lovell, February, eighteen twenty-nine."'

'Lovell was one of the anatomists charged with the dissection of William Burke. It's even likely that he pronounced Burke dead after the hanging. Less than a month later, he sat for this portrait.'

'He looks pretty happy with his lot,' Rebus commented.

Devlin's eyes sparkled. 'Doesn't he? Kennet was a craftsman too. He worked with wood, as did Deacon William Brodie, of whom you will have heard.'

'Gentleman by day, housebreaker by night,' Rebus acknowledged.

'And perhaps the model for Stevenson's *Jekyll and Hyde*. As a child, Stevenson had a wardrobe in his room, one of Brodie's creations . . .'

Rebus was still studying the portrait. Lovell had deep black eyes, a cleft chin and a profusion of dark locks of hair. He had no doubt that the painter would have flattered his subject, maybe shaved a few years and pounds from him. Still, Lovell was a handsome man.

'It's interesting about the Balfour girl,' Devlin said. Startled, Rebus turned to him. The old man, his breathing regular now, had eyes only for the painting.

'What is?' Rebus asked.

'The caskets found on Arthur's Seat . . . the way the press have brought them up again.' He turned towards Rebus. 'One notion is that they represent Burke and Hare's victims . . .'

'Yes.'

'And now another casket seems to be some memorial for young Philippa.'

Rebus turned back to the portrait. 'Lovell worked with wood?'

'The table in my dining room.' Devlin smiled. 'He made that.'

'Is that why you bought it?'

'A small memento of the early years of pathology. The history of surgery, Inspector, is the history of Edinburgh.' Devlin sniffed and then sighed. 'I miss it, you know.'

'I don't think I would.'

They were walking away from the portrait. 'It was a privilege, in its way. Endlessly fascinating, what this animal exterior can contain.' Devlin slapped his own chest to make the point. Rebus didn't feel he had anything to add. To him, a body was a body was a body. By the time it was dead, whatever it was that had made it interesting had disappeared. He almost said as much, but knew he'd fail to match the old pathologist's eloquence.

Back in the main hall, Devlin turned to him. 'Look here, you really ought to come along tonight. Plenty of time to run home and change.'

'I don't think so,' Rebus said. 'It'll be all shop talk, you said as much yourself.' And besides, he could have added, he didn't own so much as a dinner jacket, never mind the rest.

'But you'd enjoy it,' Devlin persisted. 'Bearing in mind our conversation.'

'Why's that?' Rebus asked.

'The speaker is a priest of the Roman Catholic Church. He's discussing the dichotomy between body and spirit.'

'You've lost me already,' Rebus said.

Devlin just smiled at him. 'I think you pretend to be less able than you are. Probably useful to you in your chosen career.'

Rebus admitted as much with a shrug. 'This speaker,' he said. 'It's not Father Conor Leary, is it?'

Devlin's eyes widened. 'You know him? All the more reason to join us.'

Rebus was thoughtful. 'Maybe just for a drink before dinner.'

Back at St Leonard's, Ellen Wylie was not best pleased.

'Your idea of a "break" differs somewhat from mine,' she complained.

'I bumped into someone,' he said. She didn't say anything else, but he knew she was holding back. Her face remained tense and when she snatched up the receiver it was as though with malice aforethought. She wanted something more from him: a fuller apology maybe, or some words of praise. He held off for a while, then, as she attacked the telephone again, asked:

'Is it because of that press conference?'

'What?' She slammed the receiver back down.

'Ellen,' he said, 'it's not as—'

'Don't you fucking *dare* patronise me!'

He held up his hands in surrender. 'Okay, no more first names. Sorry if it sounded patronising, DS Wylie.'

She glowered at him, then suddenly her face changed, became looser. She forced a smile from somewhere and rubbed at her cheeks with her hands.

'Sorry,' she said.

'Me too.' She looked at him. 'For being out so long. I should have called it in.' He shrugged. 'But now you know my awful secret.'

'Which is?'

'To wring an apology from John Rebus, you first have to violate a telephone.'

This time she laughed. It was far from full-blooded, and retained an edge of hysteria, but she seemed the better for it. They got back to work.

By the end of play, however, they'd achieved next to nothing. He told her not to worry, it was bound to be a rocky start. She shrugged her arms into her coat, asked if he was going for a drink.

'Previous appointment,' he told her. 'Another night though, eh?'

'Sure,' she said. But she didn't sound as if she believed it.

He drank alone: just the one before the walk to Surgeons' Hall; a Laphroaig, with the merest trickle of water to smooth its edges. He chose a pub Ellen Wylie wouldn't know, didn't like the thought of bumping into her after he'd turned her down. He'd need a few drinks in him to tell her she was wrong, that one tongue-tied press conference wasn't the end of her career. Gill Templer was down on her, no question of that, but Gill wasn't stupid enough to let it turn into a feud. Wylie was a good cop, an intelligent detective. She'd get her chance again. If Templer kept knocking her back, she herself would start to look bad.

'Another?' the barman said.

Rebus checked his watch. 'Aye, go on then.'

It suited him, this place. Small and anonymous and hidden away.

There wasn't even a name outside, nothing to identify it. It was on a corner in a back street where only the knowing would find it. Two old regulars in the corner, sitting straight-backed, eyes hypnotised by the far wall. Their dialogue was sparse and guttural. The TV had its sound turned off, but the barman watched it anyway: some American courtroom drama, with lots of pacing about and walls painted grey. Now and then there was a close-up of a woman trying to seem worried. Unwilling to rely on facial expression alone, she wrung her hands as well. Rebus handed over his money and poured the remains of his first drink into its replacement, shaking the drips out. One of the old men coughed, then sniffed. His neighbour said something, and he nodded silent agreement.

'What's going on?' Rebus couldn't help asking the barman.

'Eh?'

'The film, what's happening in it?'

'Same as always,' the barman said. It was as if each day held its identical routine, right down to the drama being played out on the screen.

'How about yourself?' the barman said. 'How's your day been?' The words sounded rusty in his mouth: small talk with the customers not part of the routine.

Rebus thought of possible answers. The potential that some serial killer was on the loose, and had been since the early seventies. A missing girl almost sure to turn up dead. A single, twisted face shared by Siamese twins.

'Ach, you know,' he said at last. The barman nodded agreement, as though it was exactly the answer he'd expected.

Rebus left the bar soon after. A short walk back on to Nicolson Street and the doors of Surgeons' Hall now, as Professor Devlin had predicted, standing open. Guests were already filtering in. Rebus had no invite to show to staff, but an explanation and his warrant card seemed to do the trick. Early arrivals were standing on the first-floor landing, drinks in hand. Rebus made his way upstairs. The banqueting hall was set for dinner, waiters scurrying around making last-minute adjustments. A trestle table just inside the doorway had been covered with a white cloth and an array of glasses and bottles. The serving staff wore black waistcoats over crisp white shirts.

'Yes, sir?'

Rebus considered another whisky. The problem was, once he had three or four under his belt, he wouldn't want to stop. And if he did stop, the thumping head would be nestling in just about the time he was due to meet Jean.

'Just an orange juice, please,' he said.

'Holy Mother, now I can die a peaceful death.'

Rebus turned towards the voice, smiling. 'And why's that?' he asked.

'Because I've seen all there is to see on this glorious planet of ours. Give the man a whisky and don't be niggardly,' he ordered the barman, who stopped halfway through pouring the orange juice. The barman looked at Rebus.

'Just the juice,' he said.

'Well now,' Father Conor Leary said. 'I can smell whisky on your breath, so I know you've not gone TT on me. But for some inexplicable reason you want to stay sober . . .' He grew thoughtful. 'Is the fairer sex involved at all?'

'You're wasted as a priest,' Rebus said.

Father Leary roared with laughter. 'I'd have made a good detective, you mean? And who's to say you're wrong?' Then, to the barman: 'Do you need to ask?' The barman didn't, and was generous with the measure. Leary nodded and took the glass from him.

'*Slainte*!' he said.

'*Slainte*.' Rebus sipped the juice. Conor Leary looked almost too well. When Rebus had last spoken with him, the old priest had been ailing, medicines jostling for space with the Guinness in his fridge.

'It's been a while,' Leary stated.

'You know how it is.'

'I know you young fellows have little enough time to visit the weak and infirm. Too busy with the sins of the flesh.'

'Been a long time since my flesh saw any sins worth reporting.'

'And by God there's plenty of it.' The priest slapped Rebus's stomach.

'Maybe that's the problem,' Rebus admitted. 'You, on the other hand . . .'

'Ah, you were expecting me to wither and die? That's not the way I'd choose. Good food, good drink and damn the consequences.'

Leary wore his clerical collar beneath a grey V-neck jumper. His trousers were navy blue, the shoes polished black. It was true he'd lost some weight, but his stomach and jowls sagged, and his thin silver hair was like spun silk, the eyes sunken beneath a Roman fringe. He held his whisky glass the way a workman would grip a flask.

'We're neither of us dressed for the occasion,' he said, looking around at the array of dinner jackets.

'At least you're in uniform,' Rebus said.

'Just barely,' Leary said. 'I've retired from active service.' Then he winked. 'It happens, you know. We're allowed to down tools. But every time I put the old collar on for something like this, I envision papal emissaries leaping forward, daggers drawn, to slice it from my neck.'

Rebus smiled. 'Like leaving the Foreign Legion?'

'Indeed! Or clipping the pigtail from a retiring Sumo.'

Both men were laughing as Donald Devlin came alongside. 'Glad you felt able to join us,' he told Rebus, before taking the priest's hand. 'I think you were the deciding factor, Father,' he said, explaining about the dinner invitation.

'The offer of which still stands,' he added. 'I'm sure you'll want to hear the Father's speech.' Rebus shook his head.

'Last thing a heathen like John needs is me telling him what's good for him,' Leary said.

'Too right,' Rebus agreed. 'And I'm sure I've heard it all before anyway.' He caught Leary's eye, and in that moment they shared a memory of the long talks in the priest's kitchen, fuelled by trips to the fridge and the drinks cabinet. Conversations about Calvin and criminals, faith and the faithless. Even when Rebus agreed with Leary, he'd try to play devil's advocate, the old priest amused by his stubbornness. Long talks they'd had, and regularly . . . until Rebus had started finding excuses to stay away. Tonight, if Leary asked why, he knew he couldn't give a reason. Maybe it was because the priest had begun to offer him certainties, and Rebus had no time for them. They'd played this game, Leary convinced he could convert 'the heathen'.

'You've got all these questions,' he'd tell Rebus. 'Why won't you let someone supply the answers?'

'Maybe because I prefer questions to answers,' Rebus had replied. And the priest had thrown up his hands in despair, before making another foray to the fridge.

Devlin was asking Leary about the theme of his talk. Rebus could see that Devlin had had a drink or two. He stood rosy-faced with hands in pockets, his smile contented but distant. Rebus was getting his OJ topped up when Gates and Curt appeared, the two pathologists dressed almost identically, making them seem more of a double-act than usual.

'Bloody hell,' Gates said, 'the gang's all here.' He caught the barman's attention. 'Whisky for me, and a glass of tonic water for this fairy here.'

Curt snorted. 'I'm not the only one.' He nodded towards Rebus's drink.

'Ye Gods, John, tell me there's vodka in that,' Gates boomed. Then: 'What the hell are you doing here anyway?' Gates was sweating, his shirt collar constricting his throat. His face had turned almost puce. Curt, as usual, looked completely at ease. He'd gained a couple of pounds but still looked slim, though his face was grey.

'I never see sunlight,' was the excuse he always gave when asked about his pallor. More than one woolly-suit at St Leonard's had taken to calling him Dracula.

'I wanted to catch the pair of you,' Rebus said now.

'The answer's no,' Gates said.

'You don't know what I was going to say.'

'That tone of voice was enough. You're going to ask a favour. You'll say it won't take long. You'll be wrong.'

'Just some old PM results. I need a second opinion.'

'We're rushed off our feet,' Curt said, looking apologetic.

'Whose are they?' Gates asked.

'I haven't got them yet. They're from Glasgow and Nairn. Maybe if you were to put in a request, it would push things along.'

Gates looked around the group. 'See what I mean?'

'University duties, John,' Curt said. 'More students and coursework, fewer people to do the teaching.'

'I appreciate that . . .' Rebus began.

Gates lifted his cummerbund and pointed to the pager hidden there. 'Even tonight, we could get a call, another body to deal with.'

'I don't think you're winning them over,' Leary said, laughing.

Rebus fixed Gates with a hard look. 'I'm serious,' he said.

'So am I. First night off I've had in ages, and you're after one of your famous "favours".'

Rebus decided there was no point pushing it, not when Gates was in a mood. Hard day at the office maybe, but then weren't they all?

Devlin cleared his throat. 'Might I perhaps . . . ?'

Leary slapped Devlin's back. 'There you are, John. A willing victim!'

'I know I've been retired a good few years, but I don't suppose the theory and practice have changed.'

Rebus looked at him. 'Actually,' he said, 'the most recent case is nineteen eighty-two.'

'Donald was still wielding the scalpel in eighty-two,' Gates said. Devlin acknowledged this truth with a small bow.

Rebus hesitated. He wanted someone with a bit of clout, someone like Gates.

'Motion carried,' Curt said, deciding the matter for him.

Siobhan Clarke sat in her living room watching TV. She'd tried cooking herself a proper dinner, but had given up halfway through chopping the red peppers, putting everything in the fridge and pulling a ready-meal from the freezer. The empty container was on the floor in front of her. She sat on the sofa with her legs tucked under her, head resting on one arm. The laptop was on the coffee table, but she'd unhooked her mobile phone. She didn't think Quizmaster would be calling again. She lifted her notepad and stared at the clue. She'd gone through dozens of sheets of paper, working out possible anagrams and meanings. Seven fins high is king . . . and mentions of the queen and 'the bust': it sounded like something from a card game, but the compendium of card games she'd borrowed from the Central Library hadn't been any help. She was just wondering if she should read it through a final time when her phone rang.

'Hello?'

'It's Grant.'

Siobhan turned the sound down on the TV. 'What's up?'

'I think maybe I've cracked it.'

Siobhan swivelled her legs so her feet were on the floor. 'Tell me,' she said.

'I'd rather show you.'

There seemed to be a lot of background noise on the line. She stood up. 'Are you on your mobile?' she asked.

'Yes.'

'Where are you?'

'Parked right outside.'

She walked over to the window and looked out. Sure enough, his Alfa was sitting in the middle of the street. Siobhan smiled. 'Find a parking space then. My buzzer's second from the top.'

By the time she'd taken the dirty dishes through to the sink, Grant was at her intercom. She checked anyway that it was him, then pressed the button to let him into the tenement. She was standing by the open door when he hauled himself up the last few steps.

'Sorry it's so late,' he said, 'but I couldn't keep it to myself.'

'Coffee?' she asked, closing the door after him.

'Thanks. Two sugars.'

They took the coffees into the living room. 'Nice place,' he said.

'I like it.'

He sat down next to her on the sofa and placed his coffee mug on the table. Then he reached into his jacket pocket and pulled out a London A–Z.

'London?' she said.

'I went through all the kings I could think of from history, then anything else to do with the word king.' He held up the book so its back cover was showing. A map of the London Underground.

'King's Cross?' she guessed.

He nodded. 'Take a look.'

She took the book from him. He could hardly sit still in his seat.

'Seven fins high is king,' he said.

'And you think the king is King's Cross?'

He slid across the sofa, his finger tracing the light blue line which went through the station. 'Do you see?' he said.

'No,' she said grimly. 'So you'd better tell me.'

'Go one stop north of King's Cross.'

'Highbury and Islington?'

'And again.'

'Finsbury Park . . . then Seven Sisters.'

'Now backwards,' he said. He was practically bouncing on the spot.

'Don't wet yourself,' she said. Then she looked at the map again. 'Seven Sisters . . . Finsbury Park . . . Highbury and Islington . . . King's Cross.' And saw it. The exact same sequence, but abbreviated. 'Seven . . . Fins . . . High Is . . . King.' She looked at Grant. He was nodding. 'Well done you,' she added, meaning it. Grant leaned over and gave her a hug, which she squirmed out of. Then he leaped from the sofa and clapped his hands together.

'I couldn't believe it myself,' he said. 'The way it just suddenly screamed at me. It's the Victoria Line.'

She nodded, couldn't think of anything to say. It was indeed a section of London Underground's Victoria Line.

'But what does it mean?' she said at last.

He sat down again, leaning forward, elbows on knees. 'That's what we have to work out next.'

She slid across the sofa a little, making some space between them, then lifted her pad and read from it. '"This queen dines well before the bust."' She looked at him, but he just shrugged.

'Could the answer be in London?' she asked.

'I don't know,' he said. 'Buckingham Palace? Queen's Park Rangers?' He shrugged. 'Could be London.'

'All these Underground stops . . . what do they mean?'

'They're all on the Victoria Line,' was all he could think to say. Then they stared at one another.

'Queen Victoria,' they said in unison.

Siobhan had a London guidebook, bought for a weekend away which she'd never taken. It took her a while to find it. Meantime Grant booted up the computer and did a search on the Internet.

'Could be the name of a pub,' he suggested. 'Like in *EastEnders*.'

'Yes,' she said, busy reading. 'Or the Victoria and Albert Museum.'

'Not forgetting Victoria Station – also on the Victoria Line. There's a coach station there too. Worst cafeteria in Britain.'

'You're speaking from experience?'

'I bussed it down there a few weekends in my teens. Didn't like it.' He was scrolling down some text.

'Didn't like the bus or didn't like London?'

'Both, I suppose. "Bust" couldn't mean a drug bust, could it?'

'Maybe. Or some stock-market crash. There was one not that long back, wasn't there? Black Monday?'

He nodded.

'Still, more likely it's a statue,' she said. 'Maybe of Queen Victoria, with a restaurant in front of it.'

They worked in silence for a while after that, until Siobhan's eyes started to hurt and she got up to make more coffee.

'Two sugars,' Grant said.

'I remember.' She looked at him, hunched over the computer screen, one knee pumping away. She wanted to say something about the hug . . . warn him off somehow . . . but she knew she'd missed her chance.

Bringing the mugs back through from the kitchen, she asked if he'd found anything.

'Tourist sites,' he said. He took the mug from her with a nod of thanks.

'Why London?' she asked.

'What do you mean?' His eyes were still on the screen.

'I mean, why not somewhere closer to home?'

'Could be Quizmaster lives in London. We don't know, do we?'

'No.'

'And who's to say Flip Balfour was the only one playing the game? Something like this, my bet is there's a website somewhere – or was.

Anyone wanting to join in could go there. They wouldn't all come from Scotland.'

She nodded. 'I'm just wondering . . . was Flip bright enough to solve this clue?'

'Obviously, or she wouldn't have gone on to the next level.'

'But maybe this is a new game,' she said. He turned his head to look at her. 'Maybe it's just for us.'

'If we ever meet the bastard, I'll be sure to ask him.'

A further half-hour later, Grant was working his way through a list of London restaurants. 'You wouldn't believe how many Victoria Roads and Victoria Streets there are in this bloody place, and half of them have restaurants on them.'

He leaned back, straightening his spine. The energy seemed to have leached out of him.

'And that's before we start looking at pubs.' Siobhan ran her fingers through her hair, pulling it back tight from her forehead. 'It's too . . .'

'What?'

'The first bit of the clue was clever. But this . . . this is just looking at lists. Does he expect us to go to London, visit every chip shop and café in the hope of finding Queen Victoria's bust?'

'He can whistle if he does.' Grant's chuckle was empty of humour.

Siobhan looked at the book of card games. She'd spent a couple of hours flicking through it, and all the time looking for the wrong thing in the wrong place. She'd only just got to the library in time. Five minutes till closing. Left her car on Victoria Street and prayed she didn't get a ticket . . .

'Victoria Street?' she said out loud.

'Take your pick, there are dozens of the buggers.'

'And some of them are right here,' she told him.

He looked up. 'Yes,' he said, 'they are.'

He went down to his car, brought back an Ordnance Survey atlas of East-Central Scotland, opened it at the index and ran his finger down the list.

'Victoria Gardens . . . there's a Victoria Hospital in Kirkcaldy . . . Victoria Street and Victoria Terrace in Edinburgh.' He looked at her. 'What do you think?'

'I think there are a couple of restaurants in Victoria Street.'

'Any statues?'

'Not on the outside.'

He checked his watch. 'They won't be open at this hour, will they?'

She shook her head. 'First thing tomorrow,' she said. 'Breakfast's on me.'

Rebus and Jean sat in the Palm Court. She was drinking a long vodka, while he nursed a ten-year-old Macallan. The waiter had brought a little glass jug of water, but Rebus hadn't disturbed it. He hadn't been inside the Balmoral Hotel in years. Back then it had been the North

British. The old place had changed a bit in the interim. Not that Jean seemed interested in her surroundings, not now she'd heard Rebus's story.

'So they might all have been murdered?' she said, her face pale. The lights in the lounge had been turned low, and a pianist was playing. Rebus kept recognising snatches of tunes; he doubted Jean had taken in any of them.

'It's possible,' he admitted.

'But you're basing all of it on the dolls?'

Her eyes met his and he nodded. 'Maybe I'm reading too much into it,' he said. 'But it needs to be investigated.'

'Where on earth will you start?'

'We're waiting for the original case notes.' He paused. 'What's the matter?'

There were tears in her eyes. She sniffed and searched her bag for a handkerchief. 'It's just the idea of it. All this time, I had those cuttings . . . Maybe if I'd given them to the police sooner . . .'

'Jean.' He took her hand. 'All you had were stories about dolls in coffins.'

'I suppose so,' she said.

'Meantime, maybe you can help.'

She hadn't found a handkerchief. Picked up her cocktail napkin and dabbed at her eyes with it. 'How?' she said.

'This whole thing goes back as far as nineteen seventy-two. I need to know who back then might have shown an interest in the Arthur's Seat exhibits. Can you do some digging for me?'

'Of course.'

He gave her hand another squeeze. 'Thanks.'

She gave a half-hearted smile and picked up her drink. The ice rattled as she finished it.

'Another?' he said.

She shook her head, looked around her. 'I get the feeling this isn't your kind of place.'

'Oh? And what is?'

'I think you feel more comfortable in small, smoky bars filled with disappointed men.'

There was a smile on her face. Rebus nodded slowly.

'You catch on quick,' he said.

Her smile faded as she looked around again. 'I was here just last week, such a happy occasion . . . It seems like a long time ago.'

'What was the occasion?'

'Gill's promotion. Do you think she's coping?'

'Gill's Gill. She'll tough it out.' He paused. 'Speaking of toughing it out, is that reporter still giving you grief?'

She managed a thin smile. 'He's persistent. Wants to know what "others" I was talking about in Bev Dodds's kitchen. That was my fault, sorry.' She seemed to have regained some composure. 'I should be getting back. I can probably find a taxi if . . .'

'I said I'd run you home.' He signalled for their waitress to bring the bill.

He'd parked the Saab on North Bridge. There was a cold wind blowing, but Jean stopped to look at the view: the Scott Monument, the Castle, and Ramsay Gardens.

'Such a beautiful city,' she said. Rebus tried to agree. He hardly saw it any more. To him, Edinburgh had become a state of mind, a juggling of criminal thoughts and baser instincts. He liked its size, its compactness. He liked its bars. But its outward show had ceased to impress him a long time ago. Jean wrapped her coat tightly around her. 'Everywhere you look, there's some story, some little piece of history.' She looked at him and he nodded agreement, but he was remembering all the suicides he'd dealt with, people who'd jumped from North Bridge maybe because they couldn't see the same city Jean did.

'I never tire of this view,' she said, turning back towards the car. He nodded again, disingenuously. To him, it wasn't a view at all. It was a crime scene waiting to happen.

When he drove off, she asked if they could have some music. He switched on the cassette-player and the car filled to bursting with Hawkwind's *In Search of Space*.

'Sorry,' he said, ejecting the tape. She found cassette boxes in the glove compartment. Hendrix, Cream and the Stones. 'Probably not your style,' he said.

She waved the Hendrix at him. 'You haven't got *Electric Ladyland* by any chance?'

Rebus looked at her and smiled.

Hendrix was the soundtrack for their drive to Portobello.

'So what made you a policeman?' she asked at one point.

'Is it such a strange career choice?'

'That doesn't answer my question.'

'True.' He glanced at her and smiled. She took the hint, nodding her understanding. Then she concentrated on the music.

Portobello was on Rebus's short-list come the move from Arden Street. It had a beach, and a main street of small local shops. At one time, it had been a fairly grand location, a place the gentry flocked to for reviving air and healthy doses of chill seawater. It wasn't quite so grand now, but the housing market dictated its rebirth. Those who couldn't afford the smart homes in the city centre were moving to 'Porty', which still had big Georgian houses, but without the premium. Jean had a house on a narrow street near the promenade. 'You own the whole thing?' he said, peering through the windscreen.

'I bought it years back. Porty wasn't so fashionable.' She hesitated. 'Do you want to come in for coffee this time?'

Their eyes met. His were questioning; hers tentative. Then their faces collapsed into smiles.

'I'd love one,' he said. Just as he was turning off the ignition, his mobile started ringing.

'I just thought you'd want to know,' Donald Devlin said. His voice trembled slightly, body likewise.

Rebus nodded. They were standing just inside the imposing front doors of Surgeons' Hall. There were people upstairs, but speaking in hushed tones. Outside, one of the grey transit vans from the mortuary was waiting, a police car standing beside it, roof-lights flashing, turning the front of the building blue every couple of seconds.

'What happened?' Rebus asked.

'Heart attack, it looks like. People were enjoying a post-prandial brandy, leaning against the railing.' Devlin pointed upwards. 'He suddenly went very pale, leaned over the rail. They thought he was going to be sick. But he just slumped, and his weight took him over.'

Rebus looked down at the marble floor. There was a smear of blood which would need cleaning. Men stood on the periphery, some outside on the lawns. They smoked and spoke of the awful shock. When Rebus looked back at Devlin, the old man seemed to be studying him, as if he were some specimen in a jar.

'Are you all right?' Devlin asked, watching as Rebus nodded. 'The two of you were pretty close, I gather.'

Rebus didn't answer. Sandy Gates walked up, mopping his face with what looked like a napkin swiped from the dining room.

'Bloody awful,' was all he said. 'Probably have to be an autopsy, too.'

The body was being stretchered away. A blanket covered the body-bag. Rebus resisted the temptation to stop the attendants and pull the zip down. He wanted his last memories of Conor Leary to be of the lively man he'd shared that drink with.

'He'd just made a fascinating speech,' Devlin said. 'A sort of ecumenical history of the human body. Everything from the sacrament to Jack the Ripper as haruspex.'

'As what?'

'Someone who foretells the truth by looking at the entrails of animals.'

Gates belched. 'Half of it was above my head,' he said.

'And the other half you slept through, Sandy,' Devlin commented with a smile. 'He did the whole thing without notes,' he added admiringly. Then he looked up at the first-floor landing again. 'The fall of man, that was his starting point.' He rummaged in his pocket for a handkerchief.

'Here,' said Gates, handing over the napkin. Devlin blew his nose loudly.

'The fall of man, and then he fell,' Devlin said. 'Perhaps Stevenson was right.'

'What about?'

'He called Edinburgh a "precipitous city". Maybe vertigo is in the nature of the place . . .'

Rebus thought he knew what Devlin meant. Precipitous city . . . each and every one of its inhabitants falling slowly, almost imperceptibly . . .

'Bloody awful meal it was, too,' Gates was saying, as though he'd have preferred to lose Conor Leary after a veritable feast. Rebus didn't doubt Conor would have felt the same.

Outside, Dr Curt was one of the smokers. Rebus joined him.

'I tried phoning you,' Curt said, 'but you were already on your way.'

'Professor Devlin caught me.'

'He said as much. I think he sensed some bond between you and Conor.' Rebus just nodded slowly. 'He'd been pretty ill, you know,' Curt continued, in that dry voice that always sounded like dictation. 'After you'd left us this evening, he talked about you.'

Rebus cleared his throat. 'What did he say?'

'He said he sometimes thought of you as a penance.' Curt flicked ash into the air. A flash of blue lit his face for a moment. 'He was laughing as he said it.'

'He was a friend,' Rebus said. Inwardly he added, *and I let him go*. So many friendships he'd pushed away, preferring his own company, the chair by the window in the darkened room. He pretended sometimes that he was doing them all a favour. People he'd let get close to him in the past, they had a habit of getting hurt, sometimes even killed. But it wasn't that. It wasn't that. He wondered about Jean, and where it might be leading. Was he ready to share himself with someone else? Ready to let her into his secrets, his darkness? He still wasn't sure. Those conversations with Conor Leary, they'd been like confessionals. He'd probably revealed more of himself to the priest than to anyone before him: wife, daughter, lovers. And now he was gone . . . up to heaven maybe, though he'd cause havoc there, no doubt about it. He'd be in dispute with the angels, looking for Guinness and a good argument.

'You okay, John?' Curt reached out a hand and touched his shoulder.

Rebus shook his head slowly, eyes squeezed shut. Curt didn't make it out the first time, so Rebus had to repeat what he said next:

'I don't believe in heaven.'

That was the horror of it. This life was the only one you got. No redemption afterwards, no chance of wiping the slate clean and starting over.

'It's all right,' Curt was saying, clearly unused to the role of comforter, the hand which touched Rebus's arm more used to easing human organs from a gaping wound. 'You'll be all right.'

'Will I?' Rebus said. 'Then there's no justice in the world.'

'You'd know more about that than I would.'

'Oh, I know all right.' Rebus took a deep breath, let it out. There was sweat beneath his shirt, the night air chilling him. 'I'll be okay,' he said quietly.

'Of course you will.' Curt finished his cigarette and pushed it into the grass with his heel. 'Like Conor said: despite rumours to the contrary, you're on the side of the angels.' He took his hand from Rebus's arm. 'Whether you like it or not.'

Donald Devlin came bustling up. 'Should I order some taxis, do you think?'

Curt looked at him. 'What does Sandy say?'

Devlin took off his glasses, made a show of wiping them. 'Told me not to be so "bloody pragmatic".' He slipped the glasses on again.

'I've got the car,' Rebus said.

'You're okay to drive?' Devlin asked.

'It's not like I've just lost my fucking dad!' Rebus exploded. Then he started to apologise.

'An emotional time for all of us,' Devlin said, waving the apology aside. Then he took his glasses off and started polishing them again, as if the world could never reveal itself too vividly for him.

7

Tuesday at eleven a.m., Siobhan Clarke and Grant Hood started working Victoria Street. They drove up George IV Bridge, forgetting that Victoria Street was one-way. Grant cursed the No Entry sign and rejoined the crawl of traffic heading for the lights at the junction with Lawnmarket.

'Just park kerbside,' Siobhan said. He shook his head. 'Why not?'

'Traffic's hopeless as it is. No use making things worse.'

She laughed. 'Do you always play by the rules, Grant?'

He glanced at her. 'What do you mean?'

'Nothing.'

He didn't say anything, just flipped on the left-turn signal as they stopped three cars back from the lights. Siobhan couldn't help but smile. He had the boy-racer car, but it was all a front, behind which sat a polite wee laddie.

'Going out with anyone just now?' she asked as the lights changed.

He considered his answer. 'Not just at the moment,' he said at last.

'For a while there, I thought maybe you and Ellen Wylie . . .'

'We worked one bloody case together!' he objected.

'Okay, okay. It's just that the pair of you seemed to hit it off.'

'We got along.'

'That's what I mean. So where was the problem?'

His face had reddened. 'What do you mean?'

'I just wondered if the difference in rank was maybe a factor. Some men can't handle it.'

'Because she's a DS and I'm a DC?'

'Yes.'

'The answer's no. Never even thought of it.'

They'd reached the roundabout outside The Hub. The right fork led to the Castle, but they took the left.

'Where are we going?' Siobhan asked.

'I'll take a left along West Port. With any luck we'll find a space in the Grassmarket.'

'And I bet you'll put money in the meter, too.'

'Unless you want the honour.'

She snorted. 'I walk on the wild side, kid,' she said.

They found a parking bay, and Grant dropped a couple of coins into the machine, peeling back the ticket and sticking it to the inside of his windscreen.

'Half an hour long enough?' he asked.

She shrugged. 'Depends what we find.'

They walked past the Last Drop pub, named for the fact that criminals had swung from Grassmarket's scaffold at one time in the city's history. Victoria Street was a steep curve back up to George IV Bridge, lined with bars and gift shops. On the far side of the street, pubs and clubs seemed to predominate. One place doubled as a Cuban bar and restaurant.

'What do you reckon?' Siobhan asked.

'Not too many statues, I wouldn't have thought, unless there's one of Castro.'

They walked the length of the street, then doubled back. Three restaurants this side, along with a cheesemonger and a shop selling nothing but brushes and string. Pierre Victoire was the first stop. Peering through the window, Siobhan could see that it was a fairly empty space with little in the way of decoration. They went in anyway, not bothering to introduce themselves. Ten seconds later they were back on the pavement.

'One down, two to go,' Grant said. He didn't sound hopeful.

Next was a place called the Grain Store, through a doorway and up a flight of stairs. The place was being readied for lunchtime trade. There were no statues.

As they descended to the street, Siobhan repeated the clue. '"This queen dines well before the bust."' She shook her head slowly. 'Maybe we've got it wrong.'

'Then the only thing we can do is send another e-mail, appeal to Quizmaster for help.'

'I don't think he's the type.'

Grant shrugged. 'Next stop, can we at least have a coffee? I skipped breakfast this morning.'

Siobhan tutted. 'What would your mum say?'

'She'd say I slept in. Then I'd tell her it's because I was up half the night trying to solve this bloody puzzle.' He paused. 'And that someone had promised me breakfast would be on them . . .'

Restaurant Bleu was their final call. It promised 'world cuisine' but had a traditional feel as they walked through the door: old varnished wood, the small window doing little to illuminate the cramped interior. Siobhan looked around, but there wasn't so much as a vase of flowers.

She turned to Grant, who pointed towards a winding staircase. 'There's an upstairs.'

'Can I help?' the assistant said.

'In a minute,' Grant assured her. He followed Siobhan up the stairs. One small room led to another. As Siobhan entered this second chamber, she gave a sigh. Grant, following her, thought the worst. Then he heard her say, 'Bingo,' in the same instant as he saw the bust. It was Queen Victoria, two and a half feet high, in black marble.

'Bloody hell,' he said, grinning. 'We cracked it!'

He looked ready to hug her, but she moved away towards the bust. It sat on a low plinth, pillars either side and sandwiched by tables. Siobhan looked all around, but couldn't see anything.

'I'll tip it,' Grant said. He took hold of Victoria by her head-dress and eased her from the plinth.

'Excuse me,' a voice said behind them. 'Is something the matter?'

Siobhan slid her hand under the bust and drew out a folded sheet of paper. She beamed at Grant, who turned towards the waitress.

'Two teas, please,' he instructed her.

'And two sugars in his,' Siobhan added.

They sat down at the nearest table. Siobhan held the note by one corner. 'Think we'd get any prints?' she asked.

'Worth a try.'

She got up and walked over to a cutlery tray in the corner, came back with a knife and fork. The waitress nearly dropped their crockery when she saw the customer attempting, as she thought, to dine on a sheet of paper.

Grant took the cups from the waitress and thanked her. Then he turned back to Siobhan. 'What does it say?'

But Siobhan looked up at the waitress. 'We found this under there,' she said, pointing to the bust. The waitress nodded. 'Any idea how it could have got there?' The waitress shook her head. She had the look of a small, frightened animal. Grant sought to reassure her.

'We're the police,' he said.

'Any chance of talking to the manager?' Siobhan added.

When the waitress had retreated, Grant repeated his earlier question.

'See for yourself,' Siobhan said, using the knife and fork to turn the sheet of paper in his direction.

B4 Scots Law sounds dear.

'Is that it?' he said.

'Your eyes are as good as mine.'

He reached up to scratch his head. 'Not much to go on, is it?'

'We didn't have much to go on last time.'

'We had more than this.'

She watched him stir sugar into his tea. 'If Quizmaster placed this clue here . . .'

'He's a local?' Grant guessed

'Either that or someone local is helping him.'

'He knows this restaurant,' Grant said, looking around. 'Not everyone who ventures in would bother coming upstairs.'

'You think he might be a regular?'

Grant shrugged. 'Look at what's nearby, on George IV Bridge. The

Central Library and the National Library. Academics and bookworms are great ones for puzzles.'

'That's a good point. The Museum's not far away either.'

'And the law courts . . . and the parliament . . .' He smiled. 'Just for a second there I thought we might be narrowing things down.'

'Maybe we are,' she said, lifting her cup as though to make a toast. 'Here's to us anyway for solving the first clue.'

'How many more till we get to Hellbank?'

Siobhan grew thoughtful. 'That's up to Quizmaster, I suppose. He told me it was the fourth stage. I'll send an e-mail when we get back, just to let him know.' She placed the sheet of paper in an evidence bag. Grant was studying the clue again. 'First thoughts?' she asked.

'I was remembering a bit of graffiti from primary school. It was in the boys' toilets.' He wrote it down on the paper serviette.

LOLO
AQIC
I82Q
B4IP

Siobhan read it aloud and smiled. 'Be-fore I pee,' she repeated. 'You think maybe that's what B4 means?'

He shrugged. 'Could be part of an address.'

'Or a coordinate . . . ?'

He looked at her. 'From a map?'

'But which one?'

'Maybe that's what the rest of the clue tells us. How's your Scots Law?'

'The exams were a while back.'

'Ditto. Is there some Latin word for "dear", maybe something to do with the law?'

'There's always the library,' she suggested. 'With a big bookshop just past it.'

He checked his watch. 'I'll go put more money in the meter,' he said.

Rebus was at his desk, five sheets of paper spread out in front of him. He'd shifted everything else on to the floor: files, memos, the lot. The office was quiet: most of the shift had headed to Gayfield Square for a briefing. They wouldn't thank him for the obstacle course he'd constructed in their absence. His computer monitor and keyboard now sat in the centre aisle between the rows of desks, just next to his multi-tiered in-tray.

And on his desk, five lives. Five victims, possibly. Caroline Farmer the youngest. Just sixteen when she'd disappeared. He'd finally got through to her mother this morning. Not an easy call to make.

'Oh my God, don't tell me there's news?' That sudden blooming of hope, wizened by his response. But he'd found out what he had to.

Caroline had never come back. There had been unconfirmed sightings in the early days, when her photo was in all the papers. But nothing since.

'We moved last year,' her mother said. 'It meant emptying her bedroom . . .'

But for the quarter-century before that, Rebus surmised, Caroline's room had been waiting for her: same posters on the walls, same early-seventies teenage girl's clothes neatly folded in the chest of drawers.

'Back at the time, they seemed to think we'd done something to her,' the mother continued. 'I mean, her own *family*.'

Rebus didn't like to say: all too often it's a father or uncle or cousin.

'Then they started picking on Ronnie.'

'Caroline's boyfriend?' Rebus guessed.

'Yes. Just a laddie.'

'They'd split up, hadn't they?'

'You know what teenagers are like.' It was as though she were talking about events from a week or two back. Rebus didn't doubt that the memories stayed fresh, always ready to torment her waking hours, maybe even the sleeping ones too.

'But he was ruled out?'

'They gave up on him, yes. But he wasn't the same after that, family moved from the area. He wrote to me for a few years . . .'

'Mrs Farmer—'

'It's Ms Colquhoun now. Joe left me.'

'I'm sorry.'

'I wasn't.'

'Did it have . . . ?' He stopped. 'Sorry, none of my business.'

'He never talked much about it,' was all she said. Rebus wondered if Caroline's father had been able to let her go, in a way her mother hadn't.

'This may seem a strange question, Ms Colquhoun, but did Dunfermline Glen have any significance for Caroline?'

'I . . . I'm not sure what you mean.'

'Me neither. It's just that something's come to our attention, and we're wondering if it might tie in with your daughter's disappearance.'

'What is it?'

He didn't suppose she'd take the coffin in the Glen as good news; resorted instead to the old cliché: 'I'm not at liberty to disclose that at present.'

There was silence on the line for a few seconds. 'She liked to walk in the Glen.'

'By herself?'

'When she felt like it.' Her voice caught. 'Is it something you've found?'

'Not the way you think, Ms Colquhoun.'

'You've dug her up, haven't you?'

'Not at all.'

'What then?' she shrieked.

'I'm not at lib—'

She'd put the phone down. He stared at the mouthpiece, then did the same.

In the men's toilets he splashed water on his face. His eyes were grey and puffy. Last night, he'd left Surgeons' Hall and driven to Portobello, parking outside Jean's house. Her lights had been off. He'd got as far as opening the car door, but had stopped. What was he planning to say to her? What was it he wanted? He'd closed the door again as quietly as he could, and just sat there, engine and headlamps off, Hendrix playing quietly: 'The Burning of the Midnight Lamp'.

Back at his desk, one of the station's civvy staff had just arrived with a large cardboard document-box. Rebus lifted the top off and peered inside. The box was actually not quite half full. He pulled out the topmost folder and examined the typed label: Paula Jennifer Gearing (née Mathieson); d.o.b. – 10.4.50; d.o.d. – 6.7.77. The Nairn drowning. Rebus sat down, pulled in his chair and started to read. About twenty minutes in, as he was scribbling another note on a lined A4 pad, Ellen Wylie arrived.

'Sorry I'm late,' she said, shedding her coat.

'We must have different ideas of a start-time,' he said. Remembering what she'd said yesterday, she reddened, but when she glanced in his direction he was smiling.

'What have you got?' she asked.

'Our friends in the north came good.'

'Paula Gearing?'

Rebus nodded. 'She was twenty-seven. Married four years to a husband who worked on a North Sea oil platform. Nice bungalow on the outskirts of town. No kids. She had a part-time job in a newsagent's . . . probably for company more than financial necessity.'

Wylie came over to his desk. 'Was foul play ruled out?'

Rebus tapped his notes. 'Nobody could ever explain it, according to what I've read so far. She didn't seem suicidal. Doesn't help that they've no idea whereabouts on the coast she actually entered the water.'

'Pathology report?'

'It's in here. Can you get on to Donald Devlin, see if he can spare us some time?'

'Professor Devlin?'

'He's the person I bumped into yesterday. He's agreed to study the autopsies for us.' He didn't say anything about the actual circumstances of Devlin's involvement, how Gates and Curt had turned him down. 'His number will be on file,' Rebus said. 'He's one of Philippa Balfour's neighbours.'

'I know. Have you seen this morning's paper?'

'No.'

She fetched it from her bag, opened it to one of the inside pages.

A photofit: the man Devlin had seen outside the tenement on the days preceding Philippa's disappearance.

'Could be anybody,' Rebus said.

Wylie nodded agreement. Short dark hair, straight nose, narrowed eyes and a thin line of a mouth. 'We're getting desperate, aren't we?' she said.

It was Rebus's turn to nod. Releasing the photofit to the media, especially one as clearly generalised as this, was an act of desperation. 'Get on to Devlin,' he said.

'Yes, sir.'

She took the newspaper with her, sat down at a spare desk and gave her head a little shake, as if clearing the cobwebs. Then she picked up the telephone, preparing to make the first call of another long day.

Rebus went back to his reading, but not for long. A name leaped out at him, the name of one of the police officers involved in the Nairn inquiry.

A detective inspector with the surname Watson.

The Farmer.

'Sorry to bother you, sir.'

The Farmer smiled, slapped a hand on Rebus's back. 'You don't have to call me "sir" any more, John.'

He gestured for Rebus to precede him down the hall. It was a farmhouse conversion just south of the bypass. The interior walls were painted a pale green and the furniture was fifties and sixties vintage. A wall had been knocked through so that the kitchen was separated from the living room only by a breakfast bar and dining area. The dining table gleamed. The kitchen's work surfaces were similarly clean, and the hob was spotless, not a dish or dirty pot in sight.

'Fancy a cuppa?' the Farmer asked.

'Some tea would go down.'

The Farmer chuckled. 'My coffee always scared you off, didn't it?'

'You got better at it towards the end.'

'Sit yourself down. I'll not be long.'

But Rebus made a circuit of the living room. Glass-fronted cabinets with china and ornaments behind. Framed photos of family. Rebus recognised a couple which until recently had graced the Farmer's office. The carpet had been vacuumed, the mirror and TV showed no signs of dust. Rebus walked over to the french doors and gazed out at a short expanse of garden which ended with a steep grassy bank.

'Maid been in today, has she?' he called.

The Farmer chuckled again, setting a tea-tray out on the worktop. 'I enjoy a bit of housework,' he called. 'Ever since Arlene passed away.'

Rebus turned, looked back at the framed photos. The Farmer and his wife at someone's wedding, and on some foreign beach, and with a gathering of grandchildren. The Farmer beaming, mouth always slightly open. His wife a little more reserved, maybe a foot shorter than him and half his weight. She'd died a few years back.

'Maybe it's my way of remembering her,' the Farmer said.

Rebus nodded: not letting go. He wondered if her clothes were still in the wardrobe, her jewellery in a box on the dressing table . . .

'How's Gill settling in?'

Rebus moved towards the kitchen. 'She's off to a flyer,' he said. 'Ordered me to take a medical, and got on the wrong side of Ellen Wylie.'

'I saw that news conference,' the Farmer admitted, studying the tray to make sure he'd not forgotten anything. 'Gill didn't give Ellen time to find her feet.'

'Purposely so,' Rebus added.

'Perhaps.'

'It's funny, not having you around, sir.' Rebus laid stress on the last word. The Farmer smiled.

'Thanks for that, John.' He walked over to the kettle, which was beginning to boil. 'All the same, I'm assuming this isn't a purely sentimental visit.'

'No. It's about a case you worked on in Nairn.'

'Nairn?' The Farmer raised an eyebrow. 'That's twenty-odd years ago. I went up there from West Lothian. I was based in Inverness.'

'Yes, but you went to Nairn to look into a drowning.'

The Farmer was thoughtful. 'Oh yes,' he said at last. 'What was her name?'

'Paula Gearing.'

'Gearing, that's right.' He snapped his fingers, keen not to seem forgetful. 'But it was cut and dried, wasn't it . . . if you'll pardon the expression.'

'I'm not so sure, sir.' Rebus watched the Farmer pour water into the teapot.

'Well, let's take this lot through to the lounge, and you can tell me all about it.'

So Rebus told the story again: the doll in Falls, then the Arthur's Seat mystery, and the cluster of drownings and disappearances from 1972 to '95. He'd brought the cuttings with him, and the Farmer studied them intently.

'I didn't even know about the doll on Nairn beach,' he admitted. 'I was back in Inverness by then. As far as I was concerned, the Gearing death was as closed as it was ever likely to get.'

'Nobody made the connection at the time. Paula's body had been washed ashore four miles out of town. If anyone thought anything of it, they probably took it as some kind of memorial to her.' He paused. 'Gill's not convinced there's a connection.'

The Farmer nodded. 'She's thinking of how it would play in a court of law. Everything you've got here is circumstantial.'

'I know.'

'All the same . . .' The Farmer leaned back. 'It's quite a set of circumstances.'

Rebus's shoulders relaxed. The Farmer seemed to notice, and smiled. 'Bad timing, isn't it, John? I manage to go into retirement just before you convince me that you may have stumbled upon something.'

'Maybe you could have a word with Gill, convince her likewise.'

The Farmer shook his head. 'I don't think she'd listen. She's in charge now . . . she knows fine well my usefulness is over.'

'That's a bit harsh.'

The Farmer looked at him. 'But you know it's true all the same. She's the one you have to convince, not an old man sitting in his slippers.'

'You're barely ten years older than me.'

'As I hope you'll live to find, John, your sixties are very different from your fifties. Maybe that medical wouldn't be such a bad idea, eh?'

'Even if I already know what he'll say?' Rebus lifted his cup and finished the tea.

The Farmer had picked up the Nairn clipping again. 'What do you want me to do?'

'You said the case was cut and dried. Maybe you could think about that, see if anything at the time jarred – anything at all, no matter how small or seemingly incidental.' He paused. 'I was also going to ask if you knew what had happened to the doll.'

'But now you know the doll's come as news to me.'

Rebus nodded.

'You want all five dolls, don't you?' the Farmer asked.

Rebus admitted as much. 'It might be the only way to prove they're connected.'

'Meaning whoever left that first one, back in nineteen seventy-two, also left one for Philippa Balfour?'

Rebus nodded again.

'If anyone can do it, John, you can. I've always had confidence in your sheer pig-headedness and inability to listen to your senior officers.'

Rebus placed his cup back on its saucer. 'I'll take that as a compliment,' he said. Looking around the room again, preparing to rise and make his farewells, he was struck by something. This house was the only thing the Farmer controlled now. He brought order to it the way he'd controlled St Leonard's. And if he ever lost the will power or the ability to keep it in shape, he'd curl up his toes and die.

'This is hopeless,' Siobhan Clarke said.

They'd spent the best part of three hours in the Central Library, followed by nearly fifty quid at a bookshop, buying maps and touring guides of Scotland. Now they were in the Elephant House coffee-shop, having commandeered a table meant for six. It was right below the window at the back of the café, and Grant Hood was staring out at the view of Greyfriars Churchyard and the Castle.

Siobhan looked at him. 'Have you switched off?'

He kept his eyes on the view. 'You have to sometimes.'

'Well, thanks for your support.' It came out more huffily than she'd expected.

'Best thing you can do,' he went on, ignoring her tone. 'There are days when I get stuck with the crossword. I don't go knocking my brains out. I just put it to one side and pick it up again later. And often I find that one or two answers come to me straight away. Thing is,' now he turned towards her, 'you fix your mind on a certain track, until eventually you can't see all the alternatives.' He got up, walked over to where the café kept its newspapers, and came back with that day's *Scotsman*. 'Peter Bee,' he said, folding it so the crossword on the back page was uppermost. 'He's cryptic, but doesn't depend on anagrams the way some of the others do.'

He handed her the paper and she saw that Peter Bee was the name of the crossword's compiler.

'Twelve across,' Grant said, 'he had me looking for the name of an old Roman weapon. But all it was in the end was an anagram.'

'Very interesting,' Siobhan said, tossing the paper on to the table, where it covered the half-dozen map-books.

'I'm just trying to explain that sometimes you have to clear your mind for a while, start again from scratch.'

She glared at him. 'Are you saying we've just wasted half the day?'

He shrugged.

'Well, thanks very much!' She pulled herself out of her chair and stomped off to the toilets. Inside, she stood leaning against the wash-bowl, staring down at its bright white surface. The sod was, she knew Grant was right. But she couldn't let go the way he could. She'd wanted to play the game, and now it had drawn her in. She wondered if Flip Balfour had become obsessed in much the same way. If she'd got stuck, would she have asked for help? Siobhan reminded herself that she had yet to ask any of Flip's friends or family about the game. No one had mentioned it in the dozens of interviews, but then why would they? Maybe to them it had just been a bit of fun, a computer game. Nothing to get worked up about . . .

Gill Templer had offered her the Press Liaison job, but only after engineering the ritual humiliation of Ellen Wylie. It would be nice to feel she'd rejected the offer out of a sense of solidarity with Wylie, but that had had nothing to do with it. Siobhan herself feared that it was more the influence of John Rebus. She'd worked beside him for several years now, coming to understand his strengths as well as his faults. And when it came down to it, like a lot of other officers she preferred the maverick approach, and wished she could be like that. But the force itself had other ideas. There could be room for only one Rebus, and meantime advancement was hers for the taking. Okay, so it would land her squarely in Gill Templer's camp: she'd follow orders, back her boss up, never take risks. And she would be safe, would continue to rise through the ranks . . . Detective Inspector, then maybe DCI by the time she was forty. She saw now that Gill had invited her to drinks and dinner that evening to show her how it was done. You cultivated the right friends, you treated them well. You were patient, and the rewards came. One lesson for Ellen Wylie, and a very different one for her.

Back out in the café, she watched as Grant Hood completed the crossword and threw the paper back down, leaning back in his seat and nonchalantly slipping his pen into his pocket. He was trying hard not to look at the table next to him, where a lone female coffee-drinker had been appraising his performance over the top of her paperback book.

Siobhan started forwards. 'Thought you'd already done that one?' she said, nodding towards the *Scotsman*.

'Easier the second time,' he answered in a voice which, had it been any more of an undertone, would have leapt up and broken into the chorus of 'Teenage Kicks'. 'Why are you grinning like that?'

The woman had gone back to her book. It was something by Muriel Spark. 'I was just remembering an old song,' Siobhan said.

Grant looked at her, but she wasn't about to enlighten him, so he reached a hand out and touched the crossword. 'Know what a homonym is?'

'No, but it sounds rude.'

'It's when a word sounds like another word. Crosswords use them all the time. There's even one in today's, and second time around it got me thinking.'

'Thinking what?'

'About our latest clue. "Sounds dear": we were thinking of "dear" meaning expensive or cherished, right?'

Siobhan nodded.

'But it could be a homonym, signalled by "sounds".'

'I'm not following.' But she'd tucked one leg beneath her and leaned forward, interested.

'It could be telling us that the word we want isn't d-e-a-r but d-e-e-r.'

She frowned. 'So we end up with "B4 Scots Law deer"? Is it just me, or does that actually make less sense than before?'

He shrugged, turned his attention to the window again. 'If you say so.'

She slapped at his leg. 'Don't be like that.'

'You think you're the only one who can take a moody?'

'I'm sorry.'

He looked at her. She was smiling again. 'That's better,' he said. 'Now . . . wasn't there some story about how Holyrood got its name? One of the ancient kings shooting arrows at a deer?'

'Search me.'

'Excuse me.' The voice came from the table next to them. 'I couldn't help overhearing.' The woman put her book down on the table. 'It was David the First, back in the twelfth century.'

'Was it now?' Siobhan said.

The woman ignored her tone. 'He was out hunting when a stag pinned him to the ground. He reached for its antlers only to find that it had vanished and in its place he was holding a cross. Holy rood means holy cross. David saw it as a sign and built the abbey of Holyrood.'

'Thank you,' Grant Hood said. The woman bowed her head and went back to her book. 'Nice to see an educated person,' he added, for Siobhan's benefit. She narrowed her eyes and wrinkled her nose at him. 'So it might have something to do with the Palace of Holyrood.'

'One of the rooms could be called B4,' Siobhan said. 'Like a school classroom.'

He saw that she wasn't being serious. 'There could be part of Scots Law relating to Holyrood – it would make another royal connection, like Victoria.'

Siobhan unfolded her arms. 'Could be,' she conceded.

'So all we have to do is find ourselves a friendly lawyer.'

'Would someone from the Procurator Fiscal's office do?' Siobhan asked. 'If so, I might know just the person . . .'

The Sheriff Court was in a new building on Chambers Street, just across from the museum complex. Grant dashed back down to Grassmarket to feed coins to the meter, despite Siobhan's protestation that it'd have been cheaper getting a fine slapped on him. She went on ahead and asked around the court until she'd located Harriet Brough. The lawyer was wearing yet another tweed two-piece with grey stockings and flat black shoes. Shapely ankles though, Siobhan couldn't help noticing.

'My dear girl, this is splendid,' Brough said, taking Siobhan's hand and working her arm as if it were a water-pump. 'Simply splendid.' Siobhan noted that the elder woman's make-up served merely to heighten her wrinkles and the folds of skin, and gave her face a garish pall.

'I hope I'm not disturbing you,' Siobhan began.

'Not in the slightest.' They were in the court's main entrance hall, busy with ushers and lawyers, security staff and worried-looking families. Elsewhere in the building, guilt and innocence were being judged, sentences handed down. 'Are you here for a trial?'

'No, I just had a question and I wondered if you might be able to help.'

'I'd be delighted to.'

'It's a note I've found. It might relate to a case, but it seems to be in some sort of code.'

The lawyer's eyes widened. 'How exciting,' she gasped. 'Let's just grab somewhere to sit and then you can tell me all about it.'

They found a free bench and sat down. Brough read the note through its polythene jacket. Siobhan watched as she mouthed the words silently, her brow creasing.

'I'm sorry,' she said at last. 'Maybe the context would help.'

'It's a missing person inquiry,' Siobhan explained. 'We think she may have been taking part in a game.'

'And you need to solve this to reach the next stage? How very curious.'

Grant Hood arrived, breathing heavily. Siobhan introduced him to Harriet Brough.

'Anything?' he asked. Siobhan just shook her head. He looked towards the lawyer. 'B4 doesn't mean anything in Scots Law? Some paragraph or sub-section?'

'My dear boy,' Brough laughed, 'there could be several hundred examples, though they'd more likely be 4B rather than B4. We use numerals first, as a general rule.'

Hood nodded. 'So it would be "paragraph 4, sub-section b"?'

'Exactly.'

'The first clue,' Siobhan added, 'had a royal connection. The answer was Victoria. We're wondering if this one might have something to do with Holyrood.' She explained her reasoning, and Brough took another look at the note.

'Well, the pair of you are cleverer than I am,' she conceded. 'Maybe my lawyer's mind is too literal.' She made to hand the note to Siobhan, but then snatched it back again. 'I wonder if the phrase "Scots Law" is there to put you off the scent.'

'How do you mean?' Siobhan asked.

'It's just that if the clue is meant to be wilfully obscure, then whoever wrote it might have been thinking laterally.'

Siobhan looked to Hood, who merely shrugged. Brough was pointing to the note.

'Something I learned from my hill-walking days,' she said, 'is that "law" is the Scots word for a hill . . .'

Rebus was on the phone to the manager of the Huntingtower Hotel.

'So it might be in storage?' he asked.

'I'm not sure,' the manager said.

'Could you take a look? Maybe ask around, see if anyone knows?'

'It could have been thrown out during a refit.'

'That's the sort of positive attitude I thrive on, Mr Ballantine.'

'Maybe the person who found it . . .'

'He says he handed it in.' Rebus had already called the *Courier* and spoken with the reporter who'd covered the case. The reporter had been curious, and Rebus had admitted that another coffin had turned up in Edinburgh, while stressing that any connection was 'the longest shot in history'. Last thing he wanted was the media sniffing around. The reporter had given him the name of the man whose dog had found the coffin. A couple of calls later, Rebus had traced the man, only to be told that he'd left the coffin at Huntingtower and had thought no more about it.

'Well,' the manager was saying now, 'I won't make any promises . . .'

'Let me know as soon as you find it,' Rebus said, repeating his name and phone number. 'It's a matter of urgency, Mr Ballantine.'

'I'll do what I can,' the manager said with a sigh.

Rebus broke the connection and looked across to the other desk, where Ellen Wylie was seated with Donald Devlin. Devlin was dressed in another old cardigan, this time with most of its buttons intact. Between the pair of them, they were trying to track down the autopsy notes from the Glasgow drowning. By the look on Wylie's face they were having little luck. Devlin, whose chair was side by side with hers, kept leaning in towards her as she spoke on the phone. He might just have been trying to catch what was being said, but Rebus could see Wylie didn't like it. She kept trying to move her chair surreptitiously, angling her body so she presented a lot of shoulder and back to the pathologist. So far, she'd avoided eye contact with Rebus.

He made a note to himself about Huntingtower, then got back on the phone. The Glasgow coffin was more awkward. The reporter who'd covered the story had moved on. Nobody at the news desk could remember anything about it. Rebus eventually got a number for the church manse and spoke to a Reverend Martine.

'Have you any idea what happened to the coffin?' Rebus asked.

'I think the journalist took it,' Reverend Martine said.

So Rebus thanked him and got back to the newspaper, where he was able eventually to speak to the editor, who wanted to hear Rebus's own story. So he explained about the 'Edinburgh coffin' and how he was working for the Department of Long Shots.

'This Edinburgh coffin, where was it found exactly?'

'Near the Castle,' Rebus said blithely. He could almost see the editor writing a note to himself, maybe thinking of following the story up.

After another minute or so, Rebus was transferred to personnel, where he was given a forwarding address for the journalist, whose name was Jenny Gabriel. It was a London address.

'She went to work for one of the broadsheets,' the personnel manager stated. 'It was what Jenny always wanted.'

So Rebus went out and bought coffee, cakes and four newspapers: *The Times, Telegraph, Guardian* and *Independent*. He went through each, studying the by-lines, but didn't find Jenny Gabriel's name. Undaunted, he called each paper and asked for her by name. At the third attempt, the switchboard asked him to hold. He glanced across to where Devlin was dropping cake crumbs on to Wylie's desk.

'Transferring you now.'

The sweetest words Rebus had heard all day. Then the call was picked up.

'News desk.'

'Jenny Gabriel, please,' Rebus said.
'Speaking.'
And it was time for the spiel again.
'My God,' the reporter said at last, 'that was twenty years ago!'
'Just about,' Rebus agreed. 'I don't suppose you still have the doll?'
'No, I don't.' Rebus felt his heart sink a little. 'When I moved south, I gave it to a friend. He'd always been fascinated by it.'
'Any chance you could put me in touch with him?'
'Hang on, I'll get his number . . .' There was a pause. Rebus spent the time working loose the mechanism of his ballpoint pen. He realised he had only the vaguest idea how such a pen worked. Spring, casing, refill . . . he could take it to pieces, put it back together again, and be none the wiser.
'He's in Edinburgh actually,' Jenny Gabriel said. Then she gave him a number. The friend's name was Dominic Mann.
'Many thanks,' Rebus said, cutting the call. Dominic Mann wasn't home, but his answering machine gave Rebus a mobile number to try. The call was picked up.
'Hello?'
'Is that Dominic Mann . . . ?' And Rebus was off again. This time getting the result he wanted. Mann still owned the coffin, and could drop it into St Leonard's later on in the day.
'I'd really appreciate that,' Rebus said. 'Funny thing to hold on to all these years . . . ?'
'I was planning to use it in one of my installations.'
'Installations?'
'I'm an artist. At least, I was. These days I run a gallery.'
'You still paint?'
'Infrequently. Just as well I didn't end up using it. It might have been wrapped in paint and bandages and sold to some collector.'
Rebus thanked the artist and put down the phone. Devlin had finished his cake. Wylie had put hers to one side, and the old man was eyeing it now. The Nairn coffin was easier: two calls got Rebus the result he wanted. He was told by a reporter that he'd do some digging, and was called back with the number of someone in Nairn, who then did some digging of their own and found the coffin stored in a neighbour's shed.
'You want me to post it to you?'
'Yes, please,' Rebus said. 'Next-day delivery.' He'd thought of sending a car, but didn't think the budget would stretch. There'd been memos flying on the subject.
'What about the postage?'
'Enclose your details and I'll see you get a refund.'
The caller thought about this. 'Seems all right, I suppose. Just have to trust you, won't I?'
'If you can't trust the police, who can you trust?'

He put down the phone and looked across to Wylie's desk again. 'Anything?' he asked.

'Getting there,' she said, her voice tired and irritated. Devlin got up, crumbs tumbling from his lap, and asked where the 'facilities' were. Rebus pointed him in the right direction. Devlin started to leave, but paused in front of Rebus.

'I can't tell you how much I'm enjoying this.'

'Glad someone's happy, Professor.'

Devlin prodded Rebus's jacket lapel with a finger. 'I think *you're* in your element.' He beamed, and shuffled out of the room. Rebus walked across to Wylie's desk.

'Better eat that cake, if you don't want him drooling.'

She considered this, then broke the cake in two and stuffed half into her mouth.

'I got a result on the dolls,' he told her. 'Two traced, with another possible.'

She took a gulp of coffee, washing down the sugary sponge. 'Doing better than us then.' She studied the remaining half of the cake, then dropped it into the bin. 'No offence,' she said.

'Professor Devlin will be gutted.'

'That's what I'm hoping.'

'He's here to help, remember?'

She stared at him. 'He smells.'

'Does he?'

'You've not noticed?'

'Can't say I have.'

She looked at him as though this comment said much about him. Then her shoulders fell. 'Why did you ask for me? I'm useless. All those reporters and TV viewers saw it. Everybody knows it. Have you got a thing about cripples or what?'

'My daughter's a cripple,' he said quietly.

Her face reddened. 'Christ, I didn't mean . . .'

'But to answer your question, the only person around here who seems to have a problem with Ellen Wylie is Ellen Wylie herself.'

Her hand had gone to her face, as if trying to force the blood back down. 'Tell that to Gill Templer,' she said at last.

'Gill ballsed things up. It's not the end of the world.' His phone was ringing. He started backing towards his desk. 'Okay?' he said. When she nodded, he turned away and answered the call. It was Huntingtower. They'd found the coffin in a cellar used for lost property. A couple of decades' worth of umbrellas and pairs of spectacles, hats and coats and cameras.

'Amazing, the stuff down there,' Mr Ballantine said. But all Rebus was interested in was the coffin.

'Can you post it next-day delivery? I'll see you get a refund . . .'

By the time Devlin came back in, Rebus was on the trail of the Dunfermline coffin, but this time he hit a wall. Nobody – local press, police – seemed to know what had happened to it. Rebus got a couple of promises that questions would be asked, but he didn't hold out much hope. Nearly thirty years had passed; unlikely it would turn up. At the other desk, Devlin was clapping his hands silently as Wylie finished another call. She looked across to Rebus.

'Post-mortem report on Hazel Gibbs is on its way,' she said. Rebus held her gaze for a few moments, then nodded slowly and smiled. His phone went again. This time it was Siobhan.

'I'm going to talk to David Costello,' she said. 'If you're not doing anything.'

'I thought you'd paired up with Grant?'

'DCS Templer has snared him for a couple of hours.'

'Has she now? Maybe she's offering him your liaison job.'

'I refuse to let you wind me up. Now, are you coming or not . . . ?'

Costello was in his flat. When he opened the door to them, he looked startled. Siobhan assured him that it wasn't bad news. He didn't seem to believe her.

'Can we come in, David?' Rebus asked. Costello looked at him for the first time, then nodded slowly. To Rebus's eyes, he was wearing the same clothes as on his last visit, and the living room didn't seem to have been tidied in the interim. The young man was growing a beard, too, but seemed self-conscious, rubbing his fingertips against its grain.

'Is there any news at all?' he asked, slumping on to the futon, while Rebus and Siobhan stayed standing.

'Bits and pieces,' Rebus said.

'But you can't go into details?' Costello kept shifting, trying to get comfortable.

'Actually, David,' Siobhan said, 'the details – some of them at least – are the reason we're here.' She handed him a sheet of paper.

'What's this?' he asked.

'It's the first clue from a game. A game we think Flip was playing.'

Costello sat forward, looked at the message again. 'What sort of game?'

'Something she found on the Internet. It's run by someone called Quizmaster. Solving each clue takes the player to a new level. Flip was working on a level called Hellbank. Maybe she'd solved it, we don't know.'

'Flip?' Costello sounded sceptical.

'You've never heard of it?'

He shook his head. 'She didn't say a word.' He looked across towards Rebus, but Rebus had picked up a poetry book.

'Was she interested in games at all?' Siobhan asked.

Costello shrugged. 'Dinner-party stuff. You know: charades and the like. Maybe Trivial Pursuit or Taboo.'

'But not fantasy games? Role-playing?'

He shook his head slowly.

'Nothing on the Internet?'

He rubbed at his bristles again. 'This is news to me.' He looked from Siobhan to Rebus and back again. 'You're *sure* this was Flip?'

'We're pretty sure,' Siobhan stated.

'And you think it has something to do with her disappearance?'

Siobhan just shrugged, and glanced in Rebus's direction, wondering if he had anything to add. But Rebus was busy with his own thoughts. He was remembering what Flip Balfour's mother had said about Costello, about how he'd turned Flip against her family. And when Rebus had asked why, she'd said: *Because of who he is.*

'Interesting poem, this,' he said, waving the book. It was more of a pamphlet really, pink cover with a line-drawing illustration. Then he recited a couple of lines:

'"You do not die for being bad, you die
For being available."'

Rebus closed the book, put it down. 'I'd never thought of it like that before,' he said, 'but it's true.' He paused to light a cigarette. 'Do you remember when we talked, David?' He inhaled, then thought to offer the packet to Costello, who shook his head. The half-bottle of whisky was empty, as were half a dozen cans of lager. Rebus could see them on the floor near the kitchen, along with mugs, plates and forks, the wrappings from takeaway food. He hadn't taken Costello for a drinker; maybe he'd have to revise that opinion. 'I asked you if Flip might have met someone, and you said something about how she'd have told you. You said she couldn't keep things to herself.'

Costello was nodding.

'And yet here's this game she was playing. Not an easy game either, lots of puzzles and word-play. She might have needed help.'

'She didn't get it from me.'

'And she never mentioned the Internet, or anyone called Quizmaster?'

He shook his head. 'Who is he anyway, this Quizmaster?'

'We don't know,' Siobhan admitted. She'd walked over to the bookshelf.

'But he should come forward, surely?'

'We'd like him to.' Siobhan lifted the toy soldier from the shelf. 'This is a gaming piece, isn't it?'

Costello turned his head to look. 'Is it?'

'You don't play?'

'I'm not even sure where it came from.'

'Been in the wars though,' Siobhan said, studying the broken musket.

Rebus looked over to where Costello's own computer – a laptop – sat ready and waiting. There were textbooks on the worktop next to it, and on the floor underneath a printer. 'I take it you're on the Internet yourself, David?' he asked.

'Isn't everybody?'

Siobhan forced a smile, put the toy soldier back. 'DI Rebus here is still wrestling with electric typewriters.'

Rebus saw what she was doing: trying to soften Costello up, using Rebus as the comedy prop.

'To me,' he said, 'the Internet is what the Milan goalie tries to defend.'

This got a smile from Costello. *Because of who he is* . . . But who was David Costello really? Rebus was beginning to wonder.

'If Flip kept this from you, David,' Siobhan was saying now, 'might there be other things she kept secret?'

Costello nodded again. He was still shifting on the futon, as if he'd never again be at rest. 'Maybe I didn't know her at all,' he conceded. He studied the clue again. 'What does it mean, do you know?'

'Siobhan worked it out,' Rebus admitted. 'But all it did was lead her to a second clue.'

Siobhan handed over the copy of the second note. 'It makes less sense than the first,' Costello said. 'I really can't believe it of Flip. It's not her sort of thing at all.' He made to hand the note back.

'What about her other friends?' Siobhan asked. 'Do any of them like games, puzzles?'

Costello's eyes fixed on her. 'You think one of them could . . . ?'

'All I'm wondering is whether Flip might have gone to anyone else for help.'

Costello was thoughtful. 'No one,' he said at last. 'No one I can think of.' Siobhan took the second note from him. 'What about this one?' he asked. 'Do you know what it means?'

She looked at the clue for maybe the fortieth time. 'No,' she admitted. 'Not yet.'

Afterwards, Siobhan drove Rebus back to St Leonard's. They were silent for the first few minutes. Traffic was bad. The evening rush hour seemed to start earlier with each passing week.

'What do you think?' Siobhan asked.

'I think we'd have been quicker walking.'

It was pretty much the response she'd expected. 'Your dolls in boxes, there's a playful quality to them, isn't there?'

'Bloody queer game, if you ask me.'

'Every bit as queer as running a quiz over the Internet.'

Rebus nodded, but didn't say anything.

'I don't want to be the one seeing a connection here,' Siobhan added.

'My department?' Rebus guessed. 'The potential's there though, isn't it?'

It was Siobhan's turn to nod. '*If* all the dolls link up.'

'Give us time,' Rebus said. 'Meanwhile, a bit of background on Mr Costello might be in order.'

'He seemed genuine enough to me. That look on his face when he answered the door, he was terrified something had happened. Besides, background check's already been done, hasn't it?'

'Doesn't mean we didn't miss anything. If I remember rightly, Hi-Ho Silvers was given the job, and that bugger's so lazy he thinks sloth's an Olympic sport.' He half turned towards her. 'What about you?'

'I try to at least *look* like I'm doing something.'

'I mean what are you going to do now?'

'I think I'm going to head home. Call it a day.'

'Better be careful, DCS Templer likes her officers to put in a full eight hours.'

'In that case she owes me . . . and you too, I shouldn't wonder. When was the last time you only worked an eight-hour shift?'

'September, nineteen eighty-six,' Rebus said, raising a smile.

'How's the flat coming on?'

'Rewiring's all but finished. The painters are moving in now.'

'Found somewhere to buy?'

He shook his head. 'It's bugging you, isn't it?'

'If you want to sell up, that's your decision.'

He gave her a sour look. 'You know what I mean.'

'Quizmaster?' She considered her answer. 'I could almost enjoy it . . .'

'If?'

'If I didn't get the sense that he's enjoying it too.'

'By manipulating you?'

Siobhan nodded. 'And if he's doing it to me, he did it to Philippa Balfour too.'

'You keep assuming it's a "he",' Rebus said.

'For convenience only.' There was the sound of a mobile. 'Mine,' Siobhan said, as Rebus reached into his own pocket. Her phone was attached to its own little charger beside the car stereo. Siobhan pressed a button, and an inbuilt microphone and speaker did the rest.

'Hands-free,' Rebus said, impressed.

'Hello?' Siobhan called out.

'Is that DC Clarke?'

She recognised the voice. 'Mr Costello? What can I do for you?'

'I was just thinking . . . what you were saying about games and stuff?'

'Yes?'

'Well, I do know someone who's into all that. Rather, Flip knows someone.'

'What's their name?'

Siobhan glanced towards Rebus, but he already had his notepad and pen ready.

David Costello said the name, but his voice broke up halfway through. 'Sorry,' Siobhan said. 'Could you give me that again?'

This time they both caught the name loud and clear: 'Ranald Marr.' Siobhan frowned, mouthing the name silently. Rebus nodded. He knew exactly who Ranald Marr was: John Balfour's business partner, the man who ran Balfour's Bank in Edinburgh.

The office was quiet. Officers had either clocked off, or were in meetings at Gayfield Square. There'd be shoe-leather patrols out there too, but scaled down now. There was almost no one left to interview. Another day without any sighting of Philippa, and no word from her, no sign that she was still alive. Credit cards and bank balance untouched, friends and family uncontacted. Nothing. Word around the station was, Bill Pryde had thrown a wobbly, sent his clipboard sailing across the open-plan office so that staff had to duck to avoid it. John Balfour had been putting the pressure on, giving media interviews critical of the lack of progress. The Chief Constable had asked for a status report from the ACC, which meant the ACC was on *everyone's* back. In the absence of any new leads, they were interviewing people for the second or third time. Everyone was jittery, frayed. Rebus tried calling Bill Pryde at Gayfield, but couldn't get through. He then placed a call to the Big House and asked to speak to Claverhouse or Ormiston in Crime Squad, Number 2 Branch. Claverhouse picked up.

'It's Rebus here. I need a favour.'

'And what makes you think I'd be daft enough to oblige?'

'Are your questions always this tough?'

'Bugger off back under your rock, Rebus.'

'Nothing I'd like better, but your mum's adopted it, says it loves her more than you ever did.' It was the only way to deal with Claverhouse: sarcasm at twelve paces.

'She's right, I'm a mean bastard at heart, which brings me back to my first question.'

'The tough one? Let's put it this way then: sooner you help me, sooner I can hit the pub and drink myself unconscious.'

'Christ, man, why didn't you say? Fire away.'

Rebus smiled into the receiver. 'I need an in.'

'Who with?'

'The *gardai* in Dublin.'

'Whatever for?'

'Philippa Balfour's boyfriend. I want a background check.'

'I put a tenner on him at two-to-one.'

'Best reason I can think of for helping me out.'

Claverhouse was thoughtful. 'Give me fifteen minutes. Don't move from that number.'

'I'll be here.'

Rebus put the phone down and sat back in his chair. Then he noticed something across the room. It was the Farmer's old chair. Gill must have turfed it out only for someone to claim it. Rebus wheeled it over to his own desk, made himself comfortable. He thought about what he'd said to Claverhouse: *sooner I can hit the pub and drink myself unconscious*. It had been part of the routine, but a large chunk of him wanted it anyway, wanted that hazy oblivion that only drink could provide. Oblivion: the name of one of Brian Auger's bands, Oblivion Express. He had their first album somewhere, *A Better Land*. A bit too jazzy for his taste. When the phone rang, he picked it up, but it was still ringing: his mobile. He fished it from his pocket, put it to his ear.

'Hello?'

'John?'

'Hello, Jean. I was meaning to call you.'

'Is this an all right time?'

'Sure. Has that journo been hassling you?' His desk phone started ringing: Claverhouse probably. Rebus got up from the Farmer's chair, walked across the office and out of the door.

'Nothing I can't handle,' Jean was saying. 'I've been doing a bit of digging, as you asked. I'm afraid I haven't found very much.'

'Never mind.'

'Well, it's taken me all day . . .'

'I'll have a look at it tomorrow, if that's all right with you.'

'Tomorrow would be fine.'

'Unless you're free tonight . . . ?'

'Oh.' She paused. 'I promised a friend I'd go see her. She's just had a baby.'

'That's nice.'

'I'm sorry.'

'Don't be. We'll meet tomorrow. Are you okay to come to the station?'

'Yes.'

They agreed a time and Rebus went back into the CID room, ending the call. He got the feeling she was pleased with him, pleased that he'd asked to meet this evening. It was what she'd been hoping for, some hint that he was still interested, that it wasn't just work for him.

Or he could be reading too much into it.

Back at his desk, he called Claverhouse.

'I'm a disappointed man,' Claverhouse said.

'I told you I wouldn't leave my desk, and I stuck to my word.'

'Then how come you didn't pick up the phone?'

'Someone caught me on my mobile.'

'Someone who means more to you than I do? Now I really am hurt.'

'It was my bookie. I owe him two hundred notes.'

Claverhouse was silent for a moment. 'This cheers me immensely,' he said. 'Right, the person you want to speak to is Declan Macmanus.'

Rebus frowned. 'Wasn't that Elvis Costello's real name?'

'Well, he obviously passed it on to someone in need.' Claverhouse gave Rebus the number in Dublin, including the international code. 'Not that I suppose the cheap bastards at St Leonard's will let you make an international call.'

'Forms will have to be filled in,' Rebus agreed. 'Thanks for your help, Claverhouse.'

'Are you going for that drink now?'

'I think I better had. Don't want to be conscious when my bookie finds me.'

'You have a point. Here's to bad horses and good whisky.'

'And vice versa,' Rebus rejoined, ending the call. Claverhouse was right: the main phones at St Leonard's were blocked for international calls, but Rebus had the feeling the Chief Super's phone would be okay. Only problem was, Gill had locked her door. Rebus thought for a second, then remembered that the Farmer had kept a spare key for emergencies. He crouched down at Gill's office door and peeled back the corner of carpet next to the jamb. Bingo: the Yale was still there. He inserted it into the lock and was inside her office, door closed after him.

He looked at her new chair but decided to stay standing, resting against the edge of her desk. He couldn't help thinking of the Three Bears: who's been sitting in my chair? And who's been making calls from my phone?

His call was answered after half a dozen rings. 'Can I speak to . . .' he suddenly realised that he didn't have a rank for Macmanus . . . 'to Declan Macmanus, please.'

'Who shall I say is calling?' The woman's voice had that seductive Irish lilt. Rebus imagined raven hair and a full body.

'Detective Inspector John Rebus, Lothian and Borders Police in Scotland.'

'Hold, please.'

While he held, the full body had become a pint of slow-poured Guinness, the beer seemingly shaped to fit its glass.

'DI Rebus?' The voice was crisp, no-nonsense.

'DI Claverhouse at the Scottish Crime Squad gave me your number.'

'That was generous of him.'

'Sometimes he just can't help himself.'

'And what can I do for you?'

'I don't know if you've heard about this case we've got, a MisPer called Philippa Balfour.'

'The banker's daughter? It's been all over the papers here.'

'Because of the connection with David Costello?'

'The Costellos are well known, Inspector, part of the Dublin social fabric, you might say.'

'You'd know better than me, which is the reason I'm calling.'

'Ah, is it now?'

'I want to know a bit more about the family.' Rebus started doodling on a sheet of paper. 'I'm sure they're blemish-free, but it would put my mind at rest if I had some evidence of that.'

'As to "blemish-free", I'm not sure I can give that guarantee.'

'Oh?'

'Every family has its dirty laundry, does it not?'

'I suppose so.'

'Maybe I could send you the Costellos' laundry list. How would that be?'

'That would be fine.'

'Do you happen to have a fax number there?'

Rebus recited it. 'You'll need the international code,' he warned.

'I think I can manage that. How confidential would this information remain?'

'As confidential as I can make it.'

'I suppose I'll have to take your word then. Are you a rugby man, Inspector?'

Rebus got the feeling he should answer yes. 'Only as a spectator.'

'I like to come to Edinburgh for the Six Nations. Maybe we'll meet for a drink next time.'

'I'd like that. Let me give you a couple of numbers.' This time he recited his office number and his mobile.

'I'll be sure to look you up.'

'You do that. I owe you a large malt.'

'I'll hold you to it.' There was a pause. 'You're not really a rugby man at all, are you?'

'No,' Rebus admitted. There was laughter on the line.

'But you're honest, and that's a start. Goodbye, Inspector.'

Rebus put the phone down. It struck him that he still didn't know Macmanus's rank, or anything much about him at all. When he looked down at the doodles covering the sheet of paper in front of him, he found he'd drawn half a dozen coffins. He waited twenty minutes for Macmanus to get back to him, but the fax machine was playing dead.

He hit the Maltings first, and followed it up with the Royal Oak, before making for Swany's. Just the one drink in each pub, starting with a pint of Guinness. It had been a while since he'd tried the stuff; it was good but filling. He knew he couldn't do too many, so switched to IPA and finally a Laphroaig with the merest drizzle of water. Then it was a taxi to the Oxford Bar, where he demolished the last corned beef and beetroot roll on the shelf and followed it with a main course of a Scotch egg. He was back on the IPA, needed something to wash down the food. A few of the regulars were in. The back room had been taken over by a party of students, and no one in the front bar was saying much, as if the sounds of enjoyment from upstairs were somehow blasphemous. Harry was behind the bar, and clearly relishing the prospect of the revellers' departure. When someone was dispatched to fetch another round, Harry kept up a steady stream of comments along the lines of 'you'll be heading off soon . . . going to a club . . . the night's young . . .' The young man, his face so shiny it might have been polished, just grinned inanely, taking none of it in. Harry shook his head in disgust. When the drinker headed off, tray laden with slopping pints, one of the regulars informed Harry that he was losing his touch. The stream of profanities which followed seemed, to everyone present, evidence to the contrary.

Rebus had come here in a vain attempt to flush all those little coffins out of his mind. He kept imagining them, seeing them as the work of one man, one killer . . . and wondering if there were any more of them, lying rotting on barren hillsides perhaps, or tucked away in crevasses, or turned into macabre ornaments in their finders' garden sheds . . . Arthur's Seat and Falls and Jean's four coffins. He saw a continuity there, and it filled him with dread. I want to be cremated, he thought, or maybe strung up in a tree the way Aborigines do it. Anything but the strict confines of a box . . . anything but that.

When the door opened, everyone turned to examine the new arrival. Rebus straightened his back, trying not to show surprise. It was Gill Templer. She saw him immediately and smiled, unbuttoning her coat and taking off her scarf.

'Thought I might find you here,' she said. 'I tried phoning, but got your machine.'

'What can I get you?'

'Gin and tonic.'

Harry had heard the order and was already reaching for a glass. 'Ice and lemon?' he asked.

'Please.'

Rebus noticed that the other drinkers had shifted a little, giving Rebus and Gill as much privacy as the cramped front bar would allow. He paid for the drink and watched Gill gulp at it.

'I needed that,' she said.

Rebus lifted his own glass and toasted her. '*Slainte*.' Then he took a sip. Gill was smiling.

'Sorry,' she said, 'rude of me to just hammer it like that.'

'Rough day?'

'I've had better.'

'So what brings you here?'

'A couple of things. As usual, you haven't been bothering to keep me up to date with any progress.'

'There's not much to report.'

'It's a dead end then?'

'I didn't say that. I just need a few more days.' He lifted his glass again.

'Then there's the small matter of your doctor's appointment.'

'Yes, I know. I'll get round to it, promise.' He nodded towards the pint. 'This is my first tonight, by the way.'

'Aye, that'll be right,' Harry muttered, busying himself drying glasses.

Gill smiled, but her eyes were on Rebus. 'How are things with Jean?'

Rebus shrugged. 'Fine. She's concentrating on the historical side.'

'Do you like her?'

Now Rebus looked at Gill. 'Does the matchmaker service come free?'

'I was just wondering.'

'And you came all this way to ask?'

'Jean's been hurt before by an alcoholic, it's how her husband went.'

'She told me. Don't worry on that score.'

She looked down at her drink. 'How's it working out with Ellen Wylie?'

'I've no complaints.'

'Has she said anything about me?'

'Not really.' Rebus had finished his drink, waved his glass to signal as much. Harry put down the tea-cloth and started pouring. Rebus felt awkward. He didn't like Gill being here like this, dropping in and catching him off-guard. He didn't like that the regulars were listening to every word. Gill seemed to sense his discomfort.

'Would you rather we did this at the office?'

He shrugged again. 'How about you?' he asked. 'Enjoying the new job?'

'I think I'll manage.'

'I'd put money on it.' He pointed to her glass, offered a refill. Gill shook her head. 'I should be going. This was just a quick one before home.'

'Same here.' Rebus made a show of checking his watch.

'I've got the car outside . . . ?'

Rebus shook his head. 'I like to walk, keeps me fit.'

Behind the bar, Harry snorted. Gill wrapped the scarf back around her neck.

'Maybe see you tomorrow then,' she said.

'You know where my office is.'

She studied her surroundings – walls the colour of a used cigarette-filter, dusty prints of Robert Burns – and began to nod. 'Yes,' she said, 'I do.' Then she gave a little wave which seemed to take in the whole bar, and was gone.

'Your boss?' Harry guessed. Rebus nodded. 'Swap you,' the barman said. The regulars started laughing. Another student appeared from the back room, the list of required drinks scribbled on the back of an envelope.

'Three IPA,' Harry began to recite, 'two lager tops, a gin, lime and soda, two Becks and a dry white wine.'

The student looked at the note, then nodded in amazement. Harry winked at his audience.

'Might be students, but they're not the only smart bastards round here.'

Siobhan sat in her living room, staring at the message on the laptop's screen. It was in response to an e-mail she'd sent to Quizmaster, informing him that she was now working on the second clue.

I forgot to tell you, from now on you're against the clock. In twenty-four hours' time, the next clue becomes void.

Siobhan got to work on the keyboard: *I think we should meet. I have some questions*. She hit 'send', then waited. His reply was prompt.

The game will answer your questions.

She hit more keys: *Did Flip have anyone helping her? Is anyone else playing the game?*

She waited for several minutes. Nothing. She was in the kitchen, pouring another half-glass of Chilean red, when she heard the laptop telling her she had a message. Wine splashed on to the back of her hand as she dashed back through.

Hello, Siobhan.

She stared at the screen. The sender's address was a series of numbers. Before she could reply, the computer told her she had another message.

Are you there? Your light's on.

She froze, the screen seeming to shimmer. He was *here*! Right outside! She walked quickly to the window. Down below, a car was parked, headlights still on.

Grant Hood's Alfa.

He waved up at her. Cursing, she ran to the front door, down the stairs and out of the tenement.

'Is that your idea of a joke?' she hissed.

Hood, easing himself from the driver's seat, seemed stunned by her reaction.

'I just had Quizmaster online,' she explained. 'I thought you were him.' She paused, narrowed her eyes. 'Just exactly how did you do that?'

Hood held up his mobile phone. 'It's a WAP,' he explained sheepishly. 'Just got it today. Sends e-mails, the lot.'

She snatched it from him and studied it. 'Jesus, Grant.'

'I'm sorry,' he said. 'I just wanted to . . .'

She handed back the phone, knowing damned well what he'd wanted: to show off his latest gadget.

'What are you doing here anyway?' she asked.

'I think I've cracked it.'

She stared at him. 'Again?' He shrugged. 'How come you always wait till late at night?'

'Maybe that's when I do my best thinking.' He glanced up at the tenement. 'So are you going to invite me in, or do we go on giving the neighbours a free show?'

She looked around. It was true that heads were silhouetted at a couple of windows. 'Come on then,' she said.

Upstairs, the first thing she did was check the laptop, but Quizmaster hadn't replied.

'I think you scared him off,' Hood said, reading the onscreen dialogue.

Siobhan fell on to the sofa and picked up her glass. 'So what have you got for us tonight, Einstein?'

'Ah, that famous Edinburgh hospitality,' Hood said, eyeing the glass.

'You're driving.'

'One glass can't hurt.'

Siobhan got up again, uttering a slight groan of protest, and headed for the kitchen. Hood reached into the bag he'd brought with him and started pulling out maps and guidebooks.

'What have you got there?' Siobhan asked, handing him a tumbler and starting to pour. She sat down, drained her own glass, refilled it, and placed what was left of the bottle on the floor.

'You're sure I'm not disturbing you?' He was teasing her – or trying to. But she wasn't in the mood.

'Just tell me what you've got.'

'Well . . . if you're absolutely sure I'm not . . .' Her glare brought him up short. He stared down at the maps. 'I got thinking about what that lawyer said.'

'Harriet?' Siobhan frowned. 'She said hills are sometimes called laws.'

Hood nodded. '"Scots Law",' he recited. 'Meaning maybe we're looking for a word that means the same thing law does in Scots.'

'Which would be . . .?'

Hood unfolded a sheet of paper and started to read aloud. 'Hill, heights, bank, brae, ben, fell, tor . . .' He turned the sheet towards her. 'The thesaurus is full of them.'

She took the paper from him and started reading the list for herself. 'We went through all the maps,' she complained.

'But we didn't know what we were looking for. Some of the guides have hills and mountains indexed at the back. For the rest, we check grid reference B4 on each page.'

'Looking for what exactly?'

'Deer Hill, Stag's Brae, Doe Bank . . .'

Siobhan nodded. 'You're assuming "sounds dear" means "d-e-e-r"?'

Hood took a sip of wine. 'I'm assuming a lot. But it's better than nothing.'

'And it couldn't wait till morning?'

'Not when Quizmaster suddenly decides we're against the clock.' Hood picked up the first map-book and flicked to the index.

Siobhan studied him over the top of her glass. Yes, she was thinking, but you didn't know there was a time element until you got here. She was also still shaken by the way he'd e-mailed her by phone. She wondered just how mobile Quizmaster was. She'd given him her name, and the city where she worked. These days, how hard would it be for him to get an address? Five minutes on the Net would probably do it.

Hood didn't seem to notice that she was still staring at him. *Maybe he's closer than you think, girl*, Siobhan thought to herself.

After half an hour, she put on some music, a Mogwai EP, about as laid-back as the band ever got. She asked Hood if he wanted coffee. He was sitting on the floor, back against the sofa, legs stretched out. He had spread an Ordnance Survey map across his thighs and was studying one of the squares. He looked up at her and blinked, as though the lighting in the room was new to him.

'Cheers,' he said.

When she came back with the mugs, she told him about Ranald Marr. The look on his face changed to a scowl.

'Keeping it a secret, were you?'

'I thought it could wait till morning.' Her answer didn't seem to satisfy him, and he took his coffee from her with only a grunt of thanks. Siobhan could feel her anger rising again. This was *her* place, *her* home. What was he doing here anyway? Work was for the office, not her living room. How come he didn't phone and tell her to go to *his* place? The more she thought about it, the more she realised that she really didn't know Grant at all. She'd worked with him before; they'd been to parties, gone out drinking and for that one meal. She didn't think he'd ever had a girlfriend. At St Leonard's a few of the CID called him Go-Go Gadget, a reference to some TV cartoon. He was both a useful officer and a figure of amusement at the same time.

He wasn't like her. He was nothing like her at all. And yet here she was sharing her free time with him. Here she was letting him turn that free time into yet more work.

She picked up another of the map books, *Handy Road Atlas Scotland*. The first page, square B4 was the Isle of Man. This really annoyed her for some reason: the Isle of Man wasn't even *in* Scotland! The next page, B4 was in the Yorkshire Dales.

'Bloody hell,' she said out loud.

'What is it?'

'This map, it's like Bonnie Prince Charlie won the war.' She flipped to the next page, where B4 was the Mull of Kintyre, but the page after that her eyes fixed on the words 'Loch Fell'. She studied the square more closely: the M74 motorway and the town of Moffat. She knew Moffat: a picture-postcard place with at least one good hotel, where she'd stopped once for lunch. At the top of square B4 she saw a small triangle, indicating a peak. The peak was called Hart Fell. It was eight hundred and eight metres high. She looked at Hood.

'A hart's a kind of deer, isn't it?'

He got up off the floor, came and sat next to her. 'Harts and hinds,' he said. 'The hart is the male.'

'Why not a stag?'

'Harts are older, I think.' He studied the map, his shoulder touching Siobhan's arm. She tried not to flinch, but it was hard work. 'Christ,' he said, 'it's the middle of nowhere.'

'Maybe it's coincidence,' she suggested.

He nodded, but she could see he was convinced. 'Square B4,' he said. 'A fell is another name for a law. A hart is a kind of deer . . .' He looked at her and shook his head. 'No coincidence.'

Siobhan switched her TV on and pressed for Teletext.

'What are you doing?' Hood asked.

'Checking the weather for tomorrow. No way I'm climbing Hart Fell in a gale.'

Rebus had dropped into St Leonard's, gathered together the notes on the four cases: Glasgow, Dunfermline, Perth and Nairn.

'All right, sir?' one of the uniforms had asked.

'Why shouldn't I be?'

He'd had a few drinks, so what? Didn't make him incapable. The taxi was waiting for him outside. Five minutes later, he was climbing the stairs to his flat. Another five after that, he was smoking a cigarette, drinking tea, and opening the first file. He sat in his chair by the window, his little oasis in the midst of chaos. He could hear a siren in the distance; sounded like an ambulance, hurtling along Melville Drive. He had photos of the four victims, culled from newspapers. They smiled at him in black and white. The snatch of poetry came back to him, and he knew all four shared the same characteristic.

They'd died because they'd been available.

He started pinning the photos to a large corkboard. He had a postcard, too, bought from the museum shop: three of the Arthur's Seat coffins in close-up, surrounded by darkness. He turned the postcard over and read: 'Carved wooden figures, with fabric clothing, in miniature coffins of pine, from a group found in a rocky niche on the north-eastern slopes of Arthur's Seat, in June 1836.' It struck him that the police of the time had probably been involved, which meant there might be paperwork somewhere. Then again, just how organised had the force been back then? He doubted there'd been anything like the modern CID. Probably they'd resorted to examining victims' eyeballs, looking for images of the murderer. Not too far removed from the witchcraft which was one theory behind the dolls. Had witches ever plied their trade on Arthur's Seat? These days, he suspected they'd get some sort of Enterprise Initiative.

He got up and put some music on. Dr John, *The Night Tripper*. Then back to the table, a fresh cigarette lit from the stub of the old. The smoke stung his eyes, and he squeezed them shut. When he opened them again, his vision was slow to focus. It was as if the photos of the four women were lying behind a layer of muslin. He blinked a couple of times, shook his head, trying to stave off weariness.

When he awoke a couple of hours later, he was still seated at the table, head resting on his arms. The photos were still there, too, restless faces which had invaded his dreams.

'I wish I could help,' he told them, getting up to go to the kitchen. He returned with a mug of tea, which he took over to the chair by the window. Here he was, getting through another night. So how come he didn't feel like celebrating?

8

Rebus and Jean Burchill were walking on Arthur's Seat. It was a bright morning, but there was a cold breeze blowing. Some people said Arthur's Seat looked like a lion about to spring. But to Rebus's mind it more resembled an elephant or mammoth, with a great bulbous head, a dip towards the neck, and an expanse of torso.

'It started life as a volcano,' Jean was explaining, 'same as Castle Rock. Later on there were farms and quarries, plus chapels.'

'People used to come here for sanctuary, didn't they?' Rebus said, keen to show off what knowledge he had.

She nodded. 'Debtors were banished here until they'd got their affairs in order. A lot of people think it's named after King Arthur.'

'You mean it isn't?'

She shook her head. 'More likely it's Gaelic: *Ard-na-Said*, "Height of the Sorrows".'

'That's a cheery name.'

She smiled. 'The park's full of them: Pulpit Rock, Powderhouse Corner.' She looked at him. 'Or how about Murder Acre and Hangman's Crag?'

'Where are they?'

'Near Duddingston Loch and the Innocent Railway.'

'Now that was named because they used horses instead of trains, right?'

She smiled again. 'Could be. There are other theories.' She pointed towards the loch. 'Samson's Ribs,' she said. 'The Romans had a fort there.' She gave him a sly glance. 'Maybe you didn't think they got this far north?'

He shrugged. 'History's never been my strong point. Do we know where the coffins were found?'

'The records from the time are vague. "The north-east range of Arthur's Seat" is how the *Scotsman* put it. A small opening in a secluded outcrop.' She shrugged. 'I've wandered all over and never found the spot. The other thing the *Scotsman* said was that the coffins were in two tiers, eight in each, and with a third tier just begun.'

'Like whoever did it had more to add?'

She held her jacket around her; Rebus got the feeling it wasn't just the wind making her shiver. He was thinking of the Innocent Railway. These days it was a walkway and cycle path. About a month back, someone had been mugged there. He didn't suppose the story would do much to cheer up his companion. He could tell her about suicides, too, and syringes left by the side of the road. Although they were walking the same path, he knew they were in different places.

'I'm afraid history's about all I have to offer,' she said suddenly. 'I've asked around, but no one seems to remember anyone showing particular interest in the coffins, except for the occasional student or tourist. They were kept in a private collection for a time, then handed over to the Society of Antiquaries, who gave them to the Museum.' She shrugged. 'I've not been very helpful, have I?'

'A case like this, Jean, everything's useful. If it doesn't rule something in, it can help rule other things out.'

'I get the feeling you've made that speech before.'

It was his turn to smile. 'Maybe I have; doesn't mean I don't mean it. Are you free later on today?'

'Why?' She was playing with her new bracelet, the one she'd bought from Bev Dodds.

'I'm taking our twentieth-century coffins to an expert. A bit of history might come in useful.' He paused, looked out over Edinburgh. 'Jesus, it's a beautiful city, isn't it?'

She studied him. 'Are you saying that because you think I want to hear it?'

'What?'

'The other night, when I stopped on North Bridge, I got the feeling you weren't impressed by the view.'

'I look, but I don't always see. I'm seeing now.' They were on the hill's west face, so not even half the city was spread below them. Climbing higher, Rebus knew he'd have a three-hundred-and-sixty-degree view. But this was enough to be going on with: the spires and chimney-pots, crow-foot gables, with the Pentland Hills to the south and the Firth of Forth to the north, the Fife coastline visible beyond.

'Maybe you are at that,' she said. And, smiling, she leaned forward, going up on her toes so she could peck his cheek. 'Best just to get that out of the way,' she said quietly. Rebus nodded, couldn't think of anything to say, until she shivered again and said she was getting cold.

'There's a café behind St Leonard's,' Rebus told her. 'And I'm buying. Not out of altruism, you understand, but because I've a huge favour to ask.'

She burst out laughing, slapped her hand to her mouth and started apologising.

'What did I say?' he asked.

'It's just that Gill told me this would happen. She said if I stuck close to you, I'd have to be prepared for "the big favour".'

'Did she now?'

'And she was right, wasn't she?'

'Not entirely. It's a *huge* favour I'm asking for, not just a big one . . .'

Siobhan was wearing a vest, polo neck and pure wool V-neck jumper. She had an old pair of thick cords on, tucked at the ankles into two pairs of socks. She'd given her old hiking boots a bit of a polish, and they seemed fine. She hadn't worn the Barbour in years, but couldn't think of a better chance to use it. Additionally, she was wearing a bobble-hat, and carrying a pack containing an umbrella, her mobile, a bottle of water and a flask of sweetened tea.

'Sure you've got enough gear?' Hood laughed. He was wearing jeans and trainers. His yellow cagoule looked brand new. He angled his face to the sun, so that the rays reflected off his sunglasses. They'd parked the car in a lay-by. There was a fence to climb, and after that a gently sloping field which then angled abruptly. The steep gradient was barren, except for occasional whin-bushes and rocks.

'What do you reckon?' Hood asked. 'An hour to the top?'

Siobhan slipped the backpack over her shoulders. 'With a bit of luck.'

Sheep watched them as they climbed the fence. There was a strand of barbed wire running along it, marked with tufts of grey wool. Hood gave Siobhan a foot up, then leaped over, using his hand on the fence-post for purchase.

'Not a bad day for it,' he said, as they started to climb. 'Reckon Flip would have done this on her ownio?'

'I don't know,' Siobhan conceded.

'I wouldn't have said she was the type. She'd have taken one look at this climb and got back into her Golf GTi.'

'Except she didn't have a car.'

'Good point. So how would she have got out here in the first place?'

Which was another good point: they really were in the middle of nowhere, with towns few and far between and only the odd cottage or farm giving signs of habitation. They were only forty miles from Edinburgh, but the city seemed already a distant memory. Siobhan guessed that few buses came this route. If Flip had come here, she'd have needed help.

'Maybe a taxi,' she said.

'Not the sort of fare you'd forget.'

'No.' Yet despite a public appeal, and plenty of photos of Flip in the papers, no taxi driver had come forward. 'Maybe a friend then, someone we haven't traced yet.'

'Could be.' But Hood sounded sceptical. She noticed that he was already breathing hard. A couple of minutes later, he'd shed the cagoule and folded it, tucking it beneath his arm.

'Don't know how you can wear that lot,' he complained. She pulled the bobble-hat from her head and unzipped the Barbour.

'Is that better?' she said.

He just shrugged.

Eventually, on the steeper climb, they were reduced to scrabbling with their hands while their feet sought purchase, the stony soil crumbling and sliding away beneath them. Siobhan stopped to rest, sitting down with her knees up, heels digging in. She took a swig of water.

'Is that you wabbit already?' Hood said, ten or so feet above her. She offered him the bottle, but he shook his head and started climbing again. She could see sweat shining in his hair.

'It's not a race, Grant,' she called out. He didn't reply. After another half-minute, she turned round and followed him. He was moving away from her. So much for team work, she thought. He was like a lot of men she'd known: driven, and yet probably unable to put the reasons into words. It was more in the way of an instinct, a basic need, going beyond the rational.

The climb was levelling off a little. Hood stood up, hands on his hips, admiring the view as he rested. Siobhan watched as he bent his head and tried to spit, but his saliva was too viscous. It hung in a strand from his mouth, refusing to drop. He got a handkerchief from his pocket and wiped it away. Catching up with him, she handed him the bottle.

'Here,' she said. He looked like he might refuse, but eventually took a mouthful. 'It's clouding over.' Siobhan was interested in the sky rather than the view. The clouds were thick and blackening. Funny how the weather could change so suddenly in Scotland. The temperature must have dropped three or four degrees, perhaps more. 'Maybe a shower,' she said. Hood just nodded, handing back the bottle.

She looked at her watch and saw that they'd been climbing for twenty minutes. That meant they were maybe fifteen from the car, reckoning the descent quicker than the climb. Peering upwards, she guessed they had another fifteen or twenty minutes to go. Hood expelled breath noisily.

'You okay?' she asked.

'Good exercise,' he said hoarsely. Then he began climbing again. There were damp patches on the back of his dark blue sweatshirt. Any minute now he'd probably take it off, and be clad only in a T-shirt as the weather turned. Sure enough, he paused to pull the sweatshirt over his head.

'It's getting cold,' she warned him.

'But I'm not.' He tied the arms of the sweatshirt around his waist.

'At least put your cagoule back on.'

'I'll bake.'

'No you won't.'

He seemed ready to argue, then changed his mind. Siobhan had already zipped up her Barbour again. The countryside around them was growing less visible, either low cloud or mist. Or maybe showers blowing in.

Five minutes on, the rain began. Drizzle at first, and then a smattering of big drops. Siobhan put her hat back on, and watched Grant pull his hood up. It was getting windy, too, gusts cutting across them. Grant lost his footing and went down on one knee, cursing. For the next few dozen steps he was limping, clutching at his leg with one hand.

'Do you want to wait?' she asked, knowing what his answer would be: silence.

The rain grew heavier, but in the distance the sky was already clearing. It wouldn't last long. All the same, Siobhan's legs were soaked, her trousers sticking to her. Grant's trainers were making squelching sounds. He had switched to auto-pilot, his eyes staring, nothing at all on his mind except reaching the summit, whatever it took.

As they clambered up the last steep incline, the land levelled off. They'd reached the summit. The rain was easing. Twenty feet away stood a cairn. Siobhan knew that sometimes hill-walkers added a rock or stone each time they ended a climb. Maybe that was how this cairn had come into being.

'What, no restaurant?' Grant said, crouching down to get his breath back. The rain had stopped, a shaft of sunshine splitting the clouds and bathing the hills around in an eerie yellow glow. He was shivering, but the rain had been pouring off his cagoule and on to his sweatshirt, soaking it. No use putting it on now. His denims had changed colour to a darker, dampened blue.

'Hot tea, if you want it,' Siobhan said. He nodded and she poured him a cup. He sipped at it, studying the cairn.

'Are we scared what we'll find?' he said.

'Maybe we won't find anything.'

He conceded as much with a nod. 'Go look,' he told her. So she screwed the top back on the flask and approached the cairn, walked round it. Just a pile of stones and pebbles. 'There's nothing here,' she said. She got down on her haunches to take a closer look.

'There must be.' Grant rose to his feet, walked towards her. 'There's got to be.'

'Well, whatever it is, it's well hidden.'

He touched a foot to the cairn, then gave a push, toppling it. Dropped to his knees, running his hands through the debris. His face was screwed up, teeth bared. Soon the pile of stones was completely flattened. Siobhan had lost interest in it, was looking around for other possibilities, seeing none. Grant thrust a hand into his cagoule pocket, pulling out the two plastic evidence bags he'd brought. She watched him stuff them under the largest rock, then begin building the cairn again. It didn't get very high before it started to fall down.

'Leave it, Grant,' Siobhan said.

'Useless piece of shit!' he cried out. She couldn't be sure who or what his words were aimed at.

'Grant,' she said quietly. 'Weather's closing in again. Let's head back.'

He seemed reluctant to go. He sat on the ground, legs stretched out, arms behind him to support himself.

'We got it wrong,' he said, almost in tears. Siobhan was looking at him, knowing she needed to coax him back down the hill. He was wet and cold and losing it. She crouched in front of him.

'I need you to be strong, Grant,' she said, her hands on his knees. 'You go to pieces on me, and that's it finished. We're a team, remember?'

'A team,' he echoed. Siobhan was nodding.

'So let's act like a team and get our arses off this hill.'

He was staring at her hands. He reached out with his own, wrapping them around hers. She started to rise, pulling him with her. 'Come on, Grant.' They were both up on their feet now, and his eyes weren't moving from her.

'Remember what you said?' he asked. 'When we were trying to get parked near Victoria Street?'

'What?'

'You asked why I always had to play by the rules . . .'

'Grant . . .' She tried for a look that was sympathetic rather than pitying. 'Let's not spoil it,' she said quietly, trying to slide her hands out from his grip.

'Spoil what?' he asked hollowly.

'We're a team,' she repeated.

'That's it?'

He was staring at her as she nodded. She kept nodding and he slowly released her hands. Siobhan turned to move away, start the descent. She hadn't gone five paces when Grant flew past her, bounding down the slope like a man possessed. He lost his footing once or twice but bounced straight back up again.

'Tell me those aren't hailstones!' he called out at one point. But they were: stinging Siobhan's face as she tried to catch up. Then Grant caught his cagoule on the barbed wire as he hurdled the fence, ripping its seam. He was swearing and red-faced as he helped Siobhan over. They got into the car and just sat there for a full minute, getting their breath back. The windscreen started steaming up, so Siobhan slid her window down. The hail had stopped. The sun was coming out again.

'Bloody Scottish weather,' Grant spat. 'Is it any wonder we've a chip on our shoulder?'

'Have we? I hadn't noticed.'

He snorted, but smiled too. Siobhan looked at him, hoping it was going to be all right between them. The way he was acting, it was as if nothing had happened up there on the summit. She took off her Barbour and tossed it into the back. Grant slipped the cagoule over his head. There was steam rising from his T-shirt. From beneath the seat,

Siobhan retrieved the laptop and plugged her mobile into it, booting the machine up. The mobile's signal was weak, but it would do.

'Tell him he's a bastard,' Grant said.

'I'm sure he'd be thrilled to hear it.' Siobhan started typing a message, Grant leaning over to watch.

Just been up Hart Fell. No sign of next clue. Did I get it wrong?

She pressed 'send' and waited, pouring herself a cup of tea. Grant was trying to prise his denims away from his skin. 'Soon as we get moving, I'll put the heater on.' She nodded, offered him some more tea, which he took. 'What time's the meeting with the banker?'

She checked her watch. 'We've a couple of hours. Time enough to go home and get changed.'

Grant looked at the screen. 'He's not there, is he?'

Siobhan shrugged, and Grant turned the Alfa's ignition. They drove in silence, the weather clearing ahead of them. It soon became clear that the rain had been localised. By Innerleithen, the road was bone dry.

'I wonder if we should have taken the A701,' Grant mused. 'Might have made for a shorter climb, the west side of the hill.'

'Doesn't matter now,' Siobhan said. She could see that in his mind he was still on Hart Fell. The laptop suddenly announced that there was post. She clicked, but it was an invitation to visit a porn site. 'That's not the first of those I've had,' she informed Grant. 'Makes me wonder what you got up to with your computer.'

'They pick names at random,' he said, his neck reddening. 'I think they have some kind of system that tells them when you're online.'

'I'll believe you,' she said.

'It's true!' His voice was rising.

'Okay, okay. I really do believe you.'

'I'd *never* do that, Siobhan.'

She nodded, but kept quiet. They had reached the outskirts of Edinburgh when the next message was announced. This time it was Quizmaster. Grant pulled up on to the verge and stopped the car.

'What's he saying?'

'Take a look.' Siobhan angled the laptop towards him. They were a team, after all . . .

Hart Fell is all I needed. You didn't need to climb it.

'Bastard,' Grant hissed.

Siobhan typed her response. *Did Flip know that?* There was nothing for a couple of minutes, then: *You're two moves away from Hellbank. Clue follows in approximately ten minutes. You have twenty-four hours to solve it. Do you wish to continue the game?*

Siobhan looked at Grant. 'Tell him yes,' he said.

'Not yet.' When he looked at her, she held his gaze. 'I think maybe he needs us as much as we need him.'

'Can we risk that?'

But she was already typing: *Need to know – did Flip have help? Who else was playing?*

His response was immediate: *Last time of asking. Do you wish to continue?*

'We don't want to lose him,' Grant warned.

'He *knew* I'd climb that hill. Probably the way he knew Flip wouldn't.' Siobhan chewed her bottom lip. 'I think we can push him a bit further.'

'We're two clues away from Hellbank. That's as far as Flip got.'

Siobhan nodded slowly, then began to type: *Continue to next level, but please, just tell me if Flip had anyone helping her.*

Grant sat back and sucked in his breath. Nothing came back. Siobhan checked her watch. 'He said ten minutes.'

'You like to gamble, don't you?'

'What's life without a bit of risk?'

'A much pleasanter, less stressful experience.'

She looked at him. 'This from the boy racer.'

He wiped the windscreen clear of condensation. 'If Flip didn't need to climb Hart Fell, I wonder if she needed to do any travelling at all. I mean, could she have solved the puzzle from her bedroom?'

'Meaning?'

'Meaning she wouldn't have gone anywhere that would have got her into trouble.'

Siobhan nodded. 'Maybe the next clue will tell us.'

'If there is a next clue.'

'You gotta have faith,' she sang.

'That's just what faith is to me: a song by George Michael.'

The laptop told them there was a message. Grant leaned over again to read it.

A corny beginning where the mason's dream ended.

While they were still taking it in, another message arrived: *I don't think Flipside had any help. Is anyone helping you, Siobhan?*

She typed 'No' and pressed 'send'.

'Why don't you want him to know?' Grant asked.

'Because he might change the rules, or even take the huff. He says Flip was on her own, I want him to think the same about me.' She glanced at him. 'Is that a problem?'

Grant thought for a moment, then shook his head. 'So what does the latest clue mean?'

'I haven't the faintest. I don't suppose you're a Mason?'

He shook his head again. 'Never quite got round to joining. Any idea where we might find one?'

Siobhan smiled. 'In the Lothian and Borders Police? I don't think we'll have too much trouble . . .'

The coffins had turned up at St Leonard's, as had the autopsy notes. There was just the one small problem: the Falls coffin was now in the possession of Steve Holly. Bev Dodds had given it to him so it could be photographed. Rebus decided he'd have to visit Holly's office. He grabbed his jacket and walked across to the desk opposite, where Ellen Wylie was looking bored as Donald Devlin pored over the contents of a slim manila file.

'I have to go out,' he explained.

'Lucky you. Need any company?'

'Look after Professor Devlin. I won't be long.'

Devlin looked up. 'And where are your peregrinations taking you?'

'There's a reporter I need to talk to.'

'Ah, our much-derided fourth estate.'

The way Devlin talked, it was getting on Rebus's nerves. And he wasn't alone, if Wylie's look was anything to go by. She always sat with her chair as far from the Professor as possible, on opposite sides of the desk if she could manage it.

'I'll be as quick as I can,' he tried to reassure her, but as he walked away he knew her eyes were following him all the way to the door.

Another thing about Devlin: he was almost too keen. Being useful again had taken years off him. He relished the autopsy reports, reciting passages aloud, and whenever Rebus was busy or trying to concentrate, you could be sure Devlin had some question to ask. Not for the first time, Rebus cursed Gates and Curt. Wylie herself had summed it up by way of a question to Rebus: 'Remind me,' she'd asked, 'is he helping us or are we helping him? I mean, if I'd wanted to be a care assistant, I'd have applied to an old folk's home . . .'

In his car, Rebus tried not to count the number of pubs he passed on his route into town.

The Glasgow tabloid had its office on the top floor of a Queen Street conversion a few doors along from the BBC. Rebus chanced his luck, parked on a single yellow line outside. The main door was wedged open, so he climbed the three flights and pulled open a glass-panelled door leading to a cramped reception area where a woman working a switchboard smiled at him as she answered the latest call.

'I'm afraid he's out for the day. Do you have his mobile number?' Her short blonde hair was tucked behind both ears. She wore a black headset consisting of earpiece and microphone. 'Thank you,' she said, terminating the call, only to press a button to take another. She didn't look at Rebus, but held up a finger telling him he hadn't been forgotten. He looked around for somewhere to sit, but there were no chairs, just an exhausted-looking cheese plant in a pot it was fast outgrowing.

'I'm afraid he's out for the day,' she told the new caller. 'Do you have his mobile number?' She gave this number, then terminated the call.

'Sorry about that,' she told Rebus.

'That's okay. I'm here to see Steve Holly, but I have the feeling I know what you're going to say.'

'He's out for the day, I'm afraid.'

Rebus nodded.

'Do you have his—'

'I do, yes.'

'Was he expecting you?'

'I don't know. I'm here to pick up the doll, if he's finished with it.'

'Ooh, that thing.' She made a show of shivering. 'He left it on my chair this morning. Steve's idea of a laugh.'

'The hours must fly.'

She smiled again, enjoying this little conspiracy against her colleague. 'I think it's in his cubicle.'

Rebus nodded. 'Photos all done?'

'Oh, yes.'

'Then maybe I could . . . ?' He pointed a thumb towards where he guessed Holly's cubicle might be.

'Don't see why not.' The switchboard was sounding again.

'I'll leave you to it then,' Rebus said, turning round as if he knew exactly where he was going.

It was easy enough. There were only four 'cubicles': desks separated by free-standing partition walls. No one was working in any of them. The small coffin was sitting next to Holly's keyboard, a couple of test Polaroids lying on top. Rebus congratulated himself: this was best-case-scenario stuff. If Holly had been here, there'd have been questions to parry, maybe a bit of grief. He took the opportunity to give the work-space a once-over. Phone numbers and news clippings pinned to the walls, a two-inch-high Scooby Doo stuck to the top of the monitor. A Simpsons desk calendar, covered with doodles, on a page three weeks out of date. A memo recorder, its battery compartment open and empty. There was a newspaper headline taped to the side of the monitor: 'Super Cally Go Ballistic, Celtic Are Atrocious'. Rebus had a little smile: it was a modern classic, referred to a football match. Maybe Holly was a Rangers fan, maybe he just appreciated a joke. As he was about to leave, he noticed Jean's name and phone number on the wall near the desk. He tore it down and pocketed it, then saw other numbers beneath . . . his own, plus Gill Templer's. Beneath these were other names: Bill Pryde, Siobhan Clarke, Ellen Wylie. The reporter had home numbers for Templer and Clarke. Rebus couldn't know if Holly had copies, but he decided to take the lot with him.

Outside, he tried Siobhan's mobile, but got a recording saying his call couldn't be connected. There was a ticket on his car, no sign of the warden. They were known around town as 'Blue Meanies' because of their uniform. Rebus, probably the only person who'd seen *Yellow Submarine* in the cinema without benefit of drugs, appreciated the name, but cursed the ticket anyway, stuffing it in his glove compartment. He smoked a cigarette on the crawl back to St Leonard's. So many of the streets now, you couldn't go the way you wanted. Unable to take a left on to Princes Street, and with traffic stalled at Waverley Bridge due to roadworks, he ended up taking The Mound, turning off down Market Street. He had Janis Joplin on the stereo, 'Buried Alive in the Blues'. Had to be better than a living death on Edinburgh's roads.

Back at the office, Ellen Wylie looked like she could sing some blues of her own.

'Fancy a little trip?' Rebus asked.

She perked up. 'Where?'

'Professor Devlin, you're invited too.'

'Sounds most intriguing.' He wasn't wearing a cardigan today, but a V-neck jumper, sagging beneath the arms but too short at the back. 'Would this be some sort of mystery tour?'

'Not exactly. We're visiting a funeral parlour.'

Wylie stared at him. 'You've got to be joking.'

But Rebus shook his head, pointing towards the coffins arranged on his desk. 'If you want an expert opinion,' he said, 'you need to ask an expert.'

'Self-evidently,' Devlin agreed.

The undertaker's was a short walk from St Leonard's. Last time Rebus had been in a funeral parlour was when his father had died. He'd walked forward, touched the old man's forehead, the way his father had taught him when his mother had died: *if you touch them, Johnny, you'll never need fear the dead*. Somewhere in the city, Conor Leary was settling into his own box. Death and taxes: shared by everyone. But Rebus had known some criminals who'd never paid a bawbee's tax in their life. It didn't matter: when the time was right, their box was still waiting.

Jean Burchill was already there. She rose from the chair in the reception area, as if glad of some company. The mood was sombre, despite the sprays of fresh-cut flowers. Idly, Rebus wondered if they got a discount from whoever did their wreaths. The walls were wood-panelled, and there was a faint smell of furniture polish. The brass doorhandles gleamed. Underfoot, the floor was tiled with marble, black and white squares like a chessboard. Rebus made the introductions. While shaking Jean's hand, Devlin asked, 'And what is it exactly that you curate?'

'Nineteenth-century,' she explained. 'Belief systems, social concerns . . .'

'Ms Burchill is helping us form a historical perspective,' Rebus said.

'I'm not sure I understand.' Devlin looked to her for help.

'I put together the display of the Arthur's Seat coffins.'

Devlin's eyebrows shot up. 'Oh, but how fascinating! And there may be some correlation with the current spate?'

'I'm not sure you could call it a "spate",' Ellen Wylie argued. 'Five coffins over a thirty-year period.'

Devlin seemed taken aback. Perhaps he wasn't often pulled up for his vocabulary. He gave Wylie a look, then turned to Rebus. 'But *is* there some historical connection?'

'We don't know. That's what we're here to find out.'

The inner door opened and a man appeared. He was in his fifties, dressed in dark suit, crisp white shirt, and grey shimmering tie. His hair was short and silver, his face long and pale.

'Mr Hodges?' Rebus asked. The man acknowledged as much with a bow. Rebus shook his hand. 'We spoke on the phone. I'm Detective Inspector Rebus.' Rebus introduced the others.

'It was,' Mr Hodges said in a near-whisper, 'one of the more remarkable requests I've received. However, Mr Patullo is waiting for you in my office. Would you care for any tea?'

Rebus assured him they'd be fine, and asked if Hodges would lead the way.

'As I explained on the phone, Inspector, these days the majority of coffins are made along what could be described as an assembly-line process. Mr Patullo is that rare woodworker who will still produce a casket to order. We've been using his services for years, certainly for as long as I've been with the firm.' The hall they trooped along was wood-panelled like the reception area, but with no exterior lighting. Hodges opened a door and ushered them inside. The office was spacious, completely lacking in clutter. Rebus didn't know what he'd expected: displays of bereavement cards, brochures for coffins maybe. But the only clue that this office belonged to an undertaker was the very lack of any outward clues. It went beyond discretion. The clients who came in here didn't want reminding of the visit's purpose, and Rebus didn't suppose it made the undertaker's job any easier if people were bursting into tears every two minutes.

'I'll leave you alone,' Hodges said, closing the door. He'd arranged enough seats for them, but Patullo was standing beside the opaque window. He carried a flat tweed cap, the brim of which he worried between the fingers of both hands. The fingers themselves were gnarled, the skin like parchment. Rebus reckoned Patullo had to be in his mid-seventies. He still had a good head of thick silver hair, and his eyes were clear, if wary. But he held himself with a stoop, and his hand trembled when Rebus made to shake it.

'Mr Patullo,' he said, 'I really appreciate you agreeing to meet us.'

Patullo shrugged, and Rebus made one more round of introductions before telling everyone to sit down. He had the coffins in a carrier bag, and brought them out now, laying them on the unblemished surface of Mr Hodges's desk. There were four of them – Perth, Nairn, Glasgow, plus the more recent one from Falls.

'I'd like you to take a look, please,' Rebus said, 'and tell us what you see.'

'I see some wee coffins.' Patullo's voice was hoarse.

'I meant in terms of craftsmanship.'

Patullo reached into his pocket for his glasses, then got up and stood in front of the display.

'Pick them up if you like,' Rebus said. Patullo did so, examining the lids and the dolls, peering closely at the nails.

'Carpet tacks and small wood nails,' he commented. 'The joints are a bit rough, but working to this scale . . .'

'What?'

'Well, you wouldn't expect to see anything as detailed as a dovetail.' He went back to his examination. 'You want to know if a coffin-maker made these?' Rebus nodded. 'I don't think so. There's a bit of skill here, but not that much. The proportions are wrong, the shape's too much of a diamond.' He turned each coffin over to examine its underside. 'See the pencil marks here where he made his outline?' Rebus nodded. 'He measured up, then he cut with a saw. Didn't do any planing, just some sandpaper.' He looked at Rebus over the top of his glasses. 'You want to know if they're all by the same hand?'

Again, Rebus nodded.

'This one's a bit cruder,' Patullo said, holding up the Glasgow coffin. 'Different wood, too. The rest are pine, this is balsa. But the joints are the same, as are the measurements.'

'So you think it's the same person?'

'As long as my life didn't depend on it.' Patullo picked up another coffin. 'Now this one, the proportions are different. Joints aren't so tidy. Either a rushed job, or my guess would be it's by someone else.'

Rebus looked at the coffin. It was the one from Falls.

'So we've got two different people responsible?' Wylie said. When Patullo nodded, she blew air from her mouth and rolled her eyes. Two culprits made for twice the work, and halved the chance of getting a result.

'A copycat?' Rebus guessed.

'I wouldn't know,' Patullo admitted.

'Which brings us to . . .' Jean Burchill dipped a hand into her shoulder-bag, produced a box, which she opened. Inside, wrapped in tissue, was one of the Arthur's Seat coffins. Rebus had asked her to bring it, and she made eye contact with him now, letting him know what she'd already told him in the café: that she was putting her job on the line. If it was discovered that she'd sneaked an artefact out of the Museum, or if anything happened to it . . . she'd be dismissed on the spot. Rebus nodded his head, letting her know he understood. She got up and placed the coffin on the desk.

'It's rather delicate,' she told Patullo. Devlin, too, had risen to his feet, and Wylie wanted a better look also.

'My goodness,' Devlin gasped, 'is that what I think it is?'

Jean just nodded. Patullo didn't pick the coffin up, but bent down so his eyes were close to the level of the desk.

'What we're wondering,' Rebus said, 'is whether you think the coffins you've just looked at could be modelled on this.'

Patullo rubbed his cheek. 'This is a much more basic design. Still well made, but the sides are a lot straighter. It's not the casket shape we'd recognise today. The lid has been decorated with iron studs.' He rubbed his cheek again, then straightened up, gripping the edge of the desk for support. 'They're not copies of it. That's about as much as I can tell you.'

'I've never seen one outside the Museum,' Devlin said, shuffling forward so he could take Patullo's place. He beamed at Jean Burchill. 'You know, I have a theory as to who made them.'

Jean raised an eyebrow. 'Who?'

Devlin turned his attention to Rebus. 'You remember that portrait I showed you? Dr Kennet Lovell?' When Rebus nodded, Devlin turned back to Jean. 'He was the anatomist who carried out Burke's autopsy. Afterwards, I think he carried a weight of guilt over the whole affair.'

Jean was interested. 'Had he been buying corpses from Burke?'

Devlin shook his head. 'There's no historical indication that such was the case. But like many an anatomist of the day, he probably bought his share of bodies without asking too many questions as to provenance. The thing is,' Devlin licked his lips, 'our Dr Lovell was also interested in carpentry.'

'Professor Devlin,' Rebus told Jean, 'owns a table he made.'

'Lovell was a good man,' Devlin was saying, 'and a good Christian.'

'He left them to commemorate the dead?' Jean asked.

Devlin shrugged, glanced around. 'I've no evidence, of course . . .' His voice tailed off, as though he realised his animation maybe looked foolish.

'It's an interesting theory,' Jean conceded, but Devlin only shrugged again, as though realising he was being patronised.

'Like I say, it's well enough made,' Patullo commented.

'There are other theories,' Jean said. 'Maybe witches or sailors made the Arthur's Seat coffins.'

Patullo nodded. 'Sailors used to be good woodworkers. In some cases it was a necessity, for others it passed a long voyage.'

'Well,' Rebus said, 'thanks again for your time, Mr Patullo. Can we get someone to drive you home?'

'I'll be fine.'

They said their goodbyes, and Rebus directed his party to the Metropole café, where they ordered coffees and squeezed into one of the booths.

'One step forward, two steps back,' Wylie said.

'How do you reckon?' Rebus asked.

'If there's no connection between the other coffins and the one at Falls, we're chasing a wild goose.'

'I don't see that,' Jean Burchill interrupted. 'I mean, maybe I'm speaking out of turn here, but it seems to me whoever left that coffin at Falls had to get the idea from somewhere.'

'Agreed,' Wylie said, 'but it's far more likely they got it from a trip to the Museum, wouldn't you say?'

Rebus was looking at Wylie. 'You're saying we should ditch the four previous cases?'

'I'm saying their only relevance here is if they connect to the Falls coffin, always supposing *it* has anything to do with the Balfour disappearance. And we can't even be sure of *that*.' Rebus started to say something, but she hadn't finished. 'If we go to DCS Templer with this – as we should – she'll say the same thing I'm saying now. We're getting further and further away from the Balfour case.' She raised her cup to her lips and sipped.

Rebus turned to Devlin, who was sitting next to him. 'What do you think, Professor?'

'I'm forced to agree, reluctant though I am to be cast back into the darkness of an old man's retirement.'

'There was nothing in the autopsy notes?'

'Nothing as yet. It looks very much as if both women were alive when they went into the water. Both bodies sustained some injuries, but that's not so unusual. The river would have rocks in it, so that the victim may have hit her head when falling. As to the victim in Nairn, the tides and sealife can do terrible things to a body, especially one that's been in the water for some time. I'm sorry I can't be more helpful.'

'Everything's useful,' Jean Burchill said. 'If it doesn't rule something in, it can help rule other things out.'

She looked to Rebus, hoping he might smile at hearing his own words paraphrased, but his mind was elsewhere. He was worried Wylie was right. Four coffins left by the same person, one by someone completely different, no connection between the two. The problem was, he felt there *was* a connection. But it wasn't something he could make someone like Wylie comprehend. There were times when instinct had to take over, no matter what the protocol. Rebus felt this was one of those times, but doubted Wylie would go along with it.

And he couldn't blame her for that.

'Maybe if you could give the notes a final look,' he asked Devlin.

'Gladly,' the old man said, bowing his head.

'And talk to the pathologists from either case. Sometimes they remember things . . .'

'Absolutely.'

Rebus turned his attention to Ellen Wylie. 'Maybe you should make your report to DCS Templer. Tell her what we've done. I'm sure there's work for you on the main investigation.'

She straightened her back. 'Meaning you're not giving up?'

Rebus gave a tired smile. 'I'm close to. Just a couple more days.'

'To do what exactly?'

'Convince myself it's a dead end.'

The way Jean looked at him across the table, he knew she wanted to offer him something, some form of comfort: a squeeze of the hand maybe, or a few well-intentioned words. He was glad there were other people present, making the gesture impossible. Otherwise he might have blurted something out, something about comfort being the last thing he needed.

Unless comfort and oblivion were the same thing.

Daytime drinking was special. In a bar, time ceased to exist, and with it the outside world. For as long as you stayed in the pub, you felt immortal and ageless. And when you stumbled back out from twilight into raging daylight, people all around you going about their afternoon's business, the world had a new shine to it. After all, people had been doing the same damned thing for centuries: plugging the holes in their consciousness with alcohol. But today . . . today Rebus was just having the two drinks. He knew he could walk out after two. To stay for three or four would mean staying either until closing time or until he keeled over. But two . . . two was a manageable number. He smiled at that word: number, with its possible other meaning – that which made you numb. Comfortably numb, as Pink Floyd would say.

Vodka and fresh orange: not his first choice, but it didn't leave a smell. He could walk back into St Leonard's and no one would know. It was just that the world would seem a little softer to him. When his mobile sounded, he thought of ignoring it, but its trilling was disturbing the other drinkers, so he pushed the button.

'Hello?'

'Let me guess,' the voice said. It was Siobhan.

'In case you're wondering, I'm not in a pub.' Which was the cue for the young guy at the bandit to hit a big win, the coins disgorging noisily.

'You were saying?'

'I'm meeting someone.'

'Do these excuses get any better?'

'What do you want anyway?'

'I need to pick a Mason's brain.'

He misheard. 'You need to pick "Amazing Grace"?'

'A *Mason*. You know, funny handshakes, trousers rolled up.'

'Can't help. I failed the audition.'

'But you must know a few?'

He thought about it. 'What's all this about anyway?'

So she told him the latest clue.

'Let me think,' he said. 'How about the Farmer?'

'Is he one?'

'Going by his handshake.'

'Do you think he'd mind me calling him?'

'Quite the opposite.' There was a pause. 'Now you're going to ask if I know his home number, and as it happens you're in luck.' He took out his notebook, recited the number.

'Thanks, John.'

'How's it going anyway?'

'Okay.'

Rebus detected a slight reticence. 'Everything all right with Grant?'

'Fine, yes.'

Rebus raised his eyes to the gantry. 'He's there with you, isn't he?'

'That's right.'

'Message received. We'll talk later. Oh, hang on.'

'What?'

'You ever had anything to do with someone called Steve Holly?'

'Who is he?'

'A local hack.'

'Oh, him. I think we might have talked once or twice.'

'He ever call you at home?'

'Don't be daft. That's one number I keep close to my chest.'

'Funny, he has it pinned to the wall in his office.' She didn't say anything. 'No idea how he could have come by it?'

'I suppose there are ways. I'm not giving him tip-offs or anything, if that's what you're implying.'

'The only thing I'm implying, Siobhan, is that he needs watching. He's as smooth as a fresh-laid turd and gives off the same smell.'

'Charming. I've got to go.'

'Yes, me too.' Rebus cut the call and drained his second drink. Right, that was that then, time to call it a day. Except there was another race coming up on TV, and he had his eye on the chestnut, Long Day's Journey. Maybe one more wouldn't do any harm . . . Then his phone rang again, and, cursing, he pushed his way outdoors, squinting into the sudden light.

'Yes?' he snapped.

'That was a bit naughty.'

'Who's this?'

'Steve Holly. We met at Bev's house.'

'Funny, I was just talking about you.'

'Only, I'm glad we met that day, or I might not have been able to place you from Margot's description.' Margot: the blonde receptionist with the earpiece. Not enough of a conspirator to resist grassing Rebus up . . .

'What do you mean?'

'Come on, Rebus. The coffin.'

'I heard you'd finished with it.'

'Is it evidence then?'

'No, I was just returning it to Ms Dodds.'

'I'll bet. Something's going on here.'

'Bright boy. That "something" is a police investigation. In fact, I'm up to my eyes in it right now, so if you wouldn't mind . . .'

'Bev said something about all these other coffins . . .'

'Did she? Maybe she misheard.'

'I don't think so.' Holly waited, but Rebus wasn't saying anything. 'Fine,' the journalist said into the silence. 'We'll talk later.' *We'll talk later*, the very words Rebus had used to Siobhan. For a split second, he wondered if Holly had been listening in. But it wasn't possible. As the phone went dead, two things struck Rebus. One was that Holly hadn't mentioned the phone numbers missing from his wall, so probably hadn't noticed them yet. The other was that he'd just called Rebus on his mobile, meaning he knew the number. Normally, Rebus gave out his pager rather than his mobile. He wondered which he had given to Bev Dodds . . .

Balfour's Bank wasn't much like a bank at all. For a start, it was sited on Charlotte Square, one of the most elegant parts of the New Town. Shoppers queued grimly for non-existent buses outside, but inside was very different: thick carpets, an imposing staircase, and a huge chandelier, walls recently given a coat of startling white. There were no cashiers, no queues. Transactions were dealt with by three members of staff seated at their own desks, far apart so that discretion was assured. The staff were young and well dressed. Other customers sat in comfortable chairs, selecting newspapers and magazines from the coffee table as they waited to be ushered into one of the private rooms. The atmosphere was rarefied: this was a place where money wasn't so much respected as worshipped. It reminded Siobhan of a temple.

'What did he say?' Grant Hood asked.

She slipped her mobile back into her pocket. 'He thinks we should talk to the Farmer.'

'Is that his number?' Grant nodded towards Siobhan's notebook.

'Yes.' She'd placed the letter F beside the number: F for Farmer. It made the various addresses and phone numbers in her notebook harder to identify, should the book fall into the wrong hands. She was annoyed that a journalist she barely knew should have access to her home number. Not that he'd called her there, but all the same . . .

'Reckon anyone here has an overdraft?' Grant asked.

'The staff might. Not so sure about their clients.'

A middle-aged woman had come from behind one of the doors, closing it softly behind her. She made no noise at all as she walked towards them.

'Mr Marr will see you now.'

They'd expected to be led back to the door, but instead the woman headed for the staircase. Her brisk pace kept her four or five steps ahead of them: no chance for conversation. At the end of the first-floor hall she knocked on a double set of doors and waited.

'Enter!' At which command she pushed open both the doors, gesturing for the two detectives to walk past her and into the room.

It was huge, with three floor-to-ceiling windows, covered by pale linen roller-blinds. There was a polished oak committee-table, laid with pens, notepads and water-jugs. It took up only a third of the available space. There was a seating area – sofa and chair, with a TV nearby showing stock-market fluctuations. Ranald Marr himself was standing behind his desk, a huge antique expanse of walnut. Marr, too, was burnished, his tan looking as though it had its roots in the Caribbean rather than a Nicolson Street sun-bed. He was tall, his salt-and-pepper hair immaculately barbered. His suit was a double-breasted pinstripe, almost certainly bespoke. He deigned to come forward to greet them.

'Ranald Marr,' he said unnecessarily. Then, to the woman: 'Thank you, Camille.'

She closed the doors after her, and Marr gestured towards the sofa. The two detectives made themselves comfortable while Marr settled into the matching leather chair. He crossed one leg over the other.

'Any news?' he asked, his face turning solicitous.

'Inquiries are progressing, sir,' Grant Hood informed him. Siobhan tried not to look askance at her colleague: *inquiries are progressing* . . . she wondered which TV show Grant had picked that up from.

'The reason we're here, Mr Marr,' Siobhan said, 'is because it looks like Philippa was involved in some sort of role-playing game.'

'Really?' Marr looked puzzled. 'But what's that got to do with me?'

'Well, sir,' Grant said, 'it's just that we've heard you like to play those sorts of games, too.'

' "Those sorts of . . ."?' Marr clapped his hands together. 'Oh, I know what you mean now. My soldiers.' He frowned. 'Is that what Flip was involved in? She never showed any interest . . .'

'This is a game where clues are given and the player has to solve each one to reach a different level.'

'Not the same thing at all.' Marr slapped his knees and rose to his feet. 'Come on,' he said, 'I'll show you.' He went to his desk and took a key from a drawer. 'This way,' he said brusquely, opening the door to the hallway. He led them back to the top of the staircase, but climbed a narrower stairwell to the second storey. 'Along here.' As he walked, Siobhan noticed a slight limp. He disguised it well, but it was there. Probably he should have been using a stick, but she doubted his vanity would allow it. She caught wafts of eau-de-Cologne. No wedding ring on show. When he made to slip the key into a lock, she saw that his wristwatch was a complicated affair with a leather strap to match his tan.

He opened the door and preceded them inside. The window had been covered with a black sheet, and he switched on the overhead lights. The room was half the size of his office, much of the space taken up with something at table height. It was a model, maybe eighteen feet long by ten wide: green rolling hills, a blue strip of river. There were trees and ruined dwellings, and, covering much of the board, two armies. Several hundred soldiers, divided into regiments. The pieces themselves were less than an inch high, but the detail on each was painstaking.

'I painted most of them myself. Tried to keep them all that little bit different, give them a personality.'

'You re-enact battles?' Grant said, picking up a cannon. Marr didn't look happy at this transgression. He nodded, lifting the piece delicately from Grant with forefinger and thumb.

'That's what I do. War-gaming, you could call it.' He placed the piece back on the board.

'I went paintballing once,' Grant told him. 'Ever done that?'

Marr allowed the officer a thin smile. 'We took the bank staff once. I can't say I was keen: too much mess. But John enjoyed himself. He's always threatening a return fixture.'

'John being Mr Balfour?' Siobhan guessed.

There was a shelf stacked with books: some on modelling, some about the battles themselves. Other shelves contained clear plastic boxes within which rested armies, waiting for their chance at victory.

'Do you ever change the outcome?' Siobhan asked.

'That's part of the strategy,' Marr explained. 'You figure out where the defeated side went wrong, and you try to alter history.' There was a new passion in his voice. Siobhan walked over to where a seamstress's dummy had been kitted out in uniform. There were other uniforms – some better preserved than others – mounted behind glass on the walls. No weapons of any kind, just the clothes the soldiers would have worn.

'The Crimea,' Marr said, pointing to one of the framed jackets.

Grant Hood interrupted with a question. 'Do you play against other people?'

'Sometimes.'

'They come here?'

'Never here, no. I have a much larger layout in the garage at my house.'

'Then why do you need a set-up here?'

Marr smiled. 'I find that it relaxes me, helps me think. And I *do* get the occasional break from the desk.' He broke off. 'You think it a childish hobby?'

'Not at all,' Siobhan said, only half truthfully. There was a certain 'toys for the boys' feel to it, and she could see the years dropping from Grant as he studied the little model armies. 'Ever play any other way?' she asked.

'How do you mean?'

She shrugged, as if the question had been a casual inquiry merely, keeping the conversation going. 'I don't know,' she said. 'Maybe moves sent by post. I've heard of chess players doing that. Or how about the Internet?'

Grant glanced at her, seeing her gist immediately.

'I know of some Internet sites,' Marr said. 'You get one of those camera thingies.'

'Web cams?' Grant offered.

'That's it. Then you can play across continents.'

'But you've never done that?'

'I'm not the most technically gifted of people.'

Siobhan turned her attention back to the bookcase. 'Ever heard of a character called Gandalf?'

'Which one?' She just looked at him. 'I mean, I know at least two. The wizard in *Lord of the Rings*, and the rather odd chap who runs the games shop on Leith Walk.'

'You've been to his shop then?'

'I've bought a few pieces from him down the years. But I mostly buy mail order.'

'And over the Internet?'

Marr nodded. 'Once or twice, yes. Look, who was it exactly who told you about this?'

'About you liking to play games?' Grant asked.

'Yes.'

'It's taken you a while to ask,' Siobhan commented.

He glowered at her. 'Well, I'm asking now.'

'I'm afraid we're not at liberty to say.'

Marr didn't like that, but refrained from making a comment. 'Am I right in thinking,' he said instead, 'that whatever game it was Flip was playing, it was nothing like this?'

Siobhan shook her head. 'Nothing at all like it, sir.'

Marr looked relieved. 'Everything all right, sir?' Grant asked.

'Everything's fine. It's just . . . it's proving such a terrible strain on all of us.'

'I'm sure that's true,' Siobhan said. Then, with a last expansive look around: 'Well, thank you for letting us see your toys, Mr Marr. We'd better let you get back to work now . . .' But having half turned away, she stopped again. 'I'm sure I've seen soldiers like these somewhere before,' she said, as if thinking aloud. 'Maybe in David Costello's flat?'

'I think I *did* give David one piece,' Marr said. 'Was it him who . . . ?' He broke off, smiled and shook his head. 'I forgot: you won't be at liberty to say.'

'Quite so, sir,' Hood told him.

As they left the building, Grant started to chuckle. 'He didn't like it when you called them "toys".'

'I know, that's why I said it.'

'Don't bother trying to open an account, I can see you being blackballed.'

She smiled. 'He knows about the Internet, Grant. And playing those sorts of games, he's probably got an analytical mind.'

'Quizmaster?'

She wrinkled her nose. 'I'm not sure. I mean, why would he do it? What's in it for him?'

Grant shrugged. 'Maybe nothing much ... apart from control of Balfour's Bank.'

'Yes, there's always that,' Siobhan said. She was thinking about the playing piece in David Costello's flat. A little gift from Ranald Marr ... only Costello had said he'd no idea where it had come from, with its broken musket and the soldier's head twisted round. Then he'd called her and told her about Marr's little hobby ...

'Meantime,' Grant was saying, 'we're no closer to solving the clue.'

He broke her train of thought. She turned towards him. 'Just promise me one thing, Grant.'

'What's that?'

'Promise you're not going to turn up outside my flat at midnight.'

'No can do,' Grant said, smiling. 'We're against the clock, remember.'

She looked at him again, remembering the way he'd been on top of Hart Fell, the way he'd gripped her hands. Right now, he looked like he was enjoying himself – the chase, the challenge – just a little too much.

'Promise,' she said again.

'Okay,' he said. 'I promise.'

Then he turned and gave her a wink.

*

Back at the station, Siobhan sat in a toilet cubicle and studied the hand which she'd brought up level with her eyes. The hand carried a slight tremble. It was curious how you could be quivering inside, yet manage not to show it. But she knew her body had other ways of manifesting outward signs: the rashes she sometimes got; the outbreaks of acne on her chin and neck; the eczema she sometimes suffered from on the thumb and forefinger of her left hand.

She was trembling now because she was having trouble focusing on what was important. It was important to do the job well; important, too, not to piss off Gill Templer. She didn't think her own hide was toughened the way Rebus's was. The case was important, and maybe Quizmaster was too. It rankled that she couldn't know for sure. She knew one thing: that the game was in danger of becoming an obsession. She kept trying to put herself in Flip Balfour's shoes, to think along the same lines. She couldn't be sure how well she was doing. Then there was Grant, who was looking more and more of a liability. Yet she couldn't have come this far without him, so maybe it was important that she stay close to him. She couldn't even be sure that Quizmaster was male. She had a gut feeling, but it was dangerous to depend on those: she'd seen Rebus screw up more than once on the strength of a gut feeling for someone's guilt or innocence.

She still wondered about the liaison job, and whether she'd burned her bridges there. Gill had succeeded only by becoming more like the male officers around her, people like ACC Carswell. She probably thought she'd played the system, but Siobhan suspected that it was the system which had played *her*, moulding her, changing her, making sure she would fit in. It meant putting up barriers, keeping your distance. It meant teaching people lessons, people like Ellen Wylie.

She heard the door to the Ladies' creak open. A moment later, there was a soft tapping on her cubicle door.

'Siobhan? That you in there?'

She recognised the voice: Dilys Gemmill, one of the WPCs. 'What's up, Dilys?' she called.

'That drink tonight, wondered if you were still on.'

It was a regular thing: four or five WPCs, plus Siobhan. A bar with loud music, plenty of gossip to go with the Moscow Mules. Siobhan an honorary member: the only non-uniform ever invited.

'I don't think I can manage it, Dilys.'

'Come on, girl . . .'

'Next time for definite, okay?'

'It's your funeral,' Gemmill said, moving away.

'I hope not,' Siobhan muttered to herself, getting up to unlock the door.

Rebus stood across the road from the church. He'd been home to change, but now that he was here he couldn't make himself go in. A taxi drew up and Dr Curt stepped out. As he stopped to button his jacket, he saw Rebus. It was a small, local church, just as Leary had wanted. He'd said as much to Rebus several times during the course of their conversations.

'Quick, clean and simple,' he'd stated. 'It's the only way I'll have it.'

The church might have been small, but the congregation looked large. The Archbishop, who'd attended the Scots College in Rome with Leary, would be leading the service, and what looked like dozens of priests and officiates had filed into the church already. 'Clean' it might be, but Rebus doubted the event would turn out either 'quick' or 'simple' . . .

Curt was crossing the street. Rebus flicked the remains of his cigarette on to the roadway and slid his hands into his pockets. He noticed some ash clinging to his sleeve, but didn't bother brushing it away.

'Nice day for it,' Curt commented, studying a sky which thick cloud had turned a bruised-looking grey. It felt claustrophobic, even outdoors. When Rebus brushed a hand across the back of his head he could feel the follicles coated with sweat. On afternoons like this, Edinburgh felt like imprisonment, a city of walls.

Curt was tugging at one of his shirt sleeves, making sure it came an inch below the jacket, exposing a hallmarked silver cuff-link. His suit was dark blue, the shirt white, his tie plain black. His black brogues had been given a polish. Always immaculately dressed. Rebus knew his own suit, though the best, the most formal he possessed, was shabby by comparison. He'd had it six, seven years, had sucked his gut in to get the trousers fastened. Hadn't even bothered trying to button the jacket. Austin Reed he'd got it from; maybe it was time for another visit. He got few invites these days to weddings and christenings, but funerals were another matter. Colleagues, drinkers he knew . . . they were falling off the perch. Only three weeks back, he'd been to the crematorium, a woolly-suit from St Leonard's who'd died less than a year after retiring. The white shirt and black tie had gone back on to the hanger afterwards. He'd checked the shirt collar this afternoon, before putting the shirt back on.

'Shall we go in then?' Curt said.

Rebus nodded. 'You go ahead.'

'What's wrong?'

Rebus shook his head. 'Nothing. I'm just not sure . . .' He took his hands from his pockets, busied himself with another cigarette. Offered one to Curt, who nodded and took it.

'Not sure of what?' the pathologist asked, as Rebus lit the cigarette for him. Rebus waited until he had his own one lit. A couple of puffs and then a loud exhaling of smoke.

'I want to remember him the way he was to me,' he said. 'If I go in there, it'll be speeches and other people's memories. It won't be the Conor I knew.'

'The pair of you were pretty close at one time,' Curt agreed. 'I didn't really know him that well.'

'Is Gates coming?' Rebus asked.

Curt shook his head. 'Prior commitment.'

'Did the pair of you do the autopsy?'

'It was a brain haemorrhage.'

More mourners were arriving, some on foot, others by car. Another taxi drew up, and Donald Devlin got out. Rebus thought he spotted a grey cardigan beneath the suit jacket. Devlin took the church steps at a brisk pace and disappeared inside.

'Was he able to help you?' Curt asked.

'Who?'

Curt nodded towards the departing taxi. 'The old-timer.'

'Not really. He gave it his best shot though.'

'Then he did as much as Gates or I could have.'

'I suppose so.' Rebus was thinking of Devlin, picturing him at the desk, poring over details, Ellen Wylie keeping her distance. 'He was married, wasn't he?' he asked.

Curt nodded again. 'Widower. Why do you ask?'

'No reason, really.'

Curt looked at his watch. 'I think I'd better go in.' He stamped the cigarette out on the pavement. 'Are you coming?'

'I don't think so.'

'What about the cemetery?'

'I think I'll give that a miss too.' Rebus looked up at the clouds. 'What the Americans would call a rain-check.'

Curt nodded. 'I'll see you later then.'

'Next time there's a homicide,' Rebus confirmed. Then he turned and walked away. His head was filling with images of the mortuary, the post-mortem examination. The wooden blocks they laid the deceased's head on. The little channels on the table which drained away the body fluids. The instruments and specimen jars . . . He thought of the jars he'd seen in the Black Museum, the way horror had mixed with fascination. One day, maybe not too far away, he knew it would be him on that table, maybe Curt and Gates preparing their day's routine. That was what he would be to them: part of the routine, just as another routine was being played out in the church behind him. He hoped some of it would be in Latin: Leary had been a great fan of the Latin mass, would recite whole passages to Rebus, knowing he couldn't understand.

'Surely in your day they taught Latin?' he'd asked one time.

'Maybe at the posh school,' Rebus had replied. 'Where I went, it was woodwork and metalwork.'

'Turning out workers for the religion of heavy industry?' And Leary had chuckled, the sound booming from deep within his chest. Those sounds were what Rebus would remember: the clucking of his tongue whenever he felt Rebus had said anything wantonly idiotic; the exaggerated groan whenever he rose to fetch more Guinness from the fridge.

'Ah, Conor,' Rebus said now, bowing his head so no passers-by would see the tears forming.

Siobhan was on the phone to the Farmer.

'It's good to hear from you, Siobhan.'

'Actually, I'm after a favour, sir. Sorry to disturb your peace and quiet.'

'There's such a thing as too much peace and quiet, you know.' The Farmer laughed, so she would assume he was joking, but she detected something behind his words.

'It's important to stay active.' She almost winced: it sounded like something from an agony column.

'That's what they say all right.' He laughed again: it sounded even more forced this time. 'Which new hobby are you suggesting?'

'I don't know.' Siobhan squirmed in her chair. This wasn't quite the conversation she'd expected. Grant Hood was sitting the other side of the desk. He'd borrowed John Rebus's chair, which looked like the one from the Farmer's old office. 'Maybe golf?'

Now Grant frowned, wondering what the hell she was talking about.

'I've always said golf spoils a good walk,' the Farmer said.

'Well, walking's good for you.'

'Is it? Thanks for reminding me.' The Farmer definitely sounded tetchy; she didn't know quite why or how she'd hit a nerve.

'About this favour . . .?' she began.

'Yes, better ask it quick, before I get my jogging shoes on.'

'It's sort of a clue to a puzzle.'

'You mean a crossword?'

'No, sir. It's something we're working on. Philippa Balfour was trying to solve all these clues, so we're doing the same.'

'And how can I help?' He'd calmed a little; sounded interested.

'Well, sir, the clue goes: "a corny beginning where the mason's dream ended". We're wondering if it might be "mason" as in "Masonic Lodge".'

'And someone told you I'm a Mason?'

'Yes.'

The Farmer was quiet for a moment. 'Let me get a pen,' he said at last. Then he had her repeat the clue while he wrote it down. 'Capital M on Mason?'

'No, sir. Does that make a difference?'

'I'm not sure. Usually I'd expect a capital.'

'So it could be a stonemason or something instead?'

'Hang on, I'm not saying you're wrong. I just need to think about it. Can you give me half an hour or so?'

'Of course.'

'Are you at St Leonard's?'

'Yes, sir.'

'Siobhan, you don't need to call me "sir" any more.'

'Understood . . . sir.' She smiled. 'Sorry, can't help it.'

The Farmer seemed to brighten a little. 'Well, I'll call you back after I've given this some thought. No nearer to finding out what happened to her?'

'We're all working flat out, sir.'

'I'm sure you are. How's Gill coping?'

'In her element, I think.'

'She could go all the way, Siobhan, mark my words. There's a lot you could learn from Gill Templer.'

'Yes, sir. I'll speak to you later.'

'Bye, Siobhan.'

She put the phone down. 'He's going to mull it over,' she told Grant.

'Great, and meantime the clock's ticking.'

'Okay then, clever-clogs, let's hear *your* great idea.'

He looked at her as if measuring the challenge, then held up a finger. 'One, it reads to me almost like a story-line. Maybe from Shakespeare or somewhere.' A second finger. 'Two, does it mean "corny" as in old-fashioned, or is it maybe to do with where corn comes from?'

'You mean where corn was first grown?'

He shrugged. 'Or how it starts off life as a seed: ever heard the expression "sowing the corn of an idea"?'

She shook her head. He held up another finger.

'Three, say it's mason as in stonemason. Could it be a gravestone? That's where all our dreams end, after all. Maybe it's a carving of a corn-stalk.' He bunched the raised fingers into a fist. 'That's what I've got so far.'

'If it's a gravestone, we need to know which cemetery.' Siobhan picked up the scrap of paper on which she'd written the clue. 'There's nothing here, no map reference or page number . . .'

Grant nodded. 'It's a different kind of clue.' He seemed to spot something else. 'Could "a corny beginning" actually be "acorny", as in like an acorn?'

Siobhan frowned. 'Where would that get us?'

'An oak tree . . . maybe oak leaves. A cemetery with "acorn" or "oak" in its name?'

She puffed out her cheeks. 'And where would this cemetery be, or do we have to check every town and city in Scotland?'

'I don't know,' Grant conceded, rubbing at his temples. Siobhan let the clue drop back on to the desk.

'Are they getting harder?' she asked. 'Or is it that my brain's packing in?'

'Maybe we just need a break,' Grant said, trying to get comfortable in the chair. 'We could even call it a day.'

Siobhan glanced up at the clock. It was true: they'd put in about ten hours already. The whole morning had been spent on a wasted trip south. She could feel her limbs aching from the climb. A long hot soak with some bath salts and a glass of Chardonnay . . . It was tempting. But she knew that when she woke up tomorrow, there'd be scant time left before the clue was void, always supposing Quizmaster stuck to his rules. The problem was, the only way to know whether he would or not was to fail to solve the clue in time. It wasn't the sort of risk she wanted to take.

The trip to Balfour's Bank . . . she wondered if that had been a waste of time too. Ranald Marr and his little soldiers . . . the tip-off coming from David Costello . . . the broken playing piece in Costello's flat. She wondered if Costello had been trying to tell her something about Marr. She couldn't think what. Skulking at the back of her mind was the possibility that this whole exercise was a waste of time, that Quizmaster really was playing with them, that the game had nothing to do with Flip's disappearance . . . Maybe that drink with the girls wasn't such a bad idea . . . When her phone went, she snatched at it.

'DC Clarke, CID,' she recited into the mouthpiece.

'DC Clarke, it's the front desk. Got someone down here wants a word.'

'Who is it?'

'A Mr Gandalf.' The speaker's voice dropped. 'Weird-looking bugger, like he got sunstroke in the Summer of Love and hasn't been right since . . .'

Siobhan went downstairs. Gandalf was holding a dark brown fedora, stroking the multicoloured feather attached to its headband. He wore a brown leather waistcoat over the same Grateful Dead T-shirt he'd worn in his shop. The pale blue cords had seen better days, as had the sand-shoes on his feet.

'Hi there,' Siobhan said.

His eyes widened as though he didn't quite recognise her.

'It's Siobhan Clarke,' she said, holding out her hand. 'We met at your shop.'

'Yes, yes,' he mumbled. He stared at her hand but didn't seem inclined to shake it, so Siobhan lowered her arm.

'What brings you here, Gandalf?'

'I said I'd see what I could find about Quizmaster.'

'That's right,' she said. 'Would you like to come upstairs? I could probably rustle us up a cup of coffee.'

He stared at the door she'd just come through, and slowly shook his head. 'Don't like police stations,' he said gravely. 'They give off a bad vibe.'

'I'm sure they do,' Siobhan agreed. 'You'd rather talk outside?' She looked out at the street. Still rush hour, the traffic nose to tail.

'There's a shop round the corner, run by some people I know . . .'

'Good vibes?' Siobhan guessed.

'Excellent,' Gandalf said, his voice animated for the first time.

'Won't it be shut?'

He shook his head. 'They're still open. I checked.'

'All right then, just give me a minute.' Siobhan walked over to the desk, where a shirtsleeved officer was watching from behind a glass shield. 'Can you buzz upstairs to DC Hood, tell him I'll be back in ten?'

The officer nodded.

'Come on then,' Siobhan told Gandalf. 'What's the shop called anyway?'

'Out of the Nomad's Tent.'

Siobhan knew the place. It was more warehouse than shop, and sold gorgeous carpets and crafts. She'd splashed out there once on a kilim, because the rug she'd coveted was out of her price range. A lot of the stuff came from India and Iran. As they walked in, Gandalf waved a greeting to the proprietor, who waved back and returned to some paperwork.

'Good vibes,' Gandalf said with a smile, and Siobhan couldn't help but smile back.

'Not sure my overdraft would agree,' she said.

'It's only money,' Gandalf told her, as though imparting some great wisdom.

She shrugged, keen to get down to business. 'So, what can you tell me about Quizmaster?'

'Not a great deal, except that he may have other names.'

'Such as?'

'Questor, Quizling, Myster, Spellbinder, OmniSent . . . How many do you want?'

'What does it all mean?'

'These are names used by people who've set challenges on the Internet.'

'Games that are happening right now?'

He reached out his hand to touch a rug hanging from the nearest wall. 'You could study this pattern for years,' he said, 'and still not wholly understand it.'

Siobhan repeated her question and he seemed to come to himself.

'No, they're old games. Some involving logic puzzles, numerology . . . others where you took on a role, like knight or apprentice wizard.' He glanced towards her. 'We're talking about the virtual world. Quizmaster could have *virtually* any number of names at his disposal.'

'And no way of tracing him?'

Gandalf shrugged. 'Maybe if you asked the CIA or the FBI . . .'

'I'll bear that in mind.'

He shifted slightly in what was almost a squirm. 'I did learn one other thing.'

'What?'

He took a sheet of paper from the back pocket of his cords, handed it to Siobhan, who unfolded it. A news cutting from three years before. It concerned a student who had disappeared from his home in Germany. A body had been found on a remote hillside in the north of Scotland. It had been lying there many weeks, even months, disturbed only by the local wildlife. Identification had proven difficult, the corpse reduced to skin and bone. Until the parents of the German student had widened their search. They became convinced the body on the hillside was that of their son, Jürgen. A revolver had been found twenty feet from the corpse. A single bullet had pierced the young man's skull. The police had it down as suicide, explained away the location of the firearm by saying a sheep or some other animal could have moved it. Plausible, Siobhan had to concede. But the parents still weren't convinced that their son hadn't been murdered. The gun wasn't his, and couldn't be traced. The bigger question was: how had he ended up in the Scottish Highlands? No one seemed to know. Then Siobhan frowned, had to read the story's final paragraph again:

Jürgen was keen on role-playing games, and spent many hours surfing the Internet. His parents think it possible that their student son became involved in some game which had tragic consequences.

Siobhan held up the clipping. 'Is this all there is?'

He nodded. 'Just the one story.'

'Where did you get it?'

'From someone I know.' He held out his hand. 'He'd like it back.'

'Why?'

'Because he's writing a book about the perils of the e-universe. Incidentally, he'd like to interview you some time, too.'

'Maybe later.' Siobhan folded the clipping but made no attempt to hand it back. 'I need to keep this, Gandalf. Your friend can have it when I'm finished with it.'

Gandalf looked disappointed in her, as though she'd failed to keep her side of some bargain.

'I promise he can have it back when I'm finished.'

'Couldn't we just photocopy it?'

Siobhan sighed. An hour from now, she hoped she'd be in that bathtub, maybe with a gin and tonic replacing the wine. 'All right,' she said. 'Come back to the station and . . .'

'They'll have a copier here.' He was pointing towards the corner where the proprietor sat.

'Okay, you win.'

Gandalf brightened at this, as though those three little words were the sweetest ones he knew.

Back at the station, having left Gandalf at Out of the Nomad's Tent, Siobhan found Grant Hood scrunching another sheet of paper into a ball and failing to hit the waste-paper bin with it.

'What's up?' she asked.

'I got wondering about anagrams.'

'And?'

'Well, if the town of Banchory didn't have that "h", it would be an anagram of "a corny b".'

Siobhan burst out laughing, slapping her hand to her mouth when she saw Grant's look.

'No,' he said, 'go ahead and laugh.'

'God, I'm sorry, Grant. I think I'm nearing a state of mild hysteria.'

'Should we try e-mailing Quizmaster, tell him we're stuck?'

'Maybe nearer the deadline.' Looking over his shoulder at the remaining sheet of paper, Siobhan saw that he was working on anagrams for 'mason's dream'.

'Call it a day?' he suggested.

'Maybe.'

He caught her tone of voice. 'You've got something?'

'Gandalf,' she said, handing over the news story. She watched him read, noticing that his lips moved slightly. She wondered if he'd always done it . . .

'Interesting,' he said at last. 'Do we follow it up?'

'I think we have to, don't you?'

He shook his head. 'Hand it over to the inquiry. We've got our work cut out with this bloody clue.'

'Hand it over . . . ?' She was aghast. 'This is *ours*, Grant. What if it turns out to be vital?'

'Christ, Siobhan, listen to yourself. It's an *inquiry*, lots of people all chipping in. It doesn't belong to us. You can't be selfish with something like this.'

'I just don't want someone else stealing our thunder.'

'Even if it means finding Flip Balfour alive?'

She paused, screwed up her face. 'Don't be stupid.'

'This all comes from John Rebus, doesn't it?'

Colour rose to her cheeks. 'What does?'

'Wanting to keep it all to yourself, like the whole investigation's down to you and you alone.'

'Bollocks.'

'You know it yourself; I can see it just by looking at you.'

'I don't believe I'm hearing this.'

He stood up to face her. They were no more than a foot apart, the office empty. 'You know it,' he repeated quietly.

'Look, all I was trying to say . . .'

'. . . was that you don't want to share, and if that doesn't sound like Rebus, I don't know what does.'

'You know your trouble?'

'I get the feeling I'm about to find out.'

'You're too chicken, always playing by the rule-book.'

'You're a cop, not a private detective.'

'And you're chicken. Blinkers on and toeing the line.'

'Chickens don't wear blinkers,' he spat back.

'They must, because *you* do!' she exploded.

'That's right,' he said, seeming to calm a little, head bobbing. 'That's right: I always play by the rules, don't I?'

'Look, all I meant was—'

He grabbed her arms, pulled her to him, his mouth seeking hers. Siobhan's body went rigid, then her face twisted away. The grip he had on her arms, she couldn't move them. She'd backed up against the desk, stuck there.

'A good close working partnership,' a voice boomed from the doorway. 'That's what I like to see.'

Grant's grip on her fell away as Rebus walked into the room.

'Don't mind me,' he continued. 'Just because I don't indulge in these new-fangled methods of policing doesn't mean I don't approve.'

'We were just . . .' Grant's voice died. Siobhan had walked round the desk and was lowering herself shakily into her chair. Rebus approached.

'Finished with this?' He meant the Farmer's chair. Grant nodded and Rebus wheeled it back towards his own desk. He noticed that on Ellen Wylie's desk, the autopsy reports were tied back up with string: conclusions reached, and of no further use. 'Did the Farmer get you a result?' he asked.

'Hasn't called back,' Siobhan said, trying to control her voice. 'I was just about to phone him.'

'But you mistook Grant's tonsils for the receiver, eh?'

'Sir,' she said, keeping her voice level, though her heart was pounding, 'I wouldn't want you to get the wrong impression about what happened here . . .'

Rebus held up a hand. 'Nothing to do with me, Siobhan. You're dead right. Let's say no more about it.'

'I think something needs to be said.' Her voice had risen. She glanced over towards where Grant was standing, body turned away from her, head twisted so his eyes were not quite on her.

But she knew he was pleading. Mr Boy-Tekky-Racer! Mr Nerdy-Well with his gadgets and flash car!

Better make that a bottle of gin, a whole crateful of gin. And sod the bath.

'Oh?' Rebus was asking, genuinely curious now.

I could finish your career right here, Grant. 'It's nothing,' she said finally. Rebus stared at her, but she kept her eyes fixed on the paperwork before her.

'Anything happening your end, Grant?' he asked blithely, settling into his chair.

'What?' Colour bloomed in Grant's cheeks.

'The latest clue: anywhere near solving it?'

'Not really, sir.' Grant was standing by one of the other desks, gripping its edge.

'How about you?' Siobhan asked, shifting in her seat.

'Me?' Rebus tapped a pen against his knuckles. 'I think today I've managed to achieve the square root of bugger all.' He threw the pen down. 'Which is why I'm buying.'

'Already had a couple of drinks?' Siobhan asked.

Rebus's eyes narrowed. 'A few. They put a friend of mine into the ground. Tonight, I was planning a private wake. If either of you would like to join me, that would be fine.'

'I need to go home,' Siobhan said.

'I don't . . .'

'Come on, Grant. It'll be good for you.'

Grant looked in Siobhan's direction, seeking guidance, or maybe permission. 'I suppose I might manage the one,' he conceded.

'Good lad,' Rebus told him. 'One drink it is.'

Having nursed his pint while Rebus downed two double whiskies and two beers, Grant was dismayed to find another half poured into his glass as soon as there was room for it.

'I have to drive home,' he warned.

'Bloody hell, Grant,' Rebus complained, 'that's about all I've heard from you.'

'Sorry.'

'And apologies make up the rest. I can't see there's any need to apologise for snogging Siobhan.'

'I don't know how it happened.'

'Don't try to analyse it.'

'I think the case just got . . .' He broke off at the sound of a dull electronic bleeping. 'Yours or mine?' he asked, already reaching into his jacket. But it was Rebus's mobile. He angled his head to let Grant know he was taking it outside.

'Hello?' Cool twilight, taxis looking for trade. A woman nearly tripped over a cracked paving slab. A young man, shaven head and nose-ring, helped her retrieve the oranges which had tumbled from her shopping bag. A small act of kindness . . . but Rebus watched until the youth moved away, just in case.

'John? It's Jean. Are you working?'

'Surveillance,' Rebus told her.

'Oh dear, do you want me to . . . ?'

'It's okay, Jean. I was joking. I'm just out having a drink.'

'How was the funeral?'

'I didn't go. I mean, I *did* go, but I couldn't face it.'

'And now you're drinking?'

'Don't start with the help-line stuff.'

She laughed. 'I wasn't going to. It's just that I'm sitting here with a bottle of wine and the TV . . .'

'And?'

'And some company would be nice.'

Rebus knew he was in no state to drive; not much of a state for anything, if it came to it. 'I don't know, Jean. You've not seen me after a drink.'

'What, you turn into Mr Hyde?' She laughed again. 'I had that with my husband. I doubt you could show me anything new.' Her voice strained for levity, but there was an edge to it. Maybe she was nervous about asking him: no one liked a rejection. Or maybe there was more to it . . .

'I suppose I could take a taxi.' He studied himself: still in the funeral suit, the tie removed and top two buttons of the shirt undone. 'Maybe I should go home and change.'

'If you like.'

He looked across the street. The woman with the shopping was waiting at the bus stop now. She kept glancing into her bag as if checking everything was there. City life: mistrust part of the armour you wore; no such thing as a simple good deed.

'I'll see you soon,' he said.

Back in the pub, Grant was standing next to his empty pint glass. As Rebus came forwards, he raised his hands in a show of surrender.

'Got to go.'

'Yes, me too,' Rebus said.

Grant looked somehow disappointed, as though he'd wanted Rebus to go on drinking, getting drunker. Rebus looked at the empty glass, wondering if the barman had been persuaded to ditch its contents.

'You all right to drive?' Rebus asked.

'I'm fine.'

'Good.' Rebus slapped Grant's shoulder. 'In that case, you can give me a lift to Portobello . . .'

Siobhan had spent the past hour trying to clear her head of anything and everything to do with the case. It wasn't working. The bath hadn't worked; the gin was refusing to kick in. The music on her hi-fi – Mutton Birds, *Envy of Angels* – wasn't cocooning her the way it usually did. The latest clue was ricocheting around her skull. And every thirty seconds or so . . . here it came again! . . . she watched a replay of Grant pinning her arms, while John Rebus – of all people! – watched from the doorway. She wondered what would have happened if he hadn't announced his presence. She wondered how long he'd been there, and whether he'd heard any of their argument.

She leaped back up from the sofa and started pacing the room again, glass in hand. No, no, no . . . as if repeating the word could make everything go away, never have happened. Because *that* was the problem. You couldn't unmake something.

'Stupid bitch,' she said aloud in a sing-song voice, repeating the phrase until the words lost their meaning.

Stupidbitchstupidbitch . . .

No no no no no no . . .

The mason's dream . . .

Flip Balfour . . . Gandalf . . . Ranald Marr . . .

Grant Hood.

Stupidbitchstupidbitch . . .

She was over by the window when the track ended. In the momentary silence, she heard a car turning into the end of her street, and instinct told her who it was. She ran to the lamp and stamped down on the floor-switch, plunging the room into darkness. There was a light on in her hallway, but she doubted it could be seen from outside. She was afraid to move, afraid she would cast a telltale shadow. The car had stopped. The next track was playing. She reached down for the remote and used it to turn off the CD player. Now she could hear the car idling. Her heart was pounding.

Then the door buzzer, telling her someone was outside and wanting in. She waited, didn't move. Her fingers were so tight around the glass that they began to cramp. She changed hands. The buzzer again.

No no no no . . .

Just leave it, Grant. Get in the Alfa and go home. Tomorrow we can start pretending it never happened.

Bzzzz bzzzz zzzz . . .

She began to hum softly to herself, a tune she was making up. Not even a tune really; just sounds to compete with the buzzer and the blood singing in her ears.

She heard a car door close, relaxed a little. Nearly dropped the glass when her phone started ringing.

She could see it by the light of the streetlamp. It was lying on the floor by the sofa. Six rings and the answering machine would kick in. Two . . . three . . . four . . .

Maybe the Farmer!

'Hello?' She slumped on to the sofa, phone to her ear.

'Siobhan? It's Grant.'

'Where are you?'

'I've just been ringing your doorbell.'

'Mustn't be working. What can I do for you?'

'Letting me in would be a start.'

'I'm tired, Grant. Just going to bed.'

'Five minutes, Siobhan.'

'I don't think so.'

'Oh.' The silence was like a third party, some huge, humourless friend only one of them had invited.

'Just go home, eh? I'll see you in the morning.'

'That might be too late for the Quizmaster.'

'Oh, you're here to talk about work?' She slid her free hand up her body, tucking it beneath the arm holding the phone.

'Not exactly,' he admitted.

'No, I didn't think so. Look, Grant, let's call it a moment of madness, eh? I think I can live with that.'

'That's what you think it was?'

'Don't you?'

'What are you scared of, Siobhan?'

'How do you mean?' Her voice hardening.

A short silence before he relented, telling her: 'Nothing. I didn't mean anything. Sorry.'

'I'll see you in the office then.'

'Right.'

'Get a good night's sleep. We'll crack the clue tomorrow.'

'If you say so.'

'I do. Goodnight, Grant.'

''Night, Shiv.'

She ended the call, didn't even take the time to tell him she hated 'Shiv': girls at school had used it. One of her boyfriends at college had liked it, too. He told her it was slang for a knife. Siobhan: even the teachers at her school in England had had trouble with her name. 'See-Oban' they'd pronounce it, and she would have to correct them.

Night, Shiv . . .

Stupidbitch . . .

She heard his car move off, watched the play of headlights across her ceiling and far wall. She sat there in the dark, finishing her drink without tasting it. When her phone rang again, she swore out loud.

'Look,' she roared into the mouthpiece, 'just let it go, okay?'

'Well . . . if you say so.' It was the Farmer's voice.

'Oh, hell, sir, I'm sorry.'

'Expecting another call?'

'No, I . . . maybe another time.'

'Fair enough. I've been doing some ringing round. There are people who know the Craft far better than I do, I thought maybe they could shed some light.'

His tone told her what she needed to know. 'No joy?'

'Not as such. But a couple of folk have still to get back to me. Nobody home, so I left messages. *Nil desperandum*: that's what they say, isn't it?'

Her smile was bleak. 'Some of them probably do, yes.' Hopeless optimists, for example.

'So you can expect another call tomorrow. What time's the cut-off?'

'Late morning.'

'Then I'll make some follow-up calls first thing.'

'Thank you, sir.'

'It's nice to feel useful again.' He paused. 'Things getting you down, Siobhan?'

'I'll cope.'

'I'd put money on it. Speak to you tomorrow.'

'Goodnight, sir.'

She put the phone down. Her drink was finished. *This all comes from John Rebus, doesn't it?* Grant's words to her during their argument. Now here she was with an empty glass in her hand, sitting in the dark, staring out the window.

'I'm not like him at all,' she said out loud, then she picked up the phone again and called his number. Got his answering machine. She knew she could try his mobile. Maybe he was out on the bevvy; almost certainly he was out on the bevvy. She could meet up with him, explore the city's late openers, each dimly lit howff protection against the dark.

But he'd want to talk about Grant, about the clinch he thought he'd found them in. It would be there between them, no matter what the conversation.

She thought about it for a minute, then called his mobile anyway, but it was switched off. Another answering service; another message not left. Last-chance saloon was his pager, but she was winding down now. A mug of tea . . . she'd take it to bed with her. She switched the kettle on, looked for the tea-bags. The box was empty. All she had were some little sachets of herbal stuff: camomile. She wondered if the petrol station at Canonmills would be open . . . maybe the chip shop on Broughton Street. Yes, that was it . . . she could see the answer to her problems! She slipped her shoes and coat on, made sure she had keys and money. When she went out, she checked that the door had locked behind her. Down the stairs and out into the night, searching for the one ally she could depend on, no matter what.

Chocolate.

9

It had just gone seven-thirty when the phone woke her up. She staggered from bed, padded through to the living room. She had one hand on her forehead; the other reached for the handset.

'Hello?'

'Good morning, Siobhan. Didn't wake you, did I?'

'No, I was just making breakfast.' She blinked a few times, then stretched her face, trying to get her eyes open. The Farmer sounded like he'd been up for hours.

'Well, I don't want to keep you, only I've just had a very interesting phone call.'

'One of your contacts?'

'Another early riser. He's in the middle of writing a book about the Knights Templar, connecting them to the Masons. That's probably why he saw it straight away.'

Siobhan was in the kitchen now. She checked there was water in the kettle and switched it on. Enough instant coffee in the jar for maybe two or three cups. She had to do a supermarket run one of these days. Crumbs of chocolate on the worktop. She pressed her finger to them, lifting them to her mouth.

'Saw what?' she said.

The Farmer started laughing. 'You're not awake yet, are you?'

'A bit groggy, that's all.'

'Late night?'

'Maybe one Rolo too many. Saw what, sir?'

'The clue. It's a reference to Rosslyn Chapel. You know where that is?'

'I was there not too long ago.' Another case; one she'd worked with Rebus.

'Then maybe you saw it: one of the windows apparently is decorated with carvings of maize.'

'I don't remember.' But she was waking up now.

'Yet the chapel was built before maize was known in Britain.'

'"A corny beginning",' she recited.

'That's right.'

'And the mason's dream?'

'Something you must have noticed in the chapel: two elaborate pillars. One is called the Mason's Pillar, the other the Apprentice Pillar. The story goes, the Master Mason decided to go abroad to study the design for the pillar he was to construct. But while he was away, one of his apprentices had a dream about the way the finished pillar should look. He got to work and created the Apprentice Pillar. When the Master Mason returned, he was so jealous he went after the apprentice and bludgeoned him to death with a mallet.'

'So the mason's dream ended with the pillar?'

'That's right.'

Siobhan went through the story in her head. 'It all fits,' she said at last. 'Thanks so much, sir.'

'Mission accomplished?'

'Well, not quite. I've got to go.'

'Call me some other time, Siobhan. I want to hear how it ends.'

'I will. Thanks again.'

She ran both hands through her hair. *A corny beginning where the mason's dream ended*. Rosslyn Chapel. It was in the village of Roslin, about six miles south of the city. Siobhan picked up her phone again, ready to call Grant . . . But then she put it down. Over at the laptop, she sent an e-mail to Quizmaster:

The Apprentice Pillar, Rosslyn Chapel.

Then she waited. She drank a cup of weak coffee, using it to wash down two paracetamol. She went into the bathroom and had a shower. She was rubbing her hair dry with a towel when she walked back into the living room. There was still no message from Quizmaster. She sat down again, chewed her bottom lip. They hadn't needed to go to Hart Fell: the name had been enough. In less than three hours, time would be up. Did Quizmaster want her to go to Roslin? She sent another e-mail:

Do I stay or do I go?

Again she waited. The second cup of coffee was weaker than the first. The jar was empty now. If she wanted anything else to drink, it would have to be camomile tea. She wondered if Quizmaster could have gone somewhere. She got the feeling he would take a laptop and mobile with him wherever he went. Maybe he'd even run it twenty-four/seven, just like she'd been doing. He'd want to know when messages came through.

So what was he playing at?

'Can't risk it,' she said out loud. One final message: *I'm going to the chapel.* Then she went to get dressed.

She got into her car, placed the laptop on the passenger seat. She thought again about calling Grant, but decided against it. She'd be all right; she could take any flak he threw at her . . .

. . . you don't want to share. And if that doesn't sound like Rebus, I don't know what does.

Grant's words to her. Yet here she was heading off to Roslin on her own. No back-up, and having alerted Quizmaster that she was coming. Before she'd reached the top of Leith Walk she'd made up her mind. She turned the car in the direction of Grant's flat.

It was just gone eight-fifteen when the phone woke Rebus up. It was his mobile. He'd plugged it into a wall socket last thing, charged it overnight. He slid from the bed and got his feet caught in the clothes strewn across the carpet. Down on hands and knees, he fumbled for the phone, held it to his ear.

'Rebus,' he said. 'And this had better be good.'

'You're late,' the voice said. Gill Templer.

'Late for what?'

'The big story.'

Still on hands and knees, Rebus glanced towards the bed. No sign of Jean. He wondered if she'd gone to work.

'What big story?'

'Your presence is requested in Holyrood Park. A body's been found on Arthur's Seat.'

'Is it her?' Rebus felt his skin suddenly go clammy.

'Hard to judge at this stage.'

'Oh, Christ.' He angled his neck, eyes to the ceiling. 'How did she die?'

'Body's been there a while.'

'Are Gates and Curt on the scene?'

'Expected shortly.'

'I'll go straight there.'

'Sorry to have disturbed you. Not at Jean's by any chance?'

'Is that a wild guess?'

'Maybe call it woman's intuition.'

'Bye, Gill.'

'Bye, John.'

As he was switching off the phone, the door swung open and Jean Burchill walked in. She was wearing a towelling robe and carrying a tray: orange juice and toast, a cafetière full of coffee.

'My,' she said, 'don't you look fetching?'

Then she saw the look on his face and her smile vanished. 'What's wrong?' she asked.

So he told her.

Grant yawned. They'd picked up a couple of beakers of coffee from a newsagent's, but even so he wasn't fully awake yet. His hair was standing up at the back, and he seemed conscious of it, kept trying to press it flat with his hand.

'Didn't get much sleep last night,' he said, glancing in Siobhan's direction. She kept her eyes on the road.

'Anything in the paper?'

He had the day's tabloid – bought along with the coffees – open across his lap. 'Not much.'

'Anything about the case?'

'I don't think so. Relegated to oblivion.' He had a sudden thought, started patting his pockets.

'What?' For a split second, she thought maybe he'd forgotten some vital medication.

'My mobile. Must've left it on the table.'

'We've got mine.'

'Yes, hooked to my ISP: what happens if someone tries calling?'

'They'll leave a message.'

'I suppose so . . . Look, about yesterday . . .'

'Let's pretend it never happened,' she said quickly.

'But it did.'

'I just wish it hadn't, all right?'

'You're the one who was always complaining I—'

'Subject closed, Grant.' She turned to him. 'I mean it. It's either closed, or I take it to the boss – your call.'

He started to say something, but stopped himself, folded his arms across his chest. Virgin AM was playing quietly on the stereo. She liked it; helped her wake up. Grant wanted something newsy, Radio Scotland or Radio Four.

'My car, my stereo,' was all she'd said to that.

Now he asked her to repeat what she'd already told him about the Farmer's call. She did, glad that they were staying off the subject of the clinch.

Grant sipped his coffee while she spoke. He was wearing sunglasses, though there was no sun. They were Ray-Bans, tortoiseshell frames.

'Sounds good,' he said when she'd finished.

'I think so,' she agreed.

'Almost too easy.'

She snorted. 'So easy we almost missed it.'

He shrugged. 'It didn't take any skill, that's what I'm saying. It's the sort of thing you either know or you don't.'

'Like you said, a different kind of clue.'

'How many Masons do you suppose Philippa Balfour knows?'

'What?'

'It's how you found out. How would *she* have worked it out?'

'She was studying art history, wasn't she?'

'True. So she might have come across Rosslyn Chapel in her studies?'

'Possibly.'

'And would Quizmaster have known that?'

'How could he?'

'Maybe she told him what she was studying.'

'Maybe.'

'Otherwise, it's just not the sort of clue she'd have been able to get. Do you see what I'm saying?'

'I think so. You're saying it needed specialist knowledge that the previous clues didn't?'

'Something like that. Of course, there is one other possibility.'

'Which is?'

'That Quizmaster knew damned fine she'd know a little of Rosslyn Chapel, whether she told him what she was studying or not.'

Siobhan saw what he was getting at. 'Someone who knows her? You're saying Quizmaster is one of her friends?'

Grant peered at her over the top of his Ray-Bans. 'Wouldn't surprise me if Ranald Marr turned out to be a Mason, man in his line of work . . .'

'No, nor me,' Siobhan said thoughtfully. 'We might just have to go back and ask him.'

They turned off the main road and drove into the village of Roslin. Siobhan parked the car beside the chapel's gift shop. The door was locked tight.

'Place doesn't open till ten,' Grant said, reading from the notice. 'How long do you reckon we've got?'

'If we wait till ten, not very long.' Siobhan was sitting in the car, checking that there were no new e-mails for her.

'There must be somebody.' Grant banged on the door with his fist. Siobhan got out of the car and studied the wall surrounding the chapel grounds.

'Any good at climbing?' she asked Grant.

'We could give it a go,' he said. 'But what if the chapel's locked too?'

'What if someone's in there giving it a quick spit and polish?'

He nodded. But then there was the sound of a bolt being drawn back. The door opened and a man stood there.

'We're not open yet,' he said sternly.

Siobhan showed him her warrant card. 'Police officers, sir. Afraid we can't wait.'

They followed him along a path towards the chapel's side door. The building itself was covered with a huge canopy. From her previous visit, Siobhan knew there was a problem with the roof. It had to dry out before work could be done on it. The chapel was small on the outside, but seemed larger inside, a trick of its ornate decoration. The ceiling itself was stunning, even if much of it was green with damp and decay. Grant stood in the central aisle, gawping much as she had done the first time she'd come here.

'It's incredible,' he said quietly, his words echoing back off the walls. There were carvings everywhere. But Siobhan knew what she was looking for, and walked straight towards the Apprentice Pillar. It was next to some steps leading down to the sacristy. The pillar was about eight feet high, carved ribbons snaking down it.

'This it?' Grant said.

'This is it.'

'So what are we looking for?'

'We'll know when we find it.' Siobhan ran her hands over the cool surface of the pillar, then crouched down. Intertwined dragons were coiled around the base. The tail of one of them, twisting back on itself, had left a small nook. She reached in with finger and thumb and brought out a small square of paper.

'Bloody hell,' Grant said.

She didn't bother with gloves or an evidence bag, knew by now that Quizmaster wouldn't have left anything useful to Forensics. It was a piece of notepaper, folded over three times. She unfolded it, Grant shifting so they could both see what was printed there.

You are the Seeker. Your next destination is Hellbank. Instructions to follow.

'I don't get it,' Grant said. 'All of this, just for *that*?' His voice was rising.

Siobhan read the message through again, turned the paper over. Its other side was blank. Grant had spun on his heels and kicked air.

'Bastard!' he called out, earning a frown from the guide. 'I bet he's having a bloody good laugh, seeing us chasing all over the place!'

'I think that's part of it, yes,' Siobhan agreed quietly.

He turned to her. 'Part of what?'

'Part of the attraction for him. He likes to see us being run ragged.'

'Yes, but he *doesn't* see us, does he?'

'I don't know. I sometimes get the feeling he might be watching.'

Grant stared at her, then walked up to the guide. 'What's your name?'

'William Eadie.'

Grant had his notebook out. 'And what's your address, Mr Eadie?' He started to take down Eadie's details.

'He's not the Quizmaster,' Siobhan stated.

'The who?' Eadie asked, his voice wavering.

'Never mind,' Siobhan said, dragging Grant away by the arm. They went back to the car, and Siobhan started typing an e-mail:

Ready for Hellbank clue.

She sent it, then sat back.

'Now what?' Grant asked. Siobhan shrugged. But then the laptop announced there was a new message. She clicked to read it.

Ready to give up? That's a surer thing.

Grant let out a hiss of breath. 'Is this a clue or a taunt?'

'Maybe both.' Another message came through:

Hellbank by six tonight.

Siobhan nodded. 'Both,' she repeated.

'Six? He's only giving us eight hours.'

'No time to waste then. What's a surer thing?'

'Not a clue.'

She looked at him. 'You don't think it's a clue?'

He forced a smile. 'That's not what I meant. Let's take another look at it.' Siobhan put the message back up on the screen. 'You know what it looks like?'

'What?'

'A crossword clue. I mean, it's not quite grammatical, is it? It almost makes sense, but doesn't.'

Siobhan nodded. 'Like it's a bit strained?'

'If it *was* a crossword clue . . .' Grant pursed his lips. A little vertical crease appeared between his eyebrows as he concentrated. 'If it was a clue, then "give up" could mean "yield", as in yielding meaning. Do you see?'

He fumbled in his pocket, brought out his notebook and pen. 'I need to see it written down,' he explained, copying out the clue. 'It's a classic crossword construction: part of it tells you what you have to do, part is the meaning you'll have if you do it.'

'Keep going. You might start making sense soon.'

He smiled again, but kept his eyes on the words in front of him. 'Let's say it's an anagram. "Ready to give up . . . that's a surer". If you give up – meaning render or use – the letters in "that's a surer", you'll get a word or words meaning a "thing".'

'What sort of thing?' Siobhan could feel a headache coming on.

'That's what we have to find out.'

'If it's an anagram.'

'If it's an anagram,' Grant conceded.

'And what's any of it got to do with Hellbank, whatever Hellbank is?'

'I don't know.'

'If it *is* an anagram, isn't that too easy?'

'Only if you know how crosswords work. Otherwise you'd read it literally, and it wouldn't mean anything at all.'

'Well, you've just explained it and it still sounds like gobbledygook to me.'

'Then aren't you lucky I'm here? Come on.' He tore off a fresh sheet of paper and handed it to her. 'See if you can unscramble "that's a surer".'

'To make a word that means a thing?'

'Word or words,' Grant corrected her. 'You've got eleven letters to play with.'

'Isn't there some computer program we could use?'

'Probably. But that would be cheating, wouldn't it?'

'Right now, cheating sounds fine to me.'

But Grant wasn't listening. He was already at work.

'I was only up here yesterday,' Rebus said. Bill Pryde had left his clipboard back at Gayfield Square. He was breathing heavily as they climbed. Uniformed officers were standing around. They held rolls of striped tape and were waiting to be told whether a cordon was necessary or practical. There was a line of parked cars on the roadway below: journalists, photographers, at least one TV crew. Word had gone around fast, and the circus had come to town.

'Anything to tell us, DI Rebus?' he'd been asked by Steve Holly as he got out of his own car.

'Just that you're annoying me.'

Now Pryde was explaining that a walker had found the body. 'In some gorse bushes. No real attempt to hide it.'

Rebus kept quiet. Two bodies never found . . . the other two found in water. Now this: a hillside. It broke the pattern.

'Is it her?' he asked.

'From the Versace T-shirt, I'd have to say yes.'

Rebus stopped, looked around. A wilderness in the middle of Edinburgh. Arthur's Seat itself was an extinct volcano, surrounded by a bird sanctuary and three lochs. 'You'd have a hard job dragging a body up here,' he said.

Pryde nodded. 'Probably killed on the spot.'

'Lured up here?'

'Or maybe just out walking.'

Rebus shook his head. 'I don't figure her for the walking type.' They'd started moving again, getting close now. A cluster of stooped forms on the hillside, white overalls and hoods: all too easy to contaminate a crime scene. Rebus recognised Professor Gates, red-faced from the exertion of the climb. Gill Templer was next to him, not talking, just listening and looking. The scene-of-crime officers were doing a rudimentary ground search – later on, when the body had been shifted, they'd bring in some of the uniforms and start a fingertip search. It wouldn't be easy: the grass was long and thick. A police photographer was adjusting his lens.

'Better not go any further than this,' Pryde said. Then he called for someone to fetch two more sets of overalls. As Rebus started pulling his on over his shoes, the thin material crackled and flapped in the strong breeze.

'Any sign of Siobhan Clarke?' he asked.

'Tried contacting her and Grant Hood,' Pryde said. 'So far, no luck.'

'Really?' Rebus had to hold back a smile.

'Something I should know about?' Pryde asked.

Rebus shook his head. 'Grim place to die, isn't it?'

'Aren't they all?' Pryde zipped up his one-piece and started forwards towards the corpse.

'Throttled,' Gill Templer informed them.

'Best guess at this stage,' Gates corrected her. 'Morning, John.'

Rebus nodded a greeting back. 'Dr Curt not with you?'

'Phoned in sick. He's been sick a lot lately.' Gates was just making conversation while his examination continued. The body lay awkwardly, legs and arms all jutting angles. The gorse bushes next to it must have hidden it well enough, Rebus guessed. Combined with the long grass, you'd need to be closer than eight feet before you'd be able to make out what it was. The clothing helped with the camouflage: light green combat trousers, khaki T-shirt, grey jacket. The clothes Flip had been wearing the day she'd gone missing.

'Parents informed?' he asked.

Gill nodded. 'They know a body's been found.'

Rebus walked around her to get a better view. The face was turned away from him. There were leaves in the hair, and a slug's shimmering trail. Her skin was mauve-coloured. Gates had probably moved the body slightly. What Rebus was seeing was lividity, the blood sinking in death, colouring the body parts nearest the ground. He'd seen dozens of corpses over the years; they never got any less sad, or made him any less depressed. Animation was the key to every living thing, its absence difficult to accept. He'd seen grieving relatives reach out to bodies on mortuary slabs and shake them, as if this would bring them back. Philippa Balfour wasn't coming back.

'The fingers have been gnawed at,' Gates stated, more for his tape recorder than his audience. 'Local wildlife most probably.'

Weasels or foxes, Rebus guessed. Facts of nature you didn't find in the TV documentaries.

'Bit of a bugger, that,' Gates went on. Rebus knew what he meant: if Philippa had fought her attacker, her fingertips might have told them a lot – bits of skin or blood beneath the nails.

'What a waste,' Pryde suddenly said. Rebus got the feeling he didn't mean Philippa's death as such, but the effort they'd expended during the days since her disappearance – the checks on airports, ferries, trains . . . working on the assumption that she was maybe – just maybe – still alive. And throughout, she'd been lying here, each day robbing them of possible evidence, possible clues.

'Lucky she was found so soon,' Gates commented, perhaps to comfort Pryde. True enough, another woman's body had been found a few months back in a different part of the park, hardly any distance at all from a popular path. Yet the body had lain there for over a month. It had turned out to be a 'domestic', that handy euphemism when victims were killed by their loved ones.

Down below, Rebus recognised one of the grey mortuary vans arriving. The body would be bagged and taken away to the Western General, where Gates would conduct his autopsy.

'Drag marks on her heels,' Gates was reciting into his tape machine. 'Not too severe. Lividity consistent with body's position, so she was either still alive or only just dead when she was dragged here.'

Gill Templer looked around. 'How far do we need to widen the search?'

'Fifty, a hundred yards maybe,' Gates told her. She glanced in Rebus's direction, and he saw that she wasn't hopeful. Unlikely they'd be able to pinpoint exactly where she was dragged from, unless she'd dropped something.

'Nothing in the pockets?' Rebus asked.

Gates shook his head. 'Jewellery on the hands, and quite an expensive watch.'

'Cartier,' Gill added.

'At least we can rule out robbery,' Rebus muttered, causing Gates to smile.

'No signs of the clothing having been disturbed,' the pathologist commented, 'so you can probably rule out a sexual motive while you're at it.'

'Better and better.' Rebus looked at Gill. 'This is going to be a cinch.'

'Hence my ear-to-ear grin,' she parried solemnly.

Back at St Leonard's, the station was buzzing with the news, but all Siobhan could feel was a dazed numbness. Playing Quizmaster's game – the way Philippa probably had – had made Siobhan feel an affinity with the missing student. Now she was no longer a MisPer, and the worst fears had been realised.

'We always knew, didn't we?' Grant said. 'It was just a matter of when the body turned up.' He dropped his notebook on to the desk in front of him. Three or four pages were covered with anagrams. He sat down and turned to a fresh sheet, pen in hand. George Silvers and Ellen Wylie were in the CID room too.

'I took my kids up Arthur's Seat just last weekend,' Silvers was saying.

Siobhan asked who found the body.

'Someone out walking,' Wylie replied. 'Middle-aged woman, I think. Daily constitutional.'

'Be a while before she takes that route again,' Silvers muttered.

'Was Flip lying there all this time?' Siobhan was looking across to where Grant was busy juggling letters. Maybe he was right to keep working, but she couldn't help feeling a certain distaste. How could he not be affected by the news? Even George Silvers – as cynical as they came – looked a bit shell-shocked.

'Arthur's Seat,' he repeated. 'Just last weekend.'

Wylie decided to answer Siobhan's question. 'Chief Super seems to think so.' As she spoke, she looked down at her desk, and rubbed her hand along it as though wiping off dust.

It hurts her, Siobhan thought . . . even saying the words 'Chief Super' reminds her of that TV appearance and hardens the sense of resentment.

When one of the phones rang, Silvers went to answer.

'No, he's not here,' he told the caller. Then: 'Hang on, I'll check.' He put his hand over the mouthpiece. 'Ellen, any idea when Rebus will be back?'

She shook her head slowly. Suddenly Siobhan knew where he was: he was on Arthur's Seat . . . while Wylie, who was supposed to be his partner, wasn't. She thought of Gill Templer, telling Rebus he was needed there. He'd have gone like a shot, leaving Wylie behind. It looked to Siobhan like a calculated snub by Templer. She would know *exactly* how Wylie would feel.

'Sorry, no idea,' Silvers said into the phone. Then: 'Hang on a sec.' He held the receiver out towards Siobhan.

'Lady wants to speak to you.'

Siobhan crossed the floor, mouthing the word 'who?', but Silvers just shrugged, handed her the phone.

'Hello, DC Clarke speaking?'

'Siobhan, it's Jean Burchill.'

'Hi, Jean, what can I do for you?'

'Have you identified her yet?'

'Not a hundred per cent. How did you know?'

'John told me, then he rushed off.'

Siobhan's lips formed a silent O. John Rebus and Jean Burchill . . . well, well. 'Do you want me to tell him you called?'

'I tried his mobile.'

'He might have it turned off: you don't always want interruptions at the locus.'

'The what?'

'The crime scene.'

'Arthur's Seat, isn't it? We were there only yesterday morning.'

Siobhan looked across to Silvers. It seemed like every other person had been on Arthur's Seat recently. When her eyes moved to Grant, she saw that he was staring at his notepad, as if mesmerised by something there.

'Do you know where on Arthur's Seat?' Jean was asking.

'Across the road from Dunsapie Loch and a bit further around towards the east.'

Siobhan was watching Grant. His eyes were on her as he got up from his chair, picking up the notebook.

'Where's that . . . ?' The question was rhetorical, Jean trying to picture the location. Grant was holding the notebook out in front of him, but still too far away for her to make out much: jumbles of letters, and then a couple of words circled. Siobhan narrowed her eyes.

'Oh,' Jean said suddenly, 'I know where you mean. Hellbank, I think it's called.'

'Hellbank?' Siobhan made sure Grant could hear her, but his mind seemed to be elsewhere.

'Quite a steep slope,' Jean was saying, 'which might explain the name, though of course the folklore prefers witches and devilry.'

'Yes,' Siobhan said, dragging the word out. 'Look, Jean, I've got to go.' She was staring at the words circled on Grant's notepad. He'd worked out the anagram. 'That's a surer' had become 'Arthur's Seat'.

Siobhan put down the phone.

'He was leading us to her,' Grant said quietly.

'Maybe.'

'What do you mean, "maybe"?'

'You're saying he knew Flip was dead. We can't know that for certain. All he was doing was taking us to the places Flip went.'

'She turned up dead at this one. And who apart from Quizmaster knew she'd be there?'

'Someone could have followed her, or even chanced upon her.'

'You don't believe that,' Grant said confidently.

'I'm playing devil's advocate, Grant, that's all.'

'He killed her.'

'Then why bother helping us play the game?'

'To fuck with our heads.' He paused. 'No, to fuck with *your* head. And maybe more than that.'

'Then he'd have killed me before now.'

'Why?'

'Because now I don't need to play the game any more. I've come as far as Flip did.'

He shook his head slowly. 'You're saying if he sends you the clue for . . . what's the next stage?'

'Stricture.'

He nodded. 'If he sends it, you won't be tempted?'

'No,' she said.

'You're lying.'

'Well, after this there's no way I'd go anywhere without back-up, and he must know that.' She had a thought. 'Stricture,' she said.

'What about it?'

'He e-mailed Flip . . . *after* she'd been killed. Why on earth would he do that if he'd killed her?'

'Because he's a psychopath.'

'I don't think so.'

'You should get online and ask him.'

'Ask if he's a psychopath?'

'Tell him what we know.'

'He could just disappear. Face it, Grant, we could walk past him in the street and not know him. He's just a name – and not even a real name.'

Grant thumped the desk. 'Well, we've got to do *something*. Any minute now he's going to hear on the radio or TV that the body's been found. He'll be expecting to hear from us.'

'You're right,' she said. The laptop was in her shoulder-bag, still hooked up to the mobile phone. She got it out and set it up, plugging both computer and phone into the floor point for a recharge.

Which gave Grant time enough to start having second thoughts. 'Hang on,' he said, 'we need to clear this with DCS Templer.'

She gave him a look. 'Back to playing by the rules, eh?'

His face reddened, but he nodded. 'Something like this, we need to tell her.'

Silvers and Wylie, who'd been listening intently throughout, had understood enough to know something important was going on.

'I'm with Siobhan,' Wylie said. 'Strike while the iron is hot and all that.'

Silvers disagreed. 'You know the score: Chief Super'll blast the pair of you if you go behind her back.'

'We're not going behind her back,' Siobhan stated, eyes on Wylie.

'Yes we are,' Grant said. 'It's a murder case now, Siobhan. The time for playing games just stopped.' He rested both hands on her desk. 'Send that e-mail, and you're on your own.'

'Maybe that's where I want to be,' she retorted, regretting the words the moment they were out.

'Nice to have a bit of plain speaking,' Grant said.

'I'm all for it,' John Rebus said from the doorway. Ellen Wylie straightened up and folded her arms. 'Speaking of which,' he went on, 'sorry, Ellen, I should have called you.'

'Forget it.' But it was clear to everyone in the room that *she* wouldn't.

When Rebus had listened to Siobhan's version of the morning's events – Grant interrupting now and then with a comment or different perspective – they all looked to him for a decision. He ran a finger along the top of the laptop's screen.

'Everything you've just told me,' he advised, 'needs to be taken to DCS Templer.'

To Siobhan's eyes, Grant didn't look so much vindicated as revoltingly smug. Ellen Wylie, meantime, looked like she was spoiling for a fight with anyone . . . about anything. As a murder team, they weren't exactly ideal.

'Okay,' she said, ready to make at least a partial peace, 'we'll go talk to the Chief Super.' And, as Rebus started nodding, she added: 'Though I'm willing to bet it's not what you would have done.'

'Me?' he said. 'I wouldn't have had the first clue, Siobhan. Know why?'

'Why?'

'Because e-mail's a black art as far as I'm concerned.'

Siobhan smiled, but there was a thread running through her mind: black art . . . coffins used in witches' spells . . . Flip's death on a hillside called Hellbank.

Witchcraft?

Six of them in the cramped office at Gayfield Square: Gill Templer and Bill Pryde; Rebus and Ellen Wylie; Siobhan and Grant. Templer was the only one sitting. Siobhan had printed off all the e-mails, and Templer was sifting through them silently. Finally she looked up.

'Is there *any* way we can identify Quizmaster?'

'Not that I know of,' Siobhan admitted.

'It's possible,' Grant added. 'I mean, I'm not sure how, but I think it's possible. Look at these viruses, somehow the Americans always seem to be able to trace them back.'

Templer nodded. 'That's true.'

'The Met has a computer crime unit, doesn't it?' Grant went on. 'They could have links to the FBI.'

Templer studied him. 'Think you're up to it, Grant?'

He shook his head. 'I like computers, but this is way out of my league. I mean, I'd be happy to liaise . . .'

'Fair enough.' Templer turned to Siobhan. 'This German student you were telling us about . . .'

'Yes?'

'I'd like a bit more detail.'

'Shouldn't be too difficult.'

Suddenly Templer's gaze shifted to Wylie. 'Can you run with that, Ellen?'

Wylie looked surprised. 'I suppose so.'

'You're splitting us up?' Rebus interrupted.

'Unless you can think of a good reason not to.'

'A doll was left at Falls, now the body's turned up. It's the same pattern as before.'

'Not according to your coffin-maker. Different workmanship altogether, I believe he said.'

'You're putting it down to coincidence?'

'I'm not putting it down to anything, and if something else crops up in connection with it, you can start back in again. But we're on a murder case now, and that changes everything.'

Rebus glanced towards Wylie. She was simmering – the transfer from dusty old autopsies to a background check on a student's curious demise . . . it wasn't exactly thrilling her. But at the same time she wasn't going to throw her weight behind Rebus – too busy working on her own sense of injustice.

'Right,' Templer said into the silence. 'For the moment, you'll be going back to the body of the investigation – and yes, I know there's a joke in there somewhere.' She tidied the sheets of paper together, made to hand them back to Siobhan. 'Can you stay behind for a sec?'

'Sure,' Siobhan said. The rest of them squeezed out of the room, glad of the fresher, cooler air. Rebus, however, loitered near Templer's door. He stared across the room to the array of information on the far wall – faxes, photos and the rest. Someone was busy dismantling the collage, now that this was no longer a MisPer inquiry. The pace of the investigation seemed already to have slowed, not from any sense of shock or out of respect for the dead, but because things had changed: there was no need to rush, no one out there whose life they might just possibly save . . .

Inside the office, Templer was asking Siobhan if she'd like to reconsider the liaison position.

'Thanks,' Siobhan replied. 'But I don't think so.'

Templer leaned back in her chair. 'Want to share the reasons with me?'

Siobhan looked around, as though seeking out the phrases that might be hidden on the bare walls. 'I can't think of any offhand,' she shrugged. 'I just don't fancy it right now.'

'I may not fancy asking again.'

'I know. Maybe I'm just too deep into this case. I want to keep working it.'

'Okay,' Templer said, dragging out the second syllable. 'I think that's us finished here.'

'Right.' Siobhan reached for the doorhandle, trying not to read too much into those words.

'Oh, could you ask Grant to pop in?'

Siobhan paused with the door an inch or two open, then nodded and left the room. Rebus stuck his head round.

'Got two seconds, Gill?'

'Just barely.'

He wandered in anyway. 'Something I forgot to mention . . .'

'Forgot?' She produced a wry smile.

He had three sheets of fax paper in his hand. 'These came through from Dublin.'

'Dublin?'

'A contact there called Declan Macmanus. I was asking about the Costellos.'

She looked up from the sheets. 'Any particular reason?'

'Just a hunch.'

'We'd already looked into the family.'

He nodded. 'Of course: a quick phone call, and back comes the news that there are no convictions. But you know as well as I do, that's often just the beginning of the story.'

And in the case of the Costellos, that story was a long one. Rebus knew he had Templer hooked. When Grant Hood knocked, she told him to come back in five minutes.

'Better make that ten,' Rebus added, winking towards the young man. Then he moved three file-boxes from the spare chair and made himself comfortable.

Macmanus had come good. David Costello had been wild in his youth: 'the result of too much money given and not enough attention', in Macmanus's phrase. Wild meant fast cars, speeding tickets, verbal warnings issued where some miscreants would have found themselves behind bars. There were fights in pubs, smashed windows and phone boxes, at least two episodes when he'd relieved himself in a public place – O'Connell Bridge, mid-afternoon. Even Rebus had been impressed by this last. It was said that the eighteen-year-old David had held a record of sorts in the number of pubs he was barred from at the same time: the Stag's Head, J. Grogan's, Davie Byrnes, O'Donoghue's, Doheny and Nesbitt's, the Shelbourne . . . eleven in total. The previous year, an ex-girlfriend complained to police that he'd punched her in the face outside a nightclub on the banks of the Liffey. Templer looked up when she reached that part.

'She'd had a few, couldn't remember the name of the nightclub,' Rebus said. 'Eventually, she let it drop.'

'You think maybe money changed hands?'

He shrugged. 'Keep reading.'

Macmanus conceded that David Costello had cleaned up his act, pinpointing the turnaround to an eighteenth birthday party, where a friend had tried to leap between two roofs for a dare, falling short, plummeting into the alley below.

He wasn't killed. But there was brain damage, spinal damage . . . not much more than a vegetable, cared for round the clock. Rebus thought back to David's flat – the half-bottle of Bell's . . . Not a drinker, he'd thought.

'Bit of a shock at that age,' Macmanus had written. 'Got David clean and sober in no seconds flat, otherwise he might have turned out not so much a chip off the old block as a bloody great boulder.'

Like son, like father. Thomas Costello had managed to write off eight cars, yet never lose his driving licence. His wife Theresa had twice called police to the home when her husband was in a rage. Both times they'd found her in the bathroom, door locked but missing some splinters where Thomas had started attacking it with a carving knife. 'Just trying to get the bloody thing open,' he'd explained to officers the first time. 'Thought she was going to do herself in.'

'It's not *me* that needs doing in!' Theresa had yelled back. (In the margins of the fax, Macmanus had added a handwritten note to the effect that Theresa had twice taken overdoses, and that everyone in the city felt sorry for her: hard-working wife, abusive and lazy husband who just happened to be hugely wealthy through no significant effort of his own.)

At the Curragh, Thomas had verbally abused a tourist visitor and been ejected by stewards. He'd threatened to cut off a bookmaker's penis after the man had asked if Mr Costello might wish finally to settle up his huge losses, losses the bookmaker had been carrying for several months.

And so it went on. The two rooms at the Caledonian made sense now . . .

'Lovely family,' Templer commented.

'Dublin's finest.'

'And all of it covered up by police.'

'Tut tut,' Rebus remarked. 'We wouldn't do that here, would we?'

'Dear me, no,' she said with a wry smile. 'And your thinking on all this is . . . ?'

'That there's a side of David Costello we didn't know about till now. And that goes for his family, too. Are they still in the city?'

'They went back to Ireland a couple of days ago.'

'But they'll be coming over again?'

She nodded. 'Now that Philippa's been found.'

'Has David Costello been told?'

'He'll have heard. If Philippa's parents haven't said, the media will have.'

'I'd like to have been there,' Rebus said to himself.

'You can't be everywhere.'

'I suppose not.'

'Okay, talk to the parents when they get here.'

'And the boyfriend?'

She nodded. 'But not too heavy . . . doesn't look good with someone who's grieving.'

He smiled. 'Always thinking of the media, eh, Gill?'

She looked at him. 'Could you send Grant in, please?'

'One impressionable young officer coming right up.' He pulled open the door. Grant was standing there, rocking on the heels of his shoes. Rebus didn't say anything, just gave another wink as he passed.

Ten minutes later, Siobhan was getting a coffee from the machine when Grant found her.

'What did Templer want?' she asked, unable to stop herself.

'Offered me liaison.'

Siobhan concentrated on stirring her drink. 'Thought it might be that.'

'I'll be on the telly!'

'I'm thrilled.'

He stared at her. 'You could try a bit harder.'

'You're right, I could.' They locked eyes. 'Thanks for helping with the clues. I couldn't have done it without you.'

Only now did he seem to realise that their partnership truly was dissolved. 'Oh . . . right,' he said. 'Look, Siobhan . . .'

'Yes?'

'What happened in the office . . . I really am sorry.'

She allowed herself a sour smile. 'Afraid I'll tell on you?'

'No . . . it's not that . . .'

But it was, and they both knew it. 'Haircut and a new suit this weekend,' she suggested.

He looked down at his jacket.

'If you're going to be on the box. Plain shirt: no stripes or checks. Oh, and Grant . . . ?'

'What?'

She reached out a finger and slipped it under his tie.

'Keep this plain, too. Cartoon characters just aren't funny.'

'That's what DCS Templer said.' He sounded surprised, angling his head to examine the little Homer Simpson heads which decorated his tie.

Grant Hood's first TV appearance took place that same afternoon. He was seated next to Gill Templer as she read out a short statement concerning the finding of the body. Ellen Wylie watched on one of the office monitors. There wasn't going to be a speaking part for Hood, but she noticed how, as the media all started asking questions, he leaned over to whisper some comment into Templer's ear, the Chief Super nodding a response. Bill Pryde was on Templer's other side, fielding most of the queries. Everyone wanted to know if the corpse was that of Philippa Balfour; everyone wanted to know the cause of death.

'We're not in a position to confirm identity as yet,' Pryde stated, his words punctuated with little coughs. He looked nervous, and Wylie knew the coughs were vocal tics. She'd been the same herself, all that throat-clearing. Gill Templer glanced towards Pryde, and Hood seemed to take this as his cue.

'Cause of death is also yet to be determined,' he said, 'with a post-mortem examination scheduled for late afternoon. As you know, another conference will take place at seven this evening, by which time we hope to have more details available.'

'But the death's being treated as suspicious?' one journalist called out.

'At this early stage, yes, we're treating the death as suspicious.'

Wylie stuck the end of her biro between her teeth and ground down on it. Hood was cool, no doubt about it. He'd changed his clothes: the ensemble looked brand new. Managed to wash his hair too, she thought.

'There's very little we can add right now,' he was telling the media, 'as you'll no doubt appreciate. If and when an identification is made, family have to be contacted and the identification confirmed.'

'Can I ask if Philippa Balfour's family are coming to Edinburgh?'

Hood gave the questioner a sour look. 'I won't deign to answer that.' Beside him, Gill Templer was nodding agreement, marking her own distaste.

'Can I ask Detective Inspector Pryde if the missing persons investigation is ongoing?'

'The investigation's ongoing,' Pryde said determinedly, picking up some confidence from Hood's performance. Wylie wanted to switch off the monitor, but others were watching with her, so instead she got up and wandered down the corridor to the drinks machine. By the time she got back, the conference was ending. Someone else turned off the monitor and put her out of her misery.

'Looked good in there, didn't he?'

She stared at the uniform who'd asked, but there was no malice apparent. 'Yes,' she confirmed. 'He did all right.'

'Better than some,' another voice said. She turned her head, but there were three officers there, all Gayfield-based. None was looking at her. She reached out a hand for her coffee, but didn't pick it up, fearing her trembling would be noticed. Instead, she turned her attention to Siobhan's notes on the German student. She could make a start, busy herself with phone calls.

Just as soon as she got the words *better than some* out of her head.

Siobhan was sending another message to Quizmaster. She'd taken twenty minutes getting it right.

Hellbank solved. Flip's body found there. Do you want to talk?

It didn't take long for him to respond.

How did you solve it?

Anagram of Arthur's Seat. Hellbank the hillside's name.

Was it you who found the body?

No. Was it you who killed her?

No.

But connected to the game. You don't think anyone was helping her?

I don't know. Do you wish to continue?

Continue?

Stricture awaits.

She stared at the screen. Did Flip's death mean so little to him?

Flip's dead. Someone killed her at Hellbank. I need you to come forward.

His reply took time coming through.

Can't help.

I think you can, Quizmaster.

Undergo Stricture. Perhaps we can meet there.

She thought for a moment. *What is the game's goal? When does it end?*

There was no answer. She was aware of a figure standing behind her: Rebus.

'What's Lover Boy saying?'

'"Lover Boy"?'

'You seem to be spending a lot of time together.'

'That's the job.'

'I suppose it is. So what's he saying?'

'He wants me to go on playing the game.'

'Tell him to sod off. You don't need him now.'

'Don't I?'

The phone rang; Siobhan picked up.

'Yes . . . that's fine . . . of course.' She looked up at Rebus, but he was sticking around. When she ended the call, he raised an eyebrow expectantly.

'The Chief Super,' she explained. 'Now that Grant's got liaison, I'm to stick with the computer angle.'

'Meaning?'

'Meaning find out if there's any way of tracing Quizmaster. What do you reckon: Crime Squad?'

'I doubt those buggers could spell "modem", never mind use one.'

'But they'll have contacts in Special Branch.'

Rebus accepted as much with a shrug.

'The other thing I need to do is canvass Flip's friends and family again.'

'Why?'

'Because I couldn't have got to Hellbank on my own.'

Rebus nodded. 'You don't think she did either?'

'She needed to know London tube lines, geography and the Scots language, Rosslyn Chapel and crossword puzzles.'

'A tall order?'

'That's my guess.'

Rebus was thoughtful. 'Whoever Quizmaster is, he needed to know all those things too.'

'Agreed.'

'And to know she had at least a chance of solving each puzzle?'

'I think maybe there were other players . . . not for me, but when Flip was playing. That would put them up against not just the clock, but each other.'

'Quizmaster won't say?'

'No.'

'I wonder why.'

Siobhan shrugged. 'I'm sure he has his reasons.'

Rebus rested his knuckles on the desk. 'I was wrong. We need him after all, don't we?'

She looked at him. '"We"?'

He held up his hands. 'All I meant was, the case needs him.'

'Good, because if I thought you were trying your usual stunt . . .'

'Which is?'

'Grabbing at every strand and calling it your own.'

'Perish the thought, Siobhan.' He paused. 'But if you're going to be talking to her friends . . .'

'Yes?'

'Would that include David Costello?'

'We already talked to him. He said he didn't know anything about the game.'

'But you're planning to talk to him again anyway?'

She almost smiled. 'Am I so easy to read?'

'It's just that maybe I could tag along. I've got a few more questions for him myself.'

'What sort of questions?'

'Let me buy you a cup of coffee and I'll tell you . . .'

That evening, John Balfour, accompanied by a family friend, made the formal identification of his daughter Philippa. His wife was waiting for him in the back of a Balfour's Bank Jaguar driven by Ranald Marr. Rather than wait in the car park, Marr had driven the car around nearby streets, returning twenty minutes later – the length of time suggested by Bill Pryde, who was there to accompany Mr Balfour on the uneasy journey to the Identification Suite.

A couple of resolute reporters were on hand, but no photographers: the Scottish press still had one or two principles left. Nobody was going to ask questions of the bereaved; all they wanted was some colour for later reports. When it was over, Pryde gave Rebus a call on his mobile to let him know.

'That's us then,' Rebus told the room. He was in the Oxford Bar with Siobhan, Ellen Wylie and Donald Devlin. Grant Hood had turned down the offer of a drink, saying he had to do a quick crash course in the media – names and faces. The conference had been moved to nine p.m., by which time it was hoped the autopsy would be complete, initial conclusions reached.

'Oh, dear,' Devlin said. He'd removed his jacket, and now bunched his fists into the capacious pockets of his cardigan. 'What a terrible shame.'

'Sorry I'm late,' Jean Burchill said, sliding her coat from her shoulders as she approached. Rebus was out of his chair, taking the coat from her, asking what she wanted to drink.

'Let me buy a round,' she said, but he shook his head.

'My invitation. That makes it my duty to get in the first round at least.'

They had colonised the back room's top table. The place wasn't busy, and the TV in the opposite corner meant they were unlikely to be overheard.

'Some sort of pow-wow?' Jean asked, after Rebus had gone.

'Or maybe a wake,' Wylie guessed.

'It's her then?' Jean asked. Their silence was answer enough.

'You work on witchcraft and stuff, don't you?' Siobhan asked Jean.

'Belief systems,' Jean corrected her, 'but, yes, witchcraft falls into it.'

'It's just that with the coffins, and Flip's body being found in a place called Hellbank . . . You said yourself there might be some connection with witchcraft.'

Jean nodded. 'It's true that Hellbank may have come by its name that way.'

'And true that the little coffins on Arthur's Seat might have been to do with witchcraft?'

Jean looked to Donald Devlin, who was following the dialogue intently. She was still debating what to say when Devlin spoke up.

'I very much doubt there's any element of witchcraft involved in the Arthur's Seat coffins. But you do propose an interesting hypothesis, in that, enlightened though we might think ourselves, we are always ready to invite such mumbo-jumbo.' He smiled at Siobhan. 'I'm impressed that a police detective should be so minded.'

'I didn't say I was,' Siobhan snapped back.

'Clutching at straws then, perhaps?'

When Rebus returned with Jean's lime and soda, he couldn't help but note the silence which had fallen over the table.

'Well,' Wylie said impatiently, 'now we're all here . . . ?'

'Now we're all here . . .' Rebus echoed, lifting his pint, 'cheers!'

He waited till they'd lifted their own glasses before putting his own to his mouth. Scotland: you couldn't refuse a toast.

'All right,' he said, putting the glass back down, 'there's a murder case needs solving, and I just want to be sure in my own mind where we all stand.'

'Isn't that what the morning briefings are for?'

He looked at Wylie. 'Then call this an unofficial briefing.'

'With the booze as a bribe?'

'I've always been a fan of incentive schemes.' He managed to force a smile from her. 'Right, here's what I think we've got so far. We've got Burke and Hare – taking things chronologically – and soon after them we've got lots of little coffins found on Arthur's Seat.' He looked towards Jean, noticing for the first time that though there was a space on the bench next to Devlin, she'd pulled a chair over from one of the other tables so she was next to Siobhan instead. 'Then, connected or not, we've got a series of similar coffins turning up in places where women happen to have disappeared or turned up dead. One such coffin is found in Falls, just after Philippa Balfour goes missing. She then turns up dead on Arthur's Seat, location of the original coffins.'

'Which is a long way from Falls,' Siobhan felt bound to point out. 'I mean, those other coffins you've got, they were found near the scene, weren't they?'

'And the Falls coffin is different from the others,' Ellen Wylie added.

'I'm not saying otherwise,' Rebus interrupted. 'I'm just trying to establish whether I'm the only one who sees possible links?'

They all looked at each other; no one said anything until Wylie lifted her Bloody Mary and, studying its red surface, mentioned the German student. 'Swords and sorcery, role-playing, ends up dead on a Scottish hillside.'

'Exactly.'

'But,' Wylie continued, 'hard to tie in with your disappearances and drownings.'

Devlin seemed persuaded by her tone. 'It's not,' he added, 'as if the drownings were considered suspicious at the time, and my examination of the pertinent details doesn't persuade me otherwise.' He had taken his hands from his pockets; they now rested on the shiny knees of his baggy grey trousers.

'Fine,' Rebus said, 'then I'm the only one who's even remotely convinced?'

This time, not even Wylie spoke up. Rebus took another long swallow of beer. 'Well,' he said, 'thanks for the vote of confidence.'

'Look, why are we here?' Wylie laid her hands on the table. 'You're trying to convince us to work as a team?'

'I'm just saying all these little details may end up being part of the same story.'

'Burke and Hare to the Quizmaster's Treasure Hunt?'

'Yes.' But Rebus looked like he was believing it less himself now. 'Christ, I don't know . . .' He ran a hand over his head.

'Look, thanks for the drink . . .' Ellen Wylie's glass was empty. She picked her shoulder-bag up from the bench, started getting to her feet.

'Ellen . . .'

She looked at him. 'Big day tomorrow, John. First full day of the murder inquiry.'

'It's not officially a murder inquiry until the pathologist pronounces,' Devlin reminded her. She looked ready to say something, but just graced him with the coldest of smiles. Then she squeezed out between two of the chairs, said a general goodbye, and was gone.

'Something connects them,' Rebus said quietly, almost to himself. 'I can't for the life of me think what it is, but it's there . . .'

'It can be detrimental,' Devlin pronounced, 'to begin obsessing – as our transatlantic cousins might say – on a case. Detrimental both to the case and to oneself.'

Rebus tried for the same smile Ellen Wylie had just given. 'I think the next round's yours,' he said.

Devlin checked his watch. 'Actually, I'm afraid I'm unable to tarry.' He seemed to find it painful rising from the table. 'I don't suppose one of the young ladies might proffer a lift?'

'You're on my way home,' Siobhan conceded at last.

Rebus's sense of desertion was softened when he saw her glance in Jean's direction: she was leaving the two of them alone, that was all.

'But I'll get a round in before I go,' Siobhan added.

'Maybe next time,' Rebus told her with a wink. He sat in silence with Jean until they'd gone, and was about to speak when Devlin came shuffling back.

'Am I right to assume,' he said, 'that my usefulness is now at an end?' Rebus nodded. 'In which case, will the files be sent back to their place of origin?'

'I'll get DS Wylie to do it first thing,' Rebus promised.

'Many thanks then.' Devlin's smile was directed at Jean. 'It's been a pleasure to have met you.'

'And you,' she said.

'I may pop into the Museum some day. Perhaps you'd do me the honour of showing me round . . .?'

'I'd love to.'

Devlin bowed his head, and started back towards the stairs again.

'I hope he doesn't,' she muttered when he'd gone.

'Why not?'

'He gives me the creeps.'

Rebus looked over his shoulder, as though some final view of Devlin might persuade him she was right. 'You're not the first to say that.' He turned back to her. 'But don't worry, you're perfectly safe with me.'

'Oh, I hope not,' she said, eyes twinkling above her glass.

They were in bed when the news came through. Rebus took the call, seated naked on the edge of the mattress, uncomfortably aware of the view he was presenting to Jean: probably two spare tyres around his middle, arms and shoulders more fat than muscle. The silver lining was: the view could only be worse from the front . . .

'Strangulation,' he told her, sliding back under the bedclothes.

'It was quick then?'

'Definitely. There's bruising on the neck just at the carotid artery. She probably passed out, then he strangled her.'

'Why would he do that?'

'Easier to kill someone when they're compliant. No struggle.'

'You're quite the expert, aren't you? Ever killed someone, John?'

'Not so you'd notice.'

'That's a lie, isn't it?'

He looked at her and nodded. She leaned over and kissed his shoulder.

'You don't want to talk about it. That's okay.'

He wrapped his arm around her, kissed her hair. There was a mirror in the room, one of those floor-standing models so you could see yourself head to foot. It faced away from the bed. Rebus wondered if that was on purpose or not, but he wasn't about to ask.

'Where's the carotid artery?' she asked.

He placed a finger on his own neck. 'Put pressure on it, the person blacks out in a matter of seconds.'

She felt her neck until she'd found it. 'Interesting,' she said. 'Does everyone except me know that?'

'Know what?'

'Where it is, what it does.'

'I don't suppose so, no. What are you getting at?'

'It's just that whoever did it was in the know.'

'Cops know about it,' he admitted. 'It's not much used these days, for obvious reasons. But there was a time it could make an unruly prisoner manageable. The Vulcan death-grip, we used to call it.'

She smiled. 'The what?'

'You know, Spock on *Star Trek*.' He pinched her shoulder blade. She wriggled free and gave his chest a slap, resting her hand there. Rebus was thinking of his army training, and how he'd been taught attack techniques, including pressure on the carotid . . .

'Would doctors know?' Jean asked.

'Probably anyone who's had medical training would.'

She looked thoughtful.

'Why?' he asked at last.

'Just something from the paper. Wasn't one of Philippa's friends a medical student, one of the ones she was going to meet that night . . . ?'

10

His name was Albert Winfield – 'Albie' to his friends. He seemed surprised that the police wanted to talk to him again, but turned up at St Leonard's at the appointed time next morning. Rebus and Siobhan left him fully fifteen minutes while they got on with other work, then made sure two burly uniforms led him to the interview room, where they left him for a further quarter of an hour. Outside the room, Siobhan and Rebus locked eyes and nodded at one another. Then Rebus pushed open the door forcefully.

'Many thanks for coming along, Mr Winfield,' he snapped. The young man almost leaped from his chair. The window was closed tight, the room stifling. Three chairs – two on one side of the narrow table, one on the other. Winfield had been facing those two empty chairs. Tape recorders and a video recorder were bolted to the wall where it met the table. There were scratched names on the table itself, evidence of time being whittled away by previous occupants called things like Shug, Jazz and Bomber. A No Smoking sign on the wall, defaced with ballpoint pen, and a video camera mounted where wall met ceiling, peering down on proceedings should anyone decide a video record was required.

Rebus ensured his chair-legs made the maximum noise as he scraped them in towards the table. He'd thrown a bulky folder down: no names on it. Winfield seemed mesmerised. He couldn't know it was full of blank sheets of paper borrowed from one of the photocopiers.

Rebus rested his hand on the folder and smiled at Winfield.

'It must have come as a terrible shock.' A quiet voice, soothing, solicitous . . . Siobhan sat down beside her thuggish colleague. 'I'm DC Clarke, by the way. This is DI Rebus.'

'What?' the young man said. Perspiration made his forehead shine. His short brown hair came to a widow's peak. There was acne on his chin.

'The news of Flip's murder,' Siobhan continued. 'It must have been a shock.'

'Y-es . . . absolutely.' He sounded English, but Rebus knew he wasn't. Private education south of the border had ironed out all trace of his Scottish roots. Father a businessman in Hong Kong until three years ago, divorced from the mother, who lived in Perthshire.

'You knew her well then?'

Winfield kept his eyes on Siobhan. 'I suppose so. I mean, she was Camille's friend really.'

'Camille's your girlfriend?' Siobhan asked.

'Foreign, is she?' Rebus barked.

'No . . .' The eyes strayed to Rebus, but only for a second. 'No, she's from Staffordshire.'

'Like I said, foreign.'

Siobhan glanced at Rebus, worried he was milking his role. As Winfield stared down at the table-top, Rebus gave Siobhan a wink of reassurance.

'Hot in here, isn't it, Albert?' Siobhan paused. 'You don't mind me calling you Albert?'

'No . . . no, that's fine.' He glanced up at her again, but whenever he did his eyes were drawn towards her neighbour.

'Would you like me to open a window?'

'Wonderful, yes.'

Siobhan looked at Rebus, who pushed his chair back with as much noise as possible. The windows were narrow, fixed high on the external wall. Rebus stood on tiptoe to open one of them, pulling it in three or four inches. The breeze swept over him.

'Better?' Siobhan asked.

'Yes, thanks.'

Rebus stayed standing, over to Winfield's left. He folded his arms and rested against the wall, directly below the camera.

'Just a few follow-up questions really,' Siobhan was saying.

'Right . . . fine.' Winfield nodded enthusiastically.

'So you wouldn't say you knew Flip that well?'

'We went out together . . . in a group, I mean. Dinner sometimes . . .'

'At her flat?'

'Once or twice. And at mine.'

'You live down near the Botanics?'

'That's right.'

'Nice part of town.'

'It's my father's place.'

'He lives there?'

'No, he's . . . I mean, he bought it for me.'

Siobhan looked towards Rebus.

'All right for some,' he muttered, arms still folded.

'I can't help it if my father has money,' Winfield complained.

'Of course you can't,' Siobhan agreed.

'What about Flip's boyfriend?' Rebus asked.

Winfield found himself looking at Rebus's shoes. 'David? What about him?'

Rebus bent down, waved a hand in Winfield's direction. 'I'm up here, son.' He straightened. Winfield held his gaze for all of three seconds.

'Just wondering if you consider him a friend,' Rebus said.

'Well, it's a bit awkward now . . . I mean, it *was* awkward. They kept splitting up, getting back together again . . .'

'And you took Flip's side?' Siobhan guessed.

'I had to, what with Camille and everything . . .'

'You say they kept splitting up. Whose fault was it?'

'I just think they had this personality clash . . . you know how opposites attract? Well, sometimes you get the inverse of that.'

'I didn't have the benefit of a university education, Mr Winfield,' Rebus said. 'Maybe you could spell that out for me.'

'I just mean that they were similar in lots of ways, and that made their relationship difficult.'

'They argued?'

'It was more that they couldn't let an argument lie. There had to be a winner and a loser, no middle ground.'

'Did these disagreements ever turn violent?'

'No.'

'But David's got a temper on him?' Rebus persisted.

'No more so than anyone else.'

Rebus walked over to the table. It only took him a couple of steps. He leaned forward so that his shadow covered Winfield. 'But you've seen him lose the rag?'

'Not really.'

'No?'

Siobhan cleared her throat, a sign that she thought Rebus had hit a wall. 'Albert,' she said, her voice like a balm, 'did you know that Flip liked to play computer games?'

'No,' he said, looking surprised.

'Do you play them?'

'I used to play Doom in first year . . . maybe pinball in the student union.'

'Computer pinball?'

'No, just pinball.'

'Flip was playing a game online, a sort of variation on a treasure hunt.' Siobhan unfolded a sheet of paper and slid it across the table. 'Do these clues mean anything to you?'

He read with a frown, then expelled some air. 'Absolutely nothing.'

'You're studying medicine, aren't you?' Rebus interrupted.

'That's right. I'm in my third year.'

'I bet it's hard work,' Siobhan said, sliding the sheet of paper back towards her.

'You wouldn't believe it,' Winfield laughed.

'I think we might,' Rebus said. 'In our line of work, we see doctors all the time.' Though some of us, he could have added, do our best to avoid them . . .

'I'm assuming you know something of the carotid artery then?' Siobhan asked.

'I know where it is,' Winfield admitted, looking puzzled.

'And what it does?'

'It's an artery in the neck. Actually, there are two of them.'

'Carrying blood to the brain?' Siobhan said.

'I had to look it up in a dictionary,' Rebus told Winfield. 'It's from the Greek, meaning sleep. Know why that is?'

'Because compression of the carotid causes you to black out.'

Rebus nodded. 'That's right, a deep sleep. And if you keep on pressing . . .'

'Christ, is that how she died?'

Siobhan shook her head. 'We think she was rendered unconscious, then strangled afterwards.'

In the silence that followed, Winfield looked wildly from one detective to the other. Then he started rising to his feet, fingers gripping the table's edge.

'Jesus Christ, you don't think . . . ? For pity's sake, you think it was *me*?'

'Sit down,' Rebus ordered. In truth, Winfield hadn't got very far up; it looked like his knees were refusing to lock.

'We know it wasn't you,' Siobhan said firmly. The student fell back on to his chair, nearly toppling it.

'We know it wasn't you because you've got an alibi: you were with everyone else in the bar that night, waiting for Flip.'

'That's right,' he said, 'that's right.'

'So you've nothing to worry about,' Rebus said, backing off from the table. 'Unless you know better.'

'No, I . . . I'm . . .'

'Anyone else in your group like to play games, Albert?' Siobhan asked.

'Nobody. I mean, Trist has a few games for his computer, Tomb Raider, that sort of thing. But probably everyone does.'

'Probably,' Siobhan admitted. 'No one else in your circle studies medicine?'

Winfield shook his head, but Siobhan could see he was having a thought. 'There's Claire,' he said. 'Claire Benzie. I've only met her once or twice at parties, but she was a friend of Flip's . . . from school days, I think.'

'And she's studying medicine?'

'Yes.'

'But you don't really know her?'

'She's a year below me, and a different specialism. God, that's right . . .' He looked up at Siobhan, then to Rebus. 'Of all the bloody things, she wants to be a pathologist . . .'

'Yes, I know Claire,' Dr Curt said, leading them down one of the corridors. They were in part of the medical faculty at the university, in a block behind McEwan Hall. Rebus had been here before: it was where both Curt and Gates had their teaching offices. But he'd never been to the lecture halls. Curt was leading them there now. Rebus had asked if he was feeling better. Gastric problems, Curt had explained. 'Very pleasant girl,' he said now, 'and a good student. I hope she stays with us.'

'How do you mean?'

'She's only in second year, she could yet change her mind.'

'Are there many female pathologists?' Siobhan asked.

'Not many, no . . . not in this country.'

'It's a weird decision to take, isn't it?' Rebus said. 'When you're that young, I mean.'

'Not really,' Curt mused. 'I was always one for dissecting the frogs at biology.' He beamed a smile. 'And I'd rather treat the deceased than the living: no anxious diagnoses, no expectant families, fewer negligence claims . . .' He stopped at a set of doors and peered through the glass upper half. 'Yes, in here.'

The lecture room was small and antiquated: wood veneer on the walls, curved wooden benches rising steeply. Curt checked his watch. 'Only another minute or two.'

Rebus peered inside. Someone he didn't know was lecturing to a few dozen students. There were fresh diagrams on the blackboard, and a podium where the lecturer stood brushing chalk from his hands.

'Not a cadaver on view,' Rebus commented.

'We tend to keep those for the practicals.'

'Are you still having to use the Western General?'

'We are, and it's a blessed nuisance with the traffic.'

The autopsy suite at the mortuary was out of commission. Fear of hepatitis allied to a ventilation system past its prime. No sign of funding for a new unit, which meant one of the city hospitals was bearing the brunt of the pathologists' needs.

'The human body is a fascinating machine,' Curt was saying. 'You only really get a sense of that *post mortem*. A hospital surgeon will concentrate on one particular area of the body, but we have the luxury of unlimited access.'

Siobhan's look said she wished he'd stop being so remorselessly cheery on the subject. 'It's an old building,' she remarked.

'Not that old really, in the context of the university. The medical school was based at Old College in earlier times.'

'That's where they took Burke's body?' Rebus added.

'Yes, after he was hanged. A tunnel led into Old College. The bodies were all brought in that way – by dead of night in some cases.' He looked to Siobhan. 'The Resurrection Men.'

'Good name for a band.'

He graced her flippancy with a scowl. 'Body-snatchers,' he said.

'And the skin was flayed from Burke's body?' Rebus went on.

'You know a bit about it.'

'I didn't until recently. Does the tunnel still exist?'

'Part of it.'

'I'd be interested to see it sometime.'

'Devlin's your man.'

'Is he?'

'Unofficial historian of the medical faculty's early days. He's written pamphlets on the subject . . . self-published, but pretty enlightening.'

'I didn't know that. I know he knows a bit about Burke and Hare. He has a theory that Dr Kennet Lovell placed the coffins on Arthur's Seat.'

'Ah, the ones that've been in the papers of late?' Curt frowned in thought. 'Lovell? Well, who's to say he isn't right?' He broke off and frowned again. 'Funny you should mention Lovell actually.'

'Why?'

'Because Claire told me recently she's descended from him.' There was a sound of movement from inside. 'Ah, Dr Easton's finished. They'll all filter out this way; we'd better stand back, lest we're stampeded to death.'

'They're keen then?' Siobhan said.

'Keen to be back in the fresh air, yes.'

Only a few of the students bothered to glance in their direction. Those who did seemed to know who Curt was, some acknowledging him with a bow, smile or word. Finally, with the hall three-quarters empty, Curt went up on to his toes.

'Claire? Could you spare a minute?'

She was tall and thin with short blonde hair and a long straight nose. Her eyes were an almost oriental shape, like tilted almonds. She carried two folders beneath one arm. There was a mobile phone in her hand. She'd been studying it on her way out of the lecture theatre: checking for messages perhaps. She came forwards with a smile.

'Hello, Dr Curt.' Her voice was almost playful.

'Claire, these police officers would like a word.'

'It's about Flip, isn't it?' Her face had fallen, all humour lost to it, and the voice had taken on a sombre tone.

Siobhan nodded slowly. 'A few follow-up questions.'

'I keep thinking maybe it wasn't her, maybe there's been a mistake . . .' She looked to the pathologist. 'Did you . . . ?'

Curt shook his head, but it was less a denial than a refusal to answer the question. Rebus and Siobhan knew Curt had been one of the pathologists at the Philippa Balfour autopsy. The other had been Professor Gates.

Claire Benzie knew it too. Her eyes were still on Dr Curt. 'Have you ever had to . . . you know . . . on someone you knew?'

Curt glanced in Rebus's direction, and Rebus knew he was thinking of Conor Leary.

'It's not a necessity,' Curt was explaining to his student. 'Something like that happens, you can be excused on compassionate grounds.'

'We're allowed compassion then?'

'The occasional handful, yes.' This put the smile back on to her face, albeit fleetingly.

'So how can I help you?' she asked Siobhan.

'You know we're treating Flip's death as homicide?'

'That's what the news said this morning.'

'Well, we just need your help to clear up a few things.'

'You can use my office,' Curt said.

As they walked, two by two, back down the corridor, Rebus watched Claire Benzie's back. She was holding her folders in front of her, discussing her recent lecture with Dr Curt. Siobhan glanced at him and frowned, wondering what he was thinking. He shook his head: not important. But all the same, he thought Claire Benzie was interesting. The morning her friend's murder is announced, and she's able to attend a lecture, talk about it afterwards, even with two detectives right behind her . . .

One explanation: displacement. She was pushing thoughts of Flip aside, replacing them with the routine. Keeping busy to keep from bursting into tears.

Another: she was self-possession itself, Flip's demise a minor intrusion in her universe.

Rebus knew which version he preferred, but he wasn't sure it was necessarily the right one . . .

Dr Curt shared a secretary with Professor Gates. They passed through the secretary's office: two doors next to one another, Curt and Gates. Curt turned the doorhandle and ushered them inside.

'I've got one or two things to do,' he said. 'Just close the door after you when you've finished.'

'Thanks,' Rebus said.

But, having brought them here, Curt seemed suddenly reluctant to leave his student alone with the two detectives.

'I'll be fine, Dr Curt,' Claire reassured him, as if she'd understood his hesitation. Curt nodded and left them. It was a cramped, airless room. A glass-fronted bookcase took up one whole wall. It was filled to overflowing. More books and documents covered every bit of shelf space, and while Rebus was sure there was a computer somewhere on the desk, he couldn't place it: more documents, files and folders, learned journals, empty envelopes . . .

'Doesn't throw much out, does he?' Claire Benzie said. 'Ironic when you think what he does to a corpse.'

The statement, so casually made, startled Siobhan Clarke.

'God, sorry,' Claire said, placing a hand over her mouth. 'They should hand out diplomas in bad taste with this course.'

Rebus was thinking of autopsies past: of innards tossed into pails, organs severed and placed on scales . . .

Siobhan was resting against the desk. Claire had dropped into the visitor's chair, which looked like a remnant from a 1970s dining-room suite. Rebus was left with standing in the middle of the floor or taking Curt's chair. He opted for the latter.

'So,' Claire said, placing her folders on the floor by her feet, 'what is it you want to know?'

'You were at school with Flip?'

'For a few years, yes.'

They'd already been through the notes from Claire Benzie's first interview. Two of the Gayfield Square contingent had talked to her, gleaning little.

'You lost touch?'

'Sort of . . . a few letters and e-mails. Then she started her history of art course and I found out I'd been accepted by Edinburgh.'

'You got in touch?'

Claire nodded. She'd tucked one leg beneath her on the chair and was playing with a bracelet on her left wrist. 'Sent her an e-mail, and we met up.'

'You saw her often after that?'

'Not that often. Different courses, different workloads.'

'Different friends?' Rebus asked.

'Some, yes,' Claire agreed.

'Did you keep in touch with anyone else from school days?'

'One or two.'

'And did Flip?'

'Not really.'

'How did she meet David Costello, do you know?' Rebus already knew the answer – they'd met at a dinner party – but was wondering how well Claire knew Costello.

'I think she said something about a party . . .'

'Did you like him?'

'David?' She was thoughtful. 'Arrogant sod, very sure of himself.'

Rebus almost came back with: *not at all like you then?* Instead, he looked to Siobhan, who reached into her jacket for the folded note.

'Claire,' she said, 'did Flip like to play games?'

'Games?'

'Role-playing . . . computer games . . . maybe on the Internet?'

She thought for a moment. Fine, except that Rebus knew you could use a pause to think up some story . . .

'We had a dungeons and dragons club at school.'

'You were both in it?'

'Until we realised it was strictly a boy thing.' She wrinkled her nose. 'Come to think of it, didn't David play at school too?'

Siobhan handed her the sheet of clues. 'Ever seen these before?'

'What do they mean?'

'Some game Flip was playing. What are you smiling at?'

'Seven fins high . . . she was so pleased with that.'

Siobhan's eyes widened. 'Sorry?'

'She came bounding up to me in some bar . . . God, I forget where. Maybe Barcelona.' She looked at Siobhan. 'It's a bar on Buccleuch Street.'

Siobhan nodded. 'Go on.'

'She just . . . she was laughing . . . and she said this.' Claire pointed to the sheet. 'Seven fins high is king. Then she asked me if I knew what it meant. I told her I hadn't the faintest. "It's the Victoria Line," she said. She seemed so pleased with herself.'

'She didn't tell you what it meant?'

'I've just said . . .'

'I mean, about it being part of a quiz clue.'

Claire shook her head. 'I thought . . . well, I don't know what I thought.'

'Was anyone else there?'

'Not at the bar, no. I was getting some drinks in when she came running up.'

'Do you think she told anyone else?'

'Not to my knowledge.'

'She didn't explain any of the others?' Siobhan gestured towards the sheet. She was feeling an intense rush of relief. Seven fins meant she'd been working out the same clues Flip had. Part of her had worried that Quizmaster was setting her new questions, questions specific to *her*. Now, she felt closer to Flip than ever . . .

'Has this game got something to do with her death?' Claire was asking.

'We don't know yet,' Rebus told her.

'And you've no suspects, no . . . leads?'

'We've plenty of leads,' Rebus was quick to assure her. 'Tell me, you said you thought David Costello was arrogant. Did it ever go beyond that?'

'How do you mean?'

'We hear there were some pretty wild fallings-out between him and Flip.'

'Flip could give as good as she got.' She stopped abruptly, stared into space. Not for the first time in his life, Rebus wished he were a mind-reader. 'She was strangled, wasn't she?'

'Yes.'

'From what I've seen on the forensics course, victims struggle. They'll scratch and kick and bite.'

'Not if they're unconscious,' Rebus said quietly.

Claire closed her eyes for a moment. When she opened them, there were tears shining there.

'Pressure on the carotid artery,' Rebus went on.

'Causing ante-mortem bruising?' Claire could have been reading from a textbook. Siobhan nodded an answer.

'Only seems like yesterday we were schoolgirls . . .'

'This was in Edinburgh?' Rebus asked, waiting till Claire had nodded. The first interview hadn't gone into her background, except as it related to Flip. 'Is that where your family live?'

'It is now. But back then, we lived in Causland.'

Rebus frowned. 'Causland?' He knew the name from somewhere.

'It's a village . . . more of a hamlet really. About a mile and a half from Falls.'

Rebus found himself gripping the arms of Dr Curt's chair. 'You know Falls then?'

'Used to.'

'And Junipers, the Balfours' house?'

She nodded. 'For a while, I was more house guest than visitor.'

'And then your family moved away?'

'Yes.'

'Why?'

'My father . . .' She broke off. 'We had to move for his work.' Rebus and Siobhan shared a look: it wasn't what she'd been about to say.

'Did you and Flip ever visit the waterfall?' Rebus asked casually.

'Do you know it?'

He nodded. 'Been there a couple of times.'

She was smiling, eyes losing focus. 'We used to play there, pretend it was our enchanted kingdom. Life Never-Ending we called it. If only we'd known . . .'

She broke down then, and Siobhan went to comfort her. Rebus walked into the outer office and asked the secretary for a glass of water. But by the time he got back with it, Claire was already recovering. Siobhan was crouching by the side of the chair, a hand on her shoulder. Rebus offered the water. Claire rubbed at her nose with a tissue.

'Thank you,' she said, compressing it to the single syllable *kyoo*.

'I think that's plenty to be going on with,' Siobhan was saying. Rebus – who privately disagreed – nodded his compliance. 'You've been a big help, Claire.'

'Really?'

It was Siobhan's turn to nod. 'We might be in touch again later, if that's all right.'

'Fine, whatever.'

Siobhan handed over her card. 'If I'm not in the office, the pager will always find me.'

'Okay.' Claire slipped the card into one of her files.

'Sure you're all right?'

Claire nodded, stood up, clutching her files to her chest. 'I've got another class,' she said. 'Don't want to miss it.'

'Dr Curt tells us you're related to Kennet Lovell?'

She looked at him. 'On my mother's side.' She paused, as if expecting a follow-up question, but Rebus didn't have one.

'Thanks again,' Siobhan said.

They watched as she started to leave. Rebus was holding the door open for her. 'Just one thing, Claire?'

She stopped beside him, staring up. 'Yes?' she said.

'You told us you used to know Falls.' Rebus waited till she'd nodded. 'Does that mean you've not been there recently?'

'I might have passed through.'

He nodded acceptance of this. She made to leave again. 'You know Beverly Dodds though,' he added.

'Who?'

'I think she made that bracelet you're wearing.'

Claire lifted her wrist. 'This?' It looked very much like the one Jean had bought: polished stones drilled and threaded. 'Flip gave it to me. Said something about it being "good magic".' She shrugged. 'Not that I believe in it, of course . . .'

Rebus watched her leave, then closed the door. 'What do you think?' he asked, turning back into the room.

'I don't know,' Siobhan admitted.

'A bit of acting going on?'

'The tears seemed real enough.'

'Isn't that what acting's all about?'

Siobhan sat down in Claire's chair. 'If a killer's hiding in there, it's buried deep.'

'Seven fin high: say Flip didn't come up to her at a bar. Say Claire already knew what it meant.'

'Because she's the Quizmaster?' Siobhan shook her head.

'Or another player,' Rebus said.

'Then why bother telling us *anything*?'

'Because . . .' But Rebus couldn't think of an answer for that.

'I'll tell you what I'm wondering.'

'Her father?' Rebus guessed.

Siobhan nodded. 'There's something she was holding back.'

'So why did her family move?'

Siobhan was thoughtful, but couldn't think of a quick answer.

'Her old school might tell us,' Rebus said. While Siobhan went to ask the secretary for a phone book, Rebus called Bev Dodds's number. She answered on the sixth ring.

'It's DI Rebus,' he said.

'Inspector, I'm a bit pushed at the moment . . .'

He could hear other voices. Tourists, he guessed, probably deciding what to buy. 'I don't think,' he said, 'I ever asked you if you knew Philippa Balfour.'

'Didn't you?'

'Do you mind if I ask you now?'

'Not at all.' She paused. 'The answer is no.'

'You never met her?'

'Never. Why do you ask?'

'A friend of hers is wearing a bracelet she says Philippa gave her. It looks to me like one of yours.'

'Quite possible.'

'But you didn't sell it to Philippa?'

'If it's one of mine, chances are she bought it in a shop. There's a craft shop in Haddington takes my work, and another in Edinburgh.'

'What's the name of the one in Edinburgh?'

'Wiccan Crafts. It's on Jeffrey Street, if you're interested. Now, if you don't mind . . .' But Rebus had already put down the phone. Siobhan was coming back in with the number for Flip's old school. Rebus made the call, putting the speaker on so Siobhan could listen. The headmistress had been one of the teachers during Flip and Claire's time there.

'Poor, poor Philippa, it's terrible news . . . and what her family must be going through,' the headmistress said.

'I'm sure they've got every support,' Rebus commiserated, trying to get as much sincerity into his voice as he could.

There was a long sigh at the other end of the line.

'But actually, I'm phoning in connection with Claire.'

'Claire?'

'Claire Benzie. It's part of the background, trying to build up a picture of Philippa. I believe she and Claire were good friends at one time.'

'Pretty good, yes.'

'They lived near one another, too?'

'That's right. Out East Lothian way.'

Rebus had a thought. 'How did they get to school?'

'Oh, Claire's father usually drove them in. Either him or Philippa's mother. A lovely lady, I do grieve for her so . . .'

'Claire's father worked in Edinburgh then?'

'Oh, yes. Some sort of lawyer.'

'Is that why the family moved? Was it to do with his work?'

'Dear me, no. I think they were evicted.'

'Evicted?'

'Well, one shouldn't gossip, but with him being deceased I don't suppose it matters.'

'We'll hold it in strictest confidence,' Rebus said, looking at Siobhan.

'Well, it's just that the poor man made some bad investments. I believe he was always a bit of a gambler, and it looks like this time he went too far, lost thousands . . . his house . . . the lot.'

'How did he die?'

'I think you've guessed. He booked into a seaside hotel quite shortly thereafter, and took an overdose of some kind of tablets. It's quite a tumble after all, isn't it, from lawyer to bankrupt . . . ?'

'Yes, it is,' Rebus agreed. 'Many thanks for that.'

'Yes, I'd better go. I've some sort of curriculum meeting to attend.'

Her tone told Rebus this was a regular occurrence, and not one to be savoured. 'Such a pity, two families torn apart by tragedy.'

'Goodbye then,' Rebus said, putting down the phone. He looked at Siobhan.

'Investments?' she echoed.

'And who would he trust if not the father of his daughter's best friend?'

Siobhan nodded. 'John Balfour's about to bury his daughter,' she reminded him.

'Then we'll talk to someone else at the bank.'

Siobhan smiled. 'I know just the man . . .'

Ranald Marr was at Junipers, so they drove out to Falls. Siobhan asked if they could stop and look at the waterfall. A couple of tourists were doing the same thing. The man was taking a photo of his wife. He asked Rebus if he'd take one of the pair of them together. His voice was Edinburgh.

'What brings you here?' Rebus asked, feigning innocence.

'Same thing as you most likely,' the man said, positioning himself next to his wife. 'Make sure you get the wee waterfall in.'

'You mean you're here because of the coffin?' Rebus said, peering through the view-finder.

'Aye, well, she's dead now, isn't she?'

'She is that,' Rebus said.

'Sure you're getting us in?' the man asked worriedly.

'Perfect,' Rebus said, pressing the button. When the film was developed, there'd be a picture of sky and trees, nothing more.

'Wee tip,' the man said, taking his camera back. He nodded towards one of the trees. 'She's the one found the coffin.'

Rebus looked. There was a crude sign pinned to the tree, advertising Bev Dodds's Pottery. A hand-drawn map showed her cottage. 'Pottery for Sale, Teas and Coffees.' She was branching out.

'Did she show you it?' Rebus asked, knowing fine well the answer. The Falls coffin was locked away with the others at St Leonard's.

The tourist shook his head in disappointment. 'Police are holding on to it.'

Rebus nodded. 'So where's your next stop?'

'Thought we'd go look at Junipers,' his wife said. 'Always supposing we can find it. Took us half an hour to find this place.' She looked at Siobhan. 'They don't believe in signposts out here, do they?'

'I know where Junipers is.' Rebus spoke authoritatively. 'You head back down the lane, left through the town. There's a housing scheme on the right called Meadowside. Drive into it and you'll see Junipers just beyond.'

The man beamed. 'Magic, thanks a lot.'

'No problem,' Rebus told him. The tourists waved their goodbyes, eager to be back on the trail.

Siobhan sidled over towards Rebus. 'Completely erroneous?'

'They'll be lucky to get out of Meadowside with four tyres still on their car.' He grinned at her. 'My good deed for the day.'

Back in the car, Rebus turned to Siobhan. 'How do you want to play this?'

'First off, I want to know if Marr's a Mason.'

Rebus nodded. 'I'll handle that.'

'Then I think we dive straight in with Hugo Benzie.'

Rebus was still nodding. 'Which one of us asks the questions?'

Siobhan sat back. 'Let's play it by ear, see which one of us Marr prefers.' Rebus looked at her. 'You don't agree?' she asked.

He shook his head. 'It's not that.'

'What then?'

'It's almost exactly what I'd have said, that's all.'

She turned towards him, held his eyes. 'Is that a good thing or a bad thing?'

Rebus's face cracked into a smile. 'I'm still trying to decide,' he said, turning the ignition.

The gates at Junipers were being protected by two uniforms, including Nicola Campbell, the WPC he'd met on his first visit. A lone reporter had parked his car on the verge across the road. He was drinking something from a flask, watched Rebus and Siobhan draw up at the gates, then went back to his crossword. Rebus wound down his window.

'No more phone taps?' he asked.

'Not now there's no kidnap,' Campbell replied.

'What about Brains?'

'Back at the Big House: something came up.'

'I see there's one vulture.' Rebus meant the reporter. 'Any ghouls?'

'A few.'

'Well, a couple more may be on their way. Who's up there?' Rebus pointed through the gates.

'DCS Templer, DC Hood.'

'Planning the next press conference,' Siobhan guessed.

'Who else?' Rebus asked Campbell.

'The parents,' she told him, 'house staff . . . someone from the funeral home. And a family friend.'

Rebus nodded. He turned to Siobhan. 'Wonder if we've talked to the staff: sometimes they see and hear things . . .' Campbell was opening the gates.

'DS Dickie interviewed them,' Siobhan said.

'Dickie?' Rebus put the car into gear, crawled through the gates. 'That clock-watching wee nyaff?'

She looked at him. 'You want to do it all yourself, don't you?'

'Because I don't trust anyone else to do it right.'

'Thanks very much.'

He took his eyes off the windscreen. 'There are exceptions,' he said.

Four cars were parked in the driveway outside the house, the same driveway Jacqueline Balfour had come stumbling down, thinking Rebus her daughter's abductor.

'Grant's Alfa,' Siobhan commented.

'Chauffeuring the boss.' Rebus guessed that the black Volvo S40 belonged to the funeral home, leaving a bronze Maserati and a green Aston Martin DB7. He couldn't decide which belonged to Ranald Marr and which to the Balfours, and said as much.

'The Aston's John Balfour's,' Siobhan told him. He looked at her.

'Is that a guess?' he asked.

She shook her head. 'It's in the notes.'

'You'll be telling me his shoe size next.'

A maid answered the door. They showed their warrant cards and were ushered into the hall. The maid headed off without saying anything. Rebus had never really seen anyone walking on tiptoe before. No voices could be heard anywhere.

'This place is straight out of Cluedo,' Siobhan murmured, studying the wood panelling, the paintings of Balfours past. There was even a suit of armour at the foot of the stairs. A stack of unopened mail sat on a table next to the armour. The same door the maid had disappeared through was opening now. A tall, middle-aged and efficient-looking woman walked towards them. Her face was composed but unsmiling.

'I'm Mr Balfour's personal assistant,' she said in a voice not much above a whisper.

'It's Mr Marr we were hoping to talk to.'

She bowed her head to acknowledge as much. 'But you must appreciate that this is an extremely difficult time . . .'

'He won't talk to us?'

'It's not a case of "won't".' She was becoming irritated.

Rebus nodded slowly. 'Tell you what then, I'll just go tell Detective Chief Superintendent Templer that Mr Marr is holding up our inquiry into Miss Balfour's murder. If you could show me the way . . ?'

She stared daggers at him, but Rebus wasn't about to blink, never mind flinch.

'If you'll wait here,' she said finally. When she spoke, Rebus saw her teeth for the first time. He managed a polite 'thank you' as she headed back towards the door.

'Impressive,' Siobhan commented.

'Her or me?'

'The general combat.'

He nodded. 'Two more minutes, I'd have been reaching for that suit of armour.'

Siobhan walked over to the table and flicked through the mail. Rebus joined her.

'Thought we'd have been opening it,' he said, 'looking for ransom demands.'

'We probably were,' Siobhan answered, studying the postmarks. 'But this is all yesterday's and today's.'

'Keeping the postman busy.' Several of the envelopes were card-sized and black-edged. 'Hope the PA opens them.'

Siobhan nodded. Ghouls again, for whom the death of someone well known was an invitation to become obsessed. You never knew who'd be sending a condolence card. 'It should be us checking them.'

'Good point.' After all, the killer could be a ghoul, too.

The door opened again. This time, Ranald Marr, in black suit and tie, white shirt, strode towards them, looking upset by the interruption.

'What is it this time?' he asked Siobhan.

'Mr Marr?' Rebus stuck out his hand. 'DI Rebus. I just want to say how sorry we are that we've had to intrude.'

Marr, accepting the apology, also accepted Rebus's hand. Rebus had never joined 'the craft', but his father had taught him the handshake one drunken night, back when Rebus had been in his teens.

'As long as it's not going to take long,' Marr said, pushing for advantage.

'Is there somewhere we could talk?'

'Along here.' Marr led them into one of two hallways. Rebus caught Siobhan's eye and nodded, answering her question. Marr was a Mason. She pursed her lips, looked thoughtful.

Marr had opened another door, leading into a large room filled with a wall-length bookcase and a full-size billiard table. When he flicked on the lights – the room, like the rest of the house, was curtained in a show of mourning – the green baize was illuminated. Two chairs sat against one wall, a small table between them. On the table sat a silver tray laid with a decanter of whisky and some crystal tumblers. Marr sat down and poured himself a drink. He gestured towards Rebus, who shook his head, Siobhan likewise. Marr raised his glass.

'Philippa, God rest her soul.' Then he drank deeply. Rebus had smelt the whisky on his breath, knew this wasn't his first of the day. Probably not the first time he'd made the toast either. If they'd been alone together, they would have exchanged information about one another's home lodge – and Rebus might have been in trouble – but with Siobhan here, he was safe. He rolled a red ball across the table, where it rebounded from the cushion.

'So,' Marr said, 'what is it you want this time?'

'Hugo Benzie,' Rebus said.

The name caught Marr by surprise. His eyebrows lifted, and he took another pull on his drink.

'You knew him?' Rebus guessed.

'Not very well. His daughter was at school with Philippa.'

'Did he bank with you?'

'You know I can't discuss the bank's business. It wouldn't be ethical.'

'You're not a doctor,' Rebus said. 'You just keep people's money for them.'

Marr's eyes narrowed. 'We do a sight more than that.'

'What? You mean lose money for them too?'

Marr leaped to his feet. 'What the hell has this got to do with Philippa's murder?'

'Just answer the question: did Hugo Benzie have his money invested with you?'

'Not with us, *through* us.'

'You advised him?'

Marr refilled his glass. Rebus glanced towards Siobhan. She knew her place in this, was keeping quiet, standing in the shadows beyond the baize.

'You advised him?' Rebus asked again.

'We advised him against taking risks.'

'But he wouldn't listen?'

'What's life without a bit of risk: that was Hugo's philosophy. He gambled . . . and lost.'

'Did he hold Balfour's responsible?'

Marr shook his head. 'I don't think so. Poor bugger just did away with himself.'

'What about his wife and daughter?'

'What about them?'

'Did they bear a grudge?'

He shook his head again. 'They knew what kind of man he was.' He put his glass down on the rim of the billiard table. 'But what's this got . . . ?' Then he seemed to realise. 'Ah, you're still looking for motives . . . and you think a dead man has risen from his grave to seek revenge on Balfour's Bank?'

Rebus rolled another ball across the table. 'Stranger things have happened.'

Siobhan walked forward now, and handed the sheet of paper to Marr. 'You remember I asked about games?'

'Yes.'

'This clue here.' She pointed to the one relating to Rosslyn Chapel. 'What do you make of it?'

He narrowed his eyes in concentration. 'Nothing at all,' he said, handing it back.

'Can I ask if you're a member of a masonic lodge, Mr Marr?'

Marr glared at her. Then his eyes flickered in Rebus's direction. 'I'm not going to dignify that question with a response.'

'You see, Philippa was given this clue to solve, and so was I. And when I saw the words "mason's dream", I had to find a member of a lodge to ask what it meant.'

'And what did it mean?'

'That's not important. What *may* be important is whether Philippa sought help along the same lines.'

'I've already told you, I knew nothing about any of this.'

'But she might have slipped something into the conversation . . . ?'

'Well, she didn't.'

'Any other Masons of her acquaintance, Mr Marr?' Rebus asked.

'I wouldn't know. Look, I really think I've given you enough time . . . today of all days.'

'Yes, sir,' Rebus said. 'Thank you for seeing us.' He held out his hand again, but this time Marr didn't take it. He walked to the door in silence, opened it, and walked out. Rebus and Siobhan followed him back down the hallway. Templer and Hood were standing in the entrance hall. Marr passed them without a word and disappeared through a door.

'What the hell are you doing here?' Templer asked in an undertone.

'Trying to catch a killer,' Rebus told her. 'How about you?'

'You looked good on the telly,' Siobhan said to Hood.

'Thanks.'

'Yes, Grant did bloody well,' Templer said, her attention deflected from Rebus on to Siobhan. 'I couldn't be more pleased.'

'Me neither,' Siobhan said with a smile.

They left the house and got into their respective cars. Templer's parting shot: 'I'll want a report explaining your presence here. And John? The doctor's waiting . . .'

'Doctor?' Siobhan asked, doing up her seat-belt.

'It's nothing,' Rebus said, turning the ignition.

'Has she got it in for you as well as me?'

Rebus turned to her. 'Gill wanted you by her side, Siobhan. You turned that down.'

'I wasn't ready.' She paused. 'You know, this is going to sound daft, but I think she's jealous.'

'Of you?'

Siobhan shook her head. 'Of *you*.'

'Me?' Rebus laughed. 'Why would she be jealous of me?'

'Because you don't play by the rules, and she has to. Because despite yourself, you always seem to get people working for you, even when they don't agree with what you're asking them to do.'

'I must be better than I think.'

She looked at him slyly. 'Oh, I think you know how good you are. At least, you think you do.'

He returned her look. 'There's an insult buried in there somewhere, but I can't quite see it.'

Siobhan sat back in her seat. 'So what now?'

'Back to Edinburgh.'

'And?'

Rebus was thoughtful as he eased the car back down the driveway. 'I don't know,' he said. 'Back there, you'd almost have thought Marr had lost his own kid . . .'

'You're not saying . . . ?'

'Did he look like her at all? I'm useless at that.'

Siobhan thought about it, gnawing her lip. 'Rich people all look the same to me. You think Marr and Mrs Balfour could have had an affair?'

Rebus shrugged. 'Hard to prove without a blood test.' He glanced in her direction. 'Better make sure Gates and Curt keep a sample.'

'And Claire Benzie?'

Rebus gave a wave to WPC Campbell. 'Claire's interesting, but we don't want to rattle her chain.'

'Why not?'

'Because a year or three from now, she could be our friendly local pathologist. I may not be around to see it, but you will, and the last thing you want is . . .'

'Bad blood?' Siobhan guessed with a smile.

'Bad blood,' Rebus agreed with a slow nod.

Siobhan was thoughtful. 'But whichever way you look at it, she has every right to feel pissed off with the Balfours.'

'Then how come she was still friends with Flip?'

'Maybe she was playing a game of her own.' As they drove back down the lane, she kept her eyes open for the tourists, but didn't see them. 'Should we check Meadowside, see if they're all right?'

Rebus shook his head. They were silent once more until they'd left Falls far behind.

'Marr's a Mason,' Siobhan said at last. 'And he likes playing games.'

'So now *he's* the Quizmaster rather than Claire Benzie?'

'I think it's more likely than him turning out to be Flip's father.'

'Sorry I spoke.' Rebus was thinking of Hugo Benzie. Before driving out to Falls, he'd rung a lawyer friend and asked about him. Benzie had specialised in wills and trusts, a quiet and efficient solicitor, part of a large practice in the city. The gambling wasn't common knowledge, and had never interfered with his work. The rumour was, he'd stuck money into Far East start-ups, guided by tip-offs and the financial pages of his favoured daily paper. If this were true, then Rebus couldn't see Balfour's as culpable. Probably all they'd done was channel the money on his instructions, then had to call time when it disappeared up the Yangtze. Benzie hadn't just lost all his money – as a lawyer he could always earn more. To Rebus's mind, he'd lost something much more substantial: his faith in himself. Having stopped believing in himself, it was probably easy to start believing in suicide as an option, and sometime thereafter as absolute necessity. Rebus had been there himself once or twice, with the bottle and the darkness for company. He knew he couldn't leap from a high place: he was scared of heights, had been ever since they'd dropped him from a helicopter during his army days. Warm bath and a razor across the wrists . . . the problem there was the mess, the thought of someone, friend or stranger, confronted with such a tableau. Booze and pills . . . it always came down to those essential drugs. Not at home, but in some anonymous hotel room, discovered by the staff. Just another lonely corpse as far as they'd be concerned.

Idle thoughts. But in Benzie's shoes . . . wife and daughter . . . he didn't think he could have done it, leaving behind a devastated family. And now Claire wanted to be a pathologist, a career filled with corpses and ventilated, windowless rooms. Would each body she dealt with be her father's image . . . ?

'Penny for them,' Siobhan said.

'No sale,' Rebus replied, fixing his eyes on the road ahead.

'Cheer up,' Hi-Ho Silvers said, 'it's Friday afternoon.'

'So what?'

He stared at Ellen Wylie. 'Don't tell me you don't have a date lined up?'

'A date?'

'You know: a meal, some dancing, then back to his place.' He started gyrating his hips.

Wylie screwed up her face. 'I'm having trouble keeping my lunch down as it is.'

The remains of the sandwich were on her desk: tuna mayonnaise with sweetcorn. There'd been a slight fizziness to the tuna, and now her stomach was sending her signals. Not that Silvers was about to take any notice.

'Must have a boyfriend though, Ellen?'

'I'll call you when desperation takes hold.'

'As long as it's not Friday or Saturday night: my drinking nights, those are.'

'I'll bear that in mind, George.'

'And Sunday afternoon, of course.'

'Of course.' Wylie couldn't help thinking that this arrangement probably suited Mrs Silvers just fine.

'Unless we get some overtime.' Silvers's mind made the switch. 'What do you reckon the chances are?'

'Depends, doesn't it?' And she knew what it depended on: media pressure, forcing the brass to look for a quick result. Or maybe John Balfour, asking another favour, twisting an arm or two. Time was, CID would work seven-day weeks, twelve-hour days on a big case, and be paid accordingly. But budgets were tighter now, along with staffing levels. She'd never seen so many happy cops as the day CHOGM – the Commonwealth Heads of Government Meeting – had rolled into town, bringing with it an overtime jamboree. But that had been a few years back now. Still she caught officers, Silvers among them, muttering the word 'chogm' under their breath, as though it were a talisman. As Silvers shrugged and moved off, overtime probably still on his mind, Wylie turned her attention to the story of the German student, Jürgen Becker. She thought of Boris Becker, her favourite tennis player at one time, and wondered idly if Jürgen might be some relation. She doubted it: a famous relly would have pulled out the stops, like with Philippa Balfour.

And yet what progress had they made? They didn't seem to be any further forward than the day the MisPer inquiry had opened. Rebus had all these ideas, but there was no focus to them. It was as if he reached out his hand and plucked possibilities from some tree or bush, expecting people to swallow them. The one time she'd worked with him before – a body found in Queensberry House, just as they were readying to knock most of it down and start building the parliament – there hadn't been a result. He'd as good as dumped her, refused to talk about the case afterwards. Nothing had come to court.

And yet . . . she'd rather be part of Rebus's team than none at all. She felt she'd burned her bridges with Gill Templer, whatever Rebus said, and she knew it was all her fault. She'd tried too hard, almost to the point of pestering Templer. It was a form of laziness: pushing to be noticed in the hope advancement would follow. And she knew Templer had rejected her precisely because she'd seen it for what it was. Gill Templer hadn't got to the top that way – she'd had to work her damnedest throughout, fighting a prejudice against women officers which was never discussed, never admitted to.

But still there.

Wylie knew she should have kept her head down and her mouth shut. That was how Siobhan Clarke worked; she never looked pushy, even though she was every inch the careerist . . . and a rival – Wylie couldn't help but see her that way. Templer's favourite from the start, which was precisely why she – Ellen Wylie – had begun campaigning overtly and, as it turned out, too strenuously. Leaving her isolated, stuck with a piece of crap like the Jürgen Becker story. On a Friday afternoon, when there'd most likely be no one around to answer her phone calls, reply to her questions. It was dead time, that was all.

Dead time.

Grant Hood had another press conference to organise. He already knew the names to put to faces, had arranged short get-to-know meetings with the 'majors', these being the more reputable journalists, crime reporters of long standing.

'Thing is, Grant,' DCS Templer had confided in him, 'there are some journos we can call our own, in that they're malleable. They'll toe the line, place a story for us if and when we want them to, while holding back stuff we don't want getting out. You already have a foundation of trust there, but it cuts both ways. We have to give them good copy, and they're hoping they get it an hour or two before the oppo.'

'The oppo, ma'am?'

'Opposition. See, they look like a solid mass when you see them in the press room, but they're not. At times they'll cooperate with each other – like sending one of their number on a thankless stake-out. He then shares whatever he gets with the rest of them. They take it in turns.'

Grant had nodded his understanding.

'But in other respects, it's dog eat dog. The hacks who're not in the loop, they're keenest of all, and not likely to be scrupulous. They'll get chequebooks out when it suits, and they'll try to win you over. Not with cash maybe, but with drinks, a bit of dinner. They'll make you feel one of the lads, and you'll start thinking: they're not so bad really. That's when you're in trouble, because all the time they'll be pumping you without you knowing it. You might let drop a hint or a teaser, just to show them you're in the know. And whatever it is you've come out with, you can guarantee they'll print it with knobs on. You'll be "a police source" or "an unnamed source close to the investigation" – that's if they're in the mood to be kind. And if they get anything on you, they'll turn the screws. They'll want chapter and verse, or they'll leave you on the rack.' She'd patted his shoulder, and finished by saying: 'Just a word to the wise.'

'Yes, ma'am. Thank you, ma'am.'

'It's okay to be on genial terms with them all, and you should introduce yourself to the ones who matter, but never forget which side you're on . . . or that there *are* sides. Okay?'

He'd nodded. Then she'd given him the list of 'majors'.

He'd stuck to coffee and orange juice in each meeting, and was relieved to see most of the journalists doing likewise.

'You might find the "elders" running on whisky and gin,' one younger reporter had said, 'but not us.'

The meeting after that had been with one of the most respected of the "elders". He'd wanted nothing more than a glass of water: 'The young ones drink like fish, but I find I can't any more. And what's your tipple of preference, DC Hood?'

'This isn't a formal occasion, Mr Gillies. Please, call me Grant.'

'Then you must call me Allan . . .'

Still Grant couldn't get Templer's warning words out of his head. As a result, he felt he'd come over as stiff and awkward at each get-to-know. Still, one definite bonus was that Templer had arranged for him to have his own office at Fettes HQ, at least for the duration of the inquiry. She'd called it 'prudent', explaining that he'd be talking to journalists every day, and it was best to keep them at a distance from the main investigation. If they happened to drop into Gayfield or St Leonard's for a briefing or even a quick chat, there was no telling what they might overhear or happen to notice.

'Good point,' he'd said, nodding.

'Same goes for phone calls,' Templer had gone on. 'If you want to call a journalist, do so from your office, door closed. That way they're not going to hear anything they shouldn't in the background. One of them phones you and catches you in CID or somewhere, say you'll call them back.'

He'd nodded again.

Thinking back, she'd probably reckoned he resembled one of those nodding dogs, the kind you got in the back of naff cars. He tried to shake the image away, focused on his screen. He was drafting a press release, copies to go to Bill Pryde, Gill Templer and ACC Carswell for their input and approval.

Carswell, the Assistant Chief Constable, was on another floor in the same building. He'd already knocked on Grant's door and come in to wish him good luck. When Grant had introduced himself as Detective Constable Hood, Carswell had nodded slowly, his eyes those of an examiner.

'Well,' he'd said, 'no cock-ups and a result on this, we'll have to see about doing something better for you, eh?'

Meaning a hike to detective sergeant. Hood knew Carswell could do it, too. He'd already taken one young CID officer under his wing – DI Derek Linford. Problem was, neither Linford nor Carswell had any time for John Rebus, which meant Hood would have to be careful. He'd already turned down one drink with Rebus and the rest of the crew, but was conscious that he'd spent some time alone with Rebus in a bar all too recently. It was the sort of thing which, leaked to Carswell, could put a real spanner in the works. He thought again of Templer's words: *if they get anything on you, they'll turn the screws* . . . Another image flashed in front of him, that clinch with Siobhan. He'd have to be careful from now on: careful who he spoke to and what he said, careful who he spent time with, careful what he did.

Careful not to make enemies.

Another knock on the door. It was one of the civilian staff. 'Something for you,' she said, handing over a carrier bag. Then she smiled and retreated. He opened it. A bottle inside: José Cuervo Gold. And along with it, a little card:

Here's wishing you well in your new post. Think of us as sleepy-headed children, who need to be told their daily story.

Your news friends, the Fourth Estate.

Grant smiled. He thought he detected the hand of Allan Gillies. Then it struck him: he'd never answered Gillies's inquiry about his favoured drink . . . yet somehow Gillies had got it right. It went beyond guesswork: someone had been talking. The smile left Grant's face. The tequila wasn't just a gift, it was a show of strength. Just then his mobile sounded. He took it from his pocket.

'Hello?'

'DC Hood?'

'Speaking.'

'Just thought I'd introduce myself, since I seemed to miss out on one of the invites.'

'Who is this?'

'My name's Steve Holly. You'll have seen my byline.'

'I've seen it.' Holly's was definitely not one of the names on Templer's list of 'majors'. Her own succinct description of him: 'a shit'.

'Well, we'll be seeing one another at all these press conferences and such like, but I thought I'd just say hello first. Did you get the bottle?'

When Grant didn't reply, Holly just laughed.

'He always does that, old Allan. Thinks it's clever, but you and I know it's just a party trick.'

'Is it?'

'I'm not the sort for rubbish like that, as you'll no doubt have noticed.'

'Noticed?' Grant frowned.

'Think about it, DC Hood.' With that, the line went dead.

Grant stared at the phone, and then it dawned on him. The journalists, all they'd had from him so far were his office phone, fax and pager. He thought hard, and was sure he hadn't given his mobile to any of them. More advice from Templer:

'Once you get to know them, there'll be one or two you really click with – it's never the same combination for any liaison officer. Those really special ones, you might want to let have your mobile number. It's a sign of trust. For the rest, forget it or your life won't be your own . . . and with them clogging the line, how can any of your colleagues hope to contact you? Us and them, Grant, us and them . . .'

And now one of 'them' had his mobile number. There was only one thing for it, he'd have to get it changed.

As for the tequila, that was going with him to the press conference. He'd hand it back to Allan Gillies, tell him he was off the alcohol these days.

He was beginning to think that might not be so far from the truth. There were a lot of changes to be made if he was going to stay the course.

Grant felt he was ready.

The CID suite at St Leonard's was emptying. Officers not involved in the murder case were clocking off for the weekend. Some would work a Saturday shift if it was offered them. Others would be on call, should a fresh case need investigating. But for most, the weekend was beginning. There was a spring in their step; they struck up choruses of old pop songs. The city had been quiet of late. A few domestics, a drug bust or two. The Drugs Squad were keeping their heads down, however, after answering a tip-off: a council house in Gracemount, silver sheeting at an upstairs bedroom window, kept closed all day and night. They'd hurtled in, ready to demolish Edinburgh's latest cannabis supply, and had instead found a teenager's bedroom, newly decorated. His mum had bought a moon blanket instead of curtains, thought it looked trendy . . .

'Bloody *Changing Rooms*,' one of the Drugs Squad had muttered.

There were other incidents, but they were isolated, hardly the stuff of a crime wave. Siobhan looked at her watch. She'd called the Crime Squad earlier, asked about computers. She hadn't even got halfway through her explanation when Claverhouse had said, 'Someone's already on it. We'll send him over.' So now she was waiting. She'd tried Claverhouse again: no answer. He was probably on his way home or to the pub. Maybe he wasn't sending anyone till Monday. She'd give it another ten minutes. After all, she had her own life, didn't she? Football tomorrow if she wanted it, though it was an away match. Sunday she could go for a drive: there were all these places she'd never been – Linlithgow Palace, Falkland Palace, Traquair. A friend she hadn't seen in months had invited her to a birthday party Saturday night. She didn't think she'd go, but the option was always there . . .

'Are you DC Clarke?'

He had a briefcase with him, which he placed on the floor. She was reminded for a second of door-to-door salesmen, cold callers. Straightening, she saw that he was overweight, most of it around the stomach. Short hair, a tuft standing up at the back of his head. He introduced himself as Eric Bain.

'I've heard of you,' Siobhan admitted. 'Don't they call you "Brains"?'

'Sometimes, but to be honest I prefer Eric.'

'Eric it is. Make yourself comfortable.'

Bain pulled over a chair. As he sat, the material of his light blue shirt stretched, opening gaps between buttons at the front, exposing areas of pale pink skin.

'So,' he said, 'what have we got?'

Siobhan explained, while Bain gave her his full concentration, his eyes fixed on hers. She noticed that his breath came in small wheezes, and wondered if there was an inhaler in one of his pockets.

She tried for eye contact, tried to relax, but his size and proximity made her uncomfortable. His fingers were pudgy and ringless. His watch had too many buttons on it. There was hair below his chin which the morning's razor had failed to find.

He didn't ask a single question throughout her speech. At the end, he asked to see the e-mails.

'Onscreen, or printed out?'

'Either will do.'

She took the sheets from her shoulder-bag. Bain moved his chair even closer so he could spread them out on the desk. He made a chronological line, working from the dates at the top of each one.

'These are just the clues,' he said.

'Yes.'

'I want all the e-mails.'

So Siobhan booted up the laptop, connecting her mobile while she was at it. 'Shall I check for new messages?'

'Why not?' he asked.

There were two from Quizmaster.

Game time is elapsing. Do you wish to continue, Seeker?

An hour later, this had been followed by:

Communication or cessation?

'Knows her vocab, doesn't she?' Bain stated. Siobhan looked at him. 'You keep saying "he",' he explained. 'Thought it might help us keep an open mind if I . . .'

'Fine,' she said, nodding. 'Whatever.'

'Do you want to reply?'

She started to shake her head, then changed it to a shrug. 'I'm not sure what I want to say.'

'Be easier to trace her if she doesn't shut down.'

She looked at Bain, then typed a reply – *Thinking about it* – and hit 'send'. 'Reckon that'll do?' she asked.

'Well, it definitely ranks as "communication".' Bain smiled. 'Now let me have those other messages.'

She hooked up to a printer, only to find there was no paper. 'Hell,' she hissed. The store cupboard was locked and she'd no idea where the key was. Then she remembered Rebus's file, the one he'd taken with him when they'd interviewed Albie the medical student. He'd made it look intimidatingly thick by padding it with sheets from the photocopier. Siobhan walked to Rebus's desk, started opening drawers. Bingo: the file was there, the half-ream still tucked inside. Two minutes later she had the history of Quizmaster's correspondence. Bain shuffled the sheets so that everything could fit on her desktop, covering it almost completely.

'See all this stuff?' he asked, pointing to the bottom halves of some of the pages. 'You probably never look at it, do you?'

Siobhan had to admit as much. Beneath the word 'Headers' lay more than a dozen lines of extra material: Return-Path, Message-ID, X-Mailer . . . It didn't mean much to her.

'This,' Bain said, drawing his lips into his mouth to moisten them, 'is the juicy stuff.'

'Can we identify Quizmaster from it?'

'Not straight away, but it's a start.'

'How come some of the messages don't have headers?' Siobhan asked.

'That,' Bain said, 'is the bad news. If a message has no headers, it means the sender is using the same ISP you are.'

'But . . .'

Bain was nodding. 'Quizmaster has more than one account.'

'He's switching ISPs?'

'It's not uncommon. I have a friend who's averse to paying for Internet access. Before the freeserves came along, he'd sign up with a different ISP every month. That way he took advantage of all those "first month free" deals. When time was up, he cancelled and went looking elsewhere. One whole year, he didn't pay a penny. What Quizmaster is doing is an extension of that.' Bain ran his finger down each list of headers, stopping at the fourth line. 'These tell you his ISP. See? Three different providers.'

'Making him harder to catch?'

'Harder, yes. But he must have set up a . . .' He noticed the look on Siobhan's face. 'What?' he asked.

'You said "he".'

'Did I?'

'Would it be simpler if we stuck to that, do you think? Not that I don't appreciate your idea of keeping an open mind.'

Bain thought about it. 'Fine,' he said. 'So, as I was saying, he – or *she* – must have set up a payment account with each one. At least, I'd think so. Even if you're on a month's free trial, they'll usually ask for some details first, including a Visa card or bank account.'

'So they can start charging you when the time comes?'

Bain nodded. 'Everyone leaves traces,' he said quietly, staring at the sheets. 'They just don't think they do.'

'It's like forensics, isn't it? A hair, a fleck of skin . . .'

'Exactly.' Bain was smiling again.

'So we need to talk to the service providers, get them to hand over his details?'

'If they'll talk to us.'

'This is a murder inquiry,' Siobhan said. 'They'll have to.'

He glanced in her direction. 'There are channels, Siobhan.'

'Channels?'

'There's a Special Branch unit deals with nothing but high-tech crime. They concentrate on hard-core mostly, track down the buyers of kiddie porn, that kind of stuff. You wouldn't believe the stories: hard disks hidden inside other hard disks, screen-savers which hide pornographic images . . .'

'We need their permission?'

Bain shook his head. 'We need their *help*.' He checked his watch. 'And it's too late tonight to do anything about it.'

'Why?'

'Because it's Friday night in London too.' He looked at her. 'Buy you a drink?'

She wasn't going to say yes: lots of excuses ready to use. But somehow she couldn't say no, and they found themselves across the road in The Maltings. Again, he placed his briefcase on the floor next to him as they stood at the bar.

'What do you keep in there?' she asked.

'What do you think?'

She shrugged. 'Laptop, mobile phone . . . gadgets and floppies . . . I don't know.'

'That's what you're supposed to think.' He hefted the briefcase on to the bar and was about to snap it open, but then paused and shook his head. 'Nah,' he said. 'Maybe when we know one another a bit better.' He placed it back beside his feet.

'Keeping secrets from me?' Siobhan said. 'That's a fine start to a working relationship.'

They both smiled as their drinks arrived: bottled lager for her, a pint of beer for him. There were no free tables.

'So what's St Leonard's like?' Bain asked.

'Much the same as any other station, I suppose.'

'It's not every station has a John Rebus in it.'

She looked at him. 'How do you mean?'

He shrugged. 'It's something Claverhouse said, about you being Rebus's apprentice.'

'Apprentice!' Even with the stereo blaring, her outburst had heads turning towards them. 'Bloody cheek!'

'Easy, easy,' Bain said. 'It's just something Claverhouse said.'

'Then you tell Claverhouse to stick his head up his arse.'

Bain started laughing.

'I'm not joking,' she said. But then she started laughing too.

After two more drinks, Bain said he felt peckish and what about seeing if Howie's had a table. She wasn't about to say yes – didn't really feel that hungry after the lager – but somehow she found herself unable to say no.

Jean Burchill was working late at the Museum. Ever since Professor Devlin had mentioned Dr Kennet Lovell, Jean had been intrigued. She'd decided to do some investigating of her own, to see if the pathologist's theory could be substantiated. She knew that she could take a short cut by talking to Devlin himself, but something stopped her. She imagined she could still smell formaldehyde on his skin and feel the cold touch of dead flesh when he took her hand. History only brought her in contact with the long-dead, and then usually as mere references in books or artefacts discovered during digs. When her husband had died, his pathology report had made for grim reading, yet whoever had written it had done so with relish, lingering on the liver abnormalities, its swollen and overtaxed nature. 'Overtaxed' was the very word the writer had used. Easy enough, she supposed, to diagnose alcoholism after death.

She thought of John Rebus's drinking. It didn't seem to her to resemble Bill's. Bill would toy with his breakfast, then head out to the garage where he kept a bottle hidden. A couple under his belt before getting into the car. She kept finding evidence: empty bourbon bottles in the cellar, and at the back of the topmost shelf of his closet. She never said anything. Bill went on being 'the life and soul', 'steady and reliable', 'a fun guy', right up until the illness stopped him working, sending him to a hospital bed instead.

She didn't think Rebus was a secret drinker in that way. He just liked to drink. If he did it alone, that was because he didn't have many friends. She'd asked Bill once why he drank, and he hadn't been able to answer her. She thought probably John Rebus had answers, though he would be reluctant to give them. They'd be to do with washing away the world, scouring his mind of the problems and questions he kept stored there.

None of which would make him a more attractive drunk than Bill had been, but then so far she hadn't seen Rebus drunk. She got the feeling he'd be a sleeper: however many drinks it took, and then crashing into unconsciousness wherever he happened to be.

When her phone rang, she was slow to pick it up.

'Jean?' It was Rebus's voice.

'Hello, John.'

'Thought you'd have left by now.'

'I'm working late.'

'I was just wondering if you . . .'

'Not tonight, John. I've a lot I want to get done.' She pinched the bridge of her nose.

'Fair enough.' He couldn't hide the disappointment in his voice.

'What about this weekend: any plans?'

'Well, that was something I wanted to tell you . . .'

'What?'

'Lou Reed at the Playhouse tomorrow night. I've got two tickets.'

'Lou Reed?'

'He could be great, could be mince. Only one way to find out.'

'I haven't listened to him in years.'

'Don't suppose he's learned how to sing in the interim.'

'No, probably not. All right then, let's do it.'

'Where shall we meet?'

'I've some shopping to do in the morning . . . how about lunch?'

'Great.'

'If you've nothing else on, we could make a weekend of it.'

'I'd like that.'

'Me too. I'm shopping in town . . . wonder if we can get a table at Café St Honore?'

'Is that just along from the Oxford Bar?'

'Yes,' she said, smiling. She thought of Edinburgh in terms of restaurants, Rebus pubs.

'I'll phone and book.'

'Make it one o'clock. If they can't fit us in, call me back.'

'They'll fit us in. The chef's a regular at the Ox.'

She asked him how the case was progressing. He was reticent, until he remembered something.

'You know Professor Devlin's anatomist?'

'Who? Kennet Lovell?'

'That's the one. I had to interview a medical student, friend of Philippa's. Turns out she's a descendant.'

'Really?' Jean tried not to sound too intrigued. 'Same name?'

'No: Claire Benzie. She's related on her mother's side.'

They chatted for another couple of minutes. When Jean put the phone down, she looked around her. Her 'office' was a small cubicle with desk and chair, filing cabinet and bookshelves. She'd stuck some postcards on the back of the door, including one from the Museum shop: the Arthur's Seat coffins. Secretarial and support staff shared a larger outer office just outside her door, but they'd all gone home. There would be cleaners busy elsewhere in the building, and a security guard doing the rounds. She'd wandered all through the Museum at night, never in the least spooked by it. Even the old museum, with its displays of stuffed animals, calmed her. Friday night, she knew the restaurant at the top of the Museum would be busy. It had its own lift, and someone on the door to make sure diners headed straight for it and didn't wander into the Museum instead.

She remembered her first meeting with Siobhan, the story of the 'bad experience'. Couldn't have had anything to do with the food, though the bill at the end could sometimes come as a shock. She wondered if she'd treat herself later. The price of a meal went down after ten p.m.; maybe they could squeeze her in. She touched her stomach. Lunch tomorrow . . . it wouldn't hurt her to skip dinner tonight. Besides, she wasn't sure she'd still be here at ten. Her investigation into the life of Kennet Lovell hadn't thrown up a surfeit of information.

Kennet: she'd first thought the name a misprint, but it kept recurring. Kennet, not Kenneth. Born 1807, in Coylton, Ayrshire, making him just twenty-one at the time of Burke's execution. His parents were farming folk, his father having employed Robert Burns's father for a time. Kennet was given an education locally, helped by the local church minister, the Reverend Kirkpatrick . . .

There was a kettle in the outer office. She got up, walked out of her room. Left the door open, so her shadow stretched across the floor. She didn't bother with the lights. Switched the kettle on and rinsed a mug under the tap. Tea-bag, powdered milk. She stood in the semi-dark, leaning against the worktop, arms folded. Through the doorway, she could see her desk and the photocopied sheets, all she'd been able to find so far on Dr Kennet Lovell, who'd assisted at a murderer's autopsy, helped flay William Burke's skin from his bones. The initial post-mortem examination had been undertaken by Dr Monro, in the presence of a select audience including a phrenologist and a sculptor, as well as the philosopher Sir William Hamilton and the surgeon Robert Liston. This was followed by a public dissection in the university's packed anatomical theatre, noisy medical students gathered around like so many vultures, hungry for knowledge, while those without tickets hammered at the doors for entry and fought with police.

She was working from history books: some about the Burke and Hare case, others about the history of medicine in Scotland. The Edinburgh Room at the Central Library had proved helpful as ever, as had a contact at the National Library. Both had done photocopying for her. She'd taken a trip to Surgeons' Hall, too, using their library and database. Hadn't told Rebus about any of this. She knew why: because she was worried. She felt that the Arthur's Seat case was a blind alley, and one down which John, with his need for answers, might go careering. Professor Devlin had been right about that: obsession was always a trap into which you could fall. This was history – ancient history, compared to the Balfour case. Whether the killer had known about the Arthur's Seat coffins or not seemed irrelevant. There was no way of telling. She was conducting this research for her own satisfaction; didn't want John reading anything more into it. He had enough on his plate without that.

There was a noise in the corridor. When the kettle clicked off, she thought no more about it. Poured the water into her mug, dunked the tea-bag a few times, then tipped it into the swing-bin. Took the mug back into her room, leaving the door open.

Kennet Lovell had arrived in Edinburgh in December 1822, aged barely fifteen. She couldn't know whether he'd taken a coach, or walked. It wasn't uncommon to walk such distances in those days, especially if money was an issue. One historian, in a book about Burke and Hare, speculated that Reverend Kirkpatrick had provided for Lovell's journey, and in addition had given him an introduction to a friend, Dr Knox, recently returned from time overseas, during which he had worked as an army surgeon at Waterloo and studied in Africa and Paris. Knox had housed young Lovell for the first year or so of his life in Edinburgh. But when Lovell had started university, the two seemed to have drifted apart, and Lovell moved to lodgings in West Port . . .

Jean sipped her tea and flipped through the photocopied sheets: no footnotes or index, nothing to indicate the provenance of these apparent 'facts'. Dealing as she did with beliefs and superstitions, she knew how hard it could be to sift out hard objective truths from the chaff of history. Hearsay and rumour could find their way into print. Mistakes, only occasionally pernicious, crept in. It galled her that she had no way of checking anything, had for the moment to rely on mere commentary. A case like Burke and Hare had thrown up any number of contemporary 'experts', who believed their testimony to be the one true and worthwhile account.

It didn't mean she had to believe it.

More frustrating still, Kennet Lovell was a bit-player in the Burke and Hare story, existing only for that one gruesome scene, while in the history of medicine in Edinburgh his role was more negligible still. Large gaps were left in his biography. By the time she'd finished reading, she knew only that he had completed his studies, moving into the field of teaching as well as practising. He had been present at the Burke autopsy. Yet three years later he seemed to be in Africa, combining much-needed medical skills with Christian missionary work. How long he spent there she couldn't say. His reappearance in

Scotland came in the late 1840s. He set up a medical practice in the New Town, his clients probably reflecting the wealth of that enclave. One historian's supposition had it that he had been bequeathed the bulk of the Reverend Kirkpatrick's estate, having 'kept in good graces with that gentleman by dint of regular correspondence down the years'. Jean would have liked to see those letters, but nobody had quoted from them in any of the books. She made a note to try tracking them down. The parish in Ayrshire might have some record, or someone at Surgeons' Hall might know. Chances were, they couldn't be recovered, either because they'd perished – been disposed of with Lovell's effects when he'd died – or had gone overseas. An awful lot of historical documentation had found its way into collections overseas – mostly Canada and the US . . . and many of those collections were private, which meant few details of their contents were available.

She'd seen many a trail go cold, frustrated by her inability to know whether some letter or document was still in existence. Then she remembered Professor Devlin, with his dining table crafted by Lovell. Lovell, who according to Devlin was an amateur woodworker . . . She sifted through the papers again, sure that there was nothing in them mentioning this hobby. Either Devlin had some book, some evidence she'd failed so far to find, or else he was myth-making. This, too, she saw all the time: people who 'just knew' that the antique in their possession had once belonged to Bonnie Prince Charlie or Sir Walter Scott. If it turned out she only had Devlin's word for it that Lovell had worked with wood, then the whole notion that he had left the coffins on Arthur's Seat would begin to crumble. She sat back, annoyed with herself. All this time, she'd been working on an assumption that could turn out to be false. Lovell had left Edinburgh in 1832; the boys had stumbled on the cave containing the coffins in June 1836. Could they have gone undetected for so long?

She lifted something from the desk-top. It was a Polaroid she'd taken in Surgeons' Hall – the portrait of Lovell. He didn't look like a man who'd suffered the ravages of Africa. His skin was pale and smooth, his face youthful. She had pencilled the artist's name on the back. She got up and left her room again, opened the door to her boss's office and switched on his light. He had a shelf of thick reference books, and she found the one she needed, turned to the painter's name, J. Scott Jauncey. 'Active in Edinburgh 1825–35,' she read, 'chiefly landscapes, but some portraiture.' After which he'd taken himself to Europe for many years before settling in Hove. So Lovell had sat for the portrait during his early years in Edinburgh, before his own travels. She wondered if such a thing was the luxury it seemed, to be afforded only by the well-off. Then she thought of Reverend Kirkpatrick . . . maybe the portrait had been at his request, something to be sent west to the Ayrshire parish, to remind the minister of his charge.

Again, there might be a clue buried deep within Surgeons' Hall, some record of the portrait's history prior to its arrival there.

'Monday,' she said out loud. It could wait till Monday. She had the weekend to look forward to . . . and a Lou Reed concert to survive.

Switching off her boss's light, she heard another noise, much closer. The door to the outer office swung open and the lights all came on. Jean took half a step back, then saw it was just the cleaner.

'You gave me a fright,' she said, putting a hand to her chest.

The cleaner just smiled and put a bin-bag down, heading back into the hallway to fetch her vacuum cleaner.

'Mind if I get started?' she asked.

'Go ahead,' Jean said. 'I'm finished here anyway.'

As she tidied her desk, she noticed that her heart was still racing, her hands shaking slightly. All her night-time walks through the museum, and this was the first time she'd been fazed. The portrait of Kennet Lovell stared at her from the Polaroid. Somehow, it seemed to her, Jauncey had failed to flatter his subject. Lovell looked young, yes, but there was a coldness to the eyes, and the mouth was set, the face full of calculation.

'Heading straight home?' the cleaner asked, coming in to empty her bin.

'Might make a pit-stop at the off-licence.'

'Kill or cure, eh?' the cleaner said.

'Something like that,' Jean replied, as an unwanted image of her husband flashed up in her mind. Then she thought of something and walked back to her desk. Lifted her pen and added a name to the notes she'd taken so far.

Claire Benzie.

11

'Jesus, that was loud,' Rebus said. They were back on the pavement outside the Playhouse, and the sky, which had still been light when they'd gone in, was now dark.

'You don't do this sort of thing often then?' she asked. Her own ears were ringing. She knew she was talking too loudly, overcompensating.

'It's been a while,' he admitted. The crowd had been a mix of teenagers, old punks, right up to people Rebus's own age . . . maybe even a year or two older. Reed had played a lot of new material, stuff Rebus hadn't recognised, but with a few of the classics stirred into the pot. The Playhouse: last time he'd been there had probably been UB40, around the time of their second album. He didn't want to think how long ago that was.

'Shall we get a drink?' Jean suggested. They'd been drinking on and off all afternoon and evening: wine with lunch, then a quick one at the Ox. A long walk down to Dean Village and along the Water of Leith. All the way down to Leith itself, with breaks on the way to park themselves on a bench and talk. Two more drinks in a pub on The Shore. They'd considered an early supper, but were still full from the Café St Honore. Walked back up Leith Walk to the Playhouse. Still early, so they'd gone into the Conan Doyle for one, then the Playhouse bar itself.

At one point Rebus had found himself saying: 'I'd have thought you'd steer clear of the drink.' Regretting the remark immediately. But Jean had just shrugged.

'You mean because of Bill? That's not the way it works. I mean, maybe it is with some people, they either become a drunk themselves or they make a pact never to touch another drop. But it's not the booze that's to blame, it's the person using it. All the time Bill had his problem, it didn't stop me indulging. I never lectured him. And it hasn't stopped me drinking . . . because I know it doesn't mean that much to me.' She'd paused. 'What about you?'

'Me?' Rebus had offered his own shrug. 'I just drink to be sociable.'

'And when does it start working?'

They'd laughed at that, and left the subject alone. Now, just g eleven on a Saturday night, the street was noisy with alcohol.

'Where do you suggest?' Jean asked. Rebus made a show of check his watch. There were plenty of bars he could think of, but th weren't places he wanted Jean to see.

'Could you stand a bit more music?'

She shrugged. 'What kind?'

'Acoustic. It'd be standing room only.'

She was thoughtful. 'Is it between here and your flat?'

He nodded. 'You know the place is a tip . . .'

'I've seen it.' Her eyes found his. 'So . . . are you going to ask?'

'You want to stay the night?'

'I want you to ask me to.'

'It's only a mattress on the floor.'

She laughed, squeezed his hand. 'Are you doing this on purpose?'

'What?'

'Trying to put me off.'

'No, it's just . . .' He shrugged. 'I just don't want you—'

She interrupted him with a kiss. 'I won't be,' she said.

He ran a hand up her arm, let it rest on her shoulder. 'Still want that drink first?'

'I think so. How far is it?'

'Just up the Bridges. Pub's called the Royal Oak.'

'Then lead me to it.'

They walked hand in hand, Rebus trying his best not to feel awkward. Still he found himself scanning faces they passed, looking for ones he recognised: colleagues or ex-cons, he couldn't have said which he'd like to meet the least.

'Do you ever relax?' Jean asked at one point.

'I thought I was doing a pretty good imitation.'

'I felt it at the concert, bits of you were elsewhere.'

'Comes with the job.'

'I don't think so. Gill manages to switch off. I'd guess most of the rest of CID do too.'

'Maybe not as much as you think.' He thought of Siobhan, imagined her sitting at home, staring into the laptop . . . and Ellen Wylie festering somewhere . . . and Grant Hood, his bed strewn with paperwork, memorising names and faces. And the Farmer, what would he be doing? Running a cloth slowly over surfaces already clean? There were some – Hi-Ho Silvers; Joe Dickie – who barely switched on when they went to work, never mind switched off at day's end. Others like Bill Pryde and Bobby Hogan worked hard, but left the job in the office, managed the magic of separating their personal lives from their careers.

Then there was Rebus himself, who for so long had put the job first . . . because it saved him having to face some home truths.

Jean broke his reverie with a question. 'Is there a twenty-four-hour shop somewhere on the route?'

'More than one. Why?'

'Breakfast: something tells me your fridge won't exactly be an Aladdin's Cave.'

Monday morning, Ellen Wylie was back at her own desk in what everyone in the force referred to as 'West End', meaning the police station on Torphichen Street. Her reasoning was that it would be easier to get work done there, space not exactly being at a premium. A couple of weekend stabbings, one mugging, three domestics and an arson . . . these were keeping her colleagues busy. When they passed her, they asked about the Balfour case. She was waiting for Reynolds and Shug Davidson in particular – the pair forming a fearsome double act – to say something about her TV appearance, but they didn't. Maybe they were taking pity on the afflicted; most likely they were just showing solidarity. Even in a city as small as Edinburgh, rivalries existed between stations. If the Balfour investigation shat on DS Ellen Wylie, it was in effect dumping on West End.

'Reassigned?' Shug Davidson guessed.

She shook her head. 'I'm following a lead. It's as easy to do it here as there.'

'Ah, but here you're a long way away from the glamour chase.'

'The what?'

He smiled. 'The big picture, the juicy inquiry, the *centre* of everything.'

'I'm at the centre of the West End,' she told him. 'That's good enough for me.' Earned herself a wink from Davidson and a round of applause from Reynolds. She smiled: she was back home.

It had niggled at her all weekend: the way she'd been sidelined – bumped from liaison and dropped off at the twilight zone in which DI John Rebus worked. And from there to this – a tourist's suicide from years back – seemed yet another snub.

So she'd come to a decision: if they didn't want her, she didn't need them. Welcome back to the West End. She'd picked up all her notes on the way in. They sat on her desk, a desk she didn't need to share with half a dozen other bodies. The telephone wasn't going constantly, Bill Pryde flapping past with his clipboard and nicotine chewing-gum. She felt safe here, and here she could safely reach the conclusion that she was on another wild-goose chase.

Now all she had to do was prove it to Gill Templer's satisfaction.

She was off to a flyer. She'd called the police station in Fort William and spoken to a very helpful sergeant called Donald Maclay, who remembered the case well.

'The upper slope of Ben Dorchory,' he told her. 'The body had been there a couple of months. It's a remote spot. A ghillie happened on the

scene; could have lain there years otherwise. We followed procedure. Nothing in the way of ID on the body. Nothing in the pockets.'

'Not even any money?'

'We didn't find any. Labels on the jacket, shirt and such-like didn't tell us anything. Talked to the B and Bs and hotels, checked the missing persons records.'

'What about the gun?'

'What about it?'

'Did you get any prints?'

'After that length of time? No, we didn't.'

'But you did check for them?'

'Oh, aye.'

Wylie was writing everything down, abbreviating most of the words. 'Gunpowder traces?'

'Sorry?'

'On the skin. He was shot in the head?'

'That's right. The pathologist didn't find any burning or residues on the scalp.'

'Isn't that unusual?'

'Not when half the head's been blown away and the local wildlife have been feeding.'

Wylie stopped writing. 'I get the picture,' she said.

'I mean, this wasn't like a body, more a scarecrow. The skin was like parchment. There's a hellish wind blows across that hill.'

'You didn't treat it as suspicious?'

'We went by the autopsy findings.'

'Any chance you can send me the file?'

'If we get a written request, sure.'

'Thanks.' She tapped her pen against the desk. 'The gun was how far away?'

'Maybe twenty feet.'

'You think an animal moved it?'

'Yes. Either that or it was a reflex thing. Put a gun to your head and pull the trigger, there's going to be a recoil, isn't there?'

'I'd think so.' She paused. 'So what happened next?'

'Well, eventually we tried facial reconstruction, then issued the composite photo.'

'And?'

'And nothing very much. Thing was, we thought he was a lot older . . . early forties maybe, and the composite reflected that. God knows how the Germans got to hear of it.'

'The mother and father?'

'That's right. Their son had been missing the best part of a year . . . maybe even a bit longer. Then we got this call from Munich, couldn't make much sense of it. Next thing, they'd turned up at the station with a translator. We showed them the clothes and they recognised a couple of things . . . the jacket, and a wristwatch.'

'You don't sound convinced.'

'To tell you the truth, I'm not. A year they'd been looking for him, going out of their minds. The jacket was just a plain green thing, nothing special about it. Same goes for the watch.'

'You think they managed to convince themselves simply because they *wanted* to believe?'

'Wanted it to be him, yes. But their son was barely twenty . . . experts told us we had the remains of someone twice that age. Then the bloody papers went and printed the story anyway.'

'How did all the sword-and-sorcery stuff come into the picture?'

'Hang on a minute, will you?' She heard Maclay put the receiver down next to his phone. He was giving instructions to someone. 'Just past the creels . . . there's a hut Aly uses when he's renting out his boat . . .' She imagined Fort William: quiet and coastal, with islands off to the west. Fishermen and tourists; gulls overhead and the tang of seaweed.

'Sorry about that,' Maclay said.

'Keeping you busy?'

'Oh, it's always hectic up this way,' he replied with a laugh. She wished she were there with him. After they'd finished talking, she could walk down to the harbour, passing those creels . . . 'Where were we?' he said.

'Sword and sorcery.'

'First we knew about that was when they put it in the paper. The parents again, they'd been talking to some reporter.'

Wylie held the photocopy in front of her. The headline: 'Did Role Game Kill in Highland Gun Mystery?' The reporter's name was Steve Holly.

Jürgen Becker was a twenty-year-old student who lived with his parents in a suburb of Hamburg. He attended the local university, specialising in psychology. He loved role-playing games, and was part of a team who played in an inter-university league on the Internet. Fellow students said that he'd been 'anxious and troubled' during the week leading up to his disappearance. When he left home for that last time, he took a backpack with him. In it, to the best of his parents' knowledge, were his passport, a couple of changes of clothes, his camera, and a portable CD player with maybe a dozen or so discs.

The parents were professionals – the father an architect, mother a lecturer – but they'd given up work to concentrate on finding their son. The story shifted into bold type for its final paragraph: 'Now, two grieving parents know they've found their son. Yet for them the mystery has only deepened. How did Jürgen come to die on a barren Scottish mountaintop? Who else was there with him? Whose was the gun . . . and who used it to end the young student's life?'

'The backpack and stuff, they never turned up?' Wylie asked.

'Never. But then if it wasn't him, you would hardly expect them to.'

She smiled. 'You've been a real help, Sergeant Maclay.'

'Just put that request in writing, and I'll let you have chapter and verse.'

'Thanks, I'll do that.' She paused. 'We've got a Maclay in Edinburgh CID, works out of Craigmillar . . .'

'Aye, we're cousins. Met him at a couple of weddings and funerals. Craigmillar's where the posh folk live?'

'Is that what he told you?'

'Was I being fed a line?'

'Come see for yourself sometime.'

Wylie was laughing when she finished the call, had to tell Shug Davidson why. He came over to her desk. The CID room wasn't big: four desks, doors leading off to walk-in cupboards where they kept old case files. Davidson picked up the photocopied news story, read it through.

'Looks like something Holly made up all by himself,' he commented.

'You know him?'

'Had a couple of run-ins with him. Holly's speciality is blowing a story up.'

She took the article from him. Sure enough, all the stuff about fantasy games and role-playing was kept ambiguous, the text peppered with conditionals: 'may have', 'could be', 'if, as it is thought . . .'

'I need to speak to him,' she stated, picking up the phone again. 'Do you know his number?'

'No, but he's based at the paper's Edinburgh office.' Davidson started back towards his own desk. 'You'll find it in Yellow Pages under "Leper Colonies" . . .'

Steve Holly was still on his way into work when his mobile sounded. He lived in the New Town, only three streets from what he'd recently called in print 'the tragic death flat'. Not that his own place was in the same league as Flip Balfour's. He was at the top of an unmodernised tenement – one of few still left in the New Town. And his street didn't have the cachet of Flip's address. Still, he'd watched the paper value of his flat soar. Four years ago, he'd decided he wanted to live in this part of town. But even then it had seemed beyond his means, until he started reading the death notices in the city's daily and evening papers. When he saw a New Town address, he'd head round there with an envelope marked 'Urgent' and addressed to 'The Owner'. The letter inside was short. He introduced himself as someone who'd been born and raised in whichever street, but whose family had moved away and encountered bad fortune since. With both parents dead, he now wished to return to a street which held such fond memories, and should the owner ever wish to consider selling . . .

And bloody hell, it had worked. An old woman – house-ridden for a decade – had died, and her niece, who was her closest living relative, had read Holly's letter, phoning him that afternoon. He'd gone to look at the place – three bedrooms, a bit smelly and dark but he knew such things could be fixed. Nearly shot himself in the foot when the niece asked which number he'd lived at, but he'd managed to fool her well enough. Then his pitch: all the estate agents and solicitors getting their cut . . . better to agree a fair price between them and cut out the middle-men.

The niece lived in the Borders, didn't seem to know what flats in Edinburgh were fetching. She'd even thrown in a lot of the old lady's furniture, for which he'd thanked her profusely, turfing out the lot his first weekend in residence.

If he sold up now he'd have a hundred grand in his pocket, a nice nest egg. In fact, only this morning he'd wondered about trying something similar with the Balfours . . . only somehow he reckoned they'd know to the last penny what Flip's place was worth. He stopped, halfway up the Dundas Street climb, and answered his mobile.

'Steve Holly speaking.'

'Mr Holly, this is Detective Sergeant Wylie, Lothian and Borders CID.'

Wylie? He tried to place her. Of course! That brilliant press conference! 'Yes, DS Wylie, and what can I do for you this morning?'

'It's about a story you ran three years or so back . . . the German student.'

'Would that be the student with the twenty-foot reach?' he asked with a grin. He was outside a small art gallery, peered in through the window, curious about the prices first, paintings second.

'That's the one, yes.'

'Don't tell me you've caught the killer?'

'No.'

'What then?'

She hesitated; he frowned in concentration. 'Some new evidence may have come to light . . .'

'What new evidence?'

'Right now, I'm afraid I can't divulge . . .'

'Yeah, yeah. Tell me something I don't hear every other day. Your lot always want something for nothing.'

'And your lot don't?'

He turned away from the window, just in time to catch a green Aston revving away from the lights: not too many about, had to be the grieving father . . . 'What's it got to do with Philippa Balfour?' he asked.

Silence on the line. 'Sorry?'

'That's not a very good answer, DS Wylie. Last time I saw you, you were attached to the Balfour case. Are you saying they've suddenly shifted you on to a case which isn't even in the Lothian and Borders remit?'

'I . . .'

'You're probably not at liberty to say, right? Me, on the other hand, I can say whatever I like.'

'The way you made up that sword-and-sorcery stuff?'

'That wasn't made up. I got it from the parents.'

'That he liked role-playing, yes, but the idea that it was some game brought him to Scotland . . . ?'

'Speculation based on the available evidence.'

'But there *was* no evidence of such a game, was there?'

'Highland mountains, all that Celtic myth rubbish . . . just the place someone like Jürgen would end up. Sent out on some quest, only there's a gun waiting for him when he gets there.'

'Yes, I read your story.'

'And somehow it ties in with Flip Balfour, but you're not going to tell me how?' Holly licked his lips; he was enjoying this.

'That's right,' Wylie said.

'It must have hurt.' His voice was almost solicitous.

'What?'

'When they pulled you from liaison. Not your fault, was it? We're like bloody savages at times. They should have prepared you better. Christ, Gill Templer worked liaison for a hundred years . . . she should have *known*.'

Another silence on the line. Holly softened his voice. 'And then they go and give it to a detective *constable*. DC Grant Hood. A shining example. Now there's one cocky little bastard if ever I saw one. Like I say, something like that's got to hurt. And what's happened to you, DS Wylie? You're stuck halfway up a Scottish mountain, scrabbling around for a reporter – one of the enemy – to put you right.'

He thought she'd gone, but then heard something which was almost a sigh.

Oh, you're good, Stevie boy, he thought to himself. You'll have the right address some day, and works of art on the walls for people to gawp at . . .

'Detective Sergeant Wylie?' he said.

'What?'

'Sorry if I hit a nerve. But, look, maybe we could meet. I think I might just have a way to help, even if only a little.'

'What is it?'

'Face to face?'

'No.' The voice hardening. 'Tell me now.'

'Well . . .' Holly angled his head towards the sun. 'Say this thing you're working on . . . it's confidential, right?' He took a breath. 'Don't answer that. We both know already. But say someone . . . a journalist, for want of a better example . . . got hold of this story. People would want to know how he got it, and do you know who they'd look to first?'

'Who?'

'The liaison officer, Detective Constable Grant Hood. He's the one with the line to the media. And if a certain journalist – the one in possession of the leak – happened to . . . well, *indicate* that his source was not a thousand miles from the liaison officer . . . I'm sorry, it probably sounds petty to you. You probably don't want to see DC Hood with a bit of mud on his new starched shirt, or the flak that would head the way of DCS Templer. It's just that sometimes when I start thinking something, I need to go the whole way. Do you know what I'm saying?'

'Yes.'

'We could still have that meeting. I'm free all morning. I've already told you what you need to know about Mountain Boy, but we could talk anyway . . .'

Rebus had been standing in front of Ellen Wylie's desk a full half-minute before she seemed to realise he was there. She was staring towards the paperwork in front of her, but Rebus didn't think she was seeing it. Then Shug Davidson wandered past, slapping Rebus on the back and saying 'Morning, John', and Wylie looked up.

'Weekend that bad, was it?' Rebus asked.

'What are you doing here?'

'Looking for you, though I'm beginning to wonder why I bothered.'

She seemed to pull herself together, ran a hand over her head and muttered something approaching an apology.

'So am I right, was it a bad weekend?'

Davidson was passing again, papers in hand. 'She was fine till ten minutes ago.' He stopped. 'Was it that wanker Holly?'

'No,' Wylie said.

'Bet it was,' Davidson stated, moving off again.

'Steve Holly?' Rebus guessed.

Wylie tapped the newspaper story. 'I had to talk to him.'

Rebus nodded. 'Just watch out for him, Ellen.'

'I can handle him, don't worry.'

He was still nodding. 'That's more like it. Now, do you feel like doing me a favour?'

'Depends what it is.'

'I got the feeling this German student thing would be driving you mental . . . Is that why you came back to West End?'

'I just thought I might get more work done here.' She threw her pen down on the desk. 'Looks like I was wrong.'

'Well, I'm here to offer you a break. I've got a couple of interviews to do, and I need a partner.'

'Who are you interviewing?'

'David Costello and his father.'

'Why me?'

'I thought I'd already explained that.'

'Charity case, am I?'

Rebus let out a long breath. 'Jesus, Ellen, you can be hard work sometimes.'

She looked at her watch. 'I have a meeting at half-eleven.'

'Me too: doctor's appointment. But this won't take long.' He paused. 'Look, if you don't want to . . .'

'All right,' she said. Her shoulders were slumped. 'Maybe you're right.'

Too late, Rebus was having second thoughts. It was as if the fight had gone out of her. He thought he knew the reason, but knew also that there was little he could do about it.

'Great,' he said.

Reynolds and Davidson were watching from one of the other desks. 'Look, Shug,' Reynolds said, 'it's the Dynamic Duo!'

It seemed to take all Ellen Wylie's effort to lift her from her chair.

He briefed her in the car. She didn't ask much, seemed more interested in the passing parade of pedestrians. Rebus left the Saab in hotel parking and walked into the Caledonian, Wylie a couple of steps behind.

The 'Caley' was an Edinburgh institution, a red-stone monolith at the west end of Princes Street. Rebus had no idea what a room cost. He'd eaten in the restaurant once, with his wife and a couple of friends of hers who were honeymooning in the city. The friends had insisted on putting dinner on their room tab, so Rebus had never known the final figure. He'd been uncomfortable all evening, right in the middle of a case and wanting to get back to it. Rhona knew, too, and excluded him from the conversation by concentrating on reminiscences she shared with her friends. The honeymooners holding hands between courses, and sometimes even while they ate. Rebus and Rhona almost strangers to one another, their marriage faltering . . .

'How the other half live,' he said to Wylie as they waited for the receptionist to call the Costellos' room. When Rebus had phoned David Costello's flat, there'd been no answer, so he'd asked around the office and been told that the parents flew into town Sunday evening, and that their son was spending the day with them.

'I don't think I've been inside before,' Wylie replied. 'It's just a hotel, after all.'

'They'd love to hear you say that.'

'Well, it's true, isn't it?'

Rebus got the feeling she wasn't thinking about what she was saying. Her mind was somewhere else, the words just filling spaces.

The receptionist smiled at them. 'Mr Costello's expecting you.' She gave them the room number and directed them towards the lifts. A liveried porter was hovering, but one look at Rebus told him there was no work for him here. As the lift glided upwards, Rebus tried to get the song 'Bell-Boy' out of his head, Keith Moon growling and wailing.

'What's that you're whistling?' Wylie asked.

'Mozart,' Rebus lied. She nodded as if she'd just placed the tune . . .

It wasn't a room after all, but a suite, with a connecting door to the suite next to it. Rebus caught a glimpse of Theresa Costello before her husband closed the door. The living area was compact: sofa, chair, table, TV . . . There was a bedroom off, and a bathroom down the hall. Rebus could smell soap and shampoo, and behind them the unaired smell you sometimes got in hotel rooms. There was a basket of fruit on the table, and David Costello, seated there, had just helped himself to an apple. He had shaved, but his hair was unwashed, lank and greasy. His grey T-shirt looked new, as did the black denims. The shoelaces on both his trainers were untied, either by accident or design.

Thomas Costello was shorter than Rebus had imagined him, a boxer's roll to his shoulders when he walked. His mauve shirt was open-necked, and his trousers were held up with pale pink braces.

'Come in, come in,' he said, 'sit yourselves down.' He gestured towards the sofa. Rebus, however, took the armchair, while Wylie stayed standing. There was nothing for the father to do but sink into the sofa himself, where he spread his arms out either side of him. But a split second later he brought his hands together in a single sharp clap and exclaimed that they needed something to drink.

'Not for us, Mr Costello,' Rebus said.

'You're sure now?' Costello looked to Ellen Wylie, who managed a slow nod.

'Well then.' The father once again arranged his arms either side of him. 'So what can we be doing for you?'

'I'm sorry we have to intrude at a time like this, Mr Costello.' Rebus glanced towards David, who was showing about as much interest in proceedings as Wylie.

'We quite understand, Inspector. You've got a job to do, and we all want to help you catch the sick bastard who did this to Philippa.' Costello clenched his fists, showing he was ready to do some damage to the culprit himself. His face was almost wider than it was long, the hair cut short and brushed straight back from the forehead. The eyes were narrowed slightly, and Rebus guessed that the man wore contact lenses, and was ever fearful of them falling out.

'Well, Mr Costello, we just have some follow-up questions . . .'

'And do you mind me staying while you ask them?'

'Not at all. It may even be that you can help.'

'Go ahead then.' His head snapped round. 'Davey! Are you listening?'

David Costello nodded, ripping another bite from the apple.

'The stage is all yours, Inspector,' the father said.

'Well, maybe I could start by asking David a couple of things.' Rebus made a show of easing the notebook from his pocket, though he knew the questions already and didn't think he'd need to write anything down. But sometimes the presence of a notebook could work a little magic. Interviewees seemed to trust the written word: if you had something in your notebook, then it had probably been verified. Additionally, if they thought their replies were going to be recorded, they gave each utterance more consideration, or else became flustered and blurted out the truth.

'You're sure you won't sit?' the father asked Wylie, patting the space on the sofa.

'I'm fine,' she answered coolly.

The exchange had somehow broken the spell; David Costello didn't look in the least bothered about the notebook.

'Fire away,' he told Rebus.

Rebus took aim and fired. 'David, we've asked you about this Internet game we think Flip might have been playing . . .'

'Yes.'

'And you said you didn't know anything about it, and didn't go much for computer games and such-like.'

'Yes.'

'But now we hear that in your schooldays you were a bit of a whizz at dungeons and dragons.'

'I remember that,' Thomas Costello interrupted. 'You and your pals, up there in your bedroom all day and all night.' He looked at Rebus. 'All *night*, Inspector, if you can believe that.'

'I've heard of grown men doing the same thing,' Rebus said. 'A few hands of poker and a big enough pot . . .'

Costello conceded as much with a smile: one gambling man to another.

'Who told you I was a "whizz"?' David asked.

'It just came up.' Rebus shrugged.

'Well, I wasn't. The D and D craze lasted about a month.'

'Flip played, too, when she was at school, did you know that?'

'I'm not sure.'

'She'd have told you though . . . I mean, the pair of you were into it.'

'Not by the time we met. I don't think the subject ever came up.'

Rebus stared into David Costello's eyes. They were red-rimmed and bloodshot.

'Then how would Flip's friend Claire have got to hear of it?'

The young man snorted. '*She* told you? Claire the Cow?'

Thomas Costello tutted.

'Well, she is,' his son snapped back. 'She was always trying to break us up, pretending she was "a friend".'

'She didn't like you?'

David considered this. 'I think it was more that she couldn't bear to see Flip happy. When I told Flip, she just laughed in my face. She couldn't see it. There was some history between her family and Claire's, and I think Flip felt guilty. Claire was a real blind spot . . .'

'Why didn't you tell us this before?'

David looked at him and laughed. 'Because Claire didn't kill Flip.'

'No?'

'Christ, you're not saying . . .' He shook his head. 'I mean, when I say Claire was vicious, it was just mind games with her . . . just words.' He paused. 'But then maybe that's what the game was, too: is that what you're thinking?'

'We're keeping an open mind,' Rebus said.

'Jesus, Davey,' the father said, 'if there's anything you need to tell these officers, get it off your chest!'

'It's *David*!' the young man spat. His father looked furious, but didn't say anything. 'I still don't think it was Claire,' David added, for Rebus's benefit.

'What about Flip's mother?' Rebus asked casually. 'How did you get on with her?'

'Fine.'

Rebus allowed the silence to linger, then repeated the word back at David, this time as a question.

'You know how mothers are with daughters,' David started to add. 'Protective and all that.'

'Rightly so, eh?' Thomas Costello winked at Rebus, who glanced towards Ellen Wylie, wondering if this would rouse her. But she was staring out of the window.

'Thing is, David,' Rebus said quietly, 'we've reason to believe there might have been a bit of friction there too.'

'How so?' Thomas Costello asked.

'Maybe David can answer that,' Rebus told him.

'Well, David?' Costello asked his son.

'I've no idea what he means.'

'I mean,' Rebus said, pretending to check his notes, 'that Mrs Balfour harboured the thought that you'd somehow poisoned Flip's mind.'

'You must have misheard the lady,' Thomas Costello said. He was bunching his fists again.

'I don't think so, sir.'

'Look at the strain she's been under . . . doesn't know what she's saying.'

'I think she knew.' Rebus was still looking at David.

'It's right enough,' he said. He'd lost all interest in the apple. It hung from his hand, the white, exposed flesh already beginning to discolour. His father gave a questioning look. 'Jacqueline had some notion that I was giving Flip ideas.'

'What sort of ideas?'

'That she hadn't had a happy childhood. That she was remembering it all wrong.'

'And did you think she was?' Rebus asked.

'It was Flip, not me,' David stated. 'She'd been having this dream. She was back in London, back at the house there, and running up and down stairs trying to get away from something. Same dream most nights for a fortnight.'

'What did you do?'

'Looked in a couple of textbooks, told her it might be to do with repressed memory.'

'The boy's lost me,' Thomas Costello admitted. His son turned his head towards him.

'Something bad that you've managed not to think about. I was quite envious, actually.' They stared at one another. Rebus thought he knew what David was talking about: growing up with Thomas Costello couldn't have been easy. Maybe it explained the son's teenage years . . .

'She never explained what that might be?' Rebus asked.

David shook his head. 'Probably it was nothing; dreams can have all sorts of meanings.'

'But Flip believed it?'

'For a little while, yes.'

'And told her mother as much?'

David nodded. 'Who then blamed the whole thing on me.'

'Bloody woman,' Thomas Costello hissed. He rubbed his forehead. 'But then she's been under a lot of strain, lot of strain . . .'

'This was before Flip went missing,' Rebus reminded him.

'I don't mean that: I mean Balfour's,' Costello growled. The slight against his son was still fresh.

Rebus frowned. 'What about it?'

'Lots of money men in Dublin. You get to hear rumours.'

'About Balfour's?'

'I don't understand it all myself: overstretched . . . liquidity ratios . . . just words to me.'

'You're saying Balfour's Bank is in trouble?'

Costello shook his head. 'Just a few stories that they might be headed that way if they don't turn things around. Problem with banking is, it's all about confidence, isn't it? Few wild stories can do a lot of damage . . .'

Rebus got the feeling Costello wouldn't have said anything, but Jacqueline Balfour's accusations against his son had tipped the balance. He made his first note of the interview: 'check Balfour's'.

He'd had a notion himself: to bring up the matter of father and son's wild days in Dublin. But David seemed calmer now, his teenage years in the past. And as for his father, well, Rebus had seen intimations of a short temper. He didn't think he needed a further lesson.

There was silence in the room again.

'Will that do you for now, Inspector?' Costello said, making show of reaching into his trousers and drawing out a pocket watch, flipping it open and snapping it closed.

'Just about,' Rebus admitted. 'Do you know when the funeral is?'

'Wednesday,' Costello said.

It was sometimes the case, in a murder inquiry, that the victim was left unburied as long as possible, just in case some new piece of evidence came to light. Rebus reckoned strings had been pulled: John Balfour again, getting his own way.

'Is it a burial?'

Costello nodded. A burial was good. With a cremation, it wasn't quite so easy to disinter the body should the need arise . . .

'Well,' he said, 'unless there's anything either of you would like to add . . . ?'

There wasn't. Rebus got to his feet. 'All right, DS Wylie?' he said. It was as if she'd been roused from sleep.

Costello insisted on seeing them to the door, shook both their hands. David didn't get up from his chair. He was lifting the apple to his mouth as Rebus said goodbye.

Outside, the door clicked shut. Rebus stood there for a moment, but couldn't make out any voices from within. He noticed the next door along was open a couple of inches, Theresa Costello peering out.

'Everything okay?' she was asking Wylie.

'Everything's fine, madam,' Wylie told her.

Before Rebus could get there, the door had closed again. He was left wondering whether Theresa Costello felt as trapped as she looked . . .

In the lift, he told Wylie he'd drop her off.

'That's okay,' she said. 'I'm walking.'

'Sure?' She nodded, and he checked his watch. 'Your half-eleven?' he guessed.

'That's right.' Her voice died away.

'Well, thanks for all your help.'

She blinked, as though having difficulty taking the words in. He stood in the main lobby and watched her make for the revolving door. A moment later, he followed her out on to the street. She was crossing Princes Street, holding her bag in front of her, almost jogging. She made her way up the side of Fraser's store, towards Charlotte Square, where Balfour's had its headquarters. He wondered where she was headed: George Street, or maybe Queen Street? Down into the New Town? The only way to find out was to follow her, but he doubted she would appreciate his curiosity.

'Oh, what the hell,' he muttered to himself, making for the crossing. He had to wait for the traffic to stop, and only caught sight of her when he reached Charlotte Square: she was over the other side, walking briskly. By the time he was on George Street, he'd lost her. He smiled to himself: some detective. Walked along as far as Castle Street, then doubled back. She could be in one of the shops or cafés. To hell with it. He unlocked the Saab and drove out of the hotel car park.

Some people had their demons. He got the feeling Ellen Wylie was among them. He was a good judge of character that way. Experience always told.

Back in St Leonard's, he phoned a contact on a Sunday newspaper's business pages.

'How sound is Balfour's?' he asked, no preamble.

'I'm assuming you mean the bank?'

'Yes.'

'What have you heard?'

'There are rumours in Dublin.'

The journalist chuckled. 'Ah, rumours, where would the world be without them?'

'Then there's no problem?'

'I didn't say that. On paper, Balfour's is ticking along as ever. But there are always margins where figures can be buried.'

'And?'

'And their half-year forecast has been revised downwards; not quite enough to give big investors the jitters, but Balfour's is a loose affiliation of smaller investors. They have a tendency towards hypochondria.'

'Bottom line, Terry?'

'Balfour's should survive, a hostile takeover notwithstanding. But if the balance sheet looks murky at year's end, there may have to be one or two ritual beheadings.'

Rebus was thoughtful. 'Who would go?'

'Ranald Marr, I should think, if only to show that Balfour himself has the ruthlessness necessary for this day and age.'

'No place for old friendships?'

'Truth be told, there never was.'

'Thanks, Terry. A large G and T will be waiting for you behind the bar of the Ox.'

'It may wait a while.'

'You on the wagon?'

'Doctor's orders. We're being picked off one by one, John.'

Rebus commiserated for a couple of minutes, thinking of his own doctor's appointment, the one he was missing yet again by making this call. When he put the phone down, he scribbled the name Marr on to his pad and circled it. Ranald Marr, with his Maserati and toy soldiers. *You'd almost have thought he'd lost a daughter* . . . Rebus was beginning to revise that opinion. He wondered if Marr knew how precarious his job was, knew that the mere thought of their savings catching a cold might spur the small investors on, demanding a sacrifice . . .

He switched to a picture of Thomas Costello, who'd never had to work in his life. What must that be like? Rebus couldn't begin to answer the question. His parents had been poor all their lives: never owned their own house. When his father had died, he'd left four hundred quid for Rebus to split with his brother. A policy had taken care of the funeral. Even back then, pocketing his share of the notes in the bank manager's office, he'd wondered . . . half his parents' life savings represented one of his week's wages.

He had money in the bank himself now: did very little with his monthly salary. The flat was paid off; neither Rhona nor Samantha ever seemed to want anything from him. Food and drink, and garage bills for the Saab. He never went on holiday, probably bought a couple of LPs or CDs a week. A couple of months back, he'd thought of buying a Linn hi-fi system, but the shop had knocked him back, told him they'd nothing in stock and would phone him when they had. They'd never phoned. The Lou Reed tickets hadn't exactly stretched him: Jean had insisted on paying for hers ... and cooked him breakfast next morning to boot.

'It's the Laughing Policeman!' Siobhan called across the office. She was seated at her desk next to Brains from Fettes. Rebus realised he had a big grin on his face. He got up and crossed the room.

'I withdraw that remark,' Siobhan said quickly, holding up her hands in surrender.

'Hello, Brains,' Rebus said.

'His name's Bain,' Siobhan corrected him. 'He likes to be called Eric.'

Rebus ignored this. 'It's like the deck of the Starship *Enterprise* in here.' He was looking at the array of computers and connections: two laptops, two PCs. He knew one of the PCs was Siobhan's, the other Flip Balfour's. 'Tell me,' he asked her, 'what do we know about Philippa's early life in London?'

She wrinkled her nose, thinking. 'Not much. Why?'

'Because the boyfriend says she was having these nightmares, running up and down the London house being chased by something.'

'Sure it was the London house?'

'What do you mean?'

She shrugged. 'Just that Junipers gave me the heebies: suits of armour and dusty old billiard rooms ... imagine growing up with that.'

'David Costello said the London house.'

'Transference?' Bain suggested. They both looked at him. 'Just a thought,' he said.

'So really it was Junipers she was scared of?' Rebus asked.

'Let's get out the ouija board and ask her.' Siobhan realised what she'd said and winced. 'Worst possible taste, sorry.'

'I've heard worse,' Rebus said. He had, too. At the murder scene, one of the woolly-suits helping with the cordon had been overheard telling a mate: 'I bet she hadn't banked on that. Get it?'

'It's kind of sub-Hitchcock, isn't it?' Bain said now. 'You know, *Marnie*, that sort of thing ...'

Rebus thought of the book of poems in David Costello's flat: *I Dream of Alfred Hitchcock*.

You do not die for being bad, you die
For being available ...

'You're probably right,' he said.

Siobhan read his tone. 'All the same, you still want the low-down on Flip's London years?'

He began to nod, then shook his head. 'No,' he said, 'you're right ... it's too far-fetched.'

As he moved away, Siobhan turned to Bain. 'That's usually right up his street,' she murmured. 'The more far-fetched it is, the better he likes it.'

Bain smiled. He had the briefcase with him again; still hadn't opened it. After the meal on Friday night they'd said their goodbyes. Siobhan had got into her car Saturday morning and headed north for the football. Didn't bother offering anyone a lift: she'd packed an overnight bag. Found herself a guest house. Good win for Hibs in the afternoon, then a bit of exploring and a spot of dinner. She'd taken her Walkman, half a dozen tapes and a couple of paperbacks with her, leaving the laptop back in her flat. A weekend without Quizmaster: just what the doctor ordered. Except that she couldn't stop thinking about him, wondering if there was a message for her. She'd made sure she was late getting back Sunday night, then busied herself with laundry.

Now the laptop sat on her desk. She was almost afraid to touch it, afraid to give in to the craving . . .

'Good weekend?' Bain asked.

'Not bad. How about you?'

'Quiet. That dinner on Friday was just about the highlight.'

She smiled, accepting the compliment. 'So what do we do now? Get on the blower to Special Branch?'

'We talk to the Crime Squad. They route our request.'

'We can't cut out the middle-man?'

'The middle-man wouldn't like that.'

Siobhan thought of Claverhouse: Bain was probably right. 'Go ahead then,' she said.

So Bain picked up the phone and had a long conversation with DI Claverhouse at the Big House. Siobhan ran her fingers over the laptop's keyboard. It was already connected to her mobile. A phone message had been waiting for her at home on Friday night: her mobile account, wondering if she knew that her usage had suddenly gone up. Yes, she knew all right. With Bain still busy explaining things to Claverhouse, she decided to connect to the Net, just to give her something to do . . .

There were three messages from Quizmaster. The first was from Friday evening, around the time she got home:

Seeker – My patience wears thin. The quest is about to close on you. Immediate response requested.

The second was from Saturday afternoon:

Siobhan? I'm disappointed in you. Your times so far have been excellent. Game is now closed.

Closed or not, he'd come back on Sunday at the stroke of midnight:

Are you busy tracing me, is that it? Do you still want to meet?

Bain ended his conversation and put down the phone. He was staring at the screen.

'You've got him rattled,' he said.

'New ISP?' Siobhan asked. Bain checked the headers and nodded.

'New name, new everything. Still, he's getting the inkling that he's not untraceable.'

'Then why doesn't he just shut down?'

'I don't know.'

'You really think the game's closed?'

'Only one way to find out . . .'

So Siobhan got busy on the keyboard:

I was away all weekend, that's all. Inquiries progress. Meantime, yes, I'd still like to meet.

She sent the message. They went and grabbed coffee, but when they came back there was no reply.

'Is he sulking?' Siobhan asked.

'Or away from his machine.'

She looked at him. 'Your bedroom, is it full of computer stuff?'

'You're angling an invite to my bedroom?'

She smiled. 'No, I was just wondering. Some of these people, they can spend all day and night at a monitor, can't they?'

'Absolutely. But I'm not one of them. Three chat rooms where I'm a regular, maybe an hour or two of surfing when I get bored.'

'What are the chat rooms?'

'Tekky stuff.' He shifted his chair towards the desk. 'Now, while we're waiting, maybe we should take a look at Ms Balfour's deleted files.' He saw the look on her face. 'You know you can undelete files?'

'Sure. We already looked at her correspondence.'

'But did you look at her e-mails?'

Siobhan was forced to admit she hadn't. Or rather, Grant hadn't known it could be done.

Bain sighed and got to work on Flip's PC. It didn't take long. Soon they were staring at a list of deleted messages, both from Flip and to her.

'How far back do they go?' Siobhan asked.

'Just over two years. When did she buy the computer?'

'It was an eighteenth birthday present,' Siobhan said.

'Not bad for some.'

Siobhan nodded. 'She got a flat, too.'

Now Bain looked at her, shook his head slowly in disbelief. 'I got a watch and a camera for mine,' he said.

'Is that the watch?' Siobhan pointed to his wrist.

Bain's mind, however, was elsewhere. 'So we've got e-mails stretching right back to when she first got started. He clicked on the one with the earliest date, but the computer told him he couldn't open it.

'Need to convert it,' he said. 'The hard disk has probably compressed it.'

Siobhan was trying to study what he was doing, but he was going too fast. In no time, they were reading the first e-mail Flip had sent on her machine. It was to her father at his office:

Just testing. Hope you get this. The PC's super! See you tonight. Flip.

'I suppose we need to read them all?' Bain guessed.

'I suppose,' Siobhan agreed. 'Which means converting them one at a time?'

'Not necessarily. If you can fetch me a tea – white, no sugar – I'll see what I can do.'

By the time she got back with the drinks, he was printing out sheets of messages. 'This way,' he said, 'you can be reading them while I'm preparing the next batch.'

Siobhan started chronologically, and it didn't take her long to find something more interesting than gossipy exchanges between Flip and her friends.

'Look at this,' she told Bain.

He read the e-mail. 'It's from Balfour's Bank,' he said. 'Someone called RAM.'

'I'm willing to bet it's Ranald Marr.' Siobhan took the note back.

Flip, Great news that at last you are part of the virtual world! I hope you have a lot of fun with it. You'll also find the Internet a great research tool, so I'm hoping it helps you with your studies . . . Yes, you're right that you can delete messages – it makes space in the memory, and allows your computer to work more quickly. But remember that deleted messages are still recoverable unless you take certain steps. Here's how to delete something completely.

The writer went on to explain the process. At the end he signed himself R. Bain ran a finger down one edge of the screen.

'Explains why there are big gaps,' he said. 'Once he'd told her how to fully delete, she started doing it.'

'Also explains why there are none of the messages to or from Quizmaster.' Siobhan was sifting through the sheets of paper. 'Not even her original message to RAM.'

'And none afterwards either.'

Siobhan rubbed at her temples. 'Why would she want everything deleted anyway?'

'I don't know. It's not something most users would think to do.'

'Shift over,' Siobhan said, sliding her chair across. She started composing a new e-mail, to RAM at Balfour's Bank.

DC Clarke here. Urgent that you get in touch.

She added the St Leonard's phone number and sent the message, then picked up a telephone and called the bank.

'Mr Marr's office, please.' She was put through to Marr's secretary. 'Is Mr Marr there?' she asked, her eyes on Bain as he sipped his tea. 'Maybe you can help me. It's Detective Constable Clarke here, CID at St Leonard's. I just sent Mr Marr an e-mail and I was wondering if he'd received it. Apparently we're having some sort of problem at our end . . .' She paused while the secretary checked.

'Oh? He's not? Could you tell me where he is then?' She paused again, listening to the secretary. 'It really is quite important.' Now her eyebrows went up. 'Prestonfield House? That's not far from here. Is there any chance you could get a message to him, asking him to drop into St Leonard's after his meeting? It'll only take five minutes. Probably more convenient than having us visit him at work . . .' She listened again. 'Thanks. And the e-mail did get through? Great, thanks.'

She put the phone down, and Bain, cup drained and binned, applauded silently.

Forty minutes later, Marr arrived at the station. Siobhan got one of the uniforms to escort him upstairs to CID. Rebus was no longer around, but the suite was busy. The uniform brought Marr to Siobhan's desk. She nodded and asked the banker to take a seat. Marr looked around: there were no spare chairs. Eyes were studying him, the other officers wondering who he was. Dressed in a crisp pinstripe suit, white shirt and pale lemon tie, he looked more like an expensive lawyer than the usual visitors to the station.

Bain got up, dragging his own chair round the desk for Marr to sit in.

'My driver's parked on a single yellow,' Marr said, making a show of looking at his watch.

'This won't take long, sir,' Siobhan said. 'Do you recognise the machine.' She tapped the computer.

'What?'

'It belonged to Philippa.'

'Did it? I wouldn't know.'

'I suppose not. But you sent e-mails to one another.'

'What?'

'RAM: that *is* you, isn't it?'

'What if it is?'

Bain stepped forward and handed Marr a sheet of paper. 'Then you sent her this,' he said. 'And it looks like Ms Balfour acted on it.'

Marr looked up from the message, his eyes on Siobhan rather than Bain. She'd winced at Bain's words, and Marr had noticed.

Big mistake, Eric! she felt like screaming. Because now Marr knew that this was the only e-mail they had between himself and Flip. Otherwise, Siobhan could have strung him along, letting him think they had others, seeing whether that bothered him or not.

'Well?' was all Marr said, having read the message.

'It's just curious,' Siobhan said, 'that your first ever e-mail to her should be all about how to delete e-mails.'

'Philippa was very private in many ways,' Marr explained. 'She *liked* her privacy. The first thing she asked me was about deleting material. This was my response. She didn't like the idea of anyone being able to read what she'd written.'

'Why not?'

Marr shrugged both elegant shoulders. 'We all have different personae, don't we? The "you" who writes to an aged relative isn't the same "you" who writes to a close friend. I know that when I'm e-mailing a war-gamer, I don't necessarily want my secretary to read it. She would see a very different "me" from the person she works for.'

Siobhan was nodding. 'I think I understand.'

'It's also the case that in my own profession, confidentiality – secrecy, if you like – is absolutely vital. Commercial subterfuge is always an issue. We shred unwanted documents, delete e-mails and so on, to protect our clients and ourselves. So when Flip mentioned the delete button, that sort of consideration was uppermost in my mind.' He paused, looked from Siobhan to Bain and back again. 'Is that all you wanted to know?'

'What else did you talk about in your e-mails?'

'We didn't correspond for long. Flip was dipping a toe in the water. She had my e-mail address and knew I was an old hand. At first she had lots of questions to ask, but she was a fast learner.'

'We're still checking the machine for deleted messages,' Siobhan led blithely. 'Any idea when your last message to or from her would have been?'

'Maybe as much as a year back.' Marr started getting to his feet. 'Now, if we're quite finished, I really must . . .'

'If you hadn't told her about deleting, we might have him by now.'

'Who?'

'Quizmaster.'

'The person she was playing this game against? You still think that had something to do with her death?'

'I'd like to know.'

Marr was standing now, smoothing his jacket. 'Is that possible, without the help of this . . . Quizmaster?'

Siobhan looked to Bain, who knew a cue when he saw one.

'Oh, yes,' he said confidently. 'It'll take a bit longer, but we'll trace him. He's left enough bits and pieces for us along the way.'

Marr looked from one detective to the other. 'Splendid,' he said with a smile. 'Well, if I can be of further assistance . . .'

'You've helped us enormously already, Mr Marr,' Siobhan said, fixing her eyes on him. 'I'll have one of the uniformed officers show you out . . .'

After he'd gone, Bain pulled his chair back around to Siobhan's side of the desk and sat down next to her.

'You think it's him, don't you?' he asked quietly.

She nodded, staring at the doorway through which Marr had just left. Then her shoulders slumped. She squeezed shut her eyes, rubbed at them. 'Truth is, I haven't a clue.'

'You also don't have any evidence.'

She nodded, eyes still closed.

'Gut feeling?' he guessed.

She opened her eyes. 'I know better than to trust it.'

'Glad to hear it.' He smiled at her. 'Some proof would be nice, wouldn't it?'

When the phone rang, Siobhan seemed in a dream, so Bain answered. It was a Special Branch officer called Black. He wanted to know if he was speaking to the right person. When Bain assured him he was, Black asked how much he knew about computers.

'I know a bit.'

'Good. Is the PC in front of you?' When Bain said that it was, Black told him what he wanted. When Bain came off the phone five minutes later, he puffed out his cheeks and exhaled noisily.

'I don't know what it is about Special Branch,' he said, 'but they always make me feel about five years old and starting my first day at school.'

'You sounded okay,' Siobhan assured him. 'What do they need?'

'Copies of all the e-mails between you and Quizmaster, plus details of Philippa Balfour's ISP account and user names, plus the same for you.'

'Except it's Grant Hood's machine,' Siobhan said, touching the laptop.

'Well, his account details then.' He paused. 'Black asked if we had any suspects.'

'You didn't tell him?'

He shook his head. 'But we could always send him Marr's name. We could even provide his e-mail address.'

'Would that help?'

'It might. You know the Americans can read e-mails using satellites? Any e-mails in the world . . .' She just stared at him, and he laughed. 'I'm not saying Special Branch have that sort of technology, but you never know, do you?'

Siobhan was thoughtful. 'Then give them what we've got. Give them Ranald Marr.'

The laptop told them they had a message. Siobhan clicked it open. Quizmaster.

Seeker – We meet on completion of Stricture. Acceptable?

'Ooh,' Bain said, 'he's actually *asking* you.'

So game isn't closed? Siobhan typed back.

Special dispensation.

She typed another message: *There are questions need answering right now.*

An immediate reply: *Ask, Seeker.*

So she asked: *Was anyone playing the game apart from Flip?*

They waited a minute for the response.

Yes.

She looked at Bain. 'He said before that there wasn't.'

'He was either lying then, or he's lying now. Fact that you asked the question again makes me think you didn't believe him first time round.'

How many? Siobhan typed.

Three.

Pitted against each other? Did they know?

They knew.

They knew who they were playing against?

A thirty-second pause. *Absolutely not.*

'Truth or lie?' Siobhan asked Bain.

'I'm busy wondering if Mr Marr's had enough time to get back to his office.'

'Someone in his profession, wouldn't surprise me if he kept a laptop and mobile in the car, just to stay ahead of the game.' She smiled at the unmeant pun.

'I could call his office . . .' Bain was already reaching for the phone. Siobhan recited the bank's number.

'Mr Marr's office, please,' Bain said into the receiver. Then: 'Is that Mr Marr's assistant? It's DS Bain here, Lothian Police. Could I have a word with Mr Marr?' He looked at Siobhan. 'Due back any minute? Thank you.' Then an afterthought. 'Oh, is there any way I could contact him in his car? He doesn't have access to e-mails there, does he?' A pause. 'No, it's okay, thank you. I'll call again later.' He put the phone down. 'No in-car e-mails.'

'As far as his assistant knows,' Siobhan said quietly.

Bain nodded.

'These days,' she went on, 'all you need is a phone.' A WAP phone, she was thinking, just like Grant's. For some reason her mind flashed to that morning in the Elephant House . . . Grant busy on a crossword he'd already completed, trying to impress the woman at the next table . . . She got to work on her next message:

Can you tell me who they were? Do you know who they are? The reply was immediate.

No.

No you can't or no you don't?

No to both. Stricture awaits.

One final thing, Master. How did you come to choose Flip?

She came to me, as you did.

But how did she find you?

Stricture clue will follow shortly.

'I think he's had enough,' Bain said. 'Probably not used to his slaves talking back.'

Siobhan thought about trying to keep the dialogue going, then nodded her agreement.

'I don't think I'm quite Grant Hood's standard,' Bain added. She frowned, not understanding. 'In the puzzle-solving department,' he explained.

'Let's wait and see about that.'

'Meantime, I can get that stuff PDQ'd to SB.'

'AOK,' Siobhan said with a smile. She was thinking of Grant again. She wouldn't have got this far without him. Yet since his transfer he hadn't shown the least curiosity, hadn't so much as called to find out if there were some new clue to be solved . . . She wondered at his ability to switch focus so completely. The Grant she saw on TV was almost unrecognisable from the one who'd paced her flat at midnight, the one who'd lost heart on Hart Fell. She knew which model she preferred; didn't think it was just professional jealousy. She thought she'd learned something about Gill Templer now. Gill was running scared, terror of her new seniority causing her to dish it out to the juniors. She was targeting the keen and the confident, maybe because she lacked confidence in herself. Siobhan hoped it was just a phase. She prayed it was.

She hoped that when Stricture came through, the busy Grant might spare a minute for his old sparring partner, whether his new sponsor liked it or not.

Grant Hood had spent the morning dealing with the press, reworking the daily news release for later in the day – hopefully this time to the satisfaction of both DCS Templer and ACC Carswell – and fielding calls from the victim's father, angry that more broadcast time wasn't being given to appeals for information.

'What about *Crimewatch*?' he'd asked several times. Secretly, Grant thought *Crimewatch* was a bloody good idea, so he'd called the BBC in Edinburgh and been given a number in Glasgow. Glasgow had then given him a number in London, and the switchboard there had put him through to a researcher who'd informed him – in a tone which said any liaison officer worth their salt would already know – that *Crimewatch* had ended its run and wouldn't be back on air for several months.

'Oh, yes, thanks,' Grant had said, putting down the phone.

He hadn't had time for lunch, and breakfast had been a bacon roll from the canteen, almost six hours ago. He was aware of politics all around him – the politics of Police HQ. Carswell and Templer might agree on some things, but never on everything, and he was poised somewhere between them, trying not to fall too fatally into either camp. Carswell was the real power, but Templer was Grant's boss, she had the means to kick him back into the wilderness. His job was to deprive her of motive and opportunity.

He knew he was coping so far, but only by dint of forgoing food, sleep and free time. On the plus side, the case was now garnering interest from further afield, not just the London media, but New York, Sydney, Singapore and Toronto. International press agencies wanted clarification of the details they had. There was talk of bringing correspondents to Edinburgh, and would DC Hood be available for a short broadcast interview?

In each case, Grant felt able to answer in the affirmative. He made sure he jotted down the details of each journalist, with contact numbers and even a note of the time difference.

'No point me sending you faxes in the middle of the night,' he'd told one news editor in New Zealand.

'I'd prefer an e-mail, mate.'

So Grant had taken those details down, too. It struck him that he needed to get his laptop back from Siobhan. Either that or invest in something more up-to-date. The case could use its own website. He'd send a memo to Carswell, copy to Templer: stating his case.

If he ever got the time . . .

Siobhan and his laptop: he hadn't thought of her in a couple of days. His 'crush' on her hadn't lasted long. Just as well they hadn't taken things any further really: his new job would have driven a wedge between them. He knew they could play down that kiss, until it would seem as if it had never happened. Rebus was the only witness, but if the pair of them denied it, called him a liar, he'd start forgetting, too.

Only two things Grant felt sure of now: that he wanted Liaison permanently, and that he was good at it.

He celebrated with the day's sixth cup of coffee, nodding to strangers in the corridors and on the stairwell. They seemed to know who he was, wanting both to know him and be known by him. His phone was ringing again when he pushed open his door – the office was small, no bigger than the cupboards in some stations, and there was no natural light. Still, it was his fiefdom. He leaned back in his chair, taking the receiver with him.

'DC Hood.'

'You sound happy.'

'Who is this, please?'

'It's Steve Holly. Remember me?'

'Sure, Steve, what can I do for you?' But the tone was immediately more professional.

'Well . . . Grant.' Holly managed to get a sneer into the word. 'I was just after a quote to go with a piece I'm running.'

'Yes?' Grant leaned forward a little in his chair, not quite so comfortable now.

'Women going missing all over Scotland . . . dolls found at the scene . . . games on the Internet . . . students dead on hillsides. Any of it ring a bell?'

Grant thought he'd squeeze the life out of the receiver. The desk, the walls . . . they'd all gone hazy. He closed his eyes, tried to shake his head clear.

'Case like this, Steve,' he said, attempting levity, 'a reporter will hear all kinds of stuff.'

'Believe you solved some of the Internet clues yourself, Grant. What do you reckon? Got to be connected to the murder, haven't they?'

'I've no comment to make on that, Mr Holly. Look, whatever you think you may know, you've got to understand that stories – true or false – can do irreparable damage to an investigation, especially one at a crucial stage.'

'Is the Balfour inquiry at a crucial stage? I hadn't heard . . .'

'All I'm trying to say is . . .'

'Look, Grant, admit it: you're fucked on this one, pardon my French. Best thing you can do is fill me in on the small print.'

'I don't think so.'

'Sure about that? Tasty new posting you've got there . . . I'd hate to see you go down in flames.'

'Something tells me you'd like nothing better, Holly.'

The telephone receiver laughed into Grant's ear. 'Steve to Mr Holly to Holly . . . you'll be calling me names next, Grant.'

'Who told you?'

'Something this big, you can never keep it watertight.'

'So who punched the hole through the hull?'

'A whisper here, a whisper there . . . you know how it is.' Holly paused. 'Oh no, that's right – you *don't* know how it is. I keep forgetting, you've only been in the job five fucking minutes, and already you think you can lord it over the likes of me.'

'I don't know what—'

'Those little individual briefings, just you and your favoured poodles. Stuff all that, Grant. It's the likes of *me* you should be looking out for. And you can take that any way you like.'

'Thanks, I will. How soon are you going to press?'

'Going to try slapping us with a two-eye?' When Grant didn't say anything, Holly laughed again. 'You don't even know the lingo!' he crowed. But Grant was a fast learner.

'It's an interim interdict,' he guessed, knowing he was right. Two i's: a court injunction, halting publication. 'Look,' he said, pinching the bridge of his nose, 'on the record, we don't know that any of the stuff you've mentioned is pertinent to the current case.'

'It's still news.'

'And possibly prejudicial.'

'So sue me.'

'People play dirty like this, I never forget it.'

'Get in the fucking queue.'

Grant was about to put down the phone, but Holly beat him to it. He got up and kicked the desk, then kicked it again, followed by the waste-bin, his briefcase (bought at the weekend), and the corner where two walls met. He rested his head against the wall.

I have to go to Carswell with this. I have to tell Gill Templer!!

Templer first . . . chain of command. Then *she'd* have to break the news to the ACC, who in turn would probably have to disturb the Chief Constable's daily routine. Mid-afternoon . . . Grant wondered how late he could leave it. Maybe Holly would call Templer or Carswell himself. If Grant sat on it till day's end, he'd be in bigger trouble. It could even be that there was still time for that two-eye.

He picked up the phone, squeezed shut his eyes once more in what, this time round, was a short and silent prayer.

Made the call.

It was late afternoon, and Rebus had been staring at the coffins for a good five minutes. Occasionally he would pick one up, examine the workmanship, comparing and contrasting with the others. His latest thought: bring in a forensic anthropologist. The tools used to make the coffins would have left tiny grooves and incisions, marks an expert could identify and explore. If the exact same chisel had been used on each joint, maybe it could be proven. Perhaps there were fibres, fingerprints . . . The scraps of cloth: could they be traced? He slid the list of victims so that it sat in front of him on the desk: 1972 . . .'77 . . .'82 and '95. The first victim, Caroline Farmer, was the youngest by far; the others were in their twenties and thirties, women in the prime of life. Drownings and disappearances. Where there was no body, it was all but impossible to prove a crime had been committed. And death by drowning . . . pathologists could tell if someone were alive or dead when they entered the water, but other than that . . . Say you knocked someone unconscious and pushed them in: even if it came to court, there'd be room for haggling, the murder charge reduced to culpable homicide. Rebus remembered a fireman once telling him the perfect way to commit murder: get the victim drunk in their kitchen, then turn the heat up under the chip-pan.

Simple and clever.

Rebus still didn't know how clever his adversary had been. Fife, Nairn, Glasgow and Perth – certainly he'd ranged far and wide. Someone who travelled. He thought of Quizmaster and the jaunts Siobhan had taken so far. Was it possible to connect Quizmaster to whoever had left the coffins? Having scribbled the words 'forensic pathologist' on to his notepad, Rebus added two more: 'offender profiling'. There were university psychologists who specialised in this, deducing aspects of a culprit's character from their MO. Rebus had never been convinced, but he felt he was banging his fists against a locked and bolted door, one he was never going to break down without help.

When Gill Templer stormed down the corridor, past the CID suite's doorway, Rebus didn't think she'd seen him. But now she was heading straight for him, her face furious.

'I thought,' she said, 'you'd been told.'

'Told what?' he asked innocently.

She pointed to the coffins. 'Told that these were a waste of time.' Her voice vibrated with anger. Her whole body was taut.

'Jesus, Gill, what's happened?'

She didn't say anything, just swung her arm across the desk, sending the coffins flying. Rebus scrambled from his chair, started picking them up, checking for damage. When he looked round, Gill was on her way to the door again, but she stopped, half turned.

'You'll find out tomorrow,' she said, making her exit.

Rebus looked around the room. Hi-Ho Silvers and one of the civilian staff had stopped the conversation they'd been having.

'She's losing it,' Silvers commented.

'What did she mean about tomorrow?' Rebus asked, but Silvers just shrugged.

'Losing it,' he said again.

Maybe he was right.

Rebus sat back down at his desk and pondered the phrase: there were lots of ways of 'losing it'. He knew he was in danger of losing it too . . . whatever *it* was.

Jean Burchill had spent much of her day trying to trace the correspondence between Kennet Lovell and the Reverend Kirkpatrick. She'd spoken to people in Alloway and Ayr – the parish minister; a local historian; one of Kirkpatrick's descendants. She'd spent over an hour on the phone to the Mitchell Library in Glasgow. She'd taken the short walk from the Museum to the National Library, and from there to the Faculty of Advocates. Finally, she'd walked back along Chambers Street and headed for Surgeons' Hall. In the museum there she'd stared long and hard at the portrait of Kennet Lovell by J. Scott Jauncey. Lovell had been a handsome young man. Often in portraits, the artist left little clues as to the character he was painting: profession, family, hobbies . . . But this was a simple execution: head and upper body. The background was plain and black, contrasting with the bright yellows and pinks of Lovell's face. The other portraits in Surgeons' Hall, they usually showed their subjects with a textbook in front of them, or some paper and a pen. Maybe standing in their library or posed with a few telling props – a skull or femur, an anatomical drawing. The sheer plainness of the Lovell portrait bothered her. Either the painter had had little enthusiasm for the commission, or else the subject had insisted on giving little enough away. She thought of Reverend Kirkpatrick, imagined him paying the artist's fee and then receiving this bland decoration. She wondered if it perhaps showed some ideal of its subject, or if it was the equivalent of a picture postcard, a mere advertisement for Lovell. This young man, hardly out of his teens, had assisted in the Burke autopsy. According to one report of the time, 'the quantity of blood that gushed out was enormous, and by the time the lecture was finished the area of the classroom had the appearance of a butcher's slaughter-house, from its flowing down and being trodden upon'. The description had made her queasy, first time she'd read it. How much more preferable to have died as one of Burke's victims, made insensible with drink and then smothered. Jean stared into Kennet Lovell's eyes again. The black pupils seemed luminous, despite the horrors they'd witnessed.

Or, she couldn't help wondering, *because* of them?

The curator wasn't able to help answer her questions, so she'd asked if she might see the bursar. But Major Bruce Cawdor, while affable and willing, wasn't able to add much to what Jean already knew.

'We don't seem to have any record,' he told her as they sat in his office, 'of how the Lovell portrait came into the College's possession. I'd presume it was a gift, perhaps to defer death duties.' He was short but distinguished-looking, well dressed and with a face shining with good health. He'd offered her tea, which she'd accepted. It was Darjeeling, each cup coming with its own silver tea-strainer.

'I'm also interested in Lovell's correspondence.'

'Yes, well, we would be, too.'

'You don't have *anything*?' She was surprised.

The bursar shook his head. 'Either Dr Lovell wasn't a great man for the pen, or else they've perished or ended up in some obscure collection.' He sighed. 'A great pity. We know so little about his time in Africa . . .'

'Or in Edinburgh, come to that.'

'He's buried here. Don't suppose his grave's of much interest to you . . . ?'

'Whereabouts is it?'

'Calton cemetery. His plot's not far from David Hume's.'

'I might as well take a look.'

'I'm sorry I can't be more help.' He thought for a moment, and his face brightened. 'Donald Devlin's supposed to have some table made by Lovell.'

'Yes, I know, though there's nothing in the literature about an interest in carpentry.'

'I'm sure it's mentioned somewhere; I seem to recall reading something . . .' But try as he might, Major Cawdor couldn't remember what or where.

That evening, she sat with John Rebus in her Portobello home. They ate Chinese takeaway, washed down with cold Chardonnay for her, bottled beer for him. Music on the hi-fi: Nick Drake, Janis Ian, Pink Floyd's *Meddle*. He seemed wrapped up in his thoughts, but she could hardly complain. After the food, they walked down to the promenade. Kids on skateboards, looking American but sounding pure Porty, swearing like troopers. One chip shop open, that childhood smell of hot fat and vinegar. They still didn't say much, which didn't make them so very different from the other couples they passed. Reticence was an Edinburgh tradition. You kept your feelings hidden and your business your own. Some people put it down to the influence of the Church and figures like John Knox – she'd heard the city called 'Fort Knox' by outsiders. But to Jean, it was more to do with Edinburgh's geography, its louring rock-faces and dark skies, the wind whipping in from the North Sea, hurtling through the canyon-like streets. At every turn you felt overwhelmed and pummelled by your surroundings. Just travelling into town from Portobello, she felt it: the bruising and bruised nature of the place.

John Rebus, too, was thinking of Edinburgh. When he moved from his flat, where would he make his next home? Was there any district he liked better than any other? Portobello itself was fine, pretty relaxed. But he could always move south or west, into the country. Some of his colleagues travelled in from as far as Falkirk and Linlithgow. He wasn't sure he was ready for that kind of commute. Portobello would be okay though. The only problem was, when they walked along the promenade, he kept looking towards the beach, as if expecting to see a little wooden coffin there, like the one they'd found in Nairn. It wouldn't matter where he went, his head would go with him, colouring his surroundings. The Falls coffin was working away at him now. He only had the carpenter's word for it that it had been made by someone else, someone who hadn't made the other four. But if the killer was being *really* clever, wouldn't he have anticipated just that, changing his work habits and tools, trying to dupe them into . . .

Oh Christ, here he went again . . . the same old dance, reeling around his skull. He sat down on the sea wall, and Jean asked if something was wrong.

'Bit of a headache,' he said.

'Isn't that supposed to be the woman's prerogative?' She was smiling, but he could see she wasn't happy.

'I should be heading back,' he told her. 'Not great company tonight.'

'Do you want to talk about it?' He raised his eyes so they met hers, and she snorted with laughter. 'Sorry, stupid question. You're a Scottish male, of course you don't want to talk about it.'

'It's not that, Jean. It's just . . .' He shrugged. 'Maybe therapy wouldn't be such a bad idea.'

He was trying to make a joke of it, so she didn't push him.

'Let's head back,' she said. 'Bloody freezing out here anyway.'

She slid her arm through his as they walked.

12

By the time Assistant Chief Constable Colin Carswell arrived at Gayfield Square police station on that underlit Tuesday morning, he was out for blood.

John Balfour had bawled him out; Balfour's lawyer had done his damage more subtly, the voice never wavering in its professional and well-educated tones. Still, Carswell felt bruised, and he wanted some measure of revenge. The Chief Constable was remaining aloof – *his* position, his unassailability, had to be maintained at all costs. This was Carswell's mess, one he'd spent all the previous evening busy surveying. He might as well have been exploring a landscape of shrapnel and broken glass, armed only with a dustpan and some tweezers.

The best minds in the Procurator Fiscal's office had pored over the problem and had concluded, in an annoyingly bland and objective way (letting Carswell know that it was no skin off *their* noses) that there was little chance of blocking the story. After all, they couldn't prove that either the dolls or the German student had anything to do with the Balfour case – most senior officers seemed to agree that a connection was unlikely at best – and so would find it difficult to persuade a judge that Holly's information could, once published, be detrimental to the inquiry.

What Balfour and his lawyer wanted to know was why the police hadn't seen fit to share with them the story of the dolls, or the information about the German student and the Internet game.

What the Chief Constable wanted to know was what Carswell intended doing about it.

And what Carswell himself wanted was blood.

His official car, driven by his acolyte DI Derek Linford, drew up in front of a station already crowded with officers. Everyone who had worked or was currently working on the Balfour case – uniforms, CID, even the forensic team from Howdenhall – had been 'requested' to attend the morning meeting. Consequently, the briefing room was packed and stifling. Outside, the morning was still recovering from overnight sleet, the pavement damp and chilling to the feet as Carswell's leather-shod soles stamped across it.

'Here he comes,' someone said, watching as Linford, having opened Carswell's door for him, now closed it and, showing a slight limp, walked back round to the driver's side. There was a sound of folding paper as the fresh tabloids – each copy the same title, each open at the same gathering of pages – were closed and put out of sight. DCS Templer, dressed as though for a funeral, dark lines under her eyes, came into the room first. She whispered something into the ear of DI Bill Pryde, who nodded and tore the corner from a notepad, spitting into it the wad of chewing gum he'd been gnawing for the past half-hour. When Carswell himself walked in, there was a ripple of movement as officers subconsciously corrected their posture or checked their attire for obvious blemishes.

'Is anyone missing?' Carswell called out. No 'good morning', no 'thank you all for coming', the usual protocols forgotten. Templer had a few names for him – minor ailments and complaints. Carswell nodded, didn't seem interested in what he was being told, and didn't wait for her to finish the roll-call.

'We've got ourselves a mole,' he bawled, loud enough to be heard down the corridor. He nodded slowly, eyes trying to take in every face in front of him. When he saw that there were people at the back, out of staring range, he walked up the aisle between the desks. Officers had to shift so he could get through, but left enough room so that there was no possibility he might brush against them.

'A mole's always an ugly little thing. It lacks vision. Sometimes it has big greedy paws. It doesn't like to be exposed.' There were flecks of saliva either side of his mouth. 'I find a mole in my garden, I put down poison. Now, some of you will say that moles can't help it. They don't know they're in someone's garden, a place of order and calm. They don't know they're making everything *ugly*. But they are, whether they know it or not. And that's why they have to be eradicated.' He paused, the silence lingering as he walked back down the aisle. Derek Linford had entered the room as if by stealth and was standing by the door, eyes searching out John Rebus, the two of them recent enemies . . .

The presence of Linford seemed only to spur Carswell on. He spun on his heels, facing his subjects again.

'Maybe it was a mistake. We all make slip-ups, can't be helped. But, by Christ, a lot of information seems to have been pushed to the surface!' Another pause. 'Maybe it was blackmail.' And now a shrug. 'Someone like Steven Holly, he's lower than a mole on the evolutionary ladder. He's pond-life. He's the scum you sometimes see there.' He waved a hand slowly in front of him, as if skimming water. 'He thinks he's made us dirty, but he hasn't. Game's not near over, we all know that. We're a *team*. That's how we *work*! Anyone who doesn't like that can always ask to be transferred back to normal duties. It's that simple, ladies and gentlemen. But just think of this, will you?' He dropped his voice. 'Think of the victim, think of her family. Think of all the upset this is going to cause them. *They're* the ones we're slogging our guts out for here, not the newspaper readers or the scribes who provide them with their daily gruel.

'You might have some grievance against me, or someone else on the team, but why the hell would you want to put *them* – the family and friends, getting ready for tomorrow's funeral – why would *anyone* want to do something like this to people like them?' He let the question hang, saw faces bow in collective shame as he scanned them. Took another deep breath, his voice rising again.

'I'm going to find whoever did this. Don't think I won't. Don't think you can trust Mr Steven Holly to protect you. He doesn't care a damn for you. If you want to stay buried, you'll have to feed him more stories, and more, and more! He's not going to let you rise back up to the world you knew before. You're different now. You're a mole. *His* mole. And he'll never let you rest, never let you forget it.'

A glance in Gill Templer's direction. She was standing by the wall, arms folded, her own eyes scanning the room.

'I know this probably all sounds like the headmaster's warning. Some pupil's smashed a window or daubed graffiti on the bike sheds.' He shook his head. 'I'm talking to all of you like this because it's important we're clear on what's at stake. Talk might not cost lives, but that doesn't mean it should be squandered. Careful what you say, who you say it to. If the person responsible wants to come forward, that's fine. You can do it now, or later. I'll be here for an hour or so, and I can always be reached at my office. Think what's at stake if you don't. Not part of a team any more, not on the side of the angels. But in a journalist's pocket. For as long as he wants you there.' This final pause seemed to last an eternity, nobody coughed or cleared their throat. Carswell slid his hands into his pockets, head angled as though inspecting his shoes. 'DCS Templer?' he said.

And now Gill Templer stepped forward, and the room relaxed a little.

'Don't go getting the holiday mood just yet!' she called out. 'Okay, there's been a leak to the press, and what we need now is some damage limitation. Nobody talks to anybody unless they run it past me first, understood?' There were murmurs of assent.

Templer went on, but Rebus wasn't listening. He hadn't wanted to listen to Carswell either, but it had been hard to block the man out. Impressive stuff really. He'd even put some thought into the image of the garden mole, almost making it work without becoming laughable.

But mostly Rebus's attention had been on the people around him. Gill and Bill Pryde were distant figures, whose discomfort he could almost ignore. Bill's big chance to shine; Gill's first major inquiry as a DCS. Hardly what either of them would have wanted . . .

And closer to home: Siobhan, concentrating hard on the ACC's speech, maybe learning something from it. She was always on the lookout for a new lesson. Grant Hood, someone else with everything to lose, dejection written into his face and shoulders, the way he held his arms across chest and stomach, as though to ward off blows. Rebus knew Grant was in trouble. A leak to the press, you looked at liaison first. They were the ones with the contacts: an unwise word; the drunk and friendly banter at the end of a good meal. Even if not to blame, a good liaison officer might have been all that was needed in the way of Gill's 'damage limitation'. With experience, you'd know how to bend a journalist's will to your own, even if it meant a bribe of some kind: first dibs on some later story or stories . . .

Rebus wondered at the extent of the damage. Quizmaster would now know what he'd probably always suspected: that it wasn't just him and Siobhan, that she was keeping her colleagues apprised. Her face didn't give anything away, but Rebus knew she was already wondering how to handle it, how to phrase her next communication with Quizmaster, supposing he wanted to keep playing . . . The Arthur's Seat coffins connection annoyed him only because Jean had been mentioned by name in the story, cited as 'the Museum's resident expert' on the case. He recalled that Holly had been persistent, leaving messages for Jean, wanting to speak to her. Could she have said something to him unwittingly? He didn't think so.

No, he had the culprit in his sights. Ellen Wylie looked like she'd been wrung out. There were tangles in her hair where she hadn't been concentrating with the brush. Her eyes had a resigned look. She kept staring at the floor during Carswell's speech, and hadn't shifted when he'd finished. She was still looking at the floor now, trying to find the will to do anything else. Rebus knew she'd spoken on the phone with Holly yesterday morning. It had been to do with the German student, but afterwards she'd seemed lifeless. Rebus had thought it was because she was working another dead end. Now he knew different. When she'd walked away from the Caledonian Hotel, she'd been heading either for Holly's office or for some wine bar or café nearby.

He'd got to her.

Maybe Shug Davidson would realise as much; maybe her colleagues at West End would remember how different she'd been after that phone call. But Rebus knew they wouldn't shop her. It was something you didn't do. Not to a colleague, a pal.

Wylie had been unravelling for days. He'd taken her into the coffin case thinking maybe he could help. But then maybe she was right – maybe he'd been treating her as just another 'cripple', someone else who might be bent to his will, do some of the hard graft on something which would always be *his* case.

Maybe he'd had ulterior motives.

Wylie had probably seen it as a way of getting back at all of them: Gill Templer, cause of her public humiliation; Siobhan, for whom Templer still had such high hopes; Grant Hood, the new golden boy, coping where Wylie had not . . . And Rebus, too, the manipulator, the user, grinding her down.

He saw her left with two alternatives: let it all out, or burst with frustration and anger. If he'd accepted her offer of a drink that night . . . maybe she'd have opened up and he'd have listened. Maybe that was all she'd needed. But he hadn't been there. He'd sneaked off to a pub by himself.

Nice one, John. Very smoothly played. For some reason an image came to mind: some old blues stalwart, turning up for 'Ellen Wylie's Blues'. Maybe John Lee Hooker or B. B. King . . . He caught himself and snapped out of it. He'd almost retreated into music, almost got to a lyric that would tide him over.

But now Carswell was reading from a list of names, and Rebus caught his own as Carswell snapped it out. DC Hood . . . DC Clarke . . . DS Wylie . . . The coffins; the German student – they'd worked those cases, and now the ACC wanted to see them. Faces turned, curious. Carswell was announcing that he'd see them in the 'boss's office', meaning the station commander's, commandeered for the occasion.

Rebus tried to catch Bill Pryde's eye as they trooped out, but with Carswell already having exited, Bill was searching his pockets for more gum, his eyes trying to locate his clipboard. Rebus was the tail of this lethargic snake, Hood in front of him, then Wylie and Siobhan. Templer and Carswell at the head. Derek Linford was standing outside the station commander's office, opened the door for them and then stood back. He tried to stare Rebus down, but Rebus wasn't having that. They were still at it when Gill Templer closed the door, breaking the spell.

Carswell was sliding his chair in towards the desk. 'You've already heard my spiel,' he told them, 'so I won't bore you again. If the leak came from anywhere, it came from one of you. That little shit Holly knew way too much.' As his mouth snapped shut his eyes looked up at them for the first time.

'Sir,' Grant Hood said, taking a half-step forward and folding his hands behind his back, 'as liaison officer it should have been my job to damp the story down. I'd just like to publicly apologise for—'

'Yes, yes, son, I got all that from you last night. What I want now is a simple confession.'

'With respect, sir,' Siobhan Clarke said, 'we're not criminals here. We've had to ask questions, put out feelers. Steve Holly could just have been putting two and two together . . .'

Carswell just stared at her, then said: 'DCS Templer?'

'Steve Holly,' Templer began, 'doesn't work that way if he can possibly help it. He's not the brightest bulb in the chandelier, but he's as sneaky as they come, and ruthless with it.' The way she spoke was telling Clarke something, was saying to her that this had all been gone over already. 'Some of the other journos, yes, I think they could take what's out there in the public domain and make something of it, but not Holly.'

'But he did work the case of the German student,' Clarke persisted.

'And shouldn't have known about the gaming connection,' Templer said, almost by rote: another argument that the senior officers had tried out between themselves.

'It was a long night,' Carswell told them, 'trust me. We've been over it time and again. And it still seems to come down to the four of you.'

'There's been outside assistance,' Grant Hood argued. 'A museum curator, a retired pathologist . . .'

Rebus laid a hand on Hood's arm, silencing him. 'It was me,' he said. Heads turned towards him. 'I think it might have been me.'

He concentrated on not looking in Ellen Wylie's direction, but was aware of her eyes burning into him.

'Early on, I was out at Falls talking to a woman called Bev Dodds. She'd found the coffin by the waterfall. Steve Holly had already been sniffing around, and she'd given him the story . . .'

'And?'

'And I let it slip that there'd been more coffins . . . let slip to her, I mean.' He was remembering the slip – a slip Jean had in fact made. 'If she yapped to Holly, he'd have been on a flyer. I had Jean Burchill with me – she's the curator. That might have given him the Arthur's Seat connection . . .'

Carswell was staring at him coldly. 'And the Internet game?'

Rebus shook his head. 'That one I can't explain, but it's not exactly a well-kept secret. We've been shoving the clues at all the victim's friends, asking if she'd asked them for help . . . any one of them could have told Holly.'

Carswell was still staring. 'You're taking the fall for this?'

'I'm saying it could be my fault. Just that one slip . . .' He turned to the others. 'I can't begin to tell you how sorry I am. I let all of us down.' His gaze skirted Wylie's face, concentrating on her hair.

'Sir,' Siobhan Clarke said, 'what DI Rebus has just admitted could go for any one of us. I'm sure I may have said a little more than I should on occasion . . .'

Carswell wafted his hand in front of him, quieting her.

'DI Rebus,' he said, 'I'm suspending you from active duty, pending further inquiries.'

'You can't do that!' Ellen Wylie blurted out.

'Shut up, Wylie!' Gill Templer hissed.

'DI Rebus knows the consequences,' Carswell was saying.

Rebus nodded. 'Someone needs to be punished.' He paused. 'For the sake of the team.'

'That's right,' Carswell said, nodding. 'Otherwise mistrust begins its corrosive influence. I don't think any of us wants that, do we?'

'No, sir.' Grant Hood's voice proved a lone one.

'Go home, DI Rebus,' Carswell said. 'Write your version down, leaving nothing out. We'll talk again later.'

'Yes, sir,' Rebus said, turning and opening the door. Linford was directly outside, and smiling with one side of his face. Rebus didn't doubt he'd been listening. It struck him suddenly that Carswell and Linford might well conspire to make the case against him look as black as possible.

He'd just given them the perfect excuse for getting rid of him for good.

His flat was ready to be put on the market, and he called the selling solicitor and told her so.

'Thursday evenings and Sunday afternoons for viewing?' she asked.

'I suppose so.' He was sitting in his chair, staring out of the window. 'Is there any way I can . . . not be here?'

'You want someone to show the flat for you?'

'Yes.'

'We have people who'll do that for a small fee.'

'Good.' He didn't want to be around when strangers were opening doors, touching things . . . He didn't think he'd make the best salesman for the place.

'We already have a photograph,' the solicitor was saying. 'So the ad could go in the ESPC guide as early as Thursday next.'

'Not the day after tomorrow?'

'I'm afraid not . . .'

When he'd finished the call, he walked into the hall. New light switches, new sockets. The place was a lot brighter, the fresh coats of paint helping. Not much clutter – he'd made three trips to the dump-site on Old Dalkeith Road: a coat-rack he'd inherited from somewhere; boxes of old magazines and newspapers; a two-bar electric fire with frayed cable; the chest of drawers from Samantha's old room, still decorated with stickers of eighties pop stars . . . The carpets were back down. A drinking acquaintance from Swany's Bar had lent a hand, asking if he wanted them nailed at the edges. Rebus hadn't seen the point.

'New owners will turf them out anyway.'

'You should've had these floors sanded, John. They'd've come up a treat . . .'

Rebus had whittled his possessions down until they wouldn't fill a one-bedroom flat, never mind the three he currently possessed. But still he had nowhere to go. He knew what the market was like in Edinburgh. If Arden Street went on the market next Thursday, it could go to a closing date the week after. Two weeks from now, he could find himself homeless.

And, come to that, jobless.

He'd been expecting phone calls, and eventually one came. It was Gill Templer.

Her opening words: 'You stupid bastard.'

'Hi there, Gill.'

'You could have kept your mouth shut.'

'I suppose I could.'

'Always the willing martyr, eh, John?' She sounded angry, tired and under pressure. He could see reasons for all three.

'I just told the truth,' he said.

'*That* would be a first . . . not that I believe it for a minute.'

'No?'

'Come on, John. Ellen Wylie practically had "guilty" stamped on her forehead.'

'You think I was shielding her?'

'I don't exactly take you for Sir Galahad. You'll have had your reasons. Maybe it was simply to piss off Carswell; you know he hates your guts.'

Rebus didn't like to concede that she might be right. 'How's everything else?' he asked.

Her anger was played out. 'Liaison's snowed under. I'm giving a helping hand.'

Rebus bet she was busy: all the other papers and media, trying to play catch-up with Steve Holly.

'What about you?' she asked.

'What about me?'

'What are you going to do?'

'I haven't really thought about it.'

'Well . . .'

'I'd better let you get back, Gill. Thanks for calling.'

'Bye, John.'

As he put the phone down, it started ringing again. Grant Hood this time.

'I just wanted to thank you for getting us off the hook like that.'

'You weren't on the hook, Grant.'

'*I* was, believe me.'

'I hear you're busy.'

'How . . . ?' Grant paused. 'Oh, DCS Templer's been on to you.'

'Is she helping out or taking over?'

'Hard to say at the minute.'

'She's not in the room with you, is she?'

'No, she's in her own office. When we came out of that meeting with the ACC . . . she was the one who looked most relieved.'

'Maybe because she has the most to lose, Grant. You probably can't see that right now, but it's true.'

'I'm sure you're right.' But he didn't sound convinced that his own survival wasn't more important in the scheme of things.

'Off you go, Grant, and thanks for finding the time to call.'

'See you around some time.'

'You never know your luck . . .'

Rebus put the phone down and waited, staring at it. But no more calls came. He went to the kitchen to make a mug of tea, and discovered he was out of tea-bags and milk. Without bothering with a jacket, he headed downstairs and out to the local deli, where he added some ham, rolls and mustard to the shopping. Back at the main door to the tenement, someone was trying one of the buzzers.

'Come on, I know you're there . . .'

'Hello, Siobhan.'

She turned towards him. 'Christ, you gave me a . . .' She put a hand to her throat. Rebus stretched an arm past her and unlocked the door.

'Because I sneaked up on you, or because you thought I was sitting upstairs with my wrists slashed?' He held the door open for her.

'What? No, that's not what I was thinking.' But the colour was rising to her cheeks.

'Well, just to stop you worrying, if I'm ever going to top myself, it'll be with a lot of drink and some pills. And by "a lot" I mean two or three days' worth, so you'll have plenty of warning.'

He preceded her up the stairs, opened his front door.

'Your lucky day,' he said. 'Not only am I not dead, but I can offer tea and rolls with ham and mustard.'

'Just tea, thanks,' she said, finally regaining some composure. 'Hey, the hall looks great!'

'Take a look around. I may as well get used to it.'

'You mean it's on the market?'

'As from next week.'

She opened a bedroom door, stuck her head round. 'Dimmer switch,' she commented, trying it out.

Rebus went into the kitchen and stuck the kettle on, found two clean mugs in the cupboard. One of them said 'World's Greatest Dad'. It wasn't his; one of the sparkies must have left it. He decided Siobhan could have her tea in it, he'd have the taller one with the poppies and the chipped rim.

'You didn't paint the living room,' she said, coming into the kitchen.

'It was done not so long ago.'

She nodded. There was something he wasn't saying, but she wasn't going to force it.

'You and Grant still an item then?' he asked.

'We never were. And that's the subject closed.'

He got the milk from the fridge. 'Better be careful, you'll be getting a rep.'

'I beg your pardon?'

'Unsuitable men. One of them was staring daggers at me all morning.'

'Oh God, Derek Linford.' She was thoughtful. 'Didn't he look awful?'

'Doesn't he always?' Rebus placed a tea-bag in each mug. 'So, are you here to check up on me or thank me for sticking my neck out?'

'I'm not about to thank you for *that*. You could have stayed quiet, and you know it. If you owned up, it was because *you* wanted to.' She broke off.

'And?' he encouraged her.

'And you'll have some agenda going.'

'Actually I don't . . . not particularly.'

'Then why did you do it?'

'It was the quickest way, the simplest. If I'd bothered to think for a moment . . . maybe I'd have kept my mouth shut.' He poured water and milk into the mugs, handed one over. Siobhan looked at the tea-bag floating there. 'Spoon it out when it's strong enough,' he suggested.

'Yummy.'

'Sure I can't tempt you with a ham roll?'

She shook her head. 'Don't let me stop you.'

'Maybe later,' he said, leading them through to the living room. 'Everything calm at base camp?'

'Say what you like about Carswell, he's a pretty good motivator. Everyone thinks it was that speech of his that made you feel guilty.'

'And they're now working harder than ever?' He waited till she'd nodded. 'A team of happy gardeners with no nasty moles to bother them.'

Siobhan grinned. 'It was pretty bloody corny, wasn't it?' She looked around. 'Where are you going to go when you sell this place?'

'Got a spare room, have you?'

'Depends for how long.'

'I'm just joking, Siobhan. I'll be fine.' He took a gulp of tea. 'So what exactly *does* bring you here?'

'You mean apart from checking up on you?'

'I'm guessing that wasn't all.'

She reached down to place her mug on the floor. 'I got another message.'

'Quizmaster?' She nodded. 'Saying what exactly?'

She unfolded some sheets from her pocket, reached over towards him with them. Their fingers touched as he took them. The first was an e-mail from Siobhan:

Still awaiting Stricture.

'I sent that first thing this morning,' she said. 'Thought maybe he wouldn't have heard.'

Rebus turned to the second sheet. It was from Quizmaster.

I'm disappointed in you, Siobhan. I'm taking my ball home now.

Then Siobhan:

Don't believe everything you read. I still want to play.

Quizmaster:

And go yapping to your bosses?

Siobhan:

You and me this time, that's a promise.

Quizmaster:

How can I trust you?

Siobhan:

I've been trusting you, haven't I? And you always know where to find me. I still don't have the first clue about you.

'I had to wait a while after that. The final sheet came in about' – she checked her watch – 'forty minutes ago.'

'And you came straight here?'

She shrugged. 'More or less.'

'You didn't show it to Brains?'

'He's off on some errand for Crime Squad.'

'Anyone else?' She shook her head. 'Why me?'

'Now that I'm here,' she said, 'I don't really know.'

'Grant's the one with the puzzle mind.'

'Right now he's too busy puzzling over how to keep his job.'

Rebus nodded slowly and re-read the final sheet:

Add Camus to ME Smith, they're boxing where the sun don't shine, and Frank Finlay's the referee.

'Well,' he said, 'you've shown me it . . .' He made to hand the sheets back. 'And it doesn't mean a thing to me.'

'No?'

He shook his head. 'Frank Finlay was an actor – might still be, for all I know. I think he played Casanova on TV, and he was in something called *Barbed Wire and Bouquets* . . . something like that.'

'*Bouquet of Barbed Wire*?'

'Could have been.' He glanced at the clue a final time. 'Camus was a French writer. I used to think it was pronounced "came as" until I heard it mentioned on the radio or the box.'

'Boxing – that's something you know about.'

'Marciano, Dempsey, Cassius Clay before he became Ali . . .' He shrugged.

'Where the sun don't shine,' Siobhan said. 'That's an American expression, isn't it?'

'It means out your arse,' Rebus confirmed. 'You think suddenly Quizmaster's American?'

She smiled, but there was no humour to it.

'Take my advice, Siobhan. Give it to Crime Squad or Special Branch or whoever's supposed to be tracking this arsehole down. Or just e-mail him back telling him to get stuffed.' He paused. 'You said he knows where to find you?'

She nodded. 'He knows my name, that I'm CID in Edinburgh.'

'But nothing about where you live? He hasn't got your phone number?' She shook her head and Rebus nodded, satisfied. He was thinking of all the numbers pinned to Steve Holly's office wall.

'Then let him go,' he said quietly.

'Is that what you'd do?'

'It's what I'd strongly advise.'

'Then you don't want to help me?'

He looked at her. 'Help you how?'

'Copy the clue, do some detecting.'

He laughed. 'You want me in even more trouble with Carswell?'

She looked down at the sheets of paper. 'You're right,' she said. 'I wasn't thinking. Thanks for the tea.'

'Stay and finish it.' He watched her get to her feet.

'I should be heading back. Lots to do.'

'Starting with handing that clue over?'

She stared at him. 'You know your advice is always important to me.'

'Is that a yes or a no?'

'Take it as a definite maybe.'

He was standing now, too. 'Thanks for coming, Siobhan.'

She turned towards the doorway. 'Linford's out to get you, isn't he? Him and Carswell both?'

'Don't fret over it.'

'But Linford's getting stronger. He'll be Chief Inspector any day.'

'For all you know, maybe I'm getting stronger too.'

She turned her head to study him, but didn't say anything, didn't need to. He followed her out into the hall, opened the door for her.

She was on the stairwell before she spoke again. 'Know what Ellen Wylie said after that meeting with Carswell?'

'What?'

'Nothing at all.' She looked at him again, one hand on the banister. 'Strange that. I was expecting a long speech about your martyr complex . . .'

Back in the flat, Rebus stood in the hall, listening to her footsteps recede. Then he walked to the living-room window and stood on tiptoe, craning his neck to watch her leave the tenement, the door closing with an echo behind her. She'd come here asking for something, and he'd turned her down. How could he tell her that he didn't want her getting hurt, the way so many people he'd let get close to him had been hurt in the past? How to tell her that she should learn her own lessons, not his, and that she'd be a better cop – as well as a better person – at the end of it?

He turned back into the room. The ghosts were faint, but visible. People he'd hurt and been hurt by, people who'd died painful, unnecessary deaths. Not for much longer. A couple more weeks and maybe he'd be free of them. He knew the phone wasn't going to ring, nor was Ellen Wylie about to pay him a visit. They understood one another well enough to render any such contact unnecessary. Maybe one day in the future they'd sit down and talk about it. Then again, maybe she'd never speak to him again. He'd stolen the moment from her, and she had stood there and let him. Defeat once again snatched from the jaws of victory. He wondered if she'd stay in Steve Holly's pocket . . . wondered just how deep and dark that pocket might be.

He walked through to the kitchen, poured Siobhan's and the rest of his tea down the sink. An inch of malt into a clean glass and a bottle of

IPA from the cupboard. Back in the living room, he sat in his chair, took pen and notebook from his pocket, and jotted down the latest clue as best he could remember it . . .

Jean Burchill's morning had consisted of a series of meetings, including one heated debate on funding levels which threatened to turn violent, with one curator walking out, slamming the door after him, and another almost bursting into tears.

By lunchtime, she felt exhausted, the stuffiness of her office contributing to a thumping head. Steve Holly had left two more messages for her, and she just knew that if she sat at her desk with a sandwich, the phone would ring again. Instead, she headed outside, joining the throng of workers released from captivity for the time it took to queue at the baker's for a filled roll or pie. The Scots had an unenviable record for heart disease and tooth decay, both the result of the national diet: saturated fats, salt and sugar. She'd wondered what it was that made Scottish people reach for the comfort foods, the chocolate, chips and fizzy drinks: was it the climate? Or could the answer lie deeper, within the nation's character? Jean decided to buck the trend, purchased some fruit and a carton of orange juice. She was heading into town down the Bridges. It was all cheap clothes shops and takeaways, with queues of buses and lorries waiting to crawl through the traffic lights at the Tron kirk. A few beggars sat in doorways, staring at the passing parade of feet. Jean paused at the lights and looked left and right along the High Street, imagining the place in the days before Princes Street: vendors hawking their wares; ill-lit howffs where business was done; the tollbooth and the gates which were closed at nightfall, locking the city into itself . . . She wondered if someone from the 1770s, somehow transported to the present, would find this part of the city so very different. The lights, the cars might shock them, but not the *feel* of the place.

She paused again on North Bridge, staring eastwards towards where the new parliament site showed no signs of progress. The *Scotsman* had moved its offices down to a shiny new building in Holyrood Road, just across from the parliament. She'd been there recently for a function, standing on the large balcony to the rear, staring out at the immensity of Salisbury Crags. Behind her now, the old *Scotsman* building was being gutted: another new hotel in the making. Further down North Bridge, where it connected with Princes Street, the old Post Office HQ sat dusty and empty, its future apparently still not decided – another hotel, the rumour went. She took a right into Waterloo Place, munching on her second apple and trying not to think of crisps and Kit-Kats. She knew where she was headed: Calton cemetery. As she entered through the wrought-iron gate, she was confronted by the obelisk known as the Martyrs' Memorial, dedicated to the memory of five men, the 'Friends of the People', who had dared in the 1790s to advocate parliamentary reform.

This at a time when fewer than forty people in the city had the power to vote in an election. The five were sentenced to transportation: a one-way ticket to Australia. Jean looked at the apple she was eating. She'd just peeled a little sticker from it, announcing its country of origin as New Zealand. She thought of the five convicts, the lives they must have led. But there was to be no counterpart to the French Revolution in Scotland, not in the 1790s.

She was reminded of some communist leader and thinker – was it Marx himself? – who had predicted that the revolution in western Europe would have Scotland as its starting-point. Another dream . . .

Jean didn't know much about David Hume, but stood in front of his monument while she attacked her carton of juice. Philosopher and essayist . . . a friend had once told her that Hume's achievement had been in making the philosophy of John Locke comprehensible, but then she didn't know anything much about Locke either.

There were other graves: Blackwood and Constable, publishers, and one of the leaders of 'the Disruption', which had led to the founding of the Free Church of Scotland. Just to the east, over the cemetery wall, was a small crenellated tower. This she knew was all that remained of the old Calton Prison. She'd seen drawings of it, taken from Calton Hill opposite: friends and family of the prisoners would gather there to shout messages and greetings. Closing her eyes, she could almost replace the traffic noises with yelps and whoops, the dialogue between loved ones echoing back along Waterloo Place . . .

When she opened her eyes again, she saw what she'd hoped to find: Dr Kennet Lovell's grave. The headstone had been set into the cemetery's eastern wall, and was now cracked and soot-blackened, its edges fallen away to reveal the sandstone beneath. It was a small thing, close to the ground. 'Dr Kennet Anderson Lovell,' Jean read, 'an eminent Physician of this City.' He'd died in 1863, aged fifty-six. There were weeds rising from ground level, obscuring much of the inscription. Jean crouched down and started pulling them away, encountering a used condom which she brushed aside with a dock leaf. She knew that there were people who used Calton Hill at night, and imagined them coupling against this wall, pressing down on the bones of Dr Lovell. How would Lovell feel about that? For a moment, she formed a picture of another coupling: herself and John Rebus. Not her type at all really. In the past she'd dated researchers, university lecturers. One brief dalliance with a sculptor in the city – a married man. He'd taken her to cemeteries, his favourite places. John Rebus probably liked cemeteries, too. When they'd first met she'd seen him as a challenge and a curiosity. Even now she had to work hard not to think of him in terms of an exhibit. There were so many secrets there, so much of him that he refused to show to the world. She knew there was digging still to be done . . .

As she cleared the weeds, she found that Lovell had married no fewer than three times, and that each wife had passed away before him. No evidence of any children . . . she wondered if the offspring might be buried elsewhere. Maybe there were no children. But then hadn't John said something about a descendant . . . ? As she examined the dates, she saw that the wives had died young, and another thought crossed her mind: they'd died in childbirth, perhaps.

His first wife: Beatrice, *née* Alexander. Aged twenty-nine.

His second wife: Alice, *née* Baxter. Aged thirty-three.

His third wife: Patricia, *née* Addison. Aged twenty-six.

An inscription read: *Passed over, to be met again so sweetly in the Lord's domain*.

Jean couldn't help thinking that it must have been some meeting, Lovell and his three wives. She had a pen in her pocket, but no notepad or paper. She looked around the cemetery, found an old envelope, torn in half. She brushed dirt and dust from it and jotted down the details.

Siobhan was back at her desk, trying to form anagrams from the letters in 'Camus' and 'ME Smith', when Eric Bain came into the office.

'All right?' he asked.

'I'll survive.'

'That good, eh?' He placed his briefcase on the floor, straightened up and looked around. 'Special Branch get back to us yet?'

'Not that I know of.' She was scoring out letters with her pen. The M and E had no space between them. Did Quizmaster mean them to be read as 'me'? Was he saying his name was Smith? ME was also a medical condition. She couldn't recall what the letters stood for . . . remembered it being called 'yuppie flu' in the newspapers. Bain had walked over to the fax machine, picked up some sheets and sifted through them.

'Ever think to check?' he said, sliding two sheets out and putting the rest back next to the machine.

Siobhan looked up. 'What is it?'

He was reading as he approached. 'Bloody marvellous,' he gasped. 'Don't ask me how they did it, but they did it.'

'What?'

'They've traced one of the accounts already.'

Siobhan's chair fell back as she got to her feet, hands grabbing at the fax. As Bain relinquished it, he asked her a simple question.

'Who's Claire Benzie?'

'You're not in custody, Claire,' Siobhan said, 'and if you want a solicitor, that's up to you. But I'd like your permission to make a tape recording.'

'Sounds serious,' Claire Benzie said. They'd picked her up at her flat in Bruntsfield, driven her to St Leonard's. She'd been compliant, not asking questions. She was wearing jeans and a pale pink turtleneck.

Her face looked scrubbed, no make-up. She sat in the interview room with arms folded while Bain fed tapes into both recording machines.

'There'll be a copy for you, and one for us,' Siobhan was saying. 'Okay?'

Benzie just shrugged.

Bain said 'okey-dokey' and set both tapes running, then eased himself into the chair next to Siobhan. Siobhan identified herself and Bain for the record, adding time and place of interview.

'If you could state your full name, Claire,' she asked.

Claire Benzie did so, adding her Bruntsfield address. Siobhan sat back for a moment, composing herself, then leaned forward again so her elbows were resting on the edge of the narrow desk.

'Claire, do you remember when I spoke to you earlier? I was with a colleague, in Dr Curt's office?'

'Yes, I remember.'

'I was asking you if you knew anything about the game Philippa Balfour had been playing?'

'It's her funeral tomorrow.'

Siobhan nodded. 'Do you remember?'

'Seven fins high is king,' Benzie said. 'I told you about it.'

'That's right. You said Philippa had come up to you at a bar . . .'

'Yes.'

'. . . and explained it to you.'

'Yes.'

'But you didn't know anything about the game itself?'

'No. I hadn't a clue till you told me.'

Siobhan sat back again, folded her own arms so that she was almost a mirror-image of Benzie. 'Then how come whoever was sending Flip those messages was using your Internet account?'

Benzie stared at her. Siobhan stared back. Eric Bain scratched his nose with his thumb.

'I want a solicitor,' Benzie said.

Siobhan nodded slowly. 'Interview ends, three-twelve p.m.' Bain switched off the tapes and Siobhan asked if Claire had anyone in mind.

'The family solicitor, I suppose,' the student said.

'And who's that?'

'My father.' When she saw the puzzled look on Siobhan's face, the corners of Benzie's mouth curled upwards. 'I mean my stepfather, DC Clarke. Don't worry, I'm not about to summon ghosts to fight my corner . . .'

News had travelled, and there was a scrum in the corridor when Siobhan came out of the interview room, just as the summoned WPC was going in. Whispered questions flew.

'Well?'

'Did she do it?'

'What's she saying?'

'Is it her?'

Siobhan ignored everyone except Gill Templer. 'She wants a solicitor, and as chance would have it there's one in her family.'

'That's handy.'

Siobhan nodded and squeezed her way into the CID office, unplugging the first free phone she came to.

'She also wants a soft drink, Diet Pepsi for preference.'

Templer looked around, eyes fixing on George Silvers. 'Hear that, George?'

'Yes, ma'am.' Silvers seemed reluctant to leave, until Gill shooed him out with her hands.

'So?' Gill was now blocking Siobhan's path.

'So,' Siobhan said, 'she's got some explaining to do. It doesn't make her the killer.'

'Be nice if she was though,' someone said.

Siobhan was remembering what Rebus had said about Claire Benzie. She met Gill Templer's gaze. 'Two or three years from now,' she said, 'if she sticks with pathology, we could end up working side by side with her. I don't think we can afford to be heavy-handed.' She wasn't sure if she was copying Rebus's words verbatim, but she knew she was pretty close. Templer was looking at her appraisingly, nodding slowly.

'DC Clarke's got a very good point,' she told the surrounding faces. Then she moved aside to let Siobhan past, murmuring something like 'Well done, Siobhan' as they were shoulder to shoulder.

Back in the interview room, Siobhan plugged the telephone into the wall and told Claire it was 9 for an outside line.

'I didn't kill her,' the student said with quiet confidence.

'Then everything's going to be okay. We just need to find out what happened.'

Claire nodded, picked up the receiver. Siobhan gestured to Bain, and they left the room together, the WPC taking over the watch.

Out in the corridor, the scrum had melted away, but the hubbub from inside the CID office was loud and excited.

'Say she didn't do it.' Siobhan spoke quietly, her words for Bain's ears only.

'Okay,' he said.

'Then how could Quizmaster be tapping into her account?'

He shook his head. 'I don't know. I mean, I suppose it's possible, but it's also highly unlikely.'

Siobhan looked at him. 'So you think it's her?'

He shrugged. 'I'd like to know who the other access accounts belong to.'

'Did Special Branch say how long it would take?'

'Maybe later today, maybe tomorrow.'

Someone walked past, patted both of them on the shoulder, gave a thumbs-up as he bounced down the corridor.

'They think we've cracked it,' Bain said.

'More fool them.'

'She had the motive, you've said so yourself.'

Siobhan nodded. She was thinking of the Stricture clue, trying to imagine it composed by a woman. Yes, it was possible; of course it was possible. The virtual world: you could pretend to be anyone you liked, either gender, any age. The newspapers were full of stories about middle-aged paedophiles who'd infiltrated children's chat rooms in the guise of teens and pre-teens. The very anonymity of the Net was what attracted people to it. She thought of Claire Benzie, of the long and careful planning it must have taken, the anger fermenting ever since her father's suicide. Maybe she'd started out wanting to know Flip again, wanting to like and forgive her, but had found rising hatred instead, hatred of Flip's easy world, her friends with fast cars, the bars and night clubs and dinner parties, the whole lifestyle enjoyed by people who'd never known pain, never lost anything in their lives that couldn't be bought again.

'I don't know,' she said, running both hands through her hair, pulling so hard that her scalp hurt. 'I just don't know.'

'That's good,' Bain said. 'Approach the interview with an open mind: textbook stuff.'

She smiled tiredly, squeezed his hand. 'Thanks, Eric.'

'You'll be fine,' he told her. She hoped he was right.

Maybe the Central Library was the right place for Rebus. Many of the customers today seemed to be the dispossessed, the tired, the unemployable. Some sat sleeping in the more comfortable chairs, the books on their laps mere props. One old man, toothless mouth gaping, sat at a desk near the telephone directories, his finger running ponderously down each column. Rebus had asked one of the staff about him.

'Been coming in here for years, never reads anything else,' he was informed.

'He could get a job with Directory Enquiries.'

'Or maybe that's where he was fired from.'

Rebus acknowledged that this was a good point, and got back to his own research. So far he'd established that Albert Camus was a French novelist and thinker, the author of novels such as *La Chute* and *La Peste*. He'd won the Nobel Prize and then died while still in his forties. The librarian had done a search for him, but this was the only Camus of note to be found.

'Unless, of course, you're talking street names.'

'What?'

'Edinburgh street names.'

Sure enough, it turned out that the city boasted a Camus Road, along with Camus Avenue, Park and Place. No one seemed to know whether they were named after the French writer; Rebus reckoned the chances were pretty good. He looked up Camus in the phone book – by luck the old man wasn't using it at the time – and found just the one. Taking a break, he thought about walking home and getting his car, maybe taking a drive out to Camus Road, but when a taxi came by he hailed it instead. Camus Road, Avenue, Park and Place turned out to be a little quartet of quiet residential streets just off Comiston Road in Fairmilehead. The taxi driver seemed bemused when Rebus told him to head back for George IV Bridge. When they hit a traffic hold-up at Greyfriars, Rebus paid the taxi off and got out. He headed straight into Sandy Bell's pub, where the afternoon crowd hadn't yet been swollen by workers on their way home. A pint and a nip. The barman knew him, told a few stories. He said that when the Infirmary moved to Petty France, they'd lose half their trade. Not the doctors and nurses, but the patients.

'Pyjamas and slippers, I'm not joking: they walk straight out the ward and in here. One guy even had the tubes hanging out his arms.'

Rebus smiled, finished his drinks. Greyfriars Kirkyard was just around the corner, so he took a wander in. He reckoned that all those Covenanting ghosts would be pretty miserable, knowing a wee dog had made the place more famous than they had. There were tours up here at night, stories of sudden chill hands clamping shoulders. He recalled that Rhona, his ex, had wanted to be married in the kirk itself. He saw graves covered with iron railings – mortsafes, protecting the deceased from the Resurrection Men. Edinburgh seemed always to have thrived on cruelty, its centuries of barbarism masked by an exterior by turns douce and strict . . .

Stricture . . . he wondered what the word had to do with the clue. He thought it meant being tied up, something along those lines, but realised that he wasn't sure. He left the kirkyard and headed on to George IV Bridge, turning in to the library. The same librarian was still on duty.

'Dictionaries?' he asked. She directed him towards the shelf he needed.

'I did that check you asked for,' she added. 'There are some books by a Mark Smith, but nothing by anyone called M. E. Smith.'

'Thanks anyway.' He started to turn away.

'I also printed you out a list of our Camus holdings.'

He took the sheet from her. 'That's great. Thank you very much.'

She smiled, as if unused to compliments, then looked more hesitant as she caught the alcohol on his breath. On his way to the shelves, he noticed that the desk by the telephone directories was vacant. He wondered if that was the old guy finished for the day; maybe it was like a nine-to-five for him. He pulled out the first dictionary he found and opened it at 'stricture': it meant binding, closure, tightness.

'Binding' made him think of mummies, or someone with their hands tied, held captive . . .

There was a clearing of the throat behind him. The librarian was standing there.

'Chucking-out time?' Rebus guessed.

'Not quite.' She pointed back towards her desk, where another member of staff was now positioned, watching them. 'My colleague . . . Kenny . . . he thinks maybe he knows who Mr Smith is.'

'Mr who?' Rebus was looking at Kenny: barely out of his teens, wearing round metal-framed glasses and a black T-shirt.

'M. E. Smith,' the librarian said. So Rebus walked over, nodded a greeting at Kenny.

'He's a singer,' Kenny said without preamble. 'At least, if it's the one I'm thinking of: Mark E. Smith. And not everyone would agree with the description "singer".'

The librarian had gone back around the desk. 'I've never heard of him, I must confess,' she said.

'Time to widen your horizons, Bridget,' Kenny said. Then he looked at Rebus, wondering at the detective's wide-eyed stare.

'Singer with The Fall?' Rebus said quietly, almost to himself.

'You know them?' Kenny seemed surprised that someone Rebus's age would have such knowledge.

'Saw them twenty years ago. A club in Abbeyhill.'

'Real noise merchants, eh?' Kenny said.

Rebus nodded distractedly. Then the other librarian, Bridget, gave voice to his thoughts.

'Funny really,' she said. Then she pointed to the sheet of paper in Rebus's hand. 'Camus' novel *La Chute* translates as "The Fall". We've a copy in the Fiction section if you'd like one . . .'

Claire Benzie's stepfather turned out to be Jack McCoist, one of the city's more able defence solicitors. He asked for ten minutes alone with her before any interview could begin. Afterwards, Siobhan entered the room again, accompanied by Gill Templer who, much to his visible annoyance, had ousted Eric Bain.

Claire's drink can was empty. McCoist had half a cup of lukewarm tea in front of him.

'I don't think we need a recording made,' McCoist stated. 'Let's just talk this through, see where it takes us. Agreed?'

He looked to Gill Templer, who nodded eventually.

'When you're ready, DC Clarke,' Templer said.

Siobhan tried for eye contact with Claire, but she was too busy with the Pepsi can, rolling it between her palms.

'Claire,' she said, 'these clues Flip was getting, one of them came from an e-mail address which we've traced back to you.'

McCoist had an A4 pad out, on which he'd already written several pages of notes in handwriting so bad it was like a personal code. Now he turned to a fresh sheet.

'Can I just ask how you came into possession of these e-mails?'

'They . . . we didn't really. Someone called Quizmaster sent Flip Balfour a message, and it came to me instead.'

'How so?' McCoist hadn't looked up from his pad. All she could see of him were blue pinstriped shoulders and the top of his head, thinning black hair showing plenty of scalp.

'Well, I was checking Ms Balfour's computer for anything that might explain her disappearance.'

'So this was *after* she'd disappeared?' He looked up now: thick black rims to his glasses and a mouth which, when not open, was a thin line of doubt.

'Yes,' Siobhan admitted.

'And this is the message you say you've traced back to my client's computer?'

'To her ISP account, yes.' Siobhan was noticing that Claire had looked up for the first time: it was that use of "my client". Claire was looking at her stepfather, studying him. Probably she'd never seen his professional side before.

'ISP being the Internet service provider?'

Siobhan nodded her answer. McCoist was letting her know that he was up on the jargon.

'Have there been subsequent messages?'

'Yes.'

'And do they belong to the same address?'

'We don't know that yet.' Siobhan had decided he didn't need to know more than one ISP was involved.

'Very well.' McCoist stabbed a full stop on the latest sheet with his pen, then sat back thoughtfully.

'Do I get to ask Claire a question now?' Siobhan asked.

McCoist peered at her over the top of his glasses. 'My client would prefer to make a short statement first.'

Claire reached into the pocket of her jeans and unfolded a sheet of paper which had obviously come from the pad on the table. The writing was different from McCoist's scrawl, but Siobhan could see scorings-out where the lawyer had suggested changes.

Claire cleared her throat. 'About a fortnight before Flip went missing, I loaned her my laptop computer. She had some essay she was writing, and I thought it might help her. I knew she didn't have a laptop of her own. I never got the chance to ask for it back. I was waiting until after the funeral to ask her family if it could be retrieved from her flat.'

'Is this laptop your only computer?' Siobhan interrupted.

Claire shook her head. 'No, but it's linked to an ISP, same account as my PC.'

Siobhan stared at her; still she didn't make eye contact. 'There was no laptop in Philippa Balfour's flat,' she said.

Eye contact at last. 'Then where is it?' Claire said.

'I'm assuming you still have the proof of purchase, something like that?'

McCoist spoke up. 'Are you accusing my daughter of lying?' She wasn't just a client any longer . . .

'I'm saying maybe it's something Claire should have told us a bit earlier.'

'I didn't know it was . . .' Claire began to say.

'DCS Templer,' McCoist began haughtily, 'I didn't think it was Lothian and Borders Police policy to accuse potential witnesses of duplicity.'

'Right now,' Templer shot back, 'your stepdaughter's a suspect rather than a witness.'

'Suspected of what exactly? Running a quiz? Since when was that an offence?'

Gill didn't have an answer for that. She glanced in Siobhan's direction, and Siobhan thought she could read at least a few of her boss's thoughts. *He's right . . . we still don't know for sure that Quizmaster has anything to do with anything . . . this is* your *hunch I'm going with, just remember that . . .*

McCoist knew the look between the two detectives meant something. He decided to press his point.

'I can't see you presenting any of this to the Procurator Fiscal. You'd be laughed back down the ranks . . . DCS Templer.' Putting the stress on those three letters. He knew she was newly promoted; knew she'd yet to prove herself . . .

Gill had already regained her composure. 'What we need from Claire, Mr McCoist, are some straight answers, otherwise her story's looking thin and we'll need to make further inquiries.'

McCoist seemed to consider this. Siobhan, meantime, was busy making a mental list. Claire Benzie had the motive all right – the role of Balfour's Bank in her father's suicide. With the role-playing game, she had the means, and luring Flip to Arthur's Seat would give the opportunity. Now she suddenly invented a loaned laptop, conveniently missing . . . Siobhan started another list, this time for Ranald Marr, who'd warned Flip early on about how to delete e-mails. Ranald Marr with his toy soldiers, second-in-command at the bank. She still didn't see what Marr would have gained from Flip's death . . .

'Claire,' she said quietly, 'those times you went to Junipers, did you ever meet Ranald Marr?'

'I don't see what that's—'

But Claire interrupted her stepfather. 'Ranald Marr, yes. I never really knew what she saw in him.'

'Who?'

'Flip. She had this crush on Ranald. Schoolgirl stuff, I suppose . . .'

'Was it reciprocated? Did it go further than a crush?'

'I think,' McCoist said, 'we're straying somewhat from the—'

But Claire was smiling at Siobhan. 'Not until later,' she was saying.

'How much later?'

'I got the feeling she was seeing him pretty much up till she went missing . . .'

'What's all the excitement?' Rebus asked.

Bain looked up from the desk he was working at. 'Brought in Claire Benzie for questioning.'

'Why?' Rebus leaned down, reached into one of the desk's drawers.

'Sorry,' Bain said, 'is this your . . .?'

He was making to get up, but Rebus stopped him. 'I'm suspended, remember? Just you keep it warm for me.' He closed the drawer, not having found anything. 'So what's Benzie doing here?'

'One of the e-mails, I got Special Branch to trace it.'

Rebus whistled. 'Claire Benzie sent it?'

'Well, it was sent from her account.'

Rebus considered this. 'Not quite the same thing?'

'Siobhan's the sceptical one.'

'Is she in with Benzie?' Rebus waited till Bain nodded. 'But you're out here?'

'DCS Templer.'

'Ah,' Rebus said, no further explanation needed.

Gill Templer burst into the CID office. 'I want Ranald Marr brought in for questioning. Who wants to fetch him?'

She got two volunteers straight away – Hi-Ho Silvers and Tommy Fleming. Others were trying to place the name, wondering what it could have to do with Claire Benzie and Quizmaster. When Gill turned round, Siobhan was standing behind her.

'That was good work in there.'

'Was it?' Siobhan asked. 'I'm not so sure.'

'How do you mean?'

'When I talk to her, it's like I'm asking her things she *wants* to be asked. It's as if *she's* in control.'

'I didn't see that.' Gill touched Siobhan's shoulder. 'Take a break. We'll let someone else have a shot at Ranald Marr.' She looked around the room. 'The rest of you, back to work.' Her eyes met those of John Rebus. 'What the hell are you doing here?'

Rebus opened another drawer, this time pulling out a pack of cigarettes and shaking them.

'Just came to collect a few personal items, ma'am.'

Gill pursed her lips, stalked out of the room. McCoist was in the corridor with Claire. The three started a short discussion. Siobhan approached Rebus.

'What the hell *are* you doing here?'

'You look shattered.'

'I see your silver tongue's as rusty as ever.'

'Boss told you to take a break, and as luck would have it, I'm buying. While you've been busy scaring wee lassies, I've been doing the important stuff . . .'

Siobhan was sticking to orange juice, and kept playing with her mobile: Bain was under strictest orders to call her if and when there was news.

'I need to get back,' she said, not for the first time. Then she checked the mobile's display again, just in case the battery needed recharging or the signal had been lost.

'Have you eaten?' Rebus asked. When she shook her head, he came back from the bar with a couple of packets of Scampi Fries, which she was devouring when she heard him say:

'That's when it struck me.'

'When what struck you?'

'Christ, Siobhan, wake up.'

'John, I feel like my head's about to explode. I honestly think it might.'

'You don't think Claire Benzie's guilty, that much I understand. And now she says Flip Balfour was getting her end away with Ranald Marr.'

'Do you believe her?'

He lit another cigarette, wafted the smoke away from Siobhan. 'I'm not allowed an opinion: suspended from duty till further notice.'

She gave him a dirty look, lifted her glass.

'It's going to be some conversation, isn't it?' Rebus asked.

'What?'

'When Balfour asks his trusted compadre what the cops wanted him for.'

'Think Marr will tell him?'

'Even if he doesn't, Balfour's sure to find out. Funeral tomorrow should be a jolly affair.' He blew more smoke ceilingwards. 'You going to be there?'

'Thinking of it. Templer and Carswell, a few others . . . they'll be going.'

'Might be needed if a fight starts.'

She looked at her watch. 'I should head back, see what Marr's been saying.'

'You were told to take a break.'

'I've had one.'

'Phone in if you really feel the need.'

'Maybe I'll do that.' She noticed that her mobile was still attached to the connector which, were the laptop not back at St Leonard's, would have given her access to the Net. She stared at the connector, then up at Rebus. 'What were you saying?'

'About what?'

'About Stricture.'

Rebus's smile widened. 'Nice to have you back with us. I was saying that I spent all afternoon in the library, and I've worked out the first bit of the puzzle.'

'Already?'

'You're dealing with quality here, Siobhan. So, do you want to hear?'

'Sure.' She noticed that his glass was almost empty. 'Should I . . . ?'

'Just listen first.' He pulled her back on to her seat. The pub was maybe half full, and most of the drinkers looked like students. Rebus reckoned he was the oldest face in the place. Standing by the bar, he might have been taken for the owner. At the corner table with Siobhan, he probably looked like a seedy boss trying to get his secretary tipsy.

'I'm all ears,' she told him.

'Albert Camus,' he began slowly, 'wrote a book called *The Fall*.' He slid a paperback copy from his coat and placed it on the table, tapping it with one finger. It wasn't from the library; he'd found it in Thin's Bookshop on his way to St Leonard's. 'Mark E. Smith is the singer with a band called The Fall.'

Siobhan frowned. 'I think I had one of their singles once.'

'So,' Rebus went on, 'we have *The Fall* and The Fall. Add one to the other and you get . . .'

'Falls?' Siobhan guessed. Rebus nodded. She picked up the book, examined its cover, then turned it to read the blurb on the back. 'You think maybe that's where Quizmaster wants to meet?'

'I think it has to do with the next clue.'

'But what about the rest of it, the boxing match and Frank Finlay?'

Rebus shrugged. 'Unlike Simple Minds, I didn't promise you a miracle.'

'No . . .' She paused, then looked up at him. 'Come to think of it, I didn't think you were that interested.'

'I changed my mind.'

'Why?'

'Ever sat at home watching paint dry?'

'I've been on dates where it would have been preferable.'

'Then maybe you know what I mean.'

She nodded, flicking the pages of the book. Then a frown appeared on her forehead, she stopped nodding, and looked up at him again. 'Actually,' she said, 'I don't have the faintest idea what you mean.'

'Good, that means you're learning.'

'Learning what?'

'John Rebus's own patented brand of existentialism.' He wagged a finger at her. 'That's a word I didn't know till today, and I've got you to thank.'

'So what does it mean?'

'I didn't say I knew what it meant, but I think it's got quite a lot to do with choosing *not* to watch paint dry . . .'

They went back to St Leonard's, but there was no news. Officers were practically bouncing off the walls. They needed a breakthrough. They needed a break. A fight had to be broken up in the toilets: two uniforms who couldn't say how it started. Rebus watched Siobhan for a few minutes. She went from one huddle to another, desperate to know things. He could see she was having trouble holding on: a head full of theories and fancies. She, too, needed the breakthrough, the break. He walked up to her. Her eyes were glistening. Rebus took hold of her arm, escorted her outside. She resisted at first.

'When did you last eat?' he asked.

'You bought me those Scampi Fries.'

'I mean a hot meal.'

'You sound like my mum . . .'

The short walk led them to an Indian restaurant on Nicolson Street. It was dark and up a flight of stairs and mostly empty. Tuesday had become the new Monday: a dead night on the town. The weekend started on Thursday as you planned how to spend your pay, and ended with a quick pint after work on the Monday so you could pick over the highlights just past. Tuesday, the sensible option was to go home, keep what cash you had.

'You know Falls better than I do,' she said now. 'What landmarks are there?'

'Well, the waterfall itself – you've seen that – and maybe Junipers – you've been there.' He shrugged. 'That's about it.'

'There's a housing scheme, right?'

He nodded. 'Meadowside. And there's a petrol station just outside town. Plus Bev Dodds's cottage and a few dozen commuters. Not even a church or a post office.'

'No boxing ring then?'

Rebus shook his head. 'And no bouquets, barbed wire or Frank Finlay House.'

Siobhan seemed to lose interest in her food. Rebus wasn't too worried: she'd already dispatched a mixed tandoori starter and the bulk of her biryani. He watched her take out her phone and try the station again. She'd called once already: no one had answered. This time someone did.

'Eric? It's Siobhan. What's happening there? Have we got Marr yet? What's he saying?' She listened, then her eyes met Rebus's. 'Really?' Her voice had risen slightly in pitch. 'That was a bit silly, wasn't it?'

For a second, Rebus thought: suicide. He drew a finger across his throat, but Siobhan shook her head.

'Okay, Eric. Thanks for that. See you later.' She ended the call, took her time placing the phone back in her bag.

'Spit it out,' Rebus said.

She scooped up another forkful of food. 'You're suspended, remember? Off the case.'

'I'll suspend you from the ceiling if you don't cough up.'

She smiled, put the fork down, food untouched. The waiter took a step forward, ready to clear the table, but Rebus waved him back.

'Well,' Siobhan said, 'they went to pick up Mr Marr at his detached home in The Grange, only he wasn't there.'

'And?'

'And the reason he wasn't there was, he'd been told they'd be coming. Gill Templer called the ACC, said they were picking up Marr for questioning. The ACC "suggested" they phone Mr Marr beforehand, as "a courtesy".'

She picked up the water jug, tipped the dregs into her glass. The same waiter started forward, ready to replace the jug, but Rebus waved him back again.

'So Marr did a runner?'

Siobhan nodded. 'Looks like it. His wife says he took the call, and two minutes later when she went to look for him, he wasn't there and neither was the Maserati.'

'Better stick one of the napkins in your pocket,' Rebus suggested. 'Looks like some egg needs wiping from Carswell's face.'

'I can't imagine he'll have fun explaining to the Chief Constable,' Siobhan agreed. Then she watched a grin light up Rebus's face. 'Just what you needed?' she guessed.

'Might help take some of the heat off.'

'Because Carswell will be too busy covering his own arse to find time to kick yours?'

'Eloquently put.'

'It's the college education.'

'So what's happening about Marr?' Rebus nodded towards the waiter, who took a hesitant step forward, unsure if he'd suddenly be expelled again. 'Two coffees,' Rebus told him. The man made a little bow and moved off.

'Not sure,' Siobhan admitted.

'Night before the funeral, could be awkward.'

'High-speed car chase . . . stop and arrest . . .' Siobhan was imagining the scenario. 'Grieving parents wondering why their best friend is suddenly in custody . . .'

'If Carswell's thinking straight, he'll do nothing till the funeral's over. Could be Marr will turn up there anyway.'

'A fond farewell to his secret lover?'

'If Claire Benzie's telling the truth.'

'Why else would he run?'

Rebus stared at her. 'I think you know the answer to that one.'

'You mean if Marr killed her?'

'I thought you had him in the frame.'

She was thoughtful. 'That was before this happened. I don't think Quizmaster would run.'

'Maybe Quizmaster didn't kill Flip Balfour.'

Siobhan nodded. 'That's my point. I had Marr in the frame for Quizmaster.'

'Meaning she was killed by someone else?'

The coffees arrived, and with them the ubiquitous mints. Siobhan dunked hers in the hot liquid, quickly hoisting it into her mouth. Without being asked, the waiter had brought the bill with their coffees.

'Split it down the middle?' Siobhan suggested. Rebus nodded, took three fivers from his pocket.

Outside, he asked how she was getting home.

'My car's at St Leonard's: need a lift?'

'Nice night for a walk,' he said, looking up at the clouds. 'Just promise me you *will* go home, take a break . . .'

'Promise, Mum.'

'And now that you've convinced yourself that Quizmaster didn't kill Flip . . .'

'Yes?'

'Well, you don't have to bother with the game any more, do you?'

She blinked, told him she supposed he was right. But he could see she didn't believe it. The game was *her* part of the case. She couldn't just let it go . . . He knew he'd have felt the same way.

They parted on the pavement, Rebus heading back to the flat. When he got in, he called Jean, but she wasn't at home. Maybe another late night at the Museum, but she wasn't answering there either. He stood in front of his dining table, staring at the case notes there. He'd pinned some sheets to the wall, detailing the four women – Jesperson, Gibbs, Gearing and Farmer. He was trying to answer a question: why would the killer leave the coffins? Okay, they were his 'signature', but that signature had not been recognised. It had taken the best part of thirty years for someone to realise that there even *was* a signature. If the killer had hoped to be identified with his crimes, wouldn't he have repeated the exercise, or tried some other method: a note to the media or the police? So say they weren't a signature as such; say his motive had been . . . what? Rebus saw them as little memorials, holding meaning only for the person who'd left them there. And couldn't the same be said for the Arthur's Seat coffins? Why had the person responsible not come forward in some form? Answer: because once found, the coffins had ceased to have meaning for their creator. They'd been memorials, never meant to be found or associated with the Burke and Hare killings . . .

Yes, there were connections between those coffins and the ones Jean had identified. Rebus was wary of adding the Falls coffin to the list, but he felt a connection there, too – a looser connection, to be sure, but still powerful.

He'd checked his answering machine, just the one message: his solicitor, concerning a retired couple who would show the flat to potential buyers, relieving him of the burden. He knew he'd have to take his little collage down before then, hide everything away, do some tidying . . .

He tried Jean's number again, but there was still no answer. Stuck a Steve Earle album on: *The Hard Way*.

Rebus didn't know of any other . . .

'You're lucky I didn't change my name,' Jan Benzie said. Jean had just explained how she'd called every Benzie in the phone book. 'I'm married to Jack McCoist these days.'

They were sitting in the drawing room of a three-storey townhouse in the city's west end, just off Palmerston Place. Jan Benzie was tall and thin, and wore a knee-length black dress with a sparkling brooch just above her right breast. The room reflected her elegance: antiques and polished surfaces, thick walls and floors muffling any sound.

'Thank you for seeing me at such short notice.'

'There's not much I can add to what I told you on the phone.' Jan Benzie sounded distracted, as if part of her was elsewhere. Maybe that was why she'd agreed to the appointment in the first place . . . 'It's been rather a strange day, Miss Burchill,' she said now.

'Oh?'

But Jan Benzie just shrugged one shoulder and asked again if Jean would like something to drink.

'I don't want to keep you. You said Patricia Lovell was a relation?'

'Great-great-grandmother . . . something like that.'

'She died very young, didn't she?'

'You probably know more about her than I do. I'd no idea she was buried at Calton Hill.'

'How many children did she have?'

'Just the one, a girl.'

'Do you know if she died in childbirth?'

'I've no idea.' Jan Benzie laughed at the absurdity of the question.

'I'm sorry,' Jean said, 'I know this must all sound a bit ghoulish . . .'

'A bit. You say you're researching Kennet Lovell?'

Jean nodded. 'Would your family have any of his papers?'

Jan Benzie shook her head. 'None.'

'You've no relatives who might . . .?'

'I really don't think so, no.' She moved an arm towards the occasional table next to her chair, lifted her cigarette packet and eased one out. 'Do you . . .?'

Jean shook her head and watched Jan Benzie light the cigarette with a slim gold lighter. The woman seemed to do everything in slow motion. It was like watching a film at the wrong speed.

'It's just that I'm looking for some correspondence between Dr Lovell and his benefactor.'

'I didn't even know there was one.'

'A kirk minister back in Ayrshire.'

'Really?' Jan Benzie said, but Jean could tell she wasn't interested.

Right now, the cigarette between her fingers meant more to her than anything else.

Jean decided to plough on. 'There's a portrait of Dr Lovell in Surgeons' Hall. I think maybe it was executed at the minister's behest.'

'Is that so?'

'Have you ever seen it?'

'Can't say that I have.'

'He had several wives, Dr Lovell, did you know that?'

'Three, wasn't it? Not so many, really, in the scheme of things.' Benzie seemed to grow thoughtful. 'I'm on my second husband . . . who's to say it'll stop there?' She examined the ash at the end of her cigarette. 'My first committed suicide, you know.'

'I didn't.'

'No reason why you should.' She paused. 'Don't suppose I can expect the same of Jack.'

Jean wasn't sure what she meant, but Jan Benzie was studying her, seeming to expect some reply. 'I suppose,' Jean said, 'it would look a bit suspicious, losing two husbands.'

'And yet Kennet Lovell can lose three wives . . . ?'

Jean's thinking exactly . . .

Jan Benzie had risen to her feet, walked over to the window. Jean took another look around the room. All the artefacts, the paintings and framed photographs, candlesticks and crystal ashtrays . . . she got the feeling none of it belonged to Benzie. It had come with her marriage to Jack McCoist, part of the baggage he brought.

'Well,' she said, 'I'd better be going. Sorry again to have . . .'

'No trouble,' Benzie said. 'I hope you find what you're looking for.'

Suddenly there were voices out in the hall, and the sound of the front door being closed. The voices began ascending the staircase, coming closer.

'Claire and my husband,' Jan said, sitting back down again, arranging herself the way an artist's model might. The door burst open and Claire Benzie stormed into the room. To Jean's eye, she bore no physical resemblance to her mother, but perhaps that was partly down to her entrance, the way she crackled with energy.

'I don't bloody care,' she was saying. 'They can lock me up if they want, throw away the bloody key!' She was pacing the room as Jack McCoist walked in. He had his wife's slow movements, but they seemed merely the result of fatigue.

'Claire, all I'm saying is . . .' He leaned down to peck his wife's cheek. 'What a bloody awful time we've had,' he informed her. 'Cops crawling over Claire like lice. Is there *any* way you can control your daughter, darling?' His words died as he straightened and saw they had a visitor. Jean was rising to her feet.

'I really should be going,' she said.

'Who the hell's this?' Claire snarled.

'Ms Burchill is from the Museum,' Jan explained. 'We've been talking about Kennet Lovell.'

'Christ, not her as well!' Claire tossed her head back, then dropped on to one of the room's two sofas.

'I'm researching his life,' Jean explained for McCoist's benefit. He was pouring himself a whisky at the drinks cabinet.

'At this time of night?' was all he said.

'His portrait's hanging in some hall somewhere,' Jan Benzie told her daughter. 'Did you know that?'

'Of course I bloody did! It's in the museum at Surgeons' Hall.' She looked at Jean. 'Is that where you're from?'

'No, actually . . .'

'Well, wherever you're from, why don't you piss off back there? I'm just out of police custody and—'

'You will *not* speak like that to a guest in this house!' Jan Benzie yelped, springing from her chair. 'Jack, tell her.'

'Look, I really should . . .' Jean's words were swamped as a three-way argument started. She backed away, heading for the door.

'You've no bloody right . . . !'

'Christ, anyone would think it was *you* they interrogated!'

'That's still no excuse for . . .'

'Just one quiet drink, is that too much to . . .'

They didn't seem to notice as Jean opened the door, closing it again behind her. She walked down the carpeted stairs on tiptoe, and opened the front door as quietly as she could, escaping into the street, where, finally, she let out a huge breath of air. Walking away, she glanced back towards the drawing-room window, but couldn't see anything. The houses here had walls so thick, they could double as padded cells, and it felt like that was just what she'd escaped from.

Claire Benzie's temper had been something to behold.

13

Wednesday morning, there was still no sign of Ranald Marr. His wife Dorothy had called Junipers and spoken to John Balfour's PA. She was reminded in no uncertain terms that the family had a funeral to see to, and that the PA didn't feel able to disturb either Mr or Mrs Balfour further until some time thereafter.

'They've lost a daughter, you know,' the PA said haughtily.

'And I've lost my fucking husband, you bitch!' Dorothy Marr spat back, recoiling ever so slightly afterwards as she realised it was probably the first time she'd used a swear-word in her adult life. But it was too late to apologise: the PA had already put down the phone and was informing a lesser member of the Balfour staff not to accept any further calls from Mrs Marr.

Junipers itself was full of people: family members and friends were gathering there. Some, having travelled far, had stayed the previous night, and were now wandering the many corridors in search of something resembling breakfast. Mrs Dolan the cook had decided that hot food would not be seemly on such a day, so her usual vapour trail of sausage, bacon and eggs or pungent kedgeree could not be followed. In the dining room sat an array of cereal packets and preserves, the latter home-made but not including Mrs Dolan's blackcurrant and apple, which had been Flip's favourite since childhood. She'd left that particular jar back in the pantry. Last time anyone had eaten some, it had been Flip herself on one of her infrequent visits.

Mrs Dolan was telling her daughter Catriona as much, as Catriona comforted her and handed over another paper handkerchief. One of the guests, sent to inquire whether coffee and cold milk might be available, put his head round the kitchen door, but withdrew again, embarrassed to be witnessing the indomitable Mrs Dolan brought low like this.

In the library, John Balfour was telling his wife that he didn't want 'any bloody police thickos' at the cemetery.

'But, John, they've all worked so hard,' his wife was saying, 'and they've asked to be there. Surely they've as much right as . . .' Her voice died away.

'As who?' His voice had grown less angry, but suddenly colder.

'Well,' his wife said, 'all these people we don't know . . .'

'You mean people *I* know? You've met them at parties, functions. Jackie, for Christ's sake, they want to pay their respects.'

His wife nodded and stayed quiet. After the funeral, there would be a buffet lunch back at Junipers, not just for close family but for all her husband's associates and acquaintances, nearly seventy of them. Jacqueline had wanted a much smaller affair, something that could be accommodated in the dining room. As it was, they'd had to order a marquee, which had been installed on the back lawn. An Edinburgh firm – run by another of her husband's clients, no doubt – was doing the catering. The lady owner was busy out there now, supervising the unloading of tables, cloths, crockery and cutlery from what seemed a never-ending series of small vans. Jacqueline's small victory so far had been to widen the circle of invitees to include Flip's own friends, though this had not been without its awkward moments. David Costello, for example, would have to be invited, along with his parents, though she'd never liked David and felt he held the family in mild distaste. She was hoping they would either fail to turn up, or would not linger.

'Silver lining, in a way,' John was droning on, hardly aware of her presence in the room. 'Something like this, it binds them all to Balfour's, makes it harder for them to make a move elsewhere . . .'

Jacqueline rose shakily to her feet.

'We're burying our daughter, John! This isn't about your bloody *business*! Flip's not part of some . . . commercial transaction!'

Balfour glanced towards the door, making sure it was closed. 'Keep your voice down, woman. It was only a . . . I didn't mean . . .' He slumped on to the sofa suddenly, face in his hands. 'You're right, I wasn't thinking . . . God help me.'

His wife sat down next to him, took his hands and lowered them from his face. 'God help both of us, John,' she said.

Steve Holly had managed to persuade his boss at the paper's Glasgow HQ that he needed to be on the scene as early as possible. He'd also, knowing the geographical illiteracy rampant in Scotland, managed to persuade him that Falls was a lot further away from Edinburgh than was actually the case, and that Greywalls Hotel would make an ideal overnight stop. He hadn't bothered explaining that Greywalls was in Gullane, and consequently wasn't much more than a half-hour's drive from Edinburgh, or that Gullane, as the crow flew, wasn't exactly between Falls and Edinburgh. But what did it matter? He'd had his overnighter, joined by his girlfriend Gina, who wasn't really his girlfriend but just someone he'd dated a few times over the previous three months. Gina had been keen, but had worried about getting to work the next morning, so then Steve had fixed a taxi for her. He knew how he'd wing it, too: he'd say his car broke down and he'd used the taxi himself to get back to town . . .

After a fabulous dinner and a walk around the garden – designed by someone called Jekyll apparently – Steve and Gina had made ample use of their ample bed before sleeping like logs, so that the first they knew of it, Gina's cab was waiting and Steve had to tuck into breakfast alone, which would have been his preference anyway. But then the first disappointment: the newspapers . . . all of them broadsheets. He'd stopped in Gullane and bought the competition on his way out to Falls, leaving them on the passenger seat and flicking through them as he drove, cars flashing and tooting at him as he took more than his share of road.

'Bollocks!' he'd yelled from his window, giving each sheep-shagger and country bumpkin the finger as he got on the mobile, wanting to make sure Tony the photographer was primed for the cemetery shoot. He knew Tony had been out to Falls a couple of times to see Bev, or 'the Potty Potter' as Steve had come to call her. He thought Tony reckoned he was in there. His advice had been simple: 'She's a nutter, mate – you might get a shag, but two-to-one you wake up with your old wotsit sliced off and lying beside you in the bed.' To which Tony had laughed and said he just wanted to persuade Bev into some 'art poses' for his 'portfolio'. So when Steve got through to Tony this morning, his first words, as usual, were:

'Got her on your potter's wheel yet, mate?'

Then, also as usual, he started laughing at his own joke, which was what he was doing when he happened to glance in the rearview and caught the cop car up his bahooky, lights flashing. No idea how long it had been there.

'Have to call you back, Tony,' he said, braking and pulling on to the verge. 'Just make sure you get to the church on time.'

'Morning, officers,' he said, stepping out of the car.

'And a good morning to you, Mr Holly,' one of the uniforms said.

Which was when Steve Holly remembered he wasn't exactly flavour of the month with the Lothian and Borders Police.

Ten minutes later, he was back on the road, the cops tailing him to prevent, as they'd put it themselves, 'further infractions'. When his mobile went, he thought about not answering, but it was Glasgow, so he mirror-signal-manoeuvred back on to the verge and took the call, watching the cops stop ten yards back.

'Yes?' he said.

'Think you're a clever little bastard, don't you, Stevie Boy?'

His boss.

'Not right this second, no,' Steve Holly said.

'Friend of mine plays golf in Gullane. It's practically *in* Edinburgh, you turd. And the same goes for Falls. So any notion you had of turning that little trip round as expenses can now be stuck well and truly up your arse.'

'No problem.'

'Where are you anyway?'

Holly looked around at fields and dry-stane dykes. There was the distant drone of a tractor.

'I'm scoping out the cemetery, waiting for Tony to turn up. I'll head to Junipers in a couple of mins, follow them to the church.'

'Oh aye? Care to confirm that?'

'Confirm what?'

'That outright fucking lie that just tripped off your tongue!'

Holly licked his lips. 'I don't follow.' What was it, did the paper have a tracking device fixed to his car?

'Tony phoned the picture editor not five minutes ago. The picture editor who happened to be standing next to my bloody desk. Guess where your missing photographer was calling from?'

Holly said nothing.

'Go on, take a wild stab, because that's what I'm going to take at you next time I see you.'

'The cemetery?' Holly said.

'That your final answer? Maybe you want to phone a friend.'

Holly felt his anger rise: best defence was attack, right? 'Look,' he hissed, 'I've just given your paper the story of the year, scooped every competitor you've got, bar none. And this is how you go and treat me? Well, stuff your miserable paper and stuff *you*. Get someone else out here to cover the funeral, someone who knows the story the way I do. Meantime I think maybe I'll be making a couple of calls to the competition – on my time, my phone bill. If that's okay with you, you chiselling bastard. And if you want to know why I'm not at the cemetery, I'll tell you. It's because I've been stopped by a couple of Lothian's finest. They won't let me shake them off now I've gone and shat on them in print. You want the patrol car's licence plate? Give me a second, maybe they'll speak to you themselves!'

Holly shut up, but made sure he was breathing hard into the mouthpiece.

'For once,' the voice from Glasgow eventually said, 'and maybe they should carve this on my tombstone, I think I may actually have heard Steve Holly tell the truth.' There was another pause, and then a chuckle. 'We've got them worried then?'

We . . . Steve Holly knew he was home and dry.

'I've got what looks like a permanent escort, just in case I'm thinking of taking a hand off the wheel to pick my nose.'

'So you're not driving as we speak?'

'Up on the verge, indicators going. And, with all due respect, boss, that's another five minutes I've just wasted talking to you . . . Not that I don't always enjoy our little tête-à-têtes.'

Another chuckle. 'Ah, fuck it, bit of steam needs to be let off now and then, eh? Tell you what, put that hotel through to accounts, okay?'

'Right, boss.'

'And get your raggedy arse back on the road.'

'Ten-four, boss. This is the shining sword of truth, signing off.' Holly cut the call, exhaled heavily, and did what he'd been told to do: got his raggedy arse back on that road . . .

The village of Falls had neither church nor cemetery, but there was a small, little-used church – more the size of a chapel, really – just off the road between Falls and Causland. The family had picked the spot and arranged everything, but secretly those friends of Flip's who'd been able to attend thought the tranquillity and isolation out of keeping with Flip's character. They couldn't help feeling she'd have wanted something livelier, somewhere in the city itself, where people walked their dogs or went for a Sunday stroll, and where, in darkness, lively biker parties and furtive couplings might take place.

The graveyard here was too neat and compact, the graves too old and looked after. Flip would have wanted wild, straggling creepers and mosses, briar bushes and long wet grass. But then, when they considered, they realised she wouldn't care one way or the other, because she was dead and that was the end of it. At that moment, perhaps for the first time, they were able to separate loss from numb shock, and to feel the pangs of a life left incomplete.

There were too many people for the church. The doors were left open so that the short service could be heard outside. The day was cool, the ground heavy with dew. Birds played in the trees, agitated at this unique invasion. Cars lined the main road, the hearse having discreetly pulled away, heading back to Edinburgh. Liveried drivers stood beside several of the vehicles, cigarettes in hands. Rollers, Mercs, Jags . . .

Nominally, the family had worshipped in a city church, and the minister had been persuaded to lead the service, though he was used to seeing the Balfours only at Christmas, and then not for the past two or three years. He was a thorough man, who had checked his script with the mother and father, asking solicitous questions whose answers would help him bulk out Flip's biography, but he was also bemused by the attentions of the media. Being used to encountering cameras only at weddings and christenings, when one was pointed in his direction for the first time, he gave a beaming smile, only afterwards realising the inappropriateness of his action. These were not carnationed relatives but journalists, keeping their distance from the solemnities and their lenses trained only so far. Though the graveyard itself could be viewed clearly from the roadway, there'd be no photos of the coffin being lowered, or the parents by the graveside. Permission had been granted for one photograph only: of the coffin being carried from the church.

Of course, once the mourners were off church property, they would be reckoned fair game again.

'Parasites,' one of the guests, a Balfour's client of long standing, had hissed. All the same, he knew he'd be buying more than one paper next morning, just to see if he figured in any of the spreads.

With the pews and side aisles being crammed, the police officers present kept their own distance, to the back of the crowd at the church doors. Assistant Chief Constable Colin Carswell stood with hands clasped in front of him, head slightly bowed. Detective Chief Superintendent Gill Templer was next to Detective Inspector Bill Pryde, just behind Carswell. Other officers were further off still, patrolling what grounds there were. Flip's killer was still out there, and so, if the two could be differentiated, was Ranald Marr. Inside the church, John Balfour kept turning his head, examining each face as if looking for someone. Only those who knew the workings of Balfour's Bank guessed who this missing face belonged to . . .

John Rebus was standing by the far wall, dressed in his good suit and a long green raincoat, its collar up. He kept thinking how bleak the surroundings were: typical bare hillside dotted with sheep; dull yellow gorse bushes. He'd read the noticeboard just inside the churchyard gate. It told him the building dated back to the seventeenth century, and that local farmers had raised the contributions necessary for its construction. At least one Templar grave had been found inside the low stone wall, leading historians to believe that a former chapel and burying place must have rested on this site.

'The headstone from this Templar grave,' he'd read, 'can now be seen in the Museum of Scotland.'

He'd thought then of Jean, who, walking in a place like this, would notice things he couldn't see, telltale signs from the past. But then Gill had come towards him, face set, hands deep in pockets, and had asked what he thought he was doing there.

'Paying my respects.'

He'd noticed Carswell move his head slightly, noting Rebus's presence.

'Unless there's a law against it,' he'd added, walking away.

Siobhan was about fifty yards from him, but so far had acknowledged his presence only with a wave of her gloved hand. Her eyes were on the hillside, as if she thought the killer might suddenly reveal himself there. Rebus had his doubts. As the service ended, the coffin was carried out, and the cameras began their short work. The journalists present were studying the scene carefully, jotting mental paragraphs, or else speaking very quietly into mobile phones. Idly, Rebus wondered which service they were using: he still couldn't get a signal out here on his.

The TV cameras, which had recorded the exit of the pall-bearers from the church, switched off and hung from their cameramen's arms. There was silence outside the churchyard walls as within, broken only by the slow crunching of feet over gravel and the occasional sob from a mourner.

John Balfour had one arm around his wife. Some of Flip's student friends were hugging each other, faces buried in shoulders and chests. Rebus recognised faces: Tristram and Tina, Albert and Camille . . . No sign of Claire Benzie. He spotted some of Flip's neighbours, too, including Professor Devlin, who had come bustling up to talk to him earlier, asking about the coffins, whether there'd been any progress. When Rebus had shaken his head, Devlin had asked how he was feeling.

'Only, I sense a certain frustration,' the old man had said.

'That's how it is sometimes.'

Devlin had studied him. 'I wouldn't have taken you for a pragmatist, Inspector.'

'I've always found pessimism a great comforter,' Rebus had told him, moving away.

Now, Rebus watched the rest of the procession. There was a smattering of politicians, including the MSP Seona Grieve. David Costello preceded his parents out of the church, blinking at the sudden light, digging sunglasses from his breast pocket and slipping them on.

Victim's eyes catching the likeness of the killer . . .

Anyone looking at David Costello would see only their own reflection. Was that precisely what Costello wanted them to see? Behind him, his mother and father walked their separate and very distinct walks, more like nodding acquaintances than spouses. As the crowd lost its shape, David found himself next to Professor Devlin. Devlin stuck out a hand for David to shake, but the young man just stared at it, until Devlin withdrew and patted his arm instead.

But now something was happening . . . A car arriving, door slamming, and a man dressed casually – woollen V-neck and grey slacks – jogging up the road and in through the churchyard gates. Rebus recognised an unshaven and bleary-eyed Ranald Marr, guessed at once that Marr had slept in his Maserati, saw Steve Holly's face crease as he wondered what was going on. The procession had just reached the graveside when Marr caught it up. He walked straight to the front and stood in front of John and Jacqueline Balfour. Balfour released his grip on his wife, hugged Marr instead, the gesture returned. Templer and Pryde were looking to Colin Carswell, who made a motion with his hands, palms down. Easy, he was saying. We go easy.

Rebus didn't think any of the reporters had noticed Carswell; too busy trying to make sense of this curious interruption. And then he saw that Siobhan was staring into the grave, eyes flickering to the coffin and back, as if she could see something there. All at once, she turned her back on proceedings and started walking between the tombstones, as if searching for something she'd dropped.

'For I am the Resurrection and the Life,' the minister was saying. Marr was standing beside John Balfour now, eyes on the coffin and nothing else. Off to one side, Siobhan was still moving between the graves. Rebus didn't think any of the reporters could see her: the mourners formed a barrier between her and them. She crouched down in front of one stubby gravestone, seemed to be reading its inscription. Then she rose to her feet again and moved off, but more slowly now, without the same sense of urgency. When she turned, she saw that Rebus was watching her. She flashed him a quick smile, which for some reason he didn't find reassuring. Then she was on the move again, round to the rear of the mourning party, and out of his immediate sight.

Carswell was muttering something to Gill Templer: instructions on how to deal with Marr. Rebus knew they'd probably let him leave the churchyard, but insist on accompanying him immediately afterwards. Maybe they'd head to Junipers, do the questioning there; more likely, Marr wouldn't be seeing the marquee and the finger buffet. Instead, it would be an interview room at Gayfield and a mug of greyish tea.

'Ashes to ashes . . .'

Rebus couldn't help it; found the first few bars of the Bowie tune bouncing through his head.

A couple of the reporters were already preparing to head off, either back to the city or up the road to Junipers, where they could make a tally of the invited guests. Rebus slipped his hands into the pockets of the raincoat, started a slow patrol of the churchyard's perimeter. Earth was raining on to Philippa Balfour's coffin, the last rain the polished wood would ever feel. Her mother sent a cry up into the sky. It was carried by the breeze towards the surrounding hills.

Rebus found himself standing in front of a small headstone. Its owner had lived from 1876 to 1937. Not quite sixty-one when he died, missing the worst of Hitler, and maybe just too old to have fought in the First World War. He'd been a carpenter, probably serving the surrounding farms. For a second, Rebus remembered the coffin-maker. Then he went back to the name on the headstone – Francis Campbell Finlay – and had to suppress a smile. Siobhan had looked at the box in which lay the remains of Flip Balfour, and she'd thought: boxing. Then she'd looked at the grave itself and realised that it was a place where the sun didn't shine. Quizmaster's clue had been leading her right here, but it was only once she'd arrived that she'd been able to work it out. She'd gone looking for Frank Finlay, and found him. Rebus wondered what else she'd found when she crouched in front of the headstone. He glanced back to where the mourners were departing the churchyard, the chauffeurs stubbing out their cigarettes and preparing to open car doors. He couldn't see Siobhan, but Carswell himself had taken Ranald Marr to one side so they could have a discussion, Carswell doing the talking, Marr responding with resigned nods of the head. When Carswell put out his hand, Marr dropped his car keys into it.

Rebus was the last to leave. Some of the cars were making three-point turns. A tractor-trailer was waiting to get past. Rebus didn't recognise the driver. Siobhan was standing on the verge, leaning her arms on her car roof, in no hurry. Rebus crossed the road, nodded a greeting.

'Thought we might see you here,' was all she said. Rebus leaned one of his own arms on the roof. 'Get a bollocking, did you?'

'Like I told Gill, it's not against the law.'

'You saw Marr arriving?'

Rebus nodded. 'What's the story?'

'Carswell's driving him up to the house. Marr wants a couple of minutes with Balfour to explain things.'

'What things?'

'We're next in line.'

'Doesn't sound to me like he's about to confess to murder.'

'No,' she said.

'I was wondering . . .' Rebus let the utterance fade.

She tore her eyes away from the spectacle of Carswell attempting a three-pointer in the Maserati. 'Yes?'

'The latest clue: Stricture. Any more ideas?' Stricture, he was thinking, as in confinement. There was nothing in life quite as confining as a coffin . . .

She blinked a couple of times, then shook her head. 'What about you?'

'I did wonder if "boxing" might mean putting things in boxes.'

'Mmm.' She looked thoughtful. 'Maybe.'

'Want me to keep trying?'

'Can't do any harm.' The Maserati was roaring down the road, Carswell having applied just too much pressure to the accelerator.

'I suppose not.' Rebus turned to face her. 'You heading on to Junipers?'

She shook her head. 'Back to St Leonard's.'

'Things to do, eh?'

She took her arms off the car roof, slid her right hand into the pocket of her black Barbour jacket. 'Things to do,' she agreed.

Rebus noticed that she held the car keys in her left hand. He wondered what was in that right-hand pocket.

'Ca' canny then, eh?' he said.

'See you back at the ranch.'

'I'm still on the blacklist, remember?'

She took her hand out of her pocket, opened her driver's-side door. 'Right,' she said, getting in. He leaned down to peer through the window. She offered him a brief smile and nothing more. He took a step back as the car came to life, wheels sliding before finding tarmac.

She'd done just what he'd have done: kept to herself whatever it was she'd found. Rebus jogged to where his own car was parked and made set to follow.

Driving back through Falls, Rebus slowed a little outside Bev Dodds's cottage. He'd half expected to see her at the funeral. The interment had brought with it a number of sightseers, though police cars each end of the road had dissuaded the casual intruder. Parking space was at a premium in the village, too, though most Wednesdays he had the feeling there'd be room to spare. The potter's makeshift sign had been replaced with something more eye-catching and professionally made. Rebus pushed a little harder on the accelerator, keeping Siobhan's car in view. The coffins were still in the bottom drawer of his desk. He knew Dodds wanted the one from Falls back in her possession. Maybe he'd be charitable, pick it up this afternoon and drop it off Thursday or Friday. One more excuse to visit the ranch, where he could have another go at Siobhan – always supposing that was where she was headed . . .

He remembered there was a half-bottle of whisky under his driver's seat. He really did feel like a drink – it was what you did after funerals. The alcohol washed away death's inevitability. 'Tempting,' he said to himself, slotting home a cassette tape. Early Alex Harvey: 'The Faith Healer'. Problem was, early Alex Harvey wasn't too far removed from late Alex Harvey. He wondered how big a part alcohol had played in the Glasgow singer's demise. You started making a line of booze deaths, it would just refuse ever to come to an end . . .

'You think I killed her, don't you?'

Three of them in the interview room. An unnatural hush outside the door: whispers and tippy-toes and phones snatched up almost before they could ring. Gill Templer, Bill Pryde, and Ranald Marr.

'Let's not jump to conclusions, Mr Marr,' Gill said.

'Isn't that what you're doing?'

'Just a few follow-up questions, sir,' Bill Pryde said.

Marr snorted, not inclined to grace such a remark with anything more.

'How long did you know Philippa Balfour, Mr Marr?'

He looked to Gill Templer. 'Since she was born. I was her godfather.'

Gill made a note of this. 'And when did the two of you start feeling a physical attraction for one another?'

'Who says we did?'

'Why did you leave home like that, Mr Marr?'

'It's been a very stressful time. Look,' Marr shifted in his chair, 'should I have a lawyer present, do you think?'

'As you were informed earlier, that's entirely up to you.'

Marr thought about it, then shrugged. 'Proceed,' he said.

'Were you having a relationship with Philippa Balfour?'

'What sort of relationship?'

Bill Pryde's voice was a bear-growl. 'The sort her dad would string you up by the balls for.'

'I think I take your meaning.' Marr looked as though he was thinking through his answer. 'Here's what I will say: I've spoken to John Balfour and he has taken a responsible attitude to that conversation. The talk we had – whatever I said to him – has no bearing on this case. And that's pretty much it.' He sat back in his chair.

'Fucking your own goddaughter,' Bill Pryde said disgustedly.

'DI Pryde!' Gill Templer said by way of warning. Then, to Marr: 'I apologise for my colleague's outburst.'

'Apology accepted.'

'It's just that he has a bit more trouble hiding his revulsion and contempt than I do.'

Marr almost smiled.

'And as to whether something does or does not have "bearing" on a case is up to us to decide, wouldn't you say, sir?'

Colour rose to Marr's cheeks, but he wasn't going to take the bait. He shrugged merely, and folded his arms to let them know that, so far as he was concerned, the discussion was now at an end.

'A moment of your time, DI Pryde,' Gill said, angling her head towards the door. As they stepped out of the room, two uniforms stepped in to stand guard. Officers were already homing in, so Gill pushed Pryde through the door marked 'Ladies', and stood with her back against the door to deter the curious.

'Well?' she asked.

'Nice place,' Pryde said, looking around. He walked over to the washbasin and fished the waste-bin out from beneath, spitting his venerable collection of gum into it and pulling two fresh sticks from their packet.

'They've stitched something up between them' he said at last, admiring his features in the mirror.

'Yes,' Gill agreed. 'We should have brought him straight here.'

'Carswell's blooper,' Pryde said, 'yet again.'

Gill nodded. 'You think he confessed to Balfour?'

'I think he probably said something. He's had all night to come up with the right way of saying it: "John, it just happened . . . it was a long time ago and just the once . . . I'm so sorry." Spouses say it all the time.'

Gill almost smiled. Pryde spoke as if from experience.

'And Balfour didn't string him up by the balls?'

Pryde shook his head slowly. 'The more I hear about John Balfour, the less I like him. Bank's looking like going down the toilet, house filled with account-holders . . . his best friend walks up and says, in so many words, that he's been getting his end away with the daughter, and what does Balfour do? He does a deal.'

'The pair of them keeping quiet, keeping the lid on it?'

It was Pryde's turn to nod. 'Because the alternative is scandal, resignation, public fisticuffs and the collapse of all they hold dearest: namely, cold hard cash.'

'Then we'll be hard pushed to get anything out of him.'

Pryde looked at her. 'Unless we push him really hard.'

'I'm not sure Mr Carswell would like that.'

'With respect, DCS Templer, Mr Carswell couldn't find his own arse if it didn't come with a label marked "Insert tongue here".'

'That's not the sort of language I can countenance,' Gill said with something approaching a grin. There was pressure on the door from outside, and she yelled for whoever was there to stop it.

'I'm desperate!' a female voice called back.

'Me too,' Bill Pryde said with a wink, 'but maybe I should head for the more rudimentary shores of the Gents'.' As Gill nodded and began to open the door, he took a final, wistful look round. 'Though it'll be in my thoughts from now on, believe me. A man could get used to luxury like this . . .'

Back in the interview room, Ranald Marr had the look of someone who knew he'd soon be back behind the wheel of his Maserati. Gill, unable to bear such palpable smugness, decided to play her last card.

'Your affair with Philippa, it lasted quite a while, didn't it?'

'God, are we back to that again,' Marr said, rolling his eyes.

'Fairly common knowledge, too. Philippa told Claire Benzie all about it.'

'Is that what Claire Benzie says? I seem to have been here before. That little madam would say anything to hurt Balfour's.'

Gill was shaking her head. 'I don't think so, because knowing what she did, she could have used it at any time: one call to John Balfour, and she'd have blown the whole secret wide open. She didn't do that, Mr Marr. I can only assume it's because Claire has some principles.'

'Or she was biding her time.'

'Maybe so.'

'Is that what this boils down to: my word against hers?'

'There's the fact that you were keen to explain to Philippa how to erase e-mails.'

'Which I've also explained to your officers.'

'Yes, but now we know the real reason why you did it.'

Marr tried staring her out, but it wasn't going to work. He couldn't know that Gill had interviewed more than a dozen killers in the course of her CID career. She'd been stared at by eyes filled with fire, eyes turned insane. He dropped his gaze and his shoulders slumped.

'Look,' he said, 'there's one thing . . .'

'We're waiting, Mr Marr,' Bill Pryde said, sitting as straight in his chair as a kirk elder.

'I . . . didn't tell the whole truth about the game Flip was involved in.'

'You haven't told the whole truth about anything,' Pryde interrupted, but Gill quietened him with a look. Not that it mattered; Marr hadn't been listening.

'I didn't know it *was* a game,' he was saying, 'not back then. It was just a question . . . maybe a crossword clue, that's what I thought.'

'So she did bring one of the clues to you?'

Marr nodded. 'The mason's dream. She thought I might know what it meant.'

'And why would she think that?'

He managed the ghost of a smile. 'She was always overestimating me. She was . . . I don't think you've been getting anything like the whole picture of the kind of person Flip was. I know what you saw at first: spoilt little rich kid, spending her university days gazing at a few paintings, then graduating and marrying someone with even more money.' He was shaking his head. 'That wasn't Flip at all. Maybe it was one side to her, but she was complex, always capable of surprising you. Like with this puzzle thing, on the one hand I was dumbstruck when I heard about it, but on the other . . . in many ways it's *so* much like Flip. She would take these sudden interests, passions in things. For years, she'd been going to the zoo once a week on her own, just about *every* week, and I only found out by chance, a few months back. I was leaving a meeting at the Posthouse Hotel and she was coming out of the zoo, practically next door.' He looked up at them. 'Do you see?'

Gill wasn't at all sure that she did, but she nodded anyway. 'Go on,' she said. But it was as though her words had broken the spell. Marr paused for breath, then seemed to lose some of his animation.

'She was . . .' His mouth opened and closed, but soundlessly. Then he shook his head. 'I'm tired and I want to go home. I have some things I need to talk about with Dorothy.'

'Are you okay to drive?' Gill asked.

'Perfectly.' He took a deep breath. But when he looked at her again, tears were welling in his eyes. 'Oh, Christ,' he said, 'I've made such an utter balls-up, haven't I? And I'd do it again and again and again if it meant I had those same moments with her.'

'Rehearsing what you're going to say to the missus?' Pryde said coolly. Only then did Gill realise that she alone had been affected by Marr's story. As if to stress his point, Pryde blew out something approaching a bubble, which popped with an audible clack.

'My God,' Marr said, almost with a sense of awe, 'I hope and pray I never grow a skin as thick as yours.'

'You're the one shagging his pal's daughter all these years. Compared to me, Mr Marr, you're a fucking armadillo.'

This time, Gill had to draw her colleague from the interview room by his arm.

Rebus walked through St Leonard's like the spectre at the feast. The feeling was, between Marr and Claire Benzie, they'd get something. Surely to hell they'd get *something*.

'Not if you haven't worked for it,' Rebus muttered. Not that anyone was listening. He found the coffins in his drawer, along with some paperwork and a used coffee beaker someone too lazy to find a bin had placed there. Easing himself into the Farmer's chair, he drew the coffins out and laid them on his desk, pushing aside more paperwork to make room. He could feel a killer slipping through his fingers. Problem was, for Rebus to get a second chance would mean some new victim turning up, and he wasn't sure he wanted that. The evidence he'd taken home, the notes pinned to his wall – he couldn't fool himself, it didn't amount to evidence at all. It was a jumble of coincidence and speculation, a thin gossamer pattern created almost from air, the merest flutter of breath beginning to snap its tensed threads. For all he knew, Betty-Anne Jesperson had eloped with her secret lover, while Hazel Gibbs had staggered drunkenly on the bank of White Cart Water and slipped in, knocking herself unconscious. Maybe Paula Gearing had hidden her depression well, walking into the sea of her own volition. And the schoolgirl Caroline Farmer, could she have started a new life in some English city, far from small-town Scottish teenage blues?

So what if someone had left coffins nearby? He couldn't even be sure it was the same person each time; only had the carpenter's word for it. And with the autopsy evidence, there was no way to prove any crime had been committed at all . . . not until the Falls coffin. Another break in the pattern: Flip Balfour was the first victim who could definitely be said to have perished at the hands of an attacker.

He held his head in his hands, felt that if he took them away it might explode. Too many ghosts, too many ifs and buts. Too much pain and grieving, loss and guilt. It was the sort of thing he'd have taken to Conor Leary once upon a night. Now, he didn't think he had anyone to turn to . . .

But it was a male voice which answered Jean's extension. 'Sorry,' the man said, 'she's been keeping her head down lately.'

'You're busy over there then?'

'Not particularly. Jean's off on one of her little mystery trips.'

'Oh?'

The man laughed. 'I don't mean a bus tour or anything. She gets these projects going from time to time. They could set off a bomb in the building and Jean would be the last to know.'

Rebus smiled: the man could have been talking about *him*. But Jean hadn't mentioned that she was busy with anything outside her normal work. Not that it was any of his business . . .

'So what's she up to this time?' he asked.

'Mmm, let me see . . . Burke and Hare, Dr Knox and all that period.'

'The Resurrectionists?'

'Curious term that, don't you think? I mean, they didn't do much resurrecting, did they, not as any good Christian would understand it?'

'True enough.' The man was annoying Rebus; something about his manner, his tone of voice. It even annoyed him that the man was giving information away so easily. He hadn't even asked who Rebus was. If Steve Holly ever managed to contact this guy, he'd have everything he could possibly want on Jean, probably down to her home address and phone number.

'But she really seemed to be focusing on this doctor who carried out the post-mortem on Burke. What's his name again . . . ?'

Rebus remembered the portrait in Surgeons' Hall. 'Kennet Lovell?' he said.

'That's right.' The man seemed slightly put out that Rebus knew. 'Are you helping Jean? Want me to leave her a message.'

'You don't happen to know where she is?'

'She doesn't always confide in me.'

Just as well, Rebus felt like saying. Instead he told the man there was no message, and put down the phone. Devlin had told Jean about Kennet Lovell, expounding his theory that Lovell had left the coffins on Arthur's Seat. Obviously she was following this up. All the same, he wondered why she hadn't said anything . . .

He stared at the desk opposite, the one Wylie had been using. It was piled high with documents. Narrowing his eyes, he rose from his desk and walked over, started lifting piles of paper from the top.

Right at the bottom were the autopsy notes from Hazel Gibbs and Paula Gearing. He'd meant to send them back. In the back room of the Ox, Professor Devlin had specified that they should be returned. Quite right, too. They weren't doing anyone any good here, and might be lost forever or mis-filed if allowed to be smothered by the paperwork generated by Flip Balfour's murder.

Rebus placed them on his own desk, then cleared all the extraneous paperwork on to the desk one along. The coffins went back into his bottom drawer, all except the one from Falls, which he placed in a Haddow's carrier bag. Over at the photocopier, he lifted a sheet of A4 from the tray – it was the only place in the whole CID suite you could ever find spare paper. On it he wrote: COULD SOMEONE PLEASE SEND THESE ON AS SPECIFIED, PREFERABLY BY FRIDAY? CHEERS, J.R.

Looking around, it struck him that although he'd followed Siobhan's car into the car park, there was no sign of her now.

'Said she was headed down Gayfield Square,' a colleague explained.

'When?'

'Five minutes ago.'

While he'd been on the phone, listening to gossip.

'Thanks,' he said, sprinting out to his car.

There was no quick route to Gayfield Square, so Rebus took a few liberties with traffic lights and junctions. Parking, he couldn't see her car. But when he dashed indoors, she was standing right there, talking to Grant Hood, who was wearing what looked like another new suit and looking suspiciously tanned.

'Been out in the sun, Grant?' Rebus asked. 'Thought that office of yours at the Big House didn't have so much as a window?'

Self-consciously, Grant put a hand to his cheek. 'I might have caught a few rays.' He made a show of spotting someone across the room. 'Sorry, got to . . .' And he was off.

'Our Grant's beginning to worry me,' Rebus said.

'What do you reckon: fake tan or one of those sun bed studios?'

Rebus shook his head slowly, unable to decide. Glancing back, catching them watching him, Grant butted into another conversation, as if these were the people he'd wanted to speak to. Rebus eased himself up on to a desk.

'Anything happening?' he asked.

'Ranald Marr's already been released. All we got out of him was that Flip *did* ask him about that masonic clue.'

'And his excuse for lying to us . . .?'

She shrugged. 'I wasn't there, so I can't say.' She seemed jumpy.

'Why don't you sit down?' She shook her head. 'Things to do?' he guessed.

'That's right.'

'Such as?'

'What?'

He repeated the question. She fixed her eyes on him. 'Excuse me,' she said, 'but for an officer under suspension, aren't you spending an awful lot of time in the office?'

'Something I forgot, I came to retrieve it.' As the words came out, he realised he *had* forgotten something: the Falls coffin, still in its carrier bag at St Leonard's. 'Is there maybe anything *you've* forgotten, Siobhan?'

'Such as?'

'Forgetting to share your find with the rest of the team.'

'I don't think so.'

'You did find something then? At Francis Finlay's grave?'

'John . . .' Her eyes were avoiding his now. 'You're off the case.'

'Maybe so. You, on the other hand, are on the case but off your trolley.'

'You've no right to say that.' She still wasn't looking at him.

'I think I have.'

'Then prove it.'

'DI Rebus!' The voice of authority: Colin Carswell, standing twenty yards away in the doorway. 'If you'd be so kind as to spare me a moment . . .'

Rebus looked at Siobhan. 'To be continued,' he said. Then he got up and left the room. Carswell was waiting for him in Gill Templer's cramped office. Gill was there too, standing with arms folded. Carswell was already making himself comfortable behind the desk, eyes showing dismay at the amount of clutter accumulated since his last visit.

'So, DI Rebus, what can we do for you?' he asked.

'Just something I had to pick up.'

'Nothing contagious, I trust.' Carswell offered a thin smile.

'That's a good one, sir,' Rebus said coldly.

'John,' Gill interrupted, 'you're supposed to be at home.'

He nodded. 'It's hard though, with all these exciting developments.' His eyes stayed on Carswell. 'Like warning Marr he was about to be picked up, and now I hear he was allowed ten minutes with John Balfour before we interviewed him. Good calls, sir.'

'Sticks and stones, Rebus,' Carswell said.

'You name the time and place.'

'John . . .' Gill Templer again. 'I don't think this is going to get us anywhere, do you?'

'I want back on the case.'

Carswell just snorted. Rebus turned to Gill.

'Siobhan's playing a wild card. I think she's back in touch with Quizmaster, maybe for a meet.'

'How do you know?'

'Call it an educated guess.' He glanced towards Carswell. 'And before you make some gag about intelligence not being my strong point, let me agree with you. But on this, I think I'm right.'

'He's sent another clue?' Gill was hooked.

'At the churchyard this morning.'

She narrowed her eyes. 'One of the mourners?'

'It could have been left any time. Thing is, Siobhan's been wanting a meeting.'

'And?'

'And she's standing around in the Inquiry Room, just biding her time.'

Gill nodded slowly. 'If it was a new clue, she'd be busy trying to work it out . . .'

'Hang on, hang on,' Carswell broke in. 'How do we know any of this? You saw her pick up some clue?'

'The last one was leading us to a particular grave. She crouched in front of the headstone . . .'

'And?'

'And that's when I think she picked up the clue.'

'You didn't see her do it?'

'She crouched down . . .'

'But you didn't see her do it?'

Sensing another confrontation brewing, Gill stepped in. 'Why don't we just bring her in here and ask her?'

Rebus nodded. 'I'll fetch her.' He paused. 'With your permission, sir?'

Carswell sighed. 'Go on then.'

But out in the Inquiry Room, there was no sign of Siobhan. Rebus walked the corridors, asking for her. At the drinks machine, someone said she'd just gone past. Rebus quickened his pace, hauled open the doors to the outside world. No sign of her on the pavement; no sign of her car. He wondered if she'd parked further away, looked to left and right. Busy Leith Walk one way, and the narrow streets of the New Town's east end the other. If he headed into the New Town, her flat was five minutes away, but instead he went back indoors.

'She's gone,' he told Gill. Catching his breath, he noticed Carswell was missing. 'Where's the ACC?'

'Summoned to the Big House. I think the Chief Constable wanted a word.'

'Gill, we've got to find her. Get some bodies out there.' He nodded towards the Inquiry Room. 'It's not like they're setting the world on fire in here.'

'Okay, John, we'll find her, don't worry. Maybe Brains knows where she's gone.' She lifted the receiver. 'We'll start with him . . .'

But Eric Bain seemed as elusive as Siobhan. He was known to be somewhere in the Big House, but nobody knew exactly where. Meantime, Rebus tried Siobhan's home number and mobile. He got her answering machine at the former, a recorded message at the latter, telling him the phone was in use. When he tried five minutes later, it was still in use. By that time, he was using his own mobile, walking downhill to Siobhan's street. He tried her buzzer, with no response. Crossed the road and stared at her window for so long that passers-by started looking up too, wondering what he could see that they couldn't. Her car wasn't parked kerbside, nor was it in any of the surrounding streets.

Gill had already left a message with Siobhan's pager, asking for an urgent call-back, but Rebus had wanted more, and eventually she'd agreed: patrols would be on the lookout for her car.

But now, standing outside her flat, it struck Rebus that she could be *anywhere*, not just inside the city boundary. Quizmaster had taken her to Hart Fell and Rosslyn Chapel. No telling where he'd choose for a rendezvous. The more isolated it was, the more danger Siobhan was in. He felt like punching himself in the face: he should have dragged her into that meeting with him, not given her the chance to do a runner . . . He tried her mobile again: still engaged. Nobody made a call that long on their mobile, way too expensive. Then, suddenly, he knew what it was: her mobile was hooked to Grant Hood's laptop. Even now, she could be telling Quizmaster she was on her way . . .

Siobhan had parked her car. Two hours yet till the time Quizmaster had suggested. She reckoned she could lie low till then. The pager message from Gill Templer had told her two things: one was that Rebus had told Gill everything; two, that if she ignored Gill's order, she'd have some explaining to do.

Explaining? She was having trouble doing that even to herself. All she knew was that the game – and she knew it wasn't *just* a game; was something potentially much more dangerous – but all the same it had gotten to her. Quizmaster, whoever he or she turned out to be, had gotten to her, to the extent that she could think of little else. The daily clues and puzzles, she missed them, would gladly take on more of them. But more than that, she wanted to *know*, know everything there was to know about Quizmaster and the game. Stricture had impressed her, because Quizmaster had to have suspected that she would be present at the funeral, and that the clue would only start making sense to her at Flip's graveside. Stricture indeed . . . but she felt the word applied to her, too, because she felt bound by the game, tied to it and to identifying its creator. And at the same time she felt almost smothered by it. Was Quizmaster present at the funeral? Had he – or *she* (remembering Bain's advice to keep an open mind) – seen Siobhan pick up the note? Maybe . . . The thought made her shiver. But then, the funeral had been announced in the media. Maybe Quizmaster had found out that way. It was the nearest cemetery to Flip's home; a good chance she'd be interred there . . .

None of which explained why she was doing what she was doing, going out on her own fragile limb like this. It was the sort of stupid thing she regularly chastised Rebus for. Maybe Grant had decided it for her, Grant who had shown himself a 'company player', with his suits and his tan, looking good on TV – good PR for the force.

One game she knew she didn't want to play.

Many times she'd crossed the line, but always crossing back again. She'd break a rule or two, but nothing important, nothing career-threatening, and then hop back into the fold. She wasn't a born outsider in the way she sensed John Rebus was, but she'd learned that she liked it on his side of the fence, liked it better than becoming a Grant or a Derek Linford . . . people who played their own games, doing anything it took to keep in with the men who mattered, men like Colin Carswell.

At one time, she'd thought maybe she could learn from Gill Templer, but Gill had become just like the others. She had her own interests to protect, whatever that took. In order to rise, she'd had to take on the worst attributes of someone like Carswell, while wrapping her own feelings inside some sort of reinforced box.

If rising through the ranks meant losing a part of herself, Siobhan didn't want it. She'd known as much back at the dinner in Hadrian's, when Gill had hinted at things to come.

Maybe that was what she was doing out here, out on her limb – proving something to herself. Maybe it wasn't really about the game and Quizmaster so much as it was about *her*.

She moved in her seat so she was facing the laptop. The line was already open, had been since she'd got into the car. No new messages, so she typed in one of her own.

Meeting accepted. See you there. Siobhan.

And clicked on 'send'.

After which, she shut down the computer, disconnected the phone and powered it down – battery needed a boost anyway. She placed both beneath the passenger seat, making sure they weren't visible to pedestrians: didn't want someone breaking in. When she got out of the car, she made sure all the doors were locked, and that the little red alarm button was flashing.

Just under two hours to go now; a little time to kill . . .

Jean Burchill had tried calling Professor Devlin, but no one ever answered. So finally she wrote him a note, asking him to contact her, and decided to deliver it by hand. In the back of the taxi, she wondered what the sense of urgency was, and realised it was because she wanted to be rid of Kennet Lovell. He was taking up too much of her waking time, and last night he'd even infected her dreams, slicing the meat from cadavers only to reveal planed wood beneath, while her colleagues from work watched and applauded, the performance turning into a stage show.

If her research into Lovell was to progress, she needed some kind of proof of his interest in woodwork. Without that, she was at a dead end. Having paid the driver, she stood in front of the Professor's tenement, note in hand. But there was no letter-box. Each flat would have its own, the postman gaining entry by pressing the buzzers until someone let him in. She supposed she could slip the note under the door, but reckoned it would lie there ignored, along with all the junk mail. So instead, she looked at the array of buzzers. Professor Devlin's just said 'D. Devlin'. She wondered if he might be back from his wanderings, and pressed the buzzer. When there was no answer, she looked at the remaining buttons, wondering which one to pick. Then the intercom crackled.

'Hello?'

'Dr Devlin? It's Jean Burchill from the Museum. I wonder if I can have a word . . .'

'Miss Burchill? This is somewhat of a surprise.'

'I've tried phoning . . .'

But the door was already signalling that it was no longer locked.

Devlin was waiting for her on his landing. He wore a white shirt, the sleeves rolled up, with thick braces holding up his trousers.

'Well, well,' he said, taking her hand.

'I'm sorry to bother you like this.'

'Not at all, young lady. Now just you come in. I'm afraid you'll find my housekeeping somewhat lacking . . .' He led her into the living room, cluttered with boxes and books.

'Separating the wheat from the chaff,' he informed her.

She picked up a case and opened it. It contained old surgical instruments. 'You're not throwing it out? Perhaps the Museum would be interested . . .'

He nodded. 'I'm in contact with the bursar at Surgeons' Hall. He thinks perhaps the exhibition there might have room for one or two pieces.'

'Major Cawdor?'

Devlin's eyebrows lifted. 'You know him?'

'I was asking him about the portrait of Kennet Lovell.'

'So you're taking my theory seriously?'

'I thought it was worth pursuing.'

'Excellent.' Devlin clapped his hands together. 'And what have you found?'

'Not a great deal. That's really why I'm here. I can't find any reference in the literature to Lovell having an interest in carpentry.'

'Oh, it's a matter of record, I assure you, though it's many years since I came across it.'

'Came across it where?'

'Some monograph or dissertation . . . I really can't recall. Could it have been a university thesis?'

Jean nodded slowly. If it had been a thesis, only the university itself would hold a copy; there'd be no record in any other library. 'I should have thought of that,' she admitted.

'But don't you agree he was a remarkable character?' Devlin asked.

'He certainly lived a very full life . . . unlike his wives.'

'You've been to his graveside?' He smiled at the idiocy of the question. 'Of course you have. And you took note of his marriages. What did you think?'

'At first, nothing . . . but then later, when I thought about it . . .'

'You began to speculate as to whether or not they had been assisted on their final journey?' He smiled again. 'It's obvious, really, isn't it?'

Jean became aware of a smell in the room: stale sweat. Perspiration was shining on Devlin's forehead, and the lenses of his spectacles looked smeared. She was amazed he could see her through them.

'Who better,' he was saying, 'than an anatomist to get away with murder?'

'You're saying he murdered them?'

He shook his head. 'Impossible to tell after all this time. I'm merely speculating.'

'But why would he do that?'

Devlin shrugged, his shoulders stretching the braces. 'Because he could? What do you think?'

'I've been wondering . . . he was very young when he assisted at Burke's autopsy; young and impressionable maybe. That might explain why he fled to Africa . . .'

'And God alone knows what horrors he encountered out there,' Devlin added.

'It would help if we had his correspondence.'

'Ah, the letters between himself and the Reverend Kirkpatrick?'

'You don't happen to know where they might be?'

'Consigned to oblivion, I'd wager. Tossed on to the pyre by some descendant of the good minister . . .'

'And here you are doing the same thing.'

Devlin looked around him at the mess. 'Indeed,' he said. 'Selecting that by which history shall judge my small endeavours.'

Jean picked up a photograph. It showed a middle-aged woman, dressed for some formal function.

'Your wife?' she guessed.

'My dear Anne. She passed away in the summer of nineteen seventy-two. Natural causes, I assure you.'

Jean looked at him. 'Why should you have to assure me?'

Devlin's smile faded. 'She meant the world to me . . . *more* than the world . . .' He clapped his hands together again. 'What can I be thinking of, not offering you something to drink. Tea perhaps?'

'Tea would be wonderful.'

'I can't promise any sense of wonder from PG tea-bags.' His smile was fixed.

'And afterwards, maybe I could see Kennet Lovell's table.'

'But of course. It's in the dining room. Bought from a reputable dealer, though I admit they couldn't be categorical about its provenance – *caveat emptor*, as they say, but they were fairly persuasive, and I was willing to believe.' He had taken his glasses off to give them a polish with his handkerchief. When he slipped them on again, his eyes seemed magnified. 'Tea,' he repeated, making for the hallway. She followed him out.

'Have you lived here long?' she asked.

'Ever since Anne passed on. The house held too many memories.'

'That's thirty years then?'

'Almost.' He was in the kitchen now. 'Won't be a minute,' he said.

'Fine.' She started to retrace her steps back to the living room. The summer of '72, his wife had died . . . She passed an open doorway: the dining room. The table filled almost the whole space. A completed jigsaw lay on top of it . . . no, not quite complete: missing just the one piece. Edinburgh, an aerial photograph. The table itself was a plain enough design. She walked into the room, studied the table's surface of polished wood. The legs were sturdy, lacking any ornamental flourishes. Utilitarian, she thought. The incomplete jigsaw must have taken hours . . . days. She crouched down, seeking the missing piece. There it was: almost completely hidden beneath one of the legs. As she reached for it, she saw that the table boasted one nice, secretive touch. Where the two leaves met in the middle, there was a central element, and into this a small cupboard had been inserted. She'd seen similar designs before, but not from as far back as the nineteenth century. She wondered if Professor Devlin had been duped into buying something from much later than Lovell's period . . . She squeezed into the narrow confines so that she could open the cupboard. It was stiff, and she almost gave up, but then it clicked open, revealing its contents.

A plane, set-square and chisels.

A small saw and some nails.

Woodwork tools.

When she looked up, Professor Devlin was filling the doorway.

'Ah, the missing piece,' was all that he said . . .

Ellen Wylie had heard reports of the funeral, how Ranald Marr had suddenly turned up and been embraced by John Balfour. The talk at West End was that Marr had been brought in for questioning but then released.

'Stitch-up,' Shug Davidson had commented. 'Somebody somewhere's pulling strings.'

He hadn't looked at her as he'd said it, but then he hadn't needed to. He knew . . . and she knew. *Pulling strings*: wasn't that what she'd thought she was doing when she met with Steve Holly? But somehow *he'd* become the puppeteer, making her the marionette. Carswell's speech to the troops had cut into her like a knife, not just nicking the skin but radiating pain through her whole body. When they'd all been called into the office, she'd half hoped her silence would give her away. But then Rebus had stepped in, taken the whole thing upon himself, leaving her feeling worse than ever.

Shug Davidson knew it . . . and though Shug was a colleague and mate, he was also a friend of Rebus's. The pair of them went way back. Now, every time he made some remark she found herself analysing it, seeking the sub-text. She couldn't concentrate, and her home station, which she'd seen so recently as a refuge, had become inhospitable and alien.

Which was why she'd made the trip to St Leonard's, only to find the CID suite all but deserted. A suit-carrier, hanging from one of the coat pegs, told her that at least one officer had been at the funeral, returning here to change back into work clothes. She guessed Rebus, but couldn't be certain. There was a plastic bag beside his desk, one of the coffins inside. All that work, and no case to show for it. The autopsy notes were sitting on the desk, waiting for someone to follow the instructions left on them. She lifted the note from the top, sat down in Rebus's chair. Without really meaning to, she found herself untying the ribbon which held the notes together. Then she opened the first file and started to read.

She'd done this before, of course; or rather, Professor Devlin had, while she'd sat by his side taking note of his findings. Slow work, yet she realised now that she'd enjoyed it – the notion that there might be some case hidden in the midst of those typewritten pages; the sense of working on the edge of things, a not-quite-investigation; and Rebus himself, as driven as the rest of them put together, biting down on a pen as he concentrated, or furrowing his brow, or stretching suddenly, unlocking his neck. He had this reputation as a loner, yet he'd been happy to delegate, happy to share the work with her. She'd accused him of pitying her, but she didn't really believe that. He did have a martyr complex, but it seemed to work for him . . . and for everyone else.

Skimming the pages now, she realised finally why she'd come: she wanted to apologise in some way he'd understand . . . And then she looked up and he was standing not four yards away, watching her.

'How long have you been there?' she asked, dropping a couple of the pages.

'What are you up to?'

'Nothing.' She picked up the sheets. 'I was just . . . I don't know, maybe one final look before it all went back into the storeroom. How was the funeral?'

'A funeral's a funeral, no matter who they're burying.'

'I heard about Marr.'

He nodded, walked into the room.

'What's wrong?' she asked.

'I was hoping Siobhan might be here.' He walked over to her desk, hoping for some clue . . . something, *anything*.

'I wanted to see you,' Ellen Wylie said.

'Oh?' He turned away from Siobhan's desk. 'Why's that then?'

'Maybe to thank you.'

Their eyes met, communicating without words.

'Don't worry about it, Ellen,' Rebus said at last. 'I mean it.'

'But I got you into trouble.'

'No, you didn't. I got myself into trouble, and maybe made things worse for you too. If I'd stayed quiet, I think you'd have spoken up.'

'Maybe,' she admitted. 'But I could have spoken up anyway.'

'I didn't make it any easier, for which I apologise.'

She had to stifle a smile. 'There you go again, turning the tables. It's *me* who's supposed to be saying sorry.'

'You're right; I can't help it.' There was nothing on or in Siobhan's desk.

'So what do I do now?' she asked. 'Talk it through with DCS Templer?'

He nodded. 'If that's what you want. Of course, you could just keep quiet about it.'

'And let you take the flak?'

'Who says I don't like it?' The phone rang and he snatched at it. 'Hello?' Suddenly his face relaxed. 'No, he's not here right now. Can I take a . . . ?' He put the receiver down. 'Someone for Silvers; no message.'

'You're expecting a call?'

He rubbed a hand against the grain of the day's stubble. 'Siobhan's gone walkabout.'

'In what sense?'

So he told her. Just as he was finishing, a phone on one of the other desks started ringing. He got up and answered it. Another message. He got a pen and a scrap of paper and started writing it down.

'Yes . . . yes,' he was saying, 'I'll stick it on his desk. No promises when he'll see it though.' While he'd been on the phone, Ellen Wylie had been flicking through the autopsy stuff again. As he put the receiver down, he saw her lower her face towards one of the files, as though trying to read something.

'Old Hi-Ho's popular today,' he said, placing the telephone message on Silvers's desk. 'What's the matter?'

She pointed to the bottom of the page. 'Can you read this signature?'

'Which one?' There were two, at the foot of an autopsy report. Date to the side of the signatures: Monday 26 April, 1982 – Hazel Gibbs, the Glasgow 'victim'. She'd died on the Friday night . . .

Typed beneath the signature were the words 'Deputising Pathologist'. The other signature – marked 'Chief Pathologist, City of Glasgow' – wasn't much clearer.

'I'm not sure,' Rebus said, examining the squiggle. 'The names should be typed on the cover-sheet.'

'That's just it,' Wylie said. 'No cover-sheet.' She turned back a few pages to confirm this. Rebus came around the desk so he was standing next to her, then bent down a little closer.

'Maybe the pages got out of order,' he suggested.

'Maybe.' She started going through them. 'But I don't think so.'

'Was it missing when the files arrived?'

'I don't know. Professor Devlin didn't say anything.'

'I think the Chief Pathologist for Glasgow back then was Ewan Stewart.'

Wylie flicked back to the signatures. 'Yep,' she said, 'I'll go with that. But it's the other one that interests me.'

'Why?'

'Well, maybe it's just me, sir, but if you sort of screw your eyes shut a little and take another look, isn't it just possible it says Donald Devlin?'

'What?' Rebus looked, blinked, looked again. 'Devlin was in Edinburgh back then.' But his voice dropped off. The word *Deputising* floated into view. 'Did you look through the report before?'

'That was Devlin's job. I was more like a secretary, remember?'

Rebus put his hand to the back of his neck, rubbed at the knot of muscle there. 'I don't get it,' he said. 'Why wouldn't Devlin say . . . ?' He grabbed the phone, hit 9 and punched a local number. 'Professor Gates, please. It's an emergency. Detective Inspector Rebus here.' A pause as the secretary put him through. 'Sandy? Yes, I know I *always* say it's an emergency, but this time I might not be stretching the truth. April nineteen eighty-two, we think we've got Donald Devlin assisting an autopsy in Glasgow. Is that possible?' He listened again. 'No, Sandy, eighty-two. Yes, April.' He nodded, making eye contact with Wylie, started relaying what he was hearing. 'Glasgow crisis . . . shortage of staff . . . gave you your first chance at being in charge here. Mm-hm, Sandy . . . is that your way of saying Devlin was in Glasgow in April nineteen eighty-two? Thanks, I'll talk to you later.' He slammed the phone down. 'Donald Devlin was *there*.'

'I don't understand,' Wylie said. 'Why didn't he say something?'

Rebus was flicking through the other report, the one from Nairn. No, neither pathologist was Donald Devlin on that occasion. All the same . . .

'He didn't want us to know,' he said at last, answering Wylie's question. 'Maybe that's why he removed the cover-sheet.'

'But *why*?'

Rebus was thinking . . . the way Devlin had returned to the back room of the Ox, anxious to see the autopsies consigned once more to history . . . the Glasgow coffin, made of balsa wood, cruder than the others, the sort of thing you might make if you didn't have access to your usual supplier, or your usual tools . . . Devlin's interest in Dr Kennet Lovell and the Arthur's Seat coffins . . .

Jean!

'I'm getting a bad feeling,' Ellen Wylie said.

'I've always been one for trusting a woman's instincts . . .' But that was just what he *hadn't* done: all those times women had reacted badly to Devlin . . . 'Your car or mine?' he said.

Jean was rising to her feet. Donald Devlin still filled the doorway, his blue eyes as cold as the North Sea, pupils reduced to black pinpoints.

'Your tools, Professor Devlin?' she guessed.

'Well, they're not Kennet Lovell's, dear lady, are they?'

Jean swallowed. 'I think I'd better be going.'

'I don't think I can let you do that.'

'Why not?'

'Because I think you know.'

'Know what?' She was looking around her, seeing nothing helpful . . .

'You know that *I* left those coffins,' the old man stated. 'I can see it in your eyes. No use pretending.'

'The first one was just after your wife died, wasn't it? You killed that poor girl in Dunfermline.'

He raised a finger. 'Untrue: I merely read about her disappearance and went there to leave a marker, a *memento mori*. There were others after that . . . God knows what happened to them.' She watched him take a step forward into the room. 'It took some time, you see, for my sense of loss to turn into something else.' The smile trembled on his lips, which glistened with moisture. 'Anne's life was just . . . *taken* . . . after whole months of agony. That seemed so unfair: no motive, no one to be found guilty . . . All those bodies I'd worked on . . . all the ones after Anne died . . . eventually I wanted some suffering to go with them.' His own hands stroked the table's edge. 'I should never have let slip about Kennet Lovell . . . a good historicist would naturally be unable to resist looking into my claim further, finding disturbing parallels between past and present, eh, Miss Burchill? And it was *you* . . . the only one who made the connection . . . all those coffins over all that time . . .'

Jean had been working hard at controlling her breathing. Now she felt strong enough not to hang on to the table. She released her grip on its edge. 'I don't understand,' she said. 'You were helping the inquiry . . .'

'Hindering, rather. And who could resist the opportunity? After all, I was investigating *myself*, watching others do the same . . .'

'You killed Philippa Balfour?'

Devlin's face creased in disgust. 'Not a bit of it.'

'But you left the coffin . . . ?'

'Of course I didn't!' he snapped.

'Then it's been five years since you last . . .' She sought the right words. 'Last *did* anything.'

He'd taken another step towards her. She thought she could hear music, and realised suddenly that it was *him*. He was humming some tune.

'You recognise it?' he asked. The corners of his mouth were flecked white. '"Swing Low, Sweet Chariot". The organist played it at Anne's funeral.' He bowed his head a little and smiled. 'Tell me, Miss Burchill: what do you do when the chariot won't swing low enough?'

She ducked, reached into the cupboard for one of the chisels. Suddenly he had hold of her hair, pulling her back up. She screamed, hands still scrabbling for a weapon. She felt a cool wooden handle. Her head felt like it was on fire. As she lost her balance and started to fall, she stabbed the chisel into his ankle. He didn't so much as flinch. She stabbed again, but now he was dragging her towards the door. She half rose to her feet and added her momentum to his, the pair of them colliding with the edge of the door, spinning out of the room and into the hall. The chisel had fallen from her grasp. She was on her hands and knees when the first blow came, spinning white lights across her vision. The whorls in the carpet seemed to form a pattern of question marks.

How ridiculous, she thought, that this was happening to her . . . She knew she had to get back on to her feet, start fighting back. He was an old man . . . Another blow made her flinch. She could see the chisel . . . only twelve feet to the front door . . . Devlin had her by the legs now, hauling her towards the living room . . . His grasp of her ankles was like a vice. Oh, Christ, she thought. Oh, Christ, oh, Christ . . . Her hands flailed, seeking purchase, or any instrument she could use . . . She screamed again. The blood was roaring in her ears; she couldn't be sure she was making any noise at all. One of Devlin's braces had come free, and his shirt-tail was hanging out.

Not like this . . . not like this . . .

John would never forgive her . . .

The area around Canonmills and Inverleith was an easy enough beat: no housing schemes, plenty of discreet wealth. The patrol car always made a point of stopping at the gates to the Botanics, just across from Inverleith Park. Arboretum Place was a double-width road which saw little traffic: perfect for the officers' mid-shift break. PC Anthony Thompson always provided the flask of tea, while his partner, Kenny Milland, brought the chocolate biscuits – either Jacob's Orange Club or, as today, Tunnock's Caramel Wafers.

'Magic,' Thompson said, though his teeth told him otherwise: there was a dull ache from one of his molars whenever it came into contact with sugar. Having not been near a dentist since the 1994 World Cup, Thompson wasn't enthusiastic about any future encounter.

Milland took sugar in his tea; Thompson didn't. That was why Milland always brought a couple of little sachets and a spoon with him. The sachets came from a burger chain where Milland's elder son worked. Not much of a job, but it had its perks, and there was talk of a significant step-up for Jason.

Thompson loved American cop films, everything from *Dirty Harry* to *Seven*, and when they stopped for their break he sometimes imagined that they were parked outside a doughnut stand, in baking heat and searing glare, with the radio about to burst into life. They'd have to leave their coffee and burn some rubber, giving chase to bank robbers or gangland killers . . .

Not much chance of either in Edinburgh. A couple of pub shootings, some pre-teen car-jackers (one of them a friend's son), and a body in a skip, these comprised the highlights of Thompson's two decades on the force. So when the radio did burst into life, detailing a car and driver, Anthony Thompson did a double-take.

'Here, Kenny, doesn't that one fit the bill?'

Milland turned and looked out of his window at the car parked next door. 'I don't know,' he admitted. 'Wasn't really listening, Tony.' He took another bite of biscuit. Thompson, however, was on the blower, asking for a repeat of the licence plate. He then opened his door and walked around the patrol car, staring down at the front of the neighbouring vehicle.

'We're only parked bloody next to it,' he told his partner. Then he got on the blower again.

The message was relayed to Gill Templer, who sent half a dozen officers from the Balfour team out to the area, then spoke to PC Thompson.

'What do you reckon, Thompson: is she in the Botanic Gardens or Inverleith Park?'

'It's for a meeting, you say?'

'We think so.'

'Well, the park's just this big flat space, easy to spot someone. The Botanics has its nooks and crannies, places you could sit down for a chat.'

'You're saying the Botanics?'

'But it'll be closing soon . . . so maybe not.'

Gill Templer expelled breath. 'You're being a big help.'

'The Botanics is a big place, ma'am. Why not send the officers in there, get some of the staff to help? Meantime my partner and me can take the park.'

Gill considered the offer. She didn't want Quizmaster scared off . . . or Siobhan Clarke for that matter. She wanted both of them back at Gayfield Square. The officers who were already on their way would pass for civvies from a distance; uniforms would not.

'No,' she said, 'that's okay. We'll start with the Botanics. You stay put, in case she comes back to her car . . .'

Back in the patrol car, Milland gave a resigned shrug. 'You can't say you didn't try, Tony.' He finished his biscuit and screwed up the wrapper.

Thompson didn't say anything. His moment had come and gone.

'That mean we're stuck here?' his partner asked. Then he held his cup out. 'Any more tea in that flask . . . ?'

They didn't call it tea in the Du Thé café. It was a 'herbal infusion': blackcurrant and ginseng to be precise. Siobhan thought it tasted all right, though she was tempted to add a spot of milk to cut the sharpness. Herbal tea and a finger of carrot cake. She'd bought an early edition of the evening paper from the newsagent's next door. There was a photo of Flip's coffin on page three, held aloft by the pall-bearers as they left the church. Smaller photos of the parents and a couple of celebs whose presence Siobhan had failed to notice at the time.

All of this after her walk through the Botanics. She hadn't meant to walk the entire length, but somehow had found herself at the eastern gate, next to Inverleith Row. Shops and cafés just along to the right, by Canonmills. Still time to spare . . . She'd thought of fetching her car, but had decided to leave it where it was. She didn't know what parking was like where she was headed. Then she remembered that her phone was tucked under the passenger seat. But by then it was too late: if she walked back through the Botanics, then either drove or walked back here, she'd have missed the meeting time. And she couldn't be sure how patient Quizmaster would be.

Her decision made, she left the paper on her table at the café and headed back towards the Botanics, but passing the entrance, staying on Inverleith Row. Just before the rugby ground at Goldenacre she took a right, the path turning into more of a track. Dusk was fast arriving as she turned a corner and approached the gates of Warriston Cemetery.

No one was answering Donald Devlin's buzzer, so Rebus hit all the others at random until someone responded. Rebus identified himself, and was buzzed into the tenement, Ellen Wylie right behind him. She actually passed him on the stairs and was first at Devlin's door, thumping it, kicking, pressing his bell, and rattling the letter-box.

'Not promising,' she admitted.

Rebus, who had caught his breath, crouched in front of the letter-box and pushed it open. 'Professor Devlin?' he called. 'It's John Rebus. I need to talk to you.' On the downstairs landing, one of the doors opened and a face peered up.

'It's okay,' Wylie assured the nervous neighbour. 'We're police officers.'

'Ssh!' Rebus hissed. He put his ear to the open letter-box.

'What is it?' Wylie whispered.

'I can hear something . . .' It sounded like the low mewling of a cat. 'Devlin didn't have any pets, did he?'

'Not that I know of.'

Rebus put his eyes to the letter-box again. The hallway was deserted. The door to the living room was at the far end, open a few inches. The curtains looked to be closed, so that he couldn't see into the room. Then his eyes widened.

'Holy Christ,' he said, getting to his feet. He stood back and launched a kick at the door, then another. The wood complained, but didn't give. He slammed his shoulder into it. No effect.

'What?' Wylie said.

'There's someone in there.'

He was about to take another run at the door when Wylie stopped him. 'Together,' she said. So that was what they did. Counted to three and hit the door at the same time. The jamb made a cracking sound. Their second assault split it, and the door opened inwards, Wylie falling through it so that she landed on all fours. When she looked up, she saw what Rebus had seen. Almost at floor level, a hand had attached itself to the living-room door and was trying to open it.

Rebus ran forward, pushed through the gap into the living room. It was Jean, bruised and beaten, her face a smear of blood and mucus, hair matted with sweat and more blood. One eye had swollen and was completely closed. Flecks of pink saliva flew from her mouth as she breathed.

'Jesus Christ,' Rebus said, dropping to his knees in front of her, eyes running over the visible damage. He didn't want to touch her, thought there might be bones broken. He didn't want her to hurt more than she already did.

Wylie was in the room now, too, surveying the scene. It looked like half the contents of the flat lay strewn across the floor, a bloody trail showing where Jean Burchill had crawled her way to the door.

'Get an ambulance,' Rebus said, voice trembling. Then: 'Jean, what did he do to you?' And watched her one good eye fill with tears.

Wylie made the call. Halfway through, she thought she heard a noise out in the hall: the nervous neighbour grown nosy perhaps. She stuck her head out, but couldn't see anything. She gave the address and stressed again that it was an emergency, then cut the call. Rebus's ear was close to Jean's face. Wylie realised she was trying to say something. Her lips were swollen, and teeth looked to have been dislodged.

Rebus looked up at Wylie, eyes widening. 'She says, did we catch him?'

Wylie caught the meaning at once, ran to the window and pulled the curtains back. Donald Devlin was scurrying across the road, dragging one leg and holding his bleeding left hand out in front of him.

'Bastard!' Wylie yelled, making for the door.

'No!' Rebus's voice was a roar. He got to his feet. 'He's mine.'

As he bounded downstairs two at a time, he realised Devlin must have been hiding in one of the other rooms. Waited till they were busy in the living room and then slipped out. They'd interrupted him. He tried not to think of what Jean's fate would have been if they hadn't . . .

By the time he reached the pavement, Devlin had disappeared from view, but the splashes of bright blood were as clear a trail as Rebus could wish for. He caught sight of him crossing Howe Street, making for St Stephen Street. Rebus was gaining, until the uneven pavement caught him, sending him over on one ankle. Devlin might be in his seventies, but that didn't mean much: he'd have the strength and determination of the possessed. Rebus had seen it before during a chase. Desperation and adrenaline made for a fearful mix . . .

Still the drops of blood showed the way. Rebus had slowed, trying to keep the weight off his twisted ankle, pictures of Jean's face filling his mind. He punched numbers into his mobile, got the sequence wrong the first time and had to start again. When the call was answered, he yelled for assistance.

'I'm keeping the line open,' he said. That way, he could let them know if Devlin suddenly flagged a taxi or boarded a bus.

He could see Devlin again now, but then he turned the corner into Kerr Street. By the time Rebus got to the corner, he'd lost him again. Deanhaugh Street and Raeburn Place were straight ahead, busy with pedestrians and traffic: the evening trawl home. With so many people around, the trail was harder to follow. Rebus crossed the road at the traffic lights and found himself on the road-bridge which crossed the Water of Leith . . . There were several routes Devlin could have taken, and the trail seemed to have stopped. Had he crossed towards Saunders Street, or maybe doubled back along Hamilton Place? Resting one arm on the parapet, taking the weight off his ankle, Rebus happened to look down at the river flowing sluggishly below.

And saw Devlin on the footpath, heading down-river towards Leith.

Rebus lifted the phone and called in his position. As he was doing so, Devlin looked back and saw him. The old man's pace quickened, but then suddenly slowed. He came to a stop, the other people on the path making a detour round him. One seemed solicitous, but Devlin shook away the offer of help. He turned back and stared at Rebus, who was walking to the end of the bridge, taking the steps down. Devlin hadn't moved. Rebus called in his position again, then put the phone in his pocket, wanting both hands free.

As he walked towards Devlin, he saw the scratches on his face, and realised that Jean had been giving almost as good as she got. Devlin was studying his bloodied hand as Rebus stopped six feet away.

'The human bite can be quite poisonous, you know,' Devlin told him. 'But at least with Miss Burchill I'm sure I needn't be concerned about hepatitis and HIV.' He looked up. 'Something struck me, seeing you on that bridge. I suddenly thought: they don't have anything.'

'What do you mean?'

'Any evidence.'

'Well, we can always make a start with attempted murder.' Rebus slipped a hand into his pocket, brought out the phone.

'Who are you going to call?' Devlin asked.

'Don't you want an ambulance?' Rebus held the phone up, took a step forwards.

'Just a couple of stitches,' Devlin commented, examining the wound again. Sweat dripped from his hair and the sides of his face. He was breathing hard, wheezily.

'You don't make the grade as a serial killer any more, do you, Professor?'

'It's been some time,' he agreed.

'Was Betty-Anne Jesperson the last?'

'I'd nothing to do with young Philippa, if that's what you're asking.'

'Someone stealing your idea?'

'Well, it wasn't exactly mine in the first place.'

'Are there any others?'

'Others?'

'Victims we don't know about.'

Devlin's smile broke open some of the cuts on his face. 'Isn't four enough?'

'You tell me.'

'It seemed . . . satisfactory. No pattern, you see. Two bodies not even found.'

'Just the coffins.'

'Which might never have been connected . . .'

Rebus nodded slowly, didn't say anything.

'Was it the autopsy?' Devlin asked at last. Rebus nodded again. 'I knew it was a risk.'

'If you'd told us at the start you'd carried out the Glasgow post-mortem, we wouldn't have thought anything of it.'

'But back then, I couldn't know what else you might find. Other connections, I mean. And by the time I saw you weren't going to come up with anything, it was too late. I could hardly say "Oh, incidentally, I was one of the pathologists", not after we'd already been through the notes . . .'

He dabbed at his face with his fingers, finding blood issuing from the cuts. Rebus held the phone a little closer.

'That ambulance . . . ?' he offered.

Devlin shook his head. 'In good time.' A middle-aged woman made to pass them, eyes widening in horror as she saw Devlin. 'A stumble down the steps,' he reassured her. 'Help is on its way.'

She quickened her pace away from the scene.

'I think I've said more than enough, don't you, DI Rebus?'

'Not for me to say, sir.'

'I do hope DS Wylie doesn't get into trouble.'

'For what?'

'Not keeping a closer eye on me when I was studying the autopsy reports.'

'I don't think she's the one that's in trouble here.'

'Uncorroborated evidence, isn't that what we're dealing with, Inspector? One woman's word against mine? I'm sure I can find some plausible motive for my fight with Miss Burchill.' He studied his hand. 'One might almost call me the victim. And let us be honest, what else do you have? Two drownings, two missing persons, no evidence.'

'Well,' Rebus corrected him, 'no evidence apart from this.' He held the phone a little higher. 'It was already on when I took it from my pocket, connected to our comms centre down in Leith.' He put the phone to his ear. Glancing back over his shoulder, he saw that uniformed officers were making their way down the steps from the bridge. 'Did you get all that?' he asked into the mouthpiece. Then he looked at Devlin and smiled.

'We record every call, you see.'

The animation left Devlin's face, his shoulders slumping. Then he turned on his heels, preparing to run. But Rebus's arm snaked out, gripping him hard by the shoulder. Devlin tried to wrestle free. One foot slipped off the walkway and he started to fall, his weight pulling Rebus with him. The two men landed heavily in the Water of Leith. It wasn't deep, and Rebus felt his own shoulder connect with a rock. When he tried standing up, his feet sank to the ankles in mud. He was still holding on to Devlin, and as the bald head appeared from below the surface, missing its spectacles, Rebus saw again the monster who had battered Jean. He reached out his free hand to the Professor's neck and forced him back under. Hands flew up, splashing, wrestling air. Fingers clawing at Rebus's arm, clutching at his jacket lapel.

He felt as calm as he ever had in his life. The water lapped around him, icy but somehow soothing, too. There were people on the bridge, staring down, and officers wading into the water nearby, and a pale lemon sun spectating from above a bruised cloud. The water seemed cleansing to him. He couldn't feel his twisted ankle any more, couldn't feel anything much. Jean would recover, and so would he. He'd move out of Arden Street, find somewhere else, somewhere nobody knew about . . . maybe near water.

His arm was wrenched from behind: one of the uniforms.

'Let go of him!'

The cry broke the spell. Rebus released his grip, and Donald Devlin rose spluttering and choking into the daylight, watery vomit dribbling from his chin . . .

They were loading Jean Burchill into the ambulance when Rebus's mobile started ringing. One of the green-suited paramedics was explaining that they couldn't rule out spinal or neck damage, which was why they'd strapped her to a stretcher and placed braces around her head and neck.

Rebus was staring at Jean, trying to take in what was being said.

'Shouldn't you answer that?' the paramedic asked.

'What?'

'Your phone.'

Rebus lifted the mobile to his ear. When he'd struggled with Devlin, it had dropped on to the walkway. It was scratched and chipped, but at least still working. 'Hello?'

'DI Rebus?'

'Yes.'

'It's Eric Bain here.'

'Yes?'

'Is something the matter?'

'Quite a lot, yes.' As the trolley slid home into the back of the ambulance, Rebus looked down at his sodden clothes. 'Any sign of Siobhan?'

'That's why I'm calling.'

'What's happened?'

'Nothing's happened. It's just that I can't reach her. They think she's in the Botanics. There are half a dozen men out there looking for her.'

'So?'

'So there's news about Quizmaster.'

'And you're bursting to tell someone?'

'I suppose so, yes.'

'I'm not sure you've got the right person, Bain, I'm a bit tied up right now.'

'Oh.'

Rebus was inside the ambulance now, seated across from the trolley. Jean had her eyes closed, but when he reached for her hand, his pressure was returned.

'Sorry?' he said, having missed what Bain had just said.

'Who should I tell then?' Bain repeated.

'I don't know.' Rebus sighed. 'Okay, tell me what it is.'

'It's Special Branch,' Bain said, the words streaming out. 'One of the e-mail addresses Quizmaster was using, it traces back to Philippa Balfour's account.'

Rebus didn't understand: was Bain trying to say that Flip Balfour had been Quizmaster . . . ?

'I think it makes sense,' Bain was saying now. 'Taken with Claire Benzie's account.'

'I'm not getting you.' Jean's eyelids were fluttering. A sudden jolt of pain, Rebus guessed. He lessened the pressure on her hand.

'If Benzie did lend her laptop to Philippa Balfour, we've got two computers in the same place, both used by Quizmaster.'

'Yes?'

'And if we rule out Ms Balfour as a suspect . . .'

'We're left with someone who had access to both?'

Silence for a moment, and then Bain: 'I think the boyfriend's back in the frame, don't you?'

'I don't know.' Rebus was having trouble concentrating. He ran the back of his hand across his forehead, feeling perspiration there.

'We could always ask him . . .'

'Siobhan's gone to meet Quizmaster,' Rebus said. Then he paused. 'She's at the Botanics, you say?'

'Yes.'

'How do we know?'

'Her car's parked right outside.'

Rebus thought for a second: Siobhan would know they were looking for her. Leaving the car in full view was too big a giveaway . . .

'What if she's not there?' he said. 'What if she's meeting him somewhere else?'

'How can we find out?'

'Maybe Costello's flat . . .' He looked down at Jean. 'Look, Bain, I really can't do this . . . not right now.'

Jean's eye opened. She mouthed something.

'Hang on, Bain,' Rebus said. Then he lowered his head to Jean's.

'Fine . . .' he heard her slur.

She was telling him she'd be okay; that he had to help Siobhan now. Rebus turned his head, his eyes meeting those of Ellen Wylie, who was standing on the roadway, waiting for the doors to close. She nodded slowly, letting him know she'd stay with Jean.

'Bain?' he said into the mobile. 'I'll meet you outside Costello's flat.'

By the time Rebus got there, Bain had climbed the winding stairs and was standing outside Costello's door.

'I don't think he's home,' Bain was saying, crouching down to look through the letter-box. A chill ran up Rebus's spine, remembering what he'd seen when he'd peered into Devlin's flat. Bain got to his feet again. 'No sign of . . . Jesus Christ, man, what happened to you?'

'Swimming lessons. I didn't have time to change.' Rebus looked at the door, then at Bain. 'Together?' he said.

Bain stared back at him. 'Isn't that illegal?'

'For Siobhan,' Rebus said simply.

They hit the door together on the count of three.

Inside, Bain knew what he was looking for: a computer. He found two in the bedroom, both of them laptops.

'Claire Benzie's,' Bain guessed, 'and either his own or someone else's.'

The screen-saver had been activated on one computer. Bain accessed Costello's ISP and opened the filing cabinet.

'No time to try for a password,' he said, almost to himself more than Rebus. 'So all we can read are the old messages.' But there were none to or from Siobhan. 'Looks like he wipes as he goes,' Bain said.

'Or else we're barking up the wrong tree.' Rebus was looking around the room: unmade bed, books scattered across the floor. Notes for an essay on the desk next to the PC. Socks, pants and T-shirts spilled from the chest of drawers, but not from the top drawer. Rebus limped over, opened it slowly. Inside: maps and guidebooks, including one about Arthur's Seat. A postcard of Rosslyn Chapel and another guidebook.

'Right tree,' he remarked simply. Bain got up, came to look.

'Everything the well-dressed Quizmaster could need.' Bain went to reach into the drawer, but Rebus slapped his hand away. 'No touching.' He tried sliding the drawer out further. Something was sticking. He took a pen from his pocket and dislodged it: an Edinburgh A–Z.

'Open at the Botanics,' Bain said, sounding relieved. If that's where David Costello was, they'd have cornered him by now.

But Rebus wasn't so sure. He was examining the rest of the page. Then he looked over towards Costello's bed. Postcards of old gravestones . . . a small framed photo of Costello with Flip Balfour, with another headstone just coming into the frame. They'd met at a dinner party . . . breakfast next morning and then a walk in Warriston Cemetery. That was what Costello had told him. Warriston Cemetery was just across the road from the Botanic Gardens. Same page of the A–Z.

'I know where he is,' Rebus said quietly. 'I know where she's meeting him. Come on.' He ran from the room, hand already reaching for his mobile. The detectives who were wandering around the Botanics, they could be at Warriston in two minutes . . .

'Hello, David.'

He still had his funeral clothes on, including the sunglasses. He grinned as she walked towards him. He was just sitting there, legs swinging from the wall. He slid down and was suddenly standing in front of her.

'You guessed,' he said.

'Sort of.'

He looked at his watch. 'You're early.'

'You're earlier.'

'I had to recce, see if you were lying.'

'I said I'd be on my own.'

'And here you are.' He looked around again.

'Plenty of escape routes,' Siobhan said, surprised by how calm she was. 'Is that why you chose it?'

'It's where I first realised I loved Flip.'

'Loved her so much you went and killed her?'

His face fell. 'I didn't know that was going to happen.'

'No?'

He shook his head. 'Right up until the moment I had my hands round her throat . . . even then I don't think I knew.'

She drew in a deep breath. 'But you did it anyway.'

He nodded. 'I suppose I did, yes.' Looked up at her. 'That's what you wanted to hear, isn't it?'

'I wanted to meet Quizmaster.'

He opened his arms. 'At your command.'

'I also want to know why.'

'Why?' He framed his lips into an O. 'How many reasons do you want? Her yah friends? Her pretensions? The way she kept teasing and picking fights, looking to break us up just so she could watch me crawling back?'

'You could have walked away.'

'But I *loved* her.' When he laughed, it was as if acknowledging his own foolishness. 'I kept telling her that, and you know what she told me back?'

'What?'

'That I wasn't the only one.'

'Ranald Marr?'

'That old goat, yes. Since before she left school. And still at it, even when *we* were together!' He stopped, swallowed. 'Enough motivation for you, Siobhan?'

'You vented your anger on Marr by disfiguring that toy soldier, and yet Flip . . . Flip you had to *kill*?' She felt calm, almost numb. 'That doesn't seem quite fair to me.'

'You wouldn't understand.'

She looked at him. 'But I think I do, David. You're a coward, pure and simple. You say you didn't know you were going to murder Flip that night – that's a lie. You had it planned all along . . . and afterwards you were Mr Calm, speaking to her worried friends not much more than an hour after you'd killed her. You knew *exactly* what you were doing, David. You were Quizmaster.' She paused. He was staring into the middle distance, soaking up every word. 'Something I don't understand . . . you sent Flip a message after she died?'

He smiled. 'That day at her flat, while Rebus was watching me and you were working on her computer . . . he told me something, said I was the only suspect.'

'You thought you'd try throwing us off the scent?'

'It was just supposed to be that one message . . . but when you replied, I couldn't resist. I was as hooked as you were, Siobhan. The game had us both.' His eyes sparkled. 'Isn't that something?'

He seemed to expect an answer, so she nodded slowly. 'Are you thinking of killing me, David?'

He shook his head briskly, irritated by the assumption. 'You know the answer to that,' he spat. 'You wouldn't have come otherwise.' He walked over to a low headstone and rested against it. 'Maybe none of it would have happened,' he said, 'without the Professor.'

Siobhan thought she must have misheard. 'Which one?'

'Donald Devlin. First time he saw me afterwards, he guessed I'd done it. That's why he came up with that story, someone loitering outside. He was trying to protect me.'

'Why would he do that, David?' It felt strange using his name. She wanted to call him Quizmaster.

'Because of everything we talked about . . . committing murder, getting away with it.'

'Professor Devlin?'

He looked at her. 'Oh yes, he's killed too, you know. Old bugger as good as said so, daring me to be like him . . . maybe he was just too good a teacher, eh?' He ran his hands over the headstone. 'We had these long talks on the stairwell. He wanted to know all about me, my early days, the angry days. I went to his flat once. He showed me these cuttings . . . people who'd disappeared or drowned. There was even one about a German student . . .'

'That's where you got the idea?'

'Maybe.' He shrugged. 'Who knows where ideas come from?' He paused. 'I helped her, you know. She was dead impressed, all those clues . . . pulling her hair out until I came along . . .' He laughed. 'Flip was never much good with computers. I gave her the name Flipside, then sent the first clue.'

'You turned up at the flat, told her you'd solved Hellbank . . .'

Costello nodded, remembering. 'She wasn't going to go with me until I promised to drop her off afterwards . . . She'd just kicked me out again – final this time, she'd piled my clothes on a chair – and after Hellbank she was heading off for a drink with all those bloody friends of hers . . .' He screwed his eyes shut for a moment, then opened them and blinked, turning his head to face Siobhan. 'Once you're there, it's hard to go back . . .' He shrugged.

'There never was a Stricture?'

He shook his head slowly. 'That clue was all for you, Siobhan . . .'

'I don't know why you kept going back to her, David, or what you thought the game would prove, but one thing I do know: you never loved her. What you wanted was to control her.' She nodded at the truth of this.

'Some people like to be controlled, Siobhan.' His eyes were staring into hers. 'Don't you?'

She thought for a moment . . . or tried to think. Opened her mouth and was about to speak, but a noise interrupted. He snapped his head round: two men approaching. And two more fifty yards beyond them. He turned slowly back to Siobhan.

'I'm disappointed in you.'

She was shaking her head. 'Not my doing.'

He leaped from the headstone, hurtled towards the wall, his hands reaching the top, feet scrabbling for purchase. The detectives were running now, one yelling, 'Stop him!' Siobhan just watched, rooted to the spot. Quizmaster . . . she'd given him her word . . . One of his feet had found a half-inch of ledge, pushing up . . .

Siobhan threw herself at the wall, grabbed the other leg with both hands and pulled. He tried kicking her off, but she held on, one hand reaching up towards his jacket, trying to haul him back. Then they were both flying backwards, his the only cry. His sunglasses seemed to float past her in slow motion. She was watching them when she hit the ground. He landed heavily on top of her, the air exploding from her lungs. She felt pain as her head connected with the grass. Costello was on his feet and running, but two of the officers had him, wrestled him back on to the ground. He managed to slide his head round so he was looking at Siobhan, the two of them only a couple of yards apart. Hatred filled his face, and he spat in her direction. The saliva hit her on the chin and hung there. Suddenly she didn't have the strength to wipe it off . . .

Jean was asleep, but the doctor assured Rebus she'd be fine: cuts and bruises, 'nothing time can't heal'.

'I very much doubt that,' he told the doctor.

Ellen Wylie was there by the bedside. Rebus walked over and stood beside her. 'I wanted to say thanks,' he told her.

'For what?'

'Helping break down Devlin's door, for one thing. I'd never have done it on my own.'

Her reply was a shrug. 'How's the ankle?' she asked.

'Ballooning nicely, thank you.'

'A week or two on the sick,' she said.

'Maybe more, if I swallowed any of the Water of Leith.'

'I hear Devlin took a good few gulps himself.' She stared at him. 'Got a good story prepared?'

He smiled. 'You offering to tell a lie or two on my behalf?'

'Just say the word.'

He nodded slowly. 'Problem is, a dozen witnesses could say otherwise.'

'But will they?'

'We'll just have to wait and see,' Rebus said.

He limped along to A&E, where Siobhan was having a couple of stitches put into a head wound. Eric Bain was there. The conversation stopped as Rebus approached.

'Eric here,' Siobhan said, 'was just explaining how you worked out where I'd be.' Rebus nodded. 'And how you gained entry to David Costello's flat.'

Rebus made an O with his lips.

'Mr Strongarm,' she went on, 'kicking in a suspect's door without authority or any sniff of a warrant.'

'Technically,' Rebus told her, 'I was on suspension. That means I wasn't a serving officer.'

'Making it even worse.' She turned to Bain. 'Eric, you're going to have to cover for him.'

'Door was open when we got there,' Bain recited. 'Botched break-in, probably . . .'

Siobhan nodded and smiled at him. Then she gave Bain's hand a squeeze . . .

Donald Devlin was under police guard in one of the Western General's private rooms. He'd half drowned in the river and was now in what the doctors were calling a coma.

'Let's hope he stays there,' ACC Colin Carswell had said. 'Save us the expense of a prosecution.'

Carswell hadn't said anything at all to Rebus. Gill said not to worry: 'He's ignoring you because he hates making apologies.'

Rebus nodded. 'I've just seen a doctor,' he told her.

She looked at him. 'So?'

'Does that count as my check-up . . . ?'

David Costello was in custody at Gayfield Square. Rebus didn't go near. He knew they'd be cracking open a few bottles of whisky and cans of beer, sounds of celebration drifting into the room where Costello was being questioned. He thought of the time he'd asked Donald Devlin whether his young neighbour was capable of killing: *not cerebral enough for David*. Well, Costello had found his method all the same, and Devlin had protected him . . . the old man sheltering the young.

When Rebus went home, he took a tour of his flat. It represented, he realised, the only fixed point of his life. All the cases he'd worked, the monsters he'd encountered . . . he dealt with them here, seated in his chair, staring out of his window. He found room for them in the bestiary of his mind, and there they stayed.

If he gave this up, what would be left? No still centre to his world, no cage for his demons . . .

Tomorrow he'd call the solicitor, tell her he wasn't moving.

Tomorrow.

For tonight, he had new cages to fill . . .

14

It was a Sunday afternoon of sharp, low sunlight, the shadows impossibly long and skewed into an elastic geometry. Trees bowed by the wind, clouds moving like oiled machines. Falls, twinned with Anguish . . . Rebus drove past the signpost, glanced towards Jean, quiet in the passenger seat. She'd been quiet all week; slow to answer her phone or come to the door. The doctor's words: *nothing time can't heal* . . .

He'd given her the option, but she'd decided to come with him. They parked next to a sparkling BMW. There were traces of soapy water in the gutters. Rebus pulled on the hand-brake and turned to Jean.

'I'll only be a minute. You want to wait here?'

She thought about it, then nodded. He reached into the back for the coffin. It was wrapped in newspaper, a front-page headline by Steven Holly. He got out of the car, leaving his door open. Knocked on the door of Wheel Cottage.

Bev Dodds answered. She had a smile fixed to her face and a frilly apron tied across her chest.

'Sorry, not a tourist,' Rebus said. Her smile faded. 'Doing a roaring trade in tea and buns?'

'What can I do for you?'

He lifted up the parcel. 'Thought you might like this back. It's yours, after all, isn't it?'

She parted the sheets of newsprint. 'Oh, thanks,' she said.

'It really *is* yours, isn't it?'

She wouldn't look at him. 'Finders keepers, I suppose . . .'

But he was shaking his head. 'I mean, you made it, Ms Dodds. This new sign of yours . . .' He nodded in its direction. 'Care to tell me who made it? I'm willing to bet you did it yourself. Nice piece of wood . . . I'm guessing you've a few chisels and such-like.'

'What do you want?' Her voice had grown chilly.

'When I brought Jean Burchill here – there she is in the car, and she's fine by the way, thanks for asking – when I brought her here, you said you often went to the Museum.'

'Yes?' She was staring over his shoulder, but averted her gaze when Jean's eyes met hers.

'Yet you'd never come across the Arthur's Seat coffins.' Rebus affected a frown. 'It should have clicked with me right there.' He stared at her, but she didn't say anything. He watched her neck redden, watched her turn the coffin in her hands. 'Still,' he said, 'brought you some extra business, eh? But I'll tell you one thing . . .'

Her eyes were liquid; she brought them up to meet his. 'What?' she asked, voice cracking.

He pointed a finger at her. 'You're lucky I didn't tag you sooner. I might have said something to Donald Devlin. And then you'd look like Jean back there, if not a damned sight worse.'

He turned away, headed back to the car. On the way, he unhooked the 'Pottery' sign and tossed it into the gutter. She was still watching from her doorway as he started the ignition. A couple of day-trippers were approaching along the pavement. Rebus knew exactly where they were headed and why. He made sure to turn the steering-wheel hard, running the sign over, front and back tyres both.

On the way back into Edinburgh, Jean asked if they were going to Portobello. He nodded, and asked if that was okay with her.

'It's fine,' she told him. 'I need someone to help me move that mirror out of the bedroom.' He looked at her. 'Just until the bruises have healed,' she said quietly.

He nodded his understanding. 'Know what I need, Jean?'

She turned towards him. 'What?'

He shook his head slowly. 'I was hoping you might tell me . . .'

Sexual repression and hysteria are what Edinburgh is all about.

Philip Kerr, 'The Unnatural History Museum'

Afterword

Firstly, a big thank-you to Mogwai, whose 'Stanley Kubrick' EP was playing in the background throughout the final draft of this book.

The collection of poetry in David Costello's flat is *I Dream of Alfred Hitchcock* by James Robertson, and the poem from which Rebus quotes is entitled 'Shower Scene'.

After the first draft of this book was written, I discovered that in 1999 the Museum of Scotland commissioned two American researchers, Dr Allen Simpson and Dr Sam Menefee of the University of Virginia, to examine the Arthur's Seat coffins and formulate a solution. They concluded that the most likely explanation was that the coffins had been made by a shoemaker acquaintance of the murderers Burke and Hare, using a shoemaker's knife and brass fittings adapted from shoe buckles, the idea being to give the victims some vestige of Christian burial, since a dissected *corpus* could not be resurrected.

The Falls is, of course, a work of fiction, a flight of fancy. Dr Kennet Lovell exists only between its pages.

In June 1996, a man's body was found near the summit of Ben Alder. He'd died of gunshot wounds. His name was Emmanuel Caillet, the son of a French merchant banker. What he was doing in Scotland was never ascertained. The report, produced from autopsy and scene-of-crime evidence, concluded that the young man had committed suicide. But there are enough discrepancies and unanswered questions to persuade his parents that this is not the real solution . . .